MIDDLEMARCH

AN AUTHORITATIVE TEXT

BACKGROUNDS

REVIEWS AND CRITICISM

A NORTON CRITICAL EDITION

GEORGE ELIOT

MIDDLEMARCH

AN AUTHORITATIVE TEXT
BACKGROUNDS
REVIEWS AND CRITICISM

Edited by

BERT G. HORNBACK

THE UNIVERSITY OF MICHIGAN

W · W · NORTON & COMPANY

New York · London

W. W. Norton & Company, Inc., 500 Fifth Avenue, New York, N.Y. 10110
W. W. Norton & Company Ltd., 37 Great Russell Street, London WC1B 3NU

Library of Congress Cataloging in Publication Data

Eliot, George, pseud., i.e. Marian Evans, afterwards
    Cross, 1819–1880.
    Middlemarch: an authoritative text, backgrounds,
reviews and criticism.

    (A Norton critical edition)
    Bibliography: p.
    I. Hornback, Bert G., 1935–   II. Title.
PZ3.E43Mi30 [PR4662]   823'.8   76–22805
ISBN 0-393-04430-0
ISBN 0-393-09210-0 pbk.

Printed in the United States of America

7 8 9 0

for Dorothe and Jay

Contents

Reviews and Criticism

Preface

Middlemarch, the sixth of George Eliot's seven novels, was originally published in eight books, between December 1871 and December 1872. Two four-volume editions from the same sheets were issued in 1872 and 1873. In 1874 the novel was revised by George Eliot, and reissued in one volume. The present text follows that of the 1874 edition, the last corrected by the author. With one exception, I have not supplied variant readings from the manuscript or the first edition of the novel. In an essay in *Middlemarch: Critical Approaches to the Novel* (see Supplementary Bibliography) Jerome Beaty remarks concerning some eight hundred such changes that "most of these revisions, of course, are relatively trivial, scarcely changing the shape or nature of the novel." Beaty discusses the few changes he doesn't consider "trivial" in his essay, to which the interested student might refer; even those changes, however, seemed not to require identification here.

The annotation in this edition is designed primarily to identify unfamiliar historical figures and explain the various historical attitudes, acts, and situations which make up so much of the fabric of this novel, in the hope that such annotation will aid the student in understanding both the world of the novel and the manner of George Eliot's art.

The background section of this edition presents selections from George Eliot's letters, journals, essays, and other works of fiction, to the end of elucidating her ideas on life and art. It also contains in their entirety her notebooks, *Quarry for "Middlemarch."* The criticism section contains contemporary reviews of *Middlemarch,* early critical commentary on George Eliot's work, and modern criticism. I have tried to choose not only interesting and significant essays, but also works which represent accurately the history of critical response to *Middlemarch.* I hope that students will be able to build from this material their own interpretations and relevant understandings of this novel. The Supplementary Bibliography suggests further biographical and critical readings.

I am grateful to M. H. Abrams, Robert A. Greenberg, and Michelle Cliff for many helpful suggestions in the preparation of this text, and to Norman D. Plumm for various assistances, involving everything from ideas to scissors and rubber cement; and to the many students who, over the years, have helped me to formulate my own thoughts about and appreciations of this great, rich novel.

BERT G. HORNBACK
ANN ARBOR, MICHIGAN

The Text of
Middlemarch

PRELUDE.

———◆———

WHO that cares much to know the history of man, and how the mysterious mixture behaves under the varying experiments of Time, has not dwelt, at least briefly, on the life of Saint Theresa, has not smiled with some gentleness at the thought of the little girl walking forth one morning hand-in-hand with her still smaller brother, to go and seek martyrdom in the country of the Moors ? [1] Out they toddled from rugged Avila, wide-eyed and helpless-looking as two fawns, but with human hearts, already beating to a national idea ; until domestic reality met them in the shape of uncles, and turned them back from their great resolve. That child-pilgrimage was a fit beginning. Theresa's passionate, ideal nature demanded an epic life : what were many-volumed romances of chivalry and the social conquests of a brilliant girl to her ? Her flame quickly burned up that light fuel ; and, fed from within, soared after some illimitable satisfaction, some object which would never justify weariness, which would reconcile self-despair with the rapturous consciousness of life beyond self. She found her epos in the reform of a religious order.

That Spanish woman who lived three hundred years ago, was certainly not the last of her kind. Many Theresas have been born who found for themselves no epic life wherein there was a constant unfolding of far-resonant action ; perhaps only a life of mistakes, the offspring of a certain spiritual grandeur ill-matched with the meanness of opportunity ; perhaps a tragic failure which found no sacred poet and sank unwept into oblivion. With dim lights and tangled circumstance they tried to shape their thought and deed in noble agreement ; but after all, to common eyes their struggles seemed mere inconsistency and formlessness ; for these later-born Theresas were helped by no coherent social faith and order which could perform the function of knowledge for the ardently willing soul. Their ardour alternated between a vague ideal and the common yearning of womanhood ; so that the one was disapproved as extravagance, and the other condemned as a lapse.

1. Saint Teresa of Avila (1515–82), Spanish saint and mystic, founder and reformer of religious communities.

Some have felt that these blundering lives are due to the inconvenient indefiniteness with which the Supreme Power has fashioned the natures of women : if there were one level of feminine incompetence as strict as the ability to count three and no more, the social lot of women might be treated with scientific certitude. Meanwhile the indefiniteness remains, and the limits of variation are really much wider than any one would imagine from the sameness of women's coiffure and the favourite love-stories in prose and verse. Here and there a cygnet is reared uneasily among the ducklings in the brown pond, and never finds the living stream in fellowship with its own oary-footed kind. Here and there is born a Saint Theresa, foundress of nothing, whose loving heart-beats and sobs after an unattained goodness tremble off and are dispersed among hindrances, instead of centering in some long-recognisable deed.

MIDDLEMARCH.

BOOK I.

MISS BROOKE.

CHAPTER I.

" Since I can do no good because a woman,
Reach constantly at something that is near it."
—*The Maid's Tragedy:* BEAUMONT AND FLETCHER.

MISS BROOKE had that kind of beauty which seems to be thrown into
relief by poor dress. Her hand and wrist were so finely formed that
she could wear sleeves not less bare of style than those in which the
Blessed Virgin appeared to Italian painters ; and her profile as well
as her stature and bearing seemed to gain the more dignity from her
plain garments, which by the side of provincial fashion gave her the
impressiveness of a fine quotation from the Bible,—or from one of
our elder poets,—in a paragraph of to-day's newspaper. She was
usually spoken of as being remarkably clever, but with the addition
that her sister Celia had more common-sense. Nevertheless, Celia
wore scarcely more trimmings ; and it was only to close observers
that her dress differed from her sister's, and had a shade of coquetry
in its arrangements ; for Miss Brooke's plain dressing was due to
mixed conditions, in most of which her sister shared. The pride of
being ladies had something to do with it : the Brooke connections,
though not exactly aristocratic, were unquestionably " good : " if you
inquired backward for a generation or two, you would not find any
yard-measuring or parcel-tying forefathers—anything lower than an
admiral or a clergyman ; and there was even an ancestor discernible
as a Puritan gentleman who served under Cromwell, but afterwards
conformed, and managed to come out of all political troubles as the
proprietor of a respectable family estate. Young women of such
birth, living in a quiet country-house, and attending a village church
hardly larger than a parlour, naturally regarded frippery as the ambition of a huckster's daughter. Then there was well-bred economy,
which in those days made show in dress the first item to be deducted

1

from, when any margin was required for expenses more distinctive of rank. Such reasons would have been enough to account for plain dress, quite apart from religious feeling; but in Miss Brooke's case, religion alone would have determined it; and Celia mildly acquiesced in all her sister's sentiments, only infusing them with that common-sense which is able to accept momentous doctrines without any eccentric agitation. Dorothea knew many passages of Pascal's *Pensées* and of Jeremy Taylor by heart; and to her the destinies of mankind, seen by the light of Christianity, made the solicitudes of feminine fashion appear an occupation for Bedlam. [2] She could not reconcile the anxieties of a spiritual life involving eternal consequences, with a keen interest in guimp and artificial protrusions of drapery. Her mind was theoretic, and yearned by its nature after some lofty conception of the world which might frankly include the parish of Tipton and her own rule of conduct there; she was enamoured of intensity and greatness, and rash in embracing whatever seemed to her to have those aspects; likely to seek martyrdom, to make retractations, and then to incur martyrdom after all in a quarter where she had not sought it. Certainly such elements in the character of a marriageable girl tended to interfere with her lot, and hinder it from being decided according to custom, by good looks, vanity, and merely canine affection. With all this, she, the elder of the sisters, was not yet twenty, and they had both been educated, since they were about twelve years old and had lost their parents, on plans at once narrow and promiscuous, first in an English family and afterwards in a Swiss family at Lausanne, their bachelor uncle and guardian trying in this way to remedy the disadvantages of their orphaned condition.

It was hardly a year since they had come to live at Tipton Grange with their uncle, a man nearly sixty, of acquiescent temper, miscellaneous opinions, and uncertain vote. He had travelled in his younger years, and was held in this part of the county to have contracted a too rambling habit of mind. Mr Brooke's conclusions were as difficult to predict as the weather: it was only safe to say that he would act with benevolent intentions, and that he would spend as little money as possible in carrying them out. For the most glutinously indefinite minds enclose some hard grains of habit; and a man has been seen lax about all his own interests except the retention of his snuffbox, concerning which he was watchful, suspicious, and greedy of clutch.

In Mr Brooke the hereditary strain of Puritan energy was clearly in abeyance; but in his niece Dorothea it glowed alike through faults and virtues, turning sometimes into impatience of her uncle's talk or his way of " letting things be " on his estate, and making her long all the more for the time when she would be of age and have some command of money for generous schemes. She was regarded as an heiress; for not only had the sisters seven hundred a-year each from their parents, but if Dorothea married and had a son, that son

---

2. Blaise Pascal (1623–62), French philosopher and mathematician; the *Pensées* were published in 1670. Jeremy Taylor (1613–67), English prelate and theological writer.

would inherit Mr Brooke's estate, presumably worth about three thousand a-year—a rental which seemed wealth to provincial families, still discussing Mr Peel's late conduct on the Catholic Question,[3] innocent of future gold-fields, and of that gorgeous plutocracy which has so nobly exalted the necessities of genteel life.

And how should Dorothea not marry ?—a girl so handsome and with such prospects ? Nothing could hinder it but her love of extremes, and her insistance on regulating life according to notions which might cause a wary man to hesitate before he made her an offer, or even might lead her at last to refuse all offers. A young lady of some birth and fortune, who knelt suddenly down on a brick floor by the side of a sick labourer and prayed fervidly as if she thought herself living in the time of the Apostles—who had strange whims of fasting like a Papist, and of sitting up at night to read old theological books ! Such a wife might awaken you some fine morning with a new scheme for the application of her income which would interfere with political economy and the keeping of saddle-horses : a man would naturally think twice before he risked himself in such fellowship. Women were expected to have weak opinions ; but the great safeguard of society and of domestic life was, that opinions were not acted on. Sane people did what their neighbours did, so that if any lunatics were at large, one might know and avoid them.

The rural opinion about the new young ladies, even among the cottagers, was generally in favour of Celia, as being so amiable and innocent-looking, while Miss Brooke's large eyes seemed, like her religion, too unusual and striking. Poor Dorothea ! compared with her, the innocent-looking Celia was knowing and worldly-wise ; so much subtler is a human mind than the outside tissues which make a sort of blazonry or clock-face for it.

Yet those who approached Dorothea, though prejudiced against her by this alarming hearsay, found that she had a charm unaccountably reconcilable with it. Most men thought her bewitching when she was on horseback. She loved the fresh air and the various aspects of the country, and when her eyes and cheeks glowed with mingled pleasure she looked very little like a devotee. Riding was an indulgence which she allowed herself in spite of conscientious qualms ; she felt that she enjoyed it in a pagan sensuous way, and always looked forward to renouncing it.

She was open, ardent, and not in the least self-admiring ; indeed, it was pretty to see how her imagination adorned her sister Celia with attractions altogether superior to her own, and if any gentleman appeared to come to the Grange from some other motive than that of seeing Mr Brooke, she concluded that he must be in love with Celia: Sir James Chettam, for example, whom she constantly considered from Celia's point of view, inwardly debating whether it would be good for Celia to accept him. That he should be regarded as a suitor

3. Robert Peel (1788–1850), home secretary in the government of the Duke of Wellington. An opponent of religious and political freedom for Catholics, Peel changed suddenly in 1829—in the face of unanimous Irish support for Daniel O'Connell and the Irish Association—to the side of Catholic emancipation. Religious and political freedom had been established for Protestant dissenters and nonconformists by the repeal of the Test Act in 1828.

to herself would have seemed to her a ridiculous irrelevance. Dorothea, with all her eagerness to know the truths of life, retained very childlike ideas about marriage. She felt sure that she would have accepted the judicious Hooker,[4] if she had been born in time to save him from that wretched mistake he made in matrimony ; or John Milton when his blindness had come on ; or any of the other great men whose odd habits it would have been glorious piety to endure ; but an amiable handsome baronet, who said " Exactly " to her remarks even when she expressed uncertainty,—how could he affect her as a lover ? The really delightful marriage must be that where your husband was a sort of father, and could teach you even Hebrew, if you wished it.

These peculiarities of Dorothea's character caused Mr Brooke to be all the more blamed in neighbouring families for not securing some middle-aged lady as guide and companion to his nieces. But he himself dreaded so much the sort of superior woman likely to be available for such a position, that he allowed himself to be dissuaded by Dorothea's objections, and was in this case brave enough to defy the world—that is to say, Mrs Cadwallader the Rector's wife, and the small group of gentry with whom he visited in the north-east corner of Loamshire. So Miss Brooke presided in her uncle's household, and did not at all dislike her new authority, with the homage that belonged to it.

Sir James Chettam was going to dine at the Grange to-day with another gentleman whom the girls had never seen, and about whom Dorothea felt some venerating expectation. This was the Reverend Edward Casaubon, noted in the county as a man of profound learning, understood for many years to be engaged on a great work concerning religious history ; also as a man of wealth enough to give lustre to his piety, and having views of his own which were to be more clearly ascertained on the publication of his book. His very name carried an impressiveness hardly to be measured without a precise chronology of scholarship.

Early in the day Dorothea had returned from the infant school which she had set going in the village, and was taking her usual place in the pretty sitting-room which divided the bedrooms of the sisters, bent on finishing a plan for some buildings (a kind of work which she delighted in), when Celia, who had been watching her with a hesitating desire to propose something, said—

" Dorothea dear, if you don't mind—if you are not very busy—suppose we looked at mamma's jewels to-day, and divided them ? It is exactly six months to-day since uncle gave them to you, and you have not looked at them yet."

Celia's face had the shadow of a pouting expression in it, the full presence of the pout being kept back by an habitual awe of Dorothea and principle ; two associated facts which might show a mysterious electricity if you touched them incautiously. To her relief, Dorothea's eyes were full of laughter as she looked up.

4. Richard Hooker (1554–1600), English theologian, author of *The Lawes of Ecclesiasticall Politie*. He was popularly believed to be unhappily married to "a clownish, silly woman."

" What a wonderful little almanac you are, Celia ! Is it six calendar or six lunar months ? "

" It is the last day of September now, and it was the first of April when uncle gave them to you. You know, he said that he had forgotten them till then. I believe you have never thought of them since you locked them up in the cabinet here."

" Well, dear, we should never wear them, you know." Dorothea spoke in a full cordial tone, half caressing, half explanatory. She had her pencil in her hand, and was making tiny side-plans on a margin.

Celia coloured, and looked very grave. " I think, dear, we are wanting in respect to mamma's memory, to put them by and take no notice of them. And," she added, after hesitating a little, with a rising sob of mortification, " necklaces are quite usual now ; and Madame Poinçon, who was stricter in some things even than you are, used to wear ornaments. And Christians generally—surely there are women in heaven now who wore jewels." Celia was conscious of some mental strength when she really applied herself to argument.

" You would like to wear them ? " exclaimed Dorothea, an air of astonished discovery animating her whole person with a dramatic action which she had caught from that very Madame Poinçon who wore the ornaments. " Of course, then, let us have them out. Why did you not tell me before ? But the keys, the keys ! " She pressed her hands against the sides of her head and seemed to despair of her memory.

" They are here," said Celia, with whom this explanation had been long meditated and prearranged.

" Pray open the large drawer of the cabinet and get out the jewel-box."

The casket was soon open before them, and the various jewels spread out, making a bright parterre on the table. It was no great collection, but a few of the ornaments were really of remarkable beauty, the finest that was obvious at first being a necklace of purple amethysts set in exquisite gold work, and a pearl cross with five brilliants in it. Dorothea immediately took up the necklace and fastened it round her sister's neck, where it fitted almost as closely as a bracelet ; but the circle suited the Henrietta-Maria style of Celia's head and neck, and she could see that it did, in the pier-glass opposite.[5]

" There, Celia ! you can wear that with your Indian muslin. But this cross you must wear with your dark dresses."

Celia was trying not to smile with pleasure. " O Dodo, you must keep the cross yourself."

" No, no, dear, no," said Dorothea, putting up her hand with careless deprecation.

" Yes, indeed you must ; it would suit you—in your black dress, now," said Celia, insistingly. " You *might* wear that."

" Not for the world, not for the world. A cross is the last thing I would wear as a trinket." Dorothea shuddered slightly.

---

5. After the style of Henrietta-Maria (1609–69), the Queen-consort of Charles I of England. She is usually pictured as wearing a choker pearl necklace around her long and slender neck.

" Then you will think it wicked in me to wear it," said Celia, uneasily.

" No, dear, no," said Dorothea, stroking her sister's cheek. " Souls have complexions too : what will suit one will not suit another."

" But you might like to keep it for mamma's sake."

" No, I have other things of mamma's — her sandal-wood box which I am so fond of—plenty of things. In fact, they are all yours, dear. We need discuss them no longer. There—take away your property."

Celia felt a little hurt. There was a strong assumption of superiority in this Puritanic toleration, hardly less trying to the blond flesh of an unenthusiastic sister than a Puritanic persecution.

" But how can I wear ornaments if you, who are the elder sister, will never wear them ? "

" Nay, Celia, that is too much to ask, that I should wear trinkets to keep you in countenance. If I were to put on such a necklace as that, I should feel as if I had been pirouetting. The world would go round with me, and I should not know how to walk."

Celia had unclasped the necklace and drawn it off. " It would be a little tight for your neck ; something to lie down and hang would suit you better," she said, with some satisfaction. The complete unfitness of the necklace from all points of view for Dorothea, made Celia happier in taking it. She was opening some ring-boxes, which disclosed a fine emerald with diamonds, and just then the sun passing beyond a cloud sent a bright gleam over the table.

" How very beautiful these gems are ! " said Dorothea, under a new current of feeling, as sudden as the gleam. " It is strange how deeply colours seem to penetrate one, like scent. I suppose that is the reason why gems are used as spiritual emblems in the Revelation of St John. They look like fragments of heaven. I think that emerald is more beautiful than any of them."

" And there is a bracelet to match it," said Celia. " We did not notice this at first."

" They are lovely," said Dorothea, slipping the ring and bracelet on her finely-turned finger and wrist, and holding them towards the window on a level with her eyes. All the while her thought was trying to justify her delight in the colours by merging them in her mystic religious joy.

" You *would* like those, Dorothea," said Celia, rather falteringly, beginning to think with wonder that her sister showed some weakness, and also that emeralds would suit her own complexion even better than purple amethysts. " You must keep that ring and bracelet—if nothing else. But see, these agates are very pretty—and quiet."

" Yes ! I will keep these—this ring and bracelet," said Dorothea. Then, letting her hand fall on the table, she said in another tone— " Yet what miserable men find such things, and work at them, and sell them ! " She paused again, and Celia thought that her sister was going to renounce the ornaments, as in consistency she ought to do.

" Yes, dear, I will keep these," said Dorothea, decidedly. " But take all the rest away, and the casket."

She took up her pencil without removing the jewels, and still looking at them. She thought of often having them by her, to feed her eye at these little fountains of pure colour.

"Shall you wear them in company?" said Celia, who was watching her with real curiosity as to what she would do.

Dorothea glanced quickly at her sister. Across all her imaginative adornment of those whom she loved, there darted now and then a keen discernment, which was not without a scorching quality. If Miss Brooke ever attained perfect meekness, it would not be for lack of inward fire.

"Perhaps," she said, rather haughtily. "I cannot tell to what level I may sink."

Celia blushed, and was unhappy: she saw that she had offended her sister, and dared not say even anything pretty about the gift of the ornaments which she put back into the box and carried away. Dorothea too was unhappy, as she went on with her plan-drawing, questioning the purity of her own feeling and speech in the scene which had ended with that little explosion.

Celia's consciousness told her that she had not been at all in the wrong: it was quite natural and justifiable that she should have asked that question, and she repeated to herself that Dorothea was inconsistent: either she should have taken her full share of the jewels, or, after what she had said, she should have renounced them altogether.

"I am sure—at least, I trust," thought Celia, "that the wearing of a necklace will not interfere with my prayers. And I do not see that I should be bound by Dorothea's opinions now we are going into society, though of course she herself ought to be bound by them. But Dorothea is not always consistent."

Thus Celia, mutely bending over her tapestry, until she heard her sister calling her.

"Here, Kitty, come and look at my plan; I shall think I am a great architect, if I have not got incompatible stairs and fireplaces."

As Celia bent over the paper, Dorothea put her cheek against her sister's arm caressingly. Celia understood the action. Dorothea saw that she had been in the wrong, and Celia pardoned her. Since they could remember, there had been a mixture of criticism and awe in the attitude of Celia's mind towards her elder sister. The younger had always worn a yoke; but is there any yoked creature without its private opinions?

CHAPTER II.

" 'Dime ; no ves aquel caballero que hácia nosotros viene sobre un caballo rucio rodado que trae puesto en la cabeza un yelmo de oro?' 'Lo que veo y columbro,' respondió Sancho, 'no es sino un hombre sobre un asno pardo como el mio, que trae sobre la cabeza una cosa que relumbra.' 'Pues ese es el yelmo de Mambrino,' dijo Don Quijote."—CERVANTES.

" 'Seest thou not yon cavalier who cometh toward us on a dapple-grey steed, and weareth a golden helmet?' 'What I see,' answered Sancho, 'is nothing but a man on a grey ass like my own, who carries something shiny on his head.' 'Just so,' answered Don Quixote : 'and that resplendent object is the helmet of Mambrino.' "

" SIR HUMPHRY DAVY ?" said Mr Brooke, over the soup, in his easy smiling way, taking up Sir James Chettam's remark that he was studying Davy's Agricultural Chemistry.[1] " Well, now, Sir Humphry Davy : I dined with him years ago at Cartwright's, and Wordsworth was there too—the poet Wordsworth, you know. Now there was something singular. I was at Cambridge when Wordsworth was there, and I never met him—and I dined with him twenty years afterwards at Cartwright's. There's an oddity in things, now. But Davy was there : he was a poet too. Or, as I may say, Wordsworth was poet one, and Davy was poet two. That was true in every sense, you know."

Dorothea felt a little more uneasy than usual. In the beginning of dinner, the party being small and the room still, these motes from the mass of a magistrate's mind fell too noticeably. She wondered how a man like Mr Casaubon would support such triviality. His manners, she thought, were very dignified ; the set of his iron-grey hair and his deep eye-sockets made him resemble the portrait of Locke. He had the spare form and the pale complexion which became a student ; as different as possible from the blooming Englishman of the red-whiskered type represented by Sir James Chettam.

" I am reading the Agricultural Chemistry," said this excellent baronet, " because I am going to take one of the farms into my own hands, and see if something cannot be done in setting a good pattern of farming among my tenants. Do you approve of that, Miss Brooke ? "

" A great mistake, Chettam," interposed Mr Brooke, " going into electrifying your land and that kind of thing, and making a parlour of your cow-house.[2] It won't do. I went into science a great deal myself at one time ; but I saw it would not do. It leads to everything ; you can let nothing alone. No, no—see that your tenants don't sell their straw, and that kind of thing ; and give them draining-tiles, you know. But your fancy-farming will not do—the most expensive sort of whistle you can buy : you may as well keep a pack of hounds."

" Surely," said Dorothea, " it is better to spend money in finding

1. Sir Humphrey Davy (1778–1829), British scientist and inventor, author of *Elements of Agricultural Chemistry* (1813).
2. Davy "found that corn sprouted much more rapidly in water positively electrified by the Voltaic instrument than in water negatively electrified" (*Agricultural Chemistry*, p. 37).

out how men can make the most of the land which supports them all, than in keeping dogs and horses only to gallop over it. It is not a sin to make yourself poor in performing experiments for the good of all."

She spoke with more energy than is expected of so young a lady, but Sir James had appealed to her. He was accustomed to do so, and she had often thought that she could urge him to many good actions when he was her brother-in-law.

Mr Casaubon turned his eyes very markedly on Dorothea while she was speaking, and seemed to observe her newly.

"Young ladies don't understand political economy, you know," said Mr Brooke, smiling towards Mr Casaubon. "I remember when we were all reading Adam Smith.[3] *There* is a book, now. I took in all the new ideas at one time—human perfectibility, now. But some say, history moves in circles ; and that may be very well argued ; I have argued it myself. The fact is, human reason may carry you a little too far—over the hedge, in fact. It carried me a good way at one time ; but I saw it would not do. I pulled up ; I pulled up in time. But not too hard. I have always been in favour of a little theory : we must have Thought ; else we shall be landed back in the dark ages. But talking of books, there is Southey's ' Peninsular War.'[4] I am reading that of a morning. You know Southey ?"

"No," said Mr Casaubon, not keeping pace with Mr Brooke's impetuous reason, and thinking of the book only. "I have little leisure for such literature just now. I have been using up my eyesight on old characters lately ; the fact is, I want a reader for my evenings ; but I am fastidious in voices, and I cannot endure listening to an imperfect reader. It is a misfortune, in some senses : I feed too much on the inward sources ; I live too much with the dead. My mind is something like the ghost of an ancient, wandering about the world and trying mentally to construct it as it used to be, in spite of ruin and confusing changes. But I find it necessary to use the utmost caution about my eyesight."

This was the first time that Mr Casaubon had spoken at any length. He delivered himself with precision, as if he had been called upon to make a public statement ; and the balanced sing-song neatness of his speech, occasionally corresponded to by a movement of his head, was the more conspicuous from its contrast with good Mr Brooke's scrappy slovenliness. Dorothea said to herself that Mr Casaubon was the most interesting man she had ever seen, not excepting even Monsieur Liret, the Vaudois clergyman who had given conferences on the history of the Waldenses.[5] To reconstruct a past world, doubtless with a view to the highest purposes of truth—what a work to be in any way present at, to assist in, though only as a lamp-holder ! This elevating thought lifted her above her annoyance at being twitted

---

3. Adam Smith (1723–90), Scottish political economist, author of *The Wealth of Nations*, a seminal work of laissez faire economics.
4. Robert Southey (1774–1843), English poet and essayist; his *History of the Peninsular War* (1823–32) was an account of the Spanish campaigns of the war with Napoleon.

5. The Waldensians—called Vaudois in France, after their founder—were adherents of a religious sect organized about 1170. Rejecting the authority of the Roman pope, the Waldensians associated themselves with the Protestant Reformation in the sixteenth century, and were aided by Cromwell in the seventeenth century.

with her ignorance of political economy, that never-explained science which was thrust as an extinguisher over all her lights.

"But you are fond of riding, Miss Brooke," Sir James presently took an opportunity of saying. "I should have thought you would enter a little into the pleasures of hunting. I wish you would let me send over a chesnut horse for you to try. It has been trained for a lady. I saw you on Saturday cantering over the hill on a nag not worthy of you. My groom shall bring Corydon for you every day, if you will only mention the time."

"Thank you, you are very good. I mean to give up riding. I shall not ride any more," said Dorothea, urged to this brusque resolution by a little annoyance that Sir James would be soliciting her attention when she wanted to give it all to Mr Casaubon.

"No, that is too hard," said Sir James, in a tone of reproach that showed strong interest. "Your sister is given to self-mortification, is she not?" he continued, turning to Celia, who sat at his right hand.

"I think she is," said Celia, feeling afraid lest she should say something that would not please her sister, and blushing as prettily as possible above her necklace. "She likes giving up."

"If that were true, Celia, my giving-up would be self-indulgence, not self-mortification. But there may be good reasons for choosing not to do what is very agreeable," said Dorothea.

Mr Brooke was speaking at the same time, but it was evident that Mr Casaubon was observing Dorothea, and she was aware of it.

"Exactly," said Sir James. "You give up from some high, generous motive."

"No, indeed, not exactly. I did not say that of myself," answered Dorothea, reddening. Unlike Celia, she rarely blushed, and only from high delight or anger. At this moment she felt angry with the perverse Sir James. Why did he not pay attention to Celia, and leave her to listen to Mr Casaubon?—if that learned man would only talk, instead of allowing himself to be talked to by Mr Brooke, who was just then informing him that the Reformation either meant something or it did not, that he himself was a Protestant to the core, but that Catholicism was a fact; and as to refusing an acre of your ground for a Romanist chapel, all men needed the bridle of religion, which, properly speaking, was the dread of a Hereafter.

"I made a great study of theology at one time," said Mr Brooke, as if to explain the insight just manifested. "I know something of all schools. I knew Wilberforce in his best days.[6] Do you know Wilberforce?"

Mr Casaubon said, "No."

"Well, Wilberforce was perhaps not enough of a thinker; but if I went into Parliament, as I have been asked to do, I should sit on the independent bench, as Wilberforce did, and work at philanthropy."

Mr Casaubon bowed, and observed that it was a wide field.

"Yes," said Mr Brooke, with an easy smile, "but I have documents. I began a long while ago to collect documents. They want arranging, but when a question has struck me, I have written to somebody and

---

6. William Wilberforce (1759–1833), English statesman, philanthropist, and religious writer; a champion of such causes as police and penal reform and the abolition of slavery.

got an answer. I have documents at my back. But now, how do you arrange your documents ?"

"In pigeon-holes partly," said Mr Casaubon, with rather a startled air of effort.

"Ah, pigeon-holes will not do. I have tried pigeon-holes, but everything gets mixed in pigeon-holes : I never know whether a paper is in A or Z."

"I wish you would let me sort your papers for you, uncle," said Dorothea. "I would letter them all, and then make a list of subjects under each letter."

Mr Casaubon gravely smiled approval, and said to Mr Brooke, "You have an excellent secretary at hand, you perceive."

"No, no," said Mr Brooke, shaking his head ; "I cannot let young ladies meddle with my documents. Young ladies are too flighty."

Dorothea felt hurt. Mr Casaubon would think that her uncle had some special reason for delivering this opinion, whereas the remark lay in his mind as lightly as the broken wing of an insect among all the other fragments there, and a chance current had sent it alighting on *her*.

When the two girls were in the drawing-room alone, Celia said—

"How very ugly Mr Casaubon is !"

"Celia ! He is one of the most distinguished-looking men I ever saw. He is remarkably like the portrait of Locke. He has the same deep eye-sockets."

"Had Locke those two white moles with hairs on them ?"

"Oh, I daresay ! when people of a certain sort looked at him," said Dorothea, walking away a little.

"Mr Casaubon is so sallow."

"All the better. I suppose you admire a man with the complexion of a *cochon de lait*." [7]

"Dodo !" exclaimed Celia, looking after her in surprise. "I never heard you make such a comparison before."

"Why should I make it before the occasion came ? It is a good comparison : the match is perfect."

Miss Brooke was clearly forgetting herself, and Celia thought so.

"I wonder you show temper, Dorothea."

"It is so painful in you, Celia, that you will look at human beings as if they were merely animals with a toilette, and never see the great soul in a man's face."

"Has Mr Casaubon a great soul ?" Celia was not without a touch of naïve malice.

"Yes, I believe he has," said Dorothea, with the full voice of decision. "Everything I see in him corresponds to his pamphlet on Biblical Cosmology."

"He talks very little," said Celia.

"There is no one for him to talk to."

Celia thought privately, "Dorothea quite despises Sir James Chettam ; I believe she would not accept him." Celia felt that this was a pity. She had never been deceived as to the object of the baronet's interest. Sometimes, indeed, she had reflected that Dodo would

---

7. Suckling pig.

perhaps not make a husband happy who had not her way of looking at things ; and stifled in the depths of her heart was the feeling that her sister was too religious for family comfort. Notions and scruples were like spilt needles, making one afraid of treading, or sitting down, or even eating.

When Miss Brooke was at the tea-table, Sir James came to sit down by her, not having felt her mode of answering him at all offensive. Why should he ? He thought it probable that Miss Brooke liked him, and manners must be very marked indeed before they cease to be interpreted by preconceptions either confident or distrustful. She was thoroughly charming to him, but of course he theorised a little about his attachment. He was made of excellent human dough, and had the rare merit of knowing that his talents, even if let loose, would not set the smallest stream in the county on fire : hence he liked the prospect of a wife to whom he could say, " What shall we do ? " about this or that ; who could help her husband out with reasons, and would also have the property qualification for doing so. As to the excessive religiousness alleged against Miss Brooke, he had a very indefinite notion of what it consisted in, and thought that it would die out with marriage. In short, he felt himself to be in love in the right place, and was ready to endure a great deal of predominance, which, after all, a man could always put down when he liked. Sir James had no idea that he should ever like to put down the predominance of this handsome girl, in whose cleverness he delighted. Why not ? A man's mind—what there is of it—has always the advantage of being masculine,—as the smallest birch-tree is of a higher kind than the most soaring palm,—and even his ignorance is of a sounder quality. Sir James might not have originated this estimate ; but a kind Providence furnishes the limpest personality with a little gum or starch in the form of tradition.

" Let me hope that you will rescind that resolution about the horse, Miss Brooke," said the persevering admirer. " I assure you, riding is the most healthy of exercises."

" I am aware of it," said Dorothea, coldly. " I think it would do Celia good—if she would take to it."

" But you are such a perfect horsewoman."

" Excuse me ; I have had very little practice, and I should be easily thrown."

" Then that is a reason for more practice. Every lady ought to be a perfect horsewoman, that she may accompany her husband."

" You see how widely we differ, Sir James. I have made up my mind that I ought not to be a perfect horsewoman, and so I should never correspond to your pattern of a lady." Dorothea looked straight before her, and spoke with cold brusquerie, very much with the air of a handsome boy, in amusing contrast with the solicitous amiability of her admirer.

" I should like to know your reasons for this cruel resolution. It is not possible that you should think horsemanship wrong."

" It is quite possible that I should think it wrong for me."

" Oh, why ? " said Sir James, in a tender tone of remonstrance.

Mr Casaubon had come up to the table, tea-cup in hand, and was listening.

"We must not inquire too curiously into motives," he interposed, in his measured way. "Miss Brooke knows that they are apt to become feeble in the utterance : the aroma is mixed with the grosser air. We must keep the germinating grain away from the light."

Dorothea coloured with pleasure, and looked up gratefully to the speaker. Here was a man who could understand the higher inward life, and with whom there could be some spiritual communion ; nay, who could illuminate principle with the widest knowledge : a man whose learning almost amounted to a proof of whatever he believed !

Dorothea's inferences may seem large ; but really life could never have gone on at any period but for this liberal allowance of conclusions, which has facilitated marriage under the difficulties of civilisation. Has any one ever pinched into its pilulous smallness the cobweb of pre-matrimonial acquaintanceship ?

"Certainly," said good Sir James. "Miss Brooke shall not be urged to tell reasons she would rather be silent upon. I am sure her reasons would do her honour."

He was not in the least jealous of the interest with which Dorothea had looked up at Mr Casaubon : it never occurred to him that a girl to whom he was meditating an offer of marriage could care for a dried bookworm towards fifty, except, indeed, in a religious sort of way, as for a clergyman of some distinction.

However, since Miss Brooke had become engaged in a conversation with Mr Casaubon about the Vaudois clergy, Sir James betook himself to Celia, and talked to her about her sister ; spoke of a house in town, and asked whether Miss Brooke disliked London. Away from her sister, Celia talked quite easily, and Sir James said to himself that the second Miss Brooke was certainly very agreeable as well as pretty, though not, as some people pretended, more clever and sensible than the elder sister. He felt that he had chosen the one who was in all respects the superior ; and a man naturally likes to look forward to having the best. He would be the very Mawworm of bachelors who pretended not to expect it. [8]

CHAPTER III.

"Say, goddess, what ensued, when Raphaël,
The affable archangel . . .
                                    Eve
The story heard attentive, and was filled
With admiration, and deep muse, to hear
Of things so high and strange."
—*Paradise Lost*, B. vii.

IF it had really occurred to Mr Casaubon to think of Miss Brooke as a suitable wife for him, the reasons that might induce her to accept him were already planted in her mind, and by the evening of the

8. Mawworm: the pious hypocrite in Isaac Bickerstaffe's play *The Hypocrite* (1769).

next day the reasons had budded and bloomed. For they had had a long conversation in the morning, while Celia, who did not like the company of Mr Casaubon's moles and sallowness, had escaped to the vicarage to play with the curate's ill-shod but merry children.

Dorothea by this time had looked deep into the ungauged reservoir of Mr Casaubon's mind, seeing reflected there in vague labyrinthine extension every quality she herself brought ; had opened much of her own experience to him, and had understood from him the scope of his great work, also of attractively labyrinthine extent. For he had been as instructive as Milton's " affable archangel ; " and with something of the archangelic manner he told her how he had undertaken to show (what indeed had been attempted before, but not with that thoroughness, justice of comparison, and effectiveness of arrangement at which Mr Casaubon aimed) that all the mythical systems or erratic mythical fragments in the world were corruptions of a tradition originally revealed. Having once mastered the true position and taken a firm footing there, the vast field of mythical constructions became intelligible, nay, luminous with the reflected light of correspondences. But to gather in this great harvest of truth was no light or speedy work. His notes already made a formidable range of volumes, but the crowning task would be to condense these voluminous still-accumulating results and bring them, like the earlier vintage of Hippocratic books, to fit a little shelf. In explaining this to Dorothea, Mr Casaubon expressed himself nearly as he would have done to a fellow-student, for he had not two styles of talking at command : it is true that when he used a Greek or Latin phrase he always gave the English with scrupulous care, but he would probably have done this in any case. A learned provincial clergyman is accustomed to think of his acquaintances as of " lords, knyghtes, and other noble and worthi men, that conne Latyn but lytille."[1]

Dorothea was altogether captivated by the wide embrace of this conception. Here was something beyond the shallows of ladies'-school literature : here was a living Bossuet, whose work would reconcile complete knowledge with devoted piety ; here was a modern Augustine who united the glories of doctor and saint.[2]

The sanctity seemed no less clearly marked than the learning, for when Dorothea was impelled to open her mind on certain themes which she could speak of to no one whom she had before seen at Tipton, especially on the secondary importance of ecclesiastical forms and articles of belief compared with that spiritual religion, that submergence of self in communion with Divine perfection which seemed to her to be expressed in the best Christian books of widely-distant ages, she found in Mr Casaubon a listener who understood her at once, who could assure her of his own agreement with that view when duly tempered with wise conformity, and could mention historical examples before unknown to her.

1. Sir John Mandeville (d. 1372), *Mandeville's Travels*, Prologue. The original—with a sense opposite to GE's quotation—reads: "But lordes & knyghtes & othere noble & worthi men that conne not latyn but lityll & han ben beyonde the see knowen & understonden yif I seye throute or non."
2. Jacques Bènigne Bossuet (1627–1704), French bishop, writer, and famous preacher.

" He thinks with me," said Dorothea to herself, " or rather, he thinks a whole world of which my thought is but a poor twopenny mirror. And his feelings too, his whole experience—what a lake compared with my little pool ! "

Miss Brooke argued from words and dispositions not less unhesitatingly than other young ladies of her age. Signs are small measurable things, but interpretations are illimitable, and in girls of sweet, ardent nature, every sign is apt to conjure up wonder, hope, belief, vast as a sky, and coloured by a diffused thimbleful of matter in the shape of knowledge. They are not always too grossly deceived ; for Sinbad himself may have fallen by good-luck on a true description, and wrong reasoning sometimes lands poor mortals in right conclusions : starting a long way off the true point, and proceeding by loops and zigzags, we now and then arrive just where we ought to be. Because Miss Brooke was hasty in her trust, it is not therefore clear that Mr Casaubon was unworthy of it.

He stayed a little longer than he had intended, on a slight pressure of invitation from Mr Brooke, who offered no bait except his own documents on machine-breaking and rick-burning.[3] Mr Casaubon was called into the library to look at these in a heap, while his host picked up first one and then the other to read aloud from in a skipping and uncertain way, passing from one unfinished passage to another with a " Yes, now, but here ! " and finally pushing them all aside to open the journal of his youthful Continental travels.

" Look here—here is all about Greece. Rhamnus, the ruins of Rhamnus—you are a great Grecian, now.[4] I don't know whether you have given much study to the topography. I spent no end of time in making out these things—Helicon, now. Here, now !—' We started the next morning for Parnassus, the double-peaked Parnassus.'[5] All this volume is about Greece, you know," Mr Brooke wound up, rubbing his thumb transversely along the edges of the leaves as he held the book forward.

Mr Casaubon made a dignified though somewhat sad audience ; bowed in the right place, and avoided looking at anything documentary as far as possible, without showing disregard or impatience ; mindful that this desultoriness was associated with the institutions of the country, and that the man who took him on this severe mental scamper was not only an amiable host, but a landholder and *custos rotulorum.*[6] Was his endurance aided also by the reflection that Mr Brooke was the uncle of Dorothea ?

Certainly he seemed more and more bent on making her talk to him, on drawing her out, as Celia remarked to herself ; and in looking at her, his face was often lit up by a smile like pale wintry sunshine. Before he left the next morning, while taking a pleasant walk with Miss Brooke along the gravelled terrace, he had mentioned to

3. Between 1811 and the time of the novel rebellious laborers had on several occasions broken up their machines in factories, and protesting tenant farmers had burned the grain they had stacked into ricks. There were serious riots of this sort in the autumn of 1830.

4. Site of two sixth century B.C. temples, to Nemesis and Themis.
5. Mountain in central Greece, sacred to the Muses.
6. A justice of the peace, who has custody of the rolls and records of the County Sessions.

her that he felt the disadvantage of loneliness, the need of that cheerful companionship with which the presence of youth can lighten or vary the serious toils of maturity. And he delivered this statement with as much careful precision as if he had been a diplomatic envoy whose words would be attended with results. Indeed, Mr Casaubon was not used to expect that he should have to repeat or revise his communications of a practical or personal kind. The inclinations which he had deliberately stated on the 2d of October he would think it enough to refer to by the mention of that date ; judging by the standard of his own memory, which was a volume where a *vide supra* could serve instead of repetitions, and not the ordinary long-used blotting-book which only tells of forgotten writing. But in this case Mr Casaubon's confidence was not likely to be falsified, for Dorothea heard and retained what he said with the eager interest of a fresh young nature to which every variety in experience is an epoch.

It was three o'clock in the beautiful breezy autumn day when Mr Casaubon drove off to his Rectory at Lowick, only five miles from Tipton ; and Dorothea, who had on her bonnet and shawl, hurried along the shrubbery and across the park that she might wander through the bordering wood with no other visible companionship than that of Monk, the Great St Bernard dog, who always took care of the young ladies in their walks. There had risen before her the girl's vision of a possible future for herself to which she looked forward with trembling hope, and she wanted to wander on in that visionary future without interruption. She walked briskly in the brisk air, the colour rose in her cheeks, and her straw-bonnet (which our contemporaries might look at with conjectural curiosity as at an obsolete form of basket) fell a little backward. She would perhaps be hardly characterised enough if it were omitted that she wore her brown hair flatly braided and coiled behind so as to expose the outline of her head in a daring manner at a time when public feeling required the meagreness of nature to be dissimulated by tall barricades of frizzed curls and bows, never surpassed by any great race except the Feejeean.[7] This was a trait of Miss Brooke's asceticism. But there was nothing of an ascetic's expression in her bright full eyes, as she looked before her, not consciously seeing, but absorbing into the intensity of her mood, the solemn glory of the afternoon with its long swathes of light between the far-off rows of limes, whose shadows touched each other.

All people, young or old (that is, all people in those ante-reform times), would have thought her an interesting object if they had referred the glow in her eyes and cheeks to the newly-awakened ordinary images of young love : the illusions of Chloe about Strephon have been sufficiently consecrated in poetry, as the pathetic loveliness of all spontaneous trust ought to be.[8] Miss Pippin adoring young Pumpkin and dreaming along endless vistas of unwearying companionship, was a little drama which never tired our fathers and mothers, and had been put into all costumes. Let but Pumpkin have

7. The inhabitants of the Fiji Islands bleached their hair, and wore it in an elaborately trained mop. Captain Cook was the first European to visit the is- lands, on his Pacific voyage in 1772–75.
8. Chloe and Strephon: conventional names for young lovers in poetry.

a figure which would sustain the disadvantages of the short-waisted swallow-tail, and everybody felt it not only natural but necessary to the perfection of womanhood, that a sweet girl should be at once convinced of his virtue, his exceptional ability, and above all, his perfect sincerity. But perhaps no persons then living—certainly none in the neighbourhood of Tipton—would have had a sympathetic understanding for the dreams of a girl whose notions about marriage took their colour entirely from an exalted enthusiasm about the ends of life, an enthusiasm which was lit chiefly by its own fire, and included neither the niceties of the *trousseau*, the pattern of plate, nor even the honours and sweet joys of the blooming matron.

It had now entered Dorothea's mind that Mr Casaubon might wish to make her his wife, and the idea that he would do so touched her with a sort of reverential gratitude. How good of him — nay, it would be almost as if a winged messenger had suddenly stood beside her path and held out his hand towards her ! For a long while she had been oppressed by the indefiniteness which hung in her mind, like a thick summer haze, over all her desire to make her life greatly effective. What could she do, what ought she to do ?—she, hardly more than a budding woman, but yet with an active conscience and a great mental need, not to be satisfied by a girlish instruction comparable to the nibblings and judgments of a discursive mouse. With some endowment of stupidity and conceit, she might have thought that a Christian young lady of fortune should find her ideal of life in village charities, patronage of the humbler clergy, the perusal of ' Female Scripture Characters,' unfolding the private experience of Sara under the Old Dispensation, and Dorcas under the New, and the care of her soul over her embroidery in her own boudoir—with a background of prospective marriage to a man who, if less strict than herself, as being involved in affairs religiously inexplicable, might be prayed for and seasonably exhorted.[9] From such contentment poor Dorothea was shut out. The intensity of her religious disposition, the coercion it exercised over her life, was but one aspect of a nature altogether ardent, theoretic, and intellectually consequent : and with such a nature, struggling in the bands of a narrow teaching, hemmed in by a social life which seemed nothing but a labyrinth of petty courses, a walled-in maze of small paths that led no whither, the outcome was sure to strike others as at once exaggeration and inconsistency. The thing which seemed to her best, she wanted to justify by the completest knowledge ; and not to live in a pretended admission of rules which were never acted on. Into this soul-hunger as yet all her youthful passion was poured ; the union which attracted her was one that would deliver her from her girlish subjection to her own ignorance, and give her the freedom of voluntary submission to a guide who would take her along the grandest path.

" I should learn everything then," she said to herself, still walking quickly along the bridle road through the wood. " It would be my duty to study that I might help him the better in his great works.

---

9. *Female Scripture Characters:* a book by Mrs. F. E. King, published in 1813. Sara was the wife of Abraham and the mother of Isaac (Gen. 9); Dorcas was a woman "full of good works and almsdeeds which she did" (Acts 9:36).

There would be nothing trivial about our lives. Everyday-things with us would mean the greatest things. It would be like marrying Pascal. I should learn to see the truth by the same light as great men have seen it by. And then I should know what to do, when I got older : I should see how it was possible to lead a grand life here —now—in England. I don't feel sure about doing good in any way now : everything seems like going on a mission to a people whose language I don't know ;—unless it were building good cottages—there can be no doubt about that. Oh, I hope I should be able to get the people well housed in Lowick ! I will draw plenty of plans while I have time."

Dorothea checked herself suddenly with self-rebuke for the presumptuous way in which she was reckoning on uncertain events, but she was spared any inward effort to change the direction of her thoughts by the appearance of a cantering horseman round a turning of the road. The well-groomed chestnut horse and two beautiful setters could leave no doubt that the rider was Sir James Chettam. He discerned Dorothea, jumped off his horse at once, and, having delivered it to his groom, advanced towards her with something white on his arm, at which the two setters were barking in an excited manner.

" How delightful to meet you, Miss Brooke," he said, raising his hat and showing his sleekly-waving blond hair. " It has hastened the pleasure I was looking forward to."

Miss Brooke was annoyed at the interruption. This amiable baronet, really a suitable husband for Celia, exaggerated the necessity of making himself agreeable to the elder sister. Even a prospective brother-in-law may be an oppression if he will always be presupposing too good an understanding with you, and agreeing with you even when you contradict him. The thought that he had made the mistake of paying his addresses to herself could not take shape : all her mental activity was used up in persuasions of another kind. But he was positively obtrusive at this moment, and his dimpled hands were quite disagreeable. Her roused temper made her colour deeply, as she returned his greeting with some haughtiness.

Sir James interpreted the heightened colour in the way most gratifying to himself, and thought he never saw Miss Brooke looking so handsome.

" I have brought a little petitioner," he said, " or rather, I have brought him to see if he will be approved before his petition is offered." He showed the white object under his arm, which was a tiny Maltese puppy, one of nature's most naïve toys.

" It is painful to me to see these creatures that are bred merely as pets," said Dorothea, whose opinion was forming itself that very moment (as opinions will) under the heat of irritation.

" Oh, why ? " said Sir James, as they walked forward.

" I believe all the petting that is given them does not make them happy. They are too helpless : their lives are too frail. A weasel or a mouse that gets its own living is more interesting. I like to think that the animals about us have souls something like our own, and either carry on their own little affairs or can be companions to us, like Monk here. Those creatures are parasitic."

" I am so glad I know that you do not like them," said good Sir James. " I should never keep them for myself, but ladies usually are fond of these Maltese dogs. Here, John, take this dog, will you ?"

The objectionable puppy, whose nose and eyes were equally black and expressive, was thus got rid of, since Miss Brooke decided that it had better not have been born. But she felt it necessary to explain.

" You must not judge of Celia's feeling from mine. I think she likes these small pets. She had a tiny terrier once, which she was very fond of. It made me unhappy, because I was afraid of treading on it. I am rather short-sighted."

" You have your own opinion about everything, Miss Brooke, and it is always a good opinion."

What answer was possible to such stupid complimenting ?

" Do you know, I envy you that," Sir James said, as they continued walking at the rather brisk pace set by Dorothea.

" I don't quite understand what you mean."

" Your power of forming an opinion. I can form an opinion of persons. I know when I like people. But about other matters, do you know, I have often a difficulty in deciding. One hears very sensible things said on opposite sides."

" Or that seem sensible. Perhaps we don't always discriminate between sense and nonsense."

Dorothea felt that she was rather rude.

" Exactly," said Sir James. " But you seem to have the power of discrimination."

" On the contrary, I am often unable to decide. But that is from ignorance. The right conclusion is there all the same, though I am unable to see it."

" I think there are few who would see it more readily. Do you know, Lovegood was telling me yesterday that you had the best notion in the world of a plan for cottages—quite wonderful for a young lady, he thought. You had a real *genus*, to use his expression. He said you wanted Mr Brooke to build a new set of cottages, but he seemed to think it hardly probable that your uncle would consent. Do you know, that is one of the things I wish to do—I mean, on my own estate. I should be so glad to carry out that plan of yours, if you would let me see it. Of course, it is sinking money ; that is why people object to it. Labourers can never pay rent to make it answer. But, after all, it is worth doing."

" Worth doing ! yes, indeed," said Dorothea, energetically, forgetting her previous small vexations. " I think we deserve to be beaten out of our beautiful houses with a scourge of small cords—all of us who let tenants live in such sties as we see round us. Life in cottages might be happier than ours, if they were real houses fit for human beings from whom we expect duties and affections."

" Will you show me your plan ?"

" Yes, certainly. I daresay it is very faulty. But I have been examining all the plans for cottages in Loudon's book, and picked out what seem the best things. [1] Oh what a happiness it would be to

<hr/>

1. John C. Loudon (1783–1843), distinguished and prolific naturalist scholar. The reference is probably to Loudon's *Observations on Laying Out Farms . . . illustrated by forty plates, descriptive of farm buildings, rural improvements, etc.* (1812). *A Manual for Cottage Gardening, Husbandry, and Agriculture* (1830), also illustrated with plans and designs, was not yet published at the time of Dorothea's conversation.

set the pattern about here ! I think, instead of Lazarus at the gate, we should put the pig-sty cottages outside the park-gate." [2]

Dorothea was in the best temper now. Sir James, as brother-in-law, building model cottages on his estate, and then, perhaps, others being built at Lowick, and more and more elsewhere in imitation— it would be as if the spirit of Oberlin had passed over the parishes to make the life of poverty beautiful ! [3]

Sir James saw all the plans, and took one away to consult upon with Lovegood. He also took away a complacent sense that he was making great progress in Miss Brooke's good opinion. The Maltese puppy was not offered to Celia ; an omission which Dorothea afterwards thought of with surprise ; but she blamed herself for it. She had been engrossing Sir James. After all, it was a relief that there was no puppy to tread upon.

Celia was present while the plans were being examined, and observed Sir James's illusion. " He thinks that Dodo cares about him, and she only cares about her plans. Yet I am not certain that she would refuse him if she thought he would let her manage everything and carry out all her notions. And how very uncomfortable Sir James would be ! I cannot bear notions."

It was Celia's private luxury to indulge in this dislike. She dared not confess it to her sister in any direct statement, for that would be laying herself open to a demonstration that she was somehow or other at war with all goodness. But on safe opportunities, she had an indirect mode of making her negative wisdom tell upon Dorothea, and calling her down from her rhapsodic mood by reminding her that people were staring, not listening. Celia was not impulsive : what she had to say could wait, and came from her always with the same quiet, staccato evenness. When people talked with energy and emphasis she watched their faces and features merely. She never could understand how well-bred persons consented to sing and open their mouths in the ridiculous manner requisite for that vocal exercise.

It was not many days before Mr Casaubon paid a morning visit, on which he was invited again for the following week to dine and stay the night. Thus Dorothea had three more conversations with him, and was convinced that her first impressions had been just. He was all she had at first imagined him to be : almost everything he had said seemed like a specimen from a mine, or the inscription on the door of a museum which might open on the treasures of past ages ; and this trust in his mental wealth was all the deeper and more effective on her inclination because it was now obvious that his visits were made for her sake. This accomplished man condescended to think of a young girl, and take the pains to talk to her, not with absurd compliment, but with an appeal to her understanding, and sometimes with instructive correction. What delightful companionship ! Mr Casaubon seemed even unconscious that trivialities existed, and never handed round that small-talk of heavy men which is as acceptable as stale bride-cake brought forth with an odour of

2. The beggar Lazarus lay at the gate of the rich man; when he died he went to heaven, but the rich man went to hell (Luke 16:20–31).

3. Johann Friedrich Oberlin (1740–1826), Alsatian Lutheran pastor and philanthropist who devoted his life to transforming his poverty-ridden parish into a wholesome and prosperous community.

cup-board. He talked of what he was interested in, or else he was silent and bowed with sad civility. To Dorothea this was adorable genuineness, and religious abstinence from that artificiality which uses up the soul in the efforts of pretence. For she looked as reverently at Mr Casaubon's religious elevation above herself as she did at his intellect and learning. He assented to her expressions of devout feeling, and usually with an appropriate quotation ; he allowed himself to say that he had gone through some spiritual conflicts in his youth ; in short, Dorothea saw that here she might reckon on understanding, sympathy, and guidance. On one—only one—of her favourite themes she was disappointed. Mr Casaubon apparently did not care about building cottages, and diverted the talk to the extremely narrow accommodation which was to be had in the dwellings of the ancient Egyptians, as if to check a too high standard. After he was gone, Dorothea dwelt with some agitation on this indifference of his ; and her mind was much exercised with arguments drawn from the varying conditions of climate which modify human needs, and from the admitted wickedness of pagan despots. Should she not urge these arguments on Mr Casaubon when he came again ? But further reflection told her that she was presumptuous in demanding his attention to such a subject ; he would not disapprove of her occupying herself with it in leisure moments, as other women expected to occupy themselves with their dress and embroidery—would not forbid it when—— Dorothea felt rather ashamed as she detected herself in these speculations. But her uncle had been invited to go to Lowick to stay a couple of days : was it reasonable to suppose that Mr Casaubon delighted in Mr Brooke's society for its own sake, either with or without documents ?

Meanwhile that little disappointment made her delight the more in Sir James Chettam's readiness to set on foot the desired improvements. He came much oftener than Mr Casaubon, and Dorothea ceased to find him disagreeable since he showed himself so entirely in earnest ; for he had already entered with much practical ability into Lovegood's estimates, and was charmingly docile. She proposed to build a couple of cottages, and transfer two families from their old cabins, which could then be pulled down, so that new ones could be built on the old sites. Sir James said, " Exactly," and she bore the word remarkably well.

Certainly these men who had so few spontaneous ideas might be very useful members of society under good feminine direction, if they were fortunate in choosing their sisters-in-law ! It is difficult to say whether there was or was not a little wilfulness in her continuing blind to the possibility that another sort of choice was in question in relation to her. But her life was just now full of hope and action : she was not only thinking of her plans, but getting down learned books from the library and reading many things hastily (that she might be a little less ignorant in talking to Mr Casaubon), all the while being visited with conscientious questionings whether she were not exalting these poor doings above measure and contemplating them with that self-satisfaction which was the last doom of ignorance and folly.

CHAPTER IV.

"1st Gent. Our deeds are fetters that we forge ourselves.
  2d Gent. Ay, truly : but I think it is the world
        That brings the iron." 1

" SIR JAMES seems determined to do everything you wish," said
Celia, as they were driving home from an inspection of the new
building-site.

" He is a good creature, and more sensible than any one would
imagine," said Dorothea, inconsiderately.

" You mean that he appears silly."

" No, no," said Dorothea, recollecting herself, and laying her hand
on her sister's a moment, " but he does not talk equally well on all
subjects."

" I should think none but disagreeable people do," said Celia, in her
usual purring way. " They must be very dreadful to live with.
Only think ! at breakfast, and always."

Dorothea laughed. " O Kitty, you are a wonderful creature !"
She pinched Celia's chin, being in the mood now to think her very
winning and lovely—fit hereafter to be an eternal cherub, and if it
were not doctrinally wrong to say so, hardly more in need of salvation
than a squirrel. " Of course people need not be always talking well.
Only one tells the quality of their minds when they try to talk well."

" You mean that Sir James tries and fails."

" I was speaking generally. Why do you catechise me about Sir
James ? It is not the object of his life to please me."

" Now, Dodo, can you really believe that ? "

" Certainly. He thinks of me as a future sister—that is all."
Dorothea had never hinted this before, waiting, from a certain shyness
on such subjects which was mutual between the sisters, until it should
be introduced by some decisive event. Celia blushed, but said at
once—

" Pray do not make that mistake any longer, Dodo. When Tantripp was brushing my hair the other day, she said that Sir James's
man knew from Mrs Cadwallader's maid that Sir James was to marry
the eldest Miss Brooke."

" How can you let Tantripp talk such gossip to you, Celia ? " said
Dorothea, indignantly, not the less angry because details asleep in her
memory were now awakened to confirm the unwelcome revelation.
" You must have asked her questions. It is degrading."

" I see no harm at all in Tantripp's talking to me. It is better to
hear what people say. You see what mistakes you make by taking
up notions. I am quite sure that Sir James means to make you an

---

1. Epigraphs otherwise unidentified are
GE's own compositions. Many of them
were written in a manuscript notebook,
now in the Yale University Library. See
Bernard J. Paris, "George Eliot's Unpublished Poetry," *Studies in Philology,*
56 (1959), 539–59, for a description of
the contents of this notebook.

offer ; and he believes that you will accept him, especially since you have been so pleased with him about the plans. And uncle too—I know he expects it. Every one can see that Sir James is very much in love with you."

The revulsion was so strong and painful in Dorothea's mind that the tears welled up and flowed abundantly. All her dear plans were embittered, and she thought with disgust of Sir James's conceiving that she recognised him as her lover. There was vexation too on account of Celia.

" How could he expect it ? " she burst forth in her most impetuous manner. " I have never agreed with him about anything but the cottages : I was barely polite to him before."

" But you have been so pleased with him since then ; he has begun to feel quite sure that you are fond of him."

" Fond of him, Celia ! How can you choose such odious expressions ? " said Dorothea, passionately.

" Dear me, Dorothea, I suppose it would be right for you to be fond of a man whom you accepted for a husband."

" It is offensive to me to say that Sir James could think I was fond of him. Besides, it is not the right word for the feeling I must have towards the man I would accept as a husband."

" Well, I am sorry for Sir James. I thought it right to tell you, because you went on as you always do, never looking just where you are, and treading in the wrong place. You always see what nobody else sees ; it is impossible to satisfy you ; yet you never see what is quite plain. That's your way, Dodo." Something certainly gave Celia unusual courage ; and she was not sparing the sister of whom she was occasionally in awe. Who can tell what just criticisms Murr the Cat may be passing on us beings of wider speculation ?

" It is very painful," said Dorothea, feeling scourged. " I can have no more to do with the cottages. I must be uncivil to him. I must tell him I will have nothing to do with them. It is very painful." Her eyes filled again with tears.

" Wait a little. Think about it. You know he is going away for a day or two to see his sister. There will be nobody besides Lovegood." Celia could not help relenting. " Poor Dodo," she went on, in an amiable staccato. " It is very hard : it is your favourite *fad* to draw plans."

" *Fad* to draw plans ! Do you think I only care about my fellow-creatures' houses in that childish way ? I may well make mistakes. How can one ever do anything nobly Christian, living among people with such petty thoughts ? "

No more was said : Dorothea was too much jarred to recover her temper and behave so as to show that she admitted any error in herself. She was disposed rather to accuse the intolerable narrowness and the purblind conscience of the society around her : and Celia was no longer the eternal cherub, but a thorn in her spirit, a pink-and-white nullifidian,[2] worse than any discouraging presence in the ' Pilgrim's Progress.' The *fad* of drawing plans ! What was life worth—what great faith was possible when the whole effect of one's actions could be withered up into such parched rubbish as that ? When she got out of the carriage, her cheeks were pale and her eye-

2. Nullifidian: skeptic.

lids red. She was an image of sorrow, and her uncle who met her in the hall would have been alarmed, if Celia had not been close to her looking so pretty and composed, that he at once concluded Dorothea's tears to have their origin in her excessive religiousness. He had returned, during their absence, from a journey to the county town, about a petition for the pardon of some criminal.

"Well, my dears," he said, kindly, as they went up to kiss him, "I hope nothing disagreeable has happened while I have been away."

"No, uncle," said Celia, "we have been to Freshitt to look at the cottages. We thought you would have been at home to lunch."

"I came by Lowick to lunch—you didn't know I came by Lowick. And I have brought a couple of pamphlets for you, Dorothea—in the library, you know; they lie on the table in the library."

It seemed as if an electric stream went through Dorothea, thrilling her from despair into expectation. They were pamphlets about the early Church. The oppression of Celia, Tantripp, and Sir James was shaken off, and she walked straight to the library. Celia went up-stairs. Mr Brooke was detained by a message, but when he re-entered the library, he found Dorothea seated and already deep in one of the pamphlets which had some marginal manuscript of Mr Casaubon's,—taking it in as eagerly as she might have taken in the scent of a fresh bouquet after a dry, hot, dreary walk.

She was getting away from Tipton and Freshitt, and her own sad liability to tread in the wrong places on her way to the New Jerusalem.

Mr Brooke sat down in his arm-chair, stretched his legs towards the wood-fire, which had fallen into a wondrous mass of glowing dice between the dogs, and rubbed his hands gently, looking very mildly towards Dorothea, but with a neutral leisurely air, as if he had nothing particular to say. Dorothea closed her pamphlet, as soon as she was aware of her uncle's presence, and rose as if to go. Usually she would have been interested about her uncle's merciful errand on behalf of the criminal, but her late agitation had made her absent-minded.

"I came back by Lowick, you know," said Mr Brooke, not as if with any intention to arrest her departure, but apparently from his usual tendency to say what he had said before. This fundamental principle of human speech was markedly exhibited in Mr Brooke. "I lunched there and saw Casaubon's library, and that kind of thing. There's a sharp air, driving. Won't you sit down, my dear? You look cold."

Dorothea felt quite inclined to accept the invitation. Sometimes, when her uncle's easy way of taking things did not happen to be exasperating, it was rather soothing. She threw off her mantle and bonnet, and sat down opposite to him, enjoying the glow, but lifting up her beautiful hands for a screen. They were not thin hands, or small hands; but powerful, feminine, maternal hands. She seemed to be holding them up in propitiation for her passionate desire to know and to think, which in the unfriendly mediums of Tipton and Freshitt had issued in crying and red eyelids.

She bethought herself now of the condemned criminal. "What news have you brought about the sheep-stealer, uncle?"

"What, poor Bunch?—well, it seems we can't get him off—he is to be hanged."

Dorothea's brow took an expression of reprobation and pity.

" Hanged, you know," said Mr Brooke, with a quiet nod. " Poor Romilly ! he would have helped us. I knew Romilly. Casaubon didn't know Romilly.[3] He is a little buried in books, you know, Casaubon is."

" When a man has great studies and is writing a great work, he must of course give up seeing much of the world. How can he go about making acquaintances ? "

" That's true. But a man mopes, you know. I have always been a bachelor too, but I have that sort of disposition that I never moped ; it was my way to go about everywhere and take in everything. I never moped : but I can see that Casaubon does, you know. He wants a companion—a companion, you know."

" It would be a great honour to any one to be his companion," said Dorothea, energetically.

" You like him, eh ? " said Mr Brooke, without showing any surprise, or other emotion. " Well, now, I've known Casaubon ten years, ever since he came to Lowick. But I never got anything out of him—any ideas, you know. However, he is a tiptop man and may be a bishop—that kind of thing, you know, if Peel stays in.[4] And he has a very high opinion of you, my dear."

Dorothea could not speak.

" The fact is, he has a very high opinion indeed of you. And he speaks uncommonly well—does Casaubon. He has deferred to me, you not being of age. In short, I have promised to speak to you, though I told him I thought there was not much chance. I was bound to tell him that. I said, my niece is very young, and that kind of thing. But I didn't think it necessary to go into everything. However, the long and the short of it is, that he has asked my permission to make you an offer of marriage—of marriage, you know," said Mr Brooke, with his explanatory nod. " I thought it better to tell you, my dear."

No one could have detected any anxiety in Mr Brooke's manner, but he did really wish to know something of his niece's mind, that, if there were any need for advice, he might give it in time. What feeling he, as a magistrate who had taken in so many ideas, could make room for, was unmixedly kind. Since Dorothea did not speak immediately, he repeated, " I thought it better to tell you, my dear."

" Thank you, uncle," said Dorothea, in a clear unwavering tone. " I am very grateful to Mr Casaubon. If he makes me an offer, I shall accept him. I admire and honour him more than any man I ever saw."

Mr Brooke paused a little, and then said in a lingering low tone, " Ah ? . . . Well ! He is a good match in some respects. But now, Chettam is a good match. And our land lies together. I shall never interfere against your wishes, my dear. People should have their own way in marriage, and that sort of thing—up to a certain point, you know. I have always said that, up to a certain point. I wish you to marry well ; and I have good reason to believe that Chettam wishes to marry you. I mention it, you know."

3. Sir Samuel Romilly (1757–1818), English statesman who worked for the reform of criminal law and the penal code.
4. The government of Peel and the Duke of Wellington fell in 1830, largely as a result of their submission to O'Connell on the Catholic Question; see above, Chapter I, note 3.

"It is impossible that I should ever marry Sir James Chettam," said Dorothea. "If he thinks of marrying me, he has made a great mistake."

"That is it, you see. One never knows. I should have thought Chettam was just the sort of man a woman would like, now."

"Pray do not mention him in that light again, uncle," said Dorothea, feeling some of her late irritation revive.

Mr Brooke wondered, and felt that women were an inexhaustible subject of study, since even he at his age was not in a perfect state of scientific prediction about them. Here was a fellow like Chettam with no chance at all.

"Well, but Casaubon, now. There is no hurry—I mean for you. It's true, every year will tell upon him. He is over five-and-forty, you know. I should say a good seven-and-twenty years older than you. To be sure,—if you like learning and standing, and that sort of thing, we can't have everything. And his income is good—he has a handsome property independent of the Church—his income is good. Still he is not young, and I must not conceal from you, my dear, that I think his health is not over-strong. I know nothing else against him."

"I should not wish to have a husband very near my own age," said Dorothea, with grave decision. "I should wish to have a husband who was above me in judgment and in all knowledge."

Mr Brooke repeated his subdued, "Ah?—I thought you had more of your own opinion than most girls. I thought you liked your own opinion—liked it, you know."

"I cannot imagine myself living without some opinions, but I should wish to have good reasons for them, and a wise man could help me to see which opinions had the best foundation, and would help me to live according to them."

"Very true. You couldn't put the thing better—couldn't put it better, beforehand, you know. But there are oddities in things," continued Mr Brooke, whose conscience was really roused to do the best he could for his niece on this occasion. "Life isn't cast in a mould—not cut out by rule and line, and that sort of thing. I never married myself, and it will be the better for you and yours. The fact is, I never loved any one well enough to put myself into a noose for them. It *is* a noose, you know. Temper, now. There is temper. And a husband likes to be master."

"I know that I must expect trials, uncle. Marriage is a state of higher duties. I never thought of it as mere personal ease," said poor Dorothea.

"Well, you are not fond of show, a great establishment, balls, dinners, that kind of thing. I can see that Casaubon's ways might suit you better than Chettam's. And you shall do as you like, my dear. I would not hinder Casaubon; I said so at once; for there is no knowing how anything may turn out. You have not the same tastes as every young lady; and a clergyman and scholar—who may be a bishop—that kind of thing—may suit you better than Chettam. Chettam is a good fellow, a good sound-hearted fellow, you know; but he doesn't go much into ideas. I did, when I was his age. But Casaubon's eyes, now. I think he has hurt them a little with too much reading."

"I should be all the happier, uncle, the more room there was for me to help him," said Dorothea, ardently.

" You have quite made up your mind, I see. Well, my dear, the fact is, I have a letter for you in my pocket." Mr Brooke handed the letter to Dorothea, but as she rose to go away, he added, " There is not too much hurry, my dear. Think about it, you know."

When Dorothea had left him, he reflected that he had certainly spoken strongly : he had put the risks of marriage before her in a striking manner. It was his duty to do so. But as to pretending to be wise for young people,—no uncle, however much he had travelled in his youth, absorbed the new ideas, and dined with celebrities now deceased, could· pretend to judge what sort of marriage would turn out well for a young girl who preferred Casaubon to Chettam. In short, woman was a problem which, since Mr Brooke's mind felt blank before it, could be hardly less complicated than the revolutions of an irregular solid.

CHAPTER V.

"Hard students are commonly troubled with gowts, catarrhs, rheums, cachexia, bradypepsia, bad eyes, stone, and collick, crudities, oppilations, vertigo, winds, consumptions, and all such diseases as come by over-much sitting : they are most part lean, dry, ill-coloured . . . and all through immoderate pains and extraordinary studies. If you will not believe the truth of this, look upon great Tostatus and Thomas Aquainas' works ; and tell me whether those men took pains."—BURTON's *Anatomy of Melancholy,* P. I. s. 2.

THIS was Mr Casaubon's letter.

MY DEAR MISS BROOKE,—I have your guardian's permission to address you on a subject than which I have none more at heart. I am not, I trust, mistaken in the recognition of some deeper correspondence than that of date in the fact that a consciousness of need in my own life had arisen contemporaneously with the possibility of my becoming acquainted with you. For in the first hour of meeting you, I had an impression of your eminent and perhaps exclusive fitness to supply that need (connected, I may say, with such activity of the affections as even the preoccupations of a work too special to be abdicated could not uninterruptedly dissimulate) ; and each succeeding opportunity for observation has given the impression an added depth by convincing me more emphatically of that fitness which I had preconceived, and thus evoking more decisively those affections to which I have but now referred. Our conversations have, I think, made sufficiently clear to you the tenor of my life and purposes : a tenor unsuited, I am aware, to the commoner order of minds. But I have discerned in you an elevation of thought and a capability of devotedness, which I had hitherto not conceived to be compatible either with the early bloom of youth or with those graces of sex that may be said at once to win and to confer distinction when combined, as they notably are in you, with the mental qualities above indicated. It was, I confess, beyond my hope to meet with this rare combination of elements both solid and attractive, adapted to supply aid in graver labours and to cast a charm over vacant hours ; and but for the event of my introduction to you (which, let me again say, I trust not to be superficially coincident with foreshadowing needs, but providentially related thereto as stages towards the completion of a life's plan), I should presumably have gone on to the last without any attempt to lighten my solitariness by a matrimonial union.

Such, my dear Miss Brooke, is the accurate statement of my feelings ; and I rely on your kind indulgence in venturing now to ask you how far your own are of a nature to confirm my happy presentiment. To be accepted by you as your husband and the earthly guardian of your welfare, I should regard as the highest of providential gifts. In return I can at least offer you an affection hitherto unwasted, and the faithful consecration of a life which, however short in the sequel, has no backward pages whereon, if you choose to turn them, you will find records such as might justly cause you either bitterness or shame. I await the expression of your sentiments with an anxiety which it would be the part of wisdom (were it possible) to divert by a more arduous labour than usual. But in this order of experience I am still young, and in looking forward to an unfavourable possibility I cannot but feel that resignation to solitude will be more difficult after the temporary illumination of hope. In any case, I shall remain, yours with sincere devotion,

EDWARD CASAUBON.

Dorothea trembled while she read this letter ; then she fell on her knees, buried her face, and sobbed. She could not pray ; under the rush of solemn emotion in which thoughts became vague and images floated uncertainly, she could but cast herself, with a childlike sense of reclining, in the lap of a divine consciousness which sustained her own. She remained in that attitude till it was time to dress for dinner.

How could it occur to her to examine the letter, to look at it critically as a profession of love? Her whole soul was possessed by the fact that a fuller life was opening before her : she was a neophyte about to enter on a higher grade of initiation. She was going to have room for the energies which stirred uneasily under the dimness and pressure of her own ignorance and the petty peremptoriness of the world's habits.

Now she would be able to devote herself to large yet definite duties ; now she would be allowed to live continually in the light of a mind that she could reverence. This hope was not unmixed with the glow of proud delight—the joyous maiden surprise that she was chosen by the man whom her admiration had chosen. All Dorothea's passion was transfused through a mind struggling towards an ideal life ; the radiance of her transfigured girlhood fell on the first object that came within its level. The impetus with which inclination became resolution was heightened by those little events of the day which had roused her discontent with the actual conditions of her life.

After dinner, when Celia was playing an " air, with variations," a small kind of tinkling which symbolised the æsthetic part of the young ladies' education, Dorothea went up to her room to answer Mr Casaubon's letter. Why should she defer the answer? She wrote it over three times, not because she wished to change the wording, but because her hand was unusually uncertain, and she could not bear that Mr Casaubon should think her handwriting bad and illegible. She piqued herself on writing a hand in which each letter was distinguishable without any large range of conjecture, and she meant to make much use of this accomplishment, to save Mr Casaubon's eyes. Three times she wrote.

MY DEAR MR CASAUBON,—I am very grateful to you for loving me, and thinking me worthy to be your wife. I can look forward to no better happiness than that which would be one with yours. If I said more, it would only be the same thing written out at greater length, for I cannot now dwell on any other thought than that I may be through life, yours devotedly,

DOROTHEA BROOKE.

Later in the evening she followed her uncle into the library to give him the letter, that he might send it in the morning. He was surprised, but his surprise only issued in a few moments' silence, during which he pushed about various objects on his writing-table, and finally stood with his back to the fire, his glasses on his nose, looking at the address of Dorothea's letter.

" Have you thought enough about this, my dear ? " he said at last.

" There was no need to think long, uncle. I know of nothing to make me vacillate. If I changed my mind, it must be because of something important and entirely new to me."

" Ah !—then you have accepted him ? Then Chettam has no chance ? Has Chettam offended you — offended you, you know ? What is it you don't like in Chettam ? "

" There is nothing that I like in him," said Dorothea, rather impetuously.

Mr Brooke threw his head and shoulders backward as if some one had thrown a light missile at him. Dorothea immediately felt some self-rebuke, and said—

" I mean in the light of a husband. He is very kind, I think—really very good about the cottages. A well-meaning man."

" But you must have a scholar, and that sort of thing ? Well, it lies a little in our family. I had it myself—that love of knowledge, and going into everything—a little too much—it took me too far ; though that sort of thing doesn't often run in the female line ; or it runs underground like the rivers in Greece, you know—it comes out in the sons. Clever sons, clever mothers. I went a good deal into that, at one time. However, my dear, I have always said that people should do as they like in these things, up to a certain point. I couldn't, as your guardian, have consented to a bad match. But Casaubon stands well : his position is good. I am afraid Chettam will be hurt, though, and Mrs Cadwallader will blame me."

That evening, of course, Celia knew nothing of what had happened. She attributed Dorothea's abstracted manner, and the evidence of further crying since they had got home, to the temper she had been in about Sir James Chettam and the buildings, and was careful not to give further offence : having once said what she wanted to say, Celia had no disposition to recur to disagreeable subjects. It had been her nature when a child never to quarrel with any one—only to observe with wonder that they quarrelled with her, and looked like turkey-cocks ; whereupon she was ready to play at cat's cradle with them whenever they recovered themselves. And as to Dorothea, it had always been her way to find something wrong in her sister's words, though Celia inwardly protested that she always said just how

things were, and nothing else : she never did and never could put
words together out of her own head. But the best of Dodo was, that
she did not keep angry for long together. Now, though they had
hardly spoken to each other all the evening, yet when Celia put by
her work, intending to go to bed, a proceeding in which she was
always much the earlier, Dorothea, who was seated on a low stool,
unable to occupy herself except in meditation, said, with the musical
intonation which in moments of deep but quiet feeling made her
speech like a fine bit of recitative—

"Celia, dear, come and kiss me," holding her arms open as she
spoke.

Celia knelt down to get the right level and gave her little butter-
fly kiss, while Dorothea encircled her with gentle arms and pressed
her lips gravely on each cheek in turn.

"Don't sit up, Dodo, you are so pale to-night : go to bed soon," said
Celia, in a comfortable way, without any touch of pathos.

"No, dear, I am very, very happy," said Dorothea, fervently.

"So much the better," thought Celia. "But how strangely Dodo
goes from one extreme to the other."

The next day, at luncheon, the butler, handing something to Mr
Brooke, said, "Jonas is come back, sir, and has brought this letter."

Mr Brooke read the letter, and then, nodding toward Dorothea, said
"Casaubon, my dear : he will be here to dinner ; he didn't wait to
write more—didn't wait, you know."

It could not seem remarkable to Celia that a dinner guest should
be announced to her sister beforehand, but, her eyes following the
same direction as her uncle's, she was struck with the peculiar effect
of the announcement on Dorothea. It seemed as if something like
the reflection of a white sunlit wing had passed across her features,
ending in one of her rare blushes. For the first time it entered into
Celia's mind that there might be something more between Mr Casaubon and her sister than his delight in bookish talk and her delight in
listening. Hitherto she had classed the admiration for this "ugly"
and learned acquaintance with the admiration for Monsieur Liret at
Lausanne, also ugly and learned. Dorothea had never been tired of
listening to old Monsieur Liret when Celia's feet were as cold as
possible, and when it had really become dreadful to see the skin of his
bald head moving about. Why then should her enthusiasm not
extend to Mr Casaubon simply in the same way as to Monsieur Liret ?
And it seemed probable that all learned men had a sort of schoolmaster's view of young people.

But now Celia was really startled at the suspicion which had
darted into her mind. She was seldom taken by surprise in this way,
her marvellous quickness in observing a certain order of signs generally preparing her to expect such outward events as she had an interest
in. Not that she now imagined Mr Casaubon to be already an
accepted lover : she had only begun to feel disgust at the possibility
that anything in Dorothea's mind could tend towards such an issue.
Here was something really to vex her about Dodo : it was all very
well not to accept Sir James Chettam, but the idea of marrying Mr
Casaubon ! Celia felt a sort of shame mingled with a sense of the
ludicrous. But perhaps Dodo, if she were really bordering on such
an extravagance, might be turned away from it : experience had often
shown that her impressibility might be calculated on. The day was

damp, and they were not going to walk out, so they both went up to their sitting-room ; and there Celia observed that Dorothea, instead of settling down with her usual diligent interest to some occupation, simply leaned her elbow on an open book and looked out of the window at the great cedar silvered with the damp. She herself had taken up the making of a toy for the curate's children, and was not going to enter on any subject too precipitately.

Dorothea was in fact thinking that it was desirable for Celia to know of the momentous change in Mr Casaubon's position since he had last been in the house : it did not seem fair to leave her in ignorance of what would necessarily affect her attitude towards him ; but it was impossible not to shrink from telling her. Dorothea accused herself of some meanness in this timidity : it was always odious to her to have any small fears or contrivances about her actions, but at this moment she was seeking the highest aid possible that she might not dread the corrosiveness of Celia's pretty carnally-minded prose. Her reverie was broken, and the difficulty of decision banished, by Celia's small and rather guttural voice speaking in its usual tone, of a remark aside or a " by the by."

" Is any one else coming to dine besides Mr Casaubon ? "

" Not that I know of."

" I hope there is some one else. Then I shall not hear him eat his soup so."

" What is there remarkable about his soup-eating ? "

" Really, Dodo, can't you hear how he scrapes his spoon ? And he always blinks before he speaks. I don't know whether Locke blinked, but I'm sure I am sorry for those who sat opposite to him if he did."

" Celia," said Dorothea, with emphatic gravity, " pray don't make any more observations of that kind."

" Why not ? They are quite true," returned Celia, who had her reasons for persevering, though she was beginning to be a little afraid.

" Many things are true which only the commonest minds observe."

" Then I think the commonest minds must be rather useful. I think it is a pity Mr Casaubon's mother had not a commoner mind : she might have taught him better." Celia was inwardly frightened, and ready to run away, now she had hurled this light javelin.

Dorothea's feelings had gathered to an avalanche, and there could be no further preparation.

" It is right to tell you, Celia, that I am engaged to marry Mr Casaubon."

Perhaps Celia had never turned so pale before. The paper man she was making would have had his leg injured, but for her habitual care of whatever she held in her hands. She laid the fragile figure down at once, and sat perfectly still for a few moments. When she spoke there was a tear gathering.

" O Dodo, I hope you will be happy." Her sisterly tenderness could not but surmount other feelings at this moment, and her fears were the fears of affection.

Dorothea was still hurt and agitated.

" It is quite decided, then ? " said Celia, in an awed undertone. " And uncle knows ? "

" I have accepted Mr Casaubon's offer. My uncle brought me the letter that contained it ; he knew about it beforehand."

" I beg your pardon, if I have said anything to hurt you, Dodo," said Celia, with a slight sob. She never could have thought that she should feel as she did. There was something funereal in the whole affair, and Mr Casaubon seemed to be the officiating clergyman, about whom it would be indecent to make remarks.

"Never mind, Kitty, do not grieve. We should never admire the same people. I often offend in something of the same way ; I am apt to speak too strongly of those who don't please me."

In spite of this magnanimity Dorothea was still smarting : perhaps as much from Celia's subdued astonishment as from her small criticisms. Of course all the world round Tipton would be out of sympathy with this marriage. Dorothea knew of no one who thought as she did about life and its best objects.

Nevertheless before the evening was at an end she was very happy. In an hour's *tête-à-tête* with Mr Casaubon she talked to him with more freedom than she had ever felt before, even pouring out her joy at the thought of devoting herself to him, and of learning how she might best share and further all his great ends. Mr Casaubon was touched with an unknown delight (what man would not have been ?) at this childlike unrestrained ardour : he was not surprised (what lover would have been ?) that he should be the object of it.

"My dear young lady—Miss Brooke—Dorothea!" he said, pressing her hand between his hands, "this is a happiness greater than I had ever imagined to be in reserve for me. That I should ever meet with a mind and person so rich in the mingled graces which could render marriage desirable, was far indeed from my conception. You have all—nay, more than all—those qualities which I have ever regarded as the characteristic excellences of womanhood. The great charm of your sex is its capability of an ardent self-sacrificing affection, and herein we see its fitness to round and complete the existence of our own. Hitherto I have known few pleasures save of the severer kind : my satisfactions have been those of the solitary student. I have been little disposed to gather flowers that would wither in my hand, but now I shall pluck them with eagerness, to place them in your bosom."

No speech could have been more thoroughly honest in its intention: the frigid rhetoric at the end was as sincere as the bark of a dog, or the cawing of an amorous rook. Would it not be rash to conclude that there was no passion behind those sonnets to Delia which strike us as the thin music of a mandolin ? [1]

Dorothea's faith supplied all that Mr Casaubon's words seemed to leave unsaid : what believer sees a disturbing omission or infelicity ? The text, whether of prophet or of poet, expands for whatever we can put into it, and even his bad grammar is sublime.

"I am very ignorant—you will quite wonder at my ignorance," said Dorothea. "I have so many thoughts that may be quite mistaken ; and now I shall be able to tell them all to you, and ask you about them. But," she added, with rapid imagination of Mr Casaubon's probable feeling, "I will not trouble you too much ; only when you are inclined to listen to me. You must often be weary with the pursuit of subjects in your own track. I shall gain enough if you will take me with you there."

1. The sonnets to Delia were a collection by Samuel Daniel (1562 – 1619), published in 1592.

" How should I be able now to persevere in any path without your companionship ? " said Mr Casaubon, kissing her candid brow, and feeling that heaven had vouchsafed him a blessing in every way suited to his peculiar wants.   He was being unconsciously wrought upon by the charms of a nature which was entirely without hidden calculations either for immediate effects or for remoter ends.   It was this which made Dorothea so childlike, and, according to some judges, so stupid, with all her reputed cleverness ; as, for example, in the present case of throwing herself, metaphorically speaking, at Mr Casaubon's feet, and kissing his unfashionable shoe-ties as if he were a Protestant Pope.   She was not in the least teaching Mr Casaubon to ask if he were good enough for her, but merely asking herself anxiously how she could be good enough for Mr Casaubon.   Before he left the next day it had been decided that the marriage should take place within six weeks.   Why not ?   Mr Casaubon's house was ready.   It was not a parsonage, but a considerable mansion, with much land attached to it.   The parsonage was inhabited by the curate, who did all the duty except preaching the morning sermon.

CHAPTER VI.

" My lady's tongue is like the meadow blades,
    That cut you stroking them with idle hand.
    Nice cutting is her function : she divides
    With spiritual edge the millet-seed,
    And makes intangible savings."

As Mr Casaubon's carriage was passing out of the gateway, it arrested the entrance of a pony phaeton driven by a lady with a servant seated behind.   It was doubtful whether the recognition had been mutual, for Mr Casaubon was looking absently before him ; but the lady was quick-eyed, and threw a nod and a " how do you do ? " in the nick of time.   In spite of her shabby bonnet and very old Indian shawl, it was plain that the lodge-keeper regarded her as an important personage, from the low curtsy which was dropped on the entrance of the small phaeton.

" Well, Mrs Fitchett, how are your fowls laying now ? " said the high-coloured, dark-eyed lady, with the clearest chiselled utterance.

" Pretty well for laying, madam, but they've ta'en to eating their eggs : I've no peace o' mind with 'em at all."

" O the cannibals !   Better sell them cheap at once.   What will you sell them a couple ?   One can't eat fowls of a bad character at a high price."

" Well, madam, half-a-crown : I couldn't let 'em go, not under."

" Half-a-crown, these times !   Come now—for the Rector's chicken-broth on a Sunday.   He has consumed all ours that I can spare. You are half paid with the sermon, Mrs Fitchett, remember that. Take a pair of tumbler-pigeons for them—little beauties.   You must come and see them.   You have no tumblers among your pigeons."

" Well, madam, Master Fitchett shall go and see 'em after work. He's very hot on new sorts : to oblige *you*."

" Oblige me !   It will be the best bargain he ever made.   A pair of church pigeons for a couple of wicked Spanish fowls that eat their own eggs ! Don't you and Fitchett boast too much, that is all ! "

The phaeton was driven onwards with the last words, leaving Mrs Fitchett laughing and shaking her head slowly, with an interjectional " Sure*ly*, sure*ly* ! "—from which it might be inferred that she would have found the country-side somewhat duller if the Rector's lady had been less free-spoken and less of a skinflint. Indeed, both the farmers and labourers in the parishes of Freshitt and Tipton would have felt a sad lack of conversation but for the stories about what Mrs Cadwallader said and did : a lady of immeasurably high birth, descended, as it were, from unknown earls, dim as the crowd of heroic shades— who pleaded poverty, pared down prices, and cut jokes in the most companionable manner, though with a turn of tongue that let you know who she was. Such a lady gave a neighbourliness to both rank and religion, and mitigated the bitterness of uncommuted tithe.[1] A much more exemplary character with an infusion of sour dignity would not have furthered their comprehension of the Thirty-nine Articles, and would have been less socially uniting.[2]

Mr Brooke, seeing Mrs Cadwallader's merits from a different point of view, winced a little when her name was announced in the library, where he was sitting alone.

" I see you have had our Lowick Cicero here," she said, seating herself comfortably, throwing back her wraps, and showing a thin but well-built figure. " I suspect you and he are brewing some bad politics, else you would not be seeing so much of the lively man. I shall inform against you : remember you are both suspicious characters since you took Peel's side about the Catholic Bill. I shall tell everybody that you are going to put up for Middlemarch on the Whig side when old Pinkerton resigns, and that Casaubon is going to help you in an underhand manner : going to bribe the voters with pamphlets, and throw open the public-houses to distribute them. Come, confess ! "

" Nothing of the sort," said Mr Brooke, smiling and rubbing his eye-glasses, but really blushing a little at the impeachment. " Casaubon and I don't talk politics much. He doesn't care much about the philanthropic side of things ; punishments, and that kind of thing. He only cares about Church questions. That is not my line of action, you know."

" Ra-a-ther too much, my friend. *I* have heard of your doings. Who was it that sold his bit of land to the Papists at Middlemarch ? I believe you bought it on purpose. You are a perfect Guy Faux. See if you are not burnt in effigy this 5th of November coming. Humphrey would not come to quarrel with you about it, so I am come." [3]

" Very good. I was prepared to be persecuted for not persecuting —not persecuting, you know."

---

1. A "tithe" is the contribution of one-tenth of one's produce or other income for the support of the church. An "uncommuted tithe" would be one required in produce or property rather than in money.

2. The articles of religion of the Church of England, subscription to which is required of all clergy of the Church of England.

3. Guy Faux (Fawkes) was the leader of the unsuccessful plot to blow up the Houses of Parliament on November 5, 1605, in retaliation against the laws against Roman Catholics. The day is celebrated in Britain with bonfires and the burning of effigies of Guy Fawkes.

" There you go ! That is a piece of clap-trap you have got ready for the hustings. Now, *do not* let them lure you to the hustings, my dear Mr Brooke. A man always makes a fool of himself, speechifying : there's no excuse but being on the right side, so that you can ask a blessing on your humming and hawing. You will lose yourself, I forewarn you. You will make a Saturday pie of all parties' opinions, and be pelted by everybody." [4]

" That is what I expect, you know," said Mr Brooke, not wishing to betray how little he enjoyed this prophetic sketch — " what I expect as an independent man. As to the Whigs, a man who goes with the thinkers is not likely to be hooked on by any party. He may go with them up to a certain point—up to a certain point, you know. But that is what you ladies never understand."

" Where your certain point is ? No. I should like to be told how a man can have any certain point when he belongs to no party—leading a roving life, and never letting his friends know his address. ' Nobody knows where Brooke will be—there's no counting on Brooke ' —that is what people say of you, to be quite frank. Now, do turn respectable. How will you like going to Sessions with everybody looking shy on you, and you with a bad conscience and an empty pocket ?" [5]

" I don't pretend to argue with a lady on politics," said Mr Brooke, with an air of smiling indifference, but feeling rather unpleasantly conscious that this attack of Mrs Cadwallader's had opened the defensive campaign to which certain rash steps had exposed him. " Your sex are not thinkers, you know—*varium et mutabile semper*— that kind of thing. [6] You don't know Virgil. I knew "—Mr Brooke reflected in time that he had not had the personal acquaintance of the Augustan poet—" I was going to say, poor Stoddart, [7] you know. That was what *he* said. You ladies are always against an independent attitude—a man's caring for nothing but truth, and that sort of thing. And there is no part of the county where opinion is narrower than it is here—I don't mean to throw stones, you know, but somebody is wanted to take the independent line ; and if I don't take it, who will ?"

" Who ? Why, any upstart who has got neither blood nor position. People of standing should consume their independent nonsense at home, not hawk it about. And you ! who are going to marry your niece, as good as your daughter, to one of our best men. Sir James would be cruelly annoyed : it will be too hard on him if you turn round now and make yourself a Whig sign-board."

Mr Brooke again winced inwardly, for Dorothea's engagement had no sooner been decided, than he had thought of Mrs Cadwallader's prospective taunts. It might have been easy for ignorant observers to say, " Quarrel with Mrs Cadwallader ; " but where is a country gentleman to go who quarrels with his oldest neighbours ? Who could taste the fine flavour in the name of Brooke if it were delivered

4. Saturday pie: a dish made from leftovers.
5. Sessions: the term of a petty court.
6. "Varium et mutabile semper femina": "a changing and inconstant thing is woman" (Virgil, *Aeneid* 4:569).

7. Probably Sir John Stoddart (1773–1856), journalist and editor of *The New Times* until 1826, who was known during his editorship as "Dr. Slop" and was the subject of several scurrilous satires.

casually, like wine without a seal? Certainly a man can only be cosmopolitan up to a certain point.

"I hope Chettam and I shall always be good friends ; but I am sorry to say there is no prospect of his marrying my niece," said Mr Brooke, much relieved to see through the window that Celia was coming in.

"Why not?" said Mrs Cadwallader, with a sharp note of surprise. "It is hardly a fortnight since you and I were talking about it."

"My niece has chosen another suitor—has chosen him, you know. I have had nothing to do with it. I should have preferred Chettam ; and I should have said Chettam was the man any girl would have chosen. But there is no accounting for these things. Your sex is capricious, you know."

"Why, whom do you mean to say that you are going to let her marry?" Mrs Cadwallader's mind was rapidly surveying the possibilities of choice for Dorothea.

But here Celia entered, blooming from a walk in the garden, and the greeting with her delivered Mr Brooke from the necessity of answering immediately. He got up hastily, and saying, "By the way, I must speak to Wright about the horses," shuffled quickly out of the room.

"My dear child, what is this?—this about your sister's engagement?" said Mrs Cadwallader.

"She is engaged to marry Mr Casaubon," said Cecilia, resorting, as usual, to the simplest statement of fact, and enjoying this opportunity of speaking to the Rector's wife alone.

"This is frightful. How long has it been going on?"

"I only knew of it yesterday. They are to be married in six weeks."

"Well, my dear, I wish you joy of your brother-in-law."

"I am so sorry for Dorothea."

"Sorry! It is her doing, I suppose."

"Yes ; she says Mr Casaubon has a great soul."

"With all my heart."

"O Mrs Cadwallader, I don't think it can be nice to marry a man with a great soul."

"Well, my dear, take warning. You know the look of one now ; when the next comes and wants to marry you, don't you accept him."

"I'm sure I never should."

"No ; one such in a family is enough. So your sister never cared about Sir James Chettam? What would you have said to *him* for a brother-in-law?"

"I should have liked that very much. I am sure he would have been a good husband. Only," Celia added, with a slight blush (she sometimes seemed to blush as she breathed), "I don't think he would have suited Dorothea."

"Not high-flown enough?"

"Dodo is very strict. She thinks so much about everything, and is so particular about what one says. Sir James never seemed to please her."

"She must have encouraged him, I am sure. That is not very creditable."

"Please don't be angry with Dodo ; she does not see things. She thought so much about the cottages, and she *was* rude to Sir James sometimes ; but he is so kind, he never noticed it."

" Well," said Mrs Cadwallader, putting on her shawl, and rising, as if in haste, " I must go straight to Sir James and break this to him. He will have brought his mother back by this time, and I must call. Your uncle will never tell him. We are all disappointed, my dear. Young people should think of their families in marrying. I set a bad example—married a poor clergyman, and made myself a pitiable object among the De Bracys—obliged to get my coals by stratagem, and pray to heaven for my salad oil. However, Casaubon has money enough ; I must do him that justice. As to his blood, I suppose the family quarterings are three cuttle-fish sable, and a commentator rampant. By the by, before I go, my dear, I must speak to your Mrs Carter about pastry. I want to send my young cook to learn of her. Poor people with four children, like us, you know, can't afford to keep a good cook. I have no doubt Mrs Carter will oblige me. Sir James's cook is a perfect dragon."

In less than an hour, Mrs Cadwallader had circumvented Mrs Carter and driven to Freshitt Hall, which was not far from her own parsonage, her husband being resident in Freshitt and keeping a curate in Tipton.

Sir James Chettam had returned from the short journey which had kept him absent for a couple of days, and had changed his dress, intending to ride over to Tipton Grange. His horse was standing at the door when Mrs Cadwallader drove up, and he immediately appeared there himself, whip in hand. Lady Chettam had not yet returned, but Mrs Cadwallader's errand could not be despatched in the presence of grooms, so she asked to be taken into the conservatory close by, to look at the new plants ; and on coming to a contemplative stand, she said—

" I have a great shock for you ; I hope you are not so far gone in love as you pretended to be."

It was of no use protesting against Mrs Cadwallader's way of putting things. But Sir James's countenance changed a little. He felt a vague alarm.

" I do believe Brooke is going to expose himself after all. I accused him of meaning to stand for Middlemarch on the Liberal side, and he looked silly and never denied it—talked about the independent line, and the usual nonsense."

" Is that all ?" said Sir James, much relieved.

" Why," rejoined Mrs Cadwallader, with a sharper note, " you don't mean to say that you would like him to turn public man in that way—making a sort of political Cheap Jack of himself ?"[8]

" He might be dissuaded, I should think. He would not like the expense."

" That is what I told him. He is vulnerable to reason there—always a few grains of common-sense in an ounce of miserliness. Miserliness is a capital quality to run in families ; it's the safe side for madness to dip on. And there must be a little crack in the Brooke family, else we should not see what we are to see."

" What ? Brooke standing for Middlemarch ?"

" Worse than that. I really feel a little responsible. I always told you Miss Brooke would be such a fine match. I knew there was a great deal of nonsense in her—a flighty sort of Methodistical

8. Cheap Jack: a hawker or peddler.

stuff. But these things wear out of girls. However, I am taken by surprise for once."

" What do you mean, Mrs Cadwallader ? " said Sir James. His fear lest Miss Brooke should have run away to join the Moravian Brethren, or some preposterous sect unknown to good society, was a little allayed by the knowledge that Mrs Cadwallader always made the worst of things. ⁹ " What has happened to Miss Brooke ? Pray speak out."

" Very well. She is engaged to be married." Mrs Cadwallader paused a few moments, observing the deeply-hurt expression in her friend's face, which he was trying to conceal by a nervous smile, while he whipped his boot ; but she soon added, " Engaged to Casaubon."

Sir James let his whip fall and stooped to pick it up. Perhaps his face had never before gathered so much concentrated disgust as when he turned to Mrs Cadwallader and repeated, " Casaubon ? "

" Even so. You know my errand now."

" Good God ! It is horrible ! He is no better than a mummy ! " (The point of view has to be allowed for, as that of a blooming and disappointed rival.)

" She says, he is a great soul.—A great bladder for dried peas to rattle in ! " said Mrs Cadwallader.

" What business has an old bachelor like that to marry ? " said Sir James. " He has one foot in the grave."

" He means to draw it out again, I suppose."

" Brooke ought not to allow it : he should insist on its being put off till she is of age. She would think better of it then. What is a guardian for ? "

" As if you could ever squeeze a resolution out of Brooke ! "

" Cadwallader might talk to him."

" Not he ! Humphrey finds everybody charming. I never can get him to abuse Casaubon. He will even speak well of the bishop, though I tell him it is unnatural in a beneficed clergyman¹: what can one do with a husband who attends so little to the decencies ? I hide it as well as I can by abusing everybody myself. Come, come, cheer up ! you are well rid of Miss Brooke, a girl who would have been requiring you to see the stars by daylight. Between ourselves, little Celia is worth two of her, and likely after all to be the better match. For this marriage to Casaubon is as good as going to a nunnery."

" Oh, on my own account—it is for Miss Brooke's sake I think her friends should try to use their influence."

" Well, Humphrey doesn't know yet. But when I tell him, you may depend on it he will say, ' Why not ? Casaubon is a good fellow —and young—young enough.' These charitable people never know vinegar from wine till they have swallowed it and got the colic. However, if I were a man I should prefer Celia, especially when Dorothea was gone. The truth is, you have been courting one and have won the other. I can see that she admires you almost as much as a man

9. The Moravian Brethren were an evangelical religious sect founded in Germany in 1722 by the followers of the Hussite tradition. The Moravian movement strongly influenced John Wesley, the founder of Methodism.

1. A beneficed clergyman was one whose position guaranteed him a fixed amount of income or property.

expects to be admired. If it were any one but me who said so, you might think it exaggeration. Good-bye!"

Sir James handed Mrs Cadwallader to the phaeton, and then jumped on his horse. He was not going to renounce his ride because of his friend's unpleasant news—only to ride the faster in some other direction than that of Tipton Grange.

Now, why on earth should Mrs Cadwallader have been at all busy about Miss Brooke's marriage; and why, when one match that she liked to think she had a hand in was frustrated, should she have straightway contrived the preliminaries of another? Was there any ingenious plot, any hide-and-seek course of action, which might be detected by a careful telescopic watch? Not at all: a telescope might have swept the parishes of Tipton and Freshitt, the whole area visited by Mrs Cadwallader in her phaeton, without witnessing any interview that could excite suspicion, or any scene from which she did not return with the same unperturbed keenness of eye and the same high natural colour. In fact, if that convenient vehicle had existed in the days of the Seven Sages, one of them would doubtless have remarked, that you can know little of women by following them about in their pony phaetons.[2] Even with a microscope directed on a water-drop we find ourselves making interpretations which turn out to be rather coarse; for whereas under a weak lens you may seem to see a creature exhibiting an active voracity into which other smaller creatures actively play as if they were so many animated tax-pennies, a stronger lens reveals to you certain tiniest hairlets which make vortices for these victims while the swallower waits passively at his receipt of custom.[3] In this way, metaphorically speaking, a strong lens applied to Mrs Cadwallader's match-making will show a play of minute causes producing what may be called thought and speech vortices to bring her the sort of food she needed.

Her life was rurally simple, quite free from secrets either foul, dangerous, or otherwise important, and not consciously affected by the great affairs of the world. All the more did the affairs of the great world interest her, when communicated in the letters of high-born relations: the way in which fascinating younger sons had gone to the dogs by marrying their mistresses; the fine old-blooded idiocy of young Lord Tapir, and the furious gouty humours of old Lord Megatherium; the exact crossing of genealogies which had brought a coronet into a new branch and widened the relations of scandal,—these were topics of which she retained details with the utmost accuracy, and reproduced them in an excellent pickle of epigrams, which she herself enjoyed the more because she believed as unquestioningly in birth and no-birth as she did in game and vermin. She would never have disowned any one on the ground of poverty: a De Bracy reduced to take his dinner in a basin would have seemed to her an example of pathos worth exaggerating, and I fear his aristocratic vices would not have horrified her. But her feeling towards the vulgar rich was a sort of religious hatred: they had probably made all their money out of high retail prices, and Mrs Cadwallader detested high prices for everything that was not paid in kind at the

---

2. The Seven Sages of ancient Greece (fl. 620–550 B.C.) were Bias, Chilon, Cleobulus, Periander, Pittacus, Solon, Thales.

3. Tax-pennies were magnetized coins.

Rectory : such people were no part of God's design in making the world ; and their accent was an affliction to the ears.   A town where such monsters abounded was hardly more than a sort of low comedy, which could not be taken account of in a well-bred scheme of the universe.   Let any lady who is inclined to be hard on Mrs Cadwallader inquire into the comprehensiveness of her own beautiful views, and be quite sure that they afford accommodation for all the lives which have the honour to coexist with hers.

With such a mind, active as phosphorus, biting everything that came near into the form that suited it, how could Mrs Cadwallader feel that the Miss Brookes and their matrimonial prospects were alien to her ? especially as it had been the habit of years for her to scold Mr Brooke with the friendliest frankness, and let him know in confidence that she thought him a poor creature.   From the first arrival of the young ladies in Tipton she had prearranged Dorothea's marriage with Sir James, and if it had taken place would have been quite sure that it was her doing : that it should not take place after she had preconceived it, caused her an irritation which every thinker will sympathise with.   She was the diplomatist of Tipton and Freshitt, and for anything to happen in spite of her was an offensive irregularity.   As to freaks like this of Miss Brooke's, Mrs Cadwallader had no patience with them, and now saw that her opinion of this girl had been infected with some of her husband's weak charitableness : those Methodistical whims, that air of being more religious than the rector and curate together, came from a deeper and more constitutional disease than she had been willing to believe.

" However," said Mrs Cadwallader, first to herself and afterwards to her husband, " I throw her over : there was a chance, if she had married Sir James, of her becoming a sane, sensible woman.   He would never have contradicted her, and when a woman is not contradicted, she has no motive for obstinacy in her absurdities.   But now I wish her joy of her hair shirt."

It followed that Mrs Cadwallader must decide on another match for Sir James, and having made up her mind that it was to be the younger Miss Brooke, there could not have been a more skilful move toward the success of her plan than her hint to the baronet that he had made an impression on Celia's heart.   For he was not one of those gentlemen who languish after the unattainable Sappho's apple that laughs from the topmost bough—the charms which[4]

> " Smile like the knot of cowslips on the cliff,
> Not to be come at by the willing hand."

He had no sonnets to write, and it could not strike him agreeably that he was not an object of preference to the woman whom he had preferred.   Already the knowledge that Dorothea had chosen Mr Casaubon had bruised his attachment and relaxed its hold.   Although Sir James was a sportsman, he had some other feelings towards women than towards grouse and foxes, and did not regard his future wife in the light of prey, valuable chiefly for the excitements of the chase.   Neither was he so well acquainted with the habits of primi-

---

4. Sappho (625–565 B.C.), Greek poet, native of the island of Lesbos. The two lines following are not from Sappho; they may, however, have been emendations attributed to her in the nineteenth century.

tive races as to feel that an ideal combat for her, tomahawk in hand,
so to speak, was necessary to the historical continuity of the marriage-
tie. On the contrary, having the amiable vanity which knits us to
those who are fond of us, and disinclines us to those who are indifferent, and also a good grateful nature, the mere idea that a woman had
a kindness towards him spun little threads of tenderness from out
his heart towards hers.

Thus it happened, that after Sir James had ridden rather fast for
half an hour in a direction away from Tipton Grange, he slackened
his pace, and at last turned into a road which would lead him back by
a shorter cut. Various feelings wrought in him the determination
after all to go to the Grange to-day as if nothing new had happened.
He could not help rejoicing that he had never made the offer and
been rejected ; mere friendly politeness required that he should call
to see Dorothea about the cottages, and now happily Mrs Cadwallader
had prepared him to offer his congratulations, if necessary, without
showing too much awkwardness. He really did not like it : giving up
Dorothea was very painful to him ; but there was something in the
resolve to make this visit forthwith and conquer all show of feeling,
which was a sort of file-biting and counter-irritant. And without his
distinctly recognising the impulse, there certainly was present in him
the sense that Celia would be there, and that he should pay her more
attention than he had done before.

We mortals, men and women, devour many a disappointment
between breakfast and dinner-time ; keep back the tears and look
a little pale about the lips, and in answer to inquiries say, " Oh,
nothing !" Pride helps us ; and pride is not a bad thing when it
only urges us to hide our own hurts—not to hurt others.

CHAPTER VII.

" Piacer e popone
Vuol la sua stagione." [1]
—*Italian Proverb.*

MR CASAUBON, as might be expected, spent a great deal of his time
at the Grange in these weeks, and the hindrance which courtship
occasioned to the progress of his great work—the Key to all Mythologies—naturally made him look forward the more eagerly to the
happy termination of courtship. But he had deliberately incurred
the hindrance, having made up his mind that it was now time for
him to adorn his life with the graces of female companionship, to
irradiate the gloom which fatigue was apt to hang over the intervals
of studious labour with the play of female fancy, and to secure in this,
his culminating age, the solace of female tendance for his declining
years. Hence he determined to abandon himself to the stream of
feeling, and perhaps was surprised to find what an exceedingly shallow
rill it was. As in droughty regions baptism by immersion could
only be performed symbolically, so Mr Casaubon found that sprink-

1. "Pleasure and melons/Want the same weather."

ling was the utmost approach to a plunge which his stream would afford him ; and he concluded that the poets had much exaggerated the force of masculine passion. Nevertheless, he observed with pleasure that Miss Brooke showed an ardent submissive affection which promised to fulfil his most agreeable previsions of marriage. It had once or twice crossed his mind that possibly there was some deficiency in Dorothea to account for the moderation of his abandonment ; but he was unable to discern the deficiency, or to figure to himself a woman who would have pleased him better ; so that there was clearly no reason to fall back upon but the exaggerations of human tradition.

"Could I not be preparing myself now to be more useful ?" said Dorothea to him, one morning, early in the time of courtship ; "could I not learn to read Latin and Greek aloud to you, as Milton's daughters did to their father, without understanding what they read ?"

"I fear that would be wearisome to you," said Mr Casaubon, smiling ; "and, indeed, if I remember rightly, the young women you have mentioned regarded that exercise in unknown tongues as a ground for rebellion against the poet."

"Yes ; but in the first place they were very naughty girls, else they would have been proud to minister to such a father ; and in the second place they might have studied privately and taught themselves to understand what they read, and then it would have been interesting. I hope you don't expect me to be naughty and stupid ?"

"I expect you to be all that an exquisite young lady can be in every possible relation of life. Certainly it might be a great advantage if you were able to copy the Greek character, and to that end it were well to begin with a little reading."

Dorothea seized this as a precious permission. She would not have asked Mr Casaubon at once to teach her the languages, dreading of all things to be tiresome instead of helpful ; but it was not entirely out of devotion to her future husband that she wished to know Latin and Greek. Those provinces of masculine knowledge seemed to her a standing-ground from which all truth could be seen more truly. As it was, she constantly doubted her own conclusions, because she felt her own ignorance : how could she be confident that one-roomed cottages were not for the glory of God, when men who knew the classics appeared to conciliate indifference to the cottages with zeal for the glory ? Perhaps even Hebrew might be necessary —at least the alphabet and a few roots—in order to arrive at the core of things, and judge soundly on the social duties of the Christian. And she had not reached that point of renunciation at which she would have been satisfied with having a wise husband : she wished, poor child, to be wise herself. Miss Brooke was certainly very naïve with all her alleged cleverness. Celia, whose mind had never been thought too powerful, saw the emptiness of other people's pretensions much more readily. To have in general but little feeling, seems to be the only security against feeling too much on any particular occasion.

However, Mr Casaubon consented to listen and teach for an hour together, like a schoolmaster of little boys, or rather like a lover, to whom a mistress's elementary ignorance and difficulties have a touching fitness. Few scholars would have disliked teaching the alphabet under such circumstances. But Dorothea herself was a little shocked and discouraged at her own stupidity, and the answers she got to some timid questions about the value of the Greek accents gave her a painful suspicion that here indeed there might be secrets not capable of explanation to a woman's reason.

Mr Brooke had no doubt on that point, and expressed himself with his usual strength upon it one day that he came into the library while the reading was going forward.

" Well, but now, Casaubon, such deep studies, classics, mathematics, that kind of thing, are too taxing for a woman—too taxing, you know."

" Dorothea is learning to read the characters simply," said Mr Casaubon, evading the question. " She had the very considerate thought of saving my eyes."

" Ah, well, without understanding, you know—that may not be so bad. But there is a lightness about the feminine mind—a touch and go—music, the fine arts, that kind of thing—they should study those up to a certain point, women should ; but in a light way, you know. A woman should be able to sit down and play you or sing you a good old English tune. That is what I like ; though I have heard most things—been at the opera in Vienna: Gluck, Mozart, everything of that sort. But I'm a conservative in music—it's not like ideas, you know. I stick to the good old tunes."

" Mr Casaubon is not fond of the piano, and I am very glad he is not," said Dorothea, whose slight regard for domestic music and feminine fine art must be forgiven her, considering the small tinkling and smearing in which they chiefly consisted at that dark period. She smiled and looked up at her betrothed with grateful eyes. If he had always been asking her to play the " Last Rose of Summer," she would have required much resignation. " He says there is only an old harpsichord at Lowick, and it is covered with books."

" Ah, there you are behind Celia, my dear. Celia, now, plays very prettily, and is always ready to play. However, since Casaubon does not like it, you are all right. But it's a pity you should not have little recreations of that sort, Casaubon : the bow always strung —that kind of thing, you know—will not do."

" I never could look on it in the light of a recreation to have my ears teased with measured noises," said Mr Casaubon. " A tune much iterated has the ridiculous effect of making the words in my mind perform a sort of minuet to keep time—an effect hardly tolerable, I imagine, after boyhood. As to the grander forms of music, worthy to accompany solemn celebrations, and even to serve as an educating influence according to the ancient conception, I say nothing, for with these we are not immediately concerned."

" No ; but music of that sort I should enjoy," said Dorothea. " When we were coming home from Lausanne my uncle took us to hear the great organ at Freiberg, and it made me sob."

" That kind of thing is not healthy, my dear," said Mr Brooke. " Casaubon, she will be in your hands now : you must teach my niece to take things more quietly, eh, Dorothea ? "

He ended with a smile, not wishing to hurt his niece, but really thinking that it was perhaps better for her to be early married to so sober a fellow as Casaubon, since she would not hear of Chettam.

" It is wonderful, though," he said to himself as he shuffled out of the room—" it is wonderful that she should have liked him. However, the match is good. I should have been travelling out of my brief to have hindered it, let Mrs Cadwallader say what she will. He is pretty certain to be a bishop, is Casaubon. That was a very seasonable pamphlet of his on the Catholic Question:—a deanery at least.[2] They owe him a deanery."

And here I must vindicate a claim to philosophical reflectiveness, by remarking that Mr Brooke on this occasion little thought of the Radical speech which, at a later period, he was led to make on the incomes of the bishops. What elegant historian would neglect a striking opportunity for pointing out that his heroes did not foresee the history of the world, or even their own actions?—For example, that Henry of Navarre, when a Protestant baby, little thought of being a Catholic monarch; or that Alfred the Great, when he measured his laborious nights with burning candles, had no idea of future gentlemen measuring their idle days with watches.[3] Here is a mine of truth, which, however vigorously it may be worked, is likely to outlast our coal.

But of Mr Brooke I make a further remark perhaps less warranted by precedent—namely, that if he had foreknown his speech, it might not have made any great difference. To think with pleasure of his niece's husband having a large ecclesiastical income was one thing—to make a Liberal speech was another thing; and it is a narrow mind which cannot look at a subject from various points of view.

CHAPTER VIII.

"Oh, rescue her! I am her brother now,
And you her father. Every gentle maid
Should have a guardian in each gentleman."

It was wonderful to Sir James Chettam how well he continued to like going to the Grange after he had once encountered the difficulty of seeing Dorothea for the first time in the light of a woman who was engaged to another man. Of course the forked lightning seemed to pass through him when he first approached her, and he remained conscious throughout the interview of hiding uneasiness; but, good as he was, it must be owned that his uneasiness was less than it would have been if he had thought his rival a brilliant and desirable match. He had no sense of being eclipsed by Mr Casaubon; he was only shocked that Dorothea was under a melancholy illusion, and his mortification lost some of its bitterness by being mingled with compassion.

Nevertheless, while Sir James said to himself that he had completely resigned her, since with the perversity of a Desdemona she had not affected a proposed match that was clearly suitable and according to nature; he could not yet be quite passive under the idea of her engagement to Mr Casaubon. On the day when he first saw them together in the light of his present knowledge, it seemed to him

---

2. Deanery: the office of the senior canon of a cathedral church.
3. Henry of Navarre (1553–1610), King of France, was educated a Protestant but converted to Catholicism in 1593 to secure his kingdom. One of the many legends which have survived concerning Alfred the Great (849–901), King of West Saxony or Wessex, is this concerning his method of measuring the hours through the night by means of burning candles.

that he had not taken the affair seriously enough. Brooke was really culpable ; he ought to have hindered it. Who could speak to him ? Something might be done perhaps even now, at least to defer the marriage. On his way home he turned into the Rectory and asked for Mr Cadwallader. Happily, the Rector was at home, and his visitor was shown into the study, where all the fishing-tackle hung. But he himself was in a little room adjoining, at work with his turning apparatus, and he called to the baronet to join him there. The two were better friends than any other landholder and clergyman in the county—a significant fact which was in agreement with the amiable expression of their faces.

Mr Cadwallader was a large man, with full lips and a sweet smile ; very plain and rough in his exterior, but with that solid imperturbable ease and good-humour which is infectious, and like great grassy hills in the sunshine, quiets even an irritated egoism, and makes it rather ashamed of itself. " Well, how are you ? " he said, showing a hand not quite fit to be grasped. " Sorry I missed you before. Is there anything particular ? You look vexed."

Sir James's brow had a little crease in it, a little depression of the eyebrow, which he seemed purposely to exaggerate as he answered.

" It is only this conduct of Brooke's. I really think somebody should speak to him."

" What ? meaning to stand ? " said Mr Cadwallader, going on with the arrangement of the reels which he had just been turning. " I hardly think he means it. But where's the harm, if he likes it ? Any one who objects to Whiggery should be glad when the Whigs don't put up the strongest fellow. They won't overturn the Constitution with our friend Brooke's head for a battering ram."

" Oh, I don't mean that," said Sir James, who, after putting down his hat and throwing himself into a chair, had begun to nurse his leg and examine the sole of his boot with much bitterness. " I mean this marriage. I mean his letting that blooming young girl marry Casaubon."

" What is the matter with Casaubon ? I see no harm in him—if the girl likes him."

" She is too young to know what she likes. Her guardian ought to interfere. He ought not to allow the thing to be done in this headlong manner. I wonder a man like you, Cadwallader—a man with daughters, can look at the affair with indifference : and with such a heart as yours ! Do think seriously about it."

" I am not joking ; I am as serious as possible," said the Rector, with a provoking little inward laugh. " You are as bad as Elinor. She has been wanting me to go and lecture Brooke ; and I have re-minded her that her friends had a very poor opinion of the match she made when she married me."

" But look at Casaubon," said Sir James, indignantly. " He must be fifty, and I don't believe he could ever have been much more than the shadow of a man. Look at his legs ! "

" Confound you handsome young fellows ! you think of having it all your own way in the world. You don't understand women. They don't admire you half so much as you admire yourselves. Elinor used to tell her sisters that she married me for my ugliness—it was so various and amusing that it had quite conquered her prudence."

" You ! it was easy enough for a woman to love you. But this is no question of beauty. I don't *like* Casaubon." This was Sir James's strongest way of implying that he thought ill of a man's character.

" Why ? what do you know against him ?" said the rector, laying down his reels, and putting his thumbs into his arm-holes with an air of attention.

Sir James paused. He did not usually find it easy to give his reasons : it seemed to him strange that people should not know them without being told, since he only felt what was reasonable. At last he said—

" Now, Cadwallader, has he got any heart ? "

" Well, yes. I don't mean of the melting sort, but a sound kernel, *that* you may be sure of. He is very good to his poor relations : pensions several of the women, and is educating a young fellow at a good deal of expense. Casaubon acts up to his sense of justice. His mother's sister made a bad match—a Pole, I think—lost herself—at any rate was disowned by her family. If it had not been for that, Casaubon would not have had so much money by half. I believe he went himself to find out his cousins, and see what he could do for them. Every man would not ring so well as that, if you tried his metal. *You* would, Chettam ; but not every man."

" l don't know," said Sir James, colouring. " I am not so sure of myself." He paused a moment, and then added, " That was a right thing for Casaubon to do. But a man may wish to do what is right, and yet be a sort of parchment code. A woman may not be happy with him. And I think when a girl is so young as Miss Brooke is, her friends ought to interfere a little to hinder her from doing anything foolish. You laugh, because you fancy I have some feeling on my own account. But upon my honour, it is not that. I should feel just the same if I were Miss Brooke's brother or uncle."

" Well, but what should you do ? "

" I should say that the marriage must not be decided on until she was of age. And depend upon it, in that case, it would never come off. I wish you saw it as I do—I wish you would talk to Brooke about it."

Sir James rose as he was finishing his sentence, for he saw Mrs Cadwallader entering from the study. She held by the hand her youngest girl, about five years old, who immediately ran to papa, and was made comfortable on his knee.

" I hear what you are talking about," said the wife. " But you will make no impression on Humphrey. As long as the fish rise to his bait, everybody is what he ought to be. Bless you, Casaubon has got a trout stream, and does not care about fishing in it himself : could there be a better fellow ? "

" Well, there is something in that," said the Rector, with his quiet, inward laugh. " It is a very good quality in a man to have a trout-stream."

" But seriously," said Sir James, whose vexation had not yet spent itself, " don't you think the Rector might do some good by speaking ? "

" Oh, I told you beforehand what he would say," answered Mrs Cadwallader, lifting up her eyebrows. " I have done what I could : I wash my hands of the marriage."

" In the first place," said the Rector, looking rather grave, " it would be nonsensical to expect that I could convince Brooke, and make him act accordingly. Brooke is a very good fellow, but pulpy; he will run into any mould, but he won't keep shape."

" He might keep shape long enough to defer the marriage," said Sir James.

" But, my dear Chettam, why should I use my influence to Casaubon's disadvantage, unless I were much surer than I am that I should be acting for the advantage of Miss Brooke ? I know no harm of Casaubon. I don't care about his Xisuthrus and Fee-fo-fum and the rest ; but then he doesn't care about my fishing-tackle.[1] As to the line he took on the Catholic Question, that was unexpected ; but he has always been civil to me, and I don't see why I should spoil his sport. For anything I can tell, Miss Brooke may be happier with him than she would be with any other man."

" Humphrey ! I have no patience with you. You know you would rather dine under the hedge than with Casaubon alone. You have nothing to say to each other."

" What has that to do with Miss Brooke's marrying him ? She does not do it for my amusement."

" He has got no good red blood in his body," said Sir James.

" No. Somebody put a drop under a magnifying-glass, and it was all semicolons and parentheses," said Mrs Cadwallader.

" Why does he not bring out his book, instead of marrying ? " said Sir James, with a disgust which he held warranted by the sound feeling of an English layman.

" Oh, he dreams footnotes, and they run away with all his brains. They say, when he was a little boy, he made an abstract of " Hop o' my Thumb,' and he has been making abstracts ever since.[2] Ugh ! And that is the man Humphrey goes on saying that a woman may be happy with."

" Well, he is what Miss Brooke likes," said the Rector. " I don't profess to understand every young lady's taste."

" But if she were your own daughter ? " said Sir James.

" That would be a different affair. She is *not* my daughter, and I don't feel called upon to interfere. Casaubon is as good as most of us. He is a scholarly clergyman, and creditable to the cloth. Some Radical fellow speechifying at Middlemarch said Casaubon was the learned straw-chopping incumbent, and Freke was the brick-and-mortar incumbent, and I was the angling incumbent. And upon my word, I don't see that one is worse or better than the other." The Rector ended with his silent laugh. He always saw the joke of any satire against himself. His conscience was large and easy, like the rest of him : it did only what it could do without any trouble.

Clearly, there would be no interference with Miss Brooke's marriage through Mr Cadwallader ; and Sir James felt with some sadness that she was to have perfect liberty of misjudgment. It was a sign of his good disposition that he did not slacken at all in his intention of carrying out Dorothea's design of the cottages. Doubtless this persistence was the best course for his own dignity : but pride only helps us to be generous ; it never makes us so, any more than vanity makes us witty. She was now enough aware of Sir James's position with regard to her, to appreciate the rectitude of his perseverance

---

1. Xisuthrus: Noah in the Babylonian flood myth. Fee-fo-fum: an ogre.

2. "Hop'o'my Thumb": a tiny hero in nursery tales, like Tom Thumb.

in a landlord's duty, to which he had at first been urged by a lover's complaisance, and her pleasure in it was great enough to count for something even in her present happiness. Perhaps she gave to Sir James Chettam's cottages all the interest she could spare from Mr Casaubon, or rather from the symphony of hopeful dreams, admiring trust, and passionate self-devotion which that learned gentleman had set playing in her soul. Hence it happened that in the good baronet's succeeding visits, while he was beginning to pay small attentions to Celia, he found himself talking with more and more pleasure to Dorothea. She was perfectly unconstrained and without irritation towards him now, and he was gradually discovering the delight there is in frank kindness and companionship between a man and a woman who have no passion to hide or confess.

CHAPTER IX.

1st *Gent.* An ancient land in ancient oracles
Is called " law-thirsty : " all the struggle there
Was after order and a perfect rule.
Pray, where lie such lands now?
2d *Gent.* Why, where they lay of old—in human souls.

MR CASAUBON's behaviour about settlements was highly satisfactory to Mr Brooke, and the preliminaries of marriage rolled smoothly along, shortening the weeks of courtship. The betrothed bride must see her future home, and dictate any changes that she would like to have made there. A woman dictates before marriage in order that she may have an appetite for submission afterwards. And certainly, the mistakes that we male and female mortals make when we have our own way might fairly raise some wonder that we are so fond of it.

On a grey but dry November morning Dorothea drove to Lowick in company with her uncle and Celia. Mr Casaubon's home was the manor-house. Close by, visible from some parts of the garden, was the little church, with the old parsonage opposite. In the beginning of his career, Mr Casaubon had only held the living, but the death of his brother had put him in possession of the manor also. It had a small park, with a fine old oak here and there, and an avenue of limes towards the south-west front, with a sunk fence between park and pleasure-ground, so that from the drawing-room windows the glance swept uninterruptedly along a slope of greensward till the limes ended in a level of corn and pastures, which often seemed to melt into a lake under the setting sun. This was the happy side of the house, for the south and east looked rather melancholy even under the brightest morning. The grounds here were more confined, the flower-beds showed no very careful tendance, and large clumps of trees, chiefly of sombre yews, had risen high, not ten yards from the windows. The building, of greenish stone, was in the old English style, not ugly, but small windowed and melancholy-looking : the sort of house that must have children, many flowers, open windows, and little vistas of bright things, to make it seem a joyous home. In this latter end of autumn, with a sparse remnant of yellow leaves falling slowly athwart the dark evergreens in a stillness without sunshine, the house too had an air of autumnal decline, and Mr Casaubon, when he presented himself, had no bloom that could be thrown into relief by that background.

"Oh dear!" Celia said to herself, "I am sure Freshitt Hall would have been pleasanter than this." She thought of the white freestone, the pillared portico, and the terrace full of flowers, Sir James smiling above them like a prince issuing from his enchantment in a rose-bush, with a handkerchief swiftly metamorphosed from the most delicately-odorous petals—Sir James, who talked so agreeably, always about things which had common-sense in them, and not about learning! Celia had those light young feminine tastes which grave and weather-worn gentlemen sometimes prefer in a wife; but happily Mr Casaubon's bias had been different, for he would have had no chance with Celia.

Dorothea, on the contrary, found the house and grounds all that she could wish : the dark book-shelves in the long library, the carpets and curtains with colours subdued by time, the curious old maps and bird's-eye views on the walls of the corridor, with here and there an old vase below, had no oppression for her, and seemed more cheerful than the casts and pictures at the Grange, which her uncle had long ago brought home from his travels—they being probably among the ideas he had taken in at one time. To poor Dorothea these severe classical nudities and smirking Renaissance-Correggiosities were painfully inexplicable, staring into the midst of her Puritanic conceptions : she had never been taught how she could bring them into any sort of relevance with her life. [1] But the owners of Lowick apparently had not been travellers, and Mr Casaubon's studies of the past were not carried on by means of such aids.

Dorothea walked about the house with delightful emotion. Everything seemed hallowed to her : this was to be the home of her wifehood, and she looked up with eyes full of confidence to Mr Casaubon when he drew her attention specially to some actual arrangement and asked her if she would like an alteration. All appeals to her taste she met gratefully, but saw nothing to alter. His efforts at exact courtesy and formal tenderness had no defect for her. She filled up all blanks with unmanifested perfections, interpreting him as she interpreted the works of Providence, and accounting for seeming discords by her own deafness to the higher harmonies. And there are many blanks left in the weeks of courtship, which a loving faith fills with happy assurance.

"Now, my dear Dorothea, I wish you to favour me by pointing out which room you would like to have as your boudoir," said Mr Casaubon, showing that his views of the womanly nature were sufficiently large to include that requirement.

"It is very kind of you to think of that," said Dorothea, "but I assure you I would rather have all those matters decided for me. I shall be much happier to take everything as it is—just as you have been used to have it, or as you will yourself choose it to be. I have no motive for wishing anything else."

"O Dodo," said Celia, "will you not have the bow-windowed room up-stairs?"

---

1. Renaissance-Correggiosities: after Antonio Correggio (1494–1534), Italian painter of the Renaissance.

Mr Casaubon led the way thither. The bow-window looked down the avenue of limes ; the furniture was all of a faded blue, and there were miniatures of ladies and gentlemen with powdered hair hanging in a group. A piece of tapestry over a door also showed a blue-green world with a pale stag in it. The chairs and tables were thin-legged and easy to upset. It was a room where one might fancy the ghost of a tight-laced lady revisiting the scene of her embroidery. A light book-case contained duodecimo volumes of polite literature in calf, completing the furniture.

" Yes," said Mr Brooke, " this would be a pretty room with some new hangings, sofas, and that sort of thing. A little bare now."

" No, uncle," said Dorothea, eagerly. " Pray do not speak of altering anything. There are so many other things in the world that want altering—I like to take these things as they are. And you like them as they are, don't you ? " she added, looking at Mr Casaubon. " Perhaps this was your mother's room when she was young."

" It was," he said, with his slow bend of the head.

" This is your mother," said Dorothea, who had turned to examine the group of miniatures. " It is like the tiny one you brought me ; only, I should think a better portrait. And this one opposite, who is this ? "

" Her elder sister. They were, like you and your sister, the only two children of their parents, who hang above them, you see."

" The sister is pretty," said Celia, implying that she thought less favourably of Mr Casaubon's mother. It was a new opening to Celia's imagination, that he came of a family who had all been young in their time—the ladies wearing necklaces.

" It is a peculiar face," said Dorothea, looking closely. " Those deep grey eyes rather near together—and the delicate irregular nose with a sort of ripple in it—and all the powdered curls hanging backward. Altogether it seems to me peculiar rather than pretty. There is not even a family likeness between her and your mother."

" No. And they were not alike in their lot."

" You did not mention her to me," said Dorothea.

" My aunt made an unfortunate marriage. I never saw her."

Dorothea wondered a little, but felt that it would be indelicate just then to ask for any information which Mr Casaubon did not proffer, and she turned to the window to admire the view. The sun had lately pierced the grey, and the avenue of limes cast shadows.

" Shall we not walk in the garden now ? " said Dorothea.

" And you would like to see the church, you know," said Mr Brooke. " It is a droll little church. And the village. It all lies in a nut-shell. By the way, it will suit you, Dorothea ; for the cottages are like a row of alms-houses—little gardens, gillyflowers, that sort of thing."

" Yes, please," said Dorothea, looking at Mr Casaubon, " I should like to see all that." She had got nothing from him more graphic about the Lowick cottages than that they were " not bad."

They were soon on a gravel walk which led chiefly between grassy borders and clumps of trees, this being the nearest way to the church, Mr Casaubon said. At the little gate leading into the churchyard there was a pause while Mr Casaubon went to the parsonage close by to fetch a key. Celia, who had been hanging a little in the rear, came up presently, when she saw that Mr Casaubon was gone away, and said in her easy staccato, which always seemed to contradict the suspicion of any malicious intent—

" Do you know, Dorothea, I saw some one quite young coming up one of the walks."

" Is that astonishing, Celia ? "

" There may be a young gardener, you know—why not ? " said Mr Brooke. " I told Casaubon he should change his gardener."

" No, not a gardener," said Celia ; " a gentleman with a sketch-book. He had light-brown curls. I only saw his back. But he was quite young."

" The curate's son, perhaps," said Mr Brooke. " Ah, there is Casaubon again, and Tucker with him. He is going to introduce Tucker. You don't know Tucker yet."

Mr Tucker was the middle-aged curate, one of the " inferior clergy," who are usually not wanting in sons. But after the introduction, the conversation did not lead to any question about his family, and the startling apparition of youthfulness was forgotten by every one but Celia. She inwardly declined to believe that the light-brown curls and slim figure could have any relationship to Mr Tucker, who was just as old and musty-looking as she would have expected Mr Casaubon's curate to be ; doubtless an excellent man who would go to heaven (for Celia wished not to be unprincipled), but the corners of his mouth were so unpleasant. Celia thought with some dismalness of the time she should have to spend as bridesmaid at Lowick, where the curate had probably no pretty little children whom she could like, irrespective of principle.

Mr Tucker was invaluable in their walk ; and perhaps Mr Casaubon had not been without foresight on this head, the curate being able to answer all Dorothea's questions about the villagers and the other parishioners. Everybody, he assured her, was well off in Lowick : not a cottager in those double cottages at a low rent but kept a pig, and the strips of garden at the back were well tended. The small boys wore excellent corduroy, the girls went out as tidy servants, or did a little straw-plaiting at home : no looms here, no Dissent ; and though the public disposition was rather towards laying by money than towards spirituality, there was not much vice.[2] The speckled fowls were so numerous that Mr Brooke observed, " Your farmers leave some barley for the women to glean, I see. The poor folks here might have a fowl in their pot, as the good French king used to wish for all his people. The French eat a good many fowls—skinny fowls, you know."

" I think it was a very cheap wish of his," said Dorothea, indignantly. " Are kings such monsters that a wish like that must be reckoned a royal virtue ? "

" And if he wished them a skinny fowl," said Celia, " that would not be nice. But perhaps he wished them to have fat fowls."

" Yes, but the word has dropped out of the text, or perhaps was *subauditum ;* that is, present in the king's mind, but not uttered," said Mr Casaubon, smiling and bending his head towards Celia, who immediately dropped backward a little, because she could not bear Mr Casaubon to blink at her.

---

2. Dissent means separation from the established church; it includes Methodism and Evangelicalism.

Dorothea sank into silence on the way back to the house. She felt some disappointment, of which she was yet ashamed, that there was nothing for her to do in Lowick ; and in the next few minutes her mind had glanced over the possibility, which she would have preferred, of finding that her home would be in a parish which had a larger share of the world's misery, so that she might have had more active duties in it. Then, recurring to the future actually before her, she made a picture of more complete devotion to Mr Casaubon's aims, in which she would await new duties. Many such might reveal themselves to the higher knowledge gained by her in that companion-ship.

Mr Tucker soon left them, having some clerical work which would not allow him to lunch at the Hall ; and as they were re-entering the garden through the little gate, Mr Casaubon said—

" You seem a little sad, Dorothea. I trust you are pleased with what you have seen. "

" I am feeling something which is perhaps foolish and wrong, " answered Dorothea, with her usual openness—" almost wishing that the people wanted more to be done for them here. I have known so few ways of making my life good for anything. Of course, my notions of usefulness must be narrow. I must learn new ways of helping people. "

" Doubtless, " said Mr Casaubon. " Each position has its corres-ponding duties. Yours, I trust, as the mistress of Lowick, will not leave any yearning unfulfilled. "

" Indeed, I believe that, " said Dorothea, earnestly. " Do not sup-pose that I am sad. "

" That is well. But, if you are not tired, we will take another way to the house than that by which we came. "

Dorothea was not at all tired, and a little circuit was made towards a fine yew-tree, the chief hereditary glory of the grounds on this side of the house. As they approached it, a figure, conspicuous on a dark background of evergreens, was seated on a bench, sketching the old tree. Mr Brooke, who was walking in front with Celia, turned his head, and said—

" Who is that youngster, Casaubon ? "

They had come very near when Mr Casaubon answered—

" That is a young relative of mine, a second cousin : the grandson, in fact, " he added, looking at Dorothea, " of the lady whose portrait you have been noticing, my aunt Julia. "

The young man had laid down his sketch-book and risen. His bushy light-brown curls, as well as his youthfulness, identified him at once with Celia's apparition.

" Dorothea, let me introduce to you my cousin, Mr Ladislaw. Will, this is Miss Brooke. "

The cousin was so close now, that, when he lifted his hat, Dorothea could see a pair of grey eyes rather near together, a delicate irregular nose with a little ripple in it, and hair falling backward ; but there was a mouth and chin of a more prominent, threatening aspect than belonged to the type of the grandmother's miniature. Young Ladis-law did not feel it necessary to smile, as if he were charmed with this introduction to his future second cousin and her relatives ; but wore rather a pouting air of discontent.

"You are an artist, I see," said Mr Brooke, taking up the sketch-book and turning it over in his unceremonious fashion.

"No, I only sketch a little. There is nothing fit to be seen there," said young Ladislaw, colouring, perhaps with temper rather than modesty.

"Oh, come, this is a nice bit, now. I did a little in this way myself at one time, you know. Look here, now; this is what I call a nice thing, done with what we used to call *brio*." [3] Mr Brooke held out towards the two girls a large coloured sketch of stony ground and trees, with a pool.

"I am no judge of these things," said Dorothea, not coldly, but with an eager deprecation of the appeal to her. "You know, uncle, I never see the beauty of those pictures which you say are so much praised. They are a language I do not understand. I suppose there is some relation between pictures and nature which I am too ignorant to feel—just as you see what a Greek sentence stands for which means nothing to me." Dorothea looked up at Mr Casaubon, who bowed his head towards her, while Mr Brooke said, smiling nonchalantly—

"Bless me, now, how different people are! But you had a bad style of teaching, you know—else this is just the thing for girls—sketching, fine art and so on. But you took to drawing plans; you don't understand *morbidezza*, and that kind of thing. [4] You will come to my house, I hope, and I will show you what I did in this way," he continued, turning to young Ladislaw, who had to be recalled from his preoccupation in observing Dorothea. Ladislaw had made up his mind that she must be an unpleasant girl, since she was going to marry Casaubon, and what she said of her stupidity about pictures would have confirmed that opinion even if he had believed her. As it was, he took her words for a covert judgment, and was certain that she thought his sketch detestable. There was too much cleverness in her apology: she was laughing both at her uncle and himself. But what a voice! It was like the voice of a soul that had once lived in an Æolian harp. [5] This must be one of Nature's inconsistencies. There could be no sort of passion in a girl who would marry Casaubon. But he turned from her, and bowed his thanks for Mr Brooke's invitation.

"We will turn over my Italian engravings together," continued that good-natured man. "I have no end of those things, that I have laid by for years. One gets rusty in this part of the country, you know. Not you, Casaubon; you stick to your studies; but my best ideas get undermost—out of use, you know. You clever young men must guard against indolence. I was too indolent, you know: else I might have been anywhere at one time."

"That is a seasonable admonition," said Mr Casaubon; "but now we will pass on to the house, lest the young ladies should be tired of standing."

When their backs were turned, young Ladislaw sat down to go on

---

3. Verve, vigor.
4. *Morbidezza* was a term popular with eighteenth-century art critics to describe that style of painting characterized by extreme delicacy and softness.
5. A wind harp or box of tuned strings played by the wind; a familiar image in Romantic poetry.

with his sketching, and as he did so his face broke into an expression of amusement which increased as he went on drawing, till at last he threw back his head and laughed aloud. Partly it was the reception of his own artistic production that tickled him ; partly the notion of his grave cousin as the lover of that girl ; and partly Mr Brooke's definition of the place he might have held but for the impediment of indolence. Mr Will Ladislaw's sense of the ludicrous lit up his features very agreeably : it was the pure enjoyment of comicality, and had no mixture of sneering and self-exaltation.

"What is your nephew going to do with himself, Casaubon ?" said Mr Brooke, as they went on.

"My cousin, you mean—not my nephew."

"Yes, yes, cousin. But in the way of a career you know."

"The answer to that question is painfully doubtful. On leaving Rugby he declined to go to an English university, where I would gladly have placed him, and chose what I must consider the anomalous course of studying at Heidelberg. And now he wants to go abroad again, without any special object, save the vague purpose of what he calls culture, preparation for he knows not what. He declines to choose a profession."

"He has no means but what you furnish, I suppose."

"I have always given him and his friends reason to understand that I would furnish in moderation what was necessary for providing him with a scholarly education, and launching him respectably. I am therefore bound to fulfil the expectation so raised," said Mr Casaubon, putting his conduct in the light of mere rectitude : a trait of delicacy which Dorothea noticed with admiration.

"He has a thirst for travelling ; perhaps he may turn out a Bruce or a Mungo Park," said Mr Brooke. [6] "I had a notion of that myself at one time."

"No, he has no bent towards exploration, or the enlargement of our geognosis : that would be a special purpose which I could recognise with some approbation, though without felicitating him on a career which so often ends in premature and violent death. But so far is he from having any desire for a more accurate knowledge of the earth's surface, that he said he should prefer not to know the sources of the Nile, and that there should be some unknown regions preserved as hunting-grounds for the poetic imagination."

"Well, there is something in that, you know," said Mr Brooke, who had certainly an impartial mind.

"It is, I fear, nothing more than a part of his general inaccuracy and indisposition to thoroughness of all kinds, which would be a bad augury for him in any profession, civil or sacred, even were he so far submissive to ordinary rule as to choose one."

"Perhaps he has conscientious scruples founded on his own unfitness," said Dorothea, who was interesting herself in finding a favourable explanation. "Because the law and medicine should be very serious professions to undertake, should they not ? People's lives and fortunes depend on them."

"Doubtless ; but I fear that my young relative Will Ladislaw is chiefly determined in his aversion to these callings by a dislike to steady application, and to that kind of acquirement which is needful

6. James Bruce (1730–94) and Mungo Park (1771–1806), British explorers of Africa.

instrumentally, but is not charming or immediately inviting to self-indulgent taste. I have insisted to him on what Aristotle has stated with admirable brevity, that for the achievement of any work regarded as an end there must be a prior exercise of many energies or acquired facilities of a secondary order, demanding patience. I have pointed to my own manuscript volumes, which represent the toil of years preparatory to a work not yet accomplished. But in vain. To careful reasoning of this kind he replies by calling himself Pegasus, and every form of prescribed work 'harness.'" [7]

Celia laughed. She was surprised to find that Mr Casaubon could say something quite amusing.

"Well, you know, he may turn out a Byron, a Chatterton, a Churchill—that sort of thing—there's no telling," said Mr Brooke[8] "Shall you let him go to Italy, or wherever else he wants to go?"

"Yes; I have agreed to furnish him with moderate supplies for a year or so; he asks no more. I shall let him be tried by the test of freedom."

"That is very kind of you," said Dorothea, looking up at Mr Casaubon with delight. "It is noble. After all, people may really have in them some vocation which is not quite plain to themselves, may they not? They may seem idle and weak because they are growing. We should be very patient with each other, I think."

"I suppose it is being engaged to be married that has made you think patience good," said Celia, as soon as she and Dorothea were alone together, taking off their wrappings.

"You mean that I am very impatient, Celia."

"Yes; when people don't do and say just what you like." Celia had become less afraid of "saying things" to Dorothea since this engagement: cleverness seemed to her more pitiable than ever.

CHAPTER X.

"He had catched a great cold, had he had no other clothes to wear than the skin of a bear not yet killed."—FULLER. [1]

YOUNG Ladislaw did not pay that visit to which Mr Brooke had invited him, and only six days afterwards Mr Casaubon mentioned that his young relative had started for the Continent, seeming by this cold vagueness to waive inquiry. Indeed, Will had declined to fix on any more precise destination than the entire area of Europe. Genius, he held, is necessarily intolerant of fetters: on the one hand it must have the utmost play for its spontaneity; on the other, it may confidently await those messages from the universe which summon it to its peculiar work, only placing itself in an attitude of receptivity towards all sublime chances. The attitudes of receptivity are various, and Will had sincerely tried many of them. He was not excessively

7. In classical mythology, Pegasus was the winged horse of poetry.
8. Lord Byron (1728–1824), English poet; Thomas Chatterton (1752–70), the "boy poet"; and probably Charles Churchill (1731–64), poet, whose grave Byron visited on the eve of his final departure from England for Italy.
1. Thomas Fuller (1608–61), English clergyman and author.

fond of wine, but he had several times taken too much, simply as an
experiment in that form of ecstasy ; he had fasted till he was faint,
and then supped on lobster ; he had made himself ill with doses of
opium. Nothing greatly original had resulted from these measures ;
and the effects of the opium had convinced him that there was an entire dissimilarity between his constitution and De Quincey's.[2] The
superadded circumstance which would evolve the genius had not yet
come ; the universe had not yet beckoned. Even Cæsar's fortune at
one time was but a grand presentiment. We know what a masquerade all development is, and what effective shapes may be disguised
in helpless embryos.—In fact, the world is full of hopeful analogies
and handsome dubious eggs called possibilities. Will saw clearly
enough the pitiable instances of long incubation producing no chick,
and but for gratitude would have laughed at Casaubon, whose plodding application, rows of note-books, and small taper of learned
theory exploring the tossed ruins of the world, seemed to enforce a
moral entirely encouraging to Will's generous reliance on the intentions of the universe with regard to himself. He held that reliance
to be a mark of genius ; and certainly it is no mark to the contrary ;
genius consisting neither in self-conceit nor in humility, but in a
power to make or do, not anything in general, but something in particular. Let him start for the Continent, then, without our pronouncing on his future. Among all forms of mistake, prophecy is
the most gratuitous.

But at present this caution against a too hasty judgment interests
me more in relation to Mr Casaubon than to his young cousin. If to
Dorothea Mr Casaubon had been the mere occasion which had set
alight the fine inflammable material of her youthful illusions, does it
follow that he was fairly represented in the minds of those less im-
passioned personages who have hitherto delivered their judgments
concerning him ? I protest against any absolute conclusion, any prejudice derived from Mrs Cadwallader's contempt for a neighbouring
clergyman's alleged greatness of soul, or Sir James Chettam's poor
opinion of his rival's legs,—from Mr Brooke's failure to elicit a companion's ideas, or from Celia's criticism of a middle-aged scholar's
personal appearance. I am not sure that the greatest man of his age,
if ever that solitary superlative existed, could escape these unfavourable reflections of himself in various small mirrors ; and even Milton,
looking for his portrait in a spoon, must submit to have the facial
angle of a bumpkin. Moreover, if Mr Casaubon, speaking for himself, has rather a chilling rhetoric, it is not therefore certain that there
is no good work or fine feeling in him. Did not an immortal physicist and interpreter of hieroglyphs write detestable verses ?[3] Has the
theory of the solar system been advanced by graceful manners and
conversational tact ? Suppose we turn from outside estimates of a
man, to wonder, with keener interest, what is the report of his own
consciousness about his doings or capacity : with what hindrances
he is carrying on his daily labours ; what fading of hopes, or what
deeper fixity of self-delusion the years are marking off within him ;
and with what spirit he wrestles against universal pressure, which

2. Thomas de Quincey (1785–1859), English essayist; his *Confessions of an English Opium Eater* was first pub-lished in 1821.
3. Thomas Young (1773–1829), physi-cian, physicist, and Egyptologist; also a classical scholar as a youth, and a poet. As a physician he did significant research on optics and the heart.

will one day be too heavy for him, and bring his heart to its final pause. Doubtless his lot is important in his own eyes; and the chief reason that we think he asks too large a place in our consideration must be our want of room for him, since we refer him to the Divine regard with perfect confidence; nay, it is even held sublime for our neighbour to expect the utmost there, however little he may have got from us. Mr Casaubon, too, was the centre of his own world; if he was liable to think that others were providentially made for him, and especially to consider them in the light of their fitness for the author of a 'Key to all Mythologies,' this trait is not quite alien to us, and, like the other mendicant hopes of mortals, claims some of our pity.

Certainly this affair of his marriage with Miss Brooke touched him more nearly than it did any one of the persons who have hitherto shown their disapproval of it, and in the present stage of things I feel more tenderly towards his experience of success than towards the disappointment of the amiable Sir James. For in truth, as the day fixed for his marriage came nearer, Mr Casaubon did not find his spirits rising; nor did the contemplation of that matrimonial garden-scene, where, as all experience showed, the path was to be bordered with flowers, prove persistently more enchanting to him than the accustomed vaults where he walked taper in hand. He did not confess to himself, still less could he have breathed to another, his surprise that though he had won a lovely and noble-hearted girl he had not won delight,—which he had also regarded as an object to be found by search. It is true that he knew all the classical passages implying the contrary; but knowing classical passages, we find, is a mode of motion, which explains why they leave so little extra force for their personal application.

Poor Mr Casaubon had imagined that his long studious bachelorhood had stored up for him a compound interest of enjoyment, and that large drafts on his affections would not fail to be honoured; for we all of us, grave or light, get our thoughts entangled in metaphors, and act fatally on the strength of them. And now he was in danger of being saddened by the very conviction that his circumstances were unusually happy: there was nothing external by which he could account for a certain blankness of sensibility which came over him just when his expectant gladness should have been most lively, just when he exchanged the accustomed dulness of his Lowick library for his visits to the Grange. Here was a weary experience in which he was as utterly condemned to loneliness as in the despair which sometimes threatened him while toiling in the morass of authorship without seeming nearer to the goal. And his was that worst loneliness which would shrink from sympathy. He could not but wish that Dorothea should think him not less happy than the world would expect her successful suitor to be; and in relation to his authorship he leaned on her young trust and veneration, he liked to draw forth her fresh interest in listening, as a means of encouragement to himself: in talking to her he presented all his performance and intention with the reflected confidence of the pedagogue, and rid himself for the time of that chilling ideal audience which crowded his laborious uncreative hours with the vaporous pressure of Tartarean shades. [4]

4. Infernal: from Tartarus, the sunless abyss, the underworld.

For to Dorothea, after that toy-box history of the world adapted to young ladies which had made the chief part of her education, Mr Casaubon's talk about his great book was full of new vistas; and this sense of revelation, this surprise of a nearer introduction to Stoics and Alexandrians, as people who had ideas not totally unlike her own, kept in abeyance for the time her usual eagerness for a binding theory which could bring her own life and doctrine into strict connection with that amazing past, and give the remotest sources of knowledge some bearing on her actions.[5] That more complete teaching would come—Mr Casaubon would tell her all that: she was looking forward to higher initiation in ideas, as she was looking forward to marriage, and blending her dim conceptions of both. It would be a great mistake to suppose that Dorothea would have cared about any share in Mr Casaubon's learning as mere accomplishment; for though opinion in the neighbourhood of Freshitt and Tipton had pronounced her clever, that epithet would not have described her to circles in whose more precise vocabulary cleverness implies mere aptitude for knowing and doing, apart from character. All her eagerness for acquirement lay within that full current of sympathetic motive in which her ideas and impulses were habitually swept along. She did not want to deck herself with knowledge—to wear it loose from the nerves and blood that fed her action; and if she had written a book she must have done it as Saint Theresa did, under the command of an authority that constrained her conscience. But something she yearned for by which her life might be filled with action at once rational and ardent; and since the time was gone by for guiding visions and spiritual directors, since prayer heightened yearning but not instruction, what lamp was there but knowledge? Surely learned men kept the only oil; and who more learned than Mr Casaubon?

Thus in these brief weeks Dorothea's joyous grateful expectation was unbroken, and however her lover might occasionally be conscious of flatness, he could never refer it to any slackening of her affectionate interest.

The season was mild enough to encourage the project of extending the wedding journey as far as Rome, and Mr Casaubon was anxious for this because he wished to inspect some manuscripts in the Vatican.

"I still regret that your sister is not to accompany us," he said one morning, some time after it had been ascertained that Celia objected to go, and that Dorothea did not wish for her companionship. "You will have many lonely hours, Dorothea, for I shall be constrained to make the utmost use of my time during our stay in Rome, and I should feel more at liberty if you had a companion."

The words "I should feel more at liberty" grated on Dorothea. For the first time in speaking to Mr Casaubon she coloured from annoyance.

"You must have misunderstood me very much," she said, "if you think I should not enter into the value of your time—if you think

---

5. Stoicism was an Athenian school of philosophy, founded c. 300 B.C. by Zeno. The Alexandrian school, which flourished in Egypt c. 30 B.C.–642 A.D., was allied in thought to later developments of Stoicism. Both taught that personal inspiration is the way to certitude in a world of universal moral and ethical doubt.

that I should not willingly give up whatever interfered with your using it to the best purpose."

" That is very amiable in you, my dear Dorothea," said Mr Casaubon, not in the least noticing that she was hurt ; " but if you had a lady as your companion, I could put you both under the care of a cicerone, and we could thus achieve two purposes in the same space of time." [6]

" I beg you will not refer to this again," said Dorothea, rather haughtily. But immediately she feared that she was wrong, and turning towards him she laid her hand on his, adding in a different tone, " Pray do not be anxious about me. I shall have so much to think of when I am alone. And Tantripp will be a sufficient companion, just to take care of me. I could not bear to have Celia : she would be miserable."

It was time to dress. There was to be a dinner-party that day, the last of the parties which were held at the Grange as proper preliminaries to the wedding, and Dorothea was glad of a reason for moving away at once on the sound of the bell, as if she needed more than her usual amount of preparation. She was ashamed of being irritated from some cause she could not define even to herself ; for though she had no intention to be untruthful, her reply had not touched the real hurt within her. Mr Casaubon's words had been quite reasonable, yet they had brought a vague instantaneous sense of aloofness on his part.

" Surely I am in a strangely selfish weak state of mind," she said to herself. " How can I have a husband who is so much above me without knowing that he needs me less than I need him ? "

Having convinced herself that Mr Casaubon was altogether right, she recovered her equanimity, and was an agreeable image of serene dignity when she came into the drawing-room in her silver-grey dress—the simple lines of her dark-brown hair parted over her brow and coiled massively behind, in keeping with the entire absence from her manner and expression of all search after mere effect. Sometimes when Dorothea was in company, there seemed to be as complete an air of repose about her as if she had been a picture of Santa Barbara looking out from her tower into the clear air ; but these intervals of quietude made the energy of her speech and emotion the more remarked when some outward appeal had touched her. [7]

She was naturally the subject of many observations this evening, for the dinner-party was large and rather more miscellaneous as to the male portion than any which had been held at the Grange since Mr Brooke's nieces had resided with him, so that the talking was done in duos and trios more or less inharmonious. There was the newly-elected mayor of Middlemarch, who happened to be a manufacturer ; the philanthropic banker his brother-in-law, who predominated so much in the town that some called him a Methodist, others a hypocrite, according to the resources of their vocabulary ; and there were various professional men. In fact, Mrs Cadwallader said that Brooke was beginning to treat the Middlemarchers, and that she pre-

6. Cicerone: a guide.
7. Saint Barbara was an early saint, supposed to have been imprisoned in a tower by her father, so that her beauty would not be contaminated by the world.

ferred the farmers at the tithe-dinner, who drank her health unpretentiously, and were not ashamed of their grandfathers' furniture. For in that part of the country, before Reform had done its notable part in developing the political consciousness, there was a clearer distinction of ranks and a dimmer distinction of parties; so that Mr Brooke's miscellaneous invitations seemed to belong to that general laxity which came from his inordinate travel and habit of taking too much in tne form of ideas.

Already, as Miss Brooke passed out of the dining-room, opportunity was found for some interjectional "asides."

"A fine woman, Miss Brooke! an uncommonly fine woman, by God!" said Mr Standish, the old lawyer, who had been so long concerned with the landed gentry that he had become landed himself, and used that oath in a deep-mouthed manner as a sort of armorial bearings, stamping the speech of a man who held a good position.

Mr Bulstrode, the banker, seemed to be addressed, but that gentleman disliked coarseness and profanity, and merely bowed. The remark was taken up by Mr Chichely, a middle-aged bachelor and coursing celebrity, who had a complexion something like an Easter egg, a few hairs carefully arranged, and a carriage implying the consciousness of a distinguished appearance. [8]

"Yes, but not my style of woman: I like a woman who lays herself out a little more to please us. There should be a little filigree about a woman—something of the coquette. A man likes a sort of challenge. The more of a dead set she makes at you the better."

"There's some truth in that," said Mr Standish, disposed to be genial. "And, by God, it's usually the way with them. I suppose it answers some wise ends: Providence made them so, eh, Bulstrode?"

"I should be disposed to refer coquetry to another source," said Mr Bulstrode. "I should rather refer it to the devil."

"Ay, to be sure, there should be a little devil in a woman," said Mr Chichely, whose study of the fair sex seemed to have been detrimental to his theology. "And I like them blond, with a certain gait, and a swan neck. Between ourselves, the mayor's daughter is more to my taste than Miss Brooke or Miss Celia either. If I were a marrying man I should choose Miss Vincy before either of them."

"Well, make up, make up," said Mr Standish, jocosely; "you see the middle-aged fellows carry the day."

Mr Chichely shook his head with much meaning: he was not going to incur the certainty of being accepted by the woman he would choose.

The Miss Vincy who had the honour of being Mr Chichely's ideal was of course not present; for Mr Brooke, always objecting to go too far, would not have chosen that his nieces should meet the daughter of a Middlemarch manufacturer, unless it were on a public occasion. The feminine part of the company included none whom Lady Chettam or Mrs Cadwallader could object to; for Mrs Renfrew, the colonel's widow, was not only unexceptionable in point of breeding, but also interesting on the ground of her complaint, which puzzled the doctors, and seemed clearly a case wherein the fulness of professional knowledge might need the supplement of quackery. Lady

8. Coursing: the sport of chasing hare or other small game with greyhounds.

Chettam, who attributed her own remarkable health to home-made bitters united with constant medical attendance, entered with much exercise of the imagination into Mrs Renfrew's account of symptoms, and into the amazing futility in her case of all strengthening medicines.

" Where can all the strength of those medicines go, my dear?" said the mild but stately dowager, turning to Mrs Cadwallader reflectively, when Mrs Renfrew's attention was called away.

" It strengthens the disease," said the Rector's wife, much too well-born not to be an amateur in medicine. " Everything depends on the constitution : some people make fat, some blood, and some bile —that's my view of the matter ; and whatever they take is a sort of grist to the mill."

" Then she ought to take medicines that would reduce—reduce the disease, you know, if you are right, my dear. And I think what you say is reasonable."

" Certainly it is reasonable. You have two sorts of potatoes, fed on the same soil. One of them grows more and more watery——"

" Ah! like this poor Mrs Renfrew—that is what I think. Dropsy! There is no swelling yet—it is inward. I should say she ought to take drying medicines, shouldn't you ?—or a dry hot-air bath. Many things might be tried, of a drying nature."

" Let her try a certain person's pamphlets," said Mrs Cadwallader in an undertone, seeing the gentlemen enter. " *He* does not want drying."

" Who, my dear ?" said Lady Chettam, a charming woman, not so quick as to nullify the pleasure of explanation.

" The bridegroom—Casaubon. He has certainly been drying up faster since the engagement : the flame of passion, I suppose."

" I should think he is far from having a good constitution," said Lady Chettam, with a still deeper undertone. " And then his studies —so very dry, as you say."

" Really, by the side of Sir James, he looks like a death's head skinned over for the occasion. Mark my words : in a year from this time that girl will hate him. She looks up to him as an oracle now, and by-and-by she will be at the other extreme. All flightiness !"

" How very shocking ! I fear she is headstrong. But tell me—you know all about him—is there anything very bad? What is the truth ?"

" The truth ? he is as bad as the wrong physic—nasty to take, and sure to disagree."

" There could not be anything worse than that," said Lady Chettam, with so vivid a conception of the physic that she seemed to have learned something exact about Mr Casaubon's disadvantages. " However, James will hear nothing against Miss Brooke. He ·says she is the mirror of women still."

" That is a generous make-believe of his. Depend upon it, he likes little Celia better, and she appreciates him. I hope you like my little Celia ?"

" Certainly ; she is fonder of geraniums, and seems more docile, though not so fine a figure. But we were talking of physic : tell me about this new young surgeon, Mr Lydgate. I am told he is wonderfully clever : he certainly looks it—a fine brow indeed."

" He is a gentleman. I heard him talking to Humphrey. He talks well."

" Yes. Mr Brooke says he is one of the Lydgates of Northumberland, really well connected. One does not expect it in a practitioner of that kind. For my own part, I like a medical man more on a footing with the servants ; they are often all the cleverer. I assure you I found poor Hicks's judgment unfailing ; I never knew him wrong. He was coarse and butcher-like, but he knew my constitution. It was a loss to me his going off so suddenly. Dear me, what a very animated conversation Miss Brooke seems to be having with this Mr Lydgate ! "

" She is talking cottages and hospitals with him," said Mrs Cadwallader, whose ears and power of interpretation were quick. " I believe he is a sort of philanthropist, so Brooke is sure to take him up."

" James," said Lady Chettam when her son came near, " bring Mr Lydgate and introduce him to me. I want to test him."

The affable dowager declared herself delighted with this opportunity of making Mr Lydgate's acquaintance, having heard of his success in treating fever on a new plan.

Mr Lydgate had the medical accomplishment of looking perfectly grave whatever nonsense was talked to him, and his dark steady eyes gave him impressiveness as a listener. He was as little as possible like the lamented Hicks, especially in a certain careless refinement about his toilette and utterance. Yet Lady Chettam gathered much confidence in him. He confirmed her view of her own constitution as being peculiar, by admitting that all constitutions might be called peculiar, and he did not deny that hers might be more peculiar than others. He did not approve of a too lowering system, including reckless cupping, nor, on the other hand, of incessant port-wine and bark. [9] He said " I think so " with an air of so much deference accompanying the insight of agreement, that she formed the most cordial opinion of his talents.

" I am quite pleased with your *protégé*," she said to Mr Brooke before going away.

" My *protégé ?*—dear me !—who is that ? " said Mr Brooke.

" This young Lydgate, the new doctor. He seems to me to understand his profession admirably."

" Oh, Lydgate ! he is not my *protégé*, you know ; only I knew an uncle of his who sent me a letter about him. However, I think he is likely to be first-rate—has studied in Paris, knew Broussais ; has ideas, you know—wants to raise the profession." [1]

" Lydgate has lots of ideas, quite new, about ventilation and diet, that sort of thing," resumed Mr Brooke, after he had handed out Lady Chettam, and had returned to be civil to a group of Middlemarchers.

" Hang it, do you think that is quite sound ?—upsetting the old treatment, which has made Englishmen what they are ? " said Mr Standish.

" Medical knowledge is at a low ebb among us," said Mr Bulstrode, who spoke in a subdued tone, and had rather a sickly air. " I, for my part, hail the advent of Mr Lydgate. I hope to find good reason for confiding the new hospital to his management."

" That is all very fine," replied Mr Standish, who was not fond of Mr Bulstrode ; " if you like him to try experiments on your hospital

9. Surgical "cupping" or blood-drawing was used to "lower" or depress fever; powdered Cinchona bark, a source of quinine, was mixed with port wine as a medicinal remedy for fever.

1. Francois Joseph Victor Broussais (1772–1838), controversial French physician and, after 1814, lecturer.

patients, and kill a few people for charity, I have no objection. But I am not going to hand money out of my purse to have experiments tried on me. I like treatment that has been tested a little."

" Well, you know, Standish, every dose you take is an experiment —an experiment, you know," said Mr Brooke, nodding towards the lawyer.

" Oh, if you talk in that sense!" said Mr Standish, with as much disgust at such non-legal quibbling as a man can well betray towards a valuable client.

" I should be glad of any treatment that would cure me without reducing me to a skeleton, like poor Grainger," said Mr Vincy, the mayor, a florid man, who would have served for a study of flesh in striking contrast with the Franciscan tints of Mr Bulstrode. " It's an uncommonly dangerous thing to be left without any padding against the shafts of disease, as somebody said,—and I think it a very good expression myself."

Mr Lydgate, of course, was out of hearing. He had quitted the party early, and would have thought it altogether tedious but for the novelty of certain introductions, especially the introduction to Miss Brooke, whose youthful bloom, with her approaching marriage to that faded scholar, and her interest in matters socially useful, gave her the piquancy of an unusual combination.

" She is a good creature—that fine girl—but a little too earnest," he thought. " It is troublesome to talk to such women. They are always wanting reasons, yet they are too ignorant to understand the merits of any question, and usually fall back on their moral sense to settle things after their own taste."

Evidently Miss Brooke was not Mr Lydgate's style of woman any more than Mr Chichely's. Considered, indeed, in relation to the latter, whose mind was matured, she was altogether a mistake, and calculated to shock his trust in final causes, including the adaptation of fine young women to purple-faced bachelors. But Lydgate was less ripe, and might possibly have experience before him which would modify his opinion as to the most excellent things in woman.

Miss Brooke, however, was not again seen by either of these gentlemen under her maiden name. Not long after that dinner-party she had become Mrs Casaubon, and was on her way to Rome.

CHAPTER XI.

" But deeds and language such as men do use,
And persons such as comedy would choose,
When she would show an image of the times,
And sport with human follies, not with crimes."
—BEN JONSON.[1]

LYDGATE, in fact, was already conscious of being fascinated by a woman strikingly different from Miss Brooke : he did not in the least suppose that he had lost his balance and fallen in love, but he

---

1. *Everyman in His Humour* (1598), Prologue.

had said of that particular woman, " She is grace itself; she is perfectly lovely and accomplished. That is what a woman ought to be : she ought to produce the effect of exquisite music." Plain women he regarded as he did the other severe facts of life, to be faced with philosophy and investigated by science. But Rosamond Vincy seemed to have the true melodic charm ; and when a man has seen the woman whom he would have chosen if he had intended to marry speedily, his remaining a bachelor will usually depend on her resolution rather than on his. Lydgate believed that he should not marry for several years : not marry until he had trodden out a good clear path for himself away from the broad road which was quite ready made. He had seen Miss Vincy above his horizon almost as long as it had taken Mr Casaubon to become engaged and married : but this learned gentleman was possessed of a fortune ; he had assembled his voluminous notes, and had made that sort of reputation which precedes performance,—often the larger part of a man's fame. He took a wife, as we have seen, to adorn the remaining quadrant of his course, and be a little moon that would cause hardly a calculable perturbation. But Lydgate was young, poor, ambitious. He had his half-century before him instead of behind him, and he had come to Middlemarch bent on doing many things that were not directly fitted to make his fortune or even secure him a good income. To a man under such circumstances, taking a wife is something more than a question of adornment, however highly he may rate this ; and Lydgate was disposed to give it the first place among wifely functions. To his taste, guided by a single conversation, here was the point on which Miss Brooke would be found wanting, notwithstanding her undeniable beauty. She did not look at things from the proper feminine angle. The society of such women was about as relaxing as going from your work to teach the second form, instead of reclining in a paradise with sweet laughs for bird-notes, and blue eyes for a heaven.

Certainly nothing at present could seem much less important to Lydgate than the turn of Miss Brooke's mind, or to Miss Brooke than the qualities of the woman who had attracted this young surgeon. But any one watching keenly the stealthy convergence of human lots, sees a slow preparation of effects from one life on another, which tells like a calculated irony on the indifference or the frozen stare with which we look at our unintroduced neighbour. Destiny stands by sarcastic with our *dramatis personæ* folded in her hand.

Old provincial society had its share of this subtle movement : had not only its striking downfalls, its brilliant young professional dandies who ended by living up an entry with a drab and six children for their establishment, but also those less marked vicissitudes which are constantly shifting the boundaries of social intercourse, and begetting new consciousness of interdependence. Some slipped a little downward, some got higher footing : people denied aspirates, gained wealth, and fastidious gentlemen stood for boroughs ; some were caught in political currents, some in ecclesiastical, and perhaps found themselves surprisingly grouped in consequence ; while a few personages or families that stood with rocky firmness amid all this fluctuation, were slowly presenting new aspects in spite of solidity, and altering with the double change of self and beholder. Municipal town and rural parish gradually made fresh threads of connection—gradually,

as the old stocking gave way to the savings-bank, and the worship of
the solar guinea became extinct; while squires and baronets, and
even lords who had once lived blamelessly afar from the civic mind,
gathered the faultiness of closer acquaintanceship.[2] Settlers, too, came
from distant counties, some with an alarming novelty of skill, others
with an offensive advantage in cunning. In fact, much the same sort
of movement and mixture went on in old England as we find in older
Herodotus, who also, in telling what had been, thought it well to take
a woman's lot for his starting-point; though Io, as a maiden apparently beguiled by attractive merchandise, was the reverse of Miss
Brooke, and in this respect perhaps bore more resemblance to Rosamond Vincy, who had excellent taste in costume, with that nymph-
like figure and pure blondness which give the largest range to choice
in the flow and colour of drapery.[3] But these things made only part
of her charm. She was admitted to be the flower of Mrs Lemon's
school, the chief school in the county, where the teaching included all
that was demanded in the accomplished female—even to extras, such
as the getting in and out of a carriage. Mrs Lemon herself had
always held up Miss Vincy as an example: no pupil, she said, exceeded that young lady for mental acquisition and propriety of speech,
while her musical execution was quite exceptional. We cannot help
the way in which people speak of us, and probably if Mrs Lemon had
undertaken to describe Juliet or Imogen, these heroines would not
have seemed poetical.[4] The first vision of Rosamond would have been
enough with most judges to dispel any prejudice excited by Mrs
Lemon's praise.

Lydgate could not be long in Middlemarch without having that
agreeable vision, or even without making the acquaintance of the
Vincy family; for though Mr Peacock, whose practice he had paid
something to enter on, had not been their doctor (Mrs Vincy not
liking the lowering system adopted by him), he had many patients
among their connections and acquaintances. For who of any consequence in Middlemarch was not connected or at least acquainted with
the Vincys? They were old manufacturers, and had kept a good
house for three generations, in which there had naturally been much
intermarrying with neighbours more or less decidedly genteel. Mr
Vincy's sister had made a wealthy match in accepting Mr Bulstrode,
who, however, as a man not born in the town, and altogether of
dimly-known origin, was considered to have done well in uniting
himself with a real Middlemarch family; on the other hand, Mr
Vincy had descended a little, having taken an innkeeper's daughter.
But on this side too there was a cheering sense of money; for Mrs
Vincy's sister had been second wife to rich old Mr Featherstone, and
had died childless years ago, so that her nephews and nieces might
be supposed to touch the affections of the widower. And it happened
that Mr Bulstrode and Mr Featherstone, two of Peacock's most im-

2. The solar guinea was a gold coin, in
use until replaced by the sovereign in
1813.

3. Herodotus (c. 484–25 B.C.), Greek
historian. His history begins with the
stories of the Phoenicians carrying Io
off into Egypt, the Greeks kidnapping
the daughter of the king of Phoenicia,
and the abduction of Helen.
Io was the daughter of Inachus, the
river god of Argos. Hera became jealous of her attraction to Zeus, and
turned her into a white heifer.

4. Juliet and Imogen are Shakespeare's
young heroines in *Romeo and Juliet* and
Cymbeline.

portant patients, had, from different causes, given an especially good reception to his successor, who had raised some partisanship as well as discussion. Mr Wrench, medical attendant to the Vincy family, very early had grounds for thinking lightly of Lydgate's professional discretion, and there was no report about him which was not retailed at the Vincys', where visitors were frequent. Mr Vincy was more inclined to general good-fellowship than to taking sides, but there was no need for him to be hasty in making any new man's acquaintance. Rosamond silently wished that her father would invite Mr Lydgate. She was tired of the faces and figures she had always been used to—the various irregular profiles and gaits and turns of phrase distinguishing those Middlemarch young men whom she had known as boys. She had been at school with girls of higher position, whose brothers, she felt sure, it would have been possible for her to be more interested in, than in these inevitable Middlemarch companions. But she would not have chosen to mention her wish to her father ; and he, for his part, was in no hurry on the subject. An alderman about to be mayor must by-and-by enlarge his dinner parties, but at present there were plenty of guests at his well-spread table.

That table often remained covered with the relics of the family breakfast long after Mr Vincy had gone with his second son to the warehouse, and when Miss Morgan was already far on in morning lessons with the younger girls in the school-room. It awaited the family laggard, who found any sort of inconvenince (to others) less disagreeable than getting up when he was called. This was the case one morning of the October in which we have lately seen Mr Casaubon visiting the Grange ; and though the room was a little over-heated with the fire, which had sent the spaniel panting to a remote corner, Rosamond, for some reason, continued to sit at her embroidery longer than usual, now and then giving herself a little shake, and laying her work on her knee to contemplate it with an air of hesitating weariness. Her mamma, who had returned from an excursion to the kitchen, sat on the other side of the small work-table with an air of more entire placidity, until, the clock again giving notice that it was going to strike, she looked up from the lace-mending which was occupying her plump fingers and rang the bell.

" Knock at Mr Fred's door again, Pritchard, and tell him it has struck half-past ten."

This was said without any change in the radiant good-humour of Mrs Vincy's face, in which forty-five years had delved neither angles nor parallels ; and pushing back her pink cap-strings, she let her work rest on her lap, while she looked admiringly at her daughter.

" Mamma," said Rosamond, " when Fred comes down I wish you would not let him have red herrings. I cannot bear the smell of them all over the house at this hour of the morning."

" Oh, my dear, you are so hard on your brothers ! It is the only fault I have to find with you. You are the sweetest temper in the world, but you are so tetchy with your brothers."

" Not tetchy, mamma : you never hear me speak in an unladylike way."

" Well, but you want to deny them things."

" Brothers are so unpleasant."

" Oh, my dear, you must allow for young men. Be thankful if

they have good hearts. A woman must learn to put up with little things. You will be married some day."

" Not to any one who is like Fred."

" Don't decry your own brother, my dear. Few young men have less against them, although he couldn't take his degree—I'm sure I can't understand why, for he seems to me most clever. And you know yourself he was thought equal to the best society at college. So particular as you are, my dear, I wonder you are not glad to have such a gentlemanly young man for a brother. You are always finding fault with Bob because he is not Fred."

" Oh no, mamma, only because he is Bob."

" Well, my dear, you will not find any Middlemarch young man who has not something against him."

" But "—here Rosamond's face broke into a smile which suddenly revealed two dimples. She herself thought unfavourably of these dimples and smiled little in general society. " But I shall not marry any Middlemarch young man."

" So it seems, my love, for you have as good as refused the pick of them ; and if there's better to be had, I'm sure there's no girl better deserves it."

" Excuse me, mamma—I wish you would not say, ' the pick of them.' "

" Why, what else are they ? "

" I mean, mamma, it is rather a vulgar expression."

" Very likely, my dear ; I never was a good speaker. What should I say ? "

" The best of them."

" Why, that seems just as plain and common. If I had had time to think, I should have said, ' the most superior young men.' But with your education you must know."

" What must Rosy know, mother ? " said Mr Fred, who had slid in unobserved through the half-open door while the ladies were bending over their work, and now going up to the fire stood with his back towards it, warming the soles of his slippers.

" Whether it's right to say ' superior young men,' " said Mrs Vincy, ringing the bell.

" Oh, there are so many superior teas and sugars now. Superior is getting to be shopkeepers' slang."

" Are you beginning to dislike slang, then ? " said Rosamond, with mild gravity.

" Only the wrong sort. All choice of words is slang. It marks a class."

" There is correct English : that is not slang."

" I beg your pardon : correct English is the slang of prigs who write history and essays. And the strongest slang of all is the slang of poets."

" You will say anything, Fred, to gain your point."

"Well, tell me whether it is slang or poetry to call an ox a *leg-plaiter*."[5]

" Of course you can call it poetry if you like."

5. The image comes from the way bovine animals walk, setting their hooves down one in front of the other and seeming thus almost to cross their legs at every step.

"Aha, Miss Rosy, you don't know Homer from slang. I shall invent a new game; I shall write bits of slang and poetry on slips, and give them to you to separate."

"Dear me, how amusing it is to hear young people talk!" said Mrs Vincy, with cheerful admiration.

"Have you got nothing else for my breakfast, Pritchard?" said Fred, to the servant who brought in coffee and buttered toast; while he walked round the table surveying the ham, potted beef, and other cold remnants, with an air of silent rejection, and polite forbearance from signs of disgust.

"Should you like eggs, sir?"

"Eggs, no! Bring me a grilled bone." [6]

"Really, Fred," said Rosamond, when the servant had left the room, "if you must have hot things for breakfast, I wish you would come down earlier. You can get up at six o'clock to go out hunting; I cannot understand why you find it so difficult to get up on other mornings."

"That is your want of understanding, Rosy. I can get up to go hunting because I like it."

"What would you think of me if I came down two hours after every one else and ordered grilled bone?"

"I should think you were an uncommonly fast young lady," said Fred, eating his toast with the utmost composure.

"I cannot see why brothers are to make themselves disagreeable, any more than sisters."

"I don't make myself disagreeable; it is you who find me so. Disagreeable is a word that describes your feelings and not my actions."

"I think it describes the smell of grilled bone."

"Not at all. It describes a sensation in your little nose associated with certain finicking notions which are the classics of Mrs Lemon's school. Look at my mother: you don't see her objecting to everything except what she does herself. She is my notion of a pleasant woman."

"Bless you both, my dears, and don't quarrel," said Mrs Vincy, with motherly cordiality. "Come, Fred, tell us all about the new doctor. How is your uncle pleased with him?"

"Pretty well, I think. He asks Lydgate all sorts of questions and then screws up his face while he hears the answers, as if they were pinching his toes. That's his way. Ah, here comes my grilled bone."

"But how came you to stay out so late, my dear? You only said you were going to your uncle's."

"Oh, I dined at Plymdale's. We had whist.[7] Lydgate was there too."

"And what do you think of him? He is very gentlemanly, I suppose. They say he is of excellent family—his relations quite county people."

"Yes," said Fred. "There was a Lydgate at John's who spent no end of money.[8] I find this man is a second cousin of his. But rich men may have very poor devils for second cousins."

"It always makes a difference, though, to be of good family," said Rosamond, with a tone of decision which showed that she had thought

6. A leftover chop with some meat on it, reheated by grilling.
7. A popular four-handed English card game, of which bridge is a descendant.
8. John's: St. John's College, Cambridge.

on this subject. Rosamond felt that she might have been happier if she had not been the daughter of a Middlemarch manufacturer. She disliked anything which reminded her that her mother's father had been an innkeeper. Certainly any one remembering the fact might think that Mrs Vincy had the air of a very handsome good-humoured landlady, accustomed to the most capricious orders of gentlemen.

" I thought it was odd his name was Tertius," said the bright-faced matron, " but of course it's a name in the family. But now, tell us exactly what sort of man he is."

" Oh, tallish, dark, clever—talks well—rather a prig, I think."

" I never can make out what you mean by a prig," said Rosamond.

" A fellow who wants to show that he has opinions."

" Why, my dear, doctors must have opinions," said Mrs Vincy. " What are they there for else ? "

" Yes, mother, the opinions they are paid for. But a prig is a fellow who is always making you a present of his opinions."

" I suppose Mary Garth admires Mr Lydgate," said Rosamond, not without a touch of innuendo.

" Really, I can't say," said Fred, rather glumly, as he left the table, and taking up a novel which he had brought down with him, threw himself into an arm-chair. " If you are jealous of her, go oftener to Stone Court yourself and eclipse her."

" I wish you would not be so vulgar, Fred. If you have finished, pray ring the bell."

" It is true, though—what your brother says, Rosamond," Mrs Vincy began, when the servant had cleared the table. " It is a thousand pities you haven't patience to go and see your uncle more, so proud of you as he is, and wanted you to live with him. There's no knowing what he might have done for you as well as for Fred. God knows, I'm fond of having you at home with me, but I can part with my children for their good. And now it stands to reason that your uncle Featherstone will do something for Mary Garth."

" Mary Garth can bear being at Stone Court, because she likes that better than being a governess," said Rosamond, folding up her work. " I would rather not have anything left to me if I must earn it by enduring much of my uncle's cough and his ugly relations."

" He can't be long for this world, my dear ; I wouldn't hasten his end, but what with asthma and that inward complaint, let us hope there is something better for him in another. And I have no ill-will towards Mary Garth, but there's justice to be thought of. And Mr Featherstone's first wife brought him no money, as my sister did. Her nieces and nephews can't have so much claim as my sister's. And I must say I think Mary Garth a dreadful plain girl—more fit for a governess."

" Every one would not agree with you there, mother," said Fred, who seemed to be able to read and listen too.

" Well, my dear," said Mrs Vincy, wheeling skilfully, " if she *had* some fortune left her,—a man marries his wife's relations, and the Garths are so poor, and live in such a small way. But I shall leave you to your studies, my dear ; for I must go and do some shopping."

" Fred's studies are not very deep," said Rosamond, rising with her mamma, " he is only reading a novel."

" Well, well, by-and-by he'll go to his Latin and things," said Mrs

Vincy, soothingly, stroking her son's head. " There's a fire in the smoking-room on purpose. It's your father's wish, you know—Fred, my dear—and I always tell him you will be good, and go to college again to take your degree."

Fred drew his mother's hand down to his lips, but said nothing.

" I suppose you are not going out riding to-day ? " said Rosamond, lingering a little after her mamma was gone.

" No ; why ? "

" Papa says I may have the chesnut to ride now."

" You can go with me to-morrow, if you like. Only I am going to Stone Court, remember."

" I want the ride so much, it is indifferent to me where we go." Rosamond really wished to go to Stone Court, of all other places.

" Oh, I say, Rosy," said Fred, as she was passing out of the room, " if you are going to the piano, let me come and play some airs with you."

" Pray do not ask me this morning."

" Why not this morning ? "

" Really, Fred, I wish you would leave off playing the flute. A man looks very silly playing the flute. And you play so out of tune."

" When next any one makes love to you, Miss Rosamond, I will tell him how obliging you are."

" Why should you expect me to oblige you by hearing you play the flute, any more than I should expect you to oblige me by not playing it ? "

" And why should you expect me to take you out riding ? "

This question led to an adjustment, for Rosamond had set her mind on that particular ride.

So Fred was gratified with nearly an hour's practice of " Ar hyd y nos," " Ye banks and braes," and other favourite airs from his " Instructor on the Flute ; " a wheezy performance, into which he threw much ambition and an irrepressible hopefulness.

CHAPTER XII.

" He had more tow on his distaffe
Than Gerveis knew."
—CHAUCER. [1]

THE ride to Stone Court, which Fred and Rosamond took the next morning, lay through a pretty bit of midland landscape, almost all meadows and pastures, with hedgerows still allowed to grow in bushy beauty and to spread out coral fruit for the birds. Little details gave each field a particular physiognomy, dear to the eyes that have looked on them from childhood : the pool in the corner where the grasses were dank and trees leaned whisperingly ; the great oak shadowing a bare place in mid-pasture ; the high bank where the ash-trees grew ; the sudden slope of the old marl-pit making a red background for the burdock ; the huddled roofs and ricks of the homestead without a

---

1. "The Miller's Tale," lines 3774–75.

traceable way of approach ; the grey gate and fences against the depths of the bordering wood ; and the stray hovel, its old, old thatch full of mossy hills and valleys with wondrous modulations of light and shadow such as we travel far to see in later life, and see larger, but not more beautiful. These are the things that make the gamut of joy in landscape to midland-bred souls—the things they toddled among, or perhaps learned by heart standing between their father's knees while he drove leisurely.

But the road, even the byroad, was excellent ; for Lowick, as we have seen, was not a parish of muddy lanes and poor tenants ; and it was into Lowick parish that Fred and Rosamond entered after a couple of miles' riding. Another mile would bring them to Stone Court, and at the end of the first half, the house was already visible, looking as if it had been arrested in its growth toward a stone mansion by an unexpected budding of farm-buildings on its left flank, which had hindered it from becoming anything more than the substantial dwelling of a gentleman farmer. It was not the less agreeable an object in the distance for the cluster of pinnacled corn-ricks which balanced the fine row of walnuts on the right.

Presently it was possible to discern something that might be a gig on the circular drive before the front door.

" Dear me," said Rosamond, " I hope none of my uncle's horrible relations are there."

" They are, though. That is Mrs Waule's gig—the last yellow gig left, I should think. When I see Mrs Waule in it, I understand how yellow can have been worn for mourning. That gig seems to me more funereal than a hearse. But then Mrs Waule always has black crape on. How does she manage it, Rosy ? Her friends can't always be dying."

" I don't know at all. And she is not in the least evangelical," said Rosamond, reflectively, as if that religious point of view would have fully accounted for perpetual crape. " And not poor," she added, after a moment's pause.

" No, by George ! They are as rich as Jews, those Waules and Featherstones ; I mean, for people like them, who don't want to spend anything. And yet they hang about my uncle like vultures, and are afraid of a farthing going away from their side of the family. But I believe he hates them all."

The Mrs Waule who was so far from being admirable in the eyes of these distant connections, had happened to say this very morning (not at all with a defiant air, but in a low, muffled, neutral tone, as of a voice heard through cotton wool) that she did not wish " to enjoy their good opinion." She was seated, as she observed, on her own brother's hearth, and had been Jane Featherstone five-and-twenty years before she had been Jane Waule, which entitled her to speak when her own brother's name had been made free with by those who had no right to it.

" What are you driving at there ?" said Mr Featherstone, holding his stick between his knees and settling his wig, while he gave her a momentary sharp glance, which seemed to react on him like a draught of cold air and set him coughing.

Mrs Waule had to defer her answer till he was quiet again, till Mary Garth had supplied him with fresh syrup, and he had begun to rub the gold knob of his stick, looking bitterly at the fire. It was a bright fire, but it made no difference to the chill-looking purplish tint of Mrs Waule's face, which was as neutral as her voice ; having mere chinks for eyes, and lips that hardly moved in speaking.

"The doctors can't master that cough, brother. It's just like what I have ; for I'm your own sister, constitution and everything. But, as I was saying, it's a pity Mrs Vincy's family can't be better conducted."

"Tchah ! you said nothing o' the sort. You said somebody had made free with my name."

"And no more than can be proved, if what everybody says is true. My brother Solomon tells me it's the talk up and down in Middlemarch how unsteady young Vincy is, and has been for ever gambling at billiards since home he came."

"Nonsense ! What's a game at billiards ? It's a good gentlemanly game ; and young Vincy is not a clodhopper. If your son John took to billiards, now, he'd make a fool of himself."

"Your nephew John never took to billiards or any other game, brother, and is far from losing hundreds of pounds, which, if what everybody says is true, must be found somewhere else than out of Mr Vincy the father's pocket. For they say he's been losing money for years, though nobody would think so, to see him go coursing and keeping open house as they do. And I've heard say Mr Bulstrode condemns Mrs Vincy beyond anything for her flightiness, and spoiling her children so."

"What's Bulstrode to me ? I don't bank with him."

"Well, Mrs Bulstrode is Mr Vincy's own sister, and they do say that Mr Vincy mostly trades on the Bank money ; and you may see yourself, brother, when a woman past forty has pink strings always flying, and that light way of laughing at everything, it's very unbecoming. But indulging your children is one thing, and finding money to pay their debts is another. And it's openly said that young Vincy has raised money on his expectations. I don't say what expectations. Miss Garth hears me, and is welcome to tell again. I know young people hang together."

"No, thank you, Mrs Waule," said Mary Garth. "I dislike hearing scandal too much to wish to repeat it."

Mr Featherstone rubbed the knob of his stick and made a brief convulsive show of laughter, which had much the same genuineness as an old whist-player's chuckle over a bad hand. Still looking at the fire, he said—

"And who pretends to say Fred Vincy hasn't got expectations ? Such a fine, spirited fellow is like enough to have 'em."

There was a slight pause before Mrs Waule replied, and when she did so, her voice seemed to be slightly moistened with tears, though her face was still dry.

"Whether or no, brother, it is naturally painful to me and my brother Solomon to hear your name made free with, and your complaint being such as may carry you off sudden, and people who are no more Featherstones than the Merry-Andrew at the fair, openly reckoning on your property coming to *them*. [2] And me your own

2. Merry-Andrew: a clown; a buffoon.

sister, and Solomon your own brother! And if that's to be it, what has it pleased the Almighty to make families for?" Here Mrs Waule's tears fell, but with moderation.

"Come, out with it, Jane!" said Mr Featherstone, looking at her. "You mean to say, Fred Vincy has been getting somebody to advance him money on what he says he knows about my will, eh?"

"I never said so, brother" (Mrs Waule's voice had again become dry and unshaken). "It was told me by my brother Solomon last night when he called coming from market to give me advice about the old wheat, me being a widow, and my son John only three-and-twenty, though steady beyond anything. And he had it from most undeniable authority, and not one, but many."

"Stuff and nonsense! I don't believe a word of it. It's all a got-up story. Go to the window, missy; I thought I heard a horse. See if the doctor's coming."

"Not got up by me, brother, nor yet by Solomon, who, whatever else he may be—and I don't deny he has oddities—has made his will and parted his property equal between such kin as he's friends with; though, for my part, I think there are times when some should be considered more than others. But Solomon makes it no secret what he means to do."

"The more fool he!" said Mr Featherstone, with some difficulty; breaking into a severe fit of coughing that required Mary Garth to stand near him, so that she did not find out whose horses they were which presently paused stamping on the gravel before the door.

Before Mr Featherstone's cough was quiet, Rosamond entered, bearing up her riding-habit with much grace. She bowed ceremoniously to Mrs Waule, who said stiffly, "How do you do, miss?" smiled and nodded silently to Mary, and remained standing till the coughing should cease, and allow her uncle to notice her.

"Heyday, miss," he said at last, "you have a fine colour. Where's Fred?"

"Seeing about the horses. He will be in presently."

"Sit down, sit down. Mrs Waule, you'd better go."

Even those neighbours who had called Peter Featherstone an old fox, had never accused him of being insincerely polite, and his sister was quite used to the peculiar absence of ceremony with which he marked his sense of blood-relationship. Indeed, she herself was accustomed to think that entire freedom from the necessity of behaving agreeably was included in the Almighty's intentions about families. She rose slowly without any sign of resentment, and said in her usual muffled monotone, "Brother, I hope the new doctor will be able to do something for you. Solomon says there's great talk of his cleverness. I'm sure it's my wish you should be spared. And there's none more ready to nurse you than your own sister and your own nieces, if you'd only say the word. There's Rebecca, and Joanna, and Elizabeth, you know."

"Ay, ay, I remember—you'll see I've remembered 'em all—all dark and ugly. They'd need have some money, eh? There never was any beauty in the women of our family; but the Featherstones have always had some money, and the Waules too. Waule had money too. A warm man was Waule. Ay, ay; money's a good egg; and if you've got money to leave behind you, lay it in a warm nest. Good-bye, Mrs Waule."

Here Mr Featherstone pulled at both sides of his wig as if he wanted to deafen himself, and his sister went away ruminating on this oracular speech of his. Notwithstanding her jealousy of the Vincys and of Mary Garth, there remained as the nethermost sediment in her mental shallows a persuasion that her brother Peter Featherstone could never leave his chief property away from his blood-relations:—else, why had the Almighty carried off his two wives both childless, after he had gained so much by manganese and things, turning up when nobody expected it?—and why was there a Lowick parish church, and the Waules and Powderells all sitting in the same pew for generations, and the Featherstone pew next to them, if, the Sunday after her brother Peter's death, everybody was to know that the property was gone out of the family? The human mind has at no period accepted a moral chaos; and so preposterous a result was not strictly conceivable. But we are frightened at much that is not strictly conceivable.

When Fred came in the old man eyed him with a peculiar twinkle, which the younger had often had reason to interpret as pride in the satisfactory details of his appearance.

"You two misses go away," said Mr Featherstone. "I want to speak to Fred."

"Come into my room, Rosamond, you will not mind the cold for a little while," said Mary. The two girls had not only known each other in childhood, but had been at the same provincial school together (Mary as an articled pupil), so that they had many memories in common, and liked very well to talk in private. Indeed, this *tête-à-tête* was one of Rosamond's objects in coming to Stone Court.

Old Featherstone would not begin the dialogue till the door had been closed. He continued to look at Fred with the same twinkle and with one of his habitual grimaces, alternately screwing and widening his mouth; and when he spoke, it was in a low tone, which might be taken for that of an informer ready to be bought off, rather than for the tone of an offended senior. He was not a man to feel any strong moral indignation even on account of trespasses against himself. It was natural that others should want to get an advantage over him, but then, he was a little too cunning for them.

"So, sir, you've been paying ten per cent for money which you've promised to pay off by mortgaging my land when I'm dead and gone, eh? You put my life at a twelvemonth, say. But I can alter my will yet."

Fred blushed. He had not borrowed money in that way, for excellent reasons. But he was conscious of having spoken with some confidence (perhaps with more than he exactly remembered) about his prospect of getting Featherstone's land as a future means of paying present debts.

"I don't know what you refer to, sir. I have certainly never borrowed any money on such an insecurity. Please to explain."

"No, sir, it's you must explain. I can alter my will yet, let me tell you. I'm of sound mind—can reckon compound interest in my head, and remember every fool's name as well as I could twenty years ago. What the deuce? I'm under eighty. I say, you must contradict this story."

"I have contradicted it, sir," Fred answered, with a touch of impatience, not remembering that his uncle did not verbally discrimi-

nate contradicting from disproving, though no one was further from
confounding the two ideas than old Featherstone, who often wondered that so many fools took his own assertions for proofs. " But I
contradict it again. The story is a silly lie."

" Nonsense! you must bring dockiments. It comes from authority."

" Name the authority, and make him name the man of whom I
borrowed the money, and then I can disprove the story."

" It's pretty good authority, I think—a man who knows most of
what goes on in Middlemarch. It's that fine, religious, charitable
uncle o' yours. Come now ! " Here Mr Featherstone had his peculiar inward shake which signified merriment.

" Mr Bulstrode ? "

" Who else, eh ? "

" Then the story has grown into this lie out of some sermonising
words he may have let fall about me. Do they pretend that he
named the man who lent me the money ? "

" If there is such a man, depend upon it Bulstrode knows him.
But, supposing you only tried to get the money lent, and didn't get
it—Bulstrode 'ud know that too. You bring me a writing from Bulstrode to say he doesn't believe you've ever promised to pay your
debts out o' my land. Come now ! "

Mr Featherstone's face required its whole scale of grimaces as a muscular outlet to his silent triumph in the soundness of his faculties.

Fred felt himself to be in a disgusting dilemma.

" You must be joking, sir. Mr Bulstrode, like other men, believes
scores of things that are not true, and he has a prejudice against me.
I could easily get him to write that he knew no facts in proof of the
report you speak of, though it might lead to unpleasantness. But I
could hardly ask him to write down what he believes or does not believe about me." Fred paused an instant, and then added, in politic
appeal to his uncle's vanity, " That is hardly a thing for a gentleman
to ask."

But he was disappointed in the result.

" Ay, I know what you mean. You'd sooner offend me than Bulstrode. And what's he ?—he's got no land hereabout that ever I
heard tell of. A speckilating fellow ! He may come down any day,
when the devil leaves off backing him. And that's what his religion
means : he wants God A'mighty to come in. That's nonsense !
There's one thing I made out pretty clear when I used to go to
church—and it's this : God A'mighty sticks to the land. He promises land, and He gives land, and He makes chaps rich with corn
and cattle. But you take the other side. You like Bulstrode and
speckilation better than Featherstone and land."

" I beg your pardon, sir," said Fred, rising, standing with his back
to the fire and beating his boot with his whip. " I like neither Bulstrode nor speculation." He spoke rather sulkily, feeling himself
stalemated.

" Well, well, you can do without *me*, that's pretty clear," said old
Featherstone, secretly disliking the possibility that Fred would show
himself at all independent. " You neither want a bit of land to
make a squire of you instead of a starving parson, nor a lift of a hundred pound by the way. It's all one to me. I can make five codicils if I like, and I shall keep my bank-notes for a nest-egg. It's all
one to me."

Fred coloured again. Featherstone had rarely given him presents of money, and at this moment it seemed almost harder to part with the immediate prospect of bank-notes than with the more distant prospect of the land.

"I am not ungrateful, sir. I never meant to show disregard for any kind intentions you might have towards me. On the contrary."

"Very good. Then prove it. You bring me a letter from Bulstrode saying he doesn't believe you've been cracking and promising to pay your debts out o' my land, and then, if there's any scrape you've got into, we'll see if I can't back you a bit. Come now! That's a bargain. Here, give me your arm. I'll try and walk round the room."

Fred, in spite of his irritation, had kindness enough in him to be a little sorry for the unloved, unvenerated old man, who with his dropsical legs looked more than usually pitiable in walking. While giving his arm, he thought that he should not himself like to be an old fellow with his constitution breaking up; and he waited good-temperedly, first before the window to hear the wonted remarks about the guinea-fowls and the weathercock, and then before the scanty book-shelves, of which the chief glories in dark calf were Josephus, Culpepper, Klopstock's ' Messiah,' and several volumes of the ' Gentleman's Magazine.' [3]

"Read me the names o' the books. Come now! you're a college man."

Fred gave him the titles.

"What did missy want with more books? What must you be bringing her more books for?"

"They amuse her, sir. She is very fond of reading."

"A little too fond," said Mr Featherstone, captiously. "She was for reading when she sat with me. But I put a stop to that. She's got the newspaper to read out loud. That's enough for one day, I should think. I can't abide to see her reading to herself. You mind and not bring her any more books, do you hear?"

"Yes, sir, I hear." Fred had received this order before, and had secretly disobeyed it. He intended to disobey it again.

"Ring the bell," said Mr Featherstone; "I want missy to come down."

Rosamond and Mary had been talking faster than their male friends. They did not think of sitting down, but stood at the toilette-table near the window while Rosamond took off her hat, adjusted her veil, and applied little touches of her finger-tips to her hair—hair of infantine fairness, neither flaxen nor yellow. Mary Garth seemed all the plainer standing at an angle between the two nymphs—the one in the glass, and the one out of it, who looked at each other with eyes of heavenly blue, deep enough to hold the most exquisite meanings an ingenious beholder could put into them, and deep enough to hide the meanings of the owner if these should happen to be less exquisite. Only a few children in Middlemarch looked

3. Flavius **Josephus** (c. 38–100), Jewish politician and historian; among his works were a history of the Jews and *Against Apion*, a defense of the Jewish people against anti-Semitism. Sir Thomas Culpepper (1578–1662) and his son of the same name (1626–97) were both writers on the subject of usury. Friedrich Gottlieb Klopstock (1724–1803) was a German poet; his *Messias* was a popular and often translated poem of the late eighteenth century.

blond by the side of Rosamond, and the slim figure displayed by her
riding-habit had delicate undulations. In fact, most men in Middlemarch, except her brothers, held that Miss Vincy was the best girl
in the world, and some called her an angel. Mary Garth, on the
contrary, had the aspect of an ordinary sinner : she was brown ; her
curly dark hair was rough and stubborn ; her stature was low ; and
it would not be true to declare, in satisfactory antithesis, that she had
all the virtues. Plainness has its peculiar temptations and vices
quite as much as beauty ; it is apt either to feign amiability, or, not
feigning it, to show all the repulsiveness of discontent : at any rate,
to be called an ugly thing in contrast with that lovely creature your
companion, is apt to produce some effect beyond a sense of fine veracity and fitness in the phrase. At the age of two-and-twenty Mary
had certainly not attained that perfect good sense and good principle
which are usually recommended to the less fortunate girl, as if they
were to be obtained in quantities ready mixed, with a flavour of resignation as required. Her shrewdness had a streak of satiric bitterness continually renewed and never carried utterly out of sight,
except by a strong current of gratitude towards those who, instead of
telling her that she ought to be contented, did something to make
her so. Advancing womanhood had tempered her plainness, which
was of a good human sort, such as the mothers of our race have very
commonly worn in all latitudes under a more or less becoming head-
gear. Rembrandt would have painted her with pleasure, and would
have made her broad features look out of the canvas with intelligent
honesty. For honesty, truth - telling fairness, was Mary's reigning
virtue : she neither tried to create illusions, nor indulged in them
for her own behoof, and when she was in a good mood she had humour enough in her to laugh at herself. When she and Rosamond
happened both to be reflected in the glass, she said, laughingly—

"What a brown patch I am by the side of you, Rosy ! You are
the most unbecoming companion."

"Oh no ! No one thinks of your appearance, you are so sensible
and useful, Mary. Beauty is of very little consequence in reality,"
said Rosamond, turning her head towards Mary, but with eyes swerving towards the new view of her neck in the glass.

"You mean *my* beauty," said Mary, rather sardonically.

Rosamond thought, "Poor Mary, she takes the kindest things ill."
Aloud she said, "What have you been doing lately ?"

"I ? Oh, minding the house—pouring out syrup—pretending to be
amiable and contented—learning to have a bad opinion of everybody."

"It is a wretched life for you."

"No," said Mary, curtly, with a little toss of her head. "I think
my life is pleasanter than your Miss Morgan's."

"Yes ; but Miss Morgan is so uninteresting, and not young."

"She is interesting to herself, I suppose ; and I am not at all sure
that everything gets easier as one gets older."

"No," said Rosamond, reflectively ; "one wonders what such
people do, without any prospect. To be sure, there is religion as a
support. But," she added, dimpling, "it is very different with you,
Mary. You may have an offer."

"Has any one told you he means to make me one ?"

"Of course not. I mean, there is a gentleman who may fall in love
with you, seeing you almost every day."

A certain change in Mary's face was chiefly determined by the resolve not to show any change.

"Does that always make people fall in love?" she answered, carelessly; "it seems to me quite as often a reason for detesting each other."

"Not when they are interesting and agreeable. I hear that Mr Lydgate is both."

"Oh, Mr Lydgate!" said Mary, with an unmistakable lapse into indifference. "You want to know something about him," she added, not choosing to indulge Rosamond's indirectness.

"Merely, how you like him."

"There is no question of liking at present. My liking always wants some little kindness to kindle it. I am not magnanimous enough to like people who speak to me without seeming to see me."

"Is he so haughty?" said Rosamond, with heightened satisfaction. "You know that he is of good family?"

"No; he did not give that as a reason."

"Mary! you are the oddest girl. But what sort of looking man is he? Describe him to me."

"How can one describe a man? I can give you an inventory: heavy eyebrows, dark eyes, a straight nose, thick dark hair, large solid white hands—and—let me see—oh, an exquisite cambric pocket-handkerchief. But you will see him. You know this is about the time of his visits."

Rosamond blushed a little, but said, meditatively, "I rather like a haughty manner. I cannot endure a rattling young man."

"I did not tell you that Mr Lydgate was haughty; but *il y en a pour tous les goûts*, as little Mamselle used to say, and if any girl can choose the particular sort of conceit she would like, I should think it is you, Rosy."[4]

"Haughtiness is not conceit; I call Fred conceited."

"I wish no one said any worse of him. He should be more careful. Mrs Waule has been telling uncle that Fred is very unsteady." Mary spoke from a girlish impulse which got the better of her judgment. There was a vague uneasiness associated with the word "unsteady" which she hoped Rosamond might say something to dissipate. But she purposely abstained from mentioning Mrs Waule's more special insinuation.

"Oh, Fred is horrid!" said Rosamond. She would not have allowed herself so unsuitable a word to any one but Mary.

"What do you mean by horrid?"

"He is so idle, and makes papa so angry, and says he will not take orders."

"I think Fred is quite right."

"How can you say he is quite right, Mary? I thought you had more sense of religion."

"He is not fit to be a clergyman."

"But he ought to be fit."

"Well, then, he is not what he ought to be. I know some other people who are in the same case."

"But no one approves of them. I should not like to marry a clergyman; but there must be clergymen."

---

4. *Il y en a pour tout les goûts:* there is something for all tastes.

" It does not follow that Fred must be one."

" But when papa has been at the expense of educating him for it ! And only suppose, if he should have no fortune left him ? "

" I can suppose that very well," said Mary, dryly.

" Then I wonder you can defend Fred," said Rosamond, inclined to push this point.

" I don't defend him," said Mary, laughing ; " I would defend any parish from having him for a clergyman."

" But of course if he were a clergyman, he must be different."

" Yes, he would be a great hypocrite ; and he is not that yet."

" It is of no use saying anything to you, Mary. You always take Fred's part."

" Why should I not take his part ? " said Mary, lighting up. " He would take mine. He is the only person who takes the least trouble to oblige me."

" You make me feel very uncomfortable, Mary," said Rosamond, with her gravest mildness ; " I would not tell mamma for the world."

" What would you not tell her ? " said Mary, angrily.

" Pray do not go into a rage, Mary," said Rosamond, mildly as ever.

" If your mamma is afraid that Fred will make me an offer, tell her that I would not marry him if he asked me. But he is not going to do so, that I am aware. He certainly never has asked me."

" Mary, you are always so violent."

" And you are always so exasperating."

" I ? What can you blame me for ? "

" Oh, blameless people are always the most exasperating. There is the bell—I think we must go down."

" I did not mean to quarrel," said Rosamond, putting on her hat.

" Quarrel ? Nonsense ; we have not quarrelled. If one is not to get into a rage sometimes, what is the good of being friends ? "

" Am I to repeat what you have said ? "

" Just as you please. I never say what I am afraid of having repeated. But let us go down."

Mr Lydgate was rather late this morning, but the visitors stayed long enough to see him ; for Mr Featherstone asked Rosamond to sing to him, and she herself was so kind as to propose a second favourite song of his—" Flow on, thou shining river"—after she had sung " Home, sweet home" (which she detested). This hard-headed old Overreach approved of the sentimental song, as the suitable garnish for girls, and also as fundamentally fine, sentiment being the right thing for a song.[5]

Mr Featherstone was still applauding the last performance, and assuring Missy that her voice was as clear as a blackbird's, when Mr Lydgate's horse passed the window.

His dull expectation of the usual disagreeable routine with an aged patient—who can hardly believe that medicine would not " set him up" if the doctor were only clever enough—added to his general disbelief in Middlemarch charms, made a doubly effective background to this vision of Rosamond, whom old Featherstone made haste ostentatiously to introduce as his niece, though he had never thought it worth while to speak of Mary Garth in that light. Nothing escaped

5. Sir Giles Overreach, extortionist villain in Philip Massinger's *A New Way to Pay Old Debts* (1633).

Lydgate in Rosamond's graceful behaviour : how delicately she waived the notice which the old man's want of taste had thrust upon her by a quiet gravity, not showing her dimples on the wrong occasion, but showing them afterwards in speaking to Mary, to whom she addressed herself with so much good-natured interest, that Lydgate, after quickly examining Mary more fully than he had done before, saw an adorable kindness in Rosamond's eyes. But Mary from some cause looked rather out of temper.

" Miss Rosy has been singing me a song—you've nothing to say against that, eh, doctor ? " said Mr Featherstone. " I like it better than your physic."

" That has made me forget how the time was going," said Rosamond, rising to reach her hat, which she had laid aside before singing, so that her flower-like head on its white stem was seen in perfection above her riding-habit. " Fred, we must really go."

" Very good," said Fred, who had his own reasons for not being in the best spirits, and wanted to get away.

" Miss Vincy is a musician ? " said Lydgate, following her with his eyes. (Every nerve and muscle in Rosamond was adjusted to the consciousness that she was being looked at. She was by nature an actress of parts that entered into her *physique:* she even acted her own character, and so well, that she did not know it to be precisely her own.)

" The best in Middlemarch, I'll be bound," said Mr Featherstone, " let the next be who she will. Eh, Fred ? Speak up for your sister."

" I'm afraid I'm out of court, sir. My evidence would be good for nothing."

" Middlemarch has not a very high standard, uncle," said Rosamond, with a pretty lightness, going towards her whip, which lay at a distance.

Lydgate was quick in anticipating her. He reached the whip before she did, and turned to present it to her. She bowed and looked at him : he of course was looking at her, and their eyes met with that peculiar meeting which is never arrived at by effort, but seems like a sudden divine clearance of haze. I think Lydgate turned a little paler than usual, but Rosamond blushed deeply and felt a certain astonishment. After that, she was really anxious to go, and did not know what sort of stupidity her uncle was talking of when she went to shake hands with him.

Yet this result, which she took to be a mutual impression, called falling in love, was just what Rosamond had contemplated beforehand. Ever since that important new arrival in Middlemarch she had woven a little future, of which something like this scene was the necessary beginning. Strangers, whether wrecked and clinging to a raft, or duly escorted and accompanied by portmanteaus, have always had a circumstantial fascination for the virgin mind, against which native merit has urged itself in vain. And a stranger was absolutely necessary to Rosamond's social romance, which had always turned on a lover and bridegroom who was not a Middlemarcher, and who had no connections at all like her own : of late, indeed, the construction seemed to demand that he should somehow be related to a baronet. Now that she and the stranger had met, reality proved much more moving than anticipation, and Rosamond could not doubt that this was the great epoch of her life. She judged of her own symptoms as those of awakening love, and she held it still more natural that Mr Lydgate should have fallen in love at first sight of her. These things happened so often at balls, and why not by the morning light, when the complexion showed all the better for it? Rosamond, though no older than Mary, was rather used to being fallen in love with; but she, for her part, had remained indifferent and fastidiously critical towards both fresh sprig and faded bachelor. And here was Mr Lydgate suddenly corresponding to her ideal, being altogether foreign to Middlemarch, carrying a certain air of distinction congruous with good family, and possessing connections which offered vistas of that middle-class heaven, rank: a man of talent, also, whom it would be especially delightful to enslave: in fact, a man who had touched her nature quite newly, and brought a vivid interest into her life which was better than any fancied "might-be" such as she was in the habit of opposing to the actual.

Thus, in riding home, both the brother and the sister were preoccupied and inclined to be silent. Rosamond, whose basis for her structure had the usual airy slightness, was of remarkably detailed and realistic imagination when the foundation had been once presupposed; and before they had ridden a mile she was far on in the costume and introductions of her wedded life, having determined on her house in Middlemarch, and foreseen the visits she would pay to her husband's high-bred relatives at a distance, whose finished manners she could appropriate as thoroughly as she had done her school accomplishments, preparing herself thus for vaguer elevations which might ultimately come. There was nothing financial, still less sordid, in her previsions: she cared about what were considered refinements, and not about the money that was to pay for them.

Fred's mind, on the other hand, was busy with an anxiety which even his ready hopefulness could not immediately quell. He saw no way of eluding Featherstone's stupid demand without incurring consequences which he liked less even than the task of fulfilling it. His father was already out of humour with him, and would be still more so if he were the occasion of any additional coolness between his own family and the Bulstrodes. Then, he himself hated having to go and speak to his uncle Bulstrode, and perhaps after drinking wine he had said many foolish things about Featherstone's property, and these had been magnified by report. Fred felt that he had made a wretched figure as a fellow who bragged about expectations from a queer old miser like Featherstone, and went to beg for certificates at his bidding. But — those expectations! He really had them, and he saw no agreeable alternative if he gave them up; besides, he had lately made a debt which galled him extremely, and old Featherstone had almost bargained to pay it off. The whole affair was miserably small: his debts were small, even his expectations were not anything so very magnificent. Fred had known men to whom he would have been ashamed of confessing the smallness of his scrapes. Such ruminations naturally produced a streak of misanthropic bitterness. To be born the son of a Middlemarch manufacturer, and inevitable heir to nothing in particular, while such men as Mainwaring and Vyan—— certainly life was a poor business, when a spirited young fellow, with a good appetite for the best of everything, had so poor an outlook.

It had not occurred to Fred that the introduction of Bulstrode's name in the matter was a fiction of old Featherstone's; nor could this have made any difference to his position. He saw plainly enough that the old man wanted to exercise his power by tormenting him a little, and also probably to get some satisfaction out of seeing him on unpleasant terms with Bulstrode. Fred fancied that he saw to the bottom of his uncle Featherstone's soul, though in reality half what he saw there was no more than the reflex of his own inclinations. The difficult task of knowing another soul is not for young gentlemen whose consciousness is chiefly made up of their own wishes.

Fred's main point of debate with himself was, whether he should tell his father, or try to get through the affair without his father's knowledge. It was probably Mrs Waule who had been talking about him ; and if Mary Garth had repeated Mrs Waule's report to Rosamond, it would be sure to reach his father, who would as surely question him about it. He said to Rosamond, as they slackened their pace—

" Rosy, did Mary tell you that Mrs Waule had said anything about me ? "

" Yes, indeed, she did."

" What ? "

" That you were very unsteady."

" Was that all ? "

" I should think that was enough, Fred."

" You are sure she said no more ? "

" Mary mentioned nothing else. But really, Fred, I think you ought to be ashamed."

" Oh, fudge ! don't lecture me. What did Mary say about it ? "

" I am not obliged to tell you. You care so very much what Mary says, and you are too rude to allow me to speak."

" Of course I care what Mary says. She is the best girl I know."

" I should never have thought she was a girl to fall in love with."

" How do you know what men would fall in love with ? Girls never know."

" At least, Fred, let me advise *you* not to fall in love with her, for she says she would not marry you if you asked her."

" She might have waited till I did ask her."

" I knew it would nettle you, Fred."

" Not at all. She would not have said so if you had not provoked her."

Before reaching home, Fred concluded that he would tell the whole affair as simply as possible to his father, who might perhaps take on himself the unpleasant business of speaking to Bulstrode.

BOOK II.

OLD AND YOUNG.

CHAPTER XIII.

1st Gent. How class your man?—as better than the most,
Or, seeming better, worse beneath that cloak?
As saint or knave, pilgrim or hypocrite?
2d Gent. Nay, tell me how you class your wealth of books,
The drifted relics of all time.   As well
Sort them at once by size and livery :
Vellum, tall copies, and the common calf
Will hardly cover more diversity
Than all your labels cunningly devised
To class your unread authors.

In consequence of what he had heard from Fred, Mr Vincy determined to speak with Mr Bulstrode in his private room at the Bank at half-past one, when he was usually free from other callers.   But a visitor had come in at one o'clock, and Mr Bulstrode had so much to say to him, that there was little chance of the interview being over in half an hour.   The banker's speech was fluent, but it was also copious, and he used up an appreciable amount of time in brief meditative pauses.   Do not imagine his sickly aspect to have been of the yellow, black-haired sort : he had a pale blond skin, thin grey-besprinkled brown hair, light-grey eyes, and a large forehead.   Loud men called his subdued tone an undertone, and sometimes implied that it was inconsistent with openness ; though there seems to be no reason why a loud man should not be given to concealment of anything except his own voice, unless it can be shown that Holy Writ has placed the seat of candour in the lungs.   Mr Bulstrode had also a deferential bending attitude in listening, and an apparently fixed attentiveness in his eyes which made those persons who thought themselves worth hearing infer that he was seeking the utmost improvement from their discourse.   Others, who expected to make no great figure, disliked this kind of moral lantern turned on them.   If you are not proud of your cellar, there is no thrill of satisfaction in seeing your guest hold up his wine-glass to the light and look judicial.   Such joys are reserved for conscious merit.   Hence Mr Bulstrode's close attention was not agreeable to the publicans and sinners in Middlemarch ; it was attributed by some to his being a Pharisee, and by others to his being Evangelical.   Less superficial reasoners among them wished to know who his father and grandfather were, observing that five-and-twenty years ago nobody had ever heard of a Bulstrode in Middlemarch.   To his present visitor, Lydgate, the scrutinising look was a matter of

indifference : he simply formed an unfavourable opinion of the banker's constitution, and concluded that he had an eager inward life with
little enjoyment of tangible things.

"I shall be ·exceedingly obliged if you will look in on me here
occasionally, Mr Lydgate," the banker observed, after a brief pause.
"If, as I dare to hope, I have the privilege of finding you a valuable
coadjutor in the interesting matter of hospital management, there
will be many questions which we shall need to discuss in private.
As to the new hospital, which is nearly finished, I shall consider
what you have said about the advantages of the special destination for
fevers. The decision will rest with me, for though Lord Medlicote
has given the land and timber for the building, he is not disposed to
give his personal attention to the object."

"There are few things better worth the pains in a provincial town
like this," said Lydgate. "A fine fever hospital in addition to the
old infirmary might be the nucleus of a medical school here, when
once we get our medical reforms ; and what would do more for medical education than the spread of such schools over the country ?
A born provincial man who has a grain of public spirit as well as a
few ideas, should do what he can to resist the rush of everything
that is a little better than common towards London. Any valid professional aims may often find a freer, if not a richer field, in the provinces."

One of Lydgate's gifts was a voice habitually deep and sonorous,
yet capable of becoming very low and gentle at the right moment.
About his ordinary bearing there was a certain fling, a fearless expectation of success, a confidence in his own powers and integrity
much fortified by contempt for petty obstacles or seductions of which
he had had no experience. But this proud openness was made lovable by an expression of unaffected good-will. Mr Bulstrode perhaps
liked him the better for the difference between them in pitch and
manners ; he certainly liked him the better, as Rosamond did, for
being a stranger in Middlemarch. One can begin so many things
with a new person !—even begin to be a better man.

"I shall rejoice to furnish your zeal with fuller opportunities," Mr
Bulstrode answered ; "I mean, by confiding to you the superintendence of my new hospital, should a maturer knowledge favour that
issue, for I am determined that so great an object shall not be
shackled by our two physicians. Indeed, I am encouraged to consider your advent to this town as a gracious indication that a more
manifest blessing is now to be awarded to my efforts, which have
hitherto been much withstood. With regard to the old infirmary, we
have gained the initial point—I mean your election. And now I
hope you will not shrink from incurring a certain amount of jealousy
and dislike from your professional brethren by presenting yourself as
a reformer."

"I will not profess bravery," said Lydgate, smiling, "but I acknowledge a good deal of pleasure in fighting, and I should not care
for my profession, if I did not believe that better methods were to be
found and enforced there as well as everywhere else."

"The standard of that profession is low in Middlemarch, my dear
sir," said the banker. "I mean in knowledge and skill ; not in social
status, for our medical men are most of them connected with respectable townspeople here. My own imperfect health has induced me to

give some attention to those palliative resources which the divine mercy has placed within our reach. I have consulted eminent men in the metropolis, and I am painfully aware of the backwardness under which medical treatment labours in our provincial districts."

"Yes ;—with our present medical rules and education, one must be satisfied now and then to meet with a fair practitioner. As to all the higher questions which determine the starting-point of a diagnosis— as to the philosophy of medical evidence—any glimmering of these can only come from a scientific culture of which country practitioners have usually no more notion than the man in the moon."

Mr Bulstrode, bending and looking intently, found the form which Lydgate had given to his agreement not quite suited to his comprehension. Under such circumstances a judicious man changes the topic and enters on ground where his own gifts may be more useful.

"I am aware," he said, "that the peculiar bias of medical ability is towards material means. Nevertheless, Mr Lydgate, I hope we shall not vary in sentiment as to a measure in which you are not likely to be actively concerned, but in which your sympathetic concurrence may be an aid to me. You recognise, I hope, the existence of spiritual interests in your patients ?"

"Certainly I do. But those words are apt to cover different meanings to different minds."

"Precisely. And on such subjects wrong teaching is as fatal as no teaching. Now a point which I have much at heart to secure is a new regulation as to clerical attendance at the old infirmary. The building stands in Mr Farebrother's parish. You know Mr Farebrother ?"

"I have seen him. He gave me his vote. I must call to thank him. He seems a very bright pleasant little fellow. And I understand he is a naturalist."

"Mr Farebrother, my dear sir, is a man deeply painful to contemplate. I suppose there is not a clergyman in this country who has greater talents." Mr Bulstrode paused and looked meditative.

"I have not yet been pained by finding any excessive talent in Middlemarch," said Lydgate, bluntly.

"What I desire," Mr Bulstrode continued, looking still more serious, "is that Mr Farebrother's attendance at the hospital should be superseded by the appointment of a chaplain—of Mr Tyke, in fact—and that no other spiritual aid should be called in."

"As a medical man I could have no opinion on such a point unless I knew Mr Tyke, and even then I should require to know the cases in which he was applied." Lydgate smiled, but he was bent on being circumspect.

"Of course you cannot enter fully into the merits of this measure at present. But"—here Mr Bulstrode began to speak with a more chiselled emphasis—"the subject is likely to be referred to the medical board of the infirmary, and what I trust I may ask of you is, that in virtue of the co-operation between us which I now look forward to, you will not, so far as you are concerned, be influenced by my opponents in this matter."

"I hope I shall have nothing to do with clerical disputes," said Lydgate. "The path I have chosen is to work well in my own profession."

"My responsibility, Mr Lydgate, is of a broader kind. With me, indeed, this question is one of sacred accountableness ; whereas with my opponents, I have good reason to say that it is an occasion for gratifying a spirit of worldly opposition. But I shall not therefore drop one iota of my convictions, or cease to identify myself with that truth which an evil generation hates. I have devoted myself to this object of hospital-improvement, but I will boldly confess to you, Mr Lydgate, that I should have no interest in hospitals if I believed that nothing more was concerned therein than the cure of mortal diseases. I have another ground of action, and in the face of persecution I will not conceal it."

Mr Bulstrode's voice had become a loud and agitated whisper as he said the last words.

"There we certainly differ," said Lydgate. But he was not sorry that the door was now opened, and Mr Vincy was announced. That florid sociable personage was become more interesting to him since he had seen Rosamond. Not that, like her, he had been weaving any future in which their lots were united ; but a man naturally remembers a charming girl with pleasure, and is willing to dine where he may see her again. Before he took leave, Mr Vincy had given that invitation which he had been "in no hurry about," for Rosamond at breakfast had mentioned that she thought her uncle Featherstone had taken the new doctor into great favour.

Mr Bulstrode, alone with his brother-in-law, poured himself out a glass of water, and opened a sandwich-box.

"I cannot persuade you to adopt my regimen, Vincy ?"

"No, no ; I've no opinion of that system. Life wants padding," said Mr Vincy, unable to omit his portable theory. "However," he went on, accenting the word, as if to dismiss all irrelevance, "what I came here to talk about was a little affair of my young scapegrace, Fred's."

"That is a subject on which you and I are likely to take quite as different views as on diet, Vincy."

"I hope not this time." (Mr Vincy was resolved to be good-humoured.) "The fact is, it's about a whim of old Featherstone's. Somebody has been cooking up a story out of spite, and telling it to the old man, to try to set him against Fred. He's very fond of Fred, and is likely to do something handsome for him ; indeed, he has as good as told Fred that he means to leave him his land, and that makes other people jealous."

"Vincy, I must repeat, that you will not get any concurrence from me as to the course you have pursued with your eldest son. It was entirely from worldly vanity that you destined him for the Church : with a family of three sons and four daughters, you were not warranted in devoting money to an expensive education which has succeeded in nothing but in giving him extravagant idle habits. You are now reaping the consequences."

To point out other people's errors was a duty that Mr Bulstrode rarely shrank from, but Mr Vincy was not equally prepared to be patient. When a man has the immediate prospect of being mayor, and is ready, in the interests of commerce, to take up a firm attitude on politics generally, he has naturally a sense of his importance to the framework of things which seems to throw questions of private conduct into the background. And this particular reproof irritated him more than any other. It was eminently superfluous to him to be told that he was reaping the consequences. But he felt his neck under Bulstrode's yoke ; and though he usually enjoyed kicking, he was anxious to refrain from that relief.

" As to that, Bulstrode, it's no use going back. I'm not one of your pattern men, and I don't pretend to be. I couldn't foresee everything in the trade ; there wasn't a finer business in Middlemarch than ours, and the lad was clever. My poor brother was in the Church, and would have done well—had got preferment already, but that stomach fever took him off : else he might have been a dean by this time. I think I was justified in what I tried to do for Fred. If you come to religion, it seems to me a man shouldn't want to carve out his meat to an ounce beforehand :—one must trust a little to Providence and be generous. It's a good British feeling to try and raise your family a little : in my opinion, it's a father's duty to give his sons a fine chance."

" I don't wish to act otherwise than as your best friend, Vincy, when I say that what you have been uttering just now is one mass of worldliness and inconsistent folly."

" Very well," said Mr Vincy, kicking in spite of resolutions, " I never professed to be anything but worldly ; and, what's more, I don't see anybody else who is not worldly. I suppose you don't conduct business on what you call unworldly principles. The only difference I see is that one worldliness is a little bit honester than another."

" This kind of discussion is unfruitful, Vincy," said Mr Bulstrode, who, finishing his sandwich, had thrown himself back in his chair, and shaded his eyes as if weary. " You had some more particular business."

" Yes, yes. The long and short of it is, somebody has told old Featherstone, giving you as the authority, that Fred has been borrowing or trying to borrow money on the prospect of his land. Of course you never said any such nonsense. But the old fellow will insist on it that Fred should bring him a denial in your handwriting ; that is, just a bit of a note saying you don't believe a word of such stuff, either of his having borrowed or tried to borrow in such a fool's way. I suppose you can have no objection to do that."

" Pardon me. I have an objection. I am by no means sure that your son, in his recklessness and ignorance—I will use no severer word—has not tried to raise money by holding out his future prospects, or even that some one may not have been foolish enough to supply him on so vague a presumption : there is plenty of such lax money-lending as of other folly in the world."

" But Fred gives me his honour that he has never borrowed money on the pretence of any understanding about his uncle's land. He is not a liar. I don't want to make him better than he is. I have blown him up well—nobody can say I wink at what he does. But he is not a liar. And I should have thought—but I may be wrong —that there was no religion to hinder a man from believing the best of a young fellow, when you don't know worse. It seems to me it would be a poor sort of religion to put a spoke in his wheel by refusing to say you don't believe such harm of him as you've got no good reason to believe."

" I am not at all sure that I should be befriending your son by smoothing his way to the future possession of Featherstone's property.

I cannot regard wealth as a blessing to those who use it simply as a harvest for this world. You do not like to hear these things, Vincy, but on this occasion I feel called upon to tell you that I have no motive for furthering such a disposition of property as that which you refer to. I do not shrink from saying that it will not tend to your son's eternal welfare or to the glory of God. Why then should you expect me to pen this kind of affidavit, which has no object but to keep up a foolish partiality and secure a foolish bequest?"

"If you mean to hinder everybody from having money but saints and evangelists, you must give up some profitable partnerships, that's all I can say," Mr Vincy burst out very bluntly. "It may be for the glory of God, but it is not for the glory of the Middlemarch trade, that Plymdale's house uses those blue and green dyes it gets from the Brassing manufactory; they rot the silk, that's all I know about it. Perhaps if other people knew so much of the profit went to the glory of God, they might like it better. But I don't mind so much about that—I could get up a pretty row, if I chose."

Mr Bulstrode paused a little before he answered. "You pain me very much by speaking in this way, Vincy. I do not expect you to understand my grounds of action—it is not an easy thing even to thread a path for principles in the intricacies of the world—still less to make the thread clear for the careless and the scoffing. You must remember, if you please, that I stretch my tolerance towards you as my wife's brother, and that it little becomes you to complain of me as withholding material help towards the worldly position of your family. I must remind you that it is not your own prudence or judgment that has enabled you to keep your place in the trade."

"Very likely not; but you have been no loser by my trade yet," said Mr Vincy, thoroughly nettled (a result which was seldom much retarded by previous resolutions). "And when you married Harriet, I don't see how you could expect that our families should not hang by the same nail. If you've changed your mind, and want my family to come down in the world, you'd better say so. I've never changed: I'm a plain Churchman now, just as I used to be before doctrines came up. I take the world as I find it, in trade and everything else. I'm contented to be no worse than my neighbours. But if you want us to come down in the world, say so. I shall know better what to do then."

"You talk unreasonably. Shall you come down in the world for want of this letter about your son?"

"Well, whether or not, I consider it very unhandsome of you to refuse it. Such doings may be lined with religion, but outside they have a nasty, dog-in-the-manger look. You might as well slander Fred: it comes pretty near to it when you refuse to say you didn't set a slander going. It's this sort of thing—this tyrannical spirit, wanting to play bishop and banker everywhere—it's this sort of thing makes a man's name stink."

"Vincy, if you insist on quarrelling with me, it will be exceedingly painful to Harriet as well as myself," said Mr Bulstrode, with a trifle more eagerness and paleness than usual.

"I don't want to quarrel. It's for my interest—and perhaps for yours too—that we should be friends. I bear you no grudge; I think no worse of you than I do of other people. A man who half starves himself, and goes the length in family prayers, and so on, that you do, believes in his religion whatever it may be : you could turn over your capital just as fast with cursing and swearing :—plenty of fellows do.   You like to be master, there's no denying that ; you must be first chop in heaven, else you won't like it much.   But you're my sister's husband, and we ought to stick together ; and if I know Harriet, she'll consider it your fault if we quarrel because you strain at a gnat in this way, and refuse to do Fred a good turn.   And I don't mean to say I shall bear it well.   I consider it unhandsome."

Mr Vincy rose, began to button his greatcoat, and looked steadily at his brother-in-law, meaning to imply a demand for a decisive answer.

This was not the first time that Mr Bulstrode had begun by admonishing Mr Vincy, and had ended by seeing a very unsatisfactory reflection of himself in the coarse unflattering mirror which that manufacturer's mind presented to the subtler lights and shadows of his fellow-men ; and perhaps his experience ought to have warned him how the scene would end.   But a full-fed fountain will be generous with its waters even in the rain, when they are worse than useless ; and a fine fount of admonition is apt to be equally irrepressible.

It was not in Mr Bulstrode's nature to comply directly in consequence of uncomfortable suggestions.   Before changing his course, he always needed to shape his motives and bring them into accordance with his habitual standard.   He said, at last—

" I will reflect a little, Vincy.   I will mention the subject to Harriet.   I shall probably send you a letter."

" Very well.   As soon as you can, please.   I hope it will all be settled before I see you to-morrow."

CHAPTER XIV.

" Follows here the strict receipt
For that sauce to dainty meat,
Named Idleness, which many eat
By preference, and call it sweet :
    First watch for morsels, like a hound,
    Mix well with buffets, stir them round
    With good thick oil of flatteries,
    And froth with mean self-lauding lies.
    Serve warm : the vessels you must choose
    To keep it in are dead men's shoes."

Mr Bulstrode's consultation of Harriet seemed to have had the effect desired by Mr Vincy, for early the next morning a letter came which Fred could carry to Mr Featherstone as the required testimony.

The old gentleman was staying in bed on account of the cold weather, and as Mary Garth was not to be seen in the sitting-room, Fred went up-stairs immediately and presented the letter to his uncle, who, propped up comfortably on a bed-rest, was not less able than usual to enjoy his consciousness of wisdom in distrusting and frustrating mankind.   He put on his spectacles to read the letter, pursing up his lips and drawing down their corners.

" *Under the circumstances I will not decline to state my conviction*—tchah ! what fine words the fellow puts ! He's as fine as an auctioneer—*that your son Frederic has not obtained any advance of money on bequests promised by Mr Featherstone*—promised? who said I had ever promised? I promise nothing—I shall make codicils as long as I like—*and that considering the nature of such a proceeding, it is unreasonable to presume that a young man of sense and character would attempt it*—ah, but the gentleman doesn't say you *are* a young man of sense and character, mark you that, sir!—' *as to my own concern with any report of such a nature, I distinctly affirm that I never made any statement to the effect that your son had borrowed money on any property that might accrue to him on Mr Featherstone's demise*'—bless my heart! 'property'—accrue—demise! Lawyer Standish is nothing to him. He couldn't speak finer if he wanted to borrow. Well," Mr Featherstone here looked over his spectacles at Fred, while he handed back the letter to him with a contemptuous gesture, "you don't suppose I believe a thing because Bulstrode writes it out fine, eh?"

Fred coloured. "You wished to have the letter, sir. I should think it very likely that Mr Bulstrode's denial is as good as the authority which told you what he denies."

"Every bit. I never said I believed either one or the other. And now what d'you expect?" said Mr Featherstone, curtly, keeping on his spectacles, but withdrawing his hands under his wraps.

"I expect nothing, sir." Fred with difficulty restrained himself from venting his irritation. "I came to bring you the letter. If you like, I will bid you good morning."

"Not yet, not yet. Ring the bell; I want missy to come."

It was a servant who came in answer to the bell.

"Tell missy to come!" said Mr Featherstone, impatiently. "What business had she to go away?" He spoke in the same tone when Mary came.

"Why couldn't you sit still here till I told you to go? I want my waistcoat now. I told you always to put it on the bed."

Mary's eyes looked rather red, as if she had been crying. It was clear that Mr Featherstone was in one of his most snappish humours this morning, and though Fred had now the prospect of receiving the much-needed present of money, he would have preferred being free to turn round on the old tyrant and tell him that Mary Garth was too good to be at his beck. Though Fred had risen as she entered the room, she had barely noticed him, and looked as if her nerves were quivering with the expectation that something would be thrown at her. But she never had anything worse than words to dread. When she went to reach the waistcoat from a peg, Fred went up to her and said, "Allow me."

"Let it alone! You bring it, missy, and lay it down here," said Mr Featherstone. "Now you go away again till I call you," he added, when the waistcoat was laid down by him. It was usual with him to season his pleasure in showing favour to one person by being especially disagreeable to another, and Mary was always at hand to furnish the condiment. When his own relatives came she was treated better. Slowly he took out a bunch of keys from the waistcoat-pocket, and slowly he drew forth a tin box which was under the bed-clothes.

"You expect I'm going to give you a little fortune, eh?" he said, looking above his spectacles and pausing in the act of opening the lid.

"Not at all, sir. You were good enough to speak of making me a present the other day, else, of course, I should not have thought of the matter." But Fred was of a hopeful disposition, and a vision had presented itself of a sum just large enough to deliver him from a certain anxiety. When Fred got into debt, it always seemed to him highly probable that something or other—he did not necessarily conceive what—would come to pass enabling him to pay in due time. And now that the providential occurrence was apparently close at hand, it would have been sheer absurdity to think that the supply would be short of the need : as absurd as a faith that believed in half a miracle for want of strength to believe in a whole one.

The deep-veined hands fingered many bank-notes one after the other, laying them down flat again, while Fred leaned back in his chair, scorning to look eager. He held himself to be a gentleman at heart, and did not like courting an old fellow for his money. At last, Mr Featherstone eyed him again over his spectacles and presented him with a little sheaf of notes : Fred could see distinctly that there were but five, as the less significant edges gaped towards him. But then, each might mean fifty pounds. He took them, saying—

"I am very much obliged to you, sir," and was going to roll them up without seeming to think of their value. But this did not suit Mr Featherstone, who was eyeing him intently.

"Come, don't you think it worth your while to count 'em ? You take money like a lord ; I suppose you lose it like one."

"I thought I was not to look a gift-horse in the mouth, sir. But I shall be very happy to count them."

Fred was not so happy, however, after he had counted them. For they actually presented the absurdity of being less than his hopefulness had decided that they must be. What can the fitness of things mean, if not their fitness to a man's expectations ? Failing this, absurdity and atheism gape behind him. The collapse for Fred was severe when he found that he held no more than five twenties, and his share in the higher education of this country did not seem to help him. Nevertheless he said, with rapid changes in his fair complexion—

"It is very handsome of you, sir."

"I should think it is," said Mr Featherstone, locking his box and replacing it, then taking off his spectacles deliberately, and at length, as if his inward meditation had more deeply convinced him, repeating, "I should think it *is* handsome."

"I assure you, sir, I am very grateful," said Fred, who had had time to recover his cheerful air.

"So you ought to be. You want to cut a figure in the world, and I reckon Peter Featherstone is the only one you've got to trust to." Here the old man's eyes gleamed with a curiously-mingled satisfaction in the consciousness that this smart young fellow relied upon him, and that the smart young fellow was rather a fool for doing so.

"Yes, indeed : I was not born to very splendid chances. Few men have been more cramped than I have been," said Fred, with some sense of surprise at his own virtue, considering how hardly he was dealt with. "It really seems a little too bad to have to ride a broken-winded hunter, and see men, who are not half such good judges as yourself, able to throw away any amount of money on buying bad bargains."

" Well, you can buy yourself a fine hunter now. Eighty pound is enough for that, I reckon—and you'll have twenty pound over to get yourself out of any little scrape," said Mr Featherstone, chuckling slightly.

" You are very good, sir," said Fred, with a fine sense of contrast between the words and his feeling.

" Ay, rather a better uncle than your fine uncle Bulstrode. You won't get much out of his spekilations, I think. He's got a pretty strong string round your father's leg, by what I hear, eh ? "

" My father never tells me anything about his affairs, sir."

" Well, he shows some sense there. But other people find 'em out without his telling. *He'll* never have much to leave you : he'll most-like die without a will—he's the sort of man to do it—let 'em make him mayor of Middlemarch as much as they like. But you won't get much by his dying without a will, though you *are* the eldest son."

Fred thought that Mr Featherstone had never been so disagreeable before. True, he had never before given him quite so much money at once.

" Shall I destroy this letter of Mr Bulstrode's, sir ? " said Fred, rising with the letter as if he would put it in the fire.

" Ay, ay, I don't want it. It's worth no money to me."

Fred carried the letter to the fire, and thrust the poker through it with much zest. He longed to get out of the room, but he was a little ashamed before his inner self, as well as before his uncle, to run away immediately after pocketing the money. Presently, the farm-bailiff came up to give his master a report, and Fred, to his unspeak-able relief, was dismissed with the injunction to come again soon.

He had longed not only to be set free from his uncle, but also to find Mary Garth. She was now in her usual place by the fire, with sewing in her hands and a book open on the little table by her side. Her eyelids had lost some of their redness now, and she had her usual air of self-command.

" Am I wanted up-stairs ? " she said, half rising as Fred entered.

" No ; I am only dismissed, because Simmons is gone up."

Mary sat down again, and resumed her work. She was certainly treating him with more indifference than usual : she did not know how affectionately indignant he had felt on her behalf up-stairs.

" May I stay here a little, Mary, or shall I bore you ? "

" Pray sit down," said Mary ; " you will not be so heavy a bore as Mr John Waule, who was here yesterday, and he sat down without asking my leave."

" Poor fellow ! I think he is in love with you."

" I am not aware of it. And to me it is one of the most odious things in a girl's life, that there must always be some supposition of falling in love coming between her and any man who is kind to her, and to whom she is grateful. I should have thought that I, at least, might have been safe from all that. I have no ground for the non-sensical vanity of fancying everybody who comes near me is in love with me."

Mary did not mean to betray any feeling, but in spite of herself she ended in a tremulous tone of vexation.

" Confound John Waule ! I did not mean to make you angry. I didn't know you had any reason for being grateful to him. I forgot what a great service you think it if any one snuffs a candle for you."

Fred also had his pride, and was not going to show that he knew what had called forth this outburst of Mary's.

"Oh, I am not angry, except with the ways of the world. I do like to be spoken to as if I had common-sense. I really often feel as if I could understand a little more than I ever hear even from young gentlemen who have been to college." Mary had recovered, and she spoke with a suppressed rippling under-current of laughter pleasant to hear.

"I don't care how merry you are at my expense this morning," said Fred, "I thought you looked so sad when you came up-stairs. It is a shame you should stay here to be bullied in that way."

"Oh, I have an easy life—by comparison. I have tried being a teacher, and I am not fit for that : my mind is too fond of wandering on its own way. I think any hardship is better than pretending to do what one is paid for, and never really doing it. Everything here I can do as well as any one else could ; perhaps better than some—Rosy, for example. Though she is just the sort of beautiful creature that is imprisoned with ogres in fairy tales."

"*Rosy !*" cried Fred, in a tone of profound brotherly scepticism.

"Come, Fred !" said Mary, emphatically ; "*you* have no right to be so critical."

"Do you mean anything particular—just now ?"

"No, I mean something general—always."

"Oh, that I am idle and extravagant. Well, I am not fit to be a poor man. I should not have made a bad fellow if I had been rich."

"You would have done your duty in that state of life to which it has not pleased God to call you," said Mary, laughing.

"Well, I couldn't do my duty as a clergyman, any more than you could do yours as a governess. You ought to have a little fellow-feeling there, Mary."

"I never said you ought to be a clergyman. There are other sorts of work. It seems to me very miserable not to resolve on some course and act accordingly."

"So I could, if——" Fred broke off, and stood up, leaning against the mantelpiece.

"If you were sure you should not have a fortune ?"

"I did not say that. You want to quarrel with me. It is too bad of you to be guided by what other people say about me."

"How can I want to quarrel with you ! I should be quarrelling with all my new books," said Mary, lifting the volume on the table. "However naughty you may be to other people, you are good to me."

"Because I like you better than any one else. But I know you despise me."

"Yes, I do—a little," said Mary, nodding, with a smile.

"You would admire a stupendous fellow, who would have wise opinions about everything."

"Yes, I should." Mary was sewing swiftly, and seemed provokingly mistress of the situation. When a conversation has taken a wrong turn for us, we only get farther and farther into the swamp of awkwardness. This was what Fred Vincy felt.

"I suppose a woman is never in love with any one she has always known—ever since she can remember ; as a man often is. It is always some new fellow who strikes a girl."

" Let me see," said Mary, the corners of her mouth curling archly ;
" I must go back on my experience. There is Juliet—she seems an
example of what you say. But then Ophelia had probably known
Hamlet a long while ; and Brenda Troil—she had known Mordaunt
Merton ever since they were children ; but then he seems to have
been an estimable young man ; and Minna was still more deeply in
love with Cleveland, who was a stranger. Waverley was new to
Flora MacIvor ; but then she did not fall in love with him.[1] And
there are Olivia and Sophia Primrose, and Corinne—they may be
said to have fallen in love with new men.[2] Altogether, my experience is rather mixed."

Mary looked up with some roguishness at Fred, and that look of
hers was very dear to him, though the eyes were nothing more than
clear windows where observation sate laughingly. He was certainly
an affectionate fellow, and as he had grown from bóy to man, he had
grown in love with his old playmate, notwithstanding that share in
the higher education of the country which had exalted his views of
rank and income.

" When a man is not loved, it is no use for him to say that he could
be a better fellow—could do anything—I mean, if he were sure of
being loved in return."

" Not of the least use in the world for him to say he *could* be better.
Might, could, would—they are contemptible auxiliaries."

" I don't see how a man is to be good for much unless he has some
one woman to love him dearly."

" I think the goodness should come before he expects that."

" You know better, Mary. Women don't love men for their goodness."

" Perhaps not. But if they love them, they never think them bad."

" It is hardly fair to say I am bad."

" I said nothing at all about you."

" I never shall be good for anything, Mary, if you will not say that
you love me—if you will not promise to marry me—I mean, when I
am able to marry."

" If I did love you, I would not marry you : I would certainly not
promise ever to marry you."

" I think that is quite wicked, Mary. If you love me, you ought
to promise to marry me."

" On the contrary, I think it would be wicked in me to marry you
even if I did love you."

" You mean, just as I am, without any means of maintaining a
wife. Of course : I am but three-and-twenty."

" In that last point you will alter. But I am not so sure of any
other alteration. My father says an idle man ought not to exist,
much less, be married."

" Then I am to blow my brains out ?"

" No ; on the whole I should think you would do better to pass

1. Brenda and Minna Troil, Mordaunt
Merton, and Clement Cleveland are
characters in Sir Walter Scott's *The
Pirate* (1822); Edward Waverley and
Flora MacIvor are in Scott's *Waverly*
(1814).

2. Olivia and Sophia Primrose are
characters in Oliver Goldsmith's *The
Vicar of Wakefield* (1766); Corinne is
the eponymous heroine of a novel by
Mme. de Staël (1807).

your examination. I have heard Mr Farebrother say it is disgracefully easy."

"That is all very fine. Anything is easy to him. Not that cleverness has anything to do with it. I am ten times cleverer than many men who pass."

"Dear me !" said Mary, unable to repress her sarcasm. "That accounts for the curates like Mr Crowse. Divide your cleverness by ten, and the quotient—dear me !—is able to take a degree. But that only shows you are ten times more idle than the others."

"Well, if I did pass, you would not want me to go into the Church ?"

"That is not the question—what I want you to do. You have a conscience of your own, I suppose. There ! there is Mr Lydgate. I must go and tell my uncle."

"Mary," said Fred, seizing her hand as she rose ; "if you will not give me some encouragement, I shall get worse instead of better."

"I will not give you any encouragement," said Mary, reddening. "Your friends would dislike it, and so would mine. My father would think it a disgrace to me if I accepted a man who got into debt, and would not work !"

Fred was stung, and released her hand. She walked to the door, but there she turned and said : "Fred, you have always been so good, so generous to me. I am not ungrateful. But never speak to me in that way again."

"Very well," said Fred, sulkily, taking up his hat and whip. His complexion showed patches of pale pink and dead white. Like many a plucked idle young gentleman, he was thoroughly in love, and with a plain girl, who had no money ! But having Mr Featherstone's land in the background, and a persuasion that, let Mary say what she would, she really did care for him, Fred was not utterly in despair.

When he got home, he gave four of the twenties to his mother, asking her to keep them for him. "I don't want to spend that money, mother. I want it to pay a debt with. So keep it safe away from my fingers."

"Bless you, my dear," said Mrs Vincy. She doated on her eldest son and her youngest girl (a child of six), whom others thought her two naughtiest children. The mother's eyes are not always deceived in their partiality : she at least can best judge who is the tender, filial-hearted child. And Fred was certainly very fond of his mother. Perhaps it was his fondness for another person also that made him particularly anxious to take some security against his own liability to spend the hundred pounds. For the creditor to whom he owed a hundred and sixty held a firmer security in the shape of a bill signed by Mary's father.

CHAPTER XV.

" Black eyes you have left, you say,
    Blue eyes fail to draw you ;
Yet you seem more rapt to-day,
    Than of old we saw you.

Oh I track the fairest fair
    · Through new haunts of pleasure ;
Footprints here and echoes there
    Guide me to my treasure :

Lo ! she turns—immortal youth
    Wrought to mortal stature,
Fresh as starlight's agèd truth—
    Many-namèd Nature !"

A GREAT historian, as he insisted on calling himself, who had the happiness to be dead a hundred and twenty years ago, and so to take his place among the colossi whose huge legs our living pettiness is observed to walk under, glories in his copious remarks and digressions as the least imitable part of his work, and especially in those initial chapters to the successive books of his history, where he seems to bring his arm-chair to the proscenium and chat with us in all the lusty ease of his fine English. [1] But Fielding lived when the days were longer (for time, like money, is measured by our needs), when summer afternoons were spacious, and the clock ticked slowly in the winter evenings. We belated historians must not linger after his example ; and if we did so, it is probable that our chat would be thin and eager, as if delivered from a camp-stool in a parrot-house. I at least have so much to do in unravelling certain human lots, and seeing how they were woven and interwoven, that all the light I can command must be concentrated on this particular web, and not dispersed over that tempting range of relevancies called the universe.

At present I have to make the new settler Lydgate better known to any one interested in him than he could possibly be even to those who had seen the most of him since his arrival in Middlemarch. For surely all must admit that a man may be puffed and belauded, envied, ridiculed, counted upon as a tool and fallen in love with, or at least selected as a future husband, and yet remain virtually unknown—known merely as a cluster of signs for his neighbours' false suppositions. There was a general impression, however, that Lydgate was not altogether a common country doctor, and in Middlemarch at that time such an impression was significant of great things being expected

1. The reference is to Henry Fielding, in *Tom Jones* (1749): "Among other good uses for which I have thought proper to institute these several introductory chapters, I have considered them as a kind of mark or stamp, which may hereafter enable a very indif- ferent reader to distinguish what is true and genuine in this historic kind of writing, from what is false and counterfeit" (Bk. IX, Ch. 1). Colossi: the Colossus of Rhodes was a giant statue of the sun god Helios; it was destroyed by earthquake in 224 B.C.

from him. For everybody's family doctor was remarkably clever, and was understood to have immeasurable skill in the management and training of the most skittish or vicious diseases. The evidence of his cleverness was of the higher intuitive order, lying in his lady-patients' immovable conviction, and was unassailable by any objection except that their intuitions were opposed by others equally strong ; each lady who saw medical truth in Wrench and "the strengthening treatment" regarding Toller and "the lowering system" as medical perdition. For the heroic times of copious bleeding and blistering had not yet departed, still less the times of thorough-going theory, when disease in general was called by some bad name, and treated accordingly without shilly-shally—as if, for example, it were to be called insurrection, which must not be fired on with blank-cartridge, but have its blood drawn at once. The strengtheners and the lowerers were all "clever" men in somebody's opinion, which is really as much as can be said for any living talents. Nobody's imagination had gone so far as to conjecture that Mr Lydgate could know as much as Dr Sprague and Dr Minchin, the two physicians, who alone could offer any hope when danger was extreme, and when the smallest hope was worth a guinea. Still, I repeat, there was a general impression that Lydgate was something rather more uncommon than any general practitioner in Middlemarch. And this was true. He was but seven-and-twenty, an age at which many men are not quite common—at which they are hopeful of achievement, resolute in avoidance, thinking that Mammon shall never put a bit in their mouths and get astride their backs, but rather that Mammon, if they have anything to do with him, shall draw their chariot. [2]

He had been left an orphan when he was fresh from a public school. [3] His father, a military man, had made but little provision for three children, and when the boy Tertius asked to have a medical education, it seemed easier to his guardians to grant his request by apprenticing him to a country practitioner than to make any objections on the score of family dignity. He was one of the rarer lads who early get a decided bent and make up their minds that there is something particular in life which they would like to do for its own sake, and not because their fathers did it. Most of us who turn to any subject with love remember some morning or evening hour when we got on a high stool to reach down an untried volume, or sat with parted lips listening to a new talker, or for very lack of books began to listen to the voices within, as the first traceable beginning of our love. Something of that sort happened to Lydgate. He was a quick fellow, and when hot from play, would toss himself in a corner, and in five minutes be deep in any sort of book that he could lay his hands on : if it were Rasselas or Gulliver, so much the better, but Bailey's Dictionary would do, or the Bible with the Apocrypha in it. [4] Something he must read, when he was not riding the pony, or running and hunting, or listening to the talk of men. All this was true

2. Mammon: the personification of riches and material wealth. See Matt. 6:24, and Luke 16:9–13.

3. I.e., a private school, in American usage.

4. Samuel Johnson's *Rasselas* (1759), Jonathan Swift's *Gulliver's Travels* (1726); Nathan Bailey published his *Dictionary* in 1721.

of him at ten years of age ; he had then read through 'Chrysal, or
the Adventures of a Guinea,' which was neither milk for babes, nor
any chalky mixture meant to pass for milk, and it had already occurred to him that books were stuff, and that life was stupid.[5] His
school studies had not much modified that opinion, for though he
" did " his classics and mathematics, he was not pre-eminent in them.
It was said of him, that Lydgate could do anything he liked, but he
had certainly not yet liked to do anything remarkable. He was a
vigorous animal with a ready understanding, but no spark had yet
kindled in him an intellectual passion ; knowledge seemed to him a
very superficial affair, easily mastered : judging from the conversation
of his elders, he had apparently got already more than was necessary
for mature life. Probably this was not an exceptional result of expensive teaching at that period of short-waisted coats, and other
fashions which have not yet recurred. But, one vacation, a wet day
sent him to the small home library to hunt once more for a book which
might have some freshness for him : in vain ! unless, indeed, he took
down a dusty row of volumes with grey-paper backs and dingy labels
—the volumes of an old Cyclopædia which he had never disturbed.
It would at least be a novelty to disturb them. They were on the
highest shelf, and he stood on a chair to get them down. But he
opened the volume which he first took from the shelf : somehow, one is
apt to read in a makeshift attitude, just where it might seem inconvenient to do so. The page he opened on was under the head of Anatomy,
and the first passage that drew his eyes was on the valves of the heart.
He was not much acquainted with valves of any sort, but he knew
that *valvæ* were folding doors, and through this crevice came a sudden
light startling him with his first vivid notion of finely-adjusted mechanism in the human frame. A liberal education had of course left
him free to read the indecent passages in the school classics, but
beyond a general sense of secrecy and obscenity in connection with
his internal structure, had left his imagination quite unbiassed, so
that for anything he knew his brains lay in small bags at his temples,
and he had no more thought of representing to himself how his blood
circulated than how paper served instead of gold. But the moment
of vocation had come, and before he got down from his chair, the
world was made new to him by a presentiment of endless processes
filling the vast spaces planked out of his sight by that wordy ignorance which he had supposed to be knowledge. From that hour Lydgate felt the growth of an intellectual passion.

We are not afraid of telling over and over again how a man comes
to fall in love with a woman and be wedded to her, or else be fatally
parted from her. Is it due to excess of poetry or of stupidity that we
are never weary of describing what King James called a woman's
" makdom and her fairnesse," never weary of listening to the twang-
ing of the old Troubadour strings, and are comparatively uninterested
in that other kind of " makdom and fairnesse " which must be wooed
with industrious thought and patient renunciation of small desires ?[6]

5. *Chrysal, or the Adventures of a
Guinea:* a satirical narrative by Charles
Johnston, published in 1760–65.
6. Makdom and fairnesse: composure

or bearing, and fairness; from James I,
*The Essayes of a Prentise, in the Divine
Art of Poesie* (1585).

In the story of this passion, too, the development varies : sometimes it is the glorious marriage, sometimes frustration and final parting. And not seldom the catastrophe is bound up with the other passion, sung by the Troubadours. For in the multitude of middle-aged men who go about their vocations in a daily course determined for them much in the same way as the tie of their cravats, there is always a good number who once meant to shape their own deeds and alter the world a little. The story of their coming to be shapen after the average and fit to be packed by the gross, is hardly ever told even in their consciousness ; for perhaps their ardour in generous unpaid toil cooled as imperceptibly as the ardour of other youthful loves, till one day their earlier self walked like a ghost in its old home and made the new furniture ghastly. Nothing in the world more subtle than the process of their gradual change ! In the beginning they inhaled it unknowingly : you and I may have sent some of our breath to-wards infecting them, when we uttered our conforming falsities or drew our silly conclusions : or perhaps it came with the vibrations from a woman's glance.

Lydgate did not mean to be one of those failures, and there was the better hope of him because his scientific interest soon took the form of a professional enthusiasm : he had a youthful belief in his bread-winning work, not to be stifled by that initiation in makeshift called his 'prentice days ; and he carried to his studies in London, Edin-burgh, and Paris, the conviction that the medical profession as it might be was the finest in the world ; presenting the most perfect interchange between science and art ; offering the most direct alliance between intellectual conquest and the social good. Lydgate's nature demanded this combination : he was an emotional creature, with a flesh-and-blood sense of fellowship which withstood all the abstrac-tions of special study. He cared not only for " cases," but for John and Elizabeth, especially Elizabeth.

There was another attraction in his profession : it wanted reform, and gave a man an opportunity for some indignant resolve to reject its venal decorations and other humbug, and to be the possessor of genuine though undemanded qualifications. He went to study in Paris with the determination that when he came home again he would settle in some provincial town as a general practitioner, and resist the irrational severance between medical and surgical knowledge in the interest of his own scientific pursuits, as well as of the general advance : he would keep away from the range of London intrigues, jealousies, and social truckling, and win celebrity, however slowly, as Jenner had done, by the independent value of his work.[7] For it must be remembered that this was a dark period ; and in spite of venerable colleges which used great efforts to secure purity of knowledge by making it scarce, and to exclude error by a rigid exclusiveness in relation to fees and appointments, it happened that very ignorant young gentlemen were promoted in town, and many more got a legal right to practise over large areas in the country. Also, the high standard held up to the public mind by the College of Physicians, which gave its peculiar sanction to the expensive and highly-rarified

7. Edward Jenner (1749–1823), English physician, discoverer of vaccination.

medical instruction obtained by graduates of Oxford and Cambridge, did not hinder quackery from having an excellent time of it ; for since professional practice chiefly consisted in giving a great many drugs, the public inferred that it might be better off with more drugs still, if they could only be got cheaply, and hence swallowed large cubic measures of physic prescribed by unscrupulous ignorance which had taken no degrees. Considering that statistics had not yet embraced a calculation as to the number of ignorant or canting doctors which absolutely must exist in the teeth of all changes, it seemed to Lydgate that a change in the units was the most direct mode of changing the numbers. He meant to be a unit who would make a certain amount of difference towards that spreading change which would one day tell appreciably upon the averages, and in the mean time have the pleasure of making an advantageous difference to the viscera of his own patients. But he did not simply aim at a more genuine kind of practice than was common. He was ambitious of a wider effect : he was fired with the possibility that he might work out the proof of an anatomical conception and make a link in the chain of discovery.

Does it seem incongruous to you that a Middlemarch surgeon should dream of himself as a discoverer ? Most of us, indeed, know little of the great originators until they have been lifted up among the constellations and already rule our fates. But that Herschel, for example, who " broke the barriers of the heavens "—did, he not once play a provincial church-organ, and give music-lessons to stumbling pianists ? [8] Each of those Shining Ones had to walk on the earth among neighbours who perhaps thought much more of his gait and his garments than of anything which was to give him a title to everlasting fame : each of them had his little local personal history sprinkled with small temptations and sordid cares, which made the retarding friction of his course towards final companionship with the immortals. Lydgate was not blind to the dangers of such friction, but he had plenty of confidence in his resolution to avoid it as far as possible : being seven-and-twenty, he felt himself experienced. And he was not going to have his vanities provoked by contact with the showy worldly successes of the capital, but to live among people who could hold no rivalry with that pursuit of a great idea which was to be a twin object with the assiduous practice of his profession. There was fascination in the hope that the two purposes would illuminate each other : the careful observation and inference which was his daily work, the use of the lens to further his judgment in special cases, would further his thought as an instrument of larger inquiry. Was not this the typical pre-eminence of his profession ? He would be a good Middlemarch doctor, and by that very means keep himself in the track of far-reaching investigation. On one point he may fairly claim approval at this particular stage of his career : he did not mean to imitate those philanthropic models who make a profit out of poisonous pickles to support themselves while they are exposing adulteration, or hold shares in a gambling-hell that they may have leisure to represent the cause of public morality. He intended to begin in his own case some particular reforms which were quite certainly within

8. Sir William Herschel (1738–1822), famous German-born English astronomer who began his career as a teacher of music.

his reach, and much less of a problem than the demonstrating of an anatomical conception. One of these reforms was to act stoutly on the strength of a recent legal decision, and simply prescribe, without dispensing drugs or taking percentage from druggists. [9] This was an innovation for one who had chosen to adopt the style of general practitioner in a country town, and would be felt as offensive criticism by his professional brethren. But Lydgate meant to innovate in his treatment also, and he was wise enough to see that the best security for his practising honestly according to his belief was to get rid of systematic temptations to the contrary.

Perhaps that was a more cheerful time for observers and theorisers than the present ; we are apt to think it the finest era of the world when America was beginning to be discovered, when a bold sailor, even if he were wrecked, might alight on a new kingdom ; and about 1829 the dark territories of Pathology were a fine America for a spirited young adventurer. Lydgate was ambitious above all to contribute towards enlarging the scientific, rational basis of his profession. The more he became interested in special questions of disease, such as the nature of fever or fevers, the more keenly he felt the need for that fundamental knowledge of structure which just at the beginning of the century had been illuminated by the brief and glorious career of Bichat,[1] who died when he was only one-and-thirty, but, like another Alexander, left a realm large enough for many heirs. That great Frenchman first carried out the conception that living bodies, fundamentally considered, are not associations of organs which can be understood by studying them first apart, and then as it were federally ; but must be regarded as consisting of certain primary webs or tissues, out of which the various organs—brain, heart, lungs, and so on—are compacted, as the various accommodations of a house are built up in various proportions of wood, iron, stone, brick, zinc, and the rest, each material having its peculiar composition and proportions. No man, one sees, can understand and estimate the entire structure or its parts—what are its frailties and what its repairs, without knowing the nature of the materials. And the conception wrought out by Bichat, with his detailed study of the different tissues, acted necessarily on medical questions as the turning of gas-light would act on a dim, oil-lit street, showing new connections and hitherto hidden facts of structure which must be taken into account in considering the symptoms of maladies and the action of medicaments. But results which depend on human conscience and intelligence work slowly, and now at the end of 1829, most medical practice was still strutting or shambling along the old paths, and there was still scientific work to be done which might have seemed to be a direct sequence of Bichat's. This great seer did not go beyond the consideration of the tissues as ultimate facts in the living organism, marking the limit of anatomical analysis ; but it was open to another mind to say, have not these structures some common basis from which they have all started, as your sarsnet, gauze, net, satin and

9. Affirming the Apothecaries Act of 1815, which licensed apothecaries to the full practice of medicine along with physicians and surgeons, the courts ruled in *Allison* v. *Haydon* that a physician may prescribe medicines, but may not charge for dispensing his own medicines.

1. Marie François Xavier Bichat (1771–1802), French anatomist and physiologist.

velvet from the raw cocoon ? Here would be another light, as of
oxy-hydrogen, showing the very grain of things, and revising all
former explanations. Of this sequence to Bichat's work, already
vibrating along many currents of the European mind, Lydgate was
enamoured ; he longed to demonstrate the more intimate relations
of living structure, and help to define men's thought more accurately
after the true order. The work had not yet been done, but only
prepared for those who knew how to use the preparation. What was
the primitive tissue ? In that way Lydgate put the question—not
quite in the way required by the awaiting answer ; but such missing
of the right word befalls many seekers. And he counted on quiet
intervals to be watchfully seized, for taking up the threads of investigation—on many hints to be won from diligent application, not only
of the scalpel, but of the microscope, which research had begun to use
again with new enthusiasm of reliance. Such was Lydgate's plan
of his future : to do good small work for Middlemarch, and great
work for the world.

He was certainly a happy fellow at this time : to be seven-and-
twenty, without any fixed vices, with a generous resolution that his
action should be beneficent, and with ideas in his brain that made
life interesting quite apart from the *cultus* of horse-flesh and other
mystic rites of costly observance, which the eight hundred pounds
left him after buying his practice would certainly not have gone far
in paying for. He was at a starting-point which makes many a
man's career a fine subject for betting, if there were any gentlemen
given to that amusement who could appreciate the complicated pro-
babilites of an arduous purpose, with all the possible thwartings and
furtherings of circumstance, all the niceties of inward balance, by
which a man swims and makes his point or else is carried headlong.
The risk would remain, even with close knowledge of Lydgate's character ; for character too is a process and an unfolding. The man was
still in the making, as much as the Middlemarch doctor and immortal discoverer, and there were both virtues and faults capable of
shrinking or expanding. The faults will not, I hope, be a reason for
the withdrawal of your interest in him. Among our valued friends
is there not some one or other who is a little too self-confident and
disdainful ; whose distinguished mind is a little spotted with commonness ; who is a little pinched here and protuberant there with
native prejudices ; or whose better energies are liable to lapse down
the wrong channel under the influence of transient solicitations ?
All these things might be alleged against Lydgate, but then, they are
the periphrases of a polite preacher, who talks of Adam, and would
not like to mention anything painful to the pew-renters. The particular faults from which these delicate generalities are distilled have
distinguishable physiognomies, diction, accent, and grimaces ; filling
up parts in very various dramas. Our vanities differ as our noses do :
all conceit is not the same conceit, but varies in correspondence with
the minutiæ of mental make in which one of us differs from another.
Lydgate's conceit was of the arrogant sort, never simpering, never impertinent, but massive in its claims and benevolently contemptuous.
He would do a great deal for noodles, being sorry for them, and feeling quite sure that they could have no power over him : he had
thought of joining the Saint Simonians when he was in Paris, in

order to turn them against some of their own doctrines.[2] All his faults were marked by kindred traits, and were those of a man who had a fine baritone, whose clothes hung well upon him, and who even in his ordinary gestures had an air of inbred distinction. Where then lay the spots of commonness ? says a young lady enamoured of that careless grace. How could there be any commonness in a man so well-bred, so ambitious of social distinction, so generous and unusual in his views of social duty ? As easily as there may be stupidity in a man of genius if you take him unawares on the wrong subject, or as many a man who has the best will to advance the social millennium might be ill-inspired in imagining its lighter pleasures ; unable to go beyond Offenbach's music, or the brilliant punning in the last burlesque.[3] Lydgate's spots of commonness lay in the complexion of his prejudices, which, in spite of noble intention and sympathy, were half of them such as are found in ordinary men of the world : that distinction of mind which belonged to his intellectual ardour, did not penetrate his feeling and judgment about furniture, or women, or the desirability of its being known (without his telling) that he was better born than other country surgeons. He did not mean to think of furniture at present ; but whenever he did so, it was to be feared that neither biology nor schemes of reform would lift him above the vulgarity of feeling that there would be an incompatibility in his furniture not being of the best.

As to women, he had once already been drawn headlong by impetuous folly, which he meant to be final, since marriage at some distant period would of course not be impetuous. For those who want to be acquainted with Lydgate it will be good to know what was that case of impetuous folly, for it may stand as an example of the fitful swerving of passion to which he was prone, together with the chivalrous kindness which helped to make him morally lovable. The story can be told without many words. It happened when he was studying in Paris, and just at the time when, over and above his other work, he was occupied with some galvanic experiments. One evening, tired with his experimenting, and not being able to elicit the facts he needed, he left his frogs and rabbits to some repose under their trying and mysterious dispensation of unexplained shocks, and went to finish his evening at the theatre of the Porte Saint Martin, where there was a melodrama which he had already seen several times; attracted, not by the ingenious work of the collaborating authors, but by an actress whose part it was to stab her lover, mistaking him for the evil-designing duke of the piece. Lydgate was in love with this actress, as a man is in love with a woman whom he never expects to speak to. She was a Provençale, with dark eyes, a Greek profile, and rounded majestic form, having that sort of beauty which carries a sweet matronliness even in youth, and her voice was a soft cooing. She had but lately come to Paris, and bore a virtuous reputation, her husband acting with her as the unfortunate lover. It was her act-

<hr />

2. Saint Simonians: after Comte de Saint-Simon (1760–1825), French philosopher; founder of French positivism, socialism, and "the new Christianity" which was intended to remake society.

3. Jacques Offenbach (1819–1880), French composer of comic opera; his first work was *Pepito* (1853), so the reference is one of the rare anachronisms in this novel.

ing which was " no better than it should be," but the public was satisfied. Lydgate's only relaxation now was to go and look at this
woman, just as he might have thrown himself under the breath of
the sweet south on a bank of violets for a while, without prejudice
to his galvanism, to which he would presently return. But this
evening the old drama had a new catastrophe. At the moment when
the heroine was to act the stabbing of her lover, and he was to fall
gracefully, the wife veritably stabbed her husband, who fell as death
willed. A wild shriek pierced the house, and the Provençale fell
swooning: a shriek and a swoon were demanded by the play, but
the swooning too was real this time. Lydgate leaped and climbed,
he hardly knew how, on to the stage, and was active in help, making
the acquaintance of his heroine by finding a contusion on her head
and lifting her gently in his arms. Paris rang with the story of this
death :—was it a murder ? Some of the actress's warmest admirers
were inclined to believe in her guilt, and liked her the better for it
(such was the taste of those times); but Lydgate was not one of these.
He vehemently contended for her innocence, and the remote impersonal passion for her beauty which he had felt before, had passed now
into personal devotion, and tender thought of her lot. The notion of
murder was absurd ; no motive was discoverable, the young couple
being understood to dote on each other ; and it was not unprecedented that an accidental slip of the foot should have brought these
grave consequences. The legal investigation ended in Madame
Laure's release. Lydgate by this time had had many interviews
with her, and found her more and more adorable. She talked little ;
but that was an additional charm. She was melancholy, and seemed
grateful ; her presence was enough, like that of the evening light.
Lydgate was madly anxious about her affection, and jealous lest any
other man than himself should win it and ask her to marry him.
But instead of re-opening her engagement at the Porte Saint Martin,
where she would have been all the more popular for the fatal episode,
she left Paris without warning, forsaking her little court of admirers.

Perhaps no one carried inquiry far except Lydgate, who felt that all
science had come to a stand-still while he imagined the unhappy
Laure, stricken by ever-wandering sorrow, herself wandering, and
finding no faithful comforter. Hidden actresses, however, are not so
difficult to find as some other hidden facts, and it was not long before
Lydgate gathered indications that Laure had taken the route to
Lyons. He found her at last acting with great success at Avignon
under the same name, looking more majestic than ever as a forsaken
wife carrying her child in her arms. He spoke to her after the play,
was received with the usual quietude which seemed to him beautiful
as clear depths of water, and obtained leave to visit her the next day ;
when he was bent on telling her that he adored her, and on asking
her to marry him. He knew that this was like the sudden impulse
of a madman—incongruous even with his habitual foibles. No matter ! It was the one thing which he was resolved to do. He had
two selves within him apparently, and they must learn to accommodate each other and bear reciprocal impediments. Strange, that
some of us, with quick alternate vision, see beyond our infatuations,
and even while we rave on the heights, behold the wide plain where
our persistent self pauses and awaits us.

To have approached Laure with any suit that was not reverentially tender would have been simply a contradiction of his whole feeling towards her.

"You have come all the way from Paris to find me ?" she said to him the next day, sitting before him with folded arms, and looking at him with eyes that seemed to wonder as an untamed ruminating animal wonders. "Are all Englishmen like that ?"

"I came because I could not live without trying to see you. You are lonely ; I love you ; I want you to consent to be my wife : I will wait, but I want you to promise that you will marry me—no one else."

Laure looked at him in silence with a melancholy radiance from under her grand eyelids, until he was full of rapturous certainty, and knelt close to her knees.

"I will tell you something," she said, in her cooing way, keeping her arms folded. "My foot really slipped."

"I know, I know," said Lydgate, deprecatingly. "It was a fatal accident—a dreadful stroke of calamity that bound me to you the more."

Again Laure paused a little and then said, slowly, "*I meant to do it.*"

Lydgate, strong man as he was, turned pale and trembled : moments seemed to pass before he rose and stood at a distance from her.

"There was a secret, then," he said at last, even vehemently. "He was brutal to you : you hated him."

"No ! he wearied me ; he was too fond : he would live in Paris, and not in my country ; that was not agreeable to me."

"Great God !" said Lydgate, in a groan of horror. "And you planned to murder him ?"

"I did not plan : it came to me in the play—*I meant to do it.*"

Lydgate stood mute, and unconsciously pressed his hat on while he looked at her. He saw this woman—the first to whom he had given his young adoration—amid the throng of stupid criminals.

"You are a good young man," she said. "But I do not like husbands. I will never have another."

Three days afterwards Lydgate was at his galvanism again in his Paris chambers, believing that illusions were at an end for him. [4] He was saved from hardening effects by the abundant kindness of his heart and his belief that human life might be made better. But he had more reason than ever for trusting his judgment, now that it was so experienced ; and henceforth he would take a strictly scientific view of woman, entertaining no expectations but such as were justified beforehand.

No one in Middlemarch was likely to have such a notion of Lydgate's past as has here been faintly shadowed, and indeed the respectable townsfolk there were not more given than mortals generally to any eager attempt at exactness in the representation to themselves of what did not come under their own senses. Not only young virgins of that town, but grey-bearded men also, were often in haste to conjecture how a new acquaintance might be wrought into their purposes, contented with very vague knowledge as to the way in which life had been shaping him for that instrumentality. Middlemarch, in fact, counted on swallowing Lydgate and assimilating him very comfortably.

4. Medical "galvanism" involves the therapeutic application of electricity to the body.

CHAPTER XVI.

" All that in woman is adored
In thy fair self I find—
For the whole sex can but afford
The handsome and the kind."
—Sir Charles Sedley. [1]

THE question whether Mr Tyke should be appointed as salaried chaplain to the hospital was an exciting topic to the Middlemarchers ; and Lydgate heard it discussed in a way that threw much light on the power exercised in the town by Mr Bulstrode.   The banker was evidently a ruler, but there was an opposition party, and even among his supporters there were some who allowed it to be seen that their support was a compromise, and who frankly stated their impression that the general scheme of things, and especially the casualties of trade, required you to hold a candle to the devil.

Mr Bulstrode's power was not due simply to his being a country banker, who knew the financial secrets of most traders in the town and could touch the springs of their credit ; it was fortified by a beneficence that was at once ready and severe—ready to confer obligations, and severe in watching the result.   He had gathered, as an industrious man always at his post, a chief share in administering the town charities, and his private charities were both minute and abundant.   He would take a great deal of pains about apprenticing Tegg the shoemaker's son, and he would watch over Tegg's churchgoing ; he would defend Mrs Strype the washerwoman against Stubbs's unjust exaction on the score of her drying-ground, and he would himself scrutinise a calumny against Mrs Strype.   His private minor loans were numerous, but he would inquire strictly into the circumstances both before and after.   In this way a man gathers a domain in his neighbours' hope and fear as well as gratitude ; and power, when once it has got into that subtle region, propagates itself, spreading out of all proportion to its external means.   It was a principle with Mr Bulstrode to gain as much power as possible, that he might use it for the glory of God.   He went through a great deal of spiritual conflict and inward argument in order to adjust his motives, and make clear to himself what God's glory required.   But, as we have seen, his motives were not always rightly appreciated.   There were many crass minds in Middlemarch whose reflective scales could only weigh things in the lump ; and they had a strong suspicion that since Mr Bulstrode could not enjoy life in their fashion, eating and drinking so little as he did, and worreting himself about everything, he must have a sort of vampire's feast in the sense of mastery.

The subject of the chaplaincy came up at Mr Vincy's table when

1. "Not, Celia, that I juster am" (1672).

Lydgate was dining there, and the family connection with Mr Bulstrode did not, he observed, prevent some freedom of remark even on the part of the host himself, though his reasons against the proposed arrangement turned entirely on his objection to Mr Tyke's sermons, which were all doctrine, and his preference for Mr Farebrother, whose sermons were free from that taint. Mr Vincy liked well enough the notion of the chaplain's having a salary, supposing it were given to Farebrother, who was as good a little fellow as ever breathed, and the best preacher anywhere, and companionable too.

" What line shall you take, then ? " said Mr Chichely, the coroner, a great coursing comrade of Mr Vincy's.

" Oh, I'm precious glad I'm not one of the Directors now. I shall vote for referring the matter to the Directors and the Medical Board together. I shall roll some of my responsibility on your shoulders, Doctor," said Mr Vincy, glancing first at Dr Sprague, the senior physician of the town, and then at Lydgate who sat opposite. " You medical gentlemen must consult which sort of black draught you will prescribe, eh, Mr Lydgate ? "

" I know little of either," said Lydgate ; " but in general, appointments are apt to be made too much a question of personal liking. The fittest man for a particular post is not always the best fellow or the most agreeable. Sometimes, if you wanted to get a reform, your only way would be to pension off the good fellows whom everybody is fond of, and put them out of the question."

Dr Sprague, who was considered the physician of most " weight," though Dr Minchin was usually said to have more " penetration," divested his large heavy face of all expression, and looked at his wine-glass while Lydgate was speaking. Whatever was not problematical and suspected about this young man—for example, a certain showiness as to foreign ideas, and a disposition to unsettle what had been settled and forgotten by his elders—was positively unwelcome to a physician whose standing had been fixed thirty years before by a treatise on Meningitis, of which at least one copy marked " own " was bound in calf. For my part I have some fellow-feeling with Dr Sprague : one's self-satisfaction is an untaxed kind of property which it is very unpleasant to find depreciated.

Lydgate's remark, however, did not meet the sense of the company. Mr Vincy said, that if he could have *his* way, he would not put disagreeable fellows anywhere.

" Hang your reforms ! " said Mr Chichely. " There's no greater humbug in the world. You never hear of a reform, but it means some trick to put in new men. I hope you are not one of the ' Lancet's '[2] men, Mr Lydgate—wanting to take the coronership out of the hands of the legal profession : your words appear to point that way."

" I disapprove of Wakley," interposed Dr Sprague, " no man more : he is an ill-intentioned fellow, who would sacrifice the respectability

2. *Lancet:* a medical journal founded by Thomas Wakley (1795–1862) in London in 1823. GE read the *Lancet* extensively in preparing to write *Middlemarch*. In her *Quarry for "Middlemarch"* she notes that the *Lancet*'s position was that the coroner's was "a medical office, only to be adequately occupied by a medical judge." See below, p. 607.

of the profession, which everybody knows depends on the London Colleges, for the sake of getting some notoriety for himself. There are men who don't mind about being kicked blue if they can only get talked about. But Wakley is right sometimes," the Doctor added, judicially. " I could mention one or two points in which Wakley is in the right."

" Oh, well," said Mr Chichely, " I blame no man for standing up in favour of his own cloth ; but, coming to argument, I should like to know how a coroner is to judge of evidence if he has not had a legal training ? "

" In my opinion," said Lydgate, " legal training only makes a man more incompetent in questions that require knowledge of another kind. People talk about evidence as if it could really be weighed in scales by a blind Justice. No man can judge what is good evidence on any particular subject, unless he knows that subject well. A lawyer is no better than an old woman at a *post-mortem* examination. How is he to know the action of a poison ? You might as well say that scanning verse will teach you to scan the potato crops."

" You are aware, I suppose, that it is not the coroner's business to conduct the *post-mortem*, but only to take the evidence of the medical witness ? " said Mr Chichely, with some scorn.

" Who is often almost as ignorant as the coroner himself," said Lydgate. " Questions of medical jurisprudence ought not to be left to the chance of decent knowledge in a medical witness, and the coroner ought not to be a man who will believe that strychnine will destroy the coats of the stomach if an ignorant practitioner happens to tell him so."

Lydgate had really lost sight of the fact that Mr Chichely was his Majesty's coroner, and ended innocently with the question, " Don't you agree with me, Dr Sprague ? "

" To a certain extent—with regard to populous districts, and in the metropolis," said the Doctor. " But I hope it will be long before this part of the country loses the services of my friend Chichely, even though it might get the best man in our profession to succeed him. I am sure Vincy will agree with me."

" Yes, yes, give me a coroner who is a good coursing man," said Mr Vincy, jovially. " And in my opinion, you're safest with a law-yer. Nobody can know everything. Most things are ' visitation of God.' And as to poisoning, why, what you want to know is the law. Come, shall we join the ladies ? "

Lydgate's private opinion was that Mr Chichely might be the very coroner without bias as to the coats of the stomach, but he had not meant to be personal. This was one of the difficulties of moving in good Middlemarch society : it was dangerous to insist on knowledge as a qualification for any salaried office. Fred Vincy had called Lyd-gate a prig, and now Mr Chichely was inclined to call him prick-eared ; especially when, in the drawing-room, he seemed to be mak-ing himself eminently agreeable to Rosamond, whom he had easily monopolised in a *tête-à-tête*, since Mrs Vincy herself sat at the tea-table. She resigned no domestic function to her daughter ; and the matron's blooming good-natured face, with the too volatile pink strings floating from her fine throat, and her cheery manners to husband and children, was certainly among the great attractions of the Vincy house—attractions which made it all the easier to fall in love with the daughter. The tinge of unpretentious, inoffensive vulgarity in Mrs Vincy gave more effect to Rosamond's refinement, which was beyond what Lydgate had expected.

Certainly, small feet and perfectly turned shoulders aid the impression of refined manners, and the right thing said seems quite astonishingly right when it is accompanied with exquisite curves of lip and eyelid. And Rosamond could say the right thing; for she was clever with that sort of cleverness which catches every tone except the humorous. Happily she never attempted to joke, and this perhaps was the most decisive mark of her cleverness.

She and Lydgate readily got into conversation. He regretted that he had not heard her sing the other day at Stone Court. The only pleasure he allowed himself during the latter part of his stay in Paris was to go and hear music.

" You have studied music, probably ? " said Rosamond.

" No, I know the notes of many birds, and I know many melodies by ear ; but the music that I don't know at all, and have no notion about, delights me—affects me. How stupid the world is that it does not make more use of such a pleasure within its reach ! "

" Yes, and you will find Middlemarch very tuneless. There are hardly any good musicians. I only know two gentlemen who sing at all well."

" I suppose it is the fashion to sing comic songs in a rhythmic way, leaving you to fancy the tune—very much as if it were tapped on a drum ? "

" Ah, you have heard Mr Bowyer," said Rosamond, with one of her rare smiles. " But we are speaking very ill of our neighbours."

Lydgate was almost forgetting that he must carry on the conversation, in thinking how lovely this creature was, her garment seeming to be made out of the faintest blue sky, herself so immaculately blond, as if the petals of some gigantic flower had just opened and disclosed her ; and yet with this infantine blondness showing so much ready, self-possessed grace. Since he had had the memory of Laure, Lydgate had lost all taste for large-eyed silence : the divine cow no longer attracted him, and Rosamond was her very opposite. But he recalled himself.

" You will let me hear some music to-night, I hope."

" I will let you hear my attempts, if you like," said Rosamond. " Papa is sure to insist on my singing. But I shall tremble before you, who have heard the best singers in Paris. I have heard very little : I have only once been to London. But our organist at St Peter's is a good musician, and I go on studying with him."

" Tell me what you saw in London."

" Very little." (A more naïve girl would have said, " Oh, everything ! " But Rosamond knew better.) " A few of the ordinary sights, such as raw country girls are always taken to."

" Do you call yourself a raw country girl ? " said Lydgate, looking at her with an involuntary emphasis of admiration, which made Rosamond blush with pleasure. But she remained simply serious, turned her long neck a little, and put up her hand to touch her wondrous hair-plaits—an habitual gesture with her as pretty as any movements of a kitten's paw. Not that Rosamond was in the least like a kitten : she was a sylph caught young and educated at Mrs Lemon's.

" I assure you my mind is raw," she said immediately ; " I pass at Middlemarch. I am not afraid of talking to our old neighbours. But I am really afraid of you."

" An accomplished woman almost always knows more than we men, though her knowledge is of a different sort. I am sure you could teach me a thousand things—as an exquisite bird could teach a bear if there were any common language between them. Happily, there is a common language between women and men, and so the bears can get taught."

" Ah, there is Fred beginning to strum ! I must go and hinder him from jarring all your nerves," said Rosamond, moving to the other side of the room, where Fred having opened the piano, at his father's desire, that Rosamond might give them some music, was parenthetically performing " Cherry Ripe !" with one hand. Able men who have passed their examinations will do these things sometimes, not less than the plucked Fred. [3]

" Fred, pray defer your practising till to-morrow ; you will make Mr Lydgate ill," said Rosamond. " He has an ear."

Fred laughed, and went on with his tune to the end.

Rosamond turned to Lydgate, smiling gently, and said, " You perceive, the bears will not always be taught."

" Now then, Rosy !" said Fred, springing from the stool and twisting it upward for her, with a hearty expectation of enjoyment. " Some good rousing tunes first."

Rosamond played admirably. Her master at Mrs Lemon's school (close to a county town with a memorable history that had its relics in church and castle) was one of those excellent musicians here and there to be found in our provinces, worthy to compare with many a noted Kapellmeister in a country which offers more plentiful conditions of musical celebrity. Rosamond, with the executant's instinct, had seized his manner of playing, and gave forth his large rendering of noble music with the precision of an echo. It was almost startling, heard for the first time. A hidden soul seemed to be flowing forth from Rosamond's fingers ; and so indeed it was, since souls live on in perpetual echoes, and to all fine expression there goes somewhere an originating activity, if it be only that of an interpreter. Lydgate was taken possession of, and began to believe in her as something exceptional. After all, he thought, one need not be surprised to find the rare conjunctions of nature under circumstances apparently unfavourable : come where they may, they always depend on conditions that are not obvious. He sat looking at her, and did not rise to pay her any compliments, leaving that to others, now that his admiration was deepened.

Her singing was less remarkable, but also well trained, and sweet to hear as a chime perfectly in tune. It is true she sang " Meet me by moonlight," and " I've been roaming ;" for mortals must share the fashions of their time, and none but the ancients can be always classical. But Rosamond could also sing " Black-eyed Susan " with

---

3. Plucked: sent down for having failed his examinations.

effect, or Haydn's canzonets, or " Voi, che sapete," or " Batti, batti "
—she only wanted to know what her audience liked.

Her father looked round at the company, delighting in their admiration. Her mother sat, like a Niobe before her troubles, with her
youngest little girl on her lap, softly beating the child's hand up and
down in time to the music.[4] And Fred, notwithstanding his general
scepticism about Rosy, listened to her music with perfect allegiance,
wishing he could do the same thing on his flute. It was the pleasantest
family party that Lydgate had seen since he came to Middlemarch.
The Vincys had the readiness to enjoy, the rejection of all anxiety,
and the belief in life as a merry lot, which made a house exceptional
in most county towns at that time, when Evangelicalism had cast
a certain suspicion as of plague-infection over the few amusements
which survived in the provinces.[5] At the Vincys' there was always
whist, and the card-tables stood ready now, making some of the
company secretly impatient of the music. Before it ceased Mr Farebrother came in—a handsome, broad-chested but otherwise small
man, about forty, whose black was very threadbare : the brilliancy
was all in his quick grey eyes. He came like a pleasant change
in the light, arresting little Louisa with fatherly nonsense as she was
being led out of the room by Miss Morgan, greeting everybody with
some special word, and seeming to condense more talk into ten
minutes than had been held all through the evening. He claimed
from Lydgate the fulfilment of a promise to come and see him. " I
can't let you off, you know, because I have some beetles to show you.
We collectors feel an interest in every new man till he has seen all
we have to show him."

But soon he swerved to the whist-table, rubbing his hands and
saying, " Come now, let us be serious ! Mr Lydgate ? not play ? Ah !
you are too young and light for this kind of thing."

Lydgate said to himself that the clergyman whose abilities were so
painful to Mr Bulstrode, appeared to have found an agreeable resort
in this certainly not erudite household. He could half understand
it : the good-humour, the good looks of elder and younger, and the
provision for passing the time without any labour of intelligence,
might make the house beguiling to people who had no particular use
for their odd hours.

Everything looked blooming and joyous except Miss Morgan, who
was brown, dull, and resigned, and altogether, as Mrs Vincy often
said, just the sort of person for a governess. Lydgate did not mean
to pay many such visits himself. They were a wretched waste of
the evenings ; and now, when he had talked a little more to Rosamond, he meant to excuse himself and go.

" You will not like us at Middlemarch, I feel sure," she said, when
the whist-players were settled. " We are very stupid, and you have
been used to something quite different."

" I suppose all country towns are pretty much alike," said Lydgate.

4. In mythology, Niobe was the proud
mother of six sons and six daughters
who boasted herself superior to Leto,
the mother of Apollo and Artemis,
whereupon Apollo and Artemis slew her
children and caused Niobe herself to
be changed into a stone.

5. Evangelism: a puritanical religious
doctrine which taught the authority of
the Scriptures over that of the institu-
tional church, and stressed the importance of personal reconciliation to God
through Christ.

" But I have noticed that one always believes one's own town to be more stupid than any other. I have made up my mind to take Middlemarch as it comes, and shall be much obliged if the town will take me in the same way. I have certainly found some charms in it which are much greater than I had expected."

" You mean the rides towards Tipton and Lowick ; every one is pleased with those," said Rosamond, with simplicity.

" No, I mean something much nearer to me."

Rosamond rose and reached her netting, and then said, " Do you care about dancing at all ? I am not quite sure whether clever men ever dance."

" I would dance with you, if you would allow me."

" Oh !" said Rosamond, with a slight deprecatory laugh. " I was only going to say that we sometimes have dancing, and I wanted to know whether you would feel insulted if you were asked to come."

" Not on the condition I mentioned."

After this chat Lydgate thought that he was going, but on moving towards the whist-tables, he got interested in watching Mr Farebrother's play, which was masterly, and also his face, which was a striking mixture of the shrewd and the mild. At ten o'clock supper was brought in (such were the customs of Middlemarch), and there was punch-drinking ; but Mr Farebrother had only a glass of water. He was winning, but there seemed to be no reason why the renewal of rubbers should end, and Lydgate at last took his leave.

But as it was not eleven o'clock, he chose to walk in the brisk air towards the tower of St Botolph's, Mr Farebrother's church, which stood out dark, square, and massive against the starlight. It was the oldest church in Middlemarch ; the living, however, was but a vicarage worth barely four hundred a-year. Lydgate had heard that, and he wondered now whether Mr Farebrother cared about the money he won at cards ; thinking, " He seems a very pleasant fellow, but Bulstrode may have his good reasons." Many things would be easier to Lydgate if it should turn out that Mr Bulstrode was generally justifiable. " What is his religious doctrine to me, if he carries some good notions along with it ? One must use such brains as are to be found."

These were actually Lydgate's first meditations as he walked away from Mr Vincy's, and on this ground I fear that many ladies will consider him hardly worthy of their attention. He thought of Rosamond and her music only in the second place ; and though, when her turn came, he dwelt on the image of her for the rest of his walk, he felt no agitation, and had no sense that any new current had set into his life. He could not marry yet ; he wished not to marry for several years ; and therefore he was not ready to entertain the notion of being in love with a girl whom he happened to admire. He did admire Rosamond exceedingly ; but that madness which had once beset him about Laure was not, he thought, likely to recur in relation to any other woman. Certainly, if falling in love had been at all in question, it would have been quite safe with a creature like this Miss Vincy, who had just the kind of intelligence one would desire in a woman —polished, refined, docile, lending itself to finish in all the delicacies of life, and enshrined in a body which expressed this with a force of demonstration that excluded the need for other evidence. Lydgate felt sure that if ever he married, his wife would have that feminine radiance, that distinctive womanhood which must be classed with flowers and music, that sort of beauty which by its very nature was virtuous, being moulded only for pure and delicate joys.

But since he did not mean to marry for the next five years— his more pressing business was to look into Louis' new book on Fever, which he was specially interested in, because he had known Louis in Paris, and had followed many anatomical demonstrations in order to ascertain the specific differences of typhus and typhoid. [6] He went home and read far into the smallest hour, bringing a much more testing vision of details and relations into this pathological study than he had ever thought it necessary to apply to the complexities of love and marriage, these being subjects on which he felt himself amply informed by literature, and that traditional wisdom which is handed down in the genial conversation of men. Whereas Fever had obscure conditions, and gave him that delightful labour of the imagination which is not mere arbitrariness, but the exercise of disciplined power—combining and constructing with the clearest eye for probabilities and the fullest obedience to knowledge ; and then, in yet more energetic alliance with impartial Nature, standing aloof to invent tests by which to try its own work.

Many men have been praised as vividly imaginative on the strength of their profuseness in indifferent drawing or cheap narration :— reports of very poor talk going on in distant orbs ; or portraits of Lucifer coming down on his bad errands as a large ugly man with bat's wings and spurts of phosphorescence ; or exaggerations of wantonness that seem to reflect life in a diseased dream. But these kinds of inspiration Lydgate regarded as rather vulgar and vinous compared with the imagination that reveals subtle actions inaccessible by any sort of lens, but tracked in that outer darkness through long pathways of necessary sequence by the inward light which is the last refinement of Energy, capable of bathing even the ethereal atoms in its ideally illuminated space. He for his part had tossed away all cheap inventions where ignorance finds itself able and at ease : he was enamoured of that arduous invention which is the very eye of research, provisionally framing its object and correcting it to more and more exactness of relation ; he wanted to pierce the obscurity of those minute processes which prepare human misery and joy, those invisible thoroughfares which are the first lurking-places of anguish, mania, and crime, that delicate poise and transition which determine the growth of happy or unhappy consciousness.

As he threw down his book, stretched his legs towards the embers in the grate, and clasped his hands at the back of his head, in that agreeable after-glow of excitement when thought lapses from examination of a specific object into a suffusive sense of its connections with all the rest of our existence—seems, as it were, to throw itself on its back after vigorous swimming and float with the repose of unexhausted strength—Lydgate felt a triumphant delight in his studies, and something like pity for those less lucky men who were not of his profession.

6. Pierre Charles Louis (1787–1872), French physician, author of *Recherches . . . sur la Fièvre Typhoide* (1828). GE's note: "the celebrated treatise of Louis, in 1829, was the first to give a complete & connected view of symptoms as well as of post-mortem lesions in the fever common in Paris" (see *Quarry* below, p. 616).

" If I had not taken that turn when I was a lad," he thought, " I might have got into some stupid draught-horse work or other, and lived always in blinkers. I should never have been happy in any profession that did not call forth the highest intellectual strain, and yet keep me in good warm contact with my neighbours. There is nothing like the medical profession for that : one can have the exclusive scientific life that touches the distance and befriend the old fogies in the parish too. It is rather harder for a clergyman : Farebrother seems to be an anomaly."

This last thought brought back the Vincys and all the pictures of the evening. They floated in his mind agreeably enough, and as he took up his bed-candle his lips were curled with that incipient smile which is apt to accompany agreeable recollections. He was an ardent fellow, but at present his ardour was absorbed in love of his work and in the ambition of making his life recognised as a factor in the better life of mankind—like other heroes of science who had nothing but an obscure country practice to begin with.

Poor Lydgate ! or shall I say, Poor Rosamond ! Each lived in a world of which the other knew nothing. It had not occurred to Lydgate that he had been a subject of eager meditation to Rosamond, who had neither any reason for throwing her marriage into distant perspective, nor any pathological studies to divert her mind from that ruminating habit, that inward repetition of looks, words, and phrases, which makes a large part in the lives of most girls. He had not meant to look at her or speak to her with more than the inevitable amount of admiration and compliment which a man must give to a beautiful girl ; indeed, it seemed to him that his enjoyment of her music had remained almost silent, for he feared falling into the rudeness of telling her his great surprise at her possession of such accomplishment. But Rosamond had registered every look and word, and estimated them as the opening incidents of a preconceived romance—incidents which gather value from the foreseen development and climax. In Rosamond's romance it was not necessary to imagine much about the inward life of the hero, or of his serious business in the world : of course, he had a profession and was clever, as well as sufficiently handsome ; but the piquant fact about Lydgate was his good birth, which distinguished him from all Middlemarch admirers, and presented marriage as a prospect of rising in rank and getting a little nearer to that celestial condition on earth in which she would have nothing to do with vulgar people, and perhaps at last associate with relatives quite equal to the county people who looked down on the Middlemarchers. It was part of Rosamond's cleverness to discern very subtly the faintest aroma of rank, and once when she had seen the Miss Brookes accompanying their uncle at the county assizes, and seated among the aristocracy, she had envied them, notwithstanding their plain dress.

If you think it incredible that to imagine Lydgate as a man of family could cause thrills of satisfaction which had anything to do with the sense that she was in love with him, I will ask you to use your power of comparison a little more effectively, and consider whether red cloth and epaulets have never had an influence of that sort. Our passions do not live apart in locked chambers, but, dressed in their small wardrobe of notions, bring their provisions to a common table and mess together, feeding out of the common store according to their appetite.

Rosamond, in fact, was entirely occupied not exactly with Tertius Lydgate as he was in himself, but with his relation to her; and it was excusable in a girl who was accustomed to hear that all young men might, could, would be, or actually were in love with her, to believe at once that Lydgate could be no exception. His looks and words meant more to her than other men's, because she cared more for them : she thought of them diligently, and diligently attended to that perfection of appearance, behaviour, sentiments, and all other elegancies, which would find in Lydgate a more adequate admirer than she had yet been conscious of.

For Rosamond, though she would never do anything that was disagreeable to her, was industrious ; and now more than ever she was active in sketching her landscapes and market-carts and portraits of friends, in practising her music, and in being from morning till night her own standard of a perfect lady, having always an audience in her own consciousness, with sometimes the not unwelcome addition of a more variable external audience in the numerous visitors of the house. She found time also to read the best novels, and even the second best, and she knew much poetry by heart. Her favourite poem was ' Lalla Rookh.' [7]

" The best girl in the world ! He will be a happy fellow who gets her !" was the sentiment of the elderly gentlemen who visited the Vincys ; and the rejected young men thought of trying again, as is the fashion in country towns where the horizon is not thick with coming rivals. But Mrs Plymdale thought that Rosamond had been educated to a ridiculous pitch, for what was the use of accomplishments which would be all laid aside as soon as she was married ? While her aunt Bulstrode, who had a sisterly faithfulness towards her brother's family, had two sincere wishes for Rosamond—that she might show a more serious turn of mind, and that she might meet with a husband whose wealth corresponded to her habits.

CHAPTER XVII.

The clerkly person smiled and said,
Promise was a pretty maid,
But being poor she died unwed.

THE Rev. Camden Farebrother, whom Lydgate went to see the next evening, lived in an old parsonage, built of stone, venerable enough to match the church which it looked out upon. All the furniture too in the house was old, but with another grade of age—that of Mr Farebrother's father and grandfather. There were painted white chairs, with gilding and wreaths on them, and some lingering red silk damask with slits in it. There were engraved portraits of Lord Chancellors and other celebrated lawyers of the last century ; and

---

7. An extremely popular but second rate poem by Thomas Moore, published in 1817.

there were old pier-glasses to reflect them, as well as the little satin-wood tables and the sofas resembling a prolongation of uneasy chairs, all standing in relief against the dark wainscot. This was the physiognomy of the drawing-room into which Lydgate was shown ; and there were three ladies to receive him, who were also old-fashioned, and of a faded but genuine respectability : Mrs Farebrother, the Vicar's white-haired mother, befrilled and kerchiefed with dainty cleanliness, upright, quick - eyed, and still under seventy ; Miss Noble, her sister, a tiny old lady of meeker aspect, with frills and kerchief decidedly more worn and mended ; and Miss Winifred Farebrother, the Vicar's elder sister, well-looking like himself, but nipped and subdued as single women are apt to be who spend their lives in uninterrupted subjection to their elders. Lydgate had not expected to see so quaint a group : knowing simply that Mr Farebrother was a bachelor, he had thought of being ushered into a snuggery where the chief furniture would probably be books and collections of natural objects. The Vicar himself seemed to wear rather a changed aspect, as most men do when acquaintances made elsewhere see them for the first time in their own homes ; some indeed showing like an actor of genial parts disadvantageously cast for the curmudgeon in a new piece. This was not the case with Mr Farebrother : he seemed a trifle milder and more silent, the chief talker being his mother, while he only put in a good-humoured moderating remark here and there. The old lady was evidently accustomed to tell her company what they ought to think, and to regard no subject as quite safe without her steering. She was afforded leisure for this function by having all her little wants attended to by Miss Winifred. Meanwhile tiny Miss Noble carried on her arm a small basket, into which she diverted a bit of sugar, which she had first dropped in her saucer as if by mistake ; looking round furtively afterwards, and reverting to her tea-cup with a small innocent noise as of a tiny timid quadruped. Pray think no ill of Miss Noble. That basket held small savings from her more portable food, destined for the children of her poor friends among whom she trotted on fine mornings ; fostering and petting all needy creatures being so spontaneous a delight to her, that she regarded it much as if it had been a pleasant vice that she was addicted to. Perhaps she was conscious of being tempted to steal from those who had much that she might give to those who had nothing, and carried in her conscience the guilt of that repressed desire. One must be poor to know the luxury of giving !

Mrs Farebrother welcomed the guest with a lively formality and precision. She presently informed him that they were not often in want of medical aid in that house. She had brought up her children to wear flannel and not to over-eat themselves, which last habit she considered the chief reason why people needed doctors. Lydgate pleaded for those whose fathers and mothers had over-eaten themselves, but Mrs Farebrother held that view of things dangerous : Nature was more just than that ; it would be easy for any felon to say that his ancestors ought to have been hanged instead of him. If those who had bad fathers and mothers were bad themselves, they were hanged for that. There was no need to go back on what you couldn't see.

" My mother is like old George the Third," said the Vicar, " she objects to metaphysics."[1]

" I object to what is wrong, Camden. I say, keep hold of a few plain truths, and make everything square with them. When I was young, Mr Lydgate, there never was any question about right and wrong. We knew our catechism, and that was enough ; we learned our creed and our duty. Every respectable Church person had the same opinions. But now, if you speak out of the Prayer-book itself, you are liable to be contradicted."

" That makes rather a pleasant time of it for those who like to maintain their own point," said Lydgate.

" But my mother always gives way," said the Vicar, slyly.

" No, no, Camden, you must not lead Mr Lydgate into a mistake about *me*. I shall never show that disrespect to my parents, to give up what they taught me. Any one may see what comes of turning. If you change once, why not twenty times ? "

" A man might see good arguments for changing once, and not see them for changing again," said Lydgate, amused with the decisive old lady.

" Excuse me there. If you go upon arguments, they are never wanting, when a man has no constancy of mind. My father never changed, and he preached plain moral sermons without arguments, and was a good man—few better. When you get me a good man made out of arguments, I will get you a good dinner with reading you the cookery-book. That's my opinion, and I think anybody's stomach will bear me out."

" About the dinner certainly, mother," said Mr Farebrother.

" It is the same thing, the dinner or the man. I am nearly seventy, Mr Lydgate, and I go upon experience. I am not likely to follow new lights, though there are plenty of them here as elsewhere. I say, they came in with the mixed stuffs that will neither wash nor wear. It was not so in my youth : a Churchman was a Churchman, and a clergyman, you might be pretty sure, was a gentleman, if nothing else. But now he may be no better than a Dissenter, and want to push aside my son on pretence of doctrine. But whoever may wish to push him aside, I am proud to say, Mr Lydgate, that he will compare with any preacher in this kingdom, not to speak of this town, which is but a low standard to go by ; at least, to my thinking, for I was born and bred at Exeter."

" A mother is never partial," said Mr Farebrother, smiling. " What do you think Tyke's mother says about him ? "

" Ah, poor creature ! what indeed ? " said Mrs Farebrother, her sharpness blunted for the moment by her confidence in maternal judgments. " She says the truth to herself, depend upon it."

" And what is the truth ? " said Lydgate. " I am curious to know."

" Oh, nothing bad at all," said Mr Farebrother. " He is a zealous

<hr />

1. When Henry Dundas (1742–1811) tried to explain to George III that his government in Parliament was not bound to agree with him on the question of Catholic emancipation, the king replied, "None of your Scotch metaphysics, Mr. Dundas" (Robert J. Mackintosh, *The Life of Sir James Mackintosh*, I: 170).

fellow : not very learned, and not very wise, I think—because I
don't agree with him."

" Why, Camden ! " said Miss Winifred, " Griffin and his wife told
me only to-day, that Mr Tyke said they should have no more coals
if they came to hear you preach."

Mrs Farebrother laid down her knitting, which she had resumed
after her small allowance of tea and toast, and looked at her son as if
to say " You hear that ? "   Miss Noble said, " Oh, poor things ! poor
things ! " in reference, probably, to the double loss of preaching and
coal.   But the Vicar answered quietly—

" That is because they are not my parishioners.   And I don't think
my sermons are worth a load of coals to them."

" Mr Lydgate," said Mrs Farebrother, who could not let this pass,
" you don't know my son : he always undervalues himself.   I tell him
he is undervaluing the God who made him, and made him a most
excellent preacher."

" That must be a hint for me to take Mr Lydgate away to my
study, mother," said the Vicar, laughing.   " I promised to show you
my collection," he added, turning to Lydgate ;   " shall we go ? "

All three ladies remonstrated.   Mr Lydgate ought not to be hurried away without being allowed to accept another cup of tea : Miss
Winifred had abundance of good tea in the pot.   Why was Camden
in such haste to take a visitor to his den ?   There was nothing but
pickled vermin, and drawers full of blue-bottles and moths, with no
carpet on the floor.   Mr Lydgate must excuse it.   A game at crib-
bage would be far better.   In short, it was plain that a vicar might
be adored by his womankind as the king of men and preachers, and
yet be held by them to stand in much need of their direction.   Lydgate, with the usual shallowness of a young bachelor, wondered that
Mr Farebrother had not taught them better.

" My mother is not used to my having visitors who can take any
interest in my hobbies," said the Vicar, as he opened the door of his
study, which was indeed as bare of luxuries for the body as the ladies
had implied, unless a short porcelain pipe and a tobacco-box were to
be excepted.

" Men of your profession don't generally smoke," he said.   Lydgate
smiled and shook his head.   " Nor of mine either, properly, I suppose.   You will hear that pipe alleged against me by Bulstrode and
Company.   They don't know how pleased the devil would be if I
gave it up."

" I understand.   You are of an excitable temper and want a seda-
tive.   I am heavier, and should get idle with it.   I should rush into
idleness, and stagnate there with all my might."

" And you mean to give it all to your work.   I am some ten or
twelve years older than you, and have come to a compromise.   I feed
a weakness or two lest they should get clamorous.   See," continued
the Vicar, opening several small drawers, " I fancy I have made an
exhaustive study of the entomology of this district.   I am going on
both with the fauna and flora ; but I have at least done my insects well.
We are singularly rich in orthoptera : I don't know whether—Ah !
you have got hold of that glass jar—you are looking into that instead
of my drawers.   You don't really care about these things ? "

" Not by the side of this lovely anencephalous monster.   I have
never had time to give myself much to natural history.   I was early

bitten with an interest in structure, and it is what lies most directly in my profession. I have no hobby besides. I have the sea to swim in there."

" Ah ! you are a happy fellow," said Mr Farebrother, turning on his heel and beginning to fill his pipe. " You don't know what it is to want spiritual tobacco—bad emendations of old texts, or small items about a variety of *Aphis Brassicæ,* with the well-known signature of Philomicron, for the ' Twaddler's Magazine ;' or a learned treatise on the entomology of the Pentateuch, including all the insects not mentioned, but probably met with by the Israelites in their passage through the desert ; with a monograph on the Ant, as treated by Solomon, showing the harmony of the Book of Proverbs with the results of modern research. [2] You don't mind my fumigating you ?"

Lydgate was more surprised at the openness of this talk than at its implied meaning—that the Vicar felt himself not altogether in the right vocation. The neat fitting-up of drawers and shelves, and the bookcase filled with expensive illustrated books on Natural History, made him think again of the winnings at cards and their destination. But he was beginning to wish that the very best construction of everything that Mr Farebrother did should be the true one. The Vicar's frankness seemed not of the repulsive sort that comes from an uneasy consciousness seeking to forestall the judgment of others, but simply the relief of a desire to do with as little pretence as possible. Apparently he was not without a sense that his freedom of speech might seem premature, for he presently said—

" I have not yet told you that I have the advantage of you, Mr Lydgate, and know you better than you know me. You remember Trawley who shared your apartment at Paris for some time ? I was a correspondent of his, and he told me a good deal about you. I was not quite sure when you first came that you were the same man. I was very glad when I found that you were. Only I don't forget that you have not had the like prologue about me."

Lydgate divined some delicacy of feeling here, but did not half understand it. " By the way," he said, " what has become of Trawley ? I have quite lost sight of him. He was hot on the French social systems, and talked of going to the Backwoods to found a sort of Pythagorean community. [3] Is he gone ?"

" Not at all. He is practising at a German bath, and has married a rich patient."

" Then my notions wear the best, so far," said Lydgate, with a short scornful laugh. " He would have it, the medical profession was an inevitable system of humbug. I said, the fault was in the men — men who truckle to lies and folly. Instead of preaching against humbug outside the walls, it might be better to set up a disinfecting apparatus within. In short—I am reporting my own conversation—you may be sure I had all the good sense on my side."

" Your scheme is a good deal more difficult to carry out than the Pythagorean community, though. You have not only got the old Adam in yourself against you, but you have got all those descendants of the original Adam who form the society around you. You see, I have

---

2. *Aphis Brassicae:* cabbage lice. Philomicron: lover of small things. Twaddler: one who writes empty, silly prose.

3. Pythagoras founded an ascetic utopian community for students at Crotona, in Italy.

paid twelve or thirteen years more than you for my knowledge of difficulties. But"—Mr Farebrother broke off a moment, and then added, " you are eyeing that glass vase again. Do you want to make an exchange ? You shall not have it without a fair barter."

" I have some sea-mice—fine specimens—in spirits. And I will throw in Robert Brown's new thing—' Microscopic Observations on the Pollen of Plants '—if you don't happen to have it already." [4]

" Why, seeing how you long for the monster, I might ask a higher price. Suppose I ask you to look through my drawers and agree with me about all my new species ? " The Vicar, while he talked in this way, alternately moved about with his pipe in his mouth, and returned to hang rather fondly over his drawers. " That would be good discipline, you know, for a young doctor who has to please his patients in Middlemarch. You must learn to be bored, remember. However, you shall have the monster on your own terms."

" Don't you think men overrate the necessity for humouring everybody's nonsense, till they get despised by the very fools they humour ? " said Lydgate, moving to Mr Farebrother's side, and look-ing rather absently at the insects ranged in fine gradation, with names subscribed in exquisite writing. " The shortest way is to make your value felt, so that people must put up with you whether you flatter them or not."

" With all my heart. But then you must be sure of having the value, and you must keep yourself independent. Very few men can do that. Either you slip out of service altogether, and become good for nothing, or you wear the harness and draw a good deal where your yoke-fellows pull you. But do look at these delicate orthop-tera ! "

Lydgate had after all to give some scrutiny to each drawer, the Vicar laughing at himself, and yet persisting in the exhibition.

" Apropos of what you said about wearing harness," Lydgate be-gan, after they had sat down, " I made up my mind some time ago to do with as little of it as possible. That was why I determined not to try anything in London, for a good many years at least. I didn't like what I saw when I was studying there—so much empty bigwiggism, and obstructive trickery. In the country, people have less pretension to knowledge, and are less of companions, but for that reason they affect one's *amour-propre* less : one makes less bad blood, and can follow one's own course more quietly." [5]

" Yes—well—you have got a good start ; you are in the right pro-fession, the work you feel yourself most fit for. Some people miss that, and repent too late. But you must not be too sure of keeping your independence."

" You mean of family ties ? " said Lydgate, conceiving that these might press rather tightly on Mr Farebrother.

" Not altogether. Of course they make many things more diffi-cult. But a good wife—a good unworldly woman—may really help a man, and keep him more independent. There's a parishioner of mine—a fine fellow, but who would hardly have pulled through as he has done without his wife. Do you know the Garths ? I think they were not Peacock's patients."

---

4. Robert Brown (1773–1858), foremost British botanist of his time; the essay

was published in 1828.
5. *Amour-propre:* self-esteem.

" No ; but there is a Miss Garth at old Featherstone's, at Lowick."

" Their daughter : an excellent girl."

" She is very quiet—I have hardly noticed her."

" She has taken notice of you, though, depend upon it."

" I don't understand," said Lydgate ; he could hardly say " Of course."

" Oh, she gauges everybody. I prepared her for confirmation—she is a favourite of mine."

Mr Farebrother puffed a few moments in silence, Lydgate not caring to know more about the Garths. At last the Vicar laid down his pipe, stretched out his legs, and turned his bright eyes with a smile towards Lydgate, saying—

" But we Middlemarchers are not so tame as you take us to be. We have our intrigues and our parties. I am a party man, for example, and Bulstrode is another. If you vote for me you will offend Bulstrode."

" What is there against Bulstrode ? " said Lydgate, emphatically.

" I did not say there was anything against him except that. If you vote against him you will make him your enemy."

" I don't know that I need mind about that," said Lydgate, rather proudly ; " but he seems to have good ideas about hospitals, and he spends large sums on useful public objects. He might help me a good deal in carrying out my ideas. As to his religious notions— why, as Voltaire said, incantations will destroy a flock of sheep if administered with a certain quantity of arsenic. I look for the man who will bring the arsenic, and don't mind about his incantations."

" Very good. But then you must not offend your arsenic-man. You will not offend me, you know," said Mr Farebrother, quite unaffectedly. " I don't translate my own convenience into other people's duties. I am opposed to Bulstrode in many ways. I don't like the set he belongs to : they are a narrow ignorant set, and do more to make their neighbours uncomfortable than to make them better. Their system is a sort of worldly-spiritual cliqueism : they really look on the rest of mankind as a doomed carcass which is to nourish them for heaven. But," he added, smilingly, " I don't say that Bulstrode's new hospital is a bad thing ; and as to his wanting to oust me from the old one—why, if he thinks me a mischievous fellow, he is only returning a compliment. And I am not a model clergyman—only a decent makeshift."

Lydgate was not at all sure that the Vicar maligned himself. A model clergyman, like a model doctor, ought to think his own profession the finest in the world, and take all knowledge as mere nourishment to his moral pathology and therapeutics. He only said, " What reason does Bulstrode give for superseding you ? "

" That I don't teach his opinions—which he calls spiritual religion ; and that I have no time to spare. Both statements are true. But then I could make time, and I should be glad of the forty pounds. That is the plain fact of the case. But let us dismiss it. I only wanted to tell you that if you vote for your arsenic-man, you are not to cut me in consequence. I can't spare you. You are a sort of circumnavigator come to settle among us, and will keep up my belief in the antipodes. Now tell me all about them in Paris."

CHAPTER XVIII.

" Oh, sir, the loftiest hopes on earth
Draw lots with meaner hopes : heroic breasts,
Breathing bad air, run risk of pestilence ;
Or, lacking lime-juice when they cross the Line,
May languish with the scurvy."

SOME weeks passed after this conversation before the question of the
chaplaincy gathered any practical import for Lydgate, and without
telling himself the reason, he deferred the predetermination on which
side he should give his vote. It would really have been a matter of
total indifference to him—that is to say, he would have taken the
more convenient side, and given his vote for the appointment of Tyke
without any hesitation—if he had not cared personally for Mr Farebrother.

But his liking for the Vicar of St Botolph's grew with growing
acquaintanceship. That, entering into Lydgate's position as a new-
comer who had his own professional objects to secure, Mr Farebrother
should have taken pains rather to warn off than to obtain his interest,
showed an unusual delicacy and generosity, which Lydgate's nature
was keenly alive to. It went along with other points of conduct in
Mr Farebrother which were exceptionally fine, and made his character
resemble those southern landscapes which seem divided between
natural grandeur and social slovenliness. Very few men could have
been as filial and chivalrous as he was to the mother, aunt, and sister,
whose dependence on him had in many ways shaped his life rather
uneasily for himself ; few men who feel the pressure of small needs
are so nobly resolute not to dress up their inevitably self-interested
desires in a pretext of better motives. In these matters he was
conscious that his life would bear the closest scrutiny ; and perhaps
the consciousness encouraged a little defiance towards the critical
strictness of persons whose celestial intimacies seemed not to improve
their domestic manners, and whose lofty aims were not needed to
account for their actions. Then, his preaching was ingenious and
pithy, like the preaching of the English Church in its robust age, and
his sermons were delivered without book. People outside his parish
went to hear him ; and, since to fill the church was always the most
difficult part of a clergyman's function, here was another ground for
a careless sense of superiority. Besides, he was a likeable man : sweet-
tempered, ready-witted, frank, without grins of suppressed bitterness or
other conversational flavours which make half of us an affliction to our
friends. Lydgate liked him heartily, and wished for his friendship.

With this feeling uppermost, he continued to waive the question
of the chaplaincy, and to persuade himself that it was not only no
proper business of his, but likely enough never to vex him with a

demand for his vote. Lydgate, at Mr Bulstrode's request, was laying down plans for the internal arrangements of the new hospital, and the two were often in consultation. The banker was always presupposing that he could count in general on Lydgate as a coadjutor, but made no special recurrence to the coming decision between Tyke and Farebrother. When the General Board of the Infirmary had met, however, and Lydgate had notice that the question of the chaplaincy was thrown on a council of the directors and medical men, to meet on the following Friday, he had a vexed sense that he must make up his mind on this trivial Middlemarch business. He could not help hearing within him the distinct declaration that Bulstrode was prime minister, and that the Tyke affair was a question of office or no office ; and he could not help an equally pronounced dislike to giving up the prospect of office. For his observation was constantly confirming Mr Farebrother's assurance that the banker would not overlook opposition. "Confound their petty politics!" was one of his thoughts for three mornings in the meditative process of shaving, when he had begun to feel that he must really hold a court of conscience on this matter. Certainly there were valid things to be said against the election of Mr Farebrother : he had too much on his hands already, especially considering how much time he spent on non-clerical occupations. Then again it was a continually repeated shock, disturbing Lydgate's esteem, that the Vicar should obviously play for the sake of money, liking the play indeed, but evidently liking some end which it served. Mr Farebrother contended on theory for the desirability of all games, and said that Englishmen's wit was stagnant for want of them ; but Lydgate felt certain that he would have played very much less but for the money. There was a billiard-room at the Green Dragon, which some anxious mothers and wives regarded as the chief temptation in Middlemarch. The Vicar was a first-rate billiard-player, and though he did not frequent the Green Dragon, there were reports that he had sometimes been there in the daytime and had won money. And as to the chaplaincy, he did not pretend that he cared for it, except for the sake of the forty pounds. Lydgate was no Puritan, but he did not care for play, and winning money at it had always seemed a meanness to him ; besides, he had an ideal of life which made this subservience of conduct to the gaining of small sums thoroughly hateful to him. Hitherto in his own life his wants had been supplied without any trouble to himself, and his first impulse was always to be liberal with half-crowns as matters of no importance to a gentleman ; it had never occurred to him to devise a plan for getting half-crowns. He had always known in a general way that he was not rich, but he had never felt poor, and he had no power of imagining the part which the want of money plays in determining the actions of men. Money had never been a motive to him. Hence he was not ready to frame excuses for this deliberate pursuit of small gains. It was altogether repulsive to him, and he never entered into any calculation of the ratio between the Vicar's income and his more or less necessary expenditure. It was possible that he would not have made such a calculation in his own case.

And now, when the question of voting had come, this repulsive fact told more strongly against Mr Farebrother than it had done before. One would know much better what to do if men's characters were more consistent, and especially if one's friends were invariably fit for any function they desired to undertake ! Lydgate was convinced that if there had been no valid objection to Mr Farebrother, he would have voted for him, whatever Bulstrode might have felt on the subject : he did not intend to be a vassal of Bulstrode's. On the other hand, there was Tyke, a man entirely given to his clerical office, who was simply curate at a chapel of ease in St Peter's parish, and had time for extra duty. Nobody had anything to say against Mr Tyke, except that they could not bear him, and suspected him of cant. Really, from his point of view, Bulstrode was thoroughly justified.

But whichever way Lydgate began to incline, there was something to make him wince ; and being a proud man, he was a little exasperated at being obliged to wince. He did not like frustrating his own best purposes by getting on bad terms with Bulstrode ; he did not like voting against Farebrother, and helping to deprive him of function and salary ; and the question occurred whether the additional forty pounds might not leave the Vicar free from that ignoble care about winning at cards. Moreover, Lydgate did not like the consciousness that in voting for Tyke he should be voting on the side obviously convenient for himself. But would the end really be his own convenience ? Other people would say so, and would allege that he was currying favour with Bulstrode for the sake of making himself important and getting on in the world. What then ? He for his own part knew that if his personal prospects simply had been concerned, he would not have cared a rotten nut for the banker's friendship or enmity. What he really cared for was a medium for his work, a vehicle for his ideas ; and after all, was he not bound to prefer the object of getting a good hospital, where he could demonstrate the specific distinctions of fever and test therapeutic results, before anything else connected with this chaplaincy ? For the first time Lydgate was feeling the hampering threadlike pressure of small social conditions, and their frustrating complexity. At the end of his inward debate, when he set out for the hospital, his hope was really in the chance that discussion might somehow give a new aspect to the question, and make the scale dip so as to exclude the necessity for voting. I think he trusted a little also to the energy which is begotten by circumstances—some feeling rushing warmly and making resolve easy, while debate in cool blood had only made it more difficult. However it was, he did not distinctly say to himself on which side he would vote ; and all the while he was inwardly resenting the subjection which had been forced upon him. It would have seemed beforehand like a ridiculous piece of bad logic that he, with his unmixed resolutions of independence and his select purposes, would find himself at the very outset in the grasp of petty alternatives, each of which was repugnant to him. In his student's chambers, he had prearranged his social action quite differently.

Lydgate was late in setting out, but Dr Sprague, the two other surgeons, and several of the directors had arrived early ; Mr Bulstrode, treasurer and chairman, being among those who were still absent. The conversation seemed to imply that the issue was problematical, and that a majority for Tyke was not so certain as had been generally supposed. The two physicians, for a wonder, turned out to be unanimous, or rather, though of different minds, they concurred in action. Dr Sprague, the rugged and weighty, was, as every one had foreseen, an adherent of Mr Farebrother. The Doctor was more than suspected of having no religion, but somehow Middlemarch tolerated this deficiency in him as if he had been a Lord Chancellor ; indeed it is probable that his professional weight was the more believed in, the world-old association of cleverness with the evil principle being still potent in the minds even of lady-patients who had the strictest ideas of frilling and sentiment. It was perhaps this negation in the Doctor which made his neighbours call him hard-headed and dry-witted ; conditions of texture which were also held favourable to the storing of judgments connected with drugs. At all events, it is certain that if any medical man had come to Middlemarch with the reputation of having very definite religious views, of being given to prayer, and of otherwise showing an active piety, there would have been a general presumption against his medical skill.

On this ground it was (professionally speaking) fortunate for Dr Minchin that his religious sympathies were of a general kind, and such as gave a distant medical sanction to all serious sentiment, whether of Church or Dissent, rather than any adhesion to particular tenets. If Mr Bulstrode insisted, as he was apt to do, on the Lutheran doctrine of justification, as that by which a Church must stand or fall, Dr Minchin in return was quite sure that man was not a mere machine or a fortuitous conjunction of atoms ; if Mrs Wimple insisted on a particular providence in relation to her stomach complaint, Dr Minchin for his part liked to keep the mental windows open and objected to fixed limits ; if the Unitarian brewer jested about the Athanasian Creed, Dr Minchin quoted Pope's 'Essay on Man.'[1] He objected to the rather free style of anecdote in which Dr Sprague indulged, preferring well-sanctioned quotations, and liking refinement of all kinds : it was generally known that he had some kinship to a bishop, and sometimes spent his holidays at " the palace."

Dr Minchin was soft-handed, pale-complexioned, and of rounded outline, not to be distinguished from a mild clergyman in appearance : whereas Dr Sprague was superfluously tall ; his trousers got creased at the knees, and showed an excess of boot at a time when straps seemed necessary to any dignity of bearing ; you heard him go in and out, and up and down, as if he had come to see after the roof-

---

1. Unitarians maintain that God is one being, not a trinity: the Athanasian Creed reasserted the orthodox Christian doctrine of the Trinity. Any number of lines from Alexander Pope's "Essay on Man" (1733) might have been used by Dr. Minchin: "Know then thyself, presume not God to scan" (ii, 1); "Tho' Man's a fool, yet God is wise" (ii, 294); "Faith, Law, Morals, all began,/ All end, in Love of God, and Love of Man" (iv, 339–40); or, most appropriately, "For Modes of Faith, let graceless zealots fight;/His can't be wrong whose life is in the right" (iii, 305–6).

ing. In short, he had weight, and might be expected to grapple with a disease and throw it ; while Dr Minchin might be better able to detect it lurking and to circumvent it. They enjoyed about equally the mysterious privilege of medical reputation, and concealed with much etiquette their contempt for each other's skill. Regarding themselves as Middlemarch institutions, they were ready to combine against all innovators, and against non-professionals given to interference. On this ground they were both in their hearts equally averse to Mr Bulstrode, though Dr Minchin had never been in open hostility with him, and never differed from him without elaborate explanation to Mrs Bulstrode, who had found that Dr Minchin alone understood her constitution. A layman who pried into the professional conduct of medical men, and was always obtruding his reforms,—though he was less directly embarrassing to the two physicians than to the surgeon-apothecaries who attended paupers by contract, was nevertheless offensive to the professional nostril as such ; and Dr Minchin shared fully in the new pique against Bulstrode, excited by his apparent determination to patronise Lydgate. The long-established practitioners, Mr Wrench and Mr Toller, were just now standing apart and having a friendly colloquy, in which they agreed that Lydgate was a jackanapes, just made to serve Bulstrode's purpose. To non-medical friends they had already concurred in praising the other young practitioner, who had come into the town on Mr Peacock's retirement without further recommendation than his own merits and such argument for solid professional acquirement as might be gathered from his having apparently wasted no time on other branches of knowledge. It was clear that Lydgate, by not dispensing drugs, intended to cast imputations on his equals, and also to obscure the limit between his own rank as a general practitioner and that of the physicians, who, in the interest of the profession, felt bound to maintain its various grades. Especially against a man who had not been to either of the English universities and enjoyed the absence of anatomical and bedside study there, but came with a libellous pretension to experience in Edinburgh and Paris, where observation might be abundant indeed, but hardly sound.

Thus it happened that on this occasion Bulstrode became identified with Lydgate, and Lydgate with Tyke ; and owing to this variety of interchangeable names for the chaplaincy question, diverse minds were enabled to form the same judgment concerning it.

Dr Sprague said at once bluntly to the group assembled when he entered, " I go for Farebrother. A salary, with all my heart. But why take it from the Vicar ? He has none too much—has to insure his life, besides keeping house, and doing a vicar's charities. Put forty pounds in his pocket and you'll do no harm. He's a good fellow, is Farebrother, with as little of the parson about him as will serve to carry orders."

" Ho, ho ! Doctor," said old Mr Powderell, a retired ironmonger of some standing—his interjection being something between a laugh and a Parliamentary disapproval. " We must let you have your say. But what we have to consider is not anybody's income—it's the souls of the poor sick people "—here Mr Powderell's voice and face had a sincere pathos in them. " He is a real Gospel preacher, is Mr Tyke. I should vote against my conscience if I voted against Mr Tyke—I should indeed."

" Mr Tyke's opponents have not asked any one to vote against his conscience, I believe," said Mr Hackbutt, a rich tanner of fluent speech, whose glittering spectacles and erect hair were turned with some severity towards innocent Mr Powderell. " But in my judgment it behoves us, as Directors, to consider whether we will regard it as our whole business to carry out propositions emanating from a single quarter. Will any member of the committee aver that he would have entertained the idea of displacing the gentleman who has always discharged the function of chaplain here, if it had not been suggested to him by parties whose disposition it is to regard every institution of this town as a machinery for carrying out their own views ? I tax no man's motives : let them lie between himself and a higher Power; but I do say, that there are influences at work here which are incompatible with genuine independence, and that a crawling servility is usually dictated by circumstances which gentlemen so conducting themselves could not afford either morally or financially to avow. I myself am a layman, but I have given no inconsiderable attention to the divisions in the Church and . . ."

" Oh, damn the divisions !" burst in Mr Frank Hawley, lawyer and town-clerk, who rarely presented himself at the board, but now looked in hurriedly, whip in hand. " We have nothing to do with them here. Farebrother has been doing the work—what there was —without pay, and if pay is to be given, it should be given to him. I call it a confounded job to take the thing away from Farebrother."

" I think it would be as well for gentlemen not to give their remarks a personal bearing," said Mr Plymdale. " I shall vote for the appointment of Mr Tyke, but I should not have known, if Mr Hackbutt hadn't hinted it, that I was a Servile Crawler."

" I disclaim any personalities. I expressly said, if I may be allowed to repeat, or even to conclude what I was about to say——"

" Ah, here's Minchin !" said Mr Frank Hawley ; at which everybody turned away from Mr Hackbutt, leaving him to feel the uselessness of superior gifts in Middlemarch. " Come, Doctor, I must have you on the right side, eh ?"

" I hope so," said Dr Minchin, nodding and shaking hands here and there. " At whatever cost to my feelings."

" If there's any feeling here, it should be feeling for the man who is turned out, I think," said Mr Frank Hawley.

" I confess I have feelings on the other side also. I have a divided esteem," said Dr Minchin, rubbing his hands. " I consider Mr Tyke an exemplary man—none more so—and I believe him to be proposed from unimpeachable motives. I, for my part, wish that I could give him my vote. But I am constrained to take a view of the case which gives the preponderance to Mr Farebrother's claims. He is an amiable man, an able preacher, and has been longer among us."

Old Mr Powderell looked on, sad and silent. Mr Plymdale settled his cravat, uneasily.

" You don't set up Farebrother as a pattern of what a clergyman ought to be, I hope," said Mr Larcher, the eminent carrier, who had just come in. " I have no ill-will towards him, but I think we owe something to the public, not to speak of anything higher, in these appointments. In my opinion Farebrother is too lax for a clergyman. I don't wish to bring up particulars against him ; but he will make a little attendance here go as far as he can."

"And a devilish deal better than too much," said Mr Hawley, whose bad language was notorious in that part of the county. "Sick people can't bear so much praying and preaching. And that methodistical sort of religion is bad for the spirits—bad for the inside, eh?" he added, turning quickly round to the four medical men who were assembled.

But any answer was dispensed with by the entrance of three gentlemen, with whom there were greetings more or less cordial. These were the Reverend Edward Thesiger, Rector of St Peter's, Mr Bulstrode, and our friend Mr Brooke of Tipton, who had lately allowed himself to be put on the board of directors in his turn, but had never before attended, his attendance now being due to Mr Bulstrode's exertions. Lydgate was the only person still expected.

Every one now sat down, Mr Bulstrode presiding, pale and self-restrained as usual. Mr Thesiger, a moderate evangelical, wished for the appointment of his friend Mr Tyke, a zealous able man, who, officiating at a chapel of ease, had not a cure of souls too extensive to leave him ample time for the new duty. It was desirable that chaplaincies of this kind should be entered on with a fervent intention : they were peculiar opportunities for spiritual influence ; and while it was good that a salary should be allotted, there was the more need for scrupulous watching lest the office should be perverted into a mere question of salary. Mr Thesiger's manner had so much quiet propriety that objectors could only simmer in silence.

Mr Brooke believed that everybody meant well in the matter. He had not himself attended to the affairs of the Infirmary, though he had a strong interest in whatever was for the benefit of Middlemarch, and was most happy to meet the gentlemen present on any public question—"any public question, you know," Mr Brooke repeated, with his nod of perfect understanding. "I am a good deal occupied as a magistrate, and in the collection of documentary evidence, but I regard my time as being at the disposal of the public—and, in short, my friends have convinced me that a chaplain with a salary—a salary, you know—is a very good thing, and I am happy to be able to come here and vote for the appointment of Mr Tyke, who, I understand, is an unexceptionable man, apostolic and eloquent and everything of that kind—and I am the last man to withhold my vote—under the circumstances, you know."

"It seems to me that you have been crammed with one side of the question, Mr Brooke," said Mr Frank Hawley, who was afraid of nobody, and was a Tory suspicious of electioneering intentions. "You don't seem to know that one of the worthiest men we have has been doing duty as chaplain here for years without pay, and that Mr Tyke is proposed to supersede him."

"Excuse me, Mr Hawley," said Mr Bulstrode. "Mr Brooke has been fully informed of Mr Farebrother's character and position."

"By his enemies," flashed out Mr Hawley.

"I trust there is no personal hostility concerned here," said Mr Thesiger.

"I'll swear there is, though," retorted Mr Hawley.

"Gentlemen," said Mr Bulstrode, in a subdued tone, "the merits of the question may be very briefly stated, and if any one present doubts that every gentleman who is about to give his vote has not been fully informed, I can now recapitulate the considerations that should weigh on either side."

" I don't see the good of that," said Mr Hawley. " I suppose we all know whom we mean to vote for. Any man who wants to do justice does not wait till the last minute to hear both sides of the question. I have no time to lose, and I propose that the matter be put to the vote at once."

A brief but still hot discussion followed before each person wrote " Tyke " or " Farebrother " on a piece of paper and slipped it into a glass tumbler ; and in the mean time Mr Bulstrode saw Lydgate enter.

" I perceive that the votes are equally divided at present," said Mr Bulstrode, in a clear biting voice. Then, looking up at Lydgate— " There is a casting-vote still to be given. It is yours, Mr Lydgate : will you be good enough to write ? "

" The thing is settled now," said Mr Wrench, rising. " We all know how Mr Lydgate will vote."

" You seem to speak with some peculiar meaning, sir," said Lydgate, rather defiantly, and keeping his pencil suspended.

" I merely mean that you are expected to vote with Mr Bulstrode. Do you regard that meaning as offensive ? "

" It may be offensive to others. But I shall not desist from voting with him on that account."

Lydgate immediately wrote down " Tyke."

So the Rev. Walter Tyke became chaplain to the Infirmary, and Lydgate continued to work with Mr Bulstrode. He was really uncertain whether Tyke were not the more suitable candidate, and yet his consciousness told him that if he had been quite free from indirect bias he should have voted for Mr Farebrother. The affair of the chaplaincy remained a sore point in his memory as a case in which this petty medium of Middlemarch had been too strong for him. How could a man be satisfied with a decision between such alternatives and under such circumstances ? No more than he can be satisfied with his hat, which he has chosen from among such shapes as the resources of the age offer him, wearing it at best with a resignation which is chiefly supported by comparison.

But Mr Farebrother met him with the same friendliness as before. The character of the publican and sinner is not always practically incompatible with that of the modern Pharisee, for the majority of us scarcely see more distinctly the faultiness of our own conduct than the faultiness of our own arguments, or the dulness of our own jokes. But the Vicar of St Botolph's had certainly escaped the slightest tincture of the Pharisee, and by dint of admitting to himself that he was too much as other men were, he had become remarkably unlike them in this—that he could excuse others for thinking slightly of him, and could judge impartially of their conduct even when it told against him.

" The world has been too strong for *me*, I know," he said one day to Lydgate. " But then I am not a mighty man—I shall never be a man of renown. The choice of Hercules is a pretty fable ; but Prodicus makes it easy work for the hero, as if the first resolves were enough. Another story says that he came to hold the distaff, and at last wore the Nessus shirt.[2] I suppose one good resolve might keep a man right if everybody else's resolve helped him."

The Vicar's talk was not always inspiriting : he had escaped being a Pharisee, but he had not escaped that low estimate of possibilities which we rather hastily arrive at as an inference from our own failure. Lydgate thought that there was a pitiable infirmity of will in Mr Farebrother.

CHAPTER XIX.

" L'altra vedete ch'ha fatto alla guancia
Della sua palma, sospirando, letto."
—*Purgatorio*, vii. [1]

WHEN George the Fourth was still reigning over the privacies of Windsor, when the Duke of Wellington was Prime Minister, and Mr Vincy was mayor of the old corporation in Middlemarch, Mrs Casaubon, born Dorothea Brooke, had taken her wedding journey to Rome. In those days the world in general was more ignorant of good and evil by forty years than it is at present. Travellers did not often carry full information on Christian art either in their heads or their pockets ; and even the most brilliant English critic of the day mistook the flower-flushed tomb of the ascended Virgin for an ornamental vase due to the painter's fancy. [2] Romanticism, which has helped to fill some dull blanks with love and knowledge, had not yet penetrated the times with its leaven and entered into everybody's food ; it was fermenting still as a distinguishable vigorous enthusiasm in certain long-haired German artists at Rome, and the youth of other nations who worked or idled near them were sometimes caught in the spreading movement. [3]

One fine morning a young man whose hair was not immoderately long, but abundant and curly, and who was otherwise English in his equipment, had just turned his back on the Belvedere Torso in the Vatican and was looking out on the magnificent view of the

---

2. Prodicus (fl. 4th century B.C.) was the author of "The Choice of Hercules," in which the hero is met at a crossing by the figures of Pleasure and Duty, the one promising him all possible enjoyments, the other a life of labor and troubles, if he will follow her. Prodicus has Hercules choose Duty. The Nessus shirt causes Hercules's death. As Hercules prepares to offer sacrifice to the gods for his successes his wife sends him his sacrificial garment steeped in the poisoned blood of the centaur Nessus, which she supposes to be a love potion.

1. "The other ye behold, who for his cheek/Makes of one hand a couch, with frequent sighs" (Henry Cary's translation [1814]).

2. William Hazlitt made the mistake alluded to, writing of Raphael's "Coronation of the Virgin" in *Notes of a Journey through France and Italy* (1826). See E. E. Duncan-Jones, "Hazlitt's Mistake," *Times Literary Supplement*, January 27, 1966, p. 68.

3. The "certain long-haired German artists in Rome" is a reference to the German Nazarene school of artists, akin to the later Pre-Raphaelites in England. Ladislaw attaches himself to one of these Nazarene artists who is at work in Rome. For a discussion of the relevance of "modern" art for the novel, see below, pp. 677–79.

mountains from the adjoining round vestibule. [4] He was sufficiently absorbed not to notice the approach of a dark-eyed, animated German who came up to him and placing a hand on his shoulder, said with a strong accent, " Come here, quick ! else she will have changed her pose."

Quickness was ready at the call, and the two figures passed lightly along by the Meleager towards the hall where the reclining Ariadne, then called the Cleopatra, lies in the marble voluptuousness of her beauty, the drapery folding around her with a petal-like ease and tenderness. [5] They were just in time to see another figure standing against a pedestal near the reclining marble : a breathing blooming girl, whose form, not shamed by the Ariadne, was clad in Quakerish grey drapery ; her long cloak, fastened at the neck, was thrown backward from her arms, and one beautiful ungloved hand pillowed her cheek, pushing somewhat backward the white beaver bonnet which made a sort of halo to her face around the simply braided dark-brown hair. She was not looking at the sculpture, probably not thinking of it : her large eyes were fixed dreamily on a streak of sunlight which fell across the floor. But she became conscious of the two strangers who suddenly paused as it to contemplate the Cleopatra, and, without looking at them, immediately turned away to join a maid-servant and courier who were loitering along the hall at a little distance off.

" What do you think of that for a fine bit of antithesis ? " said the German, searching in his friend's face for responding admiration, but going on volubly without waiting for any other answer. " There lies antique beauty, not corpse-like even in death, but arrested in the complete contentment of its sensuous perfection : and here stands beauty in its breathing life, with the consciousness of Christian centuries in its bosom. But she should be dressed as a nun ; I think she looks almost what you call a Quaker ; I would dress her as a nun in my picture. However, she is married ; I saw her wedding-ring on that wonderful left hand, otherwise I should have thought the sallow *Geistlicher* was her father. [6] I saw him parting from her a good while ago, and just now I found her in that magnificent pose. Only think ! he is perhaps rich, and would like to have her portrait taken. Ah ! it is no use looking after her—there she goes ! Let us follow her home ! "

" No, no," said his companion, with a little frown.

" You are singular, Ladislaw. You look struck together. Do you know her ? "

" I know that she is married to my cousin," said Will Ladislaw, sauntering down the hall with a preoccupied air, while his German friend kept at his side and watched him eagerly.

" What, the *Geistlicher ?* He looks more like an uncle—a more useful sort of relation."

" He is not my uncle. I tell you he is my second cousin," said Ladislaw, with some irritation.

---

4. The Belvedere Torso is the 1st century B.C. Roman fragment, possibly of Hercules, in the Vatican museum, so named from the Belvedere gallery.
5. In Greek mythology Meleager was the leader of the Caledonian boar hunt. Ariadne, the beautiful daughter of King Minos of Crete, fell in love with Theseus, and aided him in killing the Minotaur. Deserted by Theseus, Ariadne fell asleep. When she woke she met Dionysus, who made her his wife.
6. *Geistlicher:* priest or minister.

"Schön, schön.[7] Don't be snappish. You are not angry with me for thinking Mrs Second-Cousin the most perfect young Madonna I ever saw?"

"Angry? nonsense. I have only seen her once before, for a couple of minutes, when my cousin introduced her to me, just before I left England. They were not married then. I didn't know they were coming to Rome."

"But you will go to see them now—you will find out what they have for an address—since you know the name. Shall we go to the post? And you could speak about the portrait."

"Confound you, Naumann! I don't know what I shall do. I am not so brazen as you."

"Bah! that is because you are dilettantish and amateurish. If you were an artist, you would think of Mistress Second-Cousin as antique form animated by Christian sentiment—a sort of Christian Antigone—sensuous force controlled by spiritual passion."[8]

"Yes, and that your painting her was the chief outcome of her existence—the divinity passing into higher completeness and all but exhausted in the act of covering your bit of canvas. I am amateurish if you like: I do *not* think that all the universe is straining towards the obscure significance of your pictures."

"But it is, my dear!—so far as it is straining through me, Adolf Naumann: that stands firm," said the good-natured painter, putting a hand on Ladislaw's shoulder, and not in the least disturbed by the unaccountable touch of ill-humour in his tone. "See now! My existence pre-supposes the existence of the whole universe—does it *not?* and my function is to paint—and as a painter I have a conception which is altogether *genialisch*, of your great-aunt or second grandmother as a subject for a picture; therefore, the universe is straining towards that picture through that particular hook or claw which it puts forth in the shape of me—not true?"[9]

"But how if another claw in the shape of me is straining to thwart it?—the case is a little less simple then."

"Not at all: the result of the struggle is the same thing—picture or no picture—logically." Will could not resist this imperturbable temper, and the cloud in his face broke into sunshiny laughter.

"Come now, my friend—you will help?" said Naumann, in a hopeful tone.

"No; nonsense, Naumann! English ladies are not at everybody's service as models. And you want to express too much with your painting. You would only have made a better or worse portrait with a background which every connoisseur would give a different reason for or against. And what is a portrait of a woman? Your painting and Plastik are poor stuff after all. They perturb and dull conceptions instead of raising them. Language is a finer medium."

"Yes, for those who can't paint," said Naumann. "There you have perfect right. I did not recommend you to paint, my friend."

The amiable artist carried his sting, but Ladislaw did not choose to appear stung. He went on as if he had not heard.

7. Indeed, indeed.
8. Antigone was the daughter of Oedipus; for daring to bury her brother against the order of Creon she is often cited as a model of strength and courage.
9. *Genialisch:* unconventional.

"Language gives a fuller image, which is all the better for being vague. After all, the true seeing is within; and painting stares at you with an insistent imperfection. I feel that especially about representations of women. As if a woman were a mere coloured superficies! You must wait for movement and tone. There is a difference in their very breathing: they change from moment to moment.—This woman whom you have just seen, for example: how would you paint her voice, pray? But her voice is much diviner than anything you have seen of her."

"I see, I see. You are jealous. No man must presume to think that he can paint your ideal. This is serious, my friend! Your great-aunt! 'Der Neffe als Onkel' in a tragic sense—*ungeheuer!*"[1]

"You and I shall quarrel, Naumann, if you call that lady my aunt again."

"How is she to be called then?"

"Mrs Casaubon."

"Good. Suppose I get acquainted with her in spite of you, and find that she very much wishes to be painted?"

"Yes, suppose!" said Will Ladislaw, in a contemptuous under-tone, intended to dismiss the subject. He was conscious of being irritated by ridiculously small causes, which were half of his own creation. Why was he making any fuss about Mrs Casaubon? And yet he felt as if something had happened to him with regard to her. There are characters which are continually creating collisions and nodes for themselves in dramas which nobody is prepared to act with them. Their susceptibilities will clash against objects that remain innocently quiet.

CHAPTER XX.

A child forsaken, waking suddenly,
Whose gaze afeard on all things round doth rove,
And seeth only that it cannot see
The meeting eyes of love.

Two hours later, Dorothea was seated in an inner room or boudoir of a handsome apartment in the Via Sistina.

I am sorry to add that she was sobbing bitterly, with such aban-donment to this relief of an oppressed heart as a woman habitually controlled by pride on her own account and thoughtfulness for others will sometimes allow herself when she feels securely alone. And Mr Casaubon was certain to remain away for some time at the Vatican.

Yet Dorothea had no distinctly shapen grievance that she could state even to herself; and in the midst of her confused thought and passion, the mental act that was struggling forth into clearness was a self-accusing cry that her feeling of desolation was the fault of her own spiritual poverty. She had married the man of her choice, and

---

1. "'The nephew like the uncle' . . . monstrous!"

with the advantage over most girls that she had contemplated her marriage chiefly as the beginning of new duties : from the very first she had thought of Mr Casaubon as having a mind so much above her own, that he must often be claimed by studies which she could not entirely share ; moreover, after the brief narrow experience of her girlhood she was beholding Rome, the city of visible history, where the past of a whole hemisphere seems moving in funeral procession with strange ancestral images and trophies gathered from afar.

But this stupendous fragmentariness heightened the dream-like strangeness of her bridal life. Dorothea had now been five weeks in Rome, and in the kindly mornings when autumn and winter seemed to go hand in hand like a happy aged couple one of whom would presently survive in chiller loneliness, she had driven about at first with Mr Casaubon, but of late chiefly with Tantripp and their experienced courier. She had been led through the best galleries, had been taken to the chief points of view, had been shown the grandest ruins and the most glorious churches, and she had ended by oftenest choosing to drive out to the Campagna where she could feel alone with the earth and sky, away from the oppressive masquerade of ages, in which her own life too seemed to become a masque with enigmatical costumes.

To those who have looked at Rome with the quickening power of a knowledge which breathes a growing soul into all historic shapes, and traces out the suppressed transitions which unite all contrasts, Rome may still be the spiritual centre and interpreter of the world. But let them conceive one more historical contrast : the gigantic broken revelations of that Imperial and Papal city thrust abruptly on the notions of a girl who had been brought up in English and Swiss Puritanism, fed on meagre Protestant histories and on art chiefly of the hand-screen sort ; a girl whose ardent nature turned all her small allowance of knowledge into principles, fusing her actions into their mould, and whose quick emotions gave the most abstract things the quality of a pleasure or a pain ; a girl who had lately become a wife, and from the enthusiastic acceptance of untried duty found herself plunged in tumultuous preoccupation with her personal lot. The weight of unintelligible Rome might lie easily on bright nymphs to whom it formed a background for the brilliant picnic of Anglo-foreign society ; but Dorothea had no such defence against deep impressions. Ruins and basilicas, palaces and colossi, set in the midst of a sordid present, where all that was living and warm-blooded seemed sunk in the deep degeneracy of a superstition divorced from reverence ; the dimmer but yet eager Titanic life gazing and struggling on walls and ceilings ; the long vistas of white forms whose marble eyes seemed to hold the monotonous light of an alien world : all this vast wreck of ambitious ideals, sensuous and spiritual, mixed confusedly with the signs of breathing forgetfulness and degradation, at first jarred her as with an electric shock, and then urged themselves on her with that ache belonging to a glut of confused ideas which check the flow of emotion. Forms both pale and glowing took possession of her young sense, and fixed themselves in her memory even when she was not thinking of them, preparing strange associations which remained through her after-years. Our moods are apt to bring with them images which succeed each other like the

magic-lantern pictures of a doze ; and in certain states of dull for-
lornness Dorothea all her life continued to see the vastness of St
Peter's, the huge bronze canopy, the excited intention in the attitudes
and garments of the prophets and evangelists in the mosaics above,
and the red drapery which was being hung for Christmas spreading
itself everywhere like a disease of the retina.

Not that this inward amazement of Dorothea's was anything very
exceptional : many souls in their young nudity are tumbled out
among incongruities and left to " find their feet " among them, while
their elders go about their business. Nor can I suppose that when
Mrs Casaubon is discovered in a fit of weeping six weeks after her
wedding, the situation will be regarded as tragic. Some discouragement, some faintness of heart at the new real future which replaces
the imaginary, is not unusual, and we do not expect people to be
deeply moved by what is not unusual. That element of tragedy
which lies in the very fact of frequency, has not yet wrought itself
into the coarse emotion of mankind ; and perhaps our frames could
hardly bear much of it. If we had a keen vision and feeling of all
ordinary human life, it would be like hearing the grass grow and the
squirrel's heart beat, and we should die of that roar which lies on the
other side of silence. As it is, the quickest of us walk about well
wadded with stupidity.

However, Dorothea was crying, and if she had been required to
state the cause, she could only have done so in some such general
words as I have already used : to have been driven to be more particular would have been like trying to give a history of the lights
and shadows ; for that new real future which was replacing the
imaginary drew its material from the endless minutiæ by which her
view of Mr Casaubon and her wifely relation, now that she was
married to him, was gradually changing with the secret motion of a
watch-hand from what it had been in her maiden dream. It was
too early yet for her fully to recognise or at least admit the change,
still more for her to have readjusted that devotedness which was so
necessary a part of her mental life that she was almost sure sooner or
later to recover it. Permanent rebellion, the disorder of a life without
some loving reverent resolve, was not possible to her ; but she was
now in an interval when the very force of her nature heightened its
confusion. In this way, the early months of marriage often are times
of critical tumult—whether that of a shrimp-pool or of deeper waters
—which afterwards subsides into cheerful peace.

But was not Mr Casaubon just as learned as before ? Had his
forms of expression changed, or his sentiments become less laudable ?
O waywardness of womanhood ! did his chronology fail him, or his
ability to state not only a theory but the names of those who held
it ; or his provision for giving the heads of any subject on demand ?
And was not Rome the place in all the world to give free play to
such accomplishments ? Besides, had not Dorothea's enthusiasm
especially dwelt on the prospect of relieving the weight and perhaps
the sadness with which great tasks lie on him who has to achieve
them ?—And that such weight pressed on Mr Casaubon was only
plainer than before.

All these are crushing questions ; but whatever else remained the
same, the light had changed, and you cannot find the pearly dawn at
noonday. The fact is unalterable, that a fellow-mortal with whose

nature you are acquainted solely through the brief entrances and exits of a few imaginative weeks called courtship, may, when seen in the continuity of married companionship, be disclosed as something better or worse than what you have preconceived, but will certainly not appear altogether the same. And it would be astonishing to find how soon the change is felt if we had no kindred changes to compare with it. To share lodgings with a brilliant dinner-companion, or to see your favourite politician in the Ministry, may bring about changes quite as rapid : in these cases too we begin by knowing little and believing much, and we sometimes end by inverting the quantities.

Still, such comparisons might mislead, for no man was more incapable of flashy make-believe than Mr Casaubon : he was as genuine a character as any ruminant animal, and he had not actively assisted in creating any illusions about himself. How was it that in the weeks since her marriage, Dorothea had not distinctly observed but felt with a stifling depression, that the large vistas and wide fresh air which she had dreamed of finding in her husband's mind were replaced by anterooms and winding passages which seemed to lead nowhither ? I suppose it was that in courtship everything is regarded as provisional and preliminary, and the smallest sample of virtue or accomplishment is taken to guarantee delightful stores which the broad leisure of marriage will reveal. But the door-sill of marriage once crossed, expectation is concentrated on the present. Having once embarked on your marital voyage, it is impossible not to be aware that you make no way and that the sea is not within sight— that, in fact, you are exploring an enclosed basin.

In their conversation before marriage, Mr Casaubon had often dwelt on some explanation or questionable detail of which Dorothea did not see the bearing ; but such imperfect coherence seemed due to the brokenness of their intercourse, and, supported by her faith in their future, she had listened with fervid patience to a recitation of possible arguments to be brought against Mr Casaubon's entirely new view of the Philistine god Dagon and other fish-deities, thinking that hereafter she should see this subject which touched him so nearly from the same high ground whence doubtless it had become so important to him. Again, the matter-of-course statement and tone of dismissal with which he treated what to her were the most stirring thoughts, was easily accounted for as belonging to the sense of haste and preoccupation in which she herself shared during their engagement. But now, since they had been in Rome, with all the depths of her emotion roused to tumultuous activity, and with life made a new problem by new elements, she had been becoming more and more aware, with a certain terror, that her mind was continually sliding into inward fits of anger and repulsion, or else into forlorn weariness. How far the judicious Hooker or any other hero of erudition would have been the same at Mr Casaubon's time of life, she had no means of knowing, so that he could not have the advantage of comparison ; but her husband's way of commenting on the strangely impressive objects around them had begun to affect her with a sort of mental shiver : he had perhaps the best intention of acquitting himself worthily, but only of acquitting himself. What was fresh to her mind was worn out to his ; and such capacity of thought and feeling as had ever been stimulated in him by the

general life of mankind had long shrunk to a sort of dried preparation, a lifeless embalmment of knowledge.

When he said, "Does this interest you, Dorothea? Shall we stay
a little longer? I am ready to stay if you wish it,"—it seemed to her
as if going or staying were alike dreary. Or, "Should you like to go
to the Farnesina, Dorothea? It contains celebrated frescoes designed
or painted by Raphael, which most persons think it worth while to
visit."

"But do you care about them?" was always Dorothea's question.

"They are, I believe, highly esteemed. Some of them represent
the fable of Cupid and Psyche, which is probably the romantic
invention of a literary period, and cannot, I think, be reckoned as a
genuine mythical product. But if you like these wall-paintings we
can easily drive thither; and you will then, I think, have seen the
chief works of Raphael, any of which it were a pity to omit in a visit
to Rome. He is the painter who has been held to combine the most
complete grace of form with sublimity of expression. Such at least
I have gathered to be the opinion of conoscenti."

This kind of answer given in a measured official tone, as of a
clergyman reading according to the rubric, did not help to justify the
glories of the Eternal City, or to give her the hope that if she knew
more about them the world would be joyously illuminated for her.
There is hardly any contact more depressing to a young ardent
creature than that of a mind in which years full of knowledge seem
to have issued in a blank absence of interest or sympathy.

On other subjects indeed Mr Casaubon showed a tenacity of occupation and an eagerness which are usually regarded as the effect of
enthusiasm, and Dorothea was anxious to follow this spontaneous
direction of his thoughts, instead of being made to feel that she
dragged him away from it. But she was gradually ceasing to expect
with her former delightful confidence that she should see any wide
opening where she followed him. Poor Mr Casaubon himself was
lost among small closets and winding stairs, and in an agitated dimness about the Cabeiri, or in an exposure of other mythologists'
ill-considered parallels, easily lost sight of any purpose which had
prompted him to these labours. [1] With his taper stuck before him he
forgot the absence of windows, and in bitter manuscript remarks on
other men's notions about the solar deities, he had become indifferent
to the sunlight.

These characteristics, fixed and unchangeable as bone in Mr Casaubon, might have remained longer unfelt by Dorothea if she had been
encouraged to pour forth her girlish and womanly feeling—if he
would have held her hands between his and listened with the delight
of tenderness and understanding to all the little histories which made
up her experience, and would have given her the same sort of intimacy in return, so that the past life of each could be included in their
mutual knowledge and affection—or if she could have fed her affection with those childlike caresses which are the bent of every sweet
woman, who has begun by showering kisses on the hard pate of her
bald doll, creating a happy soul within that woodenness from the

---

1. Cabeiri: **Samothracian fertility gods.**

wealth of her own love. That was Dorothea's bent. With all her yearning to know what was afar from her and to be widely benignant, she had ardour enough for what was near, to have kissed Mr Casaubon's coat-sleeve, or to have caressed his shoe-latchet, if he would have made any other sign of acceptance than pronouncing her, with his unfailing propriety, to be of a most affectionate and truly feminine nature, indicating at the same time by politely reaching a chair for her that he regarded these manifestations as rather crude and startling. Having made his clerical toilette with due care in the morning, he was prepared only for those amenities of life which were suited to the well-adjusted stiff cravat of the period, and to a mind weighted with unpublished matter.

And by a sad contradiction Dorothea's ideas and resolves seemed like melting ice floating and lost in the warm flood of which they had been but another form. She was humiliated to find herself a mere victim of feeling, as if she could know nothing except through that medium : all her strength was scattered in fits of agitation, of struggle, of despondency, and then again in visions of more complete renunciation, transforming all hard conditions into duty. Poor Dorothea ! she was certainly troublesome—to herself chiefly ; but this morning for the first time she had been troublesome to Mr Casaubon.

She had begun, while they were taking coffee, with a determination to shake off what she inwardly called her selfishness, and turned a face all cheerful attention to her husband when he said, " My dear Dorothea, we must now think of all that is yet left undone, as a preliminary to our departure. I would fain have returned home earlier that we might have been at Lowick for the Christmas ; but my inquiries here have been protracted beyond their anticipated period. I trust, however, that the time here has not been passed unpleasantly to you. Among the sights of Europe, that of Rome has ever been held one of the most striking and in some respects edifying. I well remember that I considered it an epoch in my life when I visited it for the first time ; after the fall of Napoleon, an event which opened the Continent to travellers. Indeed I think it is one among several cities to which an extreme hyperbole has been applied—'See Rome and die :' but in your case I would propose an emendation and say, See Rome as a bride, and live thenceforth as a happy wife."

Mr Casaubon pronounced this little speech with the most conscientious intention, blinking a little and swaying his head up and down, and concluding with a smile. He had not found marriage a rapturous state, but he had no idea of being anything else than an irreproachable husband, who would make a charming young woman as happy as she deserved to be.

" I hope you are thoroughly satisfied with our stay—I mean, with the result so far as your studies are concerned," said Dorothea, trying to keep her mind fixed on what most affected her husband.

" Yes," said Mr Casaubon, with that peculiar pitch of voice which makes the word half a negative. " I have been led farther than I had foreseen, and various subjects for annotation have presented themselves which, though I have no direct need of them, I could not pretermit. The task, notwithstanding the assistance of my amanuensis, has been a somewhat laborious one, but your society has happily prevented me from that too continuous prosecution of thought beyond the hours of study which has been the snare of my solitary life."

"I am very glad that my presence has made any difference to you," said Dorothea, who had a vivid memory of evenings in which she had supposed that Mr Casaubon's mind had gone too deep during the day to be able to get to the surface again. I fear there was a little temper in her reply. " I hope when we get to Lowick, I shall be more useful to you, and be able to enter a little more into what interests you."

" Doubtless, my dear," said Mr Casaubon, with a slight bow. " The notes I have here made will want sifting, and you can, if you please, extract them under my direction."

" And all your notes," said Dorothea, whose heart had already burned within her on this subject, so that now she could not help speaking with her tongue. " All those rows of volumes—will you not now do what you used to speak of ?—will you not make up your mind what part of them you will use, and begin to write the book which will make your vast knowledge useful to the world ? I will write to your dictation, or I will copy and extract what you tell me : I can be of no other use." Dorothea, in a most unaccountable, darkly-feminine manner, ended with a slight sob and eyes full of tears.

The excessive feeling manifested would alone have been highly disturbing to Mr Casaubon, but there were other reasons why Dorothea's words were among the most cutting and irritating to him that she could have been impelled to use. She was as blind to his inward troubles as he to hers : she had not yet learned those hidden conflicts in her husband which claim our pity. She had not yet listened patiently to his heart-beats, but only felt that her own was beating violently. In Mr Casaubon's ear, Dorothea's voice gave loud emphatic iteration to those muffled suggestions of consciousness which it was possible to explain as mere fancy, the illusion of exaggerated sensitiveness : always when such suggestions are unmistakably repeated from without, they are resisted as cruel and unjust. We are angered even by the full acceptance of our humiliating confessions—how much more by hearing in hard distinct syllables from the lips of a near observer, those confused murmurs which we try to call morbid, and strive against as if they were the oncoming of numbness ! And this cruel outward accuser was there in the shape of a wife—nay, of a young bride, who, instead of observing his abundant pen-scratches and amplitude of paper with the uncritical awe of an elegant-minded canary-bird, seemed to present herself as a spy watching everything with a malign power of inference. Here, towards this particular point of the compass, Mr Casaubon had a sensitiveness to match Dorothea's, and an equal quickness to imagine more than the fact. He had formerly observed with approbation her capacity for worshipping the right object ; he now foresaw with sudden terror that this capacity might be replaced by presumption, this worship by the most exasperating of all criticism,—that which sees vaguely a great many fine ends, and has not the least notion what it costs to reach them.

For the first time since Dorothea had known him, Mr Casaubon's face had a quick angry flush upon it.

" My love," he said, with irritation reined in by propriety, " you may rely upon me for knowing the times and the seasons, adapted to the different stages of a work which is not to be measured by the facile conjectures of ignorant onlookers. It had been easy for me to gain a temporary effect by a mirage of baseless opinion ; but it is ever the trial of the scrupulous explorer to be saluted with the impatient scorn of chatterers who attempt only the smallest achievements, being indeed equipped for no other. And it were well if all such could be admonished to discriminate judgments of which the true subject-matter lies entirely beyond their reach, from those of which the elements may be compassed by a narrow and superficial survey."

This speech was delivered with an energy and readiness quite unusual with Mr Casaubon. It was not indeed entirely an impro-visation, but had taken shape in inward colloquy, and rushed out like the round grains from a fruit when sudden heat cracks it. Doro-thea was not only his wife : she was a personification of that shallow world which surrounds the ill-appreciated or desponding author.

Dorothea was indignant in her turn. Had she not been repressing everything in herself except the desire to enter into some fellowship with her husband's chief interests ?

" My judgment *was* a very superficial one—such as I am capable of forming," she answered, with a prompt resentment, that needed no rehearsal. " You showed me the rows of note-books—you have often spoken of them—you have often said that they wanted digesting. But I never heard you speak of the writing that is to be published. Those were very simple facts, and my judgment went no farther. I only begged you to let me be of some good to you."

Dorothea rose to leave the table and Mr Casaubon made no reply, taking up a letter which lay beside him as if to reperuse it. Both were shocked at their mutual situation — that each should have betrayed anger towards the other. If they had been at home, settled at Lowick in ordinary life among their neighbours, the clash would have been less embarrassing : but on a wedding journey, the express object of which is to isolate two people on the ground that they are all the world to each other, the sense of disagreement is, to say the least, confounding and stultifying. To have changed your longitude extensively, and placed yourselves in a moral solitude in order to have small explosions, to find conversation difficult and to hand a glass of water without looking, can hardly be regarded as satisfactory fulfilment even to the toughest minds. To Doro-thea's inexperienced sensitiveness, it seemed like a catastrophe, changing all prospects ; and to Mr Casaubon it was a new pain, he never having been on a wedding journey before, or found himself in that close union which was more of a subjection than he had been able to imagine, since this charming young bride not only obliged him to much consideration on her be-half (which he had sedulously given), but turned out to be capable of agitating him cruelly just where he most needed soothing. Instead of getting a soft fence against the cold, shadowy, unapplausive audi-ence of his life, had he only given it a more substantial presence ?

Neither of them felt it possible to speak again at present. To have reversed a previous arrangement and declined to go out would have been a show of persistent anger which Dorothea's conscience shrank from, seeing that she already began to feel herself guilty. However just her indignation might be, her ideal was not to claim justice, but to give tenderness. So when the carriage came to the door, she drove with Mr Casaubon to the Vatican, walked with him through the

stony avenue of inscriptions, and when she parted with him at the
entrance to the Library, went on through the Museum out of mere
listlessness as to what was around her. She had not spirit to turn
round and say that she would drive anywhere. It was when Mr
Casaubon was quitting her that Naumann had first seen her, and he
had entered the long gallery of sculpture at the same time with her ;
but here Naumann had to await Ladislaw with whom he was to settle
a bet of champagne about an enigmatical mediæval-looking figure
there. After they had examined the figure, and had walked on
finishing their dispute, they had parted, Ladislaw lingering behind
while Naumann had gone into the Hall of Statues where he again
saw Dorothea, and saw her in that brooding abstraction which made
her pose remarkable. She did not really see the streak of sunlight
on the floor more than she saw the statues: she was inwardly seeing
the light of years to come in her own home and over the English
fields and elms and hedge-bordered highroads; and feeling that the
way in which they might be filled with joyful devotedness was not so
clear to her as it had been. But in Dorothea's mind there was a
current into which all thought and feeling were apt sooner or later to
flow—the reaching forward of the whole consciousness towards the
fullest truth, the least partial good. There was clearly something
better than anger and despondency.

CHAPTER XXI.

" Hire facounde eke full womanly and plain,
No contrefeted termes had she
To semen wise."
—CHAUCER. [1]

IT was in that way Dorothea came to be sobbing as soon as she was
securely alone. But she was presently roused by a knock at the
door, which made her hastily dry her eyes before saying, " Come in."
Tantripp had brought a card, and said that there was a gentleman
waiting in the lobby. The courier had told him that only Mrs Casaubon was at home, but he said he was a relation of Mr Casaubon's:
would she see him ?

" Yes," said Dorothea, without pause ; " show him into the salon."
Her chief impressions about young Ladislaw were that when she had
seen him at Lowick she had been made aware of Mr Casaubon's
generosity towards him, and also that she had been interested in his
own hesitation about his career. She was alive to anything that
gave her an opportunity for active sympathy, and at this moment it
seemed as if the visit had come to shake her out of her self-absorbed
discontent—to remind her of her husband's goodness, and make her
feel that she had now the right to be his helpmate in all kind deeds.
She waited a minute or two, but when she passed into the next room

there were just signs enough that she had been crying to make her open face look more youthful and appealing than usual. She met Ladislaw with that exquisite smile of goodwill which is unmixed with vanity, and held out her hand to him. He was the elder by several years, but at that moment he looked much the younger, for his transparent complexion flushed suddenly, and he spoke with a shyness extremely unlike the ready indifference of his manner with his male companion, while Dorothea became all the calmer with a wondering desire to put him at ease.

" I was not aware that you and Mr Casaubon were in Rome, until this morning, when I saw you in the Vatican Museum," he said. " I knew you at once—but—I mean, that I concluded Mr Casaubon's address would be found at the Poste Restante, and I was anxious to pay my respects to him and you as early as possible."

" Pray sit down. He is not here now, but he will be glad to hear of you, I am sure," said Dorothea, seating herself unthinkingly between the fire and the light of the tall window, and pointing to a chair opposite, with the quietude of a benignant matron. The signs of girlish sorrow in her face were only the more striking. " Mr Casaubon is much engaged ; but you will leave your address—will you not ?—and he will write to you."

" You are very good," said Ladislaw, beginning to lose his diffidence in the interest with which he was observing the signs of weeping which had altered her face. " My address is on my card. But if you will allow me, I will call again to-morrow at an hour when Mr Casaubon is likely to be at home."

" He goes to read in the Library of the Vatican every day, and you can hardly see him except by an appointment. Especially now. We are about to leave Rome, and he is very busy. He is usually away almost from breakfast till dinner. But I am sure he will wish you to dine with us."

Will Ladislaw was struck mute for a few moments. He had never been fond of Mr Casaubon, and if it had not been for the sense of obligation, would have laughed at him as a Bat of erudition. But the idea of this dried-up pedant, this elaborator of small explanations about as important as the surplus stock of false antiquities kept in a vendor's back chamber, having first got this adorable young creature to marry him, and then passing his honeymoon away from her, groping after his mouldy futilities (Will was given to hyperbole)—this sudden picture stirred him with a sort of comic disgust : he was divided between the impulse to laugh aloud and the equally unseasonable impulse to burst into scornful invective. For an instant he felt that the struggle was causing a queer contortion of his mobile features, but with a good effort he resolved it into nothing more offensive than a merry smile.

Dorothea wondered ; but the smile was irresistible, and shone back from her face too. Will Ladislaw's smile was delightful, unless you were angry with him beforehand : it was a gush of inward light illuminating the transparent skin as well as the eyes, and playing about every curve and line as if some Ariel were touching them with a new charm, and banishing for ever the traces of moodiness. [2] The

---

2. Ariel: a spirit of the air, endowed with magical powers, like the character in Shakespeare's *The Tempest.*

reflection of that smile could not but have a little merriment in it too, even under dark eyelashes still moist, as Dorothea said inquiringly, " Something amuses you ? "

" Yes," said Will, quick in finding resources. " I am thinking of the sort of figure I cut the first time I saw you, when you annihilated my poor sketch with your criticism."

" My criticism ? " said Dorothea, wondering still more. " Surely not. I always feel particularly ignorant about painting."

" I suspected you of knowing so much, that you knew how to say just what was most cutting. You said—I daresay you don't remember it as I do—that the relation of my sketch to nature was quite hidden from you. At least, you implied that." Will could laugh now as well as smile.

" That was really my ignorance," said Dorothea, admiring Will's good-humour. " I must have said so only because I never could see any beauty in the pictures which my uncle told me all judges thought very fine. And I have gone about with just the same ignorance in Rome. There are comparatively few paintings that I can really enjoy. At first when I enter a room where the walls are covered with frescoes, or with rare pictures, I feel a kind of awe— like a child present at great ceremonies where there are grand robes and processions ; I feel myself in the presence of some higher life than my own. But when I begin to examine the pictures one by one, the life goes out of them, or else is something violent and strange to me. It must be my own dulness. I am seeing so much all at once, and not understanding half of it. That always makes one feel stupid. It is painful to be told that anything is very fine and not be able to feel that it is fine—something like being blind, while people talk of the sky."

" Oh, there is a great deal in the feeling for art which must be acquired," said Will. (It was impossible now to doubt the directness of Dorothea's confession.) " Art is an old language with a great many artificial affected styles, and sometimes the chief pleasure one gets out of knowing them is the mere sense of knowing. I enjoy the art of all sorts here immensely ; but I suppose if I could pick my enjoyment to pieces I should find it made up of many different threads. There is something in daubing a little one's self, and having an idea of the process."

" You mean perhaps to be a painter ? " said Dorothea, with a new direction of interest. " You mean to make painting your profession. Mr Casaubon will like to hear that you have chosen a profession."

" No, oh no," said Will, with some coldness. " I have quite made up my mind against it. It is too one-sided a life. I have been seeing a great deal of the German artists here : I travelled from Frankfort with one of them. Some are fine, even brilliant fellows—but I should not like to get into their way of looking at the world entirely from the studio point of view."

" That I can understand," said Dorothea, cordially. " And in Rome it seems as if there were so many things which are more wanted in the world than pictures. But if you have a genius for painting, would it not be right to take that as a guide ? Perhaps you might do better things than these—or different, so that there might not be so many pictures almost all alike in the same place."

There was no mistaking this simplicity, and Will was won by it into frankness. "A man must have a very rare genius to make changes of that sort. I am afraid mine would not carry me even to the pitch of doing well what has been done already, at least not so well as to make it worth while. And I should never succeed in anything by dint of drudgery. If things don't come easily to me I never get them."

"I have heard Mr Casaubon say that he regrets your want of patience," said Dorothea, gently. She was rather shocked at this mode of taking all life as a holiday.

"Yes, I know Mr Casaubon's opinion. He and I differ."

The slight streak of contempt in this hasty reply offended Dorothea. She was all the more susceptible about Mr Casaubon because of her morning's trouble.

"Certainly you differ," she said, rather proudly. "I did not think of comparing you : such power of persevering devoted labour as Mr Casaubon's is not common."

Will saw that she was offended, but this only gave an additional impulse to the new irritation of his latent dislike towards Mr Casaubon. It was too intolerable that Dorothea should be worshipping this husband : such weakness in a woman is pleasant to no man but the husband in question. Mortals are easily tempted to pinch the life out of their neighbour's buzzing glory, and think that such killing is no murder.

"No, indeed," he answered, promptly. "And therefore it is a pity that it should be thrown away, as so much English scholarship is, for want of knowing what is being done by the rest of the world. If Mr Casaubon read German he would save himself a great deal of trouble."

"I do not understand you," said Dorothea, startled and anxious.

"I merely mean," said Will, in an offhand way, "that the Germans have taken the lead in historical inquiries, and they laugh at results which are got by groping about in woods with a pocket-compass while they have made good roads. When I was with Mr Casaubon I saw that he deafened himself in that direction : it was almost against his will that he read a Latin treatise written by a German. I was very sorry."

Will only thought of giving a good pinch that would annihilate that vaunted laboriousness, and was unable to imagine the mode in which Dorothea would be wounded. Young Mr Ladislaw was not at all deep himself in German writers ; but very little achievement is required in order to pity another man's shortcomings.

Poor Dorothea felt a pang at the thought that the labour of her husband's life might be void, which left her no energy to spare for the question whether this young relative who was so much obliged to him ought not to have repressed his observation. She did not even speak, but sat looking at her hands, absorbed in the piteousness of that thought.

Will, however, having given that annihilating pinch, was rather ashamed, imagining from Dorothea's silence that he had offended her still more ; and having also a conscience about plucking the tail-feathers from a benefactor.

"I regretted it especially," he resumed, taking the usual course from detraction to insincere eulogy, "because of my gratitude and respect towards my cousin. It would not signify so much in a man whose talents and character were less distinguished."

Dorothea raised her eyes, brighter than usual with excited feeling, and said, in her saddest recitative, " How I wish I had learned German when I was at Lausanne ! There were plenty of German teachers. But now I can be of no use."

There was a new light, but still a mysterious light, for Will in Dorothea's last words. The question how she had come to accept Mr Casaubon—which he had dismissed when he first saw her by saying that she must be disagreeable in spite of appearances—was not now to be answered on any such short and easy method. Whatever else she might be, she was not disagreeable. She was not coldly clever and indirectly satirical, but adorably simple and full of feeling. She was an angel beguiled. It would be a unique delight to wait and watch for the melodious fragments in which her heart and soul came forth so directly and ingenuously. The Æolian harp again came into his mind.

She must have made some original romance for herself in this marriage. And if Mr Casaubon had been a dragon who had carried her off to his lair with his talons simply and without legal forms, it would have been an unavoidable feat of heroism to release her and fall at her feet. But he was something more unmanageable than a dragon : he was a benefactor with collective society at his back, and he was at that moment entering the room in all the unimpeachable correctness of his demeanour, while Dorothea was looking animated with a newly-roused alarm and regret, and Will was looking animated with his admiring speculation about her feelings.

Mr Casaubon felt a surprise which was quite unmixed with pleasure, but he did not swerve from his usual politeness of greeting, when Will rose and explained his presence. Mr Casaubon was less happy than usual, and this perhaps made him look all the dimmer and more faded ; else, the effect might easily have been produced by the contrast of his young cousin's appearance. The first impression on seeing Will was one of sunny brightness, which added to the uncertainty of his changing expression. Surely, his very features changed their form ; his jaw looked sometimes large and sometimes small ; and the little ripple in his nose was a preparation for metamorphosis. When he turned his head quickly his hair seemed to shake out light, and some persons thought they saw decided genius in this coruscation. Mr Casaubon, on the contrary, stood rayless.

As Dorothea's eyes were turned anxiously on her husband she was perhaps not insensible to the contrast, but it was only mingled with other causes in making her more conscious of that new alarm on his behalf which was the first stirring of a pitying tenderness fed by the realities of his lot and not by her own dreams. Yet it was a source of greater freedom to her that Will was there; his young equality was agreeable, and also perhaps his openness to conviction. She felt an immense need of some one to speak to, and she had never before seen any one who seemed so quick and pliable, so likely to understand everything.

Mr Casaubon gravely hoped that Will was passing his time profitably as well as pleasantly in Rome—had thought his intention was to remain in South Germany—but begged him to come and dine tomorrow, when he could converse more at large : at present he was somewhat weary. Ladislaw understood, and accepting the invitation immediately took his leave.

Dorothea's eyes followed her husband anxiously, while he sank down wearily at the end of a sofa, and resting his elbow supported his head and looked on the floor. A little flushed, and with bright eyes, she seated herself beside him, and said,

"Forgive me for speaking so hastily to you this morning. I was wrong. I fear I hurt you and made the day more burdensome."

"I am glad that you feel that, my dear," said Mr Casaubon. He spoke quietly and bowed his head a little, but there was still an uneasy feeling in his eyes as he looked at her.

"But you do forgive me?" said Dorothea, with a quick sob. In her need for some manifestation of feeling she was ready to exaggerate her own fault. Would not love see returning penitence afar off, and fall on its neck and kiss it?

"My dear Dorothea—'who with repentance is not satisfied, is not of heaven nor earth :'—you do not think me worthy to be banished by that severe sentence," said Mr Casaubon, exerting himself to make a strong statement, and also to smile faintly. [3]

Dorothea was silent, but a tear which had come up with the sob would insist on falling.

"You are excited, my dear. And I also am feeling some unpleasant consequences of too much mental disturbance," said Mr Casaubon. In fact, he had it in his thought to tell her that she ought not to have received young Ladislaw in his absence; but he abstained, partly from the sense that it would be ungracious to bring a new complaint in the moment of her penitent acknowledgment, partly because he wanted to avoid further agitation of himself by speech, and partly because he was too proud to betray that jealousy of disposition which was not so exhausted on his scholarly compeers that there was none to spare in other directions. There is a sort of jealousy which needs very little fire : it is hardly a passion, but a blight bred in the cloudy, damp despondency of uneasy egoism.

"I think it is time for us to dress," he added, looking at his watch. They both rose, and there was never any further allusion between them to what had passed on this day.

But Dorothea remembered it to the last with the vividness with which we all remember epochs in our experience when some dear expectation dies, or some new motive is born. To-day she had begun to see that she had been under a wild illusion in expecting a response to her feeling from Mr Casaubon, and she had felt the waking of a presentiment that there might be a sad consciousness in his life which made as great a need on his side as on her own.

We are all of us born in moral stupidity, taking the world as an udder to feed our supreme selves : Dorothea had early begun to emerge from that stupidity, but yet it had been easier to her to imagine how she would devote herself to Mr Casaubon, and become wise and strong in his strength and wisdom, than to conceive with that distinctness which is no longer reflection but feeling—an idea wrought back to the directness of sense, like the solidity of objects—that he had an equivalent centre of self, whence the lights and shadows must always fall with a certain difference.

3. Casaubon is quoting from Shakespeare's *Two Gentlemen of Verona*, Act V, Sc. 4, line 79.

CHAPTER XXII.

" Nous causâmes longtemps ; elle était simple et bonne.
Ne sachant pas le mal, elle faisait le bien ;
Des richesses du cœur elle me fit l'aumône,
Et tout en écoutant comme le cœur se donne,
Sans oser y penser, je lui donnai le mien ;
Elle emporta ma vie, et n'en sut jamais rien."
—ALFRED DE MUSSET. [1]

WILL LADISLAW was delightfully agreeable at dinner the next day, and gave no opportunity for Mr Casaubon to show disapprobation. On the contrary it seemed to Dorothea that Will had a happier way of drawing her husband into conversation and of deferentially listening to him than she had ever observed in any one before. To be sure, the listeners about Tipton were not highly gifted ! Will talked a good deal himself, but what he said was thrown in with such rapidity, and with such an unimportant air of saying something by the way, that it seemed a gay little chime after the great bell. If Will was not always perfect, this was certainly one of his good days. He described touches of incident among the poor people in Rome, only to be seen by one who could move about freely ; he found himself in agreement with Mr Casaubon as to the unsound opinions of Middleton concerning the relations of Judaism and Catholicism; and passed easily to a half-enthusiastic half-playful picture of the enjoyment he got out of the very miscellaneousness of Rome, which made the mind flexible with constant comparison, and saved you from seeing the world's ages as a set of box-like partitions without vital connection. [2] Mr Casaubon's studies, Will observed, had always been of too broad a kind for that, and he had perhaps never felt any such sudden effect, but for himself he confessed that Rome had given him quite a new sense of history as a whole : the fragments stimulated his imagination and made him constructive. Then occasionally, but not too often, he appealed to Dorothea, and discussed what she said, as if her sentiment were an item to be considered in the final judgment even of the Madonna di Foligno or the Laocoon. [3] A sense of contributing to form the world's opinion makes conversation particularly cheerful ; and Mr Casaubon too was not without his pride in his young wife, who spoke better than most women, as indeed he had perceived in choosing her.

Since things were going on so pleasantly, Mr Casaubon's statement

1. "We talked for a long time; she was simple and kind./Not knowing evil, she did only good;/She gave me alms from the riches of her heart,/And in sympathy with her as she gave me her heart,/Without daring to think of it I gave her mine;/Thus she possessed my life, and never even knew it" ("Une Bonne Fortune," xxxix [1834]).
2. Conyers Middleton (1683–1750), Cambridge theological controversialist.
3. The Madonna di Foligno, by Raphael, was originally done for the Church of S. Anna at Foligno and later moved to the Vatican. The Laocoön, by the Rhodian sculptors Agesander, Athenodorus, and Polydorus, depicts the deaths of Laocoön and his sons; it too is in the Vatican museums.

that his labours in the Library would be suspended for a couple of days, and that after a brief renewal he should have no further reason for staying in Rome, encouraged Will to urge that Mrs Casaubon should not go away without seeing a studio or two. Would not Mr Casaubon take her? That sort of thing ought not to be missed : it was quite special : it was a form of life that grew like a small fresh vegetation with its population of insects on huge fossils. Will would be happy to conduct them—not to anything wearisome, only to a few examples.

Mr Casaubon, seeing Dorothea look earnestly towards him, could not but ask her if she would be interested in such visits : he was now at her service during the whole day ; and it was agreed that Will should come on the morrow and drive with them.

Will could not omit Thorwaldsen, a living celebrity about whom even Mr Casaubon inquired, but before the day was far advanced he led the way to the studio of his friend Adolf Naumann, whom he mentioned as one of the chief renovators of Christian art, one of those who had not only revived but expanded that grand conception of supreme events as mysteries at which the successive ages were spectators, and in relation to which the great souls of all periods became as it were contemporaries. [4] Will added that he had made himself Naumann's pupil for the nonce.

" I have been making some oil-sketches under him," said Will. " I hate copying. I must put something of my own in. Naumann has been painting the Saints drawing the Car of the Church, and I have been making a sketch of Marlowe's Tamburlaine Driving the Conquered Kings in his Chariot. I am not so ecclesiastical as Naumann, and I sometimes twit him with his excess of meaning. But this time I mean to outdo him in breadth of intention. I take Tamburlaine in his chariot for the tremendous course of the world's physical history lashing on the harnessed dynasties. In my opinion, that is a good mythical interpretation." Will here looked at Mr Casaubon, who received this offhand treatment of symbolism very uneasily, and bowed with a neutral air.

" The sketch must be very grand, if it conveys so much," said Dorothea. " I should need some explanation even of the meaning you give. Do you intend Tamburlaine to represent earthquakes and volcanoes ? "

" O yes," said Will, laughing, " and migrations of races and clearings of forests—and America and the steam-engine. Everything you can imagine ! "

" What a difficult kind of shorthand ! " said Dorothea, smiling towards her husband. " It would require all your knowledge to be able to read it."

Mr Casaubon blinked furtively at Will. He had a suspicion that he was being laughed at. But it was not possible to include Dorothea in the suspicion.

They found Naumann painting industriously, but no model was present ; his pictures were advantageously arranged, and his own plain vivacious person set off by a dove-coloured blouse and a maroon

---

4. Albert Bertel Thorwaldsen (1770–1844), Danish sculptor, long resident in Rome, influenced by the German Naz- arene painters to reject some of his neoclassical ideas in favor of Pre-Raphaelite "purism."

velvet cap, so that everything was as fortunate as if he had expected the beautiful young English lady exactly at that time.

The painter in his confident English gave little dissertations on his finished and unfinished subjects, seeming to observe Mr Casaubon as much as he did Dorothea. Will burst in here and there with ardent words of praise, marking out particular merits in his friend's work; and Dorothea felt that she was getting quite new notions as to the significance of Madonnas seated under inexplicable canopied thrones with the simple country as a background, and of saints with architectural models in their hands, or knives accidentally wedged in their skulls. Some things which had seemed monstrous to her were gathering intelligibility and even a natural meaning; but all this was apparently a branch of knowledge in which Mr Casaubon had not interested himself.

" I think I would rather feel that painting is beautiful than have to read it as an enigma; but I should learn to understand these pictures sooner than yours with the very wide meaning," said Dorothea, speaking to Will.

" Don't speak of my painting before Naumann," said Will. " He will tell you, it is all *pfuscherei*, which is his most opprobrious word ! "[5]

" Is that true?" said Dorothea, turning her sincere eyes on Naumann, who made a slight grimace and said,

" O, he does not mean it seriously with painting. His walk must be *belles-lettres*. That is wi-ide."

Naumann's pronunciation of the vowel seemed to stretch the word satirically. Will did not half like it, but managed to laugh; and Mr Casaubon, while he felt some disgust at the artist's German accent, began to entertain a little respect for his judicious severity.

The respect was not diminished when Naumann, after drawing Will aside for a moment and looking, first at a large canvas, then at Mr Casaubon, came forward again and said,

" My friend Ladislaw thinks you will pardon me, sir, if I say that a sketch of your head would be invaluable to me for the St Thomas Aquinas in my picture there. It is too much to ask; but I so seldom see just what I want—the idealistic in the real."

"You astonish me greatly, sir," said Mr Casaubon, his looks improved with a glow of delight; " but if my poor physiognomy, which I have been accustomed to regard as of the commonest order, can be of any use to you in furnishing some traits for the angelical doctor, I shall feel honoured. That is to say, if the operation will not be a lengthy one; and if Mrs Casaubon will not object to the delay."

As for Dorothea, nothing could have pleased her more, unless it had been a miraculous voice pronouncing Mr Casaubon the wisest and worthiest among the sons of men. In that case her tottering faith would have become firm again.

Naumann's apparatus was at hand in wonderful completeness, and the sketch went on at once as well as the conversation. Dorothea sat down and subsided into calm silence, feeling happier than she had done for a long while before. Every one about her seemed good, and she said to herself that Rome, if she had only been less ignorant,

---

5. *Pfuscherei:* bungling, clumsy work.

would have been full of beauty : its sadness would have been winged with hope. No nature could be less suspicious than hers ; when she was a child she believed in the gratitude of wasps and the honourable susceptibility of sparrows, and was proportionately indignant when their baseness was made manifest.

The adroit artist was asking Mr Casaubon questions about English politics, which brought long answers, and Will meanwhile had perched himself on some steps in the background overlooking all.

Presently Naumann said—" Now if I could lay this by for half an hour and take it up again—come and look, Ladislaw—I think it is perfect so far."

Will vented those adjuring interjections which imply that admiration is too strong for syntax ; and Naumann said in a tone of piteous regret,

" Ah—now—if I could but have had more—but you have other engagements—I could not ask it—or even to come again to-morrow."

" O let us stay !" said Dorothea. " We have nothing to do to-day except to go about, have we ?" she added, looking entreatingly at Mr Casaubon. " It would be a pity not to make the head as good as possible."

" I am at your service, sir, in the matter," said Mr Casaubon, with polite condescension. " Having given up the interior of my head to idleness, it is as well that the exterior should work in this way."

" You are unspeakably good—now I am happy !" said Naumann, and then went on in German to Will, pointing here and there to the sketch as if he were considering that. Putting it aside for a moment, he looked round vaguely, as if seeking some occupation for his visitors, and afterwards turning to Mr Casaubon said,

" Perhaps the beautiful bride, the gracious lady, would not be unwilling to let me fill up the time by trying to make a slight sketch of her—not, of course, as you see, for that picture—only as a single study."

Mr Casaubon, bowing, doubted not that Mrs Casaubon would oblige him, and Dorothea said, at once, " Where shall I put myself?"

Naumann was all apologies in asking her to stand, and allow him to adjust her attitude, to which she submitted without any of the affected airs and laughs frequently thought necessary on such occasions, when the painter said, " It is as Santa Clara that I want you to stand—leaning so, with your cheek against your hand—so—looking at that stool, please, so !" [6]

Will was divided between the inclination to fall at the Saint's feet and kiss her robe, and the temptation to knock Naumann down while he was adjusting her arm. All this was impudence and desecration, and he repented that he had brought her.

The artist was diligent, and Will recovering himself moved about and occupied Mr Casaubon as ingeniously as he could ; but he did not in the end prevent the time from seeming long to that gentleman, as was clear from his expressing a fear that Mrs Casaubon would be tired. Naumann took the hint and said—

" Now, sir, if you can oblige me again, I will release the lady-wife."

---

6. St. Clare (1194–1253), converted by Francis of Assisi, insisted on taking a vow of poverty; she founded the Poor Clares, an order of medicant nuns.

So Mr Casaubon's patience held out further, and when after all it turned out that the head of Saint Thomas Aquinas would be more perfect if another sitting could be had, it was granted for the morrow. On the morrow Santa Clara too was retouched more than once. The result of all was so far from displeasing to Mr Casaubon, that he arranged for the purchase of the picture in which Saint Thomas Aquinas sat among the doctors of the Church in a disputation too abstract to be represented, but listened to with more or less attention by an audience above.[7] The Santa Clara, which was spoken of in the second place, Naumann declared himself to be dissatisfied with—he could not, in conscience, engage to make a worthy picture of it; so about the Santa Clara the arrangement was conditional.

I will not dwell on Naumann's jokes at the expense of Mr Casaubon that evening, or on his dithyrambs about Dorothea's charm, in all which Will joined, but with a difference.[8] No sooner did Naumann mention any detail of Dorothea's beauty, than Will got exasperated at his presumption : there was grossness in his choice of the most ordinary words, and what business had he to talk of her lips? She was not a woman to be spoken of as other women were. Will could not say just what he thought, but he became irritable. And yet, when after some resistance he had consented to take the Casaubons to his friend's studio, he had been allured by the gratification of his pride in being the person who could grant Naumann such an opportunity of studying her loveliness—or rather her divineness, for the ordinary phrases which might apply to mere bodily prettiness were not applicable to her. (Certainly all Tipton and its neighbourhood, as well as Dorothea herself, would have been surprised at her beauty being made so much of. In that part of the world Miss Brooke had been only a " fine young woman.")

" Oblige me by letting the subject drop, Naumann. Mrs Casaubon is not to be talked of as if she were a model," said Will. Naumann stared at him.

" Schön ! I will talk of my Aquinas. The head is not a bad type, after all. I daresay the great scholastic himself would have been flattered to have his portrait asked for. Nothing like these starchy doctors for vanity ! It was as I thought: he cared much less for her portrait than his own."

" He's a cursed white-blooded pedantic coxcomb," said Will, with gnashing impetuosity. His obligations to Mr Casaubon were not known to his hearer, but Will himself was thinking of them, and wishing that he could discharge them all by a cheque.

Naumann gave a shrug and said, " It is good they go away soon, my dear. They are spoiling your fine temper."

All Will's hope and contrivance were now concentrated on seeing Dorothea when she was alone. He only wanted her to take more emphatic notice of him ; he only wanted to be something more special in her remembrance than he could yet believe himself likely to be. He was rather impatient under that open ardent goodwill,

---

7. The painting for which Casaubon sits may be a Nazarene rendition of a similar "disputation" painting by Raphael in the Vatican.

8. Dithyrambs: enthusiastic songs. Etymologically, the reference is Dionysian; "Dithyrambus" was one of the names of Dionysius, and dithyrambs were sung in his honor.

which he saw was her usual state of feeling. The remote worship of a woman throned out of their reach plays a great part in men's lives, but in most cases the worshipper longs for some queenly recognition, some approving sign by which his soul's sovereign may cheer him without descending from her high place. That was precisely what Will wanted. But there were plenty of contradictions in his imaginative demands. It was beautiful to see how Dorothea's eyes turned with wifely anxiety and beseeching to Mr Casaubon : she would have lost some of her halo if she had been without that duteous preoccupation; and yet at the next moment the husband's sandy absorption of such nectar was too intolerable ; and Will's longing to say damaging things about him was perhaps not the less tormenting because he felt the strongest reasons for restraining it.

Will had not been invited to dine the next day. Hence he persuaded himself that he was bound to call, and that the only eligible time was the middle of the day, when Mr Casaubon would not be at home.

Dorothea, who had not been made aware that her former reception of Will had displeased her husband, had no hesitation about seeing him, especially as he might be come to pay a farewell visit. When he entered she was looking at some cameos which she had been buying for Celia. She greeted Will as if his visit were quite a matter of course, and said at once, having a cameo bracelet in her hand,

" I am so glad you are come. Perhaps you understand all about cameos, and can tell me if these are really good. I wished to have you with us in choosing them, but Mr Casaubon objected : he thought there was not time. He will finish his work to-morrow, and we shall go away in three days. I have been uneasy about these cameos. Pray sit down and look at them."

" I am not particularly knowing, but there can be no great mistake about these little Homeric bits : they are exquisitely neat. And the colour is fine : it will just suit you."

" O, they are for my sister, who has quite a different complexion. You saw her with me at Lowick : she is light-haired and very pretty —at least I think so. We were never so long away from each other in our lives before. She is a great pet, and never was naughty in her life. I found out before I came away that she wanted me to buy her some cameos, and I should be sorry for them not to be good —after their kind." Dorothea added the last words with a smile.

" You seem not to care about cameos," said Will, seating himself at some distance from her, and observing her while she closed the cases.

. " No, frankly, I don't think them a great object in life," said Dorothea.

" I fear you are a heretic about art generally. How is that ? I should have expected you to be very sensitive to the beautiful everywhere."

" I suppose I am dull about many things," said Dorothea, simply. " I should like to make life beautiful—I mean everybody's life. And then all this immense expense of art, that seems somehow to lie outside life and make it no better for the world, pains one. It spoils my enjoyment of anything when I am made to think that most people are shut out from it."

" I call that the fanaticism of sympathy," said Will, impetuously. " You might say the same of landscape, of poetry, of all refinement. If you carried it out you ought to be miserable in your own goodness, and turn evil that you might have no advantage over others. The best piety is to enjoy—when you can. You are doing the most then to save the earth's character as an agreeable planet. And enjoyment radiates. It is of no use to try and take care of all the world ; that is being taken care of when you feel delight—in art or in anything else. Would you turn all the youth of the world into a tragic chorus, wailing and moralising over misery? I suspect that you have some false belief in the virtues of misery, and want to make your life a martyrdom." Will had gone further than he intended, and checked himself. But Dorothea's thought was not taking just the same direction as his own, and she answered without any special emotion—

"Indeed you mistake me. I am not a sad, melancholy creature: I am never unhappy long together. I am angry and naughty—not like Celia : I have a great outburst, and then all seems glorious again. I cannot help believing in glorious things in a blind sort of way. I should be quite willing to enjoy the art here, but there is so much that I don't know the reason of—so much that seems to me a consecration of ugliness rather than beauty. The painting and sculpture may be wonderful, but the feeling is often low and brutal, and sometimes even ridiculous. Here and there I see what takes me at once as noble—something that I might compare with the Alban Mountains or the sunset from the Pincian Hill ; but that makes it the greater pity that there is so little of the best kind among all that mass of things over which men have toiled so."

"Of course there is always a great deal of poor work : the rarer things want that soil to grow in."

"O dear," said Dorothea, taking up that thought into the chief current of her anxiety, "I see it must be very difficult to do anything good. I have often felt since I have been in Rome that most of our lives would look much uglier and more bungling than the pictures, if they could be put on the wall."

Dorothea parted her lips again as if she were going to say more, but changed her mind and paused.

"You are too young—it is an anachronism for you to have such thoughts," said Will energetically, with a quick shake of the head habitual to him. "You talk as if you had never known any youth. It is monstrous—as if you had had a vision of Hades in your childhood, like the boy in the legend. You have been brought up in some of those horrible notions that choose the sweetest women to devour—like Minotaurs. [9] And now you will go and be shut up in that stone prison at Lowick : you will be buried alive. It makes me savage to think of it ! I would rather never have seen you than think of you with such a prospect."

Will again feared that he had gone too far ; but the meaning we attach to words depends on our feeling, and his tone of angry regret had so much kindness in it for Dorothea's heart, which had always been giving out ardour and had never been fed with much from the living beings around her, that she felt a new sense of gratitude and answered with a gentle smile.

9. The only "boy" in legend who sees Hades is Eros. His mother, Aphrodite, persuades him to shoot one of his arrows at Hades, who is then smitten with love for Persephone, whom he carries off to his underworld kingdom. The Minotaur of Crete was fed on a diet of young virgins.

" It is very good of you to be anxious about me. It is because you did not like Lowick yourself : you had set your heart on another kind of life. But Lowick is my chosen home."

The last sentence was spoken with an almost solemn cadence, and Will did not know what to say, since it would not be useful for him to embrace her slippers, and tell her that he would die for her : it was clear that she required nothing of the sort ; and they were both silent for a moment or two, when Dorothea began again with an air of saying at last what had been in her mind beforehand.

"I wanted to ask you again about something you said the other day. Perhaps it was half of it your lively way of speaking : I notice that you like to put things strongly; I myself often exaggerate when I speak hastily."

" What was it ?" said Will, observing that she spoke with a timidity quite new in her. " I have a hyperbolical tongue : it catches fire as it goes. I daresay I shall have to retract."

" I mean what you said about the necessity of knowing German— I mean, for the subjects that Mr Casaubon is engaged in. I have been thinking about it ; and it seems to me that with Mr Casaubon's learning he must have before him the same materials as German scholars—has he not ?" Dorothea's timidity was due to an indistinct consciousness that she was in the strange situation of consulting a third person about the adequacy of Mr Casaubon's learning.

" Not exactly the same materials," said Will, thinking that he would be duly reserved. " He is not an Orientalist, you know. He does not profess to have more than second-hand knowledge there."

" But there are very valuable books about antiquities which were written a long while ago by scholars who knew nothing about these modern things ; and they are still used. Why should Mr Casaubon's not be valuable, like theirs ? " said Dorothea, with more remonstrant energy. She was impelled to have the argument aloud, which she had been having in her own mind.

" That depends on the line of study taken," said Will, also getting a tone of rejoinder. " The subject Mr Casaubon has chosen is as changing as chemistry : new discoveries are constantly making new points of view. Who wants a system on the basis of the four elements, or a book to refute Paracelsus ?[1] Do you not see that it is no use now to be crawling a little way after men of the last century—men like Bryant—and correcting their mistakes?—living in a lumber-room and furbishing up broken-legged theories about Chus and Mizraim ?"[2]

" How can you bear to speak so lightly ?" said Dorothea, with a look between sorrow and anger. " If it were as you say, what could be sadder than so much ardent labour all in vain ? I wonder it does not affect you more painfully, if you really think that a man like Mr

1. Theophrastus Bombastus von Hohenheim (1493–1541), German physician and chemical theorist who wrote under the pseudonym "Paracelsus." He urged new methods of treating disease, based on both chemical and alchemical theories.
2. Jacob Bryant (1715–1804), British antiquary, wrote *A New System or an Analysis of Ancient Mythology* (1774–76), in which he traces all myths back to the descendents of Ham, through his son Chus and "the collateral branches of his family, the Mizraim, Caphtorem, and the sons of Canaan" (I, vii). GE discusses the subject in a review of R. W. Mackay's *The Progress of the Intellect* in *The Westminster Review*, 54 (1851), 353–68. Her essay is reprinted in Thomas Pinney, ed., *Essays of George Eliot* (London, 1963), pp. 27–45.

Casaubon, of so much goodness, power, and learning, should in any way fail in what has been the labour of his best years." She was beginning to be shocked that she had got to such a point of supposition, and indignant with Will for having led her to it.

"You questioned me about the matter of fact, not of feeling," said Will. "But if you wish to punish me for the fact, I submit. I am not in a position to express my feeling toward Mr Casaubon: it would be at best a pensioner's eulogy."

"Pray excuse me," said Dorothea, colouring deeply. "I am aware, as you say, that I am in fault, in having introduced the subject. Indeed, I am wrong altogether. Failure after long perseverance is much grander than never to have a striving good enough to be called a failure."

"I quite agree with you," said Will, determined to change the situation—"so much so that I have made up my mind not to run that risk of never attaining a failure. Mr Casaubon's generosity has perhaps been dangerous to me, and I mean to renounce the liberty it has given me. I mean to go back to England shortly and work my own way—depend on nobody else than myself."

"That is fine—I respect that feeling," said Dorothea, with returning kindness. "But Mr Casaubon, I am sure, has never thought of anything in the matter except what was most for your welfare."

"She has obstinacy and pride enough to serve instead of love, now she has married him," said Will to himself. Aloud he said, rising,

"I shall not see you again."

"O stay till Mr Casaubon comes," said Dorothea, earnestly. "I am so glad we met in Rome. I wanted to know you."

"And I have made you angry," said Will. "I have made you think ill of me."

"Oh no ! My sister tells me I am always angry with people who do not say just what I like. But I hope I am not given to think ill of them. In the end I am usually obliged to think ill of myself, for being so impatient."

"Still, you don't like me ; I have made myself an unpleasant thought to you."

"Not at all," said Dorothea, with the most open kindness. "I like you very much."

Will was not quite contented, thinking that he would apparently have been of more importance if he had been disliked. He said nothing, but looked dull, not to say sulky.

"And I am quite interested to see what you will do," Dorothea went on cheerfully. "I believe devoutly in a natural difference of vocation. If it were not for that belief, I suppose I should be very narrow—there are so many things, besides painting, that I am quite ignorant of. You would hardly believe how little I have taken in of music and literature, which you know so much of. I wonder what your vocation will turn out to be : perhaps you will be a poet ? "

"That depends. To be a poet is to have a soul so quick to discern that no shade of quality escapes it, and so quick to feel, that discernment is but a hand playing with finely-ordered variety on the chords of emotion—a soul in which knowledge passes instantaneously into feeling, and feeling flashes back as a new organ of knowledge. One may have that condition by fits only."

"But you leave out the poems," said Dorothea. "I think they are wanted to complete the poet. I understand what you mean about knowledge passing into feeling, for that seems to be just what I experience. But I am sure I could never produce a poem."

"You *are* a poem—and that is to be the best part of a poet—what makes up the poet's consciousness in his best moods," said Will, showing such originality as we all share with the morning and the spring-time and other endless renewals.

"I am very glad to hear it," said Dorothea, laughing out her words in a birdlike modulation, and looking at Will with playful gratitude in her eyes. "What very kind things you say to me!"

"I wish I could ever do anything that would be what you call kind —that I could ever be of the slightest service to you. I fear I shall never have the opportunity." Will spoke with fervour.

"Oh yes!" said Dorothea, cordially. "It will come ; and I shall remember how well you wish me. I quite hoped that we should be friends when I first saw you—because of your relationship to Mr Casaubon." There was a certain liquid brightness in her eyes, and Will was conscious that his own were obeying a law of nature and filling too. The allusion to Mr Casaubon would have spoiled all if anything at that moment could have spoiled the subduing power, the sweet dignity, of her noble unsuspicious inexperience.

"And there is one thing even now that you can do," said Dorothea, rising and walking a little way under the strength of a recurring impulse. "Promise me that you will not again, to any one, speak of that subject—I mean, about Mr Casaubon's writings—I mean in that kind of way. It was I who led to it. It was my fault. But promise me."

She had returned from her brief pacing and stood opposite Will, looking gravely at him.

"Certainly, I will promise you," said Will, reddening however. If he never said a cutting word about Mr Casaubon again and left off receiving favours from him, it would clearly be permissible to hate him the more. The poet must know how to hate, says Goethe ; and Will was at least ready with that accomplishment. He said that he must go now without waiting for Mr Casaubon, whom he would come to take leave of at the last moment. Dorothea gave him her hand, and they exchanged a simple " Good-bye."

But going out of the *porte cochère* he met Mr Casaubon, and that gentleman, expressing the best wishes for his cousin, politely waived the pleasure of any further leave-taking on the morrow, which would be sufficiently crowded with the preparations for departure.

"I have something to tell you about our cousin Mr Ladislaw, which I think will heighten your opinion of him," said Dorothea to her husband in the course of the evening. She had mentioned immediately on his entering that Will had just gone away, and would come again, but Mr Casaubon had said, " I met him outside, and we made our final adieux, I believe," saying this with the air and tone by which we imply that any subject, whether private or public, does not interest us enough to wish for a further remark upon it. So Dorothea had waited.

---

3. *Porte cochère:* a gateway for carriages.

" What is that, my love ? " said Mr Casaubon (he always said " my love " when his manner was the coldest).

" He has made up his mind to leave off wandering at once, and to give up his dependence on your generosity. He means soon to go back to England, and work his own way. I thought you would consider that a good sign," said Dorothea, with an appealing look into her husband's neutral face.

" Did he mention the precise order of occupation to which he would addict himself ? "

" No. But he said that he felt the danger which lay for him in your generosity. Of course he will write to you about it. Do you not think better of him for his resolve ? "

" I shall await his communication on the subject," said Mr Casaubon.

" I told him I was sure that the thing you considered in all you did for him was his own welfare. I remembered your goodness in what you said about him when I first saw him at Lowick," said Dorothea, putting her hand on her husband's.

" I had a duty towards him," said Mr Casaubon, laying his other hand on Dorothea's in conscientious acceptance of her caress, but with a glance which he could not hinder from being uneasy. " The young man, I confess, is not otherwise an object of interest to me, nor need we, I think, discuss his future course, which it is not ours to determine beyond the limits which I have sufficiently indicated."

Dorothea did not mention Will again.

BOOK III.

WAITING FOR DEATH.

CHAPTER XXIII.

"Your horses of the Sun," he said,
    "And first-rate whip Apollo!
Whate'er they be, I'll eat my head,
    But I will beat them hollow."

FRED VINCY, we have seen, had a debt on his mind, and though no such immaterial burthen could depress that buoyant-hearted young gentleman for many hours together, there were circumstances connected with this debt which made the thought of it unusually importunate. The creditor was Mr Bambridge, a horse-dealer of the neighbourhood, whose company was much sought in Middlemarch by young men understood to be "addicted to pleasure." During the vacations Fred had naturally required more amusements than he had ready money for, and Mr Bambridge had been accommodating enough not only to trust him for the hire of horses and the accidental expense of ruining a fine hunter, but also to make a small advance by which he might be able to meet some losses at billiards. The total debt was a hundred and sixty pounds. Bambridge was in no alarm about his money, being sure that young Vincy had backers; but he had required something to show for it, and Fred had at first given a bill with his own signature. Three months later he had renewed this bill with the signature of Caleb Garth. On both occasions Fred had felt confident that he should meet the bill himself, having ample funds at disposal in his own hopefulness. You will hardly demand that his confidence should have a basis in external facts; such confidence, we know, is something less coarse and materialistic: it is a comfortable disposition leading us to expect that the wisdom of providence or the folly of our friends, the mysteries of luck or the still greater mystery of our high individual value in the universe, will bring about agreeable issues, such as are consistent with our good taste in costume, and our general preference for the best style of thing. Fred felt sure that he should have a present from his uncle, that he should have a run of luck, that by dint of "swapping" he should gradually metamorphose a horse worth forty pounds into a horse that would fetch a hundred at any moment—"judgment" being always equivalent to an unspecified sum in hard cash. And in any case, even supposing negations which only a morbid distrust could imagine, Fred had always (at that time) his father's pocket as a last resource, so that his assets of hopefulness had a sort of gorgeous superfluity about them. Of what might be the capacity of his father's pocket, Fred had only a vague notion: was not trade elastic? And would not the deficiencies of one year be made up for by the surplus of another? The Vincys lived in an easy profuse way, not with any new ostentation, but according to the family habits and traditions, so that the children had no standard of economy, and the elder ones retained some of their infantine notion that their father might pay for anything if he would. Mr Vincy himself had expensive Middlemarch habits—spent money on coursing, on his cellar, and on dinner-giving, while mamma had those running accounts with tradespeople, which give a cheerful sense of getting everything one wants without any question of payment. But it was in the nature of fathers, Fred knew, to bully one about expenses : there was always a little storm over his extravagance if he had to disclose a debt, and Fred disliked bad weather within doors. He was too filial to be disrespectful to his father, and he bore the thunder with the certainty that it was transient ; but in the mean time it was disagreeable to see his mother cry, and also to be obliged to look sulky instead of having fun ; for Fred was so good-tempered that if he looked glum under scolding, it was chiefly for propriety's sake. The easier course plainly, was to renew the bill with a friend's signature. Why not? With the superfluous securities of hope at his command, there was no reason why he should not have increased other people's liabilities to any extent, but for the fact that men whose names were good for anything were usually pessimists, indisposed to believe that the universal order of things would necessarily be agreeable to an agreeable young gentleman.

With a favour to ask we review our list of friends, do justice to their more amiable qualities, forgive their little offences, and concerning each in turn, try to arrive at the conclusion that he will be eager to oblige us, our own eagerness to be obliged being as communicable as other warmth. Still there is always a certain number who are dismissed as but moderately eager until the others have refused ; and it happened that Fred checked off all his friends but one, on the ground that applying to them would be disagreeable ; being implicitly convinced that he at least (whatever might be maintained about mankind generally) had a right to be free from anything disagreeable. That he should ever fall into a thoroughly unpleasant position—wear trousers shrunk with washing, eat cold mutton, have to walk for want of a horse, or to "duck under" in any sort of way—was an absurdity irreconcilable with those cheerful intuitions implanted in him by nature. And Fred winced under the idea of being looked down upon as wanting funds for small debts. Thus it came to pass that the friend whom he chose to apply to was at once the poorest and the kindest—namely, Caleb Garth.

The Garths were very fond of Fred, as he was of them ; for when he and Rosamond were little ones, and the Garths were better off, the slight connection between the two families through Mr Featherstone's double marriage (the first to Mr Garth's sister, and the second to Mrs Vincy's) had led to an acquaintance which was carried on between the children rather than the parents : the children drank tea together out of their toy tea-cups, and spent whole days together in play. Mary was a little hoyden, and Fred at six years old thought her the nicest girl in the world, making her his wife with a brass ring which he had cut from an umbrella. Through all the stages of his education he had kept his affection for the Garths, and his habit of going to their house as a second home, though any intercourse between them and the elders of his family had long ceased. Even when Caleb Garth was prosperous, the Vincys were on condescending terms with him and his wife, for there were nice distinctions of rank in Middlemarch ; and though old manufacturers could not any more than dukes be connected with none but equals, they were conscious of an inherent social superiority which was defined with great nicety in practice, though hardly expressible theoretically. Since then Mr Garth had failed in the building business, which he had unfortunately added to his other avocations of surveyor, valuer, and agent, had conducted that business for a time entirely for the benefit of his assignees, and had been living narrowly, exerting himself to the utmost that he might after all pay twenty shillings in the pound. He had now achieved this, and from all who did not think it a bad precedent, his honourable exertions had won him due esteem ; but in no part of the world is genteel visiting founded on esteem, in the absence of suitable furniture and complete dinner-service. Mrs Vincy had never been at her ease with Mrs Garth, and frequently spoke of her as a woman who had had to work for her bread—meaning that Mrs Garth had been a teacher before her marriage ; in which case an intimacy with Lindley Murray and Mangnall's Questions was something like a draper's discrimination of calico trade-marks, or a courier's acquaintance with foreign countries : no woman who was better off needed that sort of thing. [1] And since Mary had been keeping Mr Featherstone's house, Mrs Vincy's want of liking for the Garths had been converted into something more positive, by alarm lest Fred should engage himself to this plain girl, whose parents " lived in such a small way." Fred, being aware of this, never spoke at home of his visits to Mrs Garth, which had of late become more frequent, the increasing ardour of his affection for Mary inclining him the more towards those who belonged to her.

Mr Garth had a small office in the town, and to this Fred went with his request. He obtained it without much difficulty, for a large amount of painful experience had not sufficed to make Caleb Garth cautious about his own affairs, or distrustful of his fellow-men when they had not proved themselves untrustworthy ; and he had the highest opinion of Fred, was " sure the lad would turn out well —an open affectionate fellow, with a good bottom to his character— you might trust him for anything." Such was Caleb's psychological argument. He was one of those rare men who are rigid to themselves and indulgent to others. He had a certain shame about his neighbours' errors, and never spoke of them willingly ; hence he was not likely to divert his mind from the best mode of hardening timber and other ingenious devices in order to preconceive those errors. If he had to blame any one, it was necessary for him to move all the papers within his reach, or describe various diagrams with his stick, or make calculations with the odd money in his pocket, before he could begin ; and he would rather do other men's work than find fault with their doing. I fear he was a bad disciplinarian.

When Fred stated the circumstances of his debt, his wish to meet

---

1. Lindley Murray (1745–1826) and Mrs. Richmal Mangnall (1769–1820), were authors of standard early-nineteenth-century schoolbooks.

it without troubling his father, and the certainty that the money would be forthcoming so as to cause no one any inconvenience, Caleb pushed his spectacles upward, listened, looked into his favourite's clear young eyes, and believed him, not distinguishing confidence about the future from veracity about the past; but he felt that it was an occasion for a friendly hint as to conduct, and that before giving his signature he must give a rather strong admonition. Accordingly, he took the paper and lowered his spectacles, measured the space at his command, reached his pen and examined it, dipped it in the ink and examined it again, then pushed the paper a little way from him, lifted up his spectacles again, showed a deepened depression in the outer angle of his bushy eyebrows, which gave his face a peculiar mildness (pardon these details for once—you would have learned to love them if you had known Caleb Garth), and said in a comfortable tone,

" It was a misfortune, eh, that breaking the horse's knees? And then, these exchanges, they don't answer when you have 'cute jockies to deal with. You'll be wiser another time, my boy."

Whereupon Caleb drew down his spectacles, and proceeded to write his signature with the care which he always gave to that performance; for whatever he did in the way of business he did well. He contemplated the large well-proportioned letters and final flourish, with his head a trifle on one side for an instant, then handed it to Fred, said " Good-bye," and returned forthwith to his absorption in a plan for Sir James Chettam's new farm-buildings.

Either because his interest in this work thrust the incident of the signature from his memory, or for some reason of which Caleb was more conscious, Mrs Garth remained ignorant of the affair.

Since it occurred, a change had come over Fred's sky, which altered his view of the distance, and was the reason why his uncle Featherstone's present of money was of importance enough to make his colour come and go, first with a too definite expectation, and afterwards with a proportionate disappointment. His failure in passing his examination, had made his accumulation of college debts the more unpardonable by his father, and there had been an unprecedented storm at home. Mr Vincy had sworn that if he had anything more of that sort to put up with, Fred should turn out and get his living how he could; and he had never yet quite recovered his good-humoured tone to his son, who had especially enraged him by saying at this stage of things that he did not want to be a clergyman, and would rather not " go on with that." Fred was conscious that he would have been yet more severely dealt with if his family as well as himself had not secretly regarded him as Mr Featherstone's heir; that old gentleman's pride in him, and apparent fondness for him, serving in the stead of more exemplary conduct—just as when a youthful nobleman steals jewellery we call the act kleptomania, speak of it with a philosophical smile, and never think of his being sent to the house of correction as if he were a ragged boy who had stolen turnips. In fact, tacit expectations of what would be done for him by Uncle Featherstone determined the angle at which most people viewed Fred Vincy in Middlemarch; and in his own consciousness, what Uncle Featherstone would do for him in an emergency, or what he would do simply as an incorporated luck, formed always an immeasurable depth of aërial perspective. But that present of bank-notes, once made, was measurable, and being applied to the amount of the debt, showed a deficit which had still to be filled up either by Fred's "judgment" or by luck in some other shape. For that little episode of the alleged borrowing, in which he had made his father the agent in getting the Bulstrode certificate, was a new reason against going to his father for money towards meeting his actual debt. Fred was keen enough to foresee that anger would confuse distinctions, and that his denial of having borrowed expressly on the strength of his uncle's will would be taken as a falsehood. He had gone to his father and told him one vexatious affair, and he had left another untold : in such cases the complete revelation always produces the impression of a previous duplicity. Now Fred piqued himself on keeping clear of lies, and even fibs ; he often shrugged his shoulders and made a significant grimace at what he called Rosamond's fibs (it is only brothers who can associate such ideas with a lovely girl) ; and rather than incur the accusation of falsehood he would even incur some trouble and self-restraint. It was under strong inward pressure of this kind that Fred had taken the wise step of depositing the eighty pounds with his mother. It was a pity that he had not at once given them to Mr Garth ; but he meant to make the sum complete with another sixty, and with a view to this, he had kept twenty pounds in his own pocket as a sort of seed-corn, which, planted by judgment, and watered by luck, might yield more than threefold—a very poor rate of multiplication when the field is a young gentleman's infinite soul, with all the numerals at command.

Fred was not a gambler : he had not that specific disease in which the suspension of the whole nervous energy on a chance or risk becomes as necessary as the dram to the drunkard ; he had only the tendency to that diffusive form of gambling which has no alcoholic intensity, but is carried on with the healthiest chyle-fed blood, keeping up a joyous imaginative activity which fashions events according to desire, and having no fears about its own weather, only sees the advantage there must be to others in going aboard with it.[2] Hopefulness has a pleasure in making a throw of any kind, because the prospect of success is certain ; and only a more generous pleasure in offering as many as possible a share in the stake. Fred liked play, especially billiards, as he liked hunting or riding a steeplechase ; and he only liked it the better because he wanted money and hoped to win. But the twenty pounds' worth of seed-corn had been planted in vain in the seductive green plot—all of it at least which had not been dispersed by the roadside—and Fred found himself close upon the term of payment with no money at command beyond the eighty pounds which he had deposited with his mother. The broken-winded horse which he rode represented a present which had been made to him a long while ago by his uncle Featherstone : his father always allowed him to keep a horse, Mr Vincy's own habits making him regard this as a reasonable demand even for a son who was rather exasperating. This horse, then, was Fred's property, and in his anxiety to meet the imminent bill he determined to sacrifice a possession

2. Chyle is a milky fluid containing various products of healthy digestion; it is carried by the lacteals and the thoractic duct to the veins.

without which life would certainly be worth little. He made the resolution with a sense of heroism—heroism forced on him by the dread of breaking his word to Mr Garth, by his love for Mary and awe of her opinion. He would start for Houndsley horse-fair which was to be held the next morning, and—simply sell his horse, bringing back the money by coach ?—Well, the horse would hardly fetch more than thirty pounds, and there was no knowing what might happen : it would be folly to balk himself of luck beforehand. It was a hundred to one that some good chance would fall in his way : the longer he thought of it, the less possible it seemed that he should not have a good chance, and the less reasonable that he should not equip himself with the powder and shot for bringing it down. He would ride to Houndsley with Bambridge and with Horrock "the vet," and without asking them anything expressly, he should virtually get the benefit of their opinion. Before he set out, Fred got the eighty pounds from his mother.

Most of those who saw Fred riding out of Middlemarch in company with Bambridge and Horrock, on his way of course to Houndsley horse-fair, thought that young Vincy was pleasure-seeking as usual ; and but for an unwonted consciousness of grave matters on hand, he himself would have had a sense of dissipation, and of doing what might be expected of a gay young fellow. Considering that Fred was not at all coarse, that he rather looked down on the manners and speech of young men who had not been to the university, and that he had written stanzas as pastoral and unvoluptuous as his flute-playing, his attraction towards Bambridge and Horrock was an interesting fact which even the love of horse-flesh would not wholly account for without that mysterious influence of Naming which determines so much of mortal choice. Under any other name than " pleasure" the society of Messieurs Bambridge and Horrock must certainly have been regarded as monotonous ; and to arrive with them at Houndsley on a drizzling afternoon, to get down at the Red Lion in a street shaded with coal-dust, and dine in a room furnished with a dirt-enamelled map of the county, a bad portrait of an anonymous horse in a stable, His Majesty George the Fourth with legs and cravat, and various leaden spittoons, might have seemed a hard business, but for the sustaining power of nomenclature which determined that the pursuit of these things was " gay."

In Mr Horrock there was certainly an apparent unfathomableness which offered play to the imagination. Costume, at a glance, gave him a thrilling association with horses (enough to specify the hat-brim which took the slightest upward angle just to escape the suspicion of bending downwards), and nature had given him a face which by dint of Mongolian eyes, and a nose, mouth, and chin seeming to follow his hat-brim in a moderate inclination upwards, gave the effect of a subdued unchangeable sceptical smile, of all expressions the most tyrannous over a susceptible mind, and, when accompanied by adequate silence, likely to create the reputation of an invincible understanding, an infinite fund of humour—too dry to flow, and probably in a state of immovable crust,—and a critical judgment which, if you could ever be fortunate enough to know it, would be *the* thing and no other. It is a physiognomy seen in all vocations, but perhaps it has never been more powerful over the youth of England than in a judge of horses.

Mr Horrock, at a question from Fred about his horse's fetlock, turned sideways in his saddle, and watched the horse's action for the space of three minutes, then turned forward, twitched his own bridle, and remained silent with a profile neither more nor less sceptical than it had been.

The part thus played in dialogue by Mr Horrock was terribly effective. A mixture of passions was excited in Fred—a mad desire to thrash Horrock's opinion into utterance, restrained by anxiety to retain the advantage of his friendship. There was always the chance that Horrock might say something quite invaluable at the right moment.

Mr Bambridge had more open manners, and appeared to give forth his ideas without economy. He was loud, robust, and was sometimes spoken of as being "given to indulgence"—chiefly in swearing, drinking, and beating his wife. Some people who had lost by him called him a vicious man ; but he regarded horse-dealing as the finest of the arts, and might have argued plausibly that it had nothing to do with morality. He was undeniably a prosperous man, bore his drinking better than others bore their moderation, and, on the whole, flourished like the green bay-tree. But his range of conversation was limited, and like the fine old tune, " Drops of brandy," gave you after a while a sense of returning upon itself in a way that might make weak heads dizzy. But a slight infusion of Mr Bambridge was felt to give tone and character to several circles in Middlemarch ; and he was a distinguished figure in the bar and billiard-room at the Green Dragon. He knew some anecdotes about the heroes of the turf, and various clever tricks of Marquesses and Viscounts which seemed to prove that blood asserted its pre-eminence even among blacklegs ; but the minute retentiveness of his memory was chiefly shown about the horses he had himself bought and sold ; the number of miles they would trot you in no time without turning a hair being, after the lapse of years, still a subject of passionate asseveration, in which he would assist the imagination of his hearers by solemnly swearing that they never saw anything like it. In short, Mr Bambridge was a man of pleasure and a gay companion.

Fred was subtle, and did not tell his friends that he was going to Houndsley bent on selling his horse : he wished to get indirectly at their genuine opinion of its value, not being aware that a genuine opinion was the last thing likely to be extracted from such eminent critics. It was not Mr Bambridge's weakness to be a gratuitous flatterer. He had never before been so much struck with the fact that this unfortunate bay was a roarer to a degree which required the roundest word for perdition to give you any idea of it.

" You made a bad hand at swapping when you went to anybody but me, Vincy ! Why, you never threw your leg across a finer horse than that chesnut, and you gave him for this brute. If you set him cantering, he goes on like twenty sawyers. I never heard but one worse roarer in my life, and that was a roan : it belonged to Pegwell, the corn-factor ; he used to drive him in his gig seven years ago, and he wanted me to take him, but I said, ' Thank you, Peg, I don't deal in wind-instruments.' That was what I said. It went the round of the country, that joke did. But, what the hell ! the horse was a penny trumpet to that roarer of yours."

" Why, you said just now his was worse than mine," said Fred, more irritable than usual.

"I said a lie, then," said Mr Bambridge, emphatically. "There wasn't a penny to choose between 'em."

Fred spurred his horse, and they trotted on a little way. When they slackened again, Mr Bambridge said—

"Not but what the roan was a better trotter than yours."

"I'm quite satisfied with his paces, I know," said Fred, who required all the consciousness of being in gay company to support him ; "I say, his trot is an uncommonly clean one, eh, Horrock ?"

Mr Horrock looked before him with as complete a neutrality as if he had been a portrait by a great master.

Fred gave up the fallacious hope of getting a genuine opinion ; but on reflection he saw that Bambridge's depreciation and Horrock's silence were both virtually encouraging, and indicated that they thought better of the horse than they chose to say.

That very evening, indeed, before the fair had set in, Fred thought he saw a favourable opening for disposing advantageously of his horse, but an opening which made him congratulate himself on his foresight in bringing with him his eighty pounds. A young farmer, acquainted with Mr Bambridge, came into the Red Lion, and entered into conversation about parting with a hunter, which he introduced at once as Diamond, implying that it was a public character. For himself he only wanted a useful hack, which would draw upon occasion ; being about to marry and to give up hunting. The hunter was in a friend's stable at some little distance ; there was still time for gentlemen to see it before dark. The friend's stable had to be reached through a back street where you might as easily have been poisoned without expense of drugs as in any grim street of that unsanitary period. Fred was not fortified against disgust by brandy, as his companions were, but the hope of having at last seen the horse that would enable him to make money was exhilarating enough to lead him over the same ground again the first thing in the morning. He felt sure that if he did not come to a bargain with the farmer, Bambridge would ; for the stress of circumstances, Fred felt, was sharpening his acuteness and endowing him with all the constructive power of suspicion. Bambridge had run down Diamond in a way that he never would have done (the horse being a friend's) if he had not thought of buying it ; every one who looked at the animal—even Horrock—was evidently impressed with its merit. To get all the advantage of being with men of this sort, you must know how to draw your inferences, and not be a spoon who takes things literally. The colour of the horse was a dappled grey, and Fred happened to know that Lord Medlicote's man was on the look-out for just such a horse. After all his running down, Bambridge let it out in the course of the evening, when the farmer was absent, that he had seen worse horses go for eighty pounds. Of course he contradicted himself twenty times over, but when you know what is likely to be true you can test a man's admissions. And Fred could not but reckon his own judgment of a horse as worth something. The farmer had paused over Fred's respectable though broken-winded steed long enough to show that he thought it worth consideration, and it seemed probable that he would take it, with five-and-twenty pounds in addition, as the equivalent of Diamond. In that case Fred, when he had parted with his new horse for at least eighty pounds, would be fifty-five pounds in pocket by the transaction, and would have a hundred and thirty-five pounds towards meeting the bill ; so that the deficit temporarily thrown on Mr Garth would at the utmost be twenty-five pounds.   By the time he was hurrying on his clothes in the morning, he saw so clearly the importance of not losing this rare chance, that if Bambridge and Horrock had both dissuaded him, he would not have been deluded into a direct interpretation of their purpose : he would have been aware that those deep hands held something else than a young fellow's interest. With regard to horses, distrust was your only clue.   But scepticism, as we know, can never be thoroughly applied, else life would come to a standstill : something we must believe in and do, and whatever that something may be called, it is virtually our own judgment, even when it seems like the most slavish reliance on another.   Fred believed in the excellence of his bargain, and even before the fair had well set in, had got possession of the dappled grey, at the price of his old horse and thirty pounds in addition — only five pounds more than he had expected to give.

But he felt a little worried and wearied, perhaps with mental debate, and without waiting for the further gaieties of the horse-fair, he set out alone on his fourteen miles' journey, meaning to take it very quietly and keep his horse fresh.

CHAPTER XXIV.

" The offender's sorrow brings but small relief
To him who wears the strong offence's cross."
—SHAKESPEARE : *Sonnets.* [1]

I AM sorry to say that only the third day after the propitious events at Houndsley Fred Vincy had fallen into worse spirits than he had known in his life before.   Not that he had been disappointed as to the possible market for his horse, but that before the bargain could be concluded with Lord Medlicote's man, this Diamond, in which hope to the amount of eighty pounds had been invested, had without the slightest warning exhibited in the stable a most vicious energy in kicking, had just missed killing the groom, and had ended in laming himself severely by catching his leg in a rope that overhung the stable-board.   There was no more redress for this than for the discovery of bad temper after marriage—which of course old companions were aware of before the ceremony.   For some reason or other, Fred had none of his usual elasticity under this stroke of ill-fortune : he was simply aware that he had only fifty pounds, that there was no chance of his getting any more at present, and that the bill for a hundred and sixty would be presented in five days.   Even if he had applied to his father on the plea that Mr Garth should be saved from loss, Fred felt smartingly that his father would angrily refuse to rescue Mr Garth from the consequence of what he would call encouraging extravagance and deceit.   He was so utterly downcast that he could frame no other project than to go straight to Mr Garth and tell him the sad truth, carrying with him the fifty pounds,

1. Sonnet 34.

and getting that sum at least safely out of his own hands. His father, being at the warehouse, did not yet know of the accident : when he did, he would storm about the vicious brute being brought into his stable ; and before meeting that lesser annoyance Fred wanted to get away with all his courage to face the greater. He took his father's nag, for he had made up his mind that when he had told Mr Garth, he would ride to Stone Court and confess all to Mary. In fact, it is probable that but for Mary's existence and Fred's love for her, his conscience would have been much less active both in previously urging the debt on his thought and in impelling him not to spare himself after his usual fashion by deferring an unpleasant task, but to act as directly and simply as he could. Even much stronger mortals than Fred Vincy hold half their rectitude in the mind of the being they love best. " The theatre of all my actions is fallen," said an antique personage when his chief friend was dead ; and they are fortunate who get a theatre where the audience demands their best. Certainly it would have made a considerable difference to Fred at that time if Mary Garth had had no decided notions as to what was admirable in character.

Mr Garth was not at the office, and Fred rode on to his house, which was a little way outside the town—a homely place with an orchard in front of it, a rambling, old-fashioned, half-timbered building, which before the town had spread had been a farmhouse, but was now surrounded with the private gardens of the townsmen. We get the fonder of our houses if they have a physiognomy of their own, as our friends have. The Garth family, which was rather a large one, for Mary had four brothers and one sister, were very fond of their old house, from which all the best furniture had long been sold. Fred liked it too, knowing it by heart even to the attic which smelt deliciously of apples and quinces, and until to-day he had never come to it without pleasant expectations ; but his heart beat uneasily now with the sense that he should probably have to make his confession before Mrs Garth, of whom he was rather more in awe than of her husband. Not that she was inclined to sarcasm and to impulsive sallies, as Mary was. In her present matronly age at least, Mrs Garth never committed herself by over-hasty speech ; having, as she said, borne the yoke in her youth, and learned self-control. She had that rare sense which discerns what is unalterable, and submits to it without murmuring. Adoring her husband's virtues, she had very early made up her mind to his incapacity of minding his own interests, and had met the consequences cheerfully. She had been magnanimous enough to renounce all pride in teapots or children's frilling, and had never poured any pathetic confidences into the ears of her feminine neighbours concerning Mr Garth's want of prudence and the sums he might have had if he had been like other men. Hence these fair neighbours thought her either proud or eccentric, and sometimes spoke of her to their husbands as "your fine Mrs Garth." She was not without her criticism of them in return, being more accurately instructed than most matrons in Middlemarch, and —where is the blameless woman?—apt to be a little severe towards her own sex, which in her opinion was framed to be entirely subordinate. On the other hand, she was disproportionately indulgent towards the failings of men, and was often heard to say that these were natural. Also, it must be admitted that Mrs Garth was a trifle too emphatic in her resistance to what she held to be follies : the passage from governess into housewife had wrought itself a little too strongly into her consciousness, and she rarely forgot that while her grammar and accent were above the town standard, she wore a plain cap, cooked the family dinner, and darned all the stockings. She had sometimes taken pupils in a peripatetic fashion, making them follow her about in the kitchen with their book or slate. She thought it good for them to see that she could make an excellent lather while she corrected their blunders " without looking,"—that a woman with her sleeves tucked up above her elbows might know all about the Sub-junctive Mood or the Torrid Zone—that, in short, she might possess " education " and other good things ending in " tion," and worthy to be pronounced emphatically, without being a useless doll. When she made remarks to this edifying effect, she had a firm little frown on her brow, which yet did not hinder her face from looking benevolent, and her words which came forth like a procession were uttered in a fervid agreeable contralto. Certainly, the exemplary Mrs Garth had her droll aspects, but her character sustained her oddities, as a very fine wine sustains a flavour of skin.

Towards Fred Vincy she had a motherly feeling, and had always been disposed to excuse his errors, though she would probably not have excused Mary for engaging herself to him, her daughter being included in that more rigorous judgment which she applied to her own sex. But this very fact of her exceptional indulgence towards· him made it the harder to Fred that he must now inevitably sink in her opinion. And the circumstances of his visit turned out to be still more unpleasant than he had expected ; for Caleb Garth had gone out early to look at some repairs not far off. Mrs Garth at certain hours was always in the kitchen, and this morning she was carrying on several occupations at once there—making her pies at the well-scoured deal table on one side of that airy room, observing Sally's movements at the oven and dough-tub through an open door, and giving lessons to her youngest boy and girl, who were standing oppo-site to her at the table with their books and slates before them. A tub and a clothes-horse at the other end of the kitchen indicated an intermittent wash of small things also going on.

Mrs Garth, with her sleeves turned above her elbows, deftly hand-ling her pastry—applying her rolling-pin and giving ornamental pinches, while she expounded with grammatical fervour what were the right views about the concord of verbs and pronouns with "nouns of multitude or signifying many," was a sight agreeably amusing. She was of the same curly-haired, square-faced type as Mary, but handsomer, with more delicacy of feature, a pale skin, a solid matronly figure, and a remarkable firmness of glance. In her snowy-frilled cap she reminded one of that delightful Frenchwoman whom we have all seen marketing, basket on arm. Looking at the mother, you might hope that the daughter would become like her, which is a prospective advantage equal to a dowry—the mother too often stand-ing behind the daughter like a malignant prophecy—" Such as I am, she will shortly be."

" Now let us go through that once more," said Mrs Garth, pinching an apple-puff which seemed to distract Ben, an energetic young male with a heavy brow, from due attention to the lesson. "'Not without regard to the import of the word as conveying unity or plurality of idea'—tell me again what that means, Ben."

(Mrs Garth, like more celebrated educators, had her favourite ancient paths, and in a general wreck of society would have tried to hold her 'Lindley Murray' above the waves.)

"Oh—it means—you must think what you mean," said Ben, rather peevishly. "I hate grammar. What's the use of it ?"

"To teach you to speak and write correctly, so that you can be understood," said Mrs Garth, with severe precision. "Should you like to speak as old Job does ?"

"Yes," said Ben, stoutly ; "it's funnier. He says, 'Yo goo'— that's just as good as 'You go.'"

"But he says, 'A ship's in the garden,' instead of 'a sheep,'" said Letty, with an air of superiority. "You might think he meant a ship off the sea."

"No, you mightn't, if you weren't silly," said Ben. "How could a ship off the sea come there ?"

"These things belong only to pronunciation, which is the least part of grammar," said Mrs Garth. "That apple-peel is to be eaten by the pigs, Ben ; if you eat it, I must give them your piece of pasty. Job has only to speak about very plain things. How do you think you would write or speak about anything more difficult, if you knew no more of grammar than he does ? You would use wrong words, and put words in the wrong places, and instead of making people understand you, they would turn away from you as a tiresome person. What would you do then ?"

"I shouldn't care, I should leave off," said Ben, with a sense that this was an agreeable issue where grammar was concerned.

"I see you are getting tired and stupid, Ben," said Mrs Garth, accustomed to these obstructive arguments from her male offspring. Having finished her pies, she moved towards the clothes-horse, and said, "Come here and tell me the story I told you on Wednesday, about Cincinnatus." [2]

"I know ! he was a farmer," said Ben.

"Now, Ben, he was a Roman—let *me* tell," said Letty, using her elbow contentiously.

"You silly thing, he was a Roman farmer, and he was ploughing."

"Yes, but before that—that didn't come first—people wanted him," said Letty.

"Well, but you must say what sort of a man he was first," insisted Ben. "He was a wise man, like my father, and that made the people want his advice. And he was a brave man, and could fight. And so could my father—couldn't he, mother ?"

"Now, Ben, let me tell the story straight on, as mother told it us," said Letty, frowning. "Please, mother, tell Ben not to speak."

"Letty, I am ashamed of you," said her mother, wringing out the caps from the tub. "When your brother began, you ought to have waited to see if he could not tell the story. How rude you look, pushing and frowning, as if you wanted to conquer with your

2. In 458 B.C. Lucius Quintius Cincinnatus was elected consul, and in the next year dismissed. Then, in the crisis of 456 B.C., Cincinnatus was recalled by the people of Rome, who asked him to become their dictator.

elbows ! Cincinnatus, I am sure, would have been sorry to see his daughter behave so." (Mrs Garth delivered this awful sentence with much majesty of enunciation, and Letty felt that between repressed volubility and general disesteem, that of the Romans inclusive, life was already a painful affair.) " Now, Ben."

" Well—oh—well—why, there was a great deal of fighting, and they were all blockheads, and—I can't tell it just how you told it—but they wanted a man to be captain and king and everything——"

" Dictator, now," said Letty, with injured looks, and not without a wish to make her mother repent.

" Very well, dictator !" said Ben, contemptuously. " But that isn't a good word : he didn't tell them to write on slates."

" Come, come, Ben, you are not so ignorant as that," said Mrs Garth, carefully serious. "Hark, there is a knock at the door ! Run, Letty, and open it."

The knock was Fred's ; and when Letty said that her father was not in yet, but that her mother was in the kitchen, Fred had no alternative. He could not depart from his usual practice of going to see Mrs Garth in the kitchen if she happened to be at work there. He put his arm round Letty's neck silently, and led her into the kitchen without his usual jokes and caresses.

Mrs Garth was surprised to see Fred at this hour, but surprise was not a feeling that she was given to express, and she only said, quietly continuing her work—

" You, Fred, so early in the day ? You look quite pale. Has anything happened ?"

" I want to speak to Mr Garth," said Fred, not yet ready to say more—"and to you also," he added, after a little pause, for he had no doubt that Mrs Garth knew everything about the bill, and he must in the end speak of it before her, if not to her solely.

" Caleb will be in again in a few minutes," said Mrs Garth, who imagined some trouble between Fred and his father. " He is sure not to be long, because he has some work at his desk that must be done this morning. Do you mind staying with me, while I finish my matters here ?"

" But we needn't go on about Cincinnatus, need we ?" said Ben, who had taken Fred's whip out of his hand, and was trying its efficiency on the cat.

" No, go out now. But put that whip down. How very mean of you to whip poor old Tortoise ! Pray take the whip from him, Fred."

" Come, old boy, give it me," said Fred, putting out his hand.

" Will you let me ride on your horse to-day ?" said Ben, rendering up the whip, with an air of not being obliged to do it.

" Not to-day—another time. I am not riding my own horse."

" Shall you see Mary to-day ?"

" Yes, I think so," said Fred, with an unpleasant twinge.

" Tell her to come home soon, and play at forfeits, and make fun."

" Enough, enough, Ben ! run away," said Mrs Garth, seeing that Fred was teased.

" Are Letty and Ben your only pupils now, Mrs Garth ?" said Fred, when the children were gone and it was needful to say something that would pass the time. He was not yet sure whether he should wait for Mr Garth, or use any good opportunity in conversation to confess to Mrs Garth herself, give her the money and ride away.

"One—only one. Fanny Hackbutt comes at half-past eleven. I am not getting a great income now," said Mrs Garth, smiling. "I am at a low ebb with pupils. But I have saved my little purse for Alfred's premium : I have ninety-two pounds. He can go to Mr Hanmer's now ; he is just at the right age."

This did not lead well towards the news that Mr Garth was on the brink of losing ninety-two pounds and more. Fred was silent. "Young gentlemen who go to college are rather more costly than that," Mrs Garth innocently continued, pulling out the edging on a cap-border. "And Caleb thinks that Alfred will turn out a distinguished engineer : he wants to give the boy a good chance. There he is ! I hear him coming in. We will go to him in the parlour, shall we ?"

When they entered the parlour Caleb had thrown down his hat and was seated at his desk.

"What, Fred my boy ?" he said, in a tone of mild surprise, holding his pen still undipped. "You are here betimes." But missing the usual expression of cheerful greeting in Fred's face, he immediately added, "Is there anything up at home ?—anything the matter ?"

"Yes, Mr Garth, I am come to tell something that I am afraid will give you a bad opinion of me. I am come to tell you and Mrs Garth that I can't keep my word. I can't find the money to meet the bill after all. I have been unfortunate ; I have only got these fifty pounds towards the hundred and sixty."

While Fred was speaking, he had taken out the notes and laid them on the desk before Mr Garth. He had burst forth at once with the plain fact, feeling boyishly miserable and without verbal resources. Mrs Garth was mutely astonished, and looked at her husband for an explanation. Caleb blushed, and after a little pause said—

"Oh, I didn't tell you, Susan : I put my name to a bill for Fred ; it was for a hundred and sixty pounds. He made sure he could meet it himself."

There was an evident change in Mrs Garth's face, but it was like a change below the surface of water which remains smooth. She fixed her eyes on Fred, saying—

"I suppose you have asked your father for the rest of the money and he has refused you."

"No," said Fred, biting his lip, and speaking with more difficulty ; "but I know it will be of no use to ask him ; and unless it were of use, I should not like to mention Mr Garth's name in the matter."

"It has come at an unfortunate time," said Caleb, in his hesitating way, looking down at the notes and nervously fingering the paper, "Christmas upon us—I'm rather hard up just now. You see, I have to cut out everything like a tailor with short measure. What can we do, Susan ? I shall want every farthing we have in the bank. It's a hundred and ten pounds, the deuce take it !"

"I must give you the ninety-two pounds that I have put by for Alfred's premium," said Mrs Garth, gravely and decisively, though a nice ear might have discerned a slight tremor in some of the words. "And I have no doubt that Mary has twenty pounds saved from her salary by this time. She will advance it."

Mrs Garth had not again looked at Fred, and was not in the least calculating what words she should use to cut him the most effectively. Like the eccentric woman she was, she was at present absorbed in considering what was to be done, and did not fancy that the end could be better achieved by bitter remarks or explosions. But she had made Fred feel for the first time something like the tooth of remorse. Curiously enough, his pain in the affair beforehand had consisted almost entirely in the sense that he must seem dishonourable, and sink in the opinion of the Garths : he had not occupied himself with the inconvenience and possible injury that his breach might occasion them, for this exercise of the imagination on other people's needs is not common with hopeful young gentlemen. Indeed we are most of us brought up in the notion that the highest motive for not doing a wrong is something irrespective of the beings who would suffer the wrong. But at this moment he suddenly saw himself as a pitiful rascal who was robbing two women of their savings.

"I shall certainly pay it all, Mrs Garth—ultimately," he stammered out.

"Yes, ultimately," said Mrs Garth, who having a special dislike to fine words on ugly occasions, could not now repress an epigram. "But boys cannot well be apprenticed ultimately : they should be apprenticed at fifteen." She had never been so little inclined to make excuses for Fred.

"I was the most in the wrong, Susan," said Caleb. "Fred made sure of finding the money. But I'd no business to be fingering bills. I suppose you have looked all round and tried all honest means ?" he added, fixing his merciful grey eyes on Fred. Caleb was too delicate to specify Mr Featherstone.

"Yes, I have tried everything—I really have. I should have had a hundred and thirty pounds ready but for a misfortune with a horse which I was about to sell. My uncle had given me eighty pounds, and I paid away thirty with my old horse in order to get another which I was going to sell for eighty or more—I meant to go without a horse—but now it has turned out vicious and lamed itself. I wish I and the horses too had been at the devil, before I had brought this on you. There's no one else I care so much for : you and Mrs Garth have always been so kind to me. However, it's no use saying that. You will always think me a rascal now."

Fred turned round and hurried out of the room, conscious that he was getting rather womanish, and feeling confusedly that his being sorry was not of much use to the Garths. They could see him mount, and quickly pass through the gate.

"I am disappointed in Fred Vincy," said Mrs Garth. "I would not have believed beforehand that he would have drawn you into his debts. I knew he was extravagant, but I did not think that he would be so mean as to hang his risks on his oldest friend, who could the least afford to lose."

"I was a fool, Susan."

"That you were," said the wife, nodding and smiling. "But I should not have gone to publish it in the market-place. Why should you keep such things from me ? It is just so with your buttons ; you let them burst off without telling me, and go out with your wristband hanging. If I had only known I might have been ready with some better plan."

" You are sadly cut up, I know, Susan," said Caleb, looking feelingly at her. " I can't abide your losing the money you've scraped together for Alfred."

" It is very well that I *had* scraped it together ; and it is you who will have to suffer, for you must teach the boy yourself. You must give up your bad habits. Some men take to drinking, and you have taken to working without pay. You must indulge yourself a little less in that. And you must ride over to Mary, and ask the child what money she has."

Caleb had pushed his chair back, and was leaning forward, shaking his head slowly, and fitting his finger-tips together with much nicety.

" Poor Mary ! " he said. " Susan," he went on in a lowered tone, " I'm afraid she may be fond of Fred."

" Oh no ! She always laughs at him ; and he is not likely to think of her in any other than a brotherly way."

Caleb made no rejoinder, but presently lowered his spectacles, drew up his chair to the desk, and said, " Deuce take the bill—I wish it was at Hanover ! These things are a sad interruption to business ! "

The first part of this speech comprised his whole store of maledictory expression, and was uttered with a slight snarl easy to imagine. But it would be difficult to convey to those who never heard him utter the word " business," the peculiar tone of fervid veneration, of religious regard, in which he wrapped it, as a consecrated symbol is wrapped in its gold-fringed linen.

Caleb Garth often shook his head in meditation on the value, the indispensable might of that myriad-headed, myriad-handed labour by which the social body is fed, clothed, and housed. It had laid hold of his imagination in boyhood. The echoes of the great hammer where roof or keel were a-making, the signal-shouts of the workmen, the roar of the furnace, the thunder and plash of the engine, were a sublime music to him ; the felling and lading of timber, and the huge trunk vibrating star-like in the distance along the highway, the crane at work on the wharf, the piled-up produce in warehouses, the precision and variety of muscular effort wherever exact work had to be turned out, — all these sights of his youth had acted on him as poetry without the aid of the poets, had made a philosophy for him without the aid of philosophers, a religion without the aid of theology. His early ambition had been to have as effective a share as possible in this sublime labour, which was peculiarly dignified by him with the name of " business ; " and though he had only been a short time under a surveyor, and had been chiefly his own teacher, he knew more of land, building, and mining than most of the special men in the county.

His classification of human employments was rather crude, and, like the categories of more celebrated men, would not be acceptable in these advanced times. He divided them into " business, politics, preaching, learning, and amusement." He had nothing to say against the last four ; but he regarded them as a reverential pagan regarded other gods than his own. In the same way, he thought very well of all ranks, but he would not himself have liked to be of any rank in which he had not such close contact with " business " as to get often honourably decorated with marks of dust and mortar, the damp of the engine, or the sweet soil of the woods and fields. Though he had never regarded himself as other than an orthodox Christian, and would argue on prevenient grace if the subject were proposed to him, I think his virtual divinities were good practical schemes, accurate work, and the faithful completion of undertakings : his prince of darkness was a slack workman. But there was no spirit of denial in Caleb, and the world seemed so wondrous to him that he was ready to accept any number of systems, like any number of firmaments, if they did not obviously interfere with the best land-drainage, solid building, correct measuring, and judicious boring (for coal). In fact, he had a reverential soul with a strong practical intelligence. But he could not manage finance : he knew values well, but he had no keenness of imagination for monetary results in the shape of profit and loss : and having ascertained this to his cost, he determined to give up all forms of his beloved " business " which required that talent. He gave himself up entirely to the many kinds of work which he could do without handling capital, and was one of those precious men within his own district whom everybody would choose to work for them, because he did his work well, charged very little, and often declined to charge at all. It is no wonder, then, that the Garths were poor, and "lived in a small way." However, they did not mind it.

CHAPTER XXV.

" Love seeketh not itself to please,
    Nor for itself hath any care,
But for another gives its ease,
    And builds a heaven in hell's despair.

Love seeketh only self to please,
    To bind another to its delight,
Joys in another's loss of ease,
    And builds a hell in heaven's despite."
            —W. BLAKE: *Songs of Experience.* [1]

FRED VINCY wanted to arrive at Stone Court when Mary could not expect him, and when his uncle was not down stairs : in that case she might be sitting alone in the wainscoted parlour. He left his horse in the yard to avoid making a noise on the gravel in front, and entered the parlour without other notice than the noise of the door-handle. Mary was in her usual corner, laughing over Mrs Piozzi's recollections of Johnson, and looked up with the fun still in her face.[2] It gradually faded as she saw Fred approach her without speaking, and stand before her with his elbow on the mantelpiece, looking ill. She too was silent, only raising her eyes to him inquiringly.

" Mary," he began, " I am a good-for-nothing blackguard."

" I should think one of those epithets would do at a time," said Mary, trying to smile, but feeling alarmed.

" I know you will never think well of me any more. You will think me a liar. You will think me dishonest. You will think I

---

1. "The Clod and the Pebble."
2. Hester Lynch Piozzi (1741–1821), a friend of Dr. Johnson, was the author of "Anecdotes of the Late Samuel Johnson, During the Last Twenty Years of his Life" (1786).

didn't care for you, or your father and mother. You always do make the worst of me, I know."

" I cannot deny that I shall think all that of you, Fred, if you give me good reasons. But please to tell me at once what you have done. I would rather know the painful truth than imagine it."

" I owed money—a hundred and sixty pounds. I asked your father to put his name to a bill. I thought it would not signify to him. I made sure of paying the money myself, and I have tried as hard as I could. And now, I have been so unlucky—a horse has turned out badly—I can only pay fifty pounds. And I can't ask my father for the money : he would not give me a farthing. And my uncle gave me a hundred a little while ago. So what can I do ? And now your father has no ready money to spare, and your mother will have to pay away her ninety-two pounds that she has saved, and she says your savings must go too. You see what a——"

" Oh, poor mother, poor father !" said Mary, her eyes filling with tears, and a little sob rising which she tried to repress. She looked straight before her and took no notice of Fred, all the consequences at home becoming present to her. He too remained silent for some moments, feeling more miserable than ever.

" I wouldn't have hurt you so for the world, Mary," he said at last. " You can never forgive me."

" What does it matter whether I forgive you ?" said Mary, passionately. " Would that make it any better for my mother to lose the money she has been earning by lessons for four years, that she might send Alfred to Mr Hanmer's ? Should you think all that pleasant enough if I forgave you ?"

" Say what you like, Mary. I deserve it all."

" I don't want to say anything," said Mary, more quietly ; " my anger is of no use." She dried her eyes, threw aside her book, rose and fetched her sewing.

Fred followed her with his eyes, hoping that they would meet hers, and in that way find access for his imploring penitence. But no ! Mary could easily avoid looking upward.

" I do care about your mother's money going," he said, when she was seated again and sewing quickly. " I wanted to ask you, Mary —don't you think that Mr Featherstone—if you were to tell him— tell him, I mean, about apprenticing Alfred—would advance the money ?"

" My family is not fond of begging, Fred. We would rather work for our money. Besides, you say that Mr Featherstone has lately given you a hundred pounds. He rarely makes presents ; he has never made presents to us. I am sure my father will not ask him for anything ; and even if I chose to beg of him, it would be of no use."

" I am so miserable, Mary—if you knew how miserable I am, you would be sorry for me."

" There are other things to be more sorry for than that. But selfish people always think their own discomfort of more importance than anything else in the world : I see enough of that every day."

" It is hardly fair to call me selfish. If you knew what things other young men do, you would think me a good way off the worst."

" I know that people who spend a great deal of money on themselves without knowing how they shall pay, must be selfish. They are always thinking of what they can get for themselves, and not of what other people may lose."

"Any man may be unfortunate, Mary, and find himself unable to pay when he meant it. There is not a better man in the world than your father, and yet he got into trouble."

"How dare you make any comparison between my father and you, Fred?" said Mary, in a deep tone of indignation. "He never got into trouble by thinking of his own idle pleasures, but because he was always thinking of the work he was doing for other people. And he has fared hard, and worked hard to make good everybody's loss."

"And you think that I shall never try to make good anything, Mary. It is not generous to believe the worst of a man. When you have got any power over him, I think you might try and use it to make him better; but that is what you never do. However, I'm going," Fred ended, languidly. "I shall never speak to you about anything again. I'm very sorry for all the trouble I've caused— that's all."

Mary had dropped her work out of her hand and looked up. There is often something maternal even in a girlish love, and Mary's hard experience had wrought her nature to an impressibility very different from that hard slight thing which we call girlishness. At Fred's last words she felt an instantaneous pang, something like what a mother feels at the imagined sobs or cries of her naughty truant child, which may lose itself and get harm. And when, looking up, her eyes met his dull despairing glance, her pity for him surmounted her anger and all her other anxieties.

"Oh, Fred, how ill you look! Sit down a moment. Don't go yet. Let me tell uncle that you are here. He has been wondering that he has not seen you for a whole week." Mary spoke hurriedly, saying the words that came first without knowing very well what they were, but saying them in a half-soothing half-beseeching tone, and rising as if to go away to Mr Featherstone. Of course Fred felt as if the clouds had parted and a gleam had come : he moved and stood in her way.

"Say one word, Mary, and I will do anything. Say you will not think the worst of me—will not give me up altogether."

"As if it were any pleasure to me to think ill of you," said Mary, in a mournful tone. "As if it were not very painful to me to see you an idle frivolous creature. How can you bear to be so contemptible, when others are working and striving, and there are so many things to be done—how can you bear to be fit for nothing in the world that is useful? And with so much good in your disposition, Fred,—you might be worth a great deal."

"I will try to be anything you like, Mary, if you will say that you love me."

"I should be ashamed to say that I loved a man who must always be hanging on others, and reckoning on what they would do for him. What will you be when you are forty? Like Mr Bowyer, I suppose — just as idle, living in Mrs Beck's front parlour — fat and shabby, hoping somebody will invite you to dinner—spending your morning in learning a comic song—oh no! learning a tune on the flute."

Mary's lips had begun to curl with a smile as soon as she had asked that question about Fred's future (young souls are mobile), and before she ended, her face had its full illumination of fun. To him it was like the cessation of an ache that Mary could laugh at him, and with a passive sort of smile he tried to reach her hand ; but she slipped away quickly towards the door and said, " I shall tell uncle. You *must* see him for a moment or two."

Fred secretly felt that his future was guaranteed against the fulfilment of Mary's sarcastic prophecies, apart from that " anything " which he was ready to do if she would define it. He never dared in Mary's presence to approach the subject of his expectations from Mr Featherstone, and she always ignored them, as if everything depended on himself. But if ever he actually came into the property, she must recognise the change in his position. All this passed through his mind somewhat languidly, before he went up to see his uncle. He stayed but a little while, excusing himself on the ground that he had a cold ; and Mary did not reappear before he left the house. But as he rode home, he began to be more conscious of being ill, than of being melancholy.

When Caleb Garth arrived at Stone Court soon after dusk, Mary was not surprised, although he seldom had leisure for paying her a visit, and was not at all fond of having to talk with Mr Featherstone. The old man, on the other hand, felt himself ill at ease with a brother-in-law whom he could not annoy, who did not mind about being considered poor, had nothing to ask of him, and understood all kinds of farming and mining business better than he did. But Mary had felt sure that her parents would want to see her, and if her father had not come, she would have obtained leave to go home for an hour or two the next day. After discussing prices during tea with Mr Featherstone, Caleb rose to bid him good-bye, and said, " I want to speak to you, Mary."

She took a candle into another large parlour, where there was no fire, and setting down the feeble light on the dark mahogany table, turned round to her father, and putting her arms round his neck kissed him with childish kisses which he delighted in,—the expression of his large brows softening as the expression of a great beautiful dog softens when it is caressed. Mary was his favourite child, and whatever Susan might say, and right as she was on all other subjects, Caleb thought it natural that Fred or any one else should think Mary more lovable than other girls.

" I've got something to tell you, my dear," said Caleb in his hesitating way. " No very good news ; but then it might be worse."

" About money, father ? I think I know what it is."

" Ay ? how can that be ? You see, I've been a bit of a fool again, and put my name to a bill, and now it comes to paying ; and your mother has got to part with her savings, that's the worst of it, and even they won't quite make things even. We wanted a hundred and ten pounds : your mother has ninety-two, and I have none to spare in the bank ; and she thinks that you will have some savings."

" Oh yes ; I have more than four-and-twenty pounds. I thought you would come, father, so I put it in my bag. See ! beautiful white notes and gold."

Mary took out the folded money from her reticule and put it into her father's hand.

" Well, but how—we only want eighteen—here, put the rest back, child,—but how did you know about it ? " said Caleb, who, in his unconquerable indifference to money, was beginning to be chiefly concerned about the relation the affair might have to Mary's affections.

"Fred told me this morning."

"Ah! Did he come on purpose?"

"Yes, I think so. He was a good deal distressed."

"I'm afraid Fred is not to be trusted, Mary," said the father, with hesitating tenderness. "He means better than he acts, perhaps. But I should think it a pity for anybody's happiness to be wrapped up in him, and so would your mother."

"And so should I, father," said Mary, not looking up, but putting the back of her father's hand against her cheek.

"I don't want to pry, my dear. But I was afraid there might be something between you and Fred, and I wanted to caution you. You see, Mary"—here Caleb's voice became more tender; he had been pushing his hat about on the table and looking at it, but finally he turned his eyes on his daughter—"a woman, let her be as good as she may, has got to put up with the life her husband makes for her. Your mother has had to put up with a good deal because of me."

Mary turned the back of her father's hand to her lips and smiled at him.

"Well, well, nobody's perfect, but"—here Mr Garth shook his head to help out the inadequacy of words—"what I am thinking of is —what it must be for a wife when she's never sure of her husband, when he hasn't got a principle in him to make him more afraid of doing the wrong thing by others than of getting his own toes pinched. That's the long and the short of it, Mary. Young folks may get fond of each other before they know what life is, and they may think it all holiday if they can only get together; but it soon turns into working day, my dear. However, you have more sense than most, and you haven't been kept in cotton-wool : there may be no occasion for me to say this, but a father trembles for his daughter, and you are all by yourself here."

"Don't fear for me, father," said Mary, gravely meeting her father's eyes; "Fred has always been very good to me; he is kind-hearted and affectionate, and not false, I think, with all his self-indulgence. But I will never engage myself to one who has no manly independence, and who goes on loitering away his time on the chance that others will provide for him. You and my mother have taught me too much pride for that."

"That's right—that's right. Then I am easy," said Mr Garth, taking up his hat. "But it's hard to run away with your earnings, child."

"Father!" said Mary, in her deepest tone of remonstrance. "Take pocketfuls of love besides to them all at home," was her last word before he closed the outer door on himself.

"I suppose your father wanted your earnings," said old Mr Featherstone, with his usual power of unpleasant surmise, when Mary returned to him. "He makes but a tight fit, I reckon. You're of age now; you ought to be saving for yourself."

"I consider my father and mother the best part of myself, sir," said Mary, coldly.

Mr Featherstone grunted : he could not deny that an ordinary sort of girl like her might be expected to be useful, so he thought of another rejoinder, disagreeable enough to be always apropos. "If Fred Vincy comes to-morrow, now, don't you keep him chattering: let him come up to me."

CHAPTER XXVI.

"He beats me and I rail at him: O worthy satisfaction! would it were otherwise— that I could beat him while he railed at me."—*Troilus and Cressida.* 1

BUT Fred did not go to Stone Court the next day, for reasons that were quite peremptory. From those visits to unsanitary Houndsley streets in search of Diamond, he had brought back not only a bad bargain in horse-flesh, but the further misfortune of some ailment which for a day or two had seemed mere depression and headache, but which got so much worse when he returned from his visit to Stone Court that, going into the dining-room, he threw himself on the sofa, and in answer to his mother's anxious question, said, "I feel very ill: I think you must send for Wrench."

Wrench came but did not apprehend anything serious, spoke of a "slight derangement," and did not speak of coming again on the morrow. He had a due value for the Vincys' house, but the wariest men are apt to be a little dulled by routine, and on worried mornings will sometimes go through their business with the zest of the daily bell-ringer. Mr Wrench was a small, neat, bilious man, with a well-dressed wig: he had a laborious practice, an irascible temper, a lymphatic wife and seven children; and he was already rather late before setting out on a four-miles drive to meet Dr Minchin on the other side of Tipton, the decease of Hicks, a rural practitioner, having increased Middlemarch practice in that direction. Great statesmen err, and why not small medical men? Mr Wrench did not neglect sending the usual white parcels, which this time had black and drastic contents. Their effect was not alleviating to poor Fred, who, however, unwilling as he said to believe that he was "in for an illness," rose at his usual easy hour the next morning and went downstairs meaning to breakfast, but succeeded in nothing but in sitting and shivering by the fire. Mr Wrench was again sent for, but was gone on his rounds, and Mrs Vincy seeing her darling's changed looks and general misery, began to cry and said she would send for Dr Sprague.

"Oh, nonsense, mother! It's nothing," said Fred, putting out his hot dry hand to her, "I shall soon be all right. I must have taken cold in that nasty damp ride."

"Mamma!" said Rosamond, who was seated near the window (the dining-room windows looked on that highly respectable street called Lowick Gate), "there is Mr Lydgate, stopping to speak to some one. If I were you I would call him in. He has cured Ellen Bulstrode. They say he cures every one."

Mrs Vincy sprang to the window and opened it in an instant, thinking only of Fred and not of medical etiquette. Lydgate was

1. Act II, Sc. 3, lines 3–4.

only two yards off on the other side of some iron palisading, and turned round at the sudden sound of the sash, before she called to him. In two minutes he was in the room, and Rosamond went out, after waiting just long enough to show a pretty anxiety conflicting with her sense of what was becoming.

Lydgate had to hear a narrative in which Mrs Vincy's mind insisted with remarkable instinct on every point of minor importance, especially on what Mr Wrench had said and had not said about coming again. That there might be an awkward affair with Wrench, Lydgate saw at once ; but the case was serious enough to make him dismiss that consideration : he was convinced that Fred was in the pink-skinned stage of typhoid fever, and that he had taken just the wrong medicines. He must go to bed immediately, must have a regular nurse, and various appliances and precautions must be used, about which Lydgate was particular. Poor Mrs Vincy's terror at these indications of danger found vent in such words as came most easily. She thought it " very ill usage on the part of Mr Wrench, who had attended their house so many years in preference to Mr Peacock, though Mr Peacock was equally a friend. Why Mr Wrench should neglect her children more than others, she could not for the life of her understand. He had not neglected Mrs. Larcher's when they had the measles, nor indeed would Mrs Vincy have wished that he should. And if anything should happen . . ."

Here poor Mrs Vincy's spirit quite broke down, and her Niobe-throat and good-humoured face were sadly convulsed. This was in the hall out of Fred's hearing, but Rosamond had opened the drawing-room door, and now came forward anxiously. Lydgate apologised for Mr Wrench, said that the symptoms yesterday might have been disguising, and that this form of fever was very equivocal in its beginnings : he would go immediately to the druggist's and have a prescription made up in order to lose no time, but he would write to Mr Wrench and tell him what had been done.

"But you must come again—you must go on attending Fred. I can't have my boy left to anybody who may come or not. I bear nobody ill-will, thank God, and Mr Wrench saved me in the pleurisy, but he'd better have let me die—if—if——"

" I will meet Mr Wrench here, then, shall I ? " said Lydgate, really believing that Wrench was not well prepared to deal wisely with a case of this kind.

" Pray make that arrangement, Mr Lydgate," said Rosamond, coming to her mother's aid, and supporting her arm to lead her away.

When Mr Vincy came home he was very angry with Wrench, and did not care if he never came into his house again. Lydgate should go on now, whether Wrench liked it or not. It was no joke to have fever in the house. Everybody must be sent to now, not to come to dinner on Thursday. And Pritchard needn't get up any wine : brandy was the best thing against infection. " I shall drink brandy," added Mr Vincy emphatically—as much as to say, this was not an occasion for firing with blank-cartridges. " He's an uncommonly unfortunate lad, is Fred. He'd need have some luck by-and-by to make up for all this—else I don't know who'd have an eldest son."

"Don't say so, Vincy," said the mother, with a quivering lip, " if you don't want him to be taken from me."

" It will worret you to death, Lucy ; *that* I can see," said Mr Vincy, more mildly. " However, Wrench shall know what I think of the matter." (What Mr Vincy thought confusedly was, that the fever might somehow have been hindered if Wrench had shown the proper solicitude about his—the Mayor's—family.) "I'm the last man to give in to the cry about new doctors or new parsons, either—whether they're Bulstrode's men or not. But Wrench shall know what I think, take it as he will."

Wrench did not take it at all well. Lydgate was as polite as he could be in his offhand way, but politeness in a man who has placed you at a disadvantage is only an additional exasperation, especially if he happens to have been an object of dislike beforehand. Country practitioners used to be an irritable species, susceptible on the point of honour ; and Mr Wrench was one of the most irritable among them. He did not refuse to meet Lydgate in the evening, but his temper was somewhat tried on the occasion. He had to hear Mrs Vincy say—

"Oh, Mr Wrench, what have I ever done that you should use me so ?—To go away, and never to come again ! And my boy might have been stretched a corpse ! "

Mr Vincy, who had been keeping up a sharp fire on the enemy Infection, and was a good deal heated in consequence, started up when he heard Wrench come in, and went into the hall to let him know what he thought.

" I'll tell you what, Wrench, this is beyond a joke," said the Mayor, who of late had had to rebuke offenders with an official air, and now broadened himself by putting his thumbs in his armholes.—"To let fever get unawares into a house like this. There are some things that ought to be actionable, and are not so—that's my opinion."

But irrational reproaches were easier to bear than the sense of being instructed, or rather the sense that a younger man, like Lydgate, inwardly considered him in need of instruction, for " in point of fact," Mr Wrench afterwards said, Lydgate paraded flighty, foreign notions, which would not wear. He swallowed his ire for the moment, but he afterwards wrote to decline further attendance in the case. The house might be a good one, but Mr Wrench was not going to truckle to anybody on a professional matter. He reflected, with much probability on his side, that Lydgate would by-and-by be caught tripping too, and that his ungentlemanly attempts to discredit the sale of drugs by his professional brethren would by- and - by recoil on himself. He threw out biting remarks on Lydgate's tricks, worthy only of a quack, to get himself a factitious reputation with credulous people. That cant about cures was never got up by sound practitioners.

This was a point on which Lydgate smarted as much as Wrench could desire. To be puffed by ignorance was not only humiliating, but perilous, and not more enviable than the reputation of the weather-prophet. He was impatient of the foolish expectations amidst which all work must be carried on, and likely enough to damage himself as much as Mr Wrench could wish, by an unprofessional openness.

However, Lydgate was installed as medical attendant on the Vincys, and the event was a subject of general conversation in Middlemarch. Some said, that the Vincys had behaved scandalously, that Mr Vincy had threatened Wrench, and that Mrs Vincy had accused him of poisoning her son. Others were of opinion that Mr Lydgate's passing by was providential, that he was wonderfully clever in fevers, and that Bulstrode was in the right to bring him forward. Many people believed that Lydgate's coming to the town at all was really due to Bulstrode; and Mrs Taft, who was always counting stitches and gathered her information in misleading fragments caught between the rows of her knitting, had got it into her head that Mr Lydgate was a natural son of Bulstrode's, a fact which seemed to justify her suspicions of evangelical laymen.

She one day communicated this piece of knowledge to Mrs Farebrother, who did not fail to tell her son of it, observing—

"I should not be surprised at anything in Bulstrode, but I should be sorry to think it of Mr Lydgate."

"Why, mother," said Mr Farebrother, after an explosive laugh, "you know very well that Lydgate is of a good family in the North. He never heard of Bulstrode before he came here."

"That is satisfactory so far as Mr Lydgate is concerned, Camden," said the old lady, with an air of precision. "But as to Bulstrode—the report may be true of some other son."

CHAPTER XXVII.

" Let the high Muse chant loves Olympian:
We are but mortals, and must sing of man."

An eminent philosopher among my friends, who can dignify even your ugly furniture by lifting it into the serene light of science, has shown me this pregnant little fact. Your pier-glass or extensive surface of polished steel made to be rubbed by a housemaid, will be minutely and multitudinously scratched in all directions; but place now against it a lighted candle as a centre of illumination, and lo! the scratches will seem to arrange themselves in a fine series of concentric circles round that little sun. It is demonstrable that the scratches are going everywhere impartially, and it is only your candle which produces the flattering illusion of a concentric arrangement, its light falling with an exclusive optical selection. These things are a parable. The scratches are events, and the candle is the egoism of any person now absent—of Miss Vincy, for example. Rosamond had a Providence of her own who had kindly made her more charming than other girls, and who seemed to have arranged Fred's illness and Mr Wrench's mistake in order to bring her and Lydgate within effective proximity. It would have been to contravene these arrangements if Rosamond had consented to go away to Stone Court or elsewhere, as her parents wished her to do, especially since Mr Lydgate thought the precaution needless. Therefore, while Miss Morgan and the children were sent away to a farmhouse the morning after Fred's illness had declared itself, Rosamond refused to leave papa and mamma.

Poor mamma indeed was an object to touch any creature born of woman; and Mr Vincy, who doated on his wife, was more alarmed on her account than on Fred's. But for his insistance she would have taken no rest: her brightness was all bedimmed; unconscious of her costume which had always been so fresh and gay, she was like a sick bird with languid eye and plumage ruffled, her senses dulled to the sights and sounds that used most to interest her. Fred's delirium, in which he seemed to be wandering out of her reach, tore her heart. After her first outburst against Mr Wrench she went about very quietly : her one low cry was to Lydgate. She would follow him out of the room and put her hand on his arm moaning out, " Save my boy." Once she pleaded, " He has always been good to me, Mr Lydgate : he never had a hard word for his mother,"—as if poor Fred's suffering were an accusation against him. All the deepest fibres of the mother's memory were stirred, and the young man whose voice took a gentler tone when he spoke to her, was one with the babe whom she had loved, with a love new to her, before he was born.

" I have good hope, Mrs Vincy," Lydgate would say. "Come down with me and let us talk about the food." In that way he led her to the parlour where Rosamond was, and made a change for her, surprising her into taking some tea or broth which had been prepared for her. There was a constant understanding between him and Rosamond on these matters. He almost always saw her before going to the sick-room, and she appealed to him as to what she could do for mamma. Her presence of mind and adroitness in carrying out his hints were admirable, and it is not wonderful that the idea of seeing Rosamond began to mingle itself with his interest in the case. Especially when the critical stage was passed, and he began to feel confident of Fred's recovery. In the more doubtful time, he had advised calling in Dr Sprague (who, if he could, would rather have remained neutral on Wrench's account) ; but after two consultations, the conduct of the case was left to Lydgate, and there was every reason to make him assiduous. Morning and evening he was at Mr Vincy's, and gradually the visits became cheerful as Fred became simply feeble, and lay not only in need of the utmost petting but conscious of it, so that Mrs Vincy felt as if after all the illness had made a festival for her tenderness.

Both father and mother held it an added reason for good spirits, when old Mr Featherstone sent messages by Lydgate, saying that Fred must make haste and get well, as he, Peter Featherstone, could not do without him, and missed his visits sadly. The old man himself was getting bedridden. Mrs Vincy told these messages to Fred when he could listen, and he turned towards her his delicate, pinched face, from which all the thick blond hair had been cut away, and in which the eyes seemed to have got larger, yearning for some word about Mary—wondering what she felt about his illness. No word passed his lips ; but " to hear with eyes belongs to love's rare wit," and the mother in the fulness of her heart not only divined Fred's longing, but felt ready for any sacrifice in order to satisfy him.[1]

" If I can only see my boy strong again," she said, in her loving folly ; " and who knows ?—perhaps master of Stone Court ! and he can marry anybody he likes then."

" Not if they won't have me, mother," said Fred. The illness had made him childish, and tears came as he spoke.

" Oh, take a bit of jelly, my dear," said Mrs Vincy, secretly incredulous of any such refusal.

---

1. "Oh, learn to read what silent love hath writ./To hear with eyes belongs to love's fine wit" (Shakespeare, Sonnet 23).

She never left Fred's side when her husband was not in the house, and thus Rosamond was in the unusual position of being much alone. Lydgate, naturally, never thought of staying long with her, yet it seemed that the brief impersonal conversations they had together were creating that peculiar intimacy which consists in shyness. They were obliged to look at each other in speaking, and somehow the looking could not be carried through as the matter of course which it really was. Lydgate began to feel this sort of consciousness unpleasant, and one day looked down, or anywhere, like an ill-worked puppet. But this turned out badly : the next day, Rosamond looked down, and the consequence was that when their eyes met again, both were more conscious than before. There was no help for this in science, and as Lydgate did not want to flirt, there seemed to be no help for it in folly. It was therefore a relief when neighbours no longer considered the house in quarantine, and when the chances of seeing Rosamond alone were very much reduced.

But that intimacy of mutual embarrassment, in which each feels that the other is feeling something, having once existed, its effect is not to be done away with. Talk about the weather and other well-bred topics is apt to seem a hollow device, and behaviour can hardly become easy unless it frankly recognises a mutual fascination—which of course need not mean anything deep or serious. This was the way in which Rosamond and Lydgate slid gracefully into ease, and made their intercourse lively again. Visitors came and went as usual, there was once more music in the drawing-room, and all the extra hospitality of Mr Vincy's mayoralty returned. Lydgate, whenever he could, took his seat by Rosamond's side, and lingered to hear her music, calling himself her captive—meaning, all the while, not to be her captive. The preposterousness of the notion that he could at once set up a satisfactory establishment as a married man was a sufficient guarantee against danger. This play at being a little in love was agreeable, and did not interfere with graver pursuits. Flirtation, after all, was not necessarily a singeing process. Rosamond, for her part, had never enjoyed the days so much in her life before : she was sure of being admired by some one worth captivating, and she did not distinguish flirtation from love, either in herself or in another. She seemed to be sailing with a fair wind just whither she would go, and her thoughts were much occupied with a handsome house in Lowick Gate which she hoped would by-and-by be vacant. She was quite determined, when she was married, to rid herself adroitly of all the visitors who were not agreeable to her at her father's ; and she imagined the drawing-room in her favourite house with various styles of furniture.

Certainly her thoughts were much occupied with Lydgate himself ; he seemed to her almost perfect : if he had known his notes so that his enchantment under her music had been less like an emotional elephant's, and if he had been able to discriminate better the refinements of her taste in dress, she could hardly have mentioned a deficiency in him. How different he was from young Plymdale or Mr Caius Larcher ! Those young men had not a notion of French, and could speak on no subject with striking knowledge, except perhaps the dyeing and carrying trades, which of course they were ashamed to mention ; they were Middlemarch gentry, elated with their silver-headed whips and satin stocks, but embarrassed in their manners, and timidly jocose : even Fred was above them, having at least the accent and manner of a university man. Whereas Lydgate was always listened to, bore himself with the careless politeness of conscious superiority, and seemed to have the right clothes on by a certain natural affinity, without ever having to think about them. Rosamond was proud when he entered the room, and when he approached her with a distinguishing smile, she had a delicious sense that she was the object of enviable homage. If Lydgate had been aware of all the pride he excited in that delicate bosom, he might have been just as well pleased as any other man, even the most densely ignorant of humoral pathology or fibrous tissue : he held it one of the prettiest attitudes of the feminine mind to adore a man's pre-eminence without too precise a knowledge of what it consisted in.

But Rosamond was not one of those helpless girls who betray themselves unawares, and whose behaviour is awkwardly driven by their impulses, instead of being steered by wary grace and propriety. Do you imagine that her rapid forecast and rumination concerning house-furniture and society were ever discernible in her conversation, even with her mamma ? On the contrary, she would have expressed the prettiest surprise and disapprobation if she had heard that another young lady had been detected in that immodest prematureness—indeed, would probably have disbelieved in its possibility. For Rosamond never showed any unbecoming knowledge, and was always that combination of correct sentiments, music, dancing, drawing, elegant note-writing, private album for extracted verse, and perfect blond loveliness, which made the irresistible woman for the doomed man of that date. Think no unfair evil of her, pray : she had no wicked plots, nothing sordid or mercenary ; in fact, she never thought of money except as something necessary which other people would always provide. She was not in the habit of devising falsehoods, and if her statements were no direct clue to fact, why, they were not intended in that light—they were among her elegant accomplishments, intended to please. Nature had inspired many arts in finishing Mrs Lemon's favourite pupil, who by general consent (Fred's excepted) was a rare compound of beauty, cleverness, and amiability.

Lydgate found it more and more agreeable to be with her, and there was no constraint now, there was a delightful interchange of influence in their eyes, and what they said had that superfluity of meaning for them, which is observable with some sense of flatness by a third person ; still they had no interviews or asides from which a third person need have been excluded. In fact, they flirted ; and Lydgate was secure in the belief that they did nothing else. If a man could not love and be wise, surely he could flirt and be wise at the same time ? Really, the men in Middlemarch, except Mr Farebrother, were great bores, and Lydgate did not care about commercial politics or cards : what was he to do for relaxation ? He was often invited to the Bulstrodes' ; but the girls there were hardly out of the schoolroom ; and Mrs Bulstrode's *naïve* way of conciliating piety and worldliness, the nothingness of this life and the desirability of cut glass, the consciousness at once of filthy rags and the best damask, was not a sufficient relief from the weight of her husband's invariable seriousness. The Vincys' house, with all its faults, was the pleasanter by contrast ; besides, it nourished Rosamond—sweet to look at as a half-opened blush-rose, and adorned with accomplishments for the refined amusement of man.

But he made some enemies, other than medical, by his success with Miss Vincy. One evening he came into the drawing-room rather late, when several other visitors were there. The card-table had drawn off the elders, and Mr Ned Plymdale (one of the good matches in Middlemarch, though not one of its leading minds) was in *tête-à-tête* with Rosamond. He had brought the last ' Keepsake,' the gorgeous watered-silk publication which marked modern progress at that time ; and he considered himself very fortunate that he could be the first to look over it with her, dwelling on the ladies and gentlemen with shiny copper-plate cheeks and copper-plate smiles, and pointing to comic verses as capital and sentimental stories as interesting.[2] Rosamond was gracious, and Mr Ned was satisfied that he had the very best thing in art and literature as a medium for " paying addresses "—the very thing to please a nice girl. He had also reasons, deep rather than ostensible, for being satisfied with his own appearance. To superficial observers his chin had too vanishing an aspect, looking as if it were being gradually reabsorbed. And it did indeed cause him some difficulty about the fit of his satin stocks, for which chins were at that time useful.

" I think the Honourable Mrs S. is something like you," said Mr Ned. He kept the book open at the bewitching portrait, and looked at it rather languishingly.

" Her back is very large ; she seems to have sat for that," said Rosamond, not meaning any satire, but thinking how red young Plymdale's hands were, and wondering why Lydgate did not come. She went on with her tatting all the while.

" I did not say she was as beautiful as you are," said Mr Ned, venturing to look from the portrait to its rival.

" I suspect you of being an adroit flatterer," said Rosamond, feeling sure that she should have to reject this young gentleman a second time.

But now Lydgate came in ; the book was closed before he reached Rosamond's corner, and as he took his seat with easy confidence on the other side of her, young Plymdale's jaw fell like a barometer towards the cheerless side of change. Rosamond enjoyed not only Lydgate's presence but its effect : she liked to excite jealousy.

" What a late comer you are ! " she said, as they shook hands. "Mamma had given you up a little while ago. How do you find Fred ? "

" As usual ; going on well, but slowly. I want him to go away— to Stone Court, for example. But your mamma seems to have some objection."

" Poor fellow ! " said Rosamond, prettily. " You will see Fred so changed," she added, turning to the other suitor ; " we have looked to Mr Lydgate as our guardian angel during this illness."

Mr Ned smiled nervously, while Lydgate drawing the ' Keepsake '

2. The *Keepsake* was one of a series of nineteenth-century literary annuals, consisting generally of sentimental prose and verse and inane, simperingly pretty illustrations. GE remarks on a painting of Dickens by Daniel Maclise repro- duced in John Forster's *Life of Charles Dickens* as "that keepsakey, impossible face which Maclise gave him" (Gordon S. Haight, *The George Eliot Letters* [New Haven: Yale University Press, 1954–55], v:226).

towards him and opening it, gave a short scornful laugh and tossed up his chin, as if in wonderment at human folly.

" What are you laughing at so profanely ? " said Rosamond, with bland neutrality.

" I wonder which would turn out to be the silliest—the engravings or the writing here," said Lydgate, in his most convinced tone, while he turned over the pages quickly, seeming to see all through the book in no time, and showing his large white hands to much advantage, as Rosamond thought. " Do look at this bridegroom coming out of church : did you ever see such a ' sugared invention '—as the Elizabethans used to say ? Did any haberdasher ever look so smirking ? Yet I will answer for it the story makes him one of the first gentlemen in the land."

" You are so severe, I am frightened at you," said Rosamond, keeping her amusement duly moderate. Poor young Plymdale had lingered with admiration over this very engraving, and his spirit was stirred.

" There are a great many celebrated people writing in the ' Keepsake,' at all events," he said, in a tone at once piqued and timid. " This is the first time I have heard it called silly."

" I think I shall turn round on you and accuse you of being a Goth," said Rosamond, looking at Lydgate with a smile. " I suspect you know nothing about Lady Blessington and L. E. L." [3] Rosamond herself was not without relish for these writers, but she did not readily commit herself by admiration, and was alive to the slightest hint that anything was not, according to Lydgate, in the very highest taste.

" But Sir Walter Scott—I suppose Mr Lydgate knows him," said young Plymdale, a little cheered by this advantage.

" Oh, I read no literature now," said Lydgate, shutting the book, and pushing it away. " I read so much when I was a lad, that I suppose it will last me all my life. I used to know Scott's poems by heart."

" I should like to know when you left off," said Rosamond, " because then I might be sure that I knew something which you did not know."

" Mr Lydgate would say that was not worth knowing," said Mr Ned, purposely caustic.

" On the contrary," said Lydgate, showing no smart, but smiling with exasperating confidence at Rosamond. " It would be worth knowing by the fact that Miss Vincy could tell it me."

Young Plymdale soon went to look at the whist-playing, thinking that Lydgate was one of the most conceited, unpleasant fellows it had ever been his ill-fortune to meet.

" How rash you are ! " said Rosamond, inwardly delighted " Do you see that you have given offence ? "

" What—is it Mr Plymdale's book ? I am sorry. I didn't think about it."

" I shall begin to admit what you said of yourself when you first came here—that you are a bear, and want teaching by the birds."

" Well, there is a bird who can teach me what she will. Don't I listen to her willingly ? "

3. Marguerite Power, Countess of Blessington (1789–1849), and Letitia Elizabeth Landon (1803–38), popular novelists of the 1820s and 1830s.

To Rosamond it seemed as if she and Lydgate were as good as engaged. That they were some time to be engaged had long been an idea in her mind ; and ideas, we know, tend to a more solid kind of existence, the necessary materials being at hand. It is true, Lydgate had the counter-idea of remaining unengaged ; but this was a mere negative, a shadow cast by other resolves which themselves were capable of shrinking. Circumstance was almost sure to be on the side of Rosamond's idea, which had a shaping activity and looked through watchful blue eyes, whereas Lydgate's lay blind and unconcerned as a jelly-fish which gets melted without knowing it.

That evening when he went home, he looked at his phials to see how a process of maceration was going on, with undisturbed interest ; and he wrote out his daily notes with as much precision as usual. The reveries from which it was difficult for him to detach himself were ideal constructions of something else than Rosamond's virtues, and the primitive tissue was still his fair unknown. Moreover, he was beginning to feel some zest for the growing though half-suppressed feud between him and the other medical men, which was likely to become more manifest, now that Bulstrode's method of managing the new hospital was about to be declared ; and there were various inspiriting signs that his non-acceptance by some of Peacock's patients might be counterbalanced by the impression he had produced in other quarters. Only a few days later, when he had happened to overtake Rosamond on the Lowick road and had got down from his horse to walk by her side until he had quite protected her from a passing drove, he had been stopped by a servant on horseback with a message calling him in to a house of some importance where Peacock had never attended ; and it was the second instance of this kind. The servant was Sir James Chettam's, and the house was Lowick Manor.

CHAPTER XXVIII.

> *1st Gent.* All times are good to seek your wedded home
> Bringing a mutual delight.
> *2d Gent.*   Why, true.
> The calendar hath not an evil day
> For souls made one by love, and even death
> Were sweetness, if it came like rolling waves
> While they two clasped each other, and foresaw
> No life apart.

MR and Mrs Casaubon, returning from their wedding journey, arrived at Lowick Manor in the middle of January. A light snow was falling as they descended at the door, and in the morning, when Dorothea passed from her dressing-room into the blue-green boudoir that we know of, she saw the long avenue of limes lifting their trunks from a white earth, and spreading white branches against the dun and motionless sky. The distant flat shrank in uniform whiteness and low-hanging uniformity of cloud. The very furniture in the room seemed to have shrunk since she saw it before : the stag in the tapestry looked more like a ghost in his ghostly blue-green world ; the volumes of polite literature in the bookcase looked more like immovable imitations of books. The bright fire of dry oak-boughs burning on the dogs seemed an incongruous renewal of life and glow—like the figure of Dorothea herself as she entered carrying the red-leather cases containing the cameos for Celia.

She was glowing from her morning toilette as only healthful youth can glow : there was gem-like brightness on her coiled hair and in her hazel eyes ; there was warm red life in her lips ; her throat had a breathing whiteness above the differing white of the fur which itself seemed to wind about her neck and cling down her blue-grey pelisse with a tenderness gathered from her own, a sentient commingled innocence which kept its loveliness against the crystalline purity of the out-door snow. As she laid the cameo-cases on the table in the bow-window, she unconsciously kept her hands on them, immediately absorbed in looking out on the still, white enclosure which made her visible world.

Mr Casaubon, who had risen early complaining of palpitation, was in the library giving audience to his curate Mr Tucker. By-and-by Celia would come in her quality of bridesmaid as well as sister, and through the next weeks there would be wedding visits received and given ; all in continuance of that transitional life understood to correspond with the excitement of bridal felicity, and keeping up the sense of busy ineffectiveness, as of a dream which the dreamer begins to suspect. The duties of her married life, contemplated as so great beforehand, seemed to be shrinking with the furniture and the white vapour-walled landscape. The clear heights where she expected to walk in full communion had become difficult to see even in her imagination ; the delicious repose of the soul on a complete superior had been shaken into uneasy effort and alarmed with dim presentiment. When would the days begin of that active wifely devotion which was to strengthen her husband's life and exalt her own ? Never perhaps, as she had preconceived them ; but somehow—still somehow. In this solemnly-pledged union of her life, duty would present itself in some new form of inspiration and give a new meaning to wifely love.

Meanwhile there was the snow and the low arch of dun vapour—there was the stifling oppression of that gentlewoman's world, where everything was done for her and none asked for her aid—where the sense of connection with a manifold pregnant existence had to be kept up painfully as an inward vision, instead of coming from without in claims that would have shaped her energies.—" What shall I do ? " " Whatever you please, my dear : " that had been her brief history since she had left off learning morning lessons and practising silly rhythms on the hated piano. Marriage, which was to bring guidance into worthy and imperative occupation, had not yet freed her from the gentlewoman's oppressive liberty : it had not even filled her leisure with the ruminant joy of unchecked tenderness. Her blooming full-pulsed youth stood there in a moral imprisonment which made itself one with the chill, colourless, narrowed landscape, with the shrunken furniture, the never-read books, and the ghostly stag in a pale fantastic world that seemed to be vanishing from the daylight.

In the first minutes when Dorothea looked out she felt nothing but the dreary oppression ; then came a keen remembrance, and turning away from the window she walked round the room. The ideas and hopes which were living in her mind when she first saw this room nearly three months before were present now only as memories : she judged them as we judge transient and departed things. All exist- ence seemed to beat with a lower pulse than her own, and her re- ligious faith was a solitary cry, the struggle out of a nightmare in which every object was withering and shrinking away from her. Each remembered thing in the room was disenchanted, was deadened as an unlit transparency, till her wandering gaze came to the group of miniatures, and there at last she saw something which had gathered new breath and meaning : it was the miniature of Mr Casaubon's aunt Julia, who had made the unfortunate marriage — of Will Ladislaw's grandmother. Dorothea could fancy that it was alive now —the delicate woman's face which yet had a headstrong look, a peculiarity difficult to interpret. Was it only her friends who thought her marriage unfortunate ? or did she herself find it out to be a mistake, and taste the salt bitterness of her tears in the merciful silence of the night ? What breadths of experience Dorothea seemed to have passed over since she first looked at this miniature ! She felt a new companionship with it, as if it had an ear for her and could see how she was looking at it. Here was a woman who had known some difficulty about marriage. Nay, the colours deepened, the lips and chin seemed to get larger, the hair and eyes seemed to be sending out light, the face was masculine and beamed on her with that full gaze which tells her on whom it falls that she is too interesting for the slightest movement of her eyelid to pass unnoticed and unin- terpreted. The vivid presentation came like a pleasant glow to Doro- thea : she felt herself smiling, and turning from the miniature sat down and looked up as if she were again talking to a figure in front of her. But the smile disappeared as she went on meditating, and at last she said aloud—

" Oh, it was cruel to speak so ! How sad—how dreadful ! "

She rose quickly and went out of the room, hurrying along the corridor, with the irresistible impulse to go and see her husband and inquire if she could do anything for him. Perhaps Mr Tucker was gone and Mr Casaubon was alone in the library. She felt as if all her morning's gloom would vanish if she could see her husband glad because of her presence.

But when she reached the head of the dark oak staircase, there was Celia coming up, and below there was Mr Brooke, exchanging wel- comes and congratulations with Mr Casaubon.

" Dodo ! " said Celia, in her quiet staccato ; then kissed her sister, whose arms encircled her, and said no more. I think they both cried a little in a furtive manner, while Dorothea ran down-stairs to greet her uncle.

" I need not ask how you are, my dear," said Mr Brooke, after kissing her forehead. " Rome has agreed with you, I see—happiness, frescoes, the antique—that sort of thing. Well, it's very pleasant to have you back again, and you understand all about art now, eh ? But Casaubon is a little pale, I tell him—a little pale, you know. Studying hard in his holidays is carrying it rather too far. I overdid it at one time "—Mr Brooke still held Dorothea's hand, but had turned his face to Mr Casaubon—" about topography, ruins, temples —I thought I had a clue, but I saw it would carry me too far, and nothing might have come of it. You may go any length in that sort of thing, and nothing may come of it, you know."

Dorothea's eyes also were turned up to her husband's face with some anxiety at the idea that those who saw him afresh after absence might be aware of signs which she had not noticed.

" Nothing to alarm you, my dear," said Mr Brooke, observing her expression. " A little English beef and mutton will soon make a difference. It was all very well to look pale, sitting for the portrait of Aquinas, you know—we got your letter just in time. But Aquinas, now—he was a little too subtle, wasn't he ? Does anybody read Aquinas ? "

" He is not indeed an author adapted to superficial minds," said Mr Casaubon, meeting these timely questions with dignified patience.

" You would like coffee in your own room, uncle ? " said Dorothea, coming to the rescue.

" Yes ; and you must go to Celia : she has great news to tell you, you know. I leave it all to her."

The blue-green boudoir looked much more cheerful when Celia was seated there in a pelisse exactly like her sister's, surveying the cameos with a placid satisfaction, while the conversation passed on to other topics.

" Do you think it nice to go to Rome on a wedding journey ? " said Celia, with her ready delicate blush which Dorothea was used to on the smallest occasions.

" It would not suit all—not you, dear, for example," said Dorothea, quietly. No one would ever know what she thought of a wedding journey to Rome.

" Mrs Cadwallader says it is nonsense, people going a long journey when they are married. She says they get tired to death of each other, and can't quarrel comfortably, as they would at home. And Lady Chettam says she went to Bath." Celia's colour changed again and again—seemed

> " To come and go with tidings from the heart,
>   As it a running messenger had been." [1]

It must mean more than Celia's blushing usually did.

" Celia ! has something happened ? " said Dorothea, in a tone full of sisterly feeling. " Have you really any great news to tell me ? "

" It was because you went away, Dodo. Then there was nobody but me for Sir James to talk to," said Celia, with a certain roguishness in her eyes.

" I understand. It is as I used to hope and believe," said Dorothea, taking her sister's face between her hands, and looking at her half anxiously. Celia's marriage seemed more serious than it used to do.

" It was only three days ago," said Celia. " And Lady Chettam is very kind."

" And you are very happy ? "

" Yes. We are not going to be married yet. Because everything is to be got ready. And I don't want to be married so very soon, be-

---

1. Edmund Spenser (1552–1599), *The Faerie Queene*, Canto IX, 51, 6–7.

cause I think it is nice to be engaged. And we shall be married all our lives after."

" I do believe you could not marry better, Kitty. Sir James is a good, honourable man," said Dorothea, warmly.

" He has gone on with the cottages, Dodo. He will tell you about them when he comes. Shall you be glad to see him ? "

" Of course I shall. How can you ask me ? "

" Only I was afraid you would be getting so learned," said Celia, regarding Mr Casaubon's learning as a kind of damp which might in due time saturate a neighbouring body.

CHAPTER XXIX.

" I found that no genius in another could please me. My unfortunate paradoxes had entirely dried up that source of comfort."—GOLDSMITH.

ONE morning, some weeks after her arrival at Lowick, Dorothea—but why always Dorothea ? Was her point of view the only possible one with regard to this marriage ? I protest against all our interest, all our effort at understanding being given to the young skins that look blooming in spite of trouble ; for these too will get faded, and will know the older and more eating griefs which we are helping to neglect. In spite of the blinking eyes and white moles objectionable to Celia, and the want of muscular curve which was morally painful to Sir James, Mr Casaubon had an intense consciousness within him, and was spiritually a-hungered like the rest of us. He had done nothing exceptional in marrying—nothing but what society sanctions, and considers an occasion for wreaths and bouquets. It had occurred to him that he must not any longer defer his intention of matrimony, and he had reflected that in taking a wife, a man of good position should expect and carefully choose a blooming young lady—the younger the better, because more educable and submissive—of a rank equal to his own, of religious principles, virtuous disposition, and good understanding. On such a young lady he would make handsome settlements, and he would neglect no arrangement for her happiness : in return, he should receive family pleasures and leave behind him that copy of himself which seemed so urgently required of a man—to the sonneteers of the sixteenth century. Times had altered since then, and no sonneteer had insisted on Mr Casaubon's leaving a copy of himself ; moreover, he had not yet succeeded in issuing copies of his mythological key ; but he had always intended to acquit himself by marriage, and the sense that he was fast leaving the years behind him, that the world was getting dimmer and that he felt lonely, was a reason to him for losing no more time in overtaking domestic delights before they too were left behind by the years.

And when he had seen Dorothea he believed that he had found even more than he demanded : she might really be such a helpmate to him as would enable him to dispense with a hired secretary, an aid which Mr Casaubon had never yet employed and had a suspicious dread of. (Mr Casaubon was nervously conscious that he was expected to manifest a powerful mind.) Providence, in its kindness, had supplied him with the wife he needed. A wife, a modest young lady, with the purely appreciative, unambitious abilities of her sex, is sure to think her husband's mind powerful. Whether Providence had taken equal care of Miss Brooke in presenting her with Mr Casaubon was an idea which could hardly occur to him. Society never made the preposterous demand that a man should think as much about his own qualifications for making a charming girl happy as he thinks of hers for making himself happy. As if a man could choose not only his wife but his wife's husband! Or as if he were bound to provide charms for his posterity in his own person!—When Dorothea accepted him with effusion, that was only natural ; and Mr Casaubon believed that his happiness was going to begin.

He had not had much foretaste of happiness in his previous life. To know intense joy without a strong bodily frame, one must have an enthusiastic soul. Mr Casaubon had never had a strong bodily frame, and his soul was sensitive without being enthusiastic : it was too languid to thrill out of self-consciousness into passionate delight ; it went on fluttering in the swampy ground where it was hatched, thinking of its wings and never flying. His experience was of that pitiable kind which shrinks from pity, and fears most of all that it should be known : it was that proud narrow sensitiveness which has not mass enough to spare for transformation into sympathy, and quivers thread-like in small currents of self-preoccupation or at best of an egoistic scrupulosity. And Mr Casaubon had many scruples : he was capable of a severe self-restraint ; he was resolute in being a man of honour according to the code ; he would be unimpeachable by any recognised opinion. In conduct these ends had been attained ; but the difficulty of making his Key to all Mythologies unimpeachable weighed like lead upon his mind ; and the pamphlets — or " Parerga " as he called them—by which he tested his public and deposited small monumental records of his march, were far from having been seen in all their significance.[1] He suspected the Archdeacon of not having read them ; he was in painful doubt as to what was really thought of them by the leading minds of Brasenose, and bitterly convinced that his old acquaintance Carp had been the writer of that depreciatory recension which was kept locked in a small drawer of Mr Casaubon's desk, and also in a dark closet of his verbal memory.[2] These were heavy impressions to struggle against, and brought that melancholy embitterment which is the consequence of all excessive claim : even his religious faith wavered with his wavering trust in his own authorship, and the consolations of the Christian hope in immortality seemed to lean on the immortality of the still unwritten Key to all Mythologies. For my part I am very sorry for him. It is an uneasy lot at best, to be what we call highly taught and yet not to enjoy : to be present at this great spectacle of life and never to be liberated from a small hungry shivering self—never to be fully possessed by the glory we behold, never to have our consciousness rapturously transformed into the vividness of a thought, the ardour of a passion, the energy of an action, but always to be scholarly and uninspired, ambitious and timid, scrupulous and dimsighted. Becoming a dean or even a bishop would make little difference, I fear, to Mr

1. Parerga: supplemental or secondary works.   2. Brasenose: college at Oxford.

Casaubon's uneasiness. Doubtless some ancient Greek has observed that behind the big mask and the speaking-trumpet, there must always be our poor little eyes peeping as usual and our timorous lips more or less under anxious control.

To this mental estate mapped out a quarter of a century before, to sensibilities thus fenced in, Mr Casaubon had thought of annexing happiness with a lovely young bride ; but even before marriage, as we have seen, he found himself under a new depression in the consciousness that the new bliss was not blissful to him. Inclination yearned back to its old, easier custom. And the deeper he went in domesticity the more did the sense of acquitting himself and acting with propriety predominate over any other satisfaction. Marriage, like religion and erudition, nay, like authorship itself, was fated to become an outward requirement, and Edward Casaubon was bent on fulfilling unimpeachably all requirements. Even drawing Dorothea into use in his study, according to his own intention before marriage, was an effort which he was always tempted to defer, and but for her pleading insistance it might never have begun. But she had succeeded in making it a matter of course that she should take her place at an early hour in the library and have work either of reading aloud or copying assigned her. The work had been easier to define because Mr Casaubon had adopted an immediate intention : there was to be a new Parergon, a small monograph on some lately-traced indications concerning the Egyptian mysteries whereby certain assertions of Warburton's could be corrected. [3] References were extensive even here, but not altogether shoreless ; and sentences were actually to be written in the shape wherein they would be scanned by Brasenose and a less formidable posterity. These minor monumental productions were always exciting to Mr Casaubon ; digestion was made difficult by the interference of citations, or by the rivalry of dialectical phrases ringing against each other in his brain. And from the first there was to be a Latin dedication about which everything was uncertain except that it was not to be addressed to Carp : it was a poisonous regret to Mr Casaubon that he had once addressed a dedication to Carp in which he had numbered that member of the animal kingdom among the *viros nullo œvo perituros,* a mistake which would infallibly lay the dedicator open to ridicule in the next age, and might even be chuckled over by Pike and Tench in the present. [4]

Thus Mr Casaubon was in one of his busiest epochs, and as I began to say a little while ago, Dorothea joined him early in the library where he had breakfasted alone. Celia at this time was on a second visit to Lowick, probably the last before her marriage, and was in the drawing-room expecting Sir James.

Dorothea had learned to read the signs of her husband's mood, and she saw that the morning had become more foggy there during the last hour. She was going silently to her desk when he said, in that distant tone which implied that he was discharging a disagreeable duty—

"Dorothea, here is a letter for you, which was enclosed in one addressed to me."

3. Probably William Warburton (1698–1779), bishop, literary and theological writer.

4. *Viros nullo œvo perituros:* men who will never pass away.

It was a letter of two pages, and she immediately looked at the signature.

"Mr Ladislaw ! What can he have to say to me ?" she exclaimed, in a tone of pleased surprise. "But," she added, looking at Mr Casaubon, "I can imagine what he has written to you about."

"You can, if you please, read the letter," said Mr Casaubon, severely pointing to it with his pen, and not looking at her. "But I may as well say beforehand, that I must decline the proposal it contains to pay a visit here. I trust I may be excused for desiring an interval of complete freedom from such distractions as have been hitherto inevitable, and especially from guests whose desultory vivacity makes their presence a fatigue."

There had been no clashing of temper between Dorothea and her husband since that little explosion in Rome, which had left such strong traces in her mind that it had been easier ever since to quell emotion than to incur the consequence of venting it. But this ill-tempered anticipation that she could desire visits which might be disagreeable to her husband, this gratuitous defence of himself against selfish complaint on her part, was too sharp a sting to be meditated on until after it had been resented. Dorothea had thought that she could have been patient with John Milton, but she had never imagined him behaving in this way ; and for a moment Mr Casaubon seemed to be stupidly undiscerning and odiously unjust. Pity, that "newborn babe" which was by-and-by to rule many a storm within her, did not "stride the blast" on this occasion.[5] With her first words, uttered in a tone that shook him, she startled Mr Casaubon into looking at her, and meeting the flash of her eyes.

"Why do you attribute to me a wish for anything that would annoy you ? You speak to me as if I were something you had to contend against. Wait at least till I appear to consult my own pleasure apart from yours."

"Dorothea, you are hasty," answered Mr Casaubon, nervously.

Decidedly, this woman was too young to be on the formidable level of wifehood—unless she had been pale and featureless and taken everything for granted.

"I think it was you who were first hasty in your false suppositions about my feeling," said Dorothea, in the same tone. The fire was not dissipated yet, and she thought it was ignoble in her husband not to apologise to her.

"We will, if you please, say no more on this subject, Dorothea. I have neither leisure nor energy for this kind of debate."

Here Mr Casaubon dipped his pen and made as if he would return to his writing, though his hand trembled so much that the words seemed to be written in an unknown character. There are answers which, in turning away wrath, only send it to the other end of the room, and to have a discussion coolly waived when you feel that justice is all on your own side is even more exasperating in marriage than in philosophy.

Dorothea left Ladislaw's two letters unread on her husband's writing-table and went to her own place, the scorn and indignation within her rejecting the reading of these letters, just as we hurl away any trash towards which we seem to have been suspected of mean cu-

---

5. "And pity, like a naked new-born babe,/Striding the blast . . . /Shall blow the horrid deed in every eye" (*Macbeth*, Act I, Sc. 7, lines 21–23).

pidity. She did not in the least divine the subtle sources of her husband's bad temper about these letters : she only knew that they had caused him to offend her. She began to work at once, and her hand did not tremble ; on the contrary, in writing out the quotations which had been given to her the day before, she felt that she was forming her letters beautifully, and it seemed to her that she saw the construction of the Latin she was copying, and which she was beginning to understand, more clearly than usual. In her indignation there was a sense of superiority, but it went out for the present in firmness of stroke, and did not compress itself into an inward articulate voice pronouncing the once " affable archangel" a poor creature.

There had been this apparent quiet for half an hour, and Dorothea had not looked away from her own table, when she heard the loud bang of a book on the floor, and turning quickly saw Mr Casaubon on the library-steps clinging forward as if he were in some bodily distress. She started up and bounded towards him in an instant : he was evidently in great straits for breath. Jumping on a stool she got close to his elbow and said with her whole soul melted into tender alarm—

" Can you lean on me, dear ? "

He was still for two or three minutes, which seemed endless to her, unable to speak or move, gasping for breath. When at last he descended the three steps and fell backward in the large chair which Dorothea had drawn close to the foot of the ladder, he no longer gasped but seemed helpless and about to faint. Dorothea rang the bell violently, and presently Mr Casaubon was helped to the couch : he did not faint, and was gradually reviving, when Sir James Chettam came in, having been met in the hall with the news that Mr Casaubon had " had a fit in the library."

" Good God ! this is just what might have been expected," was his immediate thought. If his prophetic soul had been urged to particularise, it seemed to him that " fits" would have been the definite expression alighted upon. He asked his informant, the butler, whether the doctor had been sent for. The butler never knew his master want the doctor before ; but would it not be right to send for a physician ?

When Sir James entered the library, however, Mr Casaubon could make some signs of his usual politeness, and Dorothea, who in the reaction from her first terror had been kneeling and sobbing by his side, now rose and herself proposed that some one should ride off for a medical man.

" I recommend you to send for Lydgate," said Sir James. " My mother has called him in, and she has found him uncommonly clever. She has had a poor opinion of the physicians since my father's death."

Dorothea appealed to her husband, and he made a silent sign of approval. So Mr Lydgate was sent for and he came wonderfully soon, for the messenger, who was Sir James Chettam's man and knew Mr Lydgate, met him leading his horse along the Lowick road and giving his arm to Miss Vincy.

Celia, in the drawing-room, had known nothing of the trouble till Sir James told her of it. After Dorothea's account, he no longer considered the illness a fit, but still something " of that nature."

"Poor dear Dodo—how dreadful!" said Celia, feeling as much grieved as her own perfect happiness would allow. Her little hands were clasped, and enclosed by Sir James's as a bud is enfolded by a liberal calyx. "It is very shocking that Mr Casaubon should be ill; but I never did like him. And I think he is not half fond enough of Dorothea; and he ought to be, for I am sure no one else would have had him—do you think they would?"

"I always thought it a horrible sacrifice of your sister," said Sir James.

"Yes. But poor Dodo never did do what other people do, and I think she never will."

"She is a noble creature," said the loyal-hearted Sir James. He had just had a fresh impression of this kind, as he had seen Dorothea stretching her tender arm under her husband's neck and looking at him with unspeakable sorrow. He did not know how much penitence there was in the sorrow.

"Yes," said Celia, thinking it was very well for Sir James to say so, but *he* would not have been comfortable with Dodo. "Shall I go to her? Could I help her, do you think?"

"I think it would be well for you just to go and see her before Lydgate comes," said Sir James, magnanimously. "Only don't stay long."

While Celia was gone, he walked up and down remembering what he had originally felt about Dorothea's engagement, and feeling a revival of his disgust at Mr Brooke's indifference. If Cadwallader—if every one else had regarded the affair as he, Sir James, had done, the marriage might have been hindered. It was wicked to let a young girl blindly decide her fate in that way, without any effort to save her. Sir James had long ceased to have any regrets on his own account: his heart was satisfied with his engagement to Celia. But he had a chivalrous nature (was not the disinterested service of woman among the ideal glories of old chivalry?): his disregarded love had not turned to bitterness; its death had made sweet odours—floating memories that clung with a consecrating effect to Dorothea. He could remain her brotherly friend, interpreting her actions with generous trustfulness.

CHAPTER XXX.

"Qui veut délasser hors de propos, lasse."—PASCAL. [1]

MR CASAUBON had no second attack of equal severity with the first, and in a few days began to recover his usual condition. But Lydgate seemed to think the case worth a great deal of attention. He not only used his stethoscope (which had not become a matter of course in practice at that time), but sat quietly by his patient and watched him. To Mr Casaubon's questions about himself, he replied that the source of the illness was the common error of intellectual men—a too eager and monotonous application: the remedy was, to be satisfied

---

1. "Who diverts himself aimlessly tires of diversion" (*Pensées*).

with moderate work, and to seek variety of relaxation. Mr Brooke, who sat by on one occasion, suggested that Mr Casaubon should go fishing, as Cadwallader did, and have a turning-room, make toys, table-legs, and that kind of thing.

"In short you recommend me to anticipate the arrival of my second childhood," said poor Mr Casaubon, with some bitterness. "These things," he added, looking at Lydgate, "would be to me such relaxation as tow-picking is to prisoners in a house of correction." [2]

"I confess," said Lydgate, smiling, "amusement is rather an unsatisfactory prescription. It is something like telling people to keep up their spirits. Perhaps I had better say, that you must submit to be mildly bored rather than to go on working."

"Yes, yes," said Mr Brooke. "Get Dorothea to play backgammon with you in the evenings. And shuttlecock, now—I don't know a finer game than shuttlecock for the daytime. I remember it all the fashion. To be sure, your eyes might not stand that, Casaubon. But you must unbend, you know. Why, you might take to some light study : conchology, now : I always think that must be a light study. Or get Dorothea to read you light things, Smollett—'Roderick Random,' 'Humphrey Clinker :' they are a little broad, but she may read anything now she's married, you know. [3] I remember they made me laugh uncommonly—there's a droll bit about a postilion's breeches. We have no such humour now. I have gone through all these things, but they might be rather new to you."

"As new as eating thistles," would have been an answer to represent Mr Casaubon's feelings. But he only bowed resignedly, with due respect to his wife's uncle, and observed that doubtless the works he mentioned had "served as a resource to a certain order of minds."

"You see," said the able magistrate to Lydgate, when they were outside the door, "Casaubon has been a little narrow : it leaves him rather at a loss when you forbid him his particular work, which I believe is something very deep indeed—in the line of research, you know. I would never give way to that ; I was always versatile. But a clergyman is tied a little tight. If they would make him a bishop, now!—he did a very good pamphlet for Peel. He would have more movement then, more show ; he might get a little flesh. But I recommend you to talk to Mrs Casaubon. She is clever enough for anything, is my niece. Tell her, her husband wants liveliness, diversion : put her on amusing tactics."

Without Mr Brooke's advice, Lydgate had determined on speaking to Dorothea. She had not been present while her uncle was throwing out his pleasant suggestions as to the mode in which life at Lowick might be enlivened, but she was usually by her husband's side, and the unaffected signs of intense anxiety in her face and voice about whatever touched his mind or health, made a drama which Lydgate was inclined to watch. He said to himself that he was only doing right in telling her the truth about her husband's probable future, but he certainly thought also that it would be interesting to talk confidentially with her. A medical man likes to make psychological observations, and sometimes in the pursuit of such studies is

<hr>

2. Tow-picking: preparing flax or hemp for use as rope; a usual occupation for prisoners.

3. Tobias Smollett, author of *Roderick Random* (1748) and *Humphrey Clinker* (1771).

too easily tempted into momentous prophecy which life and death easily set at nought. Lydgate had often been satirical on this gratuitous prediction, and he meant now to be guarded.

He asked for Mrs Casaubon, but being told that she was out walking, he was going away, when Dorothea and Celia appeared, both glowing from their struggle with the March wind. When Lydgate begged to speak with her alone, Dorothea opened the library door which happened to be the nearest, thinking of nothing at the moment but what he might have to say about Mr Casaubon. It was the first time she had entered this room since her husband had been taken ill, and the servant had chosen not to open the shutters. But there was light enough to read by from the narrow upper panes of the windows.

"You will not mind this sombre light," said Dorothea, standing in the middle of the room. "Since you forbade books, the library has been·out of the question. But Mr Casaubon will soon be here again, I hope. Is he not making progress?"

"Yes, much more rapid progress than I at first expected. Indeed, he is already nearly in his usual state of health."

"You do not fear that the illness will return?" said Dorothea, whose quick ear had detected some significance in Lydgate's tone.

"Such cases are peculiarly difficult to pronounce upon," said Lydgate. "The only point on which I can be confident is that it will be desirable to be very watchful on Mr Casaubon's account, lest he should in any way strain his nervous power."

"I beseech you to speak quite plainly," said Dorothea, in an imploring tone. "I cannot bear to think that there might be something which I did not know, and which, if I had known it, would have made me act differently." The words came out like a cry : it was evident that they were the voice of some mental experience which lay not very far off.

"Sit down," she added, placing herself on the nearest chair, and throwing off her bonnet and gloves, with an instinctive discarding of formality where a great question of destiny was concerned.

"What you say now justifies my own view," said Lydgate. "I think it is one's function as a medical man to hinder regrets of that sort as far as possible. But I beg you to observe that Mr Casaubon's case is precisely of the kind in which the issue is most difficult to pronounce upon. He may possibly live for fifteen years or more, without much worse health than he has had hitherto."

Dorothea had turned very pale, and when Lydgate paused she said in a low voice, "You mean if we are very careful."

"Yes—careful against mental agitation of all kinds, and against excessive application."

"He would be miserable, if he had to give up his work," said Dorothea, with a quick prevision of that wretchedness.

"I am aware of that. The only course is to try by all means, direct and indirect, to moderate and vary his occupations. With a happy concurrence of circumstances, there is, as I said, no immediate danger from that affection of the heart which I believe to have been the cause of his late attack. On the other hand, it is possible that the disease may develop itself more rapidly : it is one of those cases in which death is sometimes sudden. Nothing should be neglected which might be affected by such an issue."

There was silence for a few moments, while Dorothea sat as if she had been turned to marble, though the life within her was so intense that her mind had never before swept in brief time over an equal range of scenes and motives.

" Help me, pray," she said, at last, in the same low voice as before. " Tell me what I can do."

" What do you think of foreign travel ? You have been lately in Rome, I think."

The memories which made this resource utterly hopeless were a new current that shook Dorothea out of her pallid immobility.

" Oh, that would not do—that would be worse than anything," she said with a more childlike despondency, while the tears rolled down. " Nothing will be of any use that he does not enjoy."

" I wish that I could have spared you this pain," said Lydgate, deeply touched, yet wondering about her marriage. Women just like Dorothea had not entered into his traditions.

" It was right of you to tell me. I thank you for telling me the truth."

" I wish you to understand that I shall not say anything to enlighten Mr Casaubon himself. I think it desirable for him to know nothing more than that he must not overwork himself, and must observe certain rules. Anxiety of any kind would be precisely the most unfavourable condition for him."

Lydgate rose, and Dorothea mechanically rose at the same time, unclasping her cloak and throwing it off as if it stifled her. He was bowing and quitting her, when an impulse which if she had been alone would have turned into a prayer, made her say with a sob in her voice—

" Oh, you are a wise man, are you not ? You know all about life and death. Advise me. Think what I can do. He has been labouring all his life and looking forward. He minds about nothing else. And I mind about nothing else—"

For years after Lydgate remembered the impression produced in him by this involuntary appeal—this cry from soul to soul, without other consciousness than their moving with kindred natures in the same embroiled medium, the same troublous fitfully-illuminated life. But what could he say now except that he should see Mr Casaubon again to-morrow ?

When he was gone, Dorothea's tears gushed forth, and relieved her stifling oppression. Then she dried her eyes, reminded that her distress must not be betrayed to her husband ; and looked round the room thinking that she must order the servant to attend to it as usual, since Mr Casaubon might now at any moment wish to enter. On his writing-table there were letters which had lain untouched since the morning when he was taken ill, and among them, as Dorothea well remembered, there were young Ladislaw's letters, the one addressed to her still unopened. The associations of these letters had been made the more painful by that sudden attack of illness which she felt that the agitation caused by her anger might have helped to bring on : it would be time enough to read them when they were again thrust upon her, and she had had no inclination to fetch them from the library. But now it occurred to her that they should be put out of her husband's sight : whatever might have been the sources of his annoyance about them, he must, if possible, not be annoyed again ; and she ran her eyes first over the letter addressed to him to assure herself whether or not it would be necessary to write in order to hinder the offensive visit.

Will wrote from Rome, and began by saying that his obligations to Mr Casaubon were too deep for all thanks not to seem impertinent. It was plain that if he were not grateful, he must be the poorest-spirited rascal who had ever found a generous friend. To expand in wordy thanks would be like saying, " I am honest." But Will had come to perceive that his defects—defects which Mr Casaubon had himself often pointed to—needed for their correction that more strenuous position which his relative's generosity had hitherto prevented from being inevitable. He trusted that he should make the best return, if return were possible, by showing the effectiveness of the education for which he was indebted, and by ceasing in future to need any diversion towards himself of funds on which others might have a better claim. He was coming to England, to try his fortune, as many other young men were obliged to do whose only capital was in their brains. His friend Naumann had desired him to take charge of the " Dispute "— the picture painted for Mr Casaubon, with whose permission, and Mrs Casaubon's, Will would convey it to Lowick in person. A letter addressed to the Poste Restante in Paris within the fortnight would hinder him, if necessary, from arriving at an inconvenient moment. He enclosed a letter to Mrs Casaubon in which he continued a discussion about art, begun with her in Rome.

Opening her own letter Dorothea saw that it was a lively continuation of his remonstrance with her fanatical sympathy and her want of sturdy neutral delight in things as they were — an outpouring of his young vivacity which it was impossible to read just now. She had immediately to consider what was to be done about the other letter: there was still time perhaps to prevent Will from coming to Lowick. Dorothea ended by giving the letter to her uncle, who was still in the house, and begging him to let Will know that Mr Casaubon had been ill, and that his health would not allow the reception of any visitors.

No one more ready than Mr Brooke to write a letter : his only difficulty was to write a short one, and his ideas in this case expanded over the three large pages and the inward foldings. He had simply said to Dorothea—

" To be sure, I will write, my dear. He's a very clever young fellow —this young Ladislaw—I daresay will be a rising young man. It's a good letter—marks his sense of things, you know. However, I will tell him about Casaubon."

But the end of Mr Brooke's pen was a thinking organ, evolving sentences, especially of a benevolent kind, before the rest of his mind could well overtake them. It expressed regrets and proposed remedies, which, when Mr Brooke read them, seemed felicitously worded—surprisingly the right thing, and determined a sequel which he had never before thought of. In this case, his pen found it such a pity that young Ladislaw should not have come into the neighbourhood just at that time, in order that Mr Brooke might make his acquaintance more fully, and that they might go over the long-neglected Italian drawings together—it also felt such an interest in a young man who was starting in life with a stock of ideas—that by the end of the second page it had persuaded Mr Brooke to invite young Ladislaw, since he could not be received at Lowick, to come to Tipton Grange. Why not? They

could find a great many things to do together, and this was a period
of peculiar growth — the political horizon was expanding, and — in
short, Mr Brooke's pen went off into a little speech which it had
lately reported for that imperfectly-edited organ the ' Middlemarch
Pioneer.' While Mr Brooke was sealing this letter, he felt elated
with an influx of dim projects :—a young man capable of putting
ideas into form, the ' Pioneer ' purchased to clear the pathway for a
new candidate, documents utilised — who knew what might come of
it all ? Since Celia was going to marry immediately, it would be
very pleasant to have a young fellow at table with him, at least for a
time.

But he went away without telling Dorothea what he had put into
the letter, for she was engaged with her husband, and—in fact, these
things were of no importance to her.

CHAPTER XXXI.

How will you know the pitch of that great bell
Too large for you to stir ? Let but a flute
Play 'neath the fine-mixed metal : listen close
Till the right note flows forth, a silvery rill :
Then shall the huge bell tremble—then the mass
With myriad waves concurrent shall respond
In low soft unison.

LYDGATE that evening spoke to Miss Vincy of Mrs Casaubon, and
laid some emphasis on the strong feeling she appeared to have for that
formal studious man thirty years older than herself.

" Of course she is devoted to her husband," said Rosamond, implying a notion of necessary sequence which the scientific man regarded
as the prettiest possible for a woman ; but she was thinking at the
same time that it was not so very melancholy to be mistress of Lowick
Manor with a husband likely to die soon. " Do you think her very
handsome ?"

" She certainly is handsome, but I have not thought about it," said
Lydgate.

" I suppose it would be unprofessional," said Rosamond, dimpling.
" But how your practice is spreading ! You were called in before to
the Chettams, I think ; and now, the Casaubons."

" Yes," said Lydgate, in a tone of compulsory admission. " But I
don't really like attending such people so well as the poor. The cases
are more monotonous, and one has to go through more fuss and listen
more deferentially to nonsense."

" Not more than in Middlemarch," said Rosamond. " And at least
you go through wide corridors and have the scent of rose-leaves everywhere."

" That is true, Mademoiselle de Montmorenci," said Lydgate, just
bending his head to the table and lifting with his fourth finger her
delicate handkerchief which lay at the mouth of her reticule, as if to
enjoy its scent, while he looked at her with a smile. [1]

1. Probably a reference to Jeanne de
Montmorenci, heroine of Sabatier de
Castres's historical romance *La Soli-
taire des Pyrénées* (1802), who fled her
father's home rather than marry, and
devoted herself to works of Christian
charity, giving all she had to the poor.

But this agreeable holiday freedom with which Lydgate hovered about the flower of Middlemarch, could not continue indefinitely. It was not more possible to find social isolation in that town than elsewhere, and two people persistently flirting could by no means escape from " the various entanglements, weights, blows, clashings, motions, by which things severally go on." Whatever Miss Vincy did must be remarked, and she was perhaps the more conspicuous to admirers and critics because just now Mrs Vincy, after some struggle, had gone with Fred to stay a little while at Stone Court, there being no other way of at once gratifying old Featherstone and keeping watch against Mary Garth, who appeared a less tolerable daughter-in-law in proportion as Fred's illness disappeared.

Aunt Bulstrode, for example, came a little oftener into Lowick Gate to see Rosamond, now she was alone. For Mrs Bulstrode had a true sisterly feeling for her brother ; always thinking that he might have married better, but wishing well to the children. Now Mrs Bulstrode had a long-standing intimacy with Mrs Plymdale. They had nearly the same preferences in silks, patterns for underclothing, china-ware, and clergymen ; they confided their little troubles of health and household management to each other, and various little points of superiority on Mrs Bulstrode's side, namely, more decided seriousness, more admiration for mind, and a house outside the town, sometimes served to give colour to their conversation without dividing them : well-meaning women both, knowing very little of their own motives.

Mrs Bulstrode, paying a morning visit to Mrs Plymdale, happened to say that she could not stay longer, because she was going to see poor Rosamond.

" Why do you say ' poor Rosamond ' ? " said Mrs Plymdale, a round-eyed sharp little woman, liked a tamed falcon.

" She is so pretty, and has been brought up in such thoughtlessness. The mother, you know, had always that levity about her, which makes me anxious for the children."

" Well, Harriet, if I am to speak my mind," said Mrs Plymdale, with emphasis, " I must say, anybody would suppose you and Mr Bulstrode would be delighted with what has happened, for you have done everything to put Mr Lydgate forward."

" Selina, what do you mean ? " said Mrs Bulstrode in genuine surprise.

" Not but what I am truly thankful for Ned's sake," said Mrs Plymdale. " He could certainly better afford to keep such a wife than some people can ; but I should wish him to look elsewhere. Still a mother has anxieties, and some young men would take to a bad life in consequence. Besides, if I was obliged to speak, I should say I was not fond of strangers coming into a town."

" I don't know, Selina," said Mrs Bulstrode, with a little emphasis in her turn. " Mr Bulstrode was a stranger here at one time. Abraham and Moses were strangers in the land, and we are told to entertain strangers. And especially," she added, after a slight pause, " when they are unexceptionable."

" I was not speaking in a religious sense, Harriet. I spoke as a mother."

" Selina, I am sure you have never heard me say anything against a niece of mine marrying your son."

" Oh, it is pride in Miss Vincy—I am sure it is nothing else," said Mrs Plymdale, who had never before given all her confidence to " Harriet" on this subject. " No young man in Middlemarch was good enough for her : I have heard her mother say as much. That is not a Christian spirit, I think. But now, from all I hear, she has found a man as proud as herself."

" You don't mean that there is anything between Rosamond and Mr Lydgate ?" said Mrs Bulstrode, rather mortified at finding out her own ignorance.

" Is it possible you don't know, Harriet?"

" Oh, I go about so little ; and I am not fond of gossip ; I really never hear any. You see so many people that I don't see. Your circle is rather different from ours."

" Well, but your own niece and Mr Bulstrode's great favourite— and yours too, I am sure, Harriet ! I thought, at one time, you meant him for Kate, when she is a little older."

" I don't believe there can be anything serious at present," said Mrs Bulstrode. " My brother would certainly have told me."

" Well, people have different ways, but I understand that nobody can see Miss Vincy and Mr Lydgate together without taking them to be engaged. However, it is not my business. Shall I put up the pattern of mittens ?"

After this Mrs Bulstrode drove to her niece with a mind newly weighted. She was herself handsomely dressed, but she noticed with a little more regret than usual that Rosamond, who was just come in and met her in walking-dress, was almost as expensively equipped. Mrs Bulstrode was a feminine, smaller edition of her brother, and had none of her husband's low-toned pallor. She had a good honest glance and used no circumlocution.

" You are alone, I see, my dear," she said, as they entered the drawing-room together, looking round gravely. Rosamond felt sure that her aunt had something particular to say, and they sat down near each other. Nevertheless, the quilling inside Rosamond's bonnet was so charming that it was impossible not to desire the same kind of thing for Kate, and Mrs Bulstrode's eyes, which were rather fine, rolled round that ample quilled circuit, while she spoke. [2]

" I have just heard something about you that has surprised me very much, Rosamond."

" What is that, aunt?" Rosamond's eyes also were roaming over her aunt's large embroidered collar.

" I can hardly believe it—that you should be engaged without my knowing it—without your father's telling me." Here Mrs Bulstrode's eyes finally rested on Rosamond's, who blushed deeply, and said—

" I am not engaged, aunt."

" How is it that every one says so, then—that it is the town's talk ?"

" The town's talk is of very little consequence, I think," said Rosamond, inwardly gratified.

" Oh, my dear, be more thoughtful ; don't despise your neighbours so. Remember you are turned twenty-two now, and you will have no fortune : your father, I am sure, will not be able to spare you anything.

2. Quilling: ribbing.

Mr Lydgate is very intellectual and clever ; I know there is an attraction in that. I like talking to such men myself ; and your uncle finds him very useful. But the profession is a poor one here. To be sure, this life is not everything ; but it is seldom a medical man has true religious views—there is too much pride of intellect. And you are not fit to marry a poor man."

" Mr Lydgate is not a poor man, aunt. He has very high connections."

" He told me himself he was poor."

" That is because he is used to people who have a high style of living."

" My dear Rosamond, *you* must not think of living in high style."

Rosamond looked down and played with her reticule. She was not a fiery young lady and had no sharp answers, but she meant to live as she pleased.

" Then it is really true ? " said Mrs Bulstrode, looking very earnestly at her niece. " You are thinking of Mr Lydgate : there is some understanding between you, though your father doesn't know. Be open, my dear Rosamond : Mr Lydgate has really made you an offer ? "

Poor Rosamond's feelings were very unpleasant. She had been quite easy as to Lydgate's feeling and intention, but now when her aunt put this question she did not like being unable to say Yes. Her pride was hurt, but her habitual control of manner helped her.

" Pray excuse me, aunt. I would rather not speak on the subject."

" You would not give your heart to a man without a decided prospect, I trust, my dear. And think of the two excellent offers I know of that you have refused !—and one still within your reach, if you will not throw it away. I knew a very great beauty who married badly at last, by doing so. Mr Ned Plymdale is a nice young man —some might think good-looking ; and an only son ; and a large business of that kind is better than a profession. Not that marrying is everything. I would have you seek first the kingdom of God. But a girl should keep her heart within her own power."

" I should never give it to Mr Ned Plymdale, if it were. I have already refused him. If I loved, I should love at once and without change," said Rosamond, with a great sense of being a romantic heroine, and playing the part prettily.

" I see how it is, my dear," said Mrs Bulstrode, in a melancholy voice, rising to go. " You have allowed your affections to be engaged without return."

" No, indeed, aunt," said Rosamond, with emphasis.

" Then you are quite confident that Mr Lydgate has a serious attachment to you ? "

Rosamond's cheeks by this time were persistently burning, and she felt much mortification. She chose to be silent, and her aunt went away all the more convinced.

Mr Bulstrode in things worldly and indifferent was disposed to do what his wife bade him, and she now, without telling her reasons, desired him on the next opportunity to find out in conversation with Mr Lydgate whether he had any intention of marrying soon. The result was a decided negative. Mr Bulstrode, on being cross-questioned, showed that Lydgate had spoken as no man would who had any attachment that could issue in matrimony. Mrs Bulstrode now felt that she had a serious duty before her, and she soon managed to arrange a *tête-à-tête* with Lydgate, in which she passed from inquiries about Fred Vincy's health, and expressions of her sincere anxiety for her brother's large family, to general remarks on the dangers which lay before young people with regard to their settlement in life. Young men were often wild and disappointing, making little return for the money spent on them, and a girl was exposed to many circumstances which might interfere with her prospects.

"Especially when she has great attractions, and her parents see much company," said Mrs Bulstrode. "Gentlemen pay her attention, and engross her all to themselves, for the mere pleasure of the moment, and that drives off others. I think it is a heavy responsibility, Mr Lydgate, to interfere with the prospects of any girl." Here Mrs Bulstrode fixed her eyes on him, with an unmistakable purpose of warning, if not of rebuke.

"Clearly," said Lydgate, looking at her—perhaps even staring a little in return. "On the other hand, a man must be a great coxcomb to go about with a notion that he must not pay attention to a young lady lest she should fall in love with him, or lest others should think she must."

"Oh, Mr Lydgate, you know well what your advantages are. You know that our young men here cannot cope with you. Where you frequent a house it may militate very much against a girl's making a desirable settlement in life, and prevent her from accepting offers even if they are made."

Lydgate was less flattered by his advantage over the Middlemarch Orlandos[3] than he was annoyed by the perception of Mrs Bulstrode's meaning. She felt that she had spoken as impressively as it was necessary to do, and that in using the superior word "militate" she had thrown a noble drapery over a mass of particulars which were still evident enough.

Lydgate was fuming a little, pushed his hair back with one hand, felt curiously in his waistcoat-pocket with the other, and then stooped to beckon the tiny black spaniel, which had the insight to decline his hollow caresses. It would not have been decent to go away, because he had been dining with other guests, and had just taken tea. But Mrs Bulstrode, having no doubt that she had been understood, turned the conversation.

Solomon's Proverbs, I think, have omitted to say, that as the sore palate findeth grit, so an uneasy consciousness heareth innuendoes. The next day Mr Farebrother, parting from Lydgate in the street, supposed that they should meet at Vincy's in the evening. Lydgate answered curtly, no—he had work to do—he must give up going out in the evening.

"What, you are going to get lashed to the mast, eh, and are stopping your ears?" said the Vicar.[4] "Well, if you don't mean to be won by the sirens, you are right to take precautions in time."

---

3. The Roland of the Charlemagne tales, as lover, in Ariosto's *Orlando Furioso* (1532); Rosalind's lover Orlando in Shakespeare's *As You Like It* (1599).

4. Ulysses, warned by Circe, escaped the enchanting song of the Sirens by stopping the ears of his crew with wax and having himself lashed to the mast until the ship had taken him out of range of their song (*The Odyssey*, Bk. 12).

A few days before, Lydgate would have taken no notice of these words as anything more than the Vicar's usual way of putting things. They seemed now to convey an innuendo which confirmed the impression that he had been making a fool of himself and behaving so as to be misunderstood : not, he believed, by Rosamond herself ; she, he felt sure, took everything as lightly as he intended it. She had an exquisite tact and insight in relation to all points of manners ; but the people she lived among were blunderers and busybodies. However, the mistake should go no farther. He resolved — and kept his resolution — that he would not go to Mr Vincy's except on business.

Rosamond became very unhappy. The uneasiness first stirred by her aunt's questions grew and grew till at the end of ten days that she had not seen Lydgate, it grew into terror at the blank that might possibly come—into foreboding of that ready, fatal sponge which so cheaply wipes out the hopes of mortals. The world would have a new dreariness for her, as a wilderness that a magician's spells had turned for a little while into a garden. She felt that she was beginning to know the pang of disappointed love, and that no other man could be the occasion of such delightful aerial building as she had been enjoying for the last six months. Poor Rosamond lost her appetite and felt as forlorn as Ariadne—as a charming stage Ariadne left behind with all her boxes full of costumes and no hope of a coach.[5]

There are many wonderful mixtures in the world which are all alike called love, and claim the privileges of a sublime rage which is an apology for everything (in literature and the drama). Happily Rosamond did not think of committing any desperate act : she plaited her fair hair as beautifully as usual, and kept herself proudly calm. Her most cheerful supposition was that her aunt Bulstrode had interfered in some way to hinder Lydgate's visits : everything was better than a spontaneous indifference in him. Any one who imagines ten days too short a time—not for falling into leanness, lightness, or other measurable effects of passion, but — for the whole spiritual circuit of alarmed conjecture and disappointment, is ignorant of what can go on in the elegant leisure of a young lady's mind.

On the eleventh day, however, Lydgate when leaving Stone Court was requested by Mrs Vincy to let her husband know that there was a marked change in Mr Featherstone's health, and that she wished him to come to Stone Court on that day. Now Lydgate might have called at the warehouse, or might have written a message on a leaf of his pocket-book and left it at the door. Yet these simple devices apparently did not occur to him, from which we may conclude that he had no strong objection to calling at the house at an hour when Mr Vincy was not at home, and leaving the message with Miss Vincy. A man may, from various motives, decline to give his company, but perhaps not even a sage would be gratified that nobody missed him. It would be a graceful, easy way of piecing on the new habits to the old, to have a few playful words with Rosamond about his resistance to dissipation, and his firm resolve to take long fasts even from sweet

5. The reference here is to Theseus's desertion of Ariadne after he had taken her away from Crete.

sounds. It must be confessed, also, that momentary speculations as to all the possible grounds for Mrs Bulstrode's hints had managed to get woven like slight clinging hairs into the more substantial web of his thoughts.

Miss Vincy was alone, and blushed so deeply when Lydgate came in that he felt a corresponding embarrassment, and instead of any playfulness, he began at once to speak of his reason for calling, and to beg her, almost formally, to deliver the message to her father. Rosamond who at the first moment felt as if her happiness were returning, was keenly hurt by Lydgate's manner ; her blush had departed, and she assented coldly, without adding an unnecessary word, some trivial chain-work which she had in her hands enabling her to avoid looking at Lydgate higher than his chin. In all failures, the beginning is certainly the half of the whole. After sitting two long moments while he moved his whip and could say nothing, Lydgate rose to go, and Rosamond, made nervous by her struggle between mortification and the wish not to betray it, dropped her chain as if startled, and rose too, mechanically. Lydgate instantaneously stooped to pick up the chain. When he rose he was very near to a lovely little face set on a fair long neck which he had been used to see turning about under the most perfect management of self-contented grace. But as he raised his eyes now he saw a certain helpless quivering which touched him quite newly, and made him look at Rosamond with a questioning flash. At this moment she was as natural as she had ever been when she was five years old : she felt that her tears had risen, and it was no use to try to do anything else than let them stay like water on a blue flower or let them fall over her cheeks, even as they would.

That moment of naturalness was the crystallising feather-touch : it shook flirtation into love. Remember that the ambitious man who was looking at those Forget-me-nots under the water was very warm-hearted and rash. He did not know where the chain went ; an idea had thrilled through the recesses within him which had a miraculous effect in raising the power of passionate love lying buried there in no sealed sepulchre, but under the lightest, easily pierced mould. His words were quite abrupt and awkward ; but the tone made them sound like an ardent, appealing avowal.

" What is the matter ? you are distressed. Tell me—pray."

Rosamond had never been spoken to in such tones before. I am not sure that she knew what the words were ; but she looked at Lydgate and the tears fell over her cheeks. There could have been no more complete answer than that silence, and Lydgate, forgetting everything else, completely mastered by the outrush of tenderness at the sudden belief that this sweet young creature depended on him for her joy, actually put his arms round her, folding her gently and protectingly—he was used to being gentle with the weak and suffering—and kissed each of the two large tears. This was a strange way of arriving at an understanding, but it was a short way. Rosamond was not angry, but she moved backward a little in timid happiness, and Lydgate could now sit near her and speak less incompletely. Rosamond had to make her little confession, and he poured out words of gratitude and tenderness with impulsive lavishment. In half an hour he left the house an engaged man, whose soul was not his own, but the woman's to whom he had bound himself.

He came again in the evening to speak with Mr Vincy, who, just returned from Stone Court, was feeling sure that it would not be long before he heard of Mr Featherstone's demise. The felicitous word " demise," which had seasonally occurred to him, had raised his spirits even above their usual evening pitch. The right word is always a power, and communicates its definiteness to our action. Considered as a demise, old Featherstone's death assumed a merely legal aspect, so that Mr Vincy could tap his snuff-box over it and be jovial, without even an intermittent affectation of solemnity ; and Mr Vincy hated both solemnity and affectation. Who was ever awe-struck about a testator, or sang a hymn on the title to real property ? Mr Vincy was inclined to take a jovial view of all things that evening : he even observed to Lydgate that Fred had got the family constitution after all, and would soon be as fine a fellow as ever again ; and when his approbation of Rosamond's engagement was asked for, he gave it with astonishing facility, passing at once to general remarks on the desirableness of matrimony for young men and maidens, and apparently deducing from the whole the appropriateness of a little more punch.

CHAPTER XXXII.

" They'll take suggestion as a cat laps milk."
—SHAKESPEARE : *Tempest.* [1]

THE triumphant confidence of the Mayor founded on Mr Featherstone's insistent demand that Fred and his mother should not leave him, was a feeble emotion compared with all that was agitating the breasts of the old man's blood-relations, who naturally manifested more their sense of the family tie and were more visibly numerous now that he had become bedridden. Naturally : for when "poor Peter" had occupied his arm-chair in the wainscoted parlour, no assiduous beetles for whom the cook prepares boiling water could have been less welcome on a hearth which they had reasons for preferring, than those persons whose Featherstone blood was ill-nourished, not from penuriousness on their part, but from poverty. Brother Solomon and Sister Jane were rich, and the family candour and total abstinence from false politeness with which they were always received seemed to them no argument that their brother in the solemn act of making his will would overlook the superior claims of wealth. Themselves at least he had never been unnatural enough to banish from his house, and it seemed hardly eccentric that he should have kept away Brother Jonah, Sister Martha, and the rest, who had no shadow of such claims. They knew Peter's maxim, that money was a good egg, and should be laid in a warm nest.

But Brother Jonah, Sister Martha, and all the needy exiles, held a different point of view. Probabilities are as various as the faces to be seen at will in fretwork or paperhangings : every form is there, from Jupiter to Judy, if you only look with creative inclination. To the poorer and least favoured it seemed likely that since Peter had done

1. *The Tempest*, Act II, Sc. 1, line 288.

nothing for them in his life, he would remember them at the last.
Jonah argued that men liked to make a surprise of their wills, while
Martha said that nobody need be surprised if he left the best part of
his money to those who least expected it. Also it was not to be
thought but that an own brother "lying there" with dropsy in his
legs must come to feel that blood was thicker than water, and if he
didn't alter his will, he might have money by him. At any rate some
blood-relations should be on the premises and on the watch against
those who were hardly relations at all. Such things had been known
as forged wills and disputed wills, which seemed to have the golden-
hazy advantage of somehow enabling non-legatees to live out of them.
Again, those who were no blood-relations might be caught making
away with things — and poor Peter "lying there" helpless ! Somebody should be on the watch. But in this conclusion they were at
one with Solomon and Jane ; also, some nephews, nieces, and cousins,
arguing with still greater subtilty as to what might be done by a man
able to "will away" his property and give himself large treats of oddity,
felt in a handsome sort of way that there was a family interest to be
attended to, and thought of Stone Court as a place which it would be
nothing but right for them to visit. Sister Martha, otherwise Mrs
Cranch, living with some wheeziness in the Chalky Flats, could not
undertake the journey ; but her son, as being poor Peter's own
nephew, could represent her advantageously, and watch lest his uncle
Jonah should make an unfair use of the improbable things which
seemed likely to happen. In fact there was a general sense running in
the Featherstone blood that everybody must watch everybody else,
and that it would be well for everybody else to reflect that the Almighty was watching him.

Thus Stone Court continually saw one or other blood-relation
alighting or departing, and Mary Garth had the unpleasant task of
carrying their messages to Mr Featherstone, who would see none of
them, and sent her down with the still more unpleasant task of telling
them so. As manager of the household she felt bound to ask them in
good provincial fashion to stay and eat ; but she chose to consult Mrs
Vincy on the point of extra down-stairs consumption now that Mr
Featherstone was laid up.

"Oh, my dear, you must do things handsomely where there's last
illness and a property. God knows, *I* don't grudge them every ham
in the house—only, save the best for the funeral. Have some stuffed
veal always, and a fine cheese in cut. You must expect to keep open
house in these last illnesses," said liberal Mrs Vincy, once more of
cheerful note and bright plumage.

But some of the visitors alighted and did not depart after the handsome treating to veal and ham. Brother Jonah, for example (there
are such unpleasant people in most families ; perhaps even in the
highest aristocracy there are Brobdingnag[2] specimens, gigantically in
debt and bloated at greater expense)—Brother Jonah, I say, having
come down in the world, was mainly supported by a calling which
he was modest enough not to boast of, though it was much better than
swindling either on exchange or turf, but which did not require his
presence at Brassing so long as he had a good corner to sit in and a

2. Brobdingnag: the land of giants in Jonathan Swift's *Gulliver's Travels*.

supply of food. He chose the kitchen-corner, partly because he liked it best, and partly because he did not want to sit with Solomon, concerning whom he had a strong brotherly opinion. Seated in a famous arm-chair and in his best suit, constantly within sight of good cheer, he had a comfortable consciousness of being on the premises, mingled with fleeting suggestions of Sunday and the bar at the Green Man ; and he informed Mary Garth that he should not go out of reach of his brother Peter while that poor fellow was above ground. The troublesome ones in a family are usually either the wits or the idiots. Jonah was the wit among the Featherstones, and joked with the maid-servants when they came about the hearth, but seemed to consider Miss Garth a suspicious character, and followed her with cold eyes.

Mary would have borne this one pair of eyes with comparative ease, but unfortunately there was young Cranch, who, having come all the way from the Chalky Flats to represent his mother and watch his uncle Jonah, also felt it his duty to stay and to sit chiefly in the kitchen to give his uncle company. Young Cranch was not exactly the balancing point between the wit and the idiot,—verging slightly towards the latter type, and squinting so as to leave everything in doubt about his sentiments except that they were not of a forcible character. When Mary Garth entered the kitchen and Mr Jonah Featherstone began to follow her with his cold detective eyes, young Cranch turning his head in the same direction seemed to insist on it that she should remark how he was squinting, as if he did it with design, like the gypsies when Borrow read the New Testament to them. [3] This was rather too much for poor Mary ; sometimes it made her bilious, sometimes it upset her gravity. One day that she had an opportunity she could not resist describing the kitchen scene to Fred, who would not be hindered from immediately going to see it, affecting simply to pass through. But no sooner did he face the four eyes than he had to rush through the nearest door which happened to lead to the dairy, and there under the high roof and among the pans he gave way to laughter which made a hollow resonance perfectly audible in the kitchen. He fled by another doorway, but Mr Jonah who had not before seen Fred's white complexion, long legs, and pinched delicacy of face, prepared many sarcasms in which these points of appearance were wittily combined with the lowest moral attributes.

" Why, Tom, *you* don't wear such gentlemanly trousers—*you* haven't got half such fine long legs," said Jonah to his nephew, winking at the same time, to imply that there was something more in these statements than their undeniableness. Tom looked at his legs, but left it uncertain whether he preferred his moral advantages to a more vicious length of limb and reprehensible gentility of trouser.

In the large wainscoted parlour too there were constantly pairs of eyes on the watch, and own relatives eager to be " sitters-up." Many came, lunched, and departed, but Brother Solomon and the lady who had been Jane Featherstone for twenty-five years before she was Mrs

---

3. George Borrow (1803-81), English traveler, correspondent, agent for the British and Foreign Bible Society, and author. Among his books were *The Zin-* *cali: or an Account of the Gypsies in Spain* (1841) and *The Bible in Spain* (1843).

Waule found it good to be there every day for hours, without other calculable occupation than that of observing the cunning Mary Garth (who was so deep that she could be found out in nothing) and giving occasional dry wrinkly indications of crying—as if capable of torrents in a wetter season—at the thought that they were not allowed to go into Mr Featherstone's room. For the old man's dislike of his own family seemed to get stronger as he got less able to amuse himself by saying biting things to them. Too languid to sting, he had the more venom refluent in his blood.

Not fully believing the message sent through Mary Garth, they had presented themselves together within the door of the bedroom, both in black—Mrs Waule having a white handkerchief partially unfolded in her hand—and both with faces in a sort of half-mourning purple ; while Mrs Vincy with her pink cheeks and pink ribbons flying was actually administering a cordial to their own brother, and the light-complexioned Fred, his short hair curling as might be expected in a gambler's, was lolling at his ease in a large chair.

Old Featherstone no sooner caught sight of these funereal figures appearing in spite of his orders than rage came to strengthen him more successfully than the cordial. He was propped up on a bed-rest, and always had his gold-headed stick lying by him. He seized it now and swept it backwards and forwards in as large an area as he could, apparently to ban these ugly spectres, crying in a hoarse sort of screech—

"Back, back, Mrs Waule ! Back, Solomon !"

"Oh, brother Peter," Mrs Waule began—but Solomon put his hand before her repressingly. He was a large-cheeked man, nearly seventy, with small furtive eyes, and was not only of much blander temper but thought himself much deeper than his brother Peter ; indeed not likely to be deceived in any of his fellow-men, inasmuch as they could not well be more greedy and deceitful than he suspected them of being. Even the invisible powers, he thought, were likely to be soothed by a bland parenthesis here and there—coming from a man of property, who might have been as impious as others.

"Brother Peter," he said, in a wheedling yet gravely official tone, "it's nothing but right I should speak to you about the Three Crofts and the Manganese. The Almighty knows what I've got on my mind . . ."

"Then He knows more than I want to know," said Peter, laying down his stick with a show of truce which had a threat in it too, for he reversed the stick so as to make the gold handle a club in case of closer fighting, and looked hard at Solomon's bald head.

"There's things you might repent of, Brother, for want of speaking to me," said Solomon, not advancing, however. "I could sit up with you to-night, and Jane with me, willingly, and you might take your own time to speak, or let me speak."

"Yes, I shall take my own time—you needn't offer me yours," said Peter.

"But you can't take your own time to die in, Brother," began Mrs Waule, with her usual woolly tone. "And when you lie speechless you may be tired of having strangers about you, and you may think of me and my children"—— but here her voice broke under the touching thought which she was attributing to her speechless brother; the mention of ourselves being naturally affecting.

" No, I shan't," said old Featherstone, contradictiously. " I shan't think of any of you. I've made my will, I tell you, I've made my will." Here he turned his head towards Mrs Vincy, and swallowed some more of his cordial.

" Some people would be ashamed to fill up a place belonging by rights to others," said Mrs Waule, turning her narrow eyes in the same direction.

" Oh, sister," said Solomon, with ironical softness, " you and me are not fine, and handsome, and clever enough : we must be humble and let smart people push themselves before us."

Fred's spirit could not bear this : rising and looking at Mr Feather-stone, he said, " Shall my mother and I leave the room, sir, that you may be alone with your friends ?"

" Sit down, I tell you," said old Featherstone, snappishly. " Stop where you are. Good-bye, Solomon," he added, trying to wield his stick again, but failing now that he had reversed the handle. " Good-bye, Mrs Waule. Don't you come again."

" I shall be down-stairs, Brother, whether or no," said Solomon. " I shall do *my* duty, and it remains to be seen what the Almighty will allow."

" Yes, in property going out of families," said Mrs Waule, in con-tinuation,—" and where there's steady young men to carry on. But I pity them who are not such, and I pity their mothers. Good-bye, Brother Peter."

" Remember, I'm the eldest after you, Brother, and prospered from the first, just as you did, and have got land already by the name of Featherstone," said Solomon, relying much on that reflection, as one which might be suggested in the watches of the night. " But I bid you good-bye for the present."

Their exit was hastened by their seeing old Mr Featherstone pull his wig on each side and shut his eyes with his mouth-widening grimace, as if he were determined to be deaf and blind.

None the less they came to Stone Court daily and sat below at the post of duty, sometimes carrying on a slow dialogue in an undertone in which the observation and response were so far apart, that any one hearing them might have imagined himself listening to speaking auto-mata, in some doubt whether the ingenious mechanism would really work, or wind itself up for a long time in order to stick and be silent. Solomon and Jane would have been sorry to be quick : what that led to might be seen on the other side of the wall in the person of Brother Jonah.

But their watch in the wainscoted parlour was sometimes varied by the presence of other guests from far or near. Now that Peter Featherstone was up-stairs, his property could be discussed with all that local enlightenment to be found on the spot : some rural and Middlemarch neighbours expressed much agreement with the family and sympathy with their interest against the Vincys, and feminine visitors were even moved to tears, in conversation with Mrs Waule, when they recalled the fact that they themselves had been disap-pointed in times past by codicils and marriages for spite on the part of ungrateful elderly gentlemen, who, it might have been supposed, had been spared for something better. Such conversation paused suddenly, like an organ when the bellows are let drop, if Mary Garth came into the room ; and all eyes were turned on her as a possible legatee, or one who might get access to iron chests.

But the younger men who were relatives or connections of the family, were disposed to admire her in this problematic light, as a girl who showed much conduct, and who among all the chances that were flying might turn out to be at least a moderate prize. Hence she had her share of compliments and polite attentions.

Especially from Mr Borthrop Trumbull, a distinguished bachelor and auctioneer of those parts, much concerned in the sale of land and cattle : a public character, indeed, whose name was seen on widely-distributed placards, and who might reasonably be sorry for those who did not know of him. He was second cousin to Peter Featherstone, and had been treated by him with more amenity than any other relative, being useful in matters of business ; and in that programme of his funeral which the old man had himself dictated, he had been named as a Bearer. There was no odious cupidity in Mr Borthrop Trumbull—nothing more than a sincere sense of his own merit, which, he was aware, in case of rivalry might tell against competitors ; so that if Peter Featherstone, who so far as he, Trumbull, was concerned, had behaved like as good a soul as ever breathed, should have done anything handsome by him, all he could say was, that he had never fished and fawned, but had advised him to the best of his experience, which now extended over twenty years from the time of his apprenticeship at fifteen, and was likely to yield a knowledge of no surreptitious kind. His admiration was far from being confined to himself, but was accustomed professionally as well as privately to delight in estimating things at a high rate. He was an amateur of superior phrases, and never used poor language without immediately correcting himself—which was fortunate, as he was rather loud, and given to predominate, standing or walking about frequently, pulling down his waistcoat with the air of a man who is very much of his own opinion, trimming himself rapidly with his fore-finger, and marking each new series in these movements by a busy play with his large seals. There was occasionally a little fierceness in his demeanour, but it was directed chiefly against false opinion, of which there is so much to correct in the world that a man of some reading and experience necessarily has his patience tried. He felt that the Featherstone family generally was of limited understanding, but being a man of the world and a public character, took everything as a matter of course, and even went to converse with Mr Jonah and young Cranch in the kitchen, not doubting that he had impressed the latter greatly by his leading questions concerning the Chalky Flats. If anybody had observed that Mr Borthrop Trumbull, being an auctioneer, was bound to know the nature of everything, he would have smiled and trimmed himself silently with the sense that he came pretty near that. On the whole, in an auctioneering way, he was an honourable man, not ashamed of his business, and feeling that " the celebrated Peel, now Sir Robert," if introduced to him, would not fail to recognise his importance. [4]

4. Sir Robert Peel (1750–1850) acceded to the title on the death of his father on May 3, 1830.

" I don't mind if I have a slice of that ham, and a glass of that ale, Miss Garth, if you will allow me," he said, coming into the parlour at half-past eleven, after having had the exceptional privilege of seeing old Featherstone, and standing with his back to the fire between Mrs Waule and Solomon. " It's not necessary for you to go out ;—let me ring the bell."

" Thank you," said Mary, " I have an errand."

" Well, Mr Trumbull, you're highly favoured," said Mrs Waule.

" What, seeing the old man ?" said the auctioneer, playing with his seals dispassionately. " Ah, you see he has relied on me considerably." Here he pressed his lips together, and frowned meditatively.

" Might anybody ask what their brother has been saying ?" said Solomon, in a soft tone of humility, in which he had a sense of luxurious cunning, he being a rich man and not in need of it.

" Oh yes, anybody may ask," said Mr Trumbull, with loud and good-humoured though cutting sarcasm. " Anybody may interrogate. Any one may give their remarks an interrogative turn," he continued, his sonorousness rising with his style. " This is constantly done by good speakers, even when they anticipate no answer. It is what we call a figure of speech—speech at a high figure, as one may say." The eloquent auctioneer smiled at his own ingenuity.

" I shouldn't be sorry to hear he'd remembered *you*, Mr Trumbull," said Solomon. " I never was against the deserving. It's the undeserving I'm against."

" Ah, there it is, you see, there it is," said Mr Trumbull, significantly. " It can't be denied that undeserving people have been legatees, and even residuary legatees. It is so, with testamentary dispositions." Again he pursed up his lips and frowned a little.

" Do you mean to say for certain, Mr Trumbull, that my brother has left his land away from our family ?" said Mrs Waule, on whom, as an unhopeful woman, those long words had a depressing effect.

" A man might as well turn his land into charity land at once as leave it to some people," observed Solomon, his sister's question having drawn no answer.

" What, Blue-Coat land ?" said Mrs Waule, again.[5] " Oh, Mr Trumbull, you never can mean to say that. It would be flying in the face of the Almighty that's prospered him."

While Mrs Waule was speaking, Mr Borthrop Trumbull walked away from the fireplace towards the window, patrolling with his forefinger round the inside of his stock, then along his whiskers and the curves of his hair. He now walked to Miss Garth's work-table, opened a book which lay there and read the title aloud with pompous emphasis as if he were offering it for sale :

" ' Anne of Geierstein ' (pronounced Jeersteen) ' or the Maiden of the Mist, by the Author of Waverley.' " Then turning the page, he began sonorously—" The course of four centuries has well-nigh elapsed since the series of events which are related in the following chapters took place on the Continent." He pronounced the last truly admirable word with the accent on the last syllable, not as unaware

---

5. Blue-Coat land: i .e., charity-land, from the uniform—a long dark blue coat—worn by the wards of Christ's Hospital, a famous charity school founded in London in the sixteenth century.

of vulgar usage, but feeling that this novel delivery enhanced the sonorous beauty which his reading had given to the whole.

And now the servant came in with the tray, so that the moments for answering Mrs Waule's question had gone by safely, while she and Solomon, watching Mr Trumbull's movements, were thinking that high learning interfered sadly with serious affairs. Mr Borthrop Trumbull really knew nothing about old Featherstone's will ; but he could hardly have been brought to declare any ignorance unless he had been arrested for misprision of treason.

" I shall take a mere mouthful of ham and a glass of ale," he said, reassuringly. " As a man with public business, I take a snack when I can. I will back this ham," he added, after swallowing some morsels with alarming haste, " against any ham in the three kingdoms. In my opinion it is better than the hams at Freshitt Hall— and I think I am a tolerable judge."

" Some don't like so much sugar in their hams," said Mrs Waule. " But my poor brother would always have sugar."

" If any person demands better, he is at liberty to do so ; but, God bless me, what an aroma ! I should be glad to buy-in that quality, I know. There is some gratification to a gentleman "—here Mr Trumbull's voice conveyed an emotional remonstrance—" in having this kind of ham set on his table."

He pushed aside his plate, poured out his glass of ale and drew his chair a little forward, profiting by the occasion to look at the inner side of his legs, which he stroked approvingly—Mr Trumbull having all those less frivolous airs and gestures which distinguish the predominant races of the north.

" You have an interesting work there, I see, Miss Garth," he observed, when Mary re-entered. " It is by the author of ' Waverley ' : that is Sir Walter Scott. I have bought one of his works myself—a very nice thing, a very superior publication, entitled ' Ivanhoe.' You will not get any writer to beat him in a hurry, I think—he will not, in my opinion, be speedily surpassed. I have just been reading a portion at the commencement of ' Anne of Jeersteen.' It commences well." (Things never began with Mr Borthrop Trumbull : they always commenced, both in private life and on his handbills.) " You are a reader, I see. Do you subscribe to our Middlemarch library ? "

" No," said Mary. " Mr Fred Vincy brought this book."

" I am a great bookman myself," returned Mr Trumbull. " I have no less than two hundred volumes in calf, and I flatter myself they are well selected. Also pictures by Murillo, Rubens, Teniers, Titian, Vandyck, and others. I shall be happy to lend you any work you like to mention, Miss Garth."

" I am much obliged," said Mary, hastening away again, " but I have little time for reading."

" I should say my brother has done something for *her* in his will," said Mr Solomon, in a very low undertone, when she had shut the door behind her, pointing with his head towards the absent Mary.

" His first wife was a poor match for him, though," said Mrs Waule. " She brought him nothing : and this young woman is only her niece. And very proud. And my brother has always paid her wage."

" A sensible girl though, in my opinion," said Mr Trumbull, finishing his ale and starting up with an emphatic adjustment of his waistcoat. " I have observed her when she has been mixing medicine in drops. She minds what she is doing, sir. That is a great point in a woman, and a great point for our friend up-stairs, poor dear old soul. A man whose life is of any value should think of his wife as a nurse : that is what I should do, if I married ; and I believe I have lived single long enough not to make a mistake in that line. Some men must marry to elevate themselves a little, but when I am in need of that, I hope some one will tell me so—I hope some individual will apprise me of the fact. I wish you good morning, Mrs Waule. Good morning, Mr Solomon. I trust we shall meet under less melancholy auspices."

When Mr Trumbull had departed with a fine bow, Solomon, leaning forward, observed to his sister, "You may depend, Jane, my brother has left that girl a lumping sum."

"Anybody would think so, from the way Mr Trumbull talks," said Jane. Then, after a pause, "He talks as if my daughters wasn't to be trusted to give drops."

"Auctioneers talk wild," said Solomon. "Not but what Trumbull has made money."

CHAPTER XXXIII.

"Close up his eyes and draw the curtain close ;
And let us all to meditation."
—*2 Henry VI.* [1]

THAT night after twelve o'clock Mary Garth relieved the watch in Mr Featherstone's room, and sat there alone through the small hours. She often chose this task, in which she found some pleasure, notwithstanding the old man's testiness whenever he demanded her attentions. There were intervals in which she could sit perfectly still, enjoying the outer stillness and the subdued light. The red fire with its gently audible movement seemed like a solemn existence calmly independent of the petty passions, the imbecile desires, the straining after worthless uncertainties, which were daily moving her contempt. Mary was fond of her own thoughts, and could amuse herself well sitting in twilight with her hands in her lap ; for, having early had strong reason to believe that things were not likely to be arranged for her peculiar satisfaction, she wasted no time in astonishment and annoyance at that fact. And she had already come to take life very much as a comedy in which she had a proud, nay, a generous resolution not to act the mean or treacherous part. Mary might have become cynical if she had not had parents whom she honoured, and a well of affectionate gratitude within her, which was all the fuller because she had learned to make no unreasonable claims.

She sat to-night revolving, as she was wont, the scenes of the day, her lips often curling with amusement at the oddities to which her fancy added fresh drollery : people were so ridiculous with their illusions, carrying their fool's caps unawares, thinking their own lies opaque while everybody else's were transparent, making themselves

1. Act III, Sc. 3, lines 32–33.

exceptions to everything, as if when all the world looked yellow under a lamp they alone were rosy. Yet there were some illusions under Mary's eyes which were not quite comic to her. She was secretly convinced, though she had no other grounds than her close observation of old Featherstone's nature, that in spite of his fondness for having the Vincys about him, they were as likely to be disappointed as any of the relations whom he kept at a distance. She had a good deal of disdain for Mrs Vincy's evident alarm lest she and Fred should be alone together, but it did not hinder her from thinking anxiously of the way in which Fred would be affected, if it should turn out that his uncle had left him as poor as ever. She could make a butt of Fred when he was present, but she did not enjoy his follies when he was absent.

Yet she liked her thoughts: a vigorous young mind not overbalanced by passion, finds a good in making acquaintance with life, and watches its own powers with interest. Mary had plenty of merriment within.

Her thought was not veined by any solemnity or pathos about the old man on the bed : such sentiments are easier to affect than to feel about an aged creature whose life is not visibly anything but a remnant of vices. She had always seen the most disagreeable side of Mr Featherstone : he was not proud of her, and she was only useful to him. To be anxious about a soul that is always snapping at you must be left to the saints of the earth ; and Mary was not one of them. She had never returned him a harsh word, and had waited on him faithfully : that was her utmost. Old Featherstone himself was not in the least anxious about his soul, and had declined to see Mr Tucker on the subject.

To-night he had not once snapped, and for the first hour or two he lay remarkably still, until at last Mary heard him rattling his bunch of keys against the tin box which he always kept in the bed beside him. About three o'clock he said, with remarkable distinctness, " Missy, come here ! "

Mary obeyed and found that he had already drawn the tin box from under the clothes, though he usually asked to have this done for him ; and he had selected the key. He now unlocked' the box, and, drawing from it another key, looked straight at her with eyes that seemed to have recovered all their sharpness and said, " How many of 'em are in the house ? "

" You mean of your own relations, sir," said Mary, well used to the old man's way of speech. He nodded slightly and she went on.

" Mr Jonah Featherstone and young Cranch are sleeping here."

" Oh ay, they stick, do they ? and the rest—they come every day, I'll warrant—Solomon and Jane, and all the young uns ? They come peeping, and counting and casting up ? "

" Not all of them every day. Mr Solomon and Mrs Waule are here every day, and the others come often."

The old man listened with a grimace while she spoke, and then said, relaxing his face, " The more fools they. You hearken, Missy. It's three o'clock in the morning, and I've got all my faculties as well as ever I had in my life. I know all my property, and where the money's put out, and everything. And I've made everything ready to change my mind, and do as I like at the last. Do you hear, Missy ? I've got my faculties."

" Well, sir ? " said Mary, quietly.

He now lowered his tone with an air of deeper cunning. " I've made two wills, and I'm going to burn one. Now you do as I tell you. This is the key of my iron chest, in the closet there. You push well at the side of the brass plate at the top, till it goes like a bolt : then you can put the key in the front lock and turn it. See and do that ; and take out the topmost paper—Last Will and Testament—big printed."

" No, sir," said Mary, in a firm voice, " I cannot do that."

" Not do it ? I tell you, you must," said the old man, his voice beginning to shake under the shock of this resistance.

" I cannot touch your iron chest or your will. I must refuse to do anything that might lay me open to suspicion."

" I tell you, I'm in my right mind. Shan't I do as I like at the last ? I made two wills on purpose. Take the key, I say."

" No, sir, I will not," said Mary, more resolutely still. Her repulsion was getting stronger.

" I tell you, there's no time to lose."

" I cannot help that, sir. I will not let the close of your life soil the beginning of mine. I will not touch your iron chest or your will." She moved to a little distance from the bedside.

The old man paused with a blank stare for a little while, holding the one key erect on the ring ; then with an agitated jerk he began to work with his bony left hand at emptying the tin box before him.

" Missy," he began to say, hurriedly, " look here ! take the money—the notes and gold—look here—take it—you shall have it all—do as I tell you."

He made an effort to stretch out the key towards her as far as possible, and Mary again retreated.

" I will not touch your key or your money, sir. Pray don't ask me to do it again. If you do, I must go and call your brother."

He let his hand fall, and for the first time in her life Mary saw old Peter Featherstone begin to cry childishly. She said, in as gentle a tone as she could command, " Pray put up your money, sir ; " and then went away to her seat by the fire, hoping this would help to convince him that it was useless to say more. Presently he rallied and said eagerly—

" Look here, then. Call the young chap. Call Fred Vincy."

Mary's heart began to beat more quickly. Various ideas rushed through her mind as to what the burning of a second will might imply. She had to make a difficult decision in a hurry.

" I will call him, if you will let me call Mr Jonah and others with him."

" Nobody else, I say. The young chap. I shall do as I like."

" Wait till broad daylight, sir, when every one is stirring. Or let me call Simmons now, to go and fetch the lawyer. He can be here in less than two hours."

" Lawyer ? What do I want with the lawyer ? Nobody shall know—I say, nobody shall know. I shall do as I like."

" Let me call some one else, sir," said Mary, persuasively. She did not like her position—alone with the old man, who seemed to show a strange flaring of nervous energy which enabled him to speak again and again without falling into his usual cough ; yet she desired not to push unnecessarily the contradiction which agitated him. " Let me, pray, call some one else."

" You let me alone, I say. Look here, Missy. Take the money.

You'll never have the chance again. It's pretty nigh two hundred—there's more in the box, and nobody knows how much there was. Take it and do as I tell you."

Mary, standing by the fire, saw its red light falling on the old man, propped up on his pillows and bed-rest, with his bony hand holding out the key, and the money lying on the quilt before him. She never forgot that vision of a man wanting to do as he liked at the last. But the way in which he had put the offer of the money urged her to speak with harder resolution than ever.

"It is of no use, sir. I will not do it. Put up your money. I will not touch your money. I will do anything else I can to comfort you ; but I will not touch your keys or your money."

"Anything else — anything else !" said old Featherstone, with hoarse rage, which, as if in a nightmare, tried to be loud, and yet was only just audible. "I want nothing else. You come here—you come here."

Mary approached him cautiously, knowing him too well. She saw him dropping his keys and trying to grasp his stick, while he looked at her like an aged hyena, the muscles of his face getting distorted with the effort of his hand. She paused at a safe distance.

"Let me give you some cordial," she said, quietly, "and try to compose yourself. You will perhaps go to sleep. And to-morrow by daylight you can do as you like."

He lifted the stick, in spite of her being beyond his reach, and threw it with a hard effort which was but impotence. It fell, slipping over the foot of the bed. Mary let it lie, and retreated to her chair by the fire. By-and-by she would go to him with the cordial. Fatigue would make him passive. It was getting towards the chillest moment of the morning, the fire had got low, and she could see through the chink between the moreen window-curtains the light whitened by the blind. Having put some wood on the fire and thrown a shawl over her, she sat down, hoping that Mr Featherstone might now fall asleep. If she went near him the irritation might be kept up. He had said nothing after throwing the stick, but she had seen him taking his keys again and laying his right hand on the money. He did not put it up, however, and she thought that he was dropping off to sleep.

But Mary herself began to be more agitated by the remembrance of what she had gone through, than she had been by the reality—questioning those acts of hers which had come imperatively and excluded all question in the critical moment.

Presently the dry wood sent out a flame which illuminated every crevice, and Mary saw that the old man was lying quietly with his head turned a little on one side. She went towards him with inaudible steps, and thought that his face looked strangely motionless ; but the next moment the movement of the flame communicating itself to all objects made her uncertain. The violent beating of her heart rendered her perceptions so doubtful that even when she touched him and listened for his breathing, she could not trust her conclusions. She went to the window and gently propped aside the curtain and blind, so that the still light of the sky fell on the bed.

The next moment she ran to the bell and rang it energetically. In a very little while there was no longer any doubt that Peter Featherstone was dead, with his right hand clasping the keys, and his left hand lying on the heap of notes and gold.

BOOK IV.

THREE LOVE PROBLEMS.

CHAPTER XXXIV.

" *1st Gent.* Such men as this are feathers, chips, and straws,
Carry no weight, no force.
2d Gent. But levity
Is causal too, and makes the sum of weight.
For power finds its place in lack of power;
Advance is cession, and the driven ship
May run aground because the helmsman's thought
Lacked force to balance opposites."

IT was on a morning of May that Peter Featherstone was buried. In the prosaic neighbourhood of Middlemarch, May was not always warm and sunny, and on this particular morning a chill wind was blowing the blossoms from the surrounding gardens on to the green mounds of Lowick churchyard. Swiftly-moving clouds only now and then allowed a gleam to light up any object, whether ugly or beautiful, that happened to stand within its golden shower. In the churchyard the objects were remarkably various, for there was a little country crowd waiting to see the funeral. The news had spread that it was to be a "big burying;" the old gentleman had left written directions about everything and meant to have a funeral "beyond his betters." This was true; for old Featherstone had not been a Harpagon whose passions had all been devoured by the ever-lean and ever-hungry passion of saving, and who would drive a bargain with his undertaker beforehand. [1] He loved money, but he also loved to spend it in gratifying his peculiar tastes, and perhaps he loved it best of all as a means of making others feel his power more or less uncomfortably. If any one will here contend that there must have been traits of goodness in old Featherstone, I will not presume to deny this; but I must observe that goodness is of a modest nature, easily discouraged, and when much elbowed in early life by unabashed vices, is apt to retire into extreme privacy, so that it is more easily believed in by those who construct a selfish old gentleman theoretically, than by those who form the narrower judgments based on his personal acquaintance. In any case, he had been bent on having a handsome funeral, and on having persons "bid" to it who would rather have stayed at home. He had even desired that female relatives should follow him to the grave, and poor sister Martha had taken a difficult journey for this purpose from the Chalky Flats. She and Jane would have been altogether cheered (in a tearful man-

---

1. Harpagon: a miser in Moliere's play *L'Avare* (1668).

ner) by this sign that a brother who disliked seeing them while he
was living had been prospectively fond of their presence when he
should have become a testator, if the sign had not been made equivocal by being extended to Mrs Vincy, whose expense in handsome
crape seemed to imply the most presumptuous hopes, aggravated by
a bloom of complexion which told pretty plainly that she was not a
blood-relation, but of that generally objectionable class called wife's
kin.

We are all of us imaginative in some form or other, for images are
the brood of desire ; and poor old Featherstone, who laughed much at
the way in which others cajoled themselves, did not escape the fellowship of illusion. In writing the programme for his burial he certainly
did not make clear to himself that his pleasure in the little drama of
which it formed a part was confined to anticipation. In chuckling
over the vexations he could inflict by the rigid clutch of his dead
hand, he inevitably mingled his consciousness with that livid stagnant presence, and so far as he was preoccupied with a future life, it
was with one of gratification inside his coffin. Thus old Featherstone
was imaginative, after his fashion.

However, the three mourning-coaches were filled according to the
written orders of the deceased. There were pall-bearers on horseback, with the richest scarves and hatbands, and even the under-
bearers had trappings of woe which were of a good well-priced quality.
The black procession, when dismounted, looked the larger for the
smallness of the churchyard ; the heavy human faces and the black
draperies shivering in the wind seemed to tell of a world strangely
incongruous with the lightly-dropping blossoms and the gleams of
sunshine on the daisies. The clergyman who met the procession was
Mr Cadwallader—also according to the request of Peter Featherstone,
prompted as usual by peculiar reasons. Having a contempt for
curates, whom he always called understrappers, he was resolved to
be buried by a beneficed clergyman. Mr Casaubon was out of the
question, not merely because he declined duty of this sort, but because Featherstone had an especial dislike to him as the rector of his
own parish, who had a lien on the land in the shape of tithe, also as
the deliverer of morning sermons, which the old man, being in his
pew and not at all sleepy, had been obliged to sit through with an
inward snarl. He had an objection to a parson stuck up above his head
preaching to him. But his relations with Mr Cadwallader had been of
a different kind : the trout-stream which ran through Mr Casaubon's
land took its course through Featherstone's also, so that Mr Cadwallader was a parson who had had to ask a favour instead of preaching.
Moreover, he was one of the high gentry living four miles away from
Lowick, and was thus exalted to an equal sky with the sheriff of the
county and other dignities vaguely regarded as necessary to the system of things. There would be a satisfaction in being buried by Mr
Cadwallader, whose very name offered a fine opportunity for pronouncing wrongly if you liked.

This distinction conferred on the Rector of Tipton and Freshitt was
the reason why Mrs Cadwallader made one of the group that watched
old Featherstone's funeral from an upper window of the manor. She
was not fond of visiting that house, but she liked, as she said, to see
collections of strange animals such as there would be at this funeral ;

and she had persuaded Sir James and the young Lady Chettam to drive the Rector and herself to Lowick in order that the visit might be altogether pleasant.

"I will go anywhere with you, Mrs Cadwallader," Celia had said ; "but I don't like funerals."

"Oh, my dear, when you have a clergyman in your family you must accommodate your tastes : I did that very early. When I married Humphrey I made up my mind to like sermons, and I set out by liking the end very much. That soon spread to the middle and the beginning, because I couldn't have the end without them."

"No, to be sure not," said the Dowager Lady Chettam, with stately emphasis.

The upper window from which the funeral could be well seen was in the room occupied by Mr Casaubon when he had been forbidden to work ; but he had resumed nearly his habitual style of life now in spite of warnings and prescriptions, and after politely welcoming Mrs Cadwallader had slipped again into the library to chew a cud of erudite mistake about Cush and Mizraim.

But for her visitors Dorothea too might have been shut up in the library, and would not have witnessed this scene of old Featherstone's funeral, which, aloof as it seemed to be from the tenor of her life, always afterwards came back to her at the touch of certain sensitive points in memory, just as the vision of St Peter's at Rome was inwoven with moods of despondency. Scenes which make vital changes in our neighbours' lot are but the background of our own, yet, like a particular aspect of the fields and trees, they become associated for us with the epochs of our own history, and make a part of that unity which lies in the selection of our keenest consciousness.

The dream-like association of something alien and ill-understood with the deepest secrets of her experience seemed to mirror that sense of loneliness which was due to the very ardour of Dorothea's nature. The country gentry of old time lived in a rarefied social air : dotted apart on their stations up the mountain they looked down with imperfect discrimination on the belts of thicker life below. And Dorothea was not at ease in the perspective and chilliness of that height.

"I shall not look any more," said Celia, after the train had entered the church, placing herself a little behind her husband's elbow so that she could slyly touch his coat with her cheek. "I daresay Dodo likes it : she is fond of melancholy things and ugly people."

"I am fond of knowing something about the people I live among," said Dorothea, who had been watching everything with the interest of a monk on his holiday tour. "It seems to me we know nothing of our neighbours, unless they are cottagers. One is constantly wondering what sort of lives other people lead, and how they take things. I am quite obliged to Mrs Cadwallader for coming and calling me out of the library."

"Quite right to feel obliged to me," said Mrs Cadwallader. "Your rich Lowick farmers are as curious as any buffaloes or bisons, and I daresay you don't half see them at church. They are quite different from your uncle's tenants or Sir James's—monsters—farmers without landlords—one can't tell how to class them."

"Most of these followers are not Lowick people," said Sir James ;

" I suppose they are legatees from a distance, or from Middlemarch. Lovegood tells me the old fellow has left a good deal of money as well as land."

" Think of that now ! when so many younger sons can't dine at their own expense," said Mrs Cadwallader. " Ah," turning round at the sound of the opening door, " here is Mr Brooke. I felt that we were incomplete before, and here is the explanation. You are come to see this odd funeral, of course ? "

" No, I came to look after Casaubon — to see how he goes on, you know. And to bring a little news—a little news, my dear," said Mr Brooke, nodding at Dorothea as she came towards him. " I looked into the library, and I saw Casaubon over his books. I told him it wouldn't do : I said, ' This will never do, you know : think of your wife, Casaubon.' And he promised me to come up. I didn't tell him my news : I said, he must come up."

" Ah, now they are coming out of church," Mrs Cadwallader exclaimed. " Dear me, what a wonderfully mixed set ! Mr Lydgate as doctor, I suppose. But that is really a good-looking woman, and the fair young man must be her son. Who are they, Sir James, do you know ? "

" I see Vincy, the mayor of Middlemarch ; they are probably his wife and son," said Sir James, looking interrogatively at Mr Brooke, who nodded and said—

" Yes, a very decent family—a very good fellow is Vincy ; a credit to the manufacturing interest. You have seen him at my house, you know."

" Ah, yes : one of your secret committee," said Mrs Cadwallader, provokingly.

" A coursing fellow, though," said Sir James, with a fox-hunter's disgust.

" And one of those who suck the life out of the wretched handloom weavers in Tipton and Freshitt. That is how his family look so fair and sleek," said Mrs Cadwallader. " Those dark, purple-faced people are an excellent foil. Dear me, they are like a set of jugs ! Do look at Humphrey : one might fancy him an ugly archangel towering above them in his white surplice."

" It's a solemn thing, though, a funeral," said Mr Brooke, " if you take it in that light, you know."

" But I am not taking it in that light. I can't wear my solemnity too often, else it will go to rags. It was time the old man died, and none of these people are sorry."

" How piteous ! " said Dorothea. " This funeral seems to me the most dismal thing I ever saw. It is a blot on the morning. I cannot bear to think that any one should die and leave no love behind."

She was going to say more, but she saw her husband enter and seat himself a little in the background. The difference his presence made to her was not always a happy one : she felt that he often inwardly objected to her speech.

" Positively," exclaimed Mrs Cadwallader, " there is a new face come out from behind that broad man queerer than any of them : a little round head with bulging eyes—a sort of frog-face—do look. He must be of another blood, I think."

"Let me see !" said Celia, with awakened curiosity, standing be-hind Mrs Cadwallader and leaning forward over her head. "Oh, what an odd face !" Then with a quick change to another sort of surprised expression, she added, "Why, Dodo, you never told me that Mr Ladislaw was come again !"

Dorothea felt a shock of alarm : every one noticed her sudden pale-ness as she looked up immediately at her uncle, while Mr Casaubon looked at her.

"He came with me, you know ; he is my guest—puts up with me at the Grange," said Mr Brooke, in his easiest tone, nodding at Doro-thea, as if the announcement were just what she might have expected. "And we have brought the picture at the top of the carriage. I knew you would be pleased with the surprise, Casaubon. There you are to the very life — as Aquinas, you know. Quite the right sort of thing. And you will hear young Ladislaw talk about it. He talks uncommonly well — points out this, that, and the other — knows art and everything of that kind—companionable, you know—is up with you in any track—what I've been wanting a long while."

Mr Casaubon bowed with cold politeness, mastering his irritation, but only so far as to be silent. He remembered Will's letter quite as well as Dorothea did ; he had noticed that it was not among the letters which had been reserved for him on his recovery, and secretly concluding that Dorothea had sent word to Will not to come to Lowick, he had shrunk with proud sensitiveness from ever recurring to the subject. He now inferred that she had asked her uncle to invite Will to the Grange ; and she felt it impossible at that moment to enter into any explanation.

Mrs Cadwallader's eyes, diverted from the churchyard, saw a good deal of dumb show which was not so intelligible to her as she could have desired, and could not repress the question, "Who is Mr Ladis-law ?"

"A young relative of Mr Casaubon's," said Sir James, promptly. His good-nature often made him quick and clear-seeing in personal matters, and he had divined from Dorothea's glance at her husband that there was some alarm in her mind.

"A very nice young fellow — Casaubon has done everything for him," explained Mr Brooke. "He repays your expense in him, Cas-aubon," he went on, nodding encouragingly. "I hope he will stay with me a long while and we shall make something of my documents. I have plenty of ideas and facts, you know, and I can see he is just the man to put them into shape — remembers what the right quota-tions are, *omne tulit punctum,* and that sort of thing—gives subjects a kind of turn.[2] I invited him some time ago when you were ill, Cas-aubon : Dorothea said you couldn't have anybody in the house, you know, and she asked me to write."

Poor Dorothea felt that every word of her uncle's was about as

---

2. "Omne tulit punctum qui miscuit utile dulci," Horace's *Ars Poetica;* I. C. Smart's translation reads: "He who joins the instructive with the agreeable carries off the vote" (*The Works of Horace* [New York, 1857], p. 320).

pleasant as a grain of sand in the eye to Mr Casaubon. It would be altogether unfitting now to explain that she had not wished her uncle to invite Will Ladislaw. She could not in the least make clear to herself the reasons for her husband's dislike to his presence—a dislike painfully impressed on her by the scene in the library ; but she felt the unbecomingness of saying anything that might convey a notion of it to others. Mr Casaubon, indeed, had not thoroughly represented those mixed reasons to himself ; irritated feeling with him, as with all of us, seeking rather for justification than for self-knowledge. But he wished to repress outward signs, and only Dorothea could discern the changes in her husband's face before he observed with more of dignified bending and sing-song than usual—

"You are exceedingly hospitable, my dear sir ; and I owe you acknowledgments for exercising your hospitality towards a relative of mine."

The funeral was ended now, and the churchyard was being cleared.

"Now you can see him, Mrs Cadwallader," said Celia. "He is just like a miniature of Mr Casaubon's aunt that hangs in Dorothea's boudoir—quite nice-looking."

"A very pretty sprig," said Mrs Cadwallader, dryly. "What is your nephew to be, Mr Casaubon ?"

"Pardon me, he is not my nephew. He is my cousin."

"Well, you know," interposed Mr Brooke, "he is trying his wings. He is just the sort of young fellow to rise. I should be glad to give him an opportunity. He would make a good secretary, now, like Hobbes, Milton, Swift—that sort of man." [3]

"I understand," said Mrs Cadwallader. "One who can write speeches."

"I'll fetch him in now, eh, Casaubon ?" said Mr Brooke. "He wouldn't come in till I had announced him, you know. And we'll go down and look at the picture. There you are to the life : a deep subtle sort of thinker with his forefinger on the page, while Saint Bonaventure or somebody else, rather fat and florid, is looking up at the Trinity. Everything is symbolical, you know—the higher style of art : I like that up to a certain point, but not too far—it's rather straining to keep up with, you know. But you are at home in that, Casaubon. And your painter's flesh is good—solidity, transparency, everything of that sort. I went into that a great deal at one time. However, I'll go and fetch Ladislaw."

---

3. Hobbes, Milton, and Swift were all secretaries—in one or another sense of the term—as young men.

CHAPTER XXXV.

"Non, je ne comprends pas de plus charmant plaisir
Que de voir d'héritiers une troupe affligée,
Le maintien interdit, et la mine allongée,
Lire un long testament où pales, étonnés,
On leur laisse un bonsoir avec un pied de nez.
Pour voir au naturel leur tristesse profonde,
Je reviendrais, je crois, exprès de l'autre monde."
—REGNARD: *Le Légataire Universel.* [1]

WHEN the animals entered the Ark in pairs, one may imagine that allied species made much private remark on each other, and were tempted to think that so many forms feeding on the same store of fodder were eminently superfluous, as tending to diminish the rations. (I fear the part played by the vultures on that occasion would be too painful for art to represent, those birds being disadvantageously naked about the gullet, and apparently without rites and ceremonies.)

The same sort of temptation befell the Christian Carnivora who formed Peter Featherstone's funeral procession ; most of them having their minds bent on a limited store which each would have liked to get the most of. The long-recognised blood-relations and connections by marriage made already a goodly number, which, multiplied by possibilities, presented a fine range for jealous conjecture and pathetic hopefulness. Jealousy of the Vincys had created a fellowship in hostility among all persons of the Featherstone blood, so that in the absence of any decided indication that one of themselves was to have more than the rest, the dread lest that long-legged Fred Vincy should have the land was necessarily dominant, though it left abundant feeling and leisure for vaguer jealousies, such as were entertained towards Mary Garth. Solomon found time to reflect that Jonah was undeserving, and Jonah to abuse Solomon as greedy ; Jane, the elder sister, held that Martha's children ought not to expect so much as the young Waules ; and Martha, more lax on the subject of primogeniture, was sorry to think that Jane was so "having." These nearest of kin were naturally impressed with the unreasonableness of expectations in cousins and second cousins, and used their arithmetic in reckoning the large sums that small legacies might mount to, if there were too many of them. Two cousins were present to hear the will, and a second cousin besides Mr Trumbull. This second cousin was a Middlemarch mercer of polite manners and superfluous aspirates. The two cousins were

1. "No, I cannot think of a more charming pleasure/Than seeing a grieving crowd of heirs,/Dumbfounded, their faces long,/Reading·an interminable will which pales them, shocks them,/And bids them a good evening to go with their disappointment./To see thus plainly their profound sorrow/I would come again, I believe, expressly from the other world" (Jean François Regnard, *La Légataire Universel* [1700], Act I, Sc. 3).

elderly men from Brassing, one of them conscious of claims on the score
of inconvenient expense sustained by him in presents of oysters and
other eatables to his rich cousin Peter ; the other entirely saturnine,
leaning his hands and chin on a stick, and conscious of claims based on
no narrow performance but on merit generally : both blameless citizens
of Brassing, who wished that Jonah Featherstone did not live there.
The wit of a family is usually best received among strangers.

"Why, Trumbull himself is pretty sure of five hundred—*that* you
may depend,—I shouldn't wonder if my brother promised him,"
said Solomon, musing aloud with his sisters, the evening before the
funeral.

"Dear, dear !" said poor sister Martha, whose imagination of
hundreds had been habitually narrowed to the amount of her unpaid
rent.

But in the morning all the ordinary currents of conjecture were
disturbed by the presence of a strange mourner who had plashed
among them as if from the moon. This was the stranger described
by Mrs Cadwallader as frog-faced : a man perhaps about two or three
and thirty, whose prominent eyes, thin-lipped, downward-curved
mouth, and hair sleekly brushed away from a forehead that sank
suddenly above the ridge of the eyebrows, certainly gave his face a
batrachian unchangeableness of expression. [2] Here, clearly, was a new
legatee ; else why was he bidden as a mourner ? Here were new
possibilities, raising a new uncertainty, which almost checked remark
in the mourning-coaches. We are all humiliated by the sudden discovery of a fact which has existed very comfortably and perhaps been
staring at us in private while we have been making up our world
entirely without it. No one had seen this questionable stranger
before except Mary Garth, and she knew nothing more of him than
that he had twice been to Stone Court when Mr Featherstone was
down-stairs, and had sat alone with him for several hours. She had
found an opportunity of mentioning this to her father, and perhaps
Caleb's were the only eyes, except the lawyer's, which examined the
stranger with more of inquiry than of disgust or suspicion. Caleb
Garth, having little expectation and less cupidity, was interested in
the verification of his own guesses, and the calmness with which he
half-smilingly rubbed his chin and shot intelligent glances much as
if he were valuing a tree, made a fine contrast with the alarm or scorn
visible in other faces when the unknown mourner, whose name was
understood to be Rigg, entered the wainscoted parlour and took his
seat near the door to make part of the audience when the will should
be read. Just then Mr Solomon and Mr Jonah were gone up-stairs
with the lawyer to search for the will ; and Mrs Waule, seeing two
vacant seats between herself and Mr Borthrop Trumbull, had the
spirit to move next to that great authority, who was handling his
watch-seals and trimming his outlines with a determination not to
show anything so compromising to a man of ability as wonder or
surprise.

"I suppose you know everything about what my poor brother's
done, Mr Trumbull," said Mrs Waule, in the lowest of her woolly

2. Batrachian: frog-like.

tones, while she turned her crape-shadowed bonnet towards Mr Trumbull's ear.

" My good lady, whatever was told me was told in confidence," said the auctioneer, putting his hand up to screen that secret.

" Them who've made sure of their good-luck may be disappointed yet," Mrs Waule continued, finding some relief in this communication.

" Hopes are often delusive," said Mr Trumbull, still in confidence.

" Ah !" said Mrs Waule, looking across at the Vincys, and then moving back to the side of her sister Martha.

" It's wonderful how close poor Peter was," she said, in the same undertones. " We none of us know what he might have had on his mind. I only hope and trust he wasn't a worse liver than we think of, Martha."

Poor Mrs Cranch was bulky, and, breathing asthmatically, had the additional motive for making her remarks unexceptionable and giving them a general bearing, that even her whispers were loud and liable to sudden bursts like those of a deranged barrel-organ.

" I never *was* covetious, Jane," she replied ; " but I have six children and have buried three, and I didn't marry into money. The eldest, that sits there, is but nineteen—so I leave you to guess. And stock always short, and land most awkward. But if ever I've begged and prayed, it's been to God above ; though where there's one brother a bachelor and the other childless after twice marrying—anybody might think !"

Meanwhile, Mr Vincy had glanced at the passive face of Mr Rigg, and had taken out his snuff-box and tapped it, but had put it back again unopened as an indulgence which, however clarifying to the judgment, was unsuited to the occasion. " I shouldn't wonder if Featherstone had better feelings than any of us gave him credit for," he observed, in the ear of his wife. " This funeral shows a thought about everybody : it looks well when a man wants to be followed by his friends, and if they are humble, not to be ashamed of them. I should be all the better pleased if he'd left lots of small legacies. They may be uncommonly useful to fellows in a small way."

" Everything is as handsome as could be, crape and silk and every-thing," said Mrs Vincy, contentedly.

But I am sorry to say that Fred was under some difficulty in repressing a laugh, which would have been more unsuitable than his father's snuff-box. Fred had overheard Mr Jonah suggesting some-thing about a " love-child," and with this thought in his mind, the stranger's face, which happened to be opposite him, affected him too ludicrously. Mary Garth, discerning his distress in the twitchings of his mouth, and his recourse to a cough, came cleverly to his rescue by asking him to change seats with her, so that he got into a shadowy corner. Fred was feeling as good-naturedly as possible towards every-body, including Rigg ; and having some relenting towards all these people who were less lucky than he was aware of being himself, he would not for the world have behaved amiss ; still, it was particularly easy to laugh.

But the entrance of the lawyer and the two brothers drew every one's attention.

The lawyer was Mr Standish, and he had come to Stone Court this morning believing that he knew thoroughly well who would be pleased and who disappointed before the day was over. The will he expected to read was the last of three which he had drawn up for Mr Featherstone. Mr Standish was not a man who varied his manners : he behaved with the same deep-voiced, offhand-civility to everybody, as if he saw no difference in them, and talked chiefly of the hay crop, which would be "very fine, by God !" of the last bulletins concerning the King, and of the Duke of Clarence, who was a sailor every inch of him, and just the man to rule over an island like Britain.[3]

Old Featherstone had often reflected as he sat looking at the fire that Standish would be surprised some day : it is true that if he had done as he liked at the last, and burnt the will drawn up by another lawyer, he would not have secured that minor end ; still he had had his pleasure in ruminating on it. And certainly Mr Standish was surprised, but not at all sorry ; on the contrary, he rather enjoyed the zest of a little curiosity in his own mind, which the discovery of a second will added to the prospective amazement on the part of the Featherstone family.

As to the sentiments of Solomon and Jonah, they were held in utter suspense : it seemed to them that the old will would have a certain validity, and that there might be such an interlacement of poor Peter's former and latter intentions as to create endless "lawing" before anybody came by their own—an inconvenience which would have at least the advantage of going all round. Hence the brothers showed a thoroughly neutral gravity as they re-entered with Mr Standish ; but Solomon took out his white handkerchief again with a sense that in any case there would be affecting passages, and crying at funerals, however dry, was customarily served up in lawn.

Perhaps the person who felt the most throbbing excitement at this moment was Mary Garth, in the consciousness that it was she who had virtually determined the production of this second will, which might have momentous effects on the lot of some persons present. No soul except herself knew what had passed on that final night.

" The will I hold in my hand," said Mr Standish, who, seated at the table in the middle of the room, took his time about everything, including the coughs with which he showed a disposition to clear his voice, " was drawn up by myself and executed by our deceased friend on the 9th of August 1825. But I find that there is a subsequent instrument hitherto unknown to me, bearing date the 20th of July 1826, hardly a year later than the previous one. And there is farther, I see"—Mr Standish was cautiously travelling over the document with his spectacles—" a codicil to this latter will, bearing date March the first, 1828."

" Dear, dear !" said sister Martha, not meaning to be audible, but driven to some articulation under this pressure of dates.

" I shall begin by reading the earlier will," continued Mr Standish, " since such, as appears by his not having destroyed the document, was the intention of deceased."

The preamble was felt to be rather long, and several besides Solomon shook their heads pathetically, looking on the ground : all eyes avoided meeting other eyes, and were chiefly fixed either on the spots

3. George IV died on June 26, 1830, and was succeeded by the Duke of Clarence, William IV.

in the table-cloth or on Mr Standish's bald head ; excepting Mary Garth's. When all the rest were trying to look nowhere in particular, it was safe for her to look at them. And at the sound of the first " give and bequeath " she could see all complexions changing subtly, as if some faint vibration were passing through them, save that of Mr Rigg. He sat in unaltered calm, and, in fact, the company, preoccupied with more important problems, and with the complication of listening to bequests which might or might not be revoked, had ceased to think of him. Fred blushed, and Mr Vincy found it impossible to do without his snuff-box in his hand, though he kept it closed.

The small bequests came first, and even the recollection that there was another will and that poor Peter might have thought better of it, could not quell the rising disgust and indignation. One likes to be done well by in every tense, past, present, and future. And here was Peter capable five years ago of leaving only two hundred apiece to his own brothers and sisters, and only a hundred apiece to his own nephews and nieces : the Garths were not mentioned, but Mrs Vincy and Rosamond were each to have a hundred. Mr Trumbull was to have the gold-headed cane and fifty pounds ; the other second cousins and the cousins present were each to have the like handsome sum, which, as the saturnine cousin observed, was a sort of legacy that left a man nowhere ; and there was much more of such offensive dribbling in favour of persons not present—problematical, and, it was to be feared, low connections. Altogether, reckoning hastily, here were about three thousand disposed of. Where then had Peter meant the rest of the money to go—and where the land ? and what was revoked and what not revoked—and was the revocation for better or for worse ? All emotion must be conditional, and might turn out to be the wrong thing. The men were strong enough to bear up and keep quiet under this confused suspense ; some letting their lower lip fall, others pursing it up, according to the habit of their muscles. But Jane and Martha sank under the rush of questions, and began to cry ; poor Mrs Cranch being half moved with the consolation of getting any hundreds at all without working for them, and half aware that her share was scanty ; whereas Mrs Waule's mind was entirely flooded with the sense of being an own sister and getting little, while somebody else was to have much. The general expectation now was that the " much " would fall to Fred Vincy, but the Vincys themselves were surprised when ten thousand pounds in specified investments were declared to be bequeathed to him :—was the land coming too ? Fred bit his lips : it was difficult to help smiling, and Mrs Vincy felt herself the happiest of women —possible revocation shrinking out of sight in this dazzling vision.

There was still a residue of personal property as well as the land, but the whole was left to one person, and that person was—O possibilities ! O expectations founded on the favour of " close " old gentlemen ! O endless vocatives that would still leave expression slipping helpless from the measurement of mortal folly !—that residuary legatee was Joshua Rigg, who was also sole executor, and who was to take thenceforth the name of Featherstone.

There was a rustling which seemed like a shudder running round the room. Every one stared afresh at Mr Rigg, who apparently experienced no surprise.

" A most singular testamentary disposition ! " exclaimed Mr Trumbull, preferring for once that he should be considered ignorant in the past. " But there is a second will—there is a further document. We have not yet heard the final wishes of the deceased."

Mary Garth was feeling that what they had yet to hear were not the final wishes. The second will revoked everything except the legacies to the low persons before mentioned (some alterations in these being the occasion of the codicil), and the bequest of all the land lying in Lowick parish, with all the stock and household furniture, to Joshua Rigg. The residue of the property was to be devoted to the erection and endowment of almshouses for old men, to be called Featherstone's Alms-Houses, and to be built on a piece of land near Middlemarch already bought for the purpose by the testator, he wishing—so the document declared—to please God Almighty. Nobody present had a farthing ; but Mr Trumbull had the gold-headed cane. It took some time for the company to recover the power of expression. Mary dared not look at Fred.

Mr Vincy was the first to speak—after using his snuff-box energetically—and he spoke with loud indignation. " The most unaccountable will I ever heard ! I should say he was not in his right mind when he made it. I should say this last will was void," added Mr Vincy, feeling that this expression put the thing in the true light. " Eh, Standish ?"

" Our deceased friend always knew what he was about, I think," said Mr Standish. " Everything is quite regular. Here is a letter from Clemmens of Brassing tied with the will. He drew it up. A very respectable solicitor."

" I never noticed any alienation of mind — any aberration of intellect in the late Mr Featherstone," said Borthrop Trumbull, " but I call this will eccentric. I was always willingly of service to the old soul ; and he intimated pretty plainly a sense of obligation which would show itself in his will. The gold-headed cane is farcical considered as an acknowledgment to me ; but happily I am above mercenary considerations."

" There's nothing very surprising in the matter that I can see," said Caleb Garth. " Anybody might have had more reason for wondering if the will had been what you might expect from an open-minded straightforward man. For my part, I wish there was no such thing as a will."

" That's a strange sentiment to come from a Christian man, by God ! " said the lawyer. " I should like to know how you will back that up, Garth ! "   ·

" Oh," said Caleb, leaning forward, adjusting his finger-tips with nicety and looking meditatively on the ground. It always seemed to him that words were the hardest part of " business."

But here Mr Jonah Featherstone made himself heard. " Well, he always was a fine hypocrite, was my brother Peter. But this will cuts out everything. If I'd known, a waggon and six horses shouldn't have drawn me from Brassing. I'll put a white hat and drab coat on to-morrow."

" Dear, dear," wept Mrs Cranch, " and we've been at the expense of travelling, and that poor lad sitting idle here so long ! It's the first time I ever heard my brother Peter was so wishful to please God Almighty ; but if I was to be struck helpless I must say it's hard — I can think no other."

" It'll do him no good where he's gone, that's my belief," said Solomon, with a bitterness which was remarkably genuine, though his tone could not help being sly. " Peter was a bad liver, and almshouses won't cover it, when he's had the impudence to show it at the last."

" And all the while had got his own lawful family — brothers and sisters and nephews and nieces—and has sat in church with 'em whenever he thought well to come," said Mrs Waule. " And might have left his property so respectable, to them that's never been used to extravagance or unsteadiness in no manner of way—and not so poor but what they could have saved every penny and made more of it. And me—the trouble I've been at, times and times, to come here and be sisterly—and him with things on his mind all the while that might make anybody's flesh creep. But if the Almighty's allowed it, He means to punish him for it. Brother Solomon, I shall be going, if you'll drive me."

" I've no desire to put my foot on the premises again," said Solomon. " I've got land of my own and property of my own to will away."

" It's a poor tale how luck goes in the world," said Jonah. " It never answers to have a bit of spirit in you. You'd better be a dog in the manger. But those above ground might learn a lesson. One fool's will is enough in a family."

" There's more ways than one of being a fool," said Solomon. " I shan't leave my money to be poured down the sink, and I shan't leave it to fondlings from Africay. I like Featherstones that were brewed such, and not turned Featherstones with sticking the name on 'em."

Solomon addressed these remarks in a loud aside to Mrs Waule as he rose to accompany her. Brother Jonah felt himself capable of much more stinging wit than this, but he reflected that there was no use in offending the new proprietor of Stone Court, until you were certain that he was quite without intentions of hospitality towards witty men whose name he was about to bear.

Mr Joshua Rigg, in fact, appeared to trouble himself little about any innuendoes, but showed a notable change of manner, walking coolly up to Mr Standish and putting business questions with much coolness. He had a high chirping voice and a vile accent. Fred, whom he no longer moved to laughter, thought him the lowest monster he had ever seen. But Fred was feeling rather sick. The Middlemarch mercer waited for an opportunity of engaging Mr Rigg in conversation : there was no knowing how many pairs of legs the new proprietor might require hose for, and profits were more to be relied on than legacies. Also, the mercer, as a second cousin, was dispassionate enough to feel curiosity.

Mr Vincy, after his one outburst, had remained proudly silent, though too much preoccupied with unpleasant feelings to think of moving, till he observed that his wife had gone to Fred's side and was crying silently while she held her darling's hand. He rose immediately, and turning his back on the company while he said to her in an undertone,—" Don't give way, Lucy ; don't make a fool of yourself, my dear, before these people," he added in his usual loud voice —" Go and order the phaeton, Fred ; I have no time to waste."

Mary Garth had before this been getting ready to go home with her father. She met Fred in the hall, and now for the first time had the courage to look at him. He had that withered sort of paleness which will sometimes come on young faces, and his hand was very cold when she shook it. Mary too was agitated : she was conscious that fatally, without will of her own, she had perhaps made a great difference to Fred's lot.

"Good-bye," she said, with affectionate sadness. "Be brave, Fred. I do believe you are better without the money. What was the good of it to Mr Featherstone ? "

"That's all very fine," said Fred, pettishly. "What is a fellow to do ? *I must* go into the Church now." (He knew that this would vex Mary : very well ; then she must tell him what else he could do.) "And I thought I should be able to pay your father at once and make everything right. And you have not even a hundred pounds left you. What shall you do now, Mary ? "

"Take another situation, of course, as soon as I can get one. My father has enough to do to keep the rest, without me. Good-bye."

In a very short time Stone Court was cleared of well-brewed Featherstones and other long-accustomed visitors. Another stranger had been brought to settle in the neighbourhood of Middlemarch, but in the case of Mr Rigg Featherstone there was more discontent with immediate visible consequences than speculation as to the effect which his presence might have in the future. No soul was prophetic enough to have any foreboding as to what might appear on the trail of Joshua Rigg.

And here I am naturally led to reflect on the means of elevating a low subject. Historical parallels are remarkably efficient in this way. The chief objection to them is, that the diligent narrator may lack space, or (what is often the same thing) may not be able to think of them with any degree of particularity, though he may have a philosophical confidence that if known they would be illustrative. It seems an easier and shorter way to dignity, to observe that — since there never was a true story which could not be told in parables where you might put a monkey for a margrave, and *vice versa* — whatever has been or is to be narrated by me about low people, may be ennobled by being considered a parable ; so that if any bad habits and ugly consequences are brought into view, the reader may have the relief of regarding them as not more than figuratively ungenteel, and may feel himself virtually in company with persons of some style. [4] Thus while I tell the truth about loobies, my reader's imagination need not be entirely excluded from an occupation with lords ; and the petty sums which any bankrupt of high standing would be sorry to retire upon, may be lifted to the level of high commercial transactions by the inexpensive addition of proportional ciphers. [5]

As to any provincial history in which the agents are all of high moral rank, that must be of a date long posterior to the first Reform Bill, and Peter Featherstone, you perceive, was dead and buried some months before Lord Grey came into office. [6]

---

4. Margrave: marquis.
5. Loobies: clumsy louts.
6. Charles, 2nd Earl Grey (1764–1845), became prime minister in November 1830. The first great Reform Bill was introduced in the House of Commons in 1831 by Earl Grey's Whig government. It provided for an extension of the parliamentary franchise by almost 50 percent, and redistributed seats in the House of Commons to eliminate numbers of sparsely populated "rotten boroughs" and give representation to forty-two cities and towns previously without representation, among them Manchester, Birmingham, Sheffield, and Leeds. This bill was rejected by the House of Lords on October 8, 1831; then, in 1832, under pressure of near-rebellion, the Lords accepted the Bill, and it was given the royal assent by King William IV on June 7, 1832.

CHAPTER XXXVI.

" 'Tis strange to see the humours of these men,
   These great aspiring spirits, that should be wise :
         .   .   .   .   .
For being the nature of great spirits to love
To be where they may be most eminent ;
They, rating of themselves so farre above
Us in conceit, with whom they do frequent,
Imagine how we wonder and esteeme
All that they do or say ; which makes them strive
To make our admiration more extreme,
Which they suppose they cannot, 'less they give
Notice of their extreme and highest thoughts."
                    —DANIEL : *Tragedy of Philotas.* 1

MR VINCY went home from the reading of the will with his point of
view considerably changed in relation to many subjects. He was an
open-minded man, but given to indirect modes of expressing himself :
when he was disappointed in a market for his silk braids, he swore at
the groom ; when his brother-in-law Bulstrode had vexed him, he
made cutting remarks on Methodism ; and it was now apparent that
he regarded Fred's idleness with a sudden increase of severity, by his
throwing an embroidered cap out of the smoking-room on to the hall-
floor.

"Well, sir," he observed, when that young gentleman was moving
off to bed, " I hope you've made up your mind now to go up next term
and pass your examination. I've taken my resolution, so I advise
you to lose no time in taking yours."

Fred made no answer : he was too utterly depressed. Twenty-
four hours ago he had thought that instead of needing to know what
he should do, he should by this time know that he needed to do nothing :
that he should hunt in pink, have a first-rate hunter, ride to cover on
a fine hack, and be generally respected for doing so ; moreover, that
he should be able at once to pay Mr Garth, and that Mary could no
longer have any reason for not marrying him. And all this was to
have come without study or other inconvenience, purely by the favour
of providence in the shape of an old gentleman's caprice. But now, at
the end of the twenty-four hours, all those firm expectations were upset. It was "rather hard lines " that while he was smarting under
this disappointment he should be treated as if he could have helped
it. But he went away silently and his mother pleaded for him.

"Don't be hard on the poor boy, Vincy. He'll turn out well yet,
though that wicked man has deceived him. I feel as sure as I sit here,
Fred will turn out well — else why was he brought back from the
brink of the grave ? And I call it a robbery : it was like giving him
the land, to promise it ; and what is promising, if making everybody
believe is not promising ? And you see he did leave him ten thousand pounds, and then took it away again."

"Took it away again ! " said Mr Vincy, pettishly. " I tell you the lad's an unlucky lad, Lucy. And you've always spoiled him."

"Well, Vincy, he was my first, and you made a fine fuss with him when he came. You were as proud as proud," said Mrs Vincy, easily recovering her cheerful smile.

"Who knows what babies will turn to ? I was fool enough, I daresay," said the husband—more mildly, however.

"But who has handsomer, better children than ours ? Fred is far beyond other people's sons : you may hear it in his speech, that he has kept college company. And Rosamond — where is there a girl like her ? She might stand beside any lady in the land, and only look the better for it. You see — Mr Lydgate has kept the highest company and been everywhere, and he fell in love with her at once. Not but what I could have wished Rosamond had not engaged herself. She might have met somebody on a visit who would have been a far better match ; I mean at her schoolfellow Miss Willoughby's. There are relations in that family quite as high as Mr Lydgate's."

"Damn relations !" said Mr Vincy ; " I've had enough of them. I don't want a son-in-law who has got nothing but his relations to recommend him."

"Why, my dear," said Mrs Vincy, " you seemed as pleased as could be about it. It's true, I wasn't at home ; but Rosamond told me you hadn't a word to say against the engagement. And she has begun to buy in the best linen and cambric for her underclothing."

"Not by my will," said Mr Vincy. " I shall have enough to do this year, with an idle scamp of a son, without paying for wedding-clothes. The times are as tight as can be ; everybody is being ruined ; and I don't believe Lydgate has got a farthing. I shan't give my consent to their marrying. Let 'em wait, as their elders have done before 'em."

"Rosamond will take it hard, Vincy, and you know you never could bear to cross her."

"Yes, I could. The sooner the engagement's off, the better. I don't believe he'll ever make an income, the way he goes on. He makes enemies ; that's all I hear of his making."

"But he stands very high with Mr Bulstrode, my dear. The marriage would please *him,* I should think."

"Please the deuce !" said Mr Vincy. " Bulstrode won't pay for their keep. And if Lydgate thinks I'm going to give money for them to set up housekeeping, he's mistaken, that's all. I expect I shall have to put down my horses soon. You'd better tell Rosy what I say."

This was a not infrequent procedure with Mr Vincy — to be rash in jovial assent, and on becoming subsequently conscious that he had been rash, to employ others in making the offensive retractation. However, Mrs Vincy, who never willingly opposed her husband, lost no time the next morning in letting Rosamond know what he had said. Rosamond, examining some muslin-work, listened in silence, and at the end gave a certain turn of her graceful neck, of which only long experience could teach you that it meant perfect obstinacy.

"What do you say, my dear ?" said her mother, with affectionate deference.

"Papa does not mean anything of the kind," said Rosamond, quite calmly. " He has always said that he wished me to marry the man I loved. And I shall marry Mr Lydgate. It is seven weeks now since papa gave his consent. And I hope we shall have Mrs Bretton's house."

" Well, my dear, I shall leave you to manage your papa. You always do manage everybody. But if we ever do go and get damask, Sadler's is the place—far better than Hopkins's. Mrs Bretton's is very large, though : I should love you to have such a house ; but it will take a great deal of furniture—carpeting and everything, besides plate and glass. And you hear, your papa says he will give no money. Do you think Mr Lydgate expects it ? "

" You cannot imagine that I should ask him, mamma. Of course he understands his own affairs."

" But he may have been looking for money, my dear, and we all thought of your having a pretty legacy as well as Fred ;—and now everything is so dreadful — there's no pleasure in thinking of anything, with that poor boy disappointed as he is."

" That has nothing to do with my marriage, mamma. Fred must leave off being idle. I am going up-stairs to take this work to Miss Morgan : she does the open-hemming very well. Mary Garth might do some work for me now, I should think. Her sewing is exquisite ; it is the nicest thing I know about Mary. I should so like to have all my cambric frilling double-hemmed. And it takes a long time."

Mrs Vincy's belief that Rosamond could manage her papa was well founded. Apart from his dinners and his coursing, Mr Vincy, blustering as he was, had as little of his own way as if he had been a prime minister : the force of circumstances was easily too much for him, as it is for most pleasure-loving florid men ; and the circumstance called Rosamond was particularly forcible by means of that mild persistence which, as we know, enables a white soft living substance to make its way in spite of opposing rock. Papa was not a rock : he had no other fixity than that fixity of alternating impulses sometimes called habit, and this was altogether unfavourable to his taking the only decisive line of conduct in relation to his daughter's engagement— namely, to inquire thoroughly into Lydgate's circumstances, declare his own inability to furnish money, and forbid alike either a speedy marriage or an engagement which must be too lengthy. That seems very simple and easy in the statement ; but a disagreeable resolve formed in the chill hours of the morning had as many conditions against it as the early frost, and rarely persisted under the warming influences of the day. The indirect though emphatic expression of opinion to which Mr Vincy was prone suffered much restraint in this case : Lydgate was a proud man towards whom innuendoes were obviously unsafe, and throwing his hat on the floor was out of the question. Mr Vincy was a little in awe of him, a little vain that he wanted to marry Rosamond, a little indisposed to raise a question of money in which his own position was not advantageous, a little afraid of being worsted in dialogue with a man better educated and more highly bred than himself, and a little afraid of doing what his daughter would not like. The part Mr Vincy preferred playing was that of the generous host whom nobody criticises. In the earlier half of the day there was business to hinder any formal communication of an adverse resolve ; in the later there was dinner, wine, whist, and general satisfaction. And in the meanwhile the hours were each leaving their little deposit and gradually forming the final reason for inaction, namely, that action was too late.

The accepted lover spent most of his evenings in Lowick Gate, and a love-making not at all dependent on money-advances from fathers-in-law, or prospective income from a profession, went on flourishingly under Mr Vincy's own eyes. Young love-making—that gossamer web ! Even the points it clings to—the things whence its subtle interlacings are swung—are scarcely perceptible : momentary touches of finger-tips, meetings of rays from blue and dark orbs, unfinished phrases, lightest changes of cheek and lip, faintest tremors. The web itself is made of spontaneous beliefs and indefinable joys, yearnings of one life towards another, visions of completeness, indefinite trust. And Lydgate fell to spinning that web from his inward self with wonderful rapidity, in spite of experience supposed to be finished off with the drama of Laure—in spite too of medicine and biology; for the inspection of macerated muscle or of eyes presented in a dish (like Santa Lucia's), and other incidents of scientific inquiry, are observed to be less incompatible with poetic love than a native dulness or a lively addiction to the lowest prose. As for Rosamond, she was in the water-lily's expanding wonderment at its own fuller life, and she too was spinning industriously at the mutual web. All this went on in the corner of the drawing-room where the piano stood, and subtle as it was, the light made it a sort of rainbow visible to many observers besides Mr Farebrother. The certainty that Miss Vincy and Mr Lydgate were engaged became general in Middlemarch without the aid of formal announcement.

Aunt Bulstrode was again stirred to anxiety ; but this time she addressed herself to her brother, going to the warehouse expressly to avoid Mrs Vincy's volatility. His replies were not satisfactory.

"Walter, you never mean to tell me that you have allowed all this to go on without inquiry into Mr Lydgate's prospects ?" said Mrs Bulstrode, opening her eyes with wider gravity at her brother, who was in his peevish warehouse humour. "Think of this girl brought up in luxury—in too worldly a way, I am sorry to say—what will she do on a small income ?"

"Oh, confound it, Harriet ! what can I do when men come into the town without any asking of mine ? Did you shut your house up against Lydgate ? Bulstrode has pushed him forward more than anybody. I never made any fuss about the young fellow. You should go and talk to your husband about it, not me."

"Well, really, Walter, how can Mr Bulstrode be to blame ? I am sure he did not wish for the engagement."

"Oh, if Bulstrode had not taken him by the hand, I should never have invited him."

"But you called him in to attend on Fred, and I am sure that was a mercy," said Mrs Bulstrode, losing her clue in the intricacies of the subject.

"I don't know about mercy," said Mr Vincy, testily. "I know I am worried more than I like with my family. I was a good brother to you, Harriet, before you married Bulstrode, and I must say he doesn't always show that friendly spirit towards your family that might have been expected of him." Mr Vincy was very little like a Jesuit, but no accomplished Jesuit could have turned a question more adroitly.[2] Harriet had to defend her husband instead of blaming her brother, and the conversation ended at a point as far from the beginning as some recent sparring between the brothers-in-law at a vestry meeting.

Mrs Bulstrode did not repeat her brother's complaints to her husband, but in the evening she spoke to him of Lydgate and Rosamond. He did not share her warm interest, however; and only spoke with resignation of the risks attendant on the beginning of medical practice and the desirability of prudence.

"I am sure we are bound to pray for that thoughtless girl—brought up as she has been," said Mrs Bulstrode, wishing to rouse her husband's feelings.

"Truly, my dear," said Mr Bulstrode, assentingly. "Those who are not of this world can do little else to arrest the errors of the obstinately worldly. That is what we must accustom ourselves to recognise with regard to your brother's family. I could have wished that Mr Lydgate had not entered into such a union; but my relations with him are limited to that use of his gifts for God's purposes which is taught us by the divine government under each dispensation."

Mrs Bulstrode said no more, attributing some dissatisfaction which she felt to her own want of spirituality. She believed that her husband was one of those men whose memoirs should be written when they died.

As to Lydgate himself, having been accepted, he was prepared to accept all the consequences which he believed himself to foresee with perfect clearness. Of course he must be married in a year—perhaps even in half a year. This was not what he had intended; but other schemes would not be hindered : they would simply adjust themselves anew. Marriage, of course, must be prepared for in the usual way. A house must be taken instead of the rooms he at present occupied ; and Lydgate, having heard Rosamond speak with admiration of old Mrs Bretton's house (situated in Lowick Gate), took notice when it fell vacant after the old lady's death, and immediately entered into treaty for it.

He did this in an episodic way, very much as he gave orders to his tailor for every requisite of perfect dress, without any notion of being extravagant. On the contrary, he would have despised any ostentation of expense ; his profession had familiarised him with all grades of poverty, and he cared much for those who suffered hardships. He would have behaved perfectly at a table where the sauce was served in a jug with the handle off, and he would have remembered nothing about a grand dinner except that a man was there who talked well. But it had never occurred to him that he should live in any other than what he would have called an ordinary way, with green glasses

2. The Society of Jesus is a Roman Catholic religious order whose members—Jesuits—were always alleged by English prejudice to be most cunning and clever in argument.

for hock, and excellent waiting at table. In warming himself at French social theories he had brought away no smell of scorching. We may handle even extreme opinions with impunity while our furniture, our dinner-giving, and preference for armorial bearings in our own case, link us indissolubly with the established order. And Lydgate's tendency was not towards extreme opinions : he would have liked no barefooted doctrines, being particular about his boots : he was no radical in relation to anything but medical reform and the prosecution of discovery. In the rest of practical life he walked by hereditary habit ; half from that personal pride and unreflecting egoism which I have already called commonness, and half from that *naïveté* which belonged to preoccupation with favourite ideas.

Any inward debate Lydgate had as to the consequences of this engagement which had stolen upon him, turned on the paucity of time rather than of money. Certainly, being in love and being ex. pected continually by some one who always turned out to be prettier than memory could represent her to be, did interfere with the diligent use of spare hours which might serve some "plodding fellow of a German" to make the great, imminent discovery. This was really an argument for not deferring the marriage too long, as he implied to Mr Farebrother, one day that the Vicar came to his room with some pond-products which he wanted to examine under a better microscope than his own, and, finding Lydgate's tableful of apparatus and specimens in confusion, said sarcastically,

" Eros has degenerated ; he began by introducing order and harmony, and now he brings back chaos."

" Yes, at some stages," said Lydgate, lifting his brows and smiling, while he began to arrange his microscope. " But a better order will begin after."

" Soon ?" said the Vicar.

" I hope so, really. This unsettled state of affairs uses up the time, and when one has notions in science, every moment is an opportunity. I feel sure that marriage must be the best thing for a man who wants to work steadily. He has everything at home then—no teasing with personal speculations—he can get calmness and freedom."

" You are an enviable dog," said the Vicar, " to have such a prospect—Rosamond, calmness and freedom, all to your share. Here am I with nothing but my pipe and pond animalcules. Now, are you ready ?"

Lydgate did not mention to the Vicar another reason he had for wishing to shorten the period of courtship. It was rather irritating to him, even with the wine of love in his veins, to be obliged to mingle so often with the family party at the Vincys', and to enter so much into Middlemarch gossip, protracted good cheer, whist-playing, and general futility. He had to be deferential when Mr Vincy decided questions with trenchant ignorance, especially as to those liquors which were the best inward pickle, preserving you from the effects of bad air. Mrs Vincy's openness and simplicity were quite unstreaked with suspicion as to the subtle offence she might give to the taste of her intended son-in-law ; and altogether Lydgate had to confess to himself that he was descending a little in relation to Rosamond's family. But that exquisite creature herself suffered in the same sort of way :—it was at least one delightful thought that in marrying her, he could give her a much-needed transplantation.

" Dear ! " he said to her one evening, in his gentlest tone, as he sat down by her and looked closely at her face——

But I must first say that he had found her alone in the drawing-room, where the great old-fashioned window, almost as large as the side of the room, was opened to the summer scents of the garden at the back of the house. Her father and mother were gone to a party, and the rest were all out with the butterflies.

" Dear ! your eyelids are red."

" Are they ? " said Rosamond. " I wonder why." It was not in her nature to pour forth wishes or grievances. They only came forth gracefully on solicitation.

" As if you could hide it from me ! " said Lydgate, laying his hand tenderly on both of hers. " Don't I see a tiny drop on one of the lashes ? Things trouble you, and you don't tell me. That is unloving."

" Why should I tell you what you cannot alter ? They are everyday things :—perhaps they have been a little worse lately."

" Family annoyances. Don't fear speaking. I guess them."

" Papa has been more irritable lately. Fred makes him angry, and this morning there was a fresh quarrel because Fred threatens to throw his whole education away, and do something quite beneath him. And besides——"

Rosamond hesitated, and her cheeks were gathering a slight flush. Lydgate had never seen her in trouble since the morning of their engagement, and he had never felt so passionately towards her as at this moment. He kissed the hesitating lips gently, as if to encourage them.

" I feel that papa is not quite pleased about our engagement," Rosamond continued, almost in a whisper ; " and he said last night that he should certainly speak to you and say it must be given up."

" Will you give it up ? " said Lydgate, with quick energy—almost angrily.

" I never give up anything that I choose to do," said Rosamond, recovering her calmness at the touching of this cord.

" God bless you ! " said Lydgate, kissing her again. This constancy of purpose in the right place was adorable. He went on :—

" It is too late now for your father to say that our engagement must be given up. You are of age, and I claim you as mine. If anything is done to make you unhappy,—that is a reason for hastening our marriage."

An unmistakable delight shone forth from the blue eyes that met his, and the radiance seemed to light up all his future with mild sunshine. Ideal happiness (of the kind known in the Arabian Nights, in which you are invited to step from the labour and discord of the street into a paradise where everything is given to you and nothing claimed) seemed to be an affair of a few weeks' waiting, more or less.

" Why should we defer it ? " he said, with ardent insistance. " I have taken the house now : everything else can soon be got ready— can it not ? You will not mind about new clothes. Those can be bought afterwards."

" What original notions you clever men have ! " said Rosamond, dimpling with more thorough laughter than usual at this humorous incongruity. " This is the first time I ever heard of wedding-clothes being bought after marriage."

" But you don't mean to say you would insist on my waiting months for the sake of clothes ?" said Lydgate, half thinking that Rosamond was tormenting him prettily, and half fearing that she really shrank from speedy marriage. " Remember, we are looking forward to a better sort of happiness even than this—being continually together, independent of others, and ordering our lives as we will. Come, dear, tell me how soon you can be altogether mine."

There was a serious pleading in Lydgate's tone, as if he felt that she would be injuring him by any fantastic delays. Rosamond became serious too, and slightly meditative ; in fact, she was going through many intricacies of lace-edging and hosiery and petticoat-tucking, in order to give an answer that would at least be approximative.

" Six weeks would be ample—say so, Rosamond," insisted Lydgate, releasing her hands to put his arm gently round her.

One little hand immediately went to pat her hair, while she gave her neck a meditative turn, and then said seriously—

" There would be the house-linen and the furniture to be prepared. Still, mamma could see to those while we were away."

" Yes, to be sure. We must be away a week or so."

" Oh, more than that !" said Rosamond, earnestly. She was thinking of her evening dresses for the visit to Sir Godwin Lydgate's, which she had long been secretly hoping for as a delightful employment of at least one quarter of the honeymoon, even if she deferred her introduction to the uncle who was a doctor of divinity (also a pleasing though sober kind of rank, when sustained by blood). She looked at her lover with some wondering remonstrance as she spoke, and he readily understood that she might wish to lengthen the sweet time of double solitude.

" Whatever you wish, my darling, when the day is fixed. But let us take a decided course, and put an end to any discomfort you may be suffering. Six weeks !—I am sure they would be ample."

" I could certainly hasten the work," said Rosamond. " Will you, then, mention it to papa ?—I think it would be better to write to him." She blushed and looked at him as the garden flowers look at us when we walk forth happily among them in the transcendent evening light : is there not a soul beyond utterance, half-nymph, half-child, in those delicate petals which glow and breathe about the centres of deep colour ?

He touched her ear and a little bit of neck under it with his lips, and they sat quite still for many minutes which flowed by them like a small gurgling brook with the kisses of the sun upon it. Rosamond thought that no one could be more in love than she was ; and Lydgate thought that after all his wild mistakes and absurd credulity, he had found perfect womanhood—felt as if already breathed upon by exquisite wedded affection such as would be bestowed by an accomplished creature who venerated his high musings and momentous labours and would never interfere with them ; who would create order in the home and accounts with still magic, yet keep her fingers ready to touch the lute and transform life into romance at any moment; who was instructed to the true womanly limit and not a hair's-breadth beyond—docile, therefore, and ready to carry out behests which came from beyond that limit. It was plainer now than ever that his notion of remaining much longer a bachelor had been a mistake: marriage would not be an obstruction but a furtherance. And happening the next day to accompany a patient to Brassing, he saw a dinner-service there which struck him as so exactly the right thing that he bought it at once. It saved time to do these things just when you thought of them, and Lydgate hated ugly crockery. The dinner-service in question was expensive, but that might be in the nature of dinner-services. Furnishing was necessarily expensive; but then it had to be done only once.

"It must be lovely," said Mrs Vincy, when Lydgate mentioned his purchase with some descriptive touches. "Just what Rosy ought to have. I trust in heaven it won't be broken!"

"One must hire servants who will not break things," said Lydgate. (Certainly, this was reasoning with an imperfect vision of sequences. But at that period there was no sort of reasoning which was not more or less sanctioned by men of science.)

Of course it was unnecessary to defer the mention of anything to mamma, who did not readily take views that were not cheerful, and being a happy wife herself, had hardly any feeling but pride in her daughter's marriage. But Rosamond had good reasons for suggesting to Lydgate that papa should be appealed to in writing. She prepared for the arrival of the letter by walking with her papa to the warehouse the next morning, and telling him on the way that Mr Lydgate wished to be married soon.

"Nonsense, my dear," said Mr Vincy. "What has he got to marry on? You'd much better give up the engagement. I've told you so pretty plainly before this. What have you had such an education for, if you are to go and marry a poor man? It's a cruel thing for a father to see."

"Mr Lydgate is not poor, papa. He bought Mr Peacock's practice, which, they say, is worth eight or nine hundred a-year."

"Stuff and nonsense! What's buying a practice? He might as well buy next year's swallows. It'll all slip through his fingers."

"On the contrary, papa, he will increase the practice. See how he has been called in by the Chettams and Casaubons."

"I hope he knows I shan't give anything—with this disappointment about Fred, and Parliament going to be dissolved, and machine-breaking everywhere, and an election coming on——"

"Dear papa! what can that have to do with my marriage?"

"A pretty deal to do with it! We may all be ruined for what I know—the country's in that state! Some say it's the end of the world, and be hanged if I don't think it looks like it. Anyhow, it's not a time for me to be drawing money out of my business, and I should wish Lydgate to know that."

"I am sure he expects nothing, papa. And he has such very high connections: he is sure to rise in one way or another. He is engaged in making scientific discoveries."

Mr Vincy was silent.

"I cannot give up my only prospect of happiness, papa. Mr Lydgate is a gentleman. I could never love any one who was not a perfect gentleman. You would not like me to go into a consumption, as Arabella Hawley did. And you know that I never change my mind."

Again papa was silent.

"Promise me, papa, that you will consent to what we wish. We shall never give each other up ; and you know that you have always objected to long courtships and late marriages."

There was a little more urgency of this kind, till Mr Vincy said, "Well, well, child, he must write to me first before I can answer him,"—and Rosamond was certain that she had gained her point.

Mr Vincy's answer consisted chiefly in a demand that Lydgate should insure his life—a demand immediately conceded. This was a delightfully reassuring idea supposing that Lydgate died, but in the mean time not a self-supporting idea. However, it seemed to make everything comfortable about Rosamond's marriage ; and the necessary purchases went on with much spirit. Not without prudential considerations, however. A bride (who is going to visit at a baronet's) must have a few first-rate pocket-handkerchiefs ; but beyond the absolutely necessary half-dozen, Rosamond contented herself without the very highest style of embroidery and Valenciennes. [3] Lydgate also, finding that his sum of eight hundred pounds had been considerably reduced since he had come to Middlemarch, restrained his inclination for some plate of an old pattern which was shown to him when he went into Kibble's establishment at Brassing to buy forks and spoons. He was too proud to act as if he presupposed that Mr Vincy would advance money to provide furniture ; and though, since it would not be necessary to pay for everything at once, some bills would be left standing over, he did not waste time in conjecturing how much his father-in-law would give in the form of dowry, to make payment easy. He was not going to do anything extravagant, but the requisite things must be bought, and it would be bad economy to buy them of a poor quality. All these matters were by the by. Lydgate foresaw that science and his profession were the objects he should alone pursue enthusiastically ; but he could not imagine himself pursuing them in such a home as Wrench had—the doors all open, the oil-cloth worn, the children in soiled pinafores, and lunch lingering in the form of bones, black-handled knives and willow-pattern. But Wrench had a wretched lymphatic wife who made a mummy of herself indoors in a large shawl ; and he must have altogether begun with an ill-chosen domestic apparatus.

Rosamond, however, was on her side much occupied with conjectures, though her quick imitative perception warned her against betraying them too crudely.

"I shall like so much to know your family," she said one day, when the wedding-journey was being discussed. "We might perhaps take a direction that would allow us to see them as we returned. Which of your uncles do you like best ?"

"Oh,—my uncle Godwin, I think. He is a good-natured old fellow."

"You were constantly at his house at Quallingham, when you were a boy, were you not ? I should so like to see the old spot and

---

3. A kind of lace originally made at Valenciennes, in France.

everything you were used to. Does he know you are going to be married?"

"No," said Lydgate, carelessly, turning in his chair and rubbing his hair up.

"Do send him word of it, you naughty undutiful nephew. He will perhaps ask you to take me to Quallingham; and then you could show me about the grounds, and I could imagine you there when you were a boy. Remember, you see me in my home, just as it has been since I was a child. It is not fair that I should be so ignorant of yours. But perhaps you would be a little ashamed of me. I forgot that."

Lydgate smiled at her tenderly, and really accepted the suggestion that the proud pleasure of showing so charming a bride was worth some trouble. And now he came to think of it, he would like to see the old spots with Rosamond.

"I will write to him, then. But my cousins are bores."

It seemed magnificent to Rosamond to be able to speak so slightingly of a baronet's family, and she felt much contentment in the prospect of being able to estimate them contemptuously on her own account.

But mamma was near spoiling all, a day or two later, by saying—

"I hope your uncle Sir Godwin will not look down on Rosy, Mr Lydgate. I should think he would do something handsome. A thousand or two can be nothing to a baronet."

"Mamma!" said Rosamond, blushing deeply; and Lydgate pitied her so much that he remained silent and went to the other end of the room to examine a print curiously, as if he had been absent-minded. Mamma had a little filial lecture afterwards, and was docile as usual. But Rosamond reflected that if any of those high-bred cousins who were bores, should be induced to visit Middlemarch, they would see many things in her own family which might shock them. Hence it seemed desirable that Lydgate should by-and-by get some first-rate position elsewhere than in Middlemarch; and this could hardly be difficult in the case of a man who had a titled uncle and could make discoveries. Lydgate, you perceive, had talked fervidly to Rosamond of his hopes as to the highest uses of his life, and had found it delightful to be listened to by a creature who would bring him the sweet furtherance of satisfying affection—beauty—repose— such help as our thoughts get from the summer sky and the flower-fringed meadows.

Lydgate relied much on the psychological difference between what for the sake of variety I will call goose and gander: especially on the innate submissiveness of the goose as beautifully corresponding to the strength of the gander.

CHAPTER XXXVII.

"Thrice happy she that is so well assured
Unto herself, and settled so in heart,
That neither will for better be allured
Ne fears to worse with any chance to start,
But like a steddy ship doth strongly part
The raging waves, and keeps her course aright;
Ne aught for tempest doth from it depart,
Ne aught for fairer weather's false delight.
Such self-assurance need not fear the spight
Of grudging foes ; ne favour seek of friends ;
But in the stay of her own stedfast might
Neither to one herself nor other bends.
  Most happy she that most assured doth rest,
  But he most happy who such one loves best."
                                            —SPENSER.. [1]

THE doubt hinted by Mr Vincy whether it were only the general
election or the end of the world that was coming on, now that George
the Fourth was dead, Parliament dissolved, Wellington and Peel
generally depreciated and the new King apologetic, was a feeble type
of the uncertainties in provincial opinion at that time. [2] With the
glow-worm lights of country places, how could men see which were
their own thoughts in the confusion of a Tory Ministry passing Liberal
measures, of Tory nobles and electors being anxious to return Liberals
rather than friends of the recreant Ministers, and of outcries for
remedies which seemed to have a mysteriously remote bearing on
private interest, and were made suspicious by the advocacy of disagreeable neighbours ? Buyers of the Middlemarch newspapers found
themselves in an anomalous position : during the agitation on the
Catholic Question many had given up the ' Pioneer '—which had a
motto from Charles James Fox and was in the van of progress—
because it had taken Peel's side about the Papists, and had thus
blotted its Liberalism with a toleration of Jesuitry and Baal ; but they
were ill-satisfied with the ' Trumpet,' which—since its blasts against
Rome, and in the general flaccidity of the public mind (nobody
knowing who would support whom)—had become feeble in its
blowing. [3]

It was a time, according to a noticeable article in the ' Pioneer,'
when the crying needs of the country might well counteract a reluctance to public action on the part of men whose minds had from

1. *Amoretti*, LIX.
2. The Duke of Wellington and Sir
Robert Peel both declared against parliamentary reform in 1830. In 1832,
after the Lords had thrown out the
Reform Bill and Earl Grey's government had resigned, William IV appealed
to both the Duke and Sir Robert to
form a Tory government committed to
reform. Wellington agreed, but as Peel
refused, the Tories were unable to form
a government, and Lord Grey was
recalled to office.
3. Fox (1719–1806) was an English
statesman and liberal reformer; he was
the leader of the Whigs at the end of
the eighteenth century.

long experience acquired breadth as well as concentration, decision of judgment as well as tolerance, dispassionateness as well as energy—in fact, all those qualities which in the melancholy experience of mankind have been the least disposed to share lodgings.

Mr Hackbutt, whose fluent speech was at that time floating more widely than usual, and leaving much uncertainty as to its ultimate channel, was heard to say in Mr Hawley's office that the article in question " emanated" from Brooke of Tipton, and that Brooke had secretly bought the ' Pioneer' some months ago.

" That means mischief, eh ? " said Mr Hawley. " He's got the freak of being a popular man now, after dangling about like a stray tortoise. So much the worse for him. I've had my eye on him for some time. He shall be prettily pumped upon. He's a damned bad landlord. What business has an old county man to come currying favour with a low set of dark-blue freemen ?⁴ As to his paper, I only hope he may do the writing himself. It would be worth our paying for."

" I understand he has got a very brilliant young fellow to edit it, who can write the highest style of leading article, quite equal to anything in the London papers. And he means to take very high ground on Reform."

" Let Brooke reform his rent-roll. He's a cursed old screw, and the buildings all over his estate are going to rack. I suppose this young fellow is some loose fish from London."

" His name is Ladislaw. He is said to be of foreign extraction."

" I know the sort," said Mr Hawley ; "some emissary.⁵ He'll begin with flourishing about the Rights of Man and end with murdering a wench. That's the style."

" You must concede that there are abuses, Hawley," said Mr Hackbutt, foreseeing some political disagreement with his family lawyer. " I myself should never favour immoderate views—in fact I take my stand with Huskisson—but I cannot blind myself to the consideration that the non-representation of large towns——" ⁶

" Large towns be damned ! " said Mr Hawley, impatient of exposition. " I know a little too much about Middlemarch elections. Let 'em quash every pocket borough to-morrow, and bring in every mushroom town in the kingdom—they'll only increase the expense of getting into Parliament. ⁷ I go upon facts."

Mr Hawley's disgust at the notion of the ' Pioneer' being edited by an emissary, and of Brooke becoming actively political—as if a tortoise of desultory pursuits should protrude its small head ambitiously and become rampant — was hardly equal to the annoyance felt by some members of Mr Brooke's own family. The result had oozed forth gradually, like the discovery that your neighbour has set up an unpleasant kind of manufacture which will be permanently under your nostrils without legal remedy. The ' Pioneer' had been secretly

---

4. Obscure. Perhaps Oxford (dark-blue) graduates, city or town-dwellers (freemen) whose thinking and interests would presumably be different from those of a "county" man like Brooke.
5. A spy.
6. William Huskisson (1770–1830), Tory statesman of the 1820s. Like Peel, he

favored reform only when the pressures for reform were obviously going to carry it, either by law or by force of violence.
7. Pocket-borough: a borough in which the parliamentary representation was controlled by one person or one family.

bought even before Will Ladislaw's arrival, the expected opportunity having offered itself in the readiness of the proprietor to part with a valuable property which did not pay ; and in the interval since Mr Brooke had written his invitation, those germinal ideas of making his mind tell upon the world at large which had been present in him from his younger years, but had hitherto lain in some obstruction, had been sprouting under cover.

The development was much furthered by a delight in his guest which proved greater even than he had anticipated. For it seemed that Will was not only at home in all those artistic and literary subjects which Mr Brooke had gone into at one time, but that he was strikingly ready at seizing the points of the political situation, and dealing with them in that large spirit which, aided by adequate memory, lends itself to quotation and general effectiveness of treatment.

"He seems to me a kind of Shelley, you know," Mr Brooke took an opportunity of saying, for the gratification of Mr Casaubon. " I don't mean as to anything objectionable—laxities or atheism, or anything of that kind, you know—Ladislaw's sentiments in every way I am sure are good — indeed, we were talking a great deal together last night. But he has the same sort of enthusiasm for liberty, freedom, emancipation — a fine thing under guidance — under guidance, you know. I think I shall be able to put him on the right tack ; and I am the more pleased because he is a relation of yours, Casaubon."

If the right tack implied anything more precise than the rest of Mr Brooke's speech, Mr Casaubon silently hoped that it referred to some occupation at a great distance from Lowick. He had disliked Will while he helped him, but he had begun to dislike him still more now that Will had declined his help. That is the way with us when we have any uneasy jealousy in our disposition : if our talents are chiefly of the burrowing kind, our honey-sipping cousin (whom we have grave reasons for objecting to) is likely to have a secret contempt for us, and any one who admires him passes an oblique criticism on ourselves. Having the scruples of rectitude in our souls, we are above the meanness of injuring him — rather we meet all his claims on us by active benefits ; and the drawing of cheques for him, being a superiority which he must recognise, gives our bitterness a milder infusion. Now Mr Casaubon had been deprived of that superiority (as anything more than a remembrance) in a sudden, capricious manner. His antipathy to Will did not spring from the common jealousy of a winter-worn husband : it was something deeper, bred by his lifelong claims and discontents ; but Dorothea, now that she was present— Dorothea, as a young wife who herself had shown an offensive capability of criticism, necessarily gave concentration to the uneasiness which had before been vague.

Will Ladislaw on his side felt that his dislike was flourishing at the expense of his gratitude, and spent much inward discourse in justifying the dislike. Casaubon hated him — he knew that very well ; on his first entrance he could discern a bitterness in the mouth and a venom in the glance which would almost justify declaring war in spite of past benefits. He was much obliged to Casaubon in the past, but really the act of marrying this wife was a set-off against the obligation. It was a question whether gratitude which refers to what is done for one's self ought not to give way to indignation at what is done against another. And Casaubon had done a wrong to Dorothea in marrying her. A man was bound to know himself better than that, and if he chose to grow grey crunching bones in a cavern, he had no business to be luring a girl into his companionship. " It is the most horrible of virgin-sacrifices," said Will ; and he painted to himself what were Dorothea's inward sorrows as if he had been writing a choric wail. But he would never lose sight of her : he would watch over her—if he gave up everything else in life he would watch over her, and she should know that she had one slave in the world. Will had—to use Sir Thomas Browne's phrase—a "passionate prodigality" of statement both to himself and others.[8] The simple truth was that nothing then invited him so strongly as the presence of Dorothea.

Invitations of the formal kind had been wanting, however, for Will had never been asked to go to Lowick. Mr Brooke, indeed, confident of doing everything agreeable which Casaubon, poor fellow, was too much absorbed to think of, had arranged to bring Ladislaw to Lowick several times (not neglecting meanwhile to introduce him elsewhere on every opportunity as " a young relative of Casaubon's "). And though Will had not seen Dorothea alone, their interviews had been enough to restore her former sense of young companionship with one who was cleverer than herself, yet seemed ready to be swayed by her. Poor Dorothea before her marriage had never found much room in other minds for what she cared most to say ; and she had not, as we know, enjoyed her husband's superior instruction so much as she had expected. If she spoke with any keenness of interest to Mr Casaubon, he heard her with an air of patience as if she had given a quotation from the Delectus familiar to him from his tender years, and sometimes mentioned curtly what ancient sects or personages had held similar ideas, as if there were too much of that sort in stock already ; at other times he would inform her that she was mistaken, and reassert what her remark had questioned.[9]

But Will Ladislaw always seemed to see more in what she said than she herself saw. Dorothea had little vanity, but she had the ardent woman's need to rule beneficently by making the joy of another soul. Hence the mere chance of seeing Will occasionally was like a lunette opened in the wall of her prison, giving her a glimpse of the sunny air ; and this pleasure began to nullify her original alarm at what her husband might think about the introduction of Will as her uncle's guest. On this subject Mr Casaubon had remained dumb.

But Will wanted to talk with Dorothea alone, and was impatient of slow circumstance. However slight the terrestrial intercourse between Dante and Beatrice or Petrarch and Laura, time changes the proportion of things, and in later days it is preferable to have fewer sonnets and more conversation. Necessity excused stratagem, but stratagem was limited by the dread of offending Dorothea. He found out at last that he wanted to take a particular sketch at Lowick ; and one morning when Mr Brooke had to drive along the Lowick road on

8. Sir Thomas Browne (1605–82), English physician and author. "To burn the bones of the King of *Edom* for Lyme, seems no irrational ferity; But to drink of the ashes of dead relations, a passionate prodigality" (*Urn Burial*, Ch. 3 [1658]).

9. Delectus: a selection of passages from Latin and Greek authors for translation: e.g., F. S. J. Valpy's *Second Greek Delectus* (1828).

his way to the county town, Will asked to be set down with his sketch-book and camp-stool at Lowick, and without announcing himself at the Manor settled himself to sketch in a position where he must see Dorothea if she came out to walk — and he knew that she usually walked an hour in the morning.

But the stratagem was defeated by the weather. Clouds gathered with treacherous quickness, the rain came down, and Will was obliged to take shelter in the house. He intended, on the strength of relationship, to go into the drawing-room and wait there without being announced ; and seeing his old acquaintance the butler in the hall, he said, "Don't mention that I am here, Pratt; I will wait till luncheon ; I know Mr Casaubon does not like to be disturbed when he is in the library."

" Master is out, sir ; there's only Mrs Casaubon in the library. I'd better tell her you're here, sir," said Pratt, a red - cheeked man given to lively converse with Tantripp, and often agreeing with her that it must be dull for Madam.

" Oh, very well ; this confounded rain has hindered me from sketching," said Will, feeling so happy that he affected indifference with delightful ease.

In another minute he was in the library, and Dorothea was meeting him with her sweet unconstrained smile.

" Mr Casaubon has gone to the Archdeacon's," she said, at once. " I don't know whether he will be at home again long before dinner. He was uncertain how long he should be. Did you want to say anything particular to him ? "

" No ; I came to sketch, but the rain drove me in. Else I would not have disturbed you yet. I supposed that Mr Casaubon was here, and I know he dislikes interruption at this hour."

" I am indebted to the rain, then. I am so glad to see you." Dorothea uttered these common words with the simple sincerity of an unhappy child, visited at school.

" I really came for the chance of seeing you alone," said Will, mysteriously forced to be just as simple as she was. He could not stay to ask himself why not ? " I wanted to talk about things, as we did in Rome. It always makes a difference when other people are present."

" Yes," said Dorothea, in her clear full tone of assent. " Sit down." She seated herself on a dark ottoman with the brown books behind her, looking in her plain dress of some thin woollen-white material, without a single ornament on her besides her wedding-ring, as if she were under a vow to be different from all other women ; and Will sat down opposite her at two yards' distance, the light falling on his bright curls and delicate but rather petulant profile, with its defiant curves of lip and chin. Each looked at the other as if they had been two flowers which had opened then and there. Dorothea for the moment forgot her husband's mysterious irritation against Will : it seemed fresh water at her thirsty lips to speak without fear to the one person whom she had found receptive ; for in looking backward through sadness she exaggerated a past solace.

" I have often thought that I should like to talk to you again," she said, immediately. " It seems strange to me how many things I said to you."

" I remember them all," said Will, with the unspeakable content in his soul of feeling that he was in the presence of a creature worthy to be perfectly loved. I think his own feelings at that moment were perfect, for we mortals have our divine moments, when love is satisfied in the completeness of the beloved object.

"I have tried to learn a great deal since we were in Rome," said Dorothea. "I can read Latin a little, and I am beginning to understand just a little Greek. I can help Mr Casaubon better now. I can find out references for him and save his eyes in many ways. But it is very difficult to be learned; it seems as if people were worn out on the way to great thoughts, and can never enjoy them because they are too tired."

"If a man has a capacity for great thoughts, he is likely to overtake them before he is decrepit," said Will, with irrepressible quickness. But through certain sensibilities Dorothea was as quick as he, and seeing her face change, he added, immediately, "But it is quite true that the best minds have been sometimes overstrained in working out their ideas."

"You correct me," said Dorothea. "I expressed myself ill. I should have said that those who have great thoughts get too much worn in working them out. I used to feel about that, even when I was a little girl; and it always seemed to me that the use I should like to make of my life would be to help some one who did great works, so that his burthen might be lighter."

Dorothea was led on to this bit of autobiography without any sense of making a revelation. But she had never before said anything to Will which threw so strong a light on her marriage. He did not shrug his shoulders; and for want of that muscular outlet he thought the more irritably of beautiful lips kissing holy skulls and other emptinesses ecclesiastically enshrined. Also he had to take care that his speech should not betray that thought.

"But you may easily carry the help too far," he said, "and get over-wrought yourself. Are you not too much shut up? You already look paler. It would be better for Mr Casaubon to have a secretary; he could easily get a man who would do half his work for him. It would save him more effectually, and you need only help him in lighter ways."

"How can you think of that?" said Dorothea, in a tone of earnest remonstrance. "I should have no happiness if I did not help him in his work. What could I do? There is no good to be done in Lowick. The only thing I desire is to help him more. And he objects to a secretary: please not to mention that again."

"Certainly not, now I know your feeling. But I have heard both Mr Brooke and Sir James Chettam express the same wish."

"Yes," said Dorothea, "but they don't understand—they want me to be a great deal on horseback, and have the garden altered and new conservatories, to fill up my days. I thought you could understand that one's mind has other wants," she added, rather impatiently—"besides, Mr Casaubon cannot bear to hear of a secretary."

"My mistake is excusable," said Will. "In old days I used to hear Mr Casaubon speak as if he looked forward to having a secretary. Indeed he held out the prospect of that office to me. But I turned out to be—not good enough for it."

Dorothea was trying to extract out of this an excuse for her husband's evident repulsion, as she said, with a playful smile, "You were not a steady worker enough."

"No," said Will, shaking his head backward somewhat after the manner of a spirited horse. And then, the old irritable demon prompting him to give another good pinch at the moth-wings of poor Mr Casaubon's glory, he went on, "And I have seen since that Mr Casaubon does not like any one to overlook his work and know thoroughly what he is doing. He is too doubtful—too uncertain of himself. I may not be good for much, but he dislikes me because I disagree with him."

Will was not without his intentions to be always generous, but our tongues are little triggers which have usually been pulled before general intentions can be brought to bear. And it was too intolerable that Casaubon's dislike of him should not be fairly accounted for to Dorothea. Yet when he had spoken he was rather uneasy as to the effect on her.

But Dorothea was strangely quiet—not immediately indignant, as she had been on a like occasion in Rome. And the cause lay deep. She was no longer struggling against the perception of facts, but adjusting herself to their clearest perception; and now when she looked steadily at her husband's failure, still more at his possible consciousness of failure, she seemed to be looking along the one track where duty became tenderness. Will's want of reticence might have been met with more severity, if he had not already been recommended to her mercy by her husband's dislike, which must seem hard to her till she saw better reason for it.

She did not answer at once, but after looking down ruminatingly she said, with some earnestness, "Mr Casaubon must have overcome his dislike of you so far as his actions were concerned : and that is admirable."

"Yes ; he has shown a sense of justice in family matters. It was an abominable thing that my grandmother should have been disinherited because she made what they called a *mésalliance*, though there was nothing to be said against her husband except that he was a Polish refugee who gave lessons for his bread."

"I wish I knew all about her !" said Dorothea. "I wonder how she bore the change from wealth to poverty : I wonder whether she was happy with her husband ! Do you know much about them ?"

"No: only that my grandfather was a patriot—a bright fellow—could speak many languages—musical—got his bread by teaching all sorts of things. They both died rather early. And I never knew much of my father, beyond what my mother told me ; but he inherited the musical talents. I remember his slow walk and his long thin hands ; and one day remains with me when he was lying ill, and I was very hungry, and had only a little bit of bread."

"Ah, what a different life from mine !" said Dorothea, with keen interest, clasping her hands on her lap. "I have always had too much of everything. But tell me how it was—Mr Casaubon could not have known about you then."

"No ; but my father had made himself known to Mr Casaubon, and that was my last hungry day. My father died soon after, and my mother and I were well taken care of. Mr Casaubon always expressly recognised it as his duty to take care of us because of the harsh injustice which had been shown to his mother's sister. But now I am telling you what is not new to you."

In his inmost soul Will was conscious of wishing to tell Dorothea what was rather new even in his own construction of things—namely, that Mr Casaubon had never done more than pay a debt towards him. Will was much too good a fellow to be easy under the sense of being ungrateful. And when gratitude has become a matter of reasoning there are many ways of escaping from its bonds.

" No," answered Dorothea ; " Mr Casaubon has always avoided dwelling on his own honourable actions." She did not feel that her husband's conduct was depreciated ; but this notion of what justice had required in his relations with Will Ladislaw took strong hold on her mind. After a moment's pause, she added, " He had never told me that he supported your mother. Is she still living ? "

" No ; she died by an accident—a fall—four years ago. It is curious that my mother, too, ran away from her family, but not for the sake of her husband. She never would tell me anything about her family, except that she forsook them to get her own living—went on the stage, in fact. She was a dark-eyed creature, with crisp ringlets, and never seemed to be getting old. You see I come of rebellious blood on both sides," Will ended, smiling brightly at Dorothea, while she was still looking with serious intentness before her, like a child seeing a drama for the first time.

But her face, too, broke into a smile as she said, " That is your apology, I suppose, for having yourself been rather rebellious ; I mean, to Mr Casaubon's wishes. You must remember that you have not done what he thought best for you. And if he dislikes you— you were speaking of dislike a little while ago—but I should rather say, if he has shown any painful feelings towards you, you must consider how sensitive he has become from the wearing effect of study. Perhaps," she continued, getting into a pleading tone, " my uncle has not told you how serious Mr Casaubon's illness was. It would be very petty of us who are well and can bear things, to think much of small offences from those who carry a weight of trial."

" You teach me better," said Will. " I will never grumble on that subject again." There was a gentleness in his tone which came from the unutterable contentment of perceiving—what Dorothea was hardly conscious of—that she was travelling into the remoteness of pure pity and loyalty towards her husband. Will was ready to adore her pity and loyalty, if she would associate himself with her in manifesting them. " I have really sometimes been a perverse fellow," he went on, " but I will never again, if I can help it, do or say what you would disapprove."

" That is very good of you," said Dorothea, with another open smile. " I shall have a little kingdom then, where I shall give laws. But you will soon go away, out of my rule, I imagine. You will soon be tired of staying at the Grange."

" That is a point I wanted to mention to you—one of the reasons why I wished to speak to you alone. Mr Brooke proposes that I should stay in this neighbourhood. He has bought one of the Middlemarch newspapers, and he wishes me to conduct that, and also to help him in other ways."

" Would not that be a sacrifice of higher prospects for you ? " said Dorothea.

" Perhaps ; but I have always been blamed for thinking of prospects, and not settling to anything. And here is something offered to me. If you would not like me to accept it, I will give it up."

Otherwise I would rather stay in this part of the country than go away. I belong to nobody anywhere else."

"I should like you to stay very much," said Dorothea, at once, as simply and readily as she had spoken at Rome. There was not the shadow of a reason in her mind at the moment why she should not say so.

"Then I *will* stay," said Ladislaw, shaking his head backward, rising and going towards the window, as if to see whether the rain had ceased.

But the next moment, Dorothea, according to a habit which was getting continually stronger, began to reflect that her husband felt differently from herself, and she coloured deeply under the double embarrassment of having expressed what might be in opposition to her husband's feeling, and of having to suggest this opposition to Will. His face was not turned towards her, and this made it easier to say—

"But my opinion is of little consequence on such a subject. I think you should be guided by Mr Casaubon. I spoke without thinking of anything else than my own feeling, which has nothing to do with the real question. But it now occurs to me—perhaps Mr Casaubon might see that the proposal was not wise. Can you not wait now and mention it to him?"

"I can't wait to-day," said Will, inwardly scared by the possibility that Mr Casaubon would enter. "The rain is quite over now. I told Mr Brooke not to call for me : I would rather walk the five miles. I shall strike across Halsell Common, and see the gleams on the wet grass. I like that."

He approached her to shake hands quite hurriedly, longing but not daring to say, "Don't mention the subject to Mr Casaubon." No, he dared not, could not say it. To ask her to be less simple and direct would be like breathing on the crystal that you want to see the light through. And there was always the other great dread—of himself becoming dimmed and for ever ray-shorn in her eyes.

"I wish you could have stayed," said Dorothea, with a touch of mournfulness, as she rose and put out her hand. She also had her thought which she did not like to express :—Will certainly ought to lose no time in consulting Mr Casaubon's wishes, but for her to urge this might seem an undue dictation.

So they only said "Good-bye," and Will quitted the house, striking across the fields so as not to run any risk of encountering Mr Casaubon's carriage, which, however, did not appear at the gate until four o'clock. That was an unpropitious hour for coming home : it was too early to gain the moral support under *ennui* of dressing his person for dinner, and too late to undress his mind of the day's frivolous ceremony and affairs, so as to be prepared for a good plunge into the serious business of study. On such occasions he usually threw himself into an easy-chair in the library, and allowed Dorothea to read the London papers to him, closing his eyes the while. To-day, however, he declined that relief, observing that he had already had too many public details urged upon him ; but he spoke more cheerfully than usual, when Dorothea asked about his fatigue, and added with that air of formal effort which never forsook him even when he spoke without his waistcoat and cravat—

"I have had the gratification of meeting my former acquaintance,

Dr Spanning, to-day, and of being praised by one who is himself a worthy recipient of praise. He spoke very handsomely of my late tractate on the Egyptian Mysteries,—using, in fact, terms which it would not become me to repeat." In uttering the last clause, Mr Casaubon leaned over the elbow of his chair, and swayed his head up and down, apparently as a muscular outlet instead of that recapitulation which would not have been becoming.

" I am very glad you have had that pleasure," said Dorothea, delighted to see her husband less weary than usual at this hour. " Before you came I had been regretting that you happened to be out to-day."

" Why so, my dear ? " said Mr Casaubon, throwing himself backward again.

" Because Mr Ladislaw has been here ; and he has mentioned a proposal of my uncle's which I should like to know your opinion of." Her husband she felt was really concerned in this question. Even with her ignorance of the world she had a vague impression that the position offered to Will was out of keeping with his family connections, and certainly Mr Casaubon had a claim to be consulted. He did not speak, but merely bowed.

" Dear uncle, you know, has many projects. It appears that he has bought one of the Middlemarch newspapers, and he has asked Mr Ladislaw to stay in this neighbourhood and conduct the paper for him, besides helping him in other ways."

Dorothea looked at her husband while she spoke, but he had at first blinked and finally closed his eyes, as if to save them ; while his lips became more tense. " What is your opinion ? " she added, rather timidly, after a slight pause.

" Did Mr Ladislaw come on purpose to ask my opinion ? " said Mr Casaubon, opening his eyes narrowly with a knife-edged look at Dorothea. She was really uncomfortable on the point he inquired about, but she only became a little more serious, and her eyes did not swerve.

" No," she answered, immediately, " he did not say that he came to ask your opinion. But when he mentioned the proposal, he of course expected me to tell you of it."

Mr Casaubon was silent.

" I feared that you might feel some objection. But certainly a young man with so much talent might be very useful to my uncle— might help him to do good in a better way. And Mr Ladislaw wishes to have some fixed occupation. He has been blamed, he says, for not seeking something of that kind, and he would like to stay in this neighbourhood because no one cares for him elsewhere."

Dorothea felt that this was a consideration to soften her husband. However, he did not speak, and she presently recurred to Dr Spanning and the Archdeacon's breakfast. But there was no longer sunshine on these subjects.

The next morning, without Dorothea's knowledge, Mr Casaubon despatched the following letter, beginning " Dear Mr Ladislaw" (he had always before addressed him as " Will") :—

" Mrs Casaubon informs me that a proposal has been made to you, and (according to an inference by no means stretched) has on your part been in some degree entertained, which involves your residence in this neighbourhood in a capacity which I am justified in saying touches my own position in such a way as renders it not only natural and warrantable in me when that effect is viewed under the influence of legitimate feeling, but incumbent on me when the same effect is considered in the light of my responsibilities, to state at once that your acceptance of the proposal above indicated would be highly offensive to me. That I have some claim to the exercise of a veto here, would not, I believe, be denied by any reasonable person cognisant of the relations between us : relations which, though thrown into the past by your recent procedure, are not thereby annulled in their character of determining antecedents. I will not here make reflections on any person's judgment. It is enough for me to point out to yourself that there are certain social fitnesses and proprieties which should hinder a somewhat near relative of mine from becoming in anywise conspicuous in this vicinity in a status not only much beneath my own, but associated at best with the sciolism of literary or political adventurers. At any rate, the contrary issue must exclude you from further reception at my house.—Yours faithfully,

"EDWARD CASAUBON."

Meanwhile Dorothea's mind was innocently at work towards the further embitterment of her husband ; dwelling, with a sympathy that grew to agitation, on what Will had told her about his parents and grand-parents. Any private hours in her day were usually spent in her blue-green boudoir, and she had come to be very fond of its pallid quaintness. Nothing had been outwardly altered there ; but while the summer had gradually advanced over the western fields beyond the avenue of elms, the bare room had gathered within it those memories of an inward life which fill the air as with a cloud of good or bad angels, the invisible yet active forms of our spiritual triumphs or our spiritual falls. She had been so used to struggle for and to find resolve in looking along the avenue towards the arch of western light that the vision itself had gained a communicating power. Even the pale stag seemed to have reminding glances and to mean mutely, "Yes, we know." And the group of delicately-touched miniatures had made an audience as of beings no longer disturbed about their own earthly lot, but still humanly interested. Especially the mysterious "Aunt Julia" about whom Dorothea had never found it easy to question her husband.

And now, since her conversation with Will, many fresh images had gathered round that Aunt Julia who was Will's grandmother ; the presence of that delicate miniature, so like a living face that she knew, helping to concentrate her feelings. What a wrong, to cut off the girl from the family protection and inheritance only because she had chosen a man who was poor ! Dorothea, early troubling her elders with questions about the facts around her, had wrought herself into some independent clearness as to the historical, political reasons why eldest sons had superior rights, and why land should be entailed : those reasons, impressing her with a certain awe, might be weightier than she knew, but here was a question of ties which left them unin-fringed. Here was a daughter whose child—even according to the ordinary aping of aristocratic institutions by people who are no more aristocratic than retired grocers, and who have no more land to "keep together" than a lawn and a paddock—would have a prior claim.

Was inheritance a question of liking or of responsibility? All the energy of Dorothea's nature went on the side of responsibility—the fulfilment of claims founded on our own deeds, such as marriage and parentage.

It was true, she said to herself, that Mr Casaubon had a debt to the Ladislaws—that he had to pay back what the Ladislaws had been wronged of. And now she began to think of her husband's will, which had been made at the time of their marriage, leaving the bulk of his property to her, with proviso in case of her having children. That ought to be altered; and no time ought to be lost. This very question which had just arisen about Will Ladislaw's occupation, was the occasion for placing things on a new, right footing. Her husband, she felt sure, according to all his previous conduct, would be ready to take the just view, if she proposed it—she, in whose interest an unfair concentration of the property had been urged. His sense of right had surmounted and would continue to surmount anything that might be called antipathy. She suspected that her uncle's scheme was disapproved by Mr Casaubon, and this made it seem all the more opportune that a fresh understanding should be begun, so that instead of Will's starting penniless and accepting the first function that offered itself, he should find himself in possession of a rightful income which should be paid by her husband during his life, and, by an immediate alteration of the will, should be secured at his death. The vision of all this as what ought to be done seemed to Dorothea like a sudden letting in of daylight, waking her from her previous stupidity and incurious self-absorbed ignorance about her husband's relation to others. Will Ladislaw had refused Mr Casaubon's future aid on a ground that no longer appeared right to her; and Mr Casaubon had never himself seen fully what was the claim upon him. " But he will! " said Dorothea. " The great strength of his character lies here. And what are we doing with our money? We make no use of half of our income. My own money buys me nothing but an uneasy conscience."

There was a peculiar fascination for Dorothea in this division of property intended for herself, and always regarded by her as excessive. She was blind, you see, to many things obvious to others—likely to tread in the wrong places, as Celia had warned her; yet her blindness to whatever did not lie in her own pure purpose carried her safely by the side of precipices where vision would have been perilous with fear.

The thoughts which had gathered vividness in the solitude of her boudoir occupied her incessantly through the day on which Mr Casaubon had sent his letter to Will. Everything seemed hindrance to her till she could find an opportunity of opening her heart to her husband. To his preoccupied mind all subjects were to be approached gently, and she had never since his illness lost from her consciousness the dread of agitating him. But when young ardour is set brooding over the conception of a prompt deed, the deed itself seems to start forth with independent life, mastering ideal obstacles. The day passed in a sombre fashion, not unusual, though Mr Casaubon was perhaps unusually silent; but there were hours of the night which might be counted on as opportunities of conversation; for Dorothea, when aware of her husband's sleeplessness, had established the habit of rising, lighting a candle, and reading him to sleep again. And this night she was from the beginning sleepless, excited by resolves. He slept as usual for a few hours, but she had risen softly and had sat in the darkness for nearly an hour before he said—

"Dorothea, since you are up, will you light a candle?"

"Do you feel ill, dear?" was her first question, as she obeyed him.

"No, not at all; but I shall be obliged, since you are up, if you will read me a few pages of Lowth." [1]

"May I talk to you a little, instead?" said Dorothea.

"Certainly."

"I have been thinking about money all day—that I have always had too much, and especially the prospect of too much."

"These, my dear Dorothea, are providential arrangements."

"But if one has too much in consequence of others being wronged, it seems to me that the divine voice which tells us to set that wrong right must be obeyed."

"What, my love, is the bearing of your remark?"

"That you have been too liberal in arrangements for me—I mean, with regard to property; and that makes me unhappy."

"How so? I have none but comparatively distant connections."

"I have been led to think about your aunt Julia, and how she was left in poverty only because she married a poor man, an act which was not disgraceful, since he was not unworthy. It was on that ground, I know, that you educated Mr Ladislaw and provided for his mother."

Dorothea waited a few moments for some answer that would help her onward. None came, and her next words seemed the more forcible to her, falling clear upon the dark silence.

"But surely we should regard his claim as a much greater one, even to the half of that property which I know that you have destined for me. And I think he ought at once to be provided for on that understanding. It is not right that he should be in the dependence of poverty while we are rich. And if there is any objection to the proposal he mentioned, the giving him his true place and his true share would set aside any motive for his accepting it."

"Mr Ladislaw has probably been speaking to you on this subject?" said Mr Casaubon, with a certain biting quickness not habitual to him.

"Indeed, no!" said Dorothea, earnestly. "How can you imagine it, since he has so lately declined everything from you? I fear you think too hardly of him, dear. He only told me a little about his parents and grand-parents, and almost all in answer to my questions. You are so good, so just—you have done everything you thought to be right. But it seems to me clear that more than that is right; and I must speak about it, since I am the person who would get what is called benefit by that 'more' not being done."

There was a perceptible pause before Mr Casaubon replied, not quickly as before, but with a still more biting emphasis.

"Dorothea, my love, this is not the first occasion, but it were well

---

1. Either William Lowth (1660–1732), theologian and scriptural scholar, author of *A Commentary on the Prophets* (1714–25), or his son Robert Lowth (1710–1787), clergyman, poet, Greek and Hebrew scholar. One of Robert Lowth's books involved him in a controversy with William Warburton over the historical date assigned Job.

that it should be the last, on which you have assumed a judgment on subjects beyond your scope. Into the question how far conduct, especially in the matter of alliances, constitutes a forfeiture of family claims, I do not now enter. Suffice it, that you are not here qualified to discriminate. What I now wish you to understand is, that I accept no revision, still less dictation within that range of affairs which I have deliberated upon as distinctly and properly mine. It is not for you to interfere between me and Mr Ladislaw, and still less to encourage communications from him to you which constitute a criticism on my procedure."

Poor Dorothea, shrouded in the darkness, was in a tumult of conflicting emotions. Alarm at the possible effect on himself of her husband's strongly-manifested anger, would have checked any expression of her own resentment, even if she had been quite free from doubt and compunction under the consciousness that there might be some justice in his last insinuation. Hearing him breathe quickly after he had spoken, she sat listening, frightened, wretched—with a dumb inward cry for help to bear this nightmare of a life in which every energy was arrested by dread. But nothing else happened, except that they both remained a long while sleepless, without speaking again.

The next day, Mr Casaubon received the following answer from Will Ladislaw :—

" DEAR MR CASAUBON,—I have given all due consideration to your letter of yesterday, but I am unable to take precisely your view of our mutual position. With the fullest acknowledgment of your generous conduct to me in the past, I must still maintain that an obligation of this kind cannot fairly fetter me as you appear to expect that it should. Granted that a benefactor's wishes may constitute a claim ; there must always be a reservation as to the quality of those wishes. They may possibly clash with more imperative considerations. Or a benefactor's veto might impose such a negation on a man's life that the consequent blank might be more cruel than the benefaction was generous. I am merely using strong illustrations. In the present case I am unable to take your view of the bearing which my acceptance of occupation—not enriching certainly, but not dishonourable—will have on your own position, which seems to me too substantial to be affected in that shadowy manner. And though I do not believe that any change in our relations will occur (certainly none has yet occurred) which can nullify the obligations imposed on me by the past, pardon me for not seeing that those obligations should restrain me from using the ordinary freedom of living where I choose, and maintaining myself by any lawful occupation I may choose. Regretting that there exists this difference between us as to a relation in which the conferring of benefits has been entirely on your side—I remain, yours with persistent obligation,   WILL LADISLAW."

Poor Mr Casaubon felt (and must not we, being impartial, feel with him a little ?) that no man had juster cause for disgust and suspicion than he. Young Ladislaw, he was sure, meant to defy and annoy him, meant to win Dorothea's confidence and sow her mind with disrespect, and perhaps aversion, towards her husband. Some motive beneath the surface had been needed to account for Will's sudden change of course in rejecting Mr Casaubon's aid and quitting his travels ; and this defiant determination to fix himself in the neighbourhood by taking up something so much at variance with his former choice as Mr Brooke's Middlemarch projects, revealed clearly enough that the undeclared motive had relation to Dorothea. Not for one moment did Mr Casaubon suspect Dorothea of any doubleness : he had no suspicions of her, but he had (what was little less uncomfortable) the positive knowledge that her tendency to form opinions about her husband's conduct was accompanied with a disposition to regard Will Ladislaw favourably and be influenced by what he said. His own proud reticence had prevented him from ever being undeceived in the supposition that Dorothea had originally asked her uncle to invite Will to his house.

And now, on receiving Will's letter, Mr Casaubon had to consider his duty. He would never have been easy to call his action anything else than duty ; but in this case, contending motives thrust him back into negations.

Should he apply directly to Mr Brooke, and demand of that troublesome gentleman to revoke his proposal ? Or should he consult Sir James Chettam, and get him to concur in remonstrance against a step which touched the whole family ? In either case Mr Casaubon was aware that failure was just as probable as success. It was impossible for him to mention Dorothea's name in the matter, and without some alarming urgency Mr Brooke was as likely as not, after meeting all representations with apparent assent, to wind up by saying, " Never fear, Casaubon ! Depend upon it, young Ladislaw will do you credit. Depend upon it, I have put my finger on the right thing." And Mr Casaubon shrank nervously from communicating on the subject with Sir James Chettam, between whom and himself there had never been any cordiality, and who would immediately think of Dorothea without any mention of her.

Poor Mr Casaubon was distrustful of everybody's feeling towards him, especially as a husband. To let any one suppose that he was jealous would be to admit their (suspected) view of his disadvantages : to let them know that he did not find marriage particularly blissful would imply his conversion to their (probably) earlier disapproval. It would be as bad as letting Carp, and Brasenose generally, know how backward he was in organising the matter for his ' Key to all Mythologies.' All through his life Mr Casaubon had been trying not to admit even to himself the inward sores of self-doubt and jealousy. And on the most delicate of all personal subjects, the habit of proud suspicious reticence told doubly.

Thus Mr Casaubon remained proudly, bitterly silent. But he had forbidden Will to come to Lowick Manor, and he was mentally preparing other measures of frustration.

CHAPTER XXXVIII.

" C'est beaucoup que le jugement des hommes sur les actions humaines ; tôt ou tard il devient efficace."—GUIZOT. 1

SIR JAMES CHETTAM could not look with any satisfaction on Mr Brooke's new courses ; but it was easier to object than to hinder. Sir James accounted for his having come in alone one day to lunch with the Cadwalladers by saying—

" I can't talk to you as I want, before Celia : it might hurt her. Indeed, it would not be right."

" I know what you mean—the ' Pioneer' at the Grange !" darted in Mrs Cadwallader, almost before the last word was off her friend's tongue. " It is frightful—this taking to buying whistles and blowing them in everybody's hearing. Lying in bed all day and playing at dominoes, like poor Lord Plessy, would be more private and bearable."

" I see they are beginning to attack our friend Brooke in the ' Trumpet,'" said the Rector, lounging back and smiling easily, as he would have done if he had been attacked himself. " There are tremendous sarcasms against a Landlord not a hundred miles from Middlemarch, who receives his own rents, and makes no returns."

" I do wish Brooke would leave that off," said Sir James, with his little frown of annoyance.

" Is he really going to be put in nomination, though ?" said Mr Cadwallader. " I saw Farebrother yesterday—he's Whiggish himself, hoists Brougham and Useful Knowledge ; that's the worst I know of him ;—and he says that Brooke is getting up a pretty strong party. Bulstrode, the banker, is his foremost man. 2 But he thinks Brooke would come off badly at a nomination."

" Exactly," said Sir James, with earnestness. " I have been inquiring into the thing, for I've never known anything about Middlemarch politics before—the county being my business. What Brooke trusts to, is that they are going to turn out Oliver because he is a Peelite. But Hawley tells me that if they send up a Whig at all it is sure to be Bagster, one of those candidates who come from heaven knows where, but dead against Ministers, and an experienced Parliamentary man. Hawley's rather rough : he forgot that he was speaking to me. He said if Brooke wanted a pelting, he could get it cheaper than by going to the hustings."

---

1. "It is just like the judgment of men on human actions; sooner or later it becomes effective" (François Pierre Guizot [1787–1874], French historian). 2. Henry, Lord Brougham (1778–1868), British statesman and Benthamite liberal was one of the founders of *The Edinburgh Review* in 1802, and of the Society for the Diffusion of Useful knowledge in 1825.

" I warned you all of it," said Mrs Cadwallader, waving her hands outward. " I said to Humphrey long ago, Mr Brooke is going to make a splash in the mud. And now he has done it."

" Well, he might have taken it into his head to marry," said the Rector. " That would have been a graver mess than a little flirtation with politics."

" He may do that afterwards," said Mrs Cadwallader—" when he has come out on the other side of the mud with an ague."

" What I care for most is his own dignity," said Sir James. " Of course I care the more because of the family. But he's getting on in life now, and I don't like to think of his exposing himself. They will be raking up everything against him."

" I suppose it's no use trying any persuasion," said the Rector " There's such an odd mixture of obstinacy and changeableness in Brooke. Have you tried him on the subject ? "

" Well, no," said Sir James ; " I feel a delicacy in appearing to dictate. But I have been talking to this young Ladislaw that Brooke is making a factotum of. Ladislaw seems clever enough for anything. I thought it as well to hear what he had to say ; and he is against Brooke's standing this time. I think he'll turn him round : I think the nomination may be staved off."

" I know," said Mrs Cadwallader, nodding. " The independent member hasn't got his speeches well enough by heart."

" But this Ladislaw—there again is a vexatious business," said Sir James. " We have had him two or three times to dine at the Hall (you have met him, by the by) as Brooke's guest and a relation of Casaubon's, thinking he was only on a flying visit. And now I find he's in everybody's mouth in Middlemarch as the editor of the ' Pioneer.' There are stories going about him as a quill-driving alien, a foreign emissary, and what not."

" Casaubon won't like that," said the Rector.

" There *is* some foreign blood in Ladislaw," returned Sir James " I hope he won't go into extreme opinions and carry Brooke on."

" Oh, he's a dangerous young sprig, that Mr Ladislaw," said Mrs Cadwallader, " with his opera songs and his ready tongue. A sort of Byronic hero—an amorous conspirator, it strikes me. And Thomas Aquinas is not fond of him. I could see that, the day the picture was brought."

" I don't like to begin on the subject with Casaubon," said Sir James. " He has more right to interfere than I. But it's a disagreeable affair all round. What a character for anybody with decent connections to show himself in !—one of those newspaper fellows ! You have only to look at Keck, who manages the ' Trumpet.' I saw him the other day with Hawley. His writing is sound enough, I believe, but he's such a low fellow, that I wished he had been on the wrong side."

" What can you expect with these peddling Middlemarch papers ? " said the Rector. " I don't suppose you could get a high style of man anywhere to be writing up interests he doesn't really care about, and for pay that hardly keeps him in at elbows."

" Exactly : that makes it so annoying that Brooke should have put a man who has a sort of connection with the family in a position of that kind. For my part, I think Ladislaw is rather a fool for accepting."

" It is Aquinas's fault," said Mrs Cadwallader. " Why didn't he use his interest to get Ladislaw made an *attaché* or sent to India ? That is how families get rid of troublesome sprigs."

" There is no knowing to what lengths the mischief may go," said Sir James, anxiously. " But if Casaubon says nothing, what can I do ? "

" Oh, my dear Sir James," said the Rector, " don't let us make too much of all this. It is likely enough to end in mere smoke. After a month or two Brooke and this Master Ladislaw will get tired of each other ; Ladislaw will take wing ; Brooke will sell the ' Pioneer,' and everything will settle down again as usual."

" There is one good chance—that he will not like to feel his money oozing away," said Mrs Cadwallader. " If I knew the items of election expenses I could scare him. It's no use plying him with wide words like Expenditure : I wouldn't talk of phlebotomy, I would empty a pot of leeches upon him   What we good stingy people don't like, is having our sixpences sucked away from us."

" And he will not like having things raked up against him," said Sir James. " There is the management of his estate. They have begun upon that already. And it really is painful for me to see. It is a nuisance under one's very nose. I do think one is bound to do the best for one's land and tenants, especially in these hard times."

" Perhaps the ' Trumpet' may rouse him to make a change, and some good may come of it all," said the Rector. " I know I should be glad. I should hear less grumbling when my tithe is paid. I don't know what I should do if there were not a modus in Tipton." [3]

" I want him to have a proper man to look after things — I want him to take on Garth again," said Sir James. " He got rid of Garth twelve years ago, and everything has been going wrong since. I think of getting Garth to manage for me—he has made such a capital plan for my buildings ; and Lovegood is hardly up to the mark. But Garth would not undertake the Tipton estate again unless Brooke left it entirely to him."

" In the right of it too," said the Rector. " Garth is an independent fellow : an original, simple-minded fellow. One day, when he was doing some valuation for me, he told me point-blank that clergymen seldom understood anything about business, and did mischief when they meddled ; but he said it as quietly and respectfully as if he had been talking to me about sailors. He would make a different parish of Tipton, if Brooke would let him manage. I wish, by the help of the ' Trumpet,' you could bring that round."

" If Dorothea had kept near her uncle, there would have been some chance," said Sir James. " She might have got some power over him in time, and she was always uneasy about the estate. She had wonderfully good notions about such things. But now Casaubon takes

----

3. *Modus decimandi,* a money payment in lieu of tithe.

her up entirely. Celia complains a good deal. We can hardly get her to dine with us, since he had that fit." Sir James ended with a look of pitying disgust, and Mrs Cadwallader shrugged her shoulders as much as to say that *she* was not likely to see anything new in that direction.

" Poor Casaubon ! " the Rector said. " That was a nasty attack. I thought he looked shattered the other day at the Archdeacon's."

" In point of fact," resumed Sir James, not choosing to dwell on " fits," " Brooke doesn't mean badly by his tenants or any one else, but he has got that way of paring and clipping at expenses."

" Come, that's a blessing," said Mrs Cadwallader. " That helps him to find himself in a morning. He may not know his own opinions, but he does know his own pocket."

" I don't believe a man is in pocket by stinginess on his land," said Sir James.

" Oh, stinginess may be abused like other virtues : it will not do to keep one's own pigs lean," said Mrs Cadwallader, who had risen to look out of the window. " But talk of an independent politician and he will appear."

" What, Brooke ? " said her husband.

" Yes. Now, you ply him with the ' Trumpet,' Humphrey ; and I will put the leeches on him. What will you do, Sir James ? "

" The fact is, I don't like to begin about it with Brooke, in our mutual position ; the whole thing is so unpleasant. I do wish people would behave like gentlemen," said the good baronet, feeling that this was a simple and comprehensive programme for social well-being.

" Here you all are, eh ? " said Mr Brooke, shuffling round and shaking hands. " I was going up to the hall by-and-by, Chettam. But it's pleasant to find everybody, you know. Well, what do you think of things ?—going on a little fast ! It was true enough, what Lafitte said—' Since yesterday, a century has passed away : '—they're in the next century, you know, on the other side of the water.[4] Going on faster than we are."

" Why, yes," said the Rector, taking up the newspaper. " Here is the ' Trumpet ' accusing you of lagging behind—did you see ? "

" Eh ? no," said Mr Brooke, dropping his gloves into his hat and hastily adjusting his eye-glass. But Mr Cadwallader kept the paper in his hand, saying, with a smile in his eyes—

" Look here ! all this is about a landlord not a hundred miles from Middlemarch, who receives his own rents. They say he is the most retrogressive man in the county. I think you must have taught them that word in the ' Pioneer.' "

" Oh, that is Keck—an illiterate fellow, you know. Retrogressive, now ! Come, that's capital. He thinks it means destructive : they want to make me out a destructive, you know," said Mr Brooke, with that cheerfulness which is usually sustained by an adversary's ignorance.

" I think he knows the meaning of the word. Here is a sharp stroke or two. *If we had to describe a man who is retrogressive in the most evil sense of the word—we should say, he is one who would dub himself a reformer of our constitution, while every interest for which he is imme-*

4. Jacques Lafitte (1767–1844), French statesman, a leader of the revolution of 1830.

diately responsible is going to decay: a philanthropist who cannot bear one rogue to be hanged, but does not mind five honest tenants being half-starved: a man who shrieks at corruption, and keeps his farms at rack-rent: who roars himself red at rotten boroughs, and does not mind if every field on his farms has a rotten gate: a man very open-hearted to Leeds and Manchester, no doubt; he would give any number of representatives who will pay for their seats out of their own pockets: what he objects to giving, is a little return on rent-days to help a tenant to buy stock, or an outlay on repairs to keep the weather out at a tenant's barn-door or make his house look a little less like an Irish cottier's. But we all know the wag's definition of a philanthropist: a man whose charity increases directly as the square of the distance. And so on. All the rest is to show what sort of legislator a philanthropist is likely to make," ended the Rector, throwing down the paper, and clasping his hands at the back of his head, while he looked at Mr Brooke with an air of amused neutrality.

"Come, that's rather good you know," said Mr Brooke, taking up the paper and trying to bear the attack as easily as his neighbour did, but colouring and smiling rather nervously; "that about roaring himself red at rotten boroughs — I never made a speech about rotten boroughs in my life. And as to roaring myself red and that kind of thing—these men never understand what is good satire. Satire, you know, should be true up to a certain point. I recollect they said that in 'The Edinburgh' somewhere — it must be true up to a certain point."

"Well, that is really a hit about the gates," said Sir James, anxious to tread carefully. "Dagley complained to me the other day that he hadn't got a decent gate on his farm. Garth has invented a new pattern of gate — I wish you would try it. One ought to use some of one's timber in that way."

"You go in for fancy farming, you know, Chettam," said Mr Brooke, appearing to glance over the columns of the 'Trumpet.' "That's your hobby, and you don't mind the expense."

"I thought the most expensive hobby in the world was standing for Parliament," said Mrs Cadwallader. "They said the last unsuccessful candidate at Middlemarch — Giles, wasn't his name? — spent ten thousand pounds and failed because he did not bribe enough. What a bitter reflection for a man!"

"Somebody was saying," said the Rector, laughingly, "that East Retford was nothing to Middlemarch, for bribery."

"Nothing of the kind," said Mr Brooke. "The Tories bribe, you know: Hawley and his set bribe with treating, hot codlings, and that sort of thing; and they bring the voters drunk to the poll. [5] But they are not going to have it their own way in future — not in future, you know. Middlemarch is a little backward, I admit—the freemen are a little backward. But we shall educate them—we shall bring them on, you know. The best people there are on our side."

"Hawley says you have men on your side who will do you harm," remarked Sir James. "He says Bulstrode the banker will do you harm."

"And that if you got pelted," interposed Mrs Cadwallader, "half

---

5. Hot codlings: hot cinnamon apples.

the rotten eggs would mean hatred of your committee-man. Good heavens! Think what it must be to be pelted for wrong opinions. And I seem to remember a story of a man they pretended to chair and let him fall into a dust-heap on purpose!"

"Pelting is nothing to their finding holes in one's coat," said the Rector. "I confess that's what I should be afraid of, if we parsons had to stand at the hustings for preferment. I should be afraid of their reckoning up all my fishing days. Upon my word, I think the truth is the hardest missile one can be pelted with."

"The fact is," said Sir James, "if a man goes into public life he must be prepared for the consequences. He must make himself proof against calumny."

"My dear Chettam, that is all very fine, you know," said Mr Brooke. "But how will you make yourself proof against calumny? You should read history—look at ostracism, persecution, martyrdom, and that kind of thing. They always happen to the best men, you know. But what is that in Horace?—*fiat justitia, ruat . . .* something or other." [6]

"Exactly," said Sir James, with a little more heat than usual. "What I mean by being proof against calumny is being able to point to the fact as a contradiction."

"And it is not martyrdom to pay bills that one has run into one's self," said Mrs Cadwallader.

But it was Sir James's evident annoyance that most stirred Mr Brooke. "Well, you know, Chettam," he said, rising, taking up his hat and leaning on his stick, "you and I have a different system. You are all for outlay with your farms. I don't want to make out that my system is good under all circumstances — under all circumstances, you know."

"There ought to be a new valuation made from time to time," said Sir James. "Returns are very well occasionally, but I like a fair valuation. What do you say, Cadwallader?"

"I agree with you. If I were Brooke, I would choke the 'Trumpet' at once by getting Garth to make a new valuation of the farms, and giving him *carte blanche* about gates and repairs : that's my view of the political situation," said the Rector, broadening himself by sticking his thumbs in his armholes, and laughing towards Mr Brooke.

"That's a showy sort of thing to do, you know," said Mr Brooke. "But I should like you to tell me of another landlord who has distressed his tenants for arrears as little as I have. I let the old tenants stay on. I'm uncommonly easy, let me tell you—uncommonly easy. I have my own ideas, and I take my stand on them, you know. A man who does that is always charged with eccentricity, inconsistency, and that kind of thing. When I change my line of action, I shall follow my own ideas."

After that, Mr Brooke remembered that there was a packet which he had omitted to send off from the Grange, and he bade everybody hurriedly good-bye.

"I didn't want to take a liberty with Brooke," said Sir James; "I

6. "Fiat justitia et ruat mundus": "Let justice be done though the world go to ruin." The phrase is not from Horace, but became current in English in the sixteenth century.

see he is nettled. But as to what he says about old tenants, in point of fact no new tenant would take the farms on the present terms."

" I have a notion that he will be brought round in time," said the Rector. " But you were pulling one way, Elinor, and we were pulling another. You wanted to frighten him away from expense, and we want to frighten him into it. Better let him try to be popular and see that his character as a landlord stands in his way. I don't think it signifies two straws about the ' Pioneer,' or Ladislaw, or Brooke's speechifying to the Middlemarchers. But it does signify about the parishioners in Tipton being comfortable."

" Excuse me, it is you two who are on the wrong tack," said Mrs Cadwallader. " You should have proved to him that he loses money by bad management, and then we should all have pulled together. If you put him a-horseback on politics, I warn you of the consequences. It was all very well to ride on sticks at home and call them ideas."

CHAPTER XXXIX

> " If, as I have, you also doe,
>   Vertue attired in woman see,
> And dare love that, and say so too,
>   And forget the He and She ;
>
> And if this love, though placed so,
>   From prophane men you hide,
> Which will no faith on this bestow,
>   Or, if they doe, deride :
>
> Then you have done a braver thing
>   Than all the Worthies did,
> And a braver thence will spring,
>   Which is, to keep that hid."
>   —DR DONNE. [1]

SIR JAMES CHETTAM'S mind was not fruitful in devices, but his growing anxiety to " act on Brooke," once brought close to his constant belief in Dorothea's capacity for influence, became formative, and issued in a little plan ; namely, to plead Celia's indisposition as a reason for fetching Dorothea by herself to the Hall, and to leave her at the Grange with the carriage on the way, after making her fully aware of the situation concerning the management of the estate.

In this way it happened that one day near four o'clock, when Mr Brooke and Ladislaw were seated in the library, the door opened and Mrs Casaubon was announced.

Will, the moment before, had been low in the depths of boredom, and, obliged to help Mr Brooke in arranging "documents" about hanging sheep-stealers, was exemplifying the power our minds have of riding several horses at once by inwardly arranging measures towards getting a lodging for himself in Middlemarch and cutting short his constant residence at the Grange ; while there flitted through all these steadier images a tickling vision of a sheep-stealing epic written

---

1. John Donne, "The Undertaking."

with Homeric particularity. When Mrs Casaubon was announced he started up as from an electric shock, and felt a tingling at his finger-ends. Any one observing him would have seen a change in his complexion, in the adjustment of his facial muscles, in the vividness of his glance, which might have made them imagine that every molecule in his body had passed the message of a magic touch. And so it had. For effective magic is transcendent nature ; and who shall measure the subtlety of those touches which convey the quality of soul as well as body, and make a man's passion for one woman differ from his passion for another as joy in the morning light over valley and river and white mountain-top differs from joy among Chinese lanterns and glass pannels ? Will, too, was made of very impressible stuff. The bow of a violin drawn near him cleverly, would at one stroke change the aspect of the world for him, and his point of view shifted as easily as his mood. Dorothea's entrance was the freshness of morning.

"Well, my dear, this is pleasant, now," said Mr Brooke, meeting and kissing her. "You have left Casaubon with his books, I suppose. That's right. We must not have you getting too learned for a woman, you know."

"There is no fear of that, uncle," said Dorothea, turning to Will and shaking hands with open cheerfulness, while she made no other form of greeting, but went on answering her uncle. "I am very slow. When I want to be busy with books, I am often playing truant among my thoughts. I find it is not so easy to be learned as to plan cottages."

She seated herself beside her uncle opposite to Will, and was evidently preoccupied with something that made her almost unmindful of him. He was ridiculously disappointed, as if he had imagined that her coming had anything to do with him.

"Why, yes, my dear, it was quite your hobby to draw plans. But it was good to break that off a little. Hobbies are apt to run away with us, you know ; it doesn't do to be run away with. We must keep the reins. I have never let myself be run away with ; I always pulled up. That is what I tell Ladislaw. He and I are alike, you know : he likes to go into everything. We are working at capital punishment. We shall do a great deal together, Ladislaw and I."

"Yes," said Dorothea, with characteristic directness, "Sir James has been telling me that he is in hope of seeing a great change made soon in your management of the estate—that you are thinking of having the farms valued, and repairs made, and the cottages improved, so that Tipton may look quite another place. Oh, how happy !"— she went on, clasping her hands, with a return to that more childlike impetuous manner which had been subdued since her marriage. "If I were at home still, I should take to riding again, that I might go about with you and see all that ! And you are going to engage Mr Garth, who praised my cottages, Sir James says."

"Chettam is a little hasty, my dear," said Mr Brooke, colouring slightly. "A little hasty, you know. I never said I should do anything of the kind. I never said I should *not* do it, you know."

"He only feels confident that you will do it," said Dorothea, in a voice as clear and unhesitating as that of a young chorister chanting a *credo*, "because you mean to enter Parliament as a member who cares for the improvement of the people, and one of the first things to be made better is the state of the land and the labourers. Think of Kit Downes, uncle, who lives with his wife and seven children in a house with one sitting-room and one bed-room hardly larger than this table !—and those poor Dagleys, in their tumble-down farmhouse, where they live in the back kitchen and leave the other rooms to the rats ! That is one reason why I did not like the pictures here, dear uncle—which you think me stupid about. I used to come from the village with all that dirt and coarse ugliness like a pain within me, and the simpering pictures in the drawing-room seemed to me like a wicked attempt to find delight in what is false, while we don't mind how hard the truth is for the neighbours outside our walls. I think we have no right to come forward and urge wider changes for good, until we have tried to alter the evils which lie under our own hands."

Dorothea had gathered emotion as she went on, and had forgotten everything except the relief of pouring forth her feelings, unchecked : an experience once habitual with her, but hardly ever present since her marriage, which had been a perpetual struggle of energy with fear. For the moment, Will's admiration was accompanied with a chilling sense of remoteness. A man is seldom ashamed of feeling that he cannot love a woman so well when he sees a certain greatness in her : nature having intended greatness for men. But nature has sometimes made sad oversights in carrying out her intention ; as in the case of good Mr Brooke, whose masculine consciousness was at this moment in rather a stammering condition under the eloquence of his niece. He could not immediately find any other mode of expressing himself than that of rising, fixing his eye-glass, and fingering the papers before him. At last he said—

" There is something in what you say, my dear, something in what you say—but not everything—eh, Ladislaw ? You and I don't like our pictures and statues being found fault with. Young ladies are a little ardent, you know—a little one-sided, my dear. Fine art, poetry, that kind of thing, elevates a nation—*emollit mores*—you understand a little Latin now. ² But——eh, what ? "

These interrogatives were addressed to the footman who had come in to say that the keeper had found one of Dagley's boys with a leveret in his hand just killed.

" I'll come, I'll come. I shall let him off easily, you know," said Mr Brooke aside to Dorothea, shuffling away very cheerfully.

" I hope you feel how right this change is that I—that Sir James wishes for," said Dorothea to Will, as soon as her uncle was gone.

" I do, now I have heard you speak about it. I shall not forget what you have said. But can you think of something else at this moment ? I may not have another opportunity of speaking to you about what has occurred," said Will, rising with a movement of impatience, and holding the back of his chair with both hands.

" Pray tell me what it is," said Dorothea, anxiously, also rising and going to the open window, where Monk was looking in, panting and wagging his tail. She leaned her back against the window-frame, and laid her hand on the dog's head ; for though, as we know, she was not fond of pets that must be held in the hands or trodden on, she was always attentive to the feelings of dogs, and very polite if she had to decline their advances.

2. *Emollit mores:* to make manners mild or gentle.

Will followed her only with his eyes and said, " I presume you know that Mr Casaubon has forbidden me to go to his house."

" No, I did not," said Dorothea, after a moment's pause. She was evidently much moved. " I am very, very sorry," she added, mournfully. She was thinking of what Will had no knowledge of—the conversation between her and her husband in the darkness ; and she was anew smitten with hopelessness that she could influence Mr Casaubon's action. But the marked expression of her sorrow convinced Will that it was not all given to him personally, and that Dorothea had not been visited by the idea that Mr Casaubon's dislike and jealousy of him turned upon herself. He felt an odd mixture of delight and vexation : of delight that he could dwell and be cherished in her thought as in a pure home, without suspicion and without stint —of vexation because he was of too little account with her, was not formidable enough, was treated with an unhesitating benevolence which did not flatter him. But his dread of any change in Dorothea was stronger than his discontent, and he began to speak again in a tone of mere explanation.

" Mr Casaubon's reason is, his displeasure at my taking a position here which he considers unsuited to my rank as his cousin. I have told him that I cannot give way on this point. It is a little too hard on me to expect that my course in life is to be hampered by prejudices which I think ridiculous. Obligation may be stretched till it is no better than a brand of slavery stamped on us when we were too young to know its meaning. I would not have accepted the position if I had not meant to make it useful and honourable. I am not bound to regard family dignity in any other light."

Dorothea felt wretched. She thought her husband altogether in the wrong, on more grounds than Will had mentioned.

" It is better for us not to speak on the subject," she said, with a tremulousness not common in her voice, " since you and Mr Casaubon disagree. You intend to remain ?" She was looking out on the lawn, with melancholy meditation.

" Yes ; but I shall hardly ever see you now," said Will, in a tone of almost boyish complaint.

" No," said Dorothea, turning her eyes full upon him, " hardly ever. But I shall hear of you. I shall know what you are doing for my uncle."

" I shall know hardly anything about you," said Will. " No one will tell me anything."

" Oh, my life is very simple," said Dorothea, her lips curling with an exquisite smile, which irradiated her melancholy. " I am always at Lowick."

" That is a dreadful imprisonment," said Will, impetuously.

" No, don't think that," said Dorothea. " I have no longings."

He did not speak, but she replied to some change in his expression. " I mean, for myself. Except that I should like not to have so much more than my share without doing anything for others. But I have a belief of my own, and it comforts me."

" What is that ?" said Will, rather jealous of the belief.

" That by desiring what is perfectly good, even when we don't quite know what it is and cannot do what we would, we are part of the divine power against evil—widening the skirts of light and making the struggle with darkness narrower."

" That is a beautiful mysticism—it is a——"

" Please not to call it by any name," said Dorothea, putting out her hands entreatingly. " You will say it is Persian, or something else geographical. It is my life. I have found it out, and cannot part with it. I have always been finding out my religion since I was a little girl. I used to pray so much—now I hardly ever pray. I try not to have desires merely for myself, because they may not be good for others, and I have too much already. I only told you, that you might know quite well how my days go at Lowick."

" God bless you for telling me ! " said Will, ardently, and rather wondering at himself. They were looking at each other like two fond children who were talking confidentially of birds.

" What is *your* religion ? " said Dorothea. " I mean—not what you know about religion, but the belief that helps you most ? "

" To love what is good and beautiful when I see it," said Will. " But I am a rebel : I don't feel bound, as you do, to submit to what I don't like."

" But if you like what is good, that comes to the same thing," said Dorothea, smiling.

" Now you are subtle," said Will.

" Yes ; Mr Casaubon often says I am too subtle. I don't feel as if I were subtle," said Dorothea, playfully. " But how long my uncle is ! I must go and look for him. I must really go on to the Hall. Celia is expecting me."

Will offered to tell Mr Brooke, who presently came and said that he would step into the carriage and go with Dorothea as far as Dagley's, to speak about the small delinquent who had been caught with the leveret. Dorothea renewed the subject of the estate as they drove along, but Mr Brooke, not being taken unawares, got the talk under his own control.

" Chettam, now," he replied ; " he finds fault with me, my dear ; but I should not preserve my game if it were not for Chettam, and he can't say that *that* expense is for the sake of the tenants, you know. It's a little against my feeling :—poaching, now, if you come to look into it—I have often thought of getting up the subject. Not long ago, Flavell, the Methodist preacher, was brought up for knocking down a hare that came across his path when he and his wife were walking out together. He was pretty quick, and knocked it on the neck."

" That was very brutal, I think," said Dorothea.

" Well, now, it seemed rather black to me, I confess, in a Methodist preacher, you know. And Johnson said, ' You may judge what a hypo*crite* he is.' And upon my word, I thought Flavell looked very little like ' the highest style of man '—as somebody calls the Christian —Young, the poet Young, I think—you know Young ? [3] Well, now, Flavell in his shabby black gaiters, pleading that he thought the Lord had sent him and his wife a good dinner, and he had a right to knock it down, though not a mighty hunter before the Lord, as Nimrod was—I assure you it was rather comic : Fielding would have made something of it—or Scott, now—Scott might have worked it up. [4] But really, when I came to think of it, I couldn't help liking

---

3. Edward Young (1683–1765), "Night Thoughts," IV, 788.

4. Nimrod: the great-grandson of Noah, noted as a hunter.

that the fellow should have a bit of hare to say grace over. It's all a matter of prejudice—prejudice with the law on its side, you know —about the stick and the gaiters, and so on. However, it doesn't do to reason about things ; and law is law. But I got Johnson to be quiet, and I hushed the matter up. I doubt whether Chettam would not have been more severe, and yet he comes down on me as if I were the hardest man in the county. But here we are at Dagley's."

Mr Brooke got down at a farmyard-gate, and Dorothea drove on. It is wonderful how much uglier things will look when we only suspect that we are blamed for them. Even our own persons in the glass are apt to change their aspect for us after we have heard some frank remark on their less admirable points ; and on the other hand it is astonishing how pleasantly conscience takes our encroachments on those who never complain or have nobody to complain for them. Dagley's homestead never before looked so dismal to Mr Brooke as it did to-day, with his mind thus sore about the fault-finding of the ' Trumpet,' echoed by Sir James.

It is true that an observer, under that softening influence of the fine arts which makes other people's hardships picturesque, might have been delighted with this homestead called Freeman's End : the old house had dormer-windows in the dark-red roof, two of the chimneys were choked with ivy, the large porch was blocked up with bundles of sticks, and half the windows were closed with grey worm-eaten shutters about which the jasmine-boughs grew in wild luxuriance ; the mouldering garden wall with hollyhocks peeping over it was a perfect study of highly-mingled subdued colour, and there was an aged goat (kept doubtless on interesting superstitious grounds) lying against the open back-kitchen door. The mossy thatch of the cow-shed, the broken grey barn-doors, the pauper labourers in ragged breeches who had nearly finished unloading a waggon of corn into the barn ready for early thrashing ; the scanty dairy of cows being tethered for milking and leaving one half of the shed in brown emptiness ; the very pigs and white ducks seeming to wander about the uneven neglected yard as if in low spirits from feeding on a too meagre quality of rinsings—all these objects under the quiet light of a sky marbled with high clouds would have made a sort of picture which we have all paused over as a " charming bit," touching other sensibilities than those which are stirred by the depression of the agricultural interest, with the sad lack of farming capital, as seen constantly in the newspapers of that time. But these troublesome associations were just now strongly present to Mr Brooke, and spoiled the scene for him. Mr Dagley himself made a figure in the landscape, carrying a pitchfork and wearing his milking-hat—a very old beaver flattened in front. His coat and breeches were the best he had, and he would not have been wearing them on this week-day occasion if he had not been to market and returned later than usual, having given himself the rare treat of dining at the public table of the Blue Bull. How he came to fall into this extravagance would perhaps be matter of wonderment to himself on the morrow ; but before dinner something in the state of the country, a slight pause in the harvest before the Far Dips were cut, the stories about the new King and the numerous handbills on the walls, had seemed to warrant a little recklessness. It was a maxim about Middlemarch, and regarded as self-evident, that good meat should have good drink, which last Dagley interpreted as plenty of table ale well followed up by rum-and-water. These liquors have so far truth in them that they were not false enough to make poor Dagley seem merry : they only made his discontent less tongue-tied than usual. He had also taken too much in the shape of muddy political talk, a stimulant dangerously disturbing to his farming conservatism, which consisted in holding that whatever is, is bad, and any change is likely to be worse. He was flushed, and his eyes had a decidedly quarrelsome stare as he stood still grasping his pitchfork, while the landlord approached with his easy shuffling walk, one hand in his trouser-pocket and the other swinging round a thin walking-stick.

"Dagley, my good fellow," began Mr Brooke, conscious that he was going to be very friendly about the boy.

"Oh, ay, I'm a good feller, am I ? Thank ye, sir, thank ye," said Dagley, with a loud snarling irony which made Fag the sheep-dog stir from his seat and prick his ears ; but seeing Monk enter the yard after some outside loitering, Fag seated himself again in an attitude of observation. "I'm glad to hear I'm a good feller."

Mr Brooke reflected that it was market-day, and that his worthy tenant had probably been dining, but saw no reason why he should not go on, since he could take the precaution of repeating what he had to say to Mrs Dagley.

"Your little lad Jacob has been caught killing a leveret, Dagley : I have told Johnson to lock him up in the empty stable an hour or two, just to frighten him, you know. But he will be brought home by-and-by, before night : and you'll just look after him, will you, and give him a reprimand, you know ? "

"No, I woon't : I'll be dee'd if I'll leather my boy to please you or anybody else, not if you was twenty landlords istid o' one, and that a bad un."

Dagley's words were loud enough to summon his wife to the back-kitchen door—the only entrance ever used, and one always open except in bad weather—and Mr Brooke, saying soothingly, "Well, well, I'll speak to your wife—I didn't mean beating, you know," turned to walk to the house. But Dagley, only the more inclined to "have his say" with a gentleman who walked away from him, followed at once, with Fag slouching at his heels and sullenly evading some small and probably charitable advances on the part of Monk.

"How do you do, Mrs Dagley ? " said Mr Brooke, making some haste. "I came to tell you about your boy : I don't want you to give him the stick, you know." He was careful to speak quite plainly this time.

Overworked Mrs Dagley — a thin, worn woman, from whose life pleasure had so entirely vanished that she had not even any Sunday clothes which could give her satisfaction in preparing for church — had already had a misunderstanding with her husband since he had come home, and was in low spirits, expecting the worst. But her husband was beforehand in answering.

"No, nor he woon't hev the stick, whether you want it or no," pursued Dagley, throwing out his voice, as if he wanted it to hit hard. "You've got no call to come an' talk about sticks o' these primises, as you woon't give a stick tow'rt mending. Go to Middlemarch to ax for *your* charrickter."

" You'd far better hold your tongue, Dagley," said the wife, " and not kick your own trough over. When a man as is father of a family has been an' spent money at market and made himself the worse for liquor, he's done enough mischief for one day. But I should like to know what my boy's done, sir."

" Niver do you mind what he's done," said Dagley, more fiercely, " it's my business to speak, an' not yourn. An' I wull speak, too. I'll hev my say—supper or no. An' what I say is, as I've lived upo' your ground from my father and grandfather afore me, an' hev dropped our money into't, an' me an' my children might lie an' rot on the ground for top-dressin' as we can't find the money to buy, if the King wasn't to put a stop."

" My good fellow, you're drunk, you know," said Mr Brooke, confidentially but not judiciously. " Another day, another day," he added, turning as if to go.

But Dagley immediately fronted him, and Fag at his heels growled low, as his master's voice grew louder and more insulting, while Monk also drew close in silent dignified watch. The labourers on the waggon were pausing to listen, and it seemed wiser to be quite passive than to attempt a ridiculous flight pursued by a bawling man.

" I'm no more drunk nor you are, nor so much," said Dagley. " I can carry my liquor, an' I know what I meean. An' I meean as the King 'ull put a stop to't, for them say it as knows it, as there's to be a Rinform, and them landlords as never done the right thing by their tenants 'ull be treated i' that way as they'll hev to scuttle off. An' there's them i' Middlemarch knows what the Rinform is—an' as knows who'll hev to scuttle. Says they, ' I know who *your* landlord is.' An' says I, ' I hope you're the better for knowin' him, I arn't.' Says they, ' He's a close-fisted un.' ' Ay, ay,' says I. ' He's a man for the Rinform,' says they. That's what they says. An' I made out what the Rinform were—an' it were to send you an' your likes a-scuttlin' ; an' wi' pretty strong-smellin' things too. An' you may do as you like now, for I'm none afeard on you. An' you'd better let my boy aloan, an' look to yoursen, afore the Rinform has got upo' your back. That's what I'n got to say," concluded Mr Dagley, striking his fork into the ground with a firmness which proved inconvenient as he tried to draw it up again.

At this last action Monk began to bark loudly, and it was a moment for Mr Brooke to escape. He walked out of the yard as quickly as he could, in some amazement at the novelty of his situation. He had never been insulted on his own land before, and had been inclined to regard himself as a general favourite (we are all apt to do so, when we think of our own amiability more than of what other people are likely to want of us). When he had quarrelled with Caleb Garth twelve years before he had thought that the tenants would be pleased at the landlord's taking everything into his own hands.

Some who follow the narrative of his experience may wonder at the midnight darkness of Mr Dagley ; but nothing was easier in those times than for an hereditary farmer of his grade to be ignorant, in spite somehow of having a rector in the twin parish who was a gentleman to the backbone, a curate nearer at hand who preached more learnedly than the rector, a landlord who had gone into everything, especially fine art and social improvement, and all the lights of Middlemarch only three miles off. As to the facility with which mortals escape knowledge, try an average acquaintance in the intellectual blaze of London, and consider what that eligible person for a dinner-party would have been if he had learned scant skill in "summing" from the parish-clerk of Tipton, and read a chapter in the Bible with immense difficulty, because such names as Isaiah or Apollo remained unmanageable after twice spelling. Poor Dagley read a few verses sometimes on a Sunday evening, and the world was at least not darker to him than it had been before. Some things he knew thoroughly, namely, the slovenly habits of farming, and the awkwardness of weather, stock and crops, at Freeman's End—so called apparently by way of sarcasm, to imply that a man was free to quit it if he chose, but that there was no earthly "beyond" open to him.

CHAPTER XL.

Wise in his daily work was he:
To fruits of diligence,
And not to faiths or polity,
He plied his utmost sense.
These perfect in their little parts,
Whose work is all their prize—
Without them how could laws, or arts,
Or towered cities rise?

IN watching effects, if only of an electric battery, it is often necessary to change our place and examine a particular mixture or group at some distance from the point where the movement we are interested in was set up. The group I am moving towards is at Caleb Garth's breakfast-table in the large parlour where the maps and desk were: father, mother, and five of the children. Mary was just now at home waiting for a situation, while Christy, the boy next to her, was getting cheap learning and cheap fare in Scotland, having to his father's disappointment taken to books instead of that sacred calling "business."

The letters had come—nine costly letters, for which the postman had been paid three and twopence, and Mr Garth was forgetting his tea and toast while he read his letters and laid them open one above the other, sometimes swaying his head slowly, sometimes screwing up his mouth in inward debate, but not forgetting to cut off a large red seal unbroken, which Letty snatched up like an eager terrier.

The talk among the rest went on unrestrainedly, for nothing disturbed Caleb's absorption except shaking the table when he was writing.

Two letters of the nine had been for Mary. After reading them, she had passed them to her mother, and sat playing with her tea-spoon absently, till with a sudden recollection she returned to her sewing, which she had kept on her lap during breakfast.

"Oh, don't sew, Mary!" said Ben, pulling her arm down. "Make me a peacock with this bread-crumb." He had been kneading a small mass for the purpose.

"No, no, Mischief!" said Mary, good-humouredly, while she pricked his hand lightly with her needle. "Try and mould it yourself: you have seen me do it often enough. I must get this sewing done. It is for Rosamond Vincy: she is to be married next week, and she can't be married without this handkerchief." Mary ended merrily, amused with the last notion.

"Why can't she, Mary?" said Letty, seriously interested in this mystery, and pushing her head so close to her sister that Mary now turned the threatening needle toward Letty's nose.

"Because this is one of a dozen, and without it there would only be eleven," said Mary, with a grave air of explanation, so that Letty sank back with a sense of knowledge.

"Have you made up your mind, my dear," said Mrs Garth, laying the letters down.

"I shall go to the school at York," said Mary. "I am less unfit to teach in a school than in a family. I like to teach classes best. And, you see, I must teach : there is nothing else to be done."

"Teaching seems to me the most delightful work in the world," said Mrs Garth, with a touch of rebuke in her tone. "I could understand your objection to it if you had not knowledge enough, Mary, or if you disliked children."

"I suppose we never quite understand why another dislikes what we like, mother," said Mary, rather curtly. "I am not fond of a schoolroom : I like the outside world better. It is a very inconvenient fault of mine."

"It must be very stupid to be always in a girls' school," said Alfred. "Such a set of nincompoops, like Mrs Ballard's pupils walking two and two."

"And they have no games worth playing at," said Jim. "They can neither throw nor leap. I don't wonder at Mary's not liking it."

"What is that Mary doesn't like, eh?" said the father, looking over his spectacles and pausing before he opened his next letter.

"Being among a lot of nincompoop girls," said Alfred.

"Is it the situation you had heard of, Mary?" said Caleb, gently, looking at his daughter.

"Yes, father : the school at York. I have determined to take it. It is quite the best. Thirty-five pounds a-year, and extra pay for teaching the smallest strummers at the piano."

"Poor child! I wish she could stay at home with us, Susan," said Caleb, looking plaintively at his wife.

"Mary would not be happy without doing her duty," said Mrs Garth, magisterially, conscious of having done her own.

"It wouldn't make me happy to do such a nasty duty as that," said Alfred—at which Mary and her father laughed silently, but Mrs Garth said, gravely—

"Do find a fitter word than nasty, my dear Alfred, for everything that you think disagreeable. And suppose that Mary could help you to go to Mr Hanmer's with the money she gets?"

"That seems to me a great shame. But she's an old brick," said Alfred, rising from his chair, and pulling Mary's head backward to kiss her.

Mary coloured and laughed, but could not conceal that the tears were coming. Caleb, looking on over his spectacles, with the angles of his eyebrows falling, had an expression of mingled delight and sorrow as he returned to the opening of his letter ; and even Mrs Garth, her lips curling with a calm contentment, allowed that inappropriate language to pass without correction, although Ben immediately took it up, and sang, " She's an old brick, old brick, old brick ! " to a cantering measure, which he beat out with his fist on Mary's arm.

But Mrs Garth's eyes were now drawn towards her husband, who was already deep in the letter he was reading. His face had an expression of grave surprise, which alarmed her a little, but he did not like to be questioned while he was reading, and she remained anxiously watching till she saw him suddenly shaken by a little joyous laugh as he turned back to the beginning of the letter, and looking at her above his spectacles, said, in a low tone, " What do you think, Susan ? "

She went and stood behind him, putting her hand on his shoulder, while they read the letter together. It was from Sir James Chettam, offering to Mr Garth the management of the family estates at Freshitt and elsewhere, and adding that Sir James had been requested by Mr Brooke of Tipton to ascertain whether Mr Garth would be disposed at the same time to resume the agency of the Tipton property. The Baronet added in very obliging words that he himself was particularly desirous of seeing the Freshitt and Tipton estates under the same management, and he hoped to be able to show that the double agency might be held on terms agreeable to Mr Garth, whom he would be glad to see at the Hall at twelve o'clock on the following day.

" He writes handsomely, doesn't he, Susan ? " said Caleb, turning his eyes upward to his wife, who raised her hand from his shoulder to his ear, while she rested her chin on his head. " Brooke didn't like to ask me himself, I can see," he continued, laughing silently.

" Here is an honour to your father, children," said Mrs Garth, looking round at the five pair of eyes, all fixed on the parents. " He is asked to take a post again by those who dismissed him long ago. That shows that he did his work well, so that they feel the want of him."

" Like Cincinnatus—hooray ! " said Ben, riding on his chair, with a pleasant confidence that discipline was relaxed.

" Will they come to fetch him, mother ? " said Letty, thinking of the Mayor and Corporation in their robes.

Mrs Garth patted Letty's head and smiled, but seeing that her husband was gathering up his letters and likely soon to be out of reach in that sanctuary " business," she pressed his shoulder and said emphatically,

" Now, mind you ask fair pay, Caleb."

" Oh yes," said Caleb, in a deep voice of assent, as if it would be unreasonable to suppose anything else of him. " It'll come to between four and five hundred, the two together." Then with a little start of remembrance he said, " Mary, write and give up that school. Stay and help your mother. I'm as pleased as Punch, now I've thought of that."

No manner could have been less like that of Punch triumphant than Caleb's, but his talents did not lie in finding phrases, though he was very particular about his letter-writing, and regarded his wife as a treasury of correct language.

There was almost an uproar among the children now, and Mary held up the cambric embroidery towards her mother entreatingly, that it might be put out of reach while the boys dragged her into a dance. Mrs Garth, in placid joy, began to put the cups and plates together, while Caleb pushing his chair from the table, as if he were going to move to the desk, still sat holding his letters in his hand and looking on the ground meditatively, stretching out the fingers of his left hand, according to a mute language of his own. At last he said—

" It's a thousand pities Christy didn't take to business, Susan. I shall want help by-and-by. And Alfred must go off to the engineering—I've made up my mind to that." He fell into meditation and finger-rhetoric again for a little while, and then continued :—" I shall make Brooke have new agreements with the tenants, and I shall draw up a rotation of crops. And I'll lay a wager we can get fine bricks out of the clay at Bott's corner. I must look into that : it would cheapen the repairs. It's a fine bit of work, Susan ! A man without a family would be glad to do it for nothing."

" Mind you don't, though," said his wife, lifting up her finger.

" No, no ; but it's a fine thing to come to a man when he's seen into the nature of business : to have the chance of getting a bit of the country into good fettle, as they say, and putting men into the right way with their farming, and getting a bit of good contriving and solid building done—that those who are living and those who come after will be the better for. I'd sooner have it than a fortune. I hold it the most honourable work that is." Here Caleb laid down his letters, thrust his fingers between the buttons of his waistcoat, and sat upright, but presently proceeded with some awe in his voice and moving his head slowly aside—" It's a great gift of God, Susan."

" That it is, Caleb," said his wife, with answering fervour. " And it will be a blessing to your children to have had a father who did such work : a father whose good work remains though his name may be forgotten." She could not say any more to him then about the pay.

In the evening, when Caleb, rather tired with his day's work, was seated in silence with his pocket-book open on his knee, while Mrs Garth and Mary were at their sewing, and Letty in a corner was whispering a dialogue with her doll, Mr Farebrother came up the orchard walk, dividing the bright August lights and shadows with the tufted·grass and the apple-tree boughs. We know that he was fond of his parishioners the Garths, and had thought Mary worth mentioning to Lydgate. He used to the full the clergyman's privilege of disregarding the Middlemarch discrimination of ranks, and always told his mother that Mrs Garth was more of a lady than any matron in the town. Still, you see, he spent his evenings at the Vincys', where the matron, though less of a lady, presided over a well-lit drawing-room and whist. In those days human intercourse was not determined solely by respect. But the Vicar did heartily respect the Garths, and a visit from him was no surprise to that family. Nevertheless he accounted for it even while he was shaking hands, by saying, " I come as an envoy, Mrs Garth : I have something to say to you and Garth on behalf of Fred Vincy. The fact is, poor fellow," he continued, as he seated himself and looked round with his bright glance at the three who were listening to him, " he has taken me into his confidence."

Mary's heart beat rather quickly : she wondered how far Fred's confidence had gone.

"We haven't seen the lad for months," said Caleb. "I couldn't think what was become of him."

"He has been away on a visit," said the Vicar, "because home was a little too hot for him, and Lydgate told his mother that the poor fellow must not begin to study yet. But yesterday he came and poured himself out to me. I am very glad he did, because I have seen him grow up from a youngster of fourteen, and I am so much at home in the house that the children are like nephews and nieces to me. But it is a difficult case to advise upon. However, he has asked me to come and tell you that he is going away, and that he is so miserable about his debt to you, and his inability to pay, that he can't bear to come himself even to bid you good-bye."

"Tell him it doesn't signify a farthing," said Caleb, waving his hand. "We've had the pinch and have got over it. And now I'm going to be as rich as a Jew."

"Which means," said Mrs Garth, smiling at the Vicar, "that we are going to have enough to bring up the boys well and to keep Mary at home."

"What is the treasure-trove ?" said Mr Farebrother.

"I'm going to be agent for two estates, Freshitt and Tipton ; and perhaps for a pretty little bit of land in Lowick besides : it's all the same family connection, and employment spreads like water if it's once set going. It makes me very happy, Mr Farebrother"—here Caleb threw back his head a little, and spread his arms on the elbows of his chair—"that I've got an opportunity again with the letting of the land, and carrying out a notion or two with improvements. It's a most uncommonly cramping thing, as I've often told Susan, to sit on horseback and look over the hedges at the wrong thing, and not be able to put your hand to it to make it right. What people do who go into politics I can't think : it drives me almost mad to see mismanagement over only a few hundred acres."

It was seldom that Caleb volunteered so long a speech, but his happiness had the effect of mountain air : his eyes were bright, and the words came without effort.

"I congratulate you heartily, Garth," said the Vicar. "This is the best sort of news I could have had to carry to Fred Vincy, for he dwelt a good deal on the injury he had done you in causing you to part with money—robbing you of it, he said—which you wanted for other purposes. I wish Fred were not such an idle dog ; he has some very good points, and his father is a little hard upon him."

"Where is he going ?" said Mrs Garth, rather coldly.

"He means to try again for his degree, and he is going up to study before term. I have advised him to do that. I don't urge him to enter the Church—on the contrary. But if he will go and work so as to pass, that will be some guarantee that he has energy and a will ; and he is quite at sea ; he doesn't know what else to do. So far he will please his father, and I have promised in the mean time to try and reconcile Vincy to his son's adopting some other line of life. Fred says frankly he is not fit for a clergyman, and I would do anything I could to hinder a man from the fatal step of choosing the wrong profession. He quoted to me what you said, Miss Garth—do you remember it?" (Mr Farebrother used to say "Mary" instead of "Miss Garth," but it was part of his delicacy to treat her with the more deference because, according to Mrs Vincy's phrase, she worked for her bread.)

Mary felt uncomfortable, but, determined to take the matter lightly, answered at once, "I have said so many impertinent things to Fred—we are such old playfellows."

"You said, according to him, that he would be one of those ridiculous clergymen who help to make the whole clergy ridiculous. Really, that was so cutting that I felt a little cut myself."

Caleb laughed. "She gets her tongue from you, Susan," he said, with some enjoyment.

"Not its flippancy, father," said Mary, quickly, fearing that her mother would be displeased. "It is rather too bad of Fred to repeat my flippant speeches to Mr Farebrother."

"It was certainly a hasty speech, my dear," said Mrs Garth, with whom speaking evil of dignities was a high misdemeanour. "We should not value our Vicar the less because there was a ridiculous curate in the next parish."

"There's something in what she says, though," said Caleb, not disposed to have Mary's sharpness undervalued. "A bad workman of any sort makes his fellows mistrusted. Things hang together," he added, looking on the floor and moving his feet uneasily with a sense that words were scantier than thoughts.

"Clearly," said the Vicar, amused. "By being contemptible we set men's minds to the tune of contempt. I certainly agree with Miss Garth's view of the matter, whether I am condemned by it or not. But as to Fred Vincy, it is only fair he should be excused a little : old Featherstone's delusive behaviour did help to spoil him. There was something quite diabolical in not leaving him a farthing after all. But Fred has the good taste not to dwell on that. And what he cares most about is having offended you, Mrs Garth ; he supposes you will never think well of him again."

"I have been disappointed in Fred," said Mrs Garth, with decision. "But I shall be ready to think well of him again when he gives me good reason to do so."

At this point Mary went out of the room, taking Letty with her.

"Oh, we must forgive young people when they're sorry," said Caleb, watching Mary close the door. "And as you say, Mr Farebrother, there was the very devil in that old man. Now Mary's gone out, I must tell you a thing—it's only known to Susan and me, and you'll not tell it again. The old scoundrel wanted Mary to burn one of the wills the very night he died, when she was sitting up with him by herself, and he offered her a sum of money that he had in the box by him if she would do it. But Mary, you understand, could do no such thing—would not be handling his iron chest, and so on. Now, you see, the will he wanted burnt was this last, so that if Mary had done what he wanted, Fred Vincy would have had ten thousand pounds. The old man did turn to him at the last. That touches poor Mary close ; she couldn't help it—she was in the right to do what she did, but she feels, as she says, much as if she had knocked down somebody's property and broken it against her will, when she was rightfully defending herself. I feel with her, somehow, and if I could make any amends to the poor lad, instead of bearing him a grudge for the harm he did us, I should be glad to do it. Now, what is your opinion, sir? Susan doesn't agree with me. She says —tell what you say, Susan."

"Mary could not have acted otherwise, even if she had known what would be the effect on Fred," said Mrs Garth, pausing from her work, and looking at Mr Farebrother. "And she was quite ignorant of it. It seems to me, a loss which falls on another because we have done right is not to lie upon our conscience."

The Vicar did not answer immediately, and Caleb said, "It's the feeling. The child feels in that way, and I feel with her. You don't mean your horse to tread on a dog when you're backing out of the way; but it goes through you, when it's done."

"I am sure Mrs Garth would ágree with you there," said Mr Farebrother, who for some reason seemed more inclined to ruminate than to speak. "One could hardly say that the feeling you mention about Fred is wrong—or rather, mistaken—though no man ought to make a claim on such feeling."

"Well, well," said Caleb; "it's a secret. You will not tell Fred."

"Certainly not. But I shall carry the other good news—that you can afford the loss he caused you."

Mr Farebrother left the house soon after, and seeing Mary in the orchard with Letty, went to say good-bye to her. They made a pretty picture in the western light which brought out the brightness of the apples on the old scant-leaved boughs—Mary in her lavender gingham and black ribbons holding a basket, while Letty in her well-worn nankin picked up the fallen apples. If you want to know more particularly how Mary looked, ten to one you will see à face like hers in the crowded street to-morrow, if you are there on the watch: she will not be among those daughters of Zion who are haughty, and walk with stretched-out necks and wanton eyes, mincing as they go: let all those pass, and fix your eyes on some small plump brownish person of firm but quiet carriage, who looks about her, but does not suppose that anybody is looking at her. If she has a broad face and square brow, well-marked eyebrows and curly dark hair, a certain expression of amusement in her glance which her mouth keeps the secret of, and for the rest features entirely insignificant—take that ordinary but not disagreeable person for a portrait of Mary Garth. If you made her smile, she would show you perfect little teeth; if you made her angry, she would not raise her voice, but would probably say one of the bitterest things you have ever tasted the flavour of; if you did her a kindness, she would never forget it. Mary admired the keen-faced handsome little Vicar in his well-brushed threadbare clothes more than any man she had had the opportunity of knowing. She had never heard him say a foolish thing, though she knew that he did unwise ones; and perhaps foolish sayings were more objectionable to her than any of Mr Farebrother's unwise doings. At least, it was remarkable that the actual imperfections of the Vicar's clerical character never seemed to call forth the same scorn and dislike which she showed beforehand for the predicted imperfections of the clerical character sustained by Fred Vincy. These irregularities of judgment, I imagine, are found even in riper minds than Mary Garth's: our impartiality is kept for abstract merit and demerit, which none of us ever saw. Will any one guess towards which of those widely different men Mary had the peculiar woman's tenderness ?—the one she was most inclined to be severe on, or the contrary ?

"Have you any message for your old playfellow, Miss Garth ?" said the Vicar, as he took a fragrant apple from the basket which she held towards him, and put it in his pocket. "Something to soften down that harsh judgment ? I am going straight to see him."

"No," said Mary, shaking her head, and smiling. "If I were to say that he would not be ridiculous as a clergyman, I must say that he would be something worse than ridiculous. But I am very glad to hear that he is going away to work."

"On the other hand, I am very glad to hear that *you* are not going away to work. My mother, I am sure, will be all the happier if you will come to see her at the vicarage: you know she is fond of having young people to talk to, and she has a great deal to tell about old times. You will really be doing a kindness."

"I should like it very much, if I may," said Mary. "Everything seems too happy for me all at once. I thought it would always be part of my life to long for home, and losing that grievance makes me feel rather empty : I suppose it served instead of sense to fill up my mind ?"

"May I go with you, Mary ?" whispered Letty—a most inconvenient child, who listened to everything. But she was made exultant by having her chin pinched and her cheek kissed by Mr Farebrother—an incident which she narrated to her mother and father.

As the Vicar walked to Lowick, any one watching him closely might have seen him twice shrug his shoulders. I think that the rare Englishmen who have this gesture are never of the heavy type—for fear of any lumbering instance to the contrary, I will say, hardly ever ; they have usually a fine temperament and much tolerance towards the smaller errors of men (themselves inclusive). The Vicar was holding an inward dialogue in which he told himself that there was probably something more between Fred and Mary Garth than the regard of old playfellows, and replied with a question whether that bit of womanhood were not a great deal too choice for that crude young gentleman. The rejoinder to this was the first shrug. Then he laughed at himself for being likely to have felt jealous, as if he had been a man able to marry, which, added he, it is as clear as any balance-sheet that I am not. Whereupon followed the second shrug.

What could two men, so different from each other, see in this "brown patch," as Mary called herself? It was certainly not her plainness that attracted them (and let all plain young ladies be warned against the dangerous encouragement given them by Society to confide in their want of beauty). A human being in this aged nation of ours is a very wonderful whole, the slow creation of long interchanging influences ; and charm is a result of two such wholes, the one loving and the one loved.

When Mr and Mrs Garth were sitting alone, Caleb said, "Susan, guess what I'm thinking of."

"The rotation of crops," said Mrs Garth, smiling at him, above her knitting, "or else the backdoors of the Tipton cottages."

"No," said Caleb, gravely ; "I am thinking that I could do a great turn for Fred Vincy. Christy's gone, Alfred will be gone soon, and it will be five years before Jim is ready to take to business. I shall want help, and Fred might come in and learn the nature of things and act under me, and it might be the making of him into a useful man, if he gives up being a parson. What do you think ?"

" I think, there is hardly anything honest that his family would object to more," said Mrs Garth, decidedly.

" What care I about their objecting ?" said Caleb, with a sturdiness which he was apt to show when he had an opinion. " The lad is of age and must get his bread. He has sense enough and quickness enough ; he likes being on the land, and it's my belief that he could learn business well if he gave his mind to it."

" But would he ? His father and mother wanted him to be a fine gentleman, and I think he has the same sort of feeling himself. They all think us beneath them. And if the proposal came from you, I am sure Mrs Vincy would say that we wanted Fred for Mary."

" Life is a poor tale, if it is to be settled by nonsense of that sort," said Caleb, with disgust.

" Yes, but there is a certain pride which is proper, Caleb."

" I call it improper pride to let fools' notions hinder you from doing a good action. There's no sort of work," said Caleb, with fervour, putting out his hand and moving it up and down to mark his emphasis, " that could ever be done well, if you minded what fools say. You must have it inside you that your plan is right, and that plan you must follow."

" I will not oppose any plan you have set your mind on, Caleb," said Mrs Garth, who was a firm woman, but knew that there were some points on which her mild husband was yet firmer. " Still, it seems to be fixed that Fred is to go back to college : will it not be better to wait and see what he will choose to do after that ? It is not easy to keep people against their will. And you are not yet quite sure enough of your own position, or what you will want."

" Well, it may be better to wait a bit. But as to my getting plenty of work for two, I'm pretty sure of that. I've always had my hands full with scattered things, and there's always something fresh turning up. Why, only yesterday—bless me, I don't think I told you!—it was rather odd that two men should have been at me on different sides to do the same bit of valuing. And who do you think they were ?" said Caleb, taking a pinch of snuff and holding it up between his fingers, as if it were a part of his exposition. He was fond of a pinch when it occurred to him, but he usually forgot that this indulgence was at his command.

His wife held down her knitting and looked attentive.

" Why, that Rigg, or Rigg Featherstone, was one. But Bulstrode was before him, so I'm going to do it for Bulstrode. Whether it's mortgage or purchase they're going for, I can't tell yet."

" Can that man be going to sell the land just left him—which he has taken the name for ?" said Mrs Garth.

" Deuce knows," said Caleb, who never referred the knowledge of discreditable doings to any higher power than the deuce. " But Bulstrode has long been wanting to get a handsome bit of land under his fingers—that I know. And it's a difficult matter to get, in this part of the country."

Caleb scattered his snuff carefully instead of taking it, and then added, " The ins and outs of things are curious. Here is the land they've been all along expecting for Fred, which it seems the old man never meant to leave him a foot of, but left it to this side-slip of a son that he kept in the dark, and thought of his sticking there and vexing everybody as well as he could have vexed 'em himself if he could have kept alive. I say, it would be curious if it got into Bulstrode's hands after all. The old man hated him, and never would bank with him."

"What reason could the miserable creature have for hating a man whom he had nothing to do with?" said Mrs Garth.

"Pooh! where's the use of asking for such fellows' reasons? The soul of man," said Caleb, with the deep tone and grave shake of the head which always came when he used this phrase—"the soul of man, when it gets fairly rotten, will bear you all sorts of poisonous toad-stools, and no eye can see whence came the seed thereof."

It was one of Caleb's quaintnesses, that in his difficulty of finding speech for his thought, he caught, as it were, snatches of diction which he associated with various points of view or states of mind ; and whenever he had a feeling of awe, he was haunted by a sense of Biblical phraseology, though he could hardly have given a strict quotation.

CHAPTER XLI

"By swaggering could I never thrive,
For the rain it raineth every day."
—*Twelfth Night.* [1]

THE transactions referred to by Caleb Garth as having gone forward between Mr Bulstrode and Mr Joshua Rigg Featherstone concerning the land attached to Stone Court, had occasioned the interchange of a letter or two between these personages.

Who shall tell what may be the effect of writing? If it happens to have been cut in stone, though it lie face downmost for ages on a forsaken beach, or "rest quietly under the drums and tramplings of many conquests," it may end by letting us into the secret of usurpations and other scandals gossiped about long empires ago : — this world being apparently a huge whispering-gallery. [2] Such conditions are often minutely represented in our petty lifetimes. As the stone which has been kicked by generations of clowns may come by curious little links of effect under the eyes of a scholar, through whose labours it may at last fix the date of invasions and unlock religions, so a bit of ink and paper which has long been an innocent wrapping or stop-gap may at last be laid open under the one pair of eyes which have knowledge enough to turn it into the opening of a catastrophe. To Uriel watching the progress of planetary history from the Sun, the one result would be just as much of a coincidence as the other. [3]

Having made this rather lofty comparison I am less uneasy in call-

---

1. Act V, Sc. 1, lines 400–401.
2. A circular gallery—like that in the dome of St. Paul's Cathedral in London —in which low sounds carry great distances.

3. Milton's Uriel is "Regent of the Sun, and held/The sharpest-sighted Spirit of all in Heav'n" (*Paradise Lost*, III, 690–91).

ing attention to the existence of low people by whose interference, however little we may like it, the course of the world is very much determined. It would be well, certainly, if we could help to reduce their number, and something might perhaps be done by not lightly giving occasion to their existence. Socially speaking, Joshua Rigg would have been generally pronounced a superfluity. But those who like Peter Featherstone never had a copy of themselves demanded, are the very last to wait for such a request either in prose or verse. The copy in this case bore more of outside resemblance to the mother, in whose sex frog-features, accompanied with fresh-coloured cheeks and a well-rounded figure, are compatible with much charm for a certain order of admirers. The result is sometimes a frog-faced male, desirable, surely, to no order of intelligent beings. Especially when he is suddenly brought into evidence to frustrate other people's expectations — the very lowest aspect in which a social superfluity can present himself.

But Mr Rigg Featherstone's low characteristics were all of the sober, water-drinking kind. From the earliest to the latest hour of the day he was always as sleek, neat, and cool as the frog he resembled, and old Peter had secretly chuckled over an offshoot almost more calculating, and far more imperturbable, than himself. I will add that his finger-nails were scrupulously attended to, and that he meant to marry a well-educated young lady (as yet unspecified) whose person was good, and whose connections, in a solid middle-class way, were undeniable. Thus his nails and modesty were comparable to those of most gentlemen ; though his ambition had been educated only by the opportunities of a clerk and accountant in the smaller commercial houses of a seaport. He thought the rural Featherstones very simple absurd people, and they in their turn regarded his " bringing up " in a seaport town as an exaggeration of the monstrosity that their brother Peter, and still more Peter's property, should have had such belongings.

The garden and gravel approach, as seen from the two windows of the wainscoted parlour at Stone Court, were never in better trim than now, when Mr Rigg Featherstone stood, with his hands behind him, looking out on these grounds as their master. But it seemed doubtful whether he looked out for the sake of contemplation or of turning his back to a person who stood in the middle of the room, with his legs considerably apart and his hands in his trouser-pockets : a person in all respects a contrast to the sleek and cool Rigg. He was a man obviously on the way towards sixty, very florid and hairy, with much grey in his bushy whiskers and thick curly hair, a stoutish body which showed to disadvantage the somewhat worn joinings of his clothes, and the air of a swaggerer, who would aim at being noticeable even at a show of fireworks, regarding his own remarks on any other person's performance as likely to be more interesting than the performance itself.

His name was John Raffles, and he sometimes wrote jocosely W.A.G. after his signature, observing when he did so, that he was once taught by Leonard Lamb of Finsbury who wrote B.A. after his name, and that he, Raffles, originated the witticism of calling that celebrated principal Ba-Lamb. Such were the appearance and mental flavour of Mr Raffles, both of which seemed to have a stale odour of travellers' rooms in the commercial hotels of that period.

" Come, now, Josh," he was saying, in a full rumbling tone, "look
at it in this light : here is your poor mother going into the vale of
years, and you could afford something handsome now to make her
comfortable."

" Not while you live. Nothing would make her comfortable while
you live," returned Rigg, in his cool high voice. " What I give her,
you'll take."

" You bear me a grudge, Josh, that I know. But come, now — as
between man and man—without humbug—a little capital might enable me to make a first-rate thing of the shop. The tobacco trade is
growing. I should cut my own nose off in not doing the best I could
at it. I should stick to it like a flea to a fleece for my own sake. I should
always be on the spot. And nothing would make your poor mother
so happy. I've pretty well done with my wild oats—turned fifty-five.
I want to settle down in my chimney-corner. And if I once buckled
to the tobacco trade, I could bring an amount of brains and experience
to bear on it that would not be found elsewhere in a hurry. I don't
want to be bothering you one time after another, but to get things
once for all into the right channel. Consider that, Josh—as between
man and man—and with your poor mother to be made easy for her
life. I was always fond of the old woman, *by* Jove !"

" Have you done ? " said Mr Rigg, quietly, without looking away
from the window.

" Yes, *I*'ve done," said Raffles, taking hold of his hat which
stood before him on the table, and giving it a sort of oratorical
push.

" Then just listen to me. The more you say anything, the less I
shall believe it. The more you want me to do a thing, the more
reason I shall have for never doing it. Do you think I mean to forget
your kicking me when I was a lad, and eating all the best victual
away from me and my mother ? Do you think I forget your always
coming home to sell and pocket everything, and going off again leaving us in the lurch ? I should be glad to see you whipped at the
cart-tail. My mother was a fool to you : she'd no right to give me a
father-in-law, and she's been punished for it. [4] She shall have her
weekly allowance paid and no more : and that shall be stopped if you
dare to come on to these premises again, or to come into this country
after me again. The next time you show yourself inside the gates
here, you shall be driven off with the dogs and the waggoner's whip."

As Rigg pronounced the last words he turned round and looked at
Raffles with his prominent frozen eyes. The contrast was as striking
as it could have been eighteen years before, when Rigg was a most
unengaging kickable boy, and Raffles was the rather thick-set Adonis
of bar-rooms and back-parlours. But the advantage now was on the
side of Rigg, and auditors of this conversation might probably have
expected that Raffles would retire with the air of a defeated dog. Not
at all. He made a grimace which was habitual with him whenever
he was " out " in a game ; then subsided into a laugh, and drew a
brandy-flask from his pocket.

" Come, Josh," he said, in a cajoling tone, " give us a spoonful of

4. Father-in-law: stepfather.

brandy, and a sovereign to pay the way back, and I'll go. Honour bright! I'll go like a bullet, *by* Jove!"

"Mind," said Rigg, drawing out a bunch of keys, "if I ever see you again, I shan't speak to you. I don't own you any more than if I saw a crow; and if you want to own me you'll get nothing by it but a character for being what you are—a spiteful, brassy, bullying rogue."

"That's a pity, now, Josh," said Raffles, affecting to scratch his head and wrinkle his brows upward as if he were nonplussed. "I'm very fond of you; *by* Jove, I am! There's nothing I like better than plaguing you—you're so like your mother; and I must do without it. But the brandy and the sovereign's a bargain."

He jerked forward the flask and Rigg went to a fine old oaken bureau with his keys. But Raffles had reminded himself by his movement with the flask that it had become dangerously loose from its leather covering, and catching sight of a folded paper which had fallen within the fender, he took it up and shoved it under the leather so as to make the glass firm.

By that time Rigg came forward with a brandy - bottle, filled the flask, and handed Raffles a sovereign, neither looking at him nor speaking to him. After locking up the bureau again, he walked to the window and gazed out as impassibly as he had done at the beginning of the interview, while Raffles took a small allowance from the flask, screwed it up, and deposited it in his side-pocket, with provoking slowness, making a grimace at his stepson's back.

"Farewell, Josh—and if for ever!" said Raffles, turning back his head as he opened the door.

Rigg saw him leave the grounds and enter the lane. The grey day had turned to a light drizzling rain, which freshened the hedgerows and the grassy borders of the byroads, and hastened the labourers who were loading the last shocks of corn. Raffles, walking with the uneasy gait of a town loiterer obliged to do a bit of country journeying on foot, looked as incongruous amid this moist rural quiet and industry as if he had been a baboon escaped from a menagerie. But there were none to stare at him except the long-weaned calves, and none to show dislike of his appearance except the little water-rats which rustled away at his approach.

He was fortunate enough when he got on to the highroad to be overtaken by the stage-coach, which carried him to Brassing; and there he took the new-made railway, observing to his fellow-passengers that he considered it pretty well seasoned now it had done for Huskisson. [5] Mr Raffles on most occasions kept up the sense of having been educated at an academy, and being able, if he chose, to pass well everywhere; indeed, there was not one of his fellow-men whom he did not feel himself in a position to ridicule and torment, confident of the entertainment which he thus gave to all the rest of the company.

He played this part now with as much spirit as if his journey had been entirely successful, resorting at frequent intervals to his flask.

---

5. Huskisson was killed at the opening of the Manchester-Liverpool railway on September 15, 1830, when he fell from the platform in front of the incoming train. He was the first person killed in a railway accident.

The paper with which he had wedged it was a letter signed *Nicholas Bulstrode*, but Raffles was not likely to disturb it from its present useful position.

CHAPTER XLII.

" How much, methinks, I could despise this man,
Were I not bound in charity against it ! "
—SHAKESPEARE : *Henry VIII.* [1]

ONE of the professional calls made by Lydgate soon after his return from his wedding-journey was to Lowick Manor, in consequence of a letter which had requested him to fix a time for his visit.

Mr Casaubon had never put any question concerning the nature of his illness to Lydgate, nor had he even to Dorothea betrayed any anxiety as to how far it might be likely to cut short his labours or his life. On this point, as on all others, he shrank from pity ; and if the suspicion of being pitied for anything in his lot surmised or known in spite of himself was embittering, the idea of calling forth a show of compassion by frankly admitting an alarm or a sorrow was necessarily intolerable to him. Every proud mind knows something of this experience, and perhaps it is only to be overcome by a sense of fellowship deep enough to make all efforts at isolation seem mean and petty instead of exalting.

But Mr Casaubon was now brooding over something through which the question of his health and life haunted his silence with a more harassing importunity even than through the autumnal unripeness of his authorship. It is true that this last might be called his central ambition ; but there are some kinds of authorship in which by far the largest result is the uneasy susceptibility accumulated in the consciousness of the author—one knows of the river by a few streaks amid a long-gathered deposit of uncomfortable mud. That was the way with Mr Casaubon's hard intellectual labours. Their most characteristic result was not the ' Key to all Mythologies,' but a morbid consciousness that others did not give him the place which he had not demonstrably merited—a perpetual suspicious conjecture that the views entertained of him were not to his advantage—a melancholy absence of passion in his efforts at achievement, and a passionate resistance to the confession that he had achieved nothing.

Thus his intellectual ambition which seemed to others to have absorbed and dried him, was really no security against wounds, least of all against those which came from Dorothea. And he had begun now to frame possibilities for the future which were somehow more embittering to him than anything his mind had dwelt on before.

Against certain facts he was helpless : against Will Ladislaw's existence, his defiant stay in the neighbourhood of Lowick, and his flip-

---

1. Act III, Sc. 2, lines 298–99.

pant state of mind with regard to the possessors of authentic, well-stamped erudition : against Dorothea's nature, always taking on some new shape of ardent activity, and even in submission and silence covering fervid reasons which it was an irritation to think of: against certain notions and likings which had taken possession of her mind in relation to subjects that he could not possibly discuss with her. There was no denying that Dorothea was as virtuous and lovely a young lady as he could have obtained for a wife ; but a young lady turned out to be something more troublesome than he had conceived. She nursed him, she read to him, she anticipated his wants, and was solicitous about his feelings ; but there had entered into the husband's mind the certainty that she judged him, and that her wifely devotedness was like a penitential expiation of unbelieving thoughts—was accompanied with a power of comparison by which himself and his doings were seen too luminously as a part of things in general. His discontent passed vapour-like through all her gentle loving manifestations, and clung to that inappreciative world which she had only brought nearer to him.

Poor Mr Casaubon! This suffering was the harder to bear because it seemed like a betrayal: the young creature who had worshipped him with perfect trust had quickly turned into the critical wife ; and early instances of criticism and resentment had made an impression which no tenderness and submission afterwards could remove. To his suspicious interpretation Dorothea's silence now was a suppressed rebellion ; a remark from her which he had not in any way anticipated was an assertion of conscious superiority ; her gentle answers had an irritating cautiousness in them ; and when she acquiesced it was a self-approved effort of forbearance. The tenacity with which he strove to hide this inward drama made it the more vivid for him ; as we hear with the more keenness what we wish others not to hear.

Instead of wondering at this result of misery in Mr Casaubon, I think it quite ordinary. Will not a tiny speck very close to our vision blot out the glory of the world, and leave only a margin by which we see the blot? I know no speck so troublesome as self. And who, if Mr Casaubon had chosen to expound his discontents—his suspicions that he was not any longer adored without criticism—could have denied that they were founded on good reasons ? On the contrary, there was a strong reason to be added, which he had not himself taken explicitly into account—namely, that he was not unmixedly adorable. He suspected this, however, as he suspected other things, without confessing it, and like the rest of us, felt how soothing it would have been to have a companion who would never find it out.

This sore susceptibility in relation to Dorothea was thoroughly prepared before Will Ladislaw had returned to Lowick, and what had occurred since then had brought Mr Casaubon's power of suspicious construction into exasperated activity. To all the facts which he knew, he added imaginary facts both present and future which became more real to him than those, because they called up a stronger dislike, a more predominating bitterness. Suspicion and jealousy of Will Ladislaw's intentions, suspicion and jealousy of Dorothea's impressions, were constantly at their weaving work. It would be quite unjust to him to suppose that he could have entered into any coarse misinterpretation of Dorothea : his own habits of mind and conduct, quite as much as the open elevation of her nature, saved him from any such mistake. What he was jealous of was her opinion, the sway that might be given to her ardent mind in its judgments, and the future possibilities to which these might lead her. As to Will, though until his last defiant letter he had nothing definite which he would choose formally to allege against him, he felt himself warranted in believing that he was capable of any design which could fascinate a rebellious temper and an undisciplined impulsiveness. He was quite sure that Dorothea was the cause of Will's return from Rome, and his determination to settle in the neighbourhood ; and he was penetrating enough to imagine that Dorothea had innocently encouraged this course. It was as clear as possible that she was ready to be attached to Will and to be pliant to his suggestions: they had never had a *tête-à-tête* without her bringing away from it some new troublesome impression, and the last interview that Mr Casaubon was aware of (Dorothea, on returning from Freshitt Hall, had for the first time been silent about having seen Will) had led to a scene which roused an angrier feeling against them both than he had ever known before. Dorothea's outpouring. of her notions about money, in the darkness of the night, had done nothing but bring a mixture of more odious foreboding into her husband's mind.

And there was the shock lately given to his health always sadly present with him. He was certainly much revived ; he had recovered all his usual power of work : the illness might have been mere fatigue, and there might still be twenty years of achievement before him, which would justify the thirty years of preparation. That prospect was made the sweeter by a flavour of vengeance against the hasty sneers of Carp & Company ; for even when Mr Casaubon was carrying his taper among the tombs of the past, those modern figures came athwart the dim light, and interrupted his diligent exploration. To convince Carp of his mistake, so that he would have to eat his own words with a good deal of indigestion, would be an agreeable accident of triumphant authorship, which the prospect of living to future ages on earth and to all eternity in heaven could not exclude from contemplation. Since, thus, the prevision of his own unending bliss could not nullify the bitter savours of irritated jealousy and vindictiveness, it is the less surprising that the probability of a transient earthly bliss for other persons, when he himself should have entered into glory, had not a potently sweetening effect. If the truth should be that some undermining disease was at work within him, there might be large opportunity for some people to be the happier when he was gone ; and if one of those people should be Will Ladislaw, Mr Casaubon objected so strongly that it seemed as if the annoyance would make part of his disembodied existence.

This is a very bare and therefore a very incomplete way of putting the case. The human soul moves in many channels, and Mr Casaubon, we know, had a sense of rectitude and an honourable pride in satisfying the requirements of honour, which compelled him to find other reasons for his conduct than those of jealousy and vindictiveness. The way in which Mr Casaubon put the case was this :—

"In marrying Dorothea Brooke I had to care for her wellbeing in case of my death. But wellbeing is not to be secured by ample, independent possession of property ; on the contrary, occasions might arise in which such possession might expose her to the more danger. She is ready prey to any man who knows how to play adroitly either on her affectionate ardour or her Quixotic enthusiasm ; and a man stands by with that very intention in his mind—a man with no other principle than transient caprice, and who has a personal animosity towards me—I am sure of it—an animosity which is fed by the consciousness of his ingratitude, and which he has constantly vented in ridicule of which I am as well assured as if I had heard it. Even if I live I shall not be without uneasiness as to what he may attempt through indirect influence. This man has gained Dorothea's ear : he has fascinated her attention ; he has evidently tried to impress her mind with the notion that he has claims beyond anything I have done for him. If I die—and he is waiting here on the watch for that—he will persuade her to marry him. That would be calamity for her and success for him. *She* would not think it calamity : he would make her believe anything ; she has a tendency to immoderate attachment which she inwardly reproaches me for not responding to, and already her mind is occupied with his fortunes. He thinks of an easy conquest and of entering into my nest. That I will hinder ! Such a marriage would be fatal to Dorothea. Has he ever persisted in anything except from contradiction ? In knowledge he has always tried to be showy at small cost. In religion he could be, as long as it suited him, the facile echo of Dorothea's vagaries. When was sciolism ever dissociated from laxity ? I utterly distrust his morals, and it is my duty to hinder to the utmost the fulfilment of his designs."

The arrangements made by Mr Casaubon on his marriage left strong measures open to him, but in ruminating on them his mind inevitably dwelt so much on the probabilities of his own life that the longing to get the nearest possible calculation had at last overcome his proud reticence, and had determined him to ask Lydgate's opinion as to the nature of his illness.

He had mentioned to Dorothea that Lydgate was coming by appointment at half-past three, and in answer to her anxious question, whether he had felt ill, replied,—" No, I merely wish to have his opinion concerning some habitual symptoms. You need not see him, my dear. I shall give orders that he may be sent to me in the Yew-Tree walk, where I shall be taking my usual exercise."

When Lydgate entered the Yew-Tree walk he saw Mr Casaubon slowly receding with his hands behind him according to his habit, and his head bent forward. It was a lovely afternoon ; the leaves from the lofty limes were falling silently across the sombre evergreens, while the lights and shadows slept side by side : there was no sound but the cawing of the rooks, which to the accustomed ear is a lullaby, or that last solemn lullaby, a dirge. Lydgate, conscious of an energetic frame in its prime, felt some compassion when the figure which he was likely soon to overtake turned round, and in advancing towards him showed more markedly than ever the signs of premature age—the student's bent shoulders, the emaciated limbs, and the melancholy lines of the mouth. " Poor fellow," he thought, " some men with his years are like lions ; one can tell nothing of their age except that they are full grown."

" Mr Lydgate," said Mr Casaubon, with his invariably polite air, " I am exceedingly obliged to you for your punctuality. We will, if you please, carry on our conversation in walking to and fro."

" I hope your wish to see me is not due to the return of unpleasant symptoms," said Lydgate, filling up a pause.

" Not immediately—no. In order to account for that wish I must mention—what it were otherwise needless to refer to—that my life, on all collateral accounts insignificant, derives a possible importance from the incompleteness of labours which have extended through all its best years. In short, I have long had on hand a work which I would fain leave behind me in such a state, at least, that it might be committed to the press by—others. Were I assured that this is the utmost I can reasonably expect, that assurance would be a useful circumscription of my attempts, and a guide in both the positive and negative determination of my course."

Here Mr Casaubon paused, removed one hand from his back and thrust it between the buttons of his single-breasted coat. To a mind largely instructed in the human destiny hardly anything could be more interesting than the inward conflict implied in his formal measured address, delivered with the usual sing-song and motion of the head. Nay, are there many situations more sublimely tragic than the struggle of the soul with the demand to renounce a work which has been all the significance of its life—a significance which is to vanish as the waters which come and go where no man has need of them ? But there was nothing to strike others as sublime about Mr Casaubon, and Lydgate, who had some contempt at hand for futile scholarship, felt a little amusement mingling with his pity. He was at present too ill acquainted with disaster to enter into the pathos of a lot where everything is below the level of tragedy except the passionate egoism of the sufferer.

" You refer to the possible hindrances from want of health ?" he said, wishing to help forward Mr Casaubon's purpose, which seemed to be clogged by some hesitation.

" I do. You have not implied to me that the symptoms which— I am bound to testify—you watched with scrupulous care, were those of a fatal disease. But were it so, Mr Lydgate, I should desire to know the truth without reservation, and I appeal to you for an exact statement of your conclusions : I request it as a friendly service. If you can tell me that my life is not threatened by anything else than ordinary casualties, I shall rejoice, on grounds which I have already indicated. If not, knowledge of the truth is even more important to me."

" Then I can no longer hesitate as to my course," said Lydgate ; " but the first thing I must impress on you is that my conclusions are doubly uncertain—uncertain not only because of my fallibility, but because diseases of the heart are eminently difficult to found predictions on. In any case, one can hardly increase appreciably the tremendous uncertainty of life."

Mr Casaubon winced perceptibly, but bowed.

" I believe that you are suffering from what is called fatty degeneration of the heart, a disease which was first divined and explored by Laennec, the man who gave us the stethoscope, not so very many years ago.[2] A good deal of experience—a more lengthened observation—is wanting on the subject. But after what you have said, it is my duty to tell you that death from this disease is often sudden. At the same time, no such result can be predicted. Your condition may be consistent with a tolerably comfortable life for another fifteen years, or even more. I could add no information to this, beyond anatomical or medical details, which would leave expectation at precisely the same point."

Lydgate's instinct was fine enough to tell him that plain speech, quite free from ostentatious caution, would be felt by Mr Casaubon as a tribute of respect.

" I thank you, Mr Lydgate," said Mr Casaubon, after a moment's pause. " One thing more I have still to ask : did you communicate what you have now told me to Mrs Casaubon ? "

" Partly—I mean, as to the possible issues." Lydgate was going to explain why he had told Dorothea, but Mr Casaubon, with an unmistakable desire to end the conversation, waved his hand slightly, and said again, " I thank you," proceeding to remark on the rare beauty of the day.

Lydgate, certain that his patient wished to be alone, soon left him ; and the black figure with hands behind and head bent forward continued to pace the walk where the dark yew-trees gave him a mute companionship in melancholy, and the little shadows of bird or leaf that fleeted across the isles of sunlight, stole along in silence as in the presence of a sorrow. Here was a man who now for the first time found himself looking into the eyes of death—who was passing through one of those rare moments of experience when we feel the truth of a commonplace, which is as different from what we call knowing it, as the vision of waters upon the earth is different from the delirious vision of the water which cannot be had to cool the burning tongue. When the commonplace " We must all die" transforms itself suddenly into the acute consciousness " I must die—and soon," then death grapples us, and his fingers are cruel ; afterwards, he may come to fold us in his arms as our mother did, and our last moment of dim earthly discerning may be like the first. To Mr Casaubon now, it was as if he suddenly found himself on the dark river-brink and heard the plash of the oncoming oar, not discerning the forms, but expecting the summons. In such an hour the mind does not change its lifelong bias, but carries it onward in imagination to the other side of death, gazing backward—perhaps with the divine calm of beneficence, perhaps with the petty anxieties of self-assertion. What was Mr Casaubon's bias his acts will give us a clue to. He held himself to be, with some private scholarly reservations, a believing Christian, as to estimates of the present and hopes of the future. But what we strive to gratify, though we may call it a distant hope, is an immediate desire : the future estate for which men drudge up city alleys exists already in their imagination and love. And Mr Casaubon's immediate desire was not for divine communion and light

2. René Théophile Hyacinthe Laënnec (1781–1826), French physician and heart specialist. GE's note: "Laennec, First Memoir on Ausculation, 1818" (see *Quarry* below, p. 607).

divested of earthly conditions; his passionate longings, poor man, clung low and mist-like in very shady places.

Dorothea had been aware when Lydgate had ridden away, and she had stepped into the garden, with the impulse to go at once to her husband. But she hesitated, fearing to offend him by obtruding herself; for her ardour, continually repulsed, served, with her intense memory, to heighten her dread, as thwarted energy subsides into a shudder; and she wandered slowly round the nearer clumps of trees until she saw him advancing. Then she went towards him, and might have represented a heaven-sent angel coming with a promise that the short hours remaining should yet be filled with that faithful love which clings the closer to a comprehended grief. His glance in reply to hers was so chill that she felt her timidity increased; yet she turned and passed her hand through his arm.

Mr Casaubon kept his hands behind him and allowed her pliant arm to cling with difficulty against his rigid arm.

There was something horrible to Dorothea in the sensation which this unresponsive hardness inflicted on her. That is a strong word, but not too strong: it is in these acts called trivialities that the seeds of joy are for ever wasted, until men and women look round with haggard faces at the devastation their own waste has made, and say, the earth bears no harvest of sweetness—calling their denial knowledge. You may ask why, in the name of manliness, Mr Casaubon should have behaved in that way. Consider that his was a mind which shrank from pity: have you ever watched in such a mind the effect of a suspicion that what is pressing it as a grief may be really a source of contentment, either actual or future, to the being who already offends by pitying? Besides, he knew little of Dorothea's sensations, and had not reflected that on such an occasion as the present they were comparable in strength to his own sensibilities about Carp's criticisms.

Dorothea did not withdraw her arm, but she could not venture to speak. Mr Casaubon did not say, " I wish to be alone," but he directed his steps in silence towards the house, and as they entered by the glass door on this eastern side, Dorothea withdrew her arm and lingered on the matting, that she might leave her husband quite free. He entered the library and shut himself in, alone with his sorrow.

She went up to her boudoir. The open bow-window let in the serene glory of the afternoon lying in the avenue, where the lime-trees cast long shadows. But Dorothea knew nothing of the scene. She threw herself on a chair, not heeding that she was in the dazzling sun-rays: if there were discomfort in that, how could she tell that it was not part of her inward misery?

She was in the reaction of a rebellious anger stronger than any she had felt since her marriage. Instead of tears there came words:—

" What have I done—what am I—that he should treat me so? He never knows what is in my mind—he never cares. What is the use of anything I do? He wishes he had never married me."

She began to hear herself, and was checked into stillness. Like one who has lost his way and is weary, she sat and saw as in one glance all the paths of her young hope which she should never find again. And just as clearly in the miserable light she saw her own and her husband's solitude—how they walked apart so that she was obliged to survey him. If he had drawn her towards him, she would never have surveyed him—never have said, "Is he worth living for?" but would have felt him simply a part of her own life. Now she said bitterly, "It is his fault, not mine." In the jar of her whole being, Pity was overthrown. Was it her fault that she had believed in him —had believed in his worthiness?—And what, exactly, was he?—She was able enough to estimate him—she who waited on his glances with trembling, and shut her best soul in prison, paying it only hidden visits, that she might be petty enough to please him. In such a crisis as this, some women begin to hate.

The sun was low when Dorothea was thinking that she would not go down again, but would send a message to her husband saying that she was not well and preferred remaining up-stairs. She had never deliberately allowed her resentment to govern her in this way before, but she believed now that she could not see him again without telling him the truth about her feeling, and she must wait till she could do it without interruption. He might wonder and be hurt at her message. It was good that he should wonder and be hurt. Her anger said, as anger is apt to say, that God was with her—that all heaven, though it were crowded with spirits watching them, must be on her side. She had determined to ring her bell, when there came a rap at the door.

Mr Casaubon had sent to say that he would have his dinner in the library. He wished to be quite alone this evening, being much occupied.

"I shall not dine, then, Tantripp."

"Oh, madam, let me bring you a little something?"

"No ; I am not well. Get everything ready in my dressing-room, but pray do not disturb me again."

Dorothea sat almost motionless in her meditative struggle, while the evening slowly deepened into night. But the struggle changed continually, as that of a man who begins with a movement towards striking and ends with conquering his desire to strike. The energy that would animate a crime is not more than is wanted to inspire a resolved submission, when the noble habit of the soul reasserts itself. That thought with which Dorothea had gone out to meet her husband — her conviction that he had been asking about the possible arrest of all his work, and that the answer must have wrung his heart, could not be long without rising beside the image of him, like a shadowy monitor looking at her anger with sad remonstrance. It cost her a litany of pictured sorrows and of silent cries that she might be the mercy for those sorrows—but the resolved submission did come ; and when the house was still, and she knew that it was near the time when Mr Casaubon habitually went to rest, she opened her door gently and stood outside in the darkness waiting for his coming up-stairs with a light in his hand. If he did not come soon she thought that she would go down and even risk incurring another pang. She would never again expect anything else. But she did hear the library door open, and slowly the light advanced up the staircase without noise from the footsteps on the carpet. When her husband stood opposite to her, she saw that his face was more haggard. He started slightly on seeing her, and she looked up at him beseechingly, without speaking.

"Dorothea !" he said, with a gentle surprise in his tone. "Were you waiting for me ?"

"Yes, I did not like to disturb you."

"Come, my dear, come. You are young, and need not to extend your life by watching."

When the kind quiet melancholy of that speech fell on Dorothea's ears, she felt something like the thankfulness that might well up in us if we had narrowly escaped hurting a lamed creature. She put her hand into her husband's, and they went along the broad corridor together.

BOOK V.

THE DEAD HAND.

CHAPTER XLIII.

This figure hath high price: 'twas wrought with love
Ages ago in finest ivory;
Nought modish in it, pure and noble lines
Of generous womanhood that fits all time.
That too is costly ware; majolica
Of deft design, to please a lordly eye:
The smile, you see, is perfect—wonderful
As mere Faience! a table ornament
To suit the richest mounting.

DOROTHEA seldom left home without her husband, but she did occasionally drive into Middlemarch alone, on little errands of shopping or charity such as occur to every lady of any wealth when she lives within three miles of a town. Two days after that scene in the Yew-Tree Walk, she determined to use such an opportunity in order if possible to see Lydgate, and learn from him whether her husband had really felt any depressing change of symptoms which he was concealing from her, and whether he had insisted on knowing the utmost about himself. She felt almost guilty in asking for knowledge about him from another, but the dread of being without it — the dread of that ignorance which would make her unjust or hard—overcame every scruple. That there had been some crisis in her husband's mind she was certain: he had the very next day begun a new method of arranging his notes, and had associated her quite newly in carrying out his plan. Poor Dorothea needed to lay up stores of patience.

It was about four o'clock when she drove to Lydgate's house in Lowick Gate, wishing, in her immediate doubt of finding him at home, that she had written beforehand. And he was not at home.

"Is Mrs Lydgate at home?" said Dorothea, who had never, that she knew of, seen Rosamond, but now remembered the fact of the marriage. Yes, Mrs Lydgate was at home.

"I will go in and speak to her, if she will allow me. Will you ask her if she can see me—see Mrs Casaubon, for a few minutes?"

When the servant had gone to deliver that message, Dorothea could hear sounds of music through an open window — a few notes from a man's voice and then a piano bursting into roulades. But the roulades broke off suddenly, and then the servant came back saying that Mrs Lydgate would be happy to see Mrs Casaubon.

When the drawing-room door opened and Dorothea entered, there was a sort of contrast not infrequent in country life when the habits of the different ranks were less blent than now. Let those who know, tell us exactly what stuff it was that Dorothea wore in those days of mild autumn—that thin white woollen stuff soft to the touch and soft to the eye. It always seemed to have been lately washed, and to smell of the sweet hedges—was always in the shape of a pelisse with sleeves hanging all out of the fashion. Yet if she had entered before a still audience as Imogene or Cato's daughter, the dress might have seemed right enough : the grace and dignity were in her limbs and neck ; and about her simply parted hair and candid eyes the large round poke which was then in the fate of women, seemed no more odd as a head-dress than the gold trencher we call a halo. [1] By the present audience of two persons, no dramatic heroine could have been expected with more interest than Mrs Casaubon. To Rosamond she was one of those county divinities not mixing with Middlemarch mortality, whose slightest marks of manner or appearance were worthy of her study ; moreover, Rosamond was not without satisfaction that Mrs Casaubon should have an opportunity of studying *her*. What is the use of being exquisite if you are not seen by the best judges ? and since Rosamond had received the highest compliments at Sir Godwin Lydgate's, she felt quite confident of the impression she must make on people of good birth. Dorothea put out her hand with her usual simple kindness, and looked admiringly at Lydgate's lovely bride— aware that there was a gentleman standing at a distance, but seeing him merely as a coated figure at a wide angle. The gentleman was too much occupied with the presence of the one woman to reflect on the contrast between the two—a contrast that would certainly have been striking to a calm observer. They were both tall, and their eyes were on a level ; but imagine Rosamond's infantine blondness and wondrous crown of hair-plaits, with her pale-blue dress of a fit and fashion so perfect that no dressmaker could look at it without emotion, a large embroidered collar which it was to be hoped all beholders would know the price of, her small hands duly set off with rings, and that controlled self-consciousness of manner which is the expensive substitute for simplicity.

"Thank you very much for allowing me to interrupt you," said Dorothea, immediately. "I am anxious to see Mr Lydgate, if possible, before I go home, and I hoped that you might possibly tell me where I could find him, or even allow me to wait for him, if you expect him soon."

"He is at the New Hospital," said Rosamond ; "I am not sure how soon he will come home. But I can send for him."

"Will you let me go and fetch him ?" said Will Ladislaw, coming forward. He had already taken up his hat before Dorothea entered. She coloured with surprise, but put out her hand with a smile of unmistakable pleasure, saying—

"I did not know it was you : I had no thought of seeing you here."

"May I go to the Hospital and tell Mr Lydgate that you wish to see him ?" said Will.

"It would be quicker to send the carriage for him," said Doro-

---

1. Imogen is Shakespeare's heroine in *Cymbeline;* Cato's daughter, Marcia, is the heroine in Addison's *Cato*. A trencher is a round wooden plate.

thea, "if you will be kind enough to give the message to the coachman."

Will was moving to the door when Dorothea, whose mind had flashed in an instant over many connected memories, turned quickly and said, "I will go myself, thank you. I wish to lose no time before getting home again. I will drive to the Hospital and see Mr Lydgate there. Pray excuse me, Mrs Lydgate. I am very much obliged to you."

Her mind was evidently arrested by some sudden thought, and she left the room hardly conscious of what was immediately around her —hardly conscious that Will opened the door for her and offered her his arm to lead her to the carriage. She took the arm but said nothing. Will was feeling rather vexed and miserable, and found nothing to say on his side. He handed her into the carriage in silence, they said good-bye, and Dorothea drove away.

In the five minutes' drive to the Hospital she had time for some reflections that were quite new to her. Her decision to go, and her preoccupation in leaving the room, had come from the sudden sense that there would be a sort of deception in her voluntarily allowing any further intercourse between herself and Will which she was unable to mention to her husband, and already her errand in seeking Lydgate was a matter of concealment. That was all that had been explicitly in her mind; but she had been urged also by a vague discomfort. Now that she was alone in her drive, she heard the notes of the man's voice and the accompanying piano, which she had not noted much at the time, returning on her inward sense; and she found herself thinking with some wonder that Will Ladislaw was passing his time with Mrs Lydgate in her husband's absence. And then she could not help remembering that he had passed some time with her under like circumstances, so why should there be any unfitness in the fact? But Will was Mr Casaubon's relative, and one towards whom she was bound to show kindness. Still there had been signs which perhaps she ought to have understood as implying that Mr Casaubon did not like his cousin's visits during his own absence. "Perhaps I have been mistaken in many things," said poor Dorothea to herself, while the tears came rolling and she had to dry them quickly. She felt confusedly unhappy, and the image of Will which had been so clear to her before was mysteriously spoiled. But the carriage stopped at the gate of the Hospital. She was soon walking round the grass plots with Lydgate, and her feelings recovered the strong bent which had made her seek for this interview.

Will Ladislaw, meanwhile, was mortified, and knew the reason of it clearly enough. His chances of meeting Dorothea were rare; and here for the first time there had come a chance which had set him at a disadvantage. It was not only, as it had been hitherto, that she was not supremely occupied with him, but that she had seen him under circumstances in which he might appear not to be supremely occupied with her. He felt thrust to a new distance from her, amongst the circles of Middlemarchers who made no part of her life. But that was not his fault: of course, since he had taken his lodgings in the town, he had been making as many acquaintances as he could, his position requiring that he should know everybody and everything. Lydgate was really better worth knowing than any one else in the neighbourhood, and he happened to have a wife who was musical and altogether worth calling upon. Here was the whole history of the situation in which Diana had descended too unexpectedly on her worshipper. [2] It was mortifying. Will was conscious that he should not have been at Middlemarch but for Dorothea; and yet his position there was threatening to divide him from her with those barriers of habitual sentiment which are more fatal to the persistence of mutual interest than all the distance between Rome and Britain. Prejudices about rank and status were easy enough to defy in the form of a tyrannical letter from Mr Casaubon; but prejudices, like odorous bodies, have a double existence both solid and subtle—solid as the pyramids, subtle as the twentieth echo of an echo, or as the memory of hyacinths which once scented the darkness. And Will was of a temperament to feel keenly the presence of subtleties : a man of clumsier perceptions would not have felt, as he did, that for the first time some sense of unfitness in perfect freedom with him had sprung up in Dorothea's mind, and that their silence, as he conducted her to the carriage, had had a chill in it. Perhaps Casaubon, in his hatred and jealousy, had been insisting to Dorothea that Will had slid below her socially. Confound Casaubon !

Will re-entered the drawing-room, took up his hat, and looking irritated as he advanced towards Mrs Lydgate, who had seated herself at her work-table, said—

" It is always fatal to have music or poetry interrupted. May I come another day and just finish about the rendering of ' Lungi dal caro bene ' ? " [3]

" I shall be happy to be taught," said Rosamond. " But I am sure you admit that the interruption was a very beautiful one. I quite envy your acquaintance with Mrs Casaubon. Is she very clever ? She looks as if she were."

" Really, I never thought about it," said Will, sulkily.

" That is just the answer Tertius gave me, when I first asked him if she were handsome. What is it that you gentlemen are thinking of when you are with Mrs Casaubon ? "

" Herself," said Will, not indisposed to provoke the charming Mrs Lydgate. " When one sees a perfect woman, one never thinks of her attributes—one is conscious of her presence."

" I shall be jealous when Tertius goes to Lowick," said Rosamond, dimpling, and speaking with aëry lightness. " He will come back and think nothing of me."

" That does not seem to have been the effect on Lydgate hitherto. Mrs Casaubon is too unlike other women for them to be compared with her."

" You are a devout worshipper, I perceive. You often see her, I suppose."

" No," said Will, almost pettishly. " Worship is usually a matter of theory rather than of practice. But I am practising it to excess just at this moment—I must really tear myself away."

2. Presumably a reference to the story of Actaeon, who was caught by Diana watching her at her bath. She turned him into a stag, and he was killed by his own hounds. See Ovid, *Metamorphoses*, III, 138–252.

3. "Far from the well-beloved," probably the title or first line of a song. By "rendering" Will means the singing of the song, not the translation of the line.

" Pray come again some evening: Mr Lydgate will like to hear the music, and I cannot enjoy it so well without him."

When her husband was at home again, Rosamond said, standing in front of him and holding his coat-collar with both her hands, " Mr Ladislaw was here singing with me when Mrs Casaubon came in. He seemed vexed. Do you think he disliked her seeing him at our house ? Surely your position is more than equal to his—whatever may be his relation to the Casaubons."

" No, no ; it must be something else if he were really vexed. Ladislaw is a sort of gypsy ; he thinks nothing of leather and prunella." [4]

" Music apart, he is not always very agreeable. Do you like him ? "

" Yes : I think he is a good fellow : rather miscellaneous and *bric-à-brac*, but likable."

" Do you know, I think he adores Mrs Casaubon."

" Poor devil! " said Lydgate, smiling and pinching his wife's ears.

Rosamond felt herself beginning to know a great deal of the world, especially in discovering—what when she was in her un-married girlhood had been inconceivable to her except as a dim tragedy in bygone costumes—that women, even after marriage, might make conquests and enslave men. At that time young ladies in the country, even when educated at Mrs Lemon's, read little French literature later than Racine, and public prints had not cast their pre-sent magnificent illumination over the scandals of life. [5] Still, vanity, with a woman's whole mind and day to work in, can construct abun-dantly on slight hints, especially on such a hint as the possibility of indefinite conquests. How delightful to make captives from the throne of marriage with a husband as crown-prince by your side—himself in fact a subject—while the captives look up for ever hopeless, losing their rest probably, and if their appetite too, so much the better! But Rosamond's romance turned at present chiefly on her crown-prince, and it was enough to enjoy his assured subjection. When he said, " Poor devil! " she asked, with playful curiosity—

" Why so ? "

" Why, what can a man do when he takes to adoring one of you mermaids ? He only neglects his work and runs up bills."

" I am sure you do not neglect your work. You are always at the Hospital, or seeing poor patients, or thinking about some doctor's quarrel ; and then at home you always want to pore over your microscope and phials. Confess you like those things better than me."

" Haven't you ambition enough to wish that your husband should be something better than a Middlemarch doctor ? " said Lydgate, let-ting his hands fall on to his wife's shoulders, and looking at her with affectionate gravity. " I shall make you learn my favourite bit from an old poet—

---

4. "Worth makes the man, and want of it, the fellow;/The rest is all but leather or prunella" (Alexander Pope, "Essay on Man" [1733], IV, 203–4). Pope suggests that dress—the leather of the cobbler's apron, the prunella of the priest's cassock—means nothing; Lydgate says that Ladislaw knows this, and cares nothing for such irrelevant social distinctions.

5. Jean Baptiste Racine (1639–99), French dramatist.

'Why should our pride make such a stir to be
And be forgot? What good is like to this,
To do worthy the writing, and to write
Worthy the reading and the world's delight? [6]

What I want, Rosy, is to do worthy the writing,—and to write out myself what I have done. A man must work, to do that, my pet."

" Of course, I wish you to make discoveries : no one could more wish you to attain a high position in some better place than Middlemarch. You cannot say that I have ever tried to hinder you from working. But we cannot live like hermits. You are not discontented with me, Tertius ? "

" No, dear, no. I am too entirely contented."

" But what did Mrs Casaubon want to say to you ? "

" Merely to ask about her husband's health. But I think she is going to be splendid to our New Hospital : I think she will give us two hundred a-year."

CHAPTER XLIV.

I would not creep along the coast, but steer
Out in mid-sea, by guidance of the stars.

WHEN Dorothea, walking round the laurel-planted plots of the New Hospital with Lydgate, had learned from him that there were no signs of change in Mr Casaubon's bodily condition beyond the mental sign of anxiety to know the truth about his illness, she was silent for a few moments, wondering whether she had said or done anything to rouse this new anxiety. Lydgate, not willing to let slip an opportunity of furthering a favourite purpose, ventured to say—

" I don't know whether your or Mr Casaubon's attention has been drawn to the needs of our New Hospital. Circumstances have made it seem rather egotistic in me to urge the subject ; but that is not my fault : it is because there is a fight being made against it by the other medical men. I think you are generally interested in such things, for I remember that when I first had the pleasure of seeing you at Tipton Grange before your marriage, you were asking me some questions about the way in which the health of the poor was affected by their miserable housing."

" Yes, indeed," said Dorothea, brightening. " I shall be quite grateful to you if you will tell me how I can help to make things a little better. Everything of that sort has slipped away from me since I have been married. I mean," she said, after a moment's hesitation, " that the people in our village are tolerably comfortable, and my mind has been too much taken up for me to inquire further. But here—in such a place as Middlemarch—there must be a great deal to be done."

" There is everything to be done," said Lydgate, with abrupt energy. " And this Hospital is a capital piece of work, due entirely to Mr

---

6. Presumably George Eliot is the "old poet."

Bulstrode's exertions, and in a great degree to his money. But one man can't do everything in a scheme of this sort. Of course he looked forward to help. And now there's a mean, petty feud set up against the thing in the town, by certain persons who want to make it a failure."

" What can be their reasons ? " said Dorothea, with *naïve* surprise.

" Chiefly Mr Bulstrode's unpopularity, to begin with. Half the town would almost take trouble for the sake of thwarting him. In this stupid world most people never consider that a thing is good to be done unless it is done by their own set. I had no connection with Bulstrode before I came here. I look at him quite impartially, and I see that he has some notions—that he has set things on foot—which I can turn to good public purpose. If a fair number of the better educated men went to work with the belief that their observations might contribute to the reform of medical doctrine and practice, we should soon see a change for the better. That's my point of view. I hold that by refusing to work with Mr Bulstrode I should be turning my back on an opportunity of making my profession more generally serviceable."

" I quite agree with you," said Dorothea, at once fascinated by the situation sketched in Lydgate's words. " But what is there against Mr Bulstrode ? I know that my uncle is friendly with him."

" People don't like his religious tone," said Lydgate, breaking off there.

" That is all the stronger reason for despising such an opposition," said Dorothea, looking at the affairs of Middlemarch by the light of the great persecutions.

" To put the matter quite fairly, they have other objections to him : —he is masterful and rather unsociable, and he is concerned with trade, which has complaints of its own that I know nothing about. But what has that to do with the question whether it would not be a fine thing to establish here a more valuable hospital than any they have in the county ? The immediate motive to the opposition, how-ever, is the fact that Bulstrode has put the medical direction into my hands. Of course I am glad of that. It gives me an opportunity of doing some good work,—and I am aware that I have to justify his choice of me. But the consequence is, that the whole profession in Middlemarch have set themselves tooth and nail against the Hospital, and not only refuse to co-operate themselves, but try to blacken the whole affair and hinder subscriptions."

" How very petty ! " exclaimed Dorothea, indignantly.

" I suppose one must expect to fight one's way : there is hardly any-thing to be done without it. And the ignorance of people about here is stupendous. I don't lay claim to anything else than having used some opportunities which have not come within everybody's reach ; but there is no stifling the offence of being young, and a new-comer, and happening to know something more than the old inhabitants. Still, if I believe that I can set going a better method of treatment—if I believe that I can pursue certain observations and inquiries which may be a lasting benefit to medical practice, I should be a base truckler if I allowed any consideration of personal comfort to hinder me. And the course is all the clearer from there being no salary in question to put my persistence in an equivocal light."

" I am glad you have told me this, Mr Lydgate," said Dorothea, cordially. " I feel sure I can help a little. I have some money, and don't know what to do with it—that is often an uncomfortable thought to me. I am sure I can spare two hundred a-year for a grand purpose like this. How happy you must be, to know things that you feel sure will do great good ! I wish I could awake with that knowledge every morning. There seems to be so much trouble taken that one can hardly see the good of ! "

There was a melancholy cadence in Dorothea's voice as she spoke these last words. But she presently added, more cheerfully, " Pray come to Lowick and tell us more of this. I will mention the subject to Mr Casaubon. I must hasten home now."

She did mention it that evening, and said that she should like to subscribe two hundred a-year—she had seven hundred a-year as the equivalent of her own fortune, settled on her at her marriage. Mr Casaubon made no objection beyond a passing remark that the sum might be disproportionate in relation to other good objects, but when Dorothea in her ignorance resisted that suggestion, he acquiesced. He did not care himself about spending money, and was not reluctant to give it. If he ever felt keenly any question of money it was through the medium of another passion than the love of material property.

Dorothea told him that she had seen Lydgate, and recited the gist of her conversation with him about the Hospital. Mr Casaubon did not question her further, but he felt sure that she had wished to know what had passed between Lydgate and himself. " She knows that I know," said the ever-restless voice within ; but that increase of tacit knowledge only thrust further off any confidence between them. He distrusted her affection ; and what loneliness is more lonely than distrust ?

CHAPTER XLV.

" It is the humour of many heads to extol the days of their forefathers, and declaim against the wickedness of times present. Which notwithstanding they cannot handsomely do, without the borrowed help and satire of times past ; condemning the vices of their own times, by the expressions of vices in times which they commend, which cannot but argue the community of vice in both. Horace, therefore, Juvenal, and Persius, were no prophets, although their lines did seem to indigitate and point at our times."—SIR THOMAS BROWNE : *Pseudodoxia Epidemica.*

THAT opposition to the New Fever Hospital which Lydgate had sketched to Dorothea was, like other oppositions, to be viewed in many different lights. He regarded it as a mixture of jealousy and dunder-headed prejudice. Mr Bulstrode saw in it not only medical jealousy but a determination to thwart himself, prompted mainly by a hatred of that vital religion of which he had striven to be an effectual lay representative—a hatred which certainly found pretexts apart from religion such as were only too easy to find in the entanglements of human action. These might be called the ministerial views. But oppositions have the illimitable range of objections at command, which need never stop short at the boundary of knowledge, but can draw for ever on the vasts of ignorance. What the opposition in

Middlemarch said about the New Hospital and its administration had certainly a great deal of echo in it, for heaven has taken care that everybody shall not be an originator ; ·but there were differences which represented every social shade between the polished moderation of Dr Minchin and the trenchant assertion of Mrs Dollop, the landlady of the Tankard in Slaughter Lane.

Mrs Dollop became more and more convinced by her own asseveration, that Doctor Lydgate meant to let the people die in the Hospital, if not to poison them, for the sake of cutting them up without saying by your leave or with your leave ; for it was a known " fac " that he had wanted to cut up Mrs Goby, as respectable a woman as any in Parley Street, who had money in trust before her marriage—a poor tale for a doctor, who if he was good for anything should know what was the matter with you before you died, and not want to pry into your inside after you were gone.   If that was not reason, Mrs Dollop wished to know what was ; but there was a prevalent feeling in her audience that her opinion was a bulwark, and that if it were overthrown there would be no limits to the cutting-up of bodies, as had been well seen in Burke and Hare with their pitch-plaisters—such a hanging business as that was not wanted in Middlemarch ! [1]

And let it not be supposed that opinion at the Tankard in Slaughter Lane was unimportant to the medical profession : that old authentic public-house—the original Tankard, known by the name of Dollop's —was the resort of a great Benefit Club, which had some months before put to the vote whether its long-standing medical man, " Doctor Gambit," should not be cashiered in favour of " this Doctor Lydgate," who was capable of performing the most astonishing cures, and rescuing people altogether given up by other practitioners.   But the balance had been turned against Lydgate by two members, who for some private reasons held that this power of resuscitating persons as good as dead was an equivocal recommendation, and might interfere with providential favours.   In the course of the year, however, there had been a change in the public sentiment, of which the unanimity at Dollop's was an index.

A good deal more than a year ago, before anything was known of Lydgate's skill, the judgments on it had naturally been divided, depending on a sense of likelihood, situated perhaps in the pit of the stomach or in the pineal gland, and differing in its verdicts, but not the less valuable as a guide in the total deficit of evidence.   Patients who had chronic diseases or whose lives had long been worn threadbare, like old Featherstone's, had been at once inclined to try him ; also, many who did not like paying their doctor's bills, thought agreeably of opening an account with a new doctor and sending for him without stint if the children's temper wanted a dose, occasions when the old practitioners were often crusty ; and all persons thus inclined to employ Lydgate held it likely that he was clever.   Some considered that he might do more than others " where there was liver ; "—at least there would be no harm in getting a few bottles of " stuff " from him,

1. William Burke, notorious murderer, and William Hare (fl. 1820s), his accomplice, who smothered persons and sold their bodies for dissection for cholera research. Burke's name has become part of our language, "to burke" being to murder by suffocation or, in a grisly metaphor, to suppress quietly.

since if these proved useless it would still be possible to return to the Purifying Pills, which kept you alive, if they did not remove the yellowness. But these were people of minor importance. Good Middlemarch families were of course not going to change their doctor without reason shown; and everybody who had employed Mr Peacock did not feel obliged to accept a new man merely in the character of his successor, objecting that he was "not likely to be equal to Peacock."

But Lydgate had not been long in the town before there were particulars enough reported of him to breed much more specific expectations and to intensify differences into partisanship; some of the particulars being of that impressive order of which the significance is entirely hidden, like a statistical amount without a standard of comparison, but with a note of exclamation at the end. The cubic feet of oxygen yearly swallowed by a full-grown man—what a shudder they might have created in some Middlemarch circles! "Oxygen! nobody knows what that may be — is it any wonder the cholera has got to Dantzic? And yet there are people who say quarantine is no good!"

One of the facts quickly rumoured was that Lydgate did not dispense drugs. This was offensive both to the physicians whose exclusive distinction seemed infringed on, and to the surgeon-apothecaries with whom he ranged himself; and only a little while before, they might have counted on having the law on their side against a man who without calling himself a London-made M.D. dared to ask for pay except as a charge on drugs. But Lydgate had not been experienced enough to foresee that his new course would be even more offensive to the laity; and to Mr Mawmsey, an important grocer in the Top Market, who, though not one of his patients, questioned him in an affable manner on the subject, he was injudicious enough to give a hasty popular explanation of his reasons, pointing out to Mr Mawmsey that it must lower the character of practitioners, and be a constant injury to the public, if their only mode of getting paid for their work was by their making out long bills for draughts, boluses, and mixtures.

"It is in that way that hard-working medical men may come to be almost as mischievous as quacks," said Lydgate, rather thoughtlessly. "To get their own bread they must overdose the king's lieges; and that's a bad sort of treason, Mr Mawmsey—undermines the constitution in a fatal way."

Mr Mawmsey was not only an overseer (it was about a question of outdoor pay that he was having an interview with Lydgate), he was also asthmatic and had an increasing family: thus, from a medical point of view, as well as from his own, he was an important man; indeed, an exceptional grocer, whose hair was arranged in a flame-like pyramid, and whose retail deference was of the cordial, encouraging kind — jocosely complimentary, and with a certain considerate abstinence from letting out the full force of his mind. It was Mr Mawmsey's friendly jocoseness in questioning him which had set the tone of Lydgate's reply. But let the wise be warned against too great readiness at explanation: it multiplies the sources of mistake, lengthening the sum for reckoners sure to go wrong.

Lydgate smiled as he ended his speech, putting his foot into the stirrup, and Mr Mawmsey laughed more than he would have done if he had known who the king's lieges were, giving his "Good morning, sir, good morning, sir," with the air of one who saw everything clearly enough. But in truth his views were perturbed. For years he had been paying bills with strictly-made items, so that for every half-crown and eighteenpence he was certain something measurable had been delivered. He had done this with satisfaction, including it among his responsibilities as a husband and father, and regarding a longer bill than usual as a dignity worth mentioning. Moreover, in addition to the massive benefit of the drugs to " self and family," he had enjoyed the pleasure of forming an acute judgment as to their immediate effects, so as to give an intelligent statement for the guidance of Mr Gambit—a practitioner just a little lower in status than Wrench or Toller, and especially esteemed as an accoucheur, of whose ability Mr Mawmsey had the poorest opinion on all other points, but in doctoring, he was wont to say in an undertone, he placed Gambit above any of them. [2]

Here were deeper reasons than the superficial talk of a new man, which appeared still flimsier in the drawing-room over the shop, when they were recited to Mrs Mawmsey, a woman accustomed to be made much of as a fertile mother,—generally under attendance more or less frequent from Mr Gambit, and occasionally having attacks which required Dr Minchin.

" Does this Mr Lydgate mean to say there is no use in taking medicine ? " said Mrs Mawmsey, who was slightly given to drawling. " I should like him to tell me how I could bear up at Fair time, if I didn't take strengthening medicine for a month beforehand. Think of what I have to provide for calling customers, my dear ! "—here Mrs Mawmsey turned to an intimate female friend who sat by—" a large veal pie—a stuffed fillet—a round of beef—ham, tongue, *et* cetera, *et* cetera ! But what keeps me up best is the pink mixture, not the brown. I wonder, Mr Mawmsey, with *your* experience, you could have patience to listen. *I* should have told him at once that I knew a little better than that."

" No, no, no," said Mr Mawmsey ; " I was not going to tell him my opinion. Hear everything and judge for yourself is my motto. But he didn't know who he was talking to. I was not to be turned on *his* finger. People often pretend to tell me things, when they might as well say, ' Mawmsey, you're a fool.' But I smile at it : I humour everybody's weak place. If physic had done harm to self and family, I should have found it out by this time."

The next day Mr Gambit was told that Lydgate went about saying physic was of no use.

" Indeed ! " said he, lifting his eyebrows with cautious surprise. (He was a stout husky man with a large ring on his fourth finger.) " How will he cure his patients, then ? "

" That is what *I* say," returned Mrs Mawmsey, who habitually gave weight to her speech by loading her pronouns. " Does *he* suppose that people will pay him only to come and sit with them and go away again ? "

Mrs Mawmsey had had a great deal of sitting from Mr Gambit, including very full accounts of his own habits of body and other affairs ; but of course he knew there was no innuendo in her remark, since his spare time and personal narrative had never been charged for. So he replied, humorously—

2. Accoucheur: a male midwife.

" Well, Lydgate is a good-looking young fellow, you know."

" Not one that *I* would employ," said Mrs Mawmsey. " *Others* may do as they please."

Hence Mr Gambit could go away from the chief grocer's without fear of rivalry, but not without a sense that Lydgate was one of those hypocrites who try to discredit others by advertising their own honesty, and that it might be worth some people's while to show him up. Mr Gambit, however, had a satisfactory practice, much pervaded by the smells of retail trading which suggested the reduction of cash payments to a balance. And he did not think it worth his while to show Lydgate up until he knew how. He had not indeed great resources of education, and had had to work his own way against a good deal of professional contempt ; but he made none the worse accoucheur for calling the breathing apparatus " longs."

Other medical men felt themselves more capable. Mr Toller shared the highest practice in the town and belonged to an old Middlemarch family : there were Tollers in the law and everything else above the line of retail trade. Unlike our irascible friend Wrench, he had the easiest way in the world of taking things which might be supposed to annoy him, being a well-bred, quietly facetious man, who kept a good house, was very fond of a little sporting when he could get it, very friendly with Mr Hawley, and hostile to Mr Bulstrode. It may seem odd that with such pleasant habits he should have been given to the heroic treatment, bleeding and blistering and starving his patients, with a dispassionate disregard to his personal example ; but the incongruity favoured the opinion of his ability among his patients, who commonly observed that Mr Toller had lazy manners, but his treatment was as active as you could desire :—no man, said they, carried more seriousness into his profession : he was a little slow in coming, but when he came, he *did* something. He was a great favourite in his own circle, and whatever he implied to any one's disadvantage told doubly from his careless ironical tone.

He naturally got tired of smiling and saying, " Ah !" when he was told that Mr Peacock's successor did not mean to dispense medicines ; and Mr Hackbutt one day mentioning it over the wine at a dinner-party, Mr Toller said, laughingly, " Dibbitts will get rid of his stale drugs, then. I'm fond of little Dibbitts—I'm glad he's in luck."

" I see your meaning, Toller," said Mr Hackbutt, " and I am entirely of your opinion. I shall take an opportunity of expressing myself to that effect. A medical man should be responsible for the quality of the drugs consumed by his patients. That is the *rationale* of the system of charging which has hitherto obtained ; and nothing is more offensive than this ostentation of reform, where there is no real amelioration."

" Ostentation, Hackbutt ?" said Mr Toller, ironically. " I don't see that. A man can't very well be ostentatious of what nobody believes in. There's no reform in the matter : the question is, whether the profit on the drugs is paid to the medical man by the druggist or by the patient, and whether there shall be extra pay under the name of attendance."

" Ah, to be sure ; one of your damned new versions of old humbug," said Mr Hawley, passing the decanter to Mr Wrench.

Mr Wrench, generally abstemious, often drank wine rather freely at a party, getting the more irritable in consequence.

"As to humbug, Hawley," he said, "that's a word easy to fling about. But what I contend against is the way medical men are fouling their own nest, and setting up a cry about the country as if a general practitioner who dispenses drugs couldn't be a gentleman. I throw back the imputation with scorn. I say, the most ungentlemanly trick a man can be guilty of is to come among the members of his profession with innovations which are a libel on their time-honoured procedure. That is my opinion, and I am ready to maintain it against any one who contradicts me." Mr Wrench's voice had become exceedingly sharp.

"I can't oblige you there, Wrench," said Mr Hawley, thrusting his hands into his trouser-pockets.

"My dear fellow," said Mr Toller, striking in pacifically, and looking at Mr Wrench, "the physicians have their toes trodden on more than we have. If you come to dignity it is a question for Minchin and Sprague."

"Does medical jurisprudence provide nothing against these infringements ?" said Mr Hackbutt, with a disinterested desire to offer his lights. "How does the law stand, eh, Hawley ?"

"Nothing to be done there," said Mr Hawley. "I looked into it for Sprague. You'd only break your nose against a damned judge's decision."

"Pooh ! no need of law," said Mr Toller. "So far as practice is concerned the attempt is an absurdity. No patient will like it—certainly not Peacock's, who have been used to depletion. Pass the wine."

Mr Toller's prediction was partly verified. If Mr and Mrs Mawmsey, who had no idea of employing Lydgate, were made uneasy by his supposed declaration against drugs, it was inevitable that those who called him in should watch a little anxiously to see whether he did "use all the means he might use" in the case. Even good Mr Powderell, who in his constant charity of interpretation was inclined to esteem Lydgate the more for what seemed a conscientious pursuit of a better plan, had his mind disturbed with doubts during his wife's attack of erysipelas, and could not abstain from mentioning to Lydgate that Mr Peacock on a similar occasion had administered a series of boluses which were not otherwise definable than by their remarkable effect in bringing Mrs Powderell round before Michaelmas from an illness which had begun in a remarkably hot August.[3] At last, indeed, in the conflict between his desire not to hurt Lydgate and his anxiety that no "means "should be lacking, he induced his wife privately to take Widgeon's Purifying Pills, an esteemed Middlemarch medicine, which arrested every disease at the fountain by setting to work at once upon the blood. This co-operative measure was not to·be mentioned to Lydgate, and Mr Powderell himself had no certain reliance on it, only hoping that it might be attended with a blessing.

But in this doubtful stage of Lydgate's introduction he was helped by what we mortals rashly call good fortune. I suppose no doctor ever

---

3. Erysipelas: an infectious inflammation of the skin. Michaelmas is the feast of St. Michael, September 29.

came newly to a place without making cures that surprised somebody—cures which may be called fortune's testimonials, and deserve as much credit as the written or printed kind. Various patients got well while Lydgate was attending them, some even of dangerous illnesses ; and it was remarked that the new doctor with his new ways had at least the merit of bringing people back from the brink of death. The trash talked on such occasions was the more vexatious to Lydgate, because it gave precisely the sort of prestige which an incompetent and unscrupulous man would desire, and was sure to be imputed to him by the simmering dislike of the other medical men as an encouragement on his own part of ignorant puffing. But even his proud outspokenness was checked by the discernment that it was as useless to fight against the interpretations of ignorance as to whip the fog ; and "good fortune" insisted on using those interpretations.

Mrs Larcher having just become charitably concerned about alarming symptoms in her charwoman, when Dr Minchin called, asked him to see her then and there, and to give her a certificate for the Infirmary ; whereupon after examination he wrote a statement of the case as one of tumour, and recommended the bearer Nancy Nash as an outpatient. Nancy, calling at home on her way to the Infirmary, allowed the staymaker and his wife, in whose attic she lodged, to read Dr Minchin's paper, and by this means became a subject of compassionate conversation in the neighbouring shops of Churchyard Lane as being afflicted with a tumour at first declared to be as large and hard as a duck's egg, but later in the day to be about the size of "your fist." Most hearers agreed that it would have to be cut out, but one had known of oil and another of "squitchineal" as adequate to soften and reduce any lump in the body when taken enough of into the inside—the oil by gradually "soopling," the squitchineal by eating away.

Meanwhile when Nancy presented herself at the Infirmary, it happened to be one of Lydgate's days there. After questioning and examining her, Lydgate said to the house-surgeon in an undertone, "It's not tumour: it's cramp." He ordered her a blister and some steel mixture, and told her to go home and rest, giving her at the same time a note to Mrs Larcher, who, she said, was her best employer, to testify that she was in need of good food. [4]

But by-and-by Nancy, in her attic, became portentously worse, the supposed tumour having indeed given way to the blister, but only wandered to another region with angrier pain. The staymaker's wife went to fetch Lydgate, and he continued for a fortnight to attend Nancy in her own home, until under his treatment she got quite well and went to work again. But the case continued to be described as one of tumour in Churchyard Lane and other streets—nay, by Mrs Larcher also ; for when Lydgate's remarkable cure was mentioned to Dr Minchin, he naturally did not like to say, "The case was not one of tumour, and I was mistaken in describing it as such," but answered, "Indeed ! ah ! I saw it was a surgical case, not of a fatal kind." He had been inwardly annoyed, however, when he had asked at the Infirmary about the woman he had recommended two days before, to hear from the house-surgeon, a youngster who was not sorry to vex Minchin with impunity, exactly what had occurred : he privately

---

4. A blister: i.e., a vesicatory plaster, designed to raise a blister on the skin.

pronounced that it was indecent in a general practitioner to contradict a physician's diagnosis in that open manner, and afterwards agreed with Wrench that Lydgate was disagreeably inattentive to etiquette. Lydgate did not make the affair a ground for valuing himself or (very particularly) despising Minchin, such rectification of misjudgments often happening among men of equal qualifications. But report took up this amazing case of tumour, not clearly distinguished from cancer, and considered the more awful for being of the wandering sort; till much prejudice against Lydgate's method as to drugs was overcome by the proof of his marvellous skill in the speedy restoration of Nancy Nash after she had been rolling and rolling in agonies from the presence of a tumour both hard and obstinate, but nevertheless compelled to yield.

How could Lydgate help himself? It is offensive to tell a lady when she is expressing her amazement at your skill, that she is altogether mistaken and rather foolish in her amazement. And to have entered into the nature of diseases would only have added to his breaches of medical propriety. Thus he had to wince under a promise of success given by that ignorant praise which misses every valid quality.

In the case of a more conspicuous patient, Mr Borthrop Trumbull, Lydgate was conscious of having shown himself something better than an everyday doctor, though here too it was an equivocal advantage that he won. The eloquent auctioneer was seized with pneumonia, and having been a patient of Mr Peacock's, sent for Lydgate, whom he had expressed his intention to patronise. Mr Trumbull was a robust man, a good subject for trying the expectant theory upon —watching the course of an interesting disease when left as much as possible to itself, so that the stages might be noted for future guidance; and from the air with which he described his sensations Lydgate surmised that he would like to be taken into his medical man's confidence, and be represented as a partner in his own cure. The auctioneer heard, without much surprise, that his was a constitution which (always with due watching) might be left to itself, so as to offer a beautiful example of a disease with all its phases seen in clear delineation, and that he probably had the rare strength of mind voluntarily to become the test of a rational procedure, and thus make the disorder of his pulmonary functions a general benefit to society.

Mr Trumbull acquiesced at once, and entered strongly into the view that an illness of his was no ordinary occasion for medical science.

" Never fear, sir ; you are not speaking to one who is altogether ignorant of the *vis medicatrix*," said he, with his usual superiority of expression, made rather pathetic by difficulty of breathing. [5] And he went without shrinking through his abstinence from drugs, much sustained by application of the thermometer which implied the importance of his temperature, by the sense that he furnished objects for the microscope, and by learning many new words which seemed suited to the dignity of his secretions. For Lydgate was acute enough to indulge him with a little technical talk.

It may be imagined that Mr Trumbull rose from his couch with a

5. *Vis medicatrix naturae:* the healing power of nature apart from medical treatment.

disposition to speak of an illness in which he had manifested the strength of his mind as well as constitution ; and he was not backward in awarding credit to the medical man who had discerned the quality of patient he had to deal with. The auctioneer was not an ungenerous man, and liked to give others their due, feeling that he could afford it. He had caught the words " expectant method," and rang chimes on this and other learned phrases to accompany the assurance that Lydgate " knew a thing or two more than the rest of the doctors—was far better versed in the secrets of his profession than the majority of his compeers."

This had happened before the affair of Fred Vincy's illness had given to Mr Wrench's enmity towards Lydgate more definite personal ground. The new comer already threatened to be a nuisance in the shape of rivalry, and was certainly a nuisance in the shape of practical criticism or reflections on his hard-driven elders, who had had something else to do than to busy themselves with untried notions. His practice had spread in one or two quarters, and from the first the report of his high family had led to his being pretty generally invited, so that the other medical men had to meet him at dinner in the best houses ; and having to meet a man whom you dislike is not observed always to end in a mutual attachment. There was hardly ever so much unanimity among them as in the opinion that Lydgate was an arrogant young fellow, and yet ready for the sake of ultimately predominating to show a crawling subservience to Bulstrode. That Mr Farebrother, whose name was a chief flag of the anti-Bulstrode party, always defended Lydgate and made a friend of him, was referred to Farebrother's unaccountable way of fighting on both sides.

Here was plenty of preparation for the outburst of professional disgust at the announcement of the laws Mr Bulstrode was laying down for the direction of the New Hospital, which were the more exasperating because there was no present possibility of interfering with his will and pleasure, everybody except Lord Medlicote having refused help towards the building, on the ground that they preferred giving to the Old Infirmary. Mr Bulstrode met all the expenses, and had ceased to be sorry that he was purchasing the right to carry out his notions of improvement without hindrance from prejudiced coadjutors ; but he had had to spend large sums, and the building had lingered. Caleb Garth had undertaken it, had failed during its progress, and before the interior fittings were begun had retired from the management of the business ; and when referring to the Hospital he often said that however Bulstrode might ring if you tried him, he liked good solid carpentry and masonry, and had a notion both of drains and chimneys. In fact, the Hospital had become an object of intense interest to Bulstrode, and he would willingly have continued to spare a large yearly sum that he might rule it dictatorially without any Board ; but he had another favourite object which also required money for its accomplishment : he wished to buy some land in the neighbourhood of Middlemarch, and therefore he wished to get considerable contributions towards maintaining the Hospital. Meanwhile he framed his plan of management. The Hospital was to be reserved for fever in all its forms ; Lydgate was to be chief medical superintendent, that he might have free authority to pursue all comparative investigations which his studies, particularly in Paris, had shown him the importance of, the other medical visitors having a consultative influence, but no power to contravene Lydgate's ultimate decisions ; and the general management was to be lodged exclusively in the hands of five directors associated with Mr Bulstrode, who were to have votes in the ratio of their contributions, the Board itself filling up any vacancy in its numbers, and no mob of small contributors being admitted to a share of government.

There was an immediate refusal on the part of every medical man in the town to become a visitor at the Fever Hospital.

"Very well," said Lydgate to Mr Bulstrode, "we have a capital house-surgeon and dispenser, a clear-headed, neat-handed fellow ; we'll get Webbe from Crabsley, as good a country practitioner as any of them, to come over twice a-week, and in case of any exceptional operation, Protheroe will come from Brassing. I must work the harder, that's all, and I have given up my post at the Infirmary. The plan will flourish in spite of them, and then they'll be glad to come in. Things can't last as they are : there must be all sorts of reform soon, and then young fellows may be glad to come and study here." Lydgate was in high spirits.

"I shall not flinch, you may depend upon it, Mr Lydgate," said Mr Bulstrode. "While I see you carrying out high intentions with vigour, you shall have my unfailing support. And I have humble confidence that the blessing which has hitherto attended my efforts against the spirit of evil in this town will not be withdrawn. Suitable directors to assist me I have no doubt of securing. Mr Brooke of Tipton has already given me his concurrence, and a pledge to contribute yearly : he has not specified the sum—probably not a great one. But he will be a useful member of the Board."

A useful member was perhaps to be defined as one who would originate nothing, and always vote with Mr Bulstrode.

The medical aversion to Lydgate was hardly disguised now. Neither Dr Sprague nor Dr Minchin said that he disliked Lydgate's knowledge, or his disposition to improve treatment : what they disliked was his arrogance, which nobody felt to be altogether deniable. They implied that he was insolent, pretentious, and given to that reckless innovation for the sake of noise and show which was the essence of the charlatan.

The word charlatan once thrown on the air could not be let drop. In those days the world was agitated about the wondrous doings of Mr St John Long, "noblemen and gentlemen" attesting his extraction of a fluid like mercury from the temples of a patient. [6]

Mr Toller remarked one day, smilingly, to Mrs Taft, that "Bulstrode had found a man to suit him in Lydgate ; a charlatan in religion is sure to like other sorts of charlatans."

"Yes, indeed, I can imagine," said Mrs Taft, keeping the number of thirty stitches carefully in her mind all the while ; "there are so many of that sort. I remember Mr Cheshire, with his irons, trying to make people straight when the Almighty had made them crooked."

"No, no," said Mr Toller, "Cheshire was all right—all fair and above board. But there's St John Long—that's the kind of fellow

6. John St. John Long (1798–1834), medical charlatan and quack who established a practice in London in 1827; he was twice tried for manslaughter, two of his patients having died as a result of his treatment. See GE's notes on Long in *Quarry* below, pp. 610–11.

we call a charlatan, advertising cures in ways nobody knows anything about : a fellow who wants to make a noise by pretending to go deeper than other people. The other day he was pretending to tap a man's brain and get quicksilver out of it."

" Good gracious ! what dreadful trifling with people's constitutions ! " said Mrs Taft.

After this, it came to be held in various quarters that Lydgate played even with respectable constitutions for his own purposes, and how much more likely that in his flighty experimenting he should make sixes and sevens of hospital patients. Especially it was to be expected, as the landlady of the Tankard had said, that he would recklessly cut up their dead bodies. For Lydgate having attended Mrs Goby, who died apparently of a heart-disease not very clearly expressed in the symptoms, too daringly asked leave of her relatives to open the body, and thus gave an offence quickly spreading beyond Parley Street, where that lady had long resided on an income such as made this association of her body with the victims of Burke and Hare a flagrant insult to her memory.

Affairs were in this stage when Lydgate opened the subject of the Hospital to Dorothea. We see that he was bearing enmity and silly misconception with much spirit, aware that they were partly created by his good share of success.

" They will not drive me away," he said, talking confidentially in Mr Farebrother's study. " I have got a good opportunity here, for the ends I care most about ; and I am pretty sure to get income enough for our wants. By-and-by I shall go on as quietly as possible : I have no seductions now away from home and work. And I am more and more convinced that it will be possible to demonstrate the homogeneous origin of all the tissues. Raspail and others are on the same track, and I have been losing time." [7]

" I have no power of prophecy there," said Mr Farebrother, who had been puffing at his pipe thoughtfully while Lydgate talked ; " but as to the hostility in the town, you'll weather it if you are prudent."

" How am I to be prudent ? " said Lydgate, " I just do what comes before me to do. I can't help people's ignorance and spite, any more than Vesalius could. [8] It isn't possible to square one's conduct to silly conclusions which nobody can foresee."

" Quite true ; I didn't mean that. I meant only two things. One is, keep yourself as separable from Bulstrode as you can : of course, you can go on doing good work of your own by his help ; but don't get tied. Perhaps it seems like personal feeling in me to say so—and there's a good deal of that, I own—but personal feeling is not always in the wrong if you boil it down to the impressions which make it simply an opinion."

" Bulstrode is nothing to me," said Lydgate, carelessly, " except on public grounds. As to getting very closely united to him, I am not fond enough of him for that. But what was the other thing you meant ? " said Lydgate, who was nursing his leg as comfortably as possible, and feeling in no great need of advice.

---

7. François-Vincent Raspail (1794–1878), French chemist, physiologist, and radical political figure.
8. Andreas Vesalius (1514–64), founder of modern anatomy. *De Humani Corporis Fabrica* (1543), his great work, was received with hostility by Galenists.

" Why, this. Take care—*experto crede*—take care not to get hampered about money matters. [9] I know, by a word you let fall one day, that you don't like my playing at cards so much for money. You are right enough there. But try and keep clear of wanting small sums that you haven't got. I am perhaps talking rather superfluously ; but a man likes to assume superiority over himself, by holding up his bad example and sermonising on it."

Lydgate took Mr Farebrother's hints very cordially, though he would hardly have borne them from another man. He could not help remembering that he had lately made some debts, but these had seemed inevitable, and he had no intention now to do more than keep house in a simple way. The furniture for which he owed would not want renewing ; nor even the stock of wine for a long while.

Many thoughts cheered him at that time—and justly. A man conscious of enthusiasm for worthy aims is sustained under petty hostilities by the memory of great workers who had to fight their way not without wounds, and who hover in his mind as patron saints, invisibly helping. At home, that same evening when he had been chatting with Mr Farebrother, he had his long legs stretched on the sofa, his head thrown back, and his hands clasped behind it according to his favourite ruminating attitude, while Rosamond sat at the piano, and played one tune after another, of which her husband only knew (like the emotional elephant he was !) that they fell in with his mood as if they had been melodious sea-breezes.

There was something very fine in Lydgate's look just then, and any one might have been encouraged to bet on his achievement. In his dark eyes and on his mouth and brow there was that placidity which comes from the fulness of contemplative thought—the mind not searching, but beholding, and the glance seeming to be filled with what is behind it.

Presently Rosamond left the piano and seated herself on a chair close to the sofa and opposite her husband's face.

" Is that enough music for you, my lord ? " she said, folding her hands before her and putting on a little air of meekness.

" Yes, dear, if you are tired," said Lydgate, gently, turning his eyes and resting them on her, but not otherwise moving. Rosamond's presence at that moment was perhaps no more than a spoonful brought to the lake, and her woman's instinct in this matter was not dull.

" What is absorbing you ? " she said, leaning forward and bringing her face nearer to his.

He moved his hands and placed them gently behind her shoulders.

" I am thinking of a great fellow, who was about as old as I am three hundred years ago, and had already begun a new era in anatomy."

" I can't guess," said Rosamond, shaking her head. " We used to play at guessing historical characters at Mrs Lemon's, but not anatomists."

" I'll tell you. His name was Vesalius. And the only way he could get to know anatomy as he did, was by going to snatch bodies at night, from graveyards and places of execution."

" Oh ! " said Rosamond, with a look of disgust on her pretty face, " I am very glad you are not Vesalius. I should have thought he might find some less horrible way than that."

9. *Experto crede:* believe one who knows from experience.

"No, he couldn't," said Lydgate, going on too earnestly to take much notice of her answer. "He could only get a complete skeleton by snatching the whitened bones of a criminal from the gallows, and burying them, and fetching them away by bits secretly, in the dead of night."

"I hope he is not one of your great heroes," said Rosamond, half-playfully, half-anxiously, "else I shall have you getting up in the night to go to St Peter's churchyard. You know how angry you told me the people were about Mrs Goby. You have enemies enough already."

"So had Vesalius, Rosy. No wonder the medical fogies in Middlemarch are jealous, when some of the greatest doctors living were fierce upon Vesalius because they had believed in Galen, and he showed that Galen was wrong.[1] They called him a liar and a poisonous monster. But the facts of the human frame were on his side ; and so he got the better of them."

"And what happened to him afterwards?" said Rosamond, with some interest.

"Oh, he had a good deal of fighting to the last. And they did exasperate him enough at one time to make him burn a good deal of his work. Then he got shipwrecked just as he was coming from Jerusalem to take a great chair at Padua. He died rather miserably."

There was a moment's pause before Rosamond said, "Do you know, Tertius, I often wish you had not been a medical man."

"Nay, Rosy, don't say that," said Lydgate, drawing her closer to him. "That is like saying you wish you had married another man."

"Not at all ; you are clever enough for anything : you might easily have been something else. And your cousins at Quallingham all think that you have sunk below them in your choice of a profession."

"The cousins at Quallingham may go to the devil !" said Lydgate, with scorn. "It was like their impudence if they said anything of the sort to you."

"Still," said Rosamond, "I do *not* think it is a nice profession, dear." We know that she had much quiet perseverance in her opinion.

"It is the grandest profession in the world, Rosamond," said Lydgate, gravely. "And to say that you love me without loving the medical man in me, is the same sort of thing as to say that you like eating a peach but don't like its flavour. Don't say that again, dear, it pains me."

"Very well, Doctor Grave-face," said Rosy, dimpling, "I will declare in future that I dote on skeletons, and body-snatchers, and bits of things in phials, and quarrels with everybody, that end in your dying miserably."

"No, no, not so bad as that," said Lydgate, giving up remonstrance and petting her resignedly.

---

1. Galen (129–199) was a Greco-Roman physician and anatomist; his authority was unquestioned for centuries in the fields of anatomy, physiology, and pathology.

CHAPTER XLVI.

"Pues no podemos haber aquello que queremos, queramos aquello que podremos."
"Since we cannot get what we like, let us like what we can get."—*Spanish Proverb*.

WHILE Lydgate, safely married and with the Hospital under his command, felt himself struggling for Medical Reform against Middlemarch, Middlemarch was becoming more and more conscious of the national struggle for another kind of Reform.

By the time that Lord John Russell's measure was being debated in the House of Commons, there was a new political animation in Middlemarch, and a new definition of parties which might show a decided change of balance if a new election came. [1] And there were some who already predicted this event, declaring that a Reform Bill would never be carried by the actual Parliament. This was what Will Ladislaw dwelt on to Mr Brooke as a reason for congratulation that he had not yet tried his strength at the hustings.

"Things will grow and ripen as if it were a comet year," said Will. "The public temper will soon get to a cometary heat, now the question of Reform has set in. There is likely to be another election before long, and by that time Middlemarch will have got more ideas into its head. What we have to work at now is the 'Pioneer' and political meetings."

"Quite right, Ladislaw; we shall make a new thing of opinion here," said Mr Brooke. "Only I want to keep myself independent about Reform, you know : I don't want to go too far. I want to take up Wilberforce's and Romilly's line, you know, and work at Negro Emancipation, Criminal Law—that kind of thing. [2] But of course I should support Grey."

"If you go in for the principle of Reform, you must be prepared to take what the situation offers," said Will. "If everybody pulled for his own bit against everybody else, the whole question would go to tatters."

"Yes, yes, I agree with you—I quite take that point of view. I should put it in that light. I should support Grey, you know. But I don't want to change the balance of the constitution, and I don't think Grey would."

"But that is what the country wants," said Will. "Else there would be no meaning in political unions or any other movement that

1. Lord John Russell (1792–1878) was the prime sponsor of the Reform Bill of 1831–32.
2. Sir Samuel Romilly (1757–1818), law reformer, Whig member of Parliament; he favored the emancipation of Catholics and Black slaves. He was a friend of William Wiberforce (1759-1833), philanthropist and leader in Parliament of the antislavery cause from 1787 until the passage of the bill abolishing slavery and the slave trade in 1807.

knows what it's about.[3] It wants to have a house of Commons which is not weighted with nominees of the landed class, but with representatives of the other interests. And as to contending for a reform short of that, it is like asking for a bit of an avalanche which has already begun to thunder."

"That is fine, Ladislaw : that is the way to put it. Write that down, now. We must begin to get documents about the feeling of the country, as well as the machine-breaking and general distress."

"As to documents," said Will, "a two-inch card will hold plenty. A few rows of figures are enough to deduce misery from, and a few more will show the rate at which the political determination of the people is growing."

"Good : draw that out a little more at length, Ladislaw. That is an idea, now : write it out in the 'Pioneer.' Put the figures and deduce the misery, you know ; and put the other figures and deduce— and so on. You have a way of putting things. Burke, now :—when I think of Burke, I can't help wishing somebody had a pocket-borough to give you, Ladislaw.[4] You'd never get elected, you know. And we shall always want talent in the House : reform as we will, we shall always want talent. That avalanche and the thunder, now, was really a little like Burke. I want that sort of thing—not ideas, you know, but a way of putting them."

"Pocket-boroughs would be a fine thing," said Ladislaw, "if they were always in the right pocket, and there were always a Burke at hand."

Will was not displeased with that complimentary comparison, even from Mr Brooke ; for it is a little too trying to human flesh to be conscious of expressing one's self better than others and never to have it noticed, and in the general dearth of admiration for the right thing, even a chance bray of applause falling exactly in time is rather fortifying. Will felt that his literary refinements were usually beyond the limits of Middlemarch perception ; nevertheless, he was beginning thoroughly to like the work of which when he began he had said to himself rather languidly, "Why not ?"—and he studied the political situation with as ardent an interest as he had ever given to poetic metres or mediævalism.[5] It is undeniable that but for the desire to be where Dorothea was, and perhaps the want of knowing what else to do, Will would not at this time have been meditating on the needs of the English people or criticising English statesmanship : he would probably have been rambling in Italy sketching plans for several dramas, trying prose and finding it too jejune, trying verse and finding it too artificial, beginning to copy "bits" from old pictures, leaving off because they were "no good," and observing that, after all, self-culture was the principal point ; while in politics he would have been sympathising warmly with liberty and progress in general. Our sense of duty must often wait for some work which

3. Political unions: associations advocating reform.
4. Edmund Burke (1729–97), statesman and author. Burke was several times a member of Parliament thanks to the availability of pocket-boroughs at the disposal of his friends.
5. "Mediaevalism" was an interest characteristic of the German Nazarene painters and Pre-Raphaelite painters and poets.

shall take the place of dilettanteism and make us feel that the quality of our action is not a matter of indifference.

Ladislaw had now accepted his bit of work, though it was not that indeterminate loftiest thing which he had once dreamed of as alone worthy of continuous effort. His nature warmed easily in the presence of subjects which were visibly mixed with life and action, and the easily-stirred rebellion in him helped the glow of public spirit. In spite of Mr Casaubon and the banishment from Lowick, he was rather happy; getting a great deal of fresh knowledge in a vivid way and for practical purposes, and making the 'Pioneer' celebrated as far as Brassing (never mind the smallness of the area; the writing was not worse than much that reaches the four corners of the earth).

Mr Brooke was occasionally irritating; but Will's impatience was relieved by the division of his time between visits to the Grange and retreats to his Middlemarch lodgings, which gave variety to his life.

"Shift the pegs a little," he said to himself, "and Mr Brooke might be in the Cabinet, while I was Under-Secretary. That is the common order of things: the little waves make the large ones and are of the same pattern. I am better here than in the sort of life Mr Casaubon would have trained me for, where the doing would be all laid down by a precedent too rigid for me to react upon. I don't care for prestige or high pay."

As Lydgate had said of him, he was a sort of gypsy, rather enjoying the sense of belonging to no class; he had a feeling of romance in his position, and a pleasant consciousness of creating a little surprise wherever he went. That sort of enjoyment had been disturbed when he had felt some new distance between himself and Dorothea in their accidental meeting at Lydgate's, and his irritation had gone out towards Mr Casaubon, who had declared beforehand that Will would lose caste. "I never had any caste," he would have said, if that prophecy had been uttered to him, and the quick blood would have come and gone like breath in his transparent skin. But it is one thing to like defiance, and another thing to like its consequences.

Meanwhile, the town opinion about the new editor of the 'Pioneer' was tending to confirm Mr Casaubon's view. Will's relationship in that distinguished quarter did not, like Lydgate's high connections, serve as an advantageous introduction: if it was rumoured that young Ladislaw was Mr Casaubon's nephew or cousin, it was also rumoured that "Mr Casaubon would have nothing to do with him."

"Brooke has taken him up," said Mr Hawley, "because that is what no man in his senses could have expected. Casaubon has devilish good reasons, you may be sure, for turning the cold shoulder on a young fellow whose bringing-up he paid for. Just like Brooke—one of those fellows who would praise a cat to sell a horse."

And some oddities of Will's, more or less poetical, appeared to support Mr Keck, the editor of the 'Trumpet,' in asserting that Ladislaw, if the truth were known, was not only a Polish emissary but crack-brained, which accounted for the preternatural quickness and glibness of his speech when he got on to a platform—as he did whenever he had an opportunity, speaking with a facility which cast reflections on solid Englishmen generally. It was disgusting to Keck to see a strip of a fellow, with light curls round his head, get up and

speechify by the hour against institutions "which had existed when
he was in his cradle." And in a leading article of the 'Trumpet,'
Keck characterised Ladislaw's speech at a Reform meeting as "the
violence of an energumen—a miserable effort to shroud in the brilliancy of fireworks the daring of irresponsible statements and the
poverty of a knowledge which was of the cheapest and most recent
description." [6]

"That was a rattling article yesterday, Keck," said Dr Sprague,
with sarcastic intentions. "But what is an energumen?"

"Oh, a term that came up in the French Revolution," said Keck.

This dangerous aspect of Ladislaw was strangely contrasted with
other habits which became matter of remark. He had a fondness,
half artistic, half affectionate, for little children—the smaller they were
on tolerably active legs, and the funnier their clothing, the better Will
liked to surprise and please them. We know that in Rome he was
given to ramble about among the poor people, and the taste did not
quit him in Middlemarch.

He had somehow picked up a troop of droll children, little hatless
boys with their galligaskins much worn and scant shirting to hang
out, little girls who tossed their hair out of their eyes to look at him,
and guardian brothers at the mature age of seven. [7] This troop he had
led out on gypsy excursions to Halsell Wood at nutting-time, and
since the cold weather had set in he had taken them on a clear day
to gather sticks for a bonfire in the hollow of a hillside, where he
drew out a small feast of gingerbread for them, and improvised
a Punch-and-Judy drama with some private home-made puppets.
Here was one oddity. Another was, that in houses where he got
friendly, he was given to stretch himself at full length on the rug
while he talked, and was apt to be discovered in this attitude by
occasional callers for whom such an irregularity was likely to confirm
the notions of his dangerously mixed blood and general laxity.

But Will's articles and speeches naturally recommended him in
families which the new strictness of party division had marked off on
the side of Reform. He was invited to Mr Bulstrode's; but here he
could not lie down on the rug, and Mrs Bulstrode felt that his mode
of talking about Catholic countries, as if there were any truce with
Antichrist, illustrated the usual tendency to unsoundness in intellectual men.

At Mr Farebrother's, however, whom the irony of events had
brought on the same side with Bulstrode in the national movement,
Will became a favourite with the ladies; especially with little Miss
Noble, whom it was one of his oddities to escort when he met her in
the street with her little basket, giving her his arm in the eyes of the
town, and insisting on going with her to pay some call where she
distributed her small filchings from her own share of sweet things.

But the house where he visited oftenest and lay most on the rug
was Lydgate's. The two men were not at all alike, but they agreed
none the worse. Lydgate was abrupt but not irritable, taking
little notice of megrims in healthy people; and Ladislaw did not
usually throw away his susceptibilities on those who took no notice

---

6. Energumen: one possessed by an evil
spirit.

7. Galligaskins: long, loose breeches.

of them. With Rosamond, on the other hand, he pouted and was wayward—nay, often uncomplimentary, much to her inward surprise ; nevertheless he was gradually becoming necessary to her entertainment by his companionship in her music, his varied talk, and his freedom from the grave preoccupation which, with all her husband's tenderness and indulgence, often made his manners unsatisfactory to her, and confirmed her dislike of the medical profession.

Lydgate, inclined to be sarcastic on the superstitious faith of the people in the efficacy of "the bill," while nobody cared about the low state of pathology, sometimes assailed Will with troublesome questions. One evening in March, Rosamond in her cherry-coloured dress with swansdown trimming about the throat sat at the tea-table ; Lydgate, lately come in tired from his outdoor work, was seated sideways on an easy-chair by the fire with one leg over the elbow, his brow looking a little troubled as his eyes rambled over the columns of the 'Pioneer,' while Rosamond, having noticed that he was perturbed, avoided looking at him, and inwardly thanked heaven that she herself had not a moody disposition. Will Ladislaw was stretched on the rug contemplating the curtain-pole abstractedly, and humming very low the notes of "When first I saw thy face ;" while the house spaniel, also stretched out with small choice of room, looked from between his paws at the usurper of the rug with silent but strong objection.

Rosamond bringing Lydgate his cup of tea, he threw down the paper, and said to Will, who had started up and gone to the table—

"It's no use your puffing Brooke as a reforming landlord, Ladislaw : they only pick the more holes in his coat in the 'Trumpet.'"

"No matter ; those who read the 'Pioneer' don't read the 'Trumpet,'" said Will, swallowing his tea and walking about. "Do you suppose the public reads with a view to its own conversion ? We should have a witches' brewing with a vengeance then—'Mingle, mingle, mingle, mingle, You that mingle may'—and nobody would know which side he was going to take."[8]

"Farebrother says, he doesn't believe Brooke would get elected if the opportunity came : the very men who profess to be for him would bring another member out of the bag at the right moment."

"There's no harm in trying. It's good to have resident members."

"Why ?" said Lydgate, who was much given to use that inconvenient word in a curt tone.

"They represent the local stupidity better," said Will, laughing, and shaking his curls ; "and they are kept on their best behaviour in the neighbourhood. Brooke is not a bad fellow, but he has done some good things on his estate that he never would have done but for this Parliamentary bite."

"He's not fitted to be a public man," said Lydgate, with contemptuous decision. "He would disappoint everybody who counted on him : I can see that at the Hospital. Only, there Bulstrode holds the reins and drives him."

"That depends on how you fix your standard of public men," said Will. "He's good enough for the occasion : when the people have

---

8. "Mingle, mingle . . .": traditional song, appearing in Thomas Middleton's *The Witch* (c. 1610), Act V, Sc. 1; and later as an interpolated stage direction in Shakespeare's *Macbeth*, Act IV, Sc. 1.

made up their mind as they are making it up now, they don't want
a man—they only want a vote."

" That is the way with you political writers, Ladislaw—crying up
a measure as if it were a universal cure, and crying up men who are
a part of the very disease that wants curing."

" Why not? Men may help to cure themselves off the face of the
land without knowing it," said Will, who could find reasons im-
promptu, when he had not thought of a question beforehand.

" That is no excuse for encouraging the superstitious exaggeration
of hopes about this particular measure, helping the cry to swallow it
whole and to send up voting popinjays who are good for nothing but
to carry it. You go against rottenness, and there is nothing more
thoroughly rotten than making people believe that society can be
cured by a political hocus-pocus."

" That's very fine, my dear fellow. But your cure must begin
somewhere, and put it that a thousand things which debase a population can never be reformed without this particular reform to begin
with. Look what Stanley said the other day—that the House had
been tinkering long enough at small questions of bribery, inquiring
whether this or that voter has had a guinea when everybody knows
that the seats have been sold wholesale. [9] Wait for wisdom and
conscience in public agents—fiddlestick ! The only conscience we
can trust to is the massive sense of wrong in a class, and the best
wisdom that will work is the wisdom of balancing claims. That's
my text—which side is injured ? I support the man who supports
their claims ; not the virtuous upholder of the wrong."

" That general talk about a particular case is mere question-begging,
Ladislaw. When I say, I go in for the dose that cures, it doesn't
follow that I go in for opium in a given case of gout."

" I am not begging the question we are upon—whether we are to
try for nothing till we find immaculate men to work with. Should
you go on that plan ? If there were one man who would carry you a
medical reform and another who would oppose it, should you inquire
which had the better motives or even the better brains ? "

" Oh, of course," said Lydgate, seeing himself checkmated by a
move which he had often used himself, " if one did not work with
such men as are at hand, things must come to a dead-lock. Suppose
the worst opinion in the town about Bulstrode were a true one, that
would not make it less true that he has the sense and the resolution
to do what I think ought to be done in the matters I know and care
most about ; but that is the only ground on which I go with him,"
Lydgate added rather proudly, bearing in mind Mr Farebrother's
remarks. " He is nothing to me otherwise ; I would not cry him up
on any personal ground—I would keep clear of that."

" Do you mean that I cry up Brooke on any personal ground ? "
said Will Ladislaw, nettled, and turning sharp round. For the first
time he felt offended with Lydgate ; not the less so, perhaps, because
he would have declined any close inquiry into the growth of his relation to Mr Brooke.

9. Edward Stanley, 14th Earl of Derby (1799–1869), secretary for Ireland under
Earl Grey.

" Not at all," said Lydgate, " I was simply explaining my own action. I meant that a man may work for a special end with others whose motives and general course are equivocal, if he is quite sure of his personal independence, and that he is not working for his private interest—either place or money."

" Then, why don't you extend your liberality to others ?" said Will, still nettled. " My personal independence is as important to me as yours is to you. You have no more reason to imagine that I have personal expectations from Brooke, than I have to imagine that you have personal expectations from Bulstrode. Motives are points of honour, I suppose—nobody can prove them. But as to money and place in the world," Will ended, tossing back his head, " I think it is pretty clear that I am not determined by considerations of that sort."

" You quite mistake me, Ladislaw," said Lydgate, surprised. He had been preoccupied with his own vindication, and had been blind to what Ladislaw might infer on his own account. " I beg your pardon for unintentionally annoying you. In fact, I should rather attribute to you a romantic disregard of your own worldly interests. On the political question, I referred simply to intellectual bias."

" How very unpleasant you both are this evening? " said Rosamond. " I cannot conceive why money should have been referred to. Politics and medicine are sufficiently disagreeable to quarrel upon. You can both of you go on quarrelling with all the world and with each other on those two topics."

Rosamond looked mildly neutral as she said this, rising to ring the bell, and then crossing to her work-table.

"Poor Rosy !" said Lydgate, putting out his hand to her as she was passing him. "Disputation is not amusing to cherubs. Have some music. Ask Ladislaw to sing with you."

When Will was gone Rosamond said to her husband, " What put you out of temper this evening, Tertius ?"

" Me ? It was Ladislaw who was out of temper. He is like a bit of tinder."

" But I mean, before that. Something had vexed you before you came in, you looked cross. And that made you begin to dispute with Mr Ladislaw. You hurt me very much when you look so, Tertius."

" Do I ? Then I am a brute," said Lydgate, caressing her penitently.

" What vexed you ?"

" Oh, outdoor things—business."

It was really a letter insisting on the payment of a bill for furniture. But Rosamond was expecting to have a baby, and Lydgate wished to save her from any perturbation.

CHAPTER XLVII.

Was never true love loved in vain,
For truest love is highest gain.
No art can make it : it must spring
Where elements are fostering.
 So in heaven's spot and hour
Springs the little native flower,
Downward root and upward eye,
Shapen by the earth and sky.

It happened to be on a Saturday evening that Will Ladislaw had that little discussion with Lydgate. Its effect when he went to his own rooms was to make him sit up half the night, thinking over again, under a new irritation, all that he had before thought of his having settled in Middlemarch and harnessed himself with Mr Brooke. Hesitations before he had taken the step had since turned into susceptibility to every hint that he would have been wiser not to take it ; and hence came his heat towards Lydgate—a heat which still kept him restless. Was he not making a fool of himself ?—and at a time when he was more than ever conscious of being something better than a fool ? And for what end ?

Well, for no definite end. True, he had dreamy visions of possibilities: there is no human being who having both passions and thoughts does not think in consequence of his passions—does not find images rising in his mind which soothe the passion with hope or sting it with dread. But this, which happens to us all, happens to some with a wide difference ; and Will was not one of those whose wit " keeps the roadway :" he had his bypaths where there were little joys of his own choosing, such as gentlemen cantering on the highroad might have thought rather idiotic. The way in which he made a sort of happiness for himself out of his feeling for Dorothea was an example of this. It may seem strange, but it is the fact, that the ordinary vulgar vision of which Mr Casaubon suspected him—namely, that Dorothea might become a widow, and that the interest he had established in her mind might turn into acceptance of him as a husband—had no tempting, arresting power over him ; he did not live in the scenery of such an event, and follow it out, as we all do with that imagined " otherwise " which is our practical heaven. It was not only that he was unwilling to entertain thoughts which could be accused of baseness, and was already uneasy in the sense that he had to justify himself from the charge of ingratitude—the latent consciousness of many other barriers between himself and Dorothea besides the existence of her husband, had helped to turn away his imagination from speculating on what might befall Mr Casaubon. And there were yet other reasons. Will, we know, could not bear the thought of any flaw appearing in his crystal : he was at once exasperated and delighted by the calm freedom with which Dorothea looked at him and spoke to him, and there was something so exquisite in thinking of her just as she was, that he could not long for a change which must somehow change her. Do we not shun the street version of a fine melody ?— or shrink from the news that the rarity—some bit of chiselling or engraving perhaps—which we have dwelt on even with exultation in the trouble it has cost us to snatch glimpses of it, is really not an uncommon thing, and may be obtained as an everyday possession ? Our good depends on the quality and breadth of our emotion ; and to Will, a creature who cared little for what are called the solid things of life and greatly for its subtler influences, to have within him such a feeling as he had towards Dorothea, was like the inheritance of a fortune. What others might have called the futility of his passion, made an additional delight for his imagination : he was conscious of a generous movement, and of verifying in his own experience that higher love-poetry which had charmed his fancy. Dorothea, he said to himself, was for ever enthroned in his soul : no other woman could sit higher than her footstool ; and if he could have written out in immortal syllables the effect she wrought within him, he might have boasted after the example of old Drayton, that—

> " Queens hereafter might be glad to live
> Upon the alms of her superfluous praise." [1]

But this result was questionable. And what else could he do for Dorothea ? What was his devotion worth to her ? It was impossible to tell. He would not go out of her reach. He saw no creature among her friends to whom he could believe that she spoke with the same simple confidence as to him. She had once said that she would like him to stay ; and stay he would, whatever fire-breathing dragons might hiss around her.

This had always been the conclusion of Will's hesitations. But he was not without contradictoriness and rebellion even towards his own resolve. He had often got irritated, as he was on this particular night, by some outside demonstration that his public exertions with Mr Brooke as a chief could not seem as heroic as he would like them to be, and this was always associated with the other ground of irritation—that notwithstanding his sacrifice of dignity for Dorothea's sake, he could hardly ever see her. Whereupon, not being able to contradict these unpleasant facts, he contradicted his own strongest bias and said, " I am a fool."

Nevertheless, since the inward debate necessarily turned on Dorothea, he ended, as he had done before, only by getting a livelier sense of what her presence would be to him ; and suddenly reflecting that the morrow would be Sunday, he determined to go to Lowick Church and see her. He slept upon that idea, but when he was dressing in the rational morning light, Objection said—

" That will be a virtual defiance of Mr Casaubon's prohibition to visit Lowick, and Dorothea will be displeased."

1. Michael Drayton, "How Many Paltry, Foolish Things" (1594).

"Nonsense!" argued Inclination, "it would be too monstrous for him to hinder me from going out to a pretty country church on a spring morning. And Dorothea will be glad."

"It will be clear to Mr Casaubon that you have come either to annoy him or to see Dorothea."

"It is not true that I go to annoy him, and why should I not go to see Dorothea? Is he to have everything to himself and be always comfortable? Let him smart a little, as other people are obliged to do. I have always liked the quaintness of the church and congregation; besides, I know the Tuckers: I shall go into their pew."

Having silenced Objection by force of unreason, Will walked to Lowick as if he had been on the way to Paradise, crossing Halsell Common and skirting the wood, where the sunlight fell broadly under the budding boughs, bringing out the beauties of moss and lichen, and fresh green growths piercing the brown. Everything seemed to know that it was Sunday, and to approve of his going to Lowick Church. Will easily felt happy when nothing crossed his humour, and by this time the thought of vexing Mr Casaubon had become rather amusing to him, making his face break into its merry smile, pleasant to see as the breaking of sunshine on the water—though the occasion was not exemplary. But most of us are apt to settle within ourselves that the man who blocks our way is odious, and not to mind causing him a little of the disgust which his personality excites in ourselves. Will went along with a small book under his arm and a hand in each side-pocket, never reading, but chanting a little, as he made scenes of what would happen in church and coming out. He was experimenting in tunes to suit some words of his own, sometimes trying a ready-made melody, sometimes improvising The words were not exactly a hymn, but they certainly fitted his Sunday experience :—

> O me, O me, what frugal cheer
> My love doth feed upon!
> A touch, a ray, that is not here,
> A shadow that is gone:
>
> A dream of breath that might be near,
> An inly-echoed tone,
> The thought that one may think me dear,
> The place where one was known,
>
> The tremor of a banished fear,
> An ill that was not done—
> O me, O me, what frugal cheer
> My love doth feed upon!

Sometimes, when he took off his hat, shaking his head backward, and showing his delicate throat as he sang, he looked like an incarnation of the spring whose spirit filled the air—a bright creature, abundant in uncertain promises.

The bells were still ringing when he got to Lowick, and he went into the curate's pew before any one else arrived there. But he was still left alone in it when the congregation had assembled. The curate's pew was opposite the rector's at the entrance of the small chancel, and Will had time to fear that Dorothea might not come while he looked round at the group of rural faces which made the congregation from year to year within the white-washed walls and dark old pews, hardly with more change than we see in the boughs of a tree which breaks here and there with age, but yet has young shoots. Mr Rigg's frog-face was something alien and unaccountable, but notwithstanding this shock to the order of things, there were still the Waules and the rural stock of the Powderells in their pews side by side ; brother Samuel's cheek had the same purple round as ever, and the three generations of decent cottagers came as of old with a sense of duty to their betters generally—the smaller children regarding Mr Casaubon, who wore the black gown and mounted to the highest box, as probably the chief of all betters, and the one most awful if offended. Even in 1831 Lowick was at peace, not more agitated by Reform than by the solemn tenor of the Sunday sermon. The congregation had been used to seeing Will at church in former days, and no one took much note of him except the quire, who expected him to make a figure in the singing.

Dorothea did at last appear on this quaint background, walking up the short aisle in her white beaver bonnet and grey cloak—the same she had worn in the Vatican. Her face being, from her entrance, towards the chancel, even her short-sighted eyes soon discerned Will, but there was no outward show of her feeling except a slight paleness and a grave bow as she passed him. To his own surprise Will felt suddenly uncomfortable, and dared not look at her after they had bowed to each other. Two minutes later, when Mr Casaubon came out of the vestry, and, entering the pew, seated himself in face of Dorothea, Will felt his paralysis more complete. He could look nowhere except at the quire in the little gallery over the vestry-door : Dorothea was perhaps pained, and he had made a wretched blunder. It was no longer amusing to vex Mr Casaubon, who had the advantage probably of watching him and seeing that he dared not turn his head. Why had he not imagined this beforehand ?—but he could not expect that he should sit in that square pew alone, unrelieved by any Tuckers, who had apparently departed from Lowick altogether, for a new clergyman was in the desk. Still he called himself stupid now for not foreseeing that it would be impossible for him to look towards Dorothea — nay, that she might feel his coming an impertinence. There was no delivering himself from his cage, however ; and Will found his places and looked at his book as if he had been a schoolmistress, feeling that the morning service had never been so immeasurably long before, that he was utterly ridiculous, out of temper, and miserable. This was what a man got by worshipping the sight of a woman ! The clerk observed with surprise that Mr Ladislaw did not join in the tune of Hanover, and reflected that he might have a cold.

Mr Casaubon did not preach that morning, and there was no change in Will's situation until the blessing had been pronounced and every one rose. It was the fashion at Lowick for " the betters " to go out first. With a sudden determination to break the spell that was upon him, Will looked straight at Mr Casaubon. But that gentleman's eyes were on the button of the pew-door, which he opened, allowing Dorothea to pass, and following her immediately without raising his eyelids. Will's glance had caught Dorothea's as she turned out of the pew, and again she bowed, but this time with a look of agitation, as if she were repressing tears. Will walked out after them, but they went on towards the little gate leading out of the churchyard into the shrubbery, never looking round.

It was impossible for him to follow them, and he could only walk back sadly at mid-day along the same road which he had trodden hopefully in the morning. The lights were all changed for him both without and within.

CHAPTER XLVIII.

Surely the golden hours are turning grey
And dance no more, and vainly strive to run:
I see their white locks streaming in the wind—
Each face is haggard as it looks at me,
Slow turning in the constant clasping round
Storm-driven.

DOROTHEA'S distress when she was leaving the church came chiefly from the perception that Mr Casaubon was determined not to speak to his cousin, and that Will's presence at church had served to mark more strongly the alienation between them. Will's coming seemed to her quite excusable, nay, she thought it an amiable movement in him towards a reconciliation which she herself had been constantly wishing for. He had probably imagined, as she had, that if Mr Casaubon and he could meet easily, they would shake hands and friendly intercourse might return. But now Dorothea felt quite robbed of that hope. Will was banished further than ever, for Mr Casaubon must have been newly embittered by this thrusting upon him of a presence which he refused to recognise.

He had not been very well that morning, suffering from some difficulty in breathing, and had not preached in consequence ; she was not surprised, therefore, that he was nearly silent at luncheon, still less that he made no allusion to Will Ladislaw. For her own part she felt that she could never again introduce that subject. They usually spent apart the hours between luncheon and dinner on a Sunday ; Mr Casaubon in the library dozing chiefly, and Dorothea in her boudoir, where she was wont to occupy herself with some of her favourite books. There was a little heap of them on the table in the bow-window—of various sorts, from Herodotus, which she was learning to read with Mr Casaubon, to her old companion Pascal, and Keble's 'Christian Year.' [1] But to-day she opened one after another, and could read none of them. Everything seemed dreary : the portents before the birth of Cyrus—Jewish antiquities—oh dear !—devout epigrams—the sacred chime of favourite hymns—all alike were as flat as tunes beaten on wood : even the spring flowers and the grass had a dull shiver in them under the afternoon clouds that hid the sun fitfully ; even the sustaining thoughts which had become habits seemed to have in them the weariness of long future days in

---

1. Keble's "Christian Year" was an immensely popular two-volume collection of hymns, edited by John Keble (1792-1866) and first published in 1827.

which she would still live with them for her sole companions.[2] It was another or rather a fuller sort of companionship that poor Dorothea was hungering for, and the hunger had grown from the perpetual effort demanded by her married life. She was always trying to be what her husband wished, and never able to repose on his delight in what she was. The thing that she liked, that she spontaneously cared to have, seemed to be always excluded from her life; for if it was only granted and not shared by her husband it might as well have been denied. About Will Ladislaw there had been a difference between them from the first, and it had ended, since Mr Casaubon had so severely repulsed Dorothea's strong feeling about his claims on the family property, by her being convinced that she was in the right and her husband in the wrong, but that she was helpless. This afternoon the helplessness was more wretchedly benumbing than ever : she longed for objects who could be dear to her, and to whom she could be dear. She longed for work which would be directly beneficent like the sunshine and the rain, and now it appeared that she was to live more and more-in a virtual tomb, where there was the apparatus of a ghastly labour producing what would never see the light. To-day she had stood at the door of the tomb and seen Will Ladislaw receding into the distant world of warm activity and fellowship—turning his face towards her as he went.

Books were of no use. Thinking was of no use. It was Sunday, and she could not have the carriage to go to Celia, who had lately had a baby. There was no refuge now from spiritual emptinesss and discontent, and Dorothea had to bear her bad mood, as she would have borne a headache.

After dinner, at the hour when she usually began to read aloud, Mr Casaubon proposed that they should go into the library, where, he said, he had ordered a fire and lights. He seemed to have revived, and to be thinking intently.

In the library Dorothea observed that he had newly arranged a row of his note-books on a table, and now he took up and put into her hand a well-known volume, which was a table of contents to all the others.

" You will oblige me, my dear," he said, seating himself, " if instead of other reading this evening, you will go through this aloud, pencil in hand, and at each point where I say ' mark,' will make a cross with your pencil. This is the first step in a sifting process which I have long had in view, and as we go on I shall be able to indicate to you certain principles of selection whereby you will, I trust, have an intelligent participation in my purpose."

This proposal was only one more sign added to many since his memorable interview with Lydgate, that Mr Casaubon's original reluctance to let Dorothea work with him had given place to the contrary disposition, namely, to demand much interest and labour from her.

After she had read and marked for two hours, he said, " We will take the volume up-stairs—and the pencil, if you please—and in case

---

2. Herodotus records the story of Cyrus the Great's birth: that his grandfather, Astyages, had a dream that Cyrus would grow up to overthrow him, and therefore ordered the newborn infant slain. Cyrus was saved, however, and lived to fulfill the prophecy.

of reading in the night, we can pursue this task. It is not wearisome to you, I trust, Dorothea?"

" I prefer always reading what you like best to hear," said Dorothea, who told the simple truth ; for what she dreaded was to exert herself in reading or anything else which left him as joyless as ever.

It was a proof of the force with which certain characteristics in Dorothea impressed those around her, that her husband, with all his jealousy and suspicion, had gathered implicit trust in the integrity of her promises, and her power of devoting herself to her idea of the right and best. Of late he had begun to feel that these qualities were a peculiar possession for himself, and he wanted to engross them.

The reading in the night did come. Dorothea in her young weariness had slept soon and fast : she was awakened by a sense of light, which seemed to her at first like a sudden vision of sunset after she had climbed a steep hill : she opened her eyes and saw her husband wrapped in his warm gown seating himself in the arm-chair near the fire-place where the embers were still glowing. He had lit two candles, expecting that Dorothea would awake, but not liking to rouse her by more direct means.

" Are you ill, Edward?" she said, rising immediately.

" I felt some uneasiness in a reclining posture. I will sit here for a time." She threw wood on the fire, wrapped herself up, and said, " You would like me to read to you?"

" You would oblige me greatly by doing so, Dorothea," said Mr Casaubon, with a shade more meekness than usual in his polite manner. " I am wakeful : my mind is remarkably lucid."

" I fear that the excitement may be too great for you," said Dorothea, remembering Lydgate's cautions.

" No, I am not conscious of undue excitement. Thought is easy." Dorothea dared not insist, and she read for an hour or more on the same plan as she had done in the evening, but getting over the pages with more quickness. Mr Casaubon's mind was more alert, and he seemed to anticipate what was coming after a very slight verbal indication, saying, " That will do—mark that"—or " Pass on to the next head—I omit the second excursus on Crete." [3] Dorothea was amazed to think of the bird-like speed with which his mind was surveying the ground where it had been creeping for years. At last he said—

" Close the book now, my dear. We will resume our work to-morrow. I have deferred it too long, and would gladly see it completed. But you observe that the principle on which my selection is made, is to give adequate, and not disproportionate illustration to each of the theses enumerated in my introduction, as at present sketched. You have perceived that distinctly, Dorothea?"

" Yes," said Dorothea, rather tremulously. She felt sick at heart.

" And now I think that I can take some repose," said Mr Casaubon. He lay down again and begged her to put out the lights. When she had lain down too, and there was a darkness only broken by a dull glow on the hearth, he said—

---

3. The topic which Casaubon wishes to pass over here may well be that in Greek mythology concerning Paisiphae, the wife of King Minos of Crete, who became enamoured of a great bull and thus gave birth to the Minotaur. Minos kept the monster imprisoned in the labyrinth built by Daedalus until Theseus killed it.

" Before I sleep, I have a request to make, Dorothea."

" What is it ? " said Dorothea, with dread in her mind.

" It is that you will let me know, deliberately, whether, in case of my death, you will carry out my wishes : whether you will avoid doing what I should deprecate, and apply yourself to do what I should desire."

Dorothea was not taken by surprise : many incidents had been leading her to the conjecture of some intention on her husband's part which might make a new yoke for her. She did not answer immediately.

" You refuse ? " said Mr Casaubon, with more edge in his tone.

" No, I do not yet refuse," said Dorothea, in a clear voice, the need of freedom asserting itself within her ; " but it is too solemn—I think it is not right—to make a promise when I am ignorant what it will bind me to. Whatever affection prompted I would do without promising."

" But you would use your own judgment : I ask you to obey mine ; you refuse."

" No, dear, no ! " said Dorothea, beseechingly, crushed by opposing fears. " But may I wait and reflect a little while ? I desire with my whole soul to do what will comfort you ; but I cannot give any pledge suddenly—still less a pledge to do I know not what."

" You cannot then confide in the nature of my wishes ? "

" Grant me till to-morrow," said Dorothea, beseechingly.

" Till to-morrow then," said Mr Casaubon.

Soon she could hear that he was sleeping, but there was no more sleep for her. While she constrained herself to lie still lest she should disturb him, her mind was carrying on a conflict in which imagination ranged its forces first on one side and then on the other. She had no presentiment that the power which her husband wished to establish over her future action had relation to anything else than his work. But it was clear enough to her that he would expect her to devote herself to sifting those mixed heaps of material, which were to be the doubtful illustration of principles still more doubtful. The poor child had become altogether unbelieving as to the trustworthiness of that Key which had made the ambition and the labour of her husband's life. It was not wonderful that, in spite of her small instruction, her judgment in this matter was truer than his : for she looked with unbiassed comparison and healthy sense at probabilities on which he had risked all his egoism. And now she pictured to herself the days, and months, and years which she must spend in sorting what might be called shattered mummies, and fragments of a tradition which was itself a mosaic wrought from crushed ruins—sorting them as food for a theory which was already withered in the birth like an elfin child. Doubtless a vigorous error vigorously pursued has kept the embryos of truth a-breathing : the quest of gold being at the same time a questioning of substances, the body of chemistry is prepared for its soul, and Lavoisier is born. [4] But Mr Casaubon's theory of the elements which made the seed of all tradition was not likely to bruise itself unawares against discoveries : it floated among flexible conjectures no more solid than those etymologies which seemed strong

---

4. Antoine Laurent Lavoisier (1743–94), French chemist and founder of modern elemental chemistry.

because of likeness in sound, until it was shown that likeness in sound made them impossible : it was a method of interpretation which was not tested by the necessity of forming anything which had sharper collisions than an elaborate notion of Gog and Magog : it was as free from interruption as a plan for threading the stars together. [5] And Dorothea had so often had to check her weariness and impatience over this questionable riddle-guessing, as it revealed itself to her instead of the fellowship in high knowledge which was to make life worthier ! She could understand well enough now why her husband had come to cling to her, as possibly the only hope left that his labours would ever take a shape in which they could be given to the world. At first it had seemed that he wished to keep even her aloof from any close knowledge of what he was doing ; but gradually the terrible stringency of human need—the prospect of a too speedy death——

And here Dorothea's pity turned from her own future to her husband's past—nay, to his present hard struggle with a lot which had grown out of that past : the lonely labour, the ambition breathing hardly under the pressure of self-distrust ; the goal receding, and the heavier limbs ; and now at last the sword visibly trembling above him ! And had she not wished to marry him that she might help him in his life's labour ?—But she had thought the work was to be something greater, which she could serve in devoutly for its own sake. Was it right, even to soothe his grief—would it be possible, even if she promised—to work as in a treadmill fruitlessly ?

And yet, could she deny him ? Could she say, " I refuse to content this pining hunger ? " It would be refusing to do for him dead, what she was almost sure to do for him living. If he lived as Lydgate had said he might, for fifteen years or more, her life would certainly be spent in helping him and obeying him.

Still, there was a deep difference between that devotion to the living and that indefinite promise of devotion to the dead. While he lived, he could claim nothing that she would not still be free to remonstrate against, and even to refuse. But—the thought passed through her mind more than once, though she could not believe in it —might he not mean to demand something more from her than she had been able to imagine, since he wanted her pledge to carry out his wishes without telling her exactly what they were ? No ; his heart was bound up in his work only : that was the end for which his failing life was to be eked out by hers.

And now, if she were to say, " No ! if you die, I will put no finger to your work "—it seemed as if she would be crushing that bruised heart.

For four hours Dorothea lay in this conflict, till she felt ill and bewildered, unable to resolve, praying mutely. Helpless as a child which has sobbed and sought too long, she fell into a late morning sleep, and when she waked Mr Casaubon was already up. Tantripp told her that he had read prayers, breakfasted, and was in the library.

" I never saw you look so pale, madam," said Tantripp, a solid-figured woman who had been with the sisters at Lausanne.

" Was I ever high-coloured, Tantripp ? " said Dorothea, smiling faintly.

---

5. Gog and Magog: two nations led by Satan in the climactic battle at Armageddon in Rev. 20: 8.

" Well, not to say high-coloured, but with a bloom like a Chiny rose. But always smelling those leather books, what can be expected? Do rest a little this morning, madam. Let me say you are ill and not able to go into that close library."

" Oh no, no! let me make haste," said Dorothea. " Mr Casaubon wants me particularly."

When she went down she felt sure that she should promise to fulfil his wishes; but that would be later in the day—not yet.

As Dorothea entered the library, Mr Casaubon turned round from the table where he had been placing some books, and said—

" I was waiting for your appearance, my dear. I had hoped to set to work at once this morning, but I find myself under some indisposition, probably from too much excitement yesterday. I am going now to take a turn in the shrubbery, since the air is milder."

" I am glad to hear that," said Dorothea. " Your mind, I feared, was too active last night."

" I would fain have it set at rest on the point I last spoke of, Dorothea. You can now, I hope, give me an answer."

" May I come out to you in the garden presently?" said Dorothea, winning a little breathing space in that way.

" I shall be in the Yew-Tree Walk for the next half-hour," said Mr Casaubon, and then he left her.

Dorothea, feeling very weary, rang and asked Tantripp to bring her some wraps. She had been sitting still for a few minutes, but not in any renewal of the former conflict: she simply felt that she was going to say " Yes" to her own doom: she was too weak, too full of dread at the thought of inflicting a keen-edged blow on her husband, to do anything but submit completely. She sat still and let Tantripp put on her bonnet and shawl, a passivity which was unusual with her, for she liked to wait on herself.

" God bless you, madam!" said Tantripp, with an irrepressible movement of love towards the beautiful, gentle creature for whom she felt unable to do anything more, now that she had finished tying the bonnet.

This was too much for Dorothea's highly-strung feeling, and she burst into tears, sobbing against Tantripp's arm. But soon she checked herself, dried her eyes, and went out at the glass door into the shrubbery.

" I wish every book in that library was built into a caticom for your master," said Tantripp to Pratt, the butler, finding him in the breakfast-room. She had been at Rome, and visited the antiquities, as we know; and she always declined to call Mr Casaubon anything but " your master," when speaking to the other servants.

Pratt laughed. He liked his master very well, but he liked Tantripp better.

When Dorothea was out on the gravel walks, she lingered among the nearer clumps of trees, hesitating, as she had done once before, though from a different cause. Then she had feared lest her effort at fellowship should be unwelcome; now she dreaded going to the spot where she foresaw that she must bind herself to a fellowship from which she shrank. Neither law nor the world's opinion compelled her to this—only her husband's nature and her own compassion, only the ideal and not the real yoke of marriage. She saw clearly enough the whole situation, yet she was fettered: she could not smite the stricken soul that entreated hers. If that were weakness, Dorothea was weak. But the half-hour was passing, and she must not delay longer. When she entered the Yew-Tree Walk she could not see her husband ; but the walk had bends, and she went, expecting to catch sight of his figure wrapped in a blue cloak, which, with a warm velvet cap, was his outer garment on chill days for the garden. It occurred to her that he might be resting in the summer-house, towards which the path diverged a little. Turning the angle, she could see him seated on the bench, close to a stone table. His arms were resting on the table, and his brow was bowed down on them, the blue cloak being dragged forward and screening his face on each side.

" He exhausted himself last night," Dorothea said to herself, thinking at first that he was asleep, and that the summer-house was too damp a place to rest in. But then she remembered that of late she had seen him take that attitude when she was reading to him, as if he found it easier than any other ; and that he would sometimes speak, as well as listen, with his face down in that way. She went into the summer-house and said, " I am come, Edward ; I am ready."

He took no notice, and she thought that he must be fast asleep. She laid her hand on his shoulder, and repeated, " I am ready ! " Still he was motionless ; and with a sudden confused fear, she leaned down to him, took off his velvet cap, and leaned her cheek close to his head, crying in a distressed tone,

" Wake, dear, wake ! Listen to me. I am come to answer."

But Dorothea never gave her answer.

Later in the day, Lydgate was seated by her bedside, and she was talking deliriously, thinking aloud, and recalling what had gone through her mind the night before. She knew him, and called him by his name, but appeared to think it right that she should explain everything to him ; and again, and again, begged him to explain everything to her husband.

" Tell him I shall go to him soon : I am ready to promise. Only, thinking about it was so dreadful—it has made me ill. Not very ill. I shall soon be better. Go and tell him."

But the silence in her husband's ear was never more to be broken.

CHAPTER XLIX.

A task too strong for wizard spells
This squire had brought about;
'Tis easy dropping stones in wells,
But who shall get them out?

" I WISH to God we could hinder Dorothea from knowing this," said Sir James Chettam, with the little frown on his brow, and an expression of intense disgust about his mouth.

He was standing on the hearth-rug in the library at Lowick Grange, and speaking to Mr Brooke. It was the day after Mr Casaubon had been buried, and Dorothea was not yet able to leave her room.

" That would be difficult, you know, Chettam, as she is an executrix, and she likes to go into these things—property, land, that kind of thing. She has her notions, you know," said Mr Brooke, sticking his eye-glasses on nervously, and exploring the edges of a folded paper which he held in his hand; "and she would like to act—depend upon it, as an executrix Dorothea would want to act. And she was twenty-one last December, you know. I can hinder nothing."

Sir James looked at the carpet for a minute in silence, and then lifting his eyes suddenly fixed them on Mr Brooke, saying, "I will tell you what we can do. Until Dorothea is well, all business must be kept from her, and as soon as she is able to be moved she must come to us. Being with Celia and the baby will be the best thing in the world for her, and will pass away the time. And meanwhile you must get rid of Ladislaw : you must send him out of the country." Here Sir James's look of disgust returned in all its intensity.

Mr Brooke put his hands behind him, walked to the window and straightened his back with a little shake before he replied.

"That is easily said, Chettam, easily said, you know."

"My dear sir," persisted Sir James, restraining his indignation within respectful forms, "it was you who brought him here, and you who keep him here—I mean by the occupation you give him."

"Yes, but I can't dismiss him in an instant without assigning reasons, my dear Chettam. Ladislaw has been invaluable, most satisfactory. I consider that I have done this part of the country a service by bringing him—by bringing him, you know." Mr Brooke ended with a nod, turning round to give it.

"It's a pity this part of the country didn't do without him, that's all I have to say about it. At any rate, as Dorothea's brother-in-law, I feel warranted in objecting strongly to his being kept here by any action on the part of her friends. You admit, I hope, that I have a right to speak about what concerns the dignity of my wife's sister ?"

Sir James was getting warm.

"Of course, my dear Chettam, of course. But you and I have different ideas—different——"

"Not about this action of Casaubon's, I should hope," interrupted Sir James. "I say that he has most unfairly compromised Dorothea. I say that there never was a meaner, more ungentlemanly action than this—a codicil of this sort to a will which he made at the time of his marriage with the knowledge and reliance of her family—a positive insult to Dorothea !"

"Well, you know, Casaubon was a little twisted about Ladislaw. Ladislaw has told me the reason—dislike of the bent he took, you know—Ladislaw didn't think much of Casaubon's notions, Thoth and Dagon—that sort of thing : and I fancy that Casaubon didn't like the independent position Ladislaw had taken up.[1] I saw the letters between them, you know. Poor Casaubon was a little buried in books—he didn't know the world."

"It's all very well for Ladislaw to put that colour on it," said Sir James. "But I believe Casaubon was only jealous of him on Dorothea's account, and the world will suppose that she gave him some reason ; and that is what makes it so abominable—coupling her name with this young fellow's."

1. Thoth was an ancient Egyptian god of wisdom and science; Dagon was a half-man, half-fish Philistine god of fertility.

" My dear Chettam, it won't lead to anything, you know," said Mr Brooke, seating himself and sticking on his eye-glass again. " It's all of a piece with Casaubon's oddity. This paper, now, 'Synoptical Tabulation' and so on, 'for the use of Mrs Casaubon,' it was locked up in the desk with the will. I suppose he meant Dorothea to publish his researches, eh? and she'll do it, you know ; she has gone into his studies uncommonly."

" My dear sir," said Sir James, impatiently, " that is neither here nor there. The question is, whether you don't see with me the propriety of sending young Ladislaw away ?"

" Well, no, not the urgency of the thing. By-and-by, perhaps, it may come round. As to gossip, you know, sending him away won't hinder gossip. People say what they like to say, not what they have chapter and verse for," said Mr Brooke, becoming acute about the truths that lay on the side of his own wishes. " I might get rid of Ladislaw up to a certain point—take away the 'Pioneer' from him, and that sort of thing ; but I couldn't send him out of the country if he didn't choose to go—didn't choose, you know."

Mr Brooke, persisting as quietly as if he were only discussing the nature of last year's weather, and nodding at the end with his usual amenity, was an exasperating form of obstinacy.

" Good God !" said Sir James, with as much passion as he ever showed, " let us get him a post ; let us spend money on him. If he could go in the suite of some Colonial Governor ! Grampus might take him—and I could write to Fulke about it."

" But Ladislaw won't be shipped off like a head of cattle, my dear fellow ; Ladislaw has his ideas. It's my opinion that if he were to part from me to-morrow, you'd only hear the more of him in the country. With his talent for speaking and drawing up documents, there are few men who could come up to him as an agitator—an agitator, you know."

" Agitator !" said Sir James, with bitter emphasis, feeling that the syllables of this word properly repeated were a sufficient exposure of its hatefulness.

" But be reasonable, Chettam. Dorothea, now. As you say, she had better go to Celia as soon as possible. She can stay under your roof, and in the mean time things may come round quietly. Don't let us be firing off our guns in a hurry, you know. Standish will keep our counsel, and the news will be old before it's known. Twenty things may happen to carry off Ladislaw—without my doing anything, you know."

" Then I am to conclude that you decline to do anything ?"

" Decline, Chettam ?—no—I didn't say decline. But I really don't see what I could do. Ladislaw is a gentleman."

" I am glad to hear it !" said Sir James, his irritation making him forget himself a little. " I am sure Casaubon was not."

" Well, it would have been worse if he had made the codicil to hinder her from marrying again at all, you know."

" I don't know that," said Sir James. " It would have been less indelicate."

" One of poor Casaubon's freaks ! That attack upset his brain a little. It all goes for nothing. She doesn't *want* to marry Ladislaw."

" But this codicil is framed so as to make everybody believe that

she did. I don't believe anything of the sort about Dorothea," said
Sir James—then frowningly, "but I suspect Ladislaw. I tell you
frankly, I suspect Ladislaw."

"I couldn't take any immediate action on that ground, Chettam.
In fact, if it were possible to pack him off—send him to Norfolk
Island—that sort of thing—it would look all the worse for Dorothea
to those who knew about it. [2] It would seem as if we distrusted her—
distrusted her, you know."

That Mr Brooke had hit on an undeniable argument, did not tend
to soothe Sir James. He put out his hand to reach his hat, implying that he did not mean to contend further, and said, still with
some heat—

"Well, I can only say that I think Dorothea was sacrificed once,
because her friends were too careless. I shall do what I can, as her
brother, to protect her now."

"You can't do better than get her to Freshitt as soon as possible,
Chettam. I approve that plan altogether," said Mr Brooke, well
pleased that he had won the argument. It would have been highly
inconvenient to him to part with Ladislaw at that time, when a dissolution might happen any day, and electors were to be convinced of
the course by which the interests of the country would be best served.
Mr Brooke sincerely believed that this end could be secured by his
own return to Parliament : he offered the forces of his mind honestly
to the nation.

CHAPTER L.

> "'This Loller here wol prechen us somewhat.'
> 'Nay by my father's soule ! that schal he nat,'
> Sayde the Schipman, 'here schal he not preche,
> He schal no gospel glosen here ne teche.
> We leven all in the gret God,' quod he.
> He wolden sowen some diffcultee."
>
> —*Canterbury Tales.* [1]

DOROTHEA had been safe at Freshitt Hall nearly a week before she
had asked any dangerous questions. Every morning now she sat with
Celia in the prettiest of up-stairs sitting-rooms, opening into a small
conservatory—Celia all in white and lavender like a bunch of mixed
violets, watching the remarkable acts of the baby, which were so dubious to her inexperienced mind that all conversation was interrupted
by appeals for their interpretation made to the oracular nurse. Dorothea sat by in her widow's dress, with an expression which rather provoked Celia, as being much too sad ; for not only was baby quite well,
but really when a husband had been so dull and troublesome while
he lived, and besides that had—well, well ! Sir James, of course, had
told Celia everything, with a strong representation how important it
was that Dorothea should not know it sooner than was inevitable.

But Mr Brooke had been right in predicting that Dorothea would

2. Norfolk Island: a prison island.   1177–82.
1. "The   Shipman's   Prologue," lines

not long remain passive where action had been assigned to her ; she knew the purport of her husband's will made at the time of their marriage, and her mind, as soon as she was clearly conscious of her position, was silently occupied with what she ought to do as the owner of Lowick Manor with the patronage of the living attached to it.

One morning when her uncle paid his usual visit, though with an unusual alacrity in his manner which he accounted for by saying that it was now pretty certain Parliament would be dissolved forthwith, Dorothea said—

" Uncle, it is right now that I should consider who is to have the living at Lowick. After Mr Tucker had been provided for, I never heard my husband say that he had any clergyman in his mind as a successor to himself. I think I ought to have the keys now and go to Lowick to examine all my husband's papers. There may be something that would throw light on his wishes."

" No hurry, my dear," said Mr Brooke, quietly. " By-and-by, you know, you can go, if you like. But I cast my eyes over things in the desks and drawers—there was nothing—nothing but deep subjects, you know—besides the will. Everything can be done by-and-by. As to the living, I have had an application for interest already—I should say rather good. Mr Tyke has been strongly recommended to me— I had something to do with getting him an appointment before. An apostolic man, I believe—the sort of thing that would suit you, my dear." [2]

" I should like to have fuller knowledge about him, uncle, and judge for myself, if Mr Casaubon has not left any expression of his wishes. He has perhaps made some addition to his will—there may be some instructions for me," said Dorothea, who had all the while had this conjecture in her mind with relation to her husband's work.

" Nothing about the rectory, my dear—nothing." said Mr Brooke, rising to go away, and putting out his hand to his nieces : " nor about his researches, you know. Nothing in the will."

Dorothea's lip quivered.

" Come, you must not think of these things yet, my dear. By-and-by, you know."

" I am quite well now, uncle ; I wish to exert myself."

" Well, well, we shall see. But I must run away now—I have no end of work now—it's a crisis—a political crisis, you know. And here is Celia and her little man—you are an aunt, you know, now, and I am a sort of grandfather," said Mr Brooke, with placid hurry, anxious to get away and tell Chettam that it would not be his (Mr Brooke's) fault if Dorothea insisted on looking into everything.

Dorothea sank back in her chair when her uncle had left the room, and cast her eyes down meditatively on her crossed hands.

" Look, Dodo ! look at him ! Did you ever see anything like that ? " said Celia, in her comfortable staccato.

" What, Kitty ? " said Dorothea, lifting her eyes rather absently.

" What ? why, his upper lip ; see how he is drawing it down, as if he meant to make a face. Isn't it wonderful ! He may have his little thoughts. I wish nurse were here. Do look at him."

A large tear which had been for some time gathering, rolled down Dorothea's cheek as she looked up and tried to smile.

2. Apostolic man: a minister whose character, habits, and actions—particularly charitable actions—are reminiscent of the Apostles of Christ.

"Don't be sad, Dodo ; kiss baby. What are you brooding over so ? I am sure you did everything, and a great deal too much. You should be happy now."

"I wonder if Sir James would drive me to Lowick. I want to look over everything—to see if there were any words written for me."

"You are not to go till Mr Lydgate says you may go. And he has not said so yet (here you are, nurse ; take baby and walk up and down the gallery). Besides, you have got a wrong notion in your head as usual, Dodo—I can see that : it vexes me."

"Where am I wrong, Kitty ?" said Dorothea, quite meekly. She was almost ready now to think Celia wiser than herself, and was really wondering with some fear what her wrong notion was. Celia felt her advantage, and was determined to use it. None of them knew Dodo as well as she did, or knew how to manage her. Since Celia's baby was born, she had had a new sense of her mental solidity and calm wisdom. It seemed clear that where there was a baby, things were right enough, and that error, in general, was a mere lack of that central poising force.

"I can see what you are thinking of as well as can be, Dodo," said Celia. "You are wanting to find out if there is anything uncomfortable for you to do now, only because Mr Casaubon wished it. As if you had not been uncomfortable enough before. And he doesn't deserve it, and you will find that out. He has behaved very badly. James is as angry with him as can be. And I had better tell you, to prepare you."

"Celia," said Dorothea, entreatingly, "you distress me. Tell me at once what you mean." It glanced through her mind that Mr Casaubon had left the property away from her — which would not be so very distressing.

"Why, he has made a codicil to his will, to say the property was all to go away from you if you married—I mean——"

"That is of no consequence," said Dorothea, breaking in impetuously.

"But if you married Mr Ladislaw, not anybody else," Celia went on with persevering quietude. "Of course that is of no consequence in one way — you never *would* marry Mr Ladislaw ; but that only makes it worse of Mr Casaubon."

The blood rushed to Dorothea's face and neck painfully. But Celia was administering what she thought a sobering dose of fact. It was taking up notions that had done Dodo's health so much harm. So she went on in her neutral tone, as if she had been remarking on baby's robes.

"James says so. He says it is abominable, and not like a gentleman. And there never *was* a better judge than James. It is as if Mr Casaubon wanted to make people believe that you would wish to marry Mr Ladislaw—which is ridiculous. Only James says it was to hinder Mr Ladislaw from wanting to marry you for your money — just as if he ever would think of making you an offer. Mrs Cadwallader said you might as well marry an Italian with white mice ! But I must just go and look at baby," Celia added, without the least change of tone, throwing a light shawl over her, and tripping away.

Dorothea by this time had turned cold again, and now threw herself back helplessly in her chair. She might have compared her experience at that moment to the vague, alarmed consciousness that her

life was taking on a new form, that she was undergoing a metamorphosis in which memory would not adjust itself to the stirring of new
organs. Everything was changing its aspect : her husband's conduct,
her own duteous feeling towards him, every struggle between them—
and yet more, her whole relation to Will Ladislaw. Her world was
in a state of convulsive change ; the only thing she could say distinctly to herself was, that she must wait and think anew. One
change terrified her as if it had been a sin ; it was a violent shock of
repulsion from her departed husband, who had had hidden thoughts,
perhaps perverting everything she said and did. Then again she was
conscious of another change which also made her tremulous ; it was
a sudden strange yearning of heart towards Will Ladislaw. It had
never before entered her mind that he could, under any circumstances,
be her lover : conceive the effect of the sudden revelation that another had thought of him in that light—that perhaps he himself had
been conscious of such a possibility, — and this with the hurrying,
crowding vision of unfitting conditions, and questions not soon to be
solved.

It seemed a long while — she did not know how long — before she
heard Celia saying, " That will do, nurse ; he will be quiet on my lap
now. You can go to lunch, and let Garratt stay in the next room."
" What I think, Dodo," Celia went on, observing nothing more than
that Dorothea was leaning back in her chair, and likely to be passive,
" is that Mr Casaubon was spiteful. I never did like him, and James
never did. I think the corners of his mouth were dreadfully spiteful.
And now he has behaved in this way, I am sure religion does not require you to make yourself uncomfortable about him. If he has been
taken away, that is a mercy, and you ought to be grateful. *We* should
not grieve, should we, baby ? " said Celia confidentially to that unconscious centre and poise of the world, who had the most remarkable
fists all complete even to the nails, and hair enough, really, when you
took his cap off, to make—you didn't know what :—in short, he was
Bouddha in a Western form.

At this crisis Lydgate was announced, and one of the first things
he said was, " I fear you are not so well as you were, Mrs Casaubon :
have you been agitated ? allow me to feel your pulse." Dorothea's
hand was of a marble coldness.

" She wants to go to Lowick, to look over papers," said Celia. " She
ought not, ought she ? "

Lydgate did not speak for a few moments. Then he said, looking
at Dorothea, " I hardly know. In my opinion Mrs Casaubon should
do what would give her the most repose of mind. That repose will
not always come from being forbidden to act."

" Thank you," said Dorothea, exerting herself, " I am sure that is
wise. There are so many things which I ought to attend to. Why
should I sit here idle ? " Then, with an effort to recall subjects not
connected with her agitation, she added, abruptly, " You know every
one in Middlemarch, I think, Mr Lydgate. I shall ask you to tell me
a great deal. I have serious things to do now. I have a living to give
away. You know Mr Tyke and all the——" But Dorothea's effort
was too much for her ; she broke off and burst into sobs.

Lydgate made her drink a dose of sal volatile. [3]

3. An aromatic alcoholic solution of ammonium carbonate.

" Let Mrs Casaubon do as she likes," he said to Sir James, whom he asked to see before quitting the house. " She wants perfect freedom, I think, more than any other prescription."

His attendance on Dorothea while her brain was excited, had enabled him to form some true conclusions concerning the trials of her life. He felt sure that she had been suffering from the strain and conflict of self-repression ; and that she was likely now to feel herself only in another sort of pinfold than that from which she had been released.

Lydgate's advice was all the easier for Sir James to follow when he found that Celia had already told Dorothea the unpleasant fact about the will. There was no help for it now — no reason for any further delay in the execution of necessary business. And the next day Sir James complied at once with her request that he would drive her to Lowick.

" I have no wish to stay there at present," said Dorothea ; " I could hardly bear it. I am much happier at Freshitt with Celia. I shall be able to think better about what should be done at Lowick by looking at it from a distance. And I should like to be at the Grange a little while with my uncle, and go about in all the old walks and among the people in the village."

" Not yet, I think. Your uncle is having political company, and you are better out of the way of such doings," said Sir James, who at that moment thought of the Grange chiefly as a haunt of young Ladislaw's. But no word passed between him and Dorothea about the objectionable part of the will ; indeed, both of them felt that the mention of it between them would be impossible. Sir James was shy, even with men, about disagreeble subjects ; and the one thing that Dorothea would have chosen to say, if she had spoken on the matter at all, was forbidden to her at present because it seemed to be a further exposure of her husband's injustice. Yet she did wish that Sir James could know what had passed between her and her husband about Will Ladislaw's moral claim on the property : it would then, she thought, be apparent to him as it was to her, that her husband's strange indelicate proviso had been chiefly urged by his bitter resistance to that idea of claim, and not merely by personal feelings more difficult to talk about. Also, it must be admitted, Dorothea wished that this could be known for Will's sake, since her friends seemed to think of him as simply an object of Mr Casaubon's charity. Why should he be compared with an Italian carrying white mice ? That word quoted from Mrs Cadwallader seemed like a mocking travesty wrought in the dark by an impish finger.

At Lowick Dorothea searched desk and drawer—searched all her husband's places of deposit for private writing, but found no paper addressed especially to her, except that " Synoptical Tabulation " which was probably only the beginning of many intended directions for her guidance. In carrying out this bequest of labour to Dorothea, as in all else, Mr Casaubon had been slow and hesitating, oppressed in the plan of transmitting his work, as he had been in executing it, by the sense of moving heavily in a dim and clogging medium : distrust of Dorothea's competence to arrange what he had prepared was subdued only by distrust of any other redactor. But he had come at last to create a trust for himself out of Dorothea's nature : she could do what she resolved to do : and he willingly imagined her toiling under the fetters of a promise to erect a tomb with his name upon it.

(Not that Mr Casaubon called the future volumes a tomb ; he called them the Key to all Mythologies.) But the months gained on him and left his plans belated : he had only had time to ask for that promise by which he sought to keep his cold grasp on Dorothea's life.

The grasp had slipped away. Bound by a pledge given from the depths of her pity, she would have been capable of undertaking a toil which her judgment whispered was vain for all uses except that consecration of faithfulness which is a supreme use. But now her judgment, instead of being controlled by duteous devotion, was made active by the imbittering discovery that in her past union there had lurked the hidden alienation of secrecy and suspicion. The living, suffering man was no longer before her to awaken her pity : there remained only the retrospect of painful subjection to a husband whose thoughts had been lower than she had believed, whose exorbitant claims for himself had even blinded his scrupulous care for his own character, and made him defeat his own pride by shocking men of ordinary honour. As for the property which was the sign of that broken tie, she would have been glad to be free from it and have nothing more than her original fortune which had been settled on her, if there had not been duties attached to ownership, which she ought not to flinch from. About this property many troublous questions insisted on rising : had she not been right in thinking that the half of it ought to go to Will Ladislaw ?—but was it not impossible now for her to do that act of justice ? Mr Casaubon had taken a cruelly effective means of hindering her : even with indignation against him in her heart, any act that seemed a triumphant eluding of his purpose revolted her.

After collecting papers of business which she wished to examine, she locked up again the desks and drawers—all empty of personal words for her—empty of any sign that in her husband's lonely brooding his heart had gone out to her in excuse or explanation ; and she went back to Freshitt with the sense that around his last hard demand and his last injurious assertion of his power, the silence was unbroken.

Dorothea tried now to turn her thoughts towards immediate duties, and one of these was of a kind which others were determined to remind her of. Lydgate's ear had caught eagerly her mention of the living, and as soon as he could, he reopened the subject, seeing here a possibility of making amends for the casting-vote he had once given with an ill-satisfied conscience.

"Instead of telling you anything about Mr Tyke," he said, "I should like to speak of another man—Mr Farebrother, the Vicar of St Botolph's. His living is a poor one, and gives him a stinted provision for himself and his family. His mother, aunt, and sister all live with him, and depend upon him. I believe he has never married because of them. I never heard such good preaching as his—such plain, easy eloquence. He would have done to preach at St Paul's Cross after old Latimer. [4] His talk is just as good about all subjects : original, simple, clear. I think him a remarkable fellow ; he ought to have done more than he has done."

"Why has he not done more ?" said Dorothea, interested now in all who had slipped below their own intention.

---

4. Hugh Latimer (1485–1555), famous English preacher of simple, homely sermons.

" That's a hard question," said Lydgate. " I find myself that it's uncommonly difficult to make the right thing work : there are so many strings pulling at once. Farebrother often hints that he has got into the wrong profession ; he wants a wider range than that of a poor clergyman, and I suppose he has no interest to help him on. He is very fond of Natural History and various scientific matters, and he is hampered in reconciling these tastes with his position. He has no money to spare—hardly enough to use ; and that has led him into card-playing—Middlemarch is a great place for whist. He does play for money, and he wins a good deal. Of course that takes him into company a little beneath him, and makes him slack about some things ; and yet, with all that, looking at him as a whole, I think he is one of the most blameless men I ever knew. He has neither venom nor doubleness in him, and those often go with a more correct outside."

" I wonder whether he suffers in his conscience because of that habit," said Dorothea ; " I wonder whether he wishes he could leave it off."

" I have no doubt he would leave it off, if he were transplanted into plenty : he would be glad of the time for other things."

" My uncle says that Mr Tyke is spoken of as an apostolic man," said Dorothea, meditatively. She was wishing it were possible to re-store the times of primitive zeal, and yet thinking of Mr Farebrother with a strong desire to rescue him from his chance-gotten money.

" I don't pretend to say that Farebrother is apostolic," said Lyd-gate. " His position is not quite like that of the Apostles : he is only a parson among parishioners whose lives he has to try and make bet-ter. Practically I find that what is called being apostolic now, is an impatience of everything in which the parson doesn't cut the princi-pal figure. I see something of that in Mr Tyke at the Hospital : a good deal of his doctrine is a sort of pinching hard to make people uncomfortably aware of him. Besides, an apostolic man at Lowick ! —he ought to think, as St Francis did, that it is needful to preach to the birds."

" True," said Dorothea. " It is hard to imagine what sort of no-tions our farmers and labourers get from their teaching. I have been looking into a volume of sermons by Mr Tyke : such sermons would be of no use at Lowick—I mean, about imputed righteousness and the prophecies in the Apocalypse. I have always been thinking of the different ways in which Christianity is taught, and whenever I find one way that makes it a wider blessing than any other, I cling to that as the truest—I mean that which takes in the most good of all kinds, and brings in the most people as sharers in it. It is surely better to pardon too much, than to condemn too much. But I should like to see Mr Farebrother and hear him preach."

" Do," said Lydgate ; " I trust to the effect of that. He is very much beloved, but he has his enemies too : there are always people who can't forgive an able man for differing from them. And that money-winning business is really a blot. You don't, of course, see many Middlemarch people : but Mr Ladislaw, who is constantly seeing Mr Brooke, is a great friend of Mr Farebrother's old ladies, and would be glad to sing the Vicar's praises. One of the old ladies— Miss Noble, the aunt—is a wonderfully quaint picture of self-forget-ful goodness, and Ladislaw gallants her about sometimes. I met them one day in a back street : you know Ladislaw's look—a sort of Daphnis in coat and waistcoat ; and this little old maid reaching up to his arm —they looked like a couple dropped out of a romantic comedy. [5] But the best evidence about Farebrother is to see him and hear him."

Happily Dorothea was in her private sitting-room when this conversation occurred, and there was no one present to make Lydgate's innocent introduction of Ladislaw painful to her. As was usual with him in matters of personal gossip, Lydgate had quite forgotten Rosamond's remark that she thought Will adored Mrs Casaubon. At that moment he was only caring for what would recommend the Farebrother family ; and he had purposely given emphasis to the worst that could be said about the Vicar, in order to forestall objections. In the weeks since Mr Casaubon's death he had hardly seen Ladislaw, and he had heard no rumour to warn him that Mr Brooke's confidential secretary was a dangerous subject with Mrs Casaubon. When he was gone, his picture of Ladislaw lingered in her mind and disputed the ground with that question of the Lowick living. What was Will Ladislaw thinking about her ? Would he hear of that fact which made her cheeks burn as they never used to do ? And how would he feel when he heard it ?—But she could see as well as possible how he smiled down at the little old maid. An Italian with white mice !—on the contrary, he was a creature who entered into every one's feelings, and could take the pressure of their thought instead of urging his own with iron resistance.

CHAPTER LI.

Party is Nature too, and you shall see
By force of Logic how they both agree :
The Many in the One, the One in Many ;
All is not Some, nor Some the same as Any :
Genus holds species, both are great or small ;
One genus highest, one not high at all ;
Each species has its differentia too,
This is not That, and He was never You,
Though this and that are AYES, and you and he
Are like as one to one, or three to three.

No gossip about Mr Casaubon's will had yet reached Ladislaw : the air seemed to be filled with the dissolution of Parliament and the coming election, as the old wakes and fairs were filled with the rival clatter of itinerant shows ; and more private noises were taken little notice of. The famous " dry election " was at hand, in which the depths of public feeling might be measured by the low flood-mark of drink.[1] Will Ladislaw was one of the busiest at this time ; and though Dorothea's widowhood was continually in his thought, he was so far from wishing to be spoken to on the subject, that when Lydgate sought him out to tell him what had passed about the Lowick living, he answered rather waspishly—

---

5. Daphnis was the son of Hermes, raised by nymphs and taught by Pan to play the flute; he became a shepherd, and is the mythical inventor of pastoral poetry.

1. The election failed to excite much public interest nationally, and as it was not necessary for candidates to buy drinks for prospective voters, it was a "dry election."

" Why should you bring me into the matter ? I never see Mrs
Casaubon, and am not likely to see her, since she is at Freshitt. I
never go there. It is Tory ground, where I and the ' Pioneer' are no
more welcome than a poacher and his gun."

The fact was that Will had been made the more susceptible by
observing that Mr Brooke, instead of wishing him, as before, to come
to the Grange oftener than was quite agreeable to himself, seemed
now to contrive that he should go there as little as possible. This was
a shuffling concession of Mr Brooke's to Sir James Chettam's indignant
remonstrance ; and Will, awake to the slightest hint in this direction,
concluded that he was to be kept away from the Grange on Dorothea's
account. Her friends, then, regarded him with some suspicion ?
Their fears were quite superfluous : they were very much mistaken
if they imagined that he would put himself forward as a needy adventurer trying to win the favour of a rich woman.

Until now Will had never fully seen the chasm between himself
and Dorothea—until now that he was come to the brink of it, and
saw her on the other side. He began, not without some inward rage,
to think of going away from the neighbourhood : it would be impossible for him to show any further interest in Dorothea without
subjecting himself to disagreeable imputations—perhaps even in her
mind, which others might try to poison.

" We are for ever divided," said Will. " I might as well be at
Rome ; she would be no farther from me." But what we call our
despair is often only the painful eagerness of unfed hope. There
were plenty of reasons why he should not go—public reasons why he
should not quit his post at this crisis, leaving Mr Brooke in the
lurch when he needed " coaching " for the election, and when there
was so much canvassing, direct and indirect, to be carried on. Will
could not like to leave his own chessmen in the heat of a game ; and
any candidate on the right side, even if his brain and marrow had
been as soft as was consistent with a gentlemanly bearing, might help
to turn a majority. To coach Mr Brooke and keep him steadily to
the idea that he must pledge himself to vote for the actual Reform
Bill, instead of insisting on his independence and power of pulling
up in time, was not an easy task. Mr Farebrother's prophecy of a
fourth candidate " in the bag " had not yet been fulfilled, neither the
Parliamentary Candidate Society nor any other power on the watch
to secure a reforming majority seeing a worthy nodus for interference
while there was a second reforming candidate like Mr Brooke, who
might be returned at his own expense ; and the fight lay entirely
between Pinkerton the old Tory member, Bagster the new Whig
member returned at the last election, and Brooke the future independent member, who was to fetter himself for this occasion only. Mr
Hawley and his party would bend all their forces to the return of
Pinkerton, and Mr Brooke's success must depend either on plumpers
which would leave Bagster in the rear, or on the new minting of
Tory votes into reforming votes. The latter means, of course, would
be preferable.

This prospect of converting votes was a dangerous distraction to Mr
Brooke : his impression that waverers were likely to be allured by
wavering statements, and also the liability of his mind to stick afresh
at opposing arguments as they turned up in his memory, gave Will
Ladislaw much trouble.

" You know there are tactics in these things," said Mr Brooke ; " meeting people half-way—tempering your ideas—saying, ' Well now, there's something in that,' and so on. I agree with you that this is a peculiar occasion—the country with a will of its own—political unions—that sort of thing—but we sometimes cut with rather too sharp a knife, Ladislaw. These ten-pound householders, now : why ten ? [2] Draw the line somewhere—yes : but why just at ten ? That's a difficult question, now, if you go into it."

" Of course it is," said Will, impatiently. " But if you are to wait till we get a logical Bill, you must put yourself forward as a revolutionist, and then Middlemarch would not elect you, I fancy. As for trimming, this is not a time for trimming." [3]

Mr Brooke always ended by agreeing with Ladislaw, who still appeared to him a sort of Burke with a leaven of Shelley ; but after an interval the wisdom of his own methods reasserted itself, and he was again drawn into using them with much hopefulness. At this stage of affairs he was in excellent spirits, which even supported him under large advances of money ; for his powers of convincing and persuading had not yet been tested by anything more difficult than a chairman's speech introducing other orators, or a dialogue with a Middlemarch voter, from which he came away with a sense that he was a tactician by nature, and that it was a pity he had not gone earlier into this kind of thing. He was a little conscious of defeat, however, with Mr Mawmsey, a chief representative in Middlemarch of that great social power, the retail trader, and naturally one of the most doubtful voters in the borough—willing for his own part to supply an equal quality of teas and sugars to reformer and anti-reformer, as well as to agree impartially with both, and feeling like the burgesses of old that this necessity of electing members was a great burthen to a town ; for even if there were no danger in holding out hopes to all parties beforehand, there would be the painful necessity at last of disappointing respectable people whose names were on his books. He was accustomed to receive large orders from Mr Brooke of Tipton ; but then, there were many of Pinkerton's committee whose opinions had a great weight of grocery on their side. Mr Mawmsey thinking that Mr Brooke, as not too " clever in his intellects," was the more likely to forgive a grocer who gave a hostile vote under pressure, had become confidential in his back parlour.

" As to Reform, sir, put it in a family light," he said, rattling the small silver in his pocket, and smiling affably. " Will it support Mrs Mawmsey, and enable her to bring up six children when I am no more ? I put the question *fictiously*, knowing what must be the answer. Very well, sir. I ask you what, as a husband and a father, I am to do when gentlemen come to me and say, ' Do as you like, Mawmsey ; but if you vote against us, I shall get my groceries elsewhere : when I sugar my liquor I like to feel that I am benefiting the country by maintaining tradesmen of the right colour.' Those very words have been spoken to me, sir, in the very chair where you are now sitting. I don't mean by your honourable self, Mr Brooke."

2. Franchise qualification for the boroughs was the occupation of property rated for taxes at ten pounds or more a year.

3. Balancing between opinions so as to remain in favor with both sides.

"No, no, no—that's narrow, you know. Until my butler complains to me of your goods, Mr Mawmsey," said Mr Brooke, soothingly, "until I hear that you send bad sugars, spices—that sort of thing—I shall never order him to go elsewhere."

"Sir, I am your humble servant, and greatly obliged," said Mr Mawmsey, feeling that politics were clearing up a little. "There would be some pleasure in voting for a gentleman who speaks in that honourable manner."

"Well, you know, Mr Mawmsey, you would find it the right thing to put yourself on our side. This Reform will touch everybody by-and-by—a thoroughly popular measure—a sort of A, B, C, you know, that must come first before the rest can follow. I quite agree with you that you've got to look at the thing in a family light : but public spirit, now. We're all one family, you know—it's all one cupboard. Such a thing as a vote, now : why, it may help to make men's fortunes at the Cape—there's no knowing what may be the effect of a vote," Mr Brooke ended, with a sense of being a little out at sea, though finding it still enjoyable. But Mr Mawmsey answered in a tone of decisive check.

"I beg your pardon, sir, but I can't afford that. When I give a vote I must know what I'm doing ; I must look to what will be the effects on my till and ledger, speaking respectfully. Prices, I'll admit, are what nobody can know the merits of ; and the sudden falls after you've bought in currants, which are a goods that will not keep—I've never myself seen into the ins and outs there ; which is a rebuke to human pride. But as to one family, there's debtor and creditor, I hope ; they're not going to reform that away ; else I should vote for things staying as they are. Few men have less need to cry for change than I have, personally speaking—that is, for self and family. I am not one of those who have nothing to lose : I mean as to respectability both in parish and private business, and noways in respect of your honourable self and custom, which you was good enough to say you would not withdraw from me, vote or no vote, while the article sent in was satisfactory."

After this conversation Mr Mawmsey went up and boasted to his wife that he had been rather too many for Brooke of Tipton, and that he didn't mind so much now about going to the poll.

Mr Brooke on this occasion abstained from boasting of his tactics to Ladislaw, who for his part was glad enough to persuade himself that he had no concern with any canvassing except the purely argumentative sort, and that he worked no meaner engine than knowledge. Mr Brooke, necessarily, had his agents, who understood the nature of the Middlemarch voter and the means of enlisting his ignorance on the side of the Bill—which were remarkably similar to the means of enlisting it on the side against the Bill. Will stopped his ears. Occasionally Parliament, like the rest of our lives, even to our eating and apparel, could hardly go on if our imaginations were too active about processes. There were plenty of dirty-handed men in the world to do dirty business ; and Will protested to himself that his share in bringing Mr Brooke through would be quite innocent.

But whether he should succeed in that mode of contributing to the majority on the right side was very doubtful to him. He had written out various speeches and memoranda for speeches, but he had begun to perceive that Mr Brooke's mind, if it had the burthen of remembering any train of thought, would let it drop, run away in search of it, and not easily come back again. To collect documents is one mode of serving your country, and to remember the contents of a document is another. No! the only way in which Mr Brooke could be coerced into thinking of the right arguments at the right time was to be well plied with them till they took up all the room in his brain. But here there was the difficulty of finding room, so many things having been taken in beforehand. Mr Brooke himself observed that his ideas stood rather in his way when he was speaking.

However, Ladislaw's coaching was forthwith to be put to the test, for before the day of nomination Mr Brooke was to explain himself to the worthy electors of Middlemarch from the balcony of the White Hart, which looked out advantageously at an angle of the market-place, commanding a large area in front and two converging streets. It was a fine May morning, and everything seemed hopeful: there was some prospect of an understanding between Bagster's committee and Brooke's, to which Mr Bulstrode, Mr Standish as a Liberal lawyer, and such manufacturers as Mr Plymdale and Mr Vincy, gave a solidity which almost counterbalanced Mr Hawley and his associates who sat for Pinkerton at the Green Dragon. Mr Brooke, conscious of having weakened the blasts of the 'Trumpet' against him, by his reforms as a landlord in the last half year, and hearing himself cheered a little as he drove into the town, felt his heart tolerably light under his buff-coloured waistcoat. But with regard to critical occasions, it often happens that all moments seem comfortably remote until the last.

"This looks well, eh?" said Mr Brooke as the crowd gathered. "I shall have a good audience, at any rate. I like this, now—this kind of public made up of one's own neighbours, you know."

The weavers and tanners of Middlemarch, unlike Mr Mawmsey, had never thought of Mr Brooke as a neighbour, and were not more attached to him than if he had been sent in a box from London. But they listened without much disturbance to the speakers who introduced the candidate, though one of them—a political personage from Brassing, who came to tell Middlemarch its duty—spoke so fully, that it was alarming to think what the candidate could find to say after him. Meanwhile the crowd became denser, and as the political personage neared the end of his speech, Mr Brooke felt a remarkable change in his sensations while he still handled his eye-glass, trifled with documents before him, and exchanged remarks with his committee, as a man to whom the moment of summons was indifferent.

"I'll take another glass of sherry, Ladislaw," he said, with an easy air, to Will, who was close behind him, and presently handed him the supposed fortifier. It was ill-chosen; for Mr Brooke was an abstemious man, and to drink a second glass of sherry quickly at no great interval from the first was a surprise to his system which tended to scatter his energies instead of collecting them. Pray pity him: so many English gentlemen make themselves miserable by speechifying on entirely private grounds! whereas Mr Brooke wished to serve his country by standing for Parliament—which, indeed, may also be done on private grounds, but being once undertaken does absolutely demand some speechifying.

It was not about the beginning of his speech that Mr Brooke was at all anxious ; this, he felt sure, would be all right ; he should have it quite pat, cut out as neatly as a set of couplets from Pope. Embarking would be easy, but the vision of open sea that might come after was alarming. "And questions, now," hinted the demon just waking up in his stomach, "somebody may put questions about the schedules.—Ladislaw," he continued, aloud, "just hand me the memorandum of the schedules."

When Mr Brooke presented himself on the balcony, the cheers were quite loud enough to counterbalance the yells, groans, brayings, and other expressions of adverse theory, which were so moderate that Mr Standish (decidedly an old bird) observed in the ear next to him, "This looks dangerous, by God ! Hawley has got some deeper plan than this." Still, the cheers were exhilarating, and no candidate could look more amiable than Mr Brooke, with the memorandum in his breast-pocket, his left hand on the rail of the balcony, and his right trifling with his eye-glass. The striking points in his appearance were his buff waistcoat, short-clipped blond hair, and neutral physiognomy. He began with some confidence.

"Gentlemen—Electors of Middlemarch !"

This was so much the right thing that a little pause after it seemed natural.

"I'm uncommonly glad to be here—I was never so proud and happy in my life—never so happy, you know."

This was a bold figure of speech, but not exactly the right thing ; for, unhappily, the pat opening had slipped away—even couplets from Pope may be but "fallings from us, vanishings," when fear clutches us, and a glass of sherry is hurrying like smoke among our ideas. Ladislaw, who stood at the window behind the speaker, thought, " it's all up now. The only chance is that, since the best thing won't always do, floundering may answer for once." Mr Brooke, meanwhile, having lost other clues, fell back on himself and his qualifications—always an appropriate graceful subject for a candidate.

"I am a close neighbour of yours, my good friends—you've known me on the bench a good while—I've always gone a good deal into public questions—machinery, now, and machine-breaking—you're many of you concerned with machinery, and I've been going into that lately. It won't do, you know, breaking machines : everything must go on—trade, manufactures, commerce, interchange of staples—that kind of thing—since Adam Smith, that must go on. We must look all over the globe :— ' Observation with extensive view,' must look everywhere, ' from China to Peru,' as somebody says—Johnson, I think, ' The Rambler,' you know. [4] That is what I have done up to a certain point—not as far as Peru ; but I've not always stayed at home —I saw it wouldn't do. I've been in the Levant, where some of your Middlemarch goods go—and then, again, in the Baltic. The Baltic, now."

Plying among his recollections in this way, Mr Brooke might have got along, easily to himself, and would have come back from the remotest seas without trouble ; but a diabolical procedure had been set

---

4. Not from *The Rambler,* Samuel Johnson's famous series of essays, but the opening lines of his poem, "The Vanity of Human Wishes": "Let observation with extensive view/Survey mankind, from China to Peru."

up by the enemy. At one and the same moment there had risen above the shoulders of the crowd, nearly opposite Mr Brooke, and within ten yards of him, the effigy of himself ; buff-coloured waistcoat, eye-glass, and neutral physiognomy, painted on rag ; and there had arisen, apparently in the air, like the note of the cuckoo, a parrot-like, Punch-voiced echo of his words. [5] Everybody looked up at the open windows in the houses at the opposite angles of the converging streets ; but they were either blank, or filled by laughing listeners. The most innocent echo has an impish mockery in it when it follows a gravely persistent speaker, and this echo was not at all innocent ; if it did not follow with the precision of a natural echo, it had a wicked choice of the words it overtook. By the time it said, " The Baltic, now," the laugh which had been running through the audience became a general shout, and but for the sobering effects of party and that great public cause which the entanglement of things had identified with " Brooke of Tipton," the laugh might have caught his committee. Mr Bulstrode asked, reprehensively, what the new police was doing ; but a voice could not well be collared, and an attack on the effigy of the candidate would have been too equivocal, since Hawley probably meant it to be pelted.

Mr Brooke himself was not in a position to be quickly conscious of anything except a general slipping away of ideas within himself : he had even a little singing in the ears, and he was the only person who had not yet taken distinct account of the echo or discerned the image of himself. Few things hold the perceptions more thoroughly captive than anxiety about what we have got to say. Mr Brooke heard the laughter ; but he had expected some Tory efforts at disturbance, and he was at this moment additionally excited by the tickling, stinging sense that his lost exordium was coming back to fetch him from the Baltic.

" That reminds me," he went on, thrusting a hand into his side-pocket, with an easy air, " if I wanted a precedent, you know—but we never want a precedent for the right thing—but there is Chatham, now ; I can't say I should have supported Chatham, or Pitt, the younger Pitt—he was not a man of ideas, and we want ideas, you know." [6]

" Blast your ideas ! we want the Bill," said a loud rough voice from the crowd below.

Immediately the invisible Punch, who had hitherto followed Mr Brooke, repeated, " Blast your ideas ! we want the Bill." The laugh was louder than ever, and for the first time Mr Brooke being himself silent, heard distinctly the mocking echo. But it seemed to ridicule his interrupter, and in that light was encouraging ; so he replied with amenity—

" There is something in what you say, my good friend, and what do we meet for but to speak our minds—freedom of opinion, freedom of the press, liberty—that kind of thing ? The Bill, now—you shall have the Bill "—here Mr Brooke paused a moment to fix on his eye-glass and take the paper from his breast-pocket, with a sense of being practical and coming to particulars. The invisible Punch followed :—

---

5. Punch-voiced: in the ringing, bellike tone assumed by the Punch character in Punch and Judy shows.
6. William Pitt, 1st Earl of Chatham (1708–78), a great Whig statesman and orator; his second son, William Pitt (1759–1806), was prime minister from 1783–1801 and 1804–6.

" You shall have the Bill, Mr Brooke, per electioneering contest, and a seat outside Parliament as delivered, five thousand pounds, seven shillings, and fourpence."

Mr Brooke, amid the roars of laughter, turned red, let his eye-glass fall, and looking about him confusedly, saw the image of himself, which had come nearer. The next moment he saw it dolorously be-spattered with eggs. His spirit rose a little, and his voice too.

" Buffoonery, tricks, ridicule the test of truth—all that is very well " —here an unpleasant egg broke on Mr Brooke's shoulder, as the echo said, " All that is very well ; " then came a hail of eggs, chiefly aimed at the image, but occasionally hitting the original, as if by chance. There was a stream of new men pushing among the crowd; whistles, yells, bellowings, and fifes made all the greater hubbub because there was shouting and struggling to put them down. No voice would have had wing enough to rise above the uproar, and Mr Brooke, dis-agreeably anointed, stood his ground no longer. The frustration would have been less exasperating if it had been less gamesome and boyish : a serious assault of which the newspaper reporter " can aver that it endangered the learned gentleman's ribs," or can respectfully bear witness to " the soles of that gentleman's boots having been visible above the railing," has perhaps more consolations attached to it.

Mr Brooke re-entered the committee-room, saying, as carelessly as he could, " This is a little too bad, you know. I should have got the ear of the people by-and-by—but they didn't give me time. I should have gone into the Bill by-and-by, you know," he added, glancing at Ladislaw. " However, things will come all right at the nomi-nation."

But it was not resolved unanimously that things would come right ; on the contrary, the committee looked rather grim, and the political personage from Brassing was writing busily, as if he were brewing new devices.

" It was Bowyer who did it," said Mr Standish, evasively. " I know it as well as if he had been advertised. He's uncommonly good at ventriloquism, and he did it uncommonly well, by God ! Hawley has been having him to dinner lately : there's a fund of talent in Bowyer."

" Well, you know, you never mentioned him to me, Standish, else I would have invited him to dine," said poor Mr Brooke, who had gone through a great deal of inviting for the good of his country.

" There's not a more paltry fellow in Middlemarch than Bowyer," said Ladislaw, indignantly, " but it seems as if the paltry fellows were always to turn the scale."

Will was thoroughly out of temper with himself as well as with his " principal," and he went to shut himself in his rooms with a half-formed resolve to throw up the ' Pioneer ' and Mr Brooke together. Why should he stay ? If the impassable gulf between himself and Dorothea were ever to be filled up, it must rather be by his going away and getting into a thoroughly different position than by staying here and slipping into deserved contempt as an understrapper of Brooke's. Then came the young dream of wonders that he might do —in five years, for example : political writing, political speaking, would get a higher value now public life was going to be wider and more national, and they might give him such distinction that he would not seem to be asking Dorothea to step down to him. Five years :—if he could only be sure that she cared for him more than for others ; if he could only make her aware that he stood aloof until he could tell his love without lowering himself—then he could go away easily, and begin a career which at five-and-twenty seemed probable enough in the inward order of things, where talent brings fame, and fame everything else which is delightful. He could speak and he could write ; he could master any subject if he chose, and he meant always to take the side of reason and justice, on which he would carry all his ardour. Why should he not one day be lifted above the shoulders of the crowd, and feel that he had won that eminence well ? Without doubt he would leave Middlemarch, go to town, and make himself fit for celebrity by " eating his dinners." [7]

But not immediately : not until some kind of sign had passed between him and Dorothea. He could not be satisfied until she knew why, even if he were the man she would choose to marry, he would not marry her. Hence he must keep his post and bear with Mr Brooke a little longer.

But he soon had reason to suspect that Mr Brooke had anticipated him in the wish to break up their connection. Deputations without and voices within had concurred in inducing that philanthropist to take a stronger measure than usual for the good of mankind ; namely, to withdraw in favour of another candidate, to whom he left the advantages of his canvassing machinery. He himself called this a strong measure, but observed that his health was less capable of sustaining excitement than he had imagined.

" I have felt uneasy about the chest—it won't do to carry that too far," he said to Ladislaw in explaining the affair. " I must pull up. Poor Casaubon was a warning, you know. I've made some heavy advances, but I've dug a channel. It's rather coarse work—this electioneering, eh, Ladislaw ? I daresay you are tired of it. However, we have dug a channel with the ' Pioneer '—put things in a track, and so on. A more ordinary man than you might carry it on now— more ordinary, you know."

" Do you wish me to give it up ? " said Will, the quick colour coming in his face, as he rose from the writing-table, and took a turn of three steps with his hands in his pockets. " I am ready to do so whenever you wish it."

" As to wishing, my dear Ladislaw, I have the highest opinion of your powers, you know. But about the ' Pioneer,' I have been consulting a little with some of the men on our side, and they are inclined to take it into their hands—indemnify me to a certain extent—carry it on, in fact. And under the circumstances, you might like to give up—might find a better field. These people might not take that high view of you which I have always taken, as an *alter ego*, a right hand —though I always looked forward to your doing something else. I think of having a run into France. But I'll write you any letters, you know—to Althorpe and people of that kind. [8] I've met Althorpe."

---

7. Or "eating his terms": students of law were required to have dined in the hall of one of the four Inns of Court at least three times in each of twelve terms before they were called to the bar.

8. John Charles Spencer, Viscount Althorpe (1782–1845), leader of the Whig opposition to Wellington's government, 1828–30, and chancellor of the exchequer under Earl Grey, 1830–34.

" I am exceedingly obliged to you," said Ladislaw, proudly. "Since you are going to part with the 'Pioneer,' I need not trouble you about the steps I shall take. I may choose to continue here for the present."

After Mr Brooke had left him Will said to himself, " The rest of the family have been urging him to get rid of me, and he doesn't care now about my going. I shall stay as long as I like. I shall go of my own movement, and not because they are afraid of me."

CHAPTER LII.

" His heart
The lowliest duties on itself did lay."
—WORDSWORTH. [1]

ON that June evening when Mr Farebrother knew that he was to have the Lowick living, there was joy in the old-fashioned parlour, and even the portraits of the great lawyers seemed to look on with satisfaction. His mother left her tea and toast untouched, but sat with her usual pretty primness, only showing her emotion by that flush in the cheeks and brightness in the eyes which give an old woman a touching momentary identity with her far-off youthful self, and saying decisively—

" The greatest comfort, Camden, is that you have deserved it."

" When a man gets a good berth, mother, half the deserving must come after," said the son, brimful of pleasure, and not trying to conceal it. The gladness in his face was of that active kind which seems to have energy enough not only to flash outwardly, but to light up busy vision within : one seemed to see thoughts, as well as delight, in his glances.

" Now, aunt," he went on, rubbing his hands and looking at Miss Noble, who was making tender little beaver-like noises, " there shall be sugar-candy always on the table for you to steal and give to the children, and you shall have a great many new stockings to make presents of, and you shall darn your own more than ever ! "

Miss Noble nodded at her nephew with a subdued half-frightened laugh, conscious of having already dropped an additional lump of sugar into her basket on the strength of the new preferment.

" As for you, Winny "—the Vicar went on—" I shall make no difficulty about your marrying any Lowick bachelor—Mr Solomon Featherstone, for example, as soon as I find you are in love with him."

Miss Winifred, who had been looking at her brother all the while and crying heartily, which was her way of rejoicing, smiled through her tears and said, " You must set me the example, Cam : *you* must marry now."

" With all my heart. But who is in love with me ? I am a seedy old fellow," said the Vicar, rising, pushing his chair away and looking down at himself. " What do you say, mother ?"

1. "London, 1802."

" You are a handsome man, Camden : though not so fine a figure of a man as your father," said the old lady.

" I wish you would marry Miss Garth, brother," said Miss Winifred. " She would make us so lively at Lowick."

" Very fine ! You talk as if young women were tied up to be chosen, like poultry at market ; as if I had only to ask and everybody would have me," said the Vicar, not caring to specify.

" We don't want everybody," said Miss Winifred. " But *you* would like Miss Garth, mother, shouldn't you ? "

" My son's choice shall be mine," said Mrs Farebrother, with majestic discretion, " and a wife would be most welcome, Camden. You will want your whist at home when we go to Lowick, and Henrietta Noble never was a whist-player." (Mrs Farebrother always called her tiny old sister by that magnificent name.)

" I shall do without whist now, mother."

" Why so, Camden ? In my time whist was thought an undeniable amusement for a good churchman," said Mrs Farebrother, innocent of the meaning that whist had for her son, and speaking rather sharply, as at some dangerous countenancing of new doctrine.

" I shall be too busy for whist ; I shall have two parishes," said the Vicar, preferring not to discuss the virtues of that game.

He had already said to Dorothea, " I don't feel bound to give up St Botolph's. It is protest enough against the pluralism they want to reform if I give somebody else most of the money. The stronger thing is not to give up power, but to use it well."

" I have thought of that," said Dorothea. " So far as self is concerned, I think it would be easier to give up power and money than to keep them. It seems very unfitting that I should have this patronage, yet I felt that I ought not to let it be used by some one else instead of me."

" It is I who am bound to act so that you will not regret your power," said Mr Farebrother.

His was one of the natures in which conscience gets the more active when the yoke of life ceases to gall them. He made no display of humility on the subject, but in his heart he felt rather ashamed that his conduct had shown laches which others who did not get benefices were free from. [2]

" I used often to wish I had been something else than a clergyman," he said to Lydgate, " but perhaps it will be better to try and make as good a clergyman out of myself as I can. That is the well-beneficed point of view, you perceive, from which difficulties are much simplified," he ended, smiling.

The Vicar did feel then as if his share of duties would be easy. But Duty has a trick of behaving unexpectedly—something like a heavy friend whom we have amiably asked to visit us, and who breaks his leg within our gates.

Hardly a week later, Duty presented itself in his study under the disguise of Fred Vincy, now returned from Omnibus College with his bachelor's degree.

" I am ashamed to trouble you, Mr Farebrother," said Fred, whose fair open face was propitiating, " but you are the only friend I can

2. Laches: laziness, negligence.

consult. I told you everything once before, and you were so good that I can't help coming to you again."

" Sit down, Fred, I'm ready to hear and do anything I can," said the Vicar, who was busy packing some small objects for removal, and went on with his work.

"I wanted to tell you——" Fred hesitated an instant and then went on plungingly, " I might go into the Church now ; and really, look where I may, I can't see anything else to do. I don't like it, but I know it's uncommonly hard on my father to say so, after he has spent a good deal of money in educating me for it." Fred paused again an instant, and then repeated, " and I can't see anything else to do."

" I did talk to your father about it, Fred, but I made little way with him. He said it was too late. But you have got over one bridge now : what are your other difficulties ?"

" Merely that I don't like it. I don't like divinity, and preaching, and feeling obliged to look serious. I like riding across country, and doing as other men do. I don't mean that I want to be a bad fellow in any way ; but I've no taste for the sort of thing people expect of a clergyman. And yet what else am I to do ? My father can't spare me any capital, else I might go into farming. And he has no room for me in his trade. And of course I can't begin to study for law or physic now, when my father wants me to earn something. It's all very well to say I'm wrong to go into the Church ; but those who say so might as well tell me to go into the backwoods."

Fred's voice had taken a tone of grumbling remonstrance, and Mr Farebrother might have been inclined to smile if his mind had not been too busy in imagining more than Fred told him.

" Have you any difficulties about doctrines—about the Articles ?" he said, trying hard to think of the question simply for Fred's sake.

" No ; I suppose the Articles are right. I am not prepared with any arguments to disprove them, and much better, cleverer fellows than I am go in for them entirely. I think it would be rather ridiculous in me to urge scruples of that sort, as if I were a judge," said Fred, quite simply.

" I suppose, then, it has occurred to you that you might be a fair parish priest without being much of a divine ?"

" Of course, if I am obliged to be a clergyman, I shall try and do my duty, though I mayn't like it. Do you think anybody ought to blame me ?"

" For going into the Church under the circumstances ? That depends on your conscience, Fred—how far you have counted the cost, and seen what your position will require of you. I can only tell you about myself, that I have always been too lax, and have been uneasy in consequence."

" But there is another hindrance," said Fred, colouring. " I did not tell you before, though perhaps I may have said things that made you guess it. There is somebody I am very fond of : I have loved her ever since we were children."

" Miss Garth, I suppose ?" said the Vicar, examining some labels very closely.

" Yes. I shouldn't mind anything if she would have me. And I know I could be a good fellow then."

" And you think she returns the feeling ? "

" She never will say so ; and a good while ago she made me promise not to speak to her about it again. And she has set her mind especially against my being a clergyman ; I know that. But I can't give her up. I do think she cares about me. I saw Mrs Garth last night, and she said that Mary was staying at Lowick Rectory with Miss Farebrother."

" Yes, she is very kindly helping my sister. Do you wish to go there ? "

" No, I want to ask a great favour of you. I am ashamed to bother you in this way ; but Mary might listen to what you said, if you mentioned the subject to her—I mean about my going into the Church."

" That is rather a delicate task, my dear Fred. I shall have to presuppose your attachment to her ; and to enter on the subject as you wish me to do, will be asking her to tell me whether she returns it."

" That is what I want her to tell you," said Fred, bluntly. " I don't know what to do, unless I can get at her feeling."

" You mean that you would be guided by that as to your going into the Church ? "

" If Mary said she would never have me I might as well go wrong in one way as another."

" That is nonsense, Fred. Men outlive their love, but they don't outlive the consequences of their recklessness."

" Not my sort of love : I have never been without loving Mary. If I had to give her up, it would be like beginning to live on wooden legs."

" Will she not be hurt at my intrusion ? "

" No, I feel sure she will not. She respects you more than any one, and she would not put you off with fun as she does me. Of course I could not have told any one else, or asked any one else to speak to her, but you. There is no one else who could be such a friend to both of us." Fred paused a moment, and then said, rather complainingly, " And she ought to acknowledge that I have worked in order to pass. She ought to believe that I would exert myself for her sake."

There was a moment's silence before Mr Farebrother laid down his work, and putting out his hand to Fred said—

" Very well, my boy. I will do what you wish."

That very day Mr Farebrother went to Lowick parsonage on the nag which he had just set up. ."Decidedly I am an old stalk," he thought, " the young growths are pushing me aside."

He found Mary in the garden gathering roses and sprinkling the petals on a sheet. The sun was low, and tall trees sent their shadows across the grassy walks where Mary was moving without bonnet or parasol. She did not observe Mr Farebrother's approach along the grass, and had just stooped down to lecture a small black-and-tan terrier, which would persist in walking on the sheet and smelling at the rose-leaves as Mary sprinkled them. She took his fore-paws in one hand, and lifted up the forefinger of the other, while the dog wrinkled his brows and looked embarrassed. " Fly, Fly, I am ashamed of you," Mary was saying in a grave contralto. " This is not becoming in a sensible dog ; anybody would think you were a silly young gentleman."

"You are unmerciful to young gentlemen, Miss Garth," said the Vicar, within two yards of her.

Mary started up and blushed. "It always answers to reason with Fly," she said, laughingly.

"But not with young gentlemen?"

"Oh, with some, I suppose; since some of them turn into excellent men."

"I am glad of that admission, because I want at this very moment to interest you in a young gentleman."

"Not a silly one, I hope," said Mary, beginning to pluck the roses again, and feeling her heart beat uncomfortably.

"No; though perhaps wisdom is not his strong point, but rather affection and sincerity. However, wisdom lies more in those two qualities than people are apt to imagine. I hope you know by those marks what young gentleman I mean."

"Yes, I think I do," said Mary, bravely, her face getting more serious, and her hands cold; "it must be Fred Vincy."

"He has asked me to consult you about his going into the Church. I hope you will not think that I consented to take a liberty in promising to do so."

"On the contrary, Mr Farebrother," said Mary, giving up the roses, and folding her arms, but unable to look up, "whenever you have anything to say to me I feel honoured."

"But before I enter on that question, let me just touch a point on which your father took me into confidence; by the way, it was that very evening on which I once before fulfilled a mission from Fred, just after he had gone to college. Mr Garth told me what happened on the night of Featherstone's death—how you refused to burn the will; and he said that you had some heart-prickings on that subject, because you had been the innocent means of hindering Fred from getting his ten thousand pounds. I have kept that in mind, and I have heard something that may relieve you on that score—may show you that no sin-offering is demanded from you there."

Mr Farebrother paused a moment and looked at Mary. He meant to give Fred his full advantage, but it would be well, he thought, to clear her mind of any superstitions, such as women sometimes follow when they do a man the wrong of marrying him as an act of atonement. Mary's cheeks had begun to burn a little, and she was mute.

"I mean, that your action made no real difference to Fred's lot. I find that the first will would not have been legally good after the burning of the last; it would not have stood if it had been disputed, and you may be sure it would have been disputed. So, on that score, you may feel your mind free."

"Thank you, Mr Farebrother," said Mary, earnestly. "I am grateful to you for remembering my feelings."

"Well, now I may go on. Fred, you know, has taken his degree. He has worked his way so far, and now the question is, what is he to do? That question is so difficult that he is inclined to follow his father's wishes and enter the Church, though you know better than I do that he was quite set against that formerly. I have questioned him on the subject, and I confess I see no insuperable objection to his being a clergyman, as things go. He says that he could turn his mind to doing his best in that vocation, on one condition. If that condition were fulfilled I would do my utmost in helping Fred on. After a time—not, of course, at first—he might be with me as my curate, and he would have so much to do that his stipend would be nearly what I used to get as vicar. But I repeat that there is a condition without which all this good cannot come to pass. He has opened his heart to me, Miss Garth, and asked me to plead for him. The condition lies entirely in your feeling."

Mary looked so much moved, that he said after a moment, " Let us walk a little ; " and when they were walking he added, " To speak quite plainly, Fred will not take any course which would lessen the chance that you would consent to be his wife ; but with that prospect, he will try his best at anything you approve."

" I cannot possibly say that I will ever be his wife, Mr Farebrother : but I certainly never will be his wife if he becomes a clergyman. What you say is most generous and kind ; I don't mean for a moment to correct your judgment. It is only that I have my girlish, mocking way of looking at things," said Mary, with a returning sparkle of playfulness in her answer which only made its modesty more charming.

" He wishes me to report exactly what you think," said Mr Farebrother.

" I could not love a man who is ridiculous," said Mary, not choosing to go deeper. " Fred has sense and knowledge enough to make him respectable, if he likes, in some good worldly business, but I can never imagine him preaching and exhorting, and pronouncing blessings, and praying by the sick, without feeling as if I were looking at a caricature. His being a clergyman would be only for gentility's sake, and I think there is nothing more contemptible than such imbecile gentility. I used to think that of Mr Crowse, with his empty face and neat umbrella, and mincing little speeches. What right have such men to represent Christianity—as if it were an institution for getting up idiots genteelly—as if——" Mary checked herself. She had been carried along as if she had been speaking to Fred instead of Mr Farebrother.

" Young women are severe ; they don't feel the stress of action as men do, though perhaps I ought to make you an exception there. But you don't put Fred Vincy on so low a level as that ? "

" No, indeed ; he has plenty of sense, but I think he would not show it as a clergyman. He would be a piece of professional affectation."

" Then the answer is quite decided. As a clergyman he could have no hope ? "

Mary shook her head.

" But if he braved all the difficulties of getting his bread in some other way—will you give him the support of hope ? May he count on winning you ? "

" I think Fred ought not to need telling again what I have already said to him," Mary answered, with a slight resentment in her manner. " I mean that he ought not to put such questions until he has done something worthy, instead of saying that he could do it.'"

Mr Farebrother was silent for a minute or more, and then, as they turned and paused under the shadow of a maple at the end of a grassy walk, said, " I understand that you resist any attempt to fetter you, but either your feeling for Fred Vincy excludes your entertaining another attachment, or it does not : either he may count on your remaining single until he shall have earned your hand, or he may in any case be disappointed. Pardon me, Mary—you know I used to catechise you under that name—but when the state of a woman's affections touches the happiness of another life—of more lives than one—I think it would be the nobler course for her to be perfectly direct and open."

Mary in her turn was silent, wondering not at Mr Farebrother's manner but at his tone, which had a grave restrained emotion in it. When the strange idea flashed across her that his words had reference to himself, she was incredulous, and ashamed of entertaining it. She had never thought that any man could love her except Fred, who had espoused her with the umbrella ring, when she wore socks and little strapped shoes ; still less that she could be of any importance to Mr Farebrother, the cleverest man in her narrow circle. She had only time to feel that all this was hazy and perhaps illusory ; but one thing was clear and determined—her answer.

"Since you think it my duty, Mr Farebrother, I will tell you that I have too strong a feeling for Fred to give him up for any one else. I should never be quite happy if I thought he was unhappy for the loss of me. It has taken such deep root in me—my gratitude to him for always loving me best, and minding so much if I hurt myself, from the time when we were very little. I cannot imagine any new feeling coming to make that weaker. I should like better than anything to see him worthy of every one's respect. But please tell him I will not promise to marry him till then ; I should shame and grieve my father and mother. He is free to choose some one else."

"Then I have fulfilled my commission thoroughly," said Mr Farebrother, putting out his hand to Mary, "and I shall ride back to Middlemarch forthwith. With this prospect before him, we shall get Fred into the right niche somehow, and I hope I shall live to join your hands. God bless you !"

"Oh, please stay, and let me give you some tea," said Mary. Her eyes filled with tears, for something indefinable, something like the resolute suppression of a pain in Mr Farebrother's manner, made her feel suddenly miserable, as she had once felt when she saw her father's hands trembling in a moment of trouble.

"No, my dear, no. I must get back."

In three minutes the Vicar was on horseback again, having gone magnanimously through a duty much harder than the renunciation of whist, or even than the writing of penitential meditations.

CHAPTER LIII.

It is but a shallow haste which concludeth insincerity from what outsiders call inconsistency—putting a dead mechanism of "ifs" and "therefores" for the living myriad of hidden suckers whereby the belief and the conduct are wrought into mutual sustainment.

MR BULSTRODE, when he was hoping to acquire a new interest in Lowick, had naturally had an especial wish that the new clergyman should be one whom he thoroughly approved ; and he believed it to be a chastisement and admonition directed to his own shortcomings and those of the nation at large, that just about the time when he came in possession of the deeds which made him the proprietor of

Stone Court, Mr Farebrother "read himself" into the quaint little church and preached his first sermon to the congregation of farmers, labourers, and village artisans. It was not that Mr Bulstrode intended to frequent Lowick Church or to reside at Stone Court for a good while to come : he had bought the excellent farm and fine homestead simply as a retreat which he might gradually enlarge as to the land and beautify as to the dwelling, until it should be conducive to the divine glory that he should enter on it as a residence, partially withdrawing from his present exertions in the administration of business, and throwing more conspicuously on the side of Gospel truth the weight of local landed proprietorship, which Providence might increase by unforeseen occasions of purchase. A strong leading in this direction seemed to have been given in the surprising facility of getting Stone Court, when every one had expected that Mr Rigg Featherstone would have clung to it as the Garden of Eden. That was what poor old Peter himself had expected ; having often, in imagination, looked up through the sods above him, and, unobstructed by perspective, seen his frog-faced legatee enjoying the fine old place to the perpetual surprise and disappointment of other survivors.

But how little we know what would make paradise for our neighbours ! We judge from our own desires, and our neighbours themselves are not always open enough even to throw out a hint of theirs. The cool and judicious Joshua Rigg had not allowed his parent to perceive that Stone Court was anything less than the chief good in his estimation, and he had certainly wished to call it his own. But as Warren Hastings looked at gold and thought of buying Daylesford, so Joshua Rigg looked at Stone Court and thought of buying gold. He had a very distinct and intense vision of his chief good, the vigorous greed which he had inherited having taken a special form by dint of circumstance: and his chief good was to be a money-changer. From his earliest employment as an errand-boy in a seaport, he had looked through the windows of the money-changers as other boys look through the windows of the pastry-cooks ; the fascination had wrought itself gradually into a deep special passion ; he meant, when he had property, to do many things, one of them being to marry a genteel young person ; but these were all accidents and joys that imagination could dispense with. The one joy after which his soul thirsted was to have a money-changer's shop on a much-frequented quay, to have locks all round him of which he held the keys, and to look sublimely cool as he handled the breeding coins of all nations, while helpless Cupidity looked at him enviously from the other side of an iron lattice. The strength of that passion had been a power enabling him to master all the knowledge necessary to gratify it. And when others were thinking that he had settled at Stone Court for life, Joshua himself was thinking that the moment now was not far off when he should settle on the North Quay with the best appointments in safes and locks.

Enough. We are concerned with looking at Joshua Rigg's sale of his land from Mr Bulstrode's point of view, and he interpreted it as a cheering dispensation conveying perhaps a sanction to a purpose which he had for some time entertained without external encouragement ; he interpreted it thus, but not too confidently, offering up his thanksgiving in guarded phraseology. His doubts did not arise from the possible relations of the event to Joshua Rigg's destiny, which belonged to the unmapped regions not taken under the providential government, except perhaps in an imperfect colonial way; but they arose from reflecting that this dispensation too might be a chastisement for himself, as Mr Farebrother's induction to the living clearly was.

This was not what Mr Bulstrode said to any man for the sake of deceiving him : it was what he said to himself—it was as genuinely his mode of explaining events as any theory of yours may be, if you happen to disagree with him. For the egoism which enters into our theories does not affect their sincerity; rather, the more our egoism is satisfied, the more robust is our belief.

However, whether for sanction or for chastisement, Mr Bulstrode, hardly fifteen months after the death of Peter Featherstone, had become the proprietor of Stone Court, and what Peter would say " if he were worthy to know," had become an inexhaustible and consolatory subject of conversation to his disappointed relatives. The tables were now turned on that dear brother departed, and to contemplate the frustration of his cunning by the superior cunning of things in general was a cud of delight to Solomon. Mrs Waule had a melancholy triumph in the proof that it did not answer to make false Featherstones and cut off the genuine; and Sister Martha receiving the news in the Chalky Flats said, " Dear, dear ! then the Almighty could have been none so pleased with the almshouses after all."

Affectionate Mrs Bulstrode was particularly glad of the advantage which her husband's health was likely to get from the purchase of Stone Court. Few days passed without his riding thither and looking over some part of the farm with the bailiff, and the evenings were delicious in that quiet spot, when the new hay-ricks lately set up were sending forth odours to mingle with the breath of the rich old garden. One evening, while the sun was still above the horizon and burning in golden lamps among the great walnut boughs, Mr Bulstrode was pausing on horseback outside the front gate waiting for Caleb Garth, who had met him by appointment to give an opinion on a question of stable drainage, and was now advising the bailiff in the rick-yard.

Mr Bulstrode was conscious of being in a good spiritual frame and more than usually serene, under the influence of his innocent recreation. He was doctrinally convinced that there was a total absence of merit in himself; but that doctrinal conviction may be held without pain when the sense of demerit does not take a distinct shape in memory and revive the tingling of shame or the pang of remorse. Nay, it may be held with intense satisfaction when the depth of our sinning is but a measure for the depth of forgiveness, and a clenching proof that we are peculiar instruments of the divine intention. The memory has as many moods as the temper, and shifts its scenery like a diorama. At this moment Mr Bulstrode felt as if the sunshine were all one with that of far-off evenings when he was a very young man and used to go out preaching beyond Highbury. And he would willingly have had that service of exhortation in prospect now. The texts were there still, and so was his own facility in expounding them. His brief reverie was interrupted by the return of Caleb Garth, who also was on horseback, and was just shaking his bridle before starting, when he exclaimed—

" Bless my heart ! what's this fellow in black coming along the lane ? He's like one of those men one sees about after the races."

Mr Bulstrode turned his horse and looked along the lane, but made no reply. The comer was our slight acquaintance Mr Raffles, whose appearance presented no other change than such as was due to a suit of black and a crape hat-band. He was within three yards of the horsemen now, and they could see the flash of recognition in his face as he whirled his stick upward, looking all the while at Mr Bulstrode, and at last exclaiming :—

" By Jove, Nick, it's you ! I couldn't be mistaken, though the five-and-twenty years have played old Boguy with us both ! How are you, eh ? you didn't expect to see *me* here. Come, shake us by the hand."

To say that Mr Raffles' manner was rather excited would be only one mode of saying that it was evening. Caleb Garth could see that there was a moment of struggle and hesitation in Mr Bulstrode, but it ended in his putting out his hand coldly to Raffles and saying—

" I did not indeed expect to see you in this remote country place."

" Well, it belongs to a stepson of mine," said Raffles, adjusting himself in a swaggering attitude. " I came to see him here before. I'm not so surprised at seeing you, old fellow, because I picked up a letter—what you may call a providential thing. It's uncommonly fortunate I met you, though ; for I don't care about seeing my stepson : he's not affectionate, and his poor mother's gone now. To tell the truth, I came out of love to you, Nick : I came to get your address, for—look here ! " Raffles drew a crumpled paper from his pocket.

Almost any other man than Caleb Garth might have been tempted to linger on the spot for the sake of hearing all he could about a man whose acquaintance with Bulstrode seemed to imply passages in the banker's life so unlike anything that was known of him in Middlemarch that they must have the nature of a secret to pique curiosity. But Caleb was peculiar : certain human tendencies which are commonly strong were almost absent from his mind ; and one of these was curiosity about personal affairs. Especially if there was anything discreditable to be found out concerning another man, Caleb preferred not to know it ; and if he had to tell anybody under him that his evil doings were discovered, he was more embarrassed than the culprit. He now spurred his horse, and saying, " I wish you good evening, Mr Bulstrode ; I must be getting home," set off at a trot.

" You didn't put your full address to this letter," Raffles continued. " That was not like the first-rate man of business you used to be. ' The Shrubs,'—they may be anywhere : you live near at hand, eh ? —have cut the London concern altogether—perhaps turned country squire—have a rural mansion to invite me to. Lord, how many years it is ago ! The old lady must have been dead a pretty long while—gone to glory without the pain of knowing how poor her daughter was, eh ? But, by Jove ! you're very pale and pasty, Nick. Come, if you're going home, I'll walk by your side."

Mr Bulstrode's usual paleness had in fact taken an almost deathly hue. Five minutes before, the expanse of his life had been submerged in its evening sunshine which shone backward to its remembered morning : sin seemed to be a question of doctrine and inward penitence, humiliation an exercise of the closet, the bearing of his deeds a matter of private vision adjusted solely by spiritual relations and conceptions of the divine purposes. And now, as if by some hideous magic, this loud red figure had risen before him in unmanageable solidity—an incorporate past which had not entered into his imagination of chastisements. But Mr Bulstrode's thought was busy, and he was not a man to act or speak rashly.

"I was going home," he said, "but I can defer my ride a little. And you can, if you please, rest here."

"Thank you," said Raffles, making a grimace. "I don't care now about seeing my stepson. I'd rather go home with you."

"Your stepson, if Mr Rigg Featherstone was he, is here no longer. I am master here now."

Raffles opened wide eyes, and gave a long whistle of surprise, before he said, "Well then, I've no objection. I've had enough walking from the coach-road. I never was much of a walker, or rider either. What I like is a smart vehicle and a spirited cob. I was always a little heavy in the saddle. What a pleasant surprise it must be to you to see me, old fellow !" he continued, as they turned towards the house. "You don't say so ; but you never took your luck heartily—you were always thinking of improving the occasion—you'd such a gift for improving your luck."

Mr Raffles seemed greatly to enjoy his own wit, and swung his leg in a swaggering manner which was rather too much for his companion's judicious patience.

"If I remember rightly," Mr Bulstrode observed, with chill anger, "our acquaintance many years ago had not the sort of intimacy which you are now assuming, Mr Raffles. Any services you desire of me will be the more readily rendered if you will avoid a tone of familiarity which did not lie in our former intercourse, and can hardly be warranted by more than twenty years of separation."

"You don't like being called Nick ? Why, I always called you Nick in my heart, and though lost to sight, to memory dear. By Jove ! my feelings have ripened for you like fine old cognac. I hope you've got some in the house now. Josh filled my flask well the last time."

Mr Bulstrode had not yet fully learned that even the desire for cognac was not stronger in Raffles than the desire to torment, and that a hint of annoyance always served him as a fresh cue. But it was at least clear that further objection was useless, and Mr Bulstrode, in giving orders to the housekeeper for the accommodation of the guest, had a resolute air of quietude.

There was the comfort of thinking that this housekeeper had been in the service of Rigg also, and might accept the idea that Mr Bulstrode entertained Raffles merely as a friend of her former master. When there was food and drink spread before his visitor in the wainscoated parlour, and no witness in the room, Mr Bulstrode said—

"Your habits and mine are so different, Mr Raffles, that we can hardly enjoy each other's society. The wisest plan for both of us will therefore be to part as soon as possible. Since you say that you wished to meet me, you probably considered that you had some business to transact with me. But under the circumstances I will invite you to remain here for the night, and I will myself ride over here early to-morrow morning — before breakfast, in fact, when I can receive any communication you have to make to me."

"With all my heart," said Raffles ; "this is a comfortable place — a little dull for a continuance ; but I can put up with it for a night, with this good liquor and the prospect of seeing you again in the morning. You're a much better host than my stepson was ; but Josh owed me a bit of a grudge for marrying his mother ; and between you and me there was never anything but kindness."

Mr Bulstrode, hoping that the peculiar mixture of joviality and sneering in Raffles' manner was a good deal the effect of drink, had determined to wait till he was quite sober before he spent more words upon him. But he rode home with a terribly lucid vision of the difficulty there would be in arranging any result that could be permanently counted on with this man. It was inevitable that he should wish to get rid of John Raffles, though his reappearance could not be regarded as lying outside the divine plan. The spirit of evil might have sent him to threaten Mr Bulstrode's subversion as an instrument of good ; but the threat must have been permitted, and was a chastisement of a new kind. It was an hour of anguish for him very different from the hours in which his struggle had been securely private, and which had ended with a sense that his secret misdeeds were pardoned and his services accepted. Those misdeeds even when committed—had they not been half sanctified by the singleness of his desire to devote himself and all he possessed to the furtherance of the divine scheme ? And was he after all to become a mere stone of stumbling and a rock of offence ? For who would understand the work within him ? Who would not, when there was the pretext of casting disgrace upon him, confound his whole life and the truths he had espoused, in one heap of obloquy ?

In his closest meditations the life-long habit of Mr Bulstrode's mind clad his most egoistic terrors in doctrinal references to superhuman ends. But even while we are talking and meditating about the earth's orbit and the solar system, what we feel and adjust our movements to is the stable earth and the changing day. And now within all the automatic succession of theoretic phrases—distinct and inmost as the shiver and the ache of oncoming fever when we are discussing abstract pain, was the forecast of disgrace in the presence of his neighbours and of his own wife. For the pain, as well as the public estimate of disgrace, depends on the amount of previous profession. To men who only aim at escaping felony, nothing short of the prisoner's dock is disgrace. But Mr Bulstrode had aimed at being an eminent Christian.

It was not more than half-past seven in the morning when he again reached Stone Court. The fine old place never looked more like a delightful home than at that moment ; the great white lilies were in flower, the nasturtiums, their pretty leaves all silvered with dew, were running away over the low stone wall ; the very noises all around had a heart of peace within them. But everything was spoiled for the owner as he walked on the gravel in front and awaited the descent of Mr Raffles, with whom he was condemned to breakfast.

It was not long before they were seated together in the wainscoated parlour over their tea and toast, which was as much as Raffles cared to take at that early hour. The difference between his morning and evening self was not so great as his companion had imagined that it might be ; the delight in tormenting was perhaps even the stronger because his spirits were rather less highly pitched. Certainly his manners seemed more disagreeable by the morning light.

" As I have little time to spare, Mr Raffles," said the banker, who could hardly do more than sip his tea and break his toast without eating it, " I shall be obliged if you will mention at once the ground on which you wished to meet with me. I presume that you have a home elsewhere and will be glad to return to it."

" Why, if a man has got any heart, doesn't he want to see an old friend, Nick ?—I must call you Nick—we always did call you young Nick when we knew you meant to marry the old widow. Some said you had a handsome family likeness to old Nick, but that was your mother's fault, calling you Nicholas. Aren't you glad to see me again ? I expected an invite to stay with you at some pretty place. My own establishment is broken up now my wife's dead. I've no particular attachment to any spot ; I would as soon settle hereabout as anywhere."

" May I ask why you returned from America ? I considered that the strong wish you expressed to go there, when an adequate sum was furnished, was tantamount to an engagement that you would remain there for life."

" Never knew that a wish to go to a place was the same thing as a wish to stay. But I did stay a matter of ten years ; it didn't suit me to stay any longer. And I'm not going again, Nick." Here Mr Raffles winked slowly as he looked at Mr Bulstrode.

" Do you wish to be settled in any business ? What is your calling now ? "

" Thank you, my calling is to enjoy myself as much as I can. I don't care about working any more. If I did anything it would be a little travelling in the tobacco line—or something of that sort, which takes a man into agreeable company. But not without an independence to fall back upon. That's what I want : I'm not so strong as I was, Nick, though I've got more colour than you. I want an independence."

" That could be supplied to you, if you would engage to keep at a distance," said Mr Bulstrode, perhaps with a little too much eagerness in his undertone.

" That must be as it suits my convenience," said Raffles, coolly. " I see no reason why I shouldn't make a few acquaintances hereabout. I'm not ashamed of myself as company for anybody. I dropped my portmanteau at the turnpike when I got down — change of linen — genuine — honour bright ! — more than fronts and wristbands ; and with this suit of mourning, straps and everything, I should do you credit among the nobs here." Mr Raffles had pushed away his chair and looked down at himself, particularly at his straps. His chief intention was to annoy Bulstrode, but he really thought that his appearance now would produce a good effect, and that he was not only handsome and witty, but clad in a mourning style which implied solid connections.

" If you intend to rely on me in any way, Mr Raffles," said Bulstrode, after a moment's pause, " you will expect to meet my wishes."

" Ah, to be sure," said Raffles, with a mocking cordiality. " Didn't I always do it ? Lord, you made a pretty thing out of me, and I got but little. I've often thought since, I might have done better by telling the old woman that I'd found her daughter and her grandchild : it would have suited my feelings better ; I've got a soft place in my heart. But you've buried the old lady by this time, I suppose—it's all one to her now. And you've got your fortune out of that profit-

able business which had such a blessing on it. You've taken to being
a nob, buying land, being a country bashaw. Still in the Dissenting line, eh ? Still godly ? Or taken to the Church as more genteel ?"

This time Mr Raffles' slow wink and slight protrusion of his tongue
was worse than a nightmare, because it held the certitude that it was
not a nightmare, but a waking misery. Mr Bulstrode felt a shudder-
ing nausea, and did not speak, but was considering diligently whether
he should not leave Raffles to do as he would, and simply defy him as
a slanderer. The man would soon show himself disreputable enough to
make people disbelieve him. " But not when he tells any ugly-look-
ing truth about *you*," said discerning consciousness. And again : it
seemed no wrong to keep Raffles at a distance, but Mr Bulstrode
shrank from the direct falsehood of denying true statements. It
was one thing to look back on forgiven sins, nay, to explain questionable conformity to lax customs, and another to enter deliberately on
the necessity of falsehood.

But since Bulstrode did not speak, Raffles ran on, by way of using
time to the utmost.

" I've not had such fine luck as you, by Jove ! Things went confoundedly with me in New York ; those Yankees are cool hands, and
a man of gentlemanly feelings has no chance with them. I married
when I came back—a nice woman in the tobacco trade—very fond of
me—but the trade was restricted, as we say. She had been settled
there a good many years by a friend ; but there was a son too much
in the case. Josh and I never hit it off. However, I made the most
of the position, and I've always taken my glass in good company.
It's been all on the square with me ; I'm as open as the day. You
won't take it ill of me that I didn't look you up before ; I've got a
complaint that makes me a little dilatory. I thought you were trading and praying away in London still, and didn't find you there.
But you see I was sent to you, Nick—perhaps for a blessing to both
of us."

Mr Raffles ended with a jocose snuffle: no man felt his intellect
more superior to religious cant. And if the cunning which calculates
on the meanest feelings in men could be called intellect, he had his
share, for under the blurting rallying tone with which he spoke to
Bulstrode, there was an evident selection of statements, as if they had
been so many moves at chess. Meanwhile Bulstrode had determined
on his move, and he said, with gathered resolution—

" You will do well to reflect, Mr Raffles, that it is possible for a man
to overreach himself in the effort to secure undue advantage. Although
I am not in any way bound to you, I am willing to supply you with
a regular annuity—in quarterly payments—so long as you fulfil a
promise to remain at a distance from this neighbourhood. It is in
your power to choose. If you insist on remaining here, even for a
short time, you will get nothing from me. I shall decline to know
you."

" Ha, ha ! " said Raffles, with an affected explosion, " that reminds
me of a droll dog of a thief who declined to know the constable."

" Your allusions are lost on me, sir," said Bulstrode, with white
heat ; " the law has no hold on me either through your agency or any
other."

" You can't understand a joke, my good fellow. I only meant that

I should never decline to know you. But let us be serious. Your quarterly payment won't quite suit me. I like my freedom."

Here Raffles rose and stalked once or twice up and down the room, swinging his leg, and assuming an air of masterly meditation. At last he stopped opposite Bulstrode, and said, " I'll tell you what ! Give us a couple of hundreds—come, that's modest—and I'll go away —honour bright !—pick up my portmanteau and go away. But I shall not give up my liberty for a dirty annuity. I shall come and go where I like. Perhaps it may suit me to stay away, and correspond with a friend ; perhaps not. Have you the money with you ? "

" No, I have one hundred," said Bulstrode, feeling the immediate riddance too great a relief to be rejected on the ground of future uncertainties. " I will forward you the other if you will mention an address."

" No, I'll wait here till you bring it," said Raffles. " I'll take a stroll, and have a snack, and you'll be back by that time."

Mr Bulstrode's sickly body, shattered by the agitations he had gone through since the last evening, made him feel abjectly in the power of this loud invulnerable man. At that moment he snatched at a temporary repose to be won on any terms. He was rising to do what Raffles suggested, when the latter said, lifting up his finger as if with a sudden recollection—

" I did have another look after Sarah again, though I didn't tell you ; I'd a tender conscience about that pretty young woman. I didn't find her, but I found out her husband's name, and I made a note of it. But hang it, I lost my pocket-book. However, if I heard it, I should know it again. I've got my faculties as if I was in my prime, but names wear out, by Jove ! Sometimes I'm no better than a confounded tax-paper before the names are filled in. However, if I hear of her and her family, you shall know, Nick. You'd like to do something for her, now she's your step-daughter."

" Doubtless," said Mr Bulstrode, with the usual steady look of his light-grey eyes ; " though that might reduce my power of assisting you."

As he walked out of the room, Raffles winked slowly at his back, and then turned towards the window to watch the banker riding away —virtually at his command. His lips first curled with a smile and then opened with a short triumphant laugh.

" But what the deuce *was* the name ? " he presently said, half aloud, scratching his head, and wrinkling his brows horizontally. He had not really cared or thought about this point of forgetfulness until it occurred to him in his invention of annoyances for Bulstrode.

" It began with L ; it was almost all l's I fancy," he went on, with a sense that he was getting hold of the slippery name. But the hold was too slight, and he soon got tired of this mental chase ; for few men were more impatient of private occupation or more in need of making themselves continually heard than Mr Raffles. He preferred using his time in pleasant conversation with the bailiff and the housekeeper, from whom he gathered as much as he wanted to know about Mr Bulstrode's position in Middlemarch.

After all, however, there was a dull space of time which needed relieving with bread and cheese and ale, and when he was seated alone with these resources in the wainscoted parlour, he suddenly slapped his knee, and exclaimed, " Ladislaw !" That action of memory which he had tried to set going, and had abandoned in despair, had suddenly completed itself without conscious effort—a common experience, agreeable as a completed sneeze, even if the name remembered is of no value. Raffles immediately took out his pocket-book, and wrote down the name, not because he expected to use it, but merely for the sake of not being at a loss if he ever did happen to want it. He was not going to tell Bulstrode: there was no actual good in telling, and to a mind like that of Mr Raffles there is always probable good in a secret.

He was satisfied with his present success, and by three o'clock that day he had taken up his portmanteau at the turnpike and mounted the coach, relieving Mr Bulstrode's eyes of an ugly black spot on the landscape at Stone Court, but not relieving him of the dread that the black spot might reappear and become inseparable even from the vision of his hearth.

BOOK VI.

THE WIDOW AND THE WIFE.

CHAPTER LIV.

" Negli occhi porta la mia donna Amore ;
    Per che si fa gentil ciò ch'ella mira :
    Ov'ella passa, ogni uom ver lei si gira,
    E cui saluta fa tremar lo core.
Sicchè, bassando il viso, tutto smore,
    E d'ogni suo difetto allor sospira :
    Fuggon dinanzi a lei Superbia ed Ira :
    Aiutatemi, donne, a farle onore.
Ogni dolcezza, ogni pensiero umile
    Nasce nel core a chi parlar la sente ;
    Ond' è beato chi prima la vide.
Quel ch'ella par quand' un poco sorride,
    Non si può dicer, nè tener a mente,
    Si è nuovo miracolo gentile."
                    —DANTE : *La Vita Nuova.* [1]

BY that delightful morning when the hayricks at Stone Court were
scenting the air quite impartially, as if Mr Raffles had been a guest
worthy of finest incense, Dorothea had again taken up her abode at
Lowick Manor. After three months Freshitt had become rather
oppressive : to sit like a model for Saint Catherine looking rapturously at Celia's baby would not do for many hours in the day, and
to remain in that momentous babe's presence with persistent disregard was a course that could not have been tolerated in a childless
sister. Dorothea would have been capable of carrying baby joyfully
for a mile if there had been need, and of loving it the more tenderly

---

1. "My lady carries love within her
eyes;/All that she looks on is made
pleasanter;/Upon her path men turn to
gaze at her;/He whom she greeteth feels
his heart to rise,/And droops his
troubled visage, full of sighs,/And of
his evil heart is then aware;/Hate loves,
and pride becomes a worshipper./O
women, help to praise her in somewise./

Humbleness, and the hope that hopeth
well,/By speech of hers into the mind
are brought,/And who beholds is blessed
oftenwhiles./The look she hath when she
a little smiles/Cannot be said, nor
holden in the thought;/'Tis such a new
and gracious miracle" (Dante Gabriel
Rossetti's translation [1846]).

for that labour; but to an aunt who does not recognise her infant nephew as Bouddha, and has nothing to do for him but to admire, his behaviour is apt to appear monotonous, and the interest of watching him exhaustible.

This possibility was quite hidden from Celia, who felt that Dorothea's childless widowhood fell in quite prettily with the birth of little Arthur (baby was named after Mr Brooke).

"Dodo is just the creature not to mind about having anything of her own—children or anything!" said Celia to her husband. "And if she had had a baby, it never could have been such a dear as Arthur. Could it, James?"

"Not if it had been like Casaubon," said Sir James, conscious of some indirectness in his answer, and of holding a strictly private opinion as to the perfections of his first-born.

"No! just imagine? Really it was a mercy," said Celia; "and I think it is very nice for Dodo to be a widow. She can be just as fond of our baby as if it were her own, and she can have as many notions of her own as she likes."

"It is a pity she was not a queen," said the devout Sir James.

"But what should we have been then? We must have been something else," said Celia, objecting to so laborious a flight of imagination. "I like her better as she is."

Hence, when she found that Dorothea was making arrangements for her final departure to Lowick, Celia raised her eyebrows with disappointment, and in her quiet unemphatic way shot a needle-arrow of sarcasm.

"What will you do at Lowick, Dodo? You say yourself there is nothing to be done there: everybody is so clean and well off, it makes you quite melancholy. And here you have been so happy going all about Tipton with Mr Garth into the worst backyards. And now uncle is abroad, you and Mr Garth can have it all your own way; and I am sure James does everything you tell him."

"I shall often come here, and I shall see how baby grows all the better," said Dorothea.

"But you will never see him washed," said Celia: "and that is quite the best part of the day." She was almost pouting: it did seem to her very hard in Dodo to go away from the baby when she might stay.

"Dear Kitty, I will come and stay all night on purpose," said Dorothea; "but I want to be alone now, and in my own home. I wish to know the Farebrothers better, and to talk to Mr Farebrother about what there is to be done in Middlemarch."

Dorothea's native strength of will was no longer all converted into resolute submission. She had a great yearning to be at Lowick, and was simply determined to go, not feeling bound to tell all her reasons. But every one around her disapproved. Sir James was much pained, and offered that they should all migrate to Cheltenham for a few months with the sacred ark, otherwise called a cradle: at that period a man could hardly know what to propose if Cheltenham were rejected.

The Dowager Lady Chettam, just returned from a visit to her daughter in town, wished, at least, that Mrs Vigo should be written to, and invited to accept the office of companion to Mrs Casaubon : it was not credible that Dorothea as a young widow would think of living alone in the house at Lowick. Mrs Vigo had been reader and secretary to royal personages, and in point of knowledge and sentiments even Dorothea could have nothing to object to her.

Mrs Cadwallader said, privately, "You will certainly go mad in that house alone, my dear. You will see visions. We have all got to exert ourselves a little to keep sane, and call things by the same names as other people call them by. To be sure, for younger sons and women who have no money, it is a sort of provision to go mad : they are taken care of then. But you must not run into that. I daresay you are a little bored here with our good dowager ; but think what a bore you might become yourself to your fellow-creatures if you were always playing tragedy queen and taking things sublimely. Sitting alone in that library at Lowick you may fancy yourself ruling the weather ; you must get a few people round you who wouldn't believe you if you told them. That is a good lowering medicine."

"I never called everything by the same name that all the people about me did," said Dorothea, stoutly.

"But I suppose you have found out your mistake, my dear," said Mrs Cadwallader, "and that is a proof of sanity."

Dorothea was aware of the sting, but it did not hurt her. "No," she said, "I still think that the greater part of the world is mistaken about many things. Surely one may be sane and yet think so, since the greater part of the world has often had to come round from its opinion."

Mrs Cadwallader said no more on that point to Dorothea, but to her husband she remarked, "It will be well for her to marry again as soon as it is proper, if one could get her among the right people. Of course the Chettams would not wish it. But I see clearly a husband is the best thing to keep her in order. If we were not so poor I would invite Lord Triton. He will be marquis some day, and there is no denying that she would make a good marchioness : she looks handsomer than ever in her mourning."

"My dear Elinor, do let the poor woman alone. Such contrivances are of no use," said the easy Rector.

"No use ? How are matches made, except by bringing men and women together ? And it is a shame that her uncle should have run away and shut up the Grange just now. There ought to be plenty of eligible matches invited to Freshitt and the Grange. Lord Triton is precisely the man : full of plans for making the people happy in a soft-headed sort of way. That would just suit Mrs Casaubon."

"Let Mrs Casaubon choose for herself, Elinor."

"That is the nonsense you wise men talk ! How can she choose if she has no variety to choose from ? A woman's choice usually means taking the only man she can get. Mark my words, Humphrey. If her friends don't exert themselves, there will be a worse business than the Casaubon business yet."

"For heaven's sake don't touch on that topic, Elinor ! It is a very sore point with Sir James. He would be deeply offended if you entered on it to him unnecessarily."

" I have never entered on it," said Mrs Cadwallader, opening her. hands. " Celia told me all about the will at the beginning, without any asking of mine."

" Yes, yes ; but they want the thing hushed up, and I understand that the young fellow is going out of the neighbourhood."

Mrs Cadwallader said nothing, but gave her husband three significant nods, with a very sarcastic expression in her dark eyes.

Dorothea quietly persisted in spite of remonstrance and persuasion. So by the end of June the shutters were all opened at Lowick Manor, and the morning gazed calmly into the library, shining on the rows of note-books as it shines on the weary waste planted with huge stones, the mute memorial of a forgotten faith ; and the evening laden with roses entered silently into the blue-green boudoir where Dorothea chose oftenest to sit. At first she walked into every room, questioning the eighteen months of her married life, and carrying on her thoughts as if they were a speech to be heard by her husband. Then, she lingered in the library and could not be at rest till she had carefully ranged all the note-books as she imagined that he would wish to see them, in orderly sequence. The pity which had been the restraining compelling motive in her life with him still clung about his image, even while she remonstrated with him in indignant thought and told him that he was unjust. One little act of hers may perhaps be smiled at as superstitious. The *Synoptical Tabulation for the use of Mrs Casaubon*, she carefully enclosed and sealed, writing within the envelope, " *I could not use it. Do you not see now that I could not submit my soul to yours, by working hopelessly at what I have no belief in ? —Dorothea.*" Then she deposited the paper in her own desk.

That silent colloquy was perhaps only the more earnest because underneath and through it all there was always the deep longing which had really determined her to come to Lowick. The longing was to see Will Ladislaw. She did not know any good that could come of their meeting : she was helpless ; her hands had been tied from making up to him for any unfairness in his lot. But her soul thirsted to see him. How could it be otherwise ? If a princess in the days of enchantment had seen a four-footed creature from among those which live in herds come to her once and again with a human gaze which rested upon her with choice and beseeching, what would she think of in her journeying, what would she look for when the herds passed her ? Surely for the gaze which had found her, and which she would know again. Life would be no better than candle-light tinsel and daylight rubbish if our spirits were not touched by what has been, to issues of longing and constancy. It was true that Dorothea wanted to know the Farebrothers better, and especially to talk to the new rector, but also true that remembering what Lydgate had told her about Will Ladislaw and little Miss Noble, she counted on Will's coming to Lowick to see the Farebrother family. The very first Sunday, *before* she entered the church, she saw him as she had seen him the last time she was there, alone in the clergyman's pew ; but *when* she entered his figure was gone.

In the week-days when she went to see the ladies at the Rectory, she listened in vain for some word that they might let fall about

Will ; but it seemed to her that Mrs Farebrother talked of every one else in the neighbourhood and out of it.

" Probably some of Mr Farebrother's Middlemarch hearers may follow him to Lowick sometimes. Do you not think so ? " said Dorothea, rather despising herself for having a secret motive in asking the question.

" If they are wise they will, Mrs Casaubon," said the old lady. " I see that you set a right value on my son's preaching. His grandfather on my side was an excellent clergyman, but his father was in the law :—most exemplary and honest nevertheless, which is a reason for our never being rich. They say Fortune is a woman and capricious. But sometimes she is a good woman and gives to those who merit, which has been the case with you, Mrs Casaubon, who have given a living to my son."

Mrs Farebrother recurred to her knitting with a dignified satisfaction in her neat little effort at oratory, but this was not what Dorothea wanted to hear. Poor thing ! she did not even know whether Will Ladislaw was still at Middlemarch, and there was no one whom she dared to ask, unless it were Lydgate. But just now she could not see Lydgate without sending for him or going to seek him. Perhaps Will Ladislaw, having heard of that strange ban against him left by Mr Casaubon, had felt it better that he and she should not meet again, and perhaps she was wrong to wish for a meeting that others might find many good reasons against. Still " I do wish it " came at the end of those wise reflections as naturally as a sob after holding the breath. And the meeting did happen, but in a formal way quite unexpected by her.

One morning, about eleven, Dorothea was seated in her boudoir with a map of the land attached to the manor and other papers before her, which were to help her in making an exact statement for herself of her income and affairs. She had not yet applied herself to her work, but was seated with her hands folded on her lap, looking out along the avenue of limes to the distant fields. Every leaf was at rest in the sunshine, the familiar scene was changeless, and seemed to represent the prospect of her life, full of motiveless ease—motiveless, if her own energy could not seek out reasons for ardent action. The widow's cap of those times made an oval frame for the face, and had a crown standing up ; the dress was an experiment in the utmost laying on of crape ; but this heavy solemnity of clothing made her face look all the younger, with its recovered bloom, and the sweet, inquiring candour of her eyes.

Her reverie was broken by Tantripp, who came to say that Mr Ladislaw was below, and begged permission to see Madam if it were not too early.

" I will see him," ·said Dorothea, rising immediately. " Let him be shown into the drawing-room."

The drawing-room was the most neutral room in the house to her —the one least associated with the trials of her married life : the damask matched the wood-work, which was all white and gold ; there were two tall mirrors and tables with nothing on them—in brief, it was a room where you had no reason for sitting in one place rather than in another. It was below the boudoir, and had also a bow-window looking out on the avenue. But when Pratt showed Will Ladislaw into it the window was open ; and a winged visitor, buzzing in and out now and then without minding the furniture, made the room look less formal and uninhabited.

"Glad to see you here again, sir," said Pratt, lingering to adjust a blind.

"I am only come to say good-bye, Pratt," said Will, who wished even the butler to know that he was too proud to hang about Mrs Casaubon now she was a rich widow.

"Very sorry to hear it, sir," said Pratt, retiring. Of course, as a servant who was to be told nothing, he knew the fact of which Ladislaw was still ignorant, and had drawn his inferences; indeed, had not differed from his betrothed Tantripp when she said, "*Your* master was as jealous as a fiend—and no reason. Madam would look higher than Mr Ladislaw, else I don't know her. Mrs Cadwallader's maid says there's a lord coming who is to marry her when the mourning's over."

There were not many moments for Will to walk about with his hat in his hand before Dorothea entered. The meeting was very different from that first meeting in Rome when Will had been embarrassed and Dorothea calm. This time he felt miserable but determined, while she was in a state of agitation which could not be hidden. Just outside the door she had felt that this longed-for meeting was after all too difficult, and when she saw Will advancing towards her, the deep blush which was rare in her came with painful suddenness. Neither of them knew how it was, but neither of them spoke. She gave her hand for a moment, and then they went to sit down near the window, she on one settee and he on another opposite. Will was peculiarly uneasy : it seemed to him not like Dorothea that the mere fact of her being a widow should cause such a change in her manner of receiving him ; and he knew of no other condition which could have affected their previous relation to each other—except that, as his imagination at once told him, her friends might have been poisoning her mind with their suspicions of him.

"I hope I have not presumed too much in calling," said Will ; " I could not bear to leave the neighbourhood and begin a new life without seeing you to say good-bye."

"Presumed ? Surely not. I should have thought it unkind if you had not wished to see me," said Dorothea, her habit of speaking with perfect genuineness asserting itself through all her uncertainty and agitation. "Are you going away immediately ?"

"Very soon, I think. I intend to go to town and eat my dinners as a barrister, since, they say, that is the preparation for all public business. There will be a great deal of political work to be done by-and-by, and I mean to try and do some of it. Other men have managed to win an honourable position for themselves without family or money."

"And that will make it all the more honourable," said Dorothea, ardently. "Besides, you have so many talents. I have heard from my uncle how well you speak in public, so that every one is sorry when you leave off, and how clearly you can explain things. And you care that justice should be done to every one. I am so glad. When we were in Rome, I thought you only cared for poetry and art, and

the things that adorn life for us who are well off. But now I know
you think about the rest of the world."

While she was speaking Dorothea had lost her personal embarrassment, and had become like her former self. She looked at Will
with a direct glance, full of delighted confidence.

"You approve of my going away for years, then, and never coming
here again till I have made myself of some mark in the world?" said
Will, trying hard to reconcile the utmost pride with the utmost effort
to get an expression of strong feeling from Dorothea.

She was not aware how long it was before she answered. She had
turned her head and was looking out of the window on the rose-
bushes, which seemed to have in them the summers of all the years
when Will would be away. This was not judicious behaviour. But
Dorothea never thought of studying her manners: she thought only
of bowing to a sad necessity which divided her from Will. Those first
words of his about his intentions had seemed to make everything
clear to her: he knew, she supposed, all about Mr Casaubon's final
conduct in relation to him, and it had come to him with the same sort
of shock as to herself. He had never felt more than friendship for
her—had never had anything in his mind to justify what she felt to
be her husband's outrage on the feelings of both: and that friendship
he still felt. Something which may be called an inward silent sob had
gone on in Dorothea before she said with a pure voice, just trembling
in the last words as if only from its liquid flexibility—

"Yes, it must be right for you to do as you say. I shall be very
happy when I hear that you have made your value felt. But you
must have patience. It will perhaps be a long while."

Will never quite knew how it was that he saved himself from falling down at her feet, when the "long while" came forth with its
gentle tremor. He used to say that the horrible hue and surface of
her crape dress was most likely the sufficient controlling force. He
sat still, however, and only said—

"I shall never hear from you. And you will forget all about me."

"No," said Dorothea, "I shall never forget you. I have never
forgotten any one whom I once knew. My life has never been
crowded, and seems not likely to be so. And I have a great deal of
space for memory at Lowick, haven't I?" She smiled.

"Good God!" Will burst out passionately, rising, with his hat still
in his hand, and walking away to a marble table, where he suddenly
turned and leaned his back against it. The blood had mounted to his
face and neck, and he looked almost angry. It had seemed to him as
if they were like two creatures slowly turning to marble in each
other's presence, while their hearts were conscious and their eyes were
yearning. But there was no help for it. It should never be true of
him that in this meeting to which he had come with bitter resolution
he had ended by a confession which might be interpreted into asking
for her fortune. Moreover, it was actually true that he was fearful
of the effect which such confessions might have on Dorothea herself.

She looked at him from that distance in some trouble, imagining
that there might have been an offence in her words. But all the
while there was a current of thought in her about his probable want
of money, and the impossibility of her helping him. If her uncle had
been at home, something might have been done through him! It was
this preoccupation with the hardship of Will's wanting money, while

she had what ought to have been his share, which led her to say, seeing that he remained silent and looked away from her—

"I wonder whether you would like to have that miniature which
hangs up-stairs—I mean that beautiful miniature of your grandmother. I think it is not right for me to keep it, if you would wish
to have it. It is wonderfully like you."

"You are very good," said Will, irritably. "No; I don't mind
about it. It is not very consoling to have one's own likeness. It
would be more consoling if others wanted to have it."

"I thought you would like to cherish her memory—I thought——"
Dorothea broke off an instant, her imagination suddenly warning her
away from Aunt Julia's history—"you would surely like to have the
miniature as a family memorial."

"Why should I have that, when I have nothing else ! A man with
only a portmanteau for his stowage must keep his memorials in his
head."

Will spoke at random : he was merely venting his petulance ; it
was a little too exasperating to have his grandmother's portrait
offered him at that moment. But to Dorothea's feeling his words had
a peculiar sting. She rose and said with a touch of indignation as
well as hauteur—

"You are much the happier of us two, Mr Ladislaw, to have nothing."

Will was startled. Whatever the words might be, the tone seemed
like a dismissal ; and quitting his leaning posture, he walked a little
way towards her. Their eyes met, but with a strange questioning
gravity. Something was keeping their minds aloof, and each was left
to conjecture what was in the other. Will had really never thought
of himself as having a claim of inheritance on the property which was
held by Dorothea, and would have required a narrative to make him
understand her present feeling.

"I never felt it a misfortune to have nothing till now," he said.
" But poverty may be as bad as leprosy, if it divides us from what we
most care for."

The words cut Dorothea to the heart, and made her relent. She
answered in a tone of sad fellowship.

"Sorrow comes in so many ways. Two years ago I had no notion
of that—I mean of the unexpected way in which trouble comes, and
ties our hands, and makes us silent when we long to speak. I used to
despise women a little for not shaping their lives more, and doing
better things. I was very fond of doing as I liked, but I have almost
given it up," she ended, smiling playfully.

"I have not given up doing as I like, but I can very seldom do it,"
said Will. He was standing two yards from her with his mind full
of contradictory desires and resolves — desiring some unmistakable
proof that she loved him, and yet dreading the position into which
such a proof might bring him. "The thing one most longs for may
be surrounded with conditions that would be intolerable."

At this moment Pratt entered and said, "Sir James Chettam is in
the library, madam."

"Ask Sir James to come in here," said Dorothea, immediately. It
was as if the same electric shock had passed through her and Will.
Each of them felt proudly resistant, and neither looked at the other,
while they awaited Sir James's entrance.

After shaking hands with Dorothea, he bowed as slightly as possible to Ladislaw, who repaid the slightness exactly, and then going towards Dorothea, said—

"I must say good-bye, Mrs Casaubon ; and probably for a long while."

Dorothea put out her hand and said her good-bye cordially. The sense that Sir James was depreciating Will, and behaving rudely to him, roused her resolution and dignity : there was no touch of confusion in her manner. And when Will had left the room, she looked with such calm self-possession at Sir James, saying, "How is Celia?" that he was obliged to behave as if nothing had annoyed him. And what would be the use of behaving otherwise? Indeed, Sir James shrank with so much dislike from the association even in thought of Dorothea with Ladislaw as her possible lover, that he would himself have wished to avoid an outward show of displeasure which would have recognised the disagreeable possibility. If any one had asked him why he shrank in that way, I am not sure that he would at first have said anything fuller or more precise than "*that* Ladislaw !"— though on reflection he might have urged that Mr Casaubon's codicil, barring Dorothea's marriage with Will, except under a penalty, was enough to cast unfitness over any relation at all between them. His aversion was all the stronger because he felt himself unable to interfere.

But Sir James was a power in a way unguessed by himself. Entering at that moment, he was an incorporation of the strongest reasons through which Will's pride became a repellent force, keeping him asunder from Dorothea.

CHAPTER LV.

Hath she her faults ? I would you had them too.
They are the fruity must of soundest wine ;
Or say, they are regenerating fire
Such as hath turned the dense black element
Into a crystal pathway for the sun.

IF youth is the season of hope, it is often so only in the sense that our elders are hopeful about us ; for no age is so apt as youth to think its emotions, partings, and resolves are the last of their kind. Each crisis seems final, simply because it is new. We are told that the oldest inhabitants in Peru do not cease to be agitated by the earthquakes, but they probably see beyond each shock, and reflect that there are plenty more to come.

To Dorothea, still in that time of youth when the eyes with their long full lashes look out after their rain of tears unsoiled and unwearied as a freshly-opened passion-flower, that morning's parting with Will Ladislaw seemed to be the close of their personal relations. He was going away into the distance of unknown years, and if ever he came back he would be another man. The actual state of his mind —his proud resolve to give the lie beforehand to any suspicion that he would play the needy adventurer seeking a rich woman — lay quite out of her imagination, and she had interpreted all his behaviour easily enough by her supposition that Mr Casaubon's codicil seemed to him, as it did to her, a gross and cruel interdict on any active friendship between them. Their young delight in speaking to each other, and saying what no one else would care to hear, was for ever ended, and become a treasure of the past. For this very reason she dwelt on it without inward check. That unique happiness too was dead, and in its shadowed silent chamber she might vent the passionate grief which she herself wondered at. For the first time she took down the miniature from the wall and kept it before her, liking to blend the woman who had been too hardly judged with the grandson whom her own heart and judgment defended. Can any one who has rejoiced in woman's tenderness think it a reproach to her that she took the little oval picture in her palm and made a bed for it there, and leaned her cheek upon it, as if that would soothe the creatures who had suffered unjust condemnation ? She did not know then that it was Love who had come to her briefly, as in a dream before awaking, with the hues of morning on his wings—that it was Love to whom she was sobbing her farewell as his image was banished by the blameless rigour of irresistible day. She only felt that there was something irrevocably amiss and lost in her lot, and her thoughts about the future were the more readily shapen into resolve. Ardent souls, ready to construct their coming lives, are apt to commit themselves to the fulfilment of their own visions.

One day that she went to Freshitt to fulfil her promise of staying all night and seeing baby washed, Mrs Cadwallader came to dine, the Rector being gone on a fishing excursion. It was a warm evening, and even in the delightful drawing-room, where the fine old turf sloped from the open window towards a lilied pool and well-planted mounds, the heat was enough to make Celia in her white muslin and light curls reflect with pity on what Dodo must feel in her black dress and close cap. But this was not until some episodes with baby were over, and had left her mind at leisure. She had seated herself and taken up a fan for some time before she said, in her quiet guttural—

" Dear Dodo, do throw off that cap. I am sure your dress must make you feel ill."

" I am so used to the cap—it has become a sort of shell," said Dorothea, smiling. " I feel rather bare and exposed when it is off."

" I *must* see you without it ; it makes us all warm," said Celia, throwing down her fan, and going to Dorothea. It was a pretty picture to see this little lady in white muslin unfastening the widow's cap from her more majestic sister, and tossing it on to a chair. Just as the coils and braids of dark-brown hair had been set free, Sir James entered the room. He looked at the released head, and said, " Ah ! " in a tone of satisfaction.

" It was I who did it, James," said Celia. " Dodo need not make such a slavery of her mourning ; she need not wear that cap any more among her friends."

" My dear Celia," said Lady Chettam, " a widow must wear her mourning at least a year."

" Not if she marries again before the end of it," said Mrs Cadwallader, who had some pleasure in startling her good friend the Dowager. Sir James was annoyed, and leaned forward to play with Celia's Maltese dog.

" That is very rare, I hope," said Lady Chettam, in a tone intended to guard against such events. " No friend of ours ever committed herself in that way except Mrs Beevor, and it was very painful to Lord Grinsell when she did so. Her first husband was objectionable, which made it the greater wonder. And severely she was punished for it. They said Captain Beevor dragged her about by the hair, and held up loaded pistols at her."

" Oh, if she took the wrong man ! " said Mrs Cadwallader, who was in a decidedly wicked mood. " Marriage is always bad then, first or second. Priority is a poor recommendation in a husband if he has got no other. I would rather have a good second husband than an indifferent first."

" My dear, your clever tongue runs away with you," said Lady Chettam. " I am sure you would be the last woman to marry again prematurely, if our dear Rector were taken away."

" Oh, I make no vows ; it might be a necessary economy. It is lawful to marry again, I suppose ; else we might as well be Hindoos instead of Christians. Of course if a woman accepts the wrong man, she must take the consequences, and one who does it twice over deserves her fate. But if she can marry blood, beauty, and bravery— the sooner the better."

" I think the subject of our conversation is very ill-chosen," said Sir James, with a look of disgust. " Suppose we change it."

" Not on my account, Sir James," said Dorothea, determined not to lose the opportunity of freeing herself from certain oblique references to excellent matches. " If you are speaking on my behalf, I can assure you that no question can be more indifferent and impersonal to me than second marriage. It is no more to me than if you talked of women going fox-hunting : whether it is admirable in them or not, I shall not follow them. Pray let Mrs Cadwallader amuse herself on that subject as much as on any other."

" My dear Mrs Casaubon," said Lady Chettam, in her stateliest way, " you do not, I hope, think there was any allusion to you in my mentioning Mrs Beevor. It was only an instance that occurred to me. She was step-daughter to Lord Grinsell : he married Mrs Teveroy for his second wife. There could be no possible allusion to you."

" Oh no," said Celia. " Nobody chose the subject ; it all came out of Dodo's cap. Mrs Cadwallader only said what was quite true. A woman could not be married in a widow's cap, James."

" Hush, my dear ! " said Mrs Cadwallader. " I will not offend again. I will not even refer to Dido or Zenobia. [1] Only what are we to talk about ? I, for my part, object to the discussion of Human Nature, because that is the nature of rectors' wives."

Later in the evening, after Mrs Cadwallader was gone, Celia said privately to Dorothea, " Really, Dodo, taking your cap off made you like yourself again in more ways than one. You spoke up just as you used to do, when anything was said to displease you. But I could hardly make out whether it was James that you thought wrong, or Mrs Cadwallader."

" Neither," said Dorothea. " James spoke out of delicacy to me, but he was mistaken in supposing that I minded what Mrs Cadwallader said. I should only mind if there were a law obliging me to take any piece of blood and beauty that she or anybody else recommended."

1. Dido's first husband was killed; her second love was for Aeneas, who deserted her. Zenobia, Queen of Palmyra after the death of her husband, revolted against the Roman Emperor Aurelian, was defeated, and made a slave; there is no story of her second marriage.

" But you know, Dodo, if you ever did marry, it would be all the better to have blood and beauty," said Celia, reflecting that Mr Casaubon had not been richly endowed with those gifts, and that it would be well to caution Dorothea in time.

"Don't be anxious, Kitty; I have quite other thoughts about my life. I shall never marry again," said Dorothea, touching her sister's chin, and looking at her with indulgent affection. Celia was nursing her baby, and Dorothea had come to say good-night to her.

"Really—quite?" said Celia. "Not anybody at all—if he were very wonderful indeed?"

Dorothea shook her head slowly. "Not anybody at all. I have delightful plans. I should like to take a great deal of land, and drain it, and make a little colony, where everybody should work, and all the work should be done well. I should know every one of the people and be their friend. I am going to have great consultations with Mr Garth : he can tell me almost everything I want to know."

"Then you *will* be happy, if you have a plan, Dodo," said Celia. "Perhaps little Arthur will like plans when he grows up, and then he can help you."

Sir James was informed that same night that Dorothea was really quite set against marrying anybody at all, and was going to take to " all sorts of plans," just like what she used to have. Sir James made no remark. To his secret feeling, there was something repulsive in a woman's second marriage, and no match would prevent him from feeling it a sort of desecration for Dorothea. He was aware that the world would regard such a sentiment as preposterous, especially in relation to a woman of one-and-twenty ; the practice of " the world" being to treat of a young widow's second marriage as certain and probably near, and to smile with meaning if the widow acts accordingly. But if Dorothea did choose to espouse her solitude, he felt that the resolution would well become her.

CHAPTER LVI.

" How happy is he born and taught
That serveth not another's will ;
Whose armour is his honest thought,
And simple truth his only skill !

This man is freed from servile bands
Of hope to rise, or fear to fall ;
Lord of himself, though not of lands ;
And having nothing, yet hath all."
—Sir Henry Wotton. [1]

DOROTHEA's confidence in Caleb Garth's knowledge, which had begun on her hearing that he approved of her cottages, had grown fast during her stay at Freshitt, Sir James having induced her to take rides over the two estates in company with himself and Caleb, who quite returned her admiration, and told his wife that Mrs Casaubon had a

1. "The Character of a Happy Life" (1651).

head for business most uncommon in a woman. It must be remembered that by "business" Caleb never meant money transactions,
but the skilful application of labour.

"Most uncommon!" repeated Caleb. "She said a thing I often
used to think myself when I was a lad :—'Mr Garth, I should like
to feel, if I lived to be old, that I had improved a great piece of land
and built a great many good cottages, because the work is of a healthy
kind while it is being done, and after it is done, men are the better
for it.' Those were the very words : she sees into things in that way."

"But womanly, I hope," said Mrs Garth, half suspecting that Mrs
Casaubon might not hold the true principle of subordination.

"Oh, you can't think!" said Caleb, shaking his head. "You
would like to hear her speak, Susan. She speaks in such plain
words, and a voice like music. Bless me! it reminds me of bits in
the 'Messiah'—'and straightway there appeared a multitude of the
heavenly host, praising God and saying;' it has a tone with it that
satisfies your ear."

Caleb was very fond of music, and when he could afford it went to
hear an oratorio that came within his reach, returning from it with a
profound reverence for this mighty structure of tones, which made
him sit meditatively, looking on the floor and throwing much unutterable language into his outstretched hands.

With this good understanding between them, it was natural that
Dorothea asked Mr Garth to undertake any business connected with
the three farms and the numerous tenements attached to Lowick
Manor; indeed, his expectation of getting work for two was being
fast fulfilled. As he said, "Business breeds." And one form of
business which was beginning to breed just then was the construction
of railways. A projected line was to run through Lowick parish
where the cattle had hitherto grazed in a peace unbroken by astonishment; and thus it happened that the infant struggles of the railway
system entered into the affairs of Caleb Garth, and determined the
course of this history with regard to two persons who were dear to
him.

The submarine railway may have its difficulties; but the bed of
the sea is not divided among various landed proprietors with claims
for damages not only measurable but sentimental. In the hundred
to which Middlemarch belonged railways were as exciting a topic as
the Reform Bill or the imminent horrors of Cholera, and those who
held the most decided views on the subject were women and land-
holders. [2] Women both old and young regarded.travelling by steam
as presumptuous and dangerous, and argued against it by saying that
nothing should induce them to get into a railway carriage; while
proprietors, differing from each other in their arguments as much as
Mr Solomon Featherstone differed from Lord Medlicote, were yet
unanimous in the opinion that in selling land, whether to the Enemy
of mankind or to a company obliged to purchase, these pernicious
agencies must be made to pay a very high price to landowners for
permission to injure mankind.

But the slower wits, such as Mr Solomon and Mrs Waule, who
both occupied land of their own, took a long time to arrive at this

2. Hundred: a subdivision of a county.

conclusion, their minds halting at the vivid conception of what it would be to cut the Big Pasture in two, and turn it into three-cornered bits, which would be "nohow;" while accommodation-bridges and high payments were remote and incredible.

"The cows will all cast their calves, brother," said Mrs Waule, in a tone of deep melancholy, "if the railway comes across the Near Close; and I shouldn't wonder at the mare too, if she was in foal. It's a poor tale if a widow's property is to be spaded away, and the law say nothing to it. What's to hinder 'em from cutting right and left if they begin? It's well known, *I* can't fight."

"The best way would be to say nothing, and set somebody on to send 'em away with a flea in their ear, when they came spying and measuring," said Solomon. "Folks did that about Brassing, by what I can understand. It's all a pretence, if the truth was known, about their being forced to take one way. Let 'em go cutting in another parish. And I don't believe in any pay to make amends for bringing a lot of ruffians to trample your crops. Where's a company's pocket?"

"Brother Peter, God forgive him, got money out of a company," said Mrs Waule. "But that was for the manganese.[3] That wasn't for railways to blow you to pieces right and left."

"Well, there's this to be said, Jane," Mr Solomon concluded, lowering his voice in a cautious manner—"the more spokes we put in their wheel, the more they'll pay us to let 'em go on, if they must come whether or not."

This reasoning of Mr Solomon's was perhaps less thorough than he imagined, his cunning bearing about the same relation to the course of railways as the cunning of a diplomatist bears to the general chill or catarrh of the solar system. But he set about acting on his views in a thoroughly diplomatic manner, by stimulating suspicion. His side of Lowick was the most remote from the village, and the houses of the labouring people were either lone cottages or were collected in a hamlet called Frick, where a water-mill and some stone-pits made a little centre of slow, heavy-shouldered industry.

In the absence of any precise idea as to what railways were, public opinion in Frick was against them; for the human mind in that grassy corner had not the proverbial tendency to admire the unknown, holding rather that it was likely to be against the poor man, and that suspicion was the only wise attitude with regard to it. Even the rumour of Reform had not yet excited any millennial expectations in Frick, there being no definite promise in it, as of gratuitous grains to fatten Hiram Ford's pig, or of a publican at the "Weights and Scales" who would brew beer for nothing, or of an offer on the part of the three neighbouring farmers to raise wages during winter. And without distinct good of this kind in its promises, Reform seemed on a footing with the bragging of pedlars, which was a hint for distrust to every knowing person. The men of Frick were not ill-fed, and were less given to fanaticism than to a strong muscular suspicion; less inclined to believe that they were peculiarly cared for by heaven, than to regard heaven itself as rather disposed to take them in—a disposition observable in the weather.

3. A chemical element; GE has a note on its uses in *Quarry*, below, p. 621.

Thus the mind of Frick was exactly of the sort for Mr Solomon Featherstone to work upon, he having more plenteous ideas of the same order, with a suspicion of heaven and earth which was better fed and more entirely at leisure. Solomon was overseer of the roads at that time, and on his slow-paced cob often took his rounds by Frick to look at the workmen getting the stones there, pausing with a mysterious deliberation, which might have misled you into supposing that he had some other reason for staying than the mere want of impulse to move. After looking for a long while at any work that was going on, he would raise his eyes a little and look at the horizon; finally he would shake his bridle, touch his horse with the whip, and get it to move slowly onward. The hour-hand of a clock was quick by comparison with Mr Solomon, who had an agreeable sense that he could afford to be slow. He was in the habit of pausing for a cautious, vaguely-designing chat with every hedger or ditcher on his way, and was especially willing to listen even to news which he had heard before, feeling himself at an advantage over all narrators in partially disbelieving them. One day, however, he got into a dialogue with Hiram Ford, a waggoner, in which he himself contributed information. He wished to know whether Hiram had seen fellows with staves and instruments spying about: they called themselves railroad people, but there was no telling what they were, or what they meant to do. The least they pretended was that they were going to cut Lowick Parish into sixes and sevens.

"Why, there'll be no stirrin' from one pla-ace to another," said Hiram, thinking of his waggon and horses.

"Not a bit," said Mr Solomon. "And cutting up fine land such as this parish! Let 'em go into Tipton, say I. But there's no knowing what there is at the bottom of it. Traffick is what they put for'ard; but it's to do harm to the land and the poor man in the long-run."

"Why, they're Lunnon chaps, I reckon," said Hiram, who had a dim notion of London as a centre of hostility to the country.

"Ay, to be sure. And in some parts against Brassing, by what I've heard say, the folks fell on 'em when they were spying, and broke their peep-holes as they carry, and drove 'em away, so as they knew better than come again."

"It war good foon, I'd be bound," said Hiram, whose fun was much restricted by circumstances.

"Well, I wouldn't meddle with 'em myself," said Solomon. "But some say this country's seen its best days, and the sign is, as it's being overrun with these fellows trampling right and left, and wanting to cut it up into railways; and all for the big traffic to swallow up the little, so as there shan't be a team left on the land, nor a whip to crack."

"I'll crack *my* whip about their ear'n, afore they bring it to that, though," said Hiram, while Mr Solomon, shaking his bridle, moved onward.

Nettle-seed needs no digging. The ruin of this country-side by railroads was discussed, not only at the " Weights and Scales," but in the hay-field, where the muster of working hands gave opportunities for talk such as were rarely had through the rural year.

One morning, not long after that interview between Mr Farebrother and Mary Garth, in which she confessed to him her feeling for Fred Vincy, it happened that her father had some business which took him

to Yoddrell's farm in the direction of Frick : it was to measure and
value an outlying piece of land belonging to Lowick Manor, which
Caleb expected to dispose of advantageously for Dorothea (it must be
confessed that his bias was towards getting the best possible terms
from railroad companies). He put up his gig at Yoddrell's, and in
walking with his assistant and measuring-chain to the scene of his
work, he encountered the party of the company's agents, who were
adjusting their spirit-level. After a little chat he left them, observing that by-and-by they would reach him again where he was going
to measure. It was one of those grey mornings after light rains,
which become delicious about twelve o'clock, when the clouds part a
little, and the scent of the earth is sweet along the lanes and by the
hedgerows.

The scent would have been sweeter to Fred Vincy, who was coming
along the lanes on horseback, if his mind had not been worried by
unsuccessful efforts to imagine what he was to do, with his father on
one side expecting him straightway to enter the Church, with Mary
on the other threatening to forsake him if he did enter it, and with
the working-day world showing no eager need whatever of a young
gentleman without capital and generally unskilled. It was the
harder to Fred's disposition because his father, satisfied that he was
no longer rebellious, was in good humour with him, and had sent
him on this pleasant ride to see after some greyhounds. Even when
he had fixed on what he should do, there would be the task of telling his father. But it must be admitted that the fixing, which had
to come first, was the more difficult task :—what secular avocation
on earth was there for a young man (whose friends could not
get him an " appointment") which was at once gentlemanly, lucrative, and to be followed without special knowledge ? Riding along
the lanes by Frick in this mood, and slackening his pace while he
reflected whether he should venture to go round by Lowick Parsonage to call on Mary, he could see over the hedges from one field to
another. Suddenly a noise roused his attention, and on the far side
of a field on his left hand he could see six or seven men in smock-
frocks with hay-forks in their hands making an offensive approach
towards the four railway agents who were facing them, while Caleb
Garth and his assistant were hastening across the field to join the
threatened group. Fred, delayed a few moments by having to find
the gate, could not gallop up to the spot before the party in smock-
frocks, whose work of turning the hay had not been too pressing after
swallowing their mid-day beer, were driving the men in coats before
them with their hay-forks ; while Caleb Garth's assistant, a lad of
seventeen, who had snatched up the spirit-level at Caleb's order, had
been knocked down and seemed to be lying helpless. The coated men
had the advantage as runners, and Fred covered their retreat by
getting in front of the smock-frocks and charging them suddenly
enough to throw their chase into confusion. " What do you confounded fools mean ?" shouted Fred, pursuing the divided group in a
zigzag, and cutting right and left with his whip. " I'll swear to every
one of you before the magistrate. You've knocked the lad down and
killed him, for what I know. You'll every one of you be hanged at
the next assizes, if you don't mind," said Fred, who afterwards laughed
heartily as he remembered his own phrases.

The labourers had been driven through the gateway into their hay-field, and Fred had checked his horse, when Hiram Ford, observing himself at a safe challenging distance, turned back and shouted a defiance which he did not know to be Homeric.

" Yo're a coward, yo are. Yo git off your horse, young measter, and I'll have a round wi' ye, I wull. Yo daredn't come on wi'out your hoss an whip. I'd soon knock the breath out on ye, I would."

" Wait a minute, and I'll come back presently, and have a round with you all in turn, if you like," said Fred, who felt confidence in his power of boxing with his dearly-beloved brethren. But just now he wanted to hasten back to Caleb and the prostrate youth.

The lad's ankle was strained, and he was in much pain from it, but he was no further hurt, and Fred placed him on the horse that he might ride to Yoddrell's and be taken care of there.

" Let them put the horse in the stable, and tell the surveyors they can come back for their traps," said Fred. " The ground is clear now."

" No, no," said Caleb, " here's a breakage. They'll have to give up for to-day, and it will be as well. Here, take the things before you on the horse, Tom. They'll see you coming, and they'll turn back."

" I'm glad I happened to be here at the the right moment, Mr Garth," said Fred, as Tom rode away. " No knowing what might have happened if the cavalry had not come up in time."

" Ay, ay, it was lucky," said Caleb, speaking rather absently, and looking towards the spot where he had been at work at the moment of interruption. " But—deuce take it—this is what comes of men being fools—I'm hindered of my day's work. I can't get along without somebody to help me with the measuring-chain. However!" He was beginning to move towards the spot with a look of vexation, as if he had forgotten Fred's presence, but suddenly he turned round and said quickly, " What have you got to do to-day, young fellow?"

" Nothing, Mr Garth. I'll help you with pleasure—can I?" said Fred, with a sense that he should be courting Mary when he was helping her father.

" Well, you mustn't mind stooping and getting hot."

" I don't mind anything. Only I want to go first and have a round with that hulky fellow who turned to challenge me. It would be a good lesson for him. I shall not be five minutes."

" Nonsense!" said Caleb, with his most peremptory intonation. " I shall go and speak to the men myself. It's all ignorance. Somebody has been telling them lies. The poor fools don't know any better."

" I shall go with you, then," said Fred.

" No, no ; stay where you are. I don't want your young blood. I can take care of myself."

Caleb was a powerful man and knew little of any fear except the fear of hurting others and the fear of having to speechify. But he felt it his duty at this moment to try and give a little harangue. There was a striking mixture in him—which came from his having always been a hard-working man himself—of rigorous notions about workmen and practical indulgence towards them. To do a good day's work and to do it well, he held to be part of their welfare, as it was the chief part of his own happiness ; but he had a strong sense of fellowship with them. When he advanced towards the labourers they had

not gone to work again, but were standing in that form of rural grouping which consists in each turning a shoulder towards the other, at a
distance of two or three yards.   They looked rather sulkily at Caleb,
who walked quickly with one hand in his pocket and the other thrust
between the buttons of his waistcoat, and had his everyday mild air
when he paused among them.

"Why, my lads, how's this?" he began, taking as usual to brief
phrases, which seemed pregnant to himself, because he had many
thoughts lying under them, like the abundant roots of a plant that
just manages to peep above the water.   "How came you to make
such a mistake as this?   Somebody has been telling you lies.   You
thought those men up there wanted to do mischief."

"Aw!" was the answer, dropped at intervals by each according to
his degree of unreadiness.

"Nonsense!   No such thing!   They're looking out to see which
way the railroad is to take.   Now, my lads, you can't hinder the railroad: it will be made whether you like it or not.   And if you go
fighting against it, you'll get yourselves into trouble.   The law gives
those men leave to come here on the land.   The owner has nothing
to say against it, and if you meddle with them you'll have to do with
the constable and Justice Blakesley, and with the handcuffs and Middlemarch jail.   And you might be in for it now, if anybody informed
against you."

Caleb paused here, and perhaps the greatest orator could not have
chosen either his pause or his images better for the occasion.

"But come, you didn't mean any harm.   Somebody told you the
railroad was a bad thing.   That was a lie.   It may do a bit of harm
here and there, to this and to that; and so does the sun in heaven.
But the railway's a good thing."

"Aw! good for the big folks to make money out on," said old Timothy Cooper, who had stayed behind turning his hay while the others
had been gone on their spree ;—" I'n seen lots o' things turn up sin' I
war a young un—the war an' the peace, and the canells, an' the oald
King George, an' the Regen', an' the new King George, an' the new
un as has got a new ne-ame—an' it's been all aloike to the poor mon.[4]
What's the canells been t' him?   They 'n brought him neyther me-at
nor be-acon, nor wage to lay by, if he didn't save it wi' clemmin' his
own inside.[5]   Times ha' got wusser for him sin' I war a young un.
An' so it'll be wi' the railroads.   They'll on'y leave the poor mon
furder behind.   But them are fools as meddle, and so I told the chaps
here.   This is the big folks's world, this is.   But yo're for the big
folks, Muster Garth, yo are."

Timothy was a wiry old labourer, of a type lingering in those times
—who had his savings in a stocking-foot, lived in a lone cottage, and
was not to be wrought on by any oratory, having as little of the feudal
spirit, and believing as little, as if he had not been totally unacquainted
with the Age of Reason and the Rights of Man.   Caleb was in a difficulty known to any person attempting in dark times and unassisted
by miracle to reason with rustics who are in possession of an undeni-

---

4. George III was declared insane in
1811, and his eldest son was named
Regent. In 1820, when George III died,
the Prince Regent became George IV.

He was succeeded in 1830 by William
IV.

5. Clemmin': starving.

able truth which they know through a hard process of feeling, and can let it fall like a giant's club on your neatly-carved argument for a social benefit which they do *not* feel. Caleb had no cant at command, even if he could have chosen to use it ; and he had been accustomed to meet all such difficulties in no other way than by doing his " business " faithfully. He answered—

" If you don't think well of me, Tim, never mind ; that's neither here nor there now. Things may be bad for the poor man—bad they are ; but I want the lads here not to do what will make things worse for themselves. The cattle may have a heavy load, but it won't help 'em to throw it over into the roadside pit, when it's partly their own fodder."

" We war on'y for a bit o' foon," said Hiram, who was beginning to see consequences. " That war all we war arter."

" Well, promise me not to meddle again, and I'll see that nobody informs against you."

" I'n ne'er meddled, an' I'n no call to promise," said Timothy.

" No, but the rest. Come, I'm as hard at work as any of you to-day, and I can't spare much time. Say you'll be quiet without the constable."

" Aw, we wooant meddle — they may do as they loike for oos " — were the forms in which Caleb got his pledges ; and then he hastened back to Fred, who had followed him, and watched him in the gateway.

They went to work, and Fred helped vigorously. His spirits had risen, and he heartily enjoyed a good slip in the moist earth under the hedgerow, which soiled his perfect summer trousers. Was it his successful onset which had elated him, or the satisfaction of helping Mary's father ? Something more. The accidents of the morning had helped his frustrated imagination to shape an employment for himself which had several attractions. I am not sure that certain fibres in Mr Garth's mind had not resumed their old vibration towards the very end which now revealed itself to Fred. For the effective accident is but the touch of fire where there is oil and tow ; and it always appeared to Fred that the railway brought the needed touch. But they went on in silence except when their business demanded speech. At last, when they had finished and were walking away, Mr Garth said—

" A young fellow needn't be a B.A. to do this sort of work, eh, Fred ?"

" I wish I had taken to it before I had thought of being a B.A.," said Fred. He paused a moment, and then added, more hesitatingly, " Do you think I am too old to learn your business, Mr Garth?"

" My business is of many sorts, my boy," said Mr Garth, smiling. " A good deal of what I know can only come from experience : you can't learn it off as you learn things out of a book. But you are young enough to lay a foundation yet." Caleb pronounced the last sentence emphatically, but paused in some uncertainty. He had been under the impression lately that Fred had made up his mind to enter the Church.

" You do think I could do some good at it, if I were to try ?" said Fred, more eagerly.

" That depends," said Caleb, turning his head on one side and lowering his voice, with the air of a man who felt himself to be saying something deeply religious. " You must be sure of two things : you must love your work, and not be always looking over the edge of it, wanting your play to begin. And the other is, you must not be ashamed of your work, and think it would be more honourable to you to be doing something else. You must have a pride in your own work and in learning to do it well, and not be always saying, There's this and there's that—if I had this or that to do, I might make something of it. No matter what a man is—I wouldn't give twopence for him"—here Caleb's mouth looked bitter, and he snapped his fingers —"whether he was the prime minister or the rick-thatcher, if he didn't do well what he undertook to do."

" I can never feel that I should do that in being a clergyman," said Fred, meaning to take a step in argument.

" Then let it alone, my boy," said Caleb, abruptly, " else you'll never be easy. Or, if you *are* easy, you'll be a poor stick."

" That is very nearly what Mary thinks about it," said Fred, colouring. " I think you must know what I feel for Mary, Mr Garth: I hope it does not displease you that I have always loved her better than any one else, and that I shall never love any one as I love her."

The expression of Caleb's face was visibly softening while Fred spoke. But he swung his head with a solemn slowness, and said—

" That makes things more serious, Fred, if you want to take Mary's happiness into your keeping."

" I know that, Mr Garth," said Fred, eagerly, " and I would do anything for *her*. She says she will never have me if I go into the Church ; and I shall be the most miserable devil in the world if I lose all hope of Mary. Really, if I could get some other profession, business—anything that I am at all fit for, I would work hard, I would deserve your good opinion. I should like to have to do with outdoor things. I know a good deal about land and cattle already. I used to believe, you know—though you will think me rather foolish for it—that I should have land of my own. I am sure knowledge of that sort would come easily to me, especially if I could be under you in any way."

" Softly, my boy," said Caleb, having the image of " Susan " before his eyes. " What have you said to your father about all this ? "

" Nothing, yet ; but I must tell him. I am only waiting to know what I can do instead of entering the Church. I am very sorry to disappoint him, but a man ought to be allowed to judge for himself when he is four-and-twenty. How could I know when I was fifteen, what it would be right for me to do now ? My education was a mistake."

" But hearken to this, Fred," said Caleb. " Are you sure Mary is fond of you, or would ever have you ? "

" I asked Mr Farebrother to talk to her, because she had forbidden me—I didn't know what else to do," said Fred, apologetically. " And he says that I have every reason to hope, if I can put myself in an honourable position—I mean, out of the Church. I daresay you think it unwarrantable in me, Mr Garth, to be troubling you and obtruding my own wishes about Mary, before I have done anything at all for myself. Of course I have not the least claim—indeed, I have already a debt to you which will never be discharged, even when I have been able to pay it in the shape of money."

" Yes, my boy, you have a claim," said Caleb, with much feeling in his voice. " The young ones have always a claim on the old to help them forward. I was young myself once and had to do without much help ; but help would have been welcome to me, if it had been only for the fellow-feeling's sake. But I must consider. Come to me to-morrow at the office, at nine o'clock. At the office, mind."

Mr Garth would take no important step without consulting Susan, but it must be confessed that before he reached home he had taken his resolution. With regard to a large number of matters about which other men are decided or obstinate, he was the most easily manageable man in the world. He never knew what meat he would choose, and if Susan had said that they ought to live in a four-roomed cottage, in order to save, he would have said, " Let us go," without inquiring into details. But where Caleb's feeling and judgment strongly pronounced, he was a ruler ; and in spite of his mildness and timidity in reproving, every one about him knew that on the exceptional occasions when he chose, he was absolute. He never, indeed, chose to be absolute except on some one else's behalf. On ninety-nine points Mrs Garth decided, but on the hundredth she was often aware that she would have to perform the singularly difficult task of carrying out her own principle, and to make herself subordinate.

" It is come round as I thought, Susan," said Caleb, when they were seated alone in the evening. He had already narrated the adventure which had brought about Fred's sharing in his work, but had kept back the further result. " The children *are* fond of each other —I mean, Fred and Mary."

Mrs Garth laid her work on her knee, and fixed her penetrating eyes anxiously on her husband.

" After we'd done our work, Fred poured it all out to me. He can't bear to be a clergyman, and Mary says she won't have him if he is one ; and the lad would like to be under me and give his mind to business. And I've determined to take him and make a man of him."

" Caleb ! " said Mrs Garth, in a deep contralto, expressive of resigned astonishment.

" It's a fine thing to do," said Mr Garth, settling himself firmly against the back of his chair, and grasping the elbows. " I shall have trouble with him, but I think I shall carry it through. The lad loves Mary, and a true love for a good woman is a great thing, Susan. It shapes many a rough fellow."

" Has Mary spoken to you on the subject ? " said Mrs Garth, secretly a little hurt that she had to be informed on it herself.

" Not a word. I asked her about Fred once ; I gave her a bit of a warning. But she assured me she would never marry an idle, self-indulgent man—nothing since. But it seems Fred set on Mr Farebrother to talk to her, because she had forbidden him to speak himself, and Mr Farebrother has found out that she is fond of Fred, but says he must not be a clergyman. Fred's heart is fixed on Mary, that I can see : it gives me a good opinion of the lad—and we always liked him, Susan."

" It is a pity for Mary, I think," said Mrs Garth.

" Why—a pity ? "

" Because, Caleb, she might have had a man who is worth twenty Fred Vincys."

" Ah ? " said Caleb, with surprise.

" I firmly believe that Mr Farebrother is attached to her, and meant to make her an offer ; but of course, now that Fred has used him as an envoy, there is an end to that better prospect." There was a severe precision in Mrs Garth's utterance. She was vexed and disappointed, but she was bent on abstaining from useless words.

Caleb was silent a few moments under a conflict of feelings. He looked at the floor and moved his head and hands in accompaniment to some inward argumentation. At last he said—

" That would have made me very proud and happy, Susan, and I should have been glad for your sake. I've always felt that your belongings have never been on a level with you. But you took me, though I was a plain man."

" I took the best and 'cleverest man I had ever known," said Mrs Garth, convinced that *she* would never have loved any one who came short of that mark.

" Well, perhaps others thought you might have done better. But it would have been worse for me. And that is what touches me close about Fred. The lad is good at bottom, and clever enough to do, if he's put in the right way ; and he loves and honours my daughter beyond anything, and she has given him a sort of promise according to what he turns out. I say, that young man's soul is in my hand ; and I'll do the best I can for him, so help me God ! It's my duty, Susan."

Mrs Garth was not given to tears, but there was a large one rolling down her face before her husband had finished. It came from the pressure of various feelings, in which there was much affection and some vexation. She wiped it away quickly, saying—

" Few men besides you would think it a duty to add to their anxieties in that way, Caleb."

" That signifies nothing—what other men would think. I've got a clear feeling inside me, and that I shall follow ; and I hope your heart will go with me, Susan, in making everything as light as can be to Mary, poor child."

Caleb, leaning back in his chair, looked with anxious appeal towards his wife. She rose and kissed him, saying, " God bless you, Caleb ! Our children have a good father."

But she went out and had a hearty cry to make up for the suppression of her words. She felt sure that her husband's conduct would be misunderstood, and about Fred she was rational and unhopeful. Which would turn out to have the more foresight in it—her rationality or Caleb's ardent generosity ?

When Fred went to the office the next morning, there was a test to be gone through which he was not prepared for.

" Now Fred," said Caleb, " you will have some desk-work. I have always done a good deal of writing myself, but I can't do without help, and as I want you to understand the accounts and get the values into your head, I mean to do without another clerk. So you must buckle to. How are you at writing and arithmetic ?"

Fred felt an awkward movement of the heart ; he had not thought of desk-work ; but he was in a resolute mood, and not going to shrink. " I'm not afraid of arithmetic, Mr Garth : it always came easily to me. I think you know my writing."

" Let us see," said Caleb, taking up a pen, examining it carefully and handing it, well dipped, to Fred with a sheet of ruled paper. "Copy me a line or two of that valuation, with the figures at the end."

At that time the opinion existed that it was beneath a gentleman to write legibly, or with a hand in the least suitable to a clerk. Fred wrote the lines demanded in a hand as gentlemanly as that of any viscount or bishop of the day : the vowels were all alike and the consonants only distinguishable as turning up or down, the strokes had a blotted solidity and the letters disdained to keep the line—in short, it was a manuscript of that venerable kind easy to interpret when you know beforehand what the writer means.

As Caleb looked on, his visage showed a growing depression, but when Fred handed him the paper he gave something like a snarl, and wrapped the paper passionately with the back of his hand. Bad work like this dispelled all Caleb's mildness.

"The deuce !" he exclaimed, snarlingly. "To think that this is a country where a man's education may cost hundreds and hundreds, and it turns you out this !" Then in a more pathetic tone, pushing up his spectacles and looking at the unfortunate scribe, "The Lord have mercy on us, Fred, I can't put up with this !"

"What can I do, Mr Garth ?" said Fred, whose spirits had sunk very low, not only at the estimate of his handwriting, but at the vision of himself as liable to be ranked with office-clerks.

"Do ? Why, you must learn to form your letters and keep the line. What's the use of writing at all if nobody can understand it ?" asked Caleb, energetically, quite preoccupied with the bad quality of the work. "Is there so little business in the world that you must be sending puzzles over the country ? But that's the way people are brought up. I should lose no end of time with the letters some people send me, if Susan did not make them out for me. It's disgusting." Here Caleb tossed the paper from him.

Any stranger peeping into the office at that moment might have wondered what was the drama between the indignant man of business, and the fine-looking young fellow whose blond complexion was getting rather patchy as he bit his lip with mortification. Fred was struggling with many thoughts. Mr Garth had been so kind and encouraging at the beginning of their interview, that gratitude and hopefulness had been at a high pitch, and the downfall was proportionate. He had not thought of desk-work—in fact, like the majority of young gentlemen, he wanted an occupation which should be free from disagreeables. I cannot tell what might have been the consequences if he had not distinctly promised himself that he would go to Lowick to see Mary and tell her that he was engaged to work under her father. He did not like to disappoint himself there.

"I am very sorry," were all the words that he could muster. But Mr Garth was already relenting.

"We must make the best of it, Fred," he began, with a return to his usual quiet tone. "Every man can learn to write. I taught myself. Go at it with a will, and sit up at night if the day-time isn't enough. We'll be patient, my boy. Callum shall go on with the books for a bit, while you are learning. But now I must be off," said Caleb, rising. "You must let your father know our agreement. You'll save me Callum's salary, you know, when you can write ; and I can afford to give you eighty pounds for the first year, and more after."

When Fred made the necessary disclosure to his parents, the relative effect on the two was a surprise which entered very deeply into his memory. He went straight from Mr Garth's office to the warehouse, rightly feeling that the most respectful way in which he could behave to his ·father, was to make the painful communication as gravely and formally as possible. Moreover, the decision would be more certainly understood to be final, if the interview took place in his father's gravest hours, which were always those spent in his private room at the warehouse.

Fred entered on the subject directly, and declared briefly what he had done and was resolved to do, expressing at the end his regret that he should be the cause of disappointment to his father, and taking the blame on his own deficiencies. The regret was genuine, and inspired Fred with strong, simple words.

Mr Vincy listened in profound surprise without uttering even an exclamation, a silence which in his impatient temperament was a sign of unusual emotion. He had not been in good spirits about trade that morning, and the slight bitterness in his lips grew intense as he listened. When Fred had ended, there was a pause of nearly a minute, during which Mr Vincy replaced a book in his desk and turned the key emphatically. Then he looked at his son steadily, and said—

" So you've made up your mind at last, sir ? "

" Yes, father."

" Very well ; stick to it. I've no more to say. You've thrown away your education, and gone down a step in life, when I had given you the means of rising, that's all."

" I am very sorry that we differ, father. I think I can be quite as much of a gentleman at the work I have undertaken, as if I had been a curate. But I am grateful to you for wishing to do the best for me."

" Very well ; I have no more to say. I wash my hands of you. I only hope, when you have a son of your own he will make a better return for the pains you spend on him."

This was very cutting to Fred. His father was using that unfair advantage possessed by us all when we are in a pathetic situation and see our own past as if it were simply part of the pathos. In reality, Mr Vincy's wishes about his son had had a great deal of pride, inconsiderateness, and egoistic folly in them. But still the disappointed father held a strong lever ; and Fred felt as if he were being banished with a malediction.

" I hope you will not object to my remaining at home, sir ? " he said, after rising to go ; " I shall have a sufficient salary to pay for my board, as of course I should wish to do."

" Board, be hanged ! " said Mr Vincy, recovering himself in his disgust at the notion that Fred's keep would be missed at his table. " Of course your mother will want you to stay. But I shall keep no horse for you, you understand ; and you will pay your own tailor. You will do with a suit or two less, I fancy, when you have to pay for 'em."

Fred lingered ; there was still something to be said. At last it came.

" I hope you will shake hands with me, father, and forgive me the vexation I have caused you."

Mr Vincy from his chair threw a quick glance upward at his son, who had advanced near to him, and then gave his hand, saying hurriedly, " Yes, yes, let us say no more."

Fred went through much more narrative and explanation with his mother, but she was inconsolable, having before her eyes what perhaps her husband had never thought of, the certainty that Fred would marry Mary Garth, that her life would henceforth be spoiled by a perpetual infusion of Garths and their ways, and that her darling boy, with his beautiful face and stylish air " beyond anybody else's son in Middlemarch," would be sure to get like that family in plainness of appearance and carelessness about his clothes. To her it seemed that there was a Garth conspiracy to get possession of the desirable Fred, but she dared not enlarge on this opinion, because a slight hint of it had made him " fly out" at her as he had never done before. Her temper was too sweet for her to show any anger ; but she felt that her happiness had received a bruise, and for several days merely to look at Fred made her cry a little as if he were the subject of some baleful prophecy. Perhaps she was the slower to recover her usual cheerfulness because Fred had warned her that she must not reopen the sore question with his father, who had accepted his decision and forgiven him. If her husband had been vehement against Fred, she would have been urged into defence of her darling. It was the end of the fourth day when Mr Vincy said to her—

" Come, Lucy, my dear, don't be so down-hearted. You always have spoiled the boy, and you must go on spoiling him."

" Nothing ever did cut me so before, Vincy," said the wife, her fair throat and chin beginning to tremble again, " only his illness."

" Pooh, pooh, never mind ! We must expect to have trouble with our children. Don't make it worse by letting me see you out of spirits."

" Well, I won't," said Mrs Vincy, roused by this appeal and adjusting herself with a little shake as of a bird which lays down its ruffled plumage.

" It won't do to begin making a fuss about one," said Mr Vincy, wishing to combine a little grumbling with domestic cheerfulness. " There's Rosamond as well as Fred."

" Yes, poor thing. I'm sure I felt for her being disappointed of her baby ; but she got over it nicely."

" Baby, pooh ! I can see Lydgate is making a mess of his practice, and getting into debt too, by what I hear. I shall have Rosamond coming to me with a pretty tale one of these days. But they'll get no money from me, I know. Let *his* family help him. I never did like that marriage. But it's no use talking. Ring the bell for lemons, and don't look dull any more, Lucy. I'll drive you and Louisa to Riverston to-morrow."

CHAPTER LVII.

They numbered scarce eight summers when a name
   Rose on their souls and stirred such motions there
As thrill the buds and shape their hidden frame
   At penetration of the quickening air :
His name who told of loyal Evan Dhu,
   Of quaint Bradwardine, aud Vich Ian Vor,
Making the little world their childhood knew
   Large with a land of mountain, lake, and scaur,
And larger yet with wonder, love, belief
   Toward Walter Scott, who living far away
Sent them this wealth of joy and noble grief.
   The book and they must part, but day by day,
In lines that thwart like portly spiders ran,
They wrote the tale, from Tully Veolan. 1

THE evening that Fred Vincy walked to Lowick Parsonage (he had begun to see that this was a world in which even a spirited young man must sometimes walk for want of a horse to carry him) he set out at five o'clock and called on Mrs Garth by the way, wishing to assure himself that she accepted their new relations willingly.

He found the family group, dogs and cats included, under the great apple-tree in the orchard. It was a festival with Mrs Garth, for her eldest son, Christy, her peculiar joy and pride, had come home for a short holiday—Christy, who held it the most desirable thing in the world to be a tutor, to study all literatures and be a regenerate Porson, and who was an incorporate criticism on poor Fred, a sort of object-lesson given to him by the educational mother. 2 Christy himself, a square-browed, broad-shouldered masculine edition of his mother not much higher than Fred's shoulder—which made it the harder that he should be held superior—was always as simple as possible, and thought no more of Fred's disinclination to scholarship than of a giraffe's, wishing that he himself were more of the same height. He was lying on the ground now by his mother's chair, with his straw-hat laid flat over his eyes, while Jim on the other side was reading aloud from that beloved writer who has made a chief part in the happiness of many young lives. 3 The volume was ' Ivanhoe,' and Jim was in the great archery scene at the tournament, but suffered much interruption from Ben, who had fetched his own old bow and arrows, and was making himself dreadfully disagreeable, Letty thought, by begging all present to observe his random shots, which no one wished to do except Brownie, the active-minded but probably shallow mongrel, while the grizzled Newfoundland lying in the sun looked on with the dull-eyed neutrality of extreme old age. Letty herself, showing as to her mouth and pinafore some slight signs that she had been assisting at the gathering of the cherries which stood in

1. The reference is to Scott's *Waverley*, which GE was reading as a girl in 1827.
2. Richard Porson (1759–1808), English classical scholar.
3. I.e., Sir Walter Scott.

a coral-heap on the tea-table, was now seated on the grass, listening open-eyed to the reading.

But the centre of interest was changed for all by the arrival of Fred Vincy. When, seating himself on a garden-stool, he said that he was on his way to Lowick Parsonage, Ben, who had thrown down his bow, and snatched up a reluctant half-grown kitten instead, strode across Fred's outstretched leg and said, " Take me ! "

" Oh, and me too," said Letty.

" You can't keep up with Fred and me," said Ben.

" Yes, I can. Mother, please say that I am to go," urged Letty, whose life was much checkered by resistance to her depreciation as a girl.

" *I* shall stay with Christy," observed Jim ; as much as to say that he had the advantage of those simpletons ; whereupon Letty put her hand up to her head and looked with jealous indecision from the one to the other.

" Let us all go and see Mary," said Christy, opening his arms.

" No, my dear child, we must not go in a swarm to the parsonage. And that old Glasgow suit of yours would never do. Besides, your father will come home. We must let Fred go alone. He can tell Mary that you are here, and she will come back to-morrow."

Christy glanced at his own threadbare knees, and then at Fred's beautiful white trousers. Certainly Fred's tailoring suggested the advantages of an English university, and he had a graceful way even of looking warm and of pushing his hair back with his handkerchief.

" Children, run away," said Mrs Garth ; " it is too warm to hang about your friends. Take your brother and show him the rabbits."

The eldest understood, and led off the children immediately. Fred felt that Mrs Garth wished to give him an opportunity of saying anything he had to say, but he could only begin by observing—

" How glad you must be to have Christy here ! "

" Yes ; he has come sooner than I expected. He got down from the coach at nine o'clock, just after his father went out. I am longing for Caleb to come and hear what wonderful progress Christy is making. He has paid his expenses for the last year by giving lessons, carrying on hard study at the same time. He hopes soon to get a private tutorship and go abroad."

" He is a great fellow," said Fred, to whom these cheerful truths had a medicinal taste, " and no trouble to anybody." After a slight pause, he added, " But I fear you will think that I am going to be a great deal of trouble to Mr Garth."

" Caleb likes taking trouble : he is one of those men who always do more than any one would have thought of asking them to do," answered Mrs Garth. She was knitting, and could either look at Fred or not, as she chose—always an advantage when one is bent on loading speech with salutary meaning ; and though Mrs Garth intended to be duly reserved, she did wish to say something that Fred might be the better for.

" I know you think me very undeserving, Mrs Garth, and with good reason," said Fred, his spirit rising a little at the perception of something like a disposition to lecture him. " I happen to have behaved just the worst to the people I can't help wishing for the most from. But while two men like Mr Garth and Mr Farebrother have not given me up, I don't see why I should give myself up." Fred thought it might be well to suggest these masculine examples to Mrs Garth.

"Assuredly," said she, with gathering emphasis. "A young man for whom two such elders had devoted themselves would indeed be culpable if he threw himself away and made their sacrifices vain."

Fred wondered a little at this strong language, but only said, " I hope it will not be so with me, Mrs Garth, since I have some encouragement to believe that I may win Mary. Mr Garth has told you about that? You were not surprised, I daresay?" Fred ended, innocently referring only to his own love as probably evident enough.

"Not surprised that Mary has given you encouragement?" returned Mrs Garth, who thought it would be well for Fred to be more alive to the fact that Mary's friends could not possibly have wished this beforehand, whatever the Vincys might suppose. " Yes, I confess I *was* surprised."

" She never did give me any — not the least in the world, when I talked to her myself," said Fred, eager to vindicate Mary. " But when I asked Mr Farebrother to speak for me, she allowed him to tell me there was a hope."

The power of admonition which had begun to stir in Mrs Garth had not yet discharged itself. It was a little too provoking even for *her* self-control that this blooming youngster should flourish on the disappointments of sadder and wiser people—making a meal of a nightingale and never knowing it — and that all the while his family should suppose that hers was in eager need of this sprig ; and her vexation had fermented the more actively because of its total repression towards her husband. Exemplary wives will sometimes find scapegoats in this way. She now said with energetic decision, " You made a great mistake, Fred, in asking Mr Farebrother to speak for you."

" Did I ?" said Fred, reddening instantaneously. He was alarmed, but at a loss to know what Mrs Garth meant, and added, in an apologetic tone, " Mr Farebrother has always been such a friend of ours ; and Mary, I knew, would listen to him gravely ; and he took it on himself quite readily."

" Yes, young people are usually blind to everything but their own wishes, and seldom imagine how much those wishes cost others," said Mrs Garth. She did not mean to go beyond this salutary general doctrine, and threw her indignation into a needless unwinding of her worsted, knitting her brow at it with a grand air.

" I cannot conceive how it could be any pain to Mr Farebrother," said Fred, who nevertheless felt that surprising conceptions were beginning to form themselves.

" Precisely ; you cannot conceive," said Mrs Garth, cutting her words as neatly as possible.

For a moment Fred looked at the horizon with a dismayed anxiety, and then turning with a quick movement said almost sharply—

" Do you mean to say, Mrs Garth, that Mr Farebrother is in love with Mary ?"

" And if it were so, Fred, I think you are the last person who ought to be surprised," returned Mrs Garth, laying her knitting down beside her and folding her arms. It was an unwonted sign of emotion in her that she should put her work out of her hands. In fact her feelings were divided between the satisfaction of giving Fred his discipline and the sense of having gone a little too far. Fred took his hat and stick and rose quickly.

"Then you think I am standing in his way, and in Mary's too?" he said, in a tone which seemed to demand an answer.

Mrs Garth could not speak immediately. She had brought herself into the unpleasant position of being called on to say what she really felt, yet what she knew there were strong reasons for concealing. And to her the consciousness of having exceeded in words was peculiarly mortifying. Besides, Fred had given out unexpected electricity, and he now added, " Mr Garth seemed pleased that Mary should be attached to me. He could not have known anything of this."

Mrs Garth felt a severe twinge at this mention of her husband, the fear that Caleb might think her in the wrong not being easily endurable. She answered, wanting to check unintended consequences—

" I spoke from inference only. I am not aware that Mary knows anything of the matter."

But she hesitated to beg that he would keep entire silence on a subject which she had herself unnecessarily mentioned, not being used to stoop in that way ; and while she was hesitating there was already a rush of unintended consequences under the apple-tree where the tea-things stood. Ben, bouncing across the grass with Brownie at his heels, and seeing the kitten dragging the knitting by a lengthening line of wool, shouted and clapped his hands ; Brownie barked, the kitten, desperate, jumped on the tea-table and upset the milk, then jumped down again and swept half the cherries with it ; and Ben, snatching up the half-knitted sock-top, fitted it over the kitten's head as a new source of madness, while Letty arriving cried out to her mother against this cruelty — it was a history as full of sensation as "This is the house that Jack built." Mrs Garth was obliged to interfere, the other young ones came up and the *tête-à-tête* with Fred was ended. He got away as soon as he could, and Mrs Garth could only imply some retractation of her severity by saying "God bless you" when she shook hands with him.

She was unpleasantly conscious that she had been on the verge of speaking as "one of the foolish women speaketh"—telling first and entreating silence after. [4] But she had not entreated silence, and to prevent Caleb's blame she determined to blame herself and confess all to him that very night. It was curious what an awful tribunal the mild Caleb's was to her, whenever he set it up. But she meant to point out to him that the revelation might do Fred Vincy a great deal of good.

No doubt it was having a strong effect on him as he walked to Lowick. Fred's light hopeful nature had perhaps never had so much of a bruise as from this suggestion that if he had been out of the way Mary might have made a thoroughly good match. Also he was piqued that he had been what he called such a stupid lout as to ask

4. The quotation is from Job 2:10.

that intervention from Mr Farebrother. But it was not in a lover's nature—it was not in Fred's, that the new anxiety raised about Mary's feeling should not surmount every other. Notwithstanding his trust in Mr Farebrother's generosity, notwithstanding what Mary had said to him, Fred could not help feeling that he had a rival : it was a new consciousness, and he objected to it extremely, not being in the least ready to give up Mary for her good, being ready rather to fight for her with any man whatsoever. But the fighting with Mr Farebrother must be of a metaphorical kind, which was much more difficult to Fred than the muscular. Certainly this experience was a discipline for Fred hardly less sharp than his disappointment about his uncle's will. The iron had not entered into his soul, but he had begun to imagine what the sharp edge would be. It did not once occur to Fred that Mrs Garth might be mistaken about Mr Farebrother, but he suspected that she might be wrong about Mary. Mary had been staying at the parsonage lately, and her mother might know very little of what had been passing in her mind.

He did not feel easier when he found her looking cheerful with the three ladies in the drawing-room. They were in animated discussion on some subject which was dropped when he entered, and Mary was copying the labels from a heap of shallow cabinet drawers, in a minute handwriting which she was skilled in. Mr Farebrother was somewhere in the village, and the three ladies knew nothing of Fred's peculiar relation to Mary : it was impossible for either of them to propose that they should walk round the garden, and Fred predicted to himself that he should have to go away without saying a word to her in private. He told her first of Christy's arrival and then of his own engagement with her father ; and he was comforted by seeing that this latter news touched her keenly. She said hurriedly, "I am so glad," and then bent over her writing to hinder any one from noticing her face. But here was a subject which Mrs Farebrother could not let pass.

"You don't mean, my dear Miss Garth, that you are glad to hear of a young man giving up the Church for which he was educated : you only mean that things being so, you are glad that he should be under an excellent man like your father."

"No, really, Mrs Farebrother, I am glad of both, I fear," said Mary, cleverly getting rid of one rebellious tear. "I have a dreadfully secular mind. I never liked any clergyman except the Vicar of Wakefield and Mr Farebrother."

"Now why, my dear ?" said Mrs Farebrother, pausing on her large wooden knitting-needles and looking at Mary. "You have always a good reason for your opinions, but this astonishes me. Of course I put out of the question those who preach new doctrine. But why should you dislike clergymen ?"

"Oh dear," said Mary, her face breaking into merriment as she seemed to consider a moment, "I don't like their neckcloths."

"Why, you don't like Camden's, then," said Miss Winifred, in some anxiety.

"Yes, I do," said Mary. "I don't like the other clergymen's neckcloths, because it is they who wear them."

"How very puzzling !" said Miss Noble, feeling that her own intellect was probably deficient.

" My dear, you are joking. You would have better reasons than these for slighting so respectable a class of men," said Mrs Farebrother, majestically.

" Miss Garth has such severe notions of what people should be that it is difficult to satisfy her," said Fred.

" Well, I am glad at least that she makes an exception in favour of my son," said the old lady.

Mary was wondering at Fred's piqued tone, when Mr Farebrother came in and had to hear the news about the engagement under Mr Garth. At the end he said with quiet satisfaction, " *That* is right ; " and then bent to look at Mary's labels and praise her handwriting. Fred felt horribly jealous—was glad, of course, that Mr Farebrother was so estimable, but wished that he had been ugly and fat as men at forty sometimes are. It was clear what the end would be, since Mary openly placed Farebrother above everybody, and these women were all evidently encouraging the affair. He was feeling sure that he should have no chance of speaking to Mary, when Mr Farebrother said—

" Fred, help me to carry these drawers back into my study—you have never seen my fine new study. Pray come too, Miss Garth. I want you to see a stupendous spider I found this morning."

Mary at once saw the Vicar's intention. He had never since the memorable evening deviated from his old pastoral kindness towards her, and her momentary wonder and doubt had quite gone to sleep. Mary was accustomed to think rather rigorously of what was probable, and if a belief flattered her vanity she felt warned to dismiss it as ridiculous, having early had much exercise in such dismissals. It was as she had foreseen : when Fred had been asked to admire the fittings of the study, and she had been asked to admire the spider, Mr Farebrother said—

" Wait here a minute or two. I am going to look out an engraving which Fred is tall enough to hang for me. I shall be back in a few minutes." And then he went out. Nevertheless, the first word Fred said to Mary was—

" It is of no use, whatever I do, Mary. You are sure to marry Farebrother at last." There was some rage in his tone.

" What do you mean, Fred ?" Mary exclaimed indignantly, blushing deeply, and surprised out of all her readiness in reply.

" It is impossible that you should not see it all clearly enough—you who see everything."

" I only see that you are behaving very ill, Fred, in speaking so of Mr Farebrother after he has pleaded your cause in every way. How can you have taken up such an idea ?"

Fred was rather deep, in spite of his irritation. If Mary had really been unsuspicious, there was no good in telling her what Mrs Garth had said.

" It follows as a matter of course," he replied. " When you are continually seeing a man who beats me in everything, and whom you set up above everybody, I can have no fair chance."

" You are very ungrateful, Fred," said Mary. " I wish I had never told Mr Farebrother that I cared for you in the least."

" No, I am not ungrateful ; I should be the happiest fellow in the world if it were not for this. I told your father everything, and he

was very kind ; he treated me as if I were his son. I could go at
the work with a will, writing and everything, if it were not for
this."

"For this ? for what ?" said Mary, imagining now that something
specific must have been said or done.

"This dreadful certainty that I shall be bowled out by Farebrother."
Mary was appeased by her inclination to laugh.

"Fred," she said, peeping round to catch his eyes, which were
sulkily turned away from her, "you are too delightfully ridiculous.
If you were not such a charming simpleton, what a temptation this
would be to play the wicked coquette, and let you suppose that
somebody besides you has made love to me."

"Do you really like me best, Mary ?" said Fred, turning eyes full
of affection on her, and trying to take her hand.

"I don't like you at all at this moment," said Mary, retreating, and
putting her hands behind her. "I only said that no mortal ever
made love to me besides you. And that is no argument that a very
wise man ever will," she ended, merrily.

"I wish you would tell me that you could not possibly ever think
of him," said Fred.

"Never dare to mention this any more to me, Fred," said Mary,
getting serious again. "I don't know whether it is more stupid or
ungenerous in you not to see that Mr Farebrother has left us together
on purpose that we might speak freely. I am disappointed that you
should be so blind to his delicate feeling."

There was no time to say any more before Mr Farebrother came
back with the engraving ; and Fred had to return to the drawing-
room still with a jealous dread in his heart, but yet with comforting
arguments from Mary's words and manner. The result of the conversation was on the whole more painful to Mary : inevitably her
attention had taken a new attitude, and she saw the possibility of
new interpretations. She was in a position in which she seemed to
herself to be slighting Mr Farebrother, and this, in relation to a man
who is much honoured, is always dangerous to the firmness of a
grateful woman. To have a reason for going home the next day was
a relief, for Mary earnestly desired to be always clear that she loved
Fred best. When a tender affection has been storing itself in us
through many of our years, the idea that we could accept any exchange for it seems to be a cheapening of our lives. And we can set
a watch over our affections and our constancy as we can over other
treasures.

"Fred has lost all his other expectations ; he must keep this,"
Mary said to herself, with a smile curling her lips. It was impossible
to help fleeting visions of another kind—new dignities and an acknowledged value of which she had often felt the absence. But these
things with Fred outside them, Fred forsaken and looking sad for
the want of her, could never tempt her deliberate thought.

CHAPTER LVIII.

" For there can live no hatred in thine eye,
   Therefore in that I cannot know thy change :
   In many's looks the false heart's history
   Is writ in moods and frowns and wrinkles strange ;
   But Heaven in thy creation did decree
   That in thy face sweet love should ever dwell ;
   Whate'er thy thoughts or thy heart's workings be,
   Thy looks should nothing thence but sweetness tell."
              —SHAKESPEARE : *Sonnets.* 1

AT the time when Mr Vincy uttered that presentiment about Rosamond, she herself had never had the idea that she should be driven to make the sort of appeal which he foresaw. She had not yet had any anxiety about ways and means, although her domestic life had been expensive as well as eventful. Her baby had been born prematurely, and all the embroidered robes and caps had to be laid by in darkness. This misfortune was attributed entirely to her having persisted in going out on horseback one day when her husband had desired her not to do so ; but it must not be supposed that she had shown temper on the occasion, or rudely told him that she would do as she liked.

What led her particularly to desire horse-exercise was a visit from Captain Lydgate, the baronet's third son, who, I am sorry to say, was detested by our Tertius of that name as a vapid fop " parting his hair from brow to nape in a despicable fashion " (not followed by Tertius himself), and showing an ignorant security that he knew the proper thing to say on every topic. Lydgate inwardly cursed his own folly that he had drawn down this visit by consenting to go to his uncle's on the wedding-tour, and he made himself rather disagreeable to Rosamond by saying so in private. For to Rosamond this visit was a source of unprecedented but gracefully-concealed exultation. She was so intensely conscious of having a cousin who was a baronet's son staying in the house, that she imagined the knowledge of what was implied by his presence to be diffused through all other minds ; and when she introduced Captain Lydgate to her guests, she had a placid sense that his rank penetrated them as if it had been an odour. The satisfaction was enough for the time to melt away some disappointment in the conditions of marriage with a medical man even of good birth : it seemed now that her marriage was visibly as well as ideally floating her above the Middlemarch level, and the future looked bright with letters and visits to and from Quallingham, and vague advancement in consequence for Tertius. Especially as, probably at

1. Sonnet 93.

the Captain's suggestion, his married sister, Mrs Mengan, had come with her maid, and stayed two nights on her way from town. Hence it was clearly worth while for Rosamond to take pains with her music and the careful selection of her lace.

As to Captain Lydgate himself, his low brow, his aquiline nose bent on one side, and his rather heavy utterance, might have been disadvantageous in any young gentleman who had not a military bearing and mustache to give him what is doated on by some flower-like blond heads as "style." He had, moreover, that sort of high-breeding which consists in being free from the petty solicitudes of middle-class gentility, and he was a great critic of feminine charms. Rosamond delighted in his admiration now even more than she had done at Quallingham, and he found it easy to spend several hours of the day in flirting with her. The visit altogether was one of the pleasantest larks he had ever had, not the less so perhaps because he suspected that his queer cousin Tertius wished him away : though Lydgate, who would rather (hyperbolically speaking) have died than have failed in polite hospitality, suppressed his dislike, and only pretended generally not to hear what the gallant officer said, consigning the task of answering him to Rosamond. For he was not at all a jealous husband, and preferred leaving a feather-headed young gentleman alone with his wife to bearing him company.

" I wish you would talk more to the Captain at dinner, Tertius," said Rosamond, one evening when the important guest was gone to Loamford to see some brother officers stationed there. " You really look so absent sometimes—you seem to be seeing through his head into something behind it, instead of looking at him."

" My dear Rosy, you don't expect me to talk much to such a conceited ass as that, I hope," said Lydgate, brusquely. " If he got his head broken, I might look at it with interest, not before."

" I cannot conceive why you should speak of your cousin so contemptuously," said Rosamond, her fingers moving at her work while she spoke with a mild gravity which had a touch of disdain in it.

" Ask Ladislaw if he doesn't think your Captain the greatest bore he ever met with. Ladislaw has almost forsaken the house since he came."

Rosamond thought she knew perfectly well why Mr Ladislaw disliked the Captain : he was jealous, and she liked his being jealous.

" It is impossible to say what will suit eccentric persons," she answered, " but in my opinion Captain Lydgate is a thorough gentleman, and I think you ought not, out of respect to Sir Godwin, to treat him with neglect."

" No, dear ; but we have had dinners for him. And he comes in and goes out as he likes. He doesn't want me."

" Still, when he is in the room, you might show him more attention. He may not be a phœnix of cleverness in your sense ; his profession is different ; but it would be all the better for you to talk a little on his subjects. *I* think his conversation is quite agreeable. And he is anything but an unprincipled man."

" The fact is, you would wish me to be a little more like him, Rosy," said Lydgate, in a sort of resigned murmur, with a smile which was not exactly tender, and certainly not merry. Rosamond was silent and did not smile again ; but the lovely curves of her face looked good-tempered enough without smiling.

Those words of Lydgate's were like a sad milestone marking how far he had travelled from his old dreamland, in which Rosamond Vincy appeared to be that perfect piece of womanhood who would reverence her husband's mind after the fashion of an accomplished mermaid, using her comb and looking-glass and singing her song for the relaxation of his adored wisdom alone. He had begun to distinguish between that imagined adoration and the attraction towards a man's talent because it gives him prestige, and is like an order in his button-hole or an Honourable before his name.

It might have been supposed that Rosamond had travelled too, since she had found the pointless conversation of Mr Ned Plymdale perfectly wearisome; but to most mortals there is a stupidity which is unendurable and a stupidity which is altogether acceptable—else, indeed, what would become of social bonds? Captain Lydgate's stupidity was delicately scented, carried itself with " style," talked with a good accent, and was closely related to Sir Godwin. Rosamond found it quite agreeable and caught many of its phrases.

Therefore since Rosamond, as we know, was fond of horseback, there were plenty of reasons why she should be tempted to resume her riding when Captain Lydgate, who had ordered his man with two horses to follow him and put up at the " Green Dragon," begged her to go out on the grey which he warranted to be gentle and trained to carry a lady—indeed, he had bought it for his sister, and was taking it to Quallingham. Rosamond went out the first time without telling her husband, and came back before his return; but the ride had been so thorough a success, and she declared herself so much the better in consequence, that he was informed of it with full reliance on his consent that she should go riding again.

On the contrary Lydgate was more than hurt—he was utterly confounded that she had risked herself on a strange horse without referring the matter to his wish. After the first almost thundering exclamations of astonishment, which sufficiently warned Rosamond of what was coming, he was silent for some moments.

" However, you have come back safely," he said, at last, in a decisive tone. " You will not go again, Rosy; that is understood. If it were the quietest, most familiar horse in the world, there would always be the chance of accident. And you know very well that I wished you to give up riding the roan on that account."

" But there is the chance of accident indoors, Tertius."

" My darling, don't talk nonsense," said Lydgate, in an imploring tone ; " surely I am the person to judge for you. I think it is enough that I say you are not to go again."

Rosamond was arranging her hair before dinner, and the reflection of her head in the glass showed no change in its loveliness except a little turning aside of the long neck. Lydgate had been moving about with his hands in his pockets, and now paused near her, as if he awaited some assurance.

" I wish you would fasten up my plaits, dear," said Rosamond, letting her arms fall with a little sigh, so as to make a husband ashamed of standing there like a brute. Lydgate had often fastened the plaits before, being among the deftest of men with his large finely-formed fingers. He swept up the soft festoons of plaits and fastened in the tall comb (to such uses do men come !); and what could he do then but kiss the exquisite nape which was shown in all its delicate curves ? But when we do what we have done before, it is often with a difference. Lydgate was still angry, and had not forgotten his point.

" I shall tell the Captain that he ought to have known better than offer you his horse," he said, as he moved away.

" I beg you will not do anything of the kind, Tertius," said Rosamond, looking at him with something more marked than usual in her speech. " It will be treating me as if I were a child. Promise that you will leave the subject to me."

There did seem to be some truth in her objection. Lydgate said, " Very well," with a surly obedience, and thus the discussion ended with his promising Rosamond, and not with her promising him.

In fact, she had been determined not to promise. Rosamond had that victorious obstinacy which never wastes its energy in impetuous resistance. What she liked to do was to her the right thing, and all her cleverness was directed to getting the means of doing it. She meant to go out riding again on the grey, and she did go on the next opportunity of her husband's absence, not intending that he should know until it was late enough not to signify to her. The temptation was certainly great : she was very fond of the exercise, and the gratification of riding on a fine horse, with Captain Lydgate, Sir Godwin's son, on another fine horse by her side, and of being met in this position by any one but her husband, was something as good as her dreams before marriage : moreover, she was riveting the connection with the family at Quallingham, which must be a wise thing to do.

But the gentle grey, unprepared for the crash of a tree that was being felled on the edge of Halsell wood, took fright, and caused a worse fright to Rosamond, leading finally to the loss of her baby. Lydgate could not show his anger towards her, but he was rather bearish to the Captain, whose visit naturally soon came to an end.

In all future conversations on the subject, Rosamond was mildly certain that the ride had made no difference, and that if she had stayed at home the same symptoms would have come on and would have ended in the same way, because she had felt something like them before.

Lydgate could only say, " Poor, poor darling ! "—but he secretly wondered over the terrible tenacity of this mild creature. There was gathering within him an amazed sense of his powerlessness over Rosamond. His superior knowledge and mental force, instead of being, as he had imagined, a shrine to consult on all occasions, was simply set aside on every practical question. He had regarded Rosamond's cleverness as precisely of the receptive kind which became a woman. He was now beginning to find out what that cleverness was —what was the shape into which it had run as into a close network aloof and independent. No one quicker than Rosamond to see causes and effects which lay within the track of her own tastes and interests : she had seen clearly Lydgate's pre-eminence in Middlemarch society, and could go on imaginatively tracing still more agreeable social effects when his talent should have advanced him ; but for her, his professional and scientific ambition had no other relation to these desirable effects than if they had been the fortunate discovery of an ill-smelling oil. And that oil apart, with which she had nothing to do, of course she believed in her own opinion more than she did in his. Lydgate was astounded to find in numberless trifling matters, as well as in this last serious case of the riding, that affection did not make her compliant. He had no doubt that the affection was there, and had no presentiment that he had done anything to repel it. For his own part he said to himself that he loved her as tenderly as ever, and could make up his mind to her negations ; but—well ! Lydgate was much worried, and conscious of new elements in his life as noxious to him as an inlet of mud to a creature that has been used to breathe and bathe and dart after its illuminated prey in the clearest of waters.

Rosamond was soon looking lovelier than ever at her work-table, enjoying drives in her father's phaeton and thinking it likely that she might be invited to Quallingham. She knew that she was a much more exquisite ornament to the drawing-room there than any daughter of the family, and in reflecting that the gentlemen were aware of that, did not perhaps sufficiently consider whether the ladies would be eager to see themselves surpassed.

Lydgate, relieved from anxiety about her, relapsed into what she inwardly called his moodiness — a name which to her covered his thoughtful preoccupation with other subjects than herself, as well as that uneasy look of the brow and distaste for all ordinary things as if they were mixed with bitter herbs, which really made a sort of weather-glass to his vexation and foreboding. These latter states of mind had one cause amongst others, which he had generously but mistakenly avoided mentioning to Rosamond, lest it should affect her health and spirits. Between him and her indeed there was that total missing of each other's mental track, which is too evidently possible even between persons who are continually thinking of each other. To Lydgate it seemed that he had been spending month after month in sacrificing more than half of his best intent and best power to his tenderness for Rosamond ; bearing her little claims and interruptions without impatience, and, above all, bearing without betrayal of bitterness to look through less and less of interfering illusion at the blank unreflecting surface her mind presented to his ardour for the more impersonal ends of his profession and his scientific study, an ardour which he had fancied that the ideal wife must somehow worship as sublime, though not in the least knowing why. But his endurance was mingled with a self-discontent which, if we know how to be candid, we shall confess to make more than half our bitterness under grievances, wife or husband included. It always remains true that if we had been greater, circumstance would have been less strong against us. Lydgate was aware that his concessions to Rosamond were often little more than the lapse of slackening resolution, the creeping paralysis apt to seize an enthusiasm which is out of adjustment to a constant portion of our lives. And on Lydgate's enthusiasm there was constantly pressing not a simple weight of sorrow, but the biting presence of a petty degrading care, such as casts the blight of irony over all higher effort.

This was the care which he had hitherto abstained from mentioning to Rosamond ; and he believed, with some wonder, that it had never entered her mind, though certainly no difficulty could be less mysterious. It was an inference with a conspicuous handle to it, and had been easily drawn by indifferent observers, that Lydgate was in debt ; and he could not succeed in keeping out of his mind for long together that he was every day getting deeper into that swamp, which tempts men towards it with such a pretty covering of flowers and verdure.

It is wonderful how soon a man gets up to his chin there—in a condition in which, spite of himself, he is forced to think chiefly of release, though he had a scheme of the universe in his soul.

Eighteen months ago Lydgate was poor, but had never known the eager want of small sums, and felt rather a burning contempt for any one who descended a step in order to gain them. He was now experiencing something worse than a simple deficit : he was assailed by the vulgar hateful trials of a man who has bought and used a great many things which might have been done without, and which he is unable to pay for, though the demand for payment has become pressing.

How this came about may be easily seen without much arithmetic or knowledge of prices. When a man in setting up a house and preparing for marriage finds that his furniture and other initial expenses come to between four and five hundred pounds more than he has capital to pay for ; when at the end of a year it appears that his household expenses, horses and et cæteras, amount to nearly a thousand, while the proceeds of the practice reckoned from the old books to be worth eight hundred per annum have sunk like a summer pond and make hardly five hundred chiefly in unpaid entries, the plain inference is that, whether he minds it or not, he is in debt. Those were less expensive times than our own, and provincial life was comparatively modest ; but the ease with which a medical man who had lately bought a practice, who thought that he was obliged to keep two horses, whose table was supplied without stint, and who paid an insurance on his life and a high rent for house and garden, might find his expenses doubling his receipts, can be conceived by any one who does not think these details beneath his consideration. Rosamond, accustomed from her childhood to an extravagant household, thought that good housekeeping consisted simply in ordering the best of everything— nothing else " answered ; " and Lydgate supposed that " if things were done at all, they must be done properly"—he did not see how they were to live otherwise. If each head of household expenditure had been mentioned to him beforehand, he would have probably observed that " it could hardly come to much," and if any one had suggested a saving on a particular article—for example, the substitution of cheap fish for dear—it would have appeared to him simply a penny-wise, mean notion. Rosamond, even without such an occasion as Captain Lydgate's visit, was fond of giving invitations, and Lydgate, though he often thought the guests tiresome, did not interfere. This sociability seemed a necessary part of professional prudence, and the entertainment must be suitable. It is true Lydgate was constantly visiting the homes of the poor and adjusting his prescriptions of diet to their small means ; but, dear me ! has it not by this time ceased to be remarkable—is it not rather what we expect in men, that they should have numerous strands of experience lying side by side and never compare them with each other ? Expenditure —like ugliness and errors—becomes a totally new thing when we attach our own personality to it, and measure it by that wide difference which is manifest (in our own sensations) between ourselves and others. Lydgate believed himself to be careless about his dress, and he despised a man who calculated the effects of his costume ; it seemed to him only a matter of course that he had abundance of fresh garments — such things were naturally ordered in sheaves. It must be remembered that he had never hitherto felt the check of importunate debt, and he walked by habit, not by self-criticism. But the check had come.

Its novelty made it the more irritating. He was amazed, disgusted that conditions so foreign to all his purposes, so hatefully disconnected with the objects he cared to occupy himself with, should have lain in ambush and clutched him when he was unaware. And there was not only the actual debt ; there was the certainty that in his present position he must go on deepening it. Two furnishing tradesmen at Brassing, whose bills had been incurred before his marriage, and whom uncalculated current expenses had ever since prevented him from paying, had repeatedly sent him unpleasant letters which had forced themselves on his attention. This could hardly have been more galling to any disposition than to Lydgate's, with his intense pride — his dislike of asking a favour or being under an obligation to any one. He had scorned even to form conjectures about Mr Vincy's intentions on money matters, and nothing but extremity could have induced him to apply to his father-in-law, even if he had not been made aware in various indirect ways since his marriage that Mr Vincy's own affairs were not flourishing, and that the expectation of help from him would be resented. Some men easily trust in the readiness of friends ; it had never in the former part of his life occurred to Lydgate that he should need to do so : he had never thought what borrowing would be to him ; but now that the idea had entered his mind, he felt that he would rather incur any other hardship. In the mean time he had no money or prospects of money ; and his practice was not getting more lucrative.

No wonder that Lydgate had been unable to suppress all signs of inward trouble during the last few months, and now that Rosamond was regaining brilliant health, he meditated taking her entirely into confidence on his difficulties. New conversance with tradesmen's bills had forced his reasoning into a new channel of comparison : he had begun to consider from a new point of view what was necessary and unnecessary in goods ordered, and to see that there must be some change of habits. How could such a change be made without Rosamond's concurrence ? The immediate occasion of opening the disagreeable fact to her was forced upon him.

Having no money, and having privately sought advice as to what security could possibly be given by a man in his position, Lydgate had offered the one good security in his power to the less peremptory creditor, who was a silversmith and jeweller, and who consented to take on himself the upholsterer's credit also, accepting interest for a given term. The security necessary was a bill of sale on the furniture of his house, which might make a creditor easy for a reasonable time about a debt amounting to less than four hundred pounds ; and the silversmith, Mr Dover, was willing to reduce it by taking back a portion of the plate and any other article which was as good as new. " Any other article " was a phrase delicately implying jewellery, and more particularly some purple amethysts costing thirty pounds, which Lydgate had bought as a bridal present.

Opinions may be divided as to his wisdom in making this present : some may think that it was a graceful attention to be expected from a man like Lydgate, and that the fault of any troublesome consequences lay in the pinched narrowness of provincial life at that time, which offered no conveniences for professional people whose fortune was not

proportioned to their tastes ; also, in Lydgate's ridiculous fastidious-
ness about asking his friends for money.

However, it had seemed a question of no moment to him on that
fine morning when he went to give a final order for plate : in the
presence of other jewels enormously expensive, and as an addition to
orders of which the amount had not been exactly calculated, thirty
pounds for ornaments so exquisitely suited to Rosamond's neck and
arms could hardly appear excessive when there was no ready cash for
it to exceed. But at this crisis Lydgate's imagination could not help
dwelling on the possibility of letting the amethysts take their place
again among Mr Dover's stock, though he shrank from the idea of proposing this to Rosamond. Having been roused to discern consequences
which he had never been in the habit of tracing, he was preparing to
act on this discernment with some of the rigour (by no means all) that
he would have applied in pursuing experiment. He was nerving himself to this rigour as he rode from Brassing, and meditated on the
representations he must make to Rosamond.

It was evening when he got home. He was intensely miserable,
this strong man of nine-and-twenty and of many gifts. He was not
saying angrily within himself that he had made a profound mistake ;
but the mistake was at work in him like a recognised chronic disease,
mingling its uneasy importunities with every prospect, and enfeebling
every thought. As he went along the passage to the drawing-room,
he heard the piano and singing. Of course, Ladislaw was there. It
was some weeks since Will had parted from Dorothea, yet he was still
at the old post in Middlemarch. Lydgate had no objection in general
to Ladislaw's coming, but just now he was annoyed that he could not
find his hearth free. When he opened the door the two singers went
on towards the key-note, raising their eyes and looking at him indeed,
but not regarding his entrance as an interruption. To a man galled
with his harness as poor Lydgate was, it is not soothing to see two people
warbling at him, as he comes in with the sense that the painful day
has still pains in store. His face, already paler than usual, took
on a scowl as he walked across the room and flung himself into
a chair.

The singers feeling themselves excused by the fact that they had
had only three bars to sing, now turned round.

" How are you, Lydgate ? " said Will, coming forward to shake
hands.

Lydgate took his hand, but did not think it necessary to speak.

" Have you dined, Tertius ? I expected you much earlier," said
Rosamond, who had already seen that her husband was in a " horrible
humour." She seated herself in her usual place as she spoke.

" I have dined. I should like some tea, please," said Lydgate,
curtly, still scowling and looking markedly at his legs stretched out
before him.

Will was too quick to need more. " I shall be off," he said, reaching his hat.

" Tea is coming," said Rosamond ; " pray don't go."

" Yes, Lydgate is bored," said Will, who had more comprehension
of Lydgate than Rosamond had, and was not offended by his manner,
easily imagining outdoor causes of annoyance.

" There is the more need for you to stay," said Rosamond, playfully, and in her lightest accent; " he will not speak to me all the evening."

" Yes, Rosamond, I shall," said Lydgate, in his strong baritone. " I have some serious business to speak to you about."

No introduction of the business could have been less like that which Lydgate had intended ; but her indifferent manner had been too provoking.

" There ! you see," said Will. " I'm going to the meeting about the Mechanics' Institute. Good-bye ;" and he went quickly out of the room.

Rosamond did not look at her husband, but presently rose and took her place before the tea-tray. She was thinking that she had never seen him so disagreeable. Lydgate turned his dark eyes on her and watched her as she delicately handled the tea-service with her taper fingers, and looked at the objects immediately before her with no curve in her face disturbed, and yet with an ineffable protest in her air against all people with unpleasant manners. For the moment he lost the sense of his wound in a sudden speculation about this new form of feminine impassibility revealing itself in the sylph-like frame which he had once interpreted as the sign of a ready intelligent sensitiveness. His mind glancing back to Laure while he looked at Rosamond, he said inwardly, " Would *she* kill me because I wearied her ? " and then, " It is the way with all women." But this power of generalising which gives men so much the superiority in mistake over the dumb animals, was immediately thwarted by Lydgate's memory of wondering impressions from the behaviour of another woman— from Dorothea's looks and tones of emotion about her husband when Lydgate began to attend him—from her passionate cry to be taught what would best comfort that man for whose sake it seemed as if she must quell every impulse in her except the yearnings of faithfulness and compassion. These revived impressions succeeded each other quickly and dreamily in Lydgate's mind while the tea was being brewed. He had shut his eyes in the last instant of reverie while he heard Dorothea saying, " Advise me—think what I can do—he has been all his life labouring and looking forward. He minds about nothing else—and I mind about nothing else."

That voice of deep-souled womanhood had remained within him as the enkindling conceptions of dead and sceptred genius had remained within him (is there not a genius for feeling nobly which also reigns over human spirits and their conclusions ?) ; the tones were a music from which he was falling away—he had really fallen into a momentary doze, when Rosamond said in her silvery neutral way, " Here is your tea, Tertius," setting it on the small table by his side, and then moved back to her place without looking at him. Lydgate was too hasty in attributing insensibility to her ; after her own fashion, she was sensitive enough, and took lasting impressions. Her impression now was one of offence and repulsion. But then, Rosamond had no scowls and had never raised her voice : she was quite sure that no one could justly find fault with her.

Perhaps Lydgate and she had never felt so far off each other before ; but there were strong reasons for not deferring his revelation, even if he had not already begun it by that abrupt announcement ; indeed some of the angry desire to rouse her into more sensibility on his account which had prompted him to speak prematurely, still mingled with his pain in the prospect of her pain. But he waited till the tray was gone, the candles were lit, and the evening quiet might be counted on : the interval had left time for repelled tenderness to return into the old course. He spoke kindly.

" Dear Rosy, lay down your work and come to sit by me," he said, gently, pushing away the table, and stretching out his arm to draw a chair near his own.

Rosamond obeyed. As she came towards him in her drapery of transparent faintly-tinted muslin, her slim yet round figure never looked more graceful ; as she sat down by him and laid one hand on the elbow of his chair, at last looking at him and meeting his eyes, her delicate neck and cheek and purely-cut lips never had more of that untarnished beauty which touches us in spring-time and infancy and all sweet freshness. It touched Lydgate now, and mingled the early moments of his love for her with all the other memories which were stirred in this crisis of deep trouble. He laid his ample hand softly on hers, saying—

" Dear ! " with the lingering utterance which affection gives to the word. Rosamond too was still under the power of that same past, and her husband was still in part the Lydgate whose approval had stirred delight. She put his hair lightly away from his forehead, then laid her other hand on his, and was conscious of forgiving him.

" I am obliged to tell you what will hurt you, Rosy. But there are things which husband and wife must think of together. I daresay it has occurred to you already that I am short of money."

Lydgate paused ; but Rosamond turned her neck and looked at a vase on the mantelpiece.

" I was not able to pay for all the things we had to get before we were married, and there have been expenses since which I have been obliged to meet. The consequence is, there is a large debt at Brassing —three hundred and eighty pounds—which has been pressing on me a good while, and in fact we are getting deeper every day, for people don't pay me the faster because others want the money. I took pains to keep it from you while you were not well ; but now we must think together about it, and you must help me."

" What can *I* do, Tertius ? " said Rosamond, turning her eyes on him again. That little speech of four words, like so many others in all languages, is capable by varied vocal inflexions of expressing all states of mind from helpless dimness to exhaustive argumentative perception, from the completest self-devoting fellowship to the most neutral aloofness. Rosamond's thin utterance threw into the words " What can *I* do ! " as much neutrality as they could hold. They fell like a mortal chill on Lydgate's roused tenderness. He did not storm in indignation — he felt too sad a sinking of the heart. And when he spoke again it was more in the tone of a man who forces himself to fulfil a task.

" It is necessary for you to know, because I have to give security for a time, and a man must come to make an inventory of the furniture."

Rosamond coloured deeply. " Have you not asked papa for money ?" she said, as soon as she could speak.

" No."

" Then I must ask him ! " she said, releasing her hands from Lydgate's, and rising to stand at two yards' distance from him.

" No, Rosy," said Lydgate, decisively. " It is too late to do that. The inventory will be begun to-morrow. Remember it is a mere security : it will make no difference : it is a temporary affair. I insist upon it that your father shall not know, unless I choose to tell him," added Lydgate, with a more peremptory emphasis.

This certainly was unkind, but Rosamond had thrown him back on evil expectation as to what she would do in the way of quiet steady disobedience. The unkindness seemed unpardonable to her : she was not given to weeping and disliked it, but now her chin and lips began to tremble and the tears welled up. Perhaps it was not possible for Lydgate, under the double stress of outward material difficulty and of his own proud resistance to humiliating consequences, to imagine fully what this sudden trial was to a young creature who had known nothing but indulgence, and whose dreams had all been of new indulgence, more exactly to her taste. But he did wish to spare her as much as he could, and her tears cut him to the heart. He could not speak again immediately ; but Rosamond did not go on sobbing : she tried to conquer her agitation and wiped away her tears, continuing to look before her at the mantelpiece.

" Try not to grieve, darling," said Lydgate, turning his eyes up towards her. That she had chosen to move away from him in this moment of her trouble made everything harder to say, but he must absolutely go on. " We must brace ourselves to do what is necessary. It is I who have been in fault : I ought to have seen that I could not afford to live in this way. But many things have told against me in my practice, and it really just now has ebbed to a low point. I may recover it, but in the mean time we must pull up — we must change our way of living. We shall weather it. When I have given this security I shall have time to look about me ; and you are so clever that if you turn your mind to managing you will school me into carefulness. I have been a thoughtless rascal about squaring prices — but come, dear, sit down and forgive me."

Lydgate was bowing his neck under the yoke like a creature who had talons, but who had Reason too, which often reduces us to meekness. When he had spoken the last words in an imploring tone, Rosamond returned to the chair by his side. His self-blame gave her some hope that he would attend to her opinion, and she said—

" Why can you not put off having the inventory made ? You can send the men away to-morrow when they come."

" I shall not send them away," said Lydgate, the peremptoriness rising again. Was it of any use to explain ?

" If we left Middlemarch, there would of course be a sale, and that would do as well."

" But we are not going to leave Middlemarch."

" I am sure, Tertius, it would be much better to do so. Why can we not go to London ? Or near Durham, where your family is known ? "

" We can go nowhere without money, Rosamond."

" Your friends would not wish you to be without money. And surely these odious tradesmen might be made to understand that, and to wait, if you would make proper representations to them."

" This is idle, Rosamond," said Lydgate, angrily. " You must learn to take my judgment on questions you don't understand. I have made necessary arrangements, and they must be carried out. As to friends, I have no expectations whatever from them, and shall not ask them for anything."

Rosamond sat perfectly still. The thought in her mind was that if she had known how Lydgate would behave, she would never have married him.

"We have no time to waste now on unnecessary words, dear," said Lydgate, trying to be gentle again. "There are some details that I want to consider with you. Dover says he will take a good deal of the plate back again, and any of the jewellery we like. He really behaves very well."

"Are we to go without spoons and forks then ?" said Rosamond, whose very lips seemed to get thinner with the thinness of her utterance. She was determined to make no further resistance or suggestions.

"Oh no, dear !" said Lydgate. "But look here," he continued, drawing a paper from his pocket and opening it ; "here is Dover's account. See, I have marked a number of articles, which if we returned them would reduce the amount by thirty pounds and more. I have not marked any of the jewellery." Lydgate had really felt this point of the jewellery very bitter to himself ; but he had overcome the feeling by severe argument. He could not propose to Rosamond that she should return any particular present of his, but he had told himself that he was bound to put Dover's offer before her, and her inward prompting might make the affair easy.

"It is useless for me to look, Tertius," said Rosamond, calmly ; "you will return what you please." She would not turn her eyes on the paper, and Lydgate, flushing up to the roots of his hair, drew it back and let it fall on his knee. Meanwhile Rosamond quietly went out of the room, leaving Lydgate helpless and wondering. Was she not coming back ? It seemed that she had no more identified herself with him than if they had been creatures of different species and opposing interests. He tossed his head and thrust his hands deep into his pockets with a sort of vengeance. There was still science—there were still good objects to work for. He must give a tug still—all the stronger because other satisfactions were going.

But the door opened and Rosamond re-entered. She carried the leather box containing the amethysts, and a tiny ornamental basket which contained other boxes, and laying them on the chair where she had been sitting, she said, with perfect propriety in her air—

"This is all the jewellery you ever gave me. You can return what you like of it, and of the plate also. You will not, of course, expect me to stay at home to-morrow. I shall go to papa's."

To many women the look Lydgate cast at her would have been more terrible than one of anger : it had in it a despairing acceptance of the distance she was placing between them.

"And when shall you come back again ?" he said, with a bitter edge on his accent.

"Oh, in the evening. Of course I shall not mention the subject to mamma." Rosamond was convinced that no woman could behave more irreproachably than she was behaving ; and she went to sit down at her work-table. Lydgate sat meditating a minute or two, and the result was that he said, with some of the old emotion in his tone—

"Now we have been united, Rosy, you should not leave me to myself in the first trouble that has come."

"Certainly not," said Rosamond ; "I shall do everything it becomes me to do."

"It is not right that the thing should be left to servants, or that I should have to speak to them about it. And I shall be obliged to go out—I don't know how early. I understand your shrinking from the humiliation of these money affairs. But, my dear Rosamond, as a question of pride, which I feel just as much as you can, it is surely better to manage the thing ourselves, and let the servants see as little of it as possible ; and since you are my wife, there is no hindering your share in my disgraces—if there were disgraces."

Rosamond did not answer immediately, but at last she said, "Very well, I will stay at home."

"I shall not touch these jewels, Rosy. Take them away again. But I will write out a list of plate that we may return, and that can be packed up and sent at once."

"The servants will know *that*," said Rosamond, with the slightest touch of sarcasm.

"Well, we must meet some disagreeables as necessities. Where is the ink, I wonder?" said Lydgate, rising, and throwing the account on the larger table where he meant to write.

Rosamond went to reach the inkstand, and after setting it on the table was going to turn away, when Lydgate, who was standing close by, put his arm round her and drew her towards him, saying,

"Come, darling, let us make the best of things. It will only be for a time, I hope, that we shall have to be stingy and particular. Kiss me."

His native warm-heartedness took a great deal of quenching, and it is a part of manliness for a husband to feel keenly the fact that an inexperienced girl has got into trouble by marrying him. She received his kiss and returned it faintly, and in this way an appearance of accord was recovered for the time. But Lydgate could not help looking forward with dread to the inevitable future discussions about expenditure and the necessity for a complete change in their way of living.

CHAPTER LIX.

They said of old the Soul had human shape,
But smaller, subtler than the fleshly self,
So wandered forth for airing when it pleased.
And see ! beside her cherub-face there floats
A pale-lipped form aerial whispering
Its promptings in that little shell her ear.

NEWS is often dispersed as thoughtlessly and effectively as that pollen which the bées carry off (having no idea how powdery they are) when they are buzzing in search of their particular nectar. This fine comparison has reference to Fred Vincy, who on that evening at Lowick Parsonage heard a lively discussion among the ladies on the news which their old servant had got from Tantripp concerning Mr Casaubon's strange mention of Mr Ladislaw in a codicil to his will made not long before his death. Miss Winifred was astounded to find that her brother had known the fact before, and observed that Camden was the most wonderful man for knowing things and not telling them; whereupon Mary Garth said that the codicil had perhaps got mixed up with the habits of spiders, which Miss Winifred never would listen to. Mrs Farebrother considered that the news had something to do with their having only once seen Mr Ladislaw at Lowick, and Miss Noble made many small compassionate mewings.

Fred knew little and cared less about Ladislaw and the Casaubons, and his mind never recurred to that discussion till one day calling on Rosamond at his mother's request to deliver a message as he passed, he happened to see Ladislaw going away. Fred and Rosamond had little to say to each other now that marriage had removed her from collision with the unpleasantness of brothers, and especially now that he had taken what she held the stupid and even reprehensible step of giving up the Church to take to such a business as Mr Garth's. Hence Fred talked by preference of what he considered indifferent news, and "*à propos* of that young Ladislaw" mentioned what he had heard at Lowick Parsonage.

Now Lydgate, like Mr Farebrother, knew a great deal more than he told, and when he had once been set thinking about the relation between Will and Dorothea his conjectures had gone beyond the fact. He imagined that there was a passionate attachment on both sides, and this struck him as much too serious to gossip about. He remembered Will's irritability when he had mentioned Mrs Casaubon, and was the more circumspect. On the whole his surmises, in addition to what he knew of the fact, increased his friendliness and tolerance towards Ladislaw, and made him understand the vacillation which kept him at Middlemarch after he had said that he should go away. It was significant of the separateness between Lydgate's mind and Rosamond's that he had no impulse to speak to her on the subject; indeed, he did not quite trust her reticence towards Will. And he was right there; though he had no vision of the way in which her mind would act in urging her to speak.

When she repeated Fred's news to Lydgate, he said, "Take care you don't drop the faintest hint to Ladislaw, Rosy. He is likely to fly out as if you insulted him. Of course it is a painful affair."

Rosamond turned her neck and patted her hair, looking the image of placid indifference. But the next time Will came when Lydgate was away, she spoke archly about his not going to London as he had threatened.

"I know all about it. I have a confidential little bird," said she, showing very pretty airs of her head over the bit of work held high between her active fingers. "There is a powerful magnet in this neighbourhood."

"To be sure there is. Nobody knows that better than you," said Will, with light gallantry, but inwardly prepared to be angry.

"It is really the most charming romance: Mr Casaubon jealous, and foreseeing that there was no one else whom Mrs Casaubon would so much like to marry, and no one who would so much like to marry her as a certain gentleman; and then laying a plan to spoil all by making her forfeit her property if she did marry that gentleman— and then—and then—and then—oh, I have no doubt the end will be thoroughly romantic."

"Great God! what do you mean?" said Will, flushing over face and ears, his features seeming to change as if he had had a violent shake. " Don't joke ; tell me what you mean."

" You don't really know ?" said Rosamond, no longer playful, and desiring nothing better than to tell in order that she might evoke effects.

" No !" he returned, impatiently.

" Don't know that Mr Casaubon has left it in his will that if Mrs Casaubon marries you she is to forfeit all her property ?"

" How do you know that it is true ?" said Will, eagerly.

" My brother Fred heard it from the Farebrothers."

Will started up from his chair and reached his hat.

" I dare say she likes you better than the property," said Rosamond, looking at him from a distance.

" Pray don't say any more about it," said Will, in a hoarse undertone extremely unlike his usual light voice. " It is a foul insult to her and to me." Then he sat down absently, looking before him, but seeing nothing.

" Now you are angry with *me*," said Rosamond. " It is too bad to bear *me* malice. You ought to be obliged to me for telling you."

" So I am," said Will, abruptly, speaking with that kind of double soul which belongs to dreamers who answer questions.

" I expect to hear of the marriage," said Rosamond, playfully.

" Never ! You will never hear of the marriage !"

With those words uttered impetuously, Will rose, put out his hand to Rosamond, still with the air of a somnambulist, and went away.

When he was gone, Rosamond left her chair and walked to the other end of the room, leaning when she got there against a *chiffonnière*, and looking out of the window wearily. She was oppressed by ennui, and by that dissatisfaction which in women's minds is continually turning into a trivial jealousy, referring to no real claims, springing from no deeper passion than the vague exactingness of egoism, and yet capable of impelling action as well as speech. " There really is nothing to care for much," said poor Rosamond inwardly, thinking of the family at Quallingham, who did not write to her ; and that perhaps Tertius when he came home would tease her about expenses. She had already secretly disobeyed him by asking her father to help them, and he had ended decisively by saying, " I am more likely to want help myself."

CHAPTER LX.

" Good phrases are surely, and ever were, very commendable."
                                                —*Justice Shallow.* [1]

A FEW days afterwards—it was already the end of August—there was an occasion which caused some excitement in Middlemarch : the public, if it chose, was to have the advantage of buying, under the

---

1. Shakespeare, *Henry IV*, Part 2, Act III, Sc. 2, line 76.

distinguished auspices of Mr Borthrop Trumbull, the furniture, books, and pictures which anybody might see by the handbills to be the best in every kind, belonging to Edwin Larcher, Esq. This was not one of the sales indicating the depression of trade ; on the contrary, it was due to Mr Larcher's great success in the carrying business, which warranted his purchase of a mansion near Riverston already furnished in high style by an illustrious Spa physician—furnished indeed with such large framefuls of expensive flesh-painting in the dining-room, that Mrs Larcher was nervous until reassured by finding the subjects to be Scriptural. Hence the fine opportunity to purchasers which was well pointed out in the handbills of Mr Borthrop Trumbull, whose acquaintance with the history of art enabled him to state that the hall furniture, to be sold without reserve, comprised a piece of carving by a contemporary of Gibbons.[2]

At Middlemarch in those times a large sale was regarded as a kind of festival. There was a table spread with the best cold eatables, as at a superior funeral ; and facilities were offered for that generous drinking of cheerful glasses which might lead to generous and cheerful bidding for undesirable articles. Mr Larcher's sale was the more attractive in the fine weather because the house stood just at the end of the town, with a garden and stables attached, in that pleasant issue from Middlemarch called the London Road, which was also the road to the New Hospital and to Mr Bulstrode's retired residence, known as the Shrubs. In short, the auction was as good as a fair, and drew all classes with leisure at command : to some, who risked making bids in order simply to raise prices, it was almost equal to betting at the races. The second day, when the best furniture was to be sold, " everybody" was there ; even Mr Thesiger, the rector of St Peter's, had looked in for a short time, wishing to buy the carved table, and had rubbed elbows with Mr Bambridge and Mr Horrock. There was a wreath of Middlemarch ladies accommodated with seats round the large table in the dining-room, where Mr Borthrop Trumbull was mounted with desk and hammer ; but the rows chiefly of masculine faces behind were often varied by incomings and outgoings both from the door and the large bow-window opening on to the lawn.

"Everybody" that day did not include Mr Bulstrode, whose health could not well endure crowds and draughts. But Mrs Bulstrode had particularly wished to have a certain picture—a Supper at Emmaus, attributed in the catalogue to Guido ; and at the last moment before the day of the sale Mr Bulstrode had called at the office of the ' Pioneer,' of which he was now one of the proprietors, to beg of Mr Ladislaw as a great favour that he would obligingly use his remarkable knowledge of pictures on behalf of Mrs Bulstrode, and judge of the value of this particular painting—" if," added the scrupulously polite banker, " attendance at the sale would not interfere with the arrangements for your departure, which I know is imminent."[3]

This proviso might have sounded rather satirically in Will's ear if he had been in a mood to care about such satire. It referred to an understanding entered into many weeks before with the proprietors

2. Grinling Gibbons (1648–1721) was the master woodcarver to the Crown from the reign of Charles II until his death during the reign of George I.

3. Probably Guido Reni (1575–1642), Bolognese painter.

of the paper, that he should be at liberty any day he pleased to hand over the management to the sub-editor whom he had been training; since he wished finally to quit Middlemarch. But indefinite visions of ambition are weak against the ease of doing what is habitual or beguilingly agreeable; and we all know the difficulty of carrying out a resolve when we secretly long that it may turn out to be unnecessary. In such states of mind the most incredulous person has a private leaning towards miracle: impossible to conceive how our wish could be fulfilled, still—very wonderful things have happened! Will did not confess this weakness to himself, but he lingered. What was the use of going to London at that time of the year? The Rugby men who would remember him were not there; and so far as political writing was concerned, he would rather for a few weeks go on with the 'Pioneer.' At the present moment, however, when Mr Bulstrode was speaking to him, he had both a strengthened resolve to go and an equally strong resolve not to go till he had once more seen Dorothea. Hence he replied that he had reasons for deferring his departure a little, and would be happy to go to the sale.

Will was in a defiant mood, his consciousness being deeply stung with the thought that the people who looked at him probably knew a fact tantamount to an accusation against him as a fellow with low designs which were to be frustrated by a disposal of property. Like most people who assert their freedom with regard to conventional distinction, he was prepared to be sudden and quick at quarrel with any one who might hint that he had personal reasons for that assertion—that there was anything in his blood, his bearing, or his character to which he gave the mask of an opinion. When he was under an irritating impression of this kind he would go about for days with a defiant look, the colour changing in his transparent skin as if he were on the *qui vive*, watching for something which he had to dart upon.[4]

This expression was peculiarly noticeable in him at the sale, and those who had only seen him in his moods of gentle oddity or of bright enjoyment would have been struck with a contrast. He was not sorry to have this occasion for appearing in public before the Middlemarch tribes of Toller, Hackbutt, and the rest, who looked down on him as an adventurer, and were in a state of brutal ignorance about Dante—who sneered at his Polish blood, and were themselves of a breed very much in need of crossing. He stood in a conspicuous place not far from the auctioneer, with a fore-finger in each side-pocket and his head thrown backward, not caring to speak to anybody, though he had been cordially welcomed as a connoiss*ure* by Mr Trumbull, who was enjoying the utmost activity of his great faculties.

And surely among all men whose vocation requires them to exhibit their powers of speech, the happiest is a prosperous provincial auctioneer keenly alive to his own jokes and sensible of his encyclopædic knowledge. Some saturnine, sour-blooded persons might object to be constantly insisting on the merits of all articles from boot-jacks to "Berghems[5];" but Mr Borthrop Trumbull had a kindly liquid in his veins; he was an admirer by nature, and would have

---

.4. On the *qui vive*: in debt.

5. Nicolaes Berghem, or Berchem (1620–83), Danish landscape painter.

liked to have the universe under his hammer, feeling that it would go at a higher figure for his recommendation.

Meanwhile Mrs Larcher's drawing-room furniture was enough for him. When Will Ladislaw had come in, a second fender, said to have been forgotten in its right place, suddenly claimed the auctioneer's enthusiasm, which he distributed on the equitable principle of praising those things most which were most in need of praise. The fender was of polished steel, with much lancet-shaped open-work and a sharp edge.

" Now, ladies," said he, " I shall appeal to you. Here is a fender which at any other sale would hardly be offered without reserve, being, as I may say, for quality of steel and quaintness of design, a kind of thing "—here Mr Trumbull dropped his voice and became slightly nasal, trimming his outlines with his left finger—" that might not fall in with ordinary tastes. Allow me to tell you that by-and-by this style of workmanship will be the only one in vogue — half-a-crown, you said ? thank you—going at half-a-crown, this characteristic fender ; and I have particular information that the antique style is very much sought after in high quarters. Three shillings—three-and-six-pence—hold it well up, Joseph ! Look, ladies, at the chastity of the design—I have no doubt myself that it was turned out in the last century ! Four shillings, Mr Mawmsey ?—four shillings."

" It's not a thing I would put in *my* drawing-room," said Mrs Mawmsey, audibly, for the warning of the rash husband. " I wonder *at* Mrs Larcher. Every blessed child's head that fell against it would be cut in two. The edge is like a knife."

" Quite true," rejoined Mr Trumbull, quickly, " and most uncommonly useful to have a fender at hand that will cut, if you have a leather shoetie or a bit of string that wants cutting and no knife at hand : many a man has been left hanging because there was no knife to cut him down. Gentlemen, here's a fender that if you had the misfortune to hang yourselves would cut you down in no time—with astonishing celerity—four-and-sixpence—five—five-and-sixpence—an appropriate thing for a spare bedroom where there was a four-poster and a guest a little out of his mind—six shillings—thank you, Mr Clintup—going at six shillings—going—gone ! " The auctioneer's glance, which had been searching round him with a preternatural susceptibility to all signs of bidding, here dropped on the paper before him, and his voice too dropped into a tone of indifferent despatch as he said, " Mr Clintup. Be handy, Joseph."

" It was worth six shillings to have a fender you could always tell that joke on," said Mr Clintup, laughing low and apologetically to his next neighbour. He was a diffident though distinguished nurseryman, and feared that the audience might regard his bid as a foolish one.

Meanwhile Joseph had brought a trayful of small articles. " Now, ladies," said Mr Trumbull, taking up one of the articles, " this tray contains a very recherchy lot—a collection of trifles for the drawing-room table—and trifles make the sum of human things—nothing more important than trifles—(yes, Mr Ladislaw, yes, by-and-by)—but pass the tray round, Joseph—these bijoux must be examined, ladies. This I have in my hand is an ingenious contrivance—a sort of practical rebus, I may call it : here, you see, it looks like an elegant heart-shaped box, portable—for the pocket ; there, again, it becomes like a splendid double flower — an ornament for the table ; and now " — Mr Trumbull allowed the flower to fall alarmingly into strings of heart-shaped leaves—" a book of riddles! No less than five hundred printed in a beautiful red. Gentlemen, if I had less of a conscience, I should not wish you to bid high for this lot—I have a longing for it myself. What can promote innocent mirth, and I may say virtue, more than a good riddle?—it hinders profane language, and attaches a man to the society of refined females. This ingenious article itself, without the elegant domino-box, card-basket, &c., ought alone to give a high price to the lot. Carried in the pocket it might make an individual welcome in any society. Four shillings, sir?—four shillings for this remarkable collection of riddles with the et cæteras. Here is a sample : ' How must you spell honey to make it catch lady-birds? Answer—money.' You hear?—lady-birds—honey—money. This is an amusement to sharpen the intellect ; it has a sting—it has what we call satire, and wit without indecency. Four-and-sixpence—five shillings."

The bidding ran on with warming rivalry. Mr Bowyer was a bidder, and this was too exasperating. Bowyer couldn't afford it, and only wanted to hinder every other man from making a figure. The current carried even Mr Horrock with it, but this committal of himself to an opinion fell from him with so little sacrifice of his neutral expression, that the bid might not have been detected as his but for the friendly oaths of Mr Bambridge, who wanted to know what Horrock would do with blasted stuff only fit for haberdashers given over to that state of perdition which the horse-dealer so cordially recognised in the majority of earthly existences. The lot was finally knocked down at a guinea to Mr Spilkins, a young Slender of the neighbourhood, who was reckless with his pocket - money and felt his want of memory for riddles.[6]

" Come, Trumbull, this is too bad — you've been putting some old maid's rubbish into the sale," murmured Mr Toller, getting close to the auctioneer. " I want to see how the prints go, and I must be off soon."

" *Im*mediately, Mr Toller. It was only an act of benevolence which your noble heart would approve. Joseph ! quick with the prints — Lot 235. Now, gentlemen, you who are connoiss*ures*, you are going to have a treat. Here is an engraving of the Duke of Wellington surrounded by his staff on the Field of Waterloo ; and notwithstanding recent events which have, as it were, enveloped our great Hero in a cloud, I will be bold to say—for a man in my line must not be blown about by political winds—that a finer subject—of the modern order, belonging to our own time and epoch — the understanding of man could hardly conceive : angels might, perhaps, but not men, sirs, not men."[7]

" Who painted it?" said Mr Powderell, much impressed.

" It is a proof before the letter, Mr Powderell — the painter is not known," answered Trumbull, with a certain gaspingness in his last words, after which he pursed up his lips and stared round him.

" I'll bid a pound !" said Mr Powderell, in a tone of resolved emotion, as of a man ready to put himself in the breach. Whether from awe or pity, nobody raised the price on him.

Next came two Dutch prints which Mr Toller had been eager for,

---

6. Slender: Abraham Slender, a moronic young man in Shakespeare's *The Merry Wives of Windsor*.

7. The high Tories thought that Welling-ton had betrayed them in repealing the Test Act in 1828, which gave rights to dissenters, and in submitting to O'Connell and Catholic emancipation in 1829.

and after he had secured them he went away. Other prints, and afterwards some paintings, were sold to leading Middlemarchers who had come with a special desire for them, and there was a more active movement of the audience in and out ; some, who had bought what they wanted, going away, others coming in either quite newly or from a temporary visit to the refreshments which were spread under the marquee on the lawn. It was this marquee that Mr Bambridge was bent on buying, and he appeared to like looking inside it frequently, as a foretaste of its possession. On the last occasion of his return from it he was observed to bring with him a new companion, a stranger to Mr Trumbull and every one else, whose appearance, however, led to the supposition that he might be a relative of the horse-dealer's —also "given to indulgence." His large whiskers, imposing swagger, and swing of the leg, made him a striking figure ; but his suit of black, rather shabby at the edges, caused the prejudicial inference that he was not able to afford himself as much indulgence as he liked.

"Who is it you've picked up, Bam ?" said Mr Horrock, aside.

"Ask him yourself," returned Mr Bambridge. "He said he'd just turned in from the road."

Mr Horrock eyed the stranger, who was leaning back against his stick with one hand, using his toothpick with the other, and looking about him with a certain restlessness apparently under the silence imposed on him by circumstances.

At length the *Supper at Emmaus* was brought forward, to Will's immense relief, for he was getting so tired of the proceedings that he had drawn back a little and leaned his shoulder against the wall just behind the auctioneer. He now came forward again, and his eye caught the conspicuous stranger, who, rather to his surprise, was staring at him markedly. But Will was immediately appealed to by Mr Trumbull.

"Yes, Mr Ladislaw, yes ; this interests you as a connoiss*ure*, I think. It is some pleasure," the auctioneer went on with a rising fervour, "to have a picture like this to show to a company of ladies and gentlemen—a picture worth any sum to an individual whose means were on a level with his judgment. It is a painting of the Italian school —by the celebrated *Guydo*, the greatest painter in the world, the chief of the Old Masters, as they are called—I take it, because they were up to a thing or two beyond most of us—in possession of secrets now lost to the bulk of mankind. Let me tell you, gentlemen, I have seen a great many pictures by the Old Masters, and they are not all up to this mark—some of them are darker than you might like, and not family subjects. But here is a *Guydo*—the frame alone is worth pounds—which any lady might be proud to hang up—a suitable thing for what we call a refectory in a charitable institution, if any gentleman of the Corporation wished to show his muni*ficence*. Turn it a little, sir ? yes. Joseph, turn it a little towards Mr Ladislaw— Mr Ladislaw, having been abroad, understands the merit of these things, you observe."

All eyes were for a moment turned towards Will, who said, coolly, "Five pounds." The auctioneer burst out in deep remonstrance—

"Ah ! Mr Ladislaw ! the frame alone is worth that. Ladies and gentlemen, for the credit of the town ! Suppose it should be discovered hereafter that a gem of art has been amongst us in this town, and nobody in Middlemarch awake to it. Five guineas—five seven-six—five ten. Still, ladies, still ! It is a gem, and ' Full many a gem,' as the poet says, has been allowed to go at a nominal price because the public knew no better, because it was offered in circles where there was—I was going to say a low feeling, but no !—Six pounds—six guineas—a *Guydo* of the first order going at six guineas —it is an insult to religion, ladies ; it touches us all as Christians, gentlemen, that a subject like this should go at such a low figure— six pounds ten—seven——"

The bidding was brisk, and Will continued to share in it, remembering that Mrs Bulstrode had a strong wish for the picture, and thinking that he might stretch the price to twelve pounds. But it was knocked down to him at ten guineas, whereupon he pushed his way towards the bow-window and went out. He chose to go under the marquee to get a glass of water, being hot and thirsty : it was empty of other visitors, and he asked the woman in attendance to fetch him some fresh water ; but before she was well gone he was annoyed to see entering the florid stranger who had stared at him. It struck Will at this moment that the man might be one of those political parasitic insects of the bloated kind who had once or twice claimed acquaintance with him as having heard him speak on the Reform question, and who might think of getting a shilling by news. In this light his person, already rather heating to behold on a summer's day, appeared the more disagreeable ; and Will, half-seated on the elbow of a garden-chair, turned his eyes carefully away from the comer. But this signified little to our acquaintance Mr Raffles, who never hesitated to thrust himself on unwilling observation, if it suited his purpose to do so. He moved a step or two till he was in front of Will, and said with full-mouthed haste, " Excuse me, Mr Ladislaw— was your mother's name Sarah Dunkirk ?"

Will, starting to his feet, moved backward a step, frowning, and saying with some fierceness, " Yes, sir, it was. And what is that to you ?"

It was in Will's nature that the first spark it threw out was a direct answer of the question and a challenge of the consequences. To have said, " What is that to you ?" in the first instance, would have seemed like shuffling—as if he minded who knew anything about his origin !

Raffles on his side had not the same eagerness for a collision which was implied in Ladislaw's threatening air. The slim young fellow with his girl's complexion looked like a tiger-cat ready to spring on him. Under such circumstances Mr Raffles's pleasure in annoying his company was kept in abeyance.

" No offence, my good sir, no offence ! I only remember your mother—knew her when she was a girl. But it is your father that you feature, sir. I had the pleasure of seeing your father too. Parents alive, Mr Ladislaw ?"

" No !" thundered Will, in the same attitude as before.

" Should be glad to do you a service, Mr Ladislaw—by Jove, I should ! Hope to meet again."

Hereupon Raffles, who had lifted his hat with the last words, turned himself round with a swing of his leg and walked away. Will looked after him a moment, and could see that he did not re-enter the auction-room, but appeared to be walking towards the road. For an instant he thought that he had been foolish not to let the man go on talking ; — but no ! on the whole he preferred doing without knowledge from that source.

Later in the evening, however, Raffles overtook him in the street, and appearing either to have forgotten the roughness of his former reception or to intend avenging it by a forgiving familiarity, greeted him jovially and walked by his side, remarking at first on the pleasantness of the town and neighbourhood. Will suspected that the man had been drinking and was considering how to shake him off when Raffles said—

" I've been abroad myself, Mr Ladislaw—I've seen the world—used to parley-vous a little. It was at Boulogne I saw your father—a most uncommon likeness you are of him, by Jove ! mouth—nose— eyes—hair turned off your brow just like his—a little in the foreign style. John Bull doesn't do much of that. But your father was very ill when I saw him. Lord, lord ! hands you might see through. You were a small youngster then. Did he get well ? "

" No," said Will, curtly.

" Ah ! Well ! I've often wondered what became of your mother. She ran away from her friends when she was a young lass—a proud-spirited lass, and pretty, by Jove ! *I* knew the reason why she ran away," said Raffles, winking slowly as he looked sideways at Will.

" You know nothing dishonourable of her, sir," said Will, turning on him rather savagely. But Mr Raffles just now was not sensitive to shades of manner.

" Not a bit ! " said he, tossing his head decisively. " She was a little too honourable to like her friends—that was it ! " Here Raffles again winked slowly. " Lord bless you, I knew all about 'em—a little in what you may call the respectable thieving line—the high style of receiving-house—none of your holes and corners—first-rate. Slap-up shop, high profits and no mistake. But Lord ! Sarah would have known nothing about it—a dashing young lady she was—fine. boarding-school—fit for a lord's wife—only Archie Duncan threw it at her out of spite, because she would have nothing to do with him. And so she ran away from the whole concern. I travelled for 'em, sir, in a gentlemanly way—at a high salary. They didn't mind her running away at first—godly folks, sir, very godly—and she was for the stage. The son was alive then, and the daughter was at a discount. Hallo ! here we are at the Blue Bull. What do you say, Mr Ladislaw ? shall we turn in and have a glass ? "

" No, I must say good evening," said Will, dashing up a passage which led into Lowick Gate, and almost running to get out of Raffles's reach.

He walked a long while on the Lowick Road away from the town, glad of the starlit darkness when it came. He felt as if he had had dirt cast on him amidst shouts of scorn. There was this to confirm the fellow's statement—that his mother never would tell him the reason why she had run away from her family.

Well ! what was he, Will Ladislaw, the worse, supposing the truth about that family to be the ugliest ? His mother had braved hardship in order to separate herself from it. But if Dorothea's friends had known this story—if the Chettams had known it—they would have had a fine colour to give their suspicions, a welcome ground for thinking him unfit to come near her. However, let them suspect what they pleased, they would find themselves in the wrong. They would find out that the blood in his veins was as free from the taint of meanness as theirs.

CHAPTER LXI.

"'Inconsistencies,' answered Imlac, 'cannot both be right, but imputed to man they may both be true.'"—*Rasselas.*

THE same night, when Mr Bulstrode returned from a journey to Brassing on business, his good wife met him in the entrance-hall and drew him into his private sitting-room.

"Nicholas," she said, fixing her honest eyes upon him anxiously, "there has been such a disagreeable man here asking for you—it has made me quite uncomfortable."

"What kind of man, my dear," said Mr Bulstrode, dreadfully certain of the answer.

"A red-faced man with large whiskers, and most impudent in his manner. He declared he was an old friend of yours, and said you would be sorry not to see him. He wanted to wait for you here, but I told him he could see you at the Bank to-morrow morning. Most impudent he was!—stared at me, and said his friend Nick had luck in wives. I don't believe he would have gone away, if Blucher had not happened to break his chain and come running round on the gravel—for I was in the garden; so I said, 'You'd better go away—the dog is very fierce, and I can't hold him.' Do you really know anything of such a man?"

"I believe I know who he is, my dear," said Mr Bulstrode, in his usual subdued voice, "an unfortunate, dissolute wretch, whom I helped too much in days gone by. However, I presume you will not be troubled by him again. He will probably come to the Bank—to beg, doubtless."

No more was said on the subject until the next day, when Mr Bulstrode had returned from the town and was dressing for dinner. His wife, not sure that he was come home, looked into his dressing-room and saw him with his coat and cravat off, leaning one arm on a chest of drawers and staring absently at the ground. He started nervously and looked up as she entered.

"You look very ill, Nicholas. Is there anything the matter?"

"I have a good deal of pain in my head," said Mr Bulstrode, who was so frequently ailing that his wife was always ready to believe in this cause of depression.

"Sit down and let me sponge it with vinegar."

Physically Mr Bulstrode did not want the vinegar, but morally the affectionate attention soothed him. Though always polite, it was his habit to receive such services with marital coolness, as his wife's duty. But to-day, while she was bending over him, he said, "You are very good, Harriet," in a tone which had something new in it to her ear ; she did not know exactly what the novelty was, but her woman's solicitude shaped itself into a darting thought that he might be going to have an illness.

"Has anything worried you ?" she said. "Did that man come to you at the Bank ?"

"Yes ; it was as I had supposed. He is a man who at one time might have done better. But he has sunk into a drunken debauched creature."

"Is he quite gone away ?" said Mrs Bulstrode, anxiously ; but for certain reasons she refrained from adding, "It was very disagreeable to hear him calling himself a friend of yours." At that moment she would not have liked to say anything which implied her habitual consciousness that her husband's earlier connections were not quite on a level with her own. Not that she knew much about them. That her husband had at first been employed in a bank, that he had afterwards entered into what he called city business and gained a fortune before he was three-and-thirty, that he had married a widow who was much older than himself—a Dissenter, and in other ways probably of that disadvantageous quality usually perceptible in a first wife if inquired into with the dispassionate judgment of a second—was almost as much as she had cared to learn beyond the glimpses which Mr Bulstrode's narrative occasionally gave of his early bent towards religion, his inclination to be a preacher, and his association with missionary and philanthropic efforts. She believed in him as an excellent man whose piety carried a peculiar eminence in belonging to a layman, whose influence had turned her own mind towards seriousness, and whose share of perishable good had been the means of raising her own position. But she also liked to think that it was well in every sense for Mr Bulstrode to have won the hand of Harriet Vincy ; whose family was undeniable in a Middlemarch light —a better light surely than any thrown in London thoroughfares or dissenting chapel-yards. The unreformed provincial mind distrusted London ; and while true religion was everywhere saving, honest Mrs Bulstrode was convinced that to be saved in the Church was more respectable. She so much wished to ignore towards others that her husband had ever been a London Dissenter, that she liked to keep it out of sight even in talking to him. He was quite aware of this ; indeed in some respects he was rather afraid of this ingenuous wife, whose imitative piety and native worldliness were equally sincere, who had nothing to be ashamed of, and whom he had married out of a thorough inclination still subsisting. But his fears were such as belong to a man who cares to maintain his recognised supremacy : the loss of high consideration from his wife, as from every one else who did not clearly hate him out of enmity to the truth, would be as the beginning of death to him. When she said—

"Is he quite gone away ?"

"Oh, I trust so," he answered, with an effort to throw as much sober unconcern into his tone as possible.

But in truth Mr Bulstrode was very far from a state of quiet trust. In the interview at the Bank, Raffles had made it evident that his eagerness to torment was almost as strong in him as any other greed. He had frankly said that he had turned out of the way to come to

Middlemarch, just to look about him and see whether the neighbourhood would suit him to live in. He had certainly had a few debts to pay more than he expected, but the two hundred pounds were not gone yet : a cool five-and-twenty would suffice him to go away with for the present. What he had wanted chiefly was to see his friend Nick and family, and know all about the prosperity of a man to whom he was so much attached. By-and-by he might come back for a longer stay. This time Raffles declined to be " seen off the premises," as he expressed it—declined to quit Middlemarch under Bulstrode's eyes. He meant to go by coach the next day—if he chose.

Bulstrode felt himself helpless. Neither threats nor coaxing could avail : he could not count on any persistent fear nor on any promise. On the contrary, he felt a cold certainty at his heart that Raffles— unless providence sent death to hinder him—would come back to Middlemarch before long. And that certainty was a terror.

It was not that he was in danger of legal punishment or of beggary : he was in danger only of seeing disclosed to the judgment of his neighbours and the mournful perception of his wife certain facts of his past life which would render him an object of scorn and an opprobrium of the religion with which he had diligently associated himself. The terror of being judged sharpens the memory : it sends an inevitable glare over that long-unvisited past which has been habitually recalled only in general phrases. Even without memory, the life is bound into one by a zone of dependence in growth and decay ; but intense memory forces a man to own his blameworthy past. With memory set smarting like a reopened wound, a man's past is not simply a dead history, an outworn preparation of the present : it is not a repented error shaken loose from the life : it is a still quivering part of himself, bringing shudders and bitter flavours and the tinglings of a merited shame.

Into this second life Bulstrode's past had now risen, only the pleasures of it seeming to have lost their quality. Night and day, without interruption save of brief sleep which only wove retrospect and fear into a fantastic present, he felt the scenes of his earlier life coming between him and everything else, as obstinately as when we look through the window from a lighted room, the objects we turn our backs on are still before us, instead of the grass and the trees. The successive events inward and outward were there in one view : though each might be dwelt on in turn, the rest still kept their hold in the consciousness.

Once more he saw himself the young banker's clerk, with an agreeable person, as clever in figures as he was fluent in speech and fond of theological definition : an eminent though young member of a Calvinistic dissenting church at Highbury, having had striking experience in conviction of sin and sense of pardon. Again he heard himself called for as Brother Bulstrode in prayer meetings, speaking on religious platforms, preaching in private houses. Again he felt himself thinking of the ministry as possibly his vocation, and inclined towards missionary labour. That was the happiest time of his life : that was the spot he would have chosen now to awake in and find the rest a dream. The people among whom Brother Bulstrode was distinguished were very few, but they were very near to him, and stirred his satisfaction the more ; his power stretched through a narrow space, but he felt its effect the more intensely. He believed without effort in the peculiar work of grace within him, and in the signs that God intended him for special instrumentality.

Then came the moment of transition; it was with the sense of promotion he had when he, an orphan educated at a commercial charity-school, was invited to a fine villa belonging to Mr Dunkirk, the richest man in the congregation. Soon he became an intimate there, honoured for his piety by the wife, marked out for his ability by the husband, whose wealth was due to a flourishing city and west-end trade. That was the setting-in of a new current for his ambition, directing his prospects of "instrumentality" towards the uniting of distinguished religious gifts with successful business.

By-and-by came a decided external leading: a confidential sub-ordinate partner died, and nobody seemed to the principal so well fitted to fill the severely-felt vacancy as his young friend Bulstrode, if he would become confidential accountant. The offer was accepted. The business was a pawnbroker's, of the most magnificent sort both in extent and profits; and on a short acquaintance with it Bulstrode became aware that one source of magnificent profit was the easy recep-tion of any goods offered, without strict inquiry as to where they came from. But there was a branch house at the west end, and no pettiness or dinginess to give suggestions of shame.

He remembered his first moments of shrinking. They were private, and were filled with arguments; some of these taking the form of prayer. The business was established and had old roots; is it not one thing to set up a new gin-palace and another to accept an invest-ment in an old one? The profits made out of lost souls—where can the line be drawn at which they begin in human transactions? Was it not even God's way of saving His chosen? "Thou knowest,"—the young Bulstrode had said then, as the older Bulstrode was saying now—" Thou knowest how loose my soul sits from these things—how I view them all as implements for tilling Thy garden rescued here and there from the wilderness."

Metaphors and precedents were not wanting; peculiar spiritual experiences were not wanting which at last made the retention of his position seem a service demanded of him: the vista of a fortune had already opened itself, and Bulstrode's shrinking remained private. Mr Dunkirk had never expected that there would be any shrinking at all: he had never conceived that trade had anything to do with the scheme of salvation. And it was true that Bulstrode found him-self carrying on two distinct lives; his religious activity could not be incompatible with his business as soon as he had argued himself into not feeling it incompatible.

Mentally surrounded with that past again, Bulstrode had the same pleas—indeed, the years had been perpetually spinning them into intricate thickness, like masses of spider-web, padding the moral sensibility; nay, as age made egoism more eager but less enjoying, his soul had become more saturated with the belief that he did every-thing for God's sake, being indifferent to it for his own. And yet—if he could be back in that far-off spot with his youthful poverty—why, then he would choose to be a missionary.

But the train of causes in which he had locked himself went on. There was trouble in the fine villa at Highbury. Years before, the only daughter had run away, defied her parents, and gone on the stage; and now the only boy died, and after a short time Mr Dunkirk died also. The wife, a simple pious woman, left with all the wealth in and out of the magnificent trade, of which she never knew the precise nature, had come to believe in Bulstrode, and innocently adore him as women often adore their priest or " man-made" minister. It was natural that after a time marriage should have been thought of between them. But Mrs Dunkirk had qualms and yearnings about her daughter, who had long been regarded as lost both to God and her parents. It was known that the daughter had married, but she was utterly gone out of sight. The mother, having lost her boy, imagined a grandson, and wished in a double sense to reclaim her daughter. If she were found, there would be a channel for property—perhaps a wide one, in the provision for several grandchildren. Efforts to find her must be made before Mrs Dunkirk would marry again. Bulstrode concurred ; but after advertisement as well as other modes of inquiry had been tried, the mother believed that her daughter was not to be found, and consented to marry without reservation of property.

The daughter had been found ; but only one man besides Bulstrode knew it, and he was paid for keeping silence and carrying himself away.

That was the bare fact which Bulstrode was now forced to see in the rigid outline with which acts present themselves to onlookers. But for himself at that distant time, and even now in burning memory, the fact was broken into little sequences, each justified as it came by reasonings which seemed to prove it righteous. Bulstrode's course up to that time had, he thought, been sanctioned by remarkable providences, appearing to point the way for him to be the agent in making the best use of a large property and withdrawing it from perversion. Death and other striking dispositions, such as feminine trustfulness, had come ; and Bulstrode would have adopted Cromwell's words — " Do you call these bare events ? The Lord pity you ! "[1] The events were comparatively small, but the essential condition was there — namely, that they were in favour of his own ends. It was easy for him to settle what was due from him to others by inquiring what were God's intentions with regard to himself. Could it be for God's service that this fortune should in any considerable proportion go to a young woman and her husband who were given up to the lightest pursuits, and might scatter it abroad in triviality — people who seemed to lie outside the path of remarkable providences ? Bulstrode had never said to himself beforehand, " The daughter shall not be found"—nevertheless when the moment came he kept her existence hidden ; and when other moments followed, he soothed the mother with consolation in the probability that the unhappy young woman might be no more.

There were hours in which Bulstrode felt that his action was unrighteous ; but how could he go back ? He had mental exercises, called himself nought, laid hold on redemption, and went on in his course of instrumentality. And after five years Death again came to widen his path, by taking away his wife. He did gradually withdraw his capital, but he did not make the sacrifices requisite to put an end to the business, which was carried on for thirteen years afterwards before it finally collapsed. Meanwhile Nicholas Bulstrode had used his hundred thousand discreetly, and was become provincially, solidly

1. Oliver Cromwell (1599–1658), Lord Protector of Great Britain (1653–58) during the Commonwealth.

important—a banker, a Churchman, a public benefactor ; also a sleeping partner in trading concerns, in which his ability was directed to economy in the raw material, as in the case of the dyes which rotted Mr Vincy's silk. And now, when this respectability had lasted undisturbed for nearly thirty years—when all that preceded it had long lain benumbed in the consciousness—that past had risen and immersed his thought as if with the terrible irruption of a new sense overburthening the feeble being.

Meanwhile, in his conversation with Raffles, he had learned something momentous, something which entered actively into the struggle of his longings and terrors. There, he thought, lay an opening towards spiritual, perhaps towards material rescue.

The spiritual kind of rescue was a genuine need with him. There may be coarse hypocrites, who consciously affect beliefs and emotions for the sake of gulling the world, but Bulstrode was not one of them. He was simply a man whose desires had been stronger than his theoretic beliefs, and who had gradually explained the gratification of his desires into satisfactory agreement with those beliefs. If this be hypocrisy, it is a process which shows itself occasionally in us all, to whatever confession we belong, and whether we believe in the future perfection of our race or in the nearest date fixed for the end of the world ; whether we regard the earth as a putrefying nidus for a saved remnant, including ourselves, or have a passionate belief in the solidarity of mankind.

The service he could do to the cause of religion had been through life the ground he alleged to himself for his choice of action : it had been the motive which he had poured out in his prayers. Who would use money and position better than he meant to use them ? Who could surpass him in self-abhorrence and exaltation of God's cause ? And to Mr Bulstrode God's cause was something distinct from his own rectitude of conduct : it enforced a discrimination of God's enemies, who were to be used merely as instruments, and whom it would be as well if possible to keep out of money and consequent influence. Also, profitable investments in trades where the power of the prince of this world showed its most active devices, became sanctified by a right application of the profits in the hands of God's servant.

This implicit reasoning is essentially no more peculiar to evangelical belief than the use of wide phrases for narrow motives is peculiar to Englishmen. There is no general doctrine which is not capable of eating out our morality if unchecked by the deep-seated habit of direct fellow-feeling with individual fellow-men.

But a man who believes in something else than his own greed, has necessarily a conscience or standard to which he more or less adapts himself. Bulstrode's standard had been his serviceableness to God's cause : " I am sinful and nought—a vessel to be consecrated by use— but use me ! "—had been the mould into which he had constrained his immense need of being something important and predominating. And now had come a moment in which that mould seemed in danger of being broken and utterly cast away.

What, if the acts he had reconciled himself to because they made him a stronger instrument of the divine glory, were to become the pretext of the scoffer, and a darkening of that glory ? If this were to be the ruling of Providence, he was cast out from the temple as one who had brought unclean offerings.

He had long poured out utterances of repentance. But to-day a repentance had come which was of a bitterer flavour, and a threatening Providence urged him to a kind of propitiation which was not simply a doctrinal transaction. The divine tribunal had changed its aspect for him ; self-prostration was no longer enough, and he must bring restitution in his hand. It was really before his God that Bulstrode was about to attempt such restitution as seemed possible : a great dread had seized his susceptible frame, and the scorching approach of shame wrought in him a new spiritual need. Night and day, while the resurgent threatening past was making a conscience within him, he was thinking by what means he could recover peace and trust—by what sacrifice he could stay the rod. His belief in these moments of dread was, that if he spontaneously did something right, God would save him from the consequences of wrong-doing. For religion can only change when the emotions which fill it are changed ; and the religion of personal fear remains nearly at the level of the savage.

He had seen Raffles actually going away on the Brassing coach, and this was a temporary relief ; it removed the pressure of an immediate dread, but did not put an end to the spiritual conflict and the need to win protection. At last he came to a difficult resolve, and wrote a letter to Will Ladislaw, begging him to be at the Shrubs that evening for a private interview at nine o'clock. Will had felt no particular surprise at the request, and connected it with some new notions about the ' Pioneer ;' but when he was shown into Mr Bulstrode's private room, he was struck with the painfully worn look on the banker's face, and was going to say, " Are you ill ?" when, checking himself in that abruptness, he only inquired after Mrs Bulstrode, and her satisfaction with the picture bought for her.

" Thank you, she is quite satisfied ; she has gone out with her daughters this evening. I begged you to come, Mr Ladislaw, because I have a communication of a very private—indeed, I will say, of a sacredly confidential nature, which I desire to make to you. Nothing, I daresay, has been farther from your thoughts than that there had been important ties in the past which could connect your history with mine."

Will felt something like an electric shock. He was already in a state of keen sensitiveness and hardly allayed agitation on the subject of ties in the past, and his presentiments were not agreeable. It seemed like the fluctuations of a dream—as if the action begun by that loud bloated stranger were being carried on by this pale - eyed sickly-looking piece of respectability, whose subdued tone and glib formality of speech were at this moment almost as repulsive to him as their remembered contrast. He answered, with a marked change of colour—

" No, indeed, nothing."

" You see before you, Mr Ladislaw, a man who is deeply stricken. But for the urgency of conscience and the knowledge that I am before the bar of One who seeth not as man seeth, I should be under no compulsion to make the disclosure which has been my object in asking you to come here to-night. So far as human laws go, you have no claim on me whatever."

Will was even more uncomfortable than wondering. Mr Bulstrode had paused, leaning his head on his hand, and looking at the floor. But he now fixed his examining glance on Will and said—

" I am told that your mother's name was Sarah Dunkirk, and that
she ran away from her friends to go on the stage. Also, that your
father was at one time much emaciated by illness. May I ask if you
can confirm these statements ? "

" Yes, they are all true," said Will, struck with the order in which
an inquiry had come, that might have been expected to be preliminary to the banker's previous hints. But Mr Bulstrode had to-night
followed the order of his emotions ; he entertained no doubt that the
opportunity for restitution had come, and he had an overpowering
impulse towards the penitential expression by which he was deprecating chastisement.

" Do you know any particulars of your mother's family ? " he continued.

" No ; she never liked to speak of them. She was a very generous,
honourable woman," said Will, almost angrily.

" I do not wish to allege anything against her. Did she never mention her mother to you at all ?"

" I have heard her say that she thought her mother did not know
the reason of her running away. She said ' poor mother ' in a pitying
tone."

" That mother became my wife," said Bulstrode, and then paused a
moment before he added, " you have a claim on me, Mr Ladislaw :
as I said before, not a legal claim, but one which my conscience recognises. I was enriched by that marriage — a result which would probably not have taken place—certainly not to the same extent—if your
grandmother could have discovered her daughter. That daughter, I
gather, is no longer living !"

" No," said Will, feeling suspicion and repugnance rising so strongly
within him, that without quite knowing what he did, he took his hat
from the floor and stood up. The impulse within him was to reject
the disclosed connection.

"Pray be seated, Mr Ladislaw," said Bulstrode, anxiously. "Doubtless you are startled by the suddenness of this discovery. But I entreat
your patience with one who is already bowed down by inward trial."

Will reseated himself, feeling some pity which was half contempt
for this voluntary self-abasement of an elderly man.

" It is my wish, Mr Ladislaw, to make amends for the deprivation
which befell your mother. I know that you are without fortune, and
I wish to supply you adequately from a store which would have probably already been yours had your grandmother been certain of your
mother's existence and been able to find her."

Mr Bulstrode paused. He felt that he was performing a striking
piece of scrupulosity in the judgment of his auditor, and a penitential
act in the eyes of God. He had no clue to the state of Will Ladislaw's mind, smarting as it was from the clear hints of Raffles, and
with its natural quickness in construction stimulated by the expectation of discoveries which he would have been glad to conjure back
into darkness. Will made no answer for several moments, till Mr
Bulstrode, who at the end of his speech had cast his eyes on the floor,
now raised them with an examining glance, which Will met fully,
saying—

" I suppose you did know of my mother's existence, and knew
where she might have been found."

Bulstrode shrank—there was a visible quivering in his face and hands. He was totally unprepared to have his advances met in this way, or to find himself urged into more revelation than he had beforehand set down as needful. But at that moment he dared not tell a lie, and he felt suddenly uncertain of his ground which he had trodden with some confidence before.

" I will not deny that you conjecture rightly," he answered, with a faltering in his tone. " And I wish to make atonement to you as the one still remaining who has suffered a loss through me. You enter, I trust, into my purpose, Mr Ladislaw, which has a reference to higher than merely human claims, and as I have already said, is entirely independent of any legal compulsion. I am ready to narrow my own resources and the prospects of my family by binding myself to allow you five hundred pounds yearly during my life, and to leave you a proportional capital at my death—nay, to do still more, if more should be definitely necessary to any laudable project on your part." Mr Bulstrode had gone on to particulars in the expectation that these would work strongly on Ladislaw, and merge other feelings in grateful acceptance.

But Will was looking as stubborn as possible, with his lip pouting and his fingers in his side-pockets. He was not in the least touched, and said firmly—

" Before I make any reply to your proposition, Mr Bulstrode, I must beg you to answer a question or two. Were you connected with the business by which that fortune you speak of was originally made ? "

Mr Bulstrode's thought was, " Raffles has told him." How could he refuse to answer when he had volunteered what drew forth the question ? He answered, " Yes."

" And was that business—or was it not—a thoroughly dishonourable one — nay, one that, if its nature had been made public, might have ranked those concerned in it with thieves and convicts ? "

Will's tone had a cutting bitterness : he was moved to put his question as nakedly as he could.

Bulstrode reddened with irrepressible anger. He had been prepared for a scene of self-abasement, but his intense pride and his habit of supremacy overpowered penitence, and even dread, when this young man, whom he had meant to benefit, turned on him with the air of a judge.

" The business was established before I became connected with it, sir ; nor is it for you to institute an inquiry of that kind," he answered, not raising his voice, but speaking with quick defiantness.

" Yes, it is," said Will, starting up again with his hat in his hand. " It is eminently mine to ask such questions, when I have to decide whether I will have transactions with you and accept your money. My unblemished honour is important to me. It is important to me to have no stain on my birth and connections. And now I find there is a stain which I can't help. My mother felt it, and tried to keep as clear of it as she could, and so will I. You shall keep your ill-gotten money. If I had any fortune of my own, I would willingly pay it to any one who could disprove what you have told me. What I have to thank you for is that you kept the money till now, when I can refuse it. It ought to lie with a man's self that he is a gentleman. Good-night, sir."

Bulstrode was going to speak, but Will with determined quickness was out of the room in an instant, and in another the hall-door had closed behind him. He was too strongly possessed with passionate rebellion against this inherited blot which had been thrust on his knowledge to reflect at present whether he had not been too hard on Bulstrode—too arrogantly merciless towards a man of sixty, who was making efforts at retrieval when time had rendered them vain.

No third person listening could have thoroughly understood the impetuosity of Will's repulse or the bitterness of his words. No one but himself then knew how everything connected with the sentiment of his own dignity had an immediate bearing for him on his relation to Dorothea and to Mr Casaubon's treatment of him. And in the rush of impulses by which he flung back that offer of Bulstrode's, there was mingled the sense that it would have been impossible for him ever to tell Dorothea that he had accepted it.

As for Bulstrode—when Will was gone he suffered a violent reaction, and wept like a woman. It was the first time he had encountered an open expression of scorn from any man higher than Raffles ; and with that scorn hurrying like venom through his system, there was no sensibility left to consolations. But the relief of weeping had to be checked. His wife and daughters soon came home from hearing the address of an Oriental missionary, and were full of regret that papa had not heard, in the first instance, the interesting things which they tried to repeat to him.

Perhaps, through all other hidden thoughts, the one that breathed most comfort was, that Will Ladislaw at least was not likely to publish what had taken place that evening.

CHAPTER LXII.

" He was a squyer of lowe degre,
That loved the king's daughter of Hungrie."
—*Old Romance.*

WILL LADISLAW'S mind was now wholly bent on seeing Dorothea again, and forthwith quitting Middlemarch. The morning after his agitating scene with Bulstrode he wrote a brief letter to her, saying that various causes had detained him in the neighbourhood longer than he had expected, and asking her permission to call again at Lowick at some hour which she would mention on the earliest possible day, he being anxious to depart, but unwilling to do so until she had granted him an interview. He left the letter at the office, ordering the messenger to carry it to Lowick Manor, and wait for an answer.

Ladislaw felt the awkwardness of asking for more last words. His former farewell had been made in the hearing of Sir James Chettam, and had been announced as final even to the butler. It is certainly trying to a man's dignity to reappear when he is not expected to do so : a first farewell has pathos in it, but to come back for a second lends an opening to comedy, and it was possible even that there might be bitter sneers afloat about Will's motives for lingering. Still it was on the whole more satisfactory to his feeling to take the directest means of seeing Dorothea, than to use any device which might give an air of chance to a meeting of which he wished her to understand that it was what he earnestly sought. When he had parted from her before, he had been in ignorance of facts which gave a new aspect to the relation between them, and made a more absolute severance than he had then believed in. He knew nothing of Dorothea's private fortune, and being little used to reflect on such matters, took it for granted that according to Mr Casaubon's arrangement marriage to him, Will Ladislaw, would mean that she consented to be penniless. That was not what he could wish for even in his secret heart, or even if she had been ready to meet such hard contrast for his sake. And then, too, there was the fresh smart of that disclosure about his mother's family, which if known would be an added reason why Dorothea's friends should look down upon him as utterly below her. The secret hope that after some years he might come back with the sense that he had at least a personal value equal to her wealth, seemed now the dreamy continuation of a dream. This change would surely justify him in asking Dorothea to receive him once more.

But Dorothea on that morning was not at home to receive Will's note. In consequence of a letter from her uncle announcing his intention to be at home in a week, she had driven first to Freshitt to carry the news, meaning to go on to the Grange to deliver some orders with which her uncle had intrusted her—thinking, as he said, " a little mental occupation of this sort good for a widow."

If Will Ladislaw could have overheard some of the talk at Freshitt that morning, he would have felt all his suppositions confirmed as to the readiness of certain people to sneer at his lingering in the neighbourhood. Sir James, indeed, though much relieved concerning Dorothea, had been on the watch to learn Ladislaw's movements, and had an instructed informant in Mr Standish, who was necessarily in his confidence on this matter. That Ladislaw had stayed in Middlemarch nearly two months after he had declared that he was going immediately, was a fact to embitter Sir James's suspicions, or at least to justify his aversion to a " young fellow " whom he represented to himself as slight, volatile, and likely enough to show such recklessness as naturally went along with a position unriveted by family ties or a strict profession. But he had just heard something from Standish which, while it justified these surmises about Will, offered a means of nullifying all danger with regard to Dorothea.

Unwonted circumstances may make us all rather unlike ourselves : there are conditions under which the most majestic person is obliged to sneeze, and our emotions are liable to be acted on in the same incongruous manner. Good Sir James was this morning so far unlike himself that he was irritably anxious to say something to Dorothea on a subject which he usually avoided as if it had been a matter of shame to them both. He could not use Celia as a medium, because he did not choose that she should know the kind of gossip he had in his mind ; and before Dorothea happened to arrive he had been trying to imagine how, with his shyness and unready tongue, he could ever manage to introduce his communication. Her unexpected presence brought him to utter hopelessness in his own power of saying anything unpleasant ; but desperation suggested a resource ; he sent the groom on an unsaddled horse across the park with a pencilled note to Mrs Cadwallader, who already knew the gossip, and would think it no compromise of herself to repeat it as often as required.

Dorothea was detained on the good pretext that Mr Garth, whom she wanted to see, was expected at the hall within the hour, and she was still talking to Caleb on the gravel when Sir James, on the watch for the rector's wife, saw her coming and met her with the needful hints.

"Enough! I understand," said Mrs Cadwallader. "You shall be innocent. I am such a blackamoor that I cannot smirch myself."

"I don't mean that it's of any consequence," said Sir James, disliking that Mrs Cadwallader should understand too much. "Only it is desirable that Dorothea should know there are reasons why she should not receive him again; and I really can't say so to her. It will come lightly from you."

It came very lightly indeed. When Dorothea quitted Caleb and turned to meet them, it appeared that Mrs Cadwallader had stepped across the park by the merest chance in the world, just to chat with Celia in a matronly way about the baby. And so Mr Brooke was coming back? Delightful!—coming back, it was to be hoped, quite cured of Parliamentary fever and pioneering. *Apropos* of the 'Pioneer'—somebody had prophesied that it would soon be like a dying dolphin, and turn all colours for want of knowing how to help itself, because Mr Brooke's *protégé*, the brilliant young Ladislaw, was gone or going. Had Sir James heard that?

The three were walking along the gravel slowly, and Sir James, turning aside to whip a shrub, said he had heard something of that sort.

"All false!" said Mrs Cadwallader. "He is not gone, or going, apparently; the 'Pioneer' keeps its colour, and Mr Orlando Ladislaw is making a sad dark-blue scandal by warbling continually with your Mr Lydgate's wife, who they tell me is as pretty as pretty can be. It seems nobody ever goes into the house without finding this young gentleman lying on the rug or warbling at the piano. But the people in manufacturing towns are always disreputable."

"You began by saying that one report was false, Mrs Cadwallader, and I believe this is false too," said Dorothea, with indignant energy; "at least, I feel sure it is a misrepresentation. I will not hear any evil spoken of Mr Ladislaw; he has already suffered too much injustice."

Dorothea when thoroughly moved cared little what any one thought of her feelings; and even if she had been able to reflect, she would have held it petty to keep silence at injurious words about Will from fear of being herself misunderstood. Her face was flushed and her lip trembled.

Sir James, glancing at her, repented of his stratagem; but Mrs Cadwallader, equal to all occasions, spread the palms of her hands outward and said, "Heaven grant it, my dear!—I mean that all bad tales about anybody may be false. But it is a pity that young Lydgate should have married one of these Middlemarch girls. Considering he's a son of somebody, he might have got a woman with good blood in her veins, and not too young, who would have put up with his profession. There's Clara Harfager, for instance, whose friends don't know what to do with her; and she has a portion. Then we might have had her among us. However!—it's no use being wise for other people. Where is Celia? Pray let us go in."

"I am going on immediately to Tipton," said Dorothea, rather haughtily. "Good-bye."

Sir James could say nothing as he accompanied her to the carriage. He was altogether discontented with the result of a contrivance which had cost him some secret humiliation beforehand.

Dorothea drove along between the berried hedge-rows and the shorn corn-fields, not seeing or hearing anything around. The tears came and rolled down her cheeks, but she did not know it. The world, it seemed, was turning ugly and hateful, and there was no place for her trustfulness. "It is not true—it is not true!" was the voice within her that she listened to; but all the while a remembrance to which there had always clung a vague uneasiness would thrust itself on her attention—the remembrance of that day when she had found Will Ladislaw with Mrs Lydgate, and had heard his voice accompanied by the piano.

"He said he would never do anything that I disapproved—I wish I could have told him that I disapproved of that," said poor Dorothea, inwardly, feeling a strange alternation between anger with Will and the passionate defence of him. "They all try to blacken him before me; but I will care for no pain, if he is not to blame. I always believed he was good."—These were her last thoughts before she felt that the carriage was passing under the archway of the lodge-gate at the Grange, when she hurriedly pressed her handkerchief to her face and began to think of her errands. The coachman begged leave to take out the horses for half an hour as there was something wrong with a shoe; and Dorothea, having the sense that she was going to rest, took off her gloves and bonnet, while she was leaning against a statue in the entrance-hall, and talking to the housekeeper. At last she said—

"I must stay here a little, Mrs Kell. I will go into the library and write you some memoranda from my uncle's letter, if you will open the shutters for me."

"The shutters are open, madam," said Mrs Kell, following Dorothea, who had walked along as she spoke. "Mr Ladislaw is there, looking for something."

(Will had come to fetch a portfolio of his own sketches which he had missed in the act of packing his movables, and did not choose to leave behind.)

Dorothea's heart seemed to turn over as if it had had a blow, but she was not perceptibly checked: in truth, the sense that Will was there was for the moment all-satisfying to her, like the sight of something precious that one has lost. When she reached the door she said to Mrs Kell—

"Go in first, and tell him that I am here."

Will had found his portfolio, and had laid it on the table at the far end of the room, to turn over the sketches and please himself by looking at the memorable piece of art which had a relation to nature too mysterious for Dorothea. He was smiling at it still, and shaking the sketches into order with the thought that he might find a letter from her awaiting him at Middlemarch, when Mrs Kell close to his elbow said—

"Mrs Casaubon is coming in, sir."

Will turned round quickly, and the next moment Dorothea was entering. As Mrs Kell closed the door behind her they met: each was looking at the other, and consciousness was overflowed by something that suppressed utterance. It was not confusion that kept them silent, for they both felt that parting was near, and there is no shamefacedness in a sad parting.

She moved automatically towards her uncle's chair against the writing-table, and Will, after drawing it out a little for her, went a few paces off and stood opposite to her.

" Pray sit down," said Dorothea, crossing her hands on her lap ; " I am very glad you were here." Will thought that her face looked just as it did when she first shook hands with him in Rome ; for her widow's cap, fixed in her bonnet, had gone off with it, and he could see that she had lately been shedding tears. But the mixture of anger in her agitation had vanished at the sight of him ; she had been used, when they were face to face, always to feel confidence and the happy freedom which comes with mutual understanding, and how could other people's words hinder that effect on a sudden? Let the music which can take possession of our frame and fill the air with joy for us, sound once more—what does it signify that we heard it found fault with in its absence?

" I have sent a letter to Lowick Manor to-day, asking leave to see you," said Will, seating himself opposite to her. " I am going away immediately, and I could not go without speaking to you again."

" I thought we had parted when you came to Lowick many weeks ago—you thought you were going then," said Dorothea, her voice trembling a little.

" Yes ; but I was in ignorance then of things which I know now—things which have altered my feelings about the future. When I saw you before, I was dreaming that I might come back some day. I don't think I ever shall—now." Will paused here.

" You wished me to know the reasons?" said Dorothea, timidly.

" Yes," said Will, impetuously, shaking his head backward, and looking away from her with irritation in his face. " Of course I must wish it. I have been grossly insulted in your eyes and in the eyes of others. There has been a mean implication against my character. I wish you to know that under no circumstances would I have lowered myself by—under no circumstances would I have given men the chance of saying that I sought money under the pretext of seeking—something else. There was no need of other safeguard against me—the safeguard of wealth was enough."

Will rose from his chair with the last word and went—he hardly knew where ; but it was to the projecting window nearest him, which had been open as now about the same season a year ago, when he and Dorothea had stood within it and talked together. Her whole heart was going out at this moment in sympathy with Will's indignation : she only wanted to convince him that she had never done him injustice, and he seemed to have turned away from her as if she too had been part of the unfriendly world.

" It would be very unkind of you to suppose that I ever attributed any meanness to you," she began. Then in her ardent way, wanting to plead with him, she moved from her chair and went in front of him to her old place in the window, saying, " Do you suppose that I ever disbelieved in you ? "

When Will saw her there, he gave a start and moved backward out of the window, without meeting her glance. Dorothea was hurt by this movement following up the previous anger of his tone. She was ready to say that it was as hard on her as on him, and that she was helpless ; but those strange particulars of their relation which neither of them could explicitly mention kept her always in dread of saying too much. At this moment she had no belief that Will would in any case have wanted to marry her, and she feared using words which might imply such a belief. She only said earnestly, recurring to his last word—

"I am sure no safeguard was ever needed against you."

Will did not answer. In the stormy fluctuation of his feelings these words of hers seemed to him cruelly neutral, and he looked pale and miserable after his angry outburst. He went to the table and fastened up his portfolio, while Dorothea looked at him from the distance. They were wasting these last moments together in wretched silence. What could he say, since what had got obstinately uppermost in his mind was the passionate love for her which he forbade himself to utter ? What could she say, since she might offer him no help—since she was forced to keep the money that ought to have been his ?—since to-day he seemed not to respond as he used to do to her thorough trust and liking ?

But Will at last turned away from his portfolio and approached the window again.

"I must go," he said, with that peculiar look of the eyes which sometimes accompanies bitter feeling, as if they had been tired and burned with gazing too close at a light.

"What shall you do in life ?" said Dorothea, timidly. "Have your intentions remained just the same as when we said good-bye before ?"

"Yes," said Will, in a tone that seemed to waive the subject as uninteresting. "I shall work away at the first thing that offers. I suppose one gets a habit of doing without happiness or hope."

"Oh, what sad words !" said Dorothea, with a dangerous tendency to sob. Then trying to smile, she added, "We used to agree that we were alike in speaking too strongly."

"I have not spoken too strongly now," said Will, leaning back against the angle of the wall. "There are certain things which a man can only go through once in his life ; and he must know some time or other that the best is over with him. This experience has happened to me while I am very young—that is all. What I care more for than I can ever care for anything else is absolutely forbidden to me—I don't mean merely by being out of my reach, but forbidden me, even if it were within my reach, by my own pride and honour—by everything I respect myself for. Of course I shall go on living as a man might do who had seen heaven in a trance."

Will paused, imagining that it would be impossible for Dorothea to misunderstand this; indeed he felt that he was contradicting himself and offending against his self-approval in speaking to her so plainly; but still—it could not be fairly called wooing a woman to tell her that he would never woo her. It must be admitted to be a ghostly kind of wooing.

But Dorothea's mind was rapidly going over the past with quite another vision than his. The thought that she herself might be what Will most cared for did throb through her an instant, but then came doubt: the memory of the little they had lived through together turned pale and shrank before the memory which suggested how much fuller might have been the intercourse between Will and some one else with whom he had had constant companionship. Everything he had said might refer to that other relation, and whatever had passed between him and herself was thoroughly explained by what she had always regarded as their simple friendship and the cruel obstruction thrust upon it by her husband's injurious act. Dorothea stood silent, with her eyes cast down dreamily, while images crowded upon her which left the sickening certainty that Will was referring to Mrs Lydgate. But why sickening? He wanted her to know that here too his conduct should be above suspicion.

Will was not surprised at her silence. His mind also was tumultuously busy while he watched her, and he was feeling rather wildly that something must happen to hinder their parting — some miracle, clearly nothing in their own deliberate speech. Yet, after all, had she any love for him?—he could not pretend to himself that he would rather believe her to be without that pain. He could not deny that a secret longing for the assurance that she loved him was at the root of all his words.

Neither of them knew how long they stood in that way. Dorothea was raising her eyes, and was about to speak, when the door opened and her footman came to say—

"The horses are ready, madam, whenever you like to start."

"Presently," said Dorothea. Then turning to Will, she said, " I have some memoranda to write for the housekeeper."

"I must go," said Will, when the door had closed again — advancing towards her. "The day after to-morrow I shall leave Middlemarch."

"You have acted in every way rightly," said Dorothea, in a low tone, feeling a pressure at her heart which made it difficult to speak. She put out her hand, and Will took it for an instant without speaking, for her words had seemed to him cruelly cold and unlike herself. Their eyes met, but there was discontent in his, and in hers there was only sadness. He turned away and took his portfolio under his arm.

"I have never done you injustice. Please remember me," said Dorothea, repressing a rising sob.

"Why should you say that?" said Will, with irritation. "As if I were not in danger of forgetting everything else."

He had really a movement of anger against her at that moment, and it impelled him to go away without pause. It was all one flash to Dorothea — his last words — his distant bow to her as he reached the door—the sense that he was no longer there. She sank into the chair, and for a few moments sat like a statue, while images and emotions were hurrying upon her. Joy came first, in spite of the threatening train behind it—joy in the impression that it was really herself whom Will loved and was renouncing, that there was really no other love less permissible, more blameworthy, which honour was hurrying him away from. They were parted all the same, but— Dorothea drew a deep breath and felt her strength return — she could think of him unrestrainedly. At that moment the parting was easy to bear: the first sense of loving and being loved excluded sorrow. It was as if some hard icy pressure had melted, and her consciousness had room to expand : her past was come back to her with larger interpretation. The joy was not the less—perhaps it was the more complete

just then — because of the irrevocable parting ; for there was no reproach, no contemptuous wonder to imagine in any eye or from any
lips. He had acted so as to defy reproach, and make wonder respectful.

Any one watching her might have seen that there was a fortifying
thought within her. Just as when inventive power is working with
glad ease some small claim on the attention is fully met as if it were
only a cranny opened to the sunlight, it was easy now for Dorothea
to write her memoranda. She spoke her last words to the housekeeper
in cheerful tones, and when she seated herself in the carriage her eyes
were bright and her cheeks blooming under the dismal bonnet. She
threw back the heavy "weepers," and looked before her, wondering
which road Will had taken. It was in her nature to be proud that he
was blameless, and through all her feelings there ran this vein — " I
was right to defend him."

The coachman was used to drive his greys at a good pace, Mr Casaubon being unenjoying and impatient in everything away from his
desk, and wanting to get to the end of all journeys ; and Dorothea
was now bowled along quickly. Driving was pleasant, for rain in the
night had laid the dust, and the blue sky looked far off, away from
the region of the great clouds that sailed in masses. The earth looked
like a happy place under the vast heavens, and Dorothea was wishing
that she might overtake Will and see him once more.

After a turn of the road, there he was with the portfolio under his
arm ; but the next moment she was passing him while he raised his
hat, and she felt a pang at being seated there in a sort of exaltation,
leaving him behind. She could not look back at him. It was as if a
crowd of indifferent objects had thrust them asunder, and forced them
along different paths, taking them farther and farther away from each
other, and making it useless to look back. She could no more make
any sign that would seem to say, "Need we part ?" than she could
stop the carriage to wait for him. Nay, what a world of reasons
crowded upon her against any movement of her thought towards a
future that might reverse the decision of this day !

" I only wish I had known before — I wish he knew — then we
could be quite happy in thinking of each other, though we are for
ever parted. And if I could but have given him the money, and
made things easier for him ! "—were the longings that came back the
most persistently. And yet, so heavily did the world weigh on her
in spite of her independent energy, that with this idea of Will as in
need of such help and at a disadvantage with the world, there came
always the vision of that unfittingness of any closer relation between
them which lay in the opinion of every one connected with her. She
felt to the full all the imperativeness of the motives which urged Will's
conduct. How could he dream of her defying the barrier that her
husband had placed between them ?—how could she ever say to herself that she would defy it ?

Will's certainty, as the carriage grew smaller in the distance, had
much more bitterness in it. Very slight matters were enough to gall
him in his sensitive mood, and the sight of Dorothea driving past
him while he felt himself plodding along as a poor devil seeking a
position in a world which in his present temper offered him little that

he coveted, made his conduct seem a mere matter of necessity, and took away the sustainment of resolve. After all, he had no assurance that she loved him : could any man pretend that he was simply glad in such a case to have the suffering all on his own side ?

That evening Will spent with the Lydgates ; the next evening he was gone.

BOOK VII.

TWO TEMPTATIONS.

CHAPTER LXIII.

"These little things are great to little man."—GOLDSMITH. [1]

"HAVE you seen much of your scientific phœnix, Lydgate, lately?" said Mr Toller at one of his Christmas dinner-parties, speaking to Mr Farebrother on his right hand.

"Not much, I am sorry to say," answered the Vicar, accustomed to parry Mr Toller's banter about his belief in the new medical light. "I am out of the way, and he is too busy."

"Is he? I am glad to hear it," said Dr Minchin, with mingled suavity and surprise.

"He gives a great deal of time to the New Hospital," said Mr Farebrother, who had his reasons for continuing the subject: "I hear of that from my neighbour, Mrs Casaubon, who goes there often. She says Lydgate is indefatigable, and is making a fine thing of Bulstrode's institution. He is preparing a new ward in case of the cholera coming to us."

"And preparing theories of treatment to try on the patients, I suppose," said Mr Toller.

"Come, Toller, be candid," said Mr Farebrother. "You are too clever not to see the good of a bold fresh mind in medicine, as well as in everything else; and as to cholera, I fancy, none of you are very sure what you ought to do. If a man goes a little too far along a new road, it is usually himself that he harms more than any one else."

"I am sure you and Wrench ought to be obliged to him," said Dr Minchin, looking towards Toller, "for he has sent you the cream of Peacock's patients."

"Lydgate has been living at a great rate for a young beginner,"

---

said Mr Harry Toller, the brewer. " I suppose his relations in the North back him up."

" I hope so," said Mr Chichely," else he ought not to have married that nice girl we were all so fond of. Hang it, one has a grudge against a man who carries off the prettiest girl in the town."

" Ay, by God ! and the best too," said Mr Standish.

" My friend Vincy didn't half like the marriage, I know that," said Mr Chichely. " *He* wouldn't do much. How the relations on the other side may have come down I can't say." There was an emphatic kind of reticence in Mr Chichely's manner of speaking.

" Oh, I shouldn't think Lydgate ever looked to practice for a living," said Mr Toller, with a slight touch of sarcasm ; and there the subject was dropped.

This was not the first time that Mr Farebrother had heard hints of Lydgate's expenses being obviously too great to be met by his practice, but he thought it not unlikely that there were resources or expectations which excused the large outlay at the time of Lydgate's marriage, and which might hinder any bad consequences from the disappointment in his practice. One evening, when he took the pains to go to Middlemarch on purpose to have a chat with Lydgate as of old, he noticed in him an air of excited effort quite unlike his usual easy way of keeping silence or breaking it with abrupt energy whenever he had anything to say. Lydgate talked persistently when they were in his work-room, putting arguments for and against the probability of certain biological views ; but he had none of those definite things to say or to show which give the way-marks of a patient uninterrupted pursuit, such as he used himself to insist on, saying that " there must be a systole and diastole in all inquiry," and that " a man's mind must be continually expanding and shrinking between the whole human horizon and the horizon of an object-glass." [2] That evening he seemed to be talking widely for the sake of resisting any personal bearing ; and before long they went into the drawing-room, where Lydgate, having asked Rosamond to give them music, sank back in his chair in silence, but with a strange light in his eyes. " He may have been taking an opiate," was a thought that crossed Mr Farebrother's mind—" tic-douloureux perhaps—or medical worries." [3]

It did not occur to him that Lydgate's marriage was not delightful : he believed, as the rest did, that Rosamond was an amiable, docile creature, though he had always thought her rather uninteresting—a little too much the pattern-card of the finishing-school ; and his mother could not forgive Rosamond because she never seemed to see that Henrietta Noble was in the room. " However, Lydgate fell in love with her," said the Vicar to himself, " and she must be to his taste."

---

2. Systole and diastole: rhythmical contraction and dialation of the heart.

3. The first edition reads "with bright dilated eyes," instead of "a strange light in his eyes." The change was made, it seems, to eliminate the possibility of a technical medical misunderstanding. GE insisted in a letter to George D. Brown, who had questioned her on the point, that "the words 'bright dilated eyes' are not an incorrectness in relation to that stage of excitement from opium in which the subject feels and thinks vividly.. . . . The dull eyes with marked contraction of the pupils belong to a much more profound effect of opium than I meant to indicate in Lydgate's case" (Haight, *Letters*, V, 339–40). "Tic-douloureux" is facial neuralgia.

Mr Farebrother was aware that Lydgate was a proud man, but having very little corresponding fibre in himself, and perhaps too little care about personal dignity, except the dignity of not being mean or foolish, he could hardly allow enough for the way in which Lydgate shrank, as from a burn, from the utterance of any word about his private affairs. And soon after that conversation at Mr Toller's, the Vicar learned something which made him watch the more eagerly for an opportunity of indirectly letting Lydgate know that if he wanted to open himself about any difficulty there was a friendly ear ready.

The opportunity came at Mr Vincy's, where, on New Year's Day, there was a party, to which Mr Farebrother was irresistibly invited, on the plea that he must not forsake his old friends on the first new year of his being a greater man, and Rector as well as Vicar. And this party was thoroughly friendly: all the ladies of the Farebrother family were present; the Vincy children all dined at the table, and Fred had persuaded his mother that if she did not invite Mary Garth, the Farebrothers would regard it as a slight to themselves, Mary being their particular friend. Mary came, and Fred was in high spirits, though his enjoyment was of a checkered kind—triumph that his mother should see Mary's importance with the chief personages in the party being much streaked with jealousy when Mr Farebrother sat down by her. Fred used to be much more easy about his own accomplishments in the days when he had not begun to dread being " bowled out by Farebrother," and this terror was still before him. Mrs Vincy, in her fullest matronly bloom, looked at Mary's little figure, rough wavy hair, and visage quite without lilies and roses, and wondered; trying unsuccessfully to fancy herself caring about Mary's appearance in wedding clothes, or feeling complacency in grandchildren who would " feature" the Garths. However, the party was a merry one, and Mary was particularly bright; being glad, for Fred's sake, that his friends were getting kinder to her, and being also quite willing that they should see how much she was valued by others whom they must admit to be judges.

Mr Farebrother noticed that Lydgate seemed bored, and that Mr Vincy spoke as little as possible to his son-in-law. Rosamond was perfectly graceful and calm, and only a subtle observation such as the Vicar had not been roused to bestow on her would have perceived the total absence of that interest in her husband's presence which a loving wife is sure to betray, even if etiquette keeps her aloof from him. When Lydgate was taking part in the conversation, she never looked towards him any more than if she had been a sculptured Psyche modelled to look another way: and when, after being called out for an hour or two, he re-entered the room, she seemed unconscious of the fact, which eighteen months before would have had the effect of a numeral before cyphers.[4] In reality, however, she was intensely aware of Lydgate's voice and movements; and her pretty good-tempered air of unconsciousness was a studied negation by which she satisfied her inward opposition to him without compromise of propriety. When the ladies were in the drawing-room after Lydgate had been called away from the dessert, Mrs Farebrother, when Rosamond

4. Psyche was frequently represented in sculpture looking away from Eros, as in the myth he had commanded her to.

happened to be near her, said—" You have to give up a great deal of your husband's society, Mrs Lydgate."

"Yes, the life of a medical man is very arduous : especially when he is so devoted to his profession as Mr Lydgate is," said Rosamond, who was standing, and moved easily away at the end of this correct little speech.

"It is dreadfully dull for her when there is no company," said Mrs Vincy, who was seated at the old lady's side. " I am sure I thought so when Rosamond was ill, and I was staying with her. You know, Mrs Farebrother, ours is a cheerful house. I am of a cheerful disposition myself, and Mr Vincy always likes something to be going on. That is what Rosamond has been used to. Very different from a husband out at odd hours, and never knowing when he will come home, and of a close, proud disposition, *I* think"—indiscreet Mrs Vincy did lower her tone slightly with this parenthesis. " But Rosamond always had an angel of a temper ; her brothers used very often not to please her, but she was never the girl to show temper ; from a baby she was always as good as good, and with a complexion beyond anything. But my children are all good-tempered, thank God."

This was easily credible to any one looking at Mrs Vincy as she threw back her broad cap-strings, and smiled towards her three little girls, aged from seven to eleven. But in that smiling glance she was obliged to include Mary Garth, whom the three girls had got into a corner to make her tell them stories. Mary was just finishing the delicious tale of Rumpelstiltskin, which she had well by heart, because Letty was never tired of communicating it to her ignorant elders from a favourite red volume. Louisa, Mrs Vincy's darling, now ran to her with wide-eyed serious excitement, crying, " O mamma, mamma, the little man stamped so hard on the floor he couldn't get his leg out again ! "

" Bless you, my cherub !" said mamma ; " you shall tell me all about it to-morrow. Go and listen !" and then, as her eyes followed Louisa back towards the attractive corner, she thought that if Fred wished her to invite Mary again she would make no objection, the children being so pleased with her.

But presently the corner became still more animated, for Mr Farebrother came in, and seating himself behind Louisa, took her on his lap ; whereupon the girls all insisted that he must hear Rumpelstiltskin, and Mary must tell it over again. He insisted too, and Mary, without fuss, began again in her neat fashion, with precisely the same words as before. Fred, who had also seated himself near, would have felt unmixed triumph in Mary's effectiveness if Mr Farebrother had not been looking at her with evident admiration, while he dramatised an intense interest in the tale to please the children.

"You will never care any more about my one-eyed giant, Loo," said Fred at the end.

"Yes, I shall. Tell about him now," said Louisa.

"Oh, I daresay ; I am quite cut out. Ask Mr Farebrother."

"Yes," added Mary ; "ask Mr Farebrother to tell you about the ants whose beautiful house was knocked down by a giant named Tom, and he thought they didn't mind because he couldn't hear them cry, or see them use their pocket-handkerchiefs."

"Please," said Louisa, looking up at the Vicar.

"No, no, I am a grave old parson. If I try to draw a story out of my bag a sermon comes instead. Shall I preach you a sermon ?" said he, putting on his short-sighted glasses, and pursing up his lips.

"Yes," said Louisa, falteringly.

"Let me see, then. Against cakes : how cakes are bad things, especially if they are sweet and have plums in them."

Louisa took the affair rather seriously, and got down from the Vicar's knee to go to Fred.

"Ah, I see it will not do to preach on New Year's Day," said Mr Farebrother, rising and walking away. He had discovered of late that Fred had become jealous of him, and also that he himself was not losing his preference for Mary above all other women.

"A delightful young person is Miss Garth," said Mrs Farebrother, who had been watching her son's movements.

"Yes," said Mrs Vincy, obliged to reply, as the old lady turned to her expectantly. "It is a pity she is not better-looking."

"I cannot say that," said Mrs Farebrother, decisively. "I like her countenance. We must not always ask for beauty, when a good God has seen fit to make an excellent young woman without it. I put good manners first, and Miss Garth will know how to conduct herself in any station."

The old lady was a little sharp in her tone, having a prospective reference to Mary's becoming her daughter-in-law ; for there was this inconvenience in Mary's position with regard to Fred, that it was not suitable to be made public, and hence the three ladies at Lowick Parsonage were still hoping that Camden would choose Miss Garth.

New visitors entered, and the drawing-room was given up to music and games, while whist-tables were prepared in the quiet room on the other side of the hall. Mr Farebrother played a rubber to satisfy his mother, who regarded her occasional whist as a protest against scandal and novelty of opinion, in which light even a revoke had its dignity. But at the end he got Mr Chichely to take his place, and left the room. As he crossed the hall, Lydgate had just come in and was taking off his greatcoat.

"You are the man I was going to look for," said the Vicar ; and instead of entering the drawing-room, they walked along the hall and stood against the fireplace, where the frosty air helped to make a glowing bank. "You see, I can leave the whist-table easily enough," he went on, smiling at Lydgate, "now I don't play for money. I owe that to you, Mrs Casaubon says."

"How ?" said Lydgate, coldly.

"Ah, you didn't mean me to know it ; I call that ungenerous reticence. You should let a man have the pleasure of feeling that you have done him a good turn. I don't enter into some people's dislike of being under an obligation : upon my word, I prefer being under an obligation to everybody for behaving well to me."

"I can't tell what you mean," said Lydgate, "unless it is that I once spoke of you to Mrs Casaubon. But I did not think that she would break her promise not to mention that I had done so," said Lydgate, leaning his back against the corner of the mantelpiece, and showing no radiance in his face.

"It was Brooke who let it out, only the other day. He paid me the compliment of saying that he was very glad I had the living, though you had come across his tactics, and had praised me up as a

Ken and a Tillotson, and that sort of thing, till Mrs Casaubon would hear of no one else." [5]

"Oh, Brooke is such a leaky-minded fool," said Lydgate contemptuously

"Well, I was glad of the leakiness then. I don't see why you shouldn't like me to know that you wished to do me a service, my dear fellow. And you certainly have done me one. It's rather a strong check to one's self-complacency to find how much of one's right doing depends on not being in want of money. A man will not be tempted to say the Lord's Prayer backward to please the devil, if hs doesn't want the devil's services. I have no need to hang on the smiles of chance now."

"I don't see that there's any money-getting without chance," said Lydgate ; " if a man gets it in a profession, it's pretty sure to come by chance."

Mr Farebrother thought he could account for this speech, in striking contrast with Lydgate's former way of talking, as the perversity which will often spring from the moodiness of a man ill at ease in his affairs. He answered in a tone of good-humoured admission—

" Ah, there's enormous patience wanted with the way of the world. But it is the easier for a man to wait patiently when he has friends who love him, and ask for nothing better than to help him through, so far as it lies in their power."

"Oh yes," said Lydgate, in a careless tone, changing his attitude and looking at his watch. " People make much more of their difficulties than they need to do."

He knew as distinctly as possible that this was an offer of help to himself from Mr Farebrother, and he could not bear it. So strangely determined are we mortals, that, after having been long gratified with the sense that he had privately done the Vicar a service, the suggestion that the Vicar discerned his need of a service in return made him shrink into unconquerable reticence. Besides, behind all making of such offers what else must come ?—that he should " mention his case," imply that he wanted specific things. At that moment, suicide seemed easier.

Mr Farebrother was too keen a man not to know the meaning of that reply, and there was a certain massiveness in Lydgate's manner and tone, corresponding with his physique, which if he repelled your advances in the first instance seemed to put persuasive devices out of question.

" What time are you ? " said the Vicar, devouring his wounded feeling.

" After eleven," said Lydgate. And they went into the drawing-room.

5. Thomas Ken (1637–1711), English bishop, writer of devotional prose and verse; John Tillotson (1630–94), English theologian and preacher, later Archbishop of Canterbury.

CHAPTER LXIV.

1st Gent. Where lies the power, there let the blame lie too.
2d Gent. Nay, power is relative; you cannot fright
The coming pest with border fortresses,
Or catch your carp with subtle argument.
All force is twain in one: cause is not cause
Unless effect be there; and action's self
Must needs contain a passive. So command
Exists but with obedience.

EVEN if Lydgate had been inclined to be quite open about his affairs, he knew that it would have hardly been in Mr Farebrother's power to give him the help he immediately wanted. With the year's bills coming in from his tradesmen, with Dover's threatening hold on his furniture, and with nothing to depend on but slow dribbling payments from patients who must not be offended — for the handsome fees he had had from Freshitt Hall and Lowick Manor had been easily absorbed—nothing less than a thousand pounds would have freed him from actual embarrassment, and left a residue which, according to the favourite phrase of hopefulness in such circumstances, would have given him " time to look about him."

Naturally, the merry Christmas bringing the happy New Year, when fellow-citizens expect to be paid for the trouble and goods they have smilingly bestowed on their neighbours, had so tightened the pressure of sordid cares on Lydgate's mind that it was hardly possible for him to think unbrokenly of any other subject, even the most habitual and soliciting. He was not an ill-tempered man; his intellectual activity, the ardent kindness of his heart, as well as his strong frame, would always, under tolerably easy conditions, have kept him above the petty uncontrolled susceptibilities which make bad temper. But he was now a prey to that worst irritation which arises not simply from annoyances, but from the second consciousness underlying those annoyances, of wasted energy and a degrading preoccupation, which was the reverse of all his former purposes. " *This* is what I am thinking of; and *that* is what I might have been thinking of," was the bitter incessant murmur within him, making every difficulty a double goad to impatience.

Some gentlemen have made an amazing figure in literature by general discontent with the universe as a trap of dulness into which their great souls have fallen by mistake; but the sense of a stupendous self and an insignificant world may have its consolations. Lydgate's discontent was much harder to bear: it was the sense that there was a grand existence in thought and effective action lying around him, while his self was being narrowed into the miserable isolation of egoistic fears, and vulgar anxieties for events that might allay such fears. His troubles will perhaps appear miserably sordid, and beneath the attention of lofty persons who can know nothing of debt except on a magnificent scale. Doubtless they were sordid ; and for the majority, who are not lofty, there is no escape from sordidness but by being free from money-craving, with all its base hopes and temptations, its watching for death, its hinted requests, its horse-dealer's desire to make bad work pass for good, its seeking for function which ought to be another's, its compulsion often to long for Luck in the shape of a wide calamity.

It was because Lydgate writhed under the idea of getting his neck beneath this vile yoke that he had fallen into a bitter moody state which was continually widening Rosamond's alienation from him. After the first disclosure about the bill of sale, he had made many efforts to draw her into sympathy with him about possible measures for narrowing their expenses, and with the threatening approach of Christmas his propositions grew more and more definite. " We two can do with only one servant, and live on very little," he said, " and I shall manage with one horse." For Lydgate, as we have seen, had begun to reason, with a more distinct vision, about the expenses of living, and any share of pride he had given to appearances of that sort was meagre compared with the pride which made him revolt from exposure as a debtor, or from asking men to help him with their money.

" Of course you can dismiss the other two servants, if you like," said Rosamond ; " but I should have thought it would be very injurious to your position for us to live in a poor way. You must expect your practice to be lowered."

" My dear Rosamond, it is not a question of choice. We have begun too expensively. Peacock, you know, lived in a much smaller house than this. It is my fault : I ought to have known better, and I deserve a thrashing—if there were anybody who had a right to give it me—for bringing you into the necessity of living in a poorer way than you have been used to. But we married because we loved each other, I suppose. And that may help us to pull along till things get better. Come, dear, put down that work and come to me."

He was really in chill gloom about her at that moment, but he dreaded a future without affection, and was determined to resist the oncoming of division between them. Rosamond obeyed him, and he took her on his knee, but in her secret soul she was utterly aloof from him. The poor thing saw only that the world was not ordered to her liking, and Lydgate was part of that world. But he held her waist with one hand and laid the other gently on both of hers ; for this rather abrupt man had much tenderness in his manners towards women, seeming to have always present in his imagination the weakness of their frames and the delicate poise of their health both in body and mind. And he began again to speak persuasively.

" I find, now I look into things a little, Rosy, that it is wonderful what an amount of money slips away in our housekeeping. I suppose the servants are careless, and we have had a great many people coming. But there must be many in our rank who manage with much less : they must do with commoner things, I suppose, and look after the scraps. It seems, money goes but a little way in these matters, for Wrench has everything as plain as possible, and he has a very large practice."

" Oh, if you think of living as the Wrenches do ! " said Rosamond, with a little turn of her neck. " But I have heard you express your disgust at that way of living."

" Yes, they have bad taste in everything—they make economy look ugly. We needn't do that. I only meant that they avoid expenses, although Wrench has a capital practice."

" Why should not you have a good practice, Tertius ? Mr Peacock had. You should be more careful not to offend people, and you should send out medicines as the others do. I am sure you began well, and you got several good houses. It cannot answer to be eccentric ; you should think what will be generally liked," said Rosamond, in a decided little tone of admonition.

Lydgate's anger rose : he was prepared to be indulgent towards feminine weakness, but not towards feminine dictation. The shallowness of a waternixie's soul may have a charm until she becomes didactic.[1] But he controlled himself, and only said, with a touch of despotic firmness—

" What I am to do in my practice, Rosy, it is for me to judge. That is not the question between us. It is enough for you to know that our income is likely to be a very narrow one—hardly four hundred, perhaps less, for a long time to come, and we must try to rearrange our lives in accordance with that fact."

Rosamond was silent for a moment or two, looking before her, and then said, " My uncle Bulstrode ought to allow you a salary for the time you give to the Hospital : it is not right that you should work for nothing."

" It was understood from the beginning that my services would be gratuitous. That, again, need not enter into our discussion. I have pointed out what is the only probability," said Lydgate, impatiently. Then checking himself, he went on more quietly—

" I think I see one resource which would free us from a good deal of the present difficulty. I hear that young Ned Plymdale is going to be married to Miss Sophy Toller. They are rich, and it is not often that a good house is vacant in Middlemarch. I feel sure that they would be glad to take this house from us with most of our furniture, and they would be willing to pay handsomely for the lease. I can employ Trumbull to speak to Plymdale about it."

Rosamond left her husband's knee and walked slowly to the other end of the room ; when she turned round and walked towards him it was evident that the tears had come, and that she was biting her under-lip and clasping her hands to keep herself from crying. Lydgate was wretched—shaken with anger and yet feeling that it would be unmanly to vent the anger just now.

" I am very sorry, Rosamond ; I know this is painful."

" I thought, at least, when I had borne to send the plate back and have that man taking an inventory of the furniture—I should have thought *that* would suffice."

" I explained it to you at the time, dear. That was only a security and behind that security there is a debt. And that debt must be

1. Waternixie: water nymph.

paid within the next few months, else we shall have our furniture sold. If young Plymdale will take our house and most of our furniture, we shall be able to pay that debt, and some others too, and we shall be quit of a place too expensive for us. We might take a smaller house : Trumbull, I know, has a very decent one to let at thirty pounds a-year, and this is ninety." Lydgate uttered this speech in the curt hammering way with which we usually try to nail down a vague mind to imperative facts. Tears rolled silently down Rosamond's cheeks ; she just pressed her handkerchief against them, and stood looking at the large vase on the mantelpiece. It was a moment of more intense bitterness than she had ever felt before. At last, she said, without hurry and with careful emphasis—

" I never could have believed that you would like to act in that way."

" Like it ?" burst out Lydgate, rising from his chair, thrusting his hands in his pockets and stalking away from the hearth ; "it's not a question of liking. Of course, I don't like it ; it's the only thing I can do." He wheeled round there, and turned towards her.

" I should have thought there were many other means than that," said Rosamond. " Let us have a sale and leave Middlemarch altogether."

" To do what ? What is the use of my leaving my work in Middlemarch to go where I have none ? We should be just as penniless elsewhere as we are here," said Lydgate still more angrily.

" If we are to be in that position it will be entirely your own doing, Tertius," said Rosamond, turning round to speak with the fullest conviction. " You will not behave as you ought to do to your own family. You offended Captain Lydgate. Sir Godwin was very kind to me when we were at Quallingham, and I am sure if you showed proper regard to him and told him your affairs, he would do anything for you. But rather than that, you like giving up our house and furniture to Mr Ned Plymdale."

There was something like fierceness in Lydgate's eyes, as he answered with new violence, " Well then, if you will have it so, I do like it. I admit that I like it better than making a fool of myself by going to beg where it's of no use. Understand then, that it is what *I like to do.*"

There was a tone in the last sentence which was equivalent to the clutch of his strong hand on Rosamond's delicate arm. But for all that, his will was not a whit stronger than hers. She immediately walked out of the room in silence, but with an intense determination to hinder what Lydgate liked to do.

He went out of the house, but as his blood cooled he felt that the chief result of the discussion was a deposit of dread within him at the idea of opening with his wife in future subjects which might again urge him to violent speech. It was as if a fracture in delicate crystal had begun, and he was afraid of any movement that might make it fatal. His marriage would be a mere piece of bitter irony if they could not go on loving each other. He had long ago made up his mind to what he thought was her negative character — her want of sensibility, which showed itself in disregard both of his specific wishes and of his general aims. The first great disappointment had been borne : the tender devotedness and docile adoration of the ideal wife must be renounced, and life must be taken up on a lower stage of expectation, as it is by men who have lost their limbs. But the real wife had not only her claims, she had still a hold on his heart, and it was his intense desire that the hold should remain strong. In marriage, the certainty, " She will never love me much," is easier to bear than the fear, " I shall love her no more." Hence, after that outburst, his inward effort was entirely to excuse her, and to blame the hard circumstances which were partly his fault. He tried that evening, by petting her, to heal the wound he had made in the morning, and it was not in Rosamond's nature to be repellent or sulky ; indeed, she welcomed the signs that her husband loved her and was under control. But this was something quite distinct from loving *him*.

Lydgate would not have chosen soon to recur to the plan of parting with the house ; he was resolved to carry it out, and say as little more about it as possible. But Rosamond herself touched on it at breakfast by saying, mildly—

" Have you spoken to Trumbull yet ? "

" No," said Lydgate, " but I shall call on him as I go by this morning. No time must be lost." He took Rosamond's question as a sign that she withdrew her inward opposition, and kissed her head caressingly when he got up to go away.

As soon as it was late enough to make a call, Rosamond went to Mrs Plymdale, Mr Ned's mother, and entered with pretty congratulations into the subject of the coming marriage. Mrs Plymdale's maternal view was, that Rosamond might possibly now have retrospective glimpses of her own folly ; and feeling the advantages to be at present all on the side of her son, was too kind a woman not to behave graciously.

" Yes, Ned is most happy, I must say. And Sophy Toller is all I could desire in a daughter-in-law. Of course her father is able to do something handsome for her — that is only what would be expected with a brewery like his. And the connection is everything we should desire. But that is not what I look at. She is such a very nice girl — no airs, no pretensions, though on a level with the first. I don't mean with the titled aristocracy. I see very little good in people aiming out of their own sphere. I mean that Sophy is equal to the best in the town, and she is contented with that."

" I have always thought her very agreeable," said Rosamond.

" I look upon it as a reward for Ned, who never held his head too high, that he should have got into the very best connection," continued Mrs Plymdale, her native sharpness softened by a fervid sense that she was taking a correct view. " And such particular people as the Tollers are, they might have objected because some of our friends are not theirs. It is well known that your aunt Bulstrode and I have been intimate from our youth, and Mr Plymdale has been always on Mr Bulstrode's side. And I myself prefer serious opinions. But the Tollers have welcomed Ned all the same."

" I am sure he is a very deserving, well-principled young man," said Rosamond, with a neat air of patronage, in return for Mrs Plymdale's wholesome corrections.

" Oh, he has not the style of a captain in the army, or that sort of carriage as if everybody was beneath him, or that showy kind of talking, and singing, and intellectual talent. But I am thankful he has not. It is a poor preparation both for here and Hereafter."

" Oh dear, yes ; appearances have very little to do with happiness," said Rosamond. " I think there is every prospect of their being a happy couple. What house will they take ?"

" Oh, as for that, they must put up with what they can get. They have been looking at the house in St Peter's Place, next to Mr Hackbutt's ; it belongs to him, and he is putting it nicely in repair. I suppose they are not likely to hear of a better. Indeed, I think Ned will decide the matter to-day."

" I should think it is a nice house ; I like St Peter's Place."

" Well, it is near the Church, and a genteel situation. But the windows are narrow, and it is all ups and downs. You don't happen to know of any other that would be at liberty ?" said Mrs Plymdale, fixing her round black eyes on Rosamond with the animation of a sudden thought in them.

" Oh no ; I hear so little of those things."

Rosamond had not foreseen that question and answer in setting out to pay her visit ; she had simply meant to gather any information which would help her to avert the parting with her own house under circumstances thoroughly disagreeable to her. As to the untruth in her reply, she no more reflected on it than she did on the untruth there was in her saying that appearances had very little to do with happiness. Her object, she was convinced, was thoroughly justifiable : it was Lydgate whose intention was inexcusable ; and there was a plan in her mind which, when she had carried it out fully, would prove how very false a step it would have been for him to have descended from his position.

She returned home by Mr Borthrop Trumbull's office, meaning to call there. It was the first time in her life that Rosamond had thought of doing anything in the form of business, but she felt equal to the occasion. That she should be obliged to do what she intensely disliked, was an idea which turned her quiet tenacity into active invention. Here was a case in which it could not be enough simply to disobey and be serenely, placidly obstinate : she must act according to her judgment, and she said to herself that her judgment was right —" indeed, if it had not been, she would not have wished to act on it."

Mr Trumbull was in the back-room of his office, and received Rosamond with his finest manners, not only because he had much sensibility to her charms, but because the good-natured fibre in him was stirred by his certainty that Lydgate was in difficulties, and that this uncommonly pretty woman — this young lady with the highest personal attractions — was likely to feel the pinch of trouble—to find herself involved in circumstances beyond her control. He begged her to do him the honour to take a seat, and stood before her trimming and comporting himself with an eager solicitude, which was chiefly benevolent. Rosamond's first question was, whether her husband had called on Mr Trumbull that morning, to speak about disposing of their house.

" Yes, ma'am, yes, he did ; he did so," said the good auctioneer, trying to throw something soothing into his iteration. " I was about to fulfil his order, if possible, this afternoon. He wished me not to procrastinate."

" I called to tell you not to go any further, Mr Trumbull ; and I beg of you not to mention what has been said on the subject. Will you oblige me ?"

" Certainly I will, Mrs Lydgate, certainly. Confidence is sacred with me on business or any other topic. I am then to consider the commission withdrawn?" said Mr Trumbull, adjusting the long ends of his blue cravat with both hands, and looking at Rosamond deferentially.

"Yes, if you please. I find that Mr Ned Plymdale has taken a house—the one in St Peter's Place next to Mr Hackbutt's. Mr Lydgate would be annoyed that his orders should be fulfilled uselessly. And besides that, there are other circumstances which render the proposal unnecessary."

"Very good, Mrs Lydgate, very good. I am at your commands, whenever you require any service of me," said Mr Trumbull, who felt pleasure in conjecturing that some new resources had been opened. "Rely on me, I beg. The affair shall go no further."

That evening Lydgate was a little comforted by observing that Rosamond was more lively than she had usually been of late, and even seemed interested in doing what would please him without being asked. He thought, "If she will be happy and I can rub through, what does it all signify? It is only a narrow swamp that we have to pass in a long journey. If I can get my mind clear again, I shall do."

He was so much cheered that he began to search for an account of experiments which he had long ago meant to look up, and had neglected out of that creeping self-despair which comes in the train of petty anxieties. He felt again some of the old delightful absorption in a far-reaching inquiry, while Rosamond played the quiet music which was as helpful to his meditation as the plash of an oar on the evening lake. It was rather late; he had pushed away all the books, and was looking at the fire with his hands clasped behind his head in forgetfulness of everything except the construction of a new controlling experiment, when Rosamond, who had left the piano and was leaning back in her chair watching him, said—

"Mr Ned Plymdale has taken a house already."

Lydgate, startled and jarred, looked up in silence for a moment, like a man who has been disturbed in his sleep. Then flushing with an unpleasant consciousness, he asked—

"How do you know?"

"I called at Mrs Plymdale's this morning, and she told me that he had taken the house in St Peter's Place next to Mr Hackbutt's."

Lydgate was silent. He drew his hands from behind his head and pressed them against the hair which was hanging, as it was apt to do, in a mass on his forehead, while he rested his elbows on his knees. He was feeling bitter disappointment, as if he had opened a door out of a suffocating place and had found it walled up; but he also felt sure that Rosamond was pleased with the cause of his disappointment. He preferred not looking at her and not speaking, until he had got over the first spasm of vexation. After all, he said in his bitterness, what can a woman care about so much as house and furniture? a husband without them is an absurdity. When he looked up and pushed his hair aside, his dark eyes had a miserable blank non-expectance of sympathy in them, but he only said, coolly—

"Perhaps some one else may turn up. I told Trumbull to be on the look-out if he failed with Plymdale."

Rosamond made no remark. She trusted to the chance that nothing more would pass between her husband and the auctioneer until some issue should have justified her interference; at any rate, she had hindered the event which she immediately dreaded. After a pause, she said—

"How much money is it that those disagreeable people want?"

"What disagreeable people?"

"Those who took the list—and the others. I mean, how much money would satisfy them so that you need not be troubled any more?"

Lydgate surveyed her for a moment, as if he were looking for symptoms, and then said, "Oh, if I could have got six hundred from Plymdale for furniture and as premium, I might have managed. I could have paid off Dover, and given enough on account to the others to make them wait patiently, if we contracted our expenses."

"But I mean how much should you want if we stayed in this house?"

"More than I am likely to get anywhere," said Lydgate, with rather a grating sarcasm in his tone. It angered him to perceive that Rosamond's mind was wandering over impracticable wishes instead of facing possible efforts.

"Why should you not mention the sum?" said Rosamond, with a mild indication that she did not like his manners.

"Well," said Lydgate, in a guessing tone, "it would take at least a thousand to set me at ease. But," he added, incisively, "I have to consider what I shall do without it, not with it."

Rosamond said no more.

But the next day she carried out her plan of writing to Sir Godwin Lydgate. Since the Captain's visit, she had received a letter from him, and also one from Mrs Mengan, his married sister, condoling with her on the loss of her baby, and expressing vaguely the hope that they should see her again at Quallingham. Lydgate had told her that this politeness meant nothing; but she was secretly convinced that any backwardness in Lydgate's family towards him was due to his cold and contemptuous behaviour, and she had answered the letters in her most charming manner, feeling some confidence that a specific invitation would follow. But there had been total silence. The Captain evidently was not a great penman, and Rosamond reflected that the sisters might have been abroad. However, the season was come for thinking of friends at home, and at any rate Sir Godwin, who had chucked her under the chin, and pronounced her to be like the celebrated beauty, Mrs Croly, who had made a conquest of him in 1790, would be touched by any appeal from her, and would find it pleasant for her sake to behave as he ought to do towards his nephew. Rosamond was naïvely convinced of what an old gentleman ought to do to prevent her from suffering annoyance. And she wrote what she considered the most judicious letter possible —one which would strike Sir Godwin as a proof of her excellent sense—pointing out how desirable it was that Tertius should quit such a place as Middlemarch for one more fitted to his talents, how the unpleasant character of the inhabitants had hindered his professional success, and how in consequence he was in money difficulties, from which it would require a thousand pounds thoroughly to extricate him. She did not say that Tertius was unaware of her intention to write; for she had the idea that his supposed sanction of her letter would be in accordance with what she did say of his great regard for his uncle Godwin as the relative who had always been his best friend. Such was the force of poor Rosamond's tactics now she applied them to affairs.

This had happened before the party on New Year's Day, and no answer had yet come from Sir Godwin. But on the morning of that day Lydgate had to learn that Rosamond had revoked his order to Borthrop Trumbull. Feeling it necessary that she should be gradually accustomed to the idea of their quitting the house in Lowick Gate, he overcame his reluctance to speak to her again on the subject, and when they were breakfasting said—

" I shall try to see Trumbull this morning, and tell him to advertise the house in the ' Pioneer ' and the ' Trumpet.' If the thing were advertised, some one might be inclined to take it who would not otherwise have thought of a change. In these country places many people go on in their old houses when their families are too large for them, for want of knowing where they can find another. And Trumbull seems to have got no bite at all."

Rosamond knew that the inevitable moment was come. " I ordered Trumbull not to inquire further," she said, with a careful calmness which was evidently defensive.

Lydgate stared at her in mute amazement. Only half an hour before he had been fastening up her plaits for her, and talking the " little language" of affection, which Rosamond, though not returning it, accepted as if she had been a serene and lovely image, now and then miraculously dimpling towards her votary. With such fibres still astir in him, the shock he received could not at once be distinctly anger ; it was confused pain. He laid down the knife and fork with which he was carving, and throwing himself back in his chair, said at last, with a cool irony in his tone—

" May I ask when and why you did so ? "

" When I knew that the Plymdales had taken a house, I called to tell him not to mention ours to them ; and at the same time I told him not to let the affair go on any further. I knew that it would be very injurious to you if it were known that you wished to part with your house and furniture, and I had a very strong objection to it. I think that was reason enough."

" It was of no consequence then that I had told you imperative reasons of another kind ; of no consequence that I had come to a different conclusion, and given an order accordingly ? " said Lydgate, bitingly, the thunder and lightning gathering about his brow and eyes.

The effect of any one's anger on Rosamond had always been to make her shrink in cold dislike, and to become all the more calmly correct, in the conviction that she was not the person to misbehave, whatever others might do. She replied—

" I think I had a perfect right to speak on a subject which concerns me at least as much as you."

" Clearly—you had a right to speak, but only to me. You had no right to contradict my orders secretly, and treat me as if I were a fool," said Lydgate, in the same tone as before. Then with some added scorn, " Is it possible to make you understand what the consequences will be ? Is it of any use for me to tell you again why we *must* try to part with the house ? "

" It is not necessary for you to tell me again," said Rosamond, in a voice that fell and trickled like cold water-drops. " I remembered what you said. You spoke just as violently as you do now. But that does not alter my opinion that you ought to try every other means rather than take a step which is so painful to me. And as to advertising the house, I think it would be perfectly degrading to you."

" And suppose I disregard your opinion as you disregard mine ? "

" You can do so, of course. But I think you ought to have told me before we were married that you would place me in the worst position, rather than give up your own will."

Lydgate did not speak, but tossed his head on one side, and twitched the corners of his mouth in despair. Rosamond, seeing that he was not looking at her, rose and set his cup of coffee before him ; but he took no notice of it, and went on with an inward drama and argument, occasionally moving in his seat, resting one arm on the table, and rubbing his hand against his hair. There was a conflux of emotions and thoughts in him that would not let him either give thorough way to his anger or persevere with simple rigidity of resolve. Rosamond took advantage of his silence.

" When we were married every one felt that your position was very high. I could not have imagined then that you would want to sell our furniture, and take a house in Bride Street, where the rooms are like cages. If we are to live in that way let us at least leave Middlemarch."

" These would be very strong considerations," said Lydgate, half ironically—still there was a withered paleness about his lips as he looked at his coffee, and did not drink—" these would be very strong considerations if I did not happen to be in debt."

" Many persons must have been in debt in the same way, but if they are respectable, people trust them. I am sure I have heard papa say that the Torbits were in debt, and they went on very well. It cannot be good to act rashly," said Rosamond, with serene wisdom.

Lydgate sat paralysed by opposing impulses : since no reasoning he could apply to Rosamond seemed likely to conquer her assent, he wanted to smash and grind some object on which he could at least produce an impression, or else to tell her brutally that he was master, and she must obey. But he not only dreaded the effect of such extremities on their mutual life—he had a growing dread of Rosamond's quiet elusive obstinacy, which would not allow any assertion of power to be final ; and again, she had touched him in a spot of keenest feeling by implying that she had been deluded with a false vision of happiness in marrying him. As to saying that he was master, it was not the fact. The very resolution to which he had wrought himself by dint of logic and honourable pride was beginning to relax under her torpedo contact. He swallowed half his cup of coffee, and then rose to go.

" I may at least request that you will not go to Trumbull at present—until it has been seen that there are no other means," said Rosamond. Although she was not subject to much fear, she felt it safer not to betray that she had written to Sir Godwin. " Promise me that you will not go to him for a few weeks, or without telling me."

Lydgate gave a short laugh. " I think it is I who should exact a promise that you will do nothing without telling me," he said, turning his eyes sharply upon her, and then moving to the door.

" You remember that we are going to dine at papa's," said Rosamond, wishing that he should turn and make a more thorough concession to her. But he only said " Oh yes," impatiently, and went away. She held it to be very odious in him that he did not think the painful propositions he had had to make to her were enough, without showing so unpleasant a temper. And when she put the moderate request that he would defer going to Trumbull again, it was cruel in him not to assure her of what he meant to do. She was convinced of her having acted in every way for the best; and each grating or angry speech of Lydgate's served only as an addition to the register of offences in her mind. Poor Rosamond for months had begun to associate her husband with feelings of disappointment, and the terribly inflexible relation of marriage had lost its charm of encouraging delightful dreams. It had freed her from the disagreeables of her father's house, but it had not given her everything that she had wished and hoped. The Lydgate with whom she had been in love had been a group of airy conditions for her, most of which had disappeared, while their place had been taken by everyday details which must be lived through slowly from hour to hour, not floated through with a rapid selection of favourable aspects. The habits of Lydgate's profession, his home preoccupation with scientific subjects, which seemed to her almost like a morbid vampire's taste, his peculiar views of things which had never entered into the dialogue of courtship—all these continually-alienating influences, even without the fact of his having placed himself at a disadvantage in the town, and without that first shock of revelation about Dover's debt, would have made his presence dull to her. There was another presence which ever since the early days of her marriage, until four months ago, had been an agreeable excitement, but that was gone : Rosamond would not confess to herself how much the consequent blank had to do with her utter *ennui;* and it seemed to her (perhaps she was right) that an invitation to Quallingham, and an opening for Lydgate to settle elsewhere than in Middlemarch—in London, or somewhere likely to be free from unpleasantness—would satisfy her quite well, and make her indifferent to the absence of Will Ladislaw, towards whom she felt some resentment for his exaltation of Mrs Casaubon.

That was the state of things with Lydgate and Rosamond on the New Year's Day when they dined at her father's, she looking mildly neutral towards him in remembrance of his ill-tempered behaviour at breakfast, and he carrying a much deeper effect from the inward conflict in which that morning scene was only one of many epochs. His flushed effort while talking to Mr Farebrother—his effort after the cynical pretence that all ways of getting money are essentially the same, and that chance has an empire which reduces choice to a fool's illusion—was but the symptom of a wavering resolve, a benumbed response to the old stimuli of enthusiasm.

What was he to do ? He saw even more keenly than Rosamond did the dreariness of taking her into the small house in Bride Street, where she would have scanty furniture around her and discontent within : a life of privation and life with Rosamond were two images which had become more and more irreconcilable ever since the threat of privation had disclosed itself. But even if his resolves had forced the two images into combination, the useful preliminaries to that hard change were not visibly within reach. And though he had not given the promise which his wife had asked for, he did not go again to Trumbull. He even began to think of taking a rapid journey to the North and seeing Sir Godwin. He had once believed that nothing would urge him into making an application for money to his uncle, but he had not then known the full pressure of alternatives yet more disagreeable. He could not depend on the effect of a letter ; it was only in an interview, however disagreeable this might be to himself, that he could give a thorough explanation and could test the effectiveness of kinship. No sooner had Lydgate begun to represent this step to himself as the easiest than there was a reaction of anger that he— he who had long ago determined to live aloof from such abject calculations, such self-interested anxiety about the inclinations and the pockets of men with whom he had been proud to have no aims in common—should have fallen not simply to their level, but to the level of soliciting them.

CHAPTER LXV.

" One of us two must bowen douteless;
And, sith a man is more reasonable
Than woman is, ye [men] moste be suffrable."
                    —CHAUCER : *Canterbury Tales.* 1

THE bias of human nature to be slow in correspondence triumphs even over the present quickening in the general pace of things : what wonder then that in 1832 old Sir Godwin Lydgate was slow to write a letter which was of consequence to others rather than to himself ? Nearly three weeks of the new year were gone, and Rosamond, awaiting an answer to her winning appeal, was every day disappointed. Lydgate, in total ignorance of her expectations, was seeing the bills come in, and feeling that Dover's use of his advantage over other creditors was imminent. He had never mentioned to Rosamond his brooding purpose of going to Quallingham : he did not want to admit what would appear to her a concession to her wishes after indignant refusal, until the last moment ; but he was really expecting to set off soon. A slice of the railway would enable him to manage the whole journey and back in four days.

But one morning after Lydgate had gone out, a letter came addressed to him, which Rosamond saw clearly to be from Sir Godwin. She was full of hope. Perhaps there might be a particular note to her enclosed; but Lydgate was naturally addressed on the question of money or other aid, and the fact that he was written to, nay, the very delay in writing at all, seemed to certify that the answer was thoroughly compliant. She was too much excited by these thoughts to do anything but light stitching in a warm corner of the dining-room, with the outside of this momentous letter lying on the table before her. About twelve she heard her husband's step in the passage, and tripping to open the door, she said in her lightest tones, " Tertius, come in here—here is a letter for you."

" Ah ? " he said, not taking off his hat, but just turning her round within his arm to walk towards the spot where the letter lay. " My uncle Godwin ! " he exclaimed, while Rosamond reseated herself, and

1. "Wife of Bath's Prologue," lines 440–42.

watched him as he opened the letter. She had expected him to be surprised.

While Lydgate's eyes glanced rapidly over the brief letter, she saw his face, usually of a pale brown, taking on a dry whiteness ; with nostrils and lips quivering he tossed down the letter before her, and said violently—

" It will be impossible to endure life with you, if you will always be acting secretly—acting in opposition to me and hiding your actions."

He checked his speech and turned his back on her — then wheeled round and walked about, sat down, and got up again restlessly, grasping hard the objects deep down in his pockets. He was afraid of saying something irremediably cruel.

Rosamond too had changed colour as she read. The letter ran in this way :—

" DEAR TERTIUS,—Don't set your wife to write to me when you have anything to ask. It is a roundabout wheedling sort of thing which I should not have credited you with. I never choose to write to a woman on matters of business. As to my supplying you with a thousand pounds, or only half that sum, I can do nothing of the sort. My own family drains me to the last penny. With two younger sons and three daughters, I am not likely to have cash to spare. You seem to have got through your own money pretty quickly, and to have made a mess where you are ; the sooner you go somewhere else the better. But I have nothing to do with men of your profession, and can't help you there. I did the best I could for you as guardian, and let you have your own way in taking to medicine. You might have gone into the army or the Church. Your money would have held out for that, and there would have been a surer ladder before you. Your uncle Charles has had a grudge against you for not going into his profession, but not I. I have always wished you well, but you must consider yourself on your own legs entirely now.—Your affectionate uncle,
" GODWIN LYDGATE."

When Rosamond had finished reading the letter she sat quite still, with her hands folded before her, restraining any show of her keen disappointment, and intrenching herself in quiet passivity under her husband's wrath. Lydgate paused in his movements, looked at her again, and said, with biting severity—

" Will this be enough to convince you of the harm you may do by secret meddling ? Have you sense enough to recognise now your incompetence to judge and act for me—to interfere with your ignorance in affairs which it belongs to me to decide on ? "

The words were hard ; but this was not the first time that Lydgate had been frustrated by her. She did not look at him, and made no reply.

" I had nearly resolved on going to Quallingham. It would have cost me pain enough to do it, yet it might have been of some use. But it has been of no use for me to think of anything. You have always been counteracting me secretly. You delude me with a false assent, and then I am at the mercy of your devices. If you mean to resist every wish I express, say so and defy me. I shall at least know what I am doing then."

It is a terrible moment in young lives when the closeness of love's bond has turned to this power of galling. In spite of Rosamond's self-control a tear fell silently and rolled over her lips. She still said nothing ; but under that quietude was hidden an intense effect : she was in such entire disgust with her husband that she wished she had never seen him. Sir Godwin's rudeness towards her and utter want of feeling ranged him with Dover and all other creditors—disagreeable people who only thought of themselves, and did not mind how annoying they were to her. Even her father was unkind, and might have done more for them. In fact there was but one person in Rosamond's world whom she did not regard as blameworthy, and that was the graceful creature with blond plaits and with little hands crossed before her, who had never expressed herself unbecomingly, and had always acted for the best—the best naturally being what she best liked.

Lydgate pausing and looking at her began to feel that half-maddening sense of helplessness which comes over passionate people when their passion is met by an innocent-looking silence whose meek victimised air seems to put them in the wrong, and at last infects even the justest indignation with a doubt of its justice. He needed to recover the full sense that he was in the right by moderating his words.

"Can you not see, Rosamond," he began again, trying to be simply grave and not bitter, "that nothing can be so fatal as a want of openness and confidence between us ? It has happened again and again that I have expressed a decided wish, and you have seemed to assent, yet after that you have secretly disobeyed my wish. In that way I can never know what I have to trust to. There would be some hope for us if you would admit this. Am I such an unreasonable, furious brute ? Why should you not be open with me ?"

Still silence.

"Will you only say that you have been mistaken, and that I may depend on your not acting secretly in future ?" said Lydgate, urgently, but with something of request in his tone which Rosamond was quick to perceive. She spoke with coolness.

"I cannot possibly make admissions or promises in answer to such words as you have used towards me. I have not been accustomed to language of that kind. You have spoken of my 'secret meddling,' and my 'interfering ignorance,' and my 'false assent.' I have never expressed myself in that way to you, and I think that you ought to apologise. You spoke of its being impossible to live with me. Certainly you have not made my life pleasant to me of late. I think it was to be expected that I should try to avert some of the hardships which our marriage has brought on me." Another tear fell as Rosamond ceased speaking, and she pressed it away as quietly as the first.

Lydgate flung himself into a chair, feeling checkmated. What place was there in her mind for a remonstrance to lodge in ? He laid down his hat, flung an arm over the back of his chair, and looked down for some moments without speaking. Rosamond had the double purchase over him of insensibility to the point of justice in his reproach, and of sensibility to the undeniable hardships now present in her married life. Although her duplicity in the affair of the house had exceeded what he knew, and had really hindered the Plymdales from knowing of it, she had no consciousness that her action could rightly be called false. We are not obliged to identify our own acts according to a strict classification, any more than the materials of our grocery and clothes. Rosamond felt that she was aggrieved, and that this was what Lydgate had to recognise.

As for him, the need of accommodating himself to her nature, which was inflexible in proportion to its negations, held him as with pincers. He had begun to have an alarmed foresight of her irrevocable loss of love for him, and the consequent dreariness of their life. The ready fulness of his emotions made this dread alternate quickly with the first violent movements of his anger. It would assuredly have been a vain boast in him to say that he was her master.

" You have not made my life pleasant to me of late "—" the hardships which our marriage has brought on me "—these words were stinging his imagination as a pain makes an exaggerated dream. If he were not only to sink from his highest resolve, but to sink into the hideous fettering of domestic hate ?

" Rosamond," he said, turning his eyes on her with a melancholy look, " you should allow for a man's words when he is disappointed and provoked. You and I cannot have opposite interests. I cannot part my happiness from yours. If I am angry with you, it is that you seem not to see how any concealment divides us. How could I wish to make anything hard to you either by my words or conduct ? When I hurt you, I hurt part of my own life. I should never be angry with you if you would be quite open with me."

" I have only wished to prevent you from hurrying us into wretchedness without any necessity," said Rosamond, the tears coming again from a softened feeling now that her husband had softened. " It is so very hard to be disgraced here among all the people we know, and to live in such a miserable way. I wish I had died with the baby."

She spoke and wept with that gentleness which makes such words and tears omnipotent over a loving-hearted man. Lydgate drew his chair near to hers and pressed her delicate head against his cheek with his powerful tender hand. He only caressed her ; he did not say anything ; for what was there to say ? He could not promise to shield her from the dreaded wretchedness, for he could see no sure means of doing so. When he left her to go out again, he told himself that it was ten times harder for her than for him : he had a life away from home, and constant appeals to his activity on behalf of others. He wished to excuse everything in her if he could—but it was inevitable that in that excusing mood he should think of her as if she were an animal of another and feebler species. Nevertheless she had mastered him.

CHAPTER LXVI.

" 'Tis one thing to be tempted, Escalus,
 Another thing to fall."
—*Measure for Measure.*[1]

LYDGATE certainly had good reason to reflect on the service his practice did him in counteracting his personal cares. He had no longer

---

1. Act II, Sc. 1, lines 17–18.

free energy enough for spontaneous research and speculative thinking, but by the bedside of patients the direct external calls on his judgment and sympathies brought the added impulse needed to draw him out of himself. It was not simply that beneficent harness of routine which enables silly men to live respectably and unhappy men to live calmly—it was a perpetual claim on the immediate fresh application of thought, and on the consideration of another's need and trial. Many of us looking back through life would say that the kindest man we have ever known has been a medical man, or perhaps that surgeon whose fine tact, directed by deeply-informed perception, has come to us in our need with a more sublime beneficence than that of miracle-workers. Some of that twice-blessed mercy was always with Lydgate in his work at the Hospital or in private houses, serving better than any opiate to quiet and sustain him under his anxieties and his sense of mental degeneracy.

Mr Farebrother's suspicion as to the opiate was true, however. Under the first galling pressure of foreseen difficulties, and the first perception that his marriage, if it were not to be a yoked loneliness, must be a state of effort to go on loving without too much care about being loved, he had once or twice tried a dose of opium. But he had no hereditary constitutional craving after such transient escapes from the hauntings of misery. He was strong, could drink a great deal of wine, but did not care about it; and when the men round him were drinking spirits, he took sugar and water, having a contemptuous pity even for the earliest stages of excitement from drink. It was the same with gambling. He had looked on at a great deal of gambling in Paris, watching it as if it had been a disease. He was no more tempted by such winning than he was by drink. He had said to himself that the only winning he cared for must be attained by a conscious process of high, difficult combination tending towards a beneficent result. The power he longed for could not be represented by agitated fingers clutching a heap of coin, or by the half-barbarous, half-idiotic triumph in the eyes of a man who sweeps within his arms the ventures of twenty chapfallen companions.

But just as he had tried opium, so his thought now began to turn upon gambling—not with appetite for its excitement, but with a sort of wistful inward gaze after that easy way of getting money, which implied no asking and brought no responsibility. If he had been in London or Paris at that time, it is probable that such thoughts, seconded by opportunity, would have taken him into a gambling-house, no longer to watch the gamblers, but to watch with them in kindred eagerness. Repugnance would have been surmounted by the immense need to win, if chance would be kind enough to let him. An incident which happened not very long after that airy notion of getting aid from his uncle had been excluded, was a strong sign of the effect that might have followed any extant opportunity of gambling.

The billiard-room at the Green Dragon was the constant resort of a certain set, most of whom, like our acquaintance Mr Bambridge, were regarded as men of pleasure. It was here that poor Fred Vincy had made part of his memorable debt, having lost money in betting, and been obliged to borrow of that gay companion. It was generally known in Middlemarch that a good deal of money was lost and won in this way; and the consequent repute of the Green Dragon as a place of dissipation naturally heightened in some quarters the temptation to go there. Probably its regular visitants, like the initiates of freemasonry, wished that there were something a little more tremendous to keep to themselves concerning it; but they were not a closed community, and many decent seniors as well as juniors occasionally turned into the billiard-room to see what was going on. Lydgate, who had the muscular aptitude for billiards, and was fond of the game, had once or twice in the early days after his arrival in Middlemarch taken his turn with the cue at the Green Dragon; but afterwards he had no leisure for the game, and no inclination for the socialities there. One evening, however, he had occasion to seek Mr Bambridge at that resort. The horsedealer had engaged to get him a customer for his remaining good horse, for which Lydgate had determined to substitute a cheap hack, hoping by this reduction of style to get perhaps twenty pounds; and he cared now for every small sum, as a help towards feeding the patience of his tradesmen. To run up to the billiard-room, as he was passing, would save time.

Mr Bambridge was not yet come, but would be sure to arrive by-and-by, said his friend Mr Horrock; and Lydgate stayed, playing a game for the sake of passing the time. That evening he had the peculiar light in the eyes and the unusual vivacity which had been once noticed in him by Mr Farebrother. The exceptional fact of his presence was much noticed in the room, where there was a good deal of Middlemarch company; and several lookers-on, as well as some of the players, were betting with animation. Lydgate was playing well, and felt confident; the bets were dropping round him, and with a swift glancing thought of the probable gain which might double the sum he was saving from his horse, he began to bet on his own play, and won again and again. Mr Bambridge had come in, but Lydgate did not notice him. He was not only excited with his play, but visions were gleaming on him of going the next day to Brassing, where there was gambling on a grander scale to be had, and where, by one powerful snatch at the devil's bait, he might carry it off without the hook, and buy his rescue from his daily solicitings.

He was still winning when two new visitors entered. One of them was a young Hawley, just come from his law studies in town, and the other was Fred Vincy, who had spent several evenings of late at this old haunt of his. Young Hawley, an accomplished billiard-player, brought a cool fresh hand to the cue. But Fred Vincy, startled at seeing Lydgate, and astonished to see him betting with an excited air, stood aside, and kept out of the circle round the table.

Fred had been rewarding resolution by a little laxity of late. He had been working heartily for six months at all outdoor occupations under Mr Garth, and by dint of severe practice had nearly mastered the defects of his handwriting, this practice being, perhaps, a little the less severe that it was often carried on in the evening at Mr Garth's under the eyes of Mary. But the last fortnight Mary had been staying at Lowick Parsonage with the ladies there, during Mr Farebrother's residence in Middlemarch, where he was carrying out some parochial plans; and Fred, not seeing anything more agreeable to do, had turned into the Green Dragon, partly to play at billiards, partly to taste the old flavour of discourse about horses, sport, and things in general, considered from a point of view which was not strenuously correct. He had not been out hunting once this season, had had no horse of his own to ride, and had gone from place to place chiefly with Mr Garth in his gig, or on the sober cob which Mr Garth could lend him. It was a little too bad, Fred began to think, that he should be kept in the traces with more severity than if he had been a clergyman. " I will tell you what, Mistress Mary—it will be rather harder work to learn surveying and drawing plans than it would have been to write sermons," he had said, wishing her to appreciate what he went through for her sake ; "and as to Hercules and Theseus, they were nothing to me.[2] They had sport, and never learned to write a book-keeping hand." And now, Mary being out of the way for a little while, Fred, like any other strong dog who cannot slip his collar, had pulled up the staple of his chain and made a small escape, not of course meaning to go fast or far. There could be no reason why he should not play at billiards, but he was determined not to bet. As to money just now, Fred had in his mind the heroic project of saving almost all of the eighty pounds that Mr Garth offered him, and returning it, which he could easily do by giving up all futile money-spending, since he had a superfluous stock of clothes, and no expense in his board. In that way he could, in one year, go a good way towards repaying the ninety pounds of which he had deprived Mrs Garth, unhappily at a time when she needed that sum more than she did now. Nevertheless, it must be acknowledged that on this evening, which was the fifth of his recent visits to the billiard-room, Fred had, not in his pocket, but in his mind, the ten pounds which he meant to reserve for himself from his half-year's salary (having before him the pleasure of carrying thirty to Mrs Garth when Mary was likely to be come home again)—he had those ten pounds in his mind as a fund from which he might risk something, if there were a chance of a good bet. Why ? Well, when sovereigns were flying about, why shouldn't he catch a few ? He would never go far along that road again ; but a man likes to assure himself, and men of pleasure generally, what he could do in the way of mischief if he chose, and that if he abstains from making himself ill, or beggaring himself, or talking with the utmost looseness which the narrow limits of human capacity will allow, it is not because he is a spooney.[3] Fred did not enter into formal reasons, which are a very artificial, inexact way of representing the tingling returns of old habit, and the caprices of young blood : but there was lurking in him a prophetic sense that evening, that when he began to play he should also begin to bet— that he should enjoy some punch-drinking, and in general prepare himself for feeling " rather seedy " in the morning. It is in such in-definable movements that action often begins.

But the last thing likely to have entered Fred's expectation was that he should see his brother-in-law Lydgate—of whom he had never quite dropped the old opinion that he was a prig, and tremendously conscious of his superiority—looking excited and betting, just as he himself might have done. Fred felt a shock greater than he could quite account for by the vague knowledge that Lydgate was in debt, and that his father had refused to help him ; and his own inclination to enter into the play was suddenly checked. It was a strange re-

2. In Greek mythology, Hercules under-took twelve near-impossible "labors"; Theseus survived many similar trials. Both have mythical connections with Crete. Among Hercules's labors was the capture of the famous wild bull on Crete; one of Theseus's exploits was the destruction of the Minotaur.
3. A simpleton.

versal of attitudes : Fred's blond face and blue eyes, usually bright
and careless, ready to give attention to anything that held out a promise of amusement, looking involuntarily grave and almost embarrassed as if by the sight of something unfitting ; while Lydgate, who
had habitually an air of self-possessed strength, and a certain medita-
tiveness that seemed to lie behind his most observant attention, was
acting, watching, speaking with that excited narrow consciousness
which reminds one of an animal with fierce eyes and retractile claws.

Lydgate, by betting on his own strokes, had won sixteen pounds ;
but young Hawley's arrival had changed the poise of things. He
made first-rate strokes himself, and began to bet against Lydgate's
strokes, the strain of whose nerves was thus changed from simple
confidence in his own movements to defying another person's doubt
in them. The defiance was more exciting than the confidence, but it
was less sure. He continued to bet on his own play, but began often
to fail. Still he went on, for his mind was as utterly narrowed into
that precipitous crevice of play as if he had been the most ignorant
lounger there. Fred observed that Lydgate was losing fast, and found
himself in the new situation of puzzling his brains to think of some
device by which, without being offensive, he could withdraw Lydgate's attention, and perhaps suggest to him a reason for quitting the
room. He saw that others were observing Lydgate's strange unlikeness to himself, and it occurred to him that merely to touch his elbow
and call him aside for a moment might rouse him from his absorption. He could think of nothing cleverer than the daring improba-
bility of saying that he wanted to see Rosy, and wished to know if
she were at home this evening ; and he was going desperately to carry
out this weak device, when a waiter came up to him with a message,
saying that Mr Farebrother was below, and begged to speak with
him.

Fred was surprised, not quite comfortably, but sending word that
he would be down immediately, he went with a new impulse up to
Lydgate, said, "Can I speak to you a moment ?" and drew him
aside.

"Farebrother has just sent up a message to say that he wants to
speak to me. He is below. I thought you might like to know he
was there, if you had anything to say to him."

Fred had simply snatched up this pretext for speaking, because he
could not say, "You are losing confoundedly, and are making everybody stare at you ; you had better come away." But inspiration
could hardly have served him better. Lydgate had not before seen
that Fred was present, and his sudden appearance with an announcement of Mr Farebrother had the effect of a sharp concussion.

"No, no," said Lydgate ; "I have nothing particular to say to him.
But—the game is up—I must be going—I came in just to see Bambridge."

"Bambridge is over there, but he is making a row — I don't think
he's ready for business. Come down with me to Farebrother. I expect he is going to blow me up, and you will shield me," said Fred,
with some adroitness.

Lydgate felt shame, but could not bear to act as if he felt it, by refusing to see Mr Farebrother ; and he went down. They merely shook
hands, however, and spoke of the frost ; and when all three had turned
into the street, the Vicar seemed quite willing to say good-bye to

Lydgate. His present purpose was clearly to talk with Fred alone, and he said, kindly, " I disturbed you, young gentleman, because I have some pressing business with you. Walk with me to St Botolph's, will you ? "

It was a fine night, the sky thick with stars, and Mr Farebrother proposed that they should make a circuit to the old church by the London road. The next thing he said was—

" I thought Lydgate never went to the Green Dragon ? "

"So did I," said Fred. " But he said that he went to see Bambridge."

" He was not playing, then ? "

Fred had not meant to tell this, but he was obliged now to say, " Yes, he was. But I suppose it was an accidental thing. I have never seen him there before."

" You have been going often yourself, then, lately ? "

" Oh, about five or six times."

" I think you had some good reason for giving up the habit of going there ? "

" Yes. You know all about it," said Fred, not liking to be catechised in this way. " I made a clean breast to you."

" I suppose that gives me a warrant to speak about the matter now. It is understood between us, is it not ? — that we are on a footing of open friendship : I have listened to you, and you will be willing to listen to me. I may take my turn in talking a little about myself ? "

" I am under the deepest obligation to you, Mr Farebrother," said Fred, in a state of uncomfortable surmise.

" I will not affect to deny that you are under some obligation to me. But I am going to confess to you, Fred, that I have been tempted to reverse all that by keeping silence with you just now. When somebody said to me, ' Young Vincy has taken to being at the billiard-table every night again—he won't bear the curb long ; ' I was tempted to do the opposite of what I am doing—to hold my tongue and wait while you went down the ladder again, betting first and then——"

" I have not made any bets," said Fred, hastily.

" Glad to hear it. But I say, my prompting was to look on and see you take the wrong turning, wear out Garth's patience, and lose the best opportunity of your life—the opportunity which you made some rather difficult effort to secure. You can guess the feeling which raised that temptation in me—I am sure you know it. I am sure you know that the satisfaction of your affections stands in the way of mine."

There was a pause. Mr Farebrother seemed to wait for a recognition of the fact ; and the emotion perceptible in the tones of his fine voice gave solemnity to his words. But no feeling could quell Fred's alarm.

" I could not be expected to give her up," he said, after a moment's hesitation : it was not a case for any pretence of generosity.

" Clearly not, when her affection met yours. But relations of this sort, even when they are of long standing, are always liable to change. I can easily conceive that you might act in a way to loosen the tie she feels towards you—it must be remembered that she is only conditionally bound to you — and that in that case, another man, who may flatter himself that he has a hold on her regard, might succeed in winning that firm place in her love as well as respect which you had let slip. I can easily conceive such a result," repeated Mr Fare-brother, emphatically. "There is a companionship of ready sympathy, which might get the advantage even over the longest associations."

It seemed to Fred that if Mr Farebrother had had a beak and talons instead of his very capable tongue, his mode of attack could hardly be more cruel. He had a horrible conviction that behind all this hypothetic statement there was a knowledge of some actual change in Mary's feeling.

"Of course I know it might easily be all up with me," he said, in a troubled voice. "If she is beginning to compare——" He broke off, not liking to betray all he felt, and then said, by the help of a little bitterness, "But I thought you were friendly to me."

"So I am ; that is why we are here. But I have had a strong disposition to be otherwise. I have said to myself, 'If there is a likelihood of that youngster doing himself harm, why should you interfere ? Aren't you worth as much as he is, and don't your sixteen years over and above his, in which you have gone rather hungry, give you more right to satisfaction than he has ? If there's a chance of his going to the dogs, let him—perhaps you could nohow hinder it —and do you take the benefit.'"

There was a pause, in which Fred was seized by a most uncomfortable chill. What was coming next ? He dreaded to hear that something had been said to Mary—he felt as if he were listening to a threat rather than a warning. When the Vicar began again there was a change in his tone like the encouraging transition to a major key.

"But I had once meant better than that, and I am come back to my old intention. I thought that I could hardly *secure myself* in it better, Fred, than by telling you just what had gone on in me. And now, do you understand me ? I want you to make the happiness of her life and your own, and if there is any chance that a word of warning from me may turn aside any risk to the contrary—well, I have uttered it."

There was a drop in the Vicar's voice when he spoke the last words. He paused—they were standing on a patch of green where the road diverged towards St Botolph's, and he put out his hand, as if to imply that the conversation was closed. Fred was moved quite newly. Some one highly susceptible to the contemplation of a fine act has said, that it produces a sort of regenerating shudder through the frame, and makes one feel ready to begin a new life. A good degree of that effect was just then present in Fred Vincy.

"I will try to be worthy," he said, breaking off before he could say "of you as well as of her." And meanwhile Mr Farebrother had gathered the impulse to say something more.

"You must not imagine that I believe there is at present any decline in her preference of you, Fred. Set your heart at rest, that if you keep right, other things will keep right."

"I shall never forget what you have done," Fred answered. "I can't say anything that seems worth saying—only I will try that your goodness shall not be thrown away."

"That's enough. Good-bye, and God bless you."

In that way they parted. But both of them walked about a long while before they went out of the starlight. Much of Fred's rumination might be summed up in the words, " It certainly would have been a fine thing for her to marry Farebrother—but if she loves me best and I am a good husband ? "

Perhaps Mr Farebrother's might be concentrated into a single shrug and one little speech. " To think of the part one little woman can play in the life of a man, so that to renounce her may be a very good imitation of heroism, and to win her may be a discipline ! "

CHAPTER LXVII.

Now is there civil war within the soul;
Resolve is thrust from off the sacred throne
By clamorous Needs, and Pride the grand-vizier
Makes humble compact, plays the supple part
Of envoy and deft-tongued apologist
For hungry rebels.

HAPPILY Lydgate had ended by losing in the billiard-room, and brought away no encouragement to make a raid on luck. On the contrary, he felt unmixed disgust with himself the next day when he had to pay four or five pounds over and above his gains, and he carried about with him a most unpleasant vision of the figure he had made, not only rubbing elbows with the men at the Green Dragon but behaving just as they did. A philosopher fallen to betting is hardly distinguishable from a Philistine under the same circumstances : the difference will chiefly be found in his subsequent reflections, and Lydgate chewed a very disagreeable cud in that way. His reason told him how the affair might have been magnified into ruin by a slight change of scenery—if it had been a gambling-house that he had turned into, where chance could be clutched with both hands instead of being picked up with thumb and forefinger. Nevertheless, though reason strangled the desire to gamble, there remained the feeling that, with an assurance of luck to the needful amount, he would have liked to gamble, rather than take the alternative which was beginning to urge itself as inevitable.

That alternative was to apply to Mr Bulstrode. Lydgate had so many times boasted both to himself and others that he was totally independent of Bulstrode, to whose plans he had lent himself solely because they enabled him to carry out his own ideas of professional work and public benefit—he had so constantly in their personal intercourse had his pride sustained by the sense that he was making a good social use of this predominating banker, whose opinions he thought contemptible and whose motives often seemed to him an absurd mixture of contradictory impressions—that he had been creating for himself strong ideal obstacles to the proffering of any considerable request to him on his own account.

Still, early in March his affairs were at that pass in which men begin to say that their oaths were delivered in ignorance, and to perceive that the act which they had called impossible to them is becoming manifestly possible. With Dover's ugly security soon to be put in force, with the proceeds of his practice immediately absorbed in paying back-debts, and with the chance, if the worst were known, of daily supplies being refused on credit, above all with the vision of Rosamond's hopeless discontent continually haunting him, Lydgate had begun to see that he should inevitably bend himself to ask help from somebody or other. At first he had considered whether he should write to Mr Vincy; but on questioning Rosamond he found that, as he had suspected, she had already applied twice to her father, the last time being since the disappointment from Sir Godwin; and papa had said that Lydgate must look out for himself. "Papa said he had come, with one bad year after another, to trade more and more on borrowed capital, and had had to give up many indulgences: he could not spare a single hundred from the charges of his family. He said, let Lydgate ask Bulstrode: they have always been hand and glove."

Indeed, Lydgate himself had come to the conclusion that if he must end by asking for a free loan, his relations with Bulstrode, more at least than with any other man, might take the shape of a claim which was not purely personal. Bulstrode had indirectly helped to cause the failure of his practice, and had also been highly gratified by getting a medical partner in his plans:—but who among us ever reduced himself to the sort of dependence in which Lydgate now stood, without trying to believe that he had claims which diminished the humiliation of asking? It was true that of late there had seemed to be a new languor of interest in Bulstrode about the Hospital; but his health had got worse, and showed signs of a deep-seated nervous affection. In other respects he did not appear to be changed: he had always been highly polite, but Lydgate had observed in him from the first a marked coldness about his marriage and other private circumstances, a coldness which he had hitherto preferred to any warmth of familiarity between them. He deferred the intention from day to day, his habit of acting on his conclusions being made infirm by his repugnance to every possible conclusion and its consequent act. He saw Mr Bulstrode often, but he did not try to use any occasion for his private purpose. At one moment he thought, "I will write a letter: I prefer that to any circuitous talk;" at another he thought, "No; if I were talking to him, I could make a retreat before any signs of disinclination."

Still the days passed and no letter was written, no special interview sought. In his shrinking from the humiliation of a dependent attitude towards Bulstrode, he began to familiarise his imagination with another step even more unlike his remembered self. He began spontaneously to consider whether it would be possible to carry out that puerile notion of Rosamond's which had often made him angry, namely, that they should quit Middlemarch without seeing anything beyond that preface. The question came—"Would any man buy the practice of me even now, for as little as it is worth? Then the sale might happen as a necessary preparation for going away."

But against his taking this step, which he still felt to be a contemptible relinquishment of present work, a guilty turning aside from what was a real and might be a widening channel for worthy activity, to start again without any justified destination, there was this obstacle, that the purchaser, if procurable at all, might not be quickly forthcoming. And afterwards? Rosamond in a poor lodging, though in the largest city or most distant town, would not find the life that could save her from gloom, and save him from the re-

proach of having plunged her into it. For when a man is at the foot
of the hill in his fortunes, he may stay a long while there in spite of
professional accomplishment. In the British climate there is no incompatibility between scientific insight and furnished lodgings: the
incompatibility is chiefly between scientific ambition and a wife who
objects to that kind of residence.

But in the midst of his hesitation, opportunity came to decide him.
A note from Mr Bulstrode requested Lydgate to call on him at the
Bank. A hypochondriacal tendency had shown itself in the banker's
constitution of late; and a lack of sleep, which was really only a slight
exaggeration of an habitual dyspeptic symptom, had been dwelt on by
him as a sign of threatening insanity. He wanted to consult Lydgate
without delay on that particular morning, although he had nothing
to tell beyond what he had told before. He listened eagerly to what
Lydgate had to say in dissipation of his fears, though this too was
only repetition; and this moment in which Bulstrode was receiving
a medical opinion with a sense of comfort, seemed to make the
communication of a personal need to him easier than it had been
in Lydgate's contemplation beforehand. He had been insisting
that it would be well for Mr Bulstrode to relax his attention to
business.

"One sees how any mental strain, however slight, may affect a
delicate frame," said Lydgate at that stage of the consultation when
the remarks tend to pass from the personal to the general, "by
the deep stamp which anxiety will make for a time even on the
young and vigorous. I am naturally very strong; yet I have been
thoroughly shaken lately by an accumulation of trouble."

"I presume that a constitution in the susceptible state in which
mine at present is, would be especially liable to fall a victim to
cholera, if it visited our district. And since its appearance near
London, we may well besiege the Mercy-seat for our protection," said
Mr Bulstrode, not intending to evade Lydgate's allusion, but really
preoccupied with alarms about himself. [1]

"You have at all events taken your share in using good practical
precautions for the town, and that is the best mode of asking for
protection," said Lydgate, with a strong distaste for the broken
metaphor and bad logic of the banker's religion, somewhat increased
by the apparent deafness of his sympathy. But his mind had taken
up its long-prepared movement towards getting help, and was not
yet arrested. He added, "The town has done well in the way of
cleansing, and finding appliances; and I think that if the cholera
should come, even our enemies will admit that the arrangements in
the Hospital are a public good." [2]

"Truly," said Mr Bulstrode, with some coldness. "With regard
to what you say, Mr Lydgate, about the relaxation of my mental
labour, I have for some time been entertaining a purpose to that
effect—a purpose of a very decided character. I contemplate at least
a temporary withdrawal from the management of much business,
whether benevolent or commercial. Also I think of changing my
residence for a time: probably I shall close or let 'The Shrubs,'

---

1. GE notes the first appearance of
cholera in Sunderland and Newcastle in
1831, and its spread to Edinburgh,
Rotherhithe (a London suburb on the
Thames), and London in 1832 (*Quarry*,
below, pp. 611, 621).
2. Appliances: sanitary apparatuses.

and take some place near the coast—under advice, of course, as to salubrity. That would be a measure which you would recommend?"

"Oh yes," said Lydgate, falling backward in his chair, with ill-repressed impatience under the banker's pale earnest eyes and intense preoccupation with himself.

"I have for some time felt that I should open this subject with you in relation to our Hospital," continued Bulstrode. "Under the circumstances I have indicated, of course I must cease to have any personal share in the management, and it is contrary to my views of responsibility to continue a large application of means to an institution which I cannot watch over and to some extent regulate. I shall therefore, in case of my ultimate decision to leave Middlemarch, consider that I withdraw other support to the New Hospital than that which will subsist in the fact that I chiefly supplied the expenses of building it, and have contributed further large sums to its successful working."

Lydgate's thought, when Bulstrode paused according to his wont, was, "He has perhaps been losing a good deal of money." This was the most plausible explanation of a speech which had caused rather a startling change in his expectations. He said in reply—

"The loss to the Hospital can hardly be made up, I fear."

"Hardly," returned Bulstrode, in the same deliberate, silvery tone; "except by some changes of plan. The only person who may be certainly counted on as willing to increase her contributions is Mrs Casaubon. I have had an interview with her on the subject, and I have pointed out to her, as I am about to do to you, that it will be desirable to win a more general support to the New Hospital by a change of system."

Another pause, but Lydgate did not speak.

"The change I mean is an amalgamation with the Infirmary, so that the New Hospital shall be regarded as a special addition to the elder institution, having the same directing board. It will be necessary, also, that the medical management of the two shall be combined. In this way any difficulty as to the adequate maintenance of our new establishment will be removed; the benevolent interests of the town will cease to be divided."

Mr Bulstrode had lowered his eyes from Lydgate's face to the buttons of his coat as he again paused.

"No doubt that is a good device as to ways and means," said Lydgate, with an edge of irony in his tone. "But I can't be expected to rejoice in it at once, since one of the first results will be that the other medical men will upset or interrupt my methods, if it were only because they are mine."

"I myself, as you know, Mr Lydgate, highly valued the opportunity of new and independent procedure which you have diligently employed: the original plan, I confess, was one which I had much at heart, under submission to the Divine Will. But since providential indications demand a renunciation from me, I renounce."

Bulstrode showed a rather exasperating ability in this conversation. The broken metaphor and bad logic of motive which had stirred his hearer's contempt were quite consistent with a mode of putting the facts which made it difficult for Lydgate to vent his own indignation and disappointment. After some rapid reflection, he only asked,

" What did Mrs Casaubon say ? "

" That was the further statement which I wished to make to you," said Bulstrode, who had thoroughly prepared his ministerial explanation. " She is, you are aware, a woman of most munificent disposition, and happily in possession—not I presume of great wealth, but of funds which she can well spare. She has informed me that though she had destined the chief part of those funds to another purpose, she is willing to consider whether she cannot fully take my place in relation to the Hospital. But she wishes for ample time to mature her thoughts on the subject, and I have told her that there is no need for haste—that, in fact, my own plans are not yet absolute."

Lydgate was ready to say, " If Mrs Casaubon would take your place, there would be gain, instead of loss." But there was still a weight on his mind which arrested this cheerful candour. He replied, " I suppose, then, that I may enter into the subject with Mrs Casaubon."

" Precisely ; that is what she expressly desires. Her decision, she says, will much depend on what you can tell her. But not at present : she is, I believe, just setting out on a journey. I have her letter here," said Mr Bulstrode, drawing it out, and reading from it. " ' I am immediately otherwise engaged,' she says. ' I am going into Yorkshire with Sir James and Lady Chettam ; and the conclusions I come to about some land which I am to see there may affect my power of contributing to the Hospital.' Thus, Mr Lydgate, there is no haste necessary in this matter ; but I wished to apprise you beforehand of what may possibly occur."

Mr Bulstrode returned the letter to his side-pocket, and changed his attitude as if his business were closed. Lydgate, whose renewed hope about the Hospital only made him more conscious of the facts which poisoned his hope, felt that his effort after help, if made at all, must be made now and vigorously.

" I am much obliged to you for giving me full notice," he said, with a firm intention in his tone, yet with an interruptedness in his delivery which showed that he spoke unwillingly. " The highest object to me is my profession, and I had identified the Hospital with the best use I can at present make of my profession. But the best use is not always the same with monetary success. Everything which has made the Hospital unpopular has helped with other causes—I think they are all connected with my professional zeal— to make me unpopular as a practitioner. I get chiefly patients who can't pay me. I should like them best, if I had nobody to pay on my own side." Lydgate waited a little, but Bulstrode only bowed, looking at him fixedly, and he went on with the same interrupted enunciation—as if he were biting an objectionable leek.

" I have slipped into money difficulties which I can see no way out of, unless some one who trusts me and my future will advance me a sum without other security. I had very little fortune left when I came here. I have no prospects of money from my own family. My expenses, in consequence of my marriage, have been very much greater than I had expected. The result at this moment is that it would take a thousand pounds to clear me. I mean, to free me from the risk of having all my goods sold in security of my largest debt— as well as to pay my other debts—and leave anything to keep us a little beforehand with our small income. I find that it is out of the question that my wife's father should make such an advance. That is why I mention my position to—to the only other man who may be held to have some personal connection with my prosperity or ruin."

Lydgate hated to hear himself. But he had spoken now, and had spoken with unmistakable directness. Mr Bulstrode replied without haste, but also without hesitation.

" I am grieved, though, I confess, not surprised by this information, Mr Lydgate. For my own part, I regretted your alliance with my brother-in-law's family, which has always been of prodigal habits, and which has already been much indebted to me for sustainment in its present position. My advice to you, Mr Lydgate, would be, that instead of involving yourself in further obligations, and continuing a doubtful struggle, you should simply become a bankrupt."

" That would not improve my prospect," said Lydgate, rising, and speaking bitterly, " even if it were a more agreeable thing in itself."

" It is always a trial," said Mr Bulstrode ; " but trial, my dear sir, is our portion here, and is a needed corrective. I recommend you to weigh the advice I have given."

" Thank you," said Lydgate, not quite knowing what he said. " I have occupied you too long. Good-day."

CHAPTER LXVIII.

" What suit of grace hath Virtue to put on
If Vice shall wear as good, and do as well?
If Wrong, if Craft, if Indiscretion
Act as fair parts with ends as laudable?
Which all this mighty volume of events
The world, the universal map of deeds,
Strongly controls, and proves from all descents,
That the directest course still best succeeds.
For should not grave and learn'd Experience
That looks with the eyes of all the world beside,
And with all ages holds intelligence,
Go safer than Deceit without a guide !"
—DANIEL : *Musophilus.*

THAT change of plan and shifting of interest which Bulstrode stated or betrayed in his conversation with Lydgate, had been determined in him by some severe experience which he had gone through since the epoch of Mr Larcher's sale, when Raffles had recognised Will Ladislaw, and when the banker had in vain attempted an act of restitution which might move Divine Providence to arrest painful consequences.

His certainty that Raffles, unless he were dead, would return to Middlemarch before long, had been justified. On Christmas Eve he had reappeared at The Shrubs. Bulstrode was at home to receive him, and hinder his communication with the rest of the family, but he could not altogether hinder the circumstances of the visit from compromising himself and alarming his wife. Raffles proved more unmanageable than he had shown himself to be in his former appearances, his chronic state of mental restlessness, the growing effect of habitual intemperance, quickly shaking off every impression from what was said to him. He insisted on staying in the house, and Bul-

strode, weighing two sets of evils, felt that this was at least not a worse
alternative than his going into the town. He kept him in his own
room for the evening and saw him to bed, Raffles all the while amusing himself with the annoyance he was causing this decent and highly
prosperous fellow-sinner, an amusement which he facetiously expressed as sympathy with his friend's pleasure in entertaining a man
who had been serviceable to him, and who had not had all his earnings. There was a cunning calculation under this noisy joking—a
cool resolve to extract something the handsomer from Bulstrode as
payment for release from this new application of torture. But his
cunning had a little overcast its mark.

Bulstrode was indeed more tortured than the coarse fibre of Raffles
could enable him to imagine. He had told his wife that he was
simply taking care of this wretched creature, the victim of vice, who
might otherwise injure himself; he implied, without the direct form
of falsehood, that there was a family tie which bound him to this
care, and that there were signs of mental alienation in Raffles which
urged caution. He would himself drive the unfortunate being away
the next morning. In these hints he felt that he was supplying Mrs
Bulstrode with precautionary information for his daughters and
servants, and accounting for his allowing no one but himself to enter
the room even with food and drink. But he sat in an agony of fear
lest Raffles should be overheard in his loud and plain references to
past facts—lest Mrs Bulstrode should be even tempted to listen at the
door. How could he hinder her, how betray his terror by opening
the door to detect her? She was a woman of honest direct habits,
and little likely to take so low a course in order to arrive at painful knowledge; but fear was stronger than the calculation of
probabilities.

In this way Raffles had pushed the torture too far, and produced an
effect which had not been in his plan. By showing himself hopelessly unmanageable he had made Bulstrode feel that a strong defiance
was the only resource left. After taking Raffles to bed that night the
banker ordered his closed carriage to be ready at half-past seven the
next morning. At six o'clock he had already been long dressed, and
had spent some of his wretchedness in prayer, pleading his motives
for averting the worst evil if in anything he had used falsity and
spoken what was not true before God. For Bulstrode shrank from a
direct lie with an intensity disproportionate to the number of his
more indirect misdeeds. But many of these misdeeds were like the
subtle muscular movements which are not taken account of in the
consciousness, though they bring about the end that we fix our mind
on and desire. And it is only what we are vividly conscious of that
we can vividly imagine to be seen by Omniscience.

Bulstrode carried his candle to the bedside of Raffles, who was
apparently in a painful dream. He stood silent, hoping that the presence of the light would serve to waken the sleeper gradually and
gently, for he feared some noise as the consequence of a too sudden
awakening. He had watched for a couple of minutes or more the
shudderings and pantings which seemed likely to end in waking, when
Raffles, with a long half-stifled moan, started up and stared round him
in terror, trembling and gasping. But he made no further noise, and
Bulstrode, setting down the candle, awaited his recovery.

It was a quarter of an hour later before Bulstrode, with a cold peremptoriness of manner which he had not before shown, said, " I came to call you thus early, Mr Raffles, because I have ordered the carriage to be ready at half-past seven, and intend myself to conduct you as far as Ilsely, where you can either take the railway or await a coach."

Raffles was about to speak, but Bulstrode anticipated him imperiously, with the words, " Be silent, sir, and hear what I have to say. I shall supply you with money now, and I will furnish you with a reasonable sum from time to time, on your application to me by letter ; but if you choose to present yourself here again, if you return to Middlemarch, if you use your tongue in a manner injurious to me, you will have to live on such fruits as your malice can bring you, without help from me. Nobody will pay you well for blasting my name : I know the worst you can do against me, and I shall brave it if you dare to thrust yourself upon me again. Get up, sir, and do as I order you, without noise, or I will send for a policeman to take you off my premises, and you may carry your stories into every pot-house in the town, but you shall have no sixpence from me to pay your expenses there."

Bulstrode had rarely in his life spoken with such nervous energy : he had been deliberating on this speech and its probable effects through a large part of the night ; and though he did not trust to its ultimately saving him from any return of Raffles, he had concluded that it was the best throw he could make. It succeeded in enforcing submission from the jaded man this morning : his empoisoned system at this moment quailed before Bulstrode's cold, resolute bearing, and he was taken off quietly in the carriage before the family break-fast-time. The servants imagined him to be a poor relation, and were not surprised that a strict man like their master, who held his head high in the world, should be ashamed of such a cousin and want to get rid of him. The banker's drive of ten miles with his hated companion was a dreary beginning of the Christmas day ; but at the end of the drive, Raffles had recovered his spirits, and parted in a contentment for which there was the good reason that the banker had given him a hundred pounds. Various motives urged Bulstrode to this open-handedness, but he did not himself inquire closely into all of them. As he had stood watching Raffles in his uneasy sleep, it had certainly entered his mind that the man had been much shattered since the first gift of two hundred pounds.

He had taken care to repeat the incisive statement of his resolve not to be played on any more ; and had tried to penetrate Raffles with the fact that he had shown the risks of bribing him to be quite equal to the risks of defying him. But when, freed from his repulsive presence, Bulstrode returned to his quiet home, he brought with him no confidence that he had secured more than a respite. It was as if he had had a loathsome dream, and could not shake off its images with their hateful kindred of sensations—as if on all the pleasant surroundings of his life a dangerous reptile had left his slimy traces.

Who can know how much of his most inward life is made up of the thoughts he believes other men to have about him, until that fabric of opinion is threatened with ruin ?

Bulstrode was only the more conscious that there was a deposit of uneasy presentiment in his wife's mind, because she carefully avoided any allusion to it. He had been used every day to taste the flavour of supremacy and the tribute of complete deference ; and the certainty that he was watched or measured with a hidden suspicion of his having some discreditable secret, made his voice totter when he was speaking to edification. Foreseeing, to men of Bulstrode's anxious temperament, is often worse than seeing ; and his imagination continually heightened the anguish of an imminent disgrace. Yes, imminent ; for if his defiance of Raffles did not keep the man away—and though he prayed for this result he hardly hoped for it—the disgrace was certain. In vain he said to himself that, if permitted, it would be a divine visitation, a chastisement, a preparation ; he recoiled from the imagined burning ; and he judged that it must be more for the Divine glory that he should escape dishonour. That recoil had at last urged him to make preparations for quitting Middlemarch. If evil truth must be reported of him, he would then be at a less scorching distance from the contempt of his old neighbours ; and in a new scene, where his life would not have gathered the same wide sensibility, the tormentor, if he pursued him, would be less formidable. To leave the place finally would, he knew, be extremely painful to his wife, and on other grounds he would have preferred to stay where he had struck root. Hence he made his preparations at first in a conditional way, wishing to leave on all sides an opening for his return after brief absence, if any favourable intervention of Providence should dissipate his fears. He was preparing to transfer his management of the Bank, and to give up any active control of other commercial affairs in the neighbourhood, on the ground of his failing health, but without excluding his future resumption of such work. The measure would cause him some added expense and some diminution of income beyond what he had already undergone from the general depression of trade ; and the Hospital presented itself as a principal object of outlay on which he could fairly economise.

This was the experience which had determined his conversation with Lydgate. But at this time his arrangements had most of them gone no farther than a stage at which he could recall them if they proved to be unnecessary. He continually deferred the final steps ; in the midst of his fears, like many a man who is in danger of shipwreck or of being dashed from his carriage by runaway horses, he had a clinging impression that something would happen to hinder the worst, and that to spoil his life by a late transplantation might be over-hasty—especially since it was difficult to account satisfactorily to his wife for the project of their indefinite exile from the only place where she would like to live.

Among the affairs Bulstrode had to care for, was the management of the farm at Stone Court in case of his absence ; and on this as well as on all other matters connected with any houses and land he possessed in or about Middlemarch, he had consulted Caleb Garth. Like every one else who had business of that sort, he wanted to get the agent who was more anxious for his employer's interests than his own. With regard to Stone Court, since Bulstrode wished to retain his hold on the stock, and to have an arrangement by which he himself could, if he chose, resume his favourite recreation of superintendence, Caleb had advised him not to trust to a mere bailiff, but to let the land, stock, and implements yearly, and take a proportionate share of the proceeds.

"May I trust to you to find me a tenant on these terms, Mr Garth ?"

said Bulstrode. "And will you mention to me the yearly sum which would repay you for managing these affairs which we have discussed together?"

"I'll think about it," said Caleb, in his blunt away. "I'll see how I can make it out."

If it had not been that he had to consider Fred Vincy's future, Mr Garth would not probably have been glad of any addition to his work, of which his wife was always fearing an excess for him as he grew older. But on quitting Bulstrode after that conversation, a very alluring idea occurred to him about this said letting of Stone Court. What if Bulstrode would agree to his placing Fred Vincy there on the understanding that he, Caleb Garth, should be responsible for the management? It would be an excellent schooling for Fred; he might make a modest income there, and still have time left to get knowledge by helping in other business. He mentioned his notion to Mrs Garth with such evident delight that she could not bear to chill his pleasure by expressing her constant fear of his undertaking too much.

"The lad would be as happy as two," he said, throwing himself back in his chair, and looking radiant, "if I could tell him it was all settled. Think, Susan! His mind had been running on that place for years before old Featherstone died. And it would be as pretty a turn of things as could be that he should hold the place in a good industrious way after all—by his taking to business. For it's likely enough Bulstrode might let him go on, and gradually buy the stock. He hasn't made up his mind, I can see, whether or not he shall settle somewhere else as a lasting thing. I never was better pleased with a notion in my life. And then the children might be married by-and-by, Susan."

"You will not give any hint of the plan to Fred, until you are sure that Bulstrode would agree to the plan?" said Mrs Garth, in a tone of gentle caution. "And as to marriage, Caleb, we old people need not help to hasten it."

"Oh, I don't know," said Caleb, swinging his head aside. "Marriage is a taming thing. Fred would want less of my bit and bridle. However, I shall say nothing till I know the ground I'm treading on. I shall speak to Bulstrode again."

He took his earliest opportunity of doing so. Bulstrode had anything but a warm interest in his nephew Fred Vincy, but he had a strong wish to secure Mr Garth's services on many scattered points of business at which he was sure to be a considerable loser, if they were under less conscientious management. On that ground he made no objection to Mr Garth's proposal; and there was also another reason why he was not sorry to give a consent which was to benefit one of the Vincy family. It was that Mrs Bulstrode, having heard of Lydgate's debts, had been anxious to know whether her husband could not do something for poor Rosamond, and had been much troubled on learning from him that Lydgate's affairs were not easily remediable, and that the wisest plan was to let them "take their course." Mrs Bulstrode had then said for the first time, "I think you are always a little hard towards my family, Nicholas. And I am sure I have no reason to deny any of my relatives. Too worldly they may be, but no one ever had to say that they were not respectable."

"My dear Harriet," said Mr Bulstrode, wincing under his wife's eyes, which were filling with tears, " I have supplied your brother with a great deal of capital. I cannot be expected to take care of his married children."

That seemed to be true, and Mrs Bulstrode's remonstrance subsided into pity for poor Rosamond, whose extravagant education she had always foreseen the fruits of.

But remembering that dialogue, Mr Bulstrode felt that when he had to talk to his wife fully about his plan of quitting Middlemarch, he should be glad to tell her that he had made an arrangement which might be for the good of her nephew Fred. At present he had merely mentioned to her that he thought of shutting up The Shrubs for a few months, and taking a house on the Southern Coast.

Hence Mr Garth got the assurance he desired, namely, that in case of Bulstrode's departure from Middlemarch for an indefinite time, Fred Vincy should be allowed to have the tenancy of Stone Court on the terms proposed.

Caleb was so elated with his hope of this "neat turn" being given to things, that if his self-control had not been braced by a little affectionate wifely scolding, he would have betrayed everything to Mary, wanting " to give the child comfort." However, he restrained himself, and kept in strict privacy from Fred certain visits which he was making to Stone Court, in order to look more thoroughly into the state of the land and stock, and take a preliminary estimate. He was certainly more eager in these visits than the probable speed of events required him to be ; but he was stimulated by a fatherly delight in occupying his mind with this bit of probable happiness which he held in store like a hidden birthday gift for Fred and Mary.

" But suppose the whole scheme should turn out to be a castle in the air ? " said Mrs Garth.

" Well, well," replied Caleb ; " the castle will tumble about no-body's head."

CHAPTER LXIX.

" If thou hast heard a word, let it die with thee."
—*Ecclesiasticus.* [1]

Mr Bulstrode was still seated in his manager's room at the Bank, about three o'clock of the same day on which he had received Lydgate there, when the clerk entered to say that his horse was waiting, and also that Mr Garth was outside and begged to speak with him.

" By all means," said Bulstrode ; and Caleb entered. " Pray sit down, Mr Garth," continued the banker, in his suavest tone. " I am glad that you arrived just in time to find me here. I know you count your minutes."

" Oh," said Caleb, gently, with a slow swing of his head on one side, as he seated himself and laid his hat on the floor. He looked at the ground, leaning forward and letting his long fingers droop between his legs, while each finger moved in succession, as if it were sharing some thought which filled his large quiet brow.

1. Ecclesiasticus 19:10.

Mr Bulstrode, like every one else who knew Caleb, was used to his slowness in beginning to speak on any topic which he felt to be important, and rather expected that he was about to recur to the buying of some houses in Blindman's Court, for the sake of pulling them down, as a sacrifice of property which would be well repaid by the influx of air and light on that spot. It was by propositions of this kind that Caleb was sometimes troublesome to his employers ; but he had usually found Bulstrode ready to meet him in projects of improvement, and they had got on well together. When he spoke again, however, it was to say, in rather a subdued voice—

" I have just come away from Stone Court, Mr Bulstrode."

" You found nothing wrong there, I hope," said the banker ; " I was there myself yesterday. Abel has done well with the lambs this year."

" Why, yes," said Caleb, looking up gravely, " there *is* something wrong—a stranger, who is very ill, I think. He wants a doctor, and I came to tell you of that. His name is Raffles."

He saw the shock of his words passing through Bulstrode's frame. On this subject the banker had thought that his fears were too constantly on the watch to be taken by surprise ; but he had been mistaken.

" Poor wretch ! " he said in a compassionate tone, though his lips trembled a little. " Do you know how he came there ? "

" I took him myself," said Caleb, quietly — " took him up in my gig. He had got down from the coach, and was walking a little beyond the turning from the toll-house, and I overtook him. He remembered seeing me with you once before, at Stone Court, and he asked me to take him on. I saw he was ill : it seemed to me the right thing to do, to carry him under shelter. And now I think you should lose no time in getting advice for him." Caleb took up his hat from the floor as he ended, and rose slowly from his seat.

" Certainly," said Bulstrode, whose mind was very active at this moment. " Perhaps you will yourself oblige me, Mr Garth, by calling at Mr Lydgate's as you pass — or stay ! he may at this hour probably be at the Hospital. I will first send my man on the horse there with a note this instant, and then I will myself ride to Stone Court."

Bulstrode quickly wrote a note, and went out himself to give the commission to his man. When he returned, Caleb was standing as before with one hand on the back of the chair, holding his hat with the other. In Bulstrode's mind the dominant thought was, " Perhaps Raffles only spoke to Garth of his illness. Garth may wonder, as he must have done before, at this disreputable fellow's claiming intimacy with me ; but he will know nothing. And he is friendly to me—I can be of use to him."

He longed for some confirmation of this hopeful conjecture, but to have asked any question as to what Raffles had said or done would have been to betray fear.

" I am exceedingly obliged to you, Mr Garth," he said, in his usual tone of politeness. " My servant will be back in a few minutes, and I shall then go myself to see what can be done for this unfortunate man. Perhaps you had some other business with me ? If so, pray be seated."

" Thank you," said Caleb, making a slight gesture with his right hand to waive the invitation. " I wish to say, Mr Bulstrode, that I must request you to put your business into some other hands than mine. I am obliged to you for your handsome way of meeting me— about the letting of Stone Court, and all other business. But I must give it up."

A sharp certainty entered like a stab into Bulstrode's soul.

" This is sudden, Mr Garth," was all he could say at first.

" It is," said Caleb ; " but it is quite fixed. I must give it up."

He spoke with a firmness which was very gentle, and yet he could see that Bulstrode seemed to cower under that gentleness, his face looking dried and his eyes swerving away from the glance which rested on him. Caleb felt a deep pity for him, but he could have used no pretexts to account for his resolve, even if they would have been of any use.

" You have been led to this, I apprehend, by some slanders concerning me uttered by that unhappy creature," said Bulstrode, anxious now to know the utmost.

" That is true. I can't deny that I act upon what I heard from him."

" You are a conscientious man, Mr Garth—a man, I trust, who feels himself accountable to God. You would not wish to injure me by being too ready to believe a slander," said Bulstrode, casting about for pleas that might be adapted to his hearer's mind. " That is a poor reason for giving up a connection which I think I may say will be mutually beneficial."

" I would injure no man if I could help it," said Caleb ; " even if I thought God winked at it. I hope I should have a feeling for my fellow-creature. But, sir — I am obliged to believe that this Raffles has told me the truth. And I can't be happy in working with you, or profiting by you. It hurts my mind. I must beg you to seek another agent."

" Very well, Mr Garth. But I must at least claim to know the worst that he has told you. I must know what is the foul speech that I am liable to be the victim of," said Bulstrode, a certain amount of anger beginning to mingle with his humiliation before this quiet man who renounced his benefits.

" That's needless," said Caleb, waving his hand, bowing his head slightly, and not swerving from the tone which had in it the merciful intention to spare this pitiable man. " What he has said to me will never pass from my lips, unless something now unknown forces it from me. If you led a harmful life for gain, and kept others out of their rights by deceit, to get the more for yourself, I daresay you repent — you would like to go back, and can't : that must be a bitter thing "—Caleb paused a moment and shook his head—" it is not for me to make your life harder to you."

" But you do—you do make it harder to me," said Bulstrode, constrained into a genuine, pleading cry. " You make it harder to me by turning your back on me."

" That I'm forced to do," said Caleb, still more gently, lifting up his hand. " I am sorry. I don't judge you and say, he is wicked, and I am righteous. God forbid. I don't know everything. A man may do wrong, and his will may rise clear out of it, though he can't get his life clear. That's a bad punishment. If it is so with you, — well, I'm very sorry for you. But I have that feeling inside me, that I can't go on working with you. That's all, Mr Bulstrode. Everything else is buried, so far as my will goes. And I wish you good-day."

"One moment, Mr Garth!" said Bulstrode, hurriedly. "I may trust then to your solemn assurance that you will not repeat either to man or woman what — even if it have any degree of truth in it — is yet a malicious representation?"

Caleb's wrath was stirred, and he said, indignantly—

"Why should I have said it if I didn't mean it? I am in no fear of you. Such tales as that will never tempt my tongue."

"Excuse me—I am agitated—I am the victim of this abandoned man."

"Stop a bit! you have got to consider whether you didn't help to make him worse, when you profited by his vices."

"You are wronging me by too readily believing him," said Bulstrode, oppressed, as by a nightmare, with the inability to deny flatly what Raffles might have said; and yet feeling it an escape that Caleb had not so stated it to him as to ask for that flat denial.

"No," said Caleb, lifting his hand deprecatingly; "I am ready to believe better, when better is proved. I rob you of no good chance. As to speaking, I hold it a crime to expose a man's sin unless I'm clear it must be done to save the innocent. That is my way of thinking, Mr Bulstrode, and what I say, I've no need to swear. I wish you good-day."

Some hours later, when he was at home, Caleb said to his wife, incidentally, that he had had some little differences with Bulstrode, and that in consequence, he had given up all notion of taking Stone Court, and indeed had resigned doing further business for him.

"He was disposed to interfere too much, was he?" said Mrs Garth, imagining that her husband had been touched on his sensitive point, and not been allowed to do what he thought right as to materials and modes of work.

"Oh," said Caleb, bowing his head and waving his hand gravely. And Mrs Garth knew that this was a sign of his not intending to speak further on the subject.

As for Bulstrode, he had almost immediately mounted his horse and set off for Stone Court, being anxious to arrive there before Lydgate.

His mind was crowded with images and conjectures, which were a language to his hopes and fears, just as we hear tones from the vibrations which shake our whole system. The deep humiliation with which he had winced under Caleb Garth's knowledge of his past and rejection of his patronage, alternated with and almost gave way to the sense of safety in the fact that Garth, and no other, had been the man to whom Raffles had spoken. It seemed to him a sort of earnest that Providence intended his rescue from worse consequences; the way being thus left open for the hope of secrecy. That Raffles should be afflicted with illness, that he should have been led to Stone Court rather than elsewhere—Bulstrode's heart fluttered at the vision of probabilities which these events conjured up. If it should turn out that he was freed from all danger of disgrace—if he could breathe in perfect liberty—his life should be more consecrated than it had ever been before. He mentally lifted up this vow as if it would urge the result he longed for—he tried to believe in the potency of that prayerful resolution—its potency to determine death. He knew that he ought to say, "Thy will be done;" and he said it often. But the intense desire remained that the will of God might be the death of that hated man.

Yet when he arrived at Stone Court he could not see the change in Raffles without a shock. But for his pallor and feebleness, Bulstrode would have called the change in him entirely mental. Instead of his loud tormenting mood, he showed an intense, vague terror, and seemed to deprecate Bulstrode's anger, because the money was all gone—he had been robbed—it had half of it been taken from him. He had only come here because he was ill and somebody was hunting him—somebody was after him : he had told nobody anything, he had kept his mouth shut. Bulstrode, not knowing the significance of these symptoms, intepreted this new nervous susceptibility into a means of alarming Raffles into true confessions, and taxed him with falsehood in saying that he had not told anything, since he had just told the man who took him up in his gig and brought him to Stone Court. Raffles denied this with solemn adjurations ; the fact being that the links of consciousness were interrupted in him, and that his minute terror-stricken narrative to Caleb Garth had been delivered under a set of visionary impulses which had dropped back into darkness.

Bulstrode's heart sank again at this sign that he could get no grasp over the wretched man's mind, and that no word of Raffles could be trusted as to the fact which he most wanted to know, namely, whether or not he had really kept silence to every one in the neighbourhood except Caleb Garth. The housekeeper had told him without the least constraint of manner that since Mr Garth left, Raffles had asked her for beer, and after that had not spoken, seeming very ill. On that side it might be concluded that there had been no betrayal. Mrs Abel thought, like the servants at The Shrubs, that the strange man belonged to the unpleasant "kin" who are among the troubles of the rich ; she had at first referred the kinship to Mr Rigg, and where there was property left, the buzzing presence of such large blue-bottles seemed natural enough. How he could be "kin" to Bulstrode as well was not so clear, but Mrs Abel agreed with her husband that there was "no knowing," a proposition which had a great deal of mental food for her, so that she shook her head over it without further speculation.

In less than an hour Lydgate arrived. Bulstrode met him outside the wainscoted parlour, where Raffles was, and said—

"I have called you in, Mr Lydgate, to an unfortunate man who was once in my employment, many years ago. Afterwards he went to America, and returned I fear to an idle dissolute life. Being destitute, he has a claim on me. He was slightly connected with Rigg, the former owner of this place, and in consequence found his way here. I believe he is seriously ill : apparently his mind is affected. I feel bound to do the utmost for him."

Lydgate, who had the remembrance of his last conversation with Bulstrode strongly upon him, was not disposed to say an unnecessary word to him, and bowed slightly in answer to this account ; but just before entering the room he turned automatically and said, "What is his name ?"—to know names being as much a part of the medical man's accomplishment as of the practical politician's.

"Raffles, John Raffles," said Bulstrode, who hoped that whatever became of Raffles, Lydgate would never know any more of him.

When he had thoroughly examined and considered the patient,

Lydgate ordered that he should go to bed, and be kept there in as complete quiet as possible, and then went with Bulstrode into another room.

"It is a serious case, I apprehend," said the banker, before Lydgate began to speak.

"No—and yes," said Lydgate, half dubiously. "It is difficult to decide as to the possible effect of long-standing complications; but the man had a robust constitution to begin with. I should not expect this attack to be fatal, though of course the system is in a ticklish state. He should be well watched and attended to."

"I will remain here myself," said Bulstrode. "Mrs Abel and her husband are inexperienced. I can easily remain here for the night, if you will oblige me by taking a note for Mrs Bulstrode."

"I should think that is hardly necessary," said Lydgate. "He seems tame and terrified enough. He might become more unmanageable. But there is a man here—is there not?"

"I have more than once stayed here a few nights for the sake of seclusion," said Bulstrode, indifferently; "I am quite disposed to do so now. Mrs Abel and her husband can relieve or aid me, if necessary."

"Very well. Then I need give my directions only to you," said Lydgate, not feeling surprised at a little peculiarity in Bulstrode.

"You think, then, that the case is hopeful?" said Bulstrode, when Lydgate had ended giving his orders.

"Unless there turn out to be further complications, such as I have not at present detected—yes," said Lydgate. "He may pass on to a worse stage; but I should not wonder if he got better in a few days, by adhering to the treatment I have prescribed. There must be firmness. Remember, if he calls for liquors of any sort, not to give them to him. In my opinion, men in his condition are oftener killed by treatment than by the disease. Still, new symptoms may arise. I shall come again to-morrow morning."

After waiting for the note to be carried to Mrs Bulstrode, Lydgate rode away, forming no conjectures, in the first instance, about the history of Raffles, but rehearsing the whole argument, which had lately been much stirred by the publication of Dr Ware's abundant experience in America, as to the right way of treating cases of alcoholic poisoning such as this.[2] Lydgate, when abroad, had already been interested in this question: he was strongly convinced against the prevalent practice of allowing alcohol and persistently administering large doses of opium; and he had repeatedly acted on this conviction with a favourable result.

"The man is in a diseased state," he thought, "but there's a good deal of wear in him still. I suppose he is an object of charity to Bulstrode. It is curious what patches of hardness and tenderness lie side by side in men's dispositions. Bulstrode seems the most unsympathetic fellow I ever saw about some people, and yet he has taken no end of trouble, and spent a great deal of money, on benevolent

2. John Ware, M.D. (1795–1864), American physician. "Dr. Ware first dogmatically taught that *delirium tremens* is a paroxysm of poisoning by alcohol, which in a majority of cases lasts only a given time, & terminates favourably in a critical sleep" (*Quarry,* below, p. 622). GE's source is Ware's "Remarks on the History and Treatment of *Delirium Tremens*" (1831).

objects. I suppose he has some test by which he finds out whom Heaven cares for—he has made up his mind that it doesn't care for me."

This streak of bitterness came from a plenteous source, and kept widening in the current of his thought as he neared Lowick Gate. He had not been there since his first interview with Bulstrode in the morning, having been found at the Hospital by the banker's messenger ; and for the first time he was returning to his home without the vision of any expedient in the background which left him a hope of raising money enough to deliver him from the coming destitution of everything which made his married life tolerable—everything which saved him and Rosamond from that bare isolation in which they would be forced to recognise how little of a comfort they could be to each other. It was more bearable to do without tenderness for himself than to see that his own tenderness could make no amends for the lack of other things to her. The sufferings of his own pride from humiliations past and to come were keen enough, yet they were hardly distinguishable to himself from that more acute pain which dominated them—the pain of foreseeing that Rosamond would come to regard him chiefly as the cause of disappointment and unhappiness to her. He had never liked the makeshifts of poverty, and they had never before entered into his prospects for himself ; but he was beginning now to imagine how two creatures who loved each other, and had a stock of thoughts in common, might laugh over their shabby furniture, and their calculations how far they could afford butter and eggs. But the glimpse of that poetry seemed as far off from him as the carelessness of the golden age ; in poor Rosamond's mind there was not room enough for luxuries to look small in. He got down from his horse in a very sad mood, and went into the house, not expecting to be cheered except by his dinner, and reflecting that before the evening closed it would be wise to tell Rosamond of his application to Bulstrode and its failure. It would be well not to lose time in preparing her for the worst.

But his dinner waited long for him before he was able to eat it. For on entering he found that Dover's agent had already put a man in the house, and when he asked where Mrs Lydgate was, he was told that she was in her bedroom. He went up and found her stretched on the bed pale and silent, without an answer even in her face to any word or look of his. He sat down by the bed and leaning over her said with almost a cry of prayer—

"Forgive me for this misery, my poor Rosamond ! Let us only love one another."

She looked at him silently, still with the blank despair on her face ; but then the tears began to fill her blue eyes, and her lip trembled. The strong man had had too much to bear that day. He let his head fall beside hers and sobbed.

He did not hinder her from going to her father early in the morning—it seemed now that he ought not to hinder her from doing as she pleased. In half an hour she came back, and said that papa and mamma wished her to go and stay with them while things were in this miserable state. Papa said he could do nothing about the debt—if he paid this, there would be half-a-dozen more. She had better come back home again till Lydgate had got a comfortable home for her. "Do you object, Tertius ?"

" Do as you like," said Lydgate. " But things are not coming to a crisis immediately. There is no hurry."

" I should not go till to-morrow," said Rosamond ; " I shall want to pack my clothes."

" Oh I would wait a little longer than to-morrow—there is no knowing what may happen," said Lydgate, with bitter irony. " I may get my neck broken, and that may make things easier to you."

It was Lydgate's misfortune and Rosamond's too, that his tenderness towards her, which was both an emotional prompting and a well-considered resolve, was inevitably interrupted by these outbursts of indignation either ironical or remonstrant. She thought them totally unwarranted, and the repulsion which this exceptional severity excited in her was in danger of making the more persistent tenderness unacceptable.

" I see you do not wish me to go," she said, with chill mildness ; " why can you not say so, without that kind of violence ? I shall stay until you request me to do otherwise."

Lydgate said no more, but went out on his rounds. He felt bruised and shattered, and there was a dark line under his eyes which Rosamond had not seen before. She could not bear to look at him. Tertius had a way of taking things which made them a great deal worse for her.

CHAPTER LXX.

Our deeds still travel with us from afar,
And what we have been makes us what we are.

BULSTRODE'S first object after Lydgate had left Stone Court was to examine Raffles's pockets, which he imagined were sure to carry signs in the shape of hotel-bills of the places he had stopped in, if he had not told the truth in saying that he had come straight from Liverpool because he was ill and had no money. There were various bills crammed into his pocket-book, but none of a later date than Christmas at any other place, except one, which bore date that morning. This was crumpled up with a handbill about a horse-fair in one of his tail-pockets, and represented the cost of three days' stay at an inn at Bilkley, where the fair was held—a town at least forty miles from Middlemarch. The bill was heavy, and since Raffles had no luggage with him, it seemed probable that he had left his portmanteau behind in payment, in order to save money for his travelling fare ; for his purse was empty, and he had only a couple of sixpences and some loose pence in his pockets.

Bulstrode gathered a sense of safety from these indications that Raffles had really kept at a distance from Middlemarch since his memorable visit at Christmas. At a distance and among people who were strangers to Bulstrode, what satisfaction could there be to Raffles's tormenting, self-magnifying vein in telling old scandalous stories about a Middlemarch banker ? And what harm if he did talk ? The chief point now was to keep watch over him as long as there was any danger of that intelligible raving, that unaccountable impulse to tell, which seemed to have acted towards Caleb Garth ;

and Bulstrode felt much anxiety lest some such impulse should come
over him at the sight of Lydgate. He sat up alone with him through
the night, only ordering the housekeeper to lie down in her clothes,
so as to be ready when he called her, alleging his own indisposition
to sleep, and his anxiety to carry out the doctor's orders. He did
carry them out faithfully, although Raffles was incessantly asking for
brandy, and declaring that he was sinking away—that the earth was
sinking away from under him. He was restless and sleepless, but
still quailing and manageable. On the offer of the food ordered by
Lydgate, which he refused, and the denial of other things which he
demanded, he seemed to concentrate all his terror on Bulstrode, im-
ploringly deprecating his anger, his revenge on him by starvation,
and declaring with strong oaths that he had never told any mortal a
word against him. Even this Bulstrode felt that he would not have
liked Lydgate to hear ; but a more alarming sign of fitful alternation
in his delirium was, that in the morning twilight Raffles suddenly
seemed to imagine a doctor present, addressing him and declaring
that Bulstrode wanted to starve him to death out of revenge for telling, when he never had told.

Bulstrode's native imperiousness and strength of determination
served him well. This delicate-looking man, himself nervously
perturbed, found the needed stimulus in his strenuous circumstances,
and through that difficult night and morning, while he had the air of
an animated corpse returned to movement without warmth, holding
the mastery by its chill impassibility, his mind was intensely at work
thinking of what he had to guard against and what would win him
security. Whatever prayers he might lift up, whatever statements
he might inwardly make of this man's wretched spiritual condition,
and the duty he himself was under to submit to the punishment
divinely appointed for him rather than to wish for evil to another—
through all this effort to condense words into a solid mental state,
there pierced and spread with irresistible vividness the images of the
events he desired. And in the train of those images came their
apology. He could not but see the death of Raffles, and see in it his
own deliverance. What was the removal of this wretched creature ?
He was impenitent—but were not public criminals impenitent ?—
yet the law decided on their fate. Should Providence in this case
award death, there was no sin in contemplating death as the desirable
issue—if he kept his hands from hastening it—if he scrupulously did
what was prescribed. Even here there might be a mistake : human
prescriptions were fallible things : Lydgate had said that treatment
had hastened death,—why not his own method of treatment ? But
of course intention was everything in the question of right and wrong.

And Bulstrode set himself to keep his intention separate from his
desire. He inwardly declared that he intended to obey orders. Why
should he have got into any argument about the validity of these
orders ? It was only the common trick of desire—which avails itself
of any irrelevant scepticism, finding larger room for itself in all uncertainty about effects, in every obscurity that looks like the absence
of law. Still, he did obey the orders.

His anxieties continually glanced towards Lydgate, and his remembrance of what had taken place between them the morning before
was accompanied with sensibilities which had not been roused at all

during the actual scene. He had then cared but little about Lydgate's painful impressions with regard to the suggested change in the Hospital, or about the disposition towards himself which what he held to be his justifiable refusal of a rather exorbitant request might call forth. He recurred to the scene now with a perception that he had probably made Lydgate his enemy, and with an awakened desire to propitiate him, or rather to create in him a strong sense of personal obligation. He regretted that he had not at once made even an unreasonable money-sacrifice. For in case of unpleasant suspicions or even knowledge gathered from the raving of Raffles, Bulstrode would have felt that he had a defence in Lydgate's mind by having conferred a momentous benefit on him. But the regret had perhaps come too late.

Strange, piteous conflict in the soul of this unhappy man, who had longed for years to be better than he was—who had taken his selfish passions into discipline and clad them in severe robes, so that he had walked with them as a devout quire, till now that a terror had risen among them, and they could chant no longer, but threw out their common cries for safety.

It was nearly the middle of the day before Lydgate arrived : he had meant to come earlier, but had been detained, he said ; and his shattered looks were noticed by Bulstrode. But he immediately threw himself into the consideration of the patient, and inquired strictly into all that had occurred. Raffles was worse, would take hardly any food, was persistently wakeful and restlessly raving ; but still not violent. Contrary to Bulstrode's alarmed expectation, he took little notice of Lydgate's presence, and continued to talk or murmur incoherently.

" What do you think of him ? " said Bulstrode, in private.

" The symptoms are worse."

" You are less hopeful ? "

" No ; I still think he may come round. Are you going to stay here yourself ? " said Lydgate, looking at Bulstrode with an abrupt question, which made him uneasy, though in reality it was not due to any suspicious conjecture.

" Yes, I think so," said Bulstrode, governing himself and speaking with deliberation. " Mrs Bulstrode is advised of the reasons which detain me. Mrs Abel and her husband are not experienced enough to be left quite alone, and this kind of responsibility is scarcely included in their service of me. You have some fresh instructions, I presume."

The chief new instruction that Lydgate had to give was on the administration of extremely moderate doses of opium, in case of the sleeplessness continuing after several hours. He had taken the precaution of bringing opium in his pocket, and he gave minute directions to Bulstrode as to the doses, and the point at which they should cease. He insisted on the risk of not ceasing ; and repeated his order that no alcohol should be given.

" From what I see of the case," he ended, " narcotism is the only thing I should be much afraid of. He may wear through even without much food. There's a good deal of strength in him."

" You look ill yourself, Mr Lydgate—a most unusual, I may say unprecedented thing in my knowledge of you," said Bulstrode, show-

ing a solicitude as unlike his indifference the day before, as his present recklessness about his own fatigue was unlike his habitual self-
cherishing anxiety. " I fear you are harassed."

" Yes, I am," said Lydgate, brusquely, holding his hat, and ready
to go.

" Something new, I fear," said Bulstrode, inquiringly. " Pray be
seated."

" No, thank you," said Lydgate, with some *hauteur.* " I mentioned
to you yesterday what was the state of my affairs. There is nothing
to add, except that the execution has since then been actually put
into my house. One can tell a good deal of trouble in a short sentence. I will say good-morning."

" Stay, Mr Lydgate, stay," said Bulstrode ; " I have been reconsi-
dering this subject. I was yesterday taken by surprise, and saw it
superficially. Mrs Bulstrode is anxious for her niece, and I myself
should grieve at a calamitous change in your position. Claims on
me are numerous, but on reconsideration, I esteem it right that I
should incur a small sacrifice rather than leave you unaided. You
said, I think, that a thousand pounds would suffice entirely to free
you from your burthens, and enable you to recover a firm stand ? "

" Yes," said Lydgate, a great leap of joy within him surmounting
every other feeling ; " that would pay all my debts, and leave me a
little on hand. I could set about economising in our way of living.
And by-and-by my practice might look up."

" If you will wait a moment, Mr Lydgate, I will draw a cheque to
that amount. I am aware that help, to be effectual in these cases,
should be thorough."

While Bulstrode wrote, Lydgate turned to the window thinking of
his home—thinking of his life with its good start saved from frustration, its good purposes still unbroken.

" You can give me a note of hand for this, Mr Lydgate," said the
banker, advancing towards him with the cheque. " And by-and-by,
I hope, you may be in circumstances gradually to repay me. Meanwhile, I have pleasure in thinking that you will be released from
further difficulty."

" I am deeply obliged to you," said Lydgate. " You have restored
to me the prospect of working with some happiness and some chance
of good."

It appeared to him a very natural movement in Bulstrode that he
should have reconsidered his refusal : it corresponded with the more
munificent side of his character. But as he put his hack into a
canter, that he might get the sooner home, and tell the good news to
Rosamond, and get cash at the bank to pay over to Dover's agent,
there crossed his mind, with an unpleasant impression, as from a
dark-winged flight of evil augury across his vision, the thought of
that contrast in himself which a few months had brought—that he
should be overjoyed at being under a strong personal obligation—that
he should be overjoyed at getting money for himself from Bulstrode.

The banker felt that he had done something to nullify one cause
of uneasiness, and yet he was scarcely the easier. He did not measure
the quantity of diseased motive which had made him wish for Lydgate's goodwill, but the quantity was none the less actively there,
like an irritating agent in his blood. A man vows, and yet will not
cast away the means of breaking his vow. Is it that he distinctly

means to break it? Not at all; but the desires which tend to break it are at work in him dimly, and make their way into his imagination, and relax his muscles in the very moments when he is telling himself over again the reasons for his vow. Raffles, recovering quickly, returning to the free use of his odious powers—how could Bulstrode wish for that? Raffles dead was the image that brought release, and indirectly he prayed for that way of release, beseeching that, if it were possible, the rest of his days here below might be freed from the threat of an ignominy which would break him utterly as an instrument of God's service. Lydgate's opinion was not on the side of promise that this prayer would be fulfilled; and as the day advanced, Bulstrode felt himself getting irritated at the persistent life in this man, whom he would fain have seen sinking into the silence of death: imperious will stirred murderous impulses towards this brute life, over which will, by itself, had no power. He said inwardly that he was getting too much worn; he would not sit up with the patient to-night, but leave him to Mrs Abel, who, if necessary, could call her husband.

At six o'clock, Raffles, having had only fitful perturbed snatches of sleep, from which he waked with fresh restlessness and perpetual cries that he was sinking away, Bulstrode began to administer the opium according to Lydgate's directions. At the end of half an hour or more he called Mrs Abel and told her that he found himself unfit for further watching. He must now consign the patient to her care; and he proceeded to repeat to her Lydgate's directions as to the quantity of each dose. Mrs Abel had not before known anything of Lydgate's prescriptions; she had simply prepared and brought whatever Bulstrode ordered, and had done what he pointed out to her. She began now to ask what else she should do besides administering the opium.

"Nothing at present, except the offer of the soup or the soda-water: you can come to me for further directions. Unless there is any important change, I shall not come into the room again to-night. You will ask your husband for help, if necessary. I must go to bed early."

"You've much need, sir, I'm sure," said Mrs Abel, "and to take something more strengthening than what you've done."

Bulstrode went away now without anxiety as to what Raffles might say in his raving, which had taken on a muttering incoherence not likely to create any dangerous belief. At any rate he must risk this. He went down into the wainscoted parlour first, and began to consider whether he would not have his horse saddled and go home by the moonlight, and give up caring for earthly consequences. Then, he wished that he had begged Lydgate to come again that evening. Perhaps he might deliver a different opinion, and think that Raffles was getting into a less hopeful state. Should he send for Lydgate? If Raffles were really getting worse, and slowly dying, Bulstrode felt that he could go to bed and sleep in gratitude to Providence. But was he worse? Lydgate might come and simply say that he was going on as he expected, and predict that he would by-and-by fall into a good sleep, and get well. What was the use of sending for him? Bulstrode shrank from that result. No ideas or opinions could hinder him from seeing the one probability to be, that Raffles recovered would be just the same man as before, with his strength as a tormentor renewed, obliging him to drag away his wife to spend her years apart from her friends and native place, carrying an alienating suspicion against him in her heart.

He had sat an hour and a half in this conflict by the firelight only, when a sudden thought made him rise and light the bed-candle, which he had brought down with him. The thought was, that he had not told Mrs Abel when the doses of opium must cease.

He took hold of the candlestick, but stood motionless for a long while. She might already have given him more than Lydgate had prescribed. But it was excusable in him, that he should forget part of an order, in his present wearied condition. He walked up-stairs, candle in hand, not knowing whether he should straightway enter his own room and go to bed, or turn to the patient's room and rectify his omission. He paused in the passage, with his face turned towards Raffles's room, and he could hear him moaning and murmuring. He was not asleep, then. Who could know that Lydgate's prescription would not be better disobeyed than followed, since there was still no sleep?

He turned into his own room. Before he had quite undressed, Mrs Abel rapped at the door; he opened it an inch, so that he could hear her speak low.

"If you please, sir, should I have no brandy nor nothing to give the poor creetur? He feels sinking away, and nothing else will he swaller—and but little strength in it, if he did—only the opium. And he says more and more he's sinking down through the earth."

To her surprise, Mr Bulstrode did not answer. A struggle was going on within him.

"I think he must die for want o' support, if he goes on in that way. When I nursed my poor master, Mr Robisson, I had to give him port-wine and brandy constant, and a big glass at a time," added Mrs Abel, with a touch of remonstrance in her tone.

But again Mr Bulstrode did not answer immediately, and she continued, "It's not a time to spare when people are at death's door, nor would you wish it, sir, I'm sure. Else I should give him our own bottle o' rum as we keep by us. But a sitter-up so as you've been, and doing everything as laid in your power——"

Here a key was thrust through the inch of doorway, and Mr Bulstrode said huskily, "That is the key of the wine-cooler. You will find plenty of brandy there."

Early in the morning—about six—Mr Bulstrode rose and spent some time in prayer. Does any one suppose that private prayer is necessarily candid—necessarily goes to the roots of action? Private prayer is inaudible speech, and speech is representative: who can represent himself just as he is, even in his own reflections? Bulstrode had not yet unravelled in his thought the confused promptings of the last four-and-twenty hours.

He listened in the passage, and could hear hard stertorous breathing. Then he walked out in the garden, and looked at the early rime on the grass and fresh spring leaves. When he re-entered the house, he felt startled at the sight of Mrs Abel.

"How is your patient—asleep, I think?" he said, with an attempt at cheerfulness in his tone.

"He's gone very deep, sir," said Mrs Abel. "He went off gradual between three and four o'clock. Would you please to go and look at him? I thought it no harm to leave him. My man's gone afield, and the little girl's seeing to the kettles."

Bulstrode went up. At a glance he knew that Raffles was not in the sleep which brings revival, but in the sleep which streams deeper and deeper into the gulf of death.

He looked round the room and saw a bottle with some brandy in it, and the almost empty opium phial. He put the phial out of sight, and carried the brandy-bottle down-stairs with him, locking it again in the wine-cooler.

While breakfasting he considered whether he should ride to Middlemarch at once, or wait for Lydgate's arrival. He decided to wait, and told Mrs Abel that she might go about her work—he could watch in the bed-chamber.

As he sat there and beheld the enemy of his peace going irrevocably into silence, he felt more at rest than he had done for many months. His conscience was soothed by the enfolding wing of secrecy, which seemed just then like an angel sent down for his relief. He drew out his pocket-book to review various memoranda there as to the arrangements he had projected and partly carried out in the prospect of quitting Middlemarch, and considered how far he would let them stand or recall them, now that his absence would be brief. Some economies which he felt desirable might still find a suitable occasion in his temporary withdrawal from management, and he hoped still that Mrs Casaubon would take a large share in the expenses of the Hospital. In that way the moments passed, until a change in the stertorous breathing was marked enough to draw his attention wholly to the bed, and forced him to think of the departing life, which had once been subservient to his own — which he had once been glad to find base enough for him to act on as he would. It was his gladness then which impelled him now to be glad that the life was at an end.

And who could say that the death of Raffles had been hastened? Who knew what would have saved him?

Lydgate arrived at half-past ten, in time to witness the final pause of the breath. When he entered the room Bulstrode observed a sudden expression in his face, which was not so much surprise as a recognition that he had not judged correctly. He stood by the bed in silence for some time, with his eyes turned on the dying man, but with that subdued activity of expression which showed that he was carrying on an inward debate.

"When did this change begin?" said he, looking at Bulstrode.

"I did not watch by him last night," said Bulstrode. "I was overworn, and left him under Mrs Abel's care. She said that he sank into sleep between three and four o'clock. When I came in before eight he was nearly in this condition."

Lydgate did not ask another question, but watched in silence until he said, "It's all over."

This morning Lydgate was in a state of recovered hope and freedom. He had set out on his work with all his old animation, and felt himself strong enough to bear all the deficiencies of his married life. And he was conscious that Bulstrode had been a benefactor to him. But he was uneasy about this case. He had not expected it to terminate as it had done. Yet he hardly knew how to put a question on the subject to Bulstrode without appearing to insult him; and if he examined the housekeeper—why, the man was dead. There seemed to be no use in implying that somebody's ignorance or imprudence had killed him. And after all, he himself might be wrong.

He and Bulstrode rode back to Middlemarch together, talking of many things—chiefly cholera and the chances of the Reform Bill in the House of Lords, and the firm resolve of the Political Unions. Nothing was said about Raffles, except that Bulstrode mentioned the necessity of having a grave for him in Lowick churchyard, and observed that, so far as he knew, the poor man had no connections, except Rigg, whom he had stated to be unfriendly towards him.

On returning home Lydgate had a visit from Mr Farebrother. The Vicar had not been in the town the day before, but the news that there was an execution in Lydgate's house had got to Lowick by the evening, having been carried by Mr Spicer, shoemaker and parish-clerk, who had it from his brother, the respectable bell-hanger in Lowick Gate. Since that evening when Lydgate had come down from the billiard-room with Fred Vincy, Mr Farebrother's thoughts about him had been rather gloomy. Playing at the Green Dragon once or oftener might have been a trifle in another man ; but in Lydgate it was one of several signs that he was getting unlike his former self. He was beginning to do things for which he had formerly even an excessive scorn. Whatever certain dissatisfactions in marriage, which some silly tinklings of gossip had given him hints of, might have to do with this change, Mr Farebrother felt sure that it was chiefly connected with the debts which were being more and more distinctly reported, and he began to fear that any notion of Lydgate's having resources or friends in the background must be quite illusory. The rebuff he had met with in his first attempt to win Lydgate's confidence, disinclined him to a second ; but this news of the execution being actually in the house, determined the Vicar to overcome his reluctance.

Lydgate had just dismissed a poor patient, in whom he was much interested, and he came forward to put out his hand with an open cheerfulness which surprised Mr Farebrother. Could this too be a proud rejection of sympathy and help ? Never mind ; the sympathy and help should be offered.

"How are you, Lydgate ? I came to see you because I had heard something which made me anxious about you," said the Vicar, in the tone of a good brother, only that there was no reproach in it. They were both seated by this time, and Lydgate answered immediately—

"I think I know what you mean.· You had heard that there was an execution in the house ?"

"Yes ; is it true ?"

"It was true," said Lydgate, with an air of freedom, as if he did not mind talking about the affair now. "But the danger is over ; the debt is paid. I am out of my difficulties now : I shall be freed from debts, and able, I hope, to start afresh on a better plan."

"I am very thankful to hear it," said the Vicar, falling back in his chair, and speaking with that low-toned quickness which often follows the removal of a load. "I like that better than all the news in the 'Times.' I confess I came to you with a heavy heart."

"Thank you for coming," said Lydgate, cordially. "I can enjoy the kindness all the more because I am happier. I have certainly been a good deal crushed. I'm afraid I shall find the bruises still painful by-and-by," he added, smiling rather sadly ; " but just now I can only feel that the torture-screw is off."

Mr Farebrother was silent for a moment, and then said earnestly, " My dear fellow, let me ask you one question. Forgive me if I take a liberty."

" I don't believe you will ask anything that ought to offend me."

" Then—this is necessary to set my heart quite at rest—you have not—have you ?—in order to pay your debts, incurred another debt which may harass you worse hereafter ? "

" No," said Lydgate, colouring slightly. " There is no reason why I should not tell you—since the fact is so—that the person to whom I am indebted is Bulstrode. He has made me a very handsome advance—a thousand pounds—and he can afford to wait for repayment."

" Well, that is generous," said Mr Farebrother, compelling himself to approve of the man whom he disliked. His delicate feeling shrank from dwelling even in his thought on the fact that he had always urged Lydgate to avoid any personal entanglement with Bulstrode. He added immediately, " And Bulstrode must naturally feel an interest in your welfare, after you have worked with him in a way which has probably reduced your income instead of adding to it. I am glad to think that he has acted accordingly."

Lydgate felt uncomfortable under these kindly suppositions. They made more distinct within him the uneasy consciousness which had shown its first dim stirrings only a few hours before, that Bulstrode's motives for his sudden beneficence following close upon the chillest indifference might be merely selfish. He let the kindly suppositions pass. He could not tell the history of the loan, but it was more vividly present with him than ever, as well as the fact which the Vicar delicately ignored—that this relation of personal indebtedness to Bulstrode was what he had once been most resolved to avoid.

He began, instead of answering, to speak of his projected economies, and of his having come to look at his life from a different point of view.

" I shall set up a surgery," he said. " I really think I made a mistaken effort in that respect. And if Rosamond will not mind, I shall take an apprentice. I don't like these things, but if one carries them out faithfully they are not really lowering. I have had a severe galling to begin with : that will make the small rubs seem easy."

Poor Lydgate ! the " if Rosamond will not mind," which had fallen from him involuntarily as part of his thought, was a significant mark of the yoke he bore. But Mr Farebrother, whose hopes entered strongly into the same current with Lydgate's, and who knew nothing about him that could now raise a melancholy presentiment, left him with affectionate congratulation.

CHAPTER LXXI.

"*Clown.* . . . 'Twas in the Bunch of Grapes, where, indeed, you have a delight to sit, have you not?
"*Froth.* I have so ; because it is an open room, and good for winter.
"*Clo.* Why, very well then : I hope here be truths."
—*Measure for Measure.*[1]

FIVE days after the death of Raffles, Mr Bambridge was standing at his leisure under the large archway leading into the yard of the Green Dragon. He was not fond of solitary contemplation, but he had only just come out of the house, and any human figure standing at ease under the archway in the early afternoon was as certain to attract companionship as a pigeon which has found something worth pecking at. In this case there was no material object to feed upon, but the eye of reason saw a probability of mental sustenance in the shape of gossip. Mr Hopkins, the meek-mannered draper opposite, was the first to act on this inward vision, being the more ambitious of a little masculine talk because his customers were chiefly women. Mr Bambridge was rather curt to the draper, feeling that Hopkins was of course glad to talk to *him*, but that he was not going to waste much of his talk on Hopkins. Soon, however, there was a small cluster of more important listeners, who were either deposited from the passers-by, or had sauntered to the spot expressly to see if there were anything going on at the Green Dragon ; and Mr Bambridge was finding it worth his while to say many impressive things about the fine studs he had been seeing and the purchases he had made on a journey in the north from which he had just returned. Gentlemen present were assured that when they could show him anything to cut out a blood mare, a bay, rising four, which was to be seen at Doncaster if they chose to go and look at it, Mr Bambridge would gratify them by being shot "from here to Hereford." Also, a pair of blacks which he was going to put into the break recalled vividly to his mind a pair which he had sold to Faulkner in '19, for a hundred guineas, and which Faulkner had sold for a hundred and sixty two months later —any gent who could disprove this statement being offered the privilege of calling Mr Bambridge by a very ugly name until the exercise made his throat dry.

When the discourse was at this point of animation, came up **Mr Frank Hawley.** He was not a man to compromise his dignity by lounging at the Green Dragon, but happening to pass along the High Street and seeing Bambridge on the other side, he took some of his

1. Act II, Sc. 1, lines 125–30.

long strides across to ask the horse-dealer whether he had found the first-rate gig-horse which he had engaged to look for. Mr Hawley was requested to wait until he had seen a grey selected at Bilkley: if that did not meet his wishes to a hair, Bambridge did not know a horse when he saw it, which seemed to be the highest conceivable unlikelihood. Mr Hawley, standing with his back to the street, was fixing a time for looking at the grey and seeing it tried, when a horseman passed slowly by.

"Bulstrode!" said two or three voices at once in a low tone, one of them, which was the draper's, respectfully prefixing the "Mr;" but nobody having more intention in this interjectional naming than if they had said "the Riverston coach" when that vehicle appeared in the distance. Mr Hawley gave a careless glance round at Bulstrode's back, but as Bambridge's eyes followed it he made a sarcastic grimace.

"By jingo! that reminds me," he began, lowering his voice a little, "I picked up something else at Bilkley besides your gig-horse, Mr Hawley. I picked up a fine story about Bulstrode. Do you know how he came by his fortune? Any gentleman wanting a bit of curious information, I can give it him free of expense. If everybody got their deserts, Bulstrode might have had to say his prayers at Botany Bay." [2]

"What do you mean?" said Mr Hawley, thrusting his hands into his pockets, and pushing a little forward under the archway. If Bulstrode should turn out to be a rascal, Frank Hawley had a prophetic soul.

"I had it from a party who was an old chum of Bulstrode's. I'll tell you where I first picked him up," said Bambridge, with a sudden gesture of his forefinger. "He was at Larcher's sale, but I knew nothing of him then—he slipped through my fingers—was after Bulstrode, no doubt. He tells me he can tap Bulstrode to any amount, knows all his secrets. However, he blabbed to me at Bilkley: he takes a stiff glass. Damme if I think he meant to turn king's evidence; but he's that sort of bragging fellow, the bragging runs over hedge and ditch with him, till he'd brag of a spavin as if it 'ud fetch money. A man should know when to pull up." Mr Bambridge made this remark with an air of disgust, satisfied that his own bragging showed a fine sense of the marketable.

"What's the man's name? Where can he be found?" said Mr Hawley.

"As to where he is to be found, I left him to it at the Saracen's Head; but his name is Raffles."

"Raffles!" exclaimed Mr Hopkins. "I furnished his funeral yesterday. He was buried at Lowick. Mr Bulstrode followed him. A very decent funeral."

There was a strong sensation among the listeners. Mr Bambridge gave an ejaculation in which "brimstone" was the mildest word, and Mr Hawley, knitting his brows and bending his head forward, exclaimed, "What?—where did the man die?"

2. Figurative reference to the Australian penal colony at Botany Bay, near Sydney.

"At Stone Court," said the draper. "The housekeeper said he was a relation of the master's. He came there ill on Friday."

"Why, it was on Wednesday I took a glass with him," interposed Bambridge.

"Did any doctor attend him?" said Mr Hawley.

"Yes, Mr Lydgate. Mr Bulstrode sat up with him one night. He died the third morning."

"Go on, Bambridge," said Mr Hawley, insistently. "What did this fellow say about Bulstrode?"

The group had already become larger, the town-clerk's presence being a guarantee that something worth listening to was going on there; and Mr Bambridge delivered his narrative in the hearing of seven. It was mainly what we know, including the fact about Will Ladislaw, with some local colour and circumstance added: it was what Bulstrode had dreaded the betrayal of—and hoped to have buried for ever with the corpse of Raffles—it was that haunting ghost of his earlier life which as he rode past the archway of the Green Dragon he was trusting that Providence had delivered him from. Yes, Providence. He had not confessed to himself yet that he had done anything in the way of contrivance to this end; he had accepted what seemed to have been offered. It was impossible to prove that he had done anything which hastened the departure of that man's soul.

But this gossip about Bulstrode spread through Middlemarch like the smell of fire. Mr Frank Hawley followed up his information by sending a clerk whom he could trust to Stone Court on a pretext of inquiring about hay, but really to gather all that could be learned about Raffles and his illness from Mrs Abel. In this way it came to his knowledge that Mr Garth had carried the man to Stone Court in his gig; and Mr Hawley in consequence took an opportunity of seeing Caleb, calling at his office to ask whether he had time to undertake an arbitration if it were required, and then asking him incidentally about Raffles. Caleb was betrayed into no word injurious to Bulstrode beyond the fact which he was forced to admit, that he had given up acting for him within the last week. Mr Hawley drew his inferences, and feeling convinced that Raffles had told his story to Garth, and that Garth had given up Bulstrode's affairs in consequence, said so a few hours later to Mr Toller. The statement was passed on until it had quite lost the stamp of an inference, and was taken as information coming straight from Garth, so that even a diligent historian might have concluded Caleb to be the chief publisher of Bulstrode's misdemeanours.

Mr Hawley was not slow to perceive that there was no handle for the law either in the revelations made by Raffles or in the circumstances of his death. He had himself ridden to Lowick village that he might look at the register and talk over the whole matter with Mr Farebrother, who was not more surprised than the lawyer that an ugly secret should have come to light about Bulstrode, though he had always had justice enough in him to hinder his antipathy from turning into conclusions. But while they were talking another combination was silently going forward in Mr Farebrother's mind, which foreshadowed what was soon to be loudly spoken of in Middlemarch as a necessary "putting of two and two together." With the reasons which kept Bulstrode in dread of Raffles there flashed the thought

that the dread might have something to do with his munificence towards his medical man ; and though he resisted the suggestion that
it had been consciously accepted in any way as a bribe, he had a foreboding that this complication of things might be of malignant effect
on Lydgate's reputation. He perceived that Mr Hawley knew nothing
at present of the sudden relief from debt, and he himself was careful
to glide away from all approaches towards the subject.

"Well," he said, with a deep breath, wanting to wind up the illimitable discussion of what might have been, though nothing could be
legally proven, "it is a strange story. So our mercurial Ladislaw
has a queer genealogy ! A high-spirited young lady and a musical
Polish patriot made a likely enough stock for him to spring from, but
I should never have suspected a grafting of the Jew pawnbroker.
However, there's no knowing what a mixture will turn out beforehand. Some sorts of dirt serve to clarify."

"It's just what I should have expected," said Mr Hawley, mounting his horse. "Any cursed alien blood, Jew, Corsican, or Gypsy."

"I know he's one of your black sheep, Hawley. But he is really
a disinterested, unworldly fellow," said Mr Farebrother, smiling.

"Ay, ay, that is your Whiggish twist," said Mr Hawley, who had
been in the habit of saying apologetically that Farebrother was such
a damned pleasant good-hearted fellow you would mistake him for a
Tory.

Mr Hawley rode home without thinking of Lydgate's attendance
on Raffles in any other light than as a piece of evidence on the side
of Bulstrode. But the news that Lydgate had all at once become
able not only to get rid of the execution in his house but to pay all
his debts in Middlemarch was spreading fast, gathering round it conjectures and comments which gave it new body and impetus, and
soon filling the ears of other persons besides Mr Hawley, who were
not slow to see a significant relation between this sudden command
of money and Bulstrode's desire to stifle the scandal of Raffles. That
the money came from Bulstrode would infallibly have been guessed
even if there had been no direct evidence of it ; for it had beforehand entered into the gossip about Lydgate's affairs, that neither his
father-in-law nor his own family would do anything for him, and
direct evidence was furnished not only by a clerk at the Bank, but
by innocent Mrs Bulstrode herself, who mentioned the loan to Mrs
Plymdale, who mentioned it to her daughter-in-law of the house of
Toller, who mentioned it generally. The business was felt to be so
public and important that it required dinners to feed it, and many
invitations were just then issued and accepted on the strength of this
scandal concerning Bulstrode and Lydgate ; wives, widows, and
single ladies took their work and went out to tea oftener than usual ;
and all public conviviality, from the Green Dragon to Dollop's,
gathered a zest which could not be won from the question whether
the Lords would throw out the Reform Bill.

For hardly anybody doubted that some scandalous reason or other
was at the bottom of Bulstrode's liberality to Lydgate. Mr Hawley,
indeed, in the first instance, invited a select party, including the two
physicians, with Mr Toller and Mr Wrench, expressly to hold a close
discussion as to the probabilities of Raffle's illness, reciting to them
all the particulars which had been gathered from Mrs Abel in connection with Lydgate's certificate, that the death was due to *delirium*

tremens ; and the medical gentlemen, who all stood undisturbedly on the old paths in relation to this disease, declared that they could see nothing in these particulars which could be transformed into a positive ground of suspicion. But the moral grounds of suspicion remained : the strong motives Bulstrode clearly had for wishing to be rid of Raffles, and the fact that at this critical moment he had given Lydgate the help which he must for some time have known the need for ; the disposition, moreover, to believe that Bulstrode would be unscrupulous, and the absence of any indisposition to believe that Lydgate might be as easily bribed as other haughty-minded men when they have found themselves in want of money. Even if the money had been given merely to make him hold his tongue about the scandal of Bulstrode's earlier life, the fact threw an odious light on Lydgate, who had long been sneered at as making himself subservient to the banker for the sake of working himself into predominance, and discrediting the elder members of his profession. Hence, in spite of the negative as to any direct sign of guilt in relation to the death at Stone Court, Mr Hawley's select party broke up with the sense that the affair had " an ugly look."

But this vague conviction of indeterminable guilt, which was enough to keep up much head-shaking and biting innuendo even among substantial professional seniors, had for the general mind all the superior power of mystery over fact. Everybody liked better to conjecture how the thing was, than simply to know it ; for conjecture soon became more confident than knowledge, and had a more liberal allowance for the incompatible. Even the more definite scandal concerning Bulstrode's earlier life was, for some minds, melted into the mass of mystery, as so much lively metal to be poured out in dialogue, and to take such fantastic shapes as heaven pleased.

This was the tone of thought chiefly sanctioned by Mrs Dollop, the spirited landlady of the Tankard in Slaughter Lane, who had often to resist the shallow pragmatism of customers disposed to think that their reports from the outer world were of equal force with what had " come up" in her mind. How it had been brought to her she didn't know, but it was there before her as if it had been scored with the chalk on the chimney-board—" as Bulstrode should say, his inside was *that black* as if the hairs of his head knowed the thoughts of his heart, he'd tear 'em up by the roots."

" That's odd," said Mr Limp, a meditative shoemaker, with weak eyes and a piping voice. " Why, I read in the ' Trumpet' that was what the Duke of Wellington said when he turned his coat and went over to the Romans."

" Very like," said Mrs Dollop. " If one raskill said it, it's more reason why another should. But hypo*crite* as he's been, and holding things with that high hand, as there was no parson i' the country good enough for him, he was forced to take Old Harry into his counsel, and Old Harry's been too many for him."

" Ay, ay, he's a 'complice you can't send out o' the country," said Mr Crabbe the glazier, who gathered much news and groped among it dimly. " But by what I can make out, there's them says Bulstrode was for running away, for fear o' being found out, before now."

" He'll be drove away, whether or no," said Mr Dill, the barber, who had just dropped in. " I shaved Fletcher, Hawley's clerk, this morning—he's got a bad finger—and he says they're all of one mind to get rid o' Bulstrode. Mr Thesiger is turned against him, and wants him out o' the parish. And there's gentlemen in this town says they'd as soon dine with a fellow from the hulks.³ 'And a deal sooner I would,' says Fletcher; 'for what's more against one's stomach than a man coming and making himself bad company with his religion, and giving out as the Ten Commandments are not enough for him, and all the while he's worse than half the men at the tread-mill?' Fletcher said so himself."

"It'll be a bad thing for the town though, if Bulstrode's money goes out of it," said Mr Limp, quaveringly.

"Ah, there's better folks spend their money worse," said a firm-voiced dyer, whose crimson hands looked out of keeping with his good-natured face.

"But he won't keep his money, by what I can make out," said the glazier. "Don't they say as there's somebody can strip it off him? By what I can understan', they could take every penny off him, if they went to lawing."

"No such thing!" said the barber, who felt himself a little above his company at Dollop's, but liked it none the worse. "Fletcher says it's no such thing. He says they might prove over and over again whose child this young Ladislaw was, and they'd do no more than if they proved I came out of the Fens—he couldn't touch a penny."⁴

"Look you there now!" said Mrs Dollop, indignantly. "I thank the Lord he took my children to Himself, if that's all the law can do for the motherless. Then by that, it's o' no use who your father and mother is. But as to listening to what one lawyer says without asking another—I wonder at a man o' your cleverness, Mr Dill. It's well known there's always two sides, if no more; else who'd go to law, I should like to know? It's a poor tale, with all the law as there is up and down, if it's no use proving whose child you are. Fletcher may say that if he likes, but I say, don't Fletcher *me!*"

Mr Dill affected to laugh in a complimentary way at Mrs Dollop, as a woman who was more than a match for the lawyers; being disposed to submit to much twitting from a landlady who had a long score against him.

"If they come to lawing, and it's all true as folks say, there's more to be looked to nor money," said the glazier. "There's this poor creetur as is dead and gone: by what I can make out, he'd seen the day when he was a deal finer gentleman nor Bulstrode."

"Finer gentleman! I'll warrant him," said Mrs Dollop; "and a far personabler man, by what I can hear. As I said when Mr Baldwin, the tax-gatherer, comes in, a-standing where you sit, and says, 'Bulstrode got all his money as he brought into this town by thieving and swindling,'—I said, 'You don't make me no wiser, Mr Baldwin: it's set my blood a-creeping to look at him ever sin' here he came into Slaughter Lane a-wanting to buy the house over my head: folks don't look the colour o' the dough-tub and stare at you as if they wanted to see into your backbone for nothingk.' That was what I said, and Mr Baldwin can bear me witness."

"And in the rights of it too," said Mr Crabbe. "For by what I can make out, this Raffles, as they call him, was a lusty, fresh-coloured man as you'd wish to see, and the best o' company—though dead he

3. Prison ships.   4. Fens: marshes.

lies in Lowick churchyard sure enough ; and by what I can understan', there's them knows more than they *should* know about how he
got there."

" I'll believe you !" said Mrs Dollop, with a touch of scorn at Mr
Crabbe's apparent dimness. " When a man's been 'ticed to a lone
house, and there's them can pay for hospitals and nurses for half
the country-side choose to be sitters-up night and day, and nobody
to come near but a doctor as is known to stick at nothingk, and as
poor as he can hang together, and after that so flush o' money as he
can pay off Mr Byles the butcher as his bill has been running on
for the best o' joints since last Michaelmas was a twelvemonth—I
don't want anybody to come and tell me as there's been more going
on nor the Prayer-book's got a service for—I don't want to stand
winking and blinking and thinking." [5]

Mrs Dollop looked round with the air of a landlady accustomed to
dominate her company. There was a chorus of adhesion from the
more courageous ; but Mr Limp, after taking a draught, placed his
flat hands together and pressed them hard between his knees, looking
down at them with blear-eyed contemplation, as if the scorching
power of Mrs Dollop's speech had quite dried up and nullified his
wits until they could be brought round again by further moisture.

" Why shouldn't they dig the man up and have the Crowner ?" said
the dyer. " It's been done many and many's the time. If there's
been foul play they might find it out."

" Not they, Mr Jonas !" said Mrs Dollop, emphatically. " I know
what doctors are. They're a deal too cunning to be found out. And
this Dr Lydgate that's been for cutting up everybody before the
breath was well out o' their body—it's plain enough what use he
wanted to make o' looking into respectable people's insides. He
knows drugs, you may be sure, as you can neither smell nor see,
neither before they're swallowed nor after. Why, I've seen drops
myself ordered by Doctor Gambit, as is our club doctor and a good
charikter, and has brought more live children into the world nor ever
another i' Middlemarch—I say I've seen drops myself as made no
difference whether they was in the glass or out, and yet have griped
you the next day. So I'll leave your own sense to judge. Don't
tell me ! All I say is, it's a mercy they didn't take this Doctor
Lydgate on to our club. There's many a mother's child might ha'
rued it."

The heads of this discussion at " Dollop's " had been the common
theme among all classes in the town, had been carried to Lowick
Parsonage on one side and to Tipton Grange on the other, had come
fully to the ears of the Vincy family, and had been discussed with sad
reference to "poor Harriet" by all Mrs Bulstrode's friends, before
Lydgate knew distinctly why people were looking strangely at him,
and before Bulstrode himself suspected the betrayal of his secrets.
He had not been accustomed to very cordial relations with his neighbours, and hence he could not miss the signs of cordiality ; moreover,
he had been taking journeys on business of various kinds, having now
made up his mind that he need not quit Middlemarch, and feeling
able consequently to determine on matters which he had before left
in suspense.

---

5. Since Michaelmas was a twelve month: a year ago last September.

" We will make a journey to Cheltenham in the course of a month or two," he had said to his wife. " There are great spiritual advantages to be had in that town along with the air and the waters, and six weeks there will be eminently refreshing to us."

He really believed in the spiritual advantages, and meant that his life henceforth should be the more devoted because of those later sins which he represented to himself as hypothetic, praying hypothetically for their pardon :—" if I have herein transgressed."

As to the Hospital, he avoided saying anything further to Lydgate, fearing to manifest a too sudden change of plans immediately on the death of Raffles. In his secret soul he believed that Lydgate suspected his orders to have been intentionally disobeyed, and suspecting this he must also suspect a motive. But nothing had been betrayed to him as to the history of Raffles, and Bulstrode was anxious not to do anything which would give emphasis to his undefined suspicions. As to any certainty that a particular method of treatment would either save or kill, Lydgate himself was constantly arguing against such dogmatism ; he had no right to speak, and he had every motive for being silent. Hence Bulstrode felt himself providentially secured. The only incident he had strongly winced under had been an occasional encounter with Caleb Garth, who, however, had raised his hat with mild gravity.

Meanwhile, on the part of the principal townsmen a strong determination was growing against him.

A meeting was to be held in the Town-Hall on a sanitary question which had risen into pressing importance by the occurrence of a cholera case in the town. Since the Act of Parliament, which had been hurriedly passed, authorising assessments for sanitary measures, there had been a Board for the superintendence of such measures appointed in Middlemarch, and much cleansing and preparation had been concurred in by Whigs and Tories.[6] The question now was, whether a piece of ground outside the town should be secured as a burial-ground by means of assessment or by private subscription. The meeting was to be open, and almost everybody of importance in the town was expected to be there.

Mr Bulstrode was a member of the Board, and just before twelve o'clock he started from the Bank with the intention of urging the plan of private subscription. Under the hesitation of his projects, he had for some time kept himself in the background, and he felt that he should this morning resume his old position as a man of action and influence in the public affairs of the town where he expected to end his days. Among the various persons going in the same direction, he saw Lydgate ; they joined, talked over the object of the meeting, and entered it together.

It seemed that everybody of mark had been earlier than they. But there were still spaces left near the head of the large central table, and they made their way thither. Mr Farebrother sate opposite, not far from Mr Hawley ; all the medical men were there ; Mr Thesiger was in the chair, and Mr Brooke of Tipton was on his right hand.

6. "An Act to extend the Jurisdiction of the Commissions," July 15, 1828. It placed new sewers and drains under the control of the Commissioners of Woods, Forests, and Land Revenues (para. 50), and provided for assessments to pay for "making, maintaining, supporting, and keeping in repair" such sanitary facilities from the owners of the property· drained (para. 51).

Lydgate noticed a peculiar interchange of glances when he and Bulstrode took their seats.

After the business had been fully opened by the chairman, who pointed out the advantages of purchasing by subscription a piece of ground large enough to be ultimately used as a general cemetery, Mr Bulstrode, whose rather high-pitched but subdued and fluent voice the town was used to at meetings of this sort, rose and asked leave to deliver his opinion. Lydgate could see again the peculiar interchange of glances before Mr Hawley started up, and said in his firm resonant voice, " Mr Chairman, I request that before any one delivers his opinion on this point I may be permitted to speak on a question of public feeling, which not only by myself, but by many gentlemen present, is regarded as preliminary."

Mr Hawley's mode of speech, even when public decorum repressed his " awful language," was formidable in its curtness and self-possession. Mr Thesiger sanctioned the request, Mr Bulstrode sat down, and Mr Hawley continued.

" In what I have to say, Mr Chairman, I am not speaking simply on my own behalf : I am speaking with the concurrence and at the express request of no fewer than eight of my fellow-townsmen, who are immediately around us. It is our united sentiment that Mr Bulstrode should be called upon—and I do now call upon him—to resign public positions which he holds not simply as a tax-payer, but as a gentleman among gentlemen. There are practices and there are acts which, owing to circumstances, the law cannot visit, though they may be worse than many things which are legally punishable. Honest men and gentlemen, if they don't want the company of people who perpetrate such acts, have got to defend themselves as they best can, and that is what I and the friends whom I may call my clients in this affair are determined to do. I don't say that Mr Bulstrode has been guilty of shameful acts, but I call upon him either publicly to deny and confute the scandalous statements made against him by a man now dead, and who died in his house—the statement that he was for many years engaged in nefarious practices, and that he won his fortune by dishonest procedures—or else to withdraw from positions which could only have been allowed him as a gentleman among gentlemen."

All eyes in the room were turned on Mr Bulstrode, who, since the first mention of his name, had been going through a crisis of feeling almost too violent for his delicate frame to support. Lydgate, who himself was undergoing a shock as from the terrible practical interpretation of some faint augury, felt, nevertheless, that his own movement of resentful hatred was checked by that instinct of the Healer which thinks first of bringing rescue or relief to the sufferer, when he looked at the shrunken misery of Bulstrode's livid face.

The quick vision that his life was after all a failure, that he was a dishonoured man, and must quail before the glance of those towards whom he had habitually assumed the attitude of a reprover—that God had disowned him before men and left him unscreened to the triumphant scorn of those who were glad to have their hatred justified —the sense of utter futility in that equivocation with his conscience in dealing with the life of his accomplice, an equivocation which now turned venomously upon him with the full-grown fang of a discovered

lie :—all this rushed through him like the agony of terror which fails
to kill, and leaves the ears still open to the returning wave of execra-
tion.   The sudden sense of exposure after the re-established sense of
safety came—not to the coarse organisation of a criminal but—to the
susceptible nerve of a man whose intensest being lay in such mastery
and predominance as the conditions of his life had shaped for him.
But in that intense being lay the strength of reaction.   Through
all his bodily infirmity there ran a tenacious nerve of ambitious self-
preserving will, which had continually leaped out like a flame, scat-
tering all doctrinal fears, and which, even while he sat an object of
compassion for the merciful, was beginning to stir and glow under his
ashy paleness.   Before the last words were out of Mr Hawley's mouth,
Bulstrode felt that he should answer, and that his answer would be a
retort.   He dared not get up and say, " I am not guilty, the whole
story is false"—even if he had dared this, it would have seemed to
him, under his present keen sense of betrayal, as vain as to pull, for
covering to his nakedness, a frail rag which would rend at every
little strain.

For a few moments there was total silence, while every man in the
room was looking at Bulstrode.   He sat perfectly still, leaning hard
against the back of his chair; he could not venture to rise, and when
he began to speak he pressed his hands upon the seat on each side of
him.   But his voice was perfectly audible, though hoarser than
usual, and his words were distinctly pronounced, though he paused
between each sentence as if short of breath.   He said, turning first
toward Mr Thesiger, and then looking at Mr Hawley—

" I protest before you, sir, as a Christian minister, against the
sanction of proceedings towards me which are dictated by virulent
hatred.   Those who are hostile to me are glad to believe any libel
uttered by a loose tongue against me.   And their consciences become
strict against me.   Say that the evil-speaking of which I am to be
made the victim accuses me of malpractices——" here Bulstrode's voice
rose and took on a more biting accent, till it seemed a low cry—
" who shall be my accuser ?   Not men whose own lives are unchristian, nay, scandalous—not men who themselves use low instruments to carry out their ends—whose profession is a tissue of chicanery
—who have been spending their income on their own sensual enjoyments, while I have been devoting mine to advance the best objects
with regard to this life and the next."

After the word chicanery there was a growing noise, half of murmurs and half of hisses, while four persons started up at once—Mr
Hawley, Mr Toller, Mr Chichely, and Mr Hackbutt ; but Mr Hawley's
outburst was instantaneous, and left the others behind in silence.

" If you mean me, sir, I call you and every one else to the inspection of my professional life.   As to Christian or unchristian, I re-
pudiate your canting palavering Christianity ; and as to the way in
which I spend my income, it is not my principle to maintain thieves
and cheat offspring of their due inheritance in order to support religion and set myself up as a saintly Kill-joy.   I affect no niceness of
conscience—I have not found any nice standards necessary yet to
measure your actions by, sir.   And I again call upon you to enter
into satisfactory explanations concerning the scandals against you, or
else to withdraw from posts in which we at any rate decline you as a

colleague. I say, sir, we decline to co-operate with a man whose character is not cleared from infamous lights cast upon it, not only by reports but by recent actions."

"Allow me, Mr Hawley," said the chairman ; and Mr Hawley, still fuming, bowed half impatiently, and sat down with his hands thrust deep in his pockets.

"Mr Bulstrode, it is not desirable, I think, to prolong the present discussion," said Mr Thesiger, turning to the pallid trembling man ; "I must so far concur with what has fallen from Mr Hawley in expression of a general feeling, as to think it due to your Christian profession that you should clear yourself, if possible, from unhappy aspersions. I for my part should be willing to give you full opportunity and hearing. But I must say that your present attitude is painfully inconsistent with those principles which you have sought to identify yourself with, and for the honour of which I am bound to care. I recommend you at present, as your clergyman, and one who hopes for your reinstatement in respect, to quit the room, and avoid further hindrance to business."

Bulstrode, after a moment's hesitation, took his hat from the floor and slowly rose, but he grasped the corner of the chair so totteringly that Lydgate felt sure there was not strength enough in him to walk away without support. What could he do ? He could not see a man sink close to him for want of help. He rose and gave his arm to Bulstrode, and in that way led him out of the room ; yet this act, which might have been one of gentle duty and pure compassion, was at this moment unspeakably bitter to him. It seemed as if he were putting his sign-manual to that association of himself with Bulstrode, of which he now saw the full meaning as it must have presented itself to other minds. He now felt the conviction that this man who was leaning tremblingly on his arm, had given him the thousand pounds as a bribe, and that somehow the treatment of Raffles had been tampered with from an evil motive. The inferences were closely linked enough : the town knew of the loan, believed it to be a bribe, and believed that he took it as a bribe.

Poor Lydgate, his mind struggling under the terrible clutch of this revelation, was all the while morally forced to take Mr Bulstrode to the Bank, send a man off for his carriage, and wait to accompany him home.

Meanwhile the business of the meeting was despatched, and fringed off into eager discussion among various groups concerning this affair of Bulstrode—and Lydgate.

Mr Brooke, who had before heard only imperfect hints of it, and was very uneasy that he had " gone a little too far " in countenancing Bulstrode, now got himself fully informed, and felt some benevolent sadness in talking to Mr Farebrother about the ugly light in which Lydgate had come to be regarded. Mr Farebrother was going to walk back to Lowick.

"Step into my carriage," said Mr Brooke. " I am going round to see Mrs Casaubon. She was to come back from Yorkshire last night. She will like to see me, you know."

So they drove along, Mr Brooke chatting with good-natured hope that there had not really been anything black in Lydgate's behaviour —a young fellow whom he had seen to be quite above the common mark, when he brought a letter from his uncle Sir Godwin. Mr Farebrother said little : he was deeply mournful : with a keen perception of human weakness, he could not be confident that under the pressure of humiliating needs Lydgate had not fallen below himself.

When the carriage drove up to the gate of the manor, Dorothea was out on the gravel, and came to greet them.

" Well, my dear," said Mr Brooke, " we have just come from a meeting—a sanitary meeting, you know."

" Was Mr Lydgate there ? " said Dorothea, who looked full of health and animation, and stood with her head bare under the gleaming April lights. " I want to see him and have a great consultation with him about the Hospital. I have engaged with Mr Bulstrode to do so."

" Oh, my dear," said Mr Brooke, " we have been hearing bad news —bad news, you know."

They walked through the garden towards the churchyard gate, Mr Farebrother wanting to go on to the parsonage ; and Dorothea heard the whole sad story.

She listened with deep interest, and begged to hear twice over the facts and impressions concerning Lydgate. After a short silence, pausing at the churchyard gate, and addressing Mr Farebrother, she said energetically—

" You don't believe that Mr Lydgate is guilty of anything base ? I will not believe it. Let us find out the truth and clear him!"

BOOK VIII.

SUNSET AND SUNRISE,

CHAPTER LXXII.

Full souls are double mirrors, making still
An endless vista of fair things before,
Repeating things behind.

DOROTHEA'S impetuous generosity, which would have leaped at once to the vindication of Lydgate from the suspicion of having accepted money as a bribe, underwent a melancholy check when she came to consider all the circumstances of the case by the light of Mr Farebrother's experience.

"It is a delicate matter to touch," he said. "How can we begin to inquire into it? It must be either publicly by setting the magistrate and coroner to work, or privately by questioning Lydgate. As to the first proceeding there is no solid ground to go upon, else Hawley would have adopted it; and as to opening the subject with Lydgate, I confess I should shrink from it. He would probably take it as a deadly insult. I have more than once experienced the difficulty of speaking to him on personal matters. And—one should know the truth about his conduct beforehand, to feel very confident of a good result."

"I feel convinced that his conduct has not been guilty: I believe that people are almost always better than their neighbours think they are," said Dorothea. Some of her intensest experience in the last two years had set her mind strongly in opposition to any unfavourable construction of others; and for the first time she felt rather discontented with Mr Farebrother. She disliked this cautious weighing of consequences, instead of an ardent faith in efforts of justice and mercy, which would conquer by their emotional force. Two days afterwards, he was dining at the Manor with her uncle and the Chettams, and when the dessert was standing uneaten, the servants were out of the room, and Mr Brooke was nodding in a nap, she returned to the subject with renewed vivacity.

"Mr Lydgate would understand that if his friends hear a calumny about him their first wish must be to justify him. What do we live for, if it is not to make life less difficult to each other? I cannot be indifferent to the troubles of a man who advised me in *my* trouble, and attended me in my illness."

Dorothea's tone and manner were not more energetic than they had been when she was at the head of her uncle's table nearly three years before, and her experience since had given her more right to express a decided opinion. But Sir James Chettam was no longer the diffident and acquiescent suitor : he was the anxious brother-in-law, with a devout admiration for his sister, but with a constant alarm lest she should fall under some new illusion almost as bad as marrying Casaubon. He smiled much less ; when he said " Exactly" it was more often an introduction to a dissentient opinion than in those submissive bachelor days ; and Dorothea found to her surprise that she had to resolve not to be afraid of him—all the more because he was really her best friend. He disagreed with her now.

" But, Dorothea," he said, remonstrantly, " you can't undertake to manage a man's life for him in that way. Lydgate must know—at least he will soon come to know how he stands. If he can clear himself, he will. He must act for himself."

" I think his friends must wait till they find an opportunity," added Mr Farebrother. " It is possible—I have often felt so much weakness in myself that I can conceive even a man of honourable disposition, such as I have always believed Lydgate to be, succumbing to such a temptation as that of accepting money which was offered more or less indirectly as a bribe to insure his silence about scandalous facts long gone by. I say, I can conceive this, if he were under the pressure of hard circumstances—if he had been harassed as I feel sure Lydgate has been. I would not believe anything worse of him except under stringent proof. But there is the terrible Nemesis following on some errors, that it is always possible for those who like it to interpret them into a crime : there is no proof in favour of the man outside his own consciousness and assertion."

" Oh, how cruel ! " said Dorothea, clasping her hands. " And would you not like to be the one person who believed in that man's innocence, if the rest of the world belied him ? Besides, there is a man's character beforehand to speak for him."

" But, my dear Mrs Casaubon," said Mr Farebrother, smiling gently at her ardour, " character is not cut in marble—it is not something solid and unalterable. It is something living and changing, and may become diseased as our bodies do."

" Then it may be rescued and healed," said Dorothea. " I should not be afraid of asking Mr Lydgate to tell me the truth, that I might help him. Why should I be afraid ? Now that I am not to have the land, James, I might do as Mr Bulstrode proposed, and take his place in providing for the hospital ; and I have to consult Mr Lydgate, to know thoroughly what are the prospects of doing good by keeping up the present plans. There is the best opportunity in the world for me to ask for his confidence ; and he would be able to tell me things which might make all the circumstances clear. Then we would all stand by him and bring him out of his trouble. People glorify all sorts of bravery except the bravery they might show on behalf of their nearest neighbours." Dorothea's eyes had a moist brightness in them, and the changed tones of her voice roused her uncle, who began to listen.

" It is true that a woman may venture on some efforts of sympathy which would hardly succeed if we men undertook them," said Mr Farebrother, almost converted by Dorothea's ardour.

" Surely, a woman is bound to be cautious and listen to those who know the world better than she does," said Sir James, with his little frown. "Whatever you do in the end, Dorothea, you should really keep back at present, and not volunteer any meddling with this Bulstrode business. We don't know yet what may turn up. You must agree with me?" he ended, looking at Mr Farebrother.

"I do think it would be better to wait," said the latter.

"Yes, yes, my dear," said Mr Brooke, not quite knowing at what point the discussion had arrived, but coming up to it with a contribution which was generally appropriate. "It is easy to go too far, you know. You must not let your ideas run away with you. And as to being in a hurry to put money into schemes—it won't do, you know. Garth has drawn me in uncommonly with repairs, draining, that sort of thing: I'm uncommonly out of pocket with one thing or another. I must pull up. As for you, Chettam, you are spending a fortune on those oak fences round your demesne."

Dorothea, submitting uneasily to this discouragement, went with Celia into the library, which was her usual drawing-room.

"Now, Dodo, do listen to what James says," said Celia, "else you will be getting into a scrape. You always did, and you always will, when you set about doing as you please. And I think it is a mercy now after all that you have got James to think for you. He lets you have your plans, only he hinders you from being taken in. And that is the good of having a brother instead of a husband. A husband would not let you have your plans."

"As if I wanted a husband!" said Dorothea. "I only want not to have my feelings checked at every turn." Mrs Casaubon was still undisciplined enough to burst into angry tears.

"Now, really, Dodo," said Celia, with rather a deeper guttural than usual, "you *are* contradictory: first one thing and then another. You used to submit to Mr Casaubon quite shamefully: I think you would have given up ever coming to see me if he had asked you."

"Of course I submitted to him, because it was my duty; it was my feeling for him," said Dorothea, looking through the prism of her tears.

"Then why can't you think it your duty to submit a little to what James wishes?" said Celia, with a sense of stringency in her argument. "Because he only wishes what is for your own good. And, of course men know best about everything, except what women know better."

Dorothea laughed and forgot her tears.

"Well, I mean about babies and those things," explained Celia. "I should not give up to James when I knew he was wrong, as you used to do to Mr Casaubon."

CHAPTER LXXIII.

Pity the laden one; this wandering woe
May visit you and me.

WHEN Lydgate had allayed Mrs Bulstrode's anxiety by telling her that her husband had been seized with faintness at the meeting, but that he trusted soon to see him better and would call again the next

day, unless she sent for him earlier, he went directly home, got on
his horse, and rode three miles out of the town for the sake of being
out of reach.

He felt himself becoming violent and unreasonable as if raging
under the pain of stings: he was ready to curse the day on which he
had come to Middlemarch. Everything that had happened to him
there seemed a mere preparation for this hateful fatality, which had
come as a blight on his honourable ambition, and must make even
people who had only vulgar standards regard his reputation as irrevocably damaged. In such moments a man can hardly escape being
unloving. Lydgate thought of himself as the sufferer, and of others
as the agents who had injured his lot. He had meant everything to
turn out differently; and others had thrust themselves into his life
and thwarted his purposes. His marriage seemed an unmitigated
calamity; and he was afraid of going to Rosamond before he had
vented himself in this solitary rage, lest the mere sight of her should
exasperate him and make him behave unwarrantably. There are
episodes in most men's lives in which their highest qualities can only
cast a deterring shadow over the objects that fill their inward vision:
Lydgate's tender-heartedness was present just then only as a dread lest
he should offend against it, not as an emotion that swayed him to
tenderness. For he was very miserable. Only those who know the
supremacy of the intellectual life—the life which has a seed of en-
nobling thought and purpose within it—can understand the grief of
one who falls from that serene activity into the absorbing soul-wast-
ing struggle with worldly annoyances.

How was he to live on without vindicating himself among people
who suspected him of baseness? How could he go silently away
from Middlemarch as if he were retreating before a just condemnation? And yet how was he to set about vindicating himself?

For that scene at the meeting, which he had just witnessed, although it had told him no particulars, had been enough to make his
own situation thoroughly clear to him. Bulstrode had been in dread
of scandalous disclosures on the part of Raffles. Lydgate could now
construct all the probabilities of the case. "He was afraid of some
betrayal in my hearing: all he wanted was to bind me to him by a
strong obligation: that was why he passed on a sudden from hardness
to liberality. And he may have tampered with the patient—he may
have disobeyed my orders. I fear he did. But whether he did or
not, the world believes that he somehow or other poisoned the man
and that I winked at the crime, if I didn't help in it. And yet—
and yet he may not be guilty of the last offence; and it is just possible that the change towards me may have been a genuine relenting
—the effect of second thoughts such as he alleged. What we call the
'just possible' is sometimes true and the thing we find it easier to
believe is grossly false. In his last dealings with this man Bulstrode
may have kept his hands pure, in spite of my suspicion to the contrary."

There was a benumbing cruelty in his position. Even if he renounced every other consideration than that of justifying himself—
if he met shrugs, cold glances, and avoidance as an accusation, and
made a public statement of all the facts as he knew them, who would
be convinced? It would be playing the part of a fool to offer his
own testimony on behalf of himself, and say, "I did not take the

money as a bribe." The circumstances would always be stronger than his assertion. And besides, to come forward and tell everything about himself must include declarations about Bulstrode which would darken the suspicions of others against him. He must tell that he had not known of Raffles's existence when he first mentioned his pressing need of money to Bulstrode, and that he took the money innocently as a result of that communication, not knowing that a new motive for the loan might have arisen on his being called in to this man. And after all, the suspicion of Bulstrode's motives might be unjust.

But then came the question whether he should have acted in precisely the same way if he had not taken the money? Certainly, if Raffles had continued alive and susceptible of further treatment when he arrived, and he had then imagined any disobedience to his orders on the part of Bulstrode, he would have made a strict inquiry, and if his conjecture had been verified he would have thrown up the case, in spite of his recent heavy obligation. But if he had not received any money—if Bulstrode had never revoked his cold recommendation of bankruptcy—would he, Lydgate, have abstained from all inquiry even on finding the man dead?—would the shrinking from an insult to Bulstrode—would the dubiousness of all medical treatment and the argument that his own treatment would pass for the wrong with most members of his profession—have had just the same force or significance with him?

That was the uneasy corner of Lydgate's consciousness while he was reviewing the facts and resisting all reproach. If he had been independent, this matter of a patient's treatment and the distinct rule that he must do or see done that which he believed best for the life committed to him, would have been the point on which he would have been the sturdiest. As it was, he had rested in the consideration that disobedience to his orders, however it might have arisen, could not be considered a crime, that in the dominant opinion obedience to his orders was just as likely to be fatal, and that the affair was simply one of etiquette. Whereas, again and again, in his time of freedom, he had denounced the perversion of pathological doubt into moral doubt and had said—" the purest experiment in treatment may still be conscientious : my business is to take care of life, and to do the best I can think of for it. Science is properly more scrupulous than dogma. Dogma gives a charter to mistake, but the very breath of science is a contest with mistake, and must keep the conscience alive." Alas ! the scientific conscience had got into the debasing company of money obligation and selfish respects.

" Is there a medical man of them all in Middlemarch who would question himself as I do ?" said poor Lydgate, with a renewed outburst of rebellion against the oppression of his lot. " And yet they will all feel warranted in making a wide space between me and them, as if I were a leper ! My practice and my reputation are utterly damned —I can see that. Even if I could be cleared by valid evidence, it would make little difference to the blessed world here. I have been set down as tainted and should be cheapened to them all the same."

Already there had been abundant signs which had hitherto puzzled him, that just when he had been paying off his debts and getting cheerfully on his feet, the townsmen were avoiding him or looking strangely at him, and in two instances it came to his knowledge that patients of his had called in another practitioner. The reasons were too plain now. The general black-balling had begun.

No wonder that in Lydgate's energetic nature the sense of a hopeless misconstruction easily turned into a dogged resistance. The scowl which occasionally showed itself on his square brow was not a meaningless accident. Already when he was re-entering the town after that ride taken in the first hours of stinging pain, he was setting his mind on remaining in Middlemarch in spite of the worst that could be done against him. He would not retreat before calumny, as if he submitted to it. He would face it to the utmost, and no act of his should show that he was afraid. It belonged to the generosity as well as defiant force of his nature that he resolved not to shrink from showing to the full his sense of obligation to Bulstrode. It was true that the association with this man had been fatal to him—true that if he had had the thousand pounds still in his hands with all his debts unpaid he would have returned the money to Bulstrode, and taken beggary rather than the rescue which had been sullied with the suspicion of a bribe (for, remember, he was one of the proudest among the sons of men)—nevertheless, he would not turn away from this crushed fellow-mortal whose aid he had used, and make a pitiful effort to get acquittal for himself by howling against another. "I shall do as I think right, and explain to nobody. They will try to starve me out, but——" he was going on with an obstinate resolve, but he was getting near home, and the thought of Rosamond urged itself again into that chief place from which it had been thrust by the agonised struggles of wounded honour and pride.

How would Rosamond take it all? Here was another weight of chain to drag, and poor Lydgate was in a bad mood for bearing her dumb mastery. He had no impulse to tell her the trouble which must soon be common to them both. He preferred waiting for the incidental disclosure which events must soon bring about.

CHAPTER LXXIV.

"Mercifully grant that we may grow aged together."
—BOOK OF TOBIT : *Marriage Prayer.*[1]

IN Middlemarch a wife could not long remain ignorant that the town held a bad opinion of her husband. No feminine intimate might carry her friendship so far as to make a plain statement to the wife of the unpleasant fact known or believed about her husband ; but when a woman with her thoughts much at leisure got them suddenly employed on something grievously disadvantageous to her neighbours, various moral impulses were called into play which tended to stimulate utterance. Candour was one. To be candid, in Middlemarch phraseology, meant, to use an early opportunity of letting your friends know that you did not take a cheerful view of their capacity, their conduct, or their position ; and a robust candour never waited to be asked for its opinion. Then, again, there was the love of truth—a

1. Tobias 8:10.

wide phrase, but meaning in this relation, a lively objection to seeing a wife look happier than her husband's character warranted, or manifest too much satisfaction in her lot: the poor thing should have some hint given her that if she knew the truth she would have less complacency in her bonnet, and in light dishes for a supper-party. Stronger than all, there was the regard for a friend's moral improvement, sometimes called her soul, which was likely to be benefited by remarks tending to gloom, uttered with the accompaniment of pensive staring at the furniture and a manner implying that the speaker would not tell what was on her mind, from regard to the feelings of her hearer. On the whole, one might say that an ardent charity was at work setting the virtuous mind to make a neighbour unhappy for her good.

There were hardly any wives in Middlemarch whose matrimonial misfortunes would in different ways be likely to call forth more of this moral activity than Rosamond and her aunt Bulstrode. Mrs Bulstrode was not an object of dislike, and had never consciously injured any human being. Men had always thought her a handsome comfortable woman, and had reckoned it among the signs of Bulstrode's hypocrisy that he had chosen a red-blooded Vincy, instead of a ghastly and melancholy person suited to his low esteem for earthly pleasure. When the scandal about her husband was disclosed they remarked of her—" Ah, poor woman! She's as honest as the day— *she* never suspected anything wrong in him, you may depend on it." Women, who were intimate with her, talked together much of " poor Harriet," imagined what her feelings must be when she came to know everything, and conjectured how much she had already come to know. There was no spiteful disposition towards her; rather, there was a busy benevolence anxious to ascertain what it would be well for her to feel and do under the circumstances, which of course kept the imagination occupied with her character and history from the times when she was Harriet Vincy till now. With the review of Mrs Bulstrode and her position it was inevitable to associate Rosamond, whose prospects were under the same blight with her aunt's. Rosamond was more severely criticised and less pitied, though she too, as one of the good old Vincy family who had always been known in Middlemarch, was regarded as a victim to marriage with an interloper. The Vincys had their weaknesses, but then they lay on the surface: there was never anything bad to be " found out " concerning them. Mrs Bulstrode was vindicated from any resemblance to her husband. Harriet's faults were her own.

" She has always been showy," said Mrs Hackbutt, making tea for a small party, " though she has got into the way of putting her religion forward, to conform to her husband; she has tried to hold her head up above Middlemarch by making it known that she invites clergymen and heaven-knows-who from Riverston and those places."

" We can hardly blame her for that," said Mrs Sprague; " because few of the best people in the town cared to associate with Bulstrode, and she must have somebody to sit down at her table."

" Mr Thesiger has always countenanced him," said Mrs Hackbutt. " I think he must be sorry now."

" But he was never fond of him in his heart—that every one knows," said Mrs Tom Toller. " Mr Thesiger never goes into extremes. He keeps to the truth in what is evangelical. It is only clergymen like Mr Tyke, who want to use Dissenting hymn-books and that low kind of religion, who ever found Bulstrode to their taste."

" I understand, Mr Tyke is in great distress about him," said Mrs Hackbutt. " And well he may be : they say the Bulstrodes have half kept the Tyke family."

" And of course it is a discredit to his doctrines," said Mrs Sprague, who was elderly, and oldfashioned in her opinions. " People will not make a boast of being methodistical in Middlemarch for a good while to come."

" I think we must not set down people's bad actions to their religion," said falcon-faced Mrs Plymdale, who had been listening hitherto.

" Oh, my dear, we are forgetting," said Mrs Sprague. " We ought not to be talking of this before you."

" I am sure I have no reason to be partial," said Mrs Plymdale, colouring. " It's true Mr Plymdale has always been on good terms with Mr Bulstrode, and Harriet Vincy was my friend long before she married him. But I have always kept my own opinions and told her where she was wrong, poor thing. Still, in point of religion, I must say, Mr Bulstrode might have done what he has, and worse, and yet have been a man of no religion. I don't say that there has not been a little too much of that—I like moderation myself. But truth is truth. The men tried at the assizes are not all over-religious, I suppose." [2]

" Well," said Mrs Hackbutt, wheeling adroitly, " all I can say is, that I think she ought to separate from him."

" I can't say that," said Mrs Sprague. " She took him for better or worse, you know."

" But ' worse ' can never mean finding out that your husband is fit for Newgate," said Mrs Hackbutt. [3] " Fancy living with such a man ! I should expect to be poisoned."

" Yes, I think myself it is an encouragement to crime if such men are to be taken care of and waited on by good wives," said Mrs Tom Toller.

" And a good wife poor Harriet has been," said Mrs Plymdale. " She thinks her husband the first of men. It's true he has never denied her anything."

" Well, we shall see what she will do," said Mrs Hackbutt. " I suppose she knows nothing yet, poor creature. I do hope and trust I shall not see her, for I should be frightened to death lest I should say anything about her husband. Do you think any hint has reached her ? "

" I should hardly think so," said Mrs Tom Toller. " We hear that *he* is ill, and has never stirred out of the house since the meeting on Thursday ; but she was with her girls at church yesterday, and they had new Tuscan bonnets. Her own had a feather in it. I have never seen that her religion made any difference in her dress."

" She wears very neat patterns always," said Mrs Plymdale, a little stung. " And that feather I know she got dyed a pale lavender on purpose to be consistent. I must say it of Harriet that she wishes to do right."

2. The assizes: a civil or criminal trial session, conducted by the judge of a circuit court.
3. Newgate: an infamous London prison.

" As to her knowing what has happened, it can't be kept from her long," said Mrs Hackbutt. "The Vincys know, for Mr Vincy was at the meeting. It will be a great blow to him. There is his daughter as well as his sister."

"Yes, indeed," said Mrs Sprague. "Nobody supposes that Mr Lydgate can go on holding up his head in Middlemarch, things look so black about the thousand pounds he took just at that man's death. It really makes one shudder."

" Pride must have a fall," said Mrs Hackbutt.

" I am not so sorry for Rosamond Vincy that was as I am for her aunt," said Mrs Plymdale. "She needed a lesson."

" I suppose the Bulstrodes will go and live abroad somewhere," said Mrs Sprague. "That is what is generally done when there is anything disgraceful in a family."

" And a most deadly blow it will be to Harriet," said Mrs Plymdale. "If ever a woman was crushed, she will be. I pity her from my heart. And with all her faults, few women are better. From a girl she had the neatest ways, and was always good-hearted, and as open as the day. You might look into her drawers when you would —always the same. And so she has brought up Kate and Ellen. You may think how hard it will be for her to go among foreigners."

" The doctor says that is what he should recommend the Lydgates to do," said Mrs Sprague. "He says Lydgate ought to have kept among the French."

"That would suit *her* well enough, I daresay," said Mrs Plymdale ; "there is that kind of lightness about her. But she got that from her mother ; she never got it from her aunt Bulstrode, who always gave her good advice, and to my knowledge would rather have had her marry elsewhere."

Mrs Plymdale was in a situation which caused her some complication of feeling. There had been not only her intimacy with Mrs Bulstrode, but also a profitable business relation of the great Plymdale dyeing house with Mr Bulstrode, which on the one hand would have inclined her to desire that the mildest view of his character should be the true one, but on the other, made her the more afraid of seeming to palliate his culpability. Again, the late alliance of her family with the Tollers had brought her in connection with the best circle, which gratified her in every direction except in the inclination to those serious views which she believed to be the best in another sense. The sharp little woman's conscience was somewhat troubled in the adjustment of these opposing " bests," and of her griefs and satisfactions under late events, which were likely to humble those who needed humbling, but also to fall heavily on her old friend whose faults she would have preferred seeing on a background of prosperity.

Poor Mrs Bulstrode, meanwhile, had been no further shaken by the oncoming tread of calamity than in the busier stirring of that secret uneasiness which had always been present in her since the last visit of Raffles to The Shrubs. That the hateful man had come ill to Stone Court, and that her husband had chosen to remain there and watch over him, she allowed to be explained by the fact that Raffles had been employed and aided in earlier days, and that this made a tie of benevolence towards him in his degraded helplessness ; and she

had been since then innocently cheered by her husband's more hopeful speech about his own health and ability to continue his attention
to business. The calm was disturbed when Lydgate had brought
him home ill from the meeting, and in spite of comforting assurances
during the next few days, she cried in private from the conviction
that her husband was not suffering from bodily illness merely, but
from something that afflicted his mind. He would not allow her to
read to him, and scarcely to sit with him, alleging nervous susceptibility to sounds and movements ; yet she suspected that in shutting
himself up in his private room he wanted to be busy with his papers.
Something, she felt sure, had happened. Perhaps it was some great
loss of money ; and she was kept in the dark. Not daring to question her husband, she said to Lydgate, on the fifth day after the meeting, when she had not left home except to go to church—

"Mr Lydgate, pray be open with me : I like to know the truth.
Has anything happened to Mr Bulstrode ?"

"Some little nervous shock," said Lydgate, evasively. He felt that
it was not for him to make the painful revelation.

"But what brought it on ?" said Mrs Bulstrode, looking directly at
him with her large dark eyes.

"There is often something poisonous in the air of public rooms,"
said Lydgate. "Strong men can stand it, but it tells on people in
proportion to the delicacy of their systems. It is often impossible to
account for the precise moment of an attack—or rather, to say why
the strength gives way at a particular moment."

Mrs Bulstrode was not satisfied with this answer. There remained
in her the belief that some calamity had befallen her husband, of
which she was to be kept in ignorance ; and it was in her nature
strongly to object to such concealment. She begged leave for her
daughters to sit with their father, and drove into the town to pay
some visits, conjecturing that if anything were known to have gone
wrong in Mr Bulstrode's affairs, she should see or hear some sign
of it.

She called on Mrs Thesiger, who was not at home, and then drove
to Mrs Hackbutt's on the other side of the churchyard. Mrs Hackbutt saw her coming from an up-stairs window, and remembering her
former alarm lest she should meet Mrs Bulstrode, felt almost bound
in consistency to send word that she was not at home ; but against
that, there was a sudden strong desire within her for the excitement
of an interview in which she was quite determined not to make the
slightest allusion to what was in her mind.

Hence Mrs Bulstrode was shown into the drawing-room, and Mrs
Hackbutt went to her, with more tightness of lip and rubbing of her
hands than was usually observable in her, these being precautions
adopted against freedom of speech. She was resolved not to ask how
Mr Bulstrode was.

"I have not been anywhere except to church for nearly a week,"
said Mrs Bulstrode, after a few introductory remarks. "But Mr
Bulstrode was taken so ill at the meeting on Thursday that I have
not liked to leave the house."

Mrs Hackbutt rubbed the back of one hand with the palm of the
other held against her chest, and let her eyes ramble over the pattern
on the rug.

" Was Mr Hackbutt at the meeting ? " persevered Mrs Bulstrode.

" Yes, he was," said Mrs Hackbutt, with the same attitude. " The land is to be bought by subscription, I believe."

" Let us hope that there will be no more cases of cholera to be buried in it," said Mrs Bulstrode. " It is an awful visitation. But I always think Middlemarch a very healthy spot. I suppose it is being used to it from a child ; but I never saw the town I should like to live at better, and especially our end."

" I am sure I should be glad that you always should live at Middlemarch, Mrs Bulstrode," said Mrs Hackbutt, with a slight sigh. " Still, we must learn to resign ourselves, wherever our lot may be cast. Though I am sure there will always be people in this town who will wish you well."

Mrs Hackbutt longed to say, " if you take my advice you will part from your husband," but it seemed clear to her that the poor woman knew nothing of the thunder ready to bolt on her head, and she herself could do no more than prepare her a little. Mrs Bulstrode felt suddenly rather chill and trembling : there was evidently something unusual behind this speech of Mrs Hackbutt's ; but though she had set out with the desire to be fully informed, she found herself unable now to pursue her brave purpose, and turning the conversation by an inquiry about the young Hackbutts, she soon took her leave saying that she was going to see Mrs Plymdale. On her way thither she tried to imagine that there might have been some unusually warm sparring at the meeting between Mr Bulstrode and some of his frequent opponents—perhaps Mr Hackbutt might have been one of them. That would account for everything.

But when she was in conversation with Mrs Plymdale that comforting explanation seemed no longer tenable. " Selina " received her with a pathetic affectionateness and a disposition to give edifying answers on the commonest topics, which could hardly have reference to an ordinary quarrel of which the most important consequence was a perturbation of Mr Bulstrode's health. Beforehand Mrs Bulstrode had thought that she would sooner question Mrs Plymdale than any one else ; but she found to her surprise that an old friend is not always the person whom it is easiest to make a confidant of : there was the barrier of remembered communication under other circumstances—there was the dislike of being pitied and informed by one who had been long wont to allow her the superiority. For certain words of mysterious appropriateness that Mrs Plymdale let fall about her resolution never to turn her back on her friends, convinced Mrs Bulstrode that what had happened must be some kind of misfortune, and instead of being able to say with her native directness, " What is it that you have in your mind ? " she found herself anxious to get away before she had heard anything more explicit. She began to have an agitating certainty that the misfortune was something more than the mere loss of money, being keenly sensitive to the fact that Selina now, just as Mrs Hackbutt had done before, avoided noticing what she said about her husband, as they would have avoided noticing a personal blemish.

She said good-bye with nervous haste, and told the coachman to drive to Mr Vincy's warehouse. In that short drive her dread gathered so much force from the sense of darkness, that when she entered the private counting-house where her brother sat at his desk, her knees trembled and her usually florid face was deathly pale. Something of the same effect was produced in him by the sight of her : he rose from his seat to meet her, took her by the hand, and said, with his impulsive rashness—

"God help you, Harriet ! you know all."

That moment was perhaps worse than any which came after. It contained that concentrated experience which in great crises of emotion reveals the bias of a nature, and is prophetic of the ultimate act which will end an intermediate struggle. Without that memory of Raffles she might still have thought only of monetary ruin, but now along with her brother's look and words there darted into her mind the idea of some guilt in her husband—then, under the working of terror came the image of her husband exposed to disgrace—and then, after an instant of scorching shame in which she felt only the eyes ot the world, with one leap of her heart she was at his side in mournful but unreproaching fellowship with shame and isolation. All this went on within her in a mere flash of time—while she sank into the chair, and raised her eyes to her brother, who stood over her. "I know nothing, Walter. What is it ?" she said, faintly.

He told her everything, very inartificially, in slow fragments, making her aware that the scandal went much beyond proof, especially as to the end of Raffles.

"People will talk," he said. "Even if a man has been acquitted by a jury, they'll talk, and nod and wink—and as far as the world goes, a man might often as well be guilty as not. It's a breakdown blow, and it damages Lydgate as much as Bulstrode. I don't pretend to say what is the truth. I only wish we had never heard the name of either Bulstrode or Lydgate. You'd better have been a Vincy all your life, and so had Rosamond."

Mrs Bulstrode made no reply.

"But you must bear up as well as you can, Harriet. People don't blame *you*. And I'll stand by you whatever you make up your mind to do," said the brother, with rough but well-meaning affectionateness.

"Give me your arm to the carriage, Walter," said Mrs Bulstrode. "I feel very weak."

And when she got home she was obliged to say to her daughter, "I am not well, my dear ; I must go and lie down. Attend to your papa. Leave me in quiet. I shall take no dinner."

She locked herself in her room. She needed time to get used to her maimed consciousness, her poor lopped life, before she could walk steadily to the place allotted her. A new searching light had fallen on her husband's character, and she could not judge him leniently : the twenty years in which she had believed in him and venerated him by virtue of his concealments came back with particulars that made them seem an odious deceit. He had married her with that bad past life hidden behind him and she had no faith left to protest his innocence of the worst that was imputed to him. Her honest ostentatious nature made the sharing of a merited dishonour as bitter as it could be to any mortal.

But this imperfectly-taught woman, whose phrases and habits were an odd patchwork, had a loyal spirit within her. The man whose prosperity she had shared through nearly half a life, and who had unvaryingly cherished her—now that punishment had befallen him it was not possible to her in any sense to forsake him. There is a forsaking which still sits at the same board and lies on the same couch with the forsaken soul, withering it the more by unloving proximity. She knew, when she locked her door, that she should unlock it ready to go down to her unhappy husband and espouse his sorrow, and say of his guilt, I will mourn and not reproach. But she needed time to gather up her strength ; she needed to sob out her farewell to all the gladness and pride of her life. When she had resolved to go down, she prepared herself by some little acts which might seem mere folly to a hard onlooker ; they were her way of expressing to all spectators visible or invisible that she had begun a new life in which she embraced humiliation. She took off all her ornaments and put on a plain black gown, and instead of wearing her much-adorned cap and large bows of hair, she brushed her hair down and put on a plain bonnetcap, which made her look suddenly like an early Methodist.

Bulstrode, who knew that his wife had been out and had come in saying that she was not well, had spent the time in an agitation equal to hers. He had looked forward to her learning the truth from others, and had acquiesced in that probability, as something easier to him than any confession. But now that he imagined the moment of her knowledge come, he awaited the result in anguish. His daughters had been obliged to consent to leave him, and though he had allowed some food to be brought to him, he had not touched it. He felt himself perishing slowly in unpitied misery. Perhaps he should never see his wife's face with affection in it again. And if he turned to God there seemed to be no answer but the pressure of retribution.

It was eight o'clock in the evening before the door opened and his wife entered. He dared not look up at her. He sat with his eyes bent down, and as she went towards him she thought he looked smaller—he seemed so withered and shrunken. A movement of new compassion and old tenderness went through her like a great wave, and putting one hand on his which rested on the arm of the chair, and the other on his shoulder, she said, solemnly but kindly—

" Look up, Nicholas."

He raised his eyes with a little start and looked at her half amazed for a moment : her pale face, her changed, mourning dress, the trembling about her mouth, all said, " I know ; " and her hands and eyes rested gently on him. He burst out crying and they cried together, she sitting at his side. They could not yet speak to each other of the shame which she was bearing with him, or of the acts which had brought it down on them. His confession was silent, and her promise of faithfulness was silent. Open-minded as she was, she nevertheless shrank from the words which would have expressed their mutual consciousness, as she would have shrunk from flakes of fire. She could not say, " How much is only slander and false suspicion ? " and he did not say, " I am innocent."

CHAPTER LXXV.

"Le sentiment de la fausseté des plaisirs présents, et l'ignorance de la vanité des plaisirs absents, causent l'inconstance."—PASCAL. 1

ROSAMOND had a gleam of returning cheerfulness when the house was freed from the threatening figure, and when all the disagreeable creditors were paid. But she was not joyous : her married life had fulfilled none of her hopes, and had been quite spoiled for her imagination. In this brief interval of calm, Lydgate, remembering that he had often been stormy in his hours of perturbation, and mindful of the pain Rosamond had had to bear, was carefully gentle towards her ; but he, too, had lost some of his old spirit, and he still felt it necessary to refer to an economical change in their way of living as a matter of course, trying to reconcile her to it gradually, and repressing his anger when she answered by wishing that he would go to live in London. When she did not make this answer, she listened languidly, and wondered what she had that was worth living for. The hard and contemptuous words which had fallen from her husband in his anger had deeply offended that vanity which he had at first called into active enjoyment ; and what she regarded as his perverse way of looking at things, kept up a secret repulsion, which made her receive all his tenderness as a poor substitute for the happiness he had failed to give her. They were at a disadvantage with their neighbours, and there was no longer any outlook towards Quallingham—there was no outlook anywhere except in an occasional letter from Will Ladislaw. She had felt stung and disappointed by Will's resolution to quit Middlemarch, for in spite of what she knew and guessed about his admiration for Dorothea, she secretly cherished the belief that he had, or would necessarily come to have, much more admiration for herself ; Rosamond being one of those women who live much in the idea that each man they meet would have preferred them if the preference had not been hopeless. Mrs Casaubon was all very well ; but Will's interest in her dated before he knew Mrs Lydgate. Rosamond took his way of talking to herself, which was a mixture of playful fault-finding and hyperbolical gallantry, as the disguise of a deeper feeling ; and in his presence she felt that agreeable titillation of vanity and sense of romantic drama which Lydgate's presence had no longer the magic to create. She even fancied—what will not men and women fancy in these matters ?—that Will exaggerated his admiration for Mrs Casaubon in order to pique herself.

1. "Awareness of the falseness of present pleasures, and ignorance of the vanity of absent ones, causes fickleness" (*Pensées*).

In this way poor Rosamond's brain had been busy before Will's departure. He would have made, she thought, a much more suitable husband for her than she had found in Lydgate. No notion could have been falser than this, for Rosamond's discontent in her marriage was due to the conditions of marriage itself, to its demand for self-suppression and tolerance, and not to the nature of her husband ; but the easy conception of an unreal Better had a sentimental charm which diverted her ennui. She constructed a little romance which was to vary the flatness of her life : Will Ladislaw was always to be a bachelor and live near her, always to be at her command, and have an understood though never fully expressed passion for her, which would be sending out lambent flames every now and then in interesting scenes. His departure had been a proportionate disappointment, and had sadly increased her weariness of Middlemarch ; but at first she had the alternative dream of pleasures in store from her intercourse with the family at Quallingham. Since then the troubles of her married life had deepened, and the absence of other relief encouraged her regretful rumination over that thin romance which she had once fed on. Men and women make sad mistakes about their own symptoms, taking their vague uneasy longings, sometimes for genius, sometimes for religion, and oftener still for a mighty love. Will Ladislaw had written chatty letters, half to her and half to Lydgate, and she had replied : their separation, she felt, was not likely to be final, and the change she now most longed for was that Lydgate should go to live in London ; everything would be agreeable in London ; and she had set to work with quiet determination to win this result, when there came a sudden, delightful promise which inspirited her.

It came shortly before the memorable meeting at the town-hall, and was nothing less than a letter from Will Ladislaw to Lydgate, which turned indeed chiefly on his new interest in plans of colonisation, but mentioned incidentally, that he might find it necessary to pay a visit to Middlemarch within the next few weeks—a very pleasant necessity, he said, almost as good as holidays to a schoolboy. He hoped there was his old place on the rug, and a great deal of music in store for him. But he was quite uncertain as to the time. While Lydgate was reading the letter to Rosamond, her face looked like a reviving flower—it grew prettier and more blooming. There was nothing unendurable now : the debts were paid, Mr Ladislaw was coming, and Lydgate would be persuaded to leave Middlemarch and settle in London, which was "so different from a provincial town."

That was a bright bit of morning. But soon the sky became black over poor Rosamond. The presence of a new gloom in her husband, about which he was entirely reserved towards her—for he dreaded to expose his lacerated feeling to her neutrality and misconception—soon received a painfully strange explanation, alien to all her previous notions of what could affect her happiness. In the new gaiety of her spirits, thinking that Lydgate had merely a worse fit of moodiness than usual, causing him to leave her remarks unanswered, and evidently to keep out of her way as much as possible, she chose, a few days after the meeting, and without speaking to him on the subject, to send out notes of invitation for a small evening party, feeling convinced that this was a judicious step, since people seemed to have been keeping aloof from them, and wanted restoring to the old habit of intercourse. When the invitations had been accepted, she would tell Lydgate, and give him a wise admonition as to how a medical man should behave to his neighbours; for Rosamond had the gravest little airs possible about other people's duties. But all the invitations were declined, and the last answer came into Lydgate's hands.

"This is Chichely's scratch. What is he writing to you about?" said Lydgate, wonderingly, as he handed the note to her. She was obliged to let him see it, and, looking at her severely, he said—

"Why on earth have you been sending out invitations without telling me, Rosamond? I beg, I insist that you will not invite any one to this house. I suppose you have been inviting others, and they have refused too."

She said nothing.

"Do you hear me?" thundered Lydgate.

"Yes, certainly I hear you," said Rosamond, turning her head aside with the movement of a graceful long-necked bird.

Lydgate tossed his head without any grace and walked out of the room, feeling himself dangerous. Rosamond's thought was, that he was getting more and more unbearable—not that there was any new special reason for this peremptoriness. His indisposition to tell her anything in which he was sure beforehand that she would not be interested was growing into an unreflecting habit, and she was in ignorance of everything connected with the thousand pounds except that the loan had come from her uncle Bulstrode. Lydgate's odious humours and their neighbours' apparent avoidance of them had an unaccountable date for her in their relief from money difficulties. If the invitations had been accepted she would have gone to invite her mamma and the rest, whom she had seen nothing of for several days; and she now put on her bonnet to go and inquire what had become of them all, suddenly feeling as if there were a conspiracy to leave her in isolation with a husband disposed to offend everybody. It was after the dinner hour, and she found her father and mother seated together alone in the drawing-room. They greeted her with sad looks, saying, "Well, my dear!" and no more. She had never seen her father look so downcast; and seating herself near him she said—

"Is there anything the matter, papa?"

He did not answer, but Mrs Vincy said, "Oh, my dear, have you heard nothing? It won't be long before it reaches you."

"Is it anything about Tertius?" said Rosamond, turning pale. The idea of trouble immediately connected itself with what had been unaccountable to her in him.

"Oh my dear, yes. To think of your marrying into this trouble. Debt was bad enough, but this will be worse."

"Stay, stay, Lucy," said Mr Vincy. "Have you heard nothing about your uncle Bulstrode, Rosamond?"

"No, papa," said the poor thing, feeling as if trouble were not anything she had before experienced, but some invisible power with an iron grasp that made her soul faint within her.

Her father told her everything, saying at the end, "It's better for you to know, my dear. I think Lydgate must leave the town.

Things have gone against him. I daresay he couldn't help it. I don't accuse him of any harm," said Mr Vincy. He had always before been disposed to find the utmost fault with Lydgate.

The shock to Rosamond was terrible. It seemed to her that no lot could be so cruelly hard as hers—to have married a man who had become the centre of infamous suspicions. In many cases it is inevitable that the shame is felt to be the worst part of crime; and it would have required a great deal of disentangling reflection, such as had never entered into Rosamond's life, for her in these moments to feel that her trouble was less than if her husband had been certainly known to have done something criminal. All the shame seemed to be there. And she had innocently married this man with the belief that he and his family were a glory to her! She showed her usual reticence to her parents, and only said, that if Lydgate had done as she wished he would have left Middlemarch long ago.

"She bears it beyond anything," said her mother when she was gone.

"Ah, thank God!" said Mr Vincy, who was much broken down.

But Rosamond went home with a sense of justified repugnance towards her husband. What had he really done—how had he really acted? She did not know. Why had he not told her everything? He did not speak to her on the subject, and of course she could not speak to him. It came into her mind once that she would ask her father to let her go home again; but dwelling on that prospect made it seem utter dreariness to her: a married woman gone back to live with her parents—life seemed to have no meaning for her in such a position: she could not contemplate herself in it.

The next two days Lydgate observed a change in her, and believed that she had heard the bad news. Would she speak to him about it, or would she go on for ever in the silence which seemed to imply that she believed him guilty? We must remember that he was in a morbid state of mind, in which almost all contact was pain. Certainly Rosamond in this case had equal reason to complain of reserve and want of confidence on his part; but in the bitterness of his soul he excused himself;—was he not justified in shrinking from the task of telling her, since now she knew the truth she had no impulse to speak to him? But a deeper-lying consciousness that he was in fault made him restless, and the silence between them became intolerable to him; it was as if they were both adrift on one piece of wreck and looked away from each other.

He thought, "I am a fool. Haven't I given up expecting anything? I have married care, not help." And that evening he said—

"Rosamond, have you heard anything that distresses you?"

"Yes," she answered, laying down her work, which she had been carrying on with a languid semi-consciousness, most unlike her usual self.

"What have you heard?"

"Everything, I suppose. Papa told me."

"That people think me disgraced?"

"Yes," said Rosamond, faintly, beginning to sew again automatically.

There was silence. Lydgate thought, "If she has any trust in me —any notion of what I am, she ought to speak now and say that she does not believe I have deserved disgrace."

But Rosamond on her side went on moving her fingers languidly. Whatever was to be said on the subject she expected to come from Tertius. What did she know? And if he were innocent of any wrong, why did he not do something to clear himself?

This silence of hers brought a new rush of gall to that bitter mood in which Lydgate had been saying to himself that nobody believed in him—even Farebrother had not come forward. He had begun to question her with the intent that their conversation should disperse the chill fog which had gathered between them, but he felt his resolution checked by despairing resentment. Even this trouble, like the rest, she seemed to regard as if it were hers alone. He was always to her a being apart, doing what she objected to. He started from his chair with an angry impulse, and thrusting his hands in his pockets, walked up and down the room. There was an underlying consciousness all the while that he should have to master this anger, and tell her everything, and convince her of the facts. For he had almost learned the lesson that he must bend himself to her nature, and that because she came short in her sympathy, he must give the more. Soon he recurred to his intention of opening himself : the occasion must not be lost. If he could bring her to feel with some solemnity that here was a slander which must be met and not run away from, and that the whole trouble had come out of his desperate want of money, it would be a moment for urging powerfully on her that they should be one in the resolve to do with as little money as possible, so that they might weather the bad time and keep themselves independent. He would mention the definite measures which he desired to take, and win her to a willing spirit. He was bound to try this— and what else was there for him to do?

He did not know how long he had been walking uneasily backwards and forwards, but Rosamond felt that it was long, and wished that he would sit down. She too had begun to think this an opportunity for urging on Tertius what he ought to do. Whatever might be the truth about all this misery, there was one dread which asserted itself.

Lydgate at last seated himself, not in his usual chair, but in one nearer to Rosamond, leaning aside in it towards her, and looking at her gravely before he reopened the sad subject. He had conquered himself so far, and was about to speak with a sense of solemnity, as on an occasion which was not to be repeated. He had even opened his lips, when Rosamond, letting her hands fall, looked at him and said—

"Surely, Tertius——"

"Well?"

"Surely now at last you have given up the idea of staying in Middlemarch. I cannot go on living here. Let us go to London. Papa, and every one else, says you had better go. Whatever misery I have to put up with, it will be easier away from here."

Lydgate felt miserably jarred. Instead of that critical outpouring for which he had prepared himself with effort, here was the old round to be gone through again. He could not bear it. With a quick change of countenance he rose and went out of the room.

Perhaps if he had been strong enough to persist in his determination to be the more because she was less, that evening might have had a better issue. If his energy could have borne down that check, he might still have wrought on Rosamond's vision and will. We cannot be sure that any natures, however inflexible or peculiar, will resist this effect from a more massive being than their own. They may be taken by storm and for the moment converted, becoming part of the soul which enwraps them in the ardour of its movement. But poor Lydgate had a throbbing pain within him, and his energy had fallen short of its task.

The beginning of mutual understanding and resolve seemed as far off as ever ; nay, it seemed blocked out by the sense of unsuccessful effort. They lived on from day to day with their thoughts still apart, Lydgate going about what work he had in a mood of despair, and Rosamond feeling, with some justification, that he was behaving cruelly. It was of no use to say anything to Tertius ; but when Will Ladislaw came, she was determined to tell him everything. In spite of her general reticence, she needed some one who would recognise her wrongs.

CHAPTER LXXVI.

"To mercy, pity, peace, and love
  All pray in their distress,
  And to these virtues of delight,
  Return their thankfulness."

. . . .

"For Mercy has a human heart,
  Pity a human face ;
  And Love, the human form divine ;
  And Peace, the human dress."
  —WILLIAM BLAKE : *Songs of Innocence.* [1]

SOME days later, Lydgate was riding to Lowick Manor, in consequence of a summons from Dorothea. The summons had not been unexpected, since it had followed a letter from Mr Bulstrode, in which he stated that he had resumed his arrangements for quitting Middlemarch, and must remind Lydgate of his previous communications about the hospital, to the purport of which he still adhered. It had been his duty, before taking further steps, to reopen the subject with Mrs Casaubon, who now wished, as before, to discuss the question with Lydgate. " Your views may possibly have undergone some change," wrote Mr Bulstrode ; " but, in that case also, it is desirable that you should lay them before her."

Dorothea awaited his arrival with eager interest. Though, in deference to her masculine advisers, she had refrained from what Sir James had called " interfering in this Bulstrode business," the hardship of Lydgate's position was continually in her mind, and when Bulstrode applied to her again about the hospital, she felt that the opportunity was come to her which she had been hindered from hastening. In her luxurious home, wandering under the boughs of her own great trees, her thought was going out over the lot of others, and her emotions were imprisoned. The idea of some active good within her reach, " haunted her like a passion," and another's need having once

1. "The Divine Image."

come to her as a distinct image, preoccupied her desire with the yearning to give relief, and made her own ease tasteless. She was full of confident hope about this interview with Lydgate, never heeding what was said of his personal reserve ; never heeding that she was a very young woman. Nothing could have seemed more irrelevant to Dorothea than insistance on her youth and sex when she was moved to show her human fellowship.

As she sat waiting in the library, she could do nothing but live through again all the past scenes which had brought Lydgate into her memories. They all owed their significance to her marriage and its troubles—but no ; there were two occasions in which the image of Lydgate had come painfully in connection with his wife and some one else. The pain had been allayed for Dorothea, but it had left in her an awakened conjecture as to what Lydgate's marriage might be to him, a susceptibility to the slightest hint about Mrs Lydgate. These thoughts were like a drama to her, and made her eyes bright, and gave an attitude of suspense to her whole frame, though she was only looking out from the brown library on to the turf and the bright green buds which stood in relief against the dark evergreens.

When Lydgate came in, she was almost shocked at the change in his face, which was strikingly perceptible to her who had not seen him for two months. It was not the change of emaciation, but that effect which even young faces will very soon show from the persistent presence of resentment and despondency. Her cordial look, when she put out her hand to him, softened his expression, but only with melancholy.

" I have wished very much to see you for a long while, Mr Lydgate," said Dorothea when they were seated opposite each other ; " but I put off asking you to come until Mr Bulstrode applied to me again about the hospital. I know that the advantage of keeping the management of it separate from that of the Infirmary depends on you, or, at least, on the good which you are encouraged to hope for from having it under your control. And I am sure you will not refuse to tell me exactly what you think."

" You want to decide whether you should give a generous support to the hospital," said Lydgate. " I cannot conscientiously advise you to do it in dependence on any activity of mine. I may be obliged to leave the town."

He spoke curtly, feeling the ache of despair as to his being able to carry out any purpose that Rosamond had set her mind against.

" Not because there is no one to believe in you ?" said Dorothea, pouring out her words in clearness from a full heart. " I know the unhappy mistakes about you. I knew them from the first moment to be mistakes. You have never done anything vile. You would not do anything dishonourable."

It was the first assurance of belief in him that had fallen on Lydgate's ears. He drew a deep breath, and said, " Thank you." He could say no more : it was something very new and strange in his life that these few words of trust from a woman should be so much to him.

" I beseech you to tell me how everything was," said Dorothea, fearlessly. " I am sure that the truth would clear you."

Lydgate started up from his chair and went towards the window, forgetting where he was. He had so often gone over in his mind the possibility of explaining everything without aggravating appearances that would tell, perhaps unfairly, against Bulstrode, and had so often decided against it—he had so often said to himself that his assertions would not change people's impressions—that Dorothea's words sounded like a temptation to do something which in his soberness he had pronounced to be unreasonable.

"Tell me, pray," said Dorothea, with simple earnestness; "then we can consult together. It is wicked to let people think evil of any one falsely, when it can be hindered."

Lydgate turned, remembering where he was, and saw Dorothea's face looking up at him with a sweet trustful gravity. The presence of a noble nature, generous in its wishes, ardent in its charity, changes the lights for us : we begin to see things again in their larger, quieter masses, and to believe that we too can be seen and judged in the wholeness of our character. That influence was beginning to act on Lydgate, who had for many days been seeing all life as one who is dragged and struggling amid the throng. He sat down again, and felt that he was recovering his old self in the consciousness that he was with one who believed in it.

"I don't want," he said, "to bear hard on Bulstrode, who has lent me money of which I was in need—though I would rather have gone without it now. He is hunted down and miserable, and has only a poor thread of life in him. But I should like to tell you everything. It will be a comfort to me to speak where belief has gone beforehand, and where I shall not seem to be offering assertions of my own honesty. You will feel what is fair to another, as you feel what is fair to me."

"Do trust me," said Dorothea; "I will not repeat anything without your leave. But at the very least, I could say that you have made all the circumstances clear to me, and that I know you are not in any way guilty. Mr Farebrother would believe me, and my uncle, and Sir James Chettam. Nay, there are persons in Middlemarch to whom I could go ; although they don't know much of me, they would believe me. They would know that I could have no other motive than truth and justice. I would take any pains to clear you. I have very little to do. There is nothing better that I can do in the world."

Dorothea's voice, as she made this childlike picture of what she would do, might have been almost taken as a proof that she could do it effectively. The searching tenderness of her woman's tones seemed made for a defence against ready accusers. Lydgate did not stay to think that she was Quixotic : he gave himself up, for the first time in his life, to the exquisite sense of leaning entirely on a generous sympathy, without any check of proud reserve. And he told her everything, from the time when, under the pressure of his difficulties, he unwillingly made his first application to Bulstrode ; gradually, in the relief of speaking, getting into a more thorough utterance of what had gone on in his mind—entering fully into the fact that his treatment of the patient was opposed to the dominant practice, into his doubts at the last, his ideal of medical duty, and his uneasy consciousness that the acceptance of the money had made some difference in his private inclination and professional behaviour, though not in his fulfilment of any publicly recognised obligation.

"It has come to my knowledge since," he added, "that Hawley sent some one to examine the housekeeper at Stone Court, and she said that she gave the patient all the opium in the phial I left, as well as a good deal of brandy. But that would not have been opposed to ordinary prescriptions, even of first-rate men. The suspicions against me had no hold there : they are grounded on the knowledge that I took money, that Bulstrode had strong motives for wishing the man to die, and that he gave me the money as a bribe to concur in some malpractices or other against the patient—that in any case I accepted a bribe to hold my tongue. They are just the suspicions that cling the most obstinately, because they lie in people's inclination and can never be disproved. How my orders came to be disobeyed is a question to which I don't know the answer. It is still possible that Bulstrode was innocent of any criminal intention—even possible that he had nothing to do with the disobedience, and merely abstained from mentioning it. But all that has nothing to do with the public belief. It is one of those cases on which a man is condemned on the ground of his character—it is believed that he has committed a crime in some undefined way, because he had the motive for doing it ; and Bulstrode's character has enveloped me, because I took his money. I am simply blighted—like a damaged ear of corn—the business is done and can't be undone."

"Oh, it is hard !" said Dorothea. "I understand the difficulty there is in your vindicating yourself. And that all this should have come to you who had meant to lead a higher life than the common, and to find out better ways—I cannot bear to rest in this as unchangeable. I know you meant that. I remember what you said to me when you first spoke to me about the hospital. There is no sorrow I have thought more about than that—to love what is great, and try to reach it, and yet to fail."

"Yes," said Lydgate, feeling that here he had found room for the full meaning of his grief. "I had some ambition. I meant everything to be different with me. I thought I had more strength and mastery. But the most terrible obstacles are such as nobody can see except oneself."

"Suppose," said Dorothea, meditatively. "Suppose we kept on the hospital according to the present plan, and you stayed here though only with the friendship and support of a few, the evil feeling towards you would gradually die out ; there would come opportunities in which people would be forced to acknowledge that they had been unjust to you, because they would see that your purposes were pure. You may still win a great fame like the Louis and Laennec I have heard you speak of, and we shall all be proud of you," she ended, with a smile.

"That might do if I had my old trust in myself," said Lydgate, mournfully. "Nothing galls me more than the notion of turning round and running away before this slander, leaving it unchecked behind me. Still, I can't ask any one to put a great deal of money into a plan which depends on me."

"It would be quite worth my while," said Dorothea, simply. "Only think. I am very uncomfortable with my money, because they tell me I have too little for any great scheme of the sort I like best, and yet I have too much. I don't know what to do. I have seven hundred a-year of my own fortune, and nineteen hundred a-year that Mr Casaubon left me, and between three and four thousand of ready money in the bank. I wished to raise money and pay it off gradually out of my income which I don't want, to buy land with and found a village which should be a school of industry ; but Sir

James and my uncle have convinced me that the risk would be too great. So you see that what I should most rejoice at would be to have something good to do with my money : I should like it to make other people's lives better to them. It makes me very uneasy—coming all to me who don't want it."

A smile broke through the gloom of Lydgate's face. The childlike grave-eyed earnestness with which Dorothea said all this was irresistible—blent into an adorable whole with her ready understanding of high experience. (Of lower experience such as plays a great part in the world, poor Mrs Casaubon had a very blurred shortsighted knowledge, little helped by her imagination.) But she took the smile as encouragement of her plan.

" I think you see now that you spoke too scrupulously," she said, in a tone of persuasion. " The hospital would be one good ; and making your life quite whole and well again would be another."

Lydgate's smile had died away. " You have the goodness as well as the money to do all that ; if it could be done," he said. " But——"

He hesitated a little while, looking vaguely towards the window ; and she sat in silent expectation. At last he turned towards her and said impetuously—

"Why should I not tell you ?—you know what sort of bond marriage is. You will understand everything."

Dorothea felt her heart beginning to beat faster. Had he that sorrow too ? But she feared to say any word, and he went on immediately.

" It is impossible for me now to do anything—to take any step without considering my wife's happiness. The thing that I might like to do if I were alone, is become impossible to me. I can't see her miserable. She married me without knowing what she was going into, and it might have been better for her if she had not married me."

" I know, I know—you could not give her pain, if you were not obliged to do it," said Dorothea, with keen memory of her own life.

"And she has set her mind against staying. She wishes to go. The troubles she has had here have wearied her," said Lydgate, breaking off again, lest he should say too much.

" But when she saw the good that might come of staying——" said Dorothea, remonstrantly, looking at Lydgate as if he had forgotten the reasons which had just been considered. He did not speak immediately.

" She would not see it," he said at last, curtly, feeling at first that this statement must do without explanation. " And, indeed, I have lost all spirit about carrying on my life here." He paused a moment and then, following the impulse to let Dorothea see deeper into the difficulty of his life, he said, " The fact is, this trouble has come upon her confusedly. We have not been able to speak to each other about it. I am not sure what is in her mind about it : she may fear that I have really done something base. It is my fault ; I ought to be more open. But I have been suffering cruelly."

" May I go and see her ? " said Dorothea, eagerly. " Would she accept my sympathy ? I would tell her that you have not been blamable before any one's judgment but your own. I would tell her that you shall be cleared in every fair mind. I would cheer her heart. Will you ask her if I may go to see her ? I did see her once."

" I am sure you may," said Lydgate, seizing the proposition with some hope. " She would feel honoured—cheered, I think, by the proof that you at least have some respect for me. I will not speak to her about your coming—that she may not connect it with my wishes at all. I know very well that I ought not to have left anything to be told her by others, but——"

He broke off, and there was a moment's silence. Dorothea refrained from saying what was in her mind—how well she knew that there might be invisible barriers to speech between husband and wife. This was a point on which even sympathy might make a wound. She returned to the more outward aspect of Lydgate's position, saying cheerfully—

" And if Mrs Lydgate knew that there were friends who would believe in you and support you, she might then be glad that you should stay in your place and recover your hopes—and do what you meant to do. Perhaps then you would see that it was right to agree with what I proposed about your continuing at the hospital. Surely you would, if you still have faith in it as a means of making your knowledge useful ? "

Lydgate did not answer, and she saw that he was debating with himself.

" You need not decide immediately," she said, gently. " A few days hence it will be early enough for me to send my answer to Mr Bulstrode."

Lydgate still waited, but at last turned to speak in his most decisive tones.

" No ; I prefer that there should be no interval left for wavering. I am no longer sure enough of myself—I mean of what it would be possible for me to do under the changed circumstances of my life. It would be dishonourable to let others engage themselves to anything serious in dependence on me. I might be obliged to go away after all ; I see little chance of anything else. The whole thing is too problematic ; I cannot consent to be the cause of your goodness being wasted. No—let the new hospital be joined with the old infirmary, and everything go on as it might have done if I had never come. I have kept a valuable register since I have been there ; I shall send it to a man who will make use of it," he ended bitterly. " I can think of nothing for a long while but getting an income."

" It hurts me very much to hear you speak so hopelessly," said Dorothea. " It would be a happiness to your friends, who believe in your future, in your power to do great things, if you would let them save you from that. Think how much money I have ; it would be like taking a burthen from me if you took some of it every year till you got free from this fettering want of income. Why should not people do these things ? It is so difficult to make shares at all even. This is one way."

" God bless you, Mrs Casaubon ! " said Lydgate, rising as if with the same impulse that made his words energetic, and resting his arm on the back of the great leather chair he had been sitting in. " It is good that you should have such feelings. But I am not the man who ought to allow himself to benefit by them. I have not given guarantees enough. I must not at least sink into the degradation of being pensioned for work that I never achieved. It is very clear to me that I must not count on anything else than getting away from Middle-

march as soon as I can manage it. I should not be able for a long
while, at the very best, to get an income here, and—and it is easier
to make necessary changes in a new place. I must do as other men
do, and think what will please the world and bring in money; look
for a little opening in the London crowd, and push myself; set up in
a watering-place, or go to some southern town where there are plenty
of idle English, and get myself puffed,—that is the sort of shell I must
creep into and try to keep my soul alive in."

"Now that is not brave," said Dorothea,—"to give up the fight."

"No, it is not brave," said Lydgate, "but if a man is afraid of
creeping paralysis?" Then, in another tone, "Yet you have made a
great difference in my courage by believing in me. Everything seems
more bearable since I have talked to you; and if you can clear me
in a few other minds, especially in Farebrother's, I shall be deeply
grateful. The point I wish you not to mention is the fact of disobedience to my orders. That would soon get distorted. After all,
there is no evidence for me but people's opinion of me beforehand.
You can only repeat my own report of myself."

"Mr Farebrother will believe—others will believe," said Dorothea.
"I can say of you what will make it stupidity to suppose that you
would be bribed to do a wickedness."

"I don't know," said Lydgate, with something like a groan in his
voice. "I have not taken a bribe yet. But there is a pale shade of
bribery which is sometimes called prosperity. You will do me another
great kindness, then, and come to see my wife?"

"Yes, I will. I remember how pretty she is," said Dorothea, into
whose mind every impression about Rosamond had cut deep. "I
hope she will like me."

As Lydgate rode away, he thought, "This young creature has a
heart large enough for the Virgin Mary. She evidently thinks nothing of her own future, and would pledge away half her income at
once, as if she wanted nothing for herself but a chair to sit in from
which she can look down with those clear eyes at the poor mortals
who pray to her. She seems to have what I never saw in any woman
before—a fountain of friendship towards men—a man can make a
friend of her. Casaubon must have raised some heroic hallucination
in her. I wonder if she could have any other sort of passion for a
man? Ladislaw?—there was certainly an unusual feeling between
them. And Casaubon must have had a notion of it. Well—her love
might help a man more than her money."

Dorothea on her side had immediately formed a plan of relieving
Lydgate from his obligation to Bulstrode, which she felt sure was a
part, though small, of the galling pressure he had to bear. She sat
down at once under the inspiration of their interview, and wrote a
brief note, in which she pleaded that she had more claim than Mr Bulstrode had to the satisfaction of providing the money which had been
serviceable to Lydgate—that it would be unkind in Lydgate not to
grant her the position of being his helper in this small matter, the
favour being entirely to her who had so little that was plainly marked
out for her to do with her superfluous money. He might call her a
creditor or by any other name if it did but imply that he granted

her request. She enclosed a cheque for a thousand pounds, and determined to take the letter with her the next day when she went to see Rosamond.

―――――

CHAPTER LXXVII.

" And thus thy fall hath left a kind of blot,
To mark the full-fraught man and best indued
With some suspicion."
—Henry V. [1]

THE next day Lydgate had to go to Brassing, and told Rosamond that he should be away until the evening. Of late she had never gone beyond her own house and garden, except to church, and once to see her papa, to whom she said, " If Tertius goes away, you will help us to move, will you not, papa? I suppose we shall have very little money. I am sure I hope some one will help us." And Mr Vincy had said, " Yes, child, I don't mind a hundred or two. I can see the end of that." With these exceptions she had sat at home in languid melancholy and suspense, fixing her mind on Will Ladislaw's coming as the one point of hope and interest, and associating this with some new urgency on Lydgate to make immediate arrangements for leaving Middlemarch and going to London, till she felt assured that the coming would be a potent cause of the going, without at all seeing how. This way of establishing sequences is too common to be fairly regarded as a peculiar folly in Rosamond. And it is precisely this sort of sequence which causes the greatest shock when it is sundered : for to see how an effect may be produced is often to see possible missings and checks ; but to see nothing except the desirable cause, and close upon it the desirable effect, rids us of doubt and makes our minds strongly intuitive. That was the process going on in poor Rosamond, while she arranged all objects around her with the same nicety as ever, only with more slowness—or sat down to the piano, meaning to play, and then desisting, yet lingering on the music stool with her white fingers suspended on the wooden front, and looking before her in dreamy ennui. Her melancholy had become so marked that Lydgate felt a strange timidity before it, as a perpetual silent reproach, and the strong man, mastered by his keen sensibilities towards this fair fragile creature whose life he seemed somehow to have bruised, shrank from her look, and sometimes started at her approach, fear of her and fear for her rushing in only the more forcibly after it had been momentarily expelled by exasperation.

But this morning Rosamond descended from her room up-stairs— where she sometimes sat the whole day when Lydgate was out—

1. Act II, Sc. 2, lines 138–40.

equipped for a walk in the town. She had a letter to post—a letter addressed to Mr Ladislaw and written with charming discretion, but intended to hasten his arrival by a hint of trouble. The servant-maid, their sole house-servant now, noticed her coming down-stairs in her walking dress, and thought "there never did anybody look so pretty in a bonnet, poor thing."

Meanwhile Dorothea's mind was filled with her project of going to Rosamond, and with the many thoughts, both of the past and the probable future, which gathered round the idea of that visit. Until yesterday when Lydgate had opened to her a glimpse of some trouble in his married life, the image of Mrs Lydgate had always been associated for her with that of Will Ladislaw. Even in her most uneasy moments —even when she had been agitated by Mrs Cadwallader's painfully graphic report of gossip — her effort, nay, her strongest impulsive prompting, had been towards the vindication of Will from any sullying surmises ; and when, in her meeting with him afterwards, she had at first interpreted his words as a probable allusion to a feeling towards Mrs Lydgate which he was determined to cut himself off from indulging, she had had a quick, sad, excusing vision of the charm there might be in his constant opportunities of companionship with that fair creature, who most likely shared his other tastes as she evidently did his delight in music. But there had followed his parting words—the few passionate words in which he had implied that she herself was the object of whom his love held him in dread, that it was his love for her only which he was resolved not to declare but to carry away into banishment. From the time of that parting, Dorothea, believing in Will's love for her, believing with a proud delight in his delicate sense of honour and his determination that no one should impeach him justly, felt her heart quite at rest as to the regard he might have for Mrs Lydgate. She was sure that the regard was blameless.

There are natures in which, if they love us, we are conscious of having a sort of baptism and consecration : they bind us over to rectitude and purity by their pure belief about us ; and our sins become that worst kind of sacrilege which tears down the invisible altar of trust. " If you are not good, none is good "—those little words may give a terrific meaning to responsibility, may hold a vitriolic intensity for remorse.

Dorothea's nature was of that kind : her own passionate faults lay along the easily-counted open channels of her ardent character ; and while she was full of pity for the visible mistakes of others, she had not yet any material within her experience for subtle constructions and suspicions of hidden wrong. But that simplicity of hers, holding up an ideal for others in her believing conception of them, was one of the great powers of her womanhood. And it had from the first acted strongly on Will Ladislaw. He felt, when he parted from her, that the brief words by which he had tried to convey to her his feeling about herself and the division which her fortune made between them, would only profit by their brevity when Dorothea had to interpret them : he felt that in her mind he had found his highest estimate.

And he was right there. In the months since their parting Dorothea had felt a delicious though sad repose in their relation to each other, as one which was inwardly whole and without blemish. She had an active force of antagonism within her, when the antagonism turned on the defence either of plans or persons that she believed in ; and the wrongs which she felt that Will had received from her husband, and the external conditions which to others were grounds for slighting him, only gave the more tenacity to her affection and admiring judgment. And now with the disclosures about Bulstrode had come another fact affecting Will's social position, which roused afresh Dorothea's inward resistance to what was said about him in that part of her world which lay within park palings.

" Young Ladislaw the grandson of a thieving Jew pawnbroker " was a phrase which had entered emphatically into the dialogues about the Bulstrode business, at Lowick, Tipton, and Freshitt, and was a worse kind of placard on poor Will's back than the " Italian with white mice." Upright Sir James Chettam was convinced that his own satisfaction was righteous when he thought with some complacency that here was an added league to that mountainous distance between Ladislaw and Dorothea, which enabled him to dismiss any anxiety in that direction as too absurd. And perhaps there had been some pleasure in pointing Mr Brooke's attention to this ugly bit of Ladislaw's genealogy, as a fresh candle for him to see his own folly by. Dorothea had observed the animus with which Will's part in the painful story had been recalled more than once ; but she had uttered no word, being checked now, as she had not been formerly in speaking of Will, by the consciousness of a deeper relation between them which must always remain in consecrated secrecy. But her silence shrouded her resistant emotion into a more thorough glow ; and this misfortune in Will's lot which, it seemed, others were wishing to fling at his back as an opprobrium, only gave something more of enthusiasm to her clinging thought.

She entertained no visions of their ever coming into nearer union, and yet she had taken no posture of renunciation. She had accepted her whole relation to Will very simply as part of her marriage sorrows, and would have thought it very sinful in her to keep up an inward wail because she was not completely happy, being rather disposed to dwell on the superfluities of her lot. She could bear that the chief pleasures of her tenderness should lie in memory, and the idea of marriage came to her solely as a repulsive proposition from some suitor of whom she at present knew nothing, but whose merits, as seen by her friends, would be a source of torment to her :—" somebody who will manage your property for you, my dear," was Mr Brooke's attractive suggestion of suitable characteristics. " I should like to manage it myself, if I knew what to do with it," said Dorothea. No—she adhered to her declaration that she would never be married again, and in the long valley of her life, which looked so flat and empty of way-marks, guidance would come as she walked along the road, and saw her fellow-passengers by the way.

This habitual state of feeling about Will Ladislaw had been strong in all her waking hours since she had proposed to pay a visit to Mrs Lydgate, making a sort of background against which she saw Rosamond's figure presented to her without hindrances to her interest and compassion. There was evidently some mental separation, some barrier to complete confidence which had arisen between this wife and the husband who had yet made her happiness a law to him. That was a trouble which no third person must directly touch. But Dorothea thought with deep pity of the loneliness which must have come upon Rosamond from the suspicions cast on her husband ; and there would surely be help in the manifestation of respect for Lydgate and sympathy with her.

" I shall talk to her about her husband," thought Dorothea, as she was being driven towards the town. The clear spring morning, the scent of the moist earth, the fresh leaves just showing their creased-up wealth of greenery from out their half-opened sheaths, seemed part of the cheerfulness she was feeling from a long conversation with Mr Farebrother, who had joyfully accepted the justifying explanation of Lydgate's conduct. " I shall take Mrs Lydgate good news, and perhaps she will like to talk to me and make a friend of me."

Dorothea had another errand in Lowick Gate : it was about a new fine-toned bell for the school-house, and as she had to get out of her carriage very near to Lydgate's, she walked thither across the street, having told the coachman to wait for some packages. The street door was open, and the servant was taking the opportunity of looking out at the carriage which was pausing within sight when it became apparent to her that the lady who " belonged to it " was coming towards her.

" Is Mrs Lydgate at home ? " said Dorothea.

" I'm not sure, my lady ; I'll see, if you'll please to walk in," said Martha, a little confused on the score of her kitchen apron, but collected enough to be sure that " mum " was not the right title for this queenly young widow with a carriage and pair. " Will you please to walk in, and I'll go and see."

" Say that I am Mrs Casaubon," said Dorothea, as Martha moved forward intending to show her into the drawing-room and then to go up-stairs to see if Rosamond had returned from her walk.

They crossed the broader part of the entrance-hall, and turned up the passage which led to the garden. The drawing-room door was unlatched, and Martha, pushing it without looking into the room, waited for Mrs Casaubon to enter and then turned away, the door having swung open and swung back again without noise.

Dorothea had less of outward vision than usual this morning, being filled with images of things as they had been and were going to be. She found herself on the other side of the door without seeing anything remarkable, but immediately she heard a voice speaking in low tones which startled her as with a sense of dreaming in daylight, and advancing unconsciously a step or two beyond the projecting slab of a bookcase, she saw, in the terrible illumination of a certainty which filled up all outlines, something which made her pause motionless, without self-possession enough to speak.

Seated with his back towards her on a sofa which stood against the wall on a line with the door by which she had entered, she saw Will Ladislaw : close by him and turned towards him with a flushed tearfulness which gave a new brilliancy to her face sat Rosamond, her bonnet hanging back, while Will leaning towards her clasped both her upraised hands in his and spoke with low-toned fervour.

Rosamond in her agitated absorption had not noticed the silently

advancing figure ; but when Dorothea, after the first immeasurable
instant of this vision, moved confusedly backward and found herself
impeded by some piece of furniture, Rosamond was suddenly aware
of her presence, and with a spasmodic movement snatched away her
hands and rose, looking at Dorothea who was necessarily arrested.
Will Ladislaw, starting up, looked round also, and meeting Dorothea's
eyes with a new lightning in them, seemed changing to marble. But
she immediately turned them away from him to Rosamond and said
in a firm voice—

" Excuse me, Mrs Lydgate, the servant did not know that you were
here. I called to deliver an important letter for Mr Lydgate, which
I wished to put into your own hands."

She laid down the letter on the small table which had checked her
retreat, and then including Rosamond and Will in one distant glance
and bow, she went quickly out of the room, meeting in the passage
the surprised Martha, who said she was sorry the mistress was not at
home, and then showed the strange lady out with an inward reflection
that grand people were probably more impatient than others.

Dorothea walked across the street with her most elastic step and
was quickly in her carriage again.

" Drive on to Freshitt Hall," she said to the coachman, and any one
looking at her might have thought that though she was paler than
usual she was never animated by a more self-possessed energy. And
that was really her experience. It was as if she had drunk a great
draught of scorn that stimulated her beyond the susceptibility to other
feelings. She had seen something so far below her belief, that her
emotions rushed back from it and made an excited throng without an
object. She needed something active to turn her excitement out
upon. She felt power to walk and work for a day, without meat or
drink. And she would carry out the purpose with which she had
started in the morning, of going to Freshitt and Tipton to tell Sir
James and her uncle all that she wished them to know about Lydgate, whose married loneliness under his trial now presented itself to
her with new significance, and made her more ardent in readiness to
be his champion. She had never felt anything like this triumphant
power of indignation in the struggle of her married life, in which
there had always been a quickly subduing pang ; and she took it as
a sign of new strength.

"Dodo, how very bright your eyes are ! " said Celia, when Sir James
was gone out of the room. " And you don't see anything you look at,
Arthur or anything. You are going to do something uncomfortable,
I know. Is it all about Mr Lydgate, or has something else happened ? " Celia had been used to watch her sister with expectation.

" Yes, dear, a great many things have happened," said Dodo, in her
full tones.

" I wonder what," said Celia, folding her arms cozily and leaning
forward upon them.

" Oh, all the troubles of all people on the face of the earth," said
Dorothea, lifting her arms to the back of her head.

" Dear me, Dodo, are you going to have a scheme for them ? " said
Celia, a little uneasy at this Hamlet-like raving.

But Sir James came in again, ready to accompany Dorothea to the Grange, and she finished her expedition well, not swerving in her resolution until she descended at her own door.

CHAPTER LXXVIII.

Would it were yesterday and I i' the grave,
With her sweet faith above for monument.

ROSAMOND and Will stood motionless—they did not know how long—he looking towards the spot where Dorothea had stood, and she looking towards him with doubt. It seemed an endless time to Rosamond, in whose inmost soul there was hardly so much annoyance as gratification from what had just happened. Shallow natures dream of an easy sway over the emotions of others, trusting implicitly in their own petty magic to turn the deepest streams, and confident, by pretty gestures and remarks, of making the thing that is not as though it were. She knew that Will had received a severe blow, but she had been little used to imagining other people's states of mind except as a material cut into shape by her own wishes ; and she believed in her own power to soothe or subdue. Even Tertius, that most perverse of men, was always subdued in the long-run : events had been obstinate, but still Rosamond would have said now, as she did before her marriage, that she never gave up what she had set her mind on.

She put out her arm and laid the tips of her fingers on Will's coat-sleeve.

"Don't touch me !" he said, with an utterance like the cut of a lash, darting from her, and changing from pink to white and back again, as if his whole frame were tingling with the pain of the sting. He wheeled round to the other side of the room and stood opposite to her, with the tips of his fingers in his pockets and his head thrown back, looking fiercely not at Rosamond but at a point a few inches away from her.

She was keenly offended, but the signs she made of this were such as only Lydgate was used to interpret. She became suddenly quiet and seated herself, untying her hanging bonnet and laying it down with her shawl. Her little hands which she folded before her were very cold.

It would have been safer for Will in the first instance to have taken up his hat and gone away ; but he had felt no impulse to do this ; on the contrary, he had a horrible inclination to stay and shatter Rosamond with his anger. It seemed as impossible to bear the fatality she had drawn down on him without venting his fury as it would be to a panther to bear the javelin-wound without springing and biting. And yet—how could he tell a woman that he was ready to curse her ? He was fuming under a repressive law which he was forced to acknowledge : he was dangerously poised, and Rosamond's voice now brought the decisive vibration. In flute-like tones of sarcasm she said,

" You can easily go after Mrs Casaubon and explain your preference."

" Go after her ! " he burst out, with a sharp edge in his voice. " Do you think she would turn to look at me, or value any word I ever uttered to her again at more than a dirty feather ?—Explain ! How can a man explain at the expense of a woman ? "

" You can tell her what you please," said Rosamond, with more tremor.

" Do you suppose she would like me better for sacrificing you ? She is not a woman to be flattered because I made myself despicable —to believe that I must be true to her because I was a dastard to you."

He began to move about with the restlessness of a wild animal that sees prey but cannot reach it. Presently he burst out again—

" I had no hope before—not much—of anything better to come. But I had one certainty—that she believed in me. Whatever people had said or done about me, she believed in me.—That's gone ! She'll never again think me anything but a paltry pretence—too nice to take heaven except upon flattering conditions, and yet selling myself for any devil's change by the sly. She'll think of me as an incarnate insult to her, from the first moment we . . . ."

Will stopped as if he had found himself grasping something that must not be thrown and shattered. He found another vent for his rage by snatching up Rosamond's words again, as if they were reptiles to be throttled and flung off.

" Explain ! Tell a man to explain how he dropped into hell ! Explain my preference ! I never had a *preference* for her, any more than I have a preference for breathing. No other woman exists by the side of her. I would rather touch her hand if it were dead, than I would touch any other woman's living."

Rosamond, while these poisoned weapons were being hurled at her, was almost losing the sense of her identity, and seemed to be waking into some new terrible existence. She had no sense of chill resolute repulsion, of reticent self-justification such as she had known under Lydgate's most stormy displeasure : all her sensibility was turned into a bewildering novelty of pain ; she felt a new terrified recoil under a lash never experienced before. What another nature felt in opposition to her own was being burnt and bitten into her consciousness. When Will had ceased to speak she had become an image of sickened misery : her lips were pale, and her eyes had a tearless dismay in them. If it had been Tertius who stood opposite to her, that look of misery would have been a pang to him, and he would have sunk by her side to comfort her, with that strong-armed comfort which she had often held very cheap.

Let it be forgiven to Will that he had no such movement of pity. He had felt no bond beforehand to this woman who had spoiled the ideal treasure of his life, and he held himself blameless. He knew that he was cruel, but he had no relenting in him yet.

After he had done speaking, he still moved about, half in absence of mind, and Rosamond sat perfectly still. At length Will, seeming to bethink himself, took up his hat, yet stood some moments irresolute. He had spoken to her in a way that made a phrase of common politeness difficult to utter; and yet, now that he had come to the point of going away from her without further speech, he shrank from it as a brutality; he felt checked and stultified in his anger. He walked towards the mantelpiece and leaned his arm on it, and waited in silence for—he hardly knew what. The vindictive fire was still burning in him, and he could utter no word of retractation; but it was nevertheless in his mind that having come back to this hearth where he had enjoyed a caressing friendship he had found calamity seated there—he had had suddenly revealed to him a trouble that lay outside the home as well as within it. And what seemed a foreboding was pressing upon him as with slow pincers:—that his life might come to be enslaved by this helpless woman who had thrown herself upon him in the dreary sadness of her heart. But he was in gloomy rebellion against the fact that his quick apprehensiveness foreshadowed to him, and when his eyes fell on Rosamond's blighted face it seemed to him that he was the more pitiable of the two; for pain must enter into its glorified life of memory before it can turn into compassion.

And so they remained for many minutes, opposite each other, far apart, in silence; Will's face still possessed by a mute rage, and Rosamond's by a mute misery. The poor thing had no force to fling out any passion in return; the terrible collapse of the illusion towards which all her hope had been strained was a stroke which had too thoroughly shaken her: her little world was in ruins, and she felt herself tottering in the midst as a lonely bewildered consciousness.

Will wished that she would speak and bring some mitigating shadow across his own cruel speech, which seemed to stand staring at them both in mockery of any attempt at revived fellowship. But she said nothing, and at last with a desperate effort over himself, he asked, "Shall I come in and see Lydgate this evening?"

"If you like," Rosamond answered, just audibly.

And then Will went out of the house, Martha never knowing that he had been in.

After he was gone, Rosamond tried to get up from her seat, but fell back fainting. When she came to herself again, she felt too ill to make the exertion of rising to ring the bell, and she remained helpless until the girl, surprised at her long absence, thought for the first time of looking for her in all the down-stairs rooms. Rosamond said that she had felt suddenly sick and faint, and wanted to be helped up-stairs. When there she threw herself on the bed with her clothes on, and lay in apparent torpor, as she had done once before on a memorable day of grief.

Lydgate came home earlier than he had expected, about half-past five, and found her there. The perception that she was ill threw every other thought into the background. When he felt her pulse, her eyes rested on him with more persistence than they had done for a long while, as if she felt some content that he was there. He perceived the difference in a moment, and seating himself by her put his arm gently under her, and bending over her said, "My poor Rosamond! has something agitated you?" Clinging to him she fell into hysterical sobbings and cries, and for the next hour he did nothing but soothe and tend her. He imagined that Dorothea had been to see her, and that all this effect on her nervous system, which evidently involved some new turning towards himself, was due to the excitement of the new impressions which that visit had raised.

CHAPTER LXXIX.

"Now, I saw in my dream, that just as they had ended their talk, they drew nigh to a very miry slough, that was in the midst of the plain ; and they, being heedless, did both fall suddenly into the bog. The name of the slough was Despond."—BUNYAN. 1

WHEN Rosamond was quiet, and Lydgate had left her, hoping that she might soon sleep under the effect of an anodyne, he went into the drawing-room to fetch a book which he had left there, meaning to spend the evening in his work-room, and he saw on the table Dorothea's letter addressed to him. He had not ventured to ask Rosamond if Mrs Casaubon had called, but the reading of this letter assured him of the fact, for Dorothea mentioned that it was to be carried by herself.

When Will Ladislaw came in a little later, Lydgate met him with a surprise which made it clear that he had not been told of the earlier visit, and Will could not say, " Did not Mrs Lydgate tell you that I came this morning ?"

" Poor Rosamond is ill," Lydgate added immediately on his greeting.

" Not seriously, I hope," said Will.

" No—only a slight nervous shock—the effect of some agitation. She has been overwrought lately. The truth is, Ladislaw, I am an unlucky devil. We have gone through several rounds of purgatory since you left, and I have lately got on to a worse ledge of it than ever. I suppose you are only just come down—you look rather battered—you have not been long enough in the town to hear anything ?"

" I travelled all night and got to the White Hart at eight o'clock this morning. I have been shutting myself up and resting," said Will, feeling himself a sneak, but seeing no alternative to this evasion.

And then he heard Lydgate's account of the troubles which Rosamond had already depicted to him in her way. She had not mentioned the fact of Will's name being connected with the public story —this detail not immediately affecting her—and he now heard it for the first time.

" I thought it better to tell you that your name is mixed up with the disclosures," said Lydgate, who could understand better than most men how Ladislaw might be stung by the revelation. " You will be sure to hear it as soon as you turn out into the town. I suppose it is true that Raffles spoke to you."

" Yes," said Will, sardonically. " I shall be fortunate if gossip

1. *Pilgrim's Progress* (1678)

does not make me the most disreputable person in the whole affair.
I should think the latest version must be, that I plotted with Raffles
to murder Bulstrode, and ran away from Middlemarch for the
purpose."

He was thinking " Here is a new ring in the sound of my name
to recommend it in her hearing ; however—what does it signify
now ?"

But he said nothing of Bulstrode's offer to him. Will was very
open and careless about his personal affairs, but it was among the
more exquisite touches in nature's modelling of him that he had
a delicate generosity which warned him into reticence here. He
shrank from saying that he had rejected Bulstrode's money, in the moment when he was learning that it was Lydgate's misfortune to have
accepted it.

Lydgate too was reticent in the midst of his confidence. He made
no allusion to Rosamond's feeling under their trouble, and of Dorothea he only said, " Mrs Casaubon has been the one person to come
forward and say that she had no belief in any of the suspicions against
me." Observing a change in Will's face, he avoided any further
mention of her, feeling himself too ignorant of their relation to each
other not to fear that his words might have some hidden painful bearing on it. And it occurred to him that Dorothea was the real cause
of the present visit to Middlemarch.

The two men were pitying each other, but it was only Will who
guessed the extent of his companion's trouble. When Lydgate spoke
with desperate resignation of going to settle in London, and said with
a faint smile, " We shall have you again, old fellow," Will felt inex-
pressibly mournful, and said nothing. Rosamond had that morning
entreated him to urge this step on Lydgate ; and it seemed to him
as if he were beholding in a magic panorama a future where he himself was sliding into that pleasureless yielding to the small solicitations of circumstance, which is a commoner history of perdition than
any single momentous bargain.

We are on a perilous margin when we begin to look passively at
our future selves, and see our own figures led with dull consent into
insipid misdoing and shabby achievement. Poor Lydgate was inwardly groaning on that margin, and Will was arriving at it. It
seemed to him this evening as if the cruelty of his outburst to Rosamond had made an obligation for him, and he dreaded the obligation : he dreaded Lydgate's unsuspecting goodwill : he dreaded his
own distaste for his spoiled life, which would leave him in motiveless
levity.

CHAPTER LXXX.

"Stern lawgiver ! yet thou dost wear
The Godhead's most benignant grace ;
Nor know we anything so fair
As is the smile upon thy face ;
Flowers laugh before thee on their beds,
And fragrance in thy footing treads ;
Thou dost preserve the Stars from wrong ;
And the most ancient Heavens, through thee, are fresh and strong.
—WORDSWORTH : *Ode to Duty.*

WHEN Dorothea had seen Mr Farebrother in the morning, she had promised to go and dine at the parsonage on her return from Freshitt. There was a frequent interchange of visits between her and the Farebrother family, which enabled her to say that she was not at all lonely at the Manor, and to resist for the present the severe prescription of a lady companion. When she reached home and remembered her engagement, she was glad of it ; and finding that she had still an hour before she could dress for dinner, she walked straight to the schoolhouse and entered into a conversation with the master and mistress about the new bell, giving eager attention to their small details and repetitions, and getting up a dramatic sense that her life was very busy. She paused on her way back to talk to old Master Bunney who was putting in some garden-seeds, and discoursed wisely with that rural sage about the crops that would make the most return on a perch of ground, and the result of sixty years' experience as to soils—namely, that if your soil was pretty mellow it would do, but if there came wet, wet, wet to make it all of a mummy, why then——[1]

Finding that the social spirit had beguiled her into being rather late, she dressed hastily and went over to the parsonage rather earlier than was necessary. That house was never dull, Mr Farebrother, like another White of Selborne, having continually something new to tell of his inarticulate guests and *protégés,* whom he was teaching the boys not to torment ; and he had just set up a pair of beautiful goats to be pets of the village in general, and to walk at large as sacred animals.[2] The evening went by cheerfully till after tea, Dorothea talking more than usual and dilating with Mr Farebrother on the possible histories of creatures that converse compendiously with their antennæ, and for aught we know may hold reformed parliaments ; when suddenly some inarticulate little sounds were heard which called everybody's attention.

" Henrietta Noble," said Mrs Farebrother, seeing her small sister

1. Mummy: a pulpy substance.
2. White of Selborne: Gilbert White (1720–93), curate of Selborne, was a dedicated naturalist whose works were first published at the end of the eighteenth century.

moving about the furniture-legs distressfully, " what is the matter ? "

" I have lost my tortoise-shell lozenge-box. I fear the kitten has rolled it away," said the tiny old lady, involuntarily continuing her beaver-like notes.

" Is it a great treasure, aunt ? " said Mr Farebrother, putting up his glasses and looking at the carpet.

" Mr Ladislaw gave it me," said Miss Noble. " A German box— very pretty ; but if it falls it always spins away as far as it can."

" Oh, if it is Ladislaw's present," said Mr Farebrother, in a deep tone of comprehension, getting up and hunting. The box was found at last under a chiffonier, and Miss Noble grasped it with delight, saying, " it was under a fender the last time."

" That is an affair of the heart with my aunt," said Mr Farebrother, smiling at Dorothea, as he reseated himself.

" If Henrietta Noble forms an attachment to any one, Mrs Casaubon," said his mother, emphatically,—" she is like a dog—she would take their shoes for a pillow and sleep the better."

" Mr Ladislaw's shoes, I would," said Henrietta Noble.

Dorothea made an attempt at smiling in return. She was surprised and annoyed to find that her heart was palpitating violently, and that it was quite useless to try after a recovery of her former animation. Alarmed at herself—fearing some further betrayal of a change so marked in its occasion, she rose and said in a low voice with undisguised anxiety, " I must go ; I have overtired myself."

Mr Farebrother, quick in perception, rose and said, " It is true ; you must have half-exhausted yourself in talking about Lydgate. That sort of work tells upon one after the excitement is over."

He gave her his arm back to the Manor, but Dorothea did not attempt to speak, even when he said good-night.

The limit of resistance was reached, and she had sunk back helpless within the clutch of inescapable anguish. Dismissing Tantripp with a few faint words, she locked her door, and turning away from it towards the vacant room she pressed her hands hard on the top of her head, and moaned out—

" Oh, I did love him ! "

Then came the hour in which the waves of suffering shook her too thoroughly to leave any power of thought. She could only cry in loud whispers, between her sobs, after her lost belief which she had planted and kept alive from a very little seed since the days in Rome —after her lost joy of clinging with silent love and faith to one who, misprized by others, was worthy in her thought—after her lost woman's pride of reigning in his memory—after her sweet dim perspective of hope, that along some pathway they should meet with unchanged recognition and take up the backward years as a yesterday.

In that hour she repeated what the merciful eyes of solitude have looked on for ages in the spiritual struggles of man—she besought hardness and coldness and aching weariness to bring her relief from the mysterious incorporeal might of her anguish : she lay on the bare floor and let the night grow cold around her ; while her grand woman's frame was shaken by sobs as if she had been a despairing child.

There were two images—two living forms that tore her heart in two, as if it had been the heart of a mother who seems to see her child divided by the sword, and presses one bleeding half to her breast while her gaze goes forth in agony towards the half which is carried away by the lying woman that has never known the mother's pang.

Here, with the nearness of an answering smile, here within the vibrating bond of mutual speech, was the bright creature whom she had trusted—who had come to her like the spirit of morning visiting the dim vault where she sat as the bride of a worn-out life ; and now, with a full consciousness which had never awakened before, she stretched out her arms towards him and cried with bitter cries that their nearness was a parting vision : she discovered her passion to herself in the unshrinking utterance of despair.

And there, aloof, yet persistently with her, moving wherever she moved, was the Will Ladislaw who was a changed belief exhausted of hope, a detected illusion—no, a living man towards whom there could not yet struggle any wail of regretful pity, from the midst of scorn and indignation and jealous offended pride. The fire of Dorothea's anger was not easily spent, and it flamed out in fitful returns of spurning reproach. Why had he come obtruding his life into hers, hers that might have been whole enough without him ? Why had he brought his cheap regard and his lip-born words to her who had nothing paltry to give in exchange ? He knew that he was deluding her—wished, in the very moment of farewell, to make her believe that he gave her the whole price of her heart, and knew that he had spent it half before. Why had he not stayed among the crowd of whom she asked nothing—but only prayed that they might be less contemptible ?

But she lost energy at last even for her loud-whispered cries and moans : she subsided into helpless sobs, and on the cold floor she sobbed herself to sleep.

In the chill hours of the morning twilight, when all was dim around her, she awoke—not with any amazed wondering where she was or what had happened, but with the clearest consciousness that she was looking into the eyes of sorrow. She rose, and wrapped warm things around her, and seated herself in a great chair where she had often watched before. She was vigorous enough to have borne that hard night without feeling ill in body, beyond some aching and fatigue ; but she had waked to a new condition : she felt as if her soul had been liberated from its terrible conflict ; she was no longer wrestling with her grief, but could sit down with it as a lasting companion and make it a sharer in her thoughts. For now the thoughts came thickly. It was not in Dorothea's nature, for longer than the duration of a paroxysm, to sit in the narrow cell of her calamity, in the besotted misery of a consciousness that only sees another's lot as an accident of its own.

She began now to live through that yesterday morning deliberately again, forcing herself to dwell on every detail and its possible meaning. Was she alone in that scene ? Was it her event only ? She forced herself to think of it as bound up with another woman's life—

a woman towards whom she had set out with a longing to carry some clearness and comfort into her beclouded youth. In her first outleap of jealous indignation and disgust, when quitting the hateful room, she had flung away all the mercy with which she had undertaken that visit. She had enveloped both Will and Rosamond in her burning scorn, and it seemed to her as if Rosamond were burned out of her sight for ever. But that base prompting which makes a woman more cruel to a rival than to a faithless lover, could have no strength of recurrence in Dorothea when the dominant spirit of justice within her had once overcome the tumult and had once shown her the truer measure of things. All the active thought with which she had before been representing to herself the trials of Lydgate's lot, and this young marriage union which, like her own, seemed to have its hidden as well as evident troubles—all this vivid sympathetic experience returned to her now as a power : it asserted itself as acquired knowledge asserts itself and will not let us see as we saw in the day of our ignorance. She said to her own irremediable grief, that it should make her more helpful, instead of driving her back from effort.

And what sort of crisis might not this be in three lives whose contact with hers laid an obligation on her as if they had been suppliants bearing the sacred branch? The objects of her rescue were not to be sought out by her fancy : they were chosen for her. She yearned towards the perfect Right, that it might make a throne within her, and rule her errant will. "What should I do—how should I act now, this very day, if I could clutch my own pain, and compel it to silence, and think of those three?"

It had taken long for her to come to that question, and there was light piercing into the room. She opened her curtains, and looked out towards the bit of road that lay in view, with fields beyond, outside the entrance-gates. On the road there was a man with a bundle on his back and a woman carrying her baby ; in the field she could see figures moving—perhaps the shepherd with his dog. Far off in the bending sky was the pearly light ; and she felt the largeness of the world and the manifold wakings of men to labour and endurance. She was a part of that involuntary, palpitating life, and could neither look out on it from her luxurious shelter as a mere spectator, nor hide her eyes in selfish complaining.

What she would resolve to do that day did not yet seem quite clear, but something that she could achieve stirred her as with an approaching murmur which would soon gather distinctness. She took off the clothes which seemed to have some of the weariness of a hard watching in them, and began to make her toilet. Presently she rang for Tantripp, who came in her dressing-gown.

"Why, madam, you've never been in bed this blessed night," burst out Tantripp, looking first at the bed and then at Dorothea's face, which in spite of bathing had the pale cheeks and pink eyelids of a *mater dolorosa.*[3] "You'll kill yourself, you *will.* Anybody might think now you had a right to give yourself a little comfort."

"Don't be alarmed, Tantripp," said Dorothea, smiling. "I have slept ; I am not ill. I shall be glad of a cup of coffee as soon as possible. And I want you to bring me my new dress ; and most likely I shall want my new bonnet to-day."

3. "Mother of sorrows," a title of the Virgin Mary.

" They've lain there a month and more ready for you, madam, and most thankful I shall be to see you with a couple o' pounds' worth less of crape," said Tantripp, stooping to light the fire. " There's a reason in mourning, as I've always said ; and three folds at the bottom of your skirt and a plain quilling in your bonnet—and if ever anybody looked like an angel, it's you in a net quilling—is what's consistent for a second year. At least, that's *my* thinking," ended Tantripp, looking anxiously at the fire ; " and if anybody was to marry me flattering himself I should wear those hijeous weepers two years for him, he'd be deceived by his own vanity, that's all."

" The fire will do, my good Tan," said Dorothea, speaking as she used to do in the old Lausanne days, only with a very low voice ; " get me the coffee."

She folded herself in the large chair, and leaned her head against it in fatigued quiescence, while Tantripp went away wondering at this strange contrariness in her young mistress—that just the morning when she had more of a widow's face than ever, she should have asked for her lighter mourning which she had waived before. Tantripp would never have found the clue to this mystery. Dorothea wished to acknowledge that she had not the less an active life before her because she had buried a private joy ; and the tradition that fresh garments belonged to all initiation, haunting her mind, made her grasp after even that slight outward help towards calm resolve. For the resolve was not easy.

Nevertheless at eleven o'clock she was walking towards Middlemarch, having made up her mind that she would make as quietly and unnoticeably as possible her second attempt to see and save Rosamond.

CHAPTER LXXXI.

" Du Erde warst auch diese Nacht beständig,
   Und athmest neu erquickt zu meinen Füssen,
   Beginnest schon mit Lust mich zu umgeben,
   Du regst und rührst ein kräftiges Beschliessen
   Zum höchsten Dasein immerfort zu streben."
                                             —*Faust :* 2r Theil.[1]

WHEN Dorothea was again at Lydgate's door speaking to Martha, he was in the room close by with the door ajar, preparing to go out. He heard her voice, and immediately came to her.

" Do you think that Mrs Lydgate can receive me this morning ?" she said, having reflected that it would be better to leave out all allusion to her previous visit.

" I have no doubt she will," said Lydgate, suppressing his thought about Dorothea's looks, which were as much changed as Rosamond's, " if you will be kind enough to come in and let me tell her that you are here. She has not been very well since you were here yesterday, but she is better this morning, and I think it is very likely that she will be cheered by seeing you again."

1. "Thou, earth, also stood this night unshaken,/And breathe now new-refreshed before me,/Beginning already with longing to surround me;/You arouse and stir a strong resolve in me/ *Constantly to strive for the utmost of life*" (Goethe, *Faust,* Part 2, Act I, Sc. 1).

It was plain that Lydgate, as Dorothea had expected, knew nothing about the circumstances of her yesterday's visit; nay, he appeared to imagine that she had carried it out according to her intention. She had prepared a little note asking Rosamond to see her, which she would have given to the servant if he had not been in the way, but now she was in much anxiety as to the result of his announcement.

After leading her into the drawing-room, he paused to take a letter from his pocket and put it into her hands, saying, " I wrote this last night, and was going to carry it to Lowick in my ride. When one is grateful for something too good for common thanks, writing is less unsatisfactory than speech—one does not at least *hear* how inadequate the words are."

Dorothea's face brightened. " It is I who have most to thank for, since you have let me take that place. You *have* consented ? " she said, suddenly doubting.

" Yes, the cheque is going to Bulstrode to-day."

He said no more, but went up-stairs to Rosamond, who had but lately finished dressing herself, and sat languidly wondering what she should do next, her habitual industry in small things, even in the days of her sadness, prompting her to begin some kind of occupation, which she dragged through slowly or paused in from lack of interest. She looked ill, but had recovered her usual quietude of manner, and Lydgate had feared to disturb her by any questions. He had told her of Dorothea's letter containing the cheque, and afterwards he had said, " Ladislaw is come, Rosy ; he sat with me last night ; I daresay he will be here again to-day. I thought he looked rather battered and depressed." And Rosamond had made no reply.

Now, when he came up, he said to her very gently, " Rosy, dear, Mrs Casaubon is come to see you again ; you would like to see her, would you not ? " That she coloured and gave rather a startled movement did not surprise him after the agitation produced by the interview yesterday — a beneficent agitation, he thought, since it seemed to have made her turn to him again.

Rosamond dared not say no. She dared not with a tone of her voice touch the facts of yesterday. Why had Mrs Casaubon come again ? The answer was a blank which Rosamond could only fill up with dread, for Will Ladislaw's lacerating words had made every thought of Dorothea a fresh smart to her. Nevertheless, in her new humiliating uncertainty she dared do nothing but comply. She did not say yes, but she rose and let Lydgate put a light shawl over her shoulders, while he said, " I am going out immediately." Then something crossed her mind which prompted her to say, " Pray tell Martha not to bring any one else into the drawing-room." And Lydgate assented, thinking that he fully understood this wish. He led her down to the drawing-room door, and then turned away, observing to himself that he was rather a blundering husband to be dependent for his wife's trust in him on the influence of another woman.

Rosamond, wrapping her soft shawl around her as she walked towards Dorothea, was inwardly wrapping her soul in cold reserve. Had Mrs Casaubon come to say anything to her about Will ? If so, it was a liberty that Rosamond resented ; and she prepared herself to meet every word with polite impassibility. Will had bruised her pride too sorely for her to feel any compunction towards him and

Dorothea: her own injury seemed much the greater. Dorothea was not only the "preferred" woman, but had also a formidable advantage in being Lydgate's benefactor; and to poor Rosamond's pained confused vision it seemed that this Mrs Casaubon—this woman who predominated in all things concerning her—must have come now with the sense of having the advantage, and with animosity prompting her to use it. Indeed, not Rosamond only, but any one else, knowing the outer facts of the case, and not the simple inspiration on which Dorothea acted, might well have wondered why she came.

Looking like the lovely ghost of herself, her graceful slimness wrapped in her soft white shawl, the rounded infantine mouth and cheek inevitably suggesting mildness and innocence, Rosamond paused at three yards' distance from her visitor and bowed. But Dorothea, who had taken off her gloves, from an impulse which she could never resist when she wanted a sense of freedom, came forward, and with her face full of a sad yet sweet openness, put out her hand. Rosamond could not avoid meeting her glance, could not avoid putting her small hand into Dorothea's, which clasped it with gentle motherliness; and immediately a doubt of her own prepossessions began to stir within her. Rosamond's eye was quick for faces; she saw that Mrs Casaubon's face looked pale and changed since yesterday, yet gentle, and like the firm softness of her hand. But Dorothea had counted a little too much on her own strength: the clearness and intensity of her mental action this morning were the continuance of a nervous exaltation which made her frame as dangerously responsive as a bit of finest Venetian crystal; and in looking at Rosamond, she suddenly found her heart swelling, and was unable to speak—all her effort was required to keep back tears. She succeeded in that, and the emotion only passed over her face like the spirit of a sob; but it added to Rosamond's impression that Mrs Casaubon's state of mind must be something quite different from what she had imagined.

So they sat down without a word of preface on the two chairs that happened to be nearest, and happened also to be close together; though Rosamond's notion when she first bowed was that she should stay a long way off from Mrs Casaubon. But she ceased thinking how anything would turn out—merely wondering what would come. And Dorothea began to speak quite simply, gathering firmness as she went on.

"I had an errand yesterday which I did not finish; that is why I am here again so soon. You will not think me too troublesome, when I tell you that I came to talk to you about the injustice that has been shown towards Mr Lydgate. It will cheer you—will it not?—to know a great deal about him, that he may not like to speak about himself just because it is in his own vindication and to his own honour. You will like to know that your husband has warm friends, who have not left off believing in his high character? You will let me speak of this without thinking that I take a liberty?"

The cordial, pleading tones which seemed to flow with generous heedlessness above all the facts which had filled Rosamond's mind as grounds of obstruction and hatred between her and this woman, came as soothingly as a warm stream over her shrinking fears. Of course Mrs Casaubon had the facts in her mind, but she was not going to speak of anything connected with them. That relief was too great for Rosamond to feel much else at the moment. She answered prettily, in the new ease of her soul—

"I know you have been very good. I shall like to hear anything you will say to me about Tertius."

"The day before yesterday," said Dorothea, "when I had asked him to come to Lowick to give me his opinion on the affairs of the Hospital, he told me everything about his conduct and feelings in this sad event which has made ignorant people cast suspicions on him. The reason he told me was because I was very bold and asked him. I believed that he had never acted dishonourably, and I begged him to tell me the history. He confessed to me that he had never told it before, not even to you, because he had a great dislike to say, ' I was not wrong,' as if that were proof, when there are guilty people who will say so. The truth is, he knew nothing of this man Raffles, or that there were any bad secrets about him; and he thought that Mr Bulstrode offered him the money because he repented, out of kindness, of having refused it before. All his anxiety about his patient was to treat him rightly, and he was a little uncomfortable that the case did not end as he had expected; but he thought then and still thinks that there may have been no wrong in it on any one's part. And I have told Mr Farebrother, and Mr Brooke, and Sir James Chettam: they all believe in your husband. That will cheer you, will it not? That will give you courage?"

Dorothea's face had become animated, and as it beamed on Rosamond very close to her, she felt something like bashful timidity before a superior, in the presence of this self-forgetful ardour. She said, with blushing embarrassment, "Thank you: you are very kind."

"And he felt that he had been so wrong not to pour out everything about this to you. But you will forgive him. It was because he feels so much more about your happiness than anything else—he feels his life bound into one with yours, and it hurts him more than anything, that his misfortunes must hurt you. He could speak to me because I am an indifferent person. And then I asked him if I might come to see you; because I felt so much for his trouble and yours. That is why I came yesterday, and why I am come to-day. Trouble is so hard to bear, is it not?—How can we live and think that any one has trouble—piercing trouble—and we could help them, and never try?"

Dorothea, completely swayed by the feeling that she was uttering, forgot everything but that she was speaking from out the heart of her own trial to Rosamond's. The emotion had wrought itself more and more into her utterance, till the tones might have gone to one's very marrow, like a low cry from some suffering creature in the darkness. And she had unconsciously laid her hand again on the little hand that she had pressed before.

Rosamond, with an overmastering pang, as if a wound within her had been probed, burst into hysterical crying as she had done the day before when she clung to her husband. Poor Dorothea was feeling a great wave of her own sorrow returning over her—her thought being drawn to the possible share that Will Ladislaw might have in Rosamond's mental tumult. She was beginning to fear that she should not be able to suppress herself enough to the end of this meeting, and while her hand was still resting on Rosamond's lap, though the hand underneath it was withdrawn, she was struggling against her own rising sobs. She tried to master herself with the thought that this might be a turning-point in three lives—not in her own; no, there the irrevocable had happened, but—in those three lives which were touching hers with the solemn neighbourhood of danger and distress. The fragile creature who was crying close to her—there might still be time to rescue her from the misery of false incompatible bonds; and this moment was unlike any other: she and Rosamond could never be together again with the same thrilling consciousness of yesterday within them both. She felt the relation between them to be peculiar enough to give her a peculiar influence, though she had no conception that the way in which her own feelings were involved was fully known to Mrs Lydgate.

It was a newer crisis in Rosamond's experience than even Dorothea could imagine : she was under the first great shock that had shattered her dream-world in which she had been easily confident of herself and critical of others ; and this strange unexpected manifestation of feeling in a woman whom she had approached with a shrinking aversion and dread, as one who must necessarily have a jealous hatred towards her, made her soul totter all the more with a sense that she had been walking in an unknown world which had just broken in upon her.

When Rosamond's convulsed throat was subsiding into calm, and she withdrew the handkerchief with which she had been hiding her face, her eyes met Dorothea's as helplessly as if they had been blue flowers. What was the use of thinking about behaviour after this crying ? And Dorothea looked almost as childish, with the neglected trace of a silent tear. Pride was broken down between these two.

"We were talking about your husband," Dorothea said, with some timidity. "I thought his looks were sadly changed with suffering the other day. I had not seen him for many weeks before. He said he had been feeling very lonely in his trial ; but I think he would have borne it all better if he had been able to be quite open with you."

"Tertius is so angry and impatient if I say anything," said Rosamond, imagining that he had been complaining of her to Dorothea. "He ought not to wonder that I object to speak to him on painful subjects."

"It was himself he blamed for not speaking," said Dorothea. "What he said of you was, that he could not be happy in doing anything which made you unhappy—that his marriage was of course a bond which must affect his choice about everything ; and for that reason he refused my proposal that he should keep his position at the Hospital, because that would bind him to stay in Middlemarch, and he would not undertake to do anything which would be painful to you. He could say that to me, because he knows that I had much trial in my marriage, from my husband's illness, which hindered his plans and saddened him ; and he knows that I have felt how hard it is to walk always in fear of hurting another who is tied to us."

Dorothea waited a little ; she had discerned a faint pleasure stealing over Rosamond's face. But there was no answer, and she went on, with a gathering tremor, "Marriage is so unlike everything else. There is something even awful in the nearness it brings. Even if we loved some one else better than—than those we were married to, it would be no use"—poor Dorothea, in her palpitating anxiety, could only seize her language brokenly—" I mean, marriage drinks up all our power of giving or getting any blessedness in that sort of love. I know it may be very dear—but it murders our marriage—and then the marriage stays with us like a murder—and everything else is gone. And then our husband—if he loved and trusted us, and we have not helped him, but made a curse in his life . . ."

Her voice had sunk very low : there was a dread upon her of presuming too far, and of speaking as if she herself were perfection addressing error. She was too much preoccupied with her own anxiety, to be aware that Rosamond was trembling too ; and filled with the need to express pitying fellowship rather than rebuke, she put her hands on Rosamond's, and said with more agitated rapidity,—" I know, I know that the feeling may be very dear—it has taken hold of us unawares—it is so hard, it may seem like death to part with it —and we are weak—I am weak——"

The waves of her own sorrow, from out of which she was struggling to save another, rushed over Dorothea with conquering force. She stopped in speechless agitation, not crying, but feeling as if she were being inwardly grappled. Her face had become of a deathlier paleness, her lips trembled, and she pressed her hands helplessly on the hands that lay under them.

Rosamond, taken hold of by an emotion stronger than her own— hurried along in a new movement which gave all things some new, awful, undefined aspect—could find no words, but involuntarily she put her lips to Dorothea's forehead which was very near her, and then for a minute the two women clasped each other as if they had been in a shipwreck.

" You are thinking what is not true," said Rosamond, in an eager half-whisper, while she was still feeling Dorothea's arms round her —urged by a mysterious necessity to free herself from something that oppressed her as if it were blood-guiltiness.

They moved apart, looking at each other.

" When you came in yesterday—it was not as you thought," said Rosamond in the same tone.

There was a movement of surprised attention in Dorothea. She expected a vindication of Rosamond herself.

" He was telling me how he loved another woman, that I might know he could never love me," said Rosamond, getting more and more hurried as she went on. " And now I think he hates me because—because you mistook him yesterday. He says it is through me that you will think ill of him—think that he is a false person. But it shall not be through me. He has never had any love for me— I know he has not—he has always thought slightly of me. He said yesterday that no other woman existed for him beside you. The blame of what happened is entirely mine. He said he could never explain to you—because of me. He said you could never think well of him again. But now I have told you, and he cannot reproach me any more."

Rosamond had delivered her soul under impulses which she had not known before. She had begun her confession under the subduing influence of Dorothea's emotion ; and as she went on she had gathered the sense that she was repelling Will's reproaches, which were still like a knife-wound within her.

The revulsion of feeling in Dorothea was too strong to be called joy. It was a tumult in which the terrible strain of the night and morning made a resistant pain :—she could only perceive that this would be joy when she had recovered her power of feeling it. Her immediate consciousness was one of immense sympathy without check ; she cared for Rosamond without struggle now, and responded earnestly to her last words :

" No, he cannot reproach you any more."

With her usual tendency to over-estimate the good in others, she felt a great outgoing of her heart towards Rosamond for the generous effort which had redeemed her from suffering, not counting that the effort was a reflex of her own energy.

After they had been silent a little, she said—

" You are not sorry that I came this morning ? "

" No, you have been very good to me," said Rosamond. " I did not think that you would be so good. I was very unhappy. I am not happy now. Everything is so sad."

" But better days will come. Your husband will be rightly valued. And he depends on you for comfort. He loves you best. The worst loss would be to lose that—and you have not lost it," said Dorothea.

She tried to thrust away the too overpowering thought of her own relief, lest she should fail to win some sign that Rosamond's affection was yearning back towards her husband.

" Tertius did not find fault with me, then ? " said Rosamond, understanding now that Lydgate might have said anything to Mrs Casaubon, and that she certainly was different from other women. Perhaps there was a faint taste of jealousy in the question. A smile began to play over Dorothea's face as she said—

" No, indeed ! How could you imagine it ? " But here the door opened, and Lydgate entered.

" I am come back in my quality of doctor," he said. " After I went away, I was haunted by two pale faces : Mrs Casaubon looked as much in need of care as you, Rosy. And I thought that I had not done my duty in leaving you together ; so when I had been to Coleman's I came home again. I noticed that you were walking, Mrs Casaubon, and the sky has changed—I think we may have rain. May I send some one to order your carriage to come for you ? "

" Oh no ! I am strong : I need the walk," said Dorothea, rising with animation in her face. " Mrs Lydgate and I have chatted a great deal, and it is time for me to go. I have always been accused of being immoderate and saying too much."

She put out her hand to Rosamond, and they said an earnest, quiet good-bye without kiss or other show of effusion : there had been between them too much serious emotion for them to use the signs of it superficially.

As Lydgate took her to the door she said nothing of Rosamond, but told him of Mr Farebrother and the other friends who had listened with belief to his story.

When he came back to Rosamond, she had already thrown herself on the sofa, in resigned fatigue.

" Well, Rosy," he said, standing over her, and touching her hair,

" what do you think of Mrs Causabon now you have seen so much of her ? "

" I think she must be better than any one," said Rosamond, " and she is very beautiful. If you go to talk to her so often, you will be more discontented with me than ever ! "

Lydgate laughed at the " so often." " But has she made you any less discontented with me ? "

" I think she has," said Rosamond, looking up in his face. " How heavy your eyes are, Tertius—and do push your hair back." He lifted up his large white hand to obey her, and felt thankful for this little mark of interest in him. Poor Rosamond's vagrant fancy had come back terribly scourged—meek enough to nestle under the old despised shelter. And the shelter was still there : Lydgate had accepted his narrowed lot with sad resignation. He had chosen this fragile creature, and had taken the burthen of her life upon his arms. He must walk as he could, carrying that burthen pitifully.

CHAPTER LXXXII.

" My grief lies onward and my joy behind."
—SHAKESPEARE : *Sonnets*. [1]

EXILES notoriously feed much on hopes, and are unlikely to stay in banishment unless they are obliged. When Will Ladislaw exiled himself from Middlemarch he had placed no stronger obstacle to his return than his own resolve, which was by no means an iron barrier, but simply a state of mind liable to melt into a minuet with other states of mind, and to find itself bowing, smiling, and giving place with polite facility. As the months went on, it had seemed more and more difficult to him to say why he should not run down to Middlemarch—merely for the sake of hearing something about Dorothea ; and if on such a flying visit he should chance by some strange coincidence to meet with her, there was no reason for him to be ashamed of having taken an innocent journey which he had beforehand supposed that he should not take. Since he was hopelessly divided from her, he might surely venture into her neighbourhood ; and as to the suspicious friends who kept a dragon watch over her—their opinions seemed less and less important with time and change of air.

And there had come a reason quite irrespective of Dorothea, which seemed to make a journey to Middlemarch a sort of philanthropic duty. Will had given a disinterested attention to an intended settlement on a new plan in the Far West, and the need for funds in order to carry out a good design had set him on debating with himself whether it would not be a laudable use to make of his claim on Bulstrode, to urge the application of that money which had been offered to himself as a means of carrying out a scheme likely to be largely beneficial. The question seemed a very dubious one to Will, and his repugnance to again entering into any relation with the banker might have made him dismiss it quickly, if there had not arisen in his imagination the probability that his judgment might be more safely determined by a visit to Middlemarch.

That was the object which Will stated to himself as a reason for coming down. He had meant to confide in Lydgate, and discuss the money question with him, and he had meant to amuse himself for the few evenings of his stay by having a great deal of music and badinage with fair Rosamond, without neglecting his friends at Lowick Parsonage :—if the Parsonage was close to the Manor, that was no fault of his. He had neglected the Farebrothers before his departure, from a proud resistance to the possible accusation of indirectly seeking interviews with Dorothea ; but hunger tames us, and Will had become very hungry for the vision of a certain form and the sound of a certain voice. Nothing had done instead—not the opera, or the converse of zealous politicians, or the flattering reception (in dim corners) of his new hand in leading articles.

Thus he had come down, foreseeing with confidence how almost everything would be in his familiar little world ; fearing, indeed, that there would be no surprises in his visit. But he had found that humdrum world in a terribly dynamic condition, in which even badinage and lyrism had turned explosive ; and the first day of this visit had become the most fatal epoch of his life. [2] The next morning he felt so harassed with the nightmare of consequences—he dreaded so much the immediate issues before him—that seeing while he breakfasted the arrival of the Riverston coach, he went out hurriedly and took his place on it, that he might be relieved, at least for a day, from the necessity of doing or saying anything in Middlemarch. Will Ladislaw was in one of those tangled crises which are commoner in experience than one might imagine, from the shallow absoluteness of men's judgments. He had found Lydgate, for whom he had the sincerest respect, under circumstances which claimed his thorough and frankly-declared sympathy ; and the reason why, in spite of that claim, it would have been better for Will to have avoided all further intimacy, or even contact, with Lydgate, was precisely of the kind to make such a course appear impossible. To a creature of Will's susceptible temperament—without any neutral region of indifference in his nature, ready to turn everything that befell him into the collisions of a passionate drama—the revelation that Rosamond had made her happiness in any way dependent on him was a difficulty which his outburst of rage towards her had immeasurably increased for him. He hated his own cruelty, and yet he dreaded to show the fulness of his relenting : he must go to her again ; the friendship could not be put to a sudden end ; and her unhappiness was a power which he dreaded. And all the while there was no more foretaste of enjoyment in the life before him than if his limbs had been lopped off and he was making his fresh start on crutches. In the night he had debated whether he should not get on the coach, not for Riverston, but for London, leaving a note to Lydgate which would give a makeshift reason for his retreat. But there were strong cords pulling him back from that abrupt departure : the blight on his happiness in thinking of Dorothea, the crushing of that chief hope which had remained in spite of the acknowledged necessity for renunciation, was

2. **Badinage and lyrism:** playful teasing and lyric enthusiasm.

too fresh a misery for him to resign himself to it, and go straightway into a distance which was also despair.

Thus he did nothing more decided than taking the Riverston coach. He came back again by it while it was still daylight, having made up his mind that he must go to Lydgate's that evening. The Rubicon, we know, was a very insignificant stream to look at ; its significance lay entirely in certain invisible conditions. Will felt as if he were forced to cross his small boundary ditch, and what he saw beyond it was not empire, but discontented subjection.

But it is given to us sometimes even in our everyday life to witness the saving influence of a noble nature, the divine efficacy of rescue that may lie in a self-subduing act of fellowship. If Dorothea, after her night's anguish, had not taken that walk to Rosamond—why, she perhaps would have been a woman who gained a higher character for discretion, but it would certainly not have been as well for those three who were on one hearth in Lydgate's house at half-past seven that evening.

Rosamond had been prepared for Will's visit, and she received him with a languid coldness which Lydgate accounted for by her nervous exhaustion, of which he could not suppose that it had any relation to Will. And when she sat in silence bending over a bit of work, he innocently apologised for her in an indirect way by begging her to lean backward and rest. Will was miserable in the necessity for playing the part of a friend who was making his first appearance and greeting to Rosamond, while his thoughts were busy about her feeling since that scene of yesterday, which seemed still inexorably to enclose them both, like the painful vision of a double madness. It happened that nothing called Lydgate out of the room ; but when Rosamond poured out the tea, and Will came near to fetch it, she placed a tiny bit of folded paper in his saucer. He saw it and secured it quickly, but as he went back to his inn he had no eagerness to unfold the paper. What Rosamond had written to him would probably deepen the painful impressions of the evening. Still, he opened and read it by his bed-candle. There were only these few words in her neatly-flowing hand :—

" I have told Mrs Casaubon. She is not under any mistake about you. I told her because she came to see me and was very kind. You will have nothing to reproach me with now. I shall not have made any difference to you."

The effect of these words was not quite all gladness. As Will dwelt on them with excited imagination, he felt his cheeks and ears burning at the thought of what had occurred between Dorothea and Rosamond—at the uncertainty how far Dorothea might still feel her dignity wounded in having an explanation of his conduct offered to her. There might still remain in her mind a changed association with him which made an irremediable difference—a lasting flaw. With active fancy he wrought himself into a state of doubt little more easy than that of the man who has escaped from wreck by night and stands on unknown ground in the darkness. Until that wretched yesterday—except the moment of vexation long ago in the very same room and in the very same presence—all their vision, all their thought of each other, had been as in a world apart, where the sunshine fell on tall white lilies, where no evil lurked, and no other soul entered. But now—would Dorothea meet him in that world again ?

CHAPTER LXXXIII.

"And now good-morrow to our waking souls
Which watch not one another out of fear ;
For love all love of other sights controls,
And makes one little room, an everywhere."
—Dr Donne. [1]

ON the second morning after Dorothea's visit to Rosamond, she had
had two nights of sound sleep, and had not only lost all traces of fatigue, but felt as if she had a great deal of superfluous strength—that
is to say, more strength than she could manage to concentrate on any
occupation. The day before, she had taken long walks outside the
grounds, and had paid two visits to the Parsonage ; but she never in
her life told any one the reason why she spent her time in that fruitless manner, and this morning she was rather angry with herself for
her childish restlessness. To-day was to be spent quite differently.
What was there to be done in the village ? O dear ! nothing. Everybody was well and had flannel ; nobody's pig had died ; and it was
Saturday morning, when there was a general scrubbing of floors and
door-stones, and when it was useless to go into the school. But there
were various subjects that Dorothea was trying to get clear upon, and
she resolved to throw herself energetically into the gravest of all.
She sat down in the library before her particular little heap of books
on political economy and kindred matters, out of which she was trying to get light as to the best way of spending money so as not to injure one's neighbours, or—what comes to the same thing—so as to do
them the most good. Here was a weighty subject which, if she could
but lay hold of it, would certainly keep her mind steady. Unhappily
her mind slipped off it for a whole hour ; and at the end she found
herself reading sentences twice over with an intense consciousness of
many things, but not of any one thing contained in the text. This
was hopeless. Should she order the carriage and drive to Tipton ?
No ; for some reason or other she preferred staying at Lowick. But
her vagrant mind must be reduced to order : there was an art in self-
discipline ; and she walked round and round the brown library considering by what sort of manœuvre she could arrest her wandering
thoughts. Perhaps a mere task was the best means—something to
which she must go doggedly. Was there not the geography of Asia
Minor, in which her slackness had often been rebuked by Mr Casaubon ? She went to the cabinet of maps and unrolled one : this morning she might make herself finally sure that Paphlagonia was not on
the Levantine coast, and fix her total darkness about the Chalybes
firmly on the shores of the Euxine. A map was a fine thing to study
when you were disposed to think of something else, being made up of

1. John Donne, "The Good Morrow."

names that would turn into a chime if you went back upon them.[2] Dorothea set earnestly to work, bending close to her map, and uttering the names in an audible, subdued tone, which often got into a chime. She looked amusingly girlish after all her deep experience—nodding her head and marking the names off on her fingers, with a little pursing of her lip, and now and then breaking off to put her hands on each side of her face and say, " Oh dear ! oh dear ! "

There was no reason why this should end any more than a merry-go-round ; but it was at last interrupted by the opening of the door and the announcement of Miss Noble.

The little old lady, whose bonnet hardly reached Dorothea's shoulder, was warmly welcomed, but while her hand was being pressed she made many of her beaver-like noises, as if she had something difficult to say.

" Do sit down," said Dorothea, rolling a chair forward. " Am I wanted for anything? I shall be so glad if I can do anything."

" I will not stay," said Miss Noble, putting her hand into her small basket, and holding some article inside it nervously ; " I have left a friend in the churchyard." She lapsed into her inarticulate sounds, and unconsciously drew forth the article which she was fingering. It was the tortoise-shell lozenge-box, and Dorothea felt the colour mounting to her cheeks.

" Mr Ladislaw," continued the timid little woman. " He fears he has offended you, and has begged me to ask if you will see him for a few minutes."

Dorothea did not answer on the instant : it was crossing her mind that she could not receive him in this library, where her husband's prohibition seemed to dwell. She looked towards the window. Could she go out and meet him in the grounds ? The sky was heavy, and the trees had begun to shiver as at a coming storm. Besides, she shrank from going out to him.

" Do see him, Mrs Casaubon," said Miss Noble, pathetically ; " else I must go back and say No, and that will hurt him."

" Yes, I will see him," said Dorothea. " Pray tell him to come."

What else was there to be done ? There was nothing that she longed for at that moment except to see Will : the possibility of seeing him had thrust itself insistently between her and every other object ; and yet she had a throbbing excitement like an alarm upon her —a sense that she was doing something daringly defiant for his sake.

When the little lady had trotted away on her mission, Dorothea stood in the middle of the library with her hands falling clasped before her, making no attempt to compose herself in an attitude of dignified unconsciousness. What she was least conscious of just then was her own body : she was thinking of what was likely to be in Will's mind, and of the hard feelings that others had had about him. How could any duty bind her to hardness? Resistance to unjust dispraise had mingled with her feeling for him from the very first, and now in the rebound of her heart after her anguish the resistance

2. Paphlagonia, an ancient Roman province, was not on the Levantine or Mediterranean coast, but on the Black Sea; and the Chalybes, a tribe noted for its blacksmiths, lived in Pontus, on the Euxine or Black Sea coast.

was stronger than ever. " If I love him too much it is because he has been used so ill : "—there was a voice within her saying this to some imagined audience in the library, when the door was opened, and she saw Will before her.

She did not move, and he came towards her with more doubt and timidity in his face than she had ever seen before. He was in a state of uncertainty which made him afraid lest some look or word of his should condemn him to a new distance from her ; and Dorothea was afraid of her own emotion. She looked as if there were a spell upon her, keeping her motionless and hindering her from unclasping her hands, while some intense, grave yearning was imprisoned within her eyes. Seeing that she did not put out her hand as usual, Will paused a yard from her and said with embarrassment, " I am so grateful to you for seeing me."

" I wanted to see you," said Dorothea, having no other words at command. It did not occur to her to sit down, and Will did not give a cheerful interpretation to this queenly way of receiving him ; but he went on to say what he had made up his mind to say.

" I fear you think me foolish and perhaps wrong for coming back so soon. I have been punished for my impatience. You know—every one knows now—a painful story about my parentage. I knew of it before I went away, and I always meant to tell you of it if—if we ever met again."

There was a slight movement in Dorothea, and she unclasped her hands, but immediately folded them over each other.

" But the affair is matter of gossip now," Will continued. " I wished you to know that something connected with it—something which happened before I went away, helped to bring me down here again. At least I thought it excused my coming. It was the idea of getting Bulstrode to apply some money to a public purpose—some money which he had thought of giving me. Perhaps it is rather to Bulstrode's credit that he privately offered me compensation for an old injury : he offered to give me a good income to make amends ; but I suppose you know the disagreeable story ? "

Will looked doubtfully at Dorothea, but his manner was gathering some of the defiant courage with which he always thought of this fact in his destiny. He added, " You know that it must be altogether painful to me."

" Yes—yes—I know," said Dorothea, hastily.

" I did not choose to accept an income from such a source. I was sure that you would not think well of me if I did so," said Will. Why should he mind saying anything of that sort to her now ? She knew that he had avowed his love for her. " I felt that "—he broke off, nevertheless.

" You acted as I should have expected you to act," said Dorothea, her face brightening and her head becoming a little more erect on its beautiful stem.

" I did not believe that you would let any circumstance of my birth create a prejudice in you against me, though it was sure to do so in others," said Will, shaking his head backward in his old way, and looking with a grave appeal into her eyes.

"If it were a new hardship it would be a new reason for me to cling to you," said Dorothea, fervidly. "Nothing could have changed me but——" her heart was swelling, and it was difficult to go on; she made a great effort over herself to say in a low tremulous voice, "but thinking that you were different—not so good as I had believed you to be."

"You are sure to believe me better than I am in everything but one," said Will, giving way to his own feeling in the evidence of hers. "I mean, in my truth to you. When I thought you doubted of that, I didn't care about anything that was left. I thought it was all over with me, and there was nothing to try for—only things to endure."

"I don't doubt you any longer," said Dorothea, putting out her hand; a vague fear for him impelling her unutterable affection.

He took her hand and raised it to his lips with something like a sob. But he stood with his hat and gloves in the other hand, and might have done for the portrait of a Royalist. Still it was difficult to loose the hand, and Dorothea, withdrawing it in a confusion that distressed her, looked and moved away.

"See how dark the clouds have become, and how the trees are tossed," she said, walking towards the window, yet speaking and moving with only a dim sense of what she was doing.

Will followed her at a little distance, and leaned against the tall back of a leather chair, on which he ventured now to lay his hat and gloves, and free himself from the intolerable durance of formality to which he had been for the first time condemned in Dorothea's presence. It must be confessed that he felt very happy at that moment leaning on the chair. He was not much afraid of anything that she might feel now.

They stood silent, not looking at each other, but looking at the evergreens which were being tossed, and were showing the pale underside of their leaves against the blackening sky. Will never enjoyed the prospect of a storm so much: it delivered him from the necessity of going away. Leaves and little branches were hurled about, and the thunder was getting nearer. The light was more and more sombre, but there came a flash of lightning which made them start and look at each other, and then smile. Dorothea began to say what she had been thinking of.

"That was a wrong thing for you to say, that you would have had nothing to try for. If we had lost our own chief good, other people's good would remain, and that is worth trying for. Some can be happy. I seemed to see that more clearly than ever, when I was the most wretched. I can hardly think how I could have borne the trouble, if that feeling had not come to me to make strength."

"You have never felt the sort of misery I felt," said Will; "the misery of knowing that you must despise me."

"But I have felt worse—it was worse to think ill——" Dorothea had begun impetuously, but broke off.

Will coloured. He had the sense that whatever she said was uttered in the vision of a fatality that kept them apart. He was silent a moment, and then said passionately—

"We may at least have the comfort of speaking to each other without disguise. Since I must go away — since we must always be divided—you may think of me as one on the brink of the grave."

While he was speaking there came a vivid flash of lightning which lit each of them up for the other—and the light seemed to be the terror of a hopeless love. Dorothea darted instantaneously from the window ; Will followed her, seizing her hand with a spasmodic movement ; and so they stood, with their hands clasped, like two children, looking out on the storm, while the thunder gave a tremendous crack and roll above them, and the rain began to pour down. Then they turned their faces towards each other, with the memory of his last words in them, and they did not loose each other's hands.

" There is no hope for me," said Will. " Even if you loved me as well as I love you—even if I were everything to you—I shall most likely always be very poor : on a sober calculation, one can count on nothing but a creeping lot. It is impossible for us ever to belong to each other. It is perhaps base of me to have asked for a word from you. I meant to go away into silence, but I have not been able to do what I meant."

" Don't be sorry," said Dorothea, in her clear tender tones. " I would rather share all the trouble of our parting."

Her lips trembled, and so did his. It was never known which lips were the first to move towards the other lips ; but they kissed tremblingly, and then they moved apart.

The rain was dashing against the window-panes as if an angry spirit were within it, and behind it was the great swoop of the wind ; it was one of those moments in which both the busy and the idle pause with a certain awe.

Dorothea sat down on the seat nearest to her, a long low ottoman in the middle of the room, and with her hands folded over each other on her lap, looked at the drear outer world. Will stood still an instant looking at her, then seated himself beside her, and laid his hand on hers, which turned itself upward to be clasped. They sat in that way without looking at each other, until the rain abated and began to fall in stillness. Each had been full of thoughts which neither of them could begin to utter.

But when the rain was quiet, Dorothea turned to look at Will. With passionate exclamation, as if some torture-screw were threatening him, he started up and said, " It is impossible ! "

He went and leaned on the back of the chair again, and seemed to be battling with his own anger, while she looked towards him sadly.

" It is as fatal as a murder or any other horror that divides people," he burst out again ; " it is more intolerable—to have our life maimed by petty accidents."

" No—don't say that—your life need not be maimed," said Dorothea, gently.

" Yes, it must," said Will, angrily. " It is cruel of you to speak in that way—as if there were any comfort. You may see beyond the misery of it, but I don't. It is unkind—it is throwing back my love for you as if it were a trifle, to speak in that way in the face of the fact. We can never be married."

" Some time—we might," said Dorothea, in a trembling voice.

"When ?" said Will, bitterly. "What is the use of counting on any success of mine ? It is a mere toss up whether I shall ever do more than keep myself decently, unless I choose to sell myself as a mere pen and a mouthpiece. I can see that clearly enough. I could not offer myself to any woman, even if she had no luxuries to renounce."

There was silence. Dorothea's heart was full of something that she wanted to say, and yet the words were too difficult. She was wholly possessed by them : at that moment debate was mute within her. And it was very hard that she could not say what she wanted to say. Will was looking out of the window angrily. If he would have looked at her and not gone away from her side, she thought everything would have been easier. At last he turned, still resting against the chair, and stretching his hand automatically towards his hat, said with a sort of exasperation, "Good-bye."

"Oh, I cannot bear it—my heart will break," said Dorothea, start-ing from her seat, the flood of her young passion bearing down all the obstructions which had kept her silent—the great tears rising and falling in an instant : "I don't mind about poverty—I hate my wealth."

In an instant Will was close to her and had his arms round her, but she drew her head back and held his away gently that she might go on speaking, her large tear-filled eyes looking at his very simply, while she said in a sobbing childlike way, "We could live quite well on my own fortune—it is too much—seven hundred a-year —I want so little—no new clothes—and I will learn what everything costs."

CHAPTER LXXXIV.

> " Though it be songe of old and yonge,
>   That I sholde be to blame,
>   Theyrs be the charge, that spoke so large
>   In hurtynge of my name."
>   —*The Not-browne Mayde.*[1]

It was just after the Lords had thrown out the Reform Bill : that explains how Mr Cadwallader came to be walking on the slope of the lawn near the great conservatory at Freshitt Hall, holding the ' Times' in his hands behind him, while he talked with a trout-fisher's dispassionateness about the prospects of the country to Sir James Chettam. Mrs Cadwallader, the Dowager Lady Chettam, and Celia were sometimes seated on garden-chairs, sometimes walking to meet little Arthur, who was being drawn in his chariot, and, as became the infantine Bouddha, was sheltered by his sacred umbrella with hand-some silken fringe.

The ladies also talked politics, though more fitfully. Mrs Cad-wallader was strong on the intended creation of peers : she had it for certain from her cousin that Truberry had gone over to the other side entirely at the instigation of his wife, who had scented peerages in

---

1. Anonymous song, late fifteenth century, lines 109–12.

the air from the very first introduction of the Reform question, and would sign her soul away to take precedence of her younger sister, who had married a baronet. Lady Chettam thought that such conduct was very reprehensible, and remembered that Mrs Truberry's mother was a Miss Walsingham of Melspring. Celia confessed it was nicer to be " Lady" than " Mrs " and that Dodo never minded about precedence if she could have her own way. Mrs Cadwallader held that it was a poor satisfaction to take precedence when everybody about you knew that you had not a drop of good blood in your veins ; and Celia again, stopping to look at Arthur, said, " It would be very nice, though, if he were a Viscount—and his lordship's little tooth coming through ! He might have been, if James had been an Earl."

" My dear Celia," said the Dowager, " James's title is worth far more than any new earldom. I never wished his father to be anything else than Sir James."

" Oh, I only meant about Arthur's little tooth," said Celia, comfortably. " But see, he e is my uncle coming."

She tripped off to meet her uncle, while Sir James and Mr Cadwallader came forward to make one group with the ladies. Celia had slipped her arm through her uncle's, and he patted her hand with a rather melancholy " Well, my dear ! " As they approached, it was evident that Mr Brooke was looking dejected, but this was fully accounted for by the state of politics ; and as he was shaking hands all round without more greeting than a " Well, you're all here, you know," the Rector said, laughingly —

" Don't take the throwing out of the Bill so much to heart, Brooke ; you've got all the riff-raff of the country on your side."

" The Bill, eh ? ah ! " said Mr Brooke, with a mild distractedness of manner. " Thrown out, you know, eh ? The Lords are going too far, though. They'll have to pull up. Sad news, you know. I mean, here at home—sad news. But you must not blame me, Chettam."

" What is the matter ? " said Sir James. " Not another gamekeeper shot, I hope ? It's what I should expect, when a fellow like Trapping Bass is let off so easily."

" Gamekeeper ? No. Let us go in ; I can tell you all in the house, you know," said Mr Brooke, nodding at the Cadwalladers, to show that he included them in his confidence. " As to poachers like Trapping Bass, you know, Chettam," he continued, as they were entering, " when you are a magistrate, you'll not find it so easy to commit. Severity is all very well, but it's a great deal easier when you've got somebody to do it for you. You have a soft place in your heart yourself, you know—you're not a Draco, a Jeffreys, that sort of thing."[2]

Mr Brooke was evidently in a state of nervous perturbation. When he had something painful to tell, it was usually his way to introduce it among a number of disjointed particulars, as if it were a medicine that would get a milder flavour by mixing. He continued his chat with Sir James about the poachers until they were all seated, and Mrs Cadwallader, impatient of this drivelling, said—

" I'm dying to know the sad news. The gamekeeper is not shot : that is settled. What is it, then ? "

" Well, it's a very trying thing, you know," said Mr Brooke. " I'm

2. Draco (fl. 7th century B.C.), an Athenian statesman noted for the severity of his code of laws; George Jeffreys (1648–89), British judge, infamous for his severity and unjudicial conduct.

glad you and the Rector are here ; it's a family matter—but you will
help us all to bear it, Cadwallader. I've got to break it to you, my
dear." Here Mr Brooke looked at Celia—" You've no notion what
it is, you know. And, Chettam, it will annoy you uncommonly—
but, you see, you have not ben able to hinder it, any more than I
have. There's something singular in things : they come round, you
know."

" It must be about Dodo," said Celia, who had been used to think
of her sister as the dangerous part of the family machinery. She
had seated herself on a low stool against her husband's knee.

" For God's sake let us hear what it is !" said Sir James.

" Well, you know, Chettam, I couldn't help Casaubon's will : it
was a sort of will to make things worse."

" Exactly," said Sir James, hastily. " But *what* is worse ?"

" Dorothea is going to be married again, you know," said Mr Brooke,
nodding towards Celia, who immediately looked up at her husband
with a frightened glance, and put her hand on his knee.

Sir James was almost white with anger, but he did not speak.

" Merciful heaven !" said Mrs Cadwallader. " Not to young
Ladislaw ?"

Mr Brooke nodded, saying, " Yes ; to Ladislaw," and then fell into
a prudential silence.

" You see, Humphrey !" said Mrs Cadwallader, waving her arm
towards her husband. " Another time you will admit that I have
some foresight ; or rather you will contradict me and be just as blind
as ever. *You* supposed that the young gentleman was gone out of
the country."

" So he might be, and yet come back," said the Rector, quietly.

" When did you learn this ?" said Sir James, not liking to hear
any one else speak, though finding it difficult to speak himself.

" Yesterday," said Mr Brooke, meekly. " I went to Lowick.
Dorothea sent for me, you know. It had come about quite suddenly
—neither of them had any idea two days ago—not any idea, you
know. There's something singular in things. But Dorothea is quite
determined—it is no use opposing. I put it strongly to her. I did
my duty, Chettam. But she can act as she likes, you know."

" It would have been better if I had called him out and shot him a
year ago," said Sir James, not from bloody-mindedness, but because
he needed something strong to say.

" Really, James, that would have been very disagreeable," said Celia.

" Be reasonable, Chettam. Look at the affair more quietly," said
Mr Cadwallader, sorry to see his good-natured friend so overmastered
by anger.

" That is not so very easy for a man of any dignity—with any
sense of right—when the affair happens to be in his own family,"
said Sir James, still in his white indignation. " It is perfectly
scandalous. If Ladislaw had had a spark of honour he would have
gone out of the country at once, and never shown his face in it again.
However, I am not surprised. The day after Casaubon's funeral I
said what ought to be done. But I was not listened to."

" You wanted what was impossible, you know, Chettam," said Mr
Brooke. " You wanted him shipped off. I told you Ladislaw was
not to be done as we liked with : he had his ideas. He was a remarkable fellow—I always said he was a remarkable fellow."

" Yes," said Sir James, unable to repress a retort, " it is rather a pity you formed that high opinion of him. We are indebted to that for his being lodged in this neighbourhood. We are indebted to that for seeing a woman like Dorothea degrading herself by marrying him." Sir James made little stoppages between his clauses, the words not coming easily. " A man so marked out by her husband's will, that delicacy ought to have forbidden her from seeing him again—who takes her out of her proper rank—into poverty—has the meanness to accept such a sacrifice—has always had an objectionable position—a bad origin—and, *I believe*, is a man of little principle and light character. That is my opinion," Sir James ended emphatically, turning aside and crossing his leg.

" I pointed everything out to her," said Mr Brooke, apologetically —" I mean the poverty, and abandoning her position. I said, ' My dear, you don't know what it is to live on seven hundred a-year, and have no carriage, and that kind of thing, and go amongst people who don't know who you are.' I put it strongly to her. But I advise you to talk to Dorothea herself. The fact is, she has a dislike to Casaubon's property. You will hear what she says, you know."

" No—excuse me—I shall not," said Sir James, with more coolness. " I cannot bear to see her again ; it is too painful. It hurts me too much that a woman like Dorothea should have done what is wrong."

" Be just, Chettam," said the easy, large-lipped Rector, who objected to all this unnecessary discomfort. " Mrs Casaubon may be acting imprudently : she is giving up a fortune for the sake of a man, and we men have so poor an opinion of each other that we can hardly call a woman wise who does that. But I think you should not condemn it as a wrong action, in the strict sense of the word."

" Yes, I do," answered Sir James. " I think that Dorothea commits a wrong action in marrying Ladislaw."

" My dear fellow, we are rather apt to consider an act wrong because it is unpleasant to us," said the Rector, quietly. Like many men who take life easily, he had the knack of saying a home truth occasionally to those who felt themselves virtuously out of temper. Sir James took out his handkerchief and began to bite the corner.

" It is very dreadful of Dodo, though," said Celia, wishing to justify her husband. " She said she *never would* marry again—not anybody at all."

" I heard her say the same thing myself," said Lady Chettam, majestically, as if this were royal evidence.

" Oh, there is usually a silent exception in such cases," said Mrs Cadwallader. " The only wonder to me is, that any of you are surprised. You did nothing to hinder it. If you would have had Lord Triton down here to woo her with his philanthropy, he might have carried her off before the year was over. There was no safety in anything else. Mr Casaubon had prepared all this as beautifully as possible. He made himself disagreeable—or it pleased God to make him so—and then he dared her to contradict him. It's the way to make any trumpery tempting, to ticket it at a high price in that way."

" I don't know what you mean by wrong, Cadwallader," said Sir James, still feeling a little stung, and turning round in his chair towards the Rector. " He's not a man we can take into the family.

At least, I must speak for myself," he continued, carefully keeping his eyes off Mr Brooke. "I suppose others will find his society too pleasant to care about the propriety of the thing."

"Well, you know, Chettam," said Mr Brooke, good-humouredly, nursing his leg, "I can't turn my back on Dorothea. I must be a father to her up to a certain point. I said, 'My dear, I won't refuse to give you away.' I had spoken strongly before. But I can cut off the entail, you know. It will cost money and be troublesome ; but I can do it, you know."

Mr Brooke nodded at Sir James, and felt that he was both showing his own force of resolution and propitiating what was just in the Baronet's vexation. He had hit on a more ingenious mode of parrying than he was aware of. He had touched a motive of which Sir James was ashamed. The mass of his feeling about Dorothea's marriage to Ladislaw was due partly to excusable prejudice, or even justifiable opinion, partly to a jealous repugnance hardly less in Ladislaw's case than in Casaubon's. He was convinced that the marriage was a fatal one for Dorothea. But amid that mass ran a vein of which he was too good and honourable a man to like the avowal even to himself : it was undeniable that the union of the two estates—Tipton and Freshitt—lying charmingly within a ring-fence, was a prospect that flattered him for his son and heir. Hence when Mr Brooke noddingly appealed to that motive, Sir James felt a sudden embarrassment ; there was a stoppage in his throat ; he even blushed. He had found more words than usual in the first jet of his anger, but Mr Brooke's propitiation was more clogging to his tongue than Mr Cadwallader's caustic hint.

But Celia was glad to have room for speech after her uncle's suggestion of the marriage ceremony, and she said, though with as little eagerness of manner as if the question had turned on an invitation to dinner, "Do you mean that Dodo is going to be married directly, uncle ?"

"In three weeks, you know," said Mr Brooke, helplessly. "I can do nothing to hinder it, Cadwallader," he added, turning for a little countenance toward the Rector, who said—

"*I* should not make any fuss about it. If she likes to be poor, that is her affair. Nobody would have said anything if she had married the young fellow because he was rich. Plenty of beneficed clergy are poorer than they will be. Here is Elinor," continued the provoking husband ; "she vexed her friends by marrying me : I had hardly a thousand a-year—I was a lout—nobody could see anything in me—my shoes were not the right cut—all the men wondered how a woman could like me. Upon my word, I must take Ladislaw's part until I hear more harm of him."

"Humphrey, that is all sophistry, and you know it," said his wife. "Everything is all one—that is the beginning and end with you. As if you had not been a Cadwallader ! Does any one suppose that I would have taken such a monster as you by any other name ?"

"And a clergyman too," observed Lady Chettam with approbation. "Elinor cannot be said to have descended below her rank. It is difficult to say what Mr Ladislaw is, eh, James ?"

Sir James gave a small grunt, which was less respectful than his

usual mode of answering his mother. Celia looked up at him like a
thoughtful kitten.

"It must be admitted that his blood is a frightful mixture!" said
Mrs Cadwallader. "The Casaubon cuttle-fish fluid to begin with,
and then a rebellious Polish fiddler or dancing-master, was it ?—and
then an old clo——"

"Nonsense, Elinor," said the Rector, rising. "It is time for us to
go."

"After all, he is a pretty sprig," said Mrs Cadwallader, rising too,
and wishing to make amends. "He is like the fine old Crichley
portraits before the idiots came in."

"I'll go with you," said Mr Brooke, starting up with alacrity.
"You must all come and dine with me to-morrow, you know—eh,
Celia, my dear ?"

"You will, James—won't you ?" said Celia, taking her husband's
hand.

"Oh, of course, if you like," said Sir James, pulling down his
waistcoat, but unable yet to adjust his face good-humouredly. "That
is to say, if it is not to meet anybody else."

"No, no, no," said Mr Brooke, understanding the condition.
"Dorothea would not come, you know, unless you had been to see
her."

When Sir James and Celia were alone, she said, "Do you mind
about my having the carriage to go to Lowick, James ?"

"What, now, directly ?" he answered, with some surprise.

"Yes, it is very important," said Celia.

"Remember, Celia, I cannot see her," said Sir James.

"Not if she gave up marrying ?"

"What is the use of saying that ?—however, I'm going to the
stables. I'll tell Briggs to bring the carriage round."

Celia thought it was of great use, if not to say that, at least to take
a journey to Lowick in order to influence Dorothea's mind. All
through their girlhood she had felt that she could act on her sister
by a word judiciously placed—by opening a little window for the
daylight of her own understanding to enter among the strange
coloured lamps by which Dodo habitually saw. And Celia the
matron naturally felt more able to advise her childless sister. How
could any one understand Dodo so well as Celia did, or love her so
tenderly ?

Dorothea, busy in her boudoir, felt a glow of pleasure at the sight
of her sister so soon after the revelation of her intended marriage. She
had prefigured to herself, even with exaggeration, the disgust of her
friends, and she had even feared that Celia might be kept aloof from
her.

"O Kitty, I am delighted to see you!" said Dorothea, putting her
hands on Celia's shoulders, and beaming on her. "I almost thought
you would not come to me."

"I have not brought Arthur, because I was in a hurry," said Celia,
and they sat down on two small chairs opposite each other, with their
knees touching.

"You know, Dodo, it is very bad," said Celia, in her placid guttural, looking as prettily free from humours as possible. "You have

disappointed us all so. And I can't think that it ever *will* be—you never can go and live in that way. And then there are all your plans! You never can have thought of that. James would have taken any trouble for you, and you might have gone on all your life doing what you liked."

"On the contrary, dear," said Dorothea, "I never could do anything that I liked. I have never carried out any plan yet."

"Because you always wanted things that wouldn't do. But other plans would have come. And how *can* you marry Mr Ladislaw, that we none of us ever thought you *could* marry? It shocks James so dreadfully. And then it is all so different from what you have always been. You would have Mr Casaubon because he had such a great soul, and was so old and dismal and learned; and now, to think of marrying Mr Ladislaw, who has got no estate or anything. I suppose it is because you must be making yourself uncomfortable in some way or other."

Dorothea laughed.

"Well, it is very serious, Dodo," said Celia, becoming more impressive. "How will you live? and you will go away among queer people. And I shall never see you—and you won't mind about little Arthur—and I thought you always would——"

Celia's rare tears had got into her eyes, and the corners of her mouth were agitated.

"Dear Celia," said Dorothea, with tender gravity, "if you don't ever see me, it will not be my fault."

"Yes, it will," said Celia, with the same touching distortion of her small features. "How can I come to you or have you with me when James can't bear it?—that is because he thinks it is not right—he thinks you are so wrong, Dodo. But you always were wrong; only I can't help loving you. And nobody can think where you will live: where can you go?"

"I am going to London," said Dorothea.

"How can you always live in a street? And you will be so poor. I could give you half my things, only how can I, when I never see you?"

"Bless you, Kitty," said Dorothea, with gentle warmth. "Take comfort: perhaps James will forgive me some time."

"But it would be much better if you would not be married," said Celia, drying her eyes, and returning to her argument; "then there would be nothing uncomfortable. And you would not do what nobody thought you could do. James always said you ought to be a queen; but this is not at all being like a queen. You know what mistakes you have always been making, Dodo, and this is another. Nobody thinks Mr Ladislaw a proper husband for you. And you *said* you would never be married again."

"It is quite true that I might be a wiser person, Celia," said Dorothea, "and that I might have done something better, if I had been better. But this is what I am going to do. I have promised to marry Mr Ladislaw; and I am going to marry him."

The tone in which Dorothea said this was a note that Celia had long learned to recognise. She was silent a few moments, and then said, as if she had dismissed all contest, "Is he very fond of you, Dodo?"

"I hope so. I am very fond of him."

" That is nice," said Celia, comfortably. " Only I would rather you had such a sort of husband as James is, with a place very near, that I could drive to."

Dorothea smiled, and Celia looked rather meditative. Presently she said, " I cannot think how it all came about." Celia thought it would be pleasant to hear the story.

" I daresay not," said Dorothea, pinching her sister's chin. " If you knew how it came about, it would not seem wonderful to you."

" Can't you tell me ? " said Celia, settling her arms cozily.

" No, dear, you would have to feel with me, else you would never know."

CHAPTER LXXXV.

" Then went the jury out, whose names were Mr Blindman, Mr No-good, Mr Malice, Mr Love-lust, Mr Live-loose, Mr Heady, Mr High-mind, Mr Enmity, Mr Liar, Mr Cruelty, Mr Hate-light, Mr Implacable, who every one gave in his private verdict against him among themselves, and afterwards unanimously concluded to bring him in guilty before the judge. And first among themselves, Mr Blindman, the foreman, said, I see clearly that this man is a heretic. Then said Mr No-good, Away with such a fellow from the earth ! Ay, said Mr Malice, for I hate the very look of him. Then said Mr Love-lust, I could never endure him. Nor I, said Mr Live-loose ; for he would be always condemning my way. Hang him, hang him, said Mr Heady. A sorry scrub, said Mr High-mind. My heart riseth against him, said Mr Enmity. He is a rogue, said Mr Liar. Hanging is too good for him, said Mr Cruelty. Let us despatch him out of the way, said Mr Hate-light. Then said Mr Implacable, Might I have all the world given me, I could not be reconciled to him ; therefore let us forthwith bring him in guilty of death."
—*Pilgrim's Progress.*

WHEN immortal Bunyan makes his picture of the persecuting passions bringing in their verdict of guilty, who pities Faithful ? That is a rare and blessed lot which some greatest men have not attained, to know ourselves guiltless before a condemning crowd—to be sure that what we are denounced for is solely the good in us. The pitiable lot is that of the man who could not call himself a martyr even though he were to persuade himself that the men who stoned him were but ugly passions incarnate—who knows that he is stoned, not for professing the Right, but for not being the man he professed to be.

This was the consciousness that Bulstrode was withering under while he made his preparations for departing from Middlemarch, and going to end his stricken life in that sad refuge, the indifference of new faces. The duteous merciful constancy of his wife had delivered him from one dread, but it could not hinder her presence from being still a tribunal before which he shrank from confession and desired advocacy. His equivocations with himself about the death of Raffles had sustained the conception of an Omniscience whom he prayed to, yet he had a terror upon him which would not let him expose them to judgment by a full confession to his wife : the acts which he had washed and diluted with inward argument and motive, and for which it seemed comparatively easy to win invisible pardon—what name would she call them by ? That she should ever silently call his acts Murder was what he could not bear. He felt shrouded by her doubt : he got strength to face her from the sense that she could not yet feel warranted in pronouncing that worst condemnation on him. Some time, perhaps—when he was dying—he would tell her all : in the deep shadow of that time, when she held his hand in the gathering darkness, she might listen without recoiling from his touch. Perhaps : but concealment had been the habit of his life, and the impulse to confession had no power against the dread of a deeper humiliation.

He was full of timid care for his wife, not only because he deprecated any harshness of judgment from her, but because he felt a deep distress at the sight of her suffering. She had sent her daughters away to board at a school on the coast, that this crisis might be hidden from them as far as possible. Set free by their absence from the intolerable necessity of accounting for her grief or of beholding their frightened wonder, she could live unconstrainedly with the sorrow that was every day streaking her hair with whiteness and making her eyelids languid.

"Tell me anything that you would like to have me do, Harriet," Bulstrode had said to her ; "I mean with regard to arrangements of property. It is my intention not to sell the land I possess in this neighbourhood, but to leave it to you as a safe provision. If you have any wish on such subjects, do not conceal it from me."

A few days afterwards, when she had returned from a visit to her brother's, she began to speak to her husband on a subject which had for some time been in her mind.

"I *should* like to do something for my brother's family, Nicholas ; and I think we are bound to make some amends to Rosamond and her husband. Walter says Mr Lydgate must leave the town, and his practice is almost good for nothing, and they have very little left to settle anywhere with. I would rather do without something for ourselves, to make some amends to my poor brother's family."

Mrs Bulstrode did not wish to go nearer to the facts than in the phrase " make some amends ;" knowing that her husband must understand her. He had a particular reason, which she was not aware of, for wincing under her suggestion. He hesitated before he said—

"It is not possible to carry out your wish in the way you propose, my dear. Mr Lydgate has virtually rejected any further service from me. He has returned the thousand pounds which I lent him. Mrs Casaubon advanced him the sum for that purpose. Here is his letter."

The letter seemed to cut Mrs Bulstrode severely. The mention of Mrs Casaubon's loan seemed a reflection of that public feeling which held it a matter of course that every one would avoid a connection with her husband. She was silent for some time ; and the tears fell one after the other, her chin trembling as she wiped them away. Bulstrode, sitting opposite to her, ached at the sight of that grief-worn face, which two months before had been bright and blooming. It had aged to keep sad company with his own withered features. Urged into some effort at comforting her, he said—

"There is another means, Harriet, by which I might do a service to your brother's family, if you like to act in it. And it would, I think, be beneficial to you : it would be an advantageous way of managing the land which I mean to be yours."

She looked attentive.

"Garth once thought of undertaking the management of Stone Court in order to place your nephew Fred there. The stock was to remain as it is, and they were to pay a certain share of the profits instead of an ordinary rent. That would be a desirable beginning for the young man, in conjunction with his employment under Garth. Would it be a satisfaction to you?"

"Yes, it would," said Mrs Bulstrode, with some return of energy. "Poor Walter is so cast down; I would try anything in my power to do him some good before I go away. We have always been brother and sister."

"You must make the proposal to Garth yourself, Harriet," said Mr Bulstrode, not liking what he had to say, but desiring the end he had in view, for other reasons besides the consolation of his wife. "You must state to him that the land is virtually yours, and that he need have no transactions with me. Communications can be made through Standish. I mention this, because Garth gave up being my agent. I can put into your hands a paper which he himself drew up, stating conditions; and you can propose his renewed acceptance of them. I think it is not unlikely that he will accept when you propose the thing for the sake of your nephew."

<hr/>

CHAPTER LXXXVI.

"Le cœur se sature d'amour comme d'un sel divin qui le conserve ; de là l'incorruptible adhérence de ceux qui se sont aimés dès l'aube de la vie, et la fraîcheur des vielles amours prolongés. Il existe un embaumement d'amour. C'est de Daphnis et Chloë que sont faits Philémon et Baucis. Cette vieillesse là, ressemblance du soir avec l'aurore."
—Victor Hugo : *L'homme qui rit.*[1]

MRS GARTH, hearing Caleb enter the passage about tea-time, opened the parlour-door and said, "There you are, Caleb. Have you had your dinner?" (Mr Garth's meals were much subordinated to "business.")

"Oh yes, a good dinner—cold mutton and I don't know what. Where is Mary?"

"In the garden with Letty, I think."

"Fred is not come yet?"

"No. Are you going out again without taking tea, Caleb?" said Mrs Garth, seeing that her absent-minded husband was putting on again the hat which he had just taken off.

"No, no; I'm only going to Mary a minute."

Mary was in a grassy corner of the garden, where there was a swing loftily hung between two pear-trees. She had a pink kerchief tied over her head, making a little poke to shade her eyes from the level sunbeams, while she was giving a glorious swing to Letty, who laughed and screamed wildly.

Seeing her father, Mary left the swing and went to meet him, push-

<hr/>

1. "The heart is saturated with love as with a divine wit which preserves it; hence the undying attachment of those who have loved each other from the dawn of life, and the freshness of old loves which still endure. There is such a thing as the embalmment of the affections. Daphnis and Chloe become Philemon and Baucis. This, then, is old age: a resemblance of evening with the dawn" (*The Man Who Laughed* [1869], Bk. III, Ch. 9).

ing back the pink kerchief and smiling afar off at him with the involuntary smile of loving pleasure.

"I came to look for you, Mary," said Mr Garth. "Let us walk about a bit."

Mary knew quite well that her father had something particular to say: his eyebrows made their pathetic angle, and there was a tender gravity in his voice: these things had been signs to her when she was Letty's age. She put her arm within his, and they turned by the row of nut-trees.

"It will be a sad while before you can be married, Mary," said her father, not looking at her, but at the end of the stick which he held in his other hand.

"Not a sad while, father—I mean to be merry," said Mary, laughingly. "I have been single and merry for four-and-twenty years and more: I suppose it will not be quite as long again as that." Then, after a little pause, she said, more gravely, bending her face before her father's, "If you are contented with Fred?"

Caleb screwed up his mouth and turned his head aside wisely.

"Now, father, you did praise him last Wednesday. You said he had an uncommon notion of stock, and a good eye for things."

"Did I?" said Caleb, rather slyly.

"Yes, I put it all down, and the date, *anno Domini*, and everything," said Mary. "You like things to be neatly booked. And then his behaviour to you, father, is really good; he has a deep respect for you; and it is impossible to have a better temper than Fred has."

"Ay, ay; you want to coax me into thinking him a fine match."

"No, indeed, father. I don't love him because he is a fine match."

"What for, then?"

"Oh, dear, because I have always loved him. I should never like scolding any one else so well; and that is a point to be thought of in a husband."

"Your mind is quite settled, then, Mary?" said Caleb, returning to his first tone. "There's no other wish come into it since things have been going on as they have been of late?" (Caleb meant a great deal in that vague phrase;) "because, better late than never. A woman must not force her heart—she'll do a man no good by that."

"My feelings have not changed, father," said Mary, calmly. "I shall be constant to Fred as long as he is constant to me. I don't think either of us could spare the other, or like any one else better, however much we might admire them. It would make too great a difference to us—like seeing all the old places altered, and changing the name for everything. We must wait for each other a long while; but Fred knows that."

Instead of speaking immediately, Caleb stood still and screwed his stick on the grassy walk. Then he said, with emotion in his voice, "Well, I've got a bit of news. What do you think of Fred going to live at Stone Court, and managing the land there?"

"How can that ever be, father?" said Mary, wonderingly.

"He would manage it for his aunt Bulstrode. The poor woman has been to me begging and praying. She wants to do the lad good, and it might be a fine thing for him. With saving, he might gradually buy the stock, and he has a turn for farming."

"Oh Fred would be so happy? It is too good to believe."

"Ah, but mind you," said Caleb, turning his head warningly, "I

must take it on *my* shoulders, and be responsible, and see after everything ; and that will grieve your mother a bit, though she mayn't say
so. Fred had need be careful."

" Perhaps it is too much, father," said Mary, checked in her joy.
" There would be no happiness in bringing you any fresh trouble."

" Nay, nay ; work is my delight, child, when it doesn't vex your
mother. And then, if you and Fred get married," here Caleb's voice
shook just perceptibly, " he'll be steady and saving ; and you've got
your mother's cleverness, and mine too, in a woman's sort of way ;
and you'll keep him in order. He'll be coming by-and-by, so I
wanted to tell you first, because I think you'd like to tell *him* by
yourselves. After that, I could talk it well over with him, and we
could go into business and the nature of things."

" Oh, you dear good father ! " cried Mary, putting her hands round
her father's neck, while he bent his head placidly, willing to be
caressed. " I wonder if any other girl thinks her father the best man
in the world ! "

" Nonsense, child ; you'll think your husband better."

" Impossible," said Mary, relapsing into her usual tone ; " husbands
are an inferior class of men, who require keeping in order."

When they were entering the house with Letty, who had run to
join them, Mary saw Fred at the orchard-gate, and went to meet him.

" What fine clothes you wear, you extravagant youth ! " said Mary,
as Fred stood still and raised his hat to her with playful formality.
" You are not learning economy."

" Now that is too bad, Mary," said Fred. " Just look at the edges
of these coat-cuffs ! It is only by dint of good brushing that I look
respectable. I am saving up three suits—one for a wedding-suit."

" How very droll you will look !—like a gentleman in an old
fashion-book."

" Oh no, they will keep two years."

" Two years ! be reasonable, Fred," said Mary, turning to walk.
" Don't encourage flattering expectations."

" Why not ? One lives on them better than on unflattering ones.
If we can't be married in two years, the truth will be quite bad
enough when it comes."

" I have heard a story of a young gentleman who once encouraged
flattering expectations, and they did him harm."

" Mary, if you've got something discouraging to tell me, I shall
bolt ; I shall go into the house to Mr Garth. I am out of spirits. My
father is so cut up—home is not like itself. I can't bear any more
bad news."

" Should you call it bad news to be told that you were to live at
Stone Court, and manage the farm, and be remarkably prudent, and
save money every year till all the stock and furniture were your own,
and you were a distinguished agricultural character, as Mr Borthrop
Trumbull says—rather stout, I fear, and with the Greek and Latin
sadly weather-worn ? "

" You don't mean anything except nonsense, Mary ? " said Fred,
colouring slightly nevertheless.

" That is what my father has just told me of as what may happen,
and he never talks nonsense," said Mary, looking up at Fred now,
while he grasped her hand as they walked, till it rather hurt her ;
but she would not complain.

"Oh, I could be a tremendously good fellow then, Mary, and we could be married directly."

"Not so fast, sir; how do you know that I would not rather defer our marriage for some years? That would leave you time to misbehave, and then if I liked some one else better, I should have an excuse for jilting you."

"Pray don't joke, Mary," said Fred, with strong feeling. "Tell me seriously that all this is true, and that you are happy because of it—because you love me best."

"It is all true, Fred, and I am happy because of it—because I love you best," said Mary, in a tone of obedient recitation.

They lingered on the door-step under the steep-roofed porch, and Fred almost in a whisper said,—

"When we were first engaged, with the umbrella-ring, Mary, you used to——"

The spirit of joy began to laugh more decidedly in Mary's eyes, but the fatal Ben came running to the door with Brownie yapping behind him, and, bouncing against them, said—

"Fred and Mary! are you ever coming in?—or may I eat your cake?"

FINALE.

EVERY limit is a beginning as well as an ending. Who can quit young lives after being long in company with them, and not desire to know what befell them in their after-years? For the fragment of a life, however typical, is not the sample of an even web: promises may not be kept, and an ardent outset may be followed by declension; latent powers may find their long-waited opportunity; a past error may urge a grand retrieval.

Marriage, which has been the bourne of so many narratives, is still a great beginning, as it was to Adam and Eve, who kept their honey-moon in Eden, but had their first little one among the thorns and thistles of the wilderness. It is still the beginning of the home epic —the gradual conquest or irremediable loss of that complete union which makes the advancing years a climax, and age the harvest of sweet memories in common.

Some set out, like Crusaders of old, with a glorious equipment of hope and enthusiasm, and get broken by the way, wanting patience with each other and the world.

All who have cared for Fred Vincy and Mary Garth will like to know that these two made no such failure, but achieved a solid mutual happiness. Fred surprised his neighbours in various ways. He became rather distinguished in his side of the county as a theoretic and practical farmer, and produced a work on the 'Cultivation of Green Crops and the Economy of Cattle-Feeding' which won him high congratulations at agricultural meetings. In Middlemarch ad-miration was more reserved: most persons there were inclined to believe that the merit of Fred's authorship was due to his wife, since they had never expected Fred Vincy to write on turnips and mangel-wurzel.

But when Mary wrote a little book for her boys, called 'Stories of Great Men, taken from Plutarch,' and had it printed and published by Gripp & Co., Middlemarch, every one in the town was willing to give the credit of this work to Fred, observing that he had been to the University, "where the ancients were studied," and might have been a clergyman if he had chosen.

In this way it was made clear that Middlemarch had never been deceived, and that there was no need to praise anybody for writing a book, since it was always done by somebody else.

Moreover, Fred remained unswervingly steady. Some years after his marriage he told Mary that his happiness was half owing to Farebrother, who gave him a strong pull-up at the right moment. I cannot say that he was never again misled by his hopefulness : the yield of crops or the profits of a cattle sale usually fell below his estimate ; and he was always prone to believe that he could make money by the purchase of a horse which turned out badly—though this, Mary observed, was of course the fault of the horse, not of Fred's judgment. He kept his love of horsemanship, but he rarely allowed himself a day's hunting ; and when he did so, it was remarkable that he submitted to be laughed at for cowardliness at the fences, seeming to see Mary and the boys sitting on the five-barred gate, or showing their curly heads between hedge and ditch.

There were three boys : Mary was not discontented that she brought forth men-children only ; and when Fred wished to have a girl like her, she said, laughingly, "That would be too great a trial to your mother." Mrs Vincy in her declining years, and in the diminished lustre of her housekeeping, was much comforted by her perception that two at least of Fred's boys were real Vincys, and did not "feature the Garths." But Mary secretly rejoiced that the youngest of the three was very much what her father must have been when he wore a round jacket, and showed a marvellous nicety of aim in playing at marbles, or in throwing stones to bring down the mellow pears.

Ben and Letty Garth, who were uncle and aunt before they were well in their teens, disputed much as to whether nephews or nieces were more desirable ; Ben contending that it was clear girls were good for less than boys, else they would not be always in petticoats, which showed how little they were meant for ; whereupon Letty, who argued much from books, got angry in replying that God made coats of skins for both Adam and Eve alike—also it occurred to her that in the East the men too wore petticoats. But this latter argument, obscuring the majesty of the former, was one too many, for Ben answered contemptuously, "The more spooneys they !" and immediately appealed to his mother whether boys were not better than girls. Mrs Garth pronounced that both were alike naughty, but that boys were undoubtedly stronger, could run faster, and throw with more precision to a greater distance. With this oracular sentence Ben was well satisfied, not minding the naughtiness ; but Letty took it ill, her feeling of superiority being stronger than her muscles.

Fred never became rich—his hopefulness had not led him to expect that ; but he gradually saved enough to become owner of the stock and furniture at Stone Court, and the work which Mr Garth put into his hands carried him in plenty through those "bad times" which are always present with farmers. Mary, in her matronly days, became as solid in figure as her mother ; but, unlike her, gave the boys little formal teaching, so that Mrs Garth was alarmed lest they should never be well grounded in grammar and geography. Nevertheless, they were found quite forward enough when they went to school ; perhaps, because they had liked nothing so well as being with their mother. When Fred was riding home on winter evenings he had a pleasant vision beforehand of the bright hearth in the wainscoated parlour, and was sorry for other men who could not have Mary for their wife ; especially for Mr Farebrother. "He was ten times worthier of you than I was," Fred could now say to her, magnanimously. "To be sure he was," Mary answered ; "and for that reason he could do better without me. But you—I shudder to think what you would have been—a curate in debt for horse-hire and cambric pocket-handkerchiefs !"

On inquiry it might possibly be found that Fred and Mary still inhabit Stone Court—that the creeping plants still cast the foam of their blossoms over the fine stone-wall into the field where the walnut-trees stand in stately row—and that on sunny days the two lovers who were first engaged with the umbrella-ring may be seen in white-haired placidity at the open window from which Mary Garth, in the days of old Peter Featherstone, had often been ordered to look out for Mr Lydgate.

Lydgate's hair never became white. He died when he was only fifty, leaving his wife and children provided for by a heavy insurance on his life. He had gained an excellent practice, alternating, according to the season, between London and a Continental bathing-place ; having written a treatise on Gout, a disease which has a good deal of wealth on its side. His skill was relied on by many paying patients, but he always regarded himself as a failure : he had not done what he once meant to do. His acquaintances thought him enviable to have so charming a wife, and nothing happened to shake their opinion. Rosamond never committed a second compromising indiscretion. She simply continued to be mild in her temper, inflexible in her judgment, disposed to admonish her husband, and able to frustrate him by stratagem. As the years went on he opposed her less and less, whence Rosamond concluded that he had learned the value of her opinion ; on the other hand, she had a more thorough conviction of his talents now that he gained a good income, and instead of the threatened cage in Bride Street provided one all flowers and gilding, fit for the bird of paradise that she resembled. [1] In brief, Lydgate was what is called a successful man. But he died prematurely of diphtheria, and Rosamond afterwards married an elderly and wealthy physician, who took kindly to her four children. She made a very pretty show with her daughters, driving out in her carriage, and often spoke of her happiness as " a reward "—she did not say for what, but probably she meant that it was a reward for her patience with Tertius, whose temper never became faultless, and to the last occasionally let slip a bitter speech which was more memorable than the signs he made of his repentance. He once called her his basil plant ; and when she asked for an explanation, said that basil was a plant which had flourished wonderfully on a murdered man's brains. [2] Rosamond had a placid but strong answer to such speeches. Why then had he chosen her ? It was a pity he had not had Mrs Ladislaw, whom he was always praising and placing above her. And thus the conversation ended with the advantage on Rosamond's side. But it would be unjust not to tell, that she never uttered a word in depreciation of Dorothea, keeping in religious remembrance the generosity which had come to her aid in the sharpest crisis of her life.

Dorothea herself had no dreams of being praised above other women, feeling that there was always something better which she might have

1. An Indonesian bird of the family Paradisaeidae, the male (sic) of which species is noted for its ornate and colorful plumage.
2. In Boccaccio's Decameron, Lisabetta (Isabella) plants the head of her murdered lover in a pot of basil, which flourishes as she waters it with her tears. Keats wrote a poem based on Boccaccio's story, published in 1820.

done, if she had only been better and known better. Still, she never repented that she had given up position and fortune to marry Will Ladislaw, and he would have held it the greatest shame as well as sorrow to him if she had repented. They were bound to each other by a love stronger than any impulses which could have marred it. No life would have been possible to Dorothea which was not filled with emotion, and she had now a life filled also with a beneficent activity which she had not the doubtful pains of discovering and marking out for herself. Will became an ardent public man, working well in those times when reforms were begun with a young hopefulness of immediate good which has been much checked in our days, and getting at last returned to Parliament by a constituency who paid his expenses.[3] Dorothea could have liked nothing better, since wrongs existed, than that her husband should be in the thick of a struggle against them, and that she should give him wifely help. Many who knew her, thought it a pity that so substantive and rare a creature should have been absorbed into the life of another, and be only known in a certain circle as a wife and mother. But no one stated exactly what else that was in her power she ought rather to have done—not even Sir James Chettam, who went no further than the negative prescription that she ought not to have married Will Ladislaw.

But this opinion of his did not cause a lasting alienation; and the way in which the family was made whole again was characteristic of all concerned. Mr Brooke could not resist the pleasure of corresponding with Will and Dorothea; and one morning when his pen had been remarkably fluent on the prospects of Municipal Reform, it ran off into an invitation to the Grange, which, once written, could not be done away with at less cost than the sacrifice (hardly to be conceived) of the whole valuable letter. During the months of this correspondence Mr Brooke had continually, in his talk with Sir James Chettam, been presupposing or hinting that the intention of cutting off the entail was still maintained; and the day on which his pen gave the daring invitation, he went to Freshitt expressly to intimate that he had a stronger sense than ever of the reasons for taking that energetic step as a precaution against any mixture of low blood in the heir of the Brookes.

But that morning something exciting had happened at the Hall. A letter had come to Celia which made her cry silently as she read it; and when Sir James, unused to see her in tears, asked anxiously what was the matter, she burst out in a wail such as he had never heard from her before.

"Dorothea has a little boy. And you will not let me go and see her. And I am sure she wants to see me. And she will not know what to do with the baby—she will do wrong things with it. And they thought she would die. It is very dreadful! Suppose it had been me and little Arthur, and Dodo had been hindered from coming to see me! I wish you would be less unkind, James!"

"Good heavens, Celia!" said Sir James, much wrought upon, "what do you wish? I will do anything you like. I will take you to town to-morrow if you wish it." And Celia did wish it.

It was after this that Mr Brooke came, and meeting the Baronet in

3. Members of Parliament were not regularly paid until 1911.

the grounds, began to chat with him in ignorance of the news, which Sir James for some reason did not care to tell him immediately. But when the entail was touched on in the usual way, he said, "My dear sir, it is not for me to dictate to you, but for my part I would let that alone. I would let things remain as they are."

Mr Brooke felt so much surprise that he did not at once find out how much he was relieved by the sense that he was not expected to do anything in particular.

Such being the bent of Celia's heart, it was inevitable that Sir James should consent to a reconciliation with Dorothea and her husband. Where women love each other, men learn to smother their mutual dislike. Sir James never liked Ladislaw, and Will always preferred to have Sir James's company mixed with another kind : they were on a footing of reciprocal tolerance which was made quite easy only when Dorothea and Celia were present.

It became an understood thing that Mr and Mrs Ladislaw should pay at least two visits during the year to the Grange, and there came gradually a small row of cousins at Freshitt who enjoyed playing with the two cousins visiting Tipton as much as if the blood of these cousins had been less dubiously mixed.

Mr Brooke lived to a good old age, and his estate was inherited by Dorothea's son, who might have represented Middlemarch, but declined, thinking that his opinions had less chance of being stifled if he remained out of doors.

Sir James never ceased to regard Dorothea's second marriage as a mistake ; and indeed this remained the tradition concerning it in Middlemarch, where she was spoken of to a younger generation as a fine girl who married a sickly clergyman, old enough to be her father, and in little more than a year after his death gave up her estate to marry his cousin—young enough to have been his son, with no property, and not well-born. Those who had not seen anything of Dorothea usually observed that she could not have been "a nice woman," else she would not have married either the one or the other.

Certainly those determining acts of her life were not ideally beautiful. They were the mixed result of young and noble impulse struggling amidst the conditions of an imperfect social state, in which great feelings will often take the aspect of error, and great faith the aspect of illusion. [4] For there is no creature whose inward being is so strong that it is not greatly determined by what lies outside it. A new Theresa will hardly have the opportunity of reforming a conventual life, any more than a new Antigone will spend her heroic piety in daring all for the sake of a brother's burial : the medium in which their ardent deeds took shape is for ever gone. But we insig-

---

4. The first edition reads: "They were the mixed result of young and noble impulse struggling under prosaic conditions. Among the many remarks passed on her mistakes, it was never said in the neighbourhood of Middlemarch that such mistakes could not have happened if the society into which she was born had not smiled on propositions of marriage from a sickly man to a girl less than half his own age—on modes of education which make a woman's knowledge another name for motley ignorance—on rules of conduct which are in flat contradiction with its own loudly-asserted beliefs. While this is the social air in which mortals begin to breathe, there will be collisions such as those in Dorothea's life, where great feelings will take the aspect of error, and great faith the aspect of illusion."

nificant people with our daily words and acts are preparing the lives of many Dorotheas, some of which may present a far sadder sacrifice than that of the Dorothea whose story we know.

Her finely-touched spirit had still its fine issues, though they were not widely visible. Her full nature, like that river of which Cyrus broke the strength, spent itself in channels which had no great name on the earth.[5] But the effect of her being on those around her was incalculably diffusive : for the growing good of the world is partly dependent on unhistoric acts ; and that things are not so ill with you and me as they might have been, is half owing to the number who lived faithfully a hidden life, and rest in unvisited tombs.

5. Cyrus the Great of Persia. In the first edition this reads "Alexander."

Backgrounds

GEORGE ELIOT

Letter to Sara Sophia Hennell†

Foleshill, 9 October 1843

* * * The first impulse of a young and ingenuous mind is to withhold the slightest sanction from all that contains even a mixture of supposed error. When the soul is just liberated from the wretched giant's bed of dogmas on which it has been racked and stretched ever since it began to think there is a feeling of exultation and strong hope. We think we shall run well when we have the full use of our limbs and the bracing air of independence, and we believe that we shall soon obtain something positive which will not only more than compensate to us for what we have renounced, but will be so well worth offering to others that we may venture to proselyte as fast as our zeal for truth may prompt us. But a year or two of reflection and the experience of our own miserable weakness which will ill afford to part even with the crutches of superstition must, I think, effect a change. Speculative truth begins to appear but a shadow of individual minds, agreement between intellects seems unattainable, and we turn to the *truth of feeling* as the only universal bond of union. We find that the intellectual errors which we once fancied were a mere incrustation have grown into the living body and that we cannot in the majority of causes, wrench them away without destroying vitality. We begin to find that with individuals, as with nations, the only safe revolution is one arising out of the wants which their *own progress* has generated. It is the quackery of infidelity to suppose that it has a nostrum for all mankind, and to say to all and singular, 'Swallow my opinions and you shall be whole.'

If then we are debarred by such considerations from trying to reorganize opinions, are we to remain aloof from our fellow-creatures on occasions when we may fully sympathize with the feelings exercised, although our own have been melted into another mould? Ought we not on every opportunity to seek to have our feelings in harmony though not in union with those who are often richer in the fruits of faith though not in reasons, than ourselves? The results of nonconformity in a family are just an epitome of what happens on a larger scale in the world. An influential member chooses to omit an observance which in the minds of all the rest is associated with what

† From *The George Eliot Letters*, 7 vols., edited by Gordon S. Haight (New Haven: Yale University Press, 1954–55), I:162–63. Reprinted by permission of Yale University Press. Sara Sophia Hennell (1812–99) was for many years GE's most constant correspondent. They first met in 1842.

is highest and most venerable. He cannot make his reasons intelligible, and so his conduct is regarded as a relaxation of the hold that moral ties had on him previously. The rest are infected with the disease they imagine in him; all the screws by which order was maintained are loosened, and in more than one case a person's happiness may be ruined by the confusion of ideas which took the form of principles.

But it may be said how are we to do anything toward the advancement of mankind? Are we to go on cherishing superstitions out of a fear that seems inconsistent with any faith in a Supreme Being? I think the best and the only way of fulfilling our mission is to sow good seed in good i.e. prepared ground, and not to root up tares where we must inevitably gather all the wheat with them. We cannot fight and struggle enough for freedom of enquiry and we need not be idle in imparting all that is pure and lovely to children whose minds are unbespoken. Those who can write, let them do it as boldly as they like, and let no one hesitate at proper seasons to make a full *con*fession (far better than *pro*fession). St. Paul's reasoning about the conduct of the strong toward the weak in the 14 and 15 chapters of Romans, is just in point.[1] But I have not said half what I meant to say. There are so many aspects in which the subject might be presented that it is useless to attempt to exhaust it. I fear I have written very unintelligibly, for it is rather late and I am so cold that my thoughts are almost frozen.

Your affectionate
Mary Ann Evans.

GEORGE ELIOT

The Natural History of German Life†

* * *

* * * The greatest benefit we owe to the artist, whether painter, poet, or novelist, is the extension of our sympathies. Appeals founded on generalizations and statistics require a sympathy ready-made, a moral sentiment already in activity; but a picture of human life such as a great artist can give, surprises even the trivial and the selfish into that attention to what is apart from themselves, which

---

1. The argument of these chapters is that the strong must bear with the weak: "Let us not therefore judge one another any more. . . . We then that are strong ought to bear the infirmities of the weak. . . ."

† Reprinted from *The Westminster Review* LXVI (July 1856), 28–44. In this essay GE argues for a definition of morality in terms of human sympathy, and asserts then the necessity of morality in art.

may be called the raw material of moral sentiment. * * * Art is the nearest thing to life; it is a mode of amplifying experience and extending our contact with our fellow men beyond the bounds of our personal lot. All the more sacred is the task of the artist when he undertakes to paint the life of the People. Falsification here is far more pernicious than in the more artificial aspects of life. It is not so very serious that we should have false ideas about evanescent fashions—about the manners and conversation of beaux and duchesses; but it *is* serious that our sympathy with the perennial joys and struggles, the toil, the tragedy, and the humour in the life of our more heavily-laden fellow-men, should be perverted, and turned towards a false object instead of the true one.

This perversion is not the less fatal because the misrepresentation which give rise to it has what the artist considers a moral end. The thing for mankind to know is, not what are the motives and influences which the moralist thinks *ought* to act on the labourer or the artisan, but what are the motives and influences which *do* act on him. We want to be taught to feel, not for the heroic artisan or the sentimental peasant, but for the peasant in all his coarse apathy, and the artisan in all his suspicious selfishness.

* * *

If we need a true conception of the popular character to guide our sympathies rightly, we need it equally to check our theories, and direct us in their application. The tendency created by the splendid conquests of modern generalization, to believe that all social questions are merged in economical science, and that the relations of men to their neighbours may be settled by algebraic equations,—the dream that the uncultured classes are prepared for a condition which appeals principally to their moral sensibilities,—the aristocratic dilettantism which attempts to restore the "good old times" by a sort of idyllic masquerading, and to grow feudal fidelity and veneration as we grow prize turnips, by an artificial system of culture,—none of these diverging mistakes can co-exist with a real knowledge of the People, with a thorough study of their habits, their ideas, their motives. The landholder, the clergyman, the mill-owner, the mining-agent, have each an opportunity for making precious observations on different sections of the working-classes, but unfortunately their experience is too often not registered at all, or its results are too scattered to be available as a source of information and stimulus to the public mind generally. If any man of sufficient moral and intellectual breadth, whose observations would not be vitiated by a foregone conclusion, or by a professional point of view, would devote himself to studying the natural history of our social classes, especially of the small shopkeepers, artisans, and peasantry,—the degree in which they are influenced by local conditions, their maxims and habits, the points of view from which they regard their religious teachers, and the degree in which they are influenced by religious doctrines, the interaction of the various classes on each other, and what are the tendencies in their position towards disintegration or towards development,—and if, after all this study, he would give us the result of his observations in a book well nourished with specific facts, his work would be a valuable aid to the social and political reformer.

* * *

GEORGE ELIOT

Amos Barton†

Chapter V

The Rev. Amos Barton, whose sad fortunes I have undertaken to relate, was, you perceive, in no respect an ideal or exceptional character; and perhaps I am doing a bold thing to bespeak your sympathy on behalf of a man who was so very far from remarkable, —a man whose virtues were not heroic, and who had no undetected crime within his breast; who had not the slightest mystery hanging about him, but was palpably and unmistakably commonplace; who was not even in love, but had had that complaint favourably many years ago. "An utterly uninteresting character!" I think I hear a lady reader exclaim—Mrs Farthingale, for example, who prefers the ideal in fiction; to whom tragedy means ermine tippets, adultery, and murder; and comedy, the adventures of some personage who is quite a "character."

But, my dear madam, it is so very large a majority of your fellow-countrymen that are of this insignificant stamp. At least eighty out of a hundred of your adult male fellow-Britons returned in the last census are neither extraordinarily silly, nor extraordinarily wicked, nor extraordinarily wise; their eyes are neither deep and liquid with sentiment, nor sparkling with suppressed witticisms; they have probably had no hairbreadth escapes or thrilling adventures; their brains are certainly not pregnant with genius, and their passsions have not manifested themselves at all after the fashion of a volcano. They are simply men of complexions more or less muddy, whose conversation is more or less bald and disjointed. Yet these common-place people—many of them—bear a conscience, and have felt the sublime prompting to do the painful right; they have their unspoken sorrows, and their sacred joys; their hearts have perhaps gone out

---

† From *Scenes of Clerical Life* (1858), GE's first published fiction; the text here reproduced is that of the Cabinet Edition (1878).

towards their first-born, and they have mourned over the irreclaim-able dead. Nay, is there not a pathos in their very insignificance—in our comparison of their dim and narrow existence with the glorious possibilities of that human nature which they share?

Depend upon it, you would gain unspeakably if you would learn with me to see some of the poetry and the pathos, the tragedy and the comedy, lying in the experience of a human soul that looks out through dull grey eyes, and that speaks in a voice of quite ordinary tones. In that case, I should have no fear of your not caring to know what farther befell the Rev. Amos Barton, or of your thinking the homely details I have to tell at all beneath your attention. As it is, you can, if you please, decline to pursue my story farther; and you will easily find reading more to your taste, since I learn from the news-papers that many remarkable novels, full of striking situations, thrilling incidents, and eloquent writing, have appeared only within the last season.

* * *

GEORGE ELIOT

Journal, Richmond, 30 November 1858†

History of "Adam Bede"

The germ of "Adam Bede" was an anecdote told me by my Methodist Aunt Samuel (the wife of my Father's younger brother): an anecdote from her own experience. We were sitting together one afternoon during her visit to me at Griffe, probably in 1839 or 40, when it occurred to her to tell me how she had visited a condemned criminal, a very ignorant girl who had murdered her child and refused to confess—how she had stayed with her praying, through the night and how the poor creature at last broke out into tears, and confessed her crime. My Aunt afterwards went with her in the cart to the place of execution, and she described to me the great respect with which this ministry of hers was regarded by the official people about the gaol. The story, told by my aunt with great feeling, affected me deeply, and I never lost the impression of that afternoon and our talk together; but I believe I never mentioned it, through all the intervening years, till something prompted me to tell it to George[1] in December 1856, when I had begun to write the

† Reprinted from J. W. Cross, *George Eliot's Life as Related in Her Letters and Journals* (Edinburgh and New York: 1885), II:65–71.
1. George Henry Lewes (1817–78), dis-tinguished English critic and writer in many fields; he and GE first met in 1851, and lived together from 1854 until his death.

"Scenes of Clerical Life." He remarked that the scene in the prison would make a fine element in a story, and I afterwards began to think of blending this and some other recollections of my aunt in one story with some points in my father's early life and character. The problem of construction that remained was to make the unhappy girl one of the chief *dramatis personæ* and connect her with the hero. At first I thought of making the story one of the series of "Scenes," but afterwards, when several motives had induced me to close these with "Janet's Repentance," I determined on making what we always called in our conversations "My Aunt's Story," the subject of a long novel: which I accordingly began to write on the 22d October 1857.

* * *

The first volume [of *Adam Bede*] was written at Richmond and given to Blackwood[2] in March. He expressed great admiration of its freshness and vividness, but seemed to hesitate about putting it in the Magazine, which was the form of publication he, as well as myself, had previously contemplated. He still *wished* to have it for the Mag., but desired to know the course of the story; at *present*, he saw nothing to prevent its reception in Maga, but he would like to see more. I am uncertain whether his doubts rested solely on Hetty's relation to Arthur, or whether they were also dirceted towards the treatment of Methodism by the Church. I refused to tell my story beforehand, on the ground that I would not have it judged apart from my *treatment*, which alone determines the moral quality of art; and ultimately I proposed that the notion of publication in Maga should be given up, and that the novel should be published in three volumes, at Christmas, if possible. He assented.

* * *

GEORGE ELIOT

Adam Bede†

Chapter XVII

IN WHICH THE STORY PAUSES A LITTLE

"This Rector of Broxton is little better than a pagan!" I hear one of my readers exclaim. "How much more edifying it would have

---

2. John Blackwood (1818–79), son of William Blackwood the publisher, of Edinburgh. All GE's novels except *Romola* were published by Blackwood. John Blackwood was her fervent correspondent.

† *Adam Bede* was GE's first novel, published in 1859. The text here reproduced is that of the Cabinet Edition (1878–79).

been if you had made him give Arthur some truly spiritual advice!
You might have put into his mouth the most beautiful things—
quite as good as reading a sermon."

Certainly I could, if I held it the highest vocation of the novelist
to represent things as they never have been and never will be. Then,
of course, I might refashion life and character entirely after my own
liking; I might select the most unexceptionable type of clergyman,
and put my own admirable opinions into his mouth on all occasions. But it happens, on the contrary, that my strongest effort is to
avoid any such arbitrary picture, and to give a faithful account of
men and things as they have mirrored themselves in my mind. The
mirror is doubtless defective; the outlines will sometimes be disturbed, the reflection faint or confused; but I feel as much bound to
tell you as precisely as I can what that reflection is, as if I were in
the witness-box narrating my experience on oath.

Sixty years ago—it is a long time, so no wonder things have
changed—all clergymen were not zealous; indeed there is reason to
believe that the number of zealous clergymen was small, and it is
probable that if one among the small minority had owned the liv-
ings of Broxton and Hayslope in the year 1799, you would have
liked him no better than you like Mr Irwine. Ten to one, you
would have thought him a tasteless, indiscreet, methodistical man.
It is so very rarely that facts hit that nice medium required by our
own enlightened opinions and refined taste! Perhaps you will say,
"Do improve the facts a little, then; make them more accordant
with those correct views which it is our privilege to possess. The
world is not just what we like; do touch it up with a tasteful pencil,
and make believe it is not quite such a mixed entangled affair. Let
all people who hold unexceptionable opinions act unexceptionably.
Let your most faulty characters always be on the wrong side, and
your virtuous ones on the right. Then we shall see at a glance whom
we are to condemn, and whom we are to approve. Then we shall be
able to admire, without the slightest disturbance of our prepossess-
sions: we shall hate and despise with that true ruminant relish
which belongs to undoubting confidence."

But, my good friend, what will you do then with your fellow-
parishioner who opposes your husband in the vestry?—with your
newly-appointed vicar, whose style of preaching you find painfully
below that of his regretted predecessor?—with the honest servant
who worries your soul with her one failing?—with your neighbour,
Mrs Green, who was really kind to you in your last illness, but has
said several ill-natured things about you since your convalescence?
—nay, with your excellent husband himself, who has other irritating habits besides that of not wiping his shoes? These fellow-mortals,
every one, must be accepted as they are: you can neither

straighten their noses, nor brighten their wit, nor rectify their dispositions; and it is these people—amongst whom your life is passed—that it is needful you should tolerate, pity, and love: it is these more or less ugly, stupid, inconsistent people, whose movements of goodness you should be able to admire—for whom you should cherish all possible hopes, all possible patience. And I would not, even if I had the choice, be the clever novelist who could create a world so much better than this, in which we get up in the morning to do our daily work, that you would be likely to turn a harder, colder eye on the dusty streets and the common green fields—on the real breathing men and women, who can be chilled by your indifference or injured by your prejudice; who can be cheered and helped onward by your fellow-feeling, your forbearance, your outspoken, brave justice.

So I am content to tell my simple story, without trying to make things seem better than they were; dreading nothing, indeed, but falsity, which, in spite of one's best efforts, there is reason to dread. Falsehood is so easy, truth so difficult. The pencil is conscious of a delightful facility in drawing a griffin—the longer the claws, and the larger the wings, the better; but that marvellous facility which we mistook for genius is apt to forsake us when we want to draw a real unexaggerated lion. Examine your words well, and you will find that even when you have no motive to be false, it is a very hard thing to say the exact truth, even about your own immediate feelings—much harder than to say something fine about them which is *not* the exact truth.

It is for this rare, precious quality of truthfulness that I delight in many Dutch paintings, which lofty-minded people despise. I find a source of delicious sympathy in these faithful pictures of a monotonous homely existence, which has been the fate of so many more among my fellow-mortals than a life of pomp or of absolute indigence, of tragic suffering or of world-stirring actions. I turn, without shrinking, from cloud-borne angels, from prophets, sibyls, and heroic warriors, to an old woman bending over her flower-pot, or eating her solitary dinner, while the noonday light, softened, perhaps by a screen of leaves, falls on her mob-cap, and just touches the rim of her spinning-wheel, and her stone jug, and all those cheap common things which are the precious necessaries of life to her;—or I turn to that village wedding, kept between four brown walls, where an awkward bridegroom opens the dance with a high-shouldered, broad-faced bride, while elderly and middle-aged friends look on, with very irregular noses and lips, and probably with quart-pots in their hands, but with an expression of unmistakable contentment and goodwill. "Foh!" says my idealistic friend, "what vulgar details! What good is there in taking all these pains to give an exact likeness of old women and clowns? What a low phase of life!—what clumsy, ugly people!"

But bless us, things may be lovable that are not altogether handsome, I hope? I am not at all sure that the majority of the human race have not been ugly, and even among those "lords of their kind," the British, squat figures, ill-shapen nostrils, and dingy complexions are not startling exceptions. Yet there is a great deal of family love amongst us. I have a friend or two whose class of features is such that the Apollo curl on the summit of their brows would be decidedly trying; yet to my certain knowledge tender hearts have beaten for them, and their miniatures—flattering, but still not lovely—are kissed in secret by motherly lips. I have seen many an excellent matron, who could never in her best days have been handsome, and yet she had a packet of yellow love-letters in a private drawer, and sweet children showered kisses on her sallow cheeks. And I believe there have been plenty of young heroes, of middle stature and feeble beards, who have felt quite sure they could never love anything more insignificant than a Diana, and yet have found themselves in middle life happily settled with a wife who waddles. Yes! thank God; human feeling is like the mighty rivers that bless the earth: it does not wait for beauty—it flows with resistless force and brings beauty with it.

All honour and reverence to the divine beauty of form! Let us cultivate it to the utmost in men, women, and children—in our gardens and in our houses. But let us love that other beauty too, which lies in no secret of proportion, but in the secret of deep human sympathy. Paint us an angel, if you can, with a floating violet robe, and a face paled by the celestial light; paint us yet oftener a Madonna, turning her mild face upward and opening her arms to welcome the divine glory; but do not impose on us any æsthetic rules which shall banish from the region of Art those old women scraping carrots with their work-worn hands, those heavy clowns taking holiday in a dingy pot-house, those rounded backs and stupid weather-beaten faces that have bent over the spade and done the rough work of the world—those homes with their tin pans, their brown pitchers, their rough curs, and their clusters of onions. In this world there are so many of these common coarse people, who have no picturesque sentimental wretchedness! It is so needful we should remember their existence, else we may happen to leave them quite out of our religion and philosophy, and frame lofty theories which only fit a world of extremes. Therefore let Art always remind us of them; therefore let us always have men ready to give the loving pains of a life to the faithful representing of commonplace things—men who see beauty in these commonplace things, and delight in showing how kindly the light of heaven falls on them. There are few prophets in the world; few sublimely beautiful women; few heroes. I can't afford to give all my love and reverence to such rarities: I want a great deal of those feelings for my every-day fellow-men, especially for the few in the foreground of the great multitude, whose faces I know, whose hands I touch, for whom I have to make way with kindly courtesy. Neither are picturesque lazzaroni or romantic criminals half so frequent as your common labourer, who gets his own bread, and eats it vulgarly but creditably with his own pocket-knife. It is more needful that I should have a fibre of sympathy connecting me with that vulgar citizen who weighs out my sugar in a vilely-assorted cravat and waistcoat, than with the handsomest rascal in red scarf and green feathers;—more needful that my heart should swell with loving admiration at some trait of gentle goodness in the faulty people who sit at the same hearth with me, or in the clergyman of my own parish, who is perhaps rather too corpulent, and in other respects is not an Oberlin or a Tillotson, than at the deeds of heroes whom I shall never know except by hearsay, or at the sublimest abstract of all clerical graces that was ever conceived by an able novelist.

* * *

GEORGE ELIOT

Letter to Charles Bray†

Wandsworth, 5 July 1859

Dear Friend * * *

I can't tell you how much melancholy it causes me that people are, for the most part, so incapable of comprehending the state of mind which cares for that which is essentially human in all forms of belief, and desires to exhibit it under all forms with loving truthfulness. Free-thinkers are scarcely wider than the orthodox in this matter—they all want to see themselves and their own opinions held up as the true and the lovely. On the same ground that an idle woman with flirtations and flounces likes to read a French novel because she can imagine herself the heroine, grave people, with opinions, like the most admirable character in a novel to be their mouth-piece. If Art does not enlarge men's sympathies, it does nothing morally.

† From *The George Eliot Letters*, 7 vols., edited by Gordon S. Haight (New Haven: Yale University Press, 1954–55), III:110–11. Reprinted by permission of Yale University Press. Charles Bray (1811–84) married Caroline Hennell in 1836; in 1841 they first met GE, and both became close friends of hers. Bray was a rationalist much influenced in his youth by Jeremy Bentham and Jonathan Edwards.

I have had heart-cutting experience that opinions are a poor cement between human souls; and the only effect I ardently long to produce by my writings, is that those who read them should be better able to *imagine* and to *feel* the pains and the joys of those who differ from themselves in everything but the broad fact of being struggling erring human creatures.

Yours ever

G. E.

GEORGE ELIOT

Letter to Mme. Eugène Bodichon†

London, 26 December 1860

My dear Barbara

Your letter came this evening and if I were a journalist, I should say that I "hailed it with delight."

* * *

The bright point in your letter is, that you are in a happy state of mind yourself. For the rest,[1] we must wait, and not be impatient with those who have their inward trials though everything outward seems to smile on them. It seems to those who are differently placed that the time of freedom from strong ties and urgent claims must be very precious for the ends of self-culture, and good, helpful work towards the world at large. But it hardly ever is so.— As for the "forms and ceremonies," I feel no regret that any should turn to them for comfort, if they can find comfort in them: sympathetically, I enjoy them myself. But I have faith in the working-out of higher possibilities than the Catholic or any other church has presented, and those who have strength to wait and endure, are bound to accept no formula which their whole souls—their intellect as well as their emotions—do not embrace with entire reverence. The highest "calling and election" is to *do without opium* and live through all our pain with conscious, clear-eyed endurance.

* * *

God bless you, Think often of your affectionate Friend.

M. E. Lewes.

* * *

† From *The George Eliot Letters*, 7 vols., edited by Gordon S. Haight (New Haven: Yale University Press, 1954–55), III:365–67. Reprinted by permission of Yale University Press. Barbara Smith Bodichon (1827–91) first met GE in 1852. Like her cousin Florence Nightingale, she was a champion of unpopular causes, including GE's liaison with Lewes.
1. "The rest" is concerned with GE's connection with G. H. Lewes, with whom she lived from 1854 until his death in 1878.

GEORGE ELIOT

Letter to Mme. Eugène Bodichon†

London, 15 February 1862

My dear Barbara

If Miss Allen had not given me good news about you, I should have been urged to write and ask you for a letter; but I think it is a reasonable law that the one who takes wing should be the first to write—not the bird that stays in the old cage and may be supposed to be eating the usual seed and groundsel, and looking at the same slice of the world through the same wires. Miss Allen, however, kept back the sad part of the news—poor Ellen's illness, which I would rather have known; for in this as in all other cases, I think the highest and best thing is rather to suffer with real suffering than to be happy in the imagination of an unreal good. I would rather know that the beings I love are in some trouble and suffer because of it, even though I can't help them, than be fancying them happy when they are not so, and making myself comfortable on the strength of that false belief. And so I am impatient of all ignorance and concealment: I don't say, "that is wise" but simply "that is my nature." I can enter into what you have felt about Ellen, for serious illness, such as seems to bring death near makes one feel the simple human brother and sisterhood so strongly that those we were apt to think almost indifferent to us before, touch the very quick of our hearts. I suppose if one happened only to hold the hand of a hospital patient when she was dying, her face and all the memories along with it, would seem to lie deeper in our experience than all we knew of many old friends and blood relations.

* * *

† From *The George Eliot Letters*, 7 vols., edited by Gordon S. Haight (New Haven: Yale University Press, 1954–55), IV:12– 13. Reprinted by permission of Yale University Press.

GEORGE ELIOT

Letter to Frederic Harrison†

London, 15 August [1866]

My dear Mr. Harrison * * *

That is a tremendously difficult problem which you have laid before me,[1] and I think you see its difficulties, though they can hardly press upon you as they do on me, who have gone through again and again the severe effort of trying to make certain ideas thoroughly incarnate, as if they had revealed themselves to me first in the flesh and not in the spirit. I think æsthetic teaching is the highest of all teaching because it deals with life in its highest complexity. But if it ceases to be purely æsthetic—if it lapses anywhere from the picture to the diagram—it becomes the most offensive of all teaching. Avowed Utopias are not offensive, because they are understood to have a scientific and expository character: they do not pretend to work on the emotions, or couldn't do it if they did pretend. I am sure, from your own statement, that you see this quite clearly. Well then, consider the sort of agonizing labour to an English-fed imagination to make art a sufficiently real back-ground, for the desired picture, to get breathing, individual forms, and group them in the needful relations, so that the presentation will lay hold on the emotions as human experience—will, as you say, "flash" conviction on the world by means of aroused sympathy.

I took unspeakable pains in preparing to write Romola—neglecting nothing I could find that would help me to what I may call the "Idiom" of Florence, in the largest sense one could stretch the word to. And there I was only trying to give *some* out of the normal relations. I felt that the necessary idealization could only be attained by adopting the clothing of the past. And again, it is my way, (rather too much so perhaps) to <teach>[2] urge the human sanctities through tragedy—through pity and terror as well as admiration and delights.

I only say all this to show the tenfold arduousness of such a work as the one your problem demands. On the other hand, my whole

† From *The George Eliot Letters*, 7 vols., edited by Gordon S. Haight (New Haven: Yale University Press, 1954–55), IV: 300–301. Reprinted by permission of Yale University Press.
1. Harrison, a Positivist, had proposed to GE that her "destiny" was to write a great poetic drama depicting the achievement of the ideal Comtean society. "What the world yet wants to be shown," he wrote, "is the possibility in real life of healthy moral control over societies— and the infinite scope and power of wealth used morally" (*The George Eliot Letters*, IV: 284–89).
2. Word crossed out in manuscript.

soul goes with your desire that it should be done, and I shall at least keep the great possibility (or impossibility) perpetually in my mind, as something towards which I must strive, though it may be that I can do so only in a fragmentary way.

GEORGE ELIOT

Letter to Clifford Allbutt†

London [*August* 1868]

My dear Dr. Allbutt * * *

Since you refer to our conversation, I must tell you that I am always a little uneasy about my share in the talk when it has turned on religion. The weaknesses of one's mind are always taken by surprise in hasty discussion, and the chief result left in the consciousness is that of having misrepresented the dearest beliefs. My books are a form of utterance that dissatisfies me less, because they are deliberately, carefully constructed on a basis which even in my doubting mind is never shaken by a doubt, and they are not determined, as conversation inevitably is, by considerations of momentary expediency. The basis I mean is my conviction as to the relative goodness and nobleness of human dispositions and motives. And the inspiring principle which alone gives me courage to write is, that of so presenting our human life as to help my readers in getting a clearer conception and a more active admiration of those vital elements which bind men together and give a higher worthiness to their existence; and also to help them in gradually dissociating these elements from the more transient forms on which an outworn teaching tends to make them dependent.

But, since you have read my books, you must perceive that the bent of my mind is conservative rather than destructive, and that denial has been wrung from me by hard experience—not adopted as a pleasant rebellion. Still, I see clearly that we ought, each of us, not to sit down and wail, but to be heroic and constructive, if possible, like the strong souls who lived before, as in other cases [eras?] of religious decay.

I dare not enter on these wide, wide subjects in a letter—for to write a letter at all, except about necessary details, is a difficult overcoming of indolence to me; but in relation to your despairing

† Reprinted from O. Browning, *Life of George Eliot* (London: Scott, 1890), pp. 118–20. Thomas Clifford Allbutt (1836– 1925) began his acquaintance with GHL at Oxford in July 1868.

words that we seem to 'be reaching the limits of our scheme,' I wish you could thoroughly consider (if you have not already done so) whether it is probable that in a stage of society in which the ordinary standard of moral possibility, nay, of moral requirements, is still so low as I think you must recognize it to be, the highest possible religion has been evolved and accepted?

* * *

GEORGE ELIOT

Notes on Form in Art†

* * *

Form, then, as distinguished from merely massive impression, must first depend on the discrimination of wholes & then on the discrimination of parts. Fundamentally, form is unlikeness, as is seen in the philosophic use of the word Form in distinction from Matter; & in consistency with this fundamental meaning, every difference is form. Thus, sweetness is a form of sensibility, rage is a form of passion, green is a form both of light & of sensibility. But with this fundamental discrimination is born in necessary antithesis the sense of wholeness or unbroken connexion in space & time: a flash of light is a whole compared with the darkness which precedes & follows it; the taste of sourness is a whole & includes parts or degrees as it subsides. And as knowledge continues to grow by its alternating processes of distinction & combination, seeing smaller & smaller unlikenesses & grouping or associating these under a common likeness, it arrives at the conception of wholes composed of parts more & more multiplied & highly differenced, yet more & more absolutely bound together by various conditions of common likeness or mutual dependence. And the fullest example of such a whole is the highest example of Form: in other words, the relation of multiplex interdependent parts to a whole which is itself in the most varied & therefore the fullest relation to other wholes. Thus, the human organism comprises things as diverse as the finger-nails & tooth-ache, as the nervous stimulus of muscle manifested in a shout, & the discernment of a red spot on a field of snow; but all its different elements or parts of experience are bound together in a more necessary wholeness or more inseparable group of common conditions than can be found in any other existence known to us. The highest Form, then, is the highest organism, that is to say, the

† This essay, written in 1868, was first published in *Essays of George Eliot*, edited by Thomas Pinney (London: 1963); reprinted by permission of Thomas Pinney and the Beinecke Rare Book and Manuscript Library, Yale University.

most varied group of relations bound together in a wholeness which again has the most varied relations with all other phenomena.

It is only in this fundamental sense that the word Form can be applied to Art in general. Boundary or outline & visual appearance are modes of form which in music & poetry can only have a metaphorical presence. Even in the plastic arts form obviously, in its general application, means something else than mere imitation of outline, more or less correctness of drawing or modelling—just as, with reference to descriptive poetry it means something more than the bare delineation of landscape or figures. Even those who use the phrase with a very dim understanding, always have a sense that it refers to structure or composition, that is, to the impression from a work considered as a whole. And what is a structure but a set of relations selected & combined in accordance with the sequence of mental states in the constructor, or with the preconception of a whole which he has inwardly evolved? Artistic form, as distinguished from mere imitation, begins in sculpture & painting with composition or the selection of attitudes & the formation of groups, let the objects be of what order they may. In music it begins with the adjustment of tones & rhythm to a climax, apart from any direct imitation. But my concern is here chiefly with poetry which I take in its wider sense as including all literary production of which it is the prerogative & not the reproach that the choice & sequence of images & ideas—that is, of relations & groups of relations—are more or less not only determined by emotion but intended to express it. I say more or less; for even the ravings of madness include multitudinous groups & sequences which are parts of common experience; & in the range of poetry we see wide distances of degree in the combination of emotive force with sequences that are not arbitrary & individual but true & universal, just as the guiding emotion varies from an idiosyncracy only short of madness to a profoundly human passion which is or must come to be the heritage of all mankind. Sometimes the wider signification of poetry is taken to be fiction or invention as opposed to ascertained external fact or discovery. But what is fiction other than an arrangement of events or feigned correspondences according to predominant feeling? We find what destiny pleases; we make what pleases us—or what we think will please others.

Even taken in its derivative meaning of outline, what is form but the limit of that difference by which we discriminate one object from another?—a limit determined partly by the intrinsic relations or composition of the object, & partly by the extrinsic action of other bodies upon it. This is true whether the object is a rock or a man; but in the case of the inorganic body, outline is the result of a nearly equal struggle between inner constitution & the outer play of forces; while in the human organism the outline is mainly determined by the intrinsic relation of its parts, & what is called fitness, beauty or harmony in its outline & movements is dependent on the inward balance. The muscular strength which hurls, the muscular grace which gives a rhythmic movement to half a dozen balls, show a moving outline of which the chief factors are relations within the body; but the line with which a rock cuts the sky, or the shape of a boulder, may be more due to outer forces than to inner constitution. In ordinary language, the form of a stone is accidental. But the true expression of the difference is, that the wholeness of the stone depends simply on likeness of crystallization & is merely a wholeness of mass which may be broken up into other wholes; whereas the outline defining the wholeness of the human body is due to a consensus or constant interchange of effects among its parts. It is wholeness not merely of mass but of strict & manifold dependence. The word consensus expresses that fact in a complex organism by which no part can suffer increase or diminution without a participation of all other parts in the effect produced & a consequent modification of the organism as a whole.

By this light, forms of art can be called higher or lower only on the same principle as that on which we apply these words to organisms; viz. in proportion to the complexity of the parts bound up into one indissoluble whole. In Poetry—which has this superiority over all the other arts, that its medium, language, is the least imitative, & is in the most complex relation with what it expresses— Form begins in the choice of rhythms & images as signs of a mental state, for this is a process of grouping or association of a less spontaneous & more conscious order than the grouping or association which constitutes the very growth & natural history of mind. *Poetry* begins when passion weds thought by finding expression in an image; but *poetic form* begins with a choice of elements, however meagre, as the accordant expression of emotional states. The most monotonous burthen chanted by an Arab boatman on the Nile is still a beginning of poetic form.

Poetic Form was not begotten by thinking it out or framing it as a shell which should hold emotional expression, any more than the shell of an animal arises before the living creature; but emotion, by its tendency to repetition, i.e. rhythmic persistence in proportion as diversifying thought is absent, creates a form by the recurrence of its elements in adjustment with certain given conditions of sound, language, action, or environment. Just as the beautiful expanding curves of a bivalve shell are not first made for the reception of the unstable inhabitant, but grow & are limited by the simple rhythmic conditions of its growing life.

* * *

GEORGE ELIOT

Journal, London, 1 January 1869†

A bright frosty morning! And we are both well. The servants are going to have their little treat, and we are going to see Mr. and Mrs. Burne Jones and carry a Book for their little boy. I have set myself many tasks for the year—I wonder how many will be accomplished?—A Novel called Middlemarch, a long poem on Timoleon, and several minor poems.

GEORGE HENRY LEWES

Letter to John Blackwood††

Shottermill, 7 May 1871

My dear Blackwood

Here we are quietly settled for the summer and I hope you will be able to run down and see us (station Haslemere) some day and get out of the vortex of London.

Meanwhile here is something for you to turn over in your mind, and come prepared to discuss. Mrs. Lewes finds that she will require 4 volumes for her story, not 3. I winced at the idea at first, but the story must not be spoiled for want of space, and as you have more than once spoken of the desirability of inventing some mode of circumventing the Libraries and making the public *buy* instead of borrowing I have devised the following scheme, suggested by the plan Victor Hugo followed with his long *Misérables*—namely to publish it in *half-volume parts* either at intervals of one, or as I think better, two months. The eight parts at 5/-could yield the 2 £ for the four volumes, and at two month intervals would not be dearer than Maga.[1] Each part would have a certain unity and completeness in itself with separate title. Thus the work is called *Middlemarch*. Part 1 will be *Miss Brooke*.

If in a stiff paper cover—attractive but not bookstallish—(I have one in my eye) this part ought to seduce purchasers, especially if

† From *The George Eliot Letters*, 7 vols., edited by Gordon S. Haight (New Haven: Yale University Press, 1954–55), V:3. Reprinted by permission of Yale University Press.
†† From *The George Eliot Letters*, 7 vols., edited by Gordon S. Haight (New Haven: Yale University Press, 1954–55), V:145–46. Reprinted by permission of Yale University Press.
1. *Blackwood's Magazine.*

Mudie² were scant in supplies. It would be enough to furnish the town with talk for some time, and each part thus keep up and swell the general interest. *Tristram Shandy* you may remember was published at irregular intervals; and great was the desire for the continuation. Considering how slowly the public mind is brought into motion, this spreading of the publication over 16 months would be a decided advantage to the sale—especially as each part would contain as much as one ought to read at a time.

Ponder this; or suggest a better plan!

Ever your faithfully
G. H. Lewes.

JOHN BLACKWOOD

Letter to George Eliot†

St. Andrews, 20 July 1871

My Dear Mrs. Lewes

I have read the second portion of Middlemarch with the greatest admiration. It is a most wonderful study of human life and nature. You are like a great giant walking about among us and fixing every one you meet upon your canvas. In all this life like gallery that you put before us every trait in every character finds an echo or recollection in the reader's mind that tells him how true it is to Nature.

It was a disappointment at first not to find any of my old friends of the former part, all except Lydgate apparently entirely strangers, but as you beautifully express it we never know who are to influence our lives while "Destiny stands by sarcastic with our dramatis personæ folded in her hand." The elaborate picture of the formation of Lydgate's character is powerfully relieved by the tremendous French adventure into which the wise young Doctor fell. It would be endless to try to refer to all the happy hits and turns. That sylph caught young and made perfect by Mrs. Lemon is a great success, and I like poor Ned. Where did you hear those horsey men talking? Willie's room at George St. opens from my room and I often hear the mysterious words of wisdom flowing between him and his horsey yeomany friends. You have caught the very tone.

The Farebrother family are delights, a perfect picture. Reading of all the various characters in this second volume—for it is really

2. Charles Edward Mudie, proprietor of Mudie's Library.
† From *The George Eliot Letters*, 7 vols., edited by Gordon S. Haight (New Haven: Yale University Press, 1954–55), V:167–68. Reprinted by permission of Yale University Press.

almost a volume—I had quite forgotten Mr. Brooke, but I *knew his voice* the moment he came into the room at the meeting for the election of Chaplain. There is something uncommonly good about Mary Garth who has her "peculiar temptations" not to accept "good sense and good principle" "ready mixed" and does feel it hard to think that she must be called "an ugly thing" alongside of fair Rosamond.

I think our plan of publication is the right one as the two parts are almost distinct, each complete in itself. Indeed there will be complaints of the want of the continuous interest of a story, but this does not matter where all is so fresh and true to life. Each group that you introduce is a complete little book or study in itself. I return the precious M.S. registered. Have you observed how much closer and smaller you are writing? When you can spare the M.S. I should like to have the quantity calculated. I am pretty sure there is equivalent to a volume of an ordinary novel in what I now return.

* * *

John Blackwood.

GEORGE ELIOT

Letter to John Blackwood†

Redhill, 4 August [1872]

My dear Mr. Blackwood * * *

I shall send Part VII in a few days, as I wish to see it in print that I may be better able to judge of quantities. It will perhaps be desirable to make a few excisions in order to introduce a little further development and leave larger room in the last Part. Since Mr. Lewes tells me that the Spectator considers me the most melancholy of authors, it will perhaps be a welcome assurance to you that there is no unredeemed tragedy in the solution of the story.

Mr. Lewes examines the newspapers before I see them, and cuts out any criticisms which refer to me, so as to save me from these spiritual chills—though alas, he cannot save me from the physical chills which retard my work more seriously. I had hoped to have the manuscript well out of my hands before we left this place at the end of the month, but the return of my dyspeptic troubles makes me unable to reckon on such a result.

† From *The George Eliot Letters*, 7 vols., edited by Gordon S. Haight (New Haven: Yale University Press, 1954–55), V:296– 97. Reprinted by permission of Yale University Press.

It will be a good plan, I think to quicken the publication towards the end, but we feel convinced that the slow plan of publication has been of immense advantage to the book in deepening the impression it produces. Still, I shudder a little to think what a long book it will be—not so long as Vanity Fair or Pendennis, however, according to my calculation.

* * *

Always yours truly
M. E. Lewes.

GEORGE ELIOT

Letter to Harriet Beecher Stowe†

[London, October? 1872]

* * *

How good and generous you are to me! When I think how much you have lived through, the ardour of your sympathy for me, so far away as I am, seems the more wonderful and precious. True thanks, dear Friend, for every loving helpful word that you have sent me. But do not for a moment imagine that Dorothea's marriage experience is drawn from my own. Impossible to conceive any creature less like Mr. Casaubon than my warm, enthusiastic husband, who cares much more for my doing than for his own, and is a miracle of freedom from all author's jealousy and all suspicion. I fear that the Casaubon-tints are not quite foreign to my own mental complexion. At any rate I am very sorry for him.

* * *

Ever yours most gratefully and affectionately
M. E. Lewes.

GEORGE ELIOT

Journal, 1 January 1873††

January 1. 1873. At the beginning of December, the eighth and last book of Middlemarch was published, the three final numbers having been published monthly. No former book of mine has been

† From *The George Eliot Letters*, 7 vols., edited by Gordon S. Haight (New Haven: Yale University Press, 1954–55), V:321–22. Reprinted by permission of Yale University Press.

†† Reprinted from J. W. Cross, *George Eliot's Life as Related in Her Letters and Journals* (Edinburgh and New York: 1885), III:191–92.

received with more enthusiasm—not even Adam Bede, and I have received many deeply affecting assurances of its influence for good on individual minds. Hardly anything could have happened to me which I could regard as a greater blessing, than the growth of my spiritual existence when my bodily existence is decaying. The merely egoistic satisfactions of fame are easily nullified by tooth-ache, and *that* has made my chief consciousness for the last week. This morning, when I was in pain, and taking a melancholy break-fast in bed, some sweet natured creature sent a beautiful bouquet to the door for me, bound round with the written wish that "every year may be happier and happier, and that God's blessing may ever abide with the immortal author of Silas Marner." Happily my dear hus-band is well, and able to enjoy these things for me. That he rejoices in them is my most distinct personal pleasure in such tributes.

GEORGE ELIOT

Letter to Harriet Beecher Stowe†

London, 11 November 1874

My dear Friend * * *
Will you not agree with me that there is one comprehensive Church whose fellowship consists in the desire to purify and en-noble human life, and where the best members of all narrower churches may call themselves brother and sister in spite of differ-ences?

* * *

Yours affectionately
M. E. Lewes.

EMILY DAVIES

Letter to Annie Crow††

London, 24 September 1876

I mentioned that I was going to see [Mrs. Lewes] yesterday.

* * *

† Reprinted from J. W. Cross, *George Eliot's Life as Related in Her Letters and Journals* (Edinburgh and New York: 1885), III: 242–44.

†† Reprinted from Barbara Stephen, *Emily Davies and Girton College* (London: Constable, 1927), pp. 184–86. Emily Davies (1830–1921), chief founder

The talk was chiefly on Morals. * * * She spoke of truthfulness as *the* most important thing to teach—that it should be explained how important it is as the basis of mutual confidence. * * *

* * * She thought pains should be taken to avoid situations in which truth cannot be told, so as to keep up the habit of truthfulness. She thinks you are not bound to say all that you think, but would use as a test, whether your silence would lead to action being taken under a false impression. In teaching, she would ask the children to say for themselves *why* it is right to speak the truth, etc. She was anxious that my friend should impress upon them the wide, far-reaching consequences of every action, as a corrective of the common feeling that it does not signify what we do—and on the other hand how society reacts upon us, and how much we owe to it. People are always asking, Why should I do what is good for society? What is society to me? The answer is that if it were not for the accumulated result of social effort, we should be in the state of wild beasts.

Something was said about 'Assuming life to be a blessing.' I asked if we were entitled to assume that, and she said, Certainly not, in talking to people who deny it, and she knew several people who think it a curse. But she says that so long as you don't commit suicide, you must admit that there is a better life, and a worse life, and may try for the better. Some deny even this, but when you come to such stupid scepticism as that it's no use talking to them.

She hoped my friend would teach the girls not to think too much of political measures for improving society—as leading away from individual efforts to be good, I understood her to mean. I said I thought there was not much danger of that with girls. It is so much more inculcated upon them to be good and amiable than anything else. She said, was there not a great deal among girls of wanting to do some great thing and thinking it not worth while to do anything because they cannot do that? I said there might be, but I had not come across it. What I had met with more was not caring to do anything. She said, Yes, no doubt stupidity prevails more than anything. Then she hoped my friend would explain to the girls that the state of insensibility in which we are not alive to high and generous emotions is stupidity, and spoke of the mistake of supposing that stupidity is only intellectual, not a thing of the character— and of the consequent error of its being commonly assumed that goodness and cleverness don't go together, cleverness being taken to mean only the power of *knowing*. Mr. L[ewes] put in, 'and of expressing.'

---

of Girton College, Cambridge, was a pioneer in the movement to secure university education for women. She worked with Barbara Smith Bodichon in several campaigns for women's rights.

Mr. L[ewes] was taking an active part in the conversation all the time, but what I have repeated is hers, except when he said something that seemed to express her views, and in which she was concurring. At this stupidity stage I thought I had staid long enough and came away promising to try to remember to tell my friend what she had said.

GEORGE ELIOT

Leaves from a Notebook†

"Judgments on Authors"

* * *

In endeavouring to estimate a remarkable writer who aimed at more than temporary influence, we have first to consider what was his individual contribution to the spiritual wealth of mankind? Had he a new conception? Did he animate long-known but neglected truths with new vigour, and cast fresh light on their relation to other admitted truths? Did he impregnate any ideas with a fresh store of emotion, and in this way enlarge the area of moral sentiment? Did he by a wise emphasis here, and a wise disregard there, give a more useful or beautiful proportion to aims or motives? And even where his thinking was most mixed with the sort of mistake which is obvious to the majority, as well as that which can only be discerned by the instructed, or made manifest by the progress of things, has it that salt of a noble enthusiasm which should rebuke our critical discrimination if its correctness is inspired with a less admirable habit of feeling?

This is not the common or easy course to take in estimating a modern writer. It requires considerable knowledge of what he has himself done, as well as of what others had done before him, or what they were doing contemporaneously; it requires deliberate reflection as to the degree in which our own prejudices may hinder us from appreciating the intellectual or moral bearing of what on a first view offends us. * * *

* * *

† First published in *Essays and Leaves from a Notebook*, edited by Charles Lee Lewes (London and Edinburgh, 1884), pp. 353–82; Thomas Pinney has published "More Leaves from George Eliot's Notebook," *Huntington Library Quarterly* 29 (1966), 353–76. The subtitles are GE's own; the general title is Lewes's.

Story-Telling

What is the best way of telling a story? Since the standard must be the interest of the audience, there must be several or many good ways rather than one best. For we get interested in the stories life presents to us through divers orders and modes of presentation. Very commonly our first awakening to a desire of knowing a man's past or future comes from our seeing him as a stranger in some unusual or pathetic or humorous situation, or manifesting some remarkable characteristics. We make inquiries in consequence, or we become observant and attentive whenever opportunities of knowing more may happen to present themselves without our search. You have seen a refined face among the prisoners picking tow in gaol; you afterwards see the same unforgetable face in a pulpit: he must be of dull fibre who could not care to know more about a life which showed such contrasts, though he might gather his knowledge in a fragmentary and unchronological way.

Again, we have heard much, or at least something not quite common, about a man whom we have never seen, and hence we look round with curiosity when we are told that he is present; whatever he says or does before us is charged with a meaning due to our previous hearsay knowledge about him, gathered either from dialogue of which he was expressly and emphatically the subject, or from incidental remark, or from general report either in or out of print.

These indirect ways of arriving at knowledge are always the most stirring even in relation to impersonal subjects. To see a chemical experiment gives an attractiveness to a definition of chemistry, and fills it with a significance which it would never have had without the pleasant shock of an unusual sequence such as the transformation of a solid into gas, and *vice versâ*. To see a word for the first time either as substantive or adjective in a connection where we care about knowing its complete meaning, is the way to vivify its meaning in our recollection. Curiosity becomes the more eager from the incompleteness of the first information. Moreover, it is in this way that memory works in its incidental revival of events: some salient experience appears in inward vision, and in consequence the antecedent facts are retraced from what is regarded as the beginning of the episode in which that experience made a more or less strikingly memorable part. * * *

The modes of telling a story founded on these processes of outward and inward life derive their effectiveness from the superior mastery of images and pictures in grasping the attention—or, one might say with more fundamental accuracy, from the fact that our earliest, strongest impressions, our most intimate convictions, are simply images added to more or less of sensation. These are the primitive instruments of thought. Hence it is not surprising that early poetry took this way—telling a daring deed, a glorious achievement, without caring for what went before. The desire for orderly narration is a later, more reflective birth. The presence of the Jack in the box affects every child: it is the more reflective lad, the miniature philosopher, who wants to know how he got there.

The only stories life presents to us in an orderly way are those of our autobiography, or the career of our companions from our childhood upwards, or perhaps of our own children. But it is a great art to make a connected strictly relevant narrative of such careers as we can recount from the beginning. In these cases the sequence of associations is almost sure to overmaster the sense of proportion. Such narratives *ab ovo* are summer's-day stories for happy loungers; not the cup of self-forgetting excitement to the busy who can snatch an hour of entertainment.

But the simple opening of a story with a date and necessary account of places and people, passing on quietly towards the more rousing elements of narrative and dramatic presentation, without need of retrospect, has its advantages which have to be measured by the nature of the story. Spirited narrative, without more than a touch of dialogue here and there, may be made eminently interesting, and is suited to the novelette. Examples of its charm are seen in the short tales in which the French have a mastery never reached by the English, who usually demand coarser flavours than are given by that delightful gaiety which is well described by La Fontaine as not anything that provokes fits of laughter, but a certain charm, an agreeable mode of handling which lends attractiveness to all subjects even the most serious. And it is this sort of gaiety which plays around the best French novelettes. But the opening chapters of the 'Vicar of Wakefield' are as fine as anything that can be done in this way.

Why should a story not be told in the most irregular fashion that an author's idiosyncrasy may prompt, provided that he gives us what we can enjoy? The objections to Sterne's wild way of telling 'Tristram Shandy' lie more solidly in the quality of the interrupting matter than in the fact of interruption. The dear public would do well to reflect that they are often bored from the want of flexibility in their own minds. They are like the topers of 'one liquor.'

GEORGE ELIOT

Quarry for "Middlemarch" †

George Eliot gave the title *Quarry for "Middlemarch"* to a small notebook which she used throughout her planning and writing of the novel. This notebook was first published in 1950, in an edition prepared by Professor Anna T. Kitchel. As Professor Kitchel explains, the notebook is divided into two parts, which she designates *Quarry I* and *Quarry II*. *Quarry I* contains George Eliot's notes about various scientific and medical matters, historical dates, and several pages of epigraphs for chapters of the novel. *Quarry II* is mostly taken up with plans for the novel: more historical dates and corresponding dates for the action, chapter and plot sketches, "motives," and outlines of the eight parts.

Quarry One

[Flyleaf, recto]
Quarry for "Middlemarch"
George Eliot
[Flyleaf, verso]

Vicq-d'Azir, b. 1748 . . . d. 1794
Pinel, b. 1745, d. 1826   Haller died, 1777
Buffon, 3 first vols. 1749   Linneus at Paris, 1738
Bichat, born 1771, d. 1802   Galvani, d. 1798
Virey, born 1775, died 1840   Jussieu, d. 1831
Laennec, First Memoir on Auscultation, 1818
Broussais, 1772–1838   Brown d. 1788
Ambroise Paré, 1562 ecrivait
Vesalius, born 1513 or 14, died, 1564[1]

(1)

Lancet: 1830. Jan.
Triumph expressed in the Lancet at the great majority for the medical candidate for the office of Coroner of Middlesex in opposition to the attorney—"a medical office, only to be adequately occupied by a medical judge."[2]

---

† From *Nineteenth-Century Fiction*, Supplement to Volume 4, edited, with an introduction and notes by Anna T. Kitchel, © 1950 by The Regents of the University of California. Reprinted by permission. The footnotes for this selection have been renumbered. Numbers in parentheses preceding sections refer to page numbers in Eliot's manuscript notebook.

1. Names, chiefly of French scientists, taken from Renouard, *History of Medicine*, Eng. trans. (Cincinnati, 1856), or J. R. Russell, *History and Heroes of the Art of Medicine* (London, 1861). Cf. Cross, III: 83, 85. First three lines underlined.
2. *Lancet*, Sept. 11, 1830, p. 930. This "triumph" was short-lived. On Sept. 11, Wakley (the editor of the *Lancet* and the "medical candidate" referred to) was successful in the "show of hands." Sept. 18 (*Lancet*, p. 963) found the "combat . . . proceeding in a manner . . . to

Medical Reform at Paris: committee to inquire into the present state of the Hospitals, election of medical officers, public lecturers etc. Members of the Committee, M. M. Cuvier, Dubois, Duméril, etc.[3]

Foundation of the association called "Metropolitan Society of General Practitioners in Medicine, etc.[4]
Professional remuneration. Decision of Ld. Tenterden in the cause of Handey vs. Henson, 1829.[5] (Assn. dissolved, 31[6]

A letter from Derby, speaks of a self-supporting Dispensary "now getting up" where patients are to be doctored for a penny per week. Midwifery 7s. paid 2 months in advance.[7]

Death of Huskisson: his treatment criticized.[8]

(2)
Lancet, 1830
"Diary of a Physician" being published in Blackwood[9]

A writer against the College of Surgeons "fearlessly asserts that my professional education has been such as few men have been fortunate enough to enjoy . . . after having studied in the London schools of anatomy, surgery & medicine; attended as pupil & house-surgeon for two years in one of the London Hospitals; passed my examinations, & received my diploma from the College, I spent three sessions in Edinburgh, studying medicine, & one anatomical season in Dublin, & have since visited Paris:"[1]

at an inquest, giving evidence, Mr. G. Taylor, of Kingston, surgeon & M.D.[2]

Elliotson on diseases of the Heart reviewed. Laennec's discoveries as to the symptoms.[3]

Quoted from Hone's Table Book that the Empiric,

(3)
Dr Graham who appeared in London 1782 had a celestial bed, the charge for sleeping in which was £100. Several persons of high rank

---

afford unbounded satisfaction." But the *Lancet* for Oct. 2 (p. 41) announced that the medical candidate was beaten by a small majority and (pp. 43–49) discussed the contest and its importance.
3. *Lancet*, Oct. 2, 1830, p. 51.
4. *Lancet*, June 19, 1830, p. 451, announcement of the project; Oct. 2, pp. 52–54, discussion of its aims.
5. Verdict in favor of the right of a general practitioner to charge for his services [GE's note].

6. *Lancet*, Jan. 16, 1830, pp. 538–540; Jan. 23, pp. 371–373, editorial; Apr. 17, p. 85; Apr. 24, p. 132.
7. The source of this item is unidentified.
8. *Lancet*, Oct. 9, 1830, p. 69; Oct. 23, p. 129.
9. *Lancet*, Aug. 28, 1830, p. 878; Oct. 9, p. 71.
1. *Lancet*, Oct. 2, 1830, p. 60.
2. *Lancet*, Oct. 30, 1830, p. 168.
3. *Lancet*, Oct. 9, 1830, p. 84.

acceded to his terms, he pretending that it wrought miraculous effects.[4]

Medical jurisprudence, divided into medical police & Forensic Medicine. The Court of Examiners of the Company of Apothecaries have just added this subject to the curriculum.[5]

Willcocks' "Laws relating to the Medical Prof.
"Medical Law now the universal topic."[6]

A treatise on Poisons in relation to Med. Jurisprudence, by Dr Christison, Edinburgh.[7]

"From the reign of Henry VIII to Geo. IV there is neither a charter nor an act of Parlt. on the subject of Medical Polity, which would not disgrace the lowest mechanics' club."[8]

(4)

Cholera in Russia. Oct. 1830.[9]

―――――

―――――

"What are the privileges of which they (the Coll. of Physicians) can boast? That of demanding by virtue of their "charter" that no physician, if he be not a graduate of Oxford or Cambridge, shall practise in London without one of their licenses" . . . "We had well nigh forgotten another privilege & the by-law which concedes it is entirely, exclusively of their own manufacture. It is that every "fellow" of the college who shall meet in consultation any physician who may not be recognized by the charter & by-laws of the college, shall forfeit, for each offence, five pounds. This by-law applies, amongst others, to the graduates of the University of Edinburgh.[1]

"The diploma of the College of Surgeons," writes one costs 20 guineas & is of no value to the purchaser.[2]

(5)

Hôtel Dieu, Dupuytren, head surgeon: in the midst of the fighting, Nov. 1830.[3]

The decision of the house of Lords on the appeal case of Rose & Searle, conferred upon apothecaries the privilege of prescribing as well as of compounding; & the Apothecaries' Act of 1815, not only

4. William Hone, *The Table Book* (London, 1828), II:561–562.
5. *Lancet*, Oct. 16, 1830, pp. 97–103.
6. *Lancet*, Oct. 16, 1830, p. 113; Oct. 23, p. 145, editorial.
7. *Lancet*, Sept. 4, 1830, p. 906, review; Oct. 23, pp. 132–135, practical commentary continued in following numbers.

8. *Lancet*, Oct. 23, 1830, p. 145.
9. *Lancet*, Oct. 30, 1830, p. 176; Dec. 4, 1830, p. 350; Jan. 15, 1831, p. 533.
1. *Lancet*, Oct. 30, 1830, p. 180.
2. *Lancet*, Nov. 6, 1830, pp. 208–209. Letter signed "A Surgeon."
3. *Lancet*, Nov. 20, 1830, p. 257.

confirmed that privilege, but excluded the physician from any such advantage.[4]

St John Long, the quack & his trial, in question Nov, 1830[5]
Duke of Sussex, pres. of Royal Society (against Herschel)[6]

At a meeting of Derbyshire Medical & Surgical Society 10 Dec. 1830, a resolution passed that to charge less than 10/6 in midwifery cases is a "gross violation of the rules of the profession": members pledge themselves to meet no such violator, or any medical man who may have consented to meet him—except in their official situations as officers of the dispensary.[7]

(6)
Practitioners' Remuneration. Dec. 1830

A letter from Manchester proposes a scale of fees for visits, according to three grades of ability to pay in the patients. Complains that "some practitioners in this town are so dastardly in their conduct, as by sneaking, charging every patient, rich & poor alike, one shilling per visit only, & receiving those fees in weekly installments of 3d & 6d, to undersell and undermine the respectable practitioner etc.[8]

The Lancet writes about the theological prejudices against medical studies.[9]
A book on Adulteration & Slow Poisoning: or Disease & death in the Pot & the Bottle, just published. False alarms of the uninstructed on hearing that their porter is mixed with Quassia! their cheese coloured with anatto! their port wine roughened with tannin![1]

School of Edinburgh supplies the great mass of practical

(7)
physicians to England & Ireland.[2]

The Lancet protests against fixed scales of fees as futile, & injurious to young practitioners.[3]

4. *Lancet*, Nov. 20, 1830, p. 279.
5. *Lancet*, Sept. 4, 1830, p. 902; Nov. 6, pp. 200–207, full report of the trial; pp. 210–214, 276, editorials; Nov. 13, p. 248, another editorial; Nov. 27, p. 311, Long's trial in second murder case. Cf. p. 7 of *Quarry* and notes.
6. *Lancet*, Dec. 4, 1830, p. 338. This election of one of the royal dukes in preference to a leading scientist of the day caused the *Lancet's* editor to add, "The Society is rotten to the core." Cf. also, Dec. 25, p. 443.
7. *Lancet*, Jan. 1, 1831, p. 463. (Inexactly quoted.) The 1831 material really begins here, although the heading "1831"

does not occur until p. 8 of the *Quarry*, when a note of April, 1831, is given.
8. *Lancet*, Jan 1, 1831, pp. 463–464.
9. *Lancet*, Jan. 1, 1831, pp. 470–471.
1. *Lancet*, Oct. 23, 1830, book received: Jan. 8, 1831, pp. 485–487, discussion.
2. *Lancet*, Jan. 8, 1831, p. 503. Cf. D'Arcy Power, "Medicine in the British Isles," in *Clio Medica* (New York: Hoeber, 1930), p. 12. "The scots universities always more active in medical education than Oxford and Cambridge—great teachers, many students."
3. *Lancet*, Jan. 15, 1831, pp. 531–532, scale of fees suggested by the Newcastle and Gateshead Association; March 12,

"No hope of promotion in the hospitals to students in the country"—all done by Nepotism. The dons, Sir W. Halford, & Sir Astley Cooper.[4]

In 1823, bodies for dissection hardly to be obtained in London at any price "from the resurrection men." Court of Examiners would not accept certificates of dissections made in Paris, where bodies were plentiful.[5]

Fine, titled people giving their certificates as eye-witnesses to St. John Long. "Noblemen & gentlemen" attesting his extraction of a "fluid like mercury" from the temple.[6]

Proposal to establish a dispensary at Nottingham. Mr. W., cotton spinner, opposing the nomina-

(8)

tion of medical men on the committee. Lancet disapproves the Dispensary. Why should medical men always be expected to do so much work for nothing?[7]

1831

"Parishes usually send their own contracting medical pauper attendant"—who it is well known, frequently contracts at a very low salary.[8]

Meeting to advocate New College of Medicine.[9]
Certificates from County Hospitals not accepted by Coll. of Surgeons: yet says Wakley the county hospitals are better than the London: the men as eminent, the hospitals not so crowded with pupils.[1]

Cholera. About the end of March, 1832, there had been 1530 cases in London, deaths 802.
Quarantine to guard against it in England, June 13, 1831.
First cases occur at Sunderland Nov. 4. Appears at Rotherhithe,

---

1831, p. 782, comment on letter by T. M. Greenhow about the suggested scale. In the *Lancet* of Jan. 8, 1831, pp. 506–507, appears a list of fees in use in New York, taken from "Sketch of the State of Medicine in America" by Dr. Black of Bolton.
4. *Lancet*, Jan. 22, 1831, p. 567. A very condensed and rather garbled summary of a lengthy discussion.
5. *Lancet*, Jan. 29, 1831, pp. 596–598. Very much condensed note on a long editorial showing the injustice of demands by the College of Surgeons.
6. *Lancet*, Feb. 26, 1831, pp. 725–726. Long was being tried again, this time for the "murder" of Mrs. Colin Campbell Lloyd. He was acquitted.

7. *Lancet*, Feb. 26, 1831, p. 726.
8. *Lancet*, Apr. 30, 1831, pp. 151–154. This note is the first one labeled "1831," but see note 24.
9. *Lancet*, Mar. 26, 1831, p. 865. The meeting was held March 16, Wakley speaking at length and giving a sketch of the history of the three "medical corporations" afterward printed in the *Lancet*.
1. *Lancet*, Mar. 26, 1831, pp. 851–852. Some of the remarks about hospitals are quoted from W. Lawrence, M.D., *Speeches Delivered at Two Meetings of Members of the Royal College of Surgeons* (London, 1826).

Feb. 10, 1832. Again, Sept. Thanksgiving for its departure, Ap. 14, 1833.[2]

(9)
Microscopic Discovery
Cell-Theory

Untersuchungen über Phytogenesis, by Schleiden, 1837
Mikroscopische Untersuchungen. By Schwann, 1838–9
Malpighi, b. 1628 Discovered the capillary blood vessels: structure of skin, Rete Malpighii: air-vessels & nervous system of insects. Applied the microscope to embryology
Leeuwenhoek, b. 1632, gained a livelihood & his first celebrity as a glass polisher, his lenses being the best then made[3]
Contemp'y. Swammerdamm, "l'auteur le plus étonnant sur toute l'anatomie des petits animaux," says Cuvier.
Lyonnet, anatomy of the caterpillar.
Hewson: his description of the blood-discs leaves little even for moderns to improve[4]
Gleichen, precursor of Ehrenberg, invented the method of injection by feeding animalcules on coloured substances.[5]
Period between Leeuwenhoek & Ehrenberg singularly barren. Ehrenberg born 1795. Made a voyage to the east & in 1828–32 published a celebrated description of animals of N. Africa & W. Asia. His great

(10)
work on the Infusoria, in 1838. Inspired by reading, before setting out on a scientific journey in 1829, Robert Brown's just published "Brief account of microscopical observations on the particles contained in the pollen of plants, & on the general existence of active molecules in Organic & Inorganic bodies.[6]

---

2. The *Lancet* for part of 1831, most of 1832, and part of 1833 was crowded with discussions of the cholera. I find no one page or section from which this note was drawn. The *Annual Register* may have furnished some of the items. Cf. *Quarry I*, pp. 28–29 [pp. 621–22].
3. The scientists named so far on this page all appear in Huxley's essay quoted from on page 20 of the *Quarry*. In George Eliot's journal for September 10, 1869, she writes, ". . . reading on medical subjects—Encyclopedia about the Medical Colleges, 'Cullen's Life,' Russell's Heroes of Medicine,' etc." We cannot be sure that it was the *Encyclopaedia Britannica* which she referred to, but it is probable. If she found the Encyclopedia useful on the "medical colleges," she might have found it handy in straightening out the list of scientists who had made history in the use of the microscope.

Lewes could, no doubt, have furnished her with a sketch of the subject; we have to remember that she had ever at hand that source of ready information.
4. Huxley also mentions Cuvier's respect for Wolff, but does not give Cuvier's tribute to Swammerdamm quoted here. I have not found its source. Either Lewes or the Encyclopedia—or both—may have given her the facts about the 18th-century anatomists, Lyonnet and Hewson. Lyonnet appears in the *Encyclopaedia Britannica*, 8th ed., IX: 5; Hewson in II: 766. As the 8th edition of the *Britannica* came out in 1860, it would seem an up-to-date and reliable source of information.
5. Gleichen is mentioned in the *Britannica*, 8th ed., III, 208, in connection with Ehrenberg's work.
6. This paper of Robert Brown's also mentions Gleichen's work, cf. *Miscellaneous Botanical Works of Robert Brown*,

An Exposition of the state of the Medical Profession in the British Dominions, & of the injurious effects of the monopoly by usurpation of the Royal Coll. of Phys..1826.[7]

1519 College of Phys. instituted. No man to practise physic in or within seven miles of London unless by them allowed. Physicians in other places, not of the Universities, to be examined by them. £5 a month penalty for practising without admission.[8]

1540. Physicians in London were exempted from certain offices [*written in above*: services], authorized to search apothecaries' drugs & stuffs, & to *practise* surgery. In the same year Barbers forbidden to exercise surgery except in drawing teeth.[9]

(11)

By 34–35 Henry VIII, any person, being no *common* surgeon, may minister outward medicine. It shall be lawful for any person to cure outward sores, notwithstanding the statute of Henry VIII by which the Bishop's License was required for the practice of medicine or surgery.[1]

(By the original statute the College of Physicians consisted of six physicians mentioned by name, & all other persons of the same faculty within the city of London & seven miles without. There was to be elected a President, 4 Supervisors, afterwards called censors, & eight elects.)[2]

By the charter of James I, power was granted to the College to sue for penalties; to retain them for their own use; to examine & correct physicians, apothecaries, & their medicines, & to punish them by fine, imprisonment, & otherwise . . . to fine, & imprison such as practise without a license; to examine witnesses, & administer oaths; to search & destroy the drugs of apoths, & to make by-laws.[3]

published by the Ray Society, 1866, p. 477. The article in question, "A Brief Account of Microscopical Observations Made in the Months of June, July and August, 1827, . . . etc.," *Miscellaneous Works*, I: 463–486, is marked on the title page "published," but dated at the end, p. 479, "July 30, 1828." In the following article, "Additional Remarks on Active Molecules," dated July 28, 1829, Brown says, p. 479, "About twelve months ago I printed an account of Microscopical Observations made in the summer of 1827." This privately printed article or, possibly, the "Additional Remarks" must have been what "inspired" Ehrenberg before he set out on his journey of 1829. The facts cited by George Eliot on pages 9 and 10 of the *Quarry* may have been given her by

Lewes, but the passage beginning "Period between Leeuwenhoek and Ehrenberg . . ." *sounds* as if it were quoted from a book or from an article. Some day I trust this source will be found.

7. The only copy of this work available in the United States is in the library of the College of Physicians in Philadelphia. The full title adds at the end, "in London." It was published in London in the year given.

8. *Exposition*, pp. 18–19.

9. *Ibid.*, pp. 20–21.

1. *Ibid.*, p. 22. The last phrase, "by which the Bishop's License" etc., was added by George Eliot in explanation, referring to p. 18.

2. *Ibid.*, pp. 18–19.

3. *Ibid.*, pp. 24–25.

(12)

By the Charter of Charles II the college is called, President, *Fellowes*, & commonalty, the second term being added. The first 40 Fellows were nominated by the King in the body of the grant. As vacancies might happen, they were to be filled up out of "the commonalty or members"; but *not out of graduates of Oxford or Cambridge more than other members*.[4] . . . All fines, after deducting charges, to go to the poor of the parish. (Never complied with.)[5]

Curious to observe, on the one hand, the College of Physicians procuring a law enabling them to prohibit surgeons from practising physic, & on the other, a law authorizing themselves to practise surgery.[6]

In 1556, the College constituted several visitors, throughout the country, with authority not to suffer any to practise but graduates of Oxford or Cambridge, or persons licensed by themselves. All others were to enter into

(13)

recognizance, that they would not practise until they had been examined & approved; & such as refused obedience were to be imprisoned.

But as the interests of the monopoly were not so much concerned in the country, the persecutions of the College were not so well sustained, & in time they fell into disuse.[7]

———
———

"The college cannot confer the title of doctor" (apparently the title could only be given by Universities).[8] "Graduates of Oxford & Cambridge deemed by the college entitled to the exclusive privilege of the fellowship."[9]

Licentiates in a state of warfare with the college as being denied their rights of voting etc.[1] Originally no such distinction as that between Fellows & licentiates.[2]

---

4. *Ibid.*, p. 27.
5. *Ibid.*, p. 28.
6. *Ibid.*, p. 67.
7. *Ibid.*, p. 131. After "College" in line 1, George Eliot omitted "having performed prodigies against the empirics in town"; after "practise" in line 2, she omitted "physic." For the locating of this quotation and the two following I am indebted to Mr. W. B. McDaniel, II, Librarian of the College of Physicians in Philadelphia.

8. *Ibid.*, p. 175. In the *Exposition* the passage reads, ". . . by a private college, which cannot even confer the title of doctor." The parenthesis adds George Eliot's own comment.
9. *Ibid.*, pp. 175–176. The original reads, ". . . graduates of Oxford and Cambridge, since they were deemed by the college themselves to be entitled to the exclusive privilege of the fellowship."
1. *Ibid.*, p. 196.
2. *Ibid.*, p. 194.

Monopoly of the Fellowship (for gr. of Oxf. & Cam.) "It is notorious that until the middle of the last

(14)

century the persecutions of the College were as bitter against the graduates of Oxford & Cambridge as of any other universities."[3] Not till 1752, that a statute absolutely excluding from the fellowship all but the graduates of the English universities was enacted.[4] "When the choice was between the prolific & cheap seminaries of Scotland & of Leyden on the one hand, & the expensive ones of Oxford & Cambridge on the other, *in each of which not above one student graduated annually*, there was no room for hesitation. The sole object having been monopoly, the statute must be admitted to have been judiciously framed, which while it embraced only the few straggling pupils of Cam & Isis, carefully excluded the many graduates emanating from the metropolis of Scotland, which had then already attained a very high degree of celebrity" . . .[5]
"Not anywhere seminaries of education in which opportunities of obtaining medical

(15)

instruction are more scanty than in the two English universities; & that they are especially deficient in anatomical & clinical instruction."[6]

The college of Surgeons just as restrictive as the Coll. of Phys. March, 1824, the Court of Examiners decreed that the only schools of surgery they would recognize should be London, Dublin, Edinburgh, Glasgow & Aberdeen: "that certificates of attendance at lectures on anatomy, physiology, the theory & practice of surgery, & of the performance of dissections, be not received except from the appointed professors of anatomy & surgery in these above named universities; or from persons teaching in a school acknowledged by the medical establishment of one of the recognized hospitals, or from persons being physicians or surgeons to any of those hospitals."—This of course repressed the salutary competition of private with endowed teachers.[7]

(16)

Inefficiency, nay arresting action, of the Colleges in all great medical inquiries;[8] e.g. Contagion[9] & Lunacy.[1]—In Bethlem hospital it was the rule for some years to give purges & vomits, & to bleed certain classes of the patients at given periods.[2]

3. *Ibid.*, p. 221.
4. *Ibid.*, p. 222.
5. *Ibid.*, pp. 222–223.
6. *Ibid.*, p. 223.
7. *Ibid.*, pp. 238–240. The last remark is

George Eliot's own comment.
8. *Ibid.*, p. 249 ff.
9. *Ibid.*, p. 261.
1. *Ibid.*, p. 263.
2. *Ibid.*, pp. 264–265.

DISTINCTION OF TYPHUS & TYPHOID FEVERS

The dissection by Prost of Parisian Fever-patients in 1804, laid the foundations of our knowledge & turned the attention of pathologists in the direction which has led to such definite results. Petit, Serres, Pommer & Bretonneau followed up the investigations of Prost; but the celebrated treatise of Louis, in 1829, was the first to give a complete & connected view of symptoms as well as of post-mortem lesions in the fever common in Paris.

In 1835 the Academie de Medicine formally proposed the question, what are the

(17)

analogies & the differences between the typhus & typhoid fevers?" The question excited considerable interest in France, but less in England where a strong bias has always prevailed towards a belief in the doctrine of a Single Fever. But dissenters arose. Scotch, English, & American physicians, familiar with the fevers of their own countries, began to visit Paris to study fever there; & they were not long in learning to recognize the chief points of difference between the two fevers. Gerhard & Pennock of Philadelphia, in a systematic treatise were the first to indicate (1836) these differences, it having been already determined that the fever described by Louis under the name of typhoid fever existed in America.[3] Dr. Watson's[4] recommendations are

1. *Against* the old plan of "cutting short" the fever at the outset by *emetics & cold affusions.*[5]

But emetics perhaps too much neglected, being sometimes

(18)

palliative early where there is gastric disturbance.

Sponging (tepid or cold) instead of affusion. Less eligible in *typhus* than *typhoid*[6]

2. Against blood letting in typhus. He says that according to his experience the fevers which occurred in London before the cholera

---

3. W. W. Gerhard, "On the Typhus Fever Which Occurred at Philadelphia in the Spring and Summer of 1836," *American Journal of the Medical Sciences*, XIX (February, 1837): 219–322; XX (August, 1837): 289–322. Of Pennock's connection with the study Gerhard writes (p. 295 of the first article): "Our inquiries were conducted so much in concert . . . that this memoir is in most respects the expression of the results obtained by our joint labours." In the *American Journal of the Medical Sci-ences*, XV (February, 1835): 320, Dr. Gerhard had published "Reports of Cases Treated in the Medical Wards of the Pennsylvania Hospital. Part 1st. Typhus and Remittent Fevers." In this study he had identified the Philadelphia fever with the Paris fever described by Louis.

4. (Sir) Thomas Watson, *Lectures on the Principles and Practice of Physic . . .* (Philadelphia, 1844).

5. *Ibid.*, p. 856.

6. *Ibid.*, p. 857.

years 1831–32, not only bore, but required, the abstraction of blood: since then "it has been necessary to abstain wherever we could with safety, from taking blood at all: & still more necessary, even if we take away blood with one hand to uphold the patient with the other: while in the former period, wine & stimulants of all kinds seemed generally superfluous if not pernicious." "Typhoid fever I believe to have been predominant during my earlier, typhus during my later experience."[7]

3. *"Purgatives*—what are we to say in general with respect to them? Intestines should be cleared by an active aperient in the outset. . . . But if the vital power is much depressed, & when the

(19)

symptoms threaten ulceration of the intestinal glands, purgatives certainly ought not to be pressed.[8]

4. Mercury. Experience in favour of it, in the typhoid forms. Against in typhus, i.e. fever characterized by the mulberry rash.[9]

5. Cold lotion to head when the heat & aching are great. Bleeding by leeches & cupping.[1]

6. Mercury in pills, while the character of the fever is uncertain; but when it turns to the typhoid, some opium along with the mercury.

But if the fever be typhus, begin very early with beef tea, ammonia, aether, wine; & omit the mercury.[2]

6. Opiates. Require close watching in small doses.[3]

Incessant vigilance. Boerhaave, in the preface to his Aphorisms professes that he knows of nothing which can be fitly termed a remedy. "Quin solo tempestivo usu tale fiat."[4]

(20)

Bichat's work. "These old writers (Fallopius & Actuarius) were fully possessed (more so than many of their successors) with the two fundamental notions of structural & physiological biology; the 1st, that living beings may be resolved anatomically, into a comparatively small number of structural elements; the 2d, that these elementary parts possess vital properties, which depend for their manifestation only upon the existence of certain general conditions (supply of proper nutriment etc.) & are independent of all direct influence from other parts. . . . It required all the genius of Bichat to sift the wheat from the chaff amongst the great mass of facts which the observation of past ages had accumulated—& strengthen-

---

7. *Ibid.*, p. 857.
8. *Ibid.*, pp. 857–858.
9. *Ibid.*, p. 858.
1. *Ibid.*, p. 858.
2. *Ibid.*, pp. 858–859.
3. *Ibid.*, pp. 859–860. A very brief sum-

mary of a long passage. Note the repetition of the number "6."
4. *Ibid.*, p. 861. The *Quarry* note seems to read "Quia," but the "a" may be an "n." "Quin" is what Watson used, following Boerhaave correctly.

ing whatever place was weakest by new investigations—to establish
these very two propositions . . .—

Huxley, "Cell Theory"[5]

(21)

Substance membraneuse des organes Animaux

"Lorsqu'on a épuisé, par l'eau, par l'alcool, par l'éther, par les
acides et alcalis étendus, la chair musculaire, un tissu nerveux, un
organe quelconque, il reste une substance blanche comme l'al-
bumine coagulée, mais bien moins élastique, que les alcalis ou les
acides concentrés désorganisent ou dépouillent, mais ne dissolvent
jamais entièrement" . . .

. . . "C'est là la substance qui, sous le rapport anatomique, joue chez
les animaux le même rôle que celle qui forme le tissu cellulaire et
vasculaire chez les végétaux, et que je nommerai, dans le courant de
cet ouvrage, substance membraneuse, membrane ou substance molle
des tissus animaux. C'est elle qui forme la charpente des grands
organes comme des organes microscopiques, des organes mous
comme des organes solides, des muscles, des nerfs, des glandes, des
os, des cartilages, des tendons et aponévroses, des poils eux-mêmes,
enfin

(22)

de tout ce qui, dans un être anime, jouit d'une espèce de végétation,
d'un développement vital."[6]

"Les membranes de tous les organes animaux, même les plus
disparates par leur fonctions, sont donc d'une homogénéité déses-
pérante pour la physiologie, l'anatomie et la chimie microscopique.
Cependant elles peuvent se prêter à des formes capables de fournir
des caractères secondaires pour distinguer les différents organes.
Nous allons, sous ce rapport, en étudier succinctement etc.[7]

Raspail, 1833

---

5. *British and Foreign Medical and
Chirurgical Review*, **XII** (1853): 285–
314. In Leonard Huxley's biography of
T. H. Huxley (I: 152) the date of this
article is given as 1858, doubtless a
printer's error. Leonard Huxley quotes
Sir Michael Foster's remark on the inspiration which many medical students
drew from this essay. It was signed T. H.
Huxley. The names of some of the scientists mentioned in this review, i.e.,
Leuwenhock (so spelled by Huxley),
Malpighi, Schleiden, and Schwann, are
included in the list (*Quarry*, p. 9) of
those who forwarded "microscopical dis-

covery." The note on Bichat's work appears on page 289 of the review.
6. F. V. Raspail, *Nouveau système de
chimie organique fondé sur des nouvelles
méthodes d'observation*, etc. Troisième
édition, etc. (Bruxelles, 1839), I: 362.
The first edition of this work, published
in 1833, is not available in this country
at present. There are a few minor differences in wording between the 1833 text
and that of 1839, as far as we can judge
by the *Quarry* notes, but substance of the
passages remains the same.
7. *Ibid.*, p. 364.

(23)

MOTTOES[8]

"Mit kleinen thut man kleine Thaten
Mit grossen wird der Kleine gross"
GOETHE

Le sentiment de la fausseté des plaisirs présents, et l'ignorance de
la vanité des plaisirs absents causent l'inconstance

PASCAL

Whose speech Truth knows not from her thoughts
Nor love her body from her soul
G. D. ROSSETTI

"Thou art a blessed fellow to think as every man thinks; never a
man's thought in the world keeps the roadway better than thine."
SHAKESPEARE *Henry IV* (?)

Passage of the Pestilence. Villemarqué. Barsas Braiz
"For whoso seeth me first on morrow
May saine he hath met with sorrow
For I am sorrow, & sorrow is I."
CHAUCER

———

———

In all her face no wicked signe
For it was sad, simple & benigne"
CHAUCER

(24)
Wise in his daily work was he:
To fruits of diligence
And not to faith or polity
He plied his utmost sense
The perfect in their little parts
Whose work is all their prize—
Without them how could Laws or Arts
Or tower'd cities rise?[9]

8. Most of the quotations noted down on this page were not used in *Middlemarch*. They were taken from George Eliot's familiar reading. The two lines from Goethe are written above two lines which are scratched out and undecipherable. The quotation from Pascal was used for the heading of chapter 75.
9. Used at the beginning of chapter 40 in *Middlemarch*. In the *Quarry*, line 3 originally read, "not to sounding polity." The *Quarry* quote says that the verse is "From a Black Letter Inscription." But this statement is crossed out and we are left to speculate as to its source. It is hard to believe that it came from any pen but George Eliot's; certainly it has no flavor of a "Black Letter Inscription." The quotation as given in the novel has been properly punctuated; "faith" has been changed to "faiths," "*the* perfect," line 5, has been changed to "*these* perfect."

Ch. 43. This figure hath high price: 'twas wrought with love
            Ages ago in finest ivory:
            Nought modish in it, pure & noble lines
            Of generous womanhood that fits all time.
            That too is costly ware; majolica
            of deft design, to please a lordly eye:
            The smile, you see, is perfect—,wonderful
            As mere faience! A table ornament
            To suit the richest mounting.[1]

(25)

POLITICAL DATES

Birmingham political Union already founded March 11, 1830, when Mr. Huskisson & Mr. Grant contended for the transfer of representation from East Retford to Birmingham; East Retford having been guilty of bribery.[2]

"Mr O'Connell on the 28th of May moved for leave to bring in a bill to establish Triennial parliaments, universal suffrage & vote by ballot—the foundation of his system being this simple but mad proposition, that every man who pays taxes or is liable to serve in the militia is entitled to have a voice in the representation."
13 members joined him in a house of 332.[3]

   Motion to remove the disabilities of Jews, April 1831.[4]
"Mr. Owen had openly declared at a public meeting that Christianity was an imposture."[5]

ANNUAL REGISTER

(26)
How oft the sight of means to do the deeds
Makes ill deeds done!

KING JOHN[6]

(27)
Capital punishment for sheepstealing abolished 1832 (For forgery not till 1840)[7]

---

1. These lines were printed at the beginning of chapter 45 practically without change. Anyone familiar with George Eliot's ideas and verse style would, I think, be fairly confident that she wrote this very pat description herself, though the Browning tone is quite obvious.
2. *Annual Register*, LXXII (1830): 91.
3. *Annual Register*, LXXII (1830): 105.
4. One of the recurring efforts to give political equality to the Jews; for example, the *Annual Register*, LXXII (1830): 109, records one. In LXXV (1833): 226 we find another: "the Jews alone were now the only class . . . whose religion affected their rights. Mr. Grant brought in a bill to relieve them of all civil disabilities." This bill passed the Commons, but was thrown out at a second reading by the Lords.
5. *Annual Register*, LXXII (1830): 113.
6. These lines might have served at the head of chapter 70, but were rejected in favor of some which voice one of George Eliot's deepest beliefs, in the force of inner character as opposed to outer circumstance.
7. The source of this is unidentified. It could have come from any account of reform in the criminal laws.

Peruvian bark fell into total discredit in 1799, from its inability to cure the ague; & it was afterwards discovered to have been adulterated with bark of an inferior species.[8]

From Evidence on the State of the Poor Laws (blue book)
Farmer in Sussex pays £160 rent & £120 poor's rates. A good crop of wheat in that county, 4qrs per acre: average crop 2 qrs per acre.

R. Spooner says, in evidence, that the way in which Tithe is collected leads to a great evil. Men are prevented from investing their capital in the cultivation of land because they would thus make their property titheable which it had not been before.

Tithe in a parish in Norfolk—belonging to a corporation at Norwich, who farmed them

(28)

to an Anabaptist, who collected them of a Catholic population & payed £120 to a Protestant Vicar or Curate.[9]

————
————

Uses of Manganese; In dyeing & calico printing: in the colouring glass and enamel; in furnishing oxygen & chlorine. It supplies the cheapest oxygen. Also, it is used in making bleaching powder.[1]

————

Cholera. "In the end of 1831, the cholera had made its appearance in Sunderland & extended to Newcastle. Instead of moving southwards, it travelled north to Scotland, & appeared suddenly in a very fatal form at Haddington. Approaching Edinburgh it seized upon Musselburgh, six miles from the metropolis, where its ravages were the most severe that had yet been known in the island. In Edinburgh funds had been supplied by voluntary subscription, & labour & attendance by active charity, in clothing & feeding the poor, which, aided by a very vigilant police

(29)

long set the invader at defiance, & when he arrived deprived him of almost all his terror. Hitherto the legislature had been silent. All at once, without apparently having lighted on any intermediate place, the disease appeared in London, & forthwith bills were hurried through parliament (both Houses) vesting in the privy council very

8. I have not found the source of this quotation.
9. I cannot give any exact source for this quotation. Material related to it is to be found in *Reports of Commissioners*, Vol. I, *First Annual Report of the Poor Law Commissioners*, 2d ed. (London, 1836), pp. 51–55. The *Annual Register*, LXXVI (1834): 209–213, discusses the church rates. The same volume, pp. 214–219, discusses tithes, stressing (p. 217) the "tendency [of the tithe system] to check the investment of capital in the improvement of land."
1. Any dictionary or cyclopedia could have supplied this information.

ample powers to direct sanatory measures, & authorizing assessments to cover the necessary expenses. In the bill for Scotland the
house actually divided on the question whether words which spoke
of the disease being an infliction of "providence" should be part of
the preamble. Six members, headed by Mr Hume, voted for their
exclusion. They had been omitted in the preamble of the English
bill, but were inserted in the House of Lords.[2]

———

———

Remarks on the History & Treatment of Delirium Tremens. By
John Ware, M.D. Boston, 1831
    Dr Ware first dogmatically taught that *delirium tremens*

(30)

is a paroxysm of poisoning by alcohol, which in a majority of cases
lasts only a given time, & terminates favourably in a critical sleep.[3]
He says, "The natural tendency of the paroxysm is to terminate in a
spontaneous & salutary sleep at the end of a certain period—viz.
sixty to seventy-two hours; & even in the reports of cases which
have been submitted to the public as evidences of the efficacy of
various modes of practice, sleep has not actually taken place sooner
than it would have done in the natural course of the disease.[4] . . .
The termination of a paroxysm of delirium tremens is always, as
has been already mentioned, in *profound* sleep. . . . Sleep, however,
is not always to be regarded as indicating the speedy termination of
the paroxysm, since it is not uncommon for patients to sleep a
little—from a few minutes to an hour, for instance—on each day of
the delirium."[5] Dr Ware

(31)

maintained that in a large proportion of cases with-drawal of the
accustomed stimulants had nothing to do with the accessions of the
paroxysm, that the disease occurs also in individuals whose habit of

2. *Annual Register*, LXXIV (1832): 274.
The amount of space devoted to cholera
in the pages of the *Lancet* may be taken
as an indication of the anxiety with
which the medical profession regarded
the epidemic of 1832 in England. Volume II for 1830–1831 has a half column
in the index devoted to "Cholera"; Vol.
I, 1831–1832, has three and a half columns; Vol. II, 1831–1832, has *four
columns*; Vol. I, 1832–1833, has one and
a half columns; Vol. II, 1832–1833, has
less than half a column. For an account
of this epidemic see E. Ashworth Under-
wood, "The History of the 1832 Cholera
Epidemic in Yorkshire," *Proceedings of
the Royal Society of Medicine*, section
History of Medicine, 1934–1935. This

article is listed in the *Isis* bibliography
for December, 1936, p. 263, with a note
by Dr. H. R. Viets: Epidemic in the east,
1817, appeared England 1831. 1832 saw
1960 deaths in Yorkshire, one-half of
them in Leeds. In 1832 the disease was
entirely unknown to British practitioners.
Sanitary reform began shortly after this
epidemic. Full list of references to contemporary medical reports.
3. John Ware, M.D., "Remarks on the
History and Treatment of Delirium Tremens," from *Transactions of the Massachusetts Medical Society* (Boston, 1831),
p. 11.
4. *Ibid.*, p. 45. Roughly quoted; sentence
structure change to permit condensation.
5. *Ibid.*, p. 33.

drinking has never been suspended at all . . . up to the commencement of the delirium.[6]

(32)

vide. Bacon's advancement of learning
Stowe's London—medical schools?[7]

Quarry Two

[Second flyleaf, recto]
Dissolution of Parlt. April 22, 1831
General rejoicing & illuminations. Elections, May.
Parlt. Reopened, June 21.[1]

[Second flyleaf, verso]

DATES

1830 opening of Liverpool & Manchr. Railway, April
  " George IV died, June 26—Whigs come in
  " French Revolution,[2] July, 27, 28, 29,
  " Parliament Dissolved,[3] July 24
  " King & Queen decline to visit the city, Nov. 9. Funds fall.
  " Mr. Brougham's motion for Reform   Nov. 16.
  " Tory amendment carried. Machine breaking
  " x (Writs returnable for
1831 Parliament dissolved April 22 & gen. election. Reopened.
      June 21
  " x First cases of Cholera
  " (Paganini) Reform Bill thrown out by the Lords Oct. 7
  " Bristol Riots Oct. 29
      Reintrod. 3d time Dec. 12
1832 Cholera appears at Rotherhithe & London Feb. & Sep.
      R. B. read in the Lords, Mar. Motion against it carried May 7[4]

6. *Ibid.*, p. 7. On page 49 Dr. Ware writes: "There is in this disease, as in some others, a happy insensibility of the system to the action of remedies, which allows it, in a large majority of instances, to take its own course essentially unaffected by them. It may seem presumptuous to make this statement in the face of such authorities as have written of this disease. But many, if not all, have taken it for granted that it is to be treated by medicine; they have never trusted to the spontaneous efforts of nature for a cure." George Eliot must have noticed this statement. Its bearing on Lydgate's conduct of Raffles's case is obvious.

7. This note, which is on the first flyleaf at the back of the notebook, obviously belong with *Quarry I.*
1. Miscellaneous dates, probably from the *Annual Register.*
2. Charles X published the Ordinances July 26, withdrew them, 29. "Too late!" said Laffitte, "Since yesterday, a century has passed away" [GE's note].
3. Deaths from Cholera in Paris, Feb. & Mar., 1832—18,402 [GE's note].
4. King threatening to create new peers May 18   Carried in the Lords June 4 [GE's note].

" Reform Bill passed, June 7.
" Capl. Punishment for sheep & cattle stealing abolished.
" First Nos. of Chambers' Journal & Penny Mag.
1833 Reformed Parliament, election Jan.
" Thanksgiving for departure of Cholera, Ap. 14[5]

(1)

QUERIES

Periods of university examinations

	Oxford	Cambridge
Lent term	Jan. 14–April 1	Jan 13–Mar. 31
Easter	Ap. 12–May 26	April 14–June 23
Trinity	May 27–July 8	
Mich.	Oct. 10–Dec. 18	Oct. 1–Dec. 16

NOTES FROM A LETTER ON HOSPITALS

Chaplain. Chaplain at C honorary. Came when sent for & occasionally otherwise. At S. salaried £40.& had regular services &nd visitations.

Matron. At C factotum. At S. Housekeeper, with only power to report Nurses to the House Surgeon, who engaged or dismissed them.

House Surgeon. Always considered to carry out the treatment of the Surgeons & Physns, to attend urgent cases etc on his own account, & to keep the medical part of the house in order. Not allowed to attend cases out of the Hospital.

Physns. & Surgns. Attendance usually in forenoon ("At no decent institution is the term medical officer used as in C. viz. to express a license to attend medical & surgical cases—in fact to attend the Hospl as general practitioners

(2)[6]

Dr B. in 1869 refused to give a testimonial for the C. Hospital on the ground that such a state of things ought not to exist."[7]

---

5. *Annual Register* probably used here also, but the data were available in many books. The author's statements add details.

6. Page 2 is the verso of page 1. The right-hand pages are ordinarily numbered with odd numbers, the left with even; but occasionally a page is left blank and this rule is upset, e.g., page 11 is the verso of 10, and page 27 is a verso.

7. The "letter on Hospitals" was written by Mrs. Richard Congreve, whose father, Dr. Bury, had attended Robert Evans in his last illness.

MIDDLEMARCH

Directors

Mr. Plymdale, Dyer	Votes for Tyke
Mr. Powderell, Retired ironmonger	" "
Mr. Hawley, Lawyer & town clerk	" Farebrother
Mr. Hackbutt, Tanner	" Farebrother
Mr. Larcher, Carrier	Tyke
Rev. E. Thesiger, Rector of St. Peter's	Tyke
Arthur Brooke Esq. of Tipton Grange	Tyke
Nicholas Bulstrode, Esq. Banker	Tyke[8]

Lowick

o

2 miles

Middlemarch

o

3 miles

Tipton

o

o

Freshitt

[Pen-drawn lines connect the places indicated by small circles]

(3)

RELATIONS TO BE DEVELOPED

1 of Dorothea to Mr. Casaubon
2 " Lydgate to Rosamond
3 " Fred Vincy to Mary Garth
4 " The Vincys to Old Featherstone
5 " Dorothea to Will Ladislaw
6 " Lydgate to Bulstrode
7 " Bulstrode to John Raffles
8 " Celia to Sir James
9 " Ladislaw to Mr Brooke
10 " Caleb Garth to Mr Brooke etc.
11 " Mr Farebrother to all, except Sir J. & Mr Brooke

8. Votes of the directors of the Middle-march Infirmary cast in the choice of a chaplain.

(4)

PRIVATE DATES[9]

Dorothea married, 1827. Featherstone dies & Ladislaw comes to Tipton, Ap. 1830. Celia married May
Lydgate's marriage 1830—July or August
Mr Brooke tries for Parliament May 1831
Mr Casaubon's death, 1831. March
Celia's baby born, 1831—April
Dorothea's second marriage, 1832 Jan. or Feb.
Child born, 1833
Rosamond's baby born, June 1, 1831
Bulstrode buys Stone Court, June or July 1831
Raffles comes back, July 1831
Raffles dies, Aug. 1832. Two years after Lydgate's marriage.

"   "   "

Mr Casaubon's Death, March 1831
Dorothea settled at Lowick again June 1831
Bulstrode & Raffles at Stone Court, end of June 1831
Fred Vincy's adventure & choice July 1831
Lydgate's disclosure of trouble to Rosd. Aug.

(5)[1]

MIDDLEMARCH. PART I. MISS BROOKE. DECR.

Chapter 1 The two sisters pp 1–13
2 Mr Casaubon & Sir James come to dine. 13–23
3 The two suitors persevere 23–36
4 Dorothea's eyes opened. A letter arrives 36–45
5 Mr Casaubon accepted 45–57
6 Mrs Cadwallader informed, & Sir James 57–70
7. Dorothea reads with Mr Casaubon 70–75
8. Sir James appeals to the Rector 75–82
9. Dorothea sees Lowick, & Will Ladislaw 82–92
10. The marriage approaching, & a party 92–103
11 Lydgate talked of at Fred Vincy's breakfast
12 Rosamond & Fred ride to Stone Court & Mr Featherstone asks for something awkward.

Ms. 134 pp.

9. Many situations in the novel are timed to correspond with stages of the First Reform Bill; here the author gives her own timetable for important happenings in her story.

1. Page 5 begins the listing of chapters with titles. Note that chapters 11 and 12, here listed in Part I, are transferred to Part II. The lack of paging here suggests the author's indecision about the proper place for these chapters.

(6)

MIDDLEMARCH PART II. OLD AND YOUNG. FEB.

MS. 126 pp.

(7)[4]

PART III. APRIL

2. Note the changed wording of the chapter headings. The paging for these chapters, omitted on page 5, is given here.
3. The difficulty of weaving in the Fred Vincy strands is seen on pages 6, 7, and 8 of *Quarry II*. The chapters listed as 19–21 were first included in Part II, but finally formed the opening chapters of Part III, numbered 22, 23, and 24. The original chapter 20 of Part II (see *Quarry II*, p. 6) is split into two chapters, 20 and 21. The original 21 becomes 22 and concludes Part II.
4. Page 7, the verso of page 6, is a fair copy of page 8. The Vincy material is here logically and naturally interwoven with the Dorothea-Casaubon strand.

(8)[5]

PART III. APRIL

Waiting for Death

Ch.   22 Scene in the Museum of the Vatican
Tr.   23 Dorothea in tears. Is called on by a relative
to   24 Mr & Mrs Casaubon go to see a studio
pII   [25 *cancelled*]
      27 They return to Lowick
      [26 *cancelled*]
      28 Mr. Casaubon taken ill
      [27 *cancelled*]
      29 Lydgate advises, & Mr Brooke writes a letter
      [28 *cancelled*]
      25 Fred is taken ill, & Mr Wrench dismissed
  29 26 Lydgate & Rosamond in flirtation
      30. The flirtation ends in engagement
      31. The blood-relations at Stone Court
     32 Old Featherstone unable to do as he likes at the last
    ch22 Fred Vincy tries to meet his debt
     23 Has to confess to Mr & Mrs Garth
     24 Fred confesses to Mary; & her father comes.
               MS. 150 pages

(9)

MOTIVES[6]

Featherstone's burial. Arrival of Ladislaw
Will read, & Family consternation
Advent of the new stranger, Rigg
Lydgate & Rosamond married
Mr Brooke seen to be making political tentatives. Ladislaw's
relation to Dorothea & Mr Casaubon shown, a propos of appoint-
ment to edit the Pioneer.
Dismay of Sir James & the Cadwalladers.
Attacks on Mr Brooke as a Landlord.
He is induced to give the management of his estate to Caleb Garth
What Fred Vincy does.
   How Lydgate goes on medically, & in relation to Bulstrode & the
   Hospital vide P. V.
Looming of Raffles

---

5. Page 8 shows the process of working out the structure of Part III. Compare with page 7. "Dorothea Married," the original title of III, was crossed out and "Waiting for Death" substituted.

6. The heading "Motives" covers a variety of details dealing with plot and characterization.

(10)

PART IV. JUNE. THREE LOVE PROBLEMS.

Ch. 33 Featherstone buried & Ladislaw resuscitated
 " 34. The Reading of the Will.
 " 35. Lydgate & Rosamond advance toward marriage
 " 36 Ladislaw's settlement at Middlemarch, in relation
 " " to Dorothea & Mr Casaubon.
 " 37 Sir James & the Cadwalladers attack Mr Brooke about
 " " the management of the farms 249a
 " 38 Dorothea goes to the Grange, & Dagley has his say 266
 " 39 Caleb Garth at breakfast etc. 287
 " 40 Mr Raffles visits Mr Rigg 296
 " 41 Mr Casaubon in prospect of death.
        pp. 164[7]

(11)[8]

MOTIVES (IN GENERAL)

Mr Casaubon dies.
Mr Brooke stands & falls
Embarrassment of Lydgate
Raffles comes on the scene
Scandal in Middlemarch
Raffles' Death
Lydgate accepts money from Bulstrode
Further scandal
Blight on Bulstrode & Lydgate
    Rosamond's flirtation with Ladislaw
? Dorothea after severe struggles goes to Rosamond
? Action of Caleb Garth & Mr Farebrother

CONTINUATION OF PART V

1. About Mr Farebrother's appointment to Lowick
2. Mr Brooke goes to the hustings
3. Fred Vincy's choice of a career
4. Raffles' return ?
5. Drama of Will & Dorothea advanced

7. The first rough estimate of the number of pages in Part IV, "pp. 150–170," is crossed out and "pp. 164" substituted.
8. Here the "Motives (in general)" is followed by a further elaboration of Part V, previously dealt with chapter by chapter on page 12.

(12)[9]

PART V AUGUST. THE DEAD HAND

MS. pages 151

(13)

PART VI OCTOBER: THE WIDOW & THE WIFE

————

————

MS. pp. 156.

(14)

PART VII. DECEMBER

Two Temptations.

9. The first item has already been listed on page 10 as "Mr. Casaubon in prospect of death." The numbers to the left of the items are correct; the others are crossed. Note that with the renumbering of what was to have been the first chapter of Part V (originally 42, here 43) the chapters in the *Quarry* now correspond to those in the published text.

65 Sir Godwin's letter comes. 45
66 Lydgate in the Billiard Room: Fred called by Mr Farebrother 60
67 Lydgate applies to Bulstrode 72
68 Bulstrode's late experience, & consequent plans. 85
69 Caleb Garth informs Bulstrode that Raffles is at Stone Court. Lydgate called in. Goes home & finds the execution in his house.
70 Bulstrode's state of mind about Raffles—& Lydgate. Gives Lydgate the cheque for 1000. Struggles. Gives the key to the housekeeper. *Death.*
71 Scandal in Middlemarch. Mr. Hawley's outburst against Bulstrode. Dorothea enters.

MS. pp. 149

(15)

PART VIII. FEBRUARY

Sunset & Sunrise.

Ch.72 Dorothea wants to help Lydgate—.
73 Lydgate's first anguish
74 Mrs Bulstrode learns her sorrow
75 Rosamond & Lydgate
76 Lydgate & Dorothea.
77 Dorothea, Rosamond & Will Ladislaw
78 Will & Rosamond [*interlineated, underscored:* 79] afterwards Will & Lydgate
[79 *cancelled*]
80 Dorothea in her anguish. 90
81 Dorothea & Rosamond. 105
82 Will Ladislaw 112
83 Will & Dorothea 123
84 Mr Brooke carries news 138
85 Mr & Mrs Bulstrode 143
86

(16)

GARTH FAMILY

Mary 22; Christy, at Glasgow, 19, Alfred, 15
James 12; Ben, 10, Letty 8.

Bulstrode 58
Raffles 51
Joshua Rigg 32
His mother 56

(17)

SKETCH I.

Bulstrode, when young, was a banker's clerk in London & member of a dissenting church to wh. a wealthy couple living at Highbury also belonged. The husband had a business in the city, & on Bulstrode becoming an intimate offered him a place as clerk & accountant; which would be more profitable than his actual situation. Bulstrode accepted & found that the business was a pawnbroker's connected with the receipt of stolen goods.

Preliminary conversations had warned him that the wife was unacquainted with the nature of the business, & the facts were gradually opened to him as necessities which had crept into the management & could not be done away with.

Bulstrode showed ability, & became a confidential associate, winning his way at the same time with the pious wife on the ground of his gifts & divine grace.

(18)

SKETCH II.

The couple had had three children, but the two sons had died, & this bereavement made them relent towards the daughter who had run away from them to go on the stage, & had married.

But this daughter had disappeared, & they knew no means of recovering her except by advertisement, which had hitherto failed, but was persevered in.

Meanwhile, the husband died, & after a short time Bulstrode won the favour of the widow, who, however, before she made the settlements preliminary to her second marriage, was increasingly anxious to find her daughter & her daughter's possible offspring. Bulstrode, on the other hand, thought this extremely undesirable, as a possible diversion of her property into a less useful channel.

If she married him, he intended

(19)

SKETCH III.

as occasion served, to draw away the capital from the criminal business & use it more irreproachably. But the advertising could not be evaded, or an apparent sympathy with the widow's wish.

Still there was no result. But at this stage of affairs a man named Raffles who had early been in service at Highbury but was now a subordinate in the city business was sent on some occasion to Dieppe, & there saw a young couple with their child, the man apparently in a reduced state from sickness, the woman closely resembling the girl whom Raffles had known as the pawnbroker's daughter & whom he knew to have been advertised for. She was holding her baby in her arms & showed a wedding ring.

Raffles came forward & said, "I beg pardon, ma'am, but was your name

(20)

SKETCH IV.

Sarah Yorke? did your parents live at Highbury?" She coloured, was startled & said "Yes." But Raffles then drew back, saying, "I thought so," & left them. He knew that the marriage was pending between Bulstrode & the widow York, & hence debated with himself to which of the two he should carry his information. He determined for Bulstrode, conjecturing that he should get more money there for silence than in the other direction for speech, & in no case should he lose the claim for speech ultimately.

Bulstrode told Raffles that he himself would mention the matter: it was necessary to inquire into things & be cautious, for the sake of the widow's feelings. On certain hints from Raffles, he observed that R. had done a good

(21)

SKETCH V.

service which should be well rewarded if he remained silent. After this, the advertising ceased, & Bulstrode married the widow, but not before Raffles had so presented the question to Bulstrode that he had secured a large sum in acquittance & had gone off to America.

Not long after the marriage the widow died, Bulstrode wound up the business & sought a position in the provinces; having among other changes, left the dissenting body & found all the edification he needed in the evangelical party of the Establishment.

The child of that couple is Will Ladislaw whose father is the son of Mr Casaubon's aunt Julia & her Polish husband, & inherits from the latter artistic faculties. In his extremity of illness & poverty he makes himself known to Mr Casaubon, having family guarantees, & from that time

(22)

SKETCH VI.

Mr Casaubon provides for the mother & Will, the father having shortly died. Will's mother, Sarah York, had run away from home to go on the stage under peculiar circumstances, not only following a bent in opposition to her mother's dissenting tastes, but proximately determined by learning from a spiteful rejected suitor that her father's trade was dishonorable. Hence the choice of her husband's friends as sources of help, rather than her own, was doubly determined.

[The idea which governs the plot about Bulstrode is, that there is nothing which the law can lay hold of to make him responsible for: the Nemesis is wrought out by the public opinion determined against him.]

(23)

How Ladislaw goes on in Middlemarch
Initiates relation to Rosamond
Scene of Fred Vincy's choice, after Mar. 31
Ladislaw's birth known
Mr Farebrother's appointment to the living

(24)

ELEMENTS

1. Mr Casaubon makes the arrangements about his will, having been stimulated by Lydgate's answers to his inquiries about his health.
2. Lydgate again in colloquy with Dorothea, whence an occasion for her to apply some money.
3. Collision between Lydgate & medical men connected with Bulstrode.
4. Leading up to Mr Brooke's nomination in *April or May*
β 1831; his failure & loss of appetite for a public career.
5. Mr Casaubon's death. Sir James & Celia
6. Fred Vincy's debate about his career
7 δ Arrival of Raffles
8 Embarrassments of Lydgate
9 Second marriage of Dorothea
10 ε Lydgate attends Raffles' deathbed
11 Accepts money from Bulstrode
12 Scandal blighting him & Bulstrode

(25)[1]

POLITICAL DATES

After the accession of William IV. Parliament was dissolved on the 23d. July. The writs were made returnable on the 14th. of September. Parliament opened Nov. 2. Duke of Wellington's declaration against reform.

King & Queen refuse to dine in the city, Nov. 9. Government defeated on Sir H. Parnell's motion for inquiry into the Civil List, Nov. 14

Brougham, having pledged himself to his constituency to bring forward a bill for reform had on the opening of Parliament given notice of a motion to that effect. Hence, lest they should be defeated on this question also, the ministry resigned. Lord Grey as prime minister explained his policy, Nov. 22.

Parliament reassembled after Xmas, Feb. 3 1831

Lord John Russell brought forth his measure of Reform on the 1st. of March. On Ap. 21, Ministers defeated on Mr. Bankes's motion to adjourn, Ap. 22. Parliament dissolved.

(26)

ELEMENTS OF B. VI.

First meeting between Will & Dorothea after her husband's death
Will's increasing intimacy with the Lydgates
Lydgate gets more embarrassed, & moody in consequence.
Rosamond makes him angry by writing to his uncle.
Will & Dorothea meet again & part with a sense that they can't marry, Will knowing all.
Rosamond flirting with Will.
Fred Vincy choosing his career

(27)

WILL LADISLAW & DOROTHEA

An offence springs up between Mr Brooke & Will
Will, going on as editor of the Pioneer, comes to Lowick to see the Farebrothers, & has an interview with Dorothea. They part with a sense of being divided by destiny.

Dorothea has projects about filling her life: tells Sir James &

---

1. On page 25 the important events of the Reform Bill period are narrated rather than merely listed. The probable source, again, is the *Annual Register*.

Celia that she will never be married again—Celia's boy will have everything. She will go on some heroic errand of carrying away emigrants etc. Meanwhile, the cholera. Will does not go away & gets more intimate with Mrs. Lydgate. Learns the nature of Mr Casaubon's codicil; also about his mother's family from Bulstrode. There is another meeting & parting between him & Dorothea. She finds him with Mrs Lydgate. Scene between her & Will—anger, jealousy, reproach, ending in Dorothea's passionate avowal, & declaration that she will never marry him. Will reproaches Rosamond with having ruined his happiness. Rosamond alarmed lest Dorothea should tell Lydgate. Dorothea goes to R. having conquered her jealousy by pity, & hears that Will has been true to her.[2]

(28)

BULSTRODE & RAFFLES

Bulstrode buys Featherstone's land; Rigg having an ideal elsewhere. Raffles, not knowing where to find Bulstrode, his letter being dated from "The Shrubs" & containing no clue, comes again after Rigg, & finds Bulstrode riding about Stone Court. Rigg's ideal is a money-changing business.

Raffles comes again, recognizes Will & tells Bulstrode, who gets Raffles away by payment, & then under conscientious relenting offers amends to Will.

Raffles comes back the third time.

(29)[3]

SCENES

1. First interview between Will & Dorothea after her husband's death.
2. Dorothea tells Sir James & Celia that she will not marry again. Entertaining projects of usefulness.
3. Fred Vincy has an adventure.
4. In consequence seeks employment with Mr Garth.
5. Lydgate embarrassed more & more, is moody. Rosamond, discontented, writes to Sir Godwin. Sir Godwin replies to Lydgate. His anger with R.
6. Will, not going away, gets more intimate with Rosamond, & she more disposed to conquer him.

---

2. See note 3.
3. Page 29 works out in much greater detail the material outlined and then put into narrative form on pages 26 and 28.

7. Will learns the nature of Mr Casaubon's Will
8 Raffles comes back & recognizes Will
9 Raffles tells Bulstrode who Will is.
10 Bulstrode paying Raffles to go away, makes offers to Will, constained by fear & conscience.[4]
11 Will's struggles. Gets an interview with Dorothea. They part.
12 Will vacillating goes to Rosamond
13 Dorothea discovers them in emotion—together

(30)

SCENES

14 Scene of anger & jealousy between Will & Dorothea, ending in her avowal of love & resolve not to marry him
15 Will goes to Rosamond & reproaches her with having ruined his happiness.
16 Dorothea, wrought on by compassion, goes to Rosamond, & so moves her that R. tells D. how Will has been true.
17 Meeting & final reconciliation of Will & Dorothea.
18 Dorothea declares to Sir James her intention to marry Will
19. Lydgate in difficulties has half made up his mind to ask Dorothea for aid, & learns that she is going to marry Will.
20 Raffles comes back. Terror of Bulstrode. Disclosures.
21 Raffles' death. Bulstrode gives Lydgate £1000.
22 Scandal in Middlemarch. Blight on Lydgate & Bulstrode. . . .

EPILOGUE

23 Dorothea in her second married life (in London ?)

(31)

HOW TO END THE PARTS

Part VI ends with the Farebrothers telling Dorothea of Will's sudden departure—
  VII. Ends with Lydgate's bribe [*written in above:* outpouring] to Dorothea
  VIII. Epilogue of reconciliation with Dorothea's family
        "   "   "

---

4. Bulstrode expecting to be cramped for money induces Dorothea to do more for   the Hospital [GE's note].

REMAINING SCENES OF PART VI.

1. Fred goes to see the Garth Family, finds Mary still away at Lowick.
2. Fred walks to Lowick & sees Mary
3. After Will has learned the nature of Mr Casaubon's codicil.
4. Raffles returns & recognizes Will & tells Bulstrode.
5. Scene between Bulstrode & Will
6. Will's struggles
7. Interview between Will & Dorothea. Parting
8. Will gone away.

(32)

SKETCH 2.

Will declares his indifference as to what becomes of him & what career he shall pursue since the only woman he loves is debarred from him by honour. Departs.

Mrs. Cadwallader lets drop some phrase indicating some flirtation between Mrs Lydgate & Will, (in Dorothea's hearing).

Scene between Lydgate & Dorothea in which he exposes his whole life. Estrangement between him & Rosamond—her indifference to everything but Ladislaw & his singing etc.

Dorothea writes to him lending the sum: takes it herself to his house that it may fall into no other hands: also wishing to speak to Rosamond in the way of counsel—

   Meanwhile Will has returned impatient to hear something about Dorothea

   Calls on Lydgate. Rosamond who has been pining for him, overjoyed at his presence—thinks it is for her & pours out her feeling

   Means to go to Utopia.

(33)

Mr Farebrother comes to Lydgate to see if anything can be done for him. Finds him in high spirits, released from trouble. Hears him speak of Raffles' illness.

α Bambridge tells what he has heard
β Raffles identified as just buried
γ Diffusion of the scandal among the Middlemarchers in connexion with Lydgate's release from debt
δ Scandal spreads to Freshitt & Lowick
ε Mr Hawley explodes at Vestry meeting
ζ Lydgate's misery. Rosamond's repulsion
η Mrs Bulstrode

(34)
Dorothea enters. Their confusion. Will hurriedly departs. Rosamond shivering. Dorothea repressing her anguish, carries out her intended admonition, & quits Rosamond.

Scene between Will & Dorothea[5]

PART VII

1. Lydgate's affairs
2. Fred & Mary
3 Bulstrode's terrors & wish to get rid of the hospital.[6]
4 Lydgate sounds him. He is deaf. Raffles' illness & death. Loan to Lydgate.
5 Middlemarch suspicious &
6 Lydgate's misery.
7 [Outpouring to Dorothea.][7] Part VIII

---

(35)[8]
Lydgate goes to the Billiard room at G.D.
   (letter comes from Sir Godwin)
Fred Vincy is in the Billiard room
Mr Farebrother sends up for him
Walks with Fred to St Botolph's Parsonage & admonishes him that if he is not to lose Mary he must be careful.
Raffles having again been to Middlemarch—(seen by Lydgate in the billiard room) Bulstrode is meditating removal from Middlemarch going somewhere where he will have a less marked position & suffer less from the visits of Raffles. Is engaged in transferring his bank, & arranging the rest of his property for management without his personal presence. Is seeing Caleb Garth on this subject.
Hence Caleb is going to Stone Court on business. Overtakes Raffles who is ill
takes him up in his gig. Raffles tells Caleb everything about Bulstrode.
(Raffles has also told Bambridge)

(36)
1 That Raffles should tell the whole story of Bulstrode to Caleb Garth; that Caleb should remain silent on the subject even to his wife.

That Raffles should tell Bulstrode how Caleb knew all—but no one else than Caleb.

That Bulstrode sounds Caleb, who tells him his reasons for never disclosing

Caleb calls on Bulstrode tells him that Raffles is at Stone Court & in need of a doctor. Also declines to act further for Bulstrode.

Bulstrode calls in Lydgate.

Gives orders to the woman who sits up with Raffles, to administer opium & alcohol

Gives Lydgate the thousand pounds

Mr Farebrother, not knowing comes with help.

[Lydgate's anguish. Rosamond's repulsion] VIII.

Scent of outburst at a Vestry meeting in which Mr Hawley tells Bulstrode that he is known.

[Lydgate pours out to Dorothea about his misery, & she comforts him. VIII]

(37)

CONCLUSION OF PART VII.

——————

——————

The discussion at Dollop's a type of what was going on in all Middlemarch circles.

The fact of his betrayal bursts upon Bulstrode at a Vestry meeting: Returns home finds Mrs. Bulstrode partly informed: on Lydgate

 The news reaches Lowick & Freshitt

 Curtain follows on Dorothea's arrival

——————

Query: connexion of Will's return[9]

(38)

COURSE OF PART VII.

1 Mr Farebrother makes advances to Lydgate—refused.
2 Lydgate trying to get rid of his house: Rosd. thwarts him
3 Difficulties increase Sir Godwin's letter comes
4 Lydgate goes to the billiard room. Fred Vincy is there: Mr Farebrother comes to fetch him.
5 Fred Vincy & he walk together

9. The "Query" which concludes page 37 in Will's comings and goings.
emphasizes the author's difficulty in fitting

6   Lydgate begins to think of applying to Bulstrode. Bulstrode's efforts to free himself & wish to quit Middlemarch—business with Caleb Garth.

7.   Lydgate sounds Bulstrode

8   Caleb Garth picks up Raffles. Takes him to Stone Court. Raffles tells him the secrets

9   Caleb calls on Bulstrode, who tells him Raffles is there & declines further transactions. Bulstrode suspects the reasons. Caleb reassures him as to secrecy. Execution in Lydgate's house

10   Bulstrode having called in Lydgate, neglects his orders, & causes Raffles to take alcohol etc.

11   Bulstrode calls on Lydgate & gives him £1000 or £500 (?)

12   Lydgate out of his difficulties. Scandal. Outburst of Mr Hawley against Bulstrode

(39)

CONDITIONS

———
———

Return of Will Ladislaw: reasons for his return. Time at which it happens.

What becomes of Bulstrode's arrangements as to property, especially Stone Court?

  How Fred & Mary get married.

About Dorothea's money, over & above her own 700 a year.

TIMES

The death of Raffles about 21st. March
Bambridge's return 26th.
Meeting on Sanitary Reform, April 10th.
Return of Will Ladislaw

(40)

PART VIII

1   Dorothea & Lydgate

2   Dorothea goes to deliver a letter at Lydgate's
Finds Will Ladislaw there. Suspicions confirmed by their emotion.

———

1   Reasons why Dorothea does not immediately have her interview with Lydgate.

3 Mrs Bulstrode made aware of the Facts about her husband. [Their final arrangements. Fred Vincy]
Lydgate's misery [*written in above:* 2] & gloom.) Rosamond's repulsion.
Will Ladislaw's arrival & its causes

3 Lydgate's outpouring to Dorothea. She takes the money to free him, & finds Will Ladislaw with Dorothea.[1] She goes away with the impression that they are lovers. Her emotions of jealousy: making her more distinctly aware of her love.
Her struggle to overcome her selfish feeling. She goes again to R.
Will's outburst to Rosamond after Dorothea is gone away: cutting to the quick.
When Dorothea comes again to Rosamond with love, Rosamond is wrought upon to tell her that Will loves Dorothea alone.

(41)
Dorothea's motive in going to Rosamond.

(42)[2]

PART VIII

1 Dorothea wants to help Lydgate & is checked
2 Lydgate's first anguish under the sense of his position
3 Mrs Bulstrode learns her sorrow
4 Rosamond's behavior & Lydgate's towards her
5 Lydgate tells Dorothea
6 Dorothea goes to see Rosamond & take (the £1000) money for Lydgate. Finds Will with Rosamond.
7 Will's outburst of bitterness against R.
8 Dorothea's anguish & struggles. She goes to Rosamond again who tells her about Will's truth.
9 Wills interview with Dorothea: Reconciliation
10 The Garths & Fred Vincy.
11 Dorothea tells her uncle & the Chettams that she is going to marry Will
12 Mr Brooke will be father at the wedding but as a corrective proposes to cut off the entail

Finale

---

1. One of George Eliot's rare slips occurs when she writes "Dorothea" for "Rosamond" in the eighth line from the bottom.

2. The numbered, clear list of chapters in Part VIII given on page 42 should be compared with page 15.

Reviews and Criticism

Contemporary Reviews
and Criticism

SATURDAY REVIEW

Middlemarch†

If we are to call *Middlemarch* a novel at all, we may say that as a didactic novel it has scarcely been equalled. Never before have so keen and varied an observation, so deep an insight into character and motives, so strong a grasp of conceptions, such power of picturesque description, worked together to represent through the agency of fiction an author's moral and social views. But the reservation we have implied is a broad one. No talent, not genius itself, can quite overcome the inherent defect of a conspicuous, constantly prominent lesson, or bridge over the disparity between the story-teller with an ulterior aim ever before his own eyes and the reader's, and the ideal storyteller whose primary impulse is a story to tell, and human nature to portray—not human nature as supporting a theory, but human nature as he sees it. The same reader who gives himself in unreserved trust to the master of humour and pathos whose object is to please him by his art, is justified in suspecting a bias or one-sided estimate of qualities where a moral has to be worked out through human agency. His confidence is disturbed, he is at once put upon his mettle, when the same gifts seem employed to betray him into unconscious, and perhaps unwilling, admissions. Self-respect calls upon him at every turn either to renounce principles and prejudices or to stand up and defend them—attitudes of mind altogether alien from that relaxation which it is the assumed office of fiction to provide for its votaries. Not but that he must be hard to please who cannot, without overtaxing his powers of attention, derive plenty of amusement pure and simple out of *Middlemarch*—all that the ordinary novel-reader reads a novel for; but it would be unjust to so thoughtful, powerful, and earnest a writer to ignore the intention that underlies the whole. And to read such writing and thinking as they ought to be read is a real exercise of

† Reprinted from the *Saturday Review*, 7 December 1872, 733–34.

mind; especially as we own ourselves, while charmed by inimitable touches of character, and enjoying the author's graces of style and felicity of illustration and allusion, not seldom differing from her views and strictures upon society, and her suggestions for its amendment.

Of course where a moralist and satirist quarrels with society he is very sure to be able to adduce an abundance of facts on his side. The quarrel with humanity in *Middlemarch* is its selfishness, and the quarrel with society is its hollow respectability. Human nature and society are hard things to defend; but care for self up to a point is not identical with selfishness; and respectability which pays its way and conducts itself with external propriety is not hollow in any peculiar sense. And we must say that if our young ladies, repelled by the faint and "neutral" virtues of Celia on the one hand, and the powerfully drawn worldly Rosamond on the other, take to be Dorotheas, with a vow to dress differently from other women, and to regulate their own conduct on the system of a general disapproval of the state of things into which they are born, the world will be a less comfortable world without being a better one.

Dorothea is so noble and striking a character—her charm growing upon us as the story advances—she is so penetrated by a sense of duty, so ardent in her longing to make the world better and happier, that we would not introduce her as an example unfit for general imitation had the ordinary domestic type of woman with whom she is contrasted been drawn by a more friendly hand. Dorothea is born with the temper and the aspirations of a St. Theresa; to her the destinies of mankind, seen by the light of Christianity, made the solicitudes of feminine fashion appear an occupation for Bedlam. She will not ride, because all people cannot afford a horse. She takes no interest in art, because it is the delight of the few beyond the reach of material want. Her strength of opinions, and her propensity to act on them, thus put her from the first at odds with society, which, we are told, expected women to have weak opinions, "while still finding its greatest safeguard in the security that opinions were not acted on." As a foil to these high sentiments, we have her sister Celia, of whom Dorothea says that she never did anything naughty since she was born, and who really never goes contrary to our sense of what is amiable and dutiful in woman; though, not being in the good graces of the author, we are not allowed to find her attractive. Less clever than Dorothea, she has more worldly wisdom, which means perhaps more instinctive perceptions; and not feeling it her duty to subvert the world, she can take her place in it naturally. But surely it is not every girl's duty to refuse the advantages and pleasures of the condition in which she finds herself because all do not share them. She is not selfish because she is serenely happy in a happy home; and if she does her best to help and alleviate the suffering within her reach, she may comfort herself in the belief that the eye of Providence never sleeps.

* * *

We have all our especial antipathies among the vices; and the hypocrisy of seeming, the "dwelling in decencies for ever," the cant of selfishness, are the antipathies of George Eliot. As one book of this series followed another, each seemed to say, This is your benevolence, this your learning, this your family life, this your religion! The sleek trust in Providence which easy or grasping selfishness makes its boast is the particular subject of warning and contempt. The carefully elaborated character of Bulstrode, no hypocrite of the common type, but one who sincerely hopes to flatter Divine Justice into condoning the wrong done, and permitting ill-gotten gains to prosper on condition of a certain amount of service done, is a leading instance; but most of the selfishness of *Middlemarch* shelters itself under an assumed appeal from conscience to religion. Whether it be poor Celia justifying her girl's love of pretty things under the test that the necklace she longs for won't interfere with her prayers; or Mr. Brooke excusing a political move with one of his favourite summaries——"Religion, properly speaking, is the dread of a Hereafter"; or Mrs. Waule arguing that for her brother Peter to turn his property into Blue-Coat land was flying in the face of the Almighty that had prospered him, the appeal is uniformly a cover to the real thought or motive, and, as such, a fit subject for the satirist's pen. But every man's religion may be vulgarized if the alloy is too curiously sought for. We like things in groups; our preferences and convictions are tied together by association; but it is not always fair to couple the highest of these with the lowest, as though the same amount and quality of thought and conviction went to each. When we are told that Mrs. Bulstrode and Mrs. Pymdale had the same preferences in silks, patterns of undercloth ing, china ware, and clergymen, it does not prove the religion repre sented by the clergyman to be superficial and trivial, though it sounds so in such a conjunction. If *Middlemarch* is melancholy, it is due perhaps to its religion being all duty, without a sufficient admixture of hope. We miss the out-look of blue sky which is as essential to the cheerful portraiture of humanity by the moralist as a glimpse into the open is to the portraiture of art.

In so far as *Middlemarch* is an allegory Mr. Casaubon represents learning as opposed to science. Bunyan's Mr. Bat's-eyes is not more a personification of qualities than is Dorothea's first choice, with his lean person, blinking eyes, white moles, and formal phrases; with talents chiefly of the burrowing kind, carrying his taper among the tombs of the past in diligent exploration; his book, the "Key to all the Mythologies," itself a tomb. Altogether he is a striking figure, though now and then the author scarcely shows herself as entirely at home in his surroundings—for example, in his college jealousies and sorenesses—as we generally find her. As for Dorothea's sudden choice of him for a husband, it is not without precedent in real life, reminding us at once of Madame de Staël when a prodigy of fifteen gravely proposing to her parents that she should marry Gibbon; as fat a specimen of distinguished middle life as Mr. Casaubon was a lean one. The more a woman has aims of her own, and a sense of power to carry them out, the less is she guided by the common motives and aspirations of her sex. Personally we can acquiesce in her first choice more readily than in her second. There are two views of Ladislaw, who, we scarcely know on what reasonable grounds, is a great favourite with the author. He charms Dorothea by qualities exactly the reverse of her husband's; by his passionate prodigality of statement; by his ready understanding of her thoughts, which Mr. Casaubon always snubbed as long-exploded opinions, if not heresies; by the sunny brightness of his expression and hair, that seemed to shake out light when he moved his head quickly, "showing poor Mr. Casaubon by contrast altogether rayless"; by his looking an incarnation of the spring which we must suppose he typifies; by his versatility and quick transitions of mood and feeling, being made of such impressionable stuff that the bow of a violin drawn near him cleverly would at one stroke change the aspect of the world for him; by his easy unconventional manners and attitudes, and indifference to the solid goods of life. All these are doubtless attractions. Nature has done much for him, but duty —by which all the other characters of the story are tested—altogether fails in him. He does what he likes, whether right or wrong, to the end of the story; he makes no sacrifices; even his devotion to Dorothea does not preserve him from an unworthy flirtation with his friend Lydgate's wife. He is happy by luck, not desert. * * *

[SIDNEY COLVIN]

Middlemarch†

Fifteen months of pausing and recurring literary excitement are at an end; and 'Middlemarch,' the chief English book of the immediate present, lies complete before us. Now that we have the book as a whole, what place does it seem to take among the rest

† Reprinted from the *Fortnightly Review*, 19 January 1873, 142–47.

with which its illustrious writer has enriched, I will not say posterity, because for posterity every present is apt in turn to prove itself a shallow judge, but her own generation and us who delight to honour her?

In the sense in which anything is called ripe because of fullness and strength, I think the last of George Eliot's novels is also the ripest. 'Middlemarch' is extraordinarily full and strong, even among the company to which it belongs. And though I am not sure that it is the property of George Eliot's writing to satisfy, its property certainly is to rouse and attach, in proportion to its fullness and strength. There is nothing in the literature of the day so rousing—to the mind of the day there is scarcely anything so rousing in all literature—as her writing is. What she writes is so full of her time. It is observation, imagination, pathos, wit and humour, all of a high class in themselves; but what is more, all saturated with modern ideas, and poured into a language of which every word bites home with peculiar sharpness to the contemporary consciousness. That is what makes it less safe than it might seem at first sight to speak for posterity in such a case. We are afraid of exaggerating the meaning such work will have for those who come after us, for the very reason that we feel its meaning so pregnant for ourselves. If, indeed, the ideas of to-day are certain to be the ideas of to-morrow and the day after, if scientific thought and the positive synthesis are indubitably to rule the world, then any one, it should seem, might speak boldly enough to George Eliot's place. For the general definition of her work, I should say, is precisely this—that, among writers of the imagination, she has taken the lead in expressing and discussing the lives and ways of common folks—*votum, timor, ira, voluptas*[1]—in terms of scientific thought and the positive synthesis. She has walked between two epochs, upon the confines of two worlds, and has described the old in terms of the new. To the old world belong the elements of her experience, to the new world the elements of her reflection on experience. The elements of her experience are the 'English Provincial Life' before the Reform Bill—the desires and alarms, indignations and satisfactions, of the human breast in county towns and villages, farms and parsonages, manor-houses, counting-houses, surgeries, streets and lanes, shops and fields, of midlands unshaken in their prejudices and unvisited by the steam-engine. To the new world belong the elements of her reflection; the many-sided culture which looks back upon prejudice with analytical amusement; the philosophy which declares the human family deluded in its higher dreams, dependent upon itself, and bound thereby to a closer if a sadder brotherhood; the habit in regarding

---

1. Desire, fear, anger, pleasure.

and meditating physical laws, and the facts of sense and life, which leads up to that philosophy and belongs to it; the mingled depth of bitterness and tenderness in the human temper of which the philosophy becomes the spring.

Thus there is the most pointed contrast between the matter of these English tales and the manner of their telling. The matter is antiquated in our recollections, the manner seems to anticipate the future of our thoughts. Plenty of other writers have taken humdrum and narrow aspects of English life with which they were familiar, and by delicacy of perception and justness of rendering have put them together into pleasant works of literary art, without running the matter into a manner out of direct correspondence with it. But this procedure of George Eliot's is a newer thing in literature, and infinitely harder to judge of, than the gray and tranquil harmonies of that other mode of art. For no writer uses so many instruments in riveting the interest of the cultivated reader about the characters, and springs of character, which she is exhibiting. First, I say, she has the perpetual application of her own intelligence to the broad problems and conclusions of modern thought. That, for instance, when Fred Vincy, having brought losses upon the Garth family, feels his own dishonour more than their suffering, brings the reflection how '*we are most of us brought up in the notion that the highest motive for not doing a wrong is something irrespective of the beings who would suffer the wrong.*' That again, a few pages later, brings the humorous allusions to Caleb Garth's classification of human employments, into business, politics, preaching, learning, and amusement, as one which '*like the categories of more celebrated men, would not be acceptable in these more advanced times.*' And that makes it impossible to describe the roguery of a horse-dealer without suggesting that he '*regarded horse-dealing as the finest of the arts, and might have argued plausibly that it had nothing to do with morality.*'

Next, this writer possesses, in her own sympathetic insight into the workings of human nature, a psychological instrument which will be perpetually displaying its power, its subtlety and trenchancy, in passages like this which lays bare the working of poor Mrs. Bulstrode's faithful mind upon the revelation of her husband's guilt: 'Along with her brother's looks and words, there darted into her mind the idea of some guilt in her husband. Then, under the working of terror, came the image of her husband exposed to disgrace; *and then, after an instant of scorching shame in which she only felt the eyes of the world, with one leap of her heart she was at his side in mournful but unreproaching fellowship with shame and isolation.*' Of the same trenchancy and potency, equally subtle and equally sure of themselves, are a hundred other processes of analysis, whether applied to serious crises—like that prolonged one during which Bulstrode wavers before the passive murder which shall rid him of his one obstacle as an efficient servant of God—or to such trivial crises as occur in the experiences of a Mrs. Dollop or a Mrs. Taft, or others who, being their betters, still belong to the class of 'well-meaning women knowing very little of their own motives.' And this powerful knowledge of human nature is still only one of many instruments for exposing a character and turning it about. What the character itself thinks and feels, exposed by this, will receive a simultaneous commentary in what the modern analytic mind has to remark upon such thoughts and feelings: see a good instance in the account [pp. 192–93] of Mr. Casaubon's motives before marriage and experiences after it.

Then, the writer's studies in science and physiology will constantly come in to suggest for the spiritual processes of her personages an explanation here or an illustration there. For a stroke of overwhelming power in this kind, take what is said in one place of Bulstrode—that 'he shrank from a direct lie with an intensity disproportionate to the number of his more indirect misdeeds. *But many of these misdeeds were like the subtle muscular movements which are not taken account of in the consciousness; though they bring about the end that we fix in our minds and desire. And it is only what we are vividly conscious of that we can vividly imagine to be seen by Omniscience.*'

And it is yet another instrument which the writer handles when she seizes on critical points of physical look and gesture in her personages, in a way which is scientific and her own. True, there are many descriptions, and especially of the beauty and gestures of Dorothea—and these are written with a peculiarly loving and as it were watchful exquisiteness—which may be put down as belonging to the ordinary resources of art. But look at Caleb Garth; he is a complete physiognomical study in the sense of Mr. Darwin, with the 'deepened depression in the outer angle of his bushy eyebrows, which gave his face a peculiar mildness;' with his trick of 'broadening himself by putting his thumbs into his arm-holes,' and the rest. Such are Rosamond's ways of turning her neck aside and patting her hair when she is going to be obstinate. So, we are not allowed to forget 'a certain massiveness in Lydgate's manner and tone, corresponding with his physique;' nor indeed, any point of figure and physiognomy which strike the author's imagination as symptomatic. Symptomatic is the best word. There is a medical strain in the tissue of the story. There is a profound sense of the importance of physiological conditions in human life. But further still, I think, there is something like a medical habit in the writer, of examining her own creations for their symptoms, which runs through her descriptive and narrative art and gives it some of its peculiar manner.

So that, apart from the presence of rousing thought in general maxims and allusions, we know now what we mean when we speak of the fullness and strength derived, in the dramatic and narrative part of the work, from the use of so many instruments as we have seen. * * *

HENRY JAMES

George Eliot's *Middlemarch*†

Middlemarch is at once one of the strongest and one of the weakest of English novels. Its predecessors as they appeared might have been described in the same terms; *Romola* is especially a rare masterpiece, but the least *entraînant* of masterpieces. *Romola* sins by excess of analysis; there is too much description and too little drama; too much reflection (all certainly of a highly imaginative sort) and too little creation. Movement lingers in the story, and with it attention stands still in the reader. The error in *Middlemarch* is not precisely of a similar kind, but it is equally detrimental to the total aspect of the work. We can well remember how keenly we wondered, while its earlier chapters unfolded themselves, what turn in the way of form the story would take—that of an organized, moulded, balanced composition, gratifying the reader with a sense of design and construction, or a mere chain of episodes, broken into accidental lengths and unconscious of the influence of a plan. * * * *Middlemarch* is a treasure-house of details, but it is an indifferent whole.

Our objection may seem shallow and pedantic, and may even be represented as a complaint that we have had the less given us rather than the more. Certainly the greatest minds have the defects of their qualities, and as George Eliot's mind is preëminently contemplative and analytic, nothing is more natural than that her manner should be discursive and expansive. "Concentration" would doubtless have deprived us of many of the best things in the book—of Peter Featherstone's grotesquely expectant legatees, of Lydgate's medical rivals, and of Mary Garth's delightful family. The author's purpose was to be a generous rural historian, and this very redundancy of touch, born of abundant reminiscence, is one of the greatest charms of her work. It is as if her memory was crowded with antique figures, to whom for very tenderness she must grant an appearance. Her novel is a picture, vast, swarming, deep-colored, crowded with episodes, with vivid images, with lurking master-strokes, with bril-

† Reprinted from the *Galaxy*, March 1873, 424–28.

liant passages of expression; and as such we may freely accept it and enjoy it. It is not compact, doubtless; but when was a panorama compact? And yet, nominally, *Middlemarch* has a definite subject— the subject indicated in the eloquent preface. An ardent young girl was to have been the central figure, a young girl framed for a larger moral life than circumstance often affords, yearning for a motive for sustained spiritual effort and only wasting her ardor and soiling her wings against the meanness of opportunity. The author, in other words, proposed to depict the career of an obscure St. Theresa. Her success has been great, in spite of serious drawbacks. Dorothea Brooke is a genuine creation, and a most remarkable one when we consider the delicate material in which she is wrought. George Eliot's men are generally so much better than the usual trowsered offspring of the female fancy, that their merits have perhaps over-shadowed those of her women. Yet her heroines have always been of an exquisite quality, and Dorothea is only that perfect flower of conception of which her predecessors were the less unfolded blos-soms. An indefinable moral elevation is the sign of these admirable creatures; and of the representation of this quality in its superior degrees the author seems to have in English fiction a monopoly. To render the expression of a soul requires a cunning hand; but we seem to look straight into the unfathomable eyes of the beautiful spirit of Dorothea Brooke. She exhales a sort of aroma of spiritual sweetness, and we believe in her as in a woman we might providen-tially meet some fine day when we should find ourselves doubting of the immortality of the soul. By what unerring mechanism this effect is produced—whether by fine strokes or broad ones, by description or by narration, we can hardly say; it is certainly the great achieve-ment of the book. Dorothea's career is, however, but an episode, and though doubtless in intention, not distinctly enough in fact, the central one. The history of Lydgate's *ménage*, which shares honors with it, seems rather to the reader to carry off the lion's share. This is certainly a very interesting story, but on the whole it yields in dignity to the record of Dorothea's unresonant woes. The "love-problem," as the author calls it, of Mary Garth, is placed on a rather higher level than the reader willingly grants it. To the end we care less about Fred Vincy than appears to be expected of us. In so far as the writer's design has been to reproduce the total sum of life in an English village forty years ago, this commonplace young gentleman, with his somewhat meagre tribulations and his rather neutral egotism, has his proper place in the picture; but the author narrates his fortunes with a fulness of detail which the reader often finds irritating. The reader indeed is sometimes tempted to complain of a tendency which we are at loss exactly to express—a tendency to make light of the serious elements of the story and to sacrifice them to the more trivial ones. Is it an unconscious instinct or is it a deliberate plan? With its abundant and massive ingredients *Middlemarch* ought somehow to have depicted a weightier drama. Dorothea was altogether too superb a heroine to be wasted; yet she plays a narrower part than the imagination of the reader demands. She is of more consequence than the action of which she is the nominal centre. She marries enthusiastically a man whom she fancies a great thinker, and who turns out to be but an arid pedant. Here, indeed, is a disappointment with much of the dignity of tragedy; but the situation seems to us never to expand to its full capacity. It is analyzed with extraordinary penetration, but one may say of it, as of most of the situations in the book, that it is treated with too much refinement and too little breadth. It revolves too constantly on the same pivot; it abounds in fine shades, but it lacks, we think, the great dramatic *chiaroscuro*. * * * Mr. Casaubon's death befalls about the middle of the story, and from this point to the close our interest in Dorothea is restricted to the question, will she or will [she] not marry Will Ladislaw? The question is relatively trivial and the implied struggle slightly factitious. The author has depicted the struggle with a sort of elaborate solemnity which in the interviews related in the last two books tends to become almost ludicrously excessive.

The dramatic current stagnates; it runs between hero and heroine almost a game of hair-splitting. Our dissatisfaction here is provoked in a great measure by the insubstantial character of the hero. The figure of Will Ladislaw is a beautiful attempt, with many finely-completed points; but on the whole it seems to us a failure. It is the only eminent failure in the book, and its defects are therefore the more striking. It lacks sharpness of outline and depth of color; we have not found ourselves believing in Ladislaw as we believe in Dorothea, in Mary Garth, in Rosamond, in Lydgate, in Mr. Brooke and Mr. Casaubon. He is meant, indeed, to be a light creature (with a large capacity for gravity, for he finally gets into Parliament), and a light creature certainly should not be heavily drawn. The author, who is evidently very fond of him, has found for him here and there some charming and eloquent touches; but in spite of these he remains vague and impalpable to the end. He is, we may say, the one figure which a masculine intellect of the same power as George Eliot's would not have conceived with the same complacency; he is, in short, roughly speaking, a woman's man. It strikes us as an oddity in the author's scheme that she should have chosen just this figure of Ladislaw as the creature in whom Dorothea was to find her spiritual compensations. He is really, after all, not the ideal foil to Mr. Casaubon which her soul must have imperiously demanded, and if the author of the "Key to all Mythologies" sinned by lack of [ardor], Ladislaw too has not the concentrated fervor essential in the man chosen by so nobly strenuous a heroine. The impression once given that he is a *dilettante* is never properly removed, and there is slender poetic justice in Dorothea's marrying a *dilettante*. We are doubtless less content with Ladislaw, on account of the noble, almost sculptural, relief of the neighboring figure of Lydgate, the real hero of the story. It is an illustration of the generous scale of the author's picture and of the conscious power of imagination that she has given us a hero and heroine of broadly distinct interests— erected, as it were, two suns in her firmament, each with its independent solar system.

Lydgate is so richly successful a figure that we have regretted strongly at moments, for immediate interest's sake, that the current of his fortunes should not mingle more freely with the occasionally thin-flowing stream of Dorothea's. Toward the close, these two fine characters are brought into momentary contact so effectively as to suggest a wealth of dramatic possibility between them; but if this train had been followed we should have lost Rosamond Vincy—a rare psychological study. * * * A work of the liberal scope of *Middlemarch* contains a multitude of artistic intentions, some of the finest of which become clear only in the meditative after-taste of perusal. This is the case with the balanced contrast between the two histories of Lydgate and Dorothea. Each is a tale of matrimonial infelicity, but the conditions in each are so different and the circumstances so broadly opposed that the mind passes from one to the other with that supreme sense of the vastness and variety of human life, under aspects apparently similar, which it belongs only to the greatest novels to produce. The most perfectly successful passages in the book are perhaps those painful fireside scenes between Lydgate and his miserable little wife. The author's rare psychological penetration is lavished upon this veritably mulish domestic flower. There is nothing more powerfully real than these scenes in all English fiction, and nothing certainly more *intelligent*. Their impressiveness and (as regards Lydgate) their pathos, is deepened by the constantly low key in which they are pitched. It is a tragedy based on unpaid butcher's bills, and the urgent need for small economies. The author has desired to be strictly real and to adhere to the facts of the common lot, and she has given us a powerful version of that typical human drama, the struggles of an ambitious soul with sordid disappointments and vulgar embarrassments. * * *

JOSEPH JACOBS

George Eliot†

* * *

The frequent reference to psychology is significant, and indicates the dangerous tendency in George Eliot's own art which led to the psychological strain in *Middlemarch* and *Daniel Deronda,* and finally resulted in the psychological scarecrows of *Theophrastus Such.* To the novelist 'the curtain is the picture,' and if he turns to the psychologist to analyse the painting, only the canvas and frame remain intact. There is too great a tendency for the psychological novelist to regard his characters as so many *corpora vilia*[1] for his scientific theories. Luckily for George Eliot her interests were ethical rather than psychological, and if she ever does violence to art, it is in the interest of morality rather than of science.

And this leads us to discuss for a moment the need of culture for the novelist. Obviously intellectual training is not alone sufficient. George Henry Lewes was exactly on a par with George Eliot in this regard, yet his *Ranthorpe* was deservedly a failure. Nor is culture combined with observation a complete equipment for the novelist. * * * In so far as culture is real and has become instinctive and unconscious, it undoubtedly tends to give a wider background to the artistic picture and to affect us at more various points of contact. But observation, psychology, and culture can only increase the artistic value of the novel in so far as they are unconsciously applied and subordinated to the interest of character and incident. The selective principle with regard to the latter cannot be of an intellectual, conscious kind at all: it must clearly be of an emotional nature akin to the moral faculty.

It is at this point that we touch the secret spring of George Eliot's art: her whole work is imbued with ethical notions. The novel is, no less than the poem, a criticism of life; and the remarkable influence of George Eliot's novels has been mainly due to the consistent application of moral ideas to the problems set by each novel. Their stimulative effect was due to the fact that her ethical views were in consonance with some of the most advanced ideas of the age. The three chief principles which dominated her thinking were the reign of law in human affairs, the solidarity of society, and the constitution of society as incarnate history (the phrase is Riehl's). Flowing from these were the ethical laws which rule the world of her novels,

---

† Reprinted from Joseph Jacobs, *Essays and Reviews* (London, 1891), pp. 3–73.

1. Vile bodies.

the principle summed up in Novalis's words, 'Character is Fate,' the radiation of good and evil deeds throughout society, and the supreme claims of family or race. Add to these the scientific tone of impartiality, with its moral analogue, the extension of sympathy to all, and we have exhausted the *idées mères* of George Eliot's ethical system, which differentiates her novels from all others of the age.

LESLIE STEPHEN

[On *Middlemarch*] †

* * * *Middlemarch* is primarily a portrait of the circles which had been most familiar to her in youth, and its second title is "a study of provincial life." Provincial life, however, is to exemplify the results of a wider survey of contemporary society. One peculiarity of the book is appropriate to this scheme. It is not a story, but a combination of at least three stories—the love affairs of Dorothea and Casaubon, of Rosamond Vincy and Lydgate, and of Mary Garth and Fred Vincy, which again are interwoven with the story of Bulstrode. The various actions get mixed together as they would naturally do in a country town. Modern English novelists seem to have made up their mind that this kind of mixture is contrary to the rules of art. I am content to say that I used to find some old novels written on that plan very interesting. It is tiresome, of course, if a reader is to think only of the development of the plot. But when the purpose is to get a general picture of the manners and customs of a certain social stratum, and we are to be interested in all the complex play of character and the opinions of neighbours, the method is appropriate to the design. The individuals are shown as involved in the network of surrounding interests which affects their development. *Middlemarch* gives us George Eliot's most characteristic view of such matters. It is her answer to the question, What on the whole is your judgment of commonplace English life? for "provincialism" is not really confined to the provinces. Without trying to put the answer into a single formula, and it would be very unjust to her to assume that such a formula was intended, I may note one leading doctrine:—

"An eminent philosopher among my friends," she says, with a characteristically scientific illustration, "who can dignify even your ugly furniture by lifting it into the serene light of science, has

† Reprinted from Leslie Stephen, *George Eliot* (London, 1902), pp. 174–84.

shown me this pregnant little fact. Your pier-glass, an extensive surface of polished steel made to be rubbed by a housemaid, will be minutely and multitudinously scratched in all directions; but place now against it a lighted candle as a centre of illumination, and the scratches will seem to arrange themselves in a fine series of concentric circles round that little sun. It is demonstrable that the scratches are going everywhere impartially, and it is only your candle which produces the flattering illusion of a concentric arrangement, its light falling into an exclusive optical selection. These things are a parable"—showing the effect of egoism. It may also represent the effect of a novelist's mental preoccupation. Many different views of human society may be equally true to fact; but the writer, who has a particular "candle," in the shape of a favourite principle, produces a spontaneous unity by its application to the varying cases presented. The personages who carry out the various plots of *Middlemarch* may be, as I think they are, very lifelike portraits of real life, but they are seen from a particular point of view. The "prelude" gives the keynote. We are asked to remember the childish adventure of Saint Theresa setting out to seek martyrdom in the country of the Moors. Her "passionate, ideal nature demanded an epic life . . . some object which would reconcile self-despair with the rapturous consciousness of life beyond self. . . . She ultimately found her epos in the reform of a religious order." There are later-born Theresas, who had "no epic life with a constant unfolding of far-resonant action." They have had to work amid "dim lights and tangled circumstances"; they have been "helped by no coherent social faith and ardour which could perform the function of knowledge for the ardently thrilling soul." They have blundered accordingly; but "here and there is born a Saint Theresa, foundress of nothing, whose loving heart-beats and sobs after an unattained goodness tremble off, and are dispersed among hindrances, instead of centering on some long recognisable deed." We are to see how such a nature manifests itself—no longer in the remote regions of arbitrary fancy, but in the commonplace atmosphere of a modern English town. In Maggie Tulliver and in Felix Holt we have already had the struggle for an ideal; but in *Middlemarch* there is a fuller picture of the element of stupidity and insensibility which is apt to clog the wings of aspiration. The Dodsons, among whom Maggie is placed, belong to the stratum of sheer bovine indifference. They are not only without ideas, but it has never occurred to them that such things exist. In *Middlemarch* we consider the higher stratum, which reads newspapers and supports the Society for the Diffusion of Useful Knowledge, and whose notions constitute what is called enlightened public opinion. The typical representative of what it calls its mind is Mr. Brooke, who can talk about Sir Humphry Davy, and Wordsworth, and Italian art, and has a delightful facility in handling the small change of conversation which has ceased to possess any intrinsic value. Even his neighbours can see that he is a fatuous humbug, and do not care to veil their blunt commonsense by fine phrases. But he discharges the functions of the Greek chorus with a boundless supply of the platitudes which represent an indistinct foreboding of the existence of an intellectual world.

Dorothea, brought up with Mr. Brooke in place of a parent, is to be a Theresa struggling under "dim lights and entangled circumstances." She is related, of course, both to Maggie and to Romola, though she is not in danger of absolute asphyxiation in a dense bucolic atmosphere, or of martyrdom in the violent struggles of hostile creeds. Her danger is rather that of being too easily acclimatised in a comfortable state of things, where there is sufficient cultivation and no particular demand for St. Theresas. She attracts us by her perfect straightforwardness and simplicity, though we are afraid that she has even a slight touch of stupidity. We fancy that she might find satisfaction, like other young ladies, in looking after schools and the unhealthy cottages on her uncle's estate. Still, she has a real loftiness of character, and a disposition to take things seriously, which make her more or less sensible of the limitations of her circle. She has vague religious aspirations, looks down upon the excellent country gentleman, Sir James Chettam, and fancies that she would like to marry the judicious Hooker, or Milton in his blindness. We can understand, and even pardon her, when she takes the pedant Casaubon at his own valuation, and sees in him "a living Bossuet, whose work would reconcile complete knowledge with devoted piety, a modern Augustine who united the glories of doctor and saint."

Dorothea's misguided adoration is, I think, very natural, but it is undeniably painful, and many readers protested. The point is curious. George Eliot declared that she had lived in much sympathy with Casaubon's life, and was especially gratified when some one saw the pathos of his career. No doubt there is a pathos in devotion to an entirely mistaken ideal. To spend a life in researches, all thrown away from ignorance of what has been done, is a melancholy fate. One secret of Casaubon's blunder was explained to his wife during the honeymoon. He had not—as Ladislaw pointed out —read the Germans, and was therefore groping through a wood with a pocket compass where they had made carriage roads. But suppose that he had read the last authorities? Would that have really mended matters? A deeper objection is visible even to his own circle. Solid Sir James Chettam remarks that he is a man "with no good red blood in his body," and Ladislaw curses him for "a cursed white-blooded pedantic coxcomb." Their judgment is confirmed by all that we hear of him. He marries, we are told, because he wants "female tendance for his declining years. Hence he determined to abandon himself to the stream of feeling, and perhaps was surprised to find what an exceedingly shallow rill it was." His petty jealousy and steady snubbing of his wife is all in character. Now we can pity a man for making a blunder, and perhaps, in some sense, we ought to "pity" him for having neither heart nor passion. But that is a kind of pity which is not akin to love. Dorothea's mistake was not that she married a man who had not read German, but that she married a stick instead of a man. The story, the more fully we accept its truthfulness, becomes the more of a satire against young ladies who aim at lofty ideals. It implies a capacity for being imposed upon by a mere outside shell of pretence. Then we have to ask whether things are made better by her subsequent marriage to Ladislaw? That equally offended some readers, as George Eliot complained. Ladislaw is almost obtrusively a favourite with his creator. He is called "Will" for the sake of endearment; and we are to understand him as so charming that Dorothea's ability to keep him at a distance gives the most striking proof of her strong sense of wifely duty. Yet Ladislaw is scarcely more attractive to most masculine readers than the dandified Stephen Guest. He is a dabbler in art and literature; a small journalist, ready to accept employment from silly Mr. Brooke, and apparently liking to lie on a rug in the houses of his friends and flirt with their pretty wives. He certainly shows indifference to money, and behaves himself correctly to Dorothea, though he has fallen in love with her on her honeymoon. He is no doubt an amiable Bohemian, for some of whose peculiarities it would be easy to suggest a living original, and we can believe that Dorothea was quite content with her lot. But that seems to imply that a Theresa of our days has to be content with suckling fools and chronicling small beer. We are told, indeed, that Ladislaw became a reformer—apparently a "philosophical radical"—and even had the good luck to be returned by a constituency who paid his expenses. George Eliot ought to know; but I cannot believe in this conclusion. Ladislaw, I am convinced, became a brilliant journalist who could write smartly about everything, but who had not the moral force to be a leader in thought or action. I should be the last person to deny that a journalist may lead an honourable and useful life, but I cannot think the profession congenial to a lofty devotion to ideals. Dorothea was content with giving him "wifely help"; asking his friends to dinner, one supposes, and copying his ill-written manuscripts. Many lamented that "so rare a creature should be absorbed into the life of another," though no one could point out exactly what she ought to have done. That is just the pity of it. There was nothing for her to do; and I can only comfort myself by reflecting that, after all, she had a dash of stupidity, and that more successful Theresas may do a good deal of mischief.

The next pair of lovers gives a less ambiguous moral. Lydgate, we are told, though we scarcely see it, was a man of great energy, with a high purpose. His ideal is shown by his ambition to be a leader in medical science. In contrast to Casaubon, he is thoroughly familiar with the latest authorities, and has a capacity for really falling in love. Unfortunately, Rosamond Vincy is a model of one of the forms of stupidity against which the gods fight in vain. Being utterly incapable of even understanding her husband's aspirations, fixing her mind on the vulgar kind of success, and having the strength of will which comes from an absolute limitation to one aim, she is a most effective torpedo, and paralyses all Lydgate's energies. He is entangled in money difficulties; gives up his aspirations; sinks into a merely popular physician, and is sentenced to die early of diphtheria. A really strong man, such as Lydgate is supposed to be, might perhaps have made a better fight against the temptation and escaped that slavery to a pretty woman which seems to have impressed George Eliot as the great danger to the other sex. But she never, I think, showed more power than in this painful history. The skill with which Lydgate's gradual abandonment of his lofty aims is worked out without making him simply contemptible, forces us to recognise the truthfulness of the conception. It is an inimitable study of such a fascination as the snake is supposed to exert upon the bird: the slow reluctant surrender, step by step, of the higher to the lower nature, in consequence of weakness which is at least perfectly intelligible. George Eliot's "psychological analysis" is here at its best; if it is not surpassed by the power shown in Bulstrode. Bulstrode, too, has an ideal of a kind; only it is the vulgar ideal which is suggested by a low form of religion. George Eliot shows the ugly side of the beliefs in which she had more frequently emphasized the purer elements. But she still judges without bitterness; and gives, perhaps, the most satisfactory portrait of the hypocrisy which is more often treated by the method of savage caricature. If he is not as amusing as a Tartuffe or a Pecksniff, he is marvellously lifelike. Nothing can be finer than the description of the curious blending of motives and the ingenious self-deception which enables Bulstrode to maintain his own self-respect. He is afraid of exposure by the scamp who has known his past history. "At six o'clock he had already been long dressed, and had spent some of his wretchedness in prayer, pleading his motives for averting the worst evil if in anything he had used falsity and spoken what was not true before God. For Bulstrode shrank from a direct lie with an intensity disproportionate to the number of his direct misdeeds. But many of those misdeeds were like the subtle muscular movements which are not taken account of in the consciousness, though they bring about the end that we fix our mind on and desire. And it is only what we are naïvely conscious of that we can vividly imagine to be seen by Omniscience." The culminating scene in which Bulstrode comes to the edge of murder, and, though he does not kill his enemy, refrains from officiously saving life, is the practical application of the principles; and one is half inclined to think that there was some excuse for the proceeding.

It is, I think, to the force and penetration shown in such passages that *Middlemarch* owes its impressiveness. It shows George Eliot's reflective powers fully ripened and manifesting singular insight into certain intricacies of motive and character. There is, indeed, a correlative loss of the early power of attractiveness. The remaining pair of lovers, Mary Garth and Fred Vincy, the shrewd young woman and the feeble young gentleman whom she governs, do not carry us away; and Caleb Garth, though he is partly drawn from the same original as Adam Bede, is unimpeachable, but a faint duplicate of his predecessor. The moral most obviously suggested would apparently be that the desirable thing is to do your work well in the position to which Providence has assigned you, and not to bother about "ideals" at all. *Il faut cultiver notre jardin* is an excellent moral, but it comes more appropriately at the end of *Candide* than at the end of a story which is to give us a modern Theresa.

This, I think, explains the rather painful impression which is made by *Middlemarch*. It is prompted by a sympathy for the enthusiast, but turns out to be virtually a satire upon the modern world. The lofty nature is to be exhibited struggling against the circumambient element of crass stupidity and stolid selfishness. But that element comes to represent the dominant and overpowering force. Belief is in so chaotic a state that the idealist is likely to go astray after false lights. Intellectual ambition mistakes pedantry for true learning; religious aspiration tempts acquiescence in cant and superstition; the desire to carry your creed into practice makes compromise necessary, and compromise passes imperceptibly into surrender. One is tempted to ask whether this does not exaggerate one aspect of the human tragicomedy. The unity, to return to our "parable," is to be the light carried by the observer in search of an idealist. In *Middlemarch* the light shows the aspirations of the serious actors, and measures their excellence by their capacity for such a motive. The test so suggested seems to give a rather onesided view of the world. The perfect novelist, if such a being existed, looking upon human nature from a thoroughly impartial and scientific point of view, would agree that such aspirations are rare and obviously impossible for the great mass of mankind. People, indisputably, are "mostly fools," and care very little for theories of life and conduct.

But, therefore, it is idle to quarrel with the inevitable or to be disappointed at its results; and, moreover, it is easy to attach too much importance to this particular impulse. The world, somehow or other, worries along by means of very commonplace affections and very limited outlooks. George Eliot, no doubt, fully recognises that fact, but she seems to be dispirited by the contemplation. The result, however, is that she seems to be a little out of touch with the actual world, and to speak from a position of philosophical detachment which somehow exhibits her characters in a rather distorting light. For that reason *Middlemarch* seems to fall short of the great masterpieces which imply a closer contact with the world of realities and less preoccupation with certain speculative doctrines. Yet it is clearly a work of extraordinary power, full of subtle and accurate observation; and gives, if a melancholy, yet an undeniably truthful portraiture of the impression made by the society of the time upon one of the keenest observers, though upon an observer looking at the world from a certain distance, and rather too much impressed by the importance of philosophers and theorists.

Modern Criticism

WALTER ALLEN

[Character and Environment in George Eliot's Fiction]†

George Eliot has been called the first modern English novelist. The truth of the generalisation depends upon the angle from which it is approached. Some light on it, however, may be thrown by a roll call of the novels that appeared in Europe within four or five years either side of the publication of *Scenes of Clerical Life* (1858) and *Adam Bede* (1859). Turgenev's *Sportsman's Sketches* appeared in 1852 and *Rudin* in 1856, Tolstoy's *Sevastopol* and Flaubert's *Madame Bovary* in 1855, Dostoevsky's *The House of the Dead* in 1861, and Turgenev's *Fathers and Sons* in 1863. None of these novels had the slightest influence upon her; indeed, so far as one can tell, Turgenev is the only novelist among them that she read. Nevertheless, it is in the context of the European novels of her time that we read and think of her today rather than in that of her purely English contemporaries Dickens, Thackeray and Trollope.

Yet, seen formally as a novelist, it is with them that she belongs. Technically, she is the novelist as omniscient narrator, relating an action long after its conclusion as though she were God, commenting on the action, telling us which characters in it are to be admired, which to be deplored and why. It is one way of writing novels and, as the best examples show, a good one. It depends for complete artistic success, however, upon the novelist's tone of voice, for we are in this kind of novel inescapably in the presence of the story-teller telling his story. The story-teller, indeed, is almost as important as the story he tells, for it is the sense we have of him through the manner and style of his narration that mediates between us and the story he tells. He establishes the values of his story as much by his way of saying it as by what he says. In this kind of novel, we have, as it were, one foot in the personal essay, which is why the author's personal manner of speaking is so important; "writing," as Sterne said, "when properly managed, is but a different name for conversation."

In English, the great master of this kind of novel is Fielding, with

† From *George Eliot* by Walter Allen, pp. 82–85, 90–95, 185–186, Copyright © Walter Allen 1964. Reprinted with permission of Macmillan Publishing Co., Inc. (New York), Weidenfeld & Nicolson, Ltd. (London), and the author.

Thackeray, at a lower level of seriousness, following him. Fielding, in particular, has a colloquial ease of style, at once civilised and eloquent, that suggests a man of the world—but a man of the world who is something more than the phrase itself would indicate—talking familiarly with his equals. His lightness of touch does not for one moment invalidate the tremendous seriousness of the implications of what he is telling us, for the manner itself is, we feel, the expression of a temperament allied to a vast experience of life, the experience, in fact, of an unillusioned and unshockable yet deeply compassionate police-court magistrate who understands himself at least as well as the felons he meets in the dock each day.

In the last analysis, tone is a function of style; and in this regard, it is evident, in terms of the kind of novel she was writing, that George Eliot was lacking. Compared with Fielding's and Thackeray's, the authorial comment in which her stories are embodied is intrusive, indeed obtrusive. Fielding persuades us of the truth of his interpretation of what he is narrating by his appeal both to sweet reasonableness and to worldly experience; George Eliot, in contrast, lectures us and sometimes even hectors us. She lacks tact, as she lacks wit, except a ponderous irony. She gives the impression, in fact, of not quite knowing whom she is addressing. Her style is not subtle enough or easy enough; she is too self-conscious, too anxious that we should not misunderstand the point that the incidents and episodes of her novels should make themselves.

One may speculate why this should have been so. She seldom, as her letters show, when writing in her own person, wrote a sentence that gives pleasure in itself. She is, somehow, too much in the way, unable, perhaps, to distinguish between seriousness and solemnity. Over-earnest herself, she assumes her readers are over-earnest, and she has great faith in polysyllables in their own right. Admittedly, the convention in which she was writing was breaking down even while she was working in it, and she may have been half aware of this. But much of the strain seems to come from the large ends she proposed to herself in the writing of fiction.

It is these, of course, that link her with her great contemporaries in the European novel and to some extent remove her from the company of her English coevals. She would have found, for example, Wilkie Collins's formula for the writing of fiction, "Make 'em laugh, make 'em cry, make 'em wait," which is behind a great deal of Dickens's work also, quite unworthy of emulation; and though she might have accepted Trollope's description of the novel—". . . a picture of common life enlivened by humour and sweetened by pathos. To make this picture worthy of attention, the canvas should be crowded with real portraits, not of individuals known to the world or to the author, but of created personages impregnated with traits of chararacter which are known"—she would have wanted to add much more. Indeed, she did so.

In a letter written in 1861, on an article on *The Mill on the Floss*, she writes: "It is a comfort to me to read any criticism which recognises the high responsibilities of literature that undertakes to represent life. The ordinary tone about art is that the artist may do what he will, provided he pleases the public." And "the high responsibilities of literature that undertakes to represent life" she does, in fact, enlarge on in her early fiction—precisely in some of those authorial asides and comments which now seem flaws in her work.

* * *

Within the convention she followed, she was an innovator in the high seriousness which she claimed for herself as a novelist. In this respect she may be seen as the watershed between the traditional novel and the modern; after her come Hardy, James and Lawrence, who were all in one way or another indebted to her. But she was an innovator in another sense also: in her insistence upon the evolutionary forces that shape society. With the exceptions of *Romola*, a historical novel, and *Daniel Deronda*, all her fiction is set in a past that is not, indeed, remote but that, as it were, is truly over. The period of time spanned is that from the last decade of the eighteenth century to about the time of the first Reform Act, 1832, the period, in other words, of her own childhood and the twenty years before her birth. It is seen always from the vantage-point of the mid-Victorian age and slightly later in which she was writing, and by contrast with those turbulent years of rapid progress, it appears still a traditional society. Time and again, George Eliot makes great play with the contrast, the outstanding example being the prologue to *Felix Holt*. It appears the more traditional because it is a provincial society, far removed from the centre of things; even in *Middlemarch*, which is set partly in Coventry only a few years before she was living there herself, there are no characters equivalent to the Brays and the Hennells, for Lydgate, after all, is an outsider and Ladislaw a bird of passage.

To this provincial society—and it is only in *Middlemarch* that a substantial town is at its centre—George Eliot looks back with considerable nostalgia. She does so because it *is* a traditional society, in which the rhythms of life are established and duties are known. But—and this is the important thing—it is not a static society; it is one in process of being transformed by forces outside it. It would be wrong to call them revolutionary; rather, they are evolutionary. This indeed is the point of view from which George Eliot is writing.

In all these novels, the picture of society is built up slowly and leisurely, through figures who can be considered representative and whose backgrounds are presented in a sober, minute realism that can be equated with that of the seventeenth-century Dutch paintings she so much admired. She is describing, in other words, society at a moment of transition, when new evolutionary factors in society are coming into play. There is the incursion into a remote village of Methodism in *Adam Bede*; the consequences of Radical politics and of political controversy in *Felix Holt*. The disruptive, evolutionary forces that shape *Middlemarch* include not only the politics of the great debate that culminated in the first Reform Act but also the coming of the railway and new developments in medicine and public health. The world she portrays is one riven by great historical events, and this is so even when, as in *Adam Bede* and *Silas Marner*, it is a world quite marginal to the great world. * * *

There is another way in which George Eliot established the fact of change and evolution in the society she is describing. Her characters are not all of one piece. Her nostalgia is for the deeply rooted in traditional ways of life, for the Poysers and the Reverend Mr. Irwine in *Adam Bede*, for the Dodson sisters in *The Mill on the Floss*, for the Garths in *Middlemarch*. It is none the less nostalgia for its being less than total in admiration; the implicit criticism is tempered with love. Why, it is easy to see. Such characters were, one might say, the eternal verities of the lost paradise of her childhood, mellowed, transfigured by the working of memory and by the sense of what she had lost. These characters for whom she had such deep affection represented the past. They are, as it were, fixed, and George Eliot herself was not of their kind; and in some sense, in the majority of her novels, certainly in *The Mill on the Floss*, *Felix Holt* and *Middlemarch* conspicuously (from the very date of its action, *Daniel Deronda* falls outside these generalisations), George Eliot opposes to them characters of a different order of being, characters who can be described as "free spirits," to use the convenient phrase employed by C. B. Cox in his book of that name, characters for whom, as for George Eliot herself, traditional morality, however admirable, is not enough, who can be satisfied with no moral code that does not express to the full their deepest aspirations and their sense of the potentialities within them.

Their great representatives, of course, are Maggie Tulliver, in *The Mill on the Floss*,

> . . . a creature full of eager, passionate longings for all that was beautiful and glad; thirsty for all knowledge; with an ear straining after dreamy music that died away and would not come near to her; with a blind, unconscious yearning for something that would link together the wonderful impressions of this mysterious life, and give her soul a sense of home in it . . .

and Dorothea Brooke, in *Middlemarch*, a St. Theresa who found for herself "no epic life wherein there was a constant unfolding of far-resonant action." Allied to them, though seen much more from the outside, are such male characters as Felix Holt, and Lydgate and Ladislaw in *Middlemarch*. Simply because they are free spirits, living by aspiration and—in the realm of conduct—by something like experiment, these free spirits are much more vulnerable than the heirs of traditional morality such as Mrs. Poyser, Adam Bede and Mr. Garth, who, even when all seems to have gone wrong with their fortunes, can still take comfort in the fact that they have done their duty. Duty is plain to them, as it is not to the free spirits. Because it is not plain, because it may even appear as a choice between duties that seem to conflict, it is the more awful, and the obligation to follow it the more imperative. For the free spirit, indeed, the recognition of where duty lies and what it is is bound up with self-knowledge. "Great feelings," says George Eliot in her final paragraphs on Dorothea Brooke, "will often take the aspect of error, and great faith the aspect of illusion."

It was on the thoroughness and cautiousness of her investigations into the problems of conduct as they face the free spirit, who must be responsible to himself in the absence of traditional and religious sanctions felt as binding, that George Eliot's great moral authority in the nineteenth century rested. The effectiveness of these investigations is due not primarily to the seriousness with which she approached them—that alone would not have availed—but to the skill with which characters and problems are woven into the texture of the society she is describing. As much as Arnold Bennett's, her novels are saturated with the sense of the actual. It has often been pointed out that, far more than most English novels, George Eliot's describe a world at work. Hers is the workaday world in the most liberal sense; her characters are shown not "in themselves" alone but always in relation to their professions or trades, which are almost invariably sources of pride and personal fulfilment. For George Eliot and her characters, work, it might almost be said, has a sacramental quality; it is one of the factors that bind them to the community in which they live; it is the duty that is daily nearest to hand.

It is in this context of a working community that George Eliot dramatises the moral problems of her characters. These, as Joan Bennett has observed, are always concerned with the adjustment of the individual to the community, "with the discovery of a mean point between complete self-repression and unchecked self-indulgence." George Eliot sees society as a closely woven web which, touched at any point, trembles in all its parts. Hence the awful necessity of right action and the avoidance of wrong. Mr. Irwine, in *Adam Bede*, speaks for his creator when he says: "Conseqences are unpitying. Our deeds carry their terrible consequences, quite apart from any fluctuations that went before—consequences that are hardly ever confined to ourselves." The words, indeed, define the inner structure of George Eliot's novels as they do her moral view. An act of wrong-doing brings its own retribution down upon the perpetrator, but, beyond this, it affects the whole community; its consequences are incalculable. Arthur Donnithorne's thoughtless seduction of Hetty Sorrel, in *Adam Bede,* not only leads to her murder of her baby and her imprisonment and to Adam's wretchedness, it also brings shame on the Poysers and very nearly their departure from Hayslope. In other words, it disrupts a whole community. Nothing can be the same again.

The consequences of right-doing are necessarily less dramatic but just as important. * * *

Her view of morality being as stern and intransigent as it is, George Eliot's constant insistence on the necessity and beauty of self-sacrifice cannot surprise. For her, the only guide to right behaviour was the good of others. It is what the characters in her fiction who live according to traditional patterns know, as it were, by instinct; the free spirits have to learn it the hard way.

* * *

* * * V. S. Pritchett has said, "There is no real madness in George Eliot," meaning by madness the sense of the forces of the irrational, the daimonic, the incomprehensible in men's lives. This is to say that, for all her profound reverence, she is never a religious novelist; and the reality of sexual passion is also foreign to her. Her view of life was unswervingly and all the time a moral view, and nothing that existed outside the moral view, that could not be netted by it, existed for her. The loftiness of the moral view she held cannot prevent us thinking that there is a great deal in life that cannot be adequately explained or illuminated by it. The world is not primarily, as it too often seems in her novels, a gymnasium for the exercise and development of the moral faculties. Her picture of life, then, is more limited than her most fervent admirers are always willing to admit.

But her power and authority as a novelist come directly from the very passion with which she held to her moral view of life. Ben Jonson said of John Donne that he was "the first poet in the world in some things," and perhaps this is the highest praise that can be given to any imaginative writer except the very greatest, the transcendent half dozen or so. George Eliot is the first novelist in the world in some things, and they are the things that come within the scope of her moral interpretation of life. Circumscribed though it was, it was certainly not narrow; nor did she ever forget the difficulty attendant upon the moral life and the complexity that goes to its making. Indeed, it is the complexity that persuades us of its truth, the truth that reminds us that men are members one of another, linked to their fellows and to the past by innumerable fine filaments of work, habit and behaviour, to say nothing of kinship and duty.

"It is the habit of my imagination," she wrote, "to strive after as full a vision of the medium in which a character moves as of the character itself." Her novels satisfy both as detailed re-creations of specific environments and as collections of portraits of unique human beings. Because her characters are inescapably social beings —shaped by their own actions, admittedly, but shaped, too, by the pressures of the society in which they live and its history—for George Eliot, moral choice is never something in the abstract. It exists—and this is the hall-mark of her genius as a novelist—in the realm of the agonisingly personal. It is here, in her recognition of the individual's responsibility to his deepest sense of what is right, that her triumph as a novelist lies.

BERT G. HORNBACK

The Moral Imagination of George Eliot†

On 23 September, 1856, George Eliot began "Amos Barton," her first work of fiction. Just ten days earlier she had finished an essay for the *Westminster Review* with a warning to "any female reader who is in danger of adding to the number of 'silly novels by lady novelists.' "[1] It would be hard to imagine George Eliot herself ever needing to be warned against silliness; from the very beginning of her career her serious and intellectual bent was remarked by readers and critics. Yet this is not to say that her work is dry or academic or argumentative. It is didactic; but working through and from the logic of the imagination rather than the logic of reason. George Eliot never submits herself—and never asks her readers to submit themselves—to sentimental emotionalism; her style, her people, her situations, the whole of her fictions are denominated by her strength of mind. Still, such is that strength that what one comes away with is closer to "feeling" than it is to "idea"; and what I propose to explore in this essay is the nature of this "feeling," as it informs *Middlemarch*.

In a note composed sometime in the years immediately following

† From *Papers on Language and Literature* 8 (1972). Southern Illinois University at Edwardsville, publisher. Reprinted by permission of the author and publisher. Page references for this edition have been added; the author's footnotes have been renumbered.
1. "Silly Novels by Lady Novelists," *Westminster Review* 66 (October 1856): 461.

the publication of *Middlemarch* George Eliot wrote under the heading "Feeling is a sort of knowledge" that "What seems eminently wanted is a closer comparison between the knowledge which we call rational & the experience which we call emotional."[2] From this combination she thought men would derive a higher sympathy for their fellows—something much like Keats's "knowledge," which Douglas Bush defines as a "sympathetic understanding of the human condition."[3] Such an awareness is for George Eliot the highest and most noble of human pieties, the only true and relevant morality. And this is what she wanted to teach. The Puritan streak in her allowed her no room for the beautiful unless it was also good, and no room for the good unless it was also useful. F. W. H. Myers has written of what is now a famous conversation with her in 1873 in which "she, stirred somewhat beyond her wont, and taking as her text the three words which have been used so often as the inspiring trumpet-calls of men,—the words *God, Immortality, Duty*—pronounced, with a terrible earnestness, how inconceivable was the *first*, how unbelievable the *second*, and yet how peremptory and absolute the *third*."[4]

George Eliot's writings are filled with statements of this thesis. When she discarded the ardent Evangelicalism of her girlhood in her early twenties, she did not lay aside with it the ideal of relevant morality. In October of 1841 she wrote:

> Much is said about the love of the beautiful, and the idea of perfection as a characteristic of the refined mind, and as being the spring of all high attainment in the triple sisterhood, painting, poetry, and music. But there is a more important application of the terms, a moral one, which I trust we shall ever have before our mind's eye—the love of the beauty of holiness, and a continual yearning after a conformity to it, an habitual contemplation of Moral Perfection, and a dissatisfaction with all that falls short of that standard.[5]

That this art which has its source in the idea of moral perfection is also a duty is expressed in 1868:

> The inspiring principle which alone gives me courage to write is, that of so presenting our human life as to help my readers in getting a clearer conception and a more active admiration of those vital elements which bind men together and give a higher worthiness to their existence. . . . I see clearly that we ought, each of

2. Quoted in Thomas Pinney, "More Leaves from George Eliot's Notebook," *Huntington Library Quarterly* 22 (1966): 364.

3. John Keats, *Selected Poems and Letters*, ed. Douglas Bush (Cambridge, Mass., 1959), p. 338.

4. F. W. H. Myers, *Essays—Modern* (London, 1883), pp. 268–69.

5. Gordon S. Haight, ed., *The Letters of George Eliot*, 1 (New Haven, 1954–55): 118.

us, not to sit down and wail, but to be heroic and constructive, if possible, like the strong souls who lived before, as in other cases [eras?] of religious decay.[6]

This sounds much like the mental and moral point of view of Dorothea Brooke, of course, in *Middlemarch*. The young woman who introduces the almost mystical idea of beautiful failure into English fiction—and this is keyed in the expansive ironies of the "Prelude"—wants to "judge soundly on the social duties of the Christian" (p. 42), is anxious about "making my life good for anything" and learning "new ways of helping people" (p. 52). Her constant question is the would-be activist's. She asks of Lydgate, concerning Casaubon's health, "Tell me what I can do" (p. 200). Later, she asks herself "What should I do—" to help Lydgate and Rosamond (p. 544). And again, wanting to be useful at Lowick she asks "What could I do?" (p. 251). So much does she want to do something that she complains once pettishly that there is nothing wrong at Lowick: "Everybody was well and had flannel; nobody's pig had died" (p. 555).

Dorothea's desire to do something finds its best satisfaction in her assistance to Lydgate which, though it does not save him his position, at least saves him from himself. The circumstances of Raffles's death suggest some sort of moral, perhaps even criminal conspiracy between Bulstrode and Lydgate. Dorothea, however, does not accept circumstantial evidence. She is naively prejudiced for Lydgate from the beginning, sure that "to find out the truth" and to "clear him" are the same undertaking (p. 505). What is important here is not Dorothea's innocence or her prejudice, but the idea of the undertaking itself. "What do we live for," she asks, "if it is not to make life less difficult to each other?" (p. 506). To Lydgate she says: "I would take pains to clear you. I have very little to do. There is nothing better that I can do in the world" (p. 526). And to Rosamond: "How can we live and think that anyone has trouble—piercing trouble—and we could help them, and never try?" (p. 548).

This insistence on social morality and charity is the main thematic emphasis of Dorothea's story; and it is this, rather than George Eliot's realism, or her carefully precise psychological insight, which creates the feeling of beauty and of life in the novel. To help others is one thing; to sacrifice oneself for the sake of others is something else. The communication of this something is George Eliot's greatest success in *Middlemarch*. Dorothea's simple attempt to help Lydgate leads her into a situation which challenges her to sacrifice herself—her pride, her dreams—for his honor. The climax comes at the end of her night of torment, as she surrenders her own

6. See above p. 594 [*Editor*].

desires and feelings in order to help Lydgate and to save his marriage. She asks herself: "What should I do—how should I act now, this very day, if I could clutch my own pain, and compel it to silence, and think of those three?" (p. 544).

George Eliot is quite explicit in her revelation to us and to Dorothea of what it means to have asked such an heroic question as this. Immediately it is dawn, and Dorothea looks out onto a world in microcosm: "On the road there was a man with a bundle on his back and a woman carrying her baby; in the field she could see figures moving—perhaps the shepherd with his dog. Far off in the bending sky was the pearly light" (p. 544). The relevance of this symbolic scene penetrates Dorothea's sympathetic soul, and she understands:

> she felt the largeness of the world and the manifold wakings of men to labour and endurance. She was part of that involuntary, palpitating life, and could neither look out on it from her luxurious shelter as a mere spectator, nor hide her eyes in selfish complaining.
> What she would resolve to do that day did not yet seem quite clear, but something that she could achieve stirred her with an approaching murmur which would soon gather distinctness (p. 544).

What she does is make "her second attempt to see and save Rosamond" (p. 545).

Dorothea's anxiety about doing good is at once typical of and more noble than the general mood and order of action in the novel; and both of these aspects of her character must be explored in order to learn how George Eliot's moral imagination forms and informs *Middlemarch*. The world of the novel is full of reforms and reformers. Lydgate would reform the practice of medicine; Mr. Brooke—under pressure, and with Ladislaw's help—would address himself to the question of political and land reform; Sir James is engaged in economic reform on his own property; the tenant farmer Dagley threatens Mr. Brooke with "the Rinform"; and in the background of the whole novel the House of Commons debates the first great Reform Bill of 1831–32. Dorothea's plans for building cottages are her link with this world of practical reform and, at the same time, the symptom or sign of her grander spiritual ambition. In this sense, the larger world of the novel is set as a background, sometimes supportive, sometimes contrapuntal, for Dorothea's story.

In her journal for 1 January 1869 George Eliot lists "A Novel called Middlemarch" as among her plans for the year.[7] Then in 1870 she began "experimenting in a story" on "a subject which has

---

7. See above p. 598 [*Editor*].

been recorded among my possible themes ever since I began to write fiction."[8] "A Novel called Middlemarch" was probably the story of Lydgate, the Vincys, the Bulstrodes, the Farebrothers, and the Garths; the other, later story was to be called "Miss Brooke." By the spring of 1871, however, she had determined that "the work is called *Middlemarch*. Part I will be *Miss Brooke*."[9]

When George Eliot began to put Dorothea's story together with "Middlemarch" her problem was how to unite them. How could she make her heroine fit into "A Study of Provincial Life"? Dorothea scarcely belongs to the Middlemarch community in what she is or does—she would be terribly out of place, for example, at a dinner party at the Vincys'. Further, she is treated differently by her creator. Real authorial sympathy is invested in the various Middlemarch characters, certainly; but it is the condescending sympathy of a superior critical observer who is not actively involved with them. Dorothea's experience is felt much more viscerally and personally by George Eliot. This is not to say that Dorothea's experience is her creator's or that her character is autobiographically modeled. Rather, the point is that she is given more of soul, of spirit, of significant human individuality than the other characters are allowed, and this plenitude is what George Eliot responds to in writing about her. The Middlemarch people are all the subjects of a "Study"; and for all their rich vitality, they belong in a real and serious way to a research project almost as much as they do to imaginative literature. Dorothea, however, is observed, not studied. She is a creature more of "that experience which we call emotional" than of "the knowledge which we call rational" in the way she is presented. And her story is a richer, more intense experience for the reader than is the story of provincial Middlemarch.

At the center of the Middlemarch story stands Lydgate. Around him are circled Mr. Vincy, Rosamond, Fred, the Garths, Mr. Brooke, Ladislaw, Raffles, and Bulstrode. Each of them is related in some important way to Lydgate, except for Mr. Brooke and Fred, whose relationships with him are indirect, through Casaubon and Mr. Farebrother. Beyond their relationships with Lydgate, the characters of the outer circle also maintain significant relationships with their immediate neighbors: for example, Ladislaw with Brooke and Raffles, Raffles with Ladislaw and Bulstrode, and Bulstrode with Raffles and Vincy. Still, the most important relationships are with Lydgate, generally; and as each set of characters interacts with him, triangles of action are formed in the circle, segments of a web which has at its center the young doctor. It is almost as though the rest of the characters, except for Dorothea, feed from this center, dependent upon Lydgate for their action and involvement.

8. Haight, *Letters*, 5:, 124, 127.   9. See above p. 598 [*Editor*].

Lydgate is a social character as well as a character caught in society. Through most of the novel Dorothea, in contrast, has little to do with other people. When the story is concerned with Dorothea, it is usually concerned almost singly with her and ignores the other characters. All the attention is on her in her scenes with Celia, with Casaubon, with Ladislaw, and with Lydgate; they are merely her supports or foils. And her most fully realized moments are moments she spends alone. But when the scene focuses on Lydgate, it focuses on the heart of society, and suddenly all the rest of the characters appear and involve themselves with and around him in the poignantly abrasive play of life.

If this large novel is to hold together, of course, Dorothea too must become involved in the Middlemarch world. To do so, she must give up her romantic idealism and look at and work usefully among the petty but real people who live there. For all that George Eliot appreciates Dorothea's desires to do great things, she knows and remarks both their impossibility and Dorothea's fault. This is made clear in the often-discussed image of Dorothea's myopia, which is both literal and metaphorical. Dorothea tells Sir James that she is "rather short-sighted" (p. 19); and Celia complains to her, "You always see what nobody else sees . . . yet you never see what is quite plain" (p. 23). What Dorothea sees is usually the ideal vision, or the vision oriented to the ideal, that she wants to see. And busy thus blindly with her own dreams, she neither sees what is there to be seen nor does anything. At the very end of the novel she admits to Celia, "I have never carried out any plan yet" (p. 566).

Dorothea's myopia finally means that, lost in her own world, she is piously selfish and naively egoistic. She wants to marry Hooker, Locke, Milton, Pascal, or Casaubon. She rejects Sir James's suit, and determines to give up planning cottages in order to be "uncivil" with him, crying—about the cottages, not Sir James—"It is very painful" (p. 23). Celia, whom George Eliot has already established as the one who sees clearly, consoles her sister: "Poor Dodo. . . . It is very hard: it is your favorite *fad* to draw plans." But Dorothea will not accept this criticism: "How can one ever do anything nobly Christian, living among people with such petty thoughts?" she asks. And the narrator answers the rhetorical question: "Dorothea was too much jarred to recover her temper and behave so as to show that she admitted any error in herself. She was disposed rather to accuse the intolerable narrowness and the purblind conscience of the society around her" (p. 23).

As the novel progresses, Dorothea begins to see more clearly both the world and her own place in it. She is disillusioned in her dream of Casaubon and in their marriage and begins to assert that strength of character which has been lost—hidden—in the lighter tissues of her own fantasies. Her determination to clear Lydgate of suspicion in the death of Raffles leads her to the meeting with Rosamond in chapter 77. She goes to offer her sympathy to Rosamond, and to pledge her faith in Lydgate's honor. But in seeing Rosamond and Ladislaw together she is shorn of sympathy, discovering what she thinks is Ladislaw's romantic dishonesty. When Dorothea returns from Lydgate's house, Celia notices that something has happened: "Dodo, how very bright your eyes are! . . . And you don't see anything you look at." Dorothea is seeing what she thinks is her own betrayal, by Will; and Lydgate's unhappiness coupled with her own is, to her, "all the troubles of all the people on the face of the earth" (p. 535). This crisis comes as Dorothea says to herself, of Will, "Oh, I did love him" (p. 542). The act that follows is her selfless act, done for the sake of others at great cost to herself. And from this act of charity, of social morality, of heroism in truth and in Dorothea's own terms, comes her reward, and the fulfillment of George Eliot's novel.

But as many readers and critics have long said, her reward is only Will Ladislaw: a weak, unworthy, unsatisfactory, and unreal or unrealized creature with a rippling nose and coruscating hair. The key to this criticism seems to be in the term unrealized—and the result of examining what Will is realized as, may be to enable us to see him more positively. By looking carefully at how he is identified and defined in the novel and in relation to the real world upon which the novel is based we can discover why and how he can be Dorothea's reward, and why she has to sacrifice herself a second time—by giving up her future, it seems—to marry him.

One of the most remarkable aspects of *Middlemarch* has been, for many critics, its realism: the way in which the real world is woven together with the fictional. The history of England from 1828 to 1831 is an impressive part of the texture of the novel—so much so that English history and *Middlemarch* seem to be complementary. The medical education and opinions of Lydgate are real, current, and historically reliable. Dorothea's planning, Mr. Brooke's politics, Casaubon's scholarship are all drawn in reference to a real history, as has often been pointed out. But such historical realism is not in itself important to the novel or to the reader's experience of it. This historical, factual dimension becomes a part of the "feeling" that *Middlemarch* produces indirectly upon the reader, as this dimension supports the characters and gives them something like metaphysical validity and authority in their world. Their realization as characters is finally more imaginative than historical, or simply realistic.

Like most of the other characters in *Middlemarch*, Ladislaw is attached to history. Indeed, Will's attachment to historical fact is more direct and personal than that of any other character in the novel. Through this attachment, he is associated with a certain set of aesthetic, imaginative, and philosophic values which, as they are shared with Dorothea, become a kind of morality for George Eliot and provide the novel's resolution. Through these values, as through the other realistic and historical details of the novel, she creates its "feeling," the imaginative experience of the whole.

At the time in history of which she writes, George Eliot says, "Romanticism . . . was fermenting still as a distinguishable vigorous enthusiasm in certain long-haired German artists in Rome" (p. 130). Ladislaw's sketching leads him to an association with one of those artists, Adolf Naumann. Joseph Jacobs has thought Naumann's character to be suggested by that of Johann Friedrich Overbeck (1789–1869), the father of the German Nazarene school, who worked in Rome after 1810.[1] Certainly Naumann is representative of that school. He describes Dorothea not so much in the vocabulary of the German Nazarene group as in related English Pre-Raphaelite terms, seeing her as "antique form animated by Christian sentiment—a sort of Christian Antigone—sensuous force controlled by spiritual passion" (p. 132). That is to say, George Eliot is remarking on the past of forty years earlier (*Middlemarch* was published in 1871–72, and its action transpires during 1828–31) in the vocabulary familiar to, as well as from the point of view of, a contemporary of the Pre-Raphaelites. Thus, for example, a few pages later she has Will characterize Naumann as "one of the chief renovators of Christian art, one of those who [has] not only revived but expanded that grand conception of supreme events as mysteries" (p. 147)—which is to characterize him as a follower of the Nazarenes. It is not surprising that Will should be defined and situated in these terms, since from about 1850 the Nazarene school had its disciples in England in the Pre-Raphaelites, led in art and in literature by Dante Gabriel Rossetti. Will's interest in painting is influenced by Naumann's work, and he espouses something of the idea of Pre-Raphaelite poetry in saying to Naumann that "Language gives a fuller image [than painting], which [image] is all the better for being vague. After all, the true seeing is within" (p. 133).[2]

Ladislaw's role in *Middlemarch* is in part established by means of this association with Pre-Raphaelitism, as it gives him a set of basic values from which to develop his personal identity. The historical association gives authority—but not necessarily approval—to his character and his way of life. It does not prohibit George Eliot's

1. Joseph Jacobs, *Essays and Reviews* (London, 1891), p. 72.
2. George Eliot went to see some of Rossetti's paintings in January of 1870, and then received a copy of his *Poems* (1870) from him early in May (Haight, *Letters*, 5:78, 98); see also James D. Merrit, *The Pre-Raphaelite Poem* (New York, 1966), pp. 9–11.

criticizing him for being a dilettante, though even in that criticism she seems to recognize the measure of his spiritual potential. When he gives up "poetic metres" and "mediaevalism"—which is to say the Pre-Raphaelite affectation—in exchange for the chance of "sympathising warmly with liberty and progress in general" (p. 318), George Eliot comments that "Our sense of duty must often wait for some work which shall take the place of dilettanteism and make us feel that the quality of our action is not a matter of indifference" (pp. 318–19).

Of course Will has never been a petty creature, just a dilettante. His moral point of view is basically similar to Dorothea's—and to Lydgate's. His religion, he says, is "To love what is good and beautiful when I see it" (p. 271). True, by comparison with Dorothea's ambition, to *do* good for other people, Will's sounds—as his creator would have it—somewhat effetely aesthetic, "dilettanteish." And adumbrating the decadents of the 1890's, he insists to Dorothea, "I don't feel bound, as you do, to submit to what I don't like" (p. 271). Still, his point of view is important for the novel, and important for Dorothea to understand. Their confrontation in chapter 22 is a significant one. Will tells Dorothea:

> "I fear you are a heretic about art generally. How is that? I should have expected you to be very sensitive to the beautiful everywhere."
>
> "I suppose I am dull about many things," said Dorothea, simply. "I should like to make life beautiful—I mean everybody's life. And then all this immense expense of art, that seems somehow to lie outside life and make it no better for the world, pains one. . . ."
>
> "I call that the fanaticism of sympathy," said Will, impetuously. ". . . The best piety is to enjoy—when you can. You are doing the most then to save the earth as an agreeable planet. And enjoyment radiates. It is of no use to try and take care of all the world; that is being taken care of when you feel delight—in art or in anything else" (pp. 152–53).

Two similar but uncongenial idealisms meet here: the moral ideal, to which Dorothea is devoted, and the aesthetic ideal, by which Will wants to live. In the end they are reconciled by the necessary compromise which makes Will commit himself to work as "an ardent public man" and Dorothea settle for something like the "radiance" of goodness in which Will believes, so that "the effect of her being on those around her was incalculably diffusive" (p. 578).

This ending is not a triumphant one for Dorothea. She still feels "that there was always something better which she might have done" (pp. 575–76), and George Eliot concludes that her marriage to Will was not an "ideally beautiful act, but a "sacrifice" (p. 577).

And although Dorothea believes (pp. 374–75)—and George Eliot asserts (p. 576)—that Will is no longer a dilettante, he is nevertheless not Hooker, Locke, Milton, or Pascal. He is, however, real and male, a husband for Dorothea and a father for her child. And he is prepared to work in the real world at doing practical things, "working well in those times when reforms were begun with a young hopefulness of immediate good which has been much checked in our days" (p. 576). As for Dorothea, though she is happy in her life with Will, many people, according to George Eliot, "thought it a pity that so substantive and rare a creature should have been absorbed into the life of another, and be only known in a certain circle as a wife and mother. But no one stated exactly what else that was in her power she ought to have done" (p. 576). Despite the resemblances and comparisons, Dorothea is not, after all, St. Theresa, Antigone, the Virgin Mary, or a queen.

Dorothea is only real, not mythical. And in being real, in becoming a woman of responsibility in the real world, she joins the community of Middlemarch. In so doing she proves the vitality and the significance of that community. As the reader looks back now on the "Study of Provincial Life" that he has read, the various characters exhibit a new depth, a new rich dimension of humanity which was not so evident before. There is a "feeling" that "radiates" from Dorothea, affecting one's sense of the whole novel. This happens by means of example and analogue: for not only do the comparative elements in plots and characterization support Dorothea, they are themselves elevated and enhanced by what they share with her.

The simplest analogue is the story of Fred Vincy and Mary Garth. Fred's generous irresponsibility is on the side of pleasure, and Mary's goodness is bound to duty. The reform of Fred puts him to work also—and then they are married, to live happily ever after in a romanticized descant of bliss sung above the central melody of the novel. A more serious parallel, and one opposite to the subplot of Fred and Mary, is Lydgate's story. His ambition is as uncompromisingly idealistic, originally, as Dorothea's. He looks to his profession as "the most perfect interchange between science and art . . . the most direct alliance between intellectual conquest and the social good" (p. 99), and his enthusiastically conceived prospect is "to do good small work for Middlemarch, and great work for the world" (p. 102). Lydgate fails in his grand ambitions, just as Dorothea does; but unlike her, he fails completely, ruinously, fatally. Dorothea's compromise is an honorable one made with reality, whereas Lydgate's is the sacrifice of his dignity, his honor, and his honesty. He compromises his life in order to please Rosamond's weakness and vanity, and instead of doing a realistically limited but respectable good for either Middlemarch or the world, Lydgate ends his days a prostitute to the wealthy and a specialist in the treatment of gout.

The echoes of Dorothea's character and career are obvious here. Perhaps there is also some useful connection to be drawn between the Bulstrode story and Dorothea's. In physical appearance Casaubon's double, Bulstrode is an unsavory advocate of strict Evangelical living whose piety is both a terrible private penance for himself and a self-righteousness used for the moral oppression of others. His power pervades the society of Middlemarch, and is woven carefully and fully into the fabric of the novel. Yet despite his obvious corruption, the author encourages some sort of sympathy for him—moreso than for Casaubon. George Eliot allows Bulstrode to be saved by his wife's compassionate loyalty and sympathy. In the space of five chapters she sets up three parallel tests of generosity, for Dorothea, Mrs. Bulstrode, and Rosamond. Like Dorothea, Mrs. Bulstrode responds to the test selflessly, with "new compassion and old tenderness" and a silent "promise of faithfulness" (p. 518). Played against this response is Rosamond's assertion in the face of Lydgate's distress: "Whatever misery I have to put up with, it will be easier away from here" (p. 523).

In George Eliot's world happiness is a matter of the soul, and the success which the world usually recognizes is irrelevant. Early in her career she wrote, "If art does not enlarge men's sympathies, it does nothing morally."[3] The lesson of *Middlemarch* may be in the expansion of the capacity for sympathetic understanding, through the appreciation of Dorothea's story. The famous image of the pierglass, in chapter 27, is descriptive of this phenomenon as well as of the organization of the novel:

> Your pier-glass or extended surface of polished steel made to be rubbed by a housemaid, will be minutely and multitudinously scratched in all directions; but place now against it a lighted candle as a centre of illumination, and lo! the scratches will seem to arrange themselves in a fine series of concentric circles round that little sun. It is demonstrable that the scratches are going everywhere impartially, and it is only your candle which produces the flattering illusion of a concentric arrangement, its light falling with an exclusive optical selection. These things are a parable (p. 182).

In *Middlemarch*, the complicated web of character relations can be described by reference to this image. At the same time, but thought of in a different way, this "parable" of "optical selection" can be useful in explaining how the complex focus of the novel works. All

3. See above p. 590 [*Editor*].

the characters are there, and their actions and interactions are as scratches on the surface of the Middlemarch mirror. In order to organize their activity the narrator must find some pattern therein which will help make it all intelligible. The focus George Eliot chooses—where she places her candle—is one means of achieving this meaning; and the "exclusive optical selection" which results is what ordinarily is called narrative point of view.

Lydgate is the focal character for Middlemarch activity, as I have said. By looking at him George Eliot brings the rest of her characters into the "web" of the action, and describes thus the representative world of her novel. Dorothea is outside this focus, originally, and must be seen by another light. But by means of the analogy between her story and character and Lydgate's, she is associated with that other focus, and a tie is established between the two. Finally, as Dorothea commits herself to action in the world of society, the two focuses fuse, and the several stories of Middlemarch which have already been ordered and organized to fit a single structure are seen in a new depth, with a new dimension, in the light of Dorothea's radiance. This sophisticated thematic and structural organization of the novel may be what George Eliot had in mind in saying that her "ideal" in writing *Middlemarch* was "to make matter and form an inseparable truthfulness."[4]

But what this truthfulness is, exactly, is another matter. One of the long-standing arguments among readers of George Eliot's novels is about her interpretation of the nature of human experience.[5] In *The Mill on the Floss* she writes: "the tragedy of our lives is not created entirely from within. 'Character,' says Novalis, in one of his more questionable aphorisms—'character is destiny.' But not the whole of our destiny."[6] A similar argument is presented in *Middlemarch* by the epigraph to chapter 4:

4. Haight, *Letters*, 5:374.

5. The reviewers of *The Mill on the Floss* for *The Spectator* (7 April 1860) and *The Atlas* (14 April 1860) found some hint of the force of destiny governing the action of the novel. Reviewing *Middlemarch* for *The Spectator* (1 June 1872), Richard Holt Hutton called George Eliot "melancholy," "bitter," and "sceptical." For further contemporary remarks on George Eliot's philosophical position, see Edith Simcox, *"Middlemarch," The Academy* (1 January 1873), pp. 1–4, and Sidney Colvin, *"Middlemarch," The Fortnightly Review* (19 January 1873), pp. 142–47. Bernard Shaw has found that the characters of *Middlemarch* "have no more volition than billiard balls: they are moved only by circumstance and heredity": "Postscript . . . to the Preface," *Back to Methuselah, Complete Plays and Prefaces*, 2 (New York, 1963),

pp. cv–cvi. Arnold Kettle writes that "George Eliot's view of society is in the last analysis a mechanistic and determinist one" and finds this the reason for the failure of her "Study of Provincial Life": *An Introduction to the English Novel*, 1 (London, 1951):185. George Levine has written an excellent essay on "Determinism and Responsibility in the Works of George Eliot" (PMLA 77 [1962]: pp. 268–79), concluding that she shared with John Stuart Mill the position that "the world is rigidly determined, even in cases of human choice, but that man remains responsible for his actions."

6. Part 6, ch. 6. For the source of the quotation from Novalis, see W. E. Yuill, " 'Character is Fate': a Note on Thomas Hardy, George Eliot, and Novalis," *Modern Language Review* 57 (1962): 401–2.

> *1st Gent.* Our deeds are fetters that we forge ourselves.
> *2nd Gent.* Ay, truly; but I think it is the world
> That brings the iron

The idea appears again in such statements as the narrator's "Destiny stands by sarcastic with our *dramatis personae* folded in her hands" (p. 122). Will's "I take Tamburlaine in his chariot for the tremendous course of the world's physical history lashing on the harnessed dynasties" (p. 148) and the narrator's, again, in the last paragraph of the novel, "For there is no creature whose inward being is so strong that it is not greatly determined by what lies outside it" (p. 577), are similar statements. But the epigraph to chapter 70 seems to agree with the proposition that "character is destiny":

> Our deeds still travel with us from afar,
> And what we have been makes us what we are.

George Eliot seems to be of two minds about the making of man's fate. She is not a simple determinist, yet she is unsure that human choice is ever really free. There is no contradiction inherent in such a view, of course. The problem arises in the difficult adjustment of emphasis which one must make in order to find a balance, a philosophical and practical equilibrium. Perhaps the most sophisticated and satisfactory formulation of this position is Walter Pater's, in the conclusion to his essay on Winckelmann, written in 1867:

> What modern art has to do in the service of culture is so to rearrange the details of modern life, so to reflect it, that it may satisfy the spirit. And what does the spirit need in the face of modern life? The sense of freedom. That naive, rough sense of freedom, which supposes man's will to be limited, if at all, only by a will stronger than his, he can never have again. . . . For us, necessity is not, as of old, a sort of mythological personage without us, with whom we can do warfare. It is rather a magic web woven through and through us, like that magnetic system of which modern science speaks, penetrating us with a network, subtler than our subtlest nerves, yet bearing in it the central forces of the world. Can art represent men and women in these bewildering toils so as to give the spirit at least an equivalent for the sense of freedom? . . . Natural laws we shall never modify, embarrass us as they may; but there is still something in the nobler or less noble attitude with which we watch their fatal combinations. In those romances of Goethe and Victor Hugo, in some excellent work done *after* them, this entanglement, this network of law, becomes the tragic situation, in which certain groups of noble men and women work out for themselves a supreme *denouement*.[7]

7. Walter Pater, *The Renaissance*, 2nd ed. (London, 1877), pp. 224–25.

Not only is the idea here very close to George Eliot's in its balance of necessity, responsibility, and sympathy; the images, even, are hers. The concern to "satisfy the spirit" of which Pater speaks is what Henry James called George Eliot's "extensive human sympathy."[8] The artist whose work is "so to rearrange the details of modern life, so to reflect it" as to achieve that end is she who writes of the "parable" of "optical selection" in chapter 27 of *Middlemarch*. And Pater's "magic web woven through and through us," that "entanglement" or "network of law," is what George Eliot saw before her as her work: "I at least have so much to do in unravelling certain human lots, and seeing how they were woven and interwoven, that all the light I can command must be concentrated on this particular web, and not dispersed over that tempting range of relevancies called the universe." But there is enough light, finally, for *Middlemarch* to seem a universe; and for George Eliot as well as for Pater this web of ordinary life becomes "the tragic situation, in which certain groups of noble men and women work out for themselves a supreme *denouement*." For George Eliot, this *denouement* can be worked out only in terms of the moral imagination, whose end is always "to enlarge men's sympathies" with each other, and whose means to that end is "radiance." It is the "spirit" of man that needs to be saved by art; and art works through "feeling," that "sort of knowledge" which so pervades *Middlemarch* as to be its most significant truth, the truth which may lead at last to wisdom.

LEE R. EDWARDS

Women, Energy, and *Middlemarch*†

Middlemarch is a novel about imaginative energy—the mental power to envision a self and a society as yet unformed in the given world—as this force is related to will and to society. A record of the general inability of will to call up energy sufficient not just to envision but to create new social forms, it is particularly interesting in its examination of the nature and fate of energy in female characters. Contrary to her heroines, Mary Ann Evans in her own life found both energy and will sufficient to enable her to abandon her provincial home in favor of London, break with family and religion, live openly for years with a man not her husband, and, most important, transform herself into George Eliot in whose name she wrote

8. "*Felix Holt the Radical*," *Nation* (16 August 1866), p. 127.
† From the *Massachusetts Review*, 13 (1972), pp. 223–38, © 1972, reprinted by permission. The author's footnotes have been renumbered and one has been deleted.

her books, earned her living and survived the world's real or imagined hostilities. Although we do not know what psychic stress, what sense of excessive payment rendered, caused George Eliot to reject this biographical pattern to construct instead a fictional universe where nerve and personality give way before the forces of social and natural conservatism, the defensive posture of her statement, "I should wish it to be understood that I should never invite anyone to come and see me who did not ask for the invitation," perhaps gives hints.

Despite its final failures, however, energy in *Middlemarch* initially resides in many characters: in Lydgate, Fred Vincy, Rosamond, even Casaubon, and above all, in Dorothea Brooke. Indeed, it is the force of this last character's imagination, her questing nature and desire to be both wise and useful, that illuminates the book. This illumination, arising from the rare portrayal of energy and intellectual force conjoined in an admirable female character causes *Middlemarch* to be a kind of talisman for many young women. Recognizing George Eliot as a greater writer than Louisa May Alcott, we transfer our allegiance from Jo March to Dorothea. That George Eliot's view is both more complex and more ambivalent than I had first believed is what I hope to show.

* * *

Fiction, then, provides us with neither forms for an equal life shared between men and women nor even a set of moral assumptions wide enough to embrace both sexes. True, Cleopatra's essence defied the capacity of mind to conceive or tongue to express, but she was treacherous as well. To see her treachery as the highest expression of the feminine seemed to me a moral betrayal whose magnitude was as great as her beauty. Here, when young, I spoke out loud, though awkwardly I'm sure, for the critics were no help and I was not certain why it was important for me to establish Cleopatra's evil as an ethical absolute rather than the natural—and possibly wonderful—product of her sex. In denouncing Cleopatra I was willing the necessity of some single standard in whose terms all people could be judged as replacement for the traditional sexually divided and unequal codes. The experience of the class in which I voiced my discontent still haunts my nightmares. Until my face froze and my brain congealed, I was called prude and, worse yet, insensitive, since I willfully misread the play in the interest of proving a point false both to the work and in itself. Cleopatra was not immoral but wonderful because her sexuality put her beyond morality. But the world has no room for such passion. Passion destroys men, not women—Cleopatra's death immortalizes her—by distracting their attention from its proper objects. Antony should have known better. But Cleopatra? How could she? She was female.

In this context, then, it is not hard to see why *Middlemarch* became one of the "books of my life," to use the phrase Hugh Walpole used in describing his reaction to Virginia Woolf's *Jacob's Room*. I seized upon George Eliot's novel, and more particularly on the portrait of Dorothea, as indices that my imaginative life was not as lonely and unformulated as I had feared. Like Dorothea, I was a cygnet among ducklings, passionately looking for the great river whose current would carry me to others of my kind. Like her, I had great, half-formed aspirations. Like her, I felt harassed by pressures to marry some nice young man and abandon my private and no doubt weird ideas. In Rosamond, too, I thought I had found a heroine worthy of my hate, one who was condemned not for her sexuality, but for her weakness, vanity and evil, ethical categories which, in the book at least, superseded sexual definitions. I ignored Mary Garth, mentally sending her to stand at the end of the line of insipid, goody-goody heroines. And, while I noted Dorothea's second marriage, I failed to consider its implications, sanctified as it is by children and by Dorothea's reconciliation with her sister and with a world where the continuity of life is represented by the safe inheritance of entailed estates passing through the male line. I found my new fifth act, or so I thought, because I saw in Dorothea an endorsement I had found in no other book I had read of energy and social commitment on the part of a woman in combination, as I believed, with the promise that these qualities did not render the possessor either a social misfit or a danger to herself or others. In the interests of finding what I badly needed to find in some imaginative work, I had reduced the novel to a comic homily on the possibility of combining marriage with intellectual aspiration.

I also misread the book. For, while *Middlemarch* is undoubtedly a work which devotes many pages to Dorothea, she is by no means the whole novel. And while energy illuminates the work, its light seems now neither so clear nor so powerful as I once thought, or hoped, it was. For *Middlemarch* is finally not an endorsement of this energy, but first an examination and finally a condemnation of it.

In this condemnation, however, George Eliot is by no means unambivalent, as we can see if we look briefly at the structure of the book. In these terms, *Middlemarch* is peculiarly divided. Both tragic and comic, it divorces its emotional centers—Dorothea and Lydgate and their foils Casaubon and Rosamond—from its ethical pivot. It is the Garths and the other permanent residents of the town who, guaranteeing the enduring life of Middlemarch itself, also provide the moral norms of the book. In this connection it is, I think, significant to note that the action of the book, excluding the Finale, stops before the Reform Bill becomes fact, and the characters who threaten Middlemarch's values are changed (Dorothea), defeated (Lydgate), killed (Casaubon), condemned (Rosamond), or sent away, perhaps into a wider world, or merely into exile.

George Eliot sacrifices energy and personality to place and to the conservative necessities which that place dictates. But her ambivalence toward this sacrifice can be seen and felt if we notice that the book's structural anomalies are reinforced by the treatment character receives as well. The weight of the book's tragic structure is carried by a quartet of characters whose complexity George Eliot both apprehends and renders and whose stories compose the bulk of the book. The book's comic structure, on the other hand, is carried by characters who are frequently little more than caricatures, fragments of identity left over from a Jane Austen or a Dickens novel. With the exception of Mary Garth and Fred Vincy and, if one is being generous, Sir James and Celia, these characters have no stories but only scenes which take up the space between the major narratives.

It is, of course, possible that what I have defined as structural ambivalence was in fact accounted for by George Eliot when she called the book not after one of her major figures but instead *Middlemarch: A Study of Provincial Life.* In other words, the book is neither tragic nor comic but simply realistic, and what in tragic terms is annihilation is for the author, and hence for the reader who would read the book correctly, merely a realistic assessment of the best that can be done in the world, both fictional and real. Even if this position is taken, however, the particular sense of reality which the novel as a whole engenders derives from a tension—implicit and covert it is true, but nonetheless there—between truncated tragic and attenuated comic modes.

These modes are linked by the character of Dorothea who, it seems, participates in both and is, for this reason, as well as others more commonly noted, the center of the book. But the linkage is incomplete because for Dorothea to become a comic rather than a tragic heroine she must be transformed from one whose energy is so great as to constitute a threat to her society to one whose power can be contained by it. She is, in a very real sense, not the same character at the book's end that she was at its beginning. Although she leaves Middlemarch she still has a home there and, in claiming it, is herself diminished.

The image of Dorothea presented at the book's beginning is, to borrow a phrase from Simone de Beauvoir, apparently transcendent. To turn to her from Celia, Mary Garth, and Mrs. Garth is to turn from characters and women who are themselves both innately conservative and a cause of conservatism in others, who either have no energies—like Celia—or who ruthlessly suppress them—like Mrs.

Garth—who function through stasis to inspire others to return to the fold, to one for whom radical upheaval, both personal and social, seems, at least initially, possible. With her ardent nature, her intelligence, her desire not simply to be good but to discover what might be good in order to use the fruits of this discovery to change the world, Dorothea seems to be a woman whose like had not been fictively recorded in 1871 and whose imaginary history still does not exist. Even today, women readers in particular, feel in the book's opening chapters the promise of a new spiritual incarnation, possibly even an entirely new creation. We wait, almost desperately, for the author's imagination to divine a world whose shadowy existence we have long suspected, but whose reality has been perpetually denied.

But, however much we may wish it otherwise, *Middlemarch* gives very little evidence that George Eliot wished to be the god in some new machine. From Prelude to Finale, and for 86 chapters in between, she tells us instead that in the early part of the nineteenth century in England, a woman whose "passionate ideal nature demanded an epic life," whose inner "flame . . . soared after some illimitable satisfaction, some object which would never justify weariness, which would reconcile self-despair with the rapturous consciousness of life beyond self" would be defeated or, at best, deflected. George Eliot is writing not the ultimate comedy of some new incarnation, but rather the record of its failure. Seeing a world which lacked "coherent social faith and order," George Eliot either would or could not choose to create an alternative universe in her fiction. Instead, she records the dislocation which is "offspring of a certain spiritual grandeur ill-matched with the meanness of opportunity," the isolation of the cygnet who "never finds the living stream in fellowship with its own oary-footed kind."

This failure could be tragic, however, and Dorothea a tragic character, if and only if her aspirations at the book's beginnings were taken entirely seriously by the author. And they are not. Nor are Dorothea's longings as unfettered by traditional assumptions about the kinds of fulfillment open to women as a cursory reading might seem to indicate. Throughout the book, George Eliot both pities and gently mocks Dorothea. This attitude of sorrowful amusement is not merely consequent upon her marrying Casaubon, but in fact precedes the marriage and exists precisely because Dorothea is the sort of woman who would marry Casaubon in the first place. Dorothea is short-sighted, a physical defect which in this book, as in many, has its psychic implications. Moreover, George Eliot or her narrative surrogate in the book continually addresses and identifies the elder Miss Brooke as "poor Dorothea" and ranges herself regretfully but unequivocally with Celia in her assessment of

Dorothea's character. In Chapter 7, for example, it asserts that "Miss Brooke was certainly very naive with all her alleged cleverness. Celia, whose mind had never been thought too powerful, saw the emptiness of other people's pretensions much more readily." This statement, however, is less simple than it seems. Apparently, the pretensions referred to belong to Casaubon, but it is equally possible that they may secondarily refer to Dorothea as well. For, the immediately preceding sentence states that Dorothea "had not reached that point of renunciation at which she would have been satisfied with having a wise husband: she wished, poor child, to be wise herself." In other words, it is at least possible that it is not only Casaubon's knowledge which is empty pretense, but also Dorothea's desire for knowledge of her own.

If the possibility that Dorothea's quest for knowledge was, at best, misguided were raised only here, the passage would hardly be worth noting. But it is not. Indeed, George Eliot repeatedly insists on the futility and even foolishness of any desire to find an outlet for energy in the acquisition of wisdom defined narrowly as education and dissociates Dorothea from Casaubon by saying that "it would be a great mistake to suppose that Dorothea would have cared about any share in Casaubon's learning as mere accomplishment." On the contrary, she seems to be saying that Dorothea's desire for knowledge is a confused expression of her true longing for a combined moral and intellectual guidance, an analogue in the nineteenth-century world and in her own life to the force which the Catholic faith provided for Saint Theresa. Unable to find her "ideal of life" in the "walled-in maze" which constitutes the usual occupations open to a woman of the leisured class, Dorothea sees knowledge as offering the only way out of the labyrinth. But the radical implications of this vision are tempered since both Dorothea and her creator see this knowledge in terms of a "union which . . . would . . . give her the freedom of voluntary submission to a guide who would take her along the grandest path." This union is not a transcendent linking of the mind with abstract principles systematically combining wisdom and morality, but is instead mediated by physical reality and institutionalized.

Desiring to lead "a grand life here—now—in England," neither Dorothea nor George Eliot can see a way to realize this desire directly. "Since the time was gone by for guiding visions and spiritual directors, since prayer heightened yearning but not instruction," and more interestingly, since George Eliot does not even consider the possibility of educational reform as a way out of Dorothea's dilemma, marriage becomes the educating institution. In marrying Casaubon, Dorothea is mistaken merely about the contents of this knowledge, but not about the form through which such knowledge should come to her.

When Dorothea says that "people may really have in them some vocation which is not quite plain to themselves," she is speaking to Casaubon about Will. We, however, may hear her words as unwittingly self-referential and, more significantly, as revealing as well George Eliot's own bafflement with certain aspects of Dorothea's character. For, at the book's beginning, Dorothea is like Will, a character in search of a vocation, a form in which her spiritual and social energies can be harmonized and through which they can be directed in order to affect the world at large. Since, however, George Eliot has drawn Dorothea as a character to whom "permanent rebellion, the disorder of a life without some loving reverent resolve" was impossible, her search for a vocation is cut short almost before it begins. In contrast to Will, who has not only time but space in which to try on different roles. Dorothea does not. And where Will can attempt and reject a number of vocations before finding his niche as a member of Parliament, Dorothea can not. Unlike Will, Dorothea has only two alternatives: she can marry or she can remain a spinster. But even this choice is more apparent than real. Dorothea *must* marry. For unmarried and not endowed with the strength for permanent rebellion, there is no way for her even to begin to find for herself the wisdom she desires. Unmarried and untutored, she can only devise plans for cottages whose fireplaces may well interfere with their stairways. And even were her plans correct, she can not build the cottages in any case, having neither the money nor, more importantly, the courage to do so on her own. Like Kate Chopin's Edna Pontellier, she lacks the strong wings necessary for the artist: her wish for freedom is always checked by her equally strong desire to submit. And if, for whatever reasons, we ignore both sides of the equation George Eliot has set up throughout the book for defining Dorothea's character, the book's ending becomes as incomprehensible as many critics have found it to be.

Why, it is asked, does Dorothea marry Will? Because the answer to this question is most often given in terms which account for the marriage by opposing Will's presumed sensuality to Casaubon's sterility, even those posing this solution are unhappy with it and condemn the author for failing to make Dorothea's savior more sexually viable. Sexuality, however, does not provide the key to Will's significance, though the truth of this statement may indeed point to a gap in George Eliot's perceptions. Far from being an erotic radical, a pre-Lawrencian Mellors saving Dorothea by his phallic force, Will is instead a social reformer who find a vocation which can use his romantic vision when, at the book's conclusion he is transformed into "an ardent public man," and through Dorothea's adjective, into a version of Dorothea herself. Since wrongs exist and since Will is in the thick of a struggle against them, George Eliot establishes him as a husband for Dorothea, who can "give him wifely help" of just the sort she wanted to give Casaubon but could not. What *Middlemarch* is missing then is a more powerful rendering both of Ladislaw's physical presence and his social vision. We know he would reform, but what and how we know not. We know that Dorothea would help him, but don't know the exact nature of her help.

At this point, however, some real problems concerning Dorothea's second marriage do intrude themselves. The objection is not that Dorothea should have married Will but that she should have married anybody at all, that she should ultimately be denied the opportunity given Will to find her own paths and forge her energies into some new mold. Acknowledging that "many who know her, thought it a pity that so substantive and rare a creature should have been absorbed into the life of another, and be only known in a certain circle as a wife and mother," George Eliot acknowledges the fact that Dorothea is a character who might have been fulfilled in a wider world than the one she as author finally provides. But she also claims that "no one stated exactly what else that was in her power she ought rather to have done"; looking outward, George Eliot simply could not find this new and bigger world. The religion which inspired Antigone and Saint Theresa to perform their heroic deeds alone is gone. And to fill this vacuum George Eliot found it necessary to impose tradition, widening it a bit to allow Mary Garth to write a book and Dorothea to go to London, but stopping short of a full exploration of a world which would have had its birth not in reality's mirror but in the artist's will. We could perhaps have had this vision if the author held the mirror to reflect not only the world both she and Dorothea knew and left behind but also that one she forced into existence when she stopped being Mary Ann Evans and became George Eliot instead. In *Middlemarch*, however, George Eliot refuses this option and accepts a safety not entirely celebrated but rather tinged with resignation, ambivalently regarded.

It is, however, only when we draw away from Dorothea to look instead at Rosamond that the reasons for George Eliot's ambivalent attitude toward Dorothea's energy become clear. In thus moving, we are not travelling so great a distance as it might at first appear. Although Rosamond is in many ways Dorothea's opposite, they are opposed as two sides of the same coin are opposed and are centrally bonded by the common metal of their energy. It is usual to see Rosamond as simply the typical nineteenth-century heroine exposed by the persistent hostility of George Eliot's vision. This view seems to me both distorted and reductive, for it fails to take note of precisely that facet of Rosamond's character which is most interesting: the strength of her will. Like Jay Gatsby, Rosamond would spring from her own Platonic image of herself. Formed like him out of a mixed romanticism and vulgarity, her reckless will is finally even stronger than Dorothea's because it is not tempered as Dorothea's was by either the cooling winds of self-effacement or the broadening channels of social concern. What she wants is simply her own way out of Middlemarch. But her way, like Dorothea's is defined throughout the book in society's terms, though Rosamond's society is, to be sure, more limited because more narrowly class and money conscious than Dorothea's. And, like Dorothea, Rosamond cannot get her way, cannot gain both the freedom from Middlemarch's constrictions and the material perquisites she feels are due her without a husband.

In the last part of his essay *The Subjection of Women*,[1] published just two years before *Middlemarch*, John Stuart Mill provides a beautiful abstract for the Rosamond-Lydgate marriage seen against a matrix in which the woman's will to power is strengthened proportionally as her capacities for personal liberty are denied by the combined forces of social conventions both external and internal. I can do no better than to quote from the essay:

> An active and energetic mind, if denied liberty, will seek for power: refused the command of itself, it will assert its personality by attempting to control others. To allow to any human beings no existence of their own but what depends on others, is giving far too high a premium on bending others to their purposes. Where liberty cannot be hoped for, and power can, power becomes the grand object of human desire; those to whom others will not leave the undisturbed management of their own affairs, will compensate themselves, if they can, by meddling for their own purposes with the affairs of others. Hence also women's passion for personal beauty, and dress and display; and all the evils that flow from it. . . . The love of power and the love of liberty are in eternal antagonism. Where there is least liberty, the passion for power is the most ardent and unscrupulous.

Denied liberty, denied an education which would foster the formation of a personal vision which might then be tested against society's claims, Rosamond becomes, as she must, society's agent, in Mill's terms, a "hostage to Mrs. Grundy."

Like Mill, George Eliot has a powerful awareness of the destructiveness of Rosamond's energy. And, as is the case with Dorothea, she can find nothing to do with it, no place to put it once the possibility of wifely submission is denied. Thus, what I have called George Eliot's conservatism is finally both the logical conclusion to

1. The quotations from Mill are taken from the excellent *Essays on Sex Equality* by John Stuart Mill and Harriet Taylor Mill, edited and with an introductory essay by Alice S. Rossi, Chicago and London, 1970.

the problem of female energy posed in her work and, less happily, the result of the failure of her own imagination to create the sorts of alternatives Mill envisions. Middlemarch and its environs are a closed world whose survival depends on the continuing life of values cherished by the author. Her fidelity to these values, however, prevents George Eliot from arriving at a radical solution—or, indeed, any solution—to the problems of female energy the book proposes. She can only struggle to contain the energy, force the new wine back into the old bottles, as she does with Dorothea, or condemn its egotism as most hostile to the community she loves.

Only one small scene, Lydgate's memory of Madame Laure, points to the road George Eliot rejected. These passages, like no others in the book, leap from the page, demanding to be read symbolically. But as symbol of what? The traditional reading makes the scene reflect on Lydgate, showing us what he as yet can't see: that he would do well to stay unmarried. Obviously, too, Madame Laure herself reflects on Rosamond, a spiritual rather than a physical murderer. If, however, the general reading proposed here has any validity, if, that is, *Middlemarch* is significantly, even centrally, concerned with the problem that excess energy in combination with the world's conventions poses for George Eliot and her female characters, then certainly another reading is possible. When Madame Laure says, "You are a good young man. But I do not like husbands. I shall never have another," she is speaking as a woman who has literally killed a man to gain her freedom. By underscoring the violence of Laure's energy, the ruthlessness of her power, George Eliot shows clearly what she is most afraid of if she leaves her female characters generally unbridled. But we can only wonder —and perhaps regret—that this image was not pursued further and in another direction, that George Eliot did not finally create a woman who knew before the fact that she neither liked nor needed husbands since such liking would force her either to submit or to destroy. Had George Eliot been able to find some system of values by which such a woman could live, she might have succeeded in breathing life again into Saint Theresa's dessicated image.

It is illegitimate, I know, to condemn an author for what she did not choose to do. But as I have moved away from what I now believe was merely an adolescent fantasy concerning the contents and implications of *Middlemarch* to what I hope is a more true understanding of the text's attitudes toward woman, I see that it can no longer be one of the books of my life. In so seeming, I am alternately angered, puzzled, and finally depressed. Madame Laure's history without her husband, the story of Dorothea as a social force, the tale of Rosamond as a political novel, none of these have been written. If we can imagine a world or a vision that might write them, then perhaps this condition is not final and, creating our own futures, we may be consoled.

LLOYD FERNANDO

Special Pleading and Art in *Middlemarch*: The Relations between the Sexes†

Dorothea and Lydgate in George Eliot's *Middlemarch* are very frequently compared and contrasted in critical discussions, but no one has examined the fundamental reasons for considering them as a pair at all. Lydgate is even regarded as not being as important a character as Dorothea—an instance where an apparent unwillingness to benefit from our knowledge of a background social issue actually blinds us to balancing antitheses of character and theme. The issue in question was that of the revaluation of the relationship between the sexes which was the subject of much public debate in England during the second half of the nineteenth century, and which brings to light neglected aspects of Dorothea and Lydgate's relationship to each other in the novel—or as some would prefer to put it, their very lack of a living relationship with each other. To examine this question is to discover further unsuspected depths of organization in the entire novel which, while maintaining its own inner logic, was also governed by a deeply felt response to an important contemporary controversy.

Professor Barbara Hardy's essay on *Middlemarch* in her book *The Appropriate Form* was a notable advance in criticism of this novel. The advantage won in independent but converging ways by W. J. Harvey's own work besides hers was based on the premise that 'the novel holds us by its story and informs us by its moral argument, but it moves us by its individual presences and moments'[1]—which surely restores to their rightful place the things we enjoy about *Middlemarch*. The explication of a great novelist's organization of categories, parallels, and antitheses must lend a necessary aesthetic dimension to our pleasure, but we had clearly lost some flexibility through excessive preoccupation with this kind of unity. I do not know whether 'completeness,' whose claims Professor Hardy advances as an alternative critical term to 'unity', will

---

† From *Modern Language Review*, vol. 67, pp. 44–49, © 1972, reprinted by permission. The author's footnotes have been renumbered.

1. Barbara Hardy, *The Appropriate Form: An Essay on the Novel* (London, 1964), pp. 2–3.

equally satisfy us all. It does move one away from artificial notions of symmetry and towards an acceptance of her triad, story, argument, and truthful imitation of life. An awareness that aspects of these sometimes reflect contemporary social issues in detail does not inevitably produce an increase in appreciation, but there is occasionally a further gain in definition which is not to be despised. We can illustrate this point by examining the relations between the sexes in *Middlemarch* revealed by the interaction of the main characters.

But how many principal characters are there in this novel? The answer seems to be anything from one to five—which should serve to caution the unwary critic about being dogmatic on the issue. There is not neat symmetry, a final, once-for-all structure of relationships between the characters but, in Professor Hardy's words, 'a highly complex and mobile pattern'. She herself posits three, Dorothea, Casaubon, and Ladislaw. What if we gave the kaleidoscope another shake and brought in Lydgate and Rosamond, too? I do not think we have given full weight yet to Henry James's observation concerning Lydgate and Dorothea in his famous review: 'The mind passes from one to the other with that supreme sense of the vastness and variety of human life, under aspects apparently similar, which it belongs only to the greatest novels to produce.'[2] I mean we have not contrasted these two in sexual terms, believing it, I suppose, to be uncalled for. An inordinate amount of critical attention has been devoted instead to Dorothea's relationship with Ladislaw. Let us first define the basis on which her relationship with Lydgate should attract prior attention.

She is endowed with a certain largeness of conception which cannot be caught by 'realistic' nets alone. Her spiritual and cultural genealogy is affirmed with a confidence that is breathtaking: she is a modern Saint Theresa with the presence of the Blessed Virgin, the latter a comparison which Lydgate explicitly makes near the end of his own marital drama (Chapter 76). Naumann, with a painter's eye for essentials, ecstatically declared, " 'Here stands beauty in its breathing life, with the consciousness of Christian centuries in its bosom" ' (Chapter 19). One gathers she is in the mainstream of a scheme of spiritual aspiration evolving beyond doctrinal religion. It is not necessary to deny that this ambitious affiliation of such an attractive heroine with a spiritual pantheon through the ages constitutes a piece of special pleading by the author on behalf of her sex at a time when questions about the nature of woman were being vehemently discussed. W. J. Harvey suggests that a saving irony operates.[3] No doubt it does; but the religious perspective is also

2. *The House of Fiction* (London, 1957), p. 264.

3. *The Art of George Eliot* (London, 1961), p. 154.

indicative of the scope in which the character was conceived which, in numerous little touches, gives the early chapters of *Middlemarch* their compelling power.[4] By some 'unerring mechanism' this great enlargement of the portrait retains credible contact with the character in her more mundane preoccupations and contributes to what Henry James regarded as 'the great achievement of the book'. There would be no special point in noting this if it did not help to clarify Dorothea's relationships with the other principals as well.

In joining the story of the large-souled 'Miss Brooke' to the novel of Middlemarch society George Eliot removed from the scene the heroine to whom she had devoted ten full chapters and introduced the remaining principals in the next eight (Chapters 11–18). But when she returns to Dorothea in Rome (Chapters 19–22), the attempt to make a virtue of necessity is not wholly successful. Authorial reticence in one direction vies unevenly with expansiveness in another. That Casaubon is impotent and that the marriage in all probability has not been consummated are details which must be teased out by such a judicious critic as Professor Hardy. The crisis is an individual one first and most importantly—but not last. There is a kind of magic lantern projection of this hiatus against the ruins of Rome with its 'vast wreck of ambitious ideals, sensuous and spiritual' (Chapter 22). It is not surprising that there is strain here, even a slight incoherence, since the attempt is to compress into a few pages an ambitious art-history perspective for the heroine, besides her spiritual one. A piquant irony does partially save these pages, particularly where Dorothea serves as a model for a painting: the portrait of another defeated protagonist of the human spirit is added to history's wrecked ideals by—further irony—Naumann, 'one of the chief renovators of Christian art' (Chapter 22). Ironic representation is further advanced in Naumann's artifice of using Casaubon as model for his painting of Saint Thomas Aquinas 'sitting among the doctors of the Church in a disputation too abstract to be represented'. The heir of Aquinas with his influential metaphysics is Casaubon, 'elaborator of small explanations' (Chapter 21). We recognize the irony but must admit that contrivance is to the fore, and that special pleading, in the form of exaggerated female portraiture, has here produced undue rhetorical emphasis, colouring yet further the sexless romantic glow in which Dorothea and Ladislaw are bathed.

Let us now turn to Lydgate, and here W. J. Harvey's elucidation of Lydgate's intellectual interests is helpful.[5] Lydgate sees the medi-

4. I have analysed the intellectual framework behind the character of Dorothea in 'George Eliot, Feminism, and Dorothea Brooke', *Review of English Literature*, 4 (1963), 76–90.

5. W. J. Harvey, 'The Intellectual Background of the Novel: Casaubon and Lydgate', in *'Middlemarch': Critical Approaches to the Novel*, edited by Barbara Hardy (London, 1967), 25–37.

cal profession as holding out the promise of 'the most perfect interchange between science and art' (Chapter 15). That there is a
degree of error in the basic hypothesis behind his projected research
does 'place' him, as Harvey shows, but there is enough in the
quality of his thought still to make him a worthy counterpart to
Dorothea. There is an 'arts/science-syndrome' air about the way the
two complement each other, and it is tempting to argue that Lydgate is Dorothea's soul-mate, not Ladislaw. But how, one may ask,
do their careers substantiate this? In a previous essay I sought to
show that so far as George Eliot had a 'philosophy of life', it was a
scheme of such intricacy and comprehensiveness that it argued a
nature bent on preserving tradition.[6] Every endeavour had to be
devoted to promoting success in marriage, for the advancement of
life itself depended upon it. On the other hand, the histories of
Dorothea's marriage and Lydgate's show an incisive awareness of
the prevalence of marital incompatibility. There are two disadvantages in accepting the fable at the heart of *Middlemarch* as that of a
rescue into love, as Professor Hardy proposes.[7] First, we are compelled to give fuller weight than is necessary to the end result of that
rescue, the falsely romantic association of Dorothea and Ladislaw
—with the consequent dissatisfaction we have not been able to
exorcise for years now. Second and rather more seriously, we
underestimate one of the gripping successes of the major part of
Middlemarch, the impressively authentic, and artistic, representation of marital incompatibility, Dorothea's and Lydgate's with their
respective partners. After the conflation of the two separate writing
projects George Eliot had embarked upon, *Middlemarch* was no
more the story of 'Miss Brooke' alone but of Lydgate as well—he
holds the centre of the other half of the novel. And since the novel
appeared at a time when the relations between the sexes, particularly in marriage, were under searching scrutiny, it is difficult to
ignore this external resonance of the drama of their failed marriages. One does not wish to claim any particular artistic merit for
Middlemarch simply because it does analyse the disturbing reality
which was the subject of so much contemporary controversy; rather
it is that the controversy alerts us to an unsuspected basis for
comparing Dorothea with Lydgate, and thereby further defines the
core of the novel's art.

Do we not sometimes unconsciously subscribe to the conventional myth that there are such things as ideal pairs? Dorothea and
Lydgate fit that myth remarkably well. It is a moot point how far
George Eliot had the ironical intention of enticing the reader to
speculate on the course their lives would have taken had they mar-

6. 'George Eliot, Feminism, and Doro-   7. *The Appropriate Form*, p. 121.
thea Brooke'.

ried. Dorothea appeals to Lydgate before any other character for advice in her distress in marriage (Chapter 30). Exigencies of the plot in the first place—Casaubon's first attack—have brought Lydgate to Lowick, but there is a play on the parallels and differences of their natures suggested through their 'vocations', Dorothea being to Saint Theresa as Lydgate is to Vesalius. The force of the analogy does not stop here. The pair also represent the sexes in a fundamental way. Dorothea's turn to help Lydgate in his own defeat comes at the end of the novel when his marriage and career are near ruin. They are kindred natures, not in being similar, but in the status of each as the nearest ideal complement of the other. Dorothea recognizes this fact instinctively; Lydgate's awareness grows on him with each successive meeting; and the reader is stirred by this speculative attraction of contraries. At the same time it is true, as the novel stands, that their sense of kinship is not simply sexual attraction but a more inclusive, 'Promethean', kind.[8]

The novel's artistry is distinctively served, then, by keeping them, maritally speaking, apart. Their largely separate fortunes constitute a major ironic metaphor emphasizing what for the author was the most pernicious 'non-moral' fact of all: that true integration of feeling and intellect has to be sought in a stream of life so incredibly complex as to preclude worthwhile success before we even begin. An ideally successful marriage almost never comes about. In terms of George Eliot's deterministic philosophy the essential tragedy lay here. The movement of life in the mass does not, of its nature, adapt itself to the true potential of this or that particular element within it. The irony lies in the fact that meetings are rarely opportune, and in the further teasing ambiguity, creatively generated by the novel's way of showing how small circumstances go to make or unmake large events, concerning whether Lydgate and Dorothea would in fact have made a successful marriage if they had met when still uncommitted. Speculation under the latter head would pitch us straight into Professor Knights's fallacy of Lady Macbeth's children, but it is the open-ended nature of the contrast between the two which is fascinating. The largely separate paths on which these two characters are set even before they meet symbolize the fundamental divergence plaguing the successful marrying of the sexes.

But what of the marriages which do take place? How do they extend the analysis of the relations between the sexes, and further define the pattern of character-relationships in the novel? A remarkably similar rhetoric is used in portraying the courtships of Casaubon and Lydgate, with an almost identical ironical aim. Lydgate, engaged to Rosamond,

8. *George Eliot's Life as Related in her letters and Journals*, edited by J. W.   Cross, 3 vols (London and Edinburgh, 1885), III, 48.

felt as if already breathed upon by exquisite wedded affection such as would be bestowed by an accomplished creature who venerated his high musings and momentous labours and would never interfere with them; who would create order in the home and accounts with still magic, yet keep her fingers ready to touch the lute and transform life into romance at any moment; who was instructed to the true womanly limit and not a hair's breadth beyond— docile, therefore, and ready to carry out behests which came from beyond that limit. (Chapter 36)

Casaubon's expectations of happiness proceed, not surprisingly, at a sedate pace but are not different in kind from Lydgate's more ebullient imaginings. Key phrases in his letter of proposal to Dorothea (Chapter 5) strikingly echo Lydgate's thoughts in the passage above. Casaubon's labours are 'grave', Lydgate's 'momentous'; Casaubon expects that Dorothea will 'cast a charm over vacant hours', Lydgate that Rosamond will 'transform life into romance at any moment'; Dorothea is expected to 'supply' Casaubon's need, Rosamond must be 'ready to carry out [Lydgate's] behests'. Casaubon's hopes are only an older and more tired version of Lydgate's. We are told that Casaubon took a wife 'to adorn the remaining quadrant of his course, and be a little moon that would hardly cause a calculable perturbation' (Chapter 11), and the solar metaphor aptly underlines the conventional myth about relations between men and women which both men share, as did their contemporaries. The strokes of characterization even here have a resonance beyond the individual.

The crisis in each marriage consists essentially of the downfall of the man from his self-assumed position of lord, contributor to the world's knowledge, and guardian—in a way that goes near the bone. 'And all your notes', cries Dorothea, 'all those rows of volumes— will you not now do what you used to speak of?—will you not make up your mind what part of them you will use, and begin to write the book which will make your vast knowledge useful to the world?' (Chapter 20). In a marriage which thereafter hangs 'like a murder' (Chapter 81), the momentary flicker of rapport between husband and wife at the end of Chapter 42 is one of the most moving passages in the entire novel, and affords a remarkably convincing illustration of the fruits of Dorothea's womanly power. Lydgate's story is more chilling owing to the ease with which Rosamond overcomes a man of his intellectual calibre. She begins her act of destruction with 'Do you know, Tertius, I often wish you had not been a medical man' (Chapter 45); and no worthwhile affection lightens the history of this marriage. Unlike Casaubon, Lydgate is resilient enough to seek a way out of his impasse, but his appeal to Rosamond is doomed, for she replies in her most 'neutral' way,

'What can *I* do, Tertius?' (author's italics). Dorothea had addressed an almost identically worded question to Casaubon, 'What shall I do?' and the range between the two questions is the subject of authorial comment:

> That little speech [of Rosamond's] of four words, like so many others in all languages, is capable by varied vocal inflexions of expressing all states of mind from helpless dimness to exhaustive argumentative perception, from the completest self-devoting fellowship to the most neutral aloofness. (Chapter 58)

In other words, in both marriages the force of 'intellect', the traditional preserve of the man, is baffled by grinding female scepticism, aroused partly by undervalued potential.

The critical gap in the relations between Dorothea and Lydgate, then, does not present a simple unrelated contrast but is the locus of a creatively balanced interplay of character and of an organic extension of theme. To extend this line of argument to include Ladislaw, however, is admittedly much more debatable. What is clear is that against the reality of the two failed marriages which also represent a great novelist's response to issues of the day, the relationship of Dorothea and Ladislaw has a tinsel charm so incredibly at variance that it is unreasonable to interpret it as a failure of authorial distancing—and at the finishing line at that. Does it strain credulity to accept this conclusion rather as a sop to contemporary readers who had watched the dramas of married life unfold month by month over 1871–2? The implausible innocence of this pair may have been intended partly as a 'consoling lie' (to borrow a phrase from Professor Hardy), and the source of the artistic failure may well lie in an attenuation of concern for the novel's internal laws by the demands of popular publishing. Still the romantic conclusion is double-edged, and accords with my argument: by finally allying Ladislaw's limited romanticism with Dorothea's 'vigorous enthusiasm' (Chapter 19), shallow notions of romantic love are also ironically placed. The romantic ending to Dorothea's career stands in contrast to her true potential, as well as to the thorough-going analysis of love and marriage which informs most of the book. This concluding symmetrical touch, so far as it concerns Ladislaw, remains obstinately skeletal in the total pattern of character-relationships, it is true, but at the least we can see it as a failure of art, rather than of sensibility.

Of course the characterization of Dorothea was something close to the author's heart, but so too, one needs must see, was the issue so judiciously espoused and so diversely hidden. Its undeniable presence, nevertheless, makes it clear that the character of Lydgate contributes importantly to the structure of the novel. He is the lynch-pin for the intricate scientific and social world of Middle-march as Dorothea is for its best, though inarticulate, aspirations. That these two are themselves bound to each other by a profound though unnamed kinship is as much an enlightening commentary on a vexed social issue as a highly successful artistic device which unobtrusively secures the novel as a whole. W. J. Harvey was right to say that with George Eliot 'We do not leave the "real" world behind when we are confronted with the world of the novels; in fact [she] compels us to keep both worlds firmly in our minds'.[9] In doing so in this essay we discover greater consistency and, indeed, stronger evidence of 'unity', flawed, it may be, but greater than is allowed. Without being dogmatic about this term we should not refuse the evidence for it where it offers itself, even though it be in relation to a social issue—before we give the wondrous kaleidoscope which is *Middlemarch* another shake.

JEROME BEATY

History by Indirection:
The Era of Reform in *Middlemarch*†

Few readers notice how many details from the political history of a period forty years prior to the time of composition are present throughout *Middlemarch*. I wish here to give some idea of the nature and pervasiveness of those details—though indeed there are so many I cannot include them all—and to indicate how George Eliot managed to keep them, numerous as they are, from obtruding upon the fiction.

The events in *Middlemarch* are supposed to take place between 30 September 1829 and the end of May 1832. Most of the historical references in the novel therefore concern events and personalities involved in the struggle for political reform which culminated in the passage of the First Reform Bill in June 1832. For roughly the first half of this period, the Tories—under Wellington, Peel, and George IV—are in control, and though they are forced to give ground grudgingly on some issues—Catholic Emancipation, for instance—they manage to hold out against the forces of reform, even against such moderate reform as that urged by men like Huskisson. With the death of George IV in June 1830 and the assumption of power by the Whigs, under Lord Grey, in November, reform of some kind

---

9. *The Art of George Eliot*, p. 79.
† Reprinted by permission of *Victorian Studies*, I (Bloomington, Indiana, 1957–58), 173–79. The author's footnotes have been renumbered and two have been deleted.

is inevitable; interest centers on the parliamentary election of 1831 and the controversy, particularly in the House of Lords, over Lord Russell's Reform Bill.

In *Middlemarch* political events manifest themselves early, though at first only as background. In Chapter 3 Mr. Brooke is already showing Casaubon "documents" on machine-breaking and rick-burning, signs of the political discontent of the period. A few pages later, George Eliot, in one of the few historical utterances made directly to the reader in this novel, speaks of "those ante-reform times." Beginning with the very next scene political references become more specific: Mr. Brooke conjectures that Casaubon may be made a bishop "if Peel stays in," for, we later learn, Casaubon has written "a very good pamphlet for Peel" on the Catholic question. These references to Peel and Catholic Emancipation, here lumped together, are worked into the text of *Middlemarch* with the greatest of circumspection: the fact that Casaubon may hope to profit by Peel appears in Chapter 4; that he has written a pamphlet on the Catholic question appears near the end of Chapter 7; that it is this pamphlet which should put him in Peel's favor appears in Chapter 30. In none of these chapters is a date mentioned; indeed, the year 1829 is specified only once in the novel, and that not until Chapter 15.

Peel is mentioned several more times. On one occasion, during Peter Featherstone's last illness, Borthrop Trumbull notes that Peel has just inherited his father's title (Chapter 32), an event which actually took place on 3 May 1830. Two chapters later the chronology is confirmed; we are told that "It was on a morning of May that Peter Featherstone was buried."

A last mention of Peel, in Chapter 37, links his name with that of Wellington—"Wellington and Peel generally depreciated." After the first reference to Wellington as Prime Minister in Chapter 19, he is mentioned on three occasions and on all three is in disfavor. The first of these links him to Peel, as I have just noted; the second occurs at the auction, when Trumbull is trying to sell "an engraving of the Duke of Wellington surrounded by his staff on the field of Waterloo . . . notwithstanding recent events which have . . . enveloped our great Hero in a cloud . . ." (Chapter 60); the last is a remark by Mr. Limp, one of the company at Dollop's, who has read in the *Trumpet* a statement made by the Duke, "when he turned his coat and went over to the Romans" (Chapter 71).

Already we can see certain of George Eliot's techniques for handling political history: she introduces it largely through refrences to historical personages; she mentions but never explains issues; she scatters references to the same person or issue through the novel rather than lumping them in a single paragraph or chapter; she separates the event from specific dates. In other words, she presents history dramatically, within the story, as part of the lives of the characters; she rarely offers it directly to the reader as history.

About the time Peel's name disappears from the novel, a new one, that of Huskisson, is introduced. A Canningite, Huskisson lost his place in the Wellington Cabinet by trying to transfer two disenfranchised seats to growing towns, a kind of moderate reform. As a private member, in March 1830, he again supported such a move. During the summer of that year, Huskisson's name and views appear in *Middlemarch*: Hackbutt and Hawley are discussing reform, Rights of Man, the non-representation of large towns, and pocketboroughs. Hackbutt says,

> "I myself should never favour immoderate views—in fact I take my stand with Huskisson—but I cannot blind myself to the consideration that the non-representation of large towns—"
>
> "Large towns be damned!" said Mr. Hawley . . . "Let 'em quash every pocket-borough to-morrow, and bring in every mushroom town in the kingdom—they'll only increase the expense of getting into Parliament." (Chapter 37)

This is more direct and extensive than previous political references; politics is beginning to move closer to the foreground of *Middlemarch*: Mr. Brooke has bought a newspaper, has hired Will Ladislaw to edit it, and is obviously preparing to stand for Parliament. Nevertheless, this too is present in dialogue, dramatically, and there is no identification and little explanation of Huskisson.

The coming to the fore of politics in the novel actually depends to some extent on the most important historical event of the years 1829–30, the death of George IV, which seems to mark the real end of the "ante-reform" era and the beginning of the most heated period of the reform movement, leading to the passage of the First Reform Bill on 7 June 1832. George Eliot's handling of this important event is an excellent example of "history by indirection." George IV is first mentioned in 1829, the year in which the novel opens, in an overt, author-to-reader historical reference to those "good old days," "when George the Fourth was still reigning over the privacies of Windsor, when the Duke of Wellington was Prime Minister and Mr. Vincy was mayor of the old corporation in Middlemarch" (Chapter 19). In December of that year there is a picture of the monarch hanging in the inn at Houndsley (Chapter 23). In May 1830, "some months before Lord Grey came into office," Peter Featherstone dies, and everyone at the time is concerned about "the last bulletin concerning the King" (Chapter 35). The actual death of the King, however, is not introduced into the novel as news, even though its effects are felt. Indeed, Mr. Vincy is not certain that the world is not coming to an end: "The doubt hinted by Mr. Vincy whether it were only the general election or the end of the world that was coming on, now that George the Fourth was dead, Parliament dissolved, Wellington and Peel generally depreciated and the new King apologetic, was a feeble type of the uncertainties in provincial opinion at that time" (Chapter 37). Thus one of the most important historical events of the time, and one that is important as a turning point in the novel, the death of George IV, is not reported directly or immediately in the text of the novel itself. We hear of his last illness; we learn that he is dead through the effect of his death on the political (and fictional) situation; but no one rushes in with the news, no one refers to it as news.

Political history, which has pushed almost into the foreground in Chapter 37 with the events surrounding the death of George IV, quickly subsides, and does not come forward again[1] until the opening of Chapter 46:

> While Lydgate, safely married and with the Hospital under his command, felt himself struggling for Medical Reform against Middlemarch, Middlemarch was becoming more and more conscious of the national struggle for another kind of Reform.
>
> By the time that Lord John Russell's measure was being debated in the House of Commons,[2] there was a new political animation in Middlemarch, and a new definition of parties which might show a decided change of balance if a new election came. And there were some who already predicted this event, declaring that a Reform Bill would never be carried by the actual Parliament. This was what Will Ladislaw dwelt on to Mr. Brooke as a reason for congratulation that he had not yet tried his strength at the hustings.

The dissolution of Parliament "predicted" in this passage—which actually took place on 22 April 1831—is an important event, both in the history of the reform Bill and in the plot of *Middlemarch*: historically it marks the end of the last Parliament successful in blocking reform; in the novel it marks the occasion for Brooke's standing for Parliament. As in the case of the King's death, however, the historical event is heralded—"dissolution might happen any day" (Chapter 49); "certain dissolution forthwith" (Chapter 50)—and its having occurred is assumed—by Brooke's candidacy

1. There is reference to the July Revolution in France: Brooke says to Chettam, "Well, what do you think of things?— going on a little fast! It was true enough what Lafitte said—'Since yesterday, a century has passed away';—they're in the next century, you know, on the other side of the water" (Ch. 38). Lafitte's remark, made on 29 July 1830, fixes the time of the conversation. The only other references to time in this portion of the novel are in Ch. 37—"the summer had gradually advanced—and in Ch. 40—a reference to "August lights."

2. The Bill was introduced on 1 Mar. Several pages later in Ch. 46 there is reference to "an evening in March." Thus the chronology, as usual, is consistent.

—but the event itself is not specifically mentioned on, or immediately after, the day it occurred.

It is surely the subtlety and indirectness with which George Eliot introduces and uses historical dates, issues, and events which largely accounts for the average reader's impression that there are only a few minor references to political history in *Middlemarch* and his feeling that this is not in any sense a "historical novel." The major political events are forecast and have effects with no surrounding air of "momentous occasion"; they assume their natural place in the lives and actions of the characters, yet they do not distract the reader from the fiction. The death of Casaubon does not have to compete for the reader's attention with the death of George IV, for surely the fictional event would shrink in its significance should history force us to recall our willing suspension of disbelief of the fiction. Even Chapter 51, which includes Brooke's memorable speech at the hustings, the most directly political chapter in the novel, contains little or no contemporary history.

Politics and political history, which have again briefly approached the foreground of the novel, disappear almost entirely, this time for sixteen chapters, more than half a volume. When history reappears, it is already the spring of 1832 and Lord Russell's Bill has gone to the House of Lords. This is a suitable example with which to end the study of George Eliot's handling of history in *Middlemarch*, for though in part she uses some of the techniques of history by indirection, she reverses her practice, makes history obtrusive (though dramatic) and heightens the intensity of the fiction.

In Chapter 67 there is reference to "early March," and in Chapter 71 to "gleaming April lights." Twice between these references the question of the House of Lords' disposition of Lord Russell's Reform Bill is discussed in the novel: Lydgate and Bulstrode, riding back to Middlemarch after the death of Raffles, talk "of many things—chiefly cholera and the chances of the Reform Bill in the House of Lords, and the firm resolve of the political Unions" (Chapter 70); a few days later, after Bambridge has repeated Raffles' story to the Middlemarchers, the Green Dragon and Dollop's are the scenes of more discussion of the Raffles-Bulstrode-Lydgate affair than of "the question whether the Lords would throw out the Reform" (Chapter 70). This resembles the scattered, indirect references we have previously noted, but there is a new element: in the latter instance the fictional event is magnified by indicating the extent to which it overshadowed an important historical debate (or, to put it another way, it shows that the provincial mind is more concerned with the scandalous event under its nose than with the more important but remote event in London). In this case, as in that of the King's death or of the dissolution of Parliament in

1831, the political action itself does not enter the story, but here the more or less immediate reaction of characters to the event is suggested—though again with the effect of intensifying the fiction—for Chapter 84 begins: "It was just after the Lords had thrown out the Reform Bill [7 May 1832]: that explains how Mr. Cadwallader came to be walking on the slopes of the lawn . . . at Freshitt Hall, holding a 'Times' in his hand behind him, while he talked . . . about the prospects of the country to Sir James Chettam . . ." This sets the stage for Brooke's entry with a long face. Cadwallader, knowing Brooke's pro-Reform views, attributes the melancholy look to the political news:

> "Don't take the throwing out of the Bill so much to heart, Brooke; you've got all the riff-raff of the country on your side."
> "The Bill, eh? ah!" said Mr. Brooke, with a mild distractedness of manner. "Thrown out, you know, eh? The Lords are going too far, though. They'll have to pull up. Sad news, you know, I mean here at home—sad news. But you mustn't blame me, Chettam."

The news Mr. Brooke has is of Dorothea's decision to marry Will, an announcement of so much import to the gathering and to the reader, that it is no wonder the political news, important as it is, is forgotten. Thus the political event is foreshadowed and has its efect, but does not appear on stage in the novel. Here there is an interesting switch in George Eliot's use of history, however. The political event seems to be reported directly in the novel either as fresh news or as an event of historical importance; it obtrudes. Yet here it is so closely followed by the momentous fictional "news," that the reality itself is overshadowed. History is a counter in the dramatic irony: the group on the lawn is trying to console Mr. Brooke for the political news that is "good" to them though "bad" to him—they are gloating, in fact—but it is not that bad news that he is concerned with at all, but the news of Dorothea's decision to marry Will, which, if bad to him, is nearly catastrophic to Sir James and the Cadwalladers. The reader and the gathering on the lawn brush aside the political event impatiently.

After all, the Lords' rejection of the Bill is not of great historical importance. It is only the dying gasp of ante-reform England. Within a few weeks, the First Reform Bill will be finally passed. That is the great political event of the period. And, characteristically, it too occurs off the Middlemarch stage, taking place in fact after the action of the novel is finished. Indeed, there is a parallel in the fiction. The old world of Middlemarch makes a final effort to resist Dorothea's marrying an unsuitable foreigner: Casaubon's codicil to his will cuts her off; Sir James fumes and sputters; Brooke will not attend the wedding and threatens more drastic action; Celia visits Dorothea in a last effort to make her change her plans. All is in vain. Dorothea will marry Ladislaw. But the wedding, the most important fictional event of the novel, takes place off stage, after the action in the novel ends, too: it is scheduled for three weeks after the scene at Freshitt, very close to the June seventh date of the passage of the Reform Bill. This coincidence lends an air of finality or completeness to the story that began nearly three years earlier by bringing to a close a historical as well as a fictional series of events.

In *Middlemarch*, then, George Eliot uses details from the political history of the years 1829–32 accurately and extensively. On those rare occasions when she introduces relatively important political events as news directly into the novel, she so surrounds them with momentous fictional events that the history is brushed aside. Most often, however, she introduces history indirectly; she rarely addresses historical information directly to the reader, preferring to introduce it as part of the everyday affairs of the fictional characters, rarely overshadowing personal affairs, often overshadowed by them; she disperses references to a single historical person or event rather than lumping or explaining them in a single paragraph or chapter; she never mentions the historical event and the date in the same or even in adjacent passages; she does not show or immediately report the most important political events of the period (including the passage of the First Reform Bill itself) in the text of the novel. Because she skilfully uses indirection, few readers realize they are reading a novel full of documented, accurate historical information; none feels history obtrudes inorganically upon the fiction.

MARK SCHORER

Fiction and the "Matrix of Analogy"†

If the novel, as R. P. Blackmur recently proposed, is now to enjoy the kind of attention from criticism that for the past twenty years has been the privilege of poetry, criticism must begin with the simplest assertion: fiction is a literary art. It must begin with the base of language, with the word, with figurative structures, with rhetoric as skeleton and style as body of meaning. A beginning as simple as this must overcome corrupted reading habits of long

† Reprinted with the permission of Farrar, Straus & Giroux, Inc. from *The World We Imagine* by Mark Schorer, copyright © 1943, 1949, 1953, 1956, 1957, 1959, 1962, 1963, 1968 by Mark Schorer.

standing; for the novel, written in prose, bears an apparently closer resemblance to discursive forms than it does to poetry, thus easily opening itself to first questions about philosophy or politics, and, traditionally a middle-class vehicle with a reflective social function, it bears an apparently more immediate relation to life than it does to art, thus easily opening itself to first questions about conduct. Yet a novel, like a poem, is not life, it is an image of life; and the critical problem is first of all to analyse the structure of the image. Thus criticism must approach the vast and endlessly ornamented house of fiction with a willingness to do a little at a time and none of it finally, in order to suggest experiences of meaning and of feeling that may be involved in novels, and responsibilities for their style which novelists themselves may forget.

To choose, more or less at random and without premeditated end, one novel by each of only three novelists, and to examine in each only one element in the language, the dominant metaphorical quality—this, positively, is to work piecemeal, and merely to suggest. I emphasize not *metaphor* but *quality*, intending not only the explicit but the buried and the dead metaphors, and some related traits of diction generally, that whole habit of value association suggested in Scott Buchanan's phrase, the "matrix of analogy." The novels are *Persuasion, Wuthering Heights,* and *Middlemarch.*

* * *

Middlemarch is a novel written on a much grander scale than either of these others, with many points of narrative interest, a much more complex structural pattern, and an important difference in its metaphorical language. Jane Austen's metaphors are generally of the "buried" kind, submerged, woven deep in the ordinary, idiomatic fabric of the language; Emily Brontë's are generally epithetical. George Eliot's tend always to be, or to become, explicit symbols of psychological or moral conditions, and they actually function in such a way as to give symbolical value to much action, as Dorothea's pleasure in planning buildings ("a kind of work which she delighted in") and Casaubon's desire to construct a "Key to all Mythologies." Their significance lies, then, not so much in the choice of area (as, "commerce," or "natural elements" and "animals") as in the choice of function, and one tests them not by their field, their content, but by their conceptual portent. I should like to suggest a set of metaphorical qualities in *Middlemarch* which actually represents a series apparent in the thinking that underlies the dramatic structure. First of all, there are metaphors of unification; then, of antithesis; next, there are metaphors which conceive things as progressive, and then, metaphors of shaping and making, of structure and creative purpose; finally, there are metaphors of what I should call a "muted" apocalypse.

George Eliot's metaphors of unification pivot on her most characteristic verbs—these are of conciliation and reconciliation, of unification, of course, and of inclusion, of mingling, of associating, of merging and mixing, of embracing and comprehending, of connecting, allying, binding together and making room for. The elements to be brought together are as various as the universe—they may be merely "mingled pleasures" or "associated facts which . . . show a mysterious electricity if you touched them," or the relation of urban and rural areas, which "made fresh threads of connection"; again, they may be attitudes—"criticism" and "awe" *mixing*, or qualities *uniting*, as, presumably, "the glories of doctor and saint" in dreary Casaubon, or men themselves making more *energetic alliances* "with impartial nature"; or they may be those yearnings of one individual for another which find completion in love, the institution of marriage, and the literal embrace; or, most important, they may be "lofty conceptions" which embrace multitudinousness—for example, the daily life of Tipton parish and Dorothea Brooke's own "rule of conduct." If only we knew more and felt more, these metaphors insist; for there *is*, we are told, "a knowledge which . . . traces out the suppressed transitions which unite all contrasts." This is religious yearning, and it finds occasional pseudo-religious fulfilment, as after Lydgate's successful cogitations on morphology: he finds himsef "in that agreeable after-glow of excitement when thought lapses from examination of a specific object into a suffusive sense of its connections with all the rest of our existence," and one can "float with the repose of unexhausted strength."

The metaphors of unification imply the metaphors of antithesis; the first represent yearnings, the second a recognition of fact. Thus we have metaphors of reality *vs.* appearance, as: "the large vistas and wide fresh air which she had dreamed of finding in her husband's mind were replaced by anterooms and winding passages which seemed to lead no-whither"; or of chaos vs. order (humorously dramatized by Mr. Brooke's "documents," which need arranging but get mixed up in pigeon-holes) as Mary Garth's "red fire," which "seemed like a solemn existence calmly independent of the petty passions, the imbecile desires, the straining after worthless uncertainties, which were daily moving her contempt"; or of shapelessness vs. shape, as "a kind Providence furnishes the limpest personality with a little gum or starch in the form of tradition." There are other kinds, of outer *vs.* inner, for example: "so much subtler is a human mind than the outside tissues which make a sort of blazonry or clock-face for it." It is this, the outer-inner antithesis, which underscores one of George Eliot's favorite words—"inward" or "inwardly," a usage which is frequently annoying because it is tautological, applied to states which can *only* be inward under the circumstances of the fiction, but, for that reason, all the more symptomatic. There are metaphorical antitheses of fact to wish, imbalance to balance, restlessness to repose, and many other opposites. Most important, and perhaps most frequent, are the figures which oppose freedom to various forms of restraint—burdens, ties, bonds, and so on: "he replies by calling himself Pegasus, and every form of prescribed work 'harness,' " to which the answer is, "I shall let him be *tried* by the *test* of freedom." Another example of the restraint-freedom opposition illustrates the way that reported action, when conjoined with these metaphors, pushes both on to explicit symbolism: near the end, Dorothea observes on the road outside her window "a man with a bundle on his back and a woman carrying her baby," and, still nearer the end, when Lydgate has "accepted his narrowed lot," that is, the values of his child-bride, he thinks, "He had chosen this fragile creature, and had taken the burden of her life upon his arms. He must walk as he could, carrying that burden pitifully."

The oppositions in these metaphors of antithesis are the classic oppositions between Things as They Are and Things as They Should Be, between the daily realities of a community like Middlemarch and the "higher" realities of that "New Jerusalem" toward which Dorothea and others are "on the road."

Everyone and everything in this novel is moving on a "way." Life is a *progress*, and it is variously and inevitably described as road, stream, channel, avenue, way, journey, voyage, ride (either on horse or by carriage), vista, chain, line, course, path, and process. To these terms one should add the terms of *growth*, usually biological growth, which carry much the same value. There must be at least a thousand and possibly there are more metaphorical variations on the general idea of life as progress, and this progress is illimitable. At the end of the novel we are told, in words somewhat suggestive of a more orthodox religious spirit than George Eliot, that "Every limit is a beginning as well as an ending."

Everything strains forward. Consciousness is a stream. "In Dorothea's mind there was a current into which all thought and feeling were apt sooner or later to flow—the reaching forward of the whole consciousness toward the fullest truth, the least partial good." "Character, too," we are told, "is a process," and it is a process which we recognize by achievement—"the niceties of inward balance, by which man swims and makes his point or else is carried headlong." Like Leopold Bloom, George Eliot's characters think of their existence as "the stream of life in which the stream of life we trace," but with a difference: the personal life finally flows into the "gulf of death," but the general stream flows on, through vistas of endlessly unfolding good, and that good consists of individual achievements of "the fullest truth, the least partial good," of Lydgate's individually *made points*. This is a progressive, in no sense a cyclical view of human history.

These metaphors of progress, like the restraint-freedom antithesis, involve George Eliot in her many complementary metaphors of hindrance to progress. The individual purpose is sometimes confused by "a social life which seemed nothing but a labyrinth of petty courses, a walled-in maze"; sometimes by the inadequacy of the purpose itself, as Casaubon, who "was lost among small closets and winding stairs"; experience and circumstance over and over become "yokes," which slow the progress, for there are those always "who carry a weight of trials"; one may *toil* "under the fetters of a promise" or move, like Lydgate, more haltingly than one had hoped under the *burden* of a responsibility.

These hindrances are, generally speaking, social, not moral. One submits to them in the interests of the whole procession, and when one does not submit—as Dorothea, refusing to devote herself to Casaubon's scholarship after his death—it is because one has discovered that they are not in the interests of the whole procession. The particular interests of the procession are indicated by the extended metaphors drawn from nearly every known field of physical and medical science. It is by the "serene light of science" that we glimpse "a presentiment of endless processes filling the vast spaces planked out of" our "sight by that wordy ignorance which," in the past, we "had supposed to be knowledge." It is by the same light that we are able to recognize our social obligations, according to the Religion of Humanity.

Thus, quite smoothly, we come to that fourth group of prevailing metaphors, those having to do with purpose. They are of shaping, of forming, of making, of framing; they pivot on notions of pattern or rule, measure or structure. They are all words used in metaphors which, explicitly or by implication, reveal the individual directing his destiny by conscious, creative purpose toward the end of absolute human order. Opposed to them are the many metaphors of derogation of the unorganized, notably the human mind, which, at worst, like Mr. Brooke's, availing nothing perceptible in the body politic, is a *mass*.

At the end of this grand vista are the metaphors of what I have called the "muted" apocalypse. The frequency with which George Eliot uses the words *up*, *high*, and *higher* in metaphorical contexts is equalled only, perhaps, by her use of the word *light*, until one feels a special significance in "giving *up*" and in all the faces that *beam*, all the ideas that *flash* across the mind, and all the things that are all the time being "taken" in *that light* or *this light*. Fire plays a perhaps predictably important metaphorical role, and, together with light, or alternating with it, usually accompanies or is implied by those frequent metaphors in which things are *gloriously* transformed, transfused, or transfigured. Treating this complex of figures as I do, as a kind of apocalyptic drama which of course does not exist in the novel as such, but surely does in the imagination of George Eliot, we are, now, at the moment before climax, all those metaphors involving ideas of veneration and adoration, or worshipful awe; these, in my factitious series, are immediately followed by the climax itself, which is contained in endless use of the word "revelation" and figurative developments from it. Perception, in this novel, is indeed thought of as revelation, and minds and souls are always "opening" to the influx. Things are many times "manifested" or "made manifest," as if life were a perpetual epiphany. If perception is not a "revelation," it is a "divination," and for the ordinary verb, "to recognize," George Eliot usually prefers to use "to divine." It is here that we come upon her unquestionably favorite word, and the center of her most persistent metaphors. For the word "sight" or "feeling" she almost always substitutes the more portentous word "vision." Visions are of every possible kind, from *dim* to *bright* to *blinding*, from *testing* to *guiding*. The simplest sight of the physical detail may be a vision; every insight is of course a vision, usually an *inward* vision.

The experience now subsides. If perception is revelation, then it is, secondarily, nourishment, and the recurrence of metaphors in which perception is conceived as spiritual food and drink, and of all the metaphors of *fullness*, *filling*, and *fulfilment*, is perhaps predictable. It is likewise energizing, in various figurative ways, and in moments of climactic understanding, significantly, a charge of electricity flows through the human organism.

Illumination, revelation, fulfilment. One step remains in this pattern of a classic religious experience; that is expectation. Metaphors of expectation are everywhere; I will represent them in their most frequent form, a phrase so rubbed by usage that it hardly seems metaphorical at all. It is "to look forward," and it appears on nearly every page of *Middlemarch*, a commonplace there too, yet more than that: it is the clue to the whole system of metaphor I have sketched out; it is the clue to a novel, the clue to a mind.

I have separated into a series a metaphorical habit which of course always appears in conflux, and it is only because these metaphors do constantly associate themselves in the novel, that one may justifiably hit upon them as representing George Eliot's selectivity. One of many such elaborate confluences is as follows:

> . . . Mr. Casaubon's talk about his great book was *full* of *new vistas*; and this sense of *revelation*, this *surprise of a nearer intro-*

duction to Stoics and Alexandrians, as people who had ideas not totally unlike her own, kept in abeyance for the time her usual eagerness for a *binding theory* which could bring her own life and doctrine into *strict connection* with that amazing past, and give the remotest *sources* of knowledge some *bearing* on her actions . . . she was *looking forward* to *higher initiation* in ideas, as she was *looking forward* to marriage, and *blending* her *dim* conceptions of both. . . . All her eagerness for acquirement lay within that *full current of sympathetic* motive in which her ideas and impulses were habitually *swept along*. She did not want to deck herself with knowledge—to wear it loose from the *nerves and blood that fed her action*; and if she had written a book she must have done it as St. Theresa did, under the *command of an authority that constrained her conscience*. But something she yearned for by which her *life might be filled* with action at once rational and ardent: and since the time was gone by *for guiding visions* and spiritual directors, since prayer *heightened* yearning, but not instruction, *what lamp* was there but knowledge?

Here are nearly all of them: metaphors of unification, of antithesis (restraint-freedom), of progress, of the apocalypse: height, light, revelation, vision, nourishment, and, of course, the forward look. The passage is not in the least exceptional. In my analytical sketch of such persistent confluences, I separated the elements into a series to demonstrate how completely, step by step, they embody a pseudo-religious philosophy, how absolutely expressive is metaphor, even in fiction, and how systematic it can become. This is a novel of religious yearning without religious object. The unification it desires is the unification of human knowledge in the service of social ends; the antitheses that trouble it (and I observe in this otherwise classic series no antitheses either of Permanence and Change, or of Sin and Grace) are the antitheses between man as he is and man as he could be in this world; the hindrances to life as progress are man's social not his moral flaws; the purposive dedication of individuals will overcome those flaws; we see the fulfilment of all truly intellectual passions, for the greater glory of Man.

Our first observation on the function of metaphor in this novel should, then, be of its *absolutely* expressive character. The second is perhaps less evident, and we may call it the interpretive function of metaphor, the extent to which metaphor comments on subject. The subject of this novel may be Middlemarch, a community, but, as even the title metaphorically suggests, the theme is the nature of progress in what is probably meant to be the typical British community in the 19th Century. (Observe, too, these names: Brooke, a running course, and Lydgate, his progress blocked by his wife, twice-blocked by his name.) Or we can select subjects within the subject, as the clerical subject interpreted by the pseudo-religious theme: the true "religious" dedication of a Dorothea Brooke, and the characters around her falling into various "religious" postures: Casaubon as the false prophet, Bulstrode as the parody-prophet, Lydgate as the nearly true prophet—a "scientific Phoenix," he is called—somehow deflected from his prophecy; and Ladislaw as the true prophet. Indeed, given the metaphorical texture, one cannot escape the nearly systematic Christ analogy which George Eliot weaves around Ladislaw, omitting from her figure only the supremely important element of Christ's sacrifice, and the reason for which He made it. This is to be expected in a novel which is about progress without guilt. Here, even the heroic characters cannot be said to have inner struggles, for all their "inward visions." Here there is much illumination and nearly no self-doubt; much science, and never a sin. One recognizes from the metaphorical structure that this novel represents a decay of the full religious experience into that part of it which aspires alone: Christian optimism divorced from the basic human tragedy.

The metaphorical complex provides a third, and a more interesting function: a structural function. *Middlemarch* is concerned with nearly every important activity in community life—political, clerical, agricultural, industrial, professional, domestic, of course, even scholarly. It involves many different characters and groups of characters. The relations between some of these characters and even between some of these groups are often extremely tenuous, often merely accidental. The dramatic structure, in short, is not very taut, yet one feels, on finishing the book, that this is a superbly constructed work, that, indeed, as foolish Mr. Brooke observes, "We're all one family, you know—it's all one cupboard." What makes it so is thematic rather than dramatic unity.

The measure of Middlemarch is Dorothea's *sublimity*, the interpretive height from which she judges. From her sublimity, everything shades off, all the way down to garrulous Mrs. Cadwallader and villainous Mr. Bulstrode. The metaphors of unification which George Eliot enjoyed to use, those images of intermingling and embracing, are important in a double sense; they express Dorothea's ethical sentiments, and, actually, they and the others, bind the material together. They tell us *how to take* each Middlemarcher, *in what light*. They do this chiefly through the creation of symbolic echoes of the major situations in the minor ones, echoes often ironic, sometimes parodies.

Thus, in the imagery of vision, Dorothea's remark, made so early as in Chapter III, has a special ring: "I am rather shortsighted." In the imagery of human progress, Mr. Garth's question about Bulstrode, the pious fraud,—"whether he shall settle somewhere else, as a lasting thing"—has such symbolic value. Mr. Garth's own attitude

toward agriculture is a thematic parody of the exaltation of Dorothea, Lydgate, and Ladislaw: "the peculiar tone of fervid veneration, of religious regard in which he wrapped it, as a consecrated
symbol is wrapped in its gold-fringed linen." In the imagery of
structure, a special meaning seems to attach to the word "dwell,"
when it refers to characters experiencing some state of mind. Lydgate's morphological research is another such symbolic extension of
the metaphors of structure. Dorothea's avenue of limes outside her
window, leading toward the sunset, becomes, finally, a representation in the landscape of the idea of progress. The political newspapers, notably unenlightened, are called *The Pioneer* and *The
Trumpet*, and these are surely parodies, one of the progress metaphors, the other of the apocalyptic. Even that humble rural tavern,
the *Weights and Scales*, reminds us of more exalted concern, in this
novel, with justice and with metaphors of balance. And so that
wretched farm called Freeman's End, which has nearly destroyed its
tenant and his family, is an eloquent little drama of the freedom-
restraint metaphors.

"We all of us," says George Eliot, "grave or light, get our
thoughts entangled in metaphors, and act fatally on the strength of
them." If the writing of a novel is a deed, as Conrad liked to think,
she spoke truer than she knew.

* * *

HILDA M. HULME

The Language of the Novel†

Imagery

On 24 October 1871 George Eliot's publisher, John Blackwood,
had his day's work destroyed by a visit from Alexander Main, a
rhapsodic admirer of her novels ('the Gusher' as he was privately
called), who was seeking permission to prepare a volume of extracts
from George Eliot's writings.[1] Blackwood describes with some enjoyment his talk with the 'little fellow': 'He is quite an enthusiast
and told me he did "not read much but he read deep". He worships

---

† From Barbara Hardy, *"Middlemarch":
Critical Approaches to the Novel* (London, 1967), pp. 87–111. Reprinted by
permission of The Athlone Press of the
University of London and Miss Hulme.
The author's footnotes have been renumbered.

1. Subsequently published as *Wise, Witty,
and Tender Sayings of George Eliot* in
December 1871 with a second edition in
1872 which included 'sayings' from
Middlemarch. See *The George Eliot Letters*, i, lxxiv.

George Eliot as having done for the Novel what Shakespeare did for the Drama. When he wound up some glowing period by saying she was "Concrete" I was nearly upset.'[2]

The visiting linguist who seeks to examine some of the detail of the *Middlemarch* imagery in an attempt to discover whence this imagery derives its characteristic force cannot but feel certain affinities with Blackwood's guest. * * * Such an examination is necessarily experimental and there is difficulty at the outset in defining one's aim while yet preserving freedom of action. To express it in the most general terms, one would like to find out, from sources outside the novel, what kinds of imagery (perhaps also what ideas about imagery) the novelist has at her disposal and at the same time to see how, within the novel, she adapts this image-language to the purposes of her art. * * *

It may be convenient first to mention two quite considerable difficulties which have to be taken into account throughout. The would-be commentator is only too well aware that any image taken from the *Middlemarch* context loses some of its subtlety of reference and, what is worse, acquires a hardness of outline which stands out over-clearly against the general background of the writer's style and purpose; further, the meaning of an image, even within its context, is not static; its value is different for different readers. First, that is to say, the very act of selection is bound to involve a kind of falsification; any knife is used dangerously on work where 'nothing is superfluous, but all is in organic dependence, nothing is there for detached effect, but the whole is effect'.[3] These are Lewes's words (1855) on the 'perfect unity of impression' produced upon the reader by Goethe's *Iphigenia*, but George Eliot's own ideal as suggested in one of her earliest articles (1847) is very similar. Watching in a Paris studio the progress of a noble picture, the moralizing essayist (comparing life and art) loves to think how 'the perfect whole exists in the imagination of the artist, before his pencil has marked the canvass,—to observe how every minute stroke, every dismal-looking layer of colour, conduces to the ultimate effect, and how completely the creative genius which has conceived the result can calculate the necessary means'.[4] Twenty-four years later, during the writing of *Middlemarch* (while it was yet 'too early for such definite arrangements' as to where to make the break between Parts I and II of the novel), she explains to Blackwood 'I don't see how I can leave anything out,'because I hope there is nothing that will be seen to be irrelevant to my design.'[5] When a long novel is so intricately planned, the 'necessary means' so deliberately and finely

2. *George Eliot Letters*, v, 206.
3. G. H. Lewes, *The Life and Works of Goethe*, 2 vols. (London, 1855), ii, 13.
4. *Essays of George Eliot*, ed. Thomas
Pinney (New York and London, 1963), pp. 17–18.
5. *George Eliot Letters*, v, 168.

calculated, much of its minor imagery is necessarily unmarked and underemphasized. It is left, apparently, to make its own effects, and perhaps it were well, to adapt Casaubon's idiom, that it should be so left. For the 'meaning' of even the minor image is not fixed and determinable; its range of reference changes as the reader gives attention to this or that inter-relation within the novel's whole design. Jerome Beaty has shown that for George Eliot herself the writing of *Middlemarch* was 'a process of evolution and of discovery',[6] and it may well be argued that the individual reader has similarly to make his own discoveries, his view of the novel's language changing and developing as he reads. He too, it has been suggested, may prefer to 'keep the germinating grain away from the light'. One must recognize, at all events, that the interrupting commentator who selects a single image for particular examination gives that image at once an inartistic over-importance. The evolving relationship of reader and author is broken, and an outsider's exposition may well seem arbitrary, laborious, incomplete, or over-elaborate. To take one example: when Casaubon, the expected dinner-guest, is 'already an accepted lover' and Celia, in George Eliot's wonderfully extended progressiveness of tense, is feeling 'a sort of shame mingled with a sense of the ludicrous' at her own suspicion that Dodo might really be 'bordering on such an extravagance' of mind that 'could tend towards such an issue', she observes how during the afternoon 'Dorothea, instead of settling down with her usual diligent interest to some occupation, simply leaned her elbow on an open book, and looked out of the window' (Ch. 5). The author's later manuscript addition here, 'at the great cedar silvered with the damp', as well as being an accurately observed pictorial detail, might seem perhaps, at a third or fourth re-reading of the novel, an added marginal reference to Dorothea's emotional position.[7] She might, so to say, be looking out from her old life at a new opportunity; certainly she thinks of Casaubon with proud and reverential awe, and 'cedar' has obvious Biblical connotations; 'silvered' then would express the idealism of 'where your husband was a sort of father' (Ch. 1), its static beauty undiminished by her uncle's earlier warning, perhaps now recalled to the reader's consciousness, that 'every year will tell upon him' (Ch. 4). 'Damp' we find later as a Casaubon quality; it could here carry us forward to Celia's unspoken feeling (when Dorothea has returned from her wedding journey), her regarding of 'Mr Casaubon's learning as a kind of damp which might in due time saturate a neighbouring body' (Ch.

6. '*Middlemarch*' *from Notebook to Novel. A Study of George Eliot's Creative Method* (Urbana, 1960), p. 123.
7. Of Dorothea's more immediate preoccupation at this time we are given a quite precise account. She was painfully aware of the need to let Celia know 'of the momentous change in Mr Casaubon's position since he had last been in the house'.

28). It would, no doubt, be reading a little too deep to suppose from Dorothea's simply leaning her elbow on an open book, in this 'damp' context, that she shares a little ('beforehand, you know') in her sister's notion that learning may come from physical contact. Yet in a novel where physical posture and physical movement so often represent mental state and emotional change, it is hard to know what limits the author would have us set to our readiness in picking up such significances. Even the simple 'leaning' action accumulates contextual reference as the story continues. Should it be that in resting some of her weight on the open book, Dorothea has some half-conscious hope of leaning a little on her husband's openness of intellect, this hope is ended even before Celia comes to visit her on her return from her wedding-journey: already 'the delicious repose of the soul on a complete superior had been shaken into uneasy effort and alarmed with dim presentiment' (Ch. 28). It is Dorothea who, not long afterwards, supports Mr Casaubon's weight, when he is taken ill in the library (Ch. 29). This brief example will sufficiently indicate the dangers of attempting an over-clear analysis of image-'meaning'; there are no rules of procedure which lay down how strong a lens we should apply to such finely-wrought linguistic srutctures, and it is all too easy to 'find ourselves making interpretations' which, lacking George Eliot's subtle and spacious ordering, 'turn out to be rather coarse'.

A CHARACTERISTIC 'MOVEMENT' IMAGE

Many of George Eliot's readers would agree, I think, that Main's term 'Concrete' by which Blackwood's composure was nearly upset seems, now as then, precisely and totally appropriate. It has an obvious relation to the larger purposes of the novelist's art, the embodiment of general truth in a particular narrative example, and is probably also the best of single words to describe that quality on which Edith Simcox comments in an early review of *Middlemarch* (1 January 1873)—the author's gift, 'shared only, amongst contemporaries by Mr Browning, of choosing similes and illustrations, that do really illustrate the nature of the things compared'.[8] Particularly striking to the present-day observer is her ability to select and control an accurate kinaesthetic imagery, through which, in a novel-world where little is static but the furniture, the reader's whole attention can be concentrated, for a few words' space, on just that emotional energy, narrowly limited and fully charged, which 'moves' or holds the novel-character. This kind of imagery is indeed so often and so effortlessly employed that, if we measure by George

8. *Academy*, iv (1 January 1873), p. 3.

Eliot's standards, there is nothing remarkable in the following example, which tells of how Lydgate, after dining at Mr Vincy's and
for the first time enjoying Rosamond's music, went home 'and read
far into the smallest hour', bringing to a new book on fever 'a much
more testing vision of details and relations . . . than he had ever
thought it necessary to apply to the complexities of love and marriage' (Ch. 16).

> As he threw down his book, stretched his legs towards the embers
> in the grate, and clasped his hands at the back of his head, in
> that agreeable after-glow of excitement when thought lapses from
> examination of a specific object into a suffusive sense of its con-
> nections with all the rest of our existence—seems, as it were, to
> throw itself on its back after vigorous swimming and float with
> the repose of unexhausted strength—Lydgate felt a triumphal
> delight in his studies, and something like pity for those less lucky
> men who were not of his profession.

It is easy to see that this one sentence contains a three-fold series of
coincident movement patterns: there is first the account of Lydgate's actual physical movement; then the change in the process of
mental activity which is necessarily set out in abstract terms
(mainly abstract nouns) and thirdly the imagined physical movement of swimmer turning floater. Through the simply organized
interconnection of these three kinds of movement, abstract is made
concrete and the double unity of body and mind, thinker and
thought, is readily established. Lydgate the thinker changes his posture as he rests from reading; the swimmer, which is his thought,
and which has been occupied in examining a specific object—driving forward, that is to say, in a given direction—changes its posture
also, throwing itself on its back as Lydgate throws down his book.
And as Lydgate lies back in his chair, his thought also 'lapses', the
unexhausted thought-swimmer stretching out its body in the water,
with its hands, no doubt, clasped at the back of its head in Lydgate's easy attitude. The language-base on which George Eliot has
constructed the swimming-floating thought image is a part of ordinary speech; when work goes 'swimmingly' we all know what it is to
feel 'buoyed up' with confidence. The 'as it were' phrase, we may
notice, which introduces the image, is there not because the writer is
working with an unusual image range, but so that she may carry the
sentence more easily over the necessary pronoun changes; his book,
our existence, to throw itself. And it is a true observation also, as all
swimmers know, that in the effortless floating motion, as one looks
up into 'illuminated space' (the 'inward light' of Lydgate's earlier
'fever' thoughts), consciousness of an urgent separate identity is
lessened; there is the sense instead of belonging to an older, more

instinctive, liquid world: 'thought lapses . . . into a suffusive sense of its connections with all the rest of our existence'.[9]

It is interesting to note how the writer's exact economy of presentation enforces the abstract-concrete equivalence. Of Lydgate's three physical actions, 'threw down', 'stretched', 'clasped', only the first verb 'throw' is repeated in the metaphorical movement; it is left to the reader to complete the series. The only properties in the actual physical scene are Lydgate's book, which is discarded, and the 'embers in the grate'; there is not, for example, a chair in which he may lie back until my commentary provides it; all that the narrator requires him to have are what the reader is to supply for the swimmer, 'legs', 'hands' and the 'back of his head'. And even though the time is 'far into the smallest hour', no such adjective as 'dying' diminishes the embers; Lydgate's awareness of their agreeable glow after he finishes his reading is parallel, no doubt, to 'that agreeable after-glow of excitement' which follows vigorous thought and 'vigorous swimming'. As the reader, so to say, supplies the missing parts of such descriptions, he enters to some extent into the thoughts and feelings which are described. In this particular instance however we can see also that the novelist has quite deliberately set a limit to reader-character identification. Although Lydgate's existence becomes 'our' existence as thought takes on the 'sense of its connections with all the rest' of life, *we* are not grammatically present in the 'vigorous swimming'. It is clear, if we think about it, that the superlative energy of 'unexhausted strength' can belong only to part of our lives; for the rest of our existence we take our place with 'those less lucky men' (the Farebrothers of this world) for whom the vigorous swimmer feels 'something like pity'.

The placing of this incident within the narrative and the setting together of other swimming-floating images in the Lydgate context bring further correspondences and less clear cross-relations into the reader's own less active thought. Lydgate's throwing himself on his back after vigorous swimming to float with the repose of unexhausted strength seems, as a single unbroken movement, essentially a masculine and a sexual image; if, at the same time, the image is seen as two contrasted movements, such a contrast has an obvious relevance to the career-marriage opposition which is to break his intellectual strength. The reader has been warned in the previous chapter that 'that distinction of mind which belonged to his intellectual ardour did not penetrate his feeling and judgment about

9. It is interesting to compare this image with that used by Virginia Woolf in *To the Lighthouse*: 'Here, she felt, putting the spoon down, was the still space that lies about the heart of things, where one could move or rest; could wait now (they were all helped) listening; could then, like a hawk which lapses suddenly from its high station, flaunt and sink on laughter easily, resting her whole weight upon what at the other end of the table her husband was saying . . .' (I. 17).

furniture or women'. Miss Brooke he has earlier found 'a little too earnest' (Ch. 10). 'The society of such women was about as relaxing as going from your work to teach the second form, instead of reclining in a paradise.' Yet although Lydgate had quite soon been conscious of being fascinated by Miss Vincy, 'he did not in the least suppose that he had lost his balance and fallen in love' (Ch. 11). At twenty-seven and with eight hundred pounds left him after buying his practice he was, we are told, 'at a starting point which makes many a man's career a fine subject for betting' if one could appreciate 'all the niceties of inward balance, by which a man swims and makes his point or else is carried headlong' (Ch. 15). Lydgate's first intention was to swim. As he walked home from Mr Vincy's on this particular night he thought 'of Rosamond and her music only in the second place; and though, when her turn came, he dwelt on the image of her for the rest of his walk, he . . . had no sense that any new current had set into his life'.

The verb 'dwelt on' here which follows more energetic thoughts of Mr Bulstrode and the new hospital, echoes back a little to the 'reclining in a paradise' which is Lydgate's idea of relaxing after his work; it leads on also to the repose which is to be enjoyed when the book is thrown down. The agreeableness of floating is mentioned once more before Lydgate's day closes. After his reading is finished and he thinks with satisfaction of how his profession calls forth 'the highest intellectual strain' (vigorous swimming) and yet keeps him in 'good warm contact' (embers, after-glow) with his neighbours, the thought of Mr Farebrother 'brought back the Vincys and all the pictures of the evening. They floated in his mind agreeable enough.' The intricacy of the image relations forbids more detailed comment; it is clear, at least, that the particular repetition on which attention has been concentrated is very delicately handled. Some sense of it still lingers perhaps towards the end of the story, when Lydgate hears from Dorothea 'the first assurance of belief in him' and gives himself up, 'for the first time in his life, to the exquisite sense of leaning entirely on a generous sympathy, without any check of proud reserve' (Ch. 76). And it is interesting here to see with what care and intuition the writer is selecting her image-language: 'leaning' is a manuscript correction for an earlier 'throwing himself'. It seems indeed that the more vigorous action is now out of context. As Lydgate says of his time in Middlemarch, 'I had some ambition . . . I thought I had more strength and mastery . . . I have lost all spirit about carrying on my life here.'

IMAGERY FROM EVERYDAY LANGUAGE

Main's extensive admiration of George Eliot 'as having done for the Novel what Shakespeare did for the Drama' finds some echo in our present-day enthusiasm for her work; it is not without reason that we are reproached, as a modern critic has said, for thinking that every novel would be *Middlemarch* if it could. And even if we leave out of consideration what is perhaps her major 'Shakespearean' characteristic, her use of the larger image as part of the novel structure, so that relations are set up 'independently of the time-sequence which is the story',[1] certain features of her minor language, her handling of the cliché-image and her play on general linguistic expectancies have something also of the Shakespearean power to surprise, the once-only liveliness of his dramatic dialogue. The language that Shakespeare made is deeply rooted in the language that he found. George Eliot also in her minor imagery draws largely on the diction of common life, often using 'with a difference' the cliché-images of everyday language, so that a certain tension is established between generalized and individual expression. When, on occasion, the stock images appear in their ordinary form, one may deduce that the novelist is using them of deliberate intent, so as to show the 'mental flavour' of the speaker. John Raffles speaking to Mr Rigg Featherstone, 'without humbug' as he claims, uses cliché after cliché in a palpably insincere appeal which combines whining sentimentality with the pretence of shrewd self-interest. His mental flavour, we are told, 'seemed to have a stale odour of travellers' rooms in the commercial hotels of that period' (Ch. 41). Fred Vincy's mental flavour is that of the rather sulky schoolboy when he speaks to Mary of his 'dreadful certainty' that he will 'be bowled out by Farebrother'; he feels 'horribly jealous' and speaks in a 'piqued tone' with 'some rage' and irritation; he 'can have no fair chance' (Ch. 57). The cricketing image is repeated when Mr Farebrother sits down by Mary at the Vincy's New Year party, and Fred's enjoyment is 'streaked with jealousy'. He 'used to be much more easy about his own accomplishments in the days when he had not begun to dread being "bowled out by Farebrother", and this terror was still before him' (Ch. 63). This quotation from Fred's past shows something of his progress in self-knowledge but the mental flavour remains the same: life is still seen rather as a game which sportsmen play according to the rules, and a young man's cricket may be expected to improve. Fred's terror has in it no morbid self-depreciation; it is based rather on a sturdy self-interest and a friendly acceptance of his own potential.

There are many ways in which the collective experience which underlies the cliché image may be brought into play in the novel language. Sometimes, as Shakespeare so often does, George Eliot offers an old image in a new form. It seems from one or two examples that a quite simple re-phrasing can very effectively imply

1. G. Wilson Knight, *The Wheel of Fire:* (1949), p. 3.
Interpretations of Shakespearean Tragedy

frustration. When Will pays his farewell visit to Dorothea in Rome and she gently reminds him that Lowick is her chosen home, 'Will did not know what to say, since it would not be useful for him to embrace her slippers, and tell her that he would die for her: it was clear that she required nothing of the sort' (Ch. 22). Will's sense of the non-usefulness of the translated image conveys well enough his realization that all he can change are the forms of language; he can tone down and domesticate the exaggeratedness of the 'kiss her feet' image but not change at all the reality of 'that stone prison at Lowick'. A somewhat similar instance is found after the reply comes from Quallingham to Rosamond's letter, when Rosamond will not admit her 'secret meddling' and her 'false assent', and Lydgate, 'checkmated', asks himself 'What place was there in her mind for a remonstrance to lodge in?' (Ch. 65). Such a variation on the usual phrase 'How to get it into her head?' fairly indicates the speaker's frustrated sense that every 'how' has been tried and that the mind itself has no room in it for what another nature feels in opposition to its own. And although the crudity of the old proverb 'In at one ear and out at the other' has no place in the language which Rosamond and Lydgate use to each other, it may well be present in some degree to the reader's understanding. Earlier in the novel (Ch. 58) some ironic contrast may be implied between the naïve over-refinement of Rosamond's standards and the more general values of a wider, more plainly-spoken world; she suggests to Lydgate that he should talk more at dinner to their guest, his cousin, the baronet's third son. 'You really look so absent sometimes—you seem to be seeing through his head into something behind it, instead of looking at him.' Rosamond speaks as if she had no notion of someone's being 'empty-headed', and as if she had never 'seen through a person', much less 'looked straight through him'.

Many instances could be cited where the re-wording of a usual image allows a new exactness. Language seems to arise from situation, the speaker or narrator finding a new form of expression to fit the individual case. Cadwallader knows well that even if he wished to do so, he cannot influence Brooke to defer Dorothea's marriage: 'Brooke is a very good fellow, but pulpy; he will run into any mould, but he won't keep shape' (Ch. 8). This use of the active 'running into a mould' rather than the more usual passive form, 'being moulded', suggests at once the facile non-gritty compliance of Dorothea's uncle; probably also he is made the active subject of the sentence because, in the end, all would depend on his activity. Ladislaw feels a similar doubt of Mr Brooke's capacity when he is coaching him for his electoral speech (Ch. 51): 'the only way in which Mr Brooke could be coerced into thinking of the right arguments at the right time was to be well plied with them till they took up all the room in his brain. But here there was the difficulty of finding room, so many things having been taken in beforehand.' Unhappily, we are told, the 'pat opening' of Mr Brooke's speech had soon slipped away, as can so easily happen 'when fear clutches us, and a glass of sherry is hurrying like smoke among our ideas'. The author's re-wording here is obviously more telling than the blunted generality of 'fumes of wine going to one's head'. Even where no space is left, the smoke can make its way, and the added visual image blurs the eyes.

Modern linguistic theory has shown, to quote J. R. Firth, that 'a word is known by the company it keeps'; the meaning of the single word can be tightly controlled by verbal context. George Eliot's images are frequently reinforced and extended so that such words and expressions as were once metaphorical but have long since lost much of their figurative force (coming, if I may re-apply her novel metaphors, 'from the very fact of frequency' . . . 'to be shapen after the average and fit to be packed by the gross') have their original energy restored. Occasionally we can see this process in the manuscript changes made by the novelist in her final revision. Dorothea speaks to Will of her desire, even when she was a little girl, 'to help some one who did great works, so that his burthen might be lighter', and Will counters promptly within the same range of imagery 'But you may easily help too much and get over-wrought yourself' (Ch. 37). It seems to me that the 'over-wrought' of his reply is a warning to Dorothea, not from Will only but from generations of earlier speakers, that even metaphorical burdens may have real weight. This way of combining two, as it were, suspended metaphors within a simple physical image George Eliot has to perfection. In this particular instance we may observe in her final draft the result of a further slight re-thinking and re-feeling of the figurative language used; 'carry the help too far' which is substituted for the earlier 'help too much' adds a little to the load-distance physical imagery and so makes clearer the 'burthen'-'over-wrought' connection. Meanwhile however nothing is lost in simplicity of language, and the 'carry too far' abstraction is appropriately more argumentative in tone.

A number of instances are found in which, while the literal sense on which the primitive image was formed is again brought vividly into consciousness, a certain contrast is established between this individual newly-created sharpness and the dull and ordinary tone which the language unit carries in general currency. Lydgate speaks to Mr Bulstrode of 'the deep stamp which anxiety will make for a time even on the young and vigorous' (Ch. 67); Dorothea remembers how pretty is Lydgate's wife; 'every impression about Rosamond had cut deep' into her mind (Ch. 76). For the characters of the novel also these clichés have taken on a 'distinctness which is no longer reflection but feeling'. One may judge further that it is sometimes the novelist's intention so to re-word an image that it stands out with an awkward unexpectedness against the narrative background: 'It was an inference with a conspicuous handle to it, and had been easily drawn by indifferent observers, that Lydgate was in debt' (Ch. 58). As the original action involved in drawing an inference is firmly restored to the cliché-image, 'indifferent observers' are brought by casual curiosity into the movement of the story. That Lydgate has himself given a handle to his critics is suggested also through the visual image of the handle so conspicuous that it invites an experimental manipulation (Ch. 58). The author may re-word the cliché-image while at the same time extending and reinforcing it. Bulstrode, who 'had been used every day to taste the flavour of supremacy', is conscious 'that there was a deposit of uneasy presentiment in his wife's mind' (Ch. 68); his realization that she was passing beyond the stage of unsettled suspense may be combined here with the taste and flavour metaphor; there may also be in Bulstrode's mind some fear of finally drinking to the dregs the cup of humiliation. Of Dorothea we are told in the earlier part of the story (Ch. 10) that she cared nothing for learning as mere accomplishment. 'She did not want to deck herself with knowledge—to wear it loose from the nerves and blood that fed her action'—a sentence which has been revised in the manuscript, the first part written above an erasure, the second part inserted in the margin. We may judge the revision successful; form and content are finely interwoven. 'Deck herself' has a tone of literary pretentiousness which is properly set aside, while the striving for full expression within the second 'wearing' image is far removed from the crude derogation of the 'skin-deep' cliché which may seem to some readers to underlie it.

* * *

Language is enlivened and our pattern of expectancy broken by such devices as the occasional smooth 'hingeing together' of two quite ordinary images which, even though they contain an identical verbal element, belong in normal speech to wholly different situational contexts: in the Vincy's drawing-room, as Lydgate 'took his seat with easy confidence' on the other side of Rosamond, 'young Plymdale's jaw fell like a barometer towards the cheerless side of change' (Ch. 27). In this instance the word 'fell' is the hinge on which our attention pivots from the falling jaw (now a somewhat outdated image of chagrin and disappointment) to the falling mercury. Once again the simile chosen does 'really illustrate the nature' of the thing compared. Young Plymdale's expression as accurately prognosticates his evening-long dejection as might the movement of a barometer; his falling jaw is to stay fallen for some considerable time. This by-play with the forms of language can be directed to more than mere amusement: in an apparently uncontroversial authorial statement the factor of surprise may be brilliantly exploited and the generality of social judgment firmly set aside. If we have been used to think of dough as an image of lumpish ignorance or failure—knowing perhaps the proverb which Shakespeare uses, 'My cake is dough', my project has failed—such a preconception is doubly challenged. Sir James, the author tells us, 'was made of excellent human dough', the superlative-pure (excellent) and the superlative-palliative (human) both preceding the figurative noun (Ch. 2); the jolt which ends the sentence lets us know that we are not henceforward to judge so harshly the potentialities of our fellows. Subtle variations of tone may be introduced within a short series of related images. Mrs Cadwallader (Ch. 6) speaks 'with the clearest chiselled utterance'; the countryside would have been 'somewhat duller if the Rector's lady had been less . . . of a skinflint'. Everywhere there is evidence of the tact and care with which the minor imagery is handled. When Dorothea (Ch. 4) hears from her sister of the servants' talk 'that Sir James was to marry the eldest Miss Brooke' she asks indignantly, ' "How can you let Tantripp talk such gossip to you, Celia?" . . . not the less angry because she had had a stifled presentment of the fact.' But in the final manuscript copy this last clause is struck out, evidently because the concrete action of the image must be in character, and the choking back of an awareness—suffocating even an abstraction—is a negation quite foreign to Dorothea's nature. Instead of this clause there is substituted the accepting image 'details asleep in her memory were now awakened to confirm the unwelcome revelation'.[2] Here there is no repudiation or inner conflict; sleeper and waker are part of the same thinking-feeling identity; the sleep is calm, the waking judgment clear. The interest of this manuscript correction prompts one to look again at Dorothea's cry at the climax of her story, 'What should I do—how should I act now, this very day, if I could clutch my own pain, and compel it to silence, and think of these three?' (Ch. 80). In this instance also we see that there is no stifling of the feelings; the 'I' is both actor and sufferer. The compressed image 'clutch my own pain . . .' seems to suggest at once the open wound and the child whose anguish is frightening to hear; the suffering child which is the pain is accepted as no less a factor in the personal identity than the strenuously active moral sense which is its adult counterpart.

2. The MS reads: *the* [which has perhaps been deleted] *detail . . . were.*

ECONOMY OF THE IMAGE

Here as elsewhere the economy of the image intensifies the feeling, and it seems useful in this respect to compare George Eliot's practice as novelist with Herbert Spencer's notes on the theory of style and imagery (included in a review-article, 'The Philosophy of Style', published in the *Westminster Review*, of which George Eliot was then the editor, in the year 1852.[3] In this year she and Spencer were so much together that it was supposed they might be engaged).[4] Spencer has a good deal to say on the need for 'economizing the reader's or hearer's attention' and speaks of the importance of the 'choice and arrangement of the minor images out of which some larger thought is to be built'. He observes that the 'secret of producing a vivid impression' lies in selecting from a 'scene, or event described, those typical elements which carry many others along with them, and so, by saying a few things but suggesting many, to abridge the description'. Undoubtedly George Eliot has this secret. In *Middlemarch* especially the superiority of specific over general terms is constantly brought before us; a large segment of experience is represented through the single salient detail. Such a method can be very effective when the author has general comments to make: wit is a great abridgement. We are told, for example, of how within the old provincial society as the boundaries of social intercourse shifted, 'people denied aspirates, gained wealth, and fastidious gentlemen stood for boroughs' (Ch. 11). One detail of visual imagery may suffice for many: 'Lydgate's hair never became white. He died when he was only fifty, leaving his wife and children provided for by a heavy insurance on his life. He had gained an excellent practice . . .' etc. The one negative statement stands for all that follows: Lydgate does not live to be old, but he offers no appearance of being prematurely aged by sorrow at what he regards as his failure; others see him as successful in the world; his looks do not call forth that veneration which would be due to one who had given a long life to arduous medical research. Varying subjective experience of known and measurable reality can be vividly expressed in concrete terms. As the novelist compares her range with that of an earlier master, the extensiveness of earlier time is measured against an ever-increasing scale: 'Fielding lived when the days were longer . . . when summer afternoons were spacious, and the clock ticked slowly in the winter evenings (Ch. 15). For Ladislaw, on the other hand, as a child enduring poverty, the day itself is the natural unit; 'my father had made himself known to Mr Casaubon', he tells Dorothea, 'and that was my last hungry day' (Ch. 37).

3. *Westminster Review*, lviii (October 1852), 435–59. 4. *George Eliot Letters*, i, lxxv.

What a character thinks and feels about a number of complex factors within a longish narrative sequence can be very economically shown through the image which he forms of one particular moment in that sequence. Mr Brooke, in his talk to Dorothea of poaching and game-preserving, tells of how the Methodist preacher, brought up before the bench 'for knocking down a hare that came across his path' and written off as a hypocrite by one of the magistrates, pleaded comically enough 'that he thought the Lord had sent him and his wife a good dinner'. Brooke's unspoken acceptance of the sincerity of that plea is summed up in his comment, 'But really, when I came to think of it, I couldn't help liking that the fellow should have a bit of hare to say grace over' (Ch. 39). Far from supposing, for instance, that the preacher and his wife find poached hare especially tasty, Brooke's fancy stays itself at the moment of private and domestic religious ceremony with which their illegitimate meal begins.

The single adjective 'broad' in the closing phrase of a chapter, 'and they went along the broad corridor together' (Ch. 42) sums up in a final visual image Dorothea's resolution of a long and changing struggle. In this chapter Casaubon has 'for the first time found himself looking into the eyes of death' and shrinking from Dorothea's pity has 'allowed her pliant arm to cling with difficulty against his rigid arm'. In 'rebellious anger' Dorothea asks herself 'What is the use of anything I do? . . .'

> Like one who has lost his way and is weary, she sat and saw as in one glance all the paths of her young hope which she should never find again . . . she saw her own and her husband's solitude— how they walked apart so that she was obliged to survey him. If he had drawn her towards him, she would never have surveyed him—never have said, 'Is he worth living for?' but would have felt him simply a part of her own life.

Gradually the energy of her anger inspires 'a resolved submission'; 'when the house was still . . . she opened her door gently and stood outside in the darkness' waiting for Mr Casaubon. As he spoke to her 'with a gentle surprise', with a 'kind quiet melancholy', she 'put her hand into her husband's, and they went along the broad corridor together'. Lowick Manor is spacious and the corridor is broad in actuality: Rosamond Vincy has teased Lydgate about his medical visits to the house . . . 'at least you go through wide corridors and have the scent of rose-leaves everywhere' (C. 31). But clearly also, in relation to Dorothea's earlier images of the lost way, 'all the paths of her young hope' and 'how they walked apart', the 'broad corridor' is part of her subjective awareness; its width is taken note of because she and her husband are moving along it together; in their shared gentleness marriage seems purposeful and less constrict-ing.

One last point here. 'To have a specific style', says Spencer, 'is to be poor in speech.'[5] Even though the novelist seems generally to select her images in the belief (to use her own words) that 'emotion links itself with particulars, and only in a faint and secondary manner with abstractions',[6] the reader has no feeling that her talent is confined to any single method of working. There is no 'repeated production of the same effects';[7] abstractions are sometimes very simply and strikingly employed. We are told in the Prelude of how Theresa walked out from Avila one morning hand-in-hand with her still smaller brother 'until domestic reality met them in the shape of uncles, and turned them back from their great resolve'. It is difficult to comment briefly enough on the economy of this statement. The words sound friendly as the uncles, no doubt, looked friendly, but just as adults, even though recognizably uncles, can stop a child's way forward, not by talk or argument, but simply by being too big, so also (to women who are often childlike, often treated like chil-dren) 'reality' can be even more of a blockage for taking a friendly shape; the accompanying adjective 'domestic' only seems to make the reality smaller but does not really make it so. A simpler example is found when Fred Vincy agrees with Mary Garth that he is 'idle and extravagant' and tries to get from her some admission of her affection for him while she remains 'provokingly mistress of the situation'. She 'looked up with some roguishness at Fred, and that look of hers was very dear to him, though the eyes were nothing more than clear windows where observation sat laughingly' (Ch. 14). The somewhat unusual personification of this last phrase (a manuscript addition) is perfectly in context. When Dorothea comes to the summer-house to give her answer and later in the day, in her delirium, asks Lydgate to explain everything to her husband and tell him that she is ready to promise, the chapter ends, magnificently, with the sentence 'But the silence in her husband's ear was never more to be broken' (Ch. 48). Emotion and particulars are wiped out; one quality stands for a whole situation.

STRATEGIES OF INDIRECTION

Of her delight in the play of language George Eliot tells us little but she speaks often and with a certain Puritan energy of the novelist's moral purpose. From these moral pronouncements we can perhaps learn something of her theory of imagery and language. It

5. 'Philosophy of Style', p. 458.
6. 'Worldliness and Other-Worldliness: The Poet Young', *Westminster Review*,

lviii (January 1857), p. 30; *Essays*, ed. Pinney, p. 371.
7. Spencer, op. cit., p. 457.

seems that art is for her a clearer image of life; in her own words, it is 'a mode of amplifying experience and extending our contact with our fellowmen';[8] the range of vision is wider and the focus sharper; through the 'higher sensibility' of the writer our understanding and sympathy are increased.[9] She believes with Lewes that the 'true purpose of Knowledge is the regulation of our Conduct'[1] and that effective knowledge, whether gained from life or art, comes best through feeling. In 'Leaves from a Notebook' (published in 1884), when considering 'modes of telling a story' and 'the superior mastery of images and pictures in grasping the attention', she notes 'the fact that our earliest, strongest impressions, our most intimate convictions, are simply images added to more or less of sensation. These are the primitive instruments of thought'.[2] Lewes holds to the doctrine that 'all cognition is primarily emotion'[3] and she expresses a similar idea in one of her letters—'to receive deep impressions is the foundation of all true mental power'.[4] It seems, if we expand this characteristic double-cliché figure, that the strenuous, masculine, shovel-by-shovel effort towards intellectual foundation-laying works through and is complemented by the natural 'give' of human clay. Progress rests upon a willing submission to innate susceptibility of feeling. One thinks of the contrast between Dorothea at the beginning of the story, 'taking her usual place in the pretty sitting-room . . . bent on finishing a plan for some buildings (a kind of work she delighted in)' and of George Eliot when *Middlemarch* is finished, and she is 'thoroughly at peace about it', not because she is convinced that it is perfect but because she has given it what she could. 'When a subject has begun to grow in me', she writes to Alexander Main, 'I suffer terribly until it has wrought itself out—become a complete organism', and, later in the same letter, 'Nothing mars the receptivity more than eager construction, as I know to my own cost':[5] submission to the nature of the material, in life as well as in novel-writing, is evidently reckoned of greater value than over-confident efforts at quickly won control. It is scarcely necessary to emphasize the importance of imagery for the writer who believes in this way that intellectual growth rests largely on the acquiring of intuitive knowledge and who counts herself most fully successful

8. 'The Natural History of German Life', *Westminster Review*, lvi (July 1856), p. 54; *Essays*, ed. Pinney, p. 271.

9. 'If [Mr Kingsley] would confine himself to his true sphere, he might be a teacher in the sense in which every great artist is a teacher—namely, by giving us his higher sensibility as a medium, a delicate acoustic or optical instrument, bringing home to our coarser senses what would otherwise be unperceived by us.' *Westminster Review*, liv (July 1855), p. 289: *Essays*, ed. Pinney, p. 126.

1. G. H. Lewes, *The Study of Psychology* (1879), p. 39.

2. *Essays*, ed. Pinney, p. 445.

3. 12 February 1875. *George Eliot Letters*, vi, 125.

4. 20 June 1871. Ibid., v, 155.

5. 4 November 1872. Ibid., v, 324.

when 'the emotion which stirred [her] in writing is repeated in the mind of the reader'.[6]

I have suggested earlier that examination of her minor imagery enables us to see quite quickly with what subtle control she plays upon the figurative language of ordinary life so as to bring about a writer-reader communication somewhat below the level of our immediate consciousness. It is however equally clear that as regards the larger issues of this kind of moral therapy there can be few short cuts. What life or the novel teaches, the reader learns quite slowly; those truths which the novelist would wish to have most deeply felt may be better expressed in other ways than the direct verbal statement. We can be certain that she will choose those ways with care. It is even possible that the clearer image of life which she offers to the readers of *Middlemarch* is significantly different from real life as she knows it. In thus considering some few instances of her strategies of indirection it is of some interest to observe that whereas George Eliot herself can write in one of her letters of words being 'helpless borrowings and echoes, giving no description of what has gone on within the speaker',[7] the reader of *Middlemarch* is not in general required to take note of the difficulty of verbalizing complex experience. Most of the characters for much of the time show a remarkable command of words and tone; the intractability of language as a medium is considerably played down. A detailed consideration of the reasons for this would be out of place here but it seems to me to be part of George Eliot's larger image strategy not to allow us any opportunity to share in the difficulties of the novel writer. She seems consciously to have intended that whatever sense of effort is produced in the reader, whatever awareness of strain and suffering, is to come exclusively from our identification with the different characters of the story.

'Cognition is primarily emotion'; the writer's own generalizing didactic statements are not made too early and they are very carefully placed. We find, for example, that the author's realistic appraisal of that infantile egocentricity which is our common starting-point does not come until about a quarter of the way through the novel, on the day when Dorothea, in Rome

> had begun to see that she had been under a wild illusion in expecting a response to her feeling from Mr Casaubon, and she had felt the waking of a presentiment that there might be a sad consciousness in his life which made as great a need on his side as on her own.
>
> We are all of us born in moral stupidity, taking the world as an udder to feed our supreme selves: Dorothea had early begun to emerge from that stupidity, but yet it had been easier to her to

6. 11 February 1873. Ibid., v, 374.   7. 11 February 1873. Ibid., v, 373.

imagine how she would devote herself to Mr Casaubon, and become wise and strong in his strength and wisdom, than to conceive with that distinctness which is no longer reflection but feeling—an idea wrought back to the directness of sense, like the solidity of objects—that he had an equivalent centre of self, whence the lights and shadows must always fall with a certain difference. (Ch. 21)

What may well represent George Eliot's ideal in her use of imagery, to have us 'conceive with that distinctness which is no longer reflection but feeling', is here presented in an image of Dorothea's spiritual growth, a growth even now scarcely begun—the 'had' in 'yet it had been easier' seems not merely to refer to the past but to carry some tinge also of the Casaubon-style subjunctive, a distancing of future possibility. We may notice further that this impressive chapter-ending, epoch-ending sentence has been so constructed that its most important phrase, 'to conceive with that distinctness which is no longer reflection but feeling', is merely the dismissed comparison (than which daydreaming of sacrifice and of wisdom is far easier). It is not given prominence of place as subject or object of the sentence; it is not set out as a conscious aim either for Dorothea or for ourselves; the blind infant mammal cannot know the maturity towards which it moves; none of us can *think* what it is like to feel-rather-than-think in sympathy with others. And if, in some sense, the imagery of the novel is to be our training-ground, even through the placing of this didactic 'We are all' statement, a certain exercise is offered. Having watched 'poor Dorothea' acting under the wild allusion that has carried her off to Rome with one 'no better than a mummy', are we not more adept than she in our thinking-feeling relations? George Eliot's sentence order makes this doubtful: Dorothea has begun to see beyond her own needs before we are brought back to humanity's primitive condition of unlimited oral demand!

It is obvious also that long before Dorothea has begun to feel that Mr Casaubon has 'an equivalent centre of self' and long before 'we are all of us' confronted with and left to think about this summarising paragraph, we have been under subtle linguistic pressures to feel rather-than-think from many such equivalent centres. So too before we have been required to encounter any derogatory first-person plural generalizations there has been practice with a number of second-person singular hypotheses; after the interest of taking on a number of different personalities within the action of the story, the reader is ready for a certain attempt to carry over experience gained. The remarkable ease and swiftness with which George Eliot conditions us in *Middlemarch* to this habit of splitting allegiance and changing identity may be noticed especially in the opening pages of the novel: we are led, first of all, through her use of the 'you' pronoun, to adopt the attitude of the ideal reader and then, while this ideal reader follows the narrative, we take on, in addition, from time to time, the changing image of one who is living the action. The first 'you' (of sentence 5) represents a blending of the indefinite pronoun, the reader who is being given information, and the reader who, along with the author, is taking trouble to find information, to seek out reasons, in a leisurely way, for what has already, in the first twenty or so lines of the chapter, been observed, compared and differentiated—'the plain dressing' of Miss Brooke and her sister Celia: 'the Brooke connections, though not exactly aristocratic, were unquestionably "good": if you inquired backward for a generation or two, you would not find any yard-measuring or parcel-tying forefathers.'

The fourth paragraph of the chapter opens with the ringing rhetorical question 'And how should Dorothea not marry?' which at once splits the readers' allegiance, giving us two opposing sides to support in any argument that is to follow. The second 'you', nameless, male, 'wary' (essentially yard-measuring), represents one faction only in suggesting an answer to this question. He 'naturally' thinks twice before making Dorothea an offer. 'Such a wife might awaken you some fine morning with a new scheme for the application of her income. . . .' This 'you' has clearly in mind the potentially divergent interests of 'you' and 'her' and it is perhaps worth noting also with what skilful lack of emphasis the author suggests to us that this imagined marriage is considered only in its financial aspect; no sexual union forms part of the hypothetical relationship: the last clause before this 'might awaken you' sentence has the young lady 'sitting up at night to read old theological books!'

When the third 'you' comes, one page later, Dorothea, surprisingly enough, is also calculating, but rather tentatively, and not the risks, of course, but the profit of matrimony. That Sir James Chettam

> should be regarded as a suitor to herself would have seemed to her a ridiculous irrelevance . . . an amiable handsome baronet, who said, 'Exactly' to her remarks even when she expressed uncertainty,—how could he affect her as a lover? The really delightful marriage must be that where your husband was a sort of father, and could teach you even Hebrew, if you wished it.

While the 'you' and 'your' of this last sentence take the participating reader into the heart of Dorothea's unspoken 'childlike ideas', the split-off observing reader is bound to carry forward the author's question 'how could he affect her as a lover?' from the actual disregarded suitor to the imagined 'sort of father' husband. And this feminine 'you', it may be noted, does not accord to its partner separate pronoun status, does not imagine the possibility that his wishes might run counter to her own.

Little more than a page further on, as Celia is tentativly propos-ing the division of the jewels, her face 'had the shadow of a pouting expression in it, the full presence of the pout being kept back by an habitual awe of Dorothea and principle; two associated facts which might show a mysterious electricity if you touched them incau-tiously'. This single use of the 'you' pronoun involves the reader not so much in movement as in holding back from movement; watching Celia's facial expression we sense to the full the caution which controls it; our training in the kinaesthetic image has begun.

* * *

EDWIN J. KENNEY, JR.

George Eliot: Through the Looking Glass†

George Eliot's presence in her novels is too complex to be satis-factorily defined as any particular rhetorical device, such as "com-mentary," or a single characteristic tone, such as irony, or a uni-form uncomplicated vision, such as that implied by "omniscient point of view" or "the Wise Woman." The peculiar evocative qual-ity of George Eliot's fiction is created by an inward drama of the self expressed in her narrative voice, a voice that reveals George Eliot's feelings, attitudes, and ideas as she responds to the fiction she is creating, a voice that addresses the reader directly and draws him into a personal relation with the narrator and the fiction. Character, George Eliot reminds us in *Middlemarch*, is "not cut in marble"; it is "living and changing" [p. 507], and her own character in her fiction lives and changes from novel to novel and within each book itself. She exists for the reader as a living, human consciousness in action, and she forms the immediate dramatic action of the reader's experience of her fiction.

The drama of George Eliot's presence is that of the struggle of Mary Ann Evans to create, to be, George Eliot the narrator. In Matthew Arnold's phrase, this was her conception of her "best self" (*Letters*, V, 133).[1] George Eliot's narrative voice reveals the strug-gle to resolve divisions between Mary Ann Evans and George Eliot, between woman and artist, and between qualities shared by them

† Reprinted by permission of the author. Editorial additions appear in brackets. 1. All references to Eliot's letters in this essay are for the seven-volume edition by Gordon S. Haight (New Haven, 1954–55) [*Editor*].

both: intelligence and emotion, judgment and sympathy, irony and sentimentality. The effort to achieve this ideal makes George Eliot's presence in *Middlemarch* not static and removed, but vital, involved, and essential, for the drama expressed in her voice embodies the dramatic issues of the novel; George Eliot's fiction is about the struggle towards some better self, which is achieved, revealed, and defined by the quality of one's response to others. Her characters in their own different ways are forced to attempt this struggle, or at least to face up to it, and they do so in the context of the mind and voice of a narrator who responds to them and to her reader. The narrator's attempt to locate and understand her characters' centers of self is what defines her own, and it forms a process of moral self-identification that reaches out and includes the reader.

George Eliot's ideal vision of her responsibility as narrator and the design of *Middlemarch* both can be seen in the famous beginning of Chapter 27:

> Your pier-glass or extensive surface of polished steel made to be rubbed by a housemaid, will be minutely and multitudinously scratched in all directions; but place now against it a lighted candle as a centre of illumination, and lo! the scratches are going everywhere impartially, and it is only your candle which produces the flattering illusion of a concentric arrangement, its light falling with an exclusive optical selection. These things are a parable. The scratches are events, and the candle is the egoism of any person now absent—of Miss Vincy, for example. [p. 182]

This statement, characteristically addressed directly to the reader ("Your pier-glass"), reveals George Eliot's opinion that to be worthy of guiding and instructing the reader ("These things are a parable") she must be able to keep two opposing notions in her mind at once in order to function intelligently and sensitively, for this combination is her ideal. The scratches are small, multitudinous, and impartial, qualities which must be scientifically "demonstrated," and yet egoism produces the "flattering illusion of concentric arrangement." The narrator must know enough of the way things actually are to rise above the characters, who are limited by their illusion of themselves as the center of the universe, the sun. To achieve this knowledge, the narrator must not only detach herself from the characters but also transcend her own egoism, which as Mary Ann Evans she considered her "besetting sin" (*Letters*, I, 19, 251). The narrator must be objective, for only she can discern the true historical pattern of events.

The desire to know the truth of things and to call them by their right names, which enabled George Eliot to be such a fine translator, editor, and reviewer, was elevated to an important critical principle for evaluating the works of others and forming her own fiction. She said of John Ruskin's *Modern Painters*:

> The truth of infinite value that he teaches is *realism*—the doctrine that all truth and beauty are to be attained by a humble and faithful study of nature, and not by substituting vague forms, bred by imagination on the mists of feeling, in place of definite, substantial reality. The thorough acceptance of this doctrine would remould our life; and he who teaches its application to any one department of human activity with such power as Mr. Ruskin is a prophet for his generation.[2]

The goal of knowing and teaching "definite, substantial reality," the size, number, and direction of the scratches, emphasized in the choice of a "humble" household article for this parable, was an important part of George Eliot's ideal. But it was only a part; as this quotation itself suggests, with its hopeful emphasis on teaching, prophecy, and the reformation of life, realism was meant to be the condition of sympathy, the recognition of "vague forms, bred by imagination on the mists of feeling"—the "flattering illusion" created by the candle of the self.

The narrator's comprehensive and penetrating knowledge must not prevent her, and it certainly must not prevent her reader, from imaginatively sharing the characters' belief in their own illusions. On the contrary, her view of them "embroiled" in the medium of their troublous times, which they cannot apprehend objectively or historically, makes her responsible for sympathizing with them. This is what the narrator means by "impartiality" when she asks the reader about Casaubon, "must not we, being impartial, feel with him a little?" [p. 278]; true impartiality, George Eliot was aware, "is kept for abstract merit and demerit, which none of us ever saw" [p. 302], so the intellectual abstraction is tempered by the human limitations and needs that it indicates. In this sense George Eliot saw herself as "the *aesthetic*, not the doctrinal teacher," responsible for "the rousing of the nobler emotions, which make mankind desire the social right, not the prescribing of special measures" (*Letters*, VII, 44). As narrator she must establish what she called "the *truth of feeling*" and believed to be "the only universal bond of union" among them (*Letters*, I, 162 [see above, p. 581]): "If art does not enlarge men's sympathies, it does nothing morally. . . . and the only effect I ardently long to produce by my writings is that those who read them should be better able to *imagine* and to *feel* the pains and the joys of those who differ from themselves in everything but the broad fact of being struggling erring, human creatures" (*Letters*, III, 111 [see above, p. 590]). George Eliot saw human life as struggling and erring, and this view is the basis for her moral desire to understand, share, and ameliorate human suffering through the expression of her sympathy.

The pier-glass image implies that the universe of the novel is a chaos of conflicting egos and that the action of such a world is an inherently tragic action. In her "Notes on The Spanish Gypsy and Tragedy in General," George Eliot defines the general tragic situation as the "adjustment of our individual needs to the dire necessities of our lot, partly as to our natural constitution, partly as sharers of life with our fellow-beings. Tragedy consists in the terrible difficulty of this adjustment. . . . Looking at individual lots, I seemed to see in each the same story, wrought out with more or less tragedy."[3] When Lydgate warns Casaubon about the possibilities of his death, George Eliot carefully points out that Lydgate cannot yet understand and sympathize with "the pathos of a lot where everything is below the level of tragedy except the passionate egoism of the sufferer"[p. 292]. The intense suffering of the ego is the quality of emotion that George Eliot consistently sees as tragic in nature and as revealing a potentially destructive situation. But she did not and could not see all human life as finally, necessarily, leading to actual tragic ends. She believed that "The art which leaves the soul in despair is laming to the soul" (Life, III, 33), and she assured Blackwood about Middlemarch that "there is no unredeemed tragedy in the solution of the story" (Letters, V, 296 [see above, p. 600]). She seems to desire the presence of tragic emotion without the consequences of tragic action because one can respond to the human sufferer of that emotion; he remains alive, suffering and struggling, painfully "adjusted" to his lot. By manifesting her sympathy for such suffering in her own conduct as narrator, George Eliot encourages equivalent feelings in her readers and thus rouses their noblest emotions. Such sympathy, she desperately hoped, is what ultimately can prevent social chaos and irreparable, tragic collision. This was her faith and her moral action. In her novels, sympathy and understanding are what "redeem" tragedy; they "save" tragic situations from being irreparably destructive and laming to the soul, and give meaning and grandeur to ordinary—unheroic and frequent—human suffering.

George Eliot's ideal narrator, then, was to be "a noble nature"; as she says of Dorothea: "The presence of a noble nature, generous in its wishes, ardent in its charity, changes the lights for us: we begin to see things again in their larger, quieter masses, and to believe that we too can be seen and judged in the wholeness of our character" [p. 526]. Through her charity the narrator seeks to create under-

3. John W. Cross, George Eliot's Life, (London, 1885) III, p. 32. Other references to this book are cited parenthetically in the text.

standing in a world of egocentricity; she changes the lights before the pier-glass so that the reader may imagine and feel how the characters think about things, especially each other, in order to learn how he ought ideally to respond to the characters, the narrator, and ultimately his fellow-men. But the difficulties of maintaining the delicate balance between realism and sympathy in every case, of restraining her own egoism, of controlling her own ardent wishes to do good for others are revealed in George Eliot's narrative voice; they show dramatically how hard it was for her always to live up to her ideal in her conduct as narrator. Two passages describing a character's actual perception of things, Mr. Brooke's visit to Dagley farm and Fred and Rosamond Vincy's ride to Stone Court, provide the simplest examples of how George Eliot's activities raise directly the issues of response.

Mr. Brooke's conscience-stricken visit to Dagley farm in Chapter 39 calls attention to the problem of seeing things as they are so that there can be social justice. George Eliot's description of the farm buildings is designed as a criticism of the "picturesque" attitude, a tendency to sentimentalize the lost simple life, from which George Eliot and her readers are not entirely free. By discrediting this attitude as unrealistic and irresponsible, the narrator checks the possibility that her reader may see only what he expects from habit to see. George Eliot does this by first presenting Dagley farm as it might be seen by a hypothetical "observer, under that softening influence of the fine arts which makes other people's hardships picturesque"; this observer serves as a scapegoat for the reader's impulses towards the picturesque as that view is pointedly contrasted with Mr. Brooke's, which is influenced by those "troublesome associations" that makes things look uglier "when we only suspect that we are blamed for them." This contrast is achieved by the narrator's deliberate manipulation of the point of view, her changing of the lights. The picturesque view of Dagley farm contains all the elements that make up the reality of that place; it merely passes over some in its enthusiasm for others, which in the pier-glass passage is called "exclusive optical selection." So when the narrator affirms that the place may seem to be "a charming bit" if only one is *not* touched by the agricultural depression and the lack of farming capital, the reader feels that the limitations of the sentimental view have been made both clear and clearly inferior to those views determined by realistic assessment and social and moral conscience. The reader then shares the narrator's direct expression of her outrage at the idea that anyone's "aesthetic" sensibility could lead him to be "delighted" with Freeman's End, "so called apparently by way of sarcasm, to imply that a man was free to quit it if he chose, but that there was no earthly 'beyond' open to him."

What is true "wonderful" about these contradictory views of the same landscape is that they are both held by Mr. Brooke, who certainly fits the general description of one who, under the softening influence of the fine arts (which, ironically, he views just as imperceptively), does habitually see the hardships of others as "picturesque." But the attacks of the rival newspaper and the criticism of Sir James are now changing the lights for Mr. Brooke; his guilt and shame make the same homestead look dismal to him. This change in modes of perception is just the effect George Eliot the narrator has been creating in her reader; he, too, has been shamed into changing his ways of seeing, and the narrator concludes by politely extending Mr. Brooke's experience in her comment that *"Even our own persons* in the glass are apt to change their aspect for us after we have heard some frank remark on their less admirable points." To see the lives of others properly is ultimately to see ourselves anew, without "exclusive optical selection," and even in our own pier-glass.

George Eliot's description of Fred and Rosamond Vincy's ride to Stone Court in Chapter 12 shows her difficulty in sustaining this anti-sentimental, controlled attitude towards the world of her novel. George Eliot actually "takes over" for Fred and Rosamond, and the reader feels that part of the narrator's sensibilities compel her to emphasize certain sentimental and picturesque qualities of the landscape which are significant to her as Mary Ann Evans, but which her characters do not seem able to recognize, understand, or appreciate. The selfishness of these two young people, represented in the preceding breakfast scene in the Vincy home and in their preoccupying hopes for this visit, may prevent them from feeling "the gamut of joy" in the "pretty bit of midland landscape." But the narrator's response to the landscape is that of nostalgic reminiscence.

The reader is aware of her personal consciousness as it simultaneously recollects, arranges, and responds to the objects being described, and this awareness is intensified because this landscape is not a particular place, like Dagley farm. It is a composite of the "little details which gave each field a particular physiognomy," and it is assembled long after the details were perceived. The narrator is remembering the pre-Reform time when the hedgerows were "still allowed to grow in bushy beauty and to spread out coral fruit for the birds." These details are "dear" to the narrator, whose "eyes have looked on them from childhood," and who is emotionally attached to these remembered places and times. The distinctly personal tone of this passage cannot effectively be generalized; the world George Eliot is nostalgic about is that of her own past as Mary Ann Evans, when she stood between her father's knees "while he drove leisurely," a world that now seems much simpler and happier but is no more. If the reader knew nothing at all about George Eliot's childhood, he would still feel that he was listening to the personal voice of the author; and, of course, a knowledge of George Eliot's biography amplifies this feeling. The reader's experience, however, does not depend on and is not altered by biographical parallels to the literary statement; that moment, like many others in the reader's total experience of the novel, stands by itself as one meeting in the continuing, growing relation between George Eliot and her reader. It reveals that the ideal of sympathy, when applied to herself and her personal past, could be sentimental; in connection with such attacks on sentimentality as that in the Dagley farm passage, it shows George Eliot having to struggle against a part of her own temperament to achieve her ideal of the narrator as her best self, which was to be more selfless.

The affectionate treatment of Caleb Garth, who closely resembles George Eliot's father, Robert Evans, shows that George Eliot the narrator sometimes recognized but did not correct the attachments of Mary Ann Evans: "pardon these details for once—you would have learned to love them if you had known Caleb Garth" [p. 160]. Such a gesture, which alludes to a world outside of the narrator's shared experience of the fiction, excludes the reader because he cannot experience the emotion and is not likely to accept it. Caleb, as one of "those rare men who are rigid to themselves and indulgent to others" [p. 160], has a dull flatness in the novel which suggests that the narrator is remembering and idealizing, rather than creating, a man who is not vitally realized in the fiction. This is the fault not of Mary Ann Evans' love but of George Eliot's failure to control it; it is the fault of sentimentality which, as the Dagley farm passage shows, is a reductive response to the complex reality of life. In George Eliot's own critical vocabulary, the Garths function more as part of the "diagram" of the novel than of the "picture" (*Letters*, IV, 300 [see above, p. 593]). This is particularly true of Mary Garth, who has a significant thematic place in *Middlemarch* because she does seem to stand, near the narrator, outside of the immediate reference of the pier-glass image: "she neither tried to create illusions, not indulged in them for her own behoof, and when she was in a good mood she had humour in her to laugh at herself" [p. 77]. But Mary, although dramatically more successful in her homely liveliness and shrewdness, is finally limited and static in her goodness; she is not shown to possess a great enough vision to aspire, struggle, suffer, or fail. What is attractive about the world of the Garths is their apparent remove from the conflicting world of *Middlemarch*. They may represent George Eliot's old fashioned pastoral ideal of the good simple life free from any complex social, moral, or intellectual issues, but as such they are also free from any spiritual or emotional exaltation, which is what compels George Eliot the narrator's active involvement as an imaginative participant in the lives of her characters.

The act of imaginative participation, in which the narrator actually becomes one with the interior voice of her character,[4] is George Eliot's most dramatic way of expressing her belief in sympathetic understanding as a moral act. For the narrator and the reader such "knowledge" of a character is "no longer reflection but feeling," and such moments of shared response among character, narrator, and reader arise from the collisions between the self and others which alter the characters' flattering illusion of concentricity by revealing another source of illumination. Consider, for example, the following treatment of Lydgate's vacillation between giving his vote for hospital chaplain to Tyke or Farebrother:

> But which ever way Lydgate began to incline, there was something to make him wince; and being a proud man, he was a little exasperated at being obliged to wince. He did not like frustrating his own best purposes by getting on bad terms with Bulstrode; he did not like voting against Farebrother, and helping to deprive him of function and salary; and the question occurred whether the additional forty pounds might not leave the vicar free from ignoble care about winning at cards. Moreover, Lydgate did not like the consciousness that in voting for Tyke he should be voting on the side obviously convenient for himself. But would the end really be his own convenience? Other people would say so, and would allege that he was currying favour with Bulstrode for the sake of making himself important and getting on in the world. What then? He for his part knew that if his personal prospects simply had been concerned, he would not have cared a rotten nut for the banker's friendship or enmity. What he really cared for was a medium for his work, a vehicle for his ideas; and after all, was he not bound to prefer the object of getting a good hospital, where he could demonstrate the specific distinctions of fever and test therapeutic results, before anything else connected with this chaplaincy? For the first time Lydgate was feeling the hampering threadlike pressure of small social conditions, and their frustrating complexity. [p. 124]

In the first and last sentences the narrator tells the reader in a mixture of description and analysis that the proud Lydgate was exasperated at being obliged to "wince" at "the hampering threadlike pressure of small social conditions." Such a painful discovery

4. Derek Oldfield identifies this phenomenon by the term *erlebt Rede* or *oratio obliqua* in "The Language of the Novel," *"Middlemarch": Critical Approaches to the Novel*, ed. by Barbara Hardy (London, 1967), p. 81.

makes Lydgate's understanding at this moment approximate that of the narrator as it is expressed in the pier-glass passage and also in the similar metaphor of the narrator working "in unravelling certain human lots, and seeing how they were woven and interwoven" [p. 96]. In between the first and last sentences, the tone changes and the steady flow of the prose is interrupted, for the narrator expresses her shared sense of Lydgate's feelings by imitating in her own voice Lydgate's inner dialogue as he debates with himself his two alternatives and their consequences. His vacillation is represented in the balanced, antithetical structure of the prose, as in "He did not like . . . ; he did not like . . . ," to indicate two equally disagreeable possibilities. Sometimes this movement is thrown off balance by a clause which seems to suggest associated thoughts that arise from Lydgate's systematic consideration of first one alternative and then the other; sometimes it is interrupted by additional thoughts added on to one horn of the dilemma as they might have occurred to Lydgate. The sense of inner debate is further heightened by the narrator's asking questions to express Lydgate's second thoughts about his own arguments, just as he might have framed them himself as he carried on his thinking. Even the expression of not caring a "rotten nut" is appropriate to Lydgate rather than to the narrator, and it completes the temporary dramatic illusion that the reader is overhearing Lydgate's interior argument with himself. The presentation of "what he really cared for" in the form of a question indicates Lydgate's state of mind and the way his vote will finally go.

The reader respects Lydgate's "lot"—his noble aims, his faults, and his ultimate failure—because the narrator in becoming Lydgate dramatically expresses both her understanding of his conflict and her sympathy with his painful "wincing." George Eliot is in accord with Lydgate as a man who aspires "to do good small work for Middlemarch, and great work for the world" [p. 102]; she is direct in dealing with his faults and tries to anticipate the reader's reactions to them, as in the "spots of commonness" passage in Chapter 15. She readily responds to his struggle and his suffering, as she does to those of Dorothea, because these characters are themselves capable of responding to the suffering of others, and this is what she, too, feels most intensely. Her response is imaginative participation in their pained but growing consciousness.

But her response to the "lamed creatures" of unsympathetic souls, Casaubon, Rosamond, and Bulstrode, whose selfishness she cannot respect, shows how difficult it was for her to live up to her ideal. In these cases the act of imaginative participation can sometimes lead not to sympathy, but to revulsion, which takes the form of ironic criticism, or even sarcasm, that is turned back on the character's center of self. Here is George Eliot's experiencing of

Casaubon's sense that courting Dorothea is a hindrance to his "great work":

> But he had deliberately incurred the hindrance, having made up his mind that it was now time for him to adorn his life with the graces of female companionship, to irradiate the gloom which fatigue was apt to hang over the intervals of studious labour with the play of female fancy, and to secure in this, his culminating age, the solace of female tendance for his declining years. Hence he determined to abandon himself to the stream of feeling, and perhaps was surprised to find what an exceedingly shallow rill it was. As in droughty regions baptism by immersion could only be performed symbolically, so Mr. Casaubon found that sprinkling was the utmost approach to a plunge which his stream would afford him; and he concluded that the poets had much exaggerated the force of masculine passion. [pp. 41–42]

The narrator's voice here imitates Casaubon's passionless reasoning: the pragmatic conviction that courtship is a hindrance to be "deliberately incurred" in exchange for certain benefits is Casaubon's view of his relation to Dorothea, and it is his habit of mind to think and express himself in parallel clauses, "balanced sing-song neatness." This dramatic imitation of Casaubon's sensibility at first only reveals the contradiction inherent in his self-deceptions, especially his conscious "determination" to "abandon himself to the stream of feeling." But the narrator's reaction, although forestalled as long as possible, does come as a harsh and pointed judgment: "and perhaps [he] was surprised to find what an exceedingly shallow rill it was." The image of Casaubon's own inner speech is violently undercut by the narrator's metaphoric abuse of it, and her savage energy of wit reveals her temporarily restrained desire to dissociate herself from and attack Casaubon's attitude. Her indignation is indicated by the vigor with which she pursues her critical comparison: "As in droughty regions baptism by immersion could only be performed symbolically, so Mr. Casaubon found that sprinkling was the utmost approach to a plunge which his stream could afford him." The fertile energy of this simile shows the intensity of the narrator's reaction as she turns away from Casaubon's sterility.

This passage contains little active sympathy comparable to that the narrator requests from her reader in Chapter 10, when she "protests" against "any prejudice" derived from views of Casaubon presented by the other characters in the novel. That passage, cited by Quentin Anderson as an illustration of George Eliot's "judiciousness,"[5] actually suggests her awareness of her own unsympathetic,

---

5. "George Eliot in Middlemarch," *From Dickens to Hardy, The Pelican Guide to* *English Literature*, Vol 6, ed. Boris Ford (New York, 1966), p. 287.

even cruel, reaction to him. Such an obvious attempt to redress an injustice reveals to the reader the narrator's struggle to be as clear-sighted and as charitable as she desires her ideal self to be. It is as difficult for the narrator, as for anyone else, to indicate precisely the faults of her characters and the injury they cause for others and still to be able to show sympathy towards them. Yet it is just this sense of the narrator's consciousness of her ideal and her lapses from it, of her trying to achieve it, that compels the reader to respond to the narrator as she is responding to her characters: all are human beings who demand human responses.

Sometimes the reader, like the narrator, does not know exactly how to respond, as at the beginning of Chapter 29:

> One morning, some weeks after her arrival at Lowick, Dorothea —but why always Dorothea? Was her point of view the only possible one with regard to this marriage: I protest against all our interest, all our effort at understanding being given to the young skins that look blooming in spite of trouble; for these too will get faded, and will know the older and more eating griefs which we are helping to neglect. [p. 192]

What is striking about this passage is not simply the sudden shift in point of view; the point of view is always shifting in *Middlemarch*, for this is how George Eliot the narrator "changes the lights" before the pier-glass for us. Rather, what is striking here is the attitude towards the fiction and the reader which the narrator's gesture and tone display. The question "but why always Dorothea?" is naturally accepted by the reader as a question directed to him, and so, in a rhetorical sense, it is. But the narrator seems now to have become the reader, and she is criticizing the narrator, whose responsibilities she has forced the reader into accepting as his own. She is speaking as though the reader were controlling the point of view, and her speech becomes argumentative, as though she were resisting something external to herself. Although the reader may momentarily feel that he has been leading the narrator to "neglect" those "older and more eating griefs," the strong reaction expressed in the narrator's rhetoric reveals that the narrator is addressing some part of herself, the part that has been ignoring Casaubon because he is repugnant to her personal sensibilities. By assuming the role of reader and making the reader the narrator, George Eliot has externalized her own inner debate, and the alienation the reader may feel from the narrator in the midst of her transference becomes a more intense participation in the narrator's consciousness as she struggles to regain her balance. The narrator's further warnings not to accept the subjective and unfair views of Casaubon held by Celia and Sir James then seem to show the narrator's reaction to her own subjectivity, rather than detached objectivity, or "judiciousness." Her personal view of Casaubon has not been so different from theirs.

But more than her arguing with herself, the narrator's subsequent imaginative projection of herself into the "intense consciousness" of Casaubon and her emerging this time with a felt sense of his "uneasy lot" as an isolated man leads not to irony but to a direct expression of her pity:

> For my part I am very sorry for him. It is an uneasy lot at best, to be what we call highly taught and yet not to enjoy: to be present at this great spectacle of life and never to be liberated from a small hungry shivering self—never to be fully possessed by the glory we behold, never to have our consciousness rapturously transformed into the vividness of a thought, the ardour of a passion, the energy of an action, but always to be scholarly and uninspired, ambitious and timid, scrupulous and dimsighted. [p. 193]

This response comes directly from George Eliot's experience of Casaubon's thoughts as feeling, a response that reaches its height when Casaubon himself "feels the truth of the commonplace" about death: "We all must die" [p. 293].

Such a moment in the narrator's experience shared with the reader is a moment of revelation, "in which knowledge passes instantaneously into feeling, and feeling flashes back as a new organ of knowledge" [p. 155] and of power. George Eliot has to show Casaubon's ugliness, physical and psychological, and the pain and suffering he causes for others; this is his "definite substantial reality." Sometimes she responds in kind, but she manages to sympathize with him imaginatively when she isolates him, or sees him isolated, from the harm he brings to others—when he appears as another struggling and erring human being. The rather guilty shift in emphasis from Dorothea to Casaubon gives the reader a sense of George Eliot's struggle to live up to her ideal, and this sense of the struggle to overcome her own natural antipathy to Casaubon ennobles and justifies her ideal. The resolution of the struggle in the narrator's relation to Casaubon is the view that Casaubon is a man alone and paralyzed before life by the contradictions of his own nature, his "natural constitution." The narrator's final view, like Dorothea's within the novel, is that Casaubon is a "lamed creature": one who simply is what he is, who cannot be healed, and who, therefore, is not entirely responsible for his lot or his effect on another's. This is why the narrator, like Dorothea, must pity rather than attack him, even though she withholds her sympathetic approval.

George Eliot's response to Rosamond Vincy shows a similar struggle against antipathy, towards sympathy, this time stopping short of actual pity. George Eliot objects not simply to Rosamond's beauty, although Mary Ann Evans might, but to her beauty as a power which, combined with a finishing school charm that is meant to pass for culture and an impenetrable egoism that masquerades as selflessness, is destructive to those around her. In the narrator's attitude toward Rosamond, the reader is always aware of a bitterly ironic edge that seems at every moment to veer towards invective. Even when the narrator attempts to muster sympathy or to plead for it from the reader, her antipathy somehow reveals itself; in the following passage, for example, there is a fundamental and damning ambiguity about the narrator's plea for the reader's suspension of judgment and the narrator's own implied judgment:

> For Rosamond never showed any unbecoming knowledge, and was always that combination of correct sentiments, music, danc- ing, drawing, elegant note-writing, private albums for extracted verse, and perfect blond loveliness, which made the irresistible woman for the doomed man of that date. Think no unfair evil of her, pray: she had no wicked plots, nothing sordid or mercen- ary; in fact, she never thought of money except as something necessary which other people would always provide. She was not in the habit of devising falsehoods, and if her statements were no direct clue to fact, why, they were not intended in that light— they were among her elegant accomplishments, intended to please. Nature had inspired many arts in finishing Mrs. Lemons's favorite pupil, who by general consent (Fred's excepted) was a rare compound of beauty, cleverness, and amiability. [p. 185]

George Eliot is trying to understand Rosamond's "centre of self," as she does with all her characters, but she simply cannot experi- ence imaginatively the value of "elegant accomplishments" as they might be understood by the eldest daughter of a provincial manu- facturer whose business is declining. The editor of the *Westminster Review*, translator of Strauss, Feuerbach, and Spinoza, cannot con- sider "perfect blond loveliness" without irony. George Eliot is trying to be fair to Rosamond, but she cannot control the tone of her voice. She admits that Rosamond had "no wicked plots, nothing sordid or mercenary," but then undercuts that qualification: "in fact, she never thought of money except as something necessary which other people would provide." So easily the narrator slips into a mocking imitation of Rosamond's manner: "and if her statements were no direct clue to fact, why, they were not intended in that light—they were among her elegant accomplishments, intended to please." Such a brilliant parody damns Rosamond while pretending to save her, and incites George Eliot's indignation against such a mindless, self-centered nature that cannot even recognize responsi- bility and honesty. Although this is not "unfair evil," it is to George

Eliot hopelessly exasperating, for it is irremediable—and her exasperation shows.

So the narrator's final view of Rosamond is that of a child without a moral sense—"perfect blond loveliness"; it is complemented within the novel by Lydgate's opinion of Rosamond as "an animal of another and feebler species" [p. 461]. This view, and that of Casaubon as a "lamed creature," unable to move freely in life and likely to be injured by the movements around him, work to prevent final and absolute moral judgment and to evoke pity not only for Casaubon and Rosamond, but also for Dorothea and Lydgate: the less able creatures become both dependents and masters of the striving natures of Dorothea and Lydgate. The feeling of pity applies also to Mrs. Bulstrode's view of her husband as "smaller," as "withered and shrunken," after his public humiliation; Bulstrode's deception in his relations with his wife, along with his dishonest and ruthless behavior to others he has harmed, are finally seen by her, not as sins to be judged and punished, but as moral and psychological defects. Like physical defects, they must be seen for what they are, but they must be accepted and ministered to with "compassion" and "tenderness" [p. 518].

The characters' clear understanding and pity for the lamed creatures for whom they dutifully care fulfills George Eliot's design for her fiction and her own place in it: to demonstrate that realistic assessments of ugliness and meanness are necessary to the creation and the expression of fellow-feeling, or at least pity. Such a resolution of the problem of sympathy for unsympathetic characters, achieved with such difficulty, shows that George Eliot prefers to emphasize response to the sufferer, rather than the immoral conduct that causes the suffering. Since everyone suffers in one way or another, everyone may be felt with. George Eliot tends, therefore, not to make firm moral judgments, even when they may seem justified and necessary to the reader. There is a final sentimentality, after the penetrating analysis and implied judgment, in the views of Rosamond as a little girl, Casaubon as a lamed creature, and Bulstrode as a withered and shrunken old man. George Eliot was herself critical of her impulse towards that "excessive tolerance and tendency to melt off the outlines of things" (*Letters*, V, 367), which in her own nature she called "chameleon-like" (*Letters* I, 302). In *Impressions of Theophrastus Such*, she sees it as "the lunacy of fancying one's self everybody else, and being unable to play one's own part decently,—another form of the disloyal attempt to be independent of the common lot, and to live without a sharing of the pain" [Allison Library edition, New York, 189?, 4:13]. By playing one's own part decently and sharing the pain of the common lot, George Eliot seems to mean actively identifying and judging and fighting against the presence of evil; she admits that "it is undeniable that a too intense consciousness of one's kinship with all frailties and vices undermines the active heroism which battles against wrong" [*Theophrastus Such*, p. 134]. But George Eliot's intention to express sympathy, or to pity, rather than condemn, takes precedence over the intellectual and moral identification of evil. Her "keen vision and feeling of all ordinary human life" as suffering made her hear "that roar which lies on the other side of silence" [p. 135]. George Eliot's ultimate preference, therefore, is for the unifying truth of feeling over the divisive truth of discrimination and judgment; but the difficulties of making this choice and her uncertainty about it—what the tough-minded part of her would call unheroic and possibly lunatic—make up the drama of her narrative presence and give significance both to her characters and to her goal of a balanced vision, even if it remains unreached.

George Eliot's feeling for the suffering of all ordinary human life and her desire to express that feeling and do something to ameliorate the suffering also affects her treatment of Dorothea, with whom she is in sympathetic accord. Because Dorothea is struggling most ardently and painfully against the dire necessities of her lot, as George Eliot is herself as narrator, she is the character in whom George Eliot participates most imaginatively and intensely. Dorothea, from the moment of her first argument with Casaubon, is learning to feel "the waking presentiment that there might be a sad consciousness in his life which made as great a need on his side as on her own," and this is the experience of the entire novel.

> We are all of us born in moral stupidity, taking the world as an udder to feed our supreme selves: Dorothea had early begun to emerge from stupidity, but yet it had been easier to her to imagine how she would devote herself to Mr. Casaubon, and become wise and strong in his strength and wisdom, than to conceive with that distinctness which is no longer reflection but feeling—an idea wrought back to the directness of sense, like the solidity of objects—that he had an equivalent centre of self, whence the lights and shadows must always fall with a certain difference. [p. 146]

Dorothea's struggling growth to moral maturity culminates in her being able to *imagine*, by "representing to herself" the trials of the Lydgates' lot, and to *feel*: "all this vivid sympathetic experience returned to her now as a power: it asserted itself as acquired knowledge asserts itself and will not let us see as we saw in the day of our ignorance. She said to her own irremediable grief, that it should make her more helpful, instead of driving her back from effort" [p. 544]. At this point Dorothea's vision becomes that of George Eliot the narrator; instead of seeing only the self-reflective interior of her boudoir dimly illuminated by the candle of her own egotistic suffering, she now looks out her window in the light of day and feels "the largeness of the world and the manifold wakings of men to labour and endurance" and her own responsible part in that world. This is her transcendent vision of the pier-glass with all the impartiality of the scratches, and at this moment Dorothea's and George Eliot's vision and voice coalesce. There is an analagous relation between Dorothea's presence in the fictional world of Middlemarch and George Eliot's narrative presence in the novel *Middlemarch*, between Dorothea's struggle with her personal lot and George Eliot's struggle with her responsibilities as an aesthetic teacher, between their desire to become and their compromised achievements of a "noble nature." Dorothea's vision of humanity, attained through suffering, should become a power to influence the vision of others, just as George Eliot hoped that her felt sense of human suffering would influence her readers.

George Eliot's desire that Dorothea be an agent of sympathy is revealed with greatest intensity when, after her night-long struggle to gain control of her own grief at seeing Rosamond and Will together, culminating in her new vision of humanity, Dorothea again goes to see Rosamond in hopes of helping the Lydgates' marriage. Dorothea's influence on Rosamond in Chapter 81, however temporary, is remarkable, for Rosamond always remains cooly resistant to the pressures and pleas of those around her; that anyone, even a Dorothea—or the real St. Theresa—under any circumstances, could evoke a sympathetic response from her threatens to challenge the consistency of George Eliot's characterization of Rosamond. But George Eliot does want to emphasize the power of Dorothea's great nature and vision, and this emphasis here takes the form of a peculiar solemnity created by the narrator's use of religious diction. Rosamond, in all her inflexibility, will be "converted" by the appropriate "massive being" [p. 524] of Dorothea, one of those natures "in which, if they love us, we are conscious of having a sort of baptism and consecration; they bind us over to rectitude and purity by their belief about us; and our sins become that worst kind of sacrilege which tears down the invisible altar of trust" [p. 532]. George Eliot is consciously striving for sublimity; the exaltation of conversion always thrilled George Eliot, and this is the effect she wished her ardent characters and, hopefully, her best self, to produce in her fiction.

George Eliot's closing view of the two women as shipwrecked survivors clasping one another for support and comfort is another representation of her view of life as suffering made bearable by the sympathy and help that come from a sense of shared experience.

Dorothea must "save" Rosamond and herself from this shipwreck which is both of their lives, and George Eliot must attribute to Dorothea's actions a higher salvation: "it is given to us sometimes even in our everyday life to witness the saving influence of a noble nature, the divine efficacy of rescue that may lie in a self-subduing act of fellowship" [p. 554]. Like Feuerbach, George Eliot located the "divine efficacy of rescue" in a human source—in Dorothea and characters like her in the other novels, and ultimately in herself as narrator—but in its human form divinity exists more as a temporary emotion, a hope and perhaps a promise of better things, than as the actual effection of miracles. Rosamond is moved by the presence of Dorothea to emulate her self-subduing act of fellowship by giving Will back to Dorothea's dream. But this effect is only of the moment; it does not continue to influence Rosamond's conduct of her life. Without Dorothea's physical presence, Rosamond reverts to her former self; finally she is not saved, but thrives like the basil plant on Lydgate's dead brains and fortune. The reassertion of the "definite, substantial reality" of Rosamond in the Finale ironically tempers this moment and the diction which exalts it; this ironic check on spiritual conversion reveals George Eliot's uncertainty about her own presence as a moral authority in her fiction.

As George Eliot deals with moments like this, she seems to be trying to do for Dorothea what Dorothea should have been doing for her—provide a dramatic representation of a noble, sympathetic nature improving the lives of others through the quality of her vision and her speaking presence, her power as a noble nature. But George Eliot's sense of reality checks her own ardent nature; finally she cannot entirely convince herself of the reality of this hope either for Dorothea or for herself. As narrator, she too influences her readers only temporarily, only for the duration of the fiction. Yet she still must believe that this momentary experience will alter, however slightly and gradually, the reader's sensitivity for the better —will save him. In this way, too, is George Eliot mirrored through the glass of her fiction.

George Eliot says in the Finale that many who knew Dorothea "thought it a pity that so substantive and rare a creature should have been absorbed into the life of another, and be only known in a certain circle as a wife and mother. But no one stated exactly what else that was in her power she ought rather to have done" [p. 576]. This cautious remark suggests that perhaps George Eliot herself did not imagine any other possibility for Dorothea, and, consequently, restricted her interest in Will Ladislaw to that of a diagrammatic device of contrast, escape, and final compromise solution to the dilemma of "a certain spiritual grandeur ill-matched with the meanness of opportunity" [p. xiii]. And perhaps an unrealized possibility that George Eliot would have rejected—because it was not part of her conception of her best self—was to create, fifty years before the appearance of Joyce's Stephen Dedalus, *A Portrait of the Artist as a Young Woman*. Dorothea's vision and speaking presence are what George Eliot considered poetic; Dorothea possesses, like George Eliot, "a soul in which knowledge passes instantaneously into feeling, and feeling flashes back as a new organ of knowledge" [p. 155]. Such power seems to manifest itself best in communicating that vision to others, in recreating itself. This is why George Eliot was an esthetic and not doctrinal teacher, and that she did not make Dorothea into a writer shows that she was not seeking self-justification but self-transcendence. Instead, George Eliot's dramatic struggles as narrator in *Middlemarch*, reflected in the pier-glass, reveal all the difficulties implicit in the "spiritual grandeur" of her ideal vision of her best self and all the difficulties her characters experience in groping toward that pier-glass vision of human life which is at once intelligently realistic and intensely sympathetic. George Eliot's presence in the novel, as a narrator struggling against her own egoism, harshness, ardor, and limited vision, and faltering in some of her artistic accomplishments, sustains and completes this complicated human vision of imperfect human life. Her willingness to risk herself in responding to the world she is creating accounts for her success in encouraging readers to respond in the same way—"to *imagine* and to *feel* the pains and joys of those who differ from themselves in everything but the broad fact of being struggling erring human creatures."

RICHARD ELLMANN

Dorothea's Husbands†

A novelist, intent on his art, swallows into it other people along with himself. The living originals of fictional characters are elusive because they have been obliged by the writer to answer purposes not their own. It is as if they were evicted from a universe of free will into a deterministic one. The peril of confusing universes is one to which we have been alerted by fastidious critics and structuralists alike. Yet many novelists are themselves liable to this lapse, and fondly imagine that they have created characters out of people they have known. To follow them a little way is at worst devoted, and at best profitable, since the mode of translating characters from the

† From *Golden Codgers: Biographical Speculations*, copyright © 1973 by Richard Ellmann. Reprinted by permission of Oxford University Press, Inc.

one universe to the other must be close to basic movements of the mind, and so of critical as well as biographical consequence.

* * *

* * * George Eliot, contrary to T. S. Eliot, made no claims for the impersonality of the artist. She confided that her first work of fiction, *Scenes of Clerical Life*, drew upon family reminiscences, and many characters from her other books have been pursued to prototypes in her experience, often with her help. She worked from models then, probably habitually.

Like George Eliot herself, Dorothea had two husbands. Of the two, it is Mr. Casaubon who has deserved and attracted attention. He is a pedant of such Saharan aridity that the temptation to identify him has not often been resisted. Among the proffered candidates, the one most mentioned is Mark Pattison, rector of Lincoln College, Oxford. He had three points of *rapport*: an unhappy marriage with a wife much younger than himself, friendship with George Eliot, and the authorship of a life of the Swiss scholar (of the sixteenth century) Isaac Casaubon. George Eliot obviously borrowed from him the name of his subject, but other resemblances are tenuous, as if the price she paid for the one liberty was not to take others. John Sparrow, the most resolute supporter of Pattison as Casaubon's archetype, has rested his case largely on a passage in Sir Charles Dilke's unpublished autobiography, in which Dilke, later married to Mrs. Pattison, states that Casaubon's marriage proposal and Dorothea's answer were based closely on the equivalent Pattison letters. These letters have not survived. But aside from the flexibility of style and mind so notable in Pattison, so lacking in Casaubon, it is now clear, from a letter of George Eliot published in the *Times Literary Supplement* on 12 February 1971 by Professor Gordon S. Haight, that as early as 1846 she was already diverting her friends by concocting the terms of a pedant's proposal of marriage. Casaubon's letter balances precariously on the questions of whether he is seeking a wife or someone to read to him, and of whether he is actuated by love or myopia; the proposal of 'Professor Bücherwurm', which George Eliot pretends to relay to Charles Bray, similarly hinges on the ambiguity of the Professor's securing as his bride someone to translate his books from German. In 1846 George Eliot did not know Pattison, and evidently she had no need to know him in order to evolve Casaubon's letter.

To consider other possible models for Casaubon is to turn up many of George Eliot's acquaintances. Pedantry was not a scarce commodity among them. Ideally the culprit should combine arid learning with sexual insufficiency. This felicitous blend is unexpectedly hard to find. No doubt the laws of Middlemarch, rather than those of experience, demanded that Casaubon's mind symbolize his body, and his body his mind. If George Eliot drew details from models, she used more than one. For sexual low pressure, Herbert Spencer was probably the best example, and Beatrice Webb saw enough resemblance to refer to him as Casaubon. George Eliot knew Spencer well, and many have been perplexed for a time at his failure to marry anyone, herself included. But if his nubility was in doubt for her, his ability was not; it is only a later age that wishes Spencer had been Casaubon enough to finish fewer books. Besides, Spencer came to regard George Eliot as the greatest woman who ever lived, an accolade she would not have so meagrely rewarded.

For the author of the 'Key to all Mythologies', a closer prototype is Dr. R. H. Brabant. It was he whom the novelist Mrs. Eliza Lynn Linton, well acquainted with both him and George Eliot, identified positively as Casaubon. Brabant had similar difficulty in bringing a book to fruition. According to Mrs. Linton, he 'never got farther than the introductory chapter of a book which he intended to be epoch-making, and the final destroyer of superstition and theological dogma'. Under the influence of the German rationalists, Brabant presumaby intended to eliminate from all religions that supernatural element which they had eliminated from Christianity. It seems unlikely that he used the word 'key', an inappropriate one for his enterprise. Although Gordon S. Haight, George Eliot's astute and scrupulous biographer, accepts Brabant as the model, there are several obstacles to close identification with him as with Pattison. Brabant's loins were not nearly so exhausted: he did not manifest sexual indifference. He was married, he had a daughter and a son; at the age of sixty-two he squired George Eliot about in a manner which she found happily equivocal in intention, and which his blind wife acutely resented.

Moreover he was a physician, and evidently a good one; his book was a sideline, a token of intellectual community. He had a gift for companionship, and was friends with Coleridge, Moore, Landor, and others. He also had friends in Germany, notably Strauss and Paulus, and it was he who some years later introduced George Eliot, translator of *Das Leben Jesu*, to Strauss, its author. Apparently he could converse more easily in German than she could, and in this respect too he is unlike Casaubon, whose ignorance of German is scored heavily against him. Mrs. Linton describes Brabant as 'well got up and well preserved', while Casaubon is prematurely withered. He was also a man of many interests, in the theatre, art, and science, as references in George Eliot's correspondence and John Chapman's diaries confirm. Most of all, he was a man of enthusiasm, generously tendered to the work of others rather than his own.

George Eliot did feel a brief spell of veneration for Brabant, as

Dorothea did for Casaubon, but with more semblance of justification. Whatever Brabant's defects as an idol, he was in the same cultural movement as she was. If he dithered, it was not over 'Cush and Mizraim' like Mr. Casaubon, but over what George Eliot also considered the most pressing spiritual problems of the time. She followed his lead with Strauss, she borrowed his copy of Spinoza. If he was dull, he was dull in the swim. So expert a novelist would not have forgotten him—she may have derived from him not only hints for Casaubon but some for Mr. Brooke, a friend of Wordsworth and everyone else. But she was after other game than the Polonius who benignly called her, as his second daughter, 'Deutera'—an improvement on Mary Ann.

Pattison, Spencer, and Brabant hang upon Casaubon's coattails, but their intellectual interests are far afield. Comparative mythology such as Casaubon's had got off to a heady start in the eighteenth century with Jacob Bryant's *A New System: or, An Analysis of Ancient Mythology*. Mr. Haight has pointed out that George Eliot made use of Bryant's theory of 'Chus and Mizraim', Cush (so respelt by Bryant) being represented as the father of all the Scythian nations, and Mizraim as father of the Egyptians. There are further connections that can be offered: Bryant's theory of the Phoenicians (as sons of Esau) (VI, 226–39), of the ancient priests called the Cabiri (III, 341–61), and of Dagon the fish god, whom he identified both with Noah and with the Indian god Vishnu (III, 134–6; IV, 140–1; V, 236),[1] are all behind Mr. Casaubon's researches. It was as if George Eliot had Bryant ready in case she was suspected of deriding a living comparative mythologist, and she could keep him more easily in reserve because his work was evidently a familiar subject for joking between her and her friend Sara Hennell. Her concocted Professor Bücherwurm had offered the notion that Christianity was merely a late development of Buddhism, which was like making Vishnu a prior version of Noah, and Sara Hennell, in reply to her friend's comic letter about Bücherwurm's marriage proposal, quoted Bryant's favourite Egyptian source, Berosus. Yet George Eliot did have a comparative mythologist of her own day, whom she knew well, to fuse with Bryant. This was Robert William Mackay, the author of *The Progress of the Intellect as Exemplified in the Religious Development of the Greeks and Hebrews*, published by George Eliot's friend John Chapman in 1850, and at his request and Mackay's reviewed by her in her first article for the *Westminster Review*.

That Mackay was connected with Casaubon was proposed, as Mr. Haight recognizes, by Frances Power Cobbe in her 1894 *Life* of

1. References are to the third edition (1807), in six volumes.

herself (II, 110–11): 'Mr. Mackay was somewhat of an invalid and a nervous man, much absorbed in his studies. I have heard it said that he was the original of George Eliot's *Mr. Casaubon*. At all events Mrs. Lewes had met him, and taken a strong prejudice against him.' Miss Cobbe is mistaken about George Eliot's feelings towards Mackay, which were always friendly. Perhaps on this account, Mr. Haight dismisses the identification with him as hearsay. But it is not difficult to establish that Mackay contributed a small portion to *Middlemarch*. His book, unlike Brabant's unfinished one, was a revival of comparative mythology. He was more learned even than Bryant, with a dozen footnotes to the latter's one; George Eliot noted his 'industry in research', a virtue constantly claimed by Casaubon. If his search for vegetation gods is difficult to summarize, it is because, as George Eliot complained in her review, much of it seemed mere 'extracts from his commonplace book', rather than results of 'digested study'. It was such a book as Dorothea might have compiled after Casaubon's death. Some of it was manifestly absurd, but George Eliot took a benign view of his objective, which she summarized in this way:

> It is Mr. Mackay's faith that divine revelation is not contained exclusively or pre-eminently in the facts and inspirations of any one age or nation, but is co-extensive with the history of human development. . . . The master key to this revelation, is the recognition of the presence of undeviating law in the material and moral world—of that invariability of sequence which is acknowledged to be the basis of physical science, but which is still perversely ignored in our social organisation, our ethics and our religion.

Here at last is the word 'key', which Mackay himself had not used. It is his kind of locksmith that George Eliot has in mind in Casaubon's Key to all Mythologies.

There are further ties. 'Poor Mr. Casaubon himself was lost . . . in an agitated dimness about the Cabeiri' (chapter 20), and poor Mr. Mackay had followed Bryant to the extent of designating as 'Orphic or Cabiric' the primitive period of mythology (I, 276). (She noted in her article that this was an older view, but refrained from tracing it to Bryant.) If Mr. Casaubon, in dictating to Dorothea, announces, 'I omit the second excursus on Crete' (chapter 48), it is perhaps because Mr. Mackay had devoted a whole chapter to Crete and its god, 'Minos-Zeus' (II, 310–22), and Mr. Casaubon may well have felt that this first excursus was enough. If Ladislaw could say of Mr. Casaubon (chapter 22), 'He is not an Orientalist, you know. He does not profess to have more than second-hand knowledge there,' it was because Mr. Mackay had conceded in his preface

(I, viii), 'In quoting from Oriental sources the writer is under the disadvantage of ignorance of the languages; but he has taken pains to get the best possible aids.'

Mackay may have had marital designs upon George Eliot; he soon shifted them to another affective object. The resultant marriage obviously interested her. After it he appeared 'rather worse than otherwise', she reported. Following his return from a wedding trip to Weymouth, she asked him how he and his wife had liked it: 'Not at all, not at all,' he replied, 'but it was not the fault of the place.' The barrenness of Rome for the honeymooning Casaubons is at least glimpsed here.

Mackay served to update Bryant and to fill in details of Casaubon which other friends could not supply. As ultimate model for the character, he, like Brabant, is disqualified by his positive qualities. What remains to be found is the source of energy which produces both Casaubon's intensity, and the intensity of contempt, mixed with sporadic pity, which his being arouses in author and characters alike in *Middlemarch*. Mr. Haight, sensible of George Eliot's unusual venom, attributes it to her temporary infatuation with Brabant and later disillusionment with him, but so much feeling after twenty-five years of subsequent friendship, and three years after Brabant's death, seems disproportionate. Brabant was at worst one of her own follies.

Her own follies: putting these Casaubons *manqués* aside, we come to George Eliot herself. F. W. H. Myers related in the *Century Magazine* for November 1881, that when asked where she had found Casaubon, 'with a humorous solemnity, which was quite in earnest, nevertheless, she pointed to her own heart.' This remark deserves to be considered. She meant by it exactly what Flaubert had meant when he said, '*Madame Bovary, c'est moi.*' Flaubert too had his Brabants and Mackays, and secured a few useful details from actual events and persons, but in his writing he had other things to think about. What must be sought is not a Casaubon, but casaubonism, and this George Eliot found, as Flaubert found *le bovarysme*, in herself. Casaubonism is the entombing of the senses in the mind's cellarage. As a young woman George Eliot was liable to this iniquity, and all her life she was capable of what Myers calls 'almost morbid accesses of self-reproach'.

Casaubon is the only character in George Eliot's work up to this time to have a sexual problem, in the sense of being aberrant. What the problem may be is nòt easy to say definitely. Whether his marriage is consummated or not is left obscure. Living when she did, George Eliot had reason to be delicate and reticent about such a matter, but her vagueness had literary as well as Victorian causes. Impotence is a disaster, not a vice; if Casaubon cannot consummate his marriage, he is to that extent as pathetic as Ruskin. Too much sympathy would be out of order. George Eliot's fictional universe never allows her men and women to shirk moral responsibility, and Casaubon is no exception. She said that the idea of Casaubon and Dorothea had been in her mind from the time she began to write fiction, and one reason for her long delay in taking up the theme may have been the difficulty of handling Casaubon's sexual insufficiency. She finally solved the difficulty by blending impotence or near-impotence with a choice of chilliness over warmth, in which his culpability would be clear.

This can be traced in terms of one of those recurrent images which George Eliot used with minute attentiveness. At the centre of Casaubon's situation is the seed. As an image it is evoked three times. One is at dinner at Mr. Brooke's house before Dorothea's engagement. In defence of her not going out to ride, Mr. Casaubon says with sudden fervour, 'We must keep the germinating grain away from the light' (chapter 2). The association of darkness and seed is here fixed, with the residual implication that Mr. Casaubon's grain may not be of the germinating kind. Then in chapter 48 his Key to all Mythologies is unexpectedly rephrased as 'the seed of all tradition'. His inability to construct a key, or make a seed, might seem beyond his control. But his blameableness is established in a passage in chapter 42, to which Barbara Hardy has called attention. Mr. Casaubon's difficulties are here explicitly voluntary, not involuntary; as Dorothea is about to take his arms, he keeps it rigid;

> There was something horrible to Dorothea in the sensation which this unresponsive hardness inflicted on her. That is a strong word but not too strong. It is in these acts called trivialities that the seeds of joy are for ever wasted, until men and women look round with haggard faces at the devastation their own waste has made, and say, the earth bears no harvest of sweetness—calling their denial knowledge.

Mr. Casaubon chooses self-isolation like choosing self-abuse. The image of Onan is invoked to symbolize his spirit, which in turn is reflected in his physical denial.

This passage, while bold, is not quite unique in George Eliot's writings: it has one counterpart, a personal statement, in a letter she wrote in late adolescence (16 March 1839) to her old teacher Miss Lewis. The letter is startling because in it the future novelist repudiates novels, on the grounds of their effect upon her fantasy life. In this burst of candour she declares:

> . . . I venture to believe that the same causes which exist in my own breast to render novels and romances pernicious have their counterpart in that of every fellow-creature.

I am I confess not an impartial member of a jury in this case for I owe the culprits a grudge for injuries inflicted on myself. I shall carry to my grave the mental diseases with which they have contaminated me. When I was quite a little child I could not be satisfied with the things around me; I was constantly living in a world of my own creation, and was quite contented to have no companions that I might be left to my own musings and imagine scenes in which I was chief actress. Conceive what a character novels would give to these Utopias.

Not absence of feeling, but deflection of it, appears to be the charge she is levelling against herself. Mr. Haight in his biography advises against taking these statements seriously, although in his edition of the *Letters* he notes that J. W. Cross, in *George Eliot's Life*, omitted the sentence that contains 'contaminated', 'diseases', and 'to my grave'. Evidently Cross took them seriously. To use these weighty words lightly is not in character for George Eliot. If they have any serious meaning at all, then she is declaring that she has been contaminated by novels which have aroused in her erotic fantasies, as opposed to the merely megalomaniac ones of childhood. In *Felix Holt* Mrs. Transome reads French novels and so takes a lover. But George Eliot in adolescence found no such requital. Insofar as Casaubon was an expression of her own 'almost morbid accesses of self-reproach'—made vivid by her early evangelicalism—it would seem that his sexual inadequacy was a version of her struggles with adolescent sexuality, and that these struggles stirred in her sensation which remained painful even in memory.[2] The images of darkness which make up Casaubon's mental landscape would then be wincing recollections of 'the mental diseases' which she had predicted she would 'carry to my grave'. Casaubon's sexual insufficiency was an emblem for fruitless fantasies, of which she too felt victim. It was probably in this sense that he drew his strength and intensity from her nature.

The severity with which Casaubon is treated, aside from occasional remissions, would then derive from her need to exorcise this part of her experience. For a woman who prided herself on her

2. In a letter written to Miss Lewis a year later, she uses the word 'sin' to describe her oppressive fantasies: "With respect to my own state of soul of which I have said nothing for some time, I fear that my sins or rather one particular manifestation of them, have forsaken me instead of my forsaking and abhorring them. I feel that a sight of one being whom I have not beheld except passingly since the interview I last described to you would *probably* upset *all*; but as it is, the image now seldom arises in consequence of entire occupation and, I trust in some degree, desire and prayer to be free from rebelling against Him whose I am by right, whose I would be by adoption. I endeavoured to pray for the beloved object to whom I have alluded, I must still a little while say *beloved*, last night and felt soothingly melted in thinking that if mine be really prayers my acquaintance with him has probably caused the *first* to be offered up specially in his behalf. But all this I ought not to have permitted to slip from my pen." (*Letters*, I, 46–7.)

plenitude of heart, these early short-circuits of sensual emotion were painful to think on. No wonder that she makes Casaubon die of fatty degeneration of the heart. He is the repository of her inferior qualities, as Dorothea of her superior ones. She instilled her callow misimaginings, suitably shifted in clef, into old Casaubon, and her ripe affirmations into young Dorothea.

The place of Dorothea's second husband, Will Ladislaw, in this drama of George Eliot's mind is not immediately apparent. To a considerable extent Will had to be made congruent with Dorothea, even to the point of sharing or paralleling her traits. Like her, he has a somewhat undirected aspiration to achieve good and useful works, and he has a slight maliciousness to balance her mild vanity. In some ways he too radiates out from George Eliot, even in his person. His rippled nose and strong jaw are an idealization of his creator's features, and are allowed to make him handsome though she felt they made her ugly. In his indictment of Casaubon's mythological researches, he follows closely, as Thomas Pinney has noted, George Eliot's review of Mackay and particularly of her strictures on Mackay's predecessors:

> The introduction of a truly philosophic spirit into the study of mythology—an introduction for which we are chiefly indebted to the Germans—is a great step in advance of the superficial Lucian-like tone of ridicule adopted by many authors of the eighteenth century, or the orthodox prepossessions of writers such as Bryant, who saw in the Greek legends simply misrepresentations of the authentic history given in the book of Genesis.

Ladislaw says to Dorothea, 'Do you not see that it is no use now to be crawling a little way after men of the last century—men like Bryant—and correcting their mistakes?—living in a lumber-room and furbishing up broken-legged theories about Chus and Mizraim?' Yet if she modelled Ladislaw a little upon herself, she needed and found another model as well. The choice troubled her. She said that the ending of her novel might disappoint, and perhaps the main reason was that, aside from marrying Ladislaw to Dorothea (like Blake fusing Los with Enitharmon), she could not make him inevitable in the Middlemarch terrain.

Prototype hunters have left Ladislaw alone, on the assumption that George Eliot was too happily fixed in her life with Lewes to have anyone else in mind. Her commitment to Lewes was as much beyond suspicion as it was outside law. If she could not take his last name legally, she took both his last and first names extra-legally. When Harriet Beecher Stowe asked if the Casaubon marriage bore any resemblance to her own, George Eliot replied, 'Impossible to conceive any creature less like Mr. Casaubon than my warm, enthusiastic husband, who cares much more for my doing than for his own, and is a miracle of freedom from all author's jealousy and all suspicion. I fear that the Casaubon-tints are not quite foreign to my own mental complexion. At any rate I am very sorry for him.' (she echoes here her comment as author in *Middlemarch* (chapter 29), 'For my part I am very sorry for him.') Lewes was in fact one of the more engaging minds of his time, willing to tackle scientific, philosophical, and literary subjects, and with a gift of sympathy which George Eliot found indispensable to her existence as well as to her writing. If Thomas and Jane Carlyle could not refrain from calling him 'the ape', or Douglas Jerrold from calling him 'the ugliest man in London', he was not the less likeable; and George Eliot was more indulgent of his ugliness than of her own. He himself sometimes joked about playing Casaubon to his wife's Dorothea, but he had more in common with Ladislaw. He too spent some time as a young man in Germany and knew the language fairly well. He did not have 'a Jew pawnbroker' for his grandfather, an imputation made about Ladislaw, but he had Jewish associations and several times played Shylock on the stage. He had a versatility that smacked of dilettantism, so that he dissected dragonflies one moment and Comtism the next. But like Ladislaw, his variety did not prevent intensity. 'Our sense of duty', says George Eliot in chapter 46, 'must often wait for some work which shall take the place of dilettantism. . . .'

George Eliot was jealous of her husband as well as notably fond of him. Mrs. Linton quotes her as saying, 'I should not think of allowing George to stay away a night from me.' Yet sporadic deflections of erotic feeling are not inconsistent with marital content or vigilance. In her case a superabundance of amorous sentiment, beyond any immediate object, is suggested by the effusively affectionate correspondence she lavished upon women friends even though, as she had to make clear to Edith Simcox, it was men who interested her. The search for Casaubon begins with others and ends with George Eliot; the search for Ladislaw spreads out from her to her husband and beyond. In this character her critical powers, which enabled her to recognize limitations in Dorothea as in heroes outside of fiction such as Luther and Bunyan,[3] are largely suspended. He occupies a special position in her work, because he is

3. "I should imagine that neither Luther nor John Bunyan, for example, would have satisfied the modern demand for an ideal hero. . . . The real heroes, of God's making, are quite different: they have their natural heritage of love and conscience which they drew in with their mother's milk; they know one or two of those deep spiritual truths which are only to be won by long wrestling with their own sins and their own sorrows; they have earned faith and strength so far as they have done genuine work; but the rest is dry barren theory, blank prejudice, vague hearsay . . . their very deeds of self-sacrifice are sometimes only the rebound of a passionate egoism." (*Scenes of Clerical Life*, chapter x of *Janet's Repentance*.)

the first character of either sex in her novels to be irresistibly handsome and at the same time good. Early reviewers remarked upon him as constituting a new departure in George Eliot's novels. In *Adam Bede* Hetty is beautiful, but is punished for being so; she is not so good as she looks. The same is true of Tito in *Romola*. Only Ladislaw is treated with utter indulgence, even to being encouraged to toss back his curls on numerous occasions, as if George Eliot feared she had not made him fetching enough. It seems possible that she had herself been suddenly captivated by the image of a handsome young man.

The first important meeting of Dorothea and Ladislaw takes place in Rome, and since George Eliot had been to Rome just three and a half months before she began *Middlemarch*, her sojourn may be scrutinized a little. This was the second visit that she and Lewes had paid to that city, and it did not work out as well as the first. On the way there he had suffered from sciatica, and once arrived he was not in the mood to enjoy Rome. He wrote in his journal, 'I have had enough of it and want to be at home and at work again.' Mr. Casaubon had similar thoughts. But George Eliot did not share her husband's impatience. 'Here we had many days of unbroken sunshine . . .' was her summary. It was now she had the meeting which was to prove so momentous in her life, with John Walter Cross, then twenty-nine.

This meeting had long been in prospect. She had met Cross's mother two years before, thanks to Herbert Spencer, who boasted in later life that he had brought George Eliot into touch with both her husbands. At that time Mrs. Cross's other children were in England, but John was in the United States, carrying on the American side of the family's banking business. He must have been a frequent topic of discussion between the Crosses and Leweses.

On an April day in 1869 George Eliot was walking with Lewes in her beloved Pamfili Doria gardens, when she met by accident Mrs. Cross's oldest daughter and her husband, who like the Casaubons took their wedding trip to Rome. Further meetings were arranged, and when, some days later, Mrs. Cross, her son John, and another daughter arrived, they were invited on 18 April to visit the Leweses in their rooms at the Hotel Minerva—the same hotel they had stayed at on their first Roman visit in 1860. John Walter Cross shared the veneration of all members of his family for George Eliot's writings, and must have testified to that. Thanks to him, one bit of the ensuing conversation has survived: 'And I remember, many years ago, at the time of our first acquaintance, how deeply it pained her when, in reply to a direct question, I was obliged to admit that, with all my admiration for her books, I found them, on the whole, profoundly sad.' Her pain carried over into *Middle-*

march. This conversation is closely paralleled in chapter 22 when Ladislaw admonishes Dorothea, 'Would you turn all the youth of the world into a tragic chorus, wailing and moralising over misery?' She replies, as George Eliot must have replied to Cross, 'I am not a sad, melancholy creature', but he is not so easily put down, and eight chapters later has written her a letter which 'was a lively continuation of his remonstrance with her fanatical sympathy and her want of sturdy neutral delight in things as they were—an outpouring of his young vivacity. . . .'

Cross, nothing if not vivacious, had just returned from the United States, and must have been asked about his travels there. His work had been in New York, where he had invested heavily in the railroads, but, as a magazine article he wrote later confirms, he had also been to California. Something of what he said must have put George Eliot in mind of the penultimate project which she attributes to Ladislaw (before his ultimate one of marrying Dorothea), that of promoting a settlement in the 'Far West'. Cross was in fact excited about what he repeatedly called in print the 'New World'; he praised it because it 'rests on the basis of industrialism as opposed to militarism'. He thought his fellow-countrymen wrong to criticize it, and wrote later, 'One thing is certain, namely, that since all gain of *real* wealth in America *must* be of advantage to England it will surely be the first sign of impending decadence if the business men of this country, instead of putting their shoulders to the wheel to carry their chariot over all obstruction, content themselves with cherishing a vindictive feeling to rivals. . . .' This kind of imagery, natural to Cross,[4] is twitted a little in Ladislaw's projected painting of 'Tamburlaine Driving the Conquered Kings in His Chariot', intended as he says to symbolize 'the tremendous course of the world's physical history lashing on the harnessed dynasties', and to include 'migrations of races and clearings of forests—and America and the steam engine'. Cross's westward travels, the steam engine which drove the trains that carried him, the extension of the railroads to the furthest points of the New World (as he remarked in an article devoted to them), the sympathy for American energy, all found a way into George Eliot's book.

He must have delighted her. The contrast of Ladislaw's youth and Casaubon's age, of the passionate unscholarliness of the first and the uneasy ferreting of the second, would then be an idealized registration of the effect on George Eliot of her meeting with Cross. By implication it promised Dorothea in fiction something better than widow's weeds and good works after Casaubon's death, and so

4. For example, in his *The Rake's Progress in Finance* (1905), 127–8, he writes that 'the serious question is how to steer warily, for we have already pointed the nose of our ship towards State Socialism and it may be difficult now to alter the course.'

brought the whole of *Middlemarch* into focus. It can only have been a secret tribute to Cross, and one he would have appreciated, that among the misty details of Ladislaw's upbringing one fact stands out clear and is mentioned twice—he went to Rugby. So did Cross.[5]

Momentarily even the beloved Lewes must have appeared to disadvantage beside this taller, handsomer, sharper-sighted, younger banker. Cross was to prove his devotion steadily from this time on, and to be rewarded for it by having conferred upon him the title of 'nephew'. In *Middlemarch* Ladislaw, though actually Casaubon's second cousin, is often taken for his nephew. Cross was regularly and affectionately spoken of as Nephew Johnny, and in the letter George Eliot wrote to him after Lewes's death, in which she asked him to call, she addressed him as 'Dearest N.' Not that she considered for a moment infidelity to her husband; for every reason she was bound to him for life. But she was not averse to making renunciation of another cherished object a part of her bond to Lewes. As she remarks of Mary Garth's loyalty to Fred in *Middlemarch*, 'we can set a watch on our affections and our constancy as we can other treasures.' Certainly as a solution to her problems of ending *Middlemarch*, John Walter Cross had much to offer. She banked this banker in her fictional account.

The friendship of the Leweses with Cross grew deeper over the years. After Lewes's death George Eliot would not receive Cross for a time, but indicated she would do so eventually, perhaps before she received anyone else. And so it was. On the day he was asked to call, her old friend Herbert Spencer was turned away. Since Cross's mother and one of his sisters had died soon after Lewes, he and George Eliot could share each other's grief. As consolation in the next months, they read Dante's *Inferno* and *Purgatorio* together. There was no need to read the *Paradiso*, for the parallel with Beatrice required no enforcement. Cross felt Dantean about George Eliot; she was 'my ideal', 'the best', and to marry her was his 'high calling'. George Eliot did not reprove this exalted feeling; in a letter to Mrs. Burne-Jones of 5 May 1880, she wrote: 'he sees his only longed-for happiness in dedicating his life to me.'

Ladislaw objects to Casaubon's ignorance of the Germans on comparative mythology, but George Eliot is at pains to indicate that he himself has little more than vague acquaintance with these arcane books. No erudition is allowed Ladislaw, only a general interest in art, poetry, and politics. His reformist political views are close to those of Cross, who espoused a non-revolutionary amelioration

---

5. Cross entered Rugby in April 1835, at the age of fifteen. N. C. Kittermaster, the present librarian of the school, informs me that he remained for two years.

of inequity as a liberal goal.[6] A strong hint of George Eliot's sense of Cross as a Ladislaw figure comes in a patronizing (if also matronizing) letter she wrote him on 16 October 1879: 'Best loved and loving one . . . Thou dost not know anything of verbs in Hiphil and Hophal or the history of metaphysics or the position of Kepler in science, but thou knowest best things of another sort, such as belong to the manly heart—secrets of lovingness and rectitude. O I am flattering. Consider what thou wast a little time ago in Pantaloons and back hair.' (Back hair was one of Ladislaw's attributes.) By this time Cross was thirty-nine and a settled man in City banking, but he still stood for her as the embodiment of youth, almost of boyhood, with an ignorance that surpassed knowledge. No doubt these feelings had grown in George Eliot over the ten years of their friendship, but the jingled Hebrew of 'Hiphil and Hophal' suggests that from the beginning he had stood as the polar opposite of 'Cush and Mizraim'. He was also the opposite of her husband, and of most of her old friends, in knowing nothing—as she indelicately underlines—of works in ancient languages, in metaphysics, or in science. Marrying Dorothea to Ladislaw had been George Eliot's only adulterous act. Artistically it proved to be a sin. Marrying Cross as Lewes's widow legalized the fantasy. In the same way her own reconciliation with her brother Isaac validated the reconciliation of brother and sister which she had fictionally imagined, in *The Mill on the Floss*.

Now, when they married, there was a strange reversal of roles, with a sixty-year-old Dorothea marrying a forty-one-year-old Ladislaw, a disparity almost as great as that between Casaubon and his bride. Cross's own sentiments could only have been intricate, since he was her nephew, son, pupil, and reader, as well as husband. The sense of being a once independently orbited fragment drawn back now into the parent body must have been immensely disturbing. Perhaps more than sexual awkwardness or disparity of age or health was involved in Cross's pitching himself into the Grand Canal at Venice during their wedding trip. It was a solution which George Eliot had never allowed Dorothea to contemplate. Fished out, and restored to the same bedroom, he gave no further trouble.

A final witness is Eliza Lynn Linton. She had known George Eliot as a young provincial, holding her hands and arms like a kangaroo. She had been invited to call just after the decision to live with Lewes, and she met her later on too. Mrs. Linton was jealous of George Eliot's literary pre-eminence, but she acknowledged it.

6. Cross praises Dante for having seen the danger of the 'ever-increasing inequality in the distribution of wealth', and after himself opposing 'the crude spirit which would risk reducing order to chaos by violent methods', he endorses 'the spirit which is at work modifying and enlarging our ideal of possession from an individual to a social basis.' (*Impressions of Dante* . . . , 92.)

She also wrote a long essay on George Eliot's works, and had this to say about the second marriage of Dorothea in *Middlemarch*:

> And to think that to her first mistake she adds that second of marrying Will Ladislaw—the utter snob that he is! Where were George Eliot's perceptions? Or was it that in Ladislaw she had a model near at hand, whom she saw through coloured glasses, which also shed their rosy light on her reproduction, as that his copy was to her as idealized as the original, and she as ignorant of the effect produced on the clear-sighted?

In another place Mrs. Linton makes clear that she entirely disapproved of the marriage to Cross, as reducing the first marriage to a house of cards, and it is clearly Cross she has here in mind. She is unkind, but she does suggest the fictional complications for George Eliot of modelling Ladislaw on Cross, a man distinguished more for youthful ardour and amorphousness than anything else. (His skill in investment was hard to idealize.) But George Eliot chose well in making him her husband, for he was impeccably discreet in his *Life* of her, and during the more than forty years that he outlived her.

Cross did not allow his photograph to be taken, and in general he effaced himself. But he was not devoid of ambition, and he published two books. The first and more important had the ragbag title, *Impressions of Dante and of the New World with a Few Words on Bimetallism* (1893). His Dante essays provide a contrast to the worldly report on American railroads, and indicate that like Ladislaw he loved poetry. The preface perhaps gives a sense of his good-hearted and unassuming but garrulous temperament:

> 'Don't shoot the organist; he's doing his level best.' This ancient American story of a notice prominently affixed in a church in the Wild West, as a gentle appeal to the congregation, expresses the mildly deprecatory attitude that I desire to assume to my readers —if I have any—or rather the attitude that I hope they will assume to me. 'Don't shoot the essayist; he's doing his level best.' I confess that it is difficult to find a naked excuse for republishing old magazine articles, and in my own case I cannot plead that any host of admiring friends has put pressure on me to collect mine. I take it that the real reason for the republication is always the same—a desire on the part of the writer to leave some print of his footsteps, however shallow, on the sands of time. (pp. v–vi.)

This is johnnycrossism, abashed yet candid, the reverse of Casaubon's closed room which no key could unlock. After a lifetime with intellectuals, George Eliot chose a simpler love for herself as she had had Dorothea do after Casaubon's death. The Key to all Mythologies was not so hard to find. Her decision may have been sentimental, but it established the verisimilitude of Dorothea's act.

The two husbands of Dorothea have different functions in *Middlemarch*. The one is all labyrinth and darkness, the other all candour and light. George Eliot was dissatisfied with the book's ending, but she committed herself to Ladislaw in a way hard for most readers to follow. Part of the reason lies in the very different histories of the characters in her internal dialectic. To berate Casaubon, and to bury him, was to overcome in transformed state the narcissistic sensuality of her adolescence. Old feelings of self-reproach could be renewed, and the character, once stirred by this motive power, could be furnished out with details adroitly selected from people she had known either personally or through their writings. The result was a triumph, a new creature. In Ladislaw, a fantasy of middle age, indulged because innocuous, the character is deprived of her usual controls. She allows herself to idealize him, his only imperfection being what is also his chief perfection—youth. He remains a surrogate sun, lacking in energy and heat, no fiction but a figment executed in pastel colours. She had had much time to reflect on the implications of Casaubon; but, if these speculations are valid, the new image of Ladislaw took her unawares, as a result of the luxuriantly fantasied encounter in Rome with her young admirer and future husband.

George Eliot—A Chronology

1819	George Eliot born Mary Anne Evans in Warwickshire, November 22.
1844–46	Translates Strauss's *Das Leben Jesu*.
1852–54	Assistant editor of the *Westminster Review*.
1854	Translates Feuerbach's *Das Wesen des Christenthums*. Goes to Europe as the wife of G. H. Lewes.
1855–56	Translates Spinoza's *Ethics*.
1857	GE's first published fiction, *Scenes of Clerical Life*, in *Blackwood's Magazine*.
1859	*Adam Bede*.
1860	*The Mill on the Floss*.
1861	*Silas Marner*.
1862–63	*Romola* in *Cornhill Magazine*.
1866	*Felix Holt the Radical*.
1868	*The Spanish Gypsy*, a poetic narrative.
1869–71	Various poems published: "How Lisa Loved the King," "Agatha," "The Legend of Jubal," "Armgart."
1871–72	*Middlemarch*.
1876	*Daniel Deronda*.
1878	G. H. Lewes dies.
1879	*Impressions of Theophrastus Such* (essays).
1880	Marries John Walter Cross, May 6. Dies in London, December 22.

Selected Bibliography

Titles included in the preceding sections of this book are not repeated here, except in the case of general works. Items marked with an asterisk are available in paperback editions.

STUDIES IN NINETEENTH-CENTURY FICTION

* Allen, Walter. *The English Novel*. London, 1954.
* Cecil, David. *Early Victorian Novelists*. New York, 1935.
* Kettle, Arnold. *An Introduction to the English Novel*. London, 1951.
* Leavis, F. R. *The Great Tradition*. London, 1948.

STUDIES OF GEORGE ELIOT

Biographies

Cross, J. W. *George Eliot's Life as Related in Her Letters and Journals*. 3 vols. Edinburgh and New York, 1885.
Haight, Gordon S. *George Eliot: A Biography*. New York, 1968.
Kitchel, Anna T. *George Lewes and George Eliot: A Review of Records*. New York, 1933.
Redinger, Ruby V. *George Eliot: The Emergent Self*. New York, 1975.

Critical Studies

Bullett, Gerald. *George Eliot: Her Life and Books*. London, 1947.
Garrett, Peter K. *Scene and Symbol from George Eliot to James Joyce*. New Haven, 1968.
* Haight, Gordon S. *A Century of George Eliot Criticism*. Boston, 1965.
Harvey, W. J. *The Art of George Eliot*. New York, 1962.
* Holloway, John. *The Victorian Sage: Studies in Argument*. London, 1953. (Includes a chapter on GE.)
Kroeber, Karl. *Styles in Fictional Structure: The Art of Jane Austen, Charlotte Brontë, and George Eliot*. Princeton, 1971.
Mansell, Darrel, Jr. "George Eliot's Conception of Tragedy," *Nineteenth Century Fiction*, 22 (1967), 155–71.
———. "Possibilities in George Eliot's Fiction," *English Studies*, 49 1968), 193–202.
Milner, Ian. *The Structure of Values in George Eliot*. Prague, 1968. (Stimulating Marxist-socialist analysis of GE's works.)
Paris, Bernard J. *Experiments in Life*. Detroit, 1965.
———. "George Eliot's Religion of Humanity," *English Literary History*, 29 (1962), 418–43.
Pinney, Thomas. "More Leaves from George Eliot's Notebook," *Huntington Library Quarterly*, 29 (1966), 353–76.
Prest, John M. *Industrial Revolution in Coventry*. London, 1960. (Good for background information; Coventry is Middlemarch for GE.)
Stang, Richard. "The Literary Criticism of George Eliot," *PMLA*, 72 (1957), 952–61.
Stump, Reva. *Movement and Vision in George Eliot's Novels*. Seattle, 1959. (A study of imagery.)
Svaglic, Martin. "Religion in the Novels of George Eliot," *JEGP*, 53 (1954), 145–59.
Willey, Basil. *Nineteenth Century Studies*. London, 1949. (Includes a chapter on GE.)
* Woolf, Virginia. "George Eliot," *The Common Reader*. New York, 1925.

STUDIES OF *MIDDLEMARCH*

Beaty, Jerome. "*Middlemarch*" *from Notebook to Novel: A Study of George Eliot's Critical Method*. Urbana, 1960.

Bedient, Calvin. "*Middlemarch:* Touching Down," *Hudson Review*, 22 (1969), 70–84.

Carroll, D. R. "Unity through Analogy: An Interpretation of *Middlemarch*," *Victorian Studies*, 2 (1959), 305–16.

* Daiches, David. *George Eliot: "Middlemarch."* London, 1963. (A detailed, chapter-by-chapter reading of the novel.)

Damm, Robert F. "Sainthood and Dorothea Brooke," *Victorian Newsletter*, 35 (1969), 18–22.

Feltes, N. N. "George Eliot's Pier-Glass: The Development of a Metaphor," *Modern Philology*, 67 (1968), 67–71.

Griffin, Robert P. "Image and Intent: Some Observations on Style in *Middlemarch*," *Ball State University Forum*, 10 (1969), 60–63.

Hardy, Barbara, ed. *"Middlemarch": Critical Approaches to the Novel.* London, 1967. (A collection of eight useful essays.)

Hagan, John. "*Middlemarch:* Narrative Unity in the Story of Dorothea Brooke," *Nineteenth Century Fiction*, 16 (1961), 17–31.

Harvey, W. J., ed. *Middlemarch.* Baltimore, 1965. (A good general introduction to the novel.)

Stalknecht, Newton P. "Resolution and Independence: A Reading of *Middlemarch*," *Twelve Original Essays on Great English Novels*, ed. Charles Shapiro. Detroit, 1960.